2000

American Novel Explication
1969–1980

Compiled by
CATHERINE GLITSCH

Archon Books
2000

For Hans, Matthew and Peter

The American Novel Explication Series is
compiled by Catherine Glitsch and consists of
American Novel Explication 1991–1995 (1998) and
American Novel Explication 1969–1980 (2000).
Subsequent volumes will cover 1981–1985; 1986–1990;
and then go forward from 1995 in five-year increments.

Library of Congress Cataloging-in-Publication Data

Glitsch, Catherine.
American novel explication, 1969–1980 /
compiled by Catherine Glitsch.
p.   cm.
Includes bibliographical references and index.
ISBN 0-208-02479-4 (lib. bdg. : alk. paper)
1. American fiction—History and criticism—
Bibliography.   2. Canadian fiction—History and criticism—
Bibliography.   I. Title.

Z1231.F4 G56 2000
[PS371]
016.81′813009—dc21

00-033146

The paper in this publication meets the minimum
requirements of American National Standard for Information Sciences—
Permanence of Paper for Printed Library Materials, ANSI Z39.48-1984. ∞

Printed in the United States of America

Contents

Preface

The *American Novel Explication* series covers U.S. and Canadian novels from their beginnings in the eighteenth-century to the present. This volume of *American Novel Explication* covers criticism of American novels published in journals and books between the years 1969 and 1980. An "American" novelist is a writer born in the United States or Canada, or who has lived a significant portion of his or her life in the United States or Canada. Some novelists who have become identified as Canadian or U.S. authors are also included even though they do not strictly fit into these categories. For example, Frances Brooke, who was born in Great Britain and lived only a short time in Canada, is included because she is widely considered to be Canada's first novelist.

For the purposes of this bibliography, a novel is defined as a fictional prose narrative which is 150 or more pages in length. One exception to this rule is William Wells Brown's *Clotel* which, although only 100 pages in length, is considered to be the first novel by an African-American. Explication is defined as the interpretation of the *significance* and *meaning* of a novel. This includes examinations of imagery, theme and symbolism, as well as deconstructionist, linguistic, post-structuralist analyses; and, excludes discussions which are solely bibliographical studies, reception studies, publishing histories of a novel, and biographical essays on novelists. Sources consulted in the compilation of *American Novel Explication* include the *MLA Bibliography*, the *Annual Bibliography of English Language and Literature*, and *WorldCat*.

Criticism indexed is in both English and French and includes articles from journals, critical discussions from books, as well as whole books devoted to a particular novel. The body of the book is alphabetical by author with novel titles listed alphabetically within each author's entry. "See references" appear for novels known by more than one title as well as for authors known by more than one name. Pen names were chosen as main entries, with "see references" from the authors' given names. Alphabetization is word by word throughout. Authors whose names begin with Mc or Mac are interfiled.

A complete index to authors and novel titles appears at the back of the volume. Within each novelist's entry, citations to criticism are alphabetical by the author of the book, journal article, or book article. Novel titles appear in their abbreviated, but recognizable form. For example, Herman Melville's *Moby Dick, or the Whale* appears simply as *Moby Dick*. Novels written by more than one author, such as Mark Twain's and Charles Dudley Warner's *Gilded Age*, are listed under both authors, as are the citations to criticism on these novels. Main entries for novels originally written in a language other than English, appear under the original title with "see references" from the translated title.

In the main body of the volume, abbreviated titles for books of criticism are used in citations. The full citations for books cited can be found at the back of the volume in the "List of Books Indexed" section. When an article from an edited book is cited, the editor and abbreviated title of the book follow the article title and are preceded by the word "in." Books with more than one author or editor have only the first author/editor cited in the main body of the volume. Unedited books about a single novel are cited in their entirety in the main body of the bibliography, as well as appearing in the "List of Books Indexed" section. In most citations, pages cited do not refer to entire journal articles or book chapters, but to the specific section within a book or article in which a novel is discussed. Footnotes or bibliographies appearing at the end of articles are not included in the pages cited.

For ease of use, all citations to journal articles appear in full, and include the article's author, title, and a complete citation to the journal in which the article appears. When citing annual journals like *Nathaniel Hawthorne Journal* or *Fitzgerald-Hemingway Annual*, no volume number is given in the citation, only the year of publication. For the most part, journal abbreviations used are those of the Modern Language Association. A complete list of journal abbreviations appears at the front of the book in the "Journal Abbreviations" section.

Reprints are indicated when possible to further expand the retrieval of information. In the citations to articles which have been reprinted from books, the bibliographic information for the book in which the article originally appeared is cited in its entirety in the main body of the volume and does not appear in the "List of Books Indexed." Whenever possible, journal abbreviations are not used in citations for journal articles reprinted in a book.

I would like to thank the staffs of the Kendall and Robinson-Westchase libraries of the Houston Public Library system who patiently and efficiently handled the numerous books needed for the compilation of this bibliography. I would also like to thank the librarians of the Humanities department of the Houston Public Library for their invaluable reference assistance and unflagging encouragement. Thank you also to the Interlibrary Loan department of the Houston Public Library for gathering the many books used in the completion of *American Novel Explication*. Finally, I would like to thank my entire family, especially Hans, Matthew, and Peter Glitsch and Sheila Curren, for their support and encouragement in completing *American Novel Explication*. Any comments or suggestions are welcome and can be emailed to me at cathy@micronation.com or mailed to The Shoe String Press.

Houston, Texas   C.E.G
February 2000

Journal Abbreviations

AIQ	*American Indian Quarterly: A Journal of Anthropology*
AL	*American Literature: A Journal of Literary History, Criticism, and Bibliography*
ALR	*American Literary Realism*
American Imago	*American Imago: A Psychoanalytic Journal for Culture, Science, and the Arts*
AmerS	*American Studies*
ANQ	*American Notes and Queries*
AntR	*Antigonish Review*
AQ	*American Quarterly*
Ariel	*Ariel: A Review of International Literature*
ArQ	*Arizona Quarterly*
ATQ	*American Transcendental Quarterly*
BALF	*Black American Literature Forum*
BallS	*Ball State University Forum*
BoundaryII	*Boundary 2: A Journal of Postmodern Literature*
BuR	*Bucknell Review*
BW	*Black World*

Callaloo	*Callaloo: A Black South Journal of Arts and Letters*
CanL	*Canadian Literature*
CEA	*CEA Critic*
CentR	*Centennial Review*
ChildL	*Children's Literature: Annual of the Modern Language Association Seminar on Children's Literature*
Cithara	*Cithara: Essays in the Judaeo Christian Tradition*
CL	*Comparative Literature*
CLAJ	*College Language Association Journal*
CLQ	*Colby Library Quarterly*
CLS	*Comparative Literature Studies*
CMLR	*Canadian Modern Language Review/La Revue Canadienne des Langues Vivantes*
CollL	*College Literature*
Commentary	*Commentary*
ConL	*Contemporary Literature*
Crit	*Critique: Studies in Modern Fiction*
Criticism	*Criticism: A Quarterly for Literature and the Arts*
CritI	*Critical Inquiry*
CritQ	*Critical Quarterly*
DR	*Dalhousie Review*
EAL	*Early American Literature*
ECW	*Essays on Canadian Writing*
EIC	*Essays in Criticism*
EJ	*English Journal*
ELH	*ELH*

ELN	*English Language Notes*
ELWIU	*Essays in Literature*
ES	*English Studies: A Journal of English Language and Literature*
ESQ	*ESQ: A Journal of the American Renaissance*
Expl	*Explicator*
Extrapolation	*Extrapolation: A Journal of Science Fiction and Fantasy*
F-H Annual	*Fitzgerald-Hemingway Annual*
FR	*French Review*
GR	*Georgia Review*
HAR	*Humanities Association Review*
HC	*Hollins Critic*
HJR	*Henry James Review*
IFR	*International Fiction Review*
JACult	*Journal of American Culture*
JAmS	*Journal of American Studies*
JBS	*Journal of Black Studies*
JCL	*Journal of Commonwealth Literature*
JML	*Journal of Modern Literature*
JNT	*Journal of Narrative Technique*
JPC	*Journal of Popular Culture*
L&P	*Literature and Psychology*
LR	*Literary Review*
MarkR	*Markham Review*
MELUS	*MELUS: The Journal of the Society for the Study of the Multi-Ethnic Literature of the United States*

MFS	*Modern Fiction Studies*
Midamerica	*Midamerica: The Yearbook of the Society for the Study of Midwestern Literature*
MidQ	*Midwest Quarterly: A Journal of Contemporary Thought*
MissQ	*Mississippi Quarterly*
MLQ	*Modern Language Quarterly*
MLS	*Modern Language Studies*
Mosaic	*Mosaic: A Journal for the Comparative Study of Literature and Ideas*
MP	*Modern Philology*
MQR	*Michigan Quarterly Review*
MR	*Massachusetts Review: A Quarterly of Literature, the Arts and Public Affairs*
MSE	*Massachusetts Studies in English*
MTJ	*Mark Twain Journal*
N&Q	*Notes and Queries*
NALF	*Negro American Literature Forum*
NCF	*Nineteenth-Century Fiction*
NConL	*Notes on Contemporary Literature*
NDQ	*North Dakota Quarterly*
NEQ	*New England Quarterly: A Historical Review of New England Life and Letters*
NHJ	*Nathaniel Hawthorne Journal*
NLH	*New Literary History: A Journal of Theory and Interpretation*
NMW	*Notes on Mississippi Writers*
Novel	*Novel: A Forum on Fiction*

Obsidian	*Obsidian: Black Literature in Review*
Phylon	*Phylon: The Atlanta University Review of Race and Culture*
PLL	*Papers on Language and Literature: A Journal for Scholars and Critics of Language and Literature*
PMLA	*PMLA: Publications of the Modern Language Association of America*
PQ	*Philological Quarterly*
Renascence	*Renascence: Essays on Value in Literature*
RQ	*Riverside Quarterly*
SAF	*Studies in American Fiction*
SAL	*Southwestern American Literature*
SAQ	*South Atlantic Quarterly*
SCR	*South Carolina Review*
SewR	*Sewanee Review*
SFS	*Science-Fiction Studies*
SIBL	*Studies in Black Literature*
SIR	*Studies in Romanticism*
SLitI	*Studies in the Literary Imagination*
SLJ	*Southern Literary Journal*
SNNTS	*Studies in the Novel*
SoHR	*Southern Humanities Review*
SoQ	*Southern Quarterly*
SoR	*Southern Review*
SoS	*Southern Studies*
SR	*Southwest Review*
StTCL	*Studies in Twentieth Century Literature*

Studies in the Humanities	*Studies in the Humanities*
StQ	*Steinbeck Quarterly*
TCL	*Twentieth Century Literature*
TSLL	*Texas Studies in Literature and Language*
UMSE	*University of Mississippi Studies in English*
UTQ	*University of Toronto Quarterly: A Canadian Journal of the Humanities*
V&I	*Voix et Images: Littérature Québécoise*
VQR	*Virginia Quarterly Review*
WAL	*Western American Literature*
WCR	*West Coast Review*
WLWE	*World Literature Written in English*
WS	*Women's Studies: An Interdisciplinary Journal*
YR	*Yale Review: A National Quarterly*

American Novel Explication

ABBEY, EDWARD (1927–1989)

Black Sun (1971)

    McCann, Garth. *Edward Abbey*, 35–37.

    Pilkington, William T. "Edward Abbey: Western Philosopher." *Western American Literature* 9 (1974): 17–31. Rpt. in Pilkington, William T., ed. *Critical Essays on the Western American Novel*, 214–215, 217–218, 220.

Brave Cowboy (1956)

    McCann, Garth. *Edward Abbey*, 13–17, 18–19.

    Pilkington, William T. "Edward Abbey: Western Philosopher." *Western American Literature* 9 (1974): 17–31. Rpt. in Pilkington, William T., ed. *Critical Essays on the Western American Novel*, 211–212, 219.

Desert Solitaire (1968)

    McCann, Garth. *Edward Abbey*, 20–29.

    Pilkington, William T. "Edward Abbey: Western Philosopher." *Western American Literature* 9 (1974): 17–31. Rpt. in Pilkington, William T., ed. *Critical Essays on the Western American Novel*, 213–214, 216–217, 218, 219, 220.

Fire on the Mountain (1962)

    McCann, Garth. *Edward Abbey*, 17–20.

    Pilkington, William T. "Edward Abbey: Western Philosopher." *Western American Literature* 9 (1974): 17–31. Rpt. in Pilkington, William T., ed. *Critical Essays on the Western American Novel*, 212–213.

Jonathan Troy (1954)

    McCann, Garth. *Edward Abbey*, 10–13.

Monkey Wrench Gang (1975)

    McCann, Garth. *Edward Abbey*, 37–40.

ADAMS, F. COLBURN (ca. 1850–1891(?))

Justice in the By-Ways (1856)

    Woodell, Harold. "Justice Denied in the Old South: Three Novels by F. Colburn Adams." *SLJ* 11.1 (1978): 60–63.

Manuel Pereira (1853)

Woodell, Harold. "Justice Denied in the Old South: Three Novels by F. Colburn Adams." *SLJ* 11.1 (1978): 57–59, 62–63.

Our World (1855)

Woodell, Harold. "Justice Denied in the Old South: Three Novels by F. Colburn Adams." *SLJ* 11.1 (1978): 59–60, 62–63.

ADAMS, HENRY (1838–1918)

Democracy (1880)

Auchincloss, Louis. *Henry Adams*, 20–21.
Bishop, Ferman. *Henry Adams*, 54–62.
Donoghue, Denis. "American Style of Failure." *SewR* 82 (1974): 418–419.
Henderson, Harry B. *Versions of the Past*, 212–219.
Lyon, Melvin. *Symbol and Idea in Henry Adams*, 25–36, 144–145, 199.
Rowe, John Carlos. *Henry Adams and Henry James*, 55–65.
Schlereth, Thomas J. "Fiction and Facts: Henry Adams's *Democracy* and Gore Vidal's *1876*." *SoQ* 16 (1978): 209–222.
Stineback, David C. *Shifting World*, 61–74.
Wolfe, Patrick. "Revealing Fiction of Henry Adams." *NEQ* 49 (1976): 399–425.

Esther (1884)

Auchincloss, Louis. *Henry Adams*, 21–22.
Barber, David S. "Henry Adams' *Esther:* The Nature of Individuality and Immortality." *NEQ* 45 (1972): 227–240.
Bishop, Ferman. *Henry Adams*, 63–68.
Lyon, Melvin. *Symbol and Idea in Henry Adams*, 37–57, 144–146, 198–199, 205–206.
Rowe, John Carlos. *Henry Adams and Henry James*, 55–65.
Wolfe, Patrick. "Revealing Fiction of Henry Adams." *NEQ* 49 (1976): 399–425.

AGEE, JAMES (1909–1955)

Death in the Family (1957)

Coles, Robert. *Irony in the Mind's Life*, 56–106.
Kramer, Victor A. *James Agee*, 143–155.
Larsen, Erling. *James Agee*, 37–45.
Moreau, Geneviéve. *Restless Journey of James Agee*, 263–268.
Perry, J. Douglas, Jr. "Thematic Counterpoint in *A Death in the Family:* The Function of the Six Extra Scenes." *Novel* 5 (1972): 234–241.
Ruoff, Gene W. "*Death in the Family:* Agee's 'Unfinished' Novel," in French, Warren, ed. *Fifties*, 121–132.
Rupp, Richard H. *Celebration in Postwar American Fiction*, 107–110.
Ward, J. A. "*Death in the Family:* The Importance of Wordlessness." *MFS* 26 (1980–81): 597–611.
Whittier, Gayle. "Belief and Unbelief in *A Death in the Family*." *Renascence* 31 (1979): 177–192.

ALCOTT, LOUISA MAY (1832–1888)

Jo's Boys (1886)

Auerbach, Nina. "Austen and Alcott on Matriarchy: New Women or New Wives?" *Novel* 10 (1976): 25–26.

Auerbach, Nina. "Austen and Alcott on Matriarchy: New Women or New Wives?", in Spilka, Mark, ed. *Towards a Poetics of Fiction*, 285–286.

Little Men (1871)

Auerbach, Nina. "Austen and Alcott on Matriarchy: New Women or New Wives?" *Novel* 10 (1976): 24–25.

Auerbach, Nina. "Austen and Alcott on Matriarchy: New Women or New Wives?", in Spilka, Mark, ed. *Towards a Poetics of Fiction*, 284–285.

Little Women (1868)

Auerbach, Nina. "Austen and Alcott on Matriarchy: New Women or New Wives?" *Novel* 10 (1976): 17–24.

Auerbach, Nina. "Austen and Alcott on Matriarchy: New Women or New Wives?", in Spilka, Mark, ed. *Towards a Poetics of Fiction*, 277–284.

Auerbach, Nina. *Communities of Women*, 55–73.

Moers, Ellen. *Literary Women*, 87–89.

Spacks, Patricia Meyer. *Female Imagination*, 95–101.

Work (1873)

Auerbach, Nina. "Austen and Alcott on Matriarchy: New Women or New Wives?" *Novel* 10 (1976): 23.

Moers, Ellen. *Literary Women*, 86–87.

ALGER, HORATIO (1832–1899)

Jed, the Poorhouse Boy (1900)

Walters, Thomas N. "Twain's Finn and Alger's Gilman: Picaresque Counter-Directions." *MarkR* 3 (1972): 53–58.

Ragged Dick (1868)

Weiher, Carol. "Horatio Alger's Fiction: American Fairy Tales for All Ages." *CEA* 40.2 (1978): 23–27.

ALGREN, NELSON (1909–1981)

Man with the Golden Arm (1949)

Cox, Martha Heasley and Wayne Chatterton. *Nelson Algren*, 111–133.

Gelfant, Blanche Housman. *American City Novel*, 252–255.

Grebstein, Sheldon Norman. "Nelson Algren and the Whole Truth," in French, Warren, ed. *Forties*, 302–303, 305–308.

Never Come Morning (1942)

Cox, Martha Heasley and Wayne Chatterton. *Nelson Algren*, 93–110.

Grebstein, Sheldon Norman. "Nelson Algren and the Whole Truth," in French, Warren, ed. *Forties*, 302–305.

Umphlett, Wiley Lee. *Sporting Myth and the American Experience*, 102–109.

Somebody in Boots (1935)

Cox, Martha Heasley and Wayne Chatterton. *Nelson Algren*, 59–73.
Grebstein, Sheldon Norman. "Nelson Algren and the Whole Truth," in French, Warren, ed. *Forties*, 301–302.

Walk on the Wild Side (1956)

Cox, Martha Heasley and Wayne Chatterton. *Nelson Algren*, 73–92.

ANAYA, RUDOLFO (1937–)

Bless Me, Ultima (1972)

Lattin, Vernon E. "Quest for Mythic Vision in Contemporary Native American and Chicano Fiction." *AL* 50 (1979): 628–632, 637.
Mitchell, Carol. "Rudolfo Anaya's *Bless Me, Ultima:* Folk Culture in Literature." *Crit* 22.1 (1980): 55–64.
Robinson, Cecil. *Mexico and the Hispanic Southwest in American Literature*, 324–328.

ANDERSON, POUL (1926–)

Broken Sword (1954)

Miesel, Sandra. *Against Time's Arrow*, 15–24.

Operation Chaos (1971)

Miesel, Sandra. *Against Time's Arrow*, 7–15.

Tau Zero (1970)

Miesel, Sandra. *Against Time's Arrow*, 51–59.

ANDERSON, SHERWOOD (1876–1941)

Beyond Desire (1932)

Bunge, Nancy L. "Ambiguous Endings of Sherwood Anderson's Novels," in Campbell, Hilbert H. and Charles E. Modlin, eds. *Sherwood Anderson*, 252–253, 259–261.
Cook, Sylvia Jenkins. *From Tobacco Road to Route 66*, 130–135.
White, Ray Lewis. "Warmth of Desire: Sex in Anderson's Novels," in Anderson, David D., ed. *Sherwood Anderson, Dimensions of His Literary Art*, 36–38.

Dark Laughter (1925)

Bunge, Nancy L. "Ambiguous Endings of Sherwood Anderson's Novels," in Campbell, Hilbert H. and Charles E. Modlin, eds. *Sherwood Anderson*, 252, 256, 258–259.
Burbank, Rex. "Artist as Prophet," in Burbank, Rex. *Sherwood Anderson*. Boston: Twayne Publishers, Inc., 1964. 107–123. Rpt. in Rideout, Walter B., ed. *Sherwood Anderson*, 74–76.
Fanning, Michael. "Black Mystics, French Cynics, Sherwood Anderson." *BALF* 11 (1977): 49–53.
Folks, Jeffrey J. "Anderson's Satiric Portrait of William Faulkner in *Dark Laughter*." *NMW* 12 (1979): 23–29.

White, Ray Lewis. "Warmth of Desire: Sex in Anderson's Novels," in Anderson, David D., ed. *Sherwood Anderson, Dimensions of His Literary Art*, 34–36

Kit Brandon (1936)

Bunge, Nancy L. "Ambiguous Endings of Sherwood Anderson's Novels," in Campbell, Hilbert H. and Charles E. Modlin, eds. *Sherwood Anderson*, 252–253, 256.

Taylor, Welford Dunaway. *Sherwood Anderson*, 86–94.

White, Ray Lewis. "Warmth of Desire: Sex in Anderson's Novels," in Anderson, David D., ed. *Sherwood Anderson, Dimensions of His Literary Art*, 38–39.

Many Marriages (1923)

Bunge, Nancy L. "Ambiguous Endings of Sherwood Anderson's Novels," in Campbell, Hilbert H. and Charles E. Modlin, eds. *Sherwood Anderson*, 256–258.

Burbank, Rex. "Artist as Prophet," in Burbank, Rex. *Sherwood Anderson*. Boston: Twayne Publishers, Inc., 1964. 107–123. Rpt. in Rideout, Walter B., ed. *Sherwood Anderson*, 72–74.

White, Ray Lewis. "Warmth of Desire: Sex in Anderson's Novels," in Anderson, David D., ed. *Sherwood Anderson, Dimensions of His Literary Art*, 32–34.

Marching Men (1917)

Ditsky, John. "Sherwood Anderson's *Marching Men:* Unnatural Disorder and the Art of Force." *TCL* 23 (1977): 102–114.

Weber, Brom. "Sherwood Anderson," in Walcutt, Charles Child, ed. *Seven Novelists in the American Naturalist Tradition*, 179–183.

White, Ray Lewis. "Warmth of Desire: Sex in Anderson's Novels," in Anderson, David D., ed. *Sherwood Anderson, Dimensions of His Literary Art*, 27–29

Poor White (1920)

Bunge, Nancy L. "Ambiguous Endings of Sherwood Anderson's Novels," in Campbell, Hilbert H. and Charles E. Modlin, eds. *Sherwood Anderson*, 253, 254–256.

Gelfant, Blanche Housman. *American City Novel*, 99–106.

Gelfant, Blanche Housman. "A Novel of Becoming," in Gelfant, Blanche Housman. *American City Novel*. Norman, OK: University of Oklahoma Press, 1954. 99–106. Rpt. in Rideout, Walter B., ed. *Sherwood Anderson*, 59–64.

Rosenman, John B. "Anderson's *Poor White* and Faulkner's *Absalom, Absalom!*" *MissQ* 29 (1976): 437–438.

Taylor, Welford Dunaway. *Sherwood Anderson*, 75–86.

Weber, Brom. "Sherwood Anderson," in Walcutt, Charles Child, ed. *Seven Novelists in the American Naturalist Tradition*, 191–192.

White, Ray Lewis. "Warmth of Desire: Sex in Anderson's Novels," in Anderson, David D., ed. *Sherwood Anderson, Dimensions of His Literary Art*, 30–32.

Windy McPherson's Son (1919)

Bunge, Nancy L. "Ambiguous Endings of Sherwood Anderson's Novels," in Campbell, Hilbert H. and Charles E. Modlin, eds. *Sherwood Anderson*, 253–254.

Scafidel, J. R. "Sexuality in *Windy McPherson's Son*." *TCL* 23 (1977): 94–101.

Weber, Brom. "Sherwood Anderson," in Walcutt, Charles Child, ed. *Seven Novelists in the American Naturalist Tradition*, 177–179.

White, Ray Lewis. "Warmth of Desire: Sex in Anderson's Novels," in Anderson, David D., ed. *Sherwood Anderson, Dimensions of His Literary Art*, 25–27.

ANGELO, VALENTI (1897–)

Golden Gate (1939)

Green, Rose Basile. *Italian-American Novel*, 86–90.

AQUIN, HUBERT (1929–1977)

Antiphonary see *L'antiphonaire*

Blackout see *Trou de mémoire*

Hamlet's Twin see *Neige noire*

L'antiphonaire (1969)

Beausang, Michael. "Music and Medicine." *CanL* 58 (1973): 71–76.

Cagnon, Maurice. "Parody and Caricature in Hubert Aquin's *L'antiphonaire*." *Crit* 19.2 (1977): 5–12.

Chesneau, Albert. "Déchiffrons *l'antiphonaire*." *V&I* 1.1 (1975): 26–34.

Gagnon, Marcel. "Une lecture de *L'antiphonaire*," dans Boucher, Yvon, ed. *Hubert Aquin*, 105–107.

Iqbal, Françoise Maccabée. *Hubert Aquin romancier*, 169–220.

Iqbal, Françoise. "*L'antiphonaire*," dans Boucher, Yvon, ed. *Hubert Aquin*, 67–101.

La Bossière, Camille René. "Hubert Aquin's Revolutionary Commedia dell'arte of Hell: A Baroque Impasse." *Mosaic* 11.3 (1978): 122.

La Fontaine, Gilles de. *Hubert Aquin et le Québec*, 71–78.

Mélançon, Robert. "Le Téléviseur vide ou comment lire *l'antiphonaire*." *V&I* 3 (1977): 244–262.

Pelletier, Jacques. "Sur Neige noire: L'Oeuvre ouverte de Hubert Aquin." *V&I* 1.1 (1975): 20–21.

Sugden, Leonard W. "Hubert Aquin: Proteus in Despair." *ECW* 11 (1978): 73–94.

Neige noire (1974)

Houde, Christiane. "Scénario et fiction: *Neige noire*." *V&I* 2 (1977): 418–435.

La Bossière, Camille René. "Hubert Aquin's Revolutionary Commedia dell'arte of Hell: A Baroque Impasse." *Mosaic* 11.3 (1978): 122–124.

La Bossière, Camille. "Hubert Aquin's Revolutionary Commedia Dell'arte of Hell: A Baroque Impasse," in Wortley, John, ed. *Post-War Canadian Fiction*, 122–124.

La Fontaine, Gilles de. *Hubert Aquin et le Québec*, 78–91.

Maccabée-Iqbal, Françoise. *Hubert Aquin romancier*, 223–262.

Maccabée-Iqbal, Françoise. "L'appel du Nord dans *Neige noire*: La quête de Narcisse." *V&I* 5 (1980): 365–375.

Merivale, Patricia. "Chiaroscuro: *Neige noire/Hamlet's Twin*." *DR* 60 (1980): 318–330.

Pelletier, Jacques. "Sur Neige noire: L'Oeuvre ouverte de Hubert Aquin." *V&I* 1.1 (1975): 21–25.

Sugden, Leonard W. "Hubert Aquin: Proteus in Despair." *ECW* 11 (1978): 73–94.

Vuong-Riddick, Thuong. "*Neige noire*: une esthétique de la transcréativité," dans Boucher, Yvon, ed. *Hubert Aquin*, 115–119.

Point de fuite (1971)

Leduc, Jean. "Sur *Point de fuite*," dans Boucher, Yvon, ed. *Hubert Aquin*, 109–113.

Prochain épisode (1965)

Atwood, Margaret. *Survival*, 227–228.

Belleau, André. *Le romancier fictif*, 136–137.

Cohn-Sfetcu, Ofelia. "To Live in Abundance of Life: Time in Canadian Literature." *CanL* 76 (1978): 28–29.

Cohn-Sfectu, Ofelia. "To Write or to Be Written? Hubert Aquin's *Prochain épisode*." *MFS* 22 (1976): 449–456.

Dvorak, Marta. "Une analyse structurale," dans Boucher, Yvon, ed. *Hubert Aquin*, 25–31.

La Bossière, Camille René. "Hubert Aquin's Revolutionary Commedia dell'arte of Hell: A Baroque Impasse." *Mosaic* 11.3 (1978): 119–121.

La Bossière, Camille. "Hubert Aquin's Revolutionary Commedia dell'arte of Hell: A Baroque Impasse," in Wortley, John, ed. *Post-War Canadian Fiction*, 119–120.

La Fontaine, Gilles de. *Hubert Aquin et le Québec*, 59–63.

Lapierre, René. *Les masques du récit: Lecture de Prochain épisode de Hubert Aquin*. Ville LaSalle, PQ: Éditions Hurtubise HMH, Limitée, 1980.

Lasnier, Louis. "Spatio-analyse de *Prochain épisode*," dans Boucher, Yvon, ed. *Hubert Aquin*, 33–50.

Maccabée-Iqbal, Françoise. *Hubert Aquin romancier*, 11–61.

Melançon, Joseph. "Le procès métaphorique dans *Prochain épisode*," dans Boucher, Yvon, ed. *Hubert Aquin*, 15–24.

Pelletier, Jacques. "Sur Neige noire: L'Oeuvre ouverte de Hubert Aquin." *V&I* 1.1 (1975): 20.

Poulin, Gabrielle. *Romans du pays*, 195–198.

Shek, Ben-Zion. *Social Realism*, 278–279, 280–281.

Smart, Patricia. *Hubert Aquin, agent double*, 25–64.

Sugden, Leonard W. "Hubert Aquin: Proteus in Despair." *ECW* 11 (1978): 73–94.

Sutherland, Ronald. "Fourth Separatism." *CanL* 45 (1970): 9–11.

Sutherland, Ronald. *Second Image*, 16–23, 112–116.

Urbas, Jeannette. *From Thirty Acres to Modern Times*, 138–141, 143.

Trou de mémoire (1968)

Brind'Amour, Lucie. "Sur *Trou de mémoire:* Le révolutionnaire pris au piège." *V&I* 5 (1980): 557–564.

Brown, Russell M. "In Search of Lost Causes: The Canadian Novelist as Mystery Writer," in Wortley, John, ed. *Post-War Canadian Fiction*, 7–8.

La Bossière, Camille René. "Hubert Aquin's Revolutionary Commedia dell'arte of Hell: A Baroque Impasse." *Mosaic* 11.3 (1978): 121–122.

La Bossière, Camille. "Hubert Aquin's Revolutionary Commedia dell'arte of Hell: A Baroque Impasse," in Wortley, John, ed. *Post-War Canadian Fiction*, 121–122.

La Fontaine, Gilles de. *Hubert Aquin et le Québec*, 63–71.

Maccabée-Iqbal, Françoise. *Hubert Aquin romancier*, 65–165.

Martel, Jean-Pierre. "*Trou de mémoire:* un jeu formel mortel," dans Boucher, Yvon, ed. *Hubert Aquin*, 55–64.

Pelletier, Jacques. "Sur Neige noire: L'Oeuvre ouverte de Hubert Aquin." *V&I* 1.1 (1975): 20.

Shek, Ben-Zion. *Social Realism*, 279–280, 281.

Smart, Patricia. *Hubert Aquin, agent double*, 65–123.

Sugden, Leonard W. "Hubert Aquin: Proteus in Despair." *ECW* 11 (1978): 73–94.

ARCHAMBAULT, GILLES (1933–)

Les pins parasols (1976)
 Poulin, Gabrielle. *Romans du pays*, 152–156.

Umbrella Pines see *Les pins parasols*

ARLEO, JOSEPH (1933–)

Grand Street Collector (1970)
 Green, Rose Basile. *Italian-American Novel*, 277–282.

ARNOLD, JUNE (1926–1982)

Applesauce (1966)
 Morgan, Ellen. "Humanbecoming: Form & Focus in the Neo-Feminist Novel," in
 Cornillon, Susan Koppelman, ed. *Images of Women in Fiction*, 193–197.

ARNOW, HARRIETTE (1908–1986)

Dollmaker (1954)
 Eckley, Wilton. *Harriette Arnow*, 85–100.
 Hobbs, Glenda. "Portrait of the Artist as Mother: Harriette Arnow and *The Doll-
 maker*." *GR* 3 (1979): 851–866.
 Lee, Dorothy H. "Harriette Arnow's *The Dollmaker:* A Journey to Awareness."
 Crit 20.2 (1978): 92–98.
 Oates, Joyce Carol. *New Heaven, New Earth*, 99–110.

Hunter's Horn (1949)
 Eckley, Wilton. *Harriette Arnow*, 63–84.

Mountain Path (1936)
 Eckley, Wilton. *Harriette Arnow*, 45–55.

Weedkiller's Daughter (1970)
 Eckley, Wilton. *Harriette Arnow*, 110–121.

ARVONEN, HELEN

Least of All Evils (1970)
 Russ, Joanna. "Somebody's Trying to Kill Me and I Think It's My Husband: The
 Modern Gothic." *JPC* 6 (1973): 666–691.

ASCH, SHOLEM (1880–1957)

East River (1946)
 Gelfant, Blanche Housman. *American City Novel*, 246–247.

ASIMOV, ISAAC (1920–1992)

Caves of Steel (1954)
 Fiedler, Jean and Jim Mele. "Asimov's Robots," in Riley, Dick, ed. *Critical Encounters*, 13–16.

Miller, Marjorie Mithoff. "Social Science Fiction of Isaac Asimov," in Olander, Joseph D. and Martin Harry Greenberg, eds. *Isaac Asimov*, 27–28.

Milman, Fern. "Human Reactions to Technological Change in Asimov's Fiction," in Olander, Joseph D. and Martin Harry Greenberg, eds. *Isaac Asimov*, 123–124, 127–128, 133–134.

Moore, Maxine. "Use of Technical Metaphors in Asimov's Fiction," in Olander, Joseph D. and Martin Harry Greenberg, eds. *Isaac Asimov*, 79–82.

Patrouch, Joseph F., Jr. *Science Fiction of Isaac Asimov*, 159–171.

Pierce, Hazel. " 'Elementary, My Dear . . .': Asimov's Science Fiction Mysteries," in Olander, Joseph D. and Martin Harry Greenberg, eds. *Isaac Asimov*, 39–40, 43–44.

Samuelson, David. *Visions of Tomorrow*, 127–162.

Warrick, Patricia S. *Cybernetic Imagination in Science Fiction*, 61–62.

Watt, Donald. "Galaxy Full of People: Characterization in Asimov's Major Fiction," in Olander, Joseph D. and Martin Harry Greenberg, eds. *Isaac Asimov*, 144–145.

Currents of Space (1952)

Moore, Maxine. "Use of Technical Metaphors in Asimov's Fiction," in Olander, Joseph D. and Martin Harry Greenberg, eds. *Isaac Asimov*, 83.

Patrouch, Joseph F., Jr. *Science Fiction of Isaac Asimov*, 137–141.

End of Eternity (1955)

Ash, Brian. *Faces of the Future*, 155–157.

Lem, Stanislaw. "Time-Travel Story and Related Matters of SF Structuring," in Rose, Mark, ed. *Science Fiction*, 81.

Miller, Marjorie Mithoff. "Social Science Fiction of Isaac Asimov," in Olander, Joseph D. and Martin Harry Greenberg, eds. *Isaac Asimov*, 21–22.

Milman, Fern. "Human Reactions to Technological Change in Asimov's Fiction," in Olander, Joseph D. and Martin Harry Greenberg, eds. *Isaac Asimov*, 128–129, 133.

Moore, Maxine. "Asimov, Calvin and Moses," in Clareson, Thomas D., ed. *Voices for the Future* (Vol. 1), 90–91.

Moore, Maxine. "Use of Technical Metaphors in Asimov's Fiction," in Olander, Joseph D. and Martin Harry Greenberg, eds. *Isaac Asimov*, 76, 77–78.

Patrouch, Joseph F., Jr. *Science Fiction of Isaac Asimov*, 141–150.

Watt, Donald. "Galaxy Full of People: Characterization in Asimov's Major Fiction," in Olander, Joseph D. and Martin Harry Greenberg, eds. *Isaac Asimov*, 148–149.

Gods Themselves (1972)

Hark, Ina Rae. "Unity in the Composite Novel: Triadic Patterning in Asimov's *The Gods Themselves*." *SFS* 6 (1979): 281–286.

Miller, Marjorie Mithoff. "Social Science Fiction of Isaac Asimov," in Olander, Joseph D. and Martin Harry Greenberg, eds. *Isaac Asimov*, 23–24, 30.

Milman, Fern. "Human Reactions to Technological Change in Asimov's Fiction," in Olander, Joseph D. and Martin Harry Greenberg, eds. *Isaac Asimov*, 126–127.

Watt, Donald. "Galaxy Full of People: Characterization in Asimov's Major Fiction," in Olander, Joseph D. and Martin Harry Greenberg, eds. *Isaac Asimov*, 150–157.

Naked Sun (1957)

Fiedler, Jean and Jim Mele. "Asimov's Robots," in Riley, Dick, ed. *Critical Encounters*, 17–20.

Miller, Marjorie Mithoff. "Social Science Fiction of Isaac Asimov," in Olander, Joseph D. and Martin Harry Greenberg, eds. *Isaac Asimov*, 28–29.

Milman, Fern. "Human Reactions to Technological Change in Asimov's Fiction," in Olander, Joseph D. and Martin Harry Greenberg, eds. *Isaac Asimov*, 125–126, 134.

Moore, Maxine. "Asimov, Calvin and Moses," in Clareson, Thomas D., ed. *Voices for the Future* (Vol. 1), 95–101.

Moore, Maxine. "Use of Technical Metaphors in Asimov's Fiction," in Olander, Joseph D. and Martin Harry Greenberg, eds. *Isaac Asimov*, 82–83.

Patrouch, Joseph F., Jr. *Science Fiction of Isaac Asimov*, 171–180.

Pierce, Hazel. " 'Elementary, My Dear . . .': Asimov's Science Fiction Mysteries," in Olander, Joseph D. and Martin Harry Greenberg, eds. *Isaac Asimov*, 44–49.

Watt, Donald. "Galaxy Full of People: Characterization in Asimov's Major Fiction," in Olander, Joseph D. and Martin Harry Greenberg, eds. *Isaac Asimov*, 145–147.

Pebble in the Sky (1950)

Miller, Marjorie Mithoff. "Social Science Fiction of Isaac Asimov," in Olander, Joseph D. and Martin Harry Greenberg, eds. *Isaac Asimov*, 25–26, 27.

Moore, Maxine. "Use of Technical Metaphors in Asimov's Fiction," in Olander, Joseph D. and Martin Harry Greenberg, eds. *Isaac Asimov*, 83–85.

Patrouch, Joseph F., Jr. *Science Fiction of Isaac Asimov*, 115–131.

Stars Like Dust (1951)

Milman, Fern. "Human Reactions to Technological Change in Asimov's Fiction," in Olander, Joseph D. and Martin Harry Greenberg, eds. *Isaac Asimov*, 132–133.

Patrouch, Joseph F., Jr. *Science Fiction of Isaac Asimov*, 131–137.

ATHERTON, GERTRUDE (1857–1948)

American Wives and English Husbands (1898)

McClure, Charlotte S. *Gertrude Atherton*, 66–70.

Ancestors (1907)

McClure, Charlotte S. *Gertrude Atherton*, 70–76.

McClure, Charlotte S. "Gertrude Atherton's California Woman," in Lee, L. L. and Merrill Lewis, ed. *Women, Women Writers, and the West*, 106–107.

Black Oxen (1923)

McClure, Charlotte S. *Gertrude Atherton*, 99–108.

Californians (1898)

McClure, Charlotte S. *Gertrude Atherton*, 62–66.

McClure, Charlotte S. "Gertrude Atherton's California Woman," in Lee, L. L. and Merrill Lewis, ed. *Women, Women Writers, and the West*, 105–106.

Conqueror (1902)

McClure, Charlotte S. *Gertrude Atherton*, 84–87.

Dido (1929)

McClure, Charlotte S. *Gertrude Atherton*, 114–115.

Golden Peacock (1936)

McClure, Charlotte S. *Gertrude Atherton*, 115.

Horn of Life (1942)

McClure, Charlotte S. *Gertrude Atherton*, 124–128.

House of Lee (1940)

McClure, Charlotte S. *Gertrude Atherton*, 119–124.
McClure, Charlotte S. "Gertrude Atherton's California Woman," in Lee, L. L. and Merrill Lewis, ed. *Women, Women Writers, and the West*, 108.

Immortal Marriage (1927)

McClure, Charlotte S. *Gertrude Atherton*, 110–112.

Jealous Gods (1928)

McClure, Charlotte S. *Gertrude Atherton*, 112–114.

Julia France (1912)

McClure, Charlotte S. *Gertrude Atherton*, 91–95.

Patience Sparhawk (1897)

McClure, Charlotte S. *Gertrude Atherton*, 55–62.

Perch of the Devil (1914)

McClure, Charlotte S. *Gertrude Atherton*, 95–97.

Sisters-in-Law (1921)

McClure, Charlotte S. "Gertrude Atherton's California Woman," in Lee, L. L. and Merrill Lewis, ed. *Women, Women Writers, and the West*, 107–108.

Tower of Ivory (1910)

McClure, Charlotte S. *Gertrude Atherton*, 87–91.

ATTAWAY, WILLIAM (1911–1986)

Blood on the Forge (1941)

Felgar, Robert. "William Attaway's Unaccommodated Protagonists." *SIBL* 4.1 (1973): 1, 2–3.
Gayle, Addison, Jr. *Way of the New World*, 162–166.
Vaughn, Philip H. "From Pastoralism to Industrial Antipathy in William Attaway's Blood on the Forge." *Phylon* 36 (1975): 422–425.
Wade, Melvin and Margaret Wade. "Black Aesthetic in the Black Novel." *JBS* 2.4 (1972): 395.

Let Me Breathe Thunder (1939)

Felgar, Robert. "William Attaway's Unaccommodated Protagonists." *SIBL* 4.1 (1973): 1–2.
Gayle, Addison, Jr. *Way of the New World*, 160–162.

ATWOOD, MARGARET (1939–)

Edible Woman (1969)

Brown, Russell M. "Atwood's Sacred Wells." *ECW* 17 (1980): 9–10, 24–25, 32.

Dooley, D. J. *Moral Vision*, 137–147.

Grace, Sherrill. *Violent Duality*, 86–96.

Griffith, Margaret. "Verbal Terrain in the Novels of Margaret Atwood." *Crit* 21.3 (1980): 85–87.

Lauber, John. "Alice in Consumer-Land: The Self Discovery of Marian MacAlpine," in Moss, John, ed. *Here and Now*, 19–31.

Lyons, Bonnie. " 'Neither Victims nor Executioners' in Margaret Atwood's Fiction." *WLWE* 17 (1978): 182–183.

MacLulich, T. D. "Atwood's Adult Fairy Tale: Levi-Strauss, Bettelheim, and *The Edible Woman*." *ECW* 11 (1978): 111–129.

Onley, Gloria. "Power Politics in Bluebeard's Castle." *CanL* 60 (1974): 24–25, 29.

Woodcock, George. "Margaret Atwood: Poet as Novelist," in Woodcock, George, ed. *Canadian Novel*, 314–316.

Woodcock, George. *World of Canadian Writing*, 153–155.

Lady Oracle (1976)

Brown, Russell M. "Atwood's Sacred Wells." *ECW* 17 (1980): 9, 24, 32–33.

Cude, Wilfred. "Bravo Mothball! An Essay on *Lady Oracle*," in Moss, John, ed. *Here and Now*, 45–50.

Cude, Wilfred. *Due Sense of Differences*, 154–170, 203–206.

Cude, Wilfred. "The Truth Was Not Convincing: A Review of *Lady Oracle*," *Fiddlehead* (Winter, 1977): 133–137. Rpt. in Cude, Wilfred. *Due Sense of Differences*, 133–152.

Grace, Sherrill. *Violent Duality*, 111–128.

Griffith, Margaret. "Verbal Terrain in the Novels of Margaret Atwood." *Crit* 21.3 (1980): 90–93.

Irvine, Lorna. "Psychological Journey: Mothers and Daughters in English-Canadian Fiction," in Davidson, Cathy N. and E. M. Broner, eds. *Lost Tradition*, 244–245.

Jones, Anne G. "Margaret Atwood: Songs of the Transformer, Songs of the Transformed." *HC* 16.3 (1979): 13–14.

Woodcock, George. *World of Canadian Writing*, 168–169.

Life Before Man (1979)

Brown, Russell M. "Atwood's Sacred Wells." *ECW* 17 (1980): 7, 10.

Grace, Sherrill. *Violent Duality*, 135–138.

Surfacing (1972)

Boutelle, Ann. "Dorian Gray Phenomenon in Canadian Literature." *DR* 57 (1977): 270–272.

Brown, Russell M. "Atwood's Sacred Wells." *ECW* 17 (1980): 9, 24, 26–31, 32.

Brown, Russell M. "In Search of Lost Causes: The Canadian Novelist as Mystery Writer," in Wortley, John, ed. *Post-War Canadian Fiction*, 9–11.

Campbell, Josie P. "Woman as Hero in Margaret Atwood's *Surfacing*." *Mosaic* 11.3 (1978): 17–28.

Campbell, Josie P. "Woman as Hero in Margaret Atwood's *Surfacing*," in Wortley, John, ed. *Post-War Canadian Fiction*, 17–28.

Colman, S. J. "Margaret Atwood, Lucien Goldmann's Pascal, and the Meaning of 'Canada'." *UTQ* 48 (1979): 251–260.

Davidson, Arnold E. and Cathy N. Davidson. "Anatomy of Margaret Atwood's *Surfacing*." *Ariel* 10.3 (1979): 38–54.

Endres, Robin. "Marxist Literary Criticism and English Canadian Literature," in Cappon, Paul, ed. *In Our Own House*, 115, 117–119, 121–122.

Garebian, Keith. "*Surfacing:* Apocalyptic Ghost Story." *Mosaic* 9.3 (1976): 1–9.

Grace, Sherrill. *Violent Duality*, 97–110.

Griffith, Margaret. "Verbal Terrain in the Novels of Margaret Atwood." *Crit* 21.3 (1980): 87–90.

Harrison, James. "20,000,000 Solitudes of *Surfacing*." *DR* 59 (1979): 74–81.

Irvine, Lorna. "Psychological Journey: Mothers and Daughters in English-Canadian Fiction," in Davidson, Cathy N. and E. M. Broner, eds. *Lost Tradition*, 250.

Jones, Anne G. "Margaret Atwood: Songs of the Transformer, Songs of the Transformed." *HC* 16.3 (1979): 7–8, 9–13.

King, Bruce. "Margaret Atwood's *Surfacing*." *JCL* 12.1 (1977): 23–32.

Lyons, Bonnie. " 'Neither Victims nor Executioners' in Margaret Atwood's Fiction." *WLWE* 17 (1978): 183–186.

McLay, Catherine. "Divided Self: Theme and Pattern in *Surfacing*," in Moss, John, ed. *Here and Now*, 32–44.

Miller, Hugh. "Surfacing to No Purpose: Margaret Atwood's Apparent Survival." *AntR* 24 (1976): 59–61.

Moss, John. *Sex and Violence*, 123–132, 139–144, 145.

Northey, Margot. *Haunted Wilderness*, 65–69.

Onley, Gloria. "Margaret Atwood: Surfacing in the Interests of Survival." *WCR* 7.3 (1973): 52–53.

Onley, Gloria. "Power Politics in Bluebeard's Castle." *CanL* 60 (1974): 21–22, 26–32, 37–41.

Quigley, Theresia. "*Surfacing:* A Critical Study." *AntR* 34 (1978): 77–87.

Regan, Nancy. "Home of One's Own: Women's Bodies in Recent Women's Fiction." *JPC* 11 (1978): 782–784.

Rigny, Barbara Hill. *Madness and Sexual Politics in the Feminist Novel*, 93–115, 119–127.

Ross, Catherine Sheldrick. "Nancy Drew as Shaman: Atwood's *Surfacing*." *CanL* 84 (1980): 7–17.

Rubenstein, Roberta. "*Surfacing:* Margaret Atwood's Journey to the Interior." *MFS* 22 (1976): 387–399.

Schaeffer, Susan F. " 'It Is Time that Separates Us': Margaret Atwood's *Surfacing*." *CentR* 18 (1974): 319–337.

Sullivan, Rosemary. "*Surfacing* and *Deliverance*." *CanL* 67 (1976): 6–19.

Woodcock, George. "Margaret Atwood: Poet as Novelist," in Woodcock, George, ed. *Canadian Novel*, 324–327.

Woodcock, George. "Surfacing to Survive: Notes of the Recent Atwood." *Ariel* 4.3 (1973): 25–28.

Woodcock, George. *World of Canadian Writing*, 163–166.

AUBERT DE GASPÉ, PHILIPPE (1786–1871)

Les anciens Canadiens (1863)

Hathorn, Ramon. "Soldats, patrons et femmes 'fatales': Figures de l'Anglais' dans le roman québécois des XIXe et XXe siècles." *V&I* 6 (1980): 99–100.

Waterson, Elizabeth. "Politics of Conquest in Canadian Historical Fiction." *Mosaic* 3.1 (1969): 116–124.

AUBERT DE GASPÉ, PHILIPPE (1814–1841)

Le chercheur de trésors see *L'influence d'un livre*

L'influence d'un livre (1837)
  Northey, Margot. *Haunted Wilderness*, 33–41.

AUCHINCLOSS, LOUIS (1917–)

Embezzler (1966)
  Milne, Gordon. *Sense of Society*, 245.

Great World and Timothy Colt (1956)
  Milne, Gordon. *Sense of Society*, 242–243.

House of Five Talents (1960)
  Tuttleton, James W. *Novel of Manners in America*, 253–257.

Portrait in Brownstone (1962)
  Tuttleton, James W. *Novel of Manners in America*, 251–253.

Sybil (1952)
  Milne, Gordon. *Sense of Society*, 241–242.

Venus in Sparta (1958)
  Milne, Gordon. *Sense of Society*, 244.

World of Profit (1968)
  Long, Robert E. "Image of Gatsby in the Fiction of Louis Auchincloss and C.D.B. Bryan." *F-H Annual* (1972): 325–326.

BAKER, ELLIOTT (1922–)

Fine Madness (1964)
  Bryant, Jerry H. *Open Decision*, 213–215.

BALDWIN, JAMES (1924–1987)

Another Country (1962)
  Alexander, Charlotte. "The 'Stink' of Reality: Mothers and Whores in James Baldwin's Fiction." *Literature and Psychology* 18.1 (1968): 9–26. Rpt. in Kinnamon, Keneth, ed. *James Baldwin*, 83–90.
  Austen, Roger. *Playing the Game*, 201–204.
  Beja, Morris. *Epiphany in the Modern Novel*, 212–213.
  Berghahn, Marion. *Images of Africa in Black American Literature*, 178–180.
  Bone, Robert A. "James Baldwin," in Bone, Robert A. *Negro Novel in America*. Revised Edition. New Haven: Yale University Press, 1965. 215–239. Rpt. in Kinnamon, Keneth, ed. *James Baldwin*, 41–51.

Bone, Robert A. "Novels of James Baldwin." *Tri-Quarterly* 2 (Winter 1965): 3–20. Rpt. in Hemenway, Robert, ed. *Black Novelist*, 124–133.

Collier, Eugenia W. "Phrase Unbearably Repeated," in O'Daniel, Therman B., ed. *James Baldwin*, 38–46.

Davis, Arthur P. *From the Dark Tower*, 219–220.

Ferguson, Alfred R. "Black Men, White Cities: The Quest for Humanity by Black Protagonists in James Baldwin's *Another Country* and Richard Wright's *The Outsider*." *BallS* 18.2 (1977): 51–54.

Foster, David E. " 'Cause my house fell down': The Theme of the Fall in Baldwin's Novels." *Crit* 13.3 (1971): 59–62.

Gayle, Addison, Jr. *Way of the New World*, 214–220.

Gibson, Donald B. "James Baldwin: The Political Anatomy of Space," in O'Daniel, Therman B., ed. *James Baldwin*, 10–14.

Gibson, Donald B. "Ralph Ellison and James Baldwin," in Panichas, George A., ed. *Politics of Twentieth-Century Novelists*, 317–318.

Gross, Barry. " 'Uninhabitable Darkness' of Baldwin's *Another Country:* Image and Theme." *NALF* 6 (1972): 113–121.

Kent, George E. "Baldwin and the Problem of Being." *CLA Journal* 7.3 (1964): 202–214. Rpt. in Gibson, Donald B., ed. *Five Black Writers*, 155–157.

Kent, George E. "Baldwin and the Problem of Being." *CLA Journal* 7.3 (1964): 202–214. Rpt. in Kinnamon, Keneth, ed. *James Baldwin*, 25–26.

Kent, George E. "Baldwin and the Problem of Being," in O'Daniel, Therman B., ed. *James Baldwin*, 26–28.

Lash, John S. "Baldwin Beside Himself: A Study in Modern Phallicism," in O'Daniel, Therman B., ed. *James Baldwin*, 48–55.

Macebuh, Stanley. *James Baldwin*, 83–100.

MacInnes, Colin. "Dark Angel: The Writings of James Baldwin." *Encounter* 21 (1963): 22–23. Rpt. in Gibson, Donald B., ed. *Five Black Writers*, 132–136.

Newman, Charles. "Lesson of the Master: Henry James and James Baldwin." *Yale Review* 56.1 (Oct 1966): 45–59. Rpt. in Kinnamon, Keneth, ed. *James Baldwin*, 54–62.

Orsagh, Jacqueline E. "Baldwin's Female Characters: A Step Forward?" in O'Daniel, Therman B., ed. *James Baldwin*, 59–66, 68.

Pratt, Louis H. *James Baldwin*, 64–71.

Rosenblatt, Roger. *Black Fiction*, 151–158.

Rosenblatt, Roger. " 'Negro Everyman' and His Humor," in Levin, Harry, ed. *Veins of Humor*, 236.

Rupp, Richard H. *Celebration in Postwar American Fiction*, 144–148.

Schultz, Elizabeth. " 'Free in Fact and at Last': The Image of the Black Woman in Black American Fiction," in Springer, Marlene, ed. *What Manner of Woman*, 338–339.

Sylvander, Carolyn Wedin. *James Baldwin*, 52–66.

Werner, Craig. "Economic Evolution of James Baldwin." *CLAJ* 23 (1979): 23–25.

Williams, Sherley Anne. *Give Birth to Brightness*, 150–152.

Wilson, Robert N. *Writer as Social Seer*, 91–92, 94–104.

Giovanni's Room (1956)

Alexander, Charlotte. "The 'Stink' of Reality: Mothers and Whores in James Baldwin's Fiction." *Literature and Psychology* 18.1 (1968): 9–26. Rpt. in Kinnamon, Keneth, ed. *James Baldwin*, 77–83, 93–94.

Austen, Roger. *Playing the Game*, 149–152.

Bigsby, C. W. E. "From Protest to Paradox: The Black Writer at Mid Century," in French, Warren, ed. *Fifties*, 237–238.

Bone, Robert A. "James Baldwin," in Bone, Robert A. *Negro Novel in America*. Revised Edition. New Haven: Yale University Press, 1965. 215–239. Rpt. in Kinnamon, Keneth, ed. *James Baldwin*, 38–40.

Bone, Robert A. "Novels of James Baldwin." *Tri-Quarterly* 2 (Winter 1965): 3–20. Rpt. in Hemenway, Robert, ed. *Black Novelist*, 122–124.

Davis, Arthur P. *From the Dark Tower*, 218–219.

Foster, David E. " 'Cause my house fell down': The Theme of the Fall in Baldwin's Novels." *Crit* 13.3 (1971): 55–59.

Gibson, Donald B. "James Baldwin: The Political Anatomy of Space," in O'Daniel, Therman B., ed. *James Baldwin*, 8–10.

Gibson, Donald B. "Ralph Ellison and James Baldwin," in Panichas, George A., ed. *Politics of Twentieth-Century Novelists*, 316–317.

Kent, George E. "Baldwin and the Problem of Being." *CLA Journal* 7.3 (1964): 202–214. Rpt. in Gibson, Donald B., ed. *Five Black Writers*, 154–155.

Kent, George E. "Baldwin and the Problem of Being." *CLA Journal* 7.3 (1964): 202–214. Rpt. in Kinnamon, Keneth, ed. *James Baldwin*, 23–24.

Kent, George E. "Baldwin and the Problem of Being," in O'Daniel, Therman B., ed. *James Baldwin*, 25–26.

Klotman, Phyllis Rauch. *Another Man Gone*, 64–69.

Lash, John S. "Baldwin Beside Himself: A Study in Modern Phallicism," in O'Daniel, Therman B., ed. *James Baldwin*, 48–55.

Macebuh, Stanley. *James Baldwin*, 69–82.

MacInnes, Colin. "Dark Angel: The Writings of James Baldwin." *Encounter* 21 (1963): 22–23. Rpt. in Gibson, Donald B., ed. *Five Black Writers*, 126–131.

Pratt, Louis H. *James Baldwin*, 58–64.

Rupp, Richard H. *Celebration in Postwar American Fiction*, 139–144.

Sylvander, Carolyn Wedin. *James Baldwin*, 45–52, 65.

Werner, Craig. "Economic Evolution of James Baldwin." *CLAJ* 23 (1979): 21–23.

Go Tell It on the Mountain (1952)

Alexander, Charlotte. "The 'Stink' of Reality: Mothers and Whores in James Baldwin's Fiction." *Literature and Psychology* 18.1 (1968): 9–26. Rpt. in Kinnamon, Keneth, ed. *James Baldwin*, 90–93.

Allen, Shirley S. "Ironic Voice in Baldwin's *Go Tell It on the Mountain*," in O'Daniel, Therman B., ed. *James Baldwin*, 30–37.

Berghahn, Marion. *Images of Africa in Black American Literature*, 171–172, 176.

Bigsby, C. W. E. "From Protest to Paradox: The Black Writer at Mid Century," in French, Warren, ed. *Fifties*, 235–237.

Bone, Robert A. "James Baldwin," in Bone, Robert A. *Negro Novel in America*. Revised Edition. New Haven: Yale University Press, 1965. 215–239. Rpt. in Kinnamon, Keneth, ed. *James Baldwin*, 31–38.

Bone, Robert A. "Novels of James Baldwin." *Tri-Quarterly* 2 (Winter 1965): 3–20. Rpt. in Hemenway, Robert, ed. *Black Novelist*, 115–121.

Bryant, Jerry H. "Wright, Ellison, Baldwin: Exorcising the Demon." *Phylon* 37 (1976): 184–187.

Davis, Arthur P. *From the Dark Tower*, 217–218.

Emerson, O. B. "Cultural Nationalism in Afro-American Literature," in Lewald, H. Ernest, ed. *Cry of Home*, 227–230.

Fabre, Michel. "Fathers and Sons in James Baldwin's *Go Tell it on the Mountain.*" *Etudes Anglaises* 23.1 (1970): 47–61. Rpt. in Cooke, M. G., ed. *Modern Black Novelists*, 88–104.

Fabre, Michel. "Fathers and Sons in James Baldwin's *Go Tell it on the Mountain.*" *Etudes Anglaises* 23.1 (1970): 47–61. Rpt. in Kinnamon, Keneth, ed. *James Baldwin*, 120–138.

Foster, David E. " 'Cause my house fell down': The Theme of the Fall in Baldwin's Novels." *Crit* 13.3 (1971): 50–55.

Gibson, Donald B. "James Baldwin: The Political Anatomy of Space," in O'Daniel, Therman B., ed. *James Baldwin*, 5–8.

Kent, George E. "Baldwin and the Problem of Being." *CLA Journal* 7.3 (1964): 202–214. Rpt. in Gibson, Donald B., ed. *Five Black Writers*, 149–153.

Kent, George E. "Baldwin and the Problem of Being." *CLA Journal* 7.3 (1964): 202–214. Rpt. in Kinnamon, Keneth, ed. *James Baldwin*, 18–22.

Kent, George E. "Baldwin and the Problem of Being," in O'Daniel, Therman B., ed. *James Baldwin*, 20–24.

Macebuh, Stanley. *James Baldwin*, 49–67.

MacInnes, Colin. "Dark Angel: The Writings of James Baldwin." *Encounter* 21 (1963): 22–23. Rpt. in Gibson, Donald B., ed. *Five Black Writers*, 121–126.

May, John R. *Toward a New Earth*, 155–161.

May, John R., S. J. "Images of Apocalypse in the Black Novel." *Renascence* 23 (1970): 37–39.

Pratt, Louis H. *James Baldwin*, 50–58.

Rosenblatt, Roger. *Black Fiction*, 36–54.

Rupp, Richard H. *Celebration in Postwar American Fiction*, 137–139.

Scruggs, Charles. "Tale of Two Cities in James Baldwin's *Go Tell It on the Mountain.*" *AL* 52 (1980): 1–17.

Starke, Catherine Juanita. *Black Portraiture in American Fiction*, 204–207.

Sylvander, Carolyn Wedin. *James Baldwin*, 27–44.

Wade, Melvin and Margaret Wade. "Black Aesthetic in the Black Novel." *JBS* 2.4 (1972): 401–402.

Werner, Craig. "Economic Evolution of James Baldwin." *CLAJ* 23 (1979): 19–21.

Wilson, Robert N. *Writer as Social Seer*, 92–96.

If Beale Street Could Talk (1974)

Farrison, William Edward. "If Baldwin's Train Has Not Gone," in O'Daniel, Therman B., ed. *James Baldwin*, 78–81.

Harris, Trudier. "Eye as Weapon in *If Beale Street Could Talk.*" *MELUS* 5.3 (1978): 54–66.

Pratt, Louis H. *James Baldwin*, 77–80.

Schultz, Elizabeth. " 'Free in Fact and at Last': The Image of the Black Woman in Black American Fiction," in Springer, Marlene, ed. *What Manner of Woman*, 338.

Sylvander, Carolyn Wedin. *James Baldwin*, 83–88.

Werner, Craig. "Economic Evolution of James Baldwin." *CLAJ* 23 (1979): 28–30.

Just Above My Head (1979)

Sylvander, Carolyn Wedin. *James Baldwin*, 125–141.

Tell Me How Long the Train's Been Gone (1968)

Davis, Arthur P. *From the Dark Tower*, 220.

Farrison, William Edward. "If Baldwin's Train Has Not Gone," in O'Daniel, Therman B., ed. *James Baldwin*, 69–78.

Gibson, Donald B. "James Baldwin: The Political Anatomy of Space," in O'Daniel, Therman B., ed. *James Baldwin*, 14–18.

Howe, Irving. "James Baldwin: At Ease in Apocalypse." *Harper's Magazine* 237, no. 1420 (Sept 1968): 92, 95–100. Rpt. in Kinnamon, Keneth, ed. *James Baldwin*, 99–108.

Macebuh, Stanley. *James Baldwin*, 147–164.

Orsagh, Jacqueline E. "Baldwin's Female Characters: A Step Forward?" in O'Daniel, Therman B., ed. *James Baldwin*, 66–68.

Pratt, Louis H. *James Baldwin*, 71–76.

Sylvander, Carolyn Wedin. *James Baldwin*, 67–83.

Werner, Craig. "Economic Evolution of James Baldwin." *CLAJ* 23 (1979): 25–28.

BALLARD, J. G. (1930–)

Atrocity Exhibition see *Love and Napalm*

Crystal World (1966)

Franklin, H. Bruce. "What Are We to Make of J. G. Ballard's Apocalypse?" in Clareson, Thomas, ed. *Voices for the Future* (Vol. 2), 95–98.

Samuelson, David. *Visions of Tomorrow*, 339–369.

Drowned World (1962)

Franklin, H. Bruce. "What Are We to Make of J. G. Ballard's Apocalypse?" in Clareson, Thomas, ed. *Voices for the Future* (Vol. 2), 91–93, 98–99.

Love and Napalm (1970)

Franklin, H. Bruce. "What Are We to Make of J. G. Ballard's Apocalypse?" in Clareson, Thomas, ed. *Voices for the Future* (Vol. 2), 101–103.

Wind from Nowhere (1962)

Franklin, H. Bruce. "What Are We to Make of J. G. Ballard's Apocalypse?" in Clareson, Thomas, ed. *Voices for the Future* (Vol. 2), 89–91.

BALMER, EDWIN (1883–1959)

After Worlds Collide (1934)

Bendau, Clifford P. *Philip Wylie*, 16.

When Worlds Collide (1932)

Bendau, Clifford P. *Philip Wylie*, 13–16.

BARAKA, AMIRI (1934–)

System of Dante's Hell (1965)

Brown, Lloyd W. *Amiri Baraka*, 59–83.

Brown, Lloyd W. "LeRoi Jones (Imamu Amiri Baraka) as Novelist: Theme and Structure in *The System of Dante's Hell*." *NALF* 7 (1973): 132–142.

Brown, Lloyd W. "Jones (Baraka) and His Literary Heritage in *The System of Dante's Hell.*" *Obsidian* 1.1 (Spring 1975): 5–17. Rpt. in Benston, Kimberly W., ed. *Imamu Amiri Baraka (LeRoi Jones)*, 71–83.

Hudson, Theodore R. *From LeRoi Jones to Amiri Baraka*, 111–118.

May, John R., S. J. "Images of Apocalypse in the Black Novel." *Renascence* 23 (1970): 39–40.

Vickery, Olga W. "Inferno of the Moderns," in Friedman, Melvin J. and John B. Vickery, eds. *Shaken Realist*, 157.

BARNES, DJUNA (1892–1982)

Nightwood (1936)

Austen, Roger. *Playing the Game*, 82–84.

Baird, James. "Djuna Barnes and Surrealism: 'Backward Grief,' " in Baldwin, Kenneth H. and David R. Kirby, eds. *Individual and Community: Variations on a Theme in American Fiction*, 174–180.

Greiner, Donald J. "Djuna Barnes' *Nightwood* and the American Origins of Black Humor." *Crit* 17.1 (1975): 41–54.

Gunn, Edward. "Myth and Style in Djuna Barnes's *Nightwood*." *MFS* 19 (1973–74): 545–555.

Johnsen, William A. "Modern Women Novelists: *Nightwood* and the Novel of Sensibility." *BuR* 21.1 (1973): 29–42.

Kannenstine, Louis F. *Art of Djuna Barnes*, 86–126.

Littlejohn, David. *Interruptions*, 28.

Nadeau, Robert L. "*Nightwood* and the Freudian Unconscious." *IFR* 2 (1975): 159–163.

Nelson, Gerald B. *Ten Versions of America*, 93–108.

Pochoda, Elizabeth. "Style's Hoax: A Reading of Djuna Barnes's *Nightwood*." *TCL* 22 (1976): 179–191.

Scott, James B. *Djuna Barnes*, 86–119.

Spencer, Sharon. *Space, Time and Structure in the Modern Novel*, 40–43.

Ryder (1928)

Baird, James. "Djuna Barnes and Surrealism: 'Backward Grief,' " in Baldwin, Kenneth H. and David R. Kirby, eds. *Individual and Community: Variations on a Theme in American Fiction*, 168–174.

Kannenstine, Louis F. *Art of Djuna Barnes*, 34–47.

Scott, James B. *Djuna Barnes*, 61–78.

BARNES, MARGARET AYER (1886–1967)

Edna, His Wife (1935)

Taylor, Lloyd C., Jr. *Margaret Ayer Barnes*, 91–111.

Westward Passage (1931)

Taylor, Lloyd C., Jr. *Margaret Ayer Barnes*, 58–72.

Wisdom's Gate (1938)

Taylor, Lloyd C., Jr. *Margaret Ayer Barnes*, 112–128.

Within This Present (1933)

Taylor, Lloyd C., Jr. *Margaret Ayer Barnes*, 73–90.

Years of Grace (1930)

Taylor, Lloyd C., Jr. *Margaret Ayer Barnes*, 40–57.

BARR, ROBERT (1850–1912)

O'Ruddy (1903)

Nagel, James. *Stephen Crane and Literary Impressionism*, 39–40.

BARRIO, RAYMOND (1921–)

Plum Plum Pickers (1969)

Lattin, Vernon E. "Paradise and Plums: Appearance and Reality in Barrio's *The Plum Plum Pickers*." *Crit* 19.1 (1977): 49–57.

Robinson, Cecil. *Mexico and the Hispanic Southwest in American Literature*, 319–321.

BARTH, JOHN (1930–)

End of the Road (1958)

Allen, Mary. *Necessary Blankness*, 17, 20–21.

Boyers, Robert. "Attitudes Toward Sex in American 'High Culture.' " *Annals of the American Academy of Political and Social Science* (March 1968). Rpt. in Boyers, Robert. *Excursions*, 122–124.

Bryant, Jerry H. *Open Decision*, 289–293.

Davis, Cynthia. "Heroes, Earth Mothers and Muses: Gender Identity in Barth's Fiction." *CentR* 24 (1980): 309–314.

Farwell, Harold. "John Barth's Tenuous Affirmation: 'The Absurd, Unending Possibility of Love'." *Georgia Review* 28 (1974): 290–306. Rpt. in Waldmeir, Joseph J., ed. *Critical Essays on John Barth*, 57–58.

Fraustino, Daniel V. "*Country Wife* Comes to *The End of the Road:* Wycherley Bewitches Barth." *ArQ* 33 (1977): 76–86.

Gross, Beverly. "Anti-Novels of John Barth," in Waldmeir, Joseph J., ed. *Critical Essays on John Barth*, 32–33, 35–36.

Harris, Charles B. *Contemporary American Novelists of the Absurd*, 104–105.

Hauck, Richard Boyd. *Cheerful Nihilism*, 217–222.

Hendin, Josephine. *Vulnerable People*, 75–78.

Joseph, Gerhard. *John Barth*, 15–28.

Kennard, Jean E. *Number and Nightmare*, 65–67.

Kerner, David. "Psychodrama in Eden." *Chicago Review* 13 (Winter/Spring 1959): 59–67. Rpt. in Waldmeir, Joseph J., ed. *Critical Essays on John Barth*, 91–95.

Lehan, Richard. *Dangerous Crossing*, 175–177.

McConnell, Frank D. *Four Postwar American Novelists*, 126–132.

Majdiak, Daniel. "Barth and the Representation of Life." *Criticism* 12 (Winter 1970): 51–67. Rpt. in Waldmeir, Joseph J., ed. *Critical Essays on John Barth*, 96–109.

May, John R. *Toward a New Earth*, 174–180.

Morrell, David. *John Barth*, 17–26, 29–30.

Noland, Richard W. "John Barth and the Novel of Comic Nihilism." *Contemporary*

Literature 7 (Autumn 1966): 239–257. Rpt. in Waldmeir, Joseph J., ed. *Critical Essays on John Barth*, 18–20.

Purdy, Strother B. *Hole in the Fabric*, 182–185.

Rogers, Robert. *Psychoanalytic Study of the Double in Literature*, 167–171.

Schwartz, Richard Alan. "Some Formal Devices in John Barth's Early Novels." *NConL* 10.3 (1980): 7–8.

Stark, John. *Literature of Exhaustion*, 136.

Tanner, Tony. *City of Words*, 235–240.

Tharpe, Jac. *John Barth*, 24–33.

Floating Opera (1956)

Allen, Mary. *Necessary Blankness*, 18–19.

Bryant, Jerry H. *Open Decision*, 286–289.

Davis, Cynthia. "Heroes, Earth Mothers and Muses: Gender Identity in Barth's Fiction." *CentR* 24 (1980): 309–314.

Farwell, Harold. "John Barth's Tenuous Affirmation: 'The Absurd, Unending Possibility of Love'." *Georgia Review* 28 (1974): 290–306. Rpt. in Waldmeir, Joseph J., ed. *Critical Essays on John Barth*, 57.

Gross, Beverly. "Anti-Novels of John Barth," in Waldmeir, Joseph J., ed. *Critical Essays on John Barth*, 31–32, 35.

Harris, Charles B. "Todd Andrews: Ontological Insecurity, and *The Floating Opera*." *Crit* 18.2 (1976): 34–50.

Hauck, Richard Boyd. *Cheerful Nihilism*, 210–216.

Hendin, Josephine. *Vulnerable People*, 78–80.

Hyman, Stanley Edgar. "John Barth's First Novel." *New Leader* (12 April 1965). Rpt. in Waldmeir, Joseph J., ed. *Critical Essays on John Barth*, 75–78.

Joseph, Gerhard. *John Barth*, 9–15.

Kennard, Jean E. *Number and Nightmare*, 60–65.

Korkowski, Eugene. "Excremental Vision of Barth's Todd Andrews." *Crit* 18.2 (1976): 51–58.

LeClair, Thomas. "Death and Black Humor." *Crit* 17.1 (1975): 17–19.

LeClair, Thomas. "John Barth's *The Floating Opera*: Death and the Craft of Fiction." *TSLL* 14 (1972): 711–730.

Lehan, Richard. *Dangerous Crossing*, 172–175.

McConnell, Frank D. *Four Postwar American Novelists*, 119–126.

Martin, Dennis M. "Desire and Disease: The Psychological Pattern of *The Floating Opera*." *Crit* 18.2 (1976): 17–33.

Morrell, David. *John Barth*, 1–7.

Noland, Richard W. "John Barth and the Novel of Comic Nihilism." *Contemporary Literature* 7 (Autumn 1966): 239–257. Rpt. in Waldmeir, Joseph J., ed. *Critical Essays on John Barth*, 15–18.

Schwartz, Richard Alan. "Some Formal Devices in John Barth's Early Novels." *NConL* 10.3 (1980): 6–7.

Stark, John. *Literature of Exhaustion*, 135–136, 148.

Tanner, Stephen L. "John Barth's Hamlet." *SR* 56 (1971): 347–354.

Tanner, Tony. *City of Words*, 231–235.

Tatham, Campbell. "John Barth and the Aesthetics of Artifice." *ConL* 12 (1971): 64–66.

Tatham, Campbell. "John Barth and the Aesthetics of Artifice." *Contemporary*

Literature 12 (Winter 1971): 60–73. Rpt. in Waldmeir, Joseph J., ed. *Critical Essays on John Barth*, 46–47.

Tharpe, Jac. *John Barth*, 14–23.

Wallace, Ronald. *Last Laugh*, 26–44.

Giles Goat-Boy (1966)

Allen, Mary. *Necessary Blankness*, 15–16, 29–36.

Bryant, Jerry H. *Open Decision*, 299–302.

Davis, Cynthia. "Heroes, Earth Mothers and Muses: Gender Identity in Barth's Fiction." *CentR* 24 (1980): 309–314.

Farwell, Harold. "John Barth's Tenuous Affirmation: 'The Absurd, Unending Possibility of Love'." *Georgia Review* 28 (1974): 290–306. Rpt. in Waldmeir, Joseph J., ed. *Critical Essays on John Barth*, 59–60.

Gresham, James T. "*Giles Goat-Boy:* Satyr, Satire, and Tragedy Twined," in Waldmeir, Joseph J., ed. *Critical Essays on John Barth*, 157–170.

Gross, Beverly. "Anti-Novels of John Barth," in Waldmeir, Joseph J., ed. *Critical Essays on John Barth*, 33–35, 39–41.

Harris, Charles B. *Contemporary American Novelists of the Absurd*, 107–116.

Harris, Charles B. "George's Illumination: Unity in *Giles Goat-Boy.*" *SNNTS* 8 (1976): 172–184.

Hauck, Richard B. "Comic Christ and the Modern Reader," in Waldmeir, Joseph J., ed. *Critical Essays on John Barth*, 147–149.

Hauck, Richard Boyd. *Cheerful Nihilism*, 230–236.

Hendin, Josephine. *Vulnerable People*, 82–84.

Joseph, Gerhard. *John Barth*, 31–38.

Kennard, Jean E. *Number and Nightmare*, 73–78.

Kostelanetz, Richard. "American Fiction in the Sixties," in Kostelanetz, Richard, ed. *On Contemporary Literature*, 646–650.

McConnell, Frank D. *Four Postwar American Novelists*, 140–151.

Morrell, David. *John Barth*, 60–66, 71–79.

Olderman, Raymond M. *Beyond the Waste Land*, 72–93.

Rodrigues, Eusebio L. "Living Sakhyan in Barth's *Giles Goat-Boy.*" *NConL* 2.4 (1972): 7–8.

Safer, Elaine B. "Allusive Mode and Black Humor in Barth's *Giles Goat-Boy* and Pynchon's *Gravity's Rainbow.*" *Renascence* 32 (1980): 90–93.

Scholes, Robert. *Fabulation and Metafiction*, 75–102.

Schulz, Max F. *Black Humor Fiction of the Sixties*, 31–32.

Sherman, Marilyn R. "*Giles Goat-Boy:* or, 'Reality' is No Place for a Hero," in Waldmeir, Joseph J., ed. *Critical Essays on John Barth*, 172–176.

Stark, John. *Literature of Exhaustion*, 120–121, 132–133, 137–139, 142–143, 147–148, 152–154, 160, 170–171.

Stuart, Dabney. "Service to the University," in Waldmeir, Joseph J., ed. *Critical Essays on John Barth*, 150–153.

Tanner, Tony. *City of Words*, 246–253.

Tatham, Campbell. "John Barth and the Aesthetics of Artifice." *ConL* 12 (1971): 68–71.

Tatham, Campbell. "John Barth and the Aesthetics of Artifice." *Contemporary Literature* 12 (Winter 1971): 60–73. Rpt. in Waldmeir, Joseph J., ed. *Critical Essays on John Barth*, 49–53.

Tharpe, Jac. *John Barth*, 52–90.

Tilton, John W. *Cosmic Satire in the Contemporary Novel*, 43–68.

Tilton, John W. "*Giles Goat-Boy:* An Interpretation." *BuR* 18.1 (1970): 93–119.

Tilton, John W. "*Giles Goat-Boy:* Satire Given Tragic Depth," in Garvin, Harry R., ed. *Makers of the Twentieth-Century Novel*, 290–308.

Waldmeir, Joseph J. "*Giles Goat-Boy*," in Waldmeir, Joseph J., ed. *Critical Essays on John Barth*, 154–156.

Walter, James F. "Psychronology of Lust in the Menippean Tradition: *Giles Goat-Boy.*" *TCL* 21 (1975): 394–410.

Weixlmann, Joseph. "*Giles Goat-Boy* and *J.B.*." *NConL* 7.3 (1977): 6.

Ziolkowski, Theodore. *Fictional Transfigurations of Jesus*, 256–266.

Sot-Weed Factor (1960)

Allen, Mary. *Necessary Blankness*, 17–18, 21–29.

Antush, John V. "Allotropic Doubles in Barth's *Sot-Weed Factor*." *CollL* 4 (1977): 71–79.

Bryant, Jerry H. *Open Decision*, 294–299.

Davis, Cynthia. "Heroes, Earth Mothers and Muses: Gender Identity in Barth's Fiction." *CentR* 24 (1980): 309–314.

Dippie, Brian W. " 'His Visage Wild, His Form Exotick': Indian Themes and Cultural Guilt in John Barth's *The Sot-Weed Factor*." *AQ* 21 (1969): 113–121.

Donald, Miles. *American Novel in the Twentieth Century*, 127–128.

Farwell, Harold. "John Barth's Tenuous Affirmation: 'The Absurd, Unending Possibility of Love'." *Georgia Review* 28 (1974): 290–306. Rpt. in Waldmeir, Joseph J., ed. *Critical Essays on John Barth*, 58–59.

Fiedler, Leslie A. "John Barth: An Eccentric Genius." *New Leader* (13 Feb 1961). Rpt. in Kostelanetz, Richard, ed. *On Contemporary Literature*, 239–243.

Fuller, Edmund. "Joke is on Mankind." *New York Times* (21 Aug 1960). Rpt. in Waldmeir, Joseph J., ed. *Critical Essays on John Barth*, 111–112.

Gross, Beverly. "Anti-Novels of John Barth," in Waldmeir, Joseph J., ed. *Critical Essays on John Barth*, 33, 36–38.

Harris, Charles B. *Contemporary American Novelists of the Absurd*, 105–107, 116–120.

Hauck, Richard Boyd. *Cheerful Nihilism*, 222–230.

Henderson, Harry B. *Versions of the Past*, 277–278, 280–285.

Holder, Alan. " 'What Marvelous Plot . . . Was Afoot?': John Barth's *Sot-Weed Factor*," in Waldmeir, Joseph J., ed. *Critical Essays on John Barth*, 123–132.

Joseph, Gerhard. *John Barth*, 28–31.

Kennard, Jean E. *Number and Nightmare*, 67–73.

Kostelanetz, Richard. "American Fiction in the Sixties," in Kostelanetz, Richard, ed. *On Contemporary Literature*, 636–639.

Lehan, Richard. *Dangerous Crossing*, 177–179.

McConnell, Frank D. *Four Postwar American Novelists*, 132–140.

Morrell, David. *John Barth*, 27, 31–45, 49–58.

Noland, Richard W. "John Barth and the Novel of Comic Nihilism." *Contemporary Literature* 7 (Autumn 1966): 239–257. Rpt. in Waldmeir, Joseph J., ed. *Critical Essays on John Barth*, 21–26.

Puetz, Manfred. "John Barth's *The Sot-Weed Factor:* The Pitfalls of Mythopoesis." *TCL* 22 (1976): 454–466.

Puetz, Manfred. "John Barth's *The Sot-Weed Factor:* The Pitfalls of Mythopoesis," in Waldmeir, Joseph J., ed. *Critical Essays on John Barth*, 134–144.

Rovit, Earl. "Novel as Parody: John Barth." *Critique* 6.2 (Fall 1963): 77–85. Rpt. in Waldmeir, Joseph J., ed. *Critical Essays on John Barth*, 116–122.

Schulz, Max F. *Black Humor Fiction of the Sixties*, 17–18, 29–30, 87–88..

Stark, John. *Literature of Exhaustion*, 119–120, 130–131, 133–134, 137, 142–143, 144–145, 147, 148–152, 170.

Sutcliffe, Denham. "Worth a Guilty Conscience," in Waldmeir, Joseph J., ed. *Critical Essays on John Barth*, 113–115.

Tanner, Tony. *City of Words*, 241–246.

Tatham, Campbell. "John Barth and the Aesthetics of Artifice." *ConL* 12 (1971): 66–68.

Tatham, Campbell. "John Barth and the Aesthetics of Artifice." *Contemporary Literature* 12 (Winter 1971): 60–73. Rpt. in Waldmeir, Joseph J., ed. *Critical Essays on John Barth*, 47–49.

Tharpe, Jac. *John Barth*, 34–51.

Vernon, John. *Garden and the Map*, 63–65, 67–69.

BARTHELME, DONALD (1931–1989)

Dead Father (1975)

Farmer, Betty Catherine Dobson. "Mythological, Biblical, and Literary Allusions in Donald Barthelme's *The Dead Father*." *IFR* 6 (1979): 40–48.

Snow White (1967)

Harris, Charles B. *Contemporary American Novelists of the Absurd*, 124–127.

Leland, John. "Remarks Re-marked: Barthelme, What Curios of Signs!" *BoundaryII* 5 (1977): 800–810.

Longleigh, Peter J., Jr. "Donald Barthelme's *Snow White*." *Crit* 11.3 (1969): 30–34.

McCaffrey, Larry. "Barthelme's *Snow White:* The Aesthetics of Trash." *Crit* 16.3 (1975): 19–32.

BASSO, HAMILTON (1904–1964)

Cinnamon Seed (1934)

Millichap, Joseph R. *Hamilton Basso*, 39–49.

Courthouse Square (1936)

Millichap, Joseph R. *Hamilton Basso*, 56–66.

Days before Lent (1939)

Green, Rose Basile. *Italian-American Novel*, 117–121.
Millichap, Joseph R. *Hamilton Basso*, 67–76.

Greenroom (1949)

Millichap, Joseph R. *Hamilton Basso*, 91–99.

In Their Own Image (1935)

Millichap, Joseph R. *Hamilton Basso*, 49–56.

Light Infantry Ball (1959)

Millichap, Joseph R. *Hamilton Basso*, 114–122.

Relics and Angels (1929)
Millichap, Joseph R. *Hamilton Basso*, 27–38.

Sun in Capricorn (1942)
Millichap, Joseph R. *Hamilton Basso*, 83–90.

Touch of the Dragon (1964)
Millichap, Joseph R. *Hamilton Basso*, 99–105.

View from Pompey's Head (1954)
Green, Rose Basile. *Italian-American Novel*, 121–125.
Millichap, Joseph R. *Hamilton Basso*, 107–114.

Wine of the Country (1941)
Millichap, Joseph R. *Hamilton Basso*, 76–83.

BAUM, L. FRANK (1856–1919)

Emerald City of Oz (1910)
Attebery, Brian. *Fantasy Tradition in American Literature*, 85.

Land of Oz (1904)
Attebery, Brian. *Fantasy Tradition in American Literature*, 101–102, 105.

Marvelous Land of Oz (1904)
Beckwith, Osmond. "Oddness of Oz." *ChildL* 5 (1976): 78–79, 81–91.

Ozma of Oz (1907)
Beckwith, Osmond. "Oddness of Oz." *ChildL* 5 (1976): 79–91.
Sale, Roger. "Child Reading and Man Reading: Oz, Babar, and Pooh." *ChildL* 162–164.

Road to Oz (1909)
Attebery, Brian. *Fantasy Tradition in American Literature*, 85, 87.

Wonderful Wizard of Oz (1900)
Attebery, Brian. *Fantasy Tradition in American Literature*, 83–87, 88–94, 96–101, 105.
Beckwith, Osmond. "Oddness of Oz." *ChildL* 5 (1976): 76–78, 81–91.

BEACH, JOSEPH WARREN (1880–1957)

Glass Mountain (1930)
Simmons, Michael K. "Look into *The Glass Mountain*." *AL* 41 (1969): 422–425.

BEAGLE, PETER S. (1939–)

Last Unicorn (1968)
Foust, R. E. "Fabulous Paradigm: Fantasy, Meta-Fantasy, and Peter S. Beagle's *The Last Unicorn*." *Extrapolation* 21 (1980): 5–20.
Norford, Don Parry. "Reality and Illusion in Peter Beagle's *The Last Unicorn*." *Crit* 19.2 (1977): 93–104.

Olderman, Raymond M. *Beyond the Waste Land*, 220–242.

Olsen, Alexandra Hennessey. "Anti-Consolatio: Boethius and *The Last Unicorn*." *Mosaic* 13.3–4 (1980): 133–144.

Stevens, David. "Incongruity in a World of Illusion: Patterns of Humor in Peter Beagle's *The Last Unicorn*." *Extrapolation* 20 (1979): 230–237.

BEAULIEU, VICTOR-LÉVY (1945–)

Blanche forcée (1976)

Pelletier, Jacques. "Une exploration de l'enfer québécois." *V&I* 3 (1977): 221–223.

Poulin, Gabrielle. *Romans du pays*, 410–419.

Don Quichotte de la démanche (1974)

Belleau, André. *Le romancier fictif*, 138.

Pelletier, Jacques. "Une exploration de l'enfer québécois." *V&I* 3 (1977): 202–203, 218–221.

Poulin, Gabrielle. *Romans du pays*, 404–409.

Vanasse, Andre. "Analyse de textes: Rejean Ducharme et Victor-Levy Beaulieu: Les mots el les choses." *V&I* 3 (1977): 232–233, 239–242.

Don Quixote in Nighttown see *Don Quichotte de la démanche*

Grandfathers see *Les grands-pères*

Jos connaissant (1970)

Bessette, Gérard. *Trois romanciers québécois*, 15–44, 120–121.

Pelletier, Jacques. "Une exploration de l'enfer québécois." *V&I* 3 (1977): 208–211.

Poulin, Gabrielle. *Romans du pays*, 392–395.

La nuitte de Malcomm Hudd (1969)

Bessette, Gérard. *Trois romanciers québécois*, 65–78, 119–120.

Pelletier, Jacques. "Une Exploration de l'enfer québécois." *V&I* 3 (1977): 206–208.

Poulin, Gabrielle. *Romans du pays*, 387–392.

Les grands-pères (1971)

Bessette, Gérard. *Trois romanciers québécois*, 81–96, 122–125.

Michon, Jacques. "Les avatars de l'histoire: *Les grands-pères* de Victor-Lévy Beaulieu." *V&I* 5 (1980): 307–316.

Pelletier, Jacques. "Une exploration de l'enfer québécois." *V&I* 3 (1977): 212–213.

Poulin, Gabrielle. *Romans du pays*, 396–401.

Mémoires d'outre-tonneau (1968)

Bessette, Gérard. *Trois romanciers québécois*, 47–48, 114–115.

Poulin, Gabrielle. *Romans du pays*, 378–379.

Monsieur Melville (1978)

Poulin, Gabrielle. *Romans du pays*, 434–438.

Oh Miami Miami Miami (1973)

Pelletier, Jacques. "Une exploration de l'enfer québécois." *V&I* 3 (1977): 215–221.

Poulin, Gabrielle. *Romans du pays*, 402–403.

Québécois Dream see *Un rêve québécois*

Race du monde! (1969)

Bessette, Gérard. *Trois romanciers québécois*, 51–61, 116–119.
Pelletier, Jacques. "Une exploration de l'enfer québécois." *V&I* 3 (1977): 204–206.
Poulin, Gabrielle. *Romans du pays*, 379–385.
Shek, Ben-Zion. *Social Realism*, 292.

Un rêve québécois (1972)

Bessette, Gérard. *Trois romanciers québécois*, 99–106, 125–128.
Pelletier, Jacques. "Une exploration de l'enfer québécois." *V&I* 3 (1977): 214–215.
Poulin, Gabrielle. *Romans du pays*, 38–39.

BECK, ROBERT see SLIM, ICEBERG

BECKER, STEPHEN D. (1927–)

When the War Is Over (1967)

Bennett, Lee Shaw. "Modern Civil War Novels: The Still Unwritten War?" *SoS* 19 (1980): 110–112.

BECKHAM, BARRY (1944–)

Runner Mack (1972)

Klotman, Phyllis Rauch. *Another Man Gone*, 141–146.

BEDFORD, DENTON R. (1907–)

Tsali (1972)

Larson, Charles R. *American Indian Fiction*, 126–131.

BELLAMY, EDWARD (1850–1898)

Duke of Stockbridge (1879)

Henderson, Harry B. *Versions of the Past*, 199–204.

Equality (1897)

Bowman, Sylvia E. "Utopian Views of Man and the Machine." *SLitI* 6.2 (1973): 109–114.
Roemer, Kenneth M. "Sex Roles, Utopia, and Change: The Family in Late Nineteenth-Century Utopian Literature." *AmerS* 13 (1972): 37–39.

Looking Backward (1888)

Beauchamp, Gorman. "*Iron Heel* and *Looking Backward:* Two Paths to Utopia." *ALR* 9 (1976): 308–310.
Bowman, Sylvia E. "Utopian Views of Man and the Machine." *SLitI* 6.2 (1973): 109–114.
Cornet, Robert J. "Rhetorical Strategies in *Looking Backward*." *MarkR* 4 (1974): 53–58.
Ketterer, David. *New Worlds for Old*, 103–118.

Roemer, Kenneth M. "Sex Roles, Utopia, and Change: The Family in Late Nine-teenth-Century Utopian Literature." *AmerS* 13 (1972): 37–39.

Scholes, Robert and Eric S. Rabkin. *Science Fiction*, 10–11.

Strauss, Sylvia. "Women in 'Utopia'." *SAQ* 75 (1976): 116–120, 127–130.

Thomas, W. K. *Fizz Inside*, 93–96.

Wilson, R. Jackson. "Experience and Utopia: The Making of Edward Bellamy's *Looking Backward*." *JAmS* 11 (1977): 45–60.

Winters, Donald E. "Utopianism of Survival: Bellamy's *Looking Backward* and Twain's *A Connecticut Yankee*." *AmerS* 21.1 (1980): 28–29, 30–31, 33–34, 35–37.

Miss Ludington's Sister (1884)

Hogan, Robert E. "*Dr. Heidenhoff's Process* and *Miss Ludington's Sister:* Edward Bellamy's Romances of Immortality." *SAF* 8 (1980): 51–66.

BELLOW, SAUL (1915–)

Adventures of Augie March (1954)

Aldridge, John W. *Devil in the Fire*, 224–230.

Alexander, Edward. *Resonance of Dust*, 173.

Alter, Robert. *After the Tradition*, 102–104.

Bryant, Jerry H. *Open Decision*, 350–353.

Christhilf, Mark M. "Death and Deliverance in Saul Bellow's Symbolic City." *BallS* 18.2 (1977): 9–10.

Clayton, John Jacob. *Saul Bellow*, 60–61, 74–76, 83–92, 107–112, 114–115, 122–128.

Cohen, Sarah Blacher. *Saul Bellow's Enigmatic Laughter*, 64–89.

Cohen, Sarah Blacher. "Sex: Saul Bellow's Hedonistic Joke." *Studies in American Fiction* 2 (1974): 223–229. Rpt. in Trachtenberg, Stanley, ed. *Critical Essays on Saul Bellow*, 176–177.

Galloway, David D. *Absurd Hero in American Fiction*, 94–104.

Gerson, Steven M. "New American Adam in *The Adventures of Augie March*." *MFS* 25 (1979): 117–128.

Gindin, James. *Harvest of a Quiet Eye*, 314–319.

Guttmann, Allen. *Jewish Writer in America*, 189–198.

Guttmann, Allen. "Saul Bellow's Humane Comedy," in Cohen, Sara Blacher, ed. *Comic Relief*, 129–135.

Hendin, Josephine. *Vulnerable People*, 106–107.

Jones, David R. "Disappointments of Maturity: Bellow's *The Adventures of Augie March*," in French, Warren, ed. *Fifties*, 83–92.

Klein, Marcus. "Discipline of Nobility: Saul Bellow's Fiction," in Rovit, Earl, ed. *Saul Bellow*, 138–139, 140–141, 142, 144–145, 146.

Klug, M. A. "Saul Bellow: The Hero in the Middle" *DR* 56 (1976): 462–478.

Kulshrestha, Chirantan. *Saul Bellow*, 97–107.

Lehan, Richard. *Dangerous Crossing*, 115–118.

McConnell, Frank D. *Four Postwar American Novelists*, 21–28.

Malin, Irving. *Saul Bellow's Fiction*, 10–11, 13–14, 21–24, 29–31, 39, 49–52, 63–66, 77–80, 87–88, 92–93, 97, 100–101, 106–107, 111–112, 119–120, 133–134, 137–138, 141–142.

Meyers, Jeffrey. "Brueghel and Augie March." *AL* 49 (1977): 113–119.

Meyers, Jeffrey. "Brueghel and Augie March." *American Literature* 49 (1977): 113–119. Rpt. in Trachtenberg, Stanley, ed. *Critical Essays on Saul Bellow*, 83–87.

Opdahl, Keith. " 'Stillness in the Midst of Chaos': Plot in the Novels of Saul Bellow." *MFS* 25 (1979): 15–28.

Porter, M. Gilbert. *Whence the Power?*, 61–101.

Rupp, Richard H. *Celebration in Postwar American Fiction*, 195–199.

Scheer-Schäzler, Brigitte. *Saul Bellow*, 33–58.

Schulz, Max F. *Radical Sophistication*, 110–125, 145, 146, 150–151.

Scott, Nathan A., Jr. *Three American Moralists*, 119–122.

Tanner, Tony. *City of Words*, 64–72.

Zietlow, E. R. "Saul Bellow: The Theater of the Soul." *Ariel* 4.4 (1973): 45.

Dangling Man (1944)

Abbott, H. Porter. "Saul Bellow and the 'Lost Cause' of Character." *Novel* 13 (1980): 265–271.

Alexander, Edward. *Resonance of Dust*, 171.

Alter, Robert. *After the Tradition*, 98–100.

Berets, Ralph. "Saul Bellow's Fiction: Repudiation and Reality Instruction in Saul Bellow's Fiction." *CentR* 20 (1976): 76–80.

Bryant, Jerry H. *Open Decision*, 342–344.

Christhilf, Mark M. "Death and Deliverance in Saul Bellow's Symbolic City." *BallS* 18.2 (1977): 10.

Clayton, John Jacob. *Saul Bellow*, 56–59, 61–69, 77–83, 97–105, 114, 115–122.

Cohen, Sarah Blacher. *Saul Bellow's Enigmatic Laughter*, 22–39.

Donoghue, Denis. *"Dangling Man,"* in Rovit, Earl, ed. *Saul Bellow*, 19–30.

Galloway, David D. *Absurd Hero in American Fiction*, 82–89.

Gindin, James. *Harvest of a Quiet Eye*, 305–309.

Glenday, Michael K. " 'The Consummating Glimpse': *Dangling Man*'s Treacherous Reality." *MFS* 25 (1979): 139–148.

Guttmann, Allen. *Jewish Writer in America*, 178–183.

Guttmann, Allen. "Saul Bellow's Humane Comedy," in Cohen, Sara Blacher, ed. *Comic Relief*, 128.

Hendin, Josephine. *Vulnerable People*, 107–109.

Klein, Marcus. "Discipline of Nobility: Saul Bellow's Fiction," in Rovit, Earl, ed. *Saul Bellow*, 136, 137.

Klug, M. A. "Saul Bellow: The Hero in the Middle" *DR* 56 (1976): 462–478.

Kulshrestha, Chirantan. *Saul Bellow*, 64–77.

Lehan, Richard. *Dangerous Crossing*, 109–111.

McConnell, Frank D. *Four Postwar American Novelists*, 11–15.

Malin, Irving. *Saul Bellow's Fiction*, 10, 11, 13, 16, 17–20, 26–28, 36–37, 46–48, 57–59, 71–74, 85–86, 90, 95, 98–100, 104, 109, 116–118, 128–129, 130–131, 135–136, 139–140.

May, Keith M. *Out of the Maelstrom*, 95–96.

Opdahl, Keith. " 'Stillness in the Midst of Chaos': Plot in the Novels of Saul Bellow." *MFS* 25 (1979): 15–28.

Porter, M. Gilbert. *Whence the Power?*, 6–28.

Rupp, Richard H. *Celebration in Postwar American Fiction*, 189–192.

Scheer-Schäzler, Brigitte. *Saul Bellow*, 8–17.

Schulz, Max F. *Radical Sophistication*, 148–150.

Scott, Nathan A., Jr. *Three American Moralists*, 114–116.

Henderson the Rain King (1959)

Alter, Robert. *After the Tradition*, 105–107.

Alter, Robert. "Jewish Humor and the Domestication of Myth," in Levin, Harry, ed. *Veins of Humor*, 257–260.

Axelrod, Robert. "Jewishness of Bellow's Henderson." *AL* 47 (1975): 439–443.

Berets, Ralph. "Saul Bellow's Fiction: Repudiation and Reality Instruction in Saul Bellow's Fiction." *CentR* 20 (1976): 88–91.

Borrus, Bruce J. "Bellow's Critique of the Intellect." *MFS* 25 (1979): 32–36.

Bryant, Jerry H. *Open Decision*, 353–357.

Campbell, Jeff H. "Bellow's Intimations of Immorality: *Henderson the Rain King*." *SNNTS* 1 (1969): 323–333.

Clayton, John Jacob. *Saul Bellow*, 166–185.

Cohen, Sarah Blacher. *Saul Bellow's Enigmatic Laughter*, 115–142.

Dougherty, David C. "Finding before Seeking: Theme in *Henderson the Rain King* and *Humboldt's Gift*." *MFS* 25 (1979): 93–101.

Edwards, Duane. "Quest for Reality in *Henderson the Rain King*." *DR* 53 (1973): 246–255.

Galloway, David D. *Absurd Hero in American Fiction*, 110–123.

Gindin, James. *Harvest of a Quiet Eye*, 322–326.

Guttmann, Allen. *Jewish Writer in America*, 201–210.

Guttmann, Allen. "Saul Bellow's Humane Comedy," in Cohen, Sara Blacher, ed. *Comic Relief*, 135–142.

Hays, Peter L. *Limping Hero*, 57–59.

Hendin, Josephine. *Vulnerable People*, 106–107.

Hull, Byron D. "*Henderson the Rain King* and William James." *Criticism* 13 (1971): 402–414.

Kehler, Joel R. "Henderson's Sacred Science." *CentR* 24 (1980): 232–247.

Klein, Marcus. "Discipline of Nobility: Saul Bellow's Fiction," in Rovit, Earl, ed. *Saul Bellow*, 136–137, 139–140, 142–144, 145–146, 149–152.

Klug, M. A. "Saul Bellow: The Hero in the Middle" *DR* 56 (1976): 462–478.

Knipp, Thomas R. "Cost of Henderson's Quest." *BallS* 10.2 (1969): 37–39.

Lehan, Richard. *Dangerous Crossing*, 121–125.

Lutwack, Leonard. *Heroic Fiction*, 100–121.

McConnell, Frank D. *Four Postwar American Novelists*, 30–36.

Malin, Irving. *Saul Bellow's Fiction*, 25–26, 33–35, 42–44, 53–54, 69–71, 81–84, 89–90, 93–95, 98, 103–104, 107–108, 114–116, 121, 129–130, 129–130, 133–134.

Majdiak, Daniel. "Romantic Self and *Henderson the Rain King*," in Garvin, Harry R., ed. *Makers of the Twentieth-Century Novel*, 276–289.

Markos, Donald W. "Life Against Death in *Henderson the Rain King*." *MFS* 17 (1971): 193–205.

Opdahl, Keith. " 'Stillness in the Midst of Chaos': Plot in the Novels of Saul Bellow." *MFS* 25 (1979): 15–28.

Pearce, Richard. "Ambiguous Assault of Henderson and Herzog," in Rovit, Earl, ed. *Saul Bellow*, 72–75, 79.

Pearce, Richard. *Stages of the Clown*, 103–116.

Pearson, Carol. "Bellow's *Henderson the Rain King* and the Myth of the King, the Fool, and the Hero." *NConL* 5.5 (1975): 8–11.

Porter, M. Gilbert. *Whence the Power?*, 127–145.

Rodrigues, Eusebio L. "Bellow's Africa." *AL* 43 (1971): 242–256.

Rodrigues, Eusebio L. "Reference to 'Joxi' in *Henderson the Rain King*." *NConL* 8.4 (1978): 9–10.

Rodrigues, Eusebio L. "Reichianism in *Henderson the Rain King*." *Criticism* 15 (1973): 212–233.

Rodrigues, Eusebio L. "Saul Bellow's Henderson as America." *CentR* 20 (1976): 189–195.

Rupp, Richard H. *Celebration in Postwar American Fiction*, 201–204.

Scheer-Schäzler, Brigitte. *Saul Bellow*, 78–89.

Schulz, Max F. *Radical Sophistication*, 110–125, 146.

Scott, Nathan A., Jr. *Three American Moralists*, 127–130.

Stout, Janis P. "Possibility of Affirmation in *Heart of Darkness* and *Henderson the Rain King*." *PQ* 57 (1978): 115–129.

Sullivan, Victoria. "Battle of the Sexes in Three Bellow Novels," in Rovit, Earl, ed. *Saul Bellow*, 107–114.

Toth, Susan A. "*Henderson the Rain King*, Eliot, and Browning." *NConL* 1.5 (1971): 6–8.

Towner, Daniel. "Brill's Ruins and Henderson's Rain." *Crit* 17.3 (1976): 96–101.

Zietlow, E. R. "Saul Bellow: The Theater of the Soul." *Ariel* 4.4 (1973): 45–47.

Herzog (1964)

Abbott, H. Porter. "Saul Bellow and the 'Lost Cause' of Character." *Novel* 13 (1980): 278–280.

Adams, Timothy Dow. "La Petite Madeleine: Proust and *Herzog*." *NConL* 8.1 (1978): 11.

Aldridge, John W. *Devil in the Fire*, 231–234.

Alter, Robert. *After the Tradition*, 107–109, 111–115.

Bailey, Jennifer M. "Qualified Affirmation of Saul Bellow's Recent Work." *JAmS* 7 (1973): 67–71, 75–76.

Berets, Ralph. "Saul Bellow's Fiction: Repudiation and Reality Instruction in Saul Bellow's Fiction." *CentR* 20 (1976): 91–95.

Bluefarb, Sam. "Middle-Aged Man in Contemporary Literature: Bloom to Herzog." *CLAJ* 20 (1976): 11–13.

Bryant, Jerry H. *Open Decision*, 357–363.

Christhilf, Mark M. "Death and Deliverance in Saul Bellow's Symbolic City." *BallS* 18.2 (1977): 17–20.

Clayton, John Jacob. *Saul Bellow*, 186–229.

Cohen, Sarah Blacher. *Saul Bellow's Enigmatic Laughter*, 143–175.

Cohen, Sarah Blacher. "Sex: Saul Bellow's Hedonistic Joke." *Studies in American Fiction* 2 (1974): 223–229. Rpt. in Trachtenberg, Stanley, ed. *Critical Essays on Saul Bellow*, 177–178.

Donald, Miles. *American Novel in the Twentieth Century*, 171–174.

Fuchs, Daniel. "*Herzog*: The Making of a Novel," in Trachtenberg, Stanley, ed. *Critical Essays on Saul Bellow*, 101–120.

Galloway, David D. *Absurd Hero in American Fiction*, 123–139.

Gindin, James. *Harvest of a Quiet Eye*, 326–334.

Guttmann, Allen. *Jewish Writer in America*, 210–217.

Guttmann, Allen. "Saul Bellow's Humane Comedy," in Cohen, Sara Blacher, ed. *Comic Relief*, 142–147.

Hays, Peter L. *Limping Hero*, 109–113.

Hendin, Josephine. *Vulnerable People*, 100–103.

Josipovici, Gabriel. *World and the Book*, 221–235.

Kulshrestha, Chirantan. *Saul Bellow*, 114–132.

Landor, Mikhail. "Centaur-Novels," in Proffer, Carl R., ed. and trans. *Soviet Criticism of American Literature in the Sixties*, 49–54.

Lehan, Richard. *Dangerous Crossing*, 125–130.

Lutwack, Leonard. *Heroic Fiction*, 91–100, 117–121.

McConnell, Frank D. *Four Postwar American Novelists*, 36–42.

Malin, Irving. *Saul Bellow's Fiction*, 145–162.

Masinton, Martha and Charles G. Masinton. "Second-class Citizenship: The Status of Women in Contemporary American Fiction," in Springer, Marlene, ed. *What Manner of Woman*, 302–304.

Opdahl, Keith. " 'Stillness in the Midst of Chaos': Plot in the Novels of Saul Bellow." *MFS* 25 (1979): 15–28.

Ousby, Ian. *Reader's Guide to Fifty American Novels*, 338–341.

Pearce, Richard. "Ambiguous Assault of Henderson and Herzog," in Rovit, Earl, ed. *Saul Bellow*, 75–80.

Pinsker, Sanford. "Saul Bellow, Soren Kierkegaard and the Question of Boredom." *CentR* 24 (1980): 121–122.

Porter, M. Gilbert. *Whence the Power?*, 146–159.

Rahv, Philip. *Essays on Literature and Politics*, 62–66.

Rahv, Philip. *Literature and the Sixth Sense*, 392–397.

Richter, David H. *Fable's End*, 185–192.

Rupp, Richard H. *Celebration in Postwar American Fiction*, 204–208.

Scheer-Schäzler, Brigitte. *Saul Bellow*, 92–115.

Schueler, Mary D. "Figure of Madeleine in *Herzog*." *NConL* 1.3 (1971): 5–7.

Schulz, Max F. *Radical Sophistication*, 110–125, 131–144, 145–149, 151–152.

Scott, Nathan A., Jr. *Three American Moralists*, 130–134.

Sullivan, Victoria. "Battle of the Sexes in Three Bellow Novels," in Rovit, Earl, ed. *Saul Bellow*, 102–105, 111–114.

Tanner, Tony. *City of Words*, 299–305.

Wisse, Ruth R. "Schlemiel as Liberal Humanist," in Wisse, Ruth R. *Schlemiel as Modern Hero*. Chicago: University of Chicago Press, 1971. Rpt. in Rovit, Earl, ed. *Saul Bellow*, 90–100.

Zietlow, E. R. "Saul Bellow: The Theater of the Soul." *Ariel* 4.4 (1973): 47–49.

Humboldt's Gift (1975)

Borrus, Bruce J. "Bellow's Critique of the Intellect." *MFS* 25 (1979): 29–31, 38–39.

Chavkin, Allan. "Baron Humboldt and Bellow's Von Humboldt Fleisher: Success and Failure in *Humboldt's Gift*." *NConL* 10.2 (1980): 11–12.

Christhilf, Mark M. "Death and Deliverance in Saul Bellow's Symbolic City." *BallS* 18.2 (1977): 9–10, 16, 22.

Clayton, John Jacob. *Saul Bellow*, 262–284.

Cohen, Sarah Blacher. "Comedy and Guilt in *Humboldt's Gift*." *MFS* 25 (1979): 47–57.

Dougherty, David C. "Finding before Seeking: Theme in *Henderson the Rain King* and *Humboldt's Gift*." *MFS* 25 (1979): 93–101.

Hendin, Josephine. *Vulnerable People*, 110.

McConnell, Frank D. *Four Postwar American Novelists*, 47–57.

Nault, Marianne. "Humboldt the First." *ANQ* 15 (1977): 88–89.

Pinsker, Sanford. "Saul Bellow, Soren Kierkegaard and the Question of Boredom." *CentR* 24 (1980): 122–125.

Rosenberg, Ruth. "Three Jewish Narrative Strategies in *Humboldt's Gift*." *MELUS* 6.4 (1979): 59–66.

Siegel, Ben. "Artists and Opportunists in Saul Bellow's *Humboldt's Gift*." *ConL* 19 (1978): 143–164.

Siegel, Ben. "Artists and Opportunists in Saul Bellow's *Humboldt's Gift*." *Contemporary Literature* (Spring 1978): 143–164. Rpt. in Trachtenberg, Stanley, ed. *Critical Essays on Saul Bellow*, 158–172.

Mr. Sammler's Planet (1970)

Alexander, Edward. *Resonance of Dust*, 171–192.

Bailey, Jennifer M. "Qualified Affirmation of Saul Bellow's Recent Work." *JAmS* 7 (1973): 71–76.

Berets, Ralph. "Saul Bellow's Fiction: Repudiation and Reality Instruction in Saul Bellow's Fiction." *CentR* 20 (1976): 95–100.

Borrus, Bruce J. "Bellow's Critique of the Intellect." *MFS* 25 (1979): 36–38.

Boyers, Robert. *Excursions*, 25–46.

Boyers, Robert. "Nature and Social Reality in Bellow's *Sammler*." *Critical Quarterly* 15 (1973): 251–271. Rpt. in Trachtenberg, Stanley, ed. *Critical Essays on Saul Bellow*, 122–140.

Bryant, Jerry H. *Open Decision*, 363–369.

Christhilf, Mark M. "Death and Deliverance in Saul Bellow's Symbolic City." *BallS* 18.2 (1977): 10, 20–22.

Clayton, John Jacob. *Saul Bellow*, 230–250.

Cohen, Sarah Blacher. *Saul Bellow's Enigmatic Laughter*, 176–210.

Cohen, Sarah Blacher. "Sex: Saul Bellow's Hedonistic Joke." *Studies in American Fiction* 2 (1974): 223–229. Rpt. in Trachtenberg, Stanley, ed. *Critical Essays on Saul Bellow*, 178–180.

Cushman, Keith. "Mr. Bellow's *Sammler:* The Evolution of a Contemporary Text." *SNNTS* 7 (1975): 425–444.

Cushman, Keith. "Mr. Bellow's *Sammler:* The Evolution of a Contemporary Text." *Studies in the Novel* 7 (1975): 425–444. Rpt. in Trachtenberg, Stanley, ed. *Critical Essays on Saul Bellow*, 141–157.

Donald, Miles. *American Novel in the Twentieth Century*, 171–172, 173.

Galloway, David. "*Mr. Sammler's Planet:* Bellow's Failure of Nerve." *MFS* 19 (1973): 17–28.

Gindin, James. *Harvest of a Quiet Eye*, 334–336.

Guttmann, Allen. *Jewish Writer in America*, 217–221.

Guttmann, Allen. "Saul Bellow's Humane Comedy," in Cohen, Sara Blacher, ed. *Comic Relief*, 148–151.

Guttmann, Allen. "Saul Bellow's Mr. Sammler." *ConL* 14 (1973): 157–168.

Klug, M. A. "Saul Bellow: The Hero in the Middle" *DR* 56 (1976): 462–478.

Kulshrestha, Chirantan. *Saul Bellow*, 132–149.

Kuna, F. M. "European Culture Game: Mr. Bellow's Planet." *ES* 53 (1972): 531–544.

LeClair, Thomas. "Death and Black Humor." *Crit* 17.1 (1975): 9–11.

Lehan, Richard. *Dangerous Crossing*, 130–133.

McConnell, Frank D. *Four Postwar American Novelists*, 42–47.

Maloney, Stephen R. "Half-way to Byzantium: *Mr. Sammler's Planet* and the Modern Tradition." *SCR* 6.1 (1973): 31–40.

Porter, M. Gilbert. *Whence the Power?*, 160–180.

Scheer-Schäzler, Brigitte. *Saul Bellow*, 118–128.

Scheik, William J. "Circle Sailing in Bellow's *Mr. Sammler's Planet*." *ELWIU* 5 (1978): 95–101.

Schulz, Max F. "Mr. Bellow's Perigee, Or, The Lowered Horizon of *Mr. Sammler's Planet*," in Malin, Irving, ed. *Contemporary American-Jewish Literature*, 117–132.

Scott, Nathan A., Jr. *Three American Moralists*, 136–146.

Siegel, Ben. "Saul Bellow and Mr. Sammler: Absurd Seekers of High Qualities," in Rovit, Earl, ed. *Saul Bellow*, 125–134.

Vernier, Jean-Pierre. "Mr Sammler's Lesson," in Johnson, Ira D. and Christiane Johnson, eds. *Les Américanistes*, 16–36.

Wirth-Nesher, Hana and Andrea Cohen Malamut. "Jewish and Human Survival on Bellow's Planet." *MFS* 25 (1979): 59–74.

Zietlow, E. R. "Saul Bellow: The Theater of the Soul." *Ariel* 4.4 (1973): 44, 49–57.

Victim (1947)

Berets, Ralph. "Saul Bellow's Fiction: Repudiation and Reality Instruction in Saul Bellow's Fiction." *CentR* 20 (1976): 80–85.

Bryant, Jerry H. *Open Decision*, 344–348.

Chavkin, Allan. "Ivan Karamazov's Rebellion and Bellow's *The Victim*." *PLL* 16 (1980): 316–320.

Christhilf, Mark M. "Death and Deliverance in Saul Bellow's Symbolic City." *BallS* 18.2 (1977): 10–13.

Clayton, John Jacob. *Saul Bellow*, 139–165.

Clayton, John J. "*The Victim*," in Clayton, John J. *Saul Bellow: In Defense of Man*. Bloomington, IN: Indiana University Press, 1968. Rpt. in Rovit, Earl, ed. *Saul Bellow*, 31–51.

Cohen, Sarah Blacher. *Saul Bellow's Enigmatic Laughter*, 40–62.

Galloway, David D. *Absurd Hero in American Fiction*, 89–94.

Gindin, James. *Harvest of a Quiet Eye*, 309–314.

Gordon, Andrew. " 'Pushy Jew': Leventhal in *The Victim*." *MFS* 25 (1979): 129–138.

Guttmann, Allen. *Jewish Writer in America*, 183–189.

Guttmann, Allen. "Saul Bellow's Humane Comedy," in Cohen, Sara Blacher, ed. *Comic Relief*, 128–129.

Hendin, Josephine. *Vulnerable People*, 105–106.

Klein, Marcus. "Discipline of Nobility: Saul Bellow's Fiction," in Rovit, Earl, ed. *Saul Bellow*, 136, 137, 138, 141–142.

Klug, M. A. "Saul Bellow: The Hero in the Middle" *DR* 56 (1976): 462–478.

Lehan, Richard. *Dangerous Crossing*, 111–115.

McConnell, Frank D. *Four Postwar American Novelists*, 15–19.

Malin, Irving. *Saul Bellow's Fiction*, 11, 13, 20–21, 28–29, 37–39, 48–49, 59–63,

74–76, 86–87, 91–92, 96, 100, 104–106, 109–110, 118–119, 129, 131–132, 136–137, 140–141.

May, Keith M. *Out of the Maelstrom*, 96.

Opdahl, Keith. " 'Stillness in the Midst of Chaos': Plot in the Novels of Saul Bellow." *MFS* 25 (1979): 15–28.

Porter, M. Gilbert. *Whence the Power?*, 29–60.

Rupp, Richard H. *Celebration in Postwar American Fiction*, 192–195.

Scheer-Schäzler, Brigitte. *Saul Bellow*, 17–28.

Scott, Nathan A., Jr. *Three American Moralists*, 116–119.

BENASUTTI, MARION (1908–1992)

No Steady Job for Papa (1966)

Green, Rose Basile. *Italian-American Novel*, 194–198.

BENOÎT, JACQUES (1941–)

Les voleurs (1969)

Shek, Ben-Zion. *Social Realism*, 291.

Sugden, Leonard W. "Man as Monster, Dog and Prince: A Critique of *Les voleurs* by Jacques Benoît." *Mosaic* 11.3 (1978): 153–163.

Sugden, Leonard W. "Man as Monster, Dog and Prince: A Critique of *Les voleurs* by Jacques Benoît," in Wortley, John, ed. *Post-War Canadian Fiction*, 153–163.

Patience et Firlipon (1970)

Poulin, Gabrielle. *Romans du pays*, 259–262.

BERGER, THOMAS (1924–)

Crazy in Berlin (1958)

Hughes, Douglas A. "Schlemiel as Humanist: Thomas Berger's Carlo Reinhart." *Cithara* 15.1 (1975): 5–10.

Little Big Man (1964)

Cleary, Michael. "Finding the Center of the Earth: Satire, History, and Myth in *Little Big Man*." *WAL* 15 (1980): 195–211.

Fetrow, Fred M. "Function of the External Narrator in Thomas Berger's *Little Big Man*." *JNT* 5 (1975): 57–65.

Harris, Charles B. *Contemporary American Novelists of the Absurd*, 129–131.

Oliva, Leo E. "Thomas Berger's *Little Big Man* as History." *WAL* 8 (1973): 33–54.

Royot, Daniel. "Aspects of the American Picaresque in *Little Big Man*," in Johnson, Ira D. and Christiane Johnson, eds. *Les Américanistes*, 37–52.

Schulz, Max F. *Black Humor Fiction of the Sixties*, 72–77.

Trachtenberg, Stanley. "Berger and Barth: The Comedy of Decomposition," in Cohen, Sara Blacher, ed. *Comic Relief*, 48–51.

Turner, Frederick W., III. "Melville and Thomas Berger: The Novelist as Cultural Anthropologist." *CentR* 13 (1969): 113–120.

Reinhart in Love (1962)

Hughes, Douglas A. "Schlemiel as Humanist: Thomas Berger's Carlo Reinhart." *Cithara* 15.1 (1975): 11–16.

Vital Parts (1970)

> Hughes, Douglas A. "Schlemiel as Humanist: Thomas Berger's Carlo Reinhart." *Cithara* 15.1 (1975): 16–20.
> Trachtenberg, Stanley. "Berger and Barth: The Comedy of Decomposition," in Cohen, Sara Blacher, ed. *Comic Relief*, 54–60.

BERGMAN, ANDREW (1945–)

Big Kiss-Off of 1944 (1974)

> Geherin, David. *Sons of Sam Spade*, 130–140.

Hollywood and Levine (1975)

> Geherin, David. *Sons of Sam Spade*, 140–153.

BERRY, DON (1932–)

Moontrap (1962)

> Love, Glen A. *Don Berry*, 20–29, 36.

To Build a Ship (1963)

> Love, Glen A. *Don Berry*, 29–34.

Trask (1960)

> Love, Glen A. *Don Berry*, 9–20, 35.

BESSETTE, GÉRARD (1920–)

Brawl see *La bagarre*

La bagarre (1958)

> Belleau, André. *Le romancier fictif*, 115–130.
> Iqbal, Françoise. "Précieux et préciosité chez Bessette: demi-mesure et démesure." *V&I* 1 (1976): 338, 340–344.
> Shek, Ben Z. "Gerard Bessette and Social Realism." *CMLR* 31 (1975): 292–295.
> Shek, Ben-Zion. *Social Realism*, 230–234.
> Sutherland, Ronald. "Brawling with Gerard Bessette." *Ariel* 4.3 (1973): 32–37.
> Sutherland, Ronald. *New Hero*, 57–63.
> Sutherland, Ronald. *Second Image*, 11–16.

La commensale (1975)

> Fisette, Jean. "L'Écriture comme pratique fantastique: *La commensale* de Gerard Bessette." *V&I* 329–336.
> Iqbal, Françoise. "Précieux et préciosité chez Bessette: demi-mesure et démesure." *V&I* 1 (1976): 361–363.

Le cycle (1971)

> Iqbal, Françoise. "Précieux et préciosité chez Bessette: demi-mesure et démesure." *V&I* 1 (1976): 339–340, 355–361.
> Poulin, Gabrielle. *Romans du pays*, 141–151.
> Sugden, Leonard W. "Unending Cycle." *CanL* 63 (1975): 64–71.

Le libraire (1960)

Iqbal, Françoise. "Précieux et préciosité chez Bessette: demi-mesure et démesure." *V&I* 1 (1976): 338, 344–347.

Shek, Ben Z. "Gerard Bessette and Social Realism." *CMLR* 31 (1975): 296–298.

Shek, Ben-Zion. *Social Realism*, 282–285.

Urbas, Jeannette. *From Thirty Acres to Modern Times*, 85–89.

Les pédagogues (1961)

Iqbal, Françoise. "Précieux et préciosité chez Bessette: demi-mesure et démesure." *V&I* 1 (1976): 338, 348–352.

Shek, Ben Z. "Gerard Bessette and Social Realism." *CMLR* 31 (1975): 294–295.

L'incubation (1965)

Iqbal, Françoise. "Précieux et préciosité chez Bessette: demi-mesure et démesure." *V&I* 1 (1976): 338–339, 352–355.

Leduc, Renée. "L'Incubation 'psychologique' ou *L'incubation*, roman à suspense." *V&I* 3 (1978): 421–431.

Shek, Ben Z. "Gerard Bessette and Social Realism." *CMLR* 31 (1975): 298–299.

Shek, Ben-Zion. *Social Realism*, 285–287.

Urbas, Jeannette. *From Thirty Acres to Modern Times*, 130–133.

Not for Every Eye see *Le libraire*

BESTER, ALFRED (1913–1987)

Stars My Destination (1956)

Scholes, Robert and Eric S. Rabkin. *Science Fiction*, 67–68.

BETHEA, JACK (1892–1928)

Cotton (1928)

Cook, Sylvia Jenkins. *From Tobacco Road to Route 66*, 28–30.

BIRD, ROBERT MONTGOMERY (1806–1854)

Nick of the Woods (1837)

Martin, Terence. "Surviving on the Frontier: The Doubled Consciousness of Natty Bumppo." *SAQ* 75 (1975): 450, 454, 455.

Sweeney, Gerard M. "Strong Family Likeness: The Love Plot of *Nick of the Woods*." *MarkR* 9 (1980): 48–52.

BIRNEY, EARLE (1904–1995)

Down the Long Table (1955)

Aichinger, Peter. *Earle Birney*, 59–60, 73–74, 76, 110–111, 113, 145, 157–158.

Davey, Frank. *Earle Birney*, 38–43.

Dooley, D. J. "Satiric Novel in Canada Today: *Down the Long Table*." *Queen's Quarterly* 64 (1958): 584–585. Rpt. in Nesbitt, Bruce, ed. *Earle Birney*, 95–96.

Nesbitt, Bruce. "*Down the Long Table*: A Retrospective Review." *WCR* 9.3 (1975): 35–39.

Woodcock, George. "Earle Birney: *Down the Long Table.*" Vinson, James, ed. *Contemporary Novelists.* New York: St. Martins Press, 1972. 125–126. Rpt. in Nesbitt, Bruce, ed. *Earle Birney*, 99.
Woodcock, George. *World of Canadian Writing*, 294.

Turvey (1949)
Aichinger, Peter. *Earle Birney*, 60–67, 91, 145.
Davey, Frank. *Earle Birney*, 29–37.
Dooley, D. J. "Satiric Novel in Canada Today: *Turvey.*" *Queen's Quarterly* 64 (1958): 580–584. Rpt. in Nesbitt, Bruce, ed. *Earle Birney*, 76–79.
Weaver, Robert. "Introduction to *Strange Fugitive.*" Callaghan, Morley. *Strange Fugitive.* Edmonton, AL: M.G. Hurtig, 1970. Rpt. in Conron, Brandon, ed. *Morley Callaghan*, 27–33.
Woodcock, George. *Odysseus Ever Returning*, 124–129.
Woodcock, George. *World of Canadian Writing*, 293–294.

BISHOP, LEONARD (1922–)
Down All Your Streets (1952)
Gelfant, Blanche Housman. *American City Novel*, 259–263.

BISHOP, WILLIAM H. (1847–1928)
Garden of Eden (1895)
Roemer, Kenneth M. "Sex Roles, Utopia, and Change: The Family in Late Nineteenth-Century Utopian Literature." *AmerS* 13 (1972): 40–41, 43.

BLAIS, MARIE-CLAIRE (1939–)
David Sterne (1967)
Ahmed, Maroussia. "La technique de l'inversion dans les romans de Marie-Claire Blais." *CMLR* 31 (1975): 380–385.
Gordon, Jan B. " 'Incandescence of Suffering': The Fiction of Marie-Claire Blais." *MFS* 22 (1976): 482.

La belle bête (1959)
Fabi, Thérèse. *Le monde perturbé*, 55–59.
Gordon, Jan B. " 'Incandescence of Suffering': The Fiction of Marie-Claire Blais." *MFS* 22 (1976): 468, 471–472, 481.
Legris, Maurice R. "Modern French-Canadian Novel." *TCL* 16 (1970): 172.
Northey, Margot. *Haunted Wilderness*, 70–78.
Serafin, Bruce. "Marie-Claire Blais' *La belle bête.*" *ECW* 7–8 (1977): 63–73.
Stratford, Philip. *Marie-Claire Blais*, 9–16.
. Urbas, Jeannette. *From Thirty Acres to Modern Times*, 111–112.

Le loup (1972)
Ahmed, Maroussia. "La technique de l'inversion dans les romans de Marie-Claire Blais." *CMLR* 31 (1975): 382–385.
Gordon, Jan B. " 'Incandescence of Suffering': The Fiction of Marie-Claire Blais." *MFS* 22 (1976): 482–483.
Urbas, Jeannette. *From Thirty Acres to Modern Times*, 116–117.

Les apparences (1970)

> Ahmed, Maroussia. "La technique de l'inversion dans les romans de Marie-Claire Blais." *CMLR* 31 (1975): 383–385.
>
> Fabi, Thérèse. *Le monde perturbé*, 109–113.

Les nuits de l'underground (1978)

> Poulin, Gabrielle. *Romans du pays*, 321–325.

Literary Affair see *Une liason parisienne*

Mad Shadows see *La belle bête*

Manuscipts of Pauline Archange see *Manuscrits de Pauline Archange*

Manuscrits de Pauline Archange (1968)

> Ahmed, Maroussia. "La technique de l'inversion dans les romans de Marie-Claire Blais." *CMLR* 31 (1975): 380–385.
>
> Dawson, Anthony B. "Coming of Age in Canada." *Mosaic* 11.3 (1978): 59–62.
>
> Fabi, Thérèse. *Le monde perturbé*, 95–99.
>
> Gordon, Jan B. " 'Incandescence of Suffering': The Fiction of Marie-Claire Blais." *MFS* 22 (1976): 469–470, 477–478, 479.
>
> Kraft, James. "Fiction as Autobiography in Quebec: Notes on Pierre Vallieres and Marie-Claire Blais." *Novel* 6 (1972): 75–78.
>
> Stratford, Philip. *Marie-Claire Blais*, 55–60.

Nights in the Underground see *Les nuits de l'underground*

St. Lawrence Blues see *Un joualonias sa joualonie*

Season in the Life of Emmanuel see *Une saison dans la vie d'Emmanuel*

Tête blanche (1960)

> Fabi, Thérèse. *Le monde perturbé*, 61–66.
>
> Gordon, Jan B. " 'Incandescence of Suffering': The Fiction of Marie-Claire Blais." *MFS* 22 (1976): 474–475, 477.
>
> Urbas, Jeannette. *From Thirty Acres to Modern Times*, 112.

Un joualonais sa joualonie (1973)

> Gordon, Jan B. " 'Incandescence of Suffering': The Fiction of Marie-Claire Blais." *MFS* 22 (1976): 475, 478–479, 480, 481.

Une liaison parisienne (1975)

> Poulin, Gabrielle. *Romans du pays*, 314–320.

Une saison dans la vie d'Emmanuel (1965)

> Ahmed, Maroussia. "La technique de l'inversion dans les romans de Marie-Claire Blais." *CMLR* 31 (1975): 380–385.
>
> Atwood, Margaret. *Survival*, 225–226.
>
> Fabi, Thérèse. *Le monde perturbé*, 71–73.
>
> Gordon, Jan B. " 'Incandescence of Suffering': The Fiction of Marie-Claire Blais." *MFS* 22 (1976): 470–471, 473.
>
> Lecker, Robert A. "Aesthetics of Deception: Marie-Claire Blais' *A Season in the Life of Emmanuel*." *ECW* 4 (1976): 42–55.
>
> Marcotte, Gilles. "La dialectique de l'ancien et du nouveau chez Marie-Claire Blais, Jacques Ferron et Rejean Ducharme." *V&I* 6 (1980): 63, 65–67.

Mitterand, Henri. "Coup de pistolet dans un concert: *Une saison dans la vie d'Emmanuel.*" *V&I* 2 (1977): 407–417.
Nadeau, Vincent. *Marie-Claire Blais*, 9–73.
Shek, Ben-Zion. *Social Realism*, 287–290.
Stratford, Philip. *Marie-Claire Blais*, 36–45.
Urbas, Jeannette. *From Thirty Acres to Modern Times*, 112–116.
Viswanathan, Jacqueline. *"Une saison dans la vie d'Emmanuel* de Marie-Claire Blais: introduction à l'analyse du personnage romanesque." *FR* 52 (1979): 755–758.

Vivre! Vivre! (1969)

Ahmed, Maroussia. "La technique de l'inversion dans les romans de Marie-Claire Blais." *CMLR* 31 (1975): 384–385.
Fabi, Thérèse. *Le monde perturbé*, 103–107.
Stratford, Philip. *Marie-Claire Blais*, 60–65.

BLAND, ALDEN (1911–)

Behold a Cry (1947)

Fleming, Robert E. "Overshadowed by Richard Wright: Three Black Chicago Novelists." *NALF* 7 (1973): 76–77, 79.

BLATTY, WILLIAM PETER (1928–)

Exorcist (1971)

Beit-Hallahmi, Benjamin. " 'Turn of the Screw' and *The Exorcist:* Demoniacal Possession and Childhood Purity." *American Imago* 33 (1976): 296–303.

BLECHMAN, BURT (1932–)

War of Camp Omongo (1963)

Guttmann, Allen. *Jewish Writer in America*, 77–78.

BLISH, JAMES (1921–1975)

Case of Conscience (1958)

Eckley, Grace. "Finnegans Wake in the Work of James Blish." *Extrapolation* 20 (1979): 334–341.
Reilly, Robert. "Discerning Conscience." *Extrapolation* 18 (1977): 176–180.

BODENHEIM, MAXWELL (1892–1954)

Blackguard (1923)
Moore, Jack B. *Maxwell Bodenheim*, 74–79.
Crazy Man (1924)
Moore, Jack B. *Maxwell Bodenheim*, 79–86.
Georgie May (1928
Moore, Jack B. *Maxwell Bodenheim*, 110–116.

Naked on Roller Skates (1930)
    Moore, Jack B. *Maxwell Bodenheim*, 125–130.
Ninth Avenue (1926)
    Moore, Jack B. *Maxwell Bodenheim*, 95–101.
Run, Sheep, Run (1932)
    Moore, Jack B. *Maxwell Bodenheim*, 142–148.
Sixty Seconds (1929)
    Moore, Jack B. *Maxwell Bodenheim*, 116–121.
Slow Vision (1934)
    Moore, Jack B. *Maxwell Bodenheim*, 149–155.
Virtuous Girl (1930)
    Moore, Jack B. *Maxwell Bodenheim*, 121–125.

BONENFANT, JOSEPH (1934–)

Repère (1979)
    Poulin, Gabrielle. *Romans du pays*, 364–370.

BONNER, SHERWOOD (1849–1883)

Like Unto Like (1878)
    Frank, William L. *Sherwood Bonner (Catherine McDowell)*, 119–129.

BONTEMPS, ARNA (1902–1973)

Black Thunder (1936)
    Davis, Arthur P. *From the Dark Tower*, 87–89.
    Wade, Melvin and Margaret Wade. "Black Aesthetic in the Black Novel." *JBS* 2.4 (1972): 403.
    Williams, Sherley Anne. *Give Birth to Brightness*, 78–79.
Drums at Dusk (1939)
    Isani, Mukhtar Ali. "Exotic and Protest in Earlier Black Literature: The Use of Alien Setting and Character." *SIBL* 5.2 (1974): 13–14.
God Sends Sunday (1931)
    Perry, Margaret. *Silence to the Drums*, 102–105.

BORLAND, HAL (1900–1978)

When the Legends Die (1963)
    Barry, Nora Baker. "Bear's Son Folk Tale in *When the Legends Die* and *House Made of Dawn*." *WAL* 12 (1978): 274–281.
    Kelty, Jean McClure. "Cult of Kill in Adolescent Fiction." *EJ* 64.2 (1975): 60.

BOSTON, LUCY (1882–1990)

Children of Green Knowe (1955)

Rosenthal, Lynne. "Development of Consciousness in Lucy Boston's *The Children of Green Knowe." ChildL* 8 (1979): 83–67.

BOTSFORD, MARGARET (fl. 1812–1830)

Adelaide (1816)

Petter, Henri. *Early American Novel*, 186–199.

BOUCHETTE, ERROL (1863–1912)

Robert Lozé (1903)

Hathorn, Ramon. "Soldats, patrons et femmes 'fatales': Figures de l'"Anglais' dans le roman québécois des XIXe et XXe siècles." *V&I* 6 (1980): 103–104.

BOURJAILY, VANCE (1922–)

Brill among the Ruins (1970)

Towner, Daniel. "Brill's Ruins and Henderson's Rain." *Crit* 17.3 (1976): 96–97, 101–104.

Confessions of a Spent Youth (1960)

Muste, John M. "Fractional Man as Hero: Bourjaily's *Confessions of a Spent Youth." Crit* 17.3 (1976): 73–85.

Muste, John M. "Second Major Subwar: Four Novels by Vance Bourjaily," in Friedman, Melvin J. and John B. Vickery, eds. *Shaken Realist*, 319–320, 323–325.

End of My Life (1947)

Muste, John M. "Second Major Subwar: Four Novels by Vance Bourjaily," in Friedman, Melvin J. and John B. Vickery, eds. *Shaken Realist*, 313–315.

Waldmeir, Joseph J. *American Novels of the Second World War*, 20–23.

Hound of Earth (1955)

Francis, William A. "Motif of Names of Bourjaily's *The Hound of Earth." Crit* 17.3 (1976): 64–72.

Muste, John M. "Second Major Subwar: Four Novels by Vance Bourjaily," in Friedman, Melvin J. and John B. Vickery, eds. *Shaken Realist*, 315–319.

Man Who Knew Kennedy (1967)

McMillen, William. "Public Man and the Private Novel: Bourjaily's *The Man Who Knew Kennedy." Crit* 17.3 (1976): 86–95.

Violated (1958)

Muste, John M. "Second Major Subwar: Four Novels by Vance Bourjaily," in Friedman, Melvin J. and John B. Vickery, eds. *Shaken Realist*, 319–323.

BOWLES, PAUL (1910–1999)

Let It Come Down (1952)

Stewart, Lawrence D. *Paul Bowles*, 87–98.

Sheltering Sky (1949)
  Stewart, Lawrence D. *Paul Bowles*, 49–72.

Spider's House (1955)
  Stewart, Lawrence D. *Paul Bowles*, 103–110.

BOYD, JOHN (1919–)

Last Starship from Earth (1968)
  Hipolito, Jane. "The Last and First Starship from Earth," in Clareson, Thomas D.,
    ed. *SF: The Other Side of Realism*, 186–192.
  Ketterer, David. *New Worlds for Old*, 236–242.
  Warrick, Patricia S. *Cybernetic Imagination in Science Fiction*, 188–191.

BOYD, THOMAS (1898–1935)

Through the Wheat (1923)
  Jones, Peter G. *War and the Novelist*, 9–10.

BOYESEN, HJALMAR HJORTH (1848–1895)

Daughter of the Philistines (1883)
  Fredrickson, Robert S. *Hjalmar Hjorth Boyesen*, 97–99.

Falconberg (1879)
  Fredrickson, Robert S. *Hjalmar Hjorth Boyesen*, 59–65.

Golden Calf (1892)
  Fredrickson, Robert S. *Hjalmar Hjorth Boyesen*, 139–146.

Gunnar (1874)
  Fredrickson, Robert S. *Hjalmar Hjorth Boyesen*, 32–43.

Light of Her Countenance (1889)
  Fredrickson, Robert S. *Hjalmar Hjorth Boyesen*, 85–92.

Mammon of Unrighteousness (1891)
  Fredrickson, Robert S. *Hjalmar Hjorth Boyesen*, 128–139.

Norseman's Pilgrimage (1874)
  Fredrickson, Robert S. *Hjalmar Hjorth Boyesen*, 52–59.

Social Strugglers (1893)
  Fredrickson, Robert S. *Hjalmar Hjorth Boyesen*, 146–152.

BOYLE, KAY (1902–1992)

Generation without Farewell (1960)
  Moore, Harry T. "Kay Boyle's Fiction." *Kenyon Review* (Spring 1960). Rpt. in
    Moore, Harry T. *Age of the Modern*, 34–36.

BRACKENRIDGE, HUGH HENRY (1748–1816)

Modern Chivalry (1797)

Gilmore, Michael T. "Eighteenth-Century Oppositional Ideology and Hugh Henry Brackenridge's *Modern Chivalry.*" *EAL* 13 (1978): 181–192.

Haims, Lynn. "Of Indians and Irishmen: A Note on Brackenridge's Use of Sources for Satire in *Modern Chivalry.*" *EAL* 10 (1975): 88–92.

Harkey, Joseph H. "Don Quixote of the Frontier: Brackenridge's *Modern Chivalry.*" *EAL* 8 (1973) 193–203.

Hirsch, David H. *Reality and Idea in the Early American Novel,* 51–73.

Martin, Wendy. "Rogue and the Rational Man: Hugh Henry Brackenridge's Study of a Con Man in *Modern Chivalry.*" *EAL* 8 (1973): 179–192.

Spengemann, William C. *Adventurous Muse,* 94–96.

Whittle, Amberys R. "*Modern Chivalry:* The Frontier as Crucible." *EAL* 6 (1971): 263–270.

BRACKETT, LEIGH (1915–1978)

Long Tomorrow (1955)

Wolfe, Gary K. *Known and the Unknown,* 134–137.

BRADBURY, RAY (1920–)

Dandelion Wine (1957)

Diskin, Lahna. "Bradbury on Children," in Greenberg, Martin Harry and Joseph D. Olander, eds. *Ray Bradbury,* 127–129, 130–134, 135–142.

Johnson, Wayne L. *Ray Bradbury,* 91–102.

Mengeling, Marvin E. "Ray Bradbury's *Dandelion Wine:* Themes, Sources, and Styles." *EJ* 60 (1971): 877–887.

Stupple, A. James. "Past, The Future, and Ray Bradbury," in Greenberg, Martin Harry and Joseph D. Olander, eds. *Ray Bradbury,* 26–30.

Stupple, A. James. "Past, The Future, and Ray Bradbury," in Clareson, Thomas D., ed. *Voices for the Future* (Vol. 1), 178–181.

Fahrenheit 451 (1953)

Ash, Brian. *Faces of the Future,* 98–99.

Colmer, John. *Coleridge to Catch-22,* 200–204.

Johnson, Wayne L. *Ray Bradbury,* 85–88.

McNelly, Willis E. "Ray Bradbury – Past, Present, and Future," in Greenberg, Martin Harry and Joseph D. Olander, eds. *Ray Bradbury,* 19, 21–23.

McNelly, Willis E. "Ray Bradbury – Past, Present, and Future," in Clareson, Thomas D., ed. *Voices for the Future* (Vol. 1), 169–170, 172–175.

Watt, Donald. "Burning Bright: *Fahrenheit 451* as Symbolic Dystopia," in Greenberg, Martin Harry and Joseph D. Olander, eds. *Ray Bradbury,* 195–213.

Watt, Donald J. "Hearth or Salamander: Uses of Fire in Bradbury's *Fahrenheit 451.*" *NConL* 1.2 (1971): 13–14.

Something Wicked This Way Comes (1963)

Attebery, Brian. *Fantasy Tradition in American Literature,* 136–141.

Diskin, Lahna. "Bradbury on Children," in Greenberg, Martin Harry and Joseph D. Olander, eds. *Ray Bradbury,* 128–129, 131, 144–151.

Johnson, Wayne L. "Invasion Stories of Ray Bradbury," in Riley, Dick, ed. *Critical Encounters*, 29–30.

Johnson, Wayne L. *Ray Bradbury*, 101–104.

Pierce, Hazel. "Ray Bradbury and the Gothic Tradition," in Greenberg, Martin Harry and Joseph D. Olander, eds. *Ray Bradbury*, 176–182.

BRADLEY, EMILY (1827–1863)

Coopers (1858)

Baym, Nina. *Woman's Fiction*, 245–246.

BRALY, MALCOLM (1925–1980)

It's Cold Out There (1966)

Franklin, H. Bruce. *Victim as Criminal and Artist*, 193–198.

On the Yard (1968)

Franklin, H. Bruce. *Victim as Criminal and Artist*, 198–205.

Shake Him Till He Rattles (1963)

Franklin, H. Bruce. *Victim as Criminal and Artist*, 187–191.

BRAUTIGAN, RICHARD (1935–1984)

Abortion (1971)

Malley, Terence. *Richard Brautigan*, 65–89.

Schmitz, Neil. "Richard Brautigan and the Modern Pastoral." *MFS* 19 (1973): 111, 112–115, 116.

Confederate General from Big Sur (1964)

Malley, Terence. *Richard Brautigan*, 90–114.

Schmitz, Neil. "Richard Brautigan and the Modern Pastoral." *MFS* 19 (1973): 112, 115–116.

Trout Fishing in America (1967)

Donald, Miles. *American Novel in the Twentieth Century*, 126–127.

Malley, Terence. *Richard Brautigan*, 143–181.

Mellard, James M. *Exploded Form*, 155–168.

Schmitz, Neil. "Richard Brautigan and the Modern Pastoral." *MFS* 19 (1973): 109, 120–125.

BRINIG, MYRON (1897–1991)

This Man Is My Brother (1932)

Austen, Roger. *Playing the Game*, 74–75.

BRODEUR, PAUL (1931–)

Stunt Man (1970)

Saltzman, Arthur M. "Betrayal of the Imagination: Paul Brodeur's *The Stunt Man* and Tim O'Brien's *Going after Cacciato*." *Crit* 22.1 (1980): 32–35.

Scholes, Robert. *Fabulation and Metafiction*, 128–130.

BROOKE, FRANCES (1724–1789)

History of Emily Montague (1769)

Edwards, Mary Jane. "Frances Brooke's Politics and *The History of Emily Montague*," in Moss, John, ed. *Beginnings*, 19–26.

MacAndrew, Elizabeth. *Gothic Tradition in Fiction*, 33–34.

Moss, John. *Patterns of Isolation*, 24–34.

New, William H. "Frances Brooke's Chequered Gardens." *CanL* 52 (1972): 24–38.

Shohet, Linda. "Essay on *The History of Emily Montague*," in Moss, John, ed. *Beginnings*, 28–34.

BROOKS, JOHN (1920–1993)

Big Wheel (1949)

Bryant, Jerry H. *Open Decision*, 194–196.

Man Who Broke Things (1958)

Bryant, Jerry H. *Open Decision*, 196–198.

BROSSARD, CHANDLER (1922–1993)

Bold Saboteurs (1953)

Bryant, Jerry H. *Open Decision*, 219–221.

BROSSARD, JACQUES (1933–   )

Le sang du souvenir (1976)

Poulin, Gabrielle. *Romans du pays*, 240–245.

BROWN, ALICE (1857–1948)

Dear Old Templeton (1927)

Walker, Dorothea. *Alice Brown*, 119–123.

John Winterbourne's Family (1910)

Walker, Dorothea. *Alice Brown*, 115–119.

Kings End (1901)

Walker, Dorothea. *Alice Brown*, 95–99.

Margaret Warrener (1901)

Walker, Dorothea. *Alice Brown*, 91–95.

My Love and I (1912)

Walker, Dorothea. *Alice Brown*, 86–91.

Old Crow (1922)

Walker, Dorothea. *Alice Brown*, 99–106.

Rose MacLeod (1908)

Walker, Dorothea. *Alice Brown*, 107–111.

Story of Thyrza (1909)

Walker, Dorothea. *Alice Brown*, 107–108, 111–115.

BROWN, CHARLES BROCKDEN (1771–1810)

Arthur Mervyn (1800)

Bell, Michael D. " 'The Double-Tongued Deceiver': Sincerity and Duplicity in the Novels of Charles Brockden Brown." *EAL* 9 (1974): 154–158.

Bell, Michael Davitt. *Development of American Romance*, 55–59.

Bernard, Kenneth. "Charles Brockden Brown," in Hoyt, Charles Alva, ed. *Minor American Novelists*, 7.

Butler, David L. *Dissecting a Human Heart*, 63–69.

Cleman, John. "Ambiguous Evil: A Study of Villains and Heroes in Charles Brockden Brown's Major Novels." *EAL* 10 (1975): 192, 194–195, 198–200, 211–217.

Ferguson, Robert A. "Literature and Vocation in the Early Republic: The Example of Charles Brockden Brown." *MP* 78 (1980): 146–152.

Hedges, William. "Charles Brockden Brown and the Culture of Contradictions." *EAL* 9 (1974): 109–111, 112–113, 123–130, 134–138.

Hedges, William L. "Benjamin Rush, Charles Brockden Brown, and the American Plague Year." *EAL* 7 (1973): 304–307.

Hume, Robert D. "Charles Brockden Brown and the Use of Gothicism: A Reassessment." *ESQ* 66 (1972): 16.

McAlexander, Patricia Jewell. "*Arthur Mervyn* and the Sentimental Love Tradition." *SLitI* 9.2 (1976): 31–41.

Micklus, Robert. "Charles Brockden Brown's Curiosity Shop." *EAL* 15 (1980): 180–184.

Petter, Henri. *Early American Novel*, 334–340.

Ringe, Donald A. "Charles Brockden Brown," in Emerson, Everett, ed. *Major Writers*, 288–292.

Rose, Alan H. "Sin and the City: The Uses of Disorder in the Urban Novel." *CentR* 16 (1972): 204–207.

Spengemann, William C. *Adventurous Muse*, 98–106.

Stout, Janis P. *Sodoms in Eden*, 46–50.

Caleb Williams (1794)

Hirsch, David H. *Reality and Idea in the Early American Novel*, 83–84.

Clara Howard (1801)

Butler, David L. *Dissecting a Human Heart*, 71–75.

Petter, Henri. *Early American Novel*, 174–177.

Witherington, Paul. "Charles Brown's Other Novels: *Clara Howard* and *Jane Talbot*." *NCF* 29 (1974): 257–272.

Edgar Huntly (1799)

Bell, Michael D. " 'The Double-Tongued Deceiver': Sincerity and Duplicity in the Novels of Charles Brockden Brown." *EAL* 9 (1974): 151–154.

Bell, Michael Davitt. *Development of American Romance*, 52–55.

Bernard, Kenneth. "Charles Brockden Brown," in Hoyt, Charles Alva, ed. *Minor American Novelists*, 7–8.

Butler, David L. *Dissecting a Human Heart*, 49–55.

Cleman, John. "Ambiguous Evil: A Study of Villains and Heroes in Charles Brockden Brown's Major Novels." *EAL* 10 (1975): 192–194, 204–217.

Ferguson, Robert A. "Literature and Vocation in the Early Republic: The Example of Charles Brockden Brown." *MP* 78 (1980): 146–152.

Hedges, William. "Charles Brockden Brown and the Culture of Contradictions." *EAL* 9 (1974): 122–123, 131–134, 138.

Hughes, Philip R. "Archetypal Patterns in *Edgar Huntly.*" *SNNTS* 5 (1973): 176–190.

Hume, Robert D. "Charles Brockden Brown and the Use of Gothicism: A Reassessment." *ESQ* 66 (1972): 15–16.

Micklus, Robert. "Charles Brockden Brown's Curiosity Shop." *EAL* 15 (1980): 178–180.

Petter, Henri. *Early American Novel*, 353–359.

Ringe, Donald A. "Charles Brockden Brown," in Emerson, Everett, ed. *Major Writers*, 281–284.

Schulz, Dieter. "*Edgar Huntly* as Quest Romance." *AL* 43 (1971): 323–335.

Jane Talbot (1801)

Butler, David L. *Dissecting a Human Heart*, 77–83.

Petter, Henri. *Early American Novel*, 192–196.

Witherington, Paul. "Charles Brown's Other Novels: *Clara Howard* and *Jane Talbot.*" *NCF* 29 (1974): 257–272.

Ormond (1799)

Bell, Michael D. " 'The Double-Tongued Deceiver': Sincerity and Duplicity in the Novels of Charles Brockden Brown." *EAL* 9 (1974): 148–151.

Bell, Michael Davitt. *Development of American Romance*, 48–51.

Bernard, Kenneth. "Charles Brockden Brown," in Hoyt, Charles Alva, ed. *Minor American Novelists*, 4–6.

Butler, David L. *Dissecting a Human Heart*, 57–62.

Christopherson, Bill. "Charles Brockden Brown's *Ormond:* The Secret Witness as Ironic Motif." *MLS* 10.2 (1980): 37–41.

Cleman, John. "Ambiguous Evil: A Study of Villains and Heroes in Charles Brockden Brown's Major Novels." *EAL* 10 (1975): 194, 195–198, 206–217.

Ferguson, Robert A. "Literature and Vocation in the Early Republic: The Example of Charles Brockden Brown." *MP* 78 (1980): 146–152.

Hedges, William. "Charles Brockden Brown and the Culture of Contradictions." *EAL* 9 (1974): 116–119.

Hirsch, David H. *Reality and Idea in the Early American Novel*, 81–82, 92–100.

Hume, Robert D. "Charles Brockden Brown and the Use of Gothicism: A Reassessment." *ESQ* 66 (1972): 14–15.

Krause, Sydney J. "*Ormond:* How Rapidly and How Well 'Composed, Arranged and Delivered'." *EAL* 13 (1978): 238–249.

Krause, Sydney J. "*Ormond:* Seduction in a New Key." *AL* 44 (1973): 570–584.

Levine, Robert S. "Villainy and the Fear of Conspiracy in Charles Brockden Brown's *Ormond.*" *EAL* 15 (1980): 124–140.

Micklus, Robert. "Charles Brockden Brown's Curiosity Shop." *EAL* 15 (1980): 173–175.

Nelson, Carl. "Just Reading of Charles Brockden Brown's *Ormond.*" *EAL* 8 (1973): 163–178.

Petter, Henri. *Early American Novel*, 340–346.

Ringe, Donald A. "Charles Brockden Brown," in Emerson, Everett, ed. *Major Writers*, 277–279.

Rodgers, Paul C., Jr. "Brown's *Ormond:* The Fruits of Improvisation." *AQ* 26 (1974): 4–22.

Stout, Janis P. *Sodoms in Eden*, 46–50.

Witherington, Paul. "Charles Brockden Brown's *Ormond:* The American Artist and His Masquerades." *SAF* 4 (1976): 111–119.

Wieland (1798)

Bell, Michael D. " 'The Double-Tongued Deceiver': Sincerity and Duplicity in the Novels of Charles Brockden Brown." *EAL* 9 (1974): 146–148.

Bell, Michael Davitt. *Development of American Romance*, 46–48.

Bernard, Kenneth. "Charles Brockden Brown," in Hoyt, Charles Alva, ed. *Minor American Novelists*, 7.

Bredahl, A. Carl, Jr. "Transformations in *Wieland*." *EAL* 12 (1977): 177–192.

Butler, David L. *Dissecting a Human Heart*, 39–48.

Butler, Michael D. "Charles Brockden Brown's *Wieland:* Method and Meaning." *SAF* 4 (1976): 127–142.

Cleman, John. "Ambiguous Evil: A Study of Villains and Heroes in Charles Brockden Brown's Major Novels." *EAL* 10 (1975): 194, 195–198, 206–217.

Ferguson, Robert A. "Literature and Vocation in the Early Republic: The Example of Charles Brockden Brown." *MP* 78 (1980): 146–152.

Franklin, Wayne. "Tragedy and Comedy in Brown's *Wieland*." *Novel* 8 (1975): 147–163.

Gilmore, Michael T. "Calvinism and Gothicism: The Example of Brown's *Wieland*." *SNNTS* 9 (1977): 107–118.

Hedges, William. "Charles Brockden Brown and the Culture of Contradictions." *EAL* 9 (1974): 111–112, 119–121.

Hirsch, David H. *Reality and Idea in the Early American Novel*, 79–80, 84–92.

Hobson, Robert W. "Voices of Carwin and Other Mysteries in Charles Brockden Brown's *Wieland*." *EAL* 10 (1975): 307–309.

Hume, Robert D. "Charles Brockden Brown and the Use of Gothicism: A Reassessment." *ESQ* 66 (1972): 13–14, 15.

Ketterer, David. *New Worlds for Old*, 167–181.

Krause, Sydney J. "Romanticism in *Wieland:* Brown and the Reconciliation of Opposites," in DeMott, Robert J. and Sanford E. Marovitz, eds. *Artful Thunder*, 13–24.

Micklus, Robert. "Charles Brockden Brown's Curiosity Shop." *EAL* 15 (1980): 175–178.

Mulqueen, James E. "Plea for a Deistic Education in Charles Brockden Brown's *Wieland*." *BallS* 10.2 (1969): 70–77.

Ousby, Ian. *Reader's Guide to Fifty American Novels*, 23–25.

Petter, Henri. *Early American Novel*, 347–353.

Ridgely, J. V. "Empty World of *Wieland*," in Baldwin, Kenneth H. and David R. Kirby, eds. *Individual and Community: Variations on a Theme in American Fiction*, 3–16.

Ringe, Donald A. "Charles Brockden Brown," in Emerson, Everett, ed. *Major Writers*, 275, 276, 284–288.

Seltzer, Mark. "Saying Makes It So: Language and Event in Brown's *Wieland*." *EAL* 13 (1978): 81–91.

Soldati, Joseph A. "Americanization of Faust: A Study of Charles Brockden Brown's *Wieland*." *ESQ* no.74 (1974): 1–14.

Wilson, James D. "Incest and American Romantic Fiction." *SLitI* 7.1 (1974): 37–40.

Yarbrough, Stephen R. "Tragedy of Isolation: Fictional Technique and Environmentalism in *Wieland*." *SAF* 8 (1980): 98–105.

BROWN, CLAUDE (1937–)

Manchild in the Promised Land (1965)

Rosenblatt, Roger. *Black Fiction*, 118–126.

Wade, Melvin and Margaret Wade. "Black Aesthetic in the Black Novel." *JBS* 2.4 (1972): 399.

BROWN, FORNAN see MEEKER, RICHARD

BROWN, FRANK LONDON (1927–1962)

Trumbull Park (1959)

Fleming, Robert E. "Overshadowed by Richard Wright: Three Black Chicago Novelists." *NALF* 7 (1973): 77–79.

BROWN, HARRY (1917–1986)

Walk in the Sun (1944)

Jones, Peter G. *War and the Novelist*, 186–189, 197.

BROWN, JAMES COOKE (1921–)

Troika Incident (1970)

Meyers, Walter E. *Aliens and Linguists*, 194–198.

BROWN, RITA MAE (1944–)

Rubyfruit Jungle (1973)

Rosinsky, Natalie M. "Mothers and Daughters: Another Minority Group," in Davidson, Cathy N. and E. M. Broner, eds. *Lost Tradition*, 286–287.

BROWN, WILLIAM HILL (1765–1793)

Ira or Isabella (1807)

Stein, Roger B. "Pulled Out of the Bay: American Fiction in the Eighteenth Century." *SAF* 2 (1974): 19–20.

Power of Sympathy (1789)

Arner, Robert D. "Sentiment and Sensibility: The Role of Emotion and William Hill Brown's *The Power of Sympathy*." *SAF* 1 (1973): 121–132.

Davidson, Cathy N. *"Power of Sympathy* Reconsidered: William Hill Brown as Literary Craftsman." *EAL* 10 (1975): 14–29.
Wilson, James D. "Incest and American Romantic Fiction." *SLitI* 7.1 (1974): 33–36.

BROWN, WILLIAM WELLS (1816(?)–1884)

Clotel (1853)

Christian, Barbara. *Black Women Novelists*, 22–24.
Elder, Arlene A. *"Hindered Hand"*, 12, 17, 18, 19, 20–21, 22, 23–25, 26, 29–30, 47, 48–49, 57–58, 59.
Farrison, William Edward. *William Wells Brown*, 218–227.
Fleming, Robert E. "Humor in the Early Black Novel." *CLAJ* 17 (1973): 255.
Gayle, Addison, Jr. *Way of the New World*, 7–10.
Isani, Mukhtar Ali. "Exotic and Protest in Earlier Black Literature: The Use of Alien Setting and Character." *SIBL* 5.2 (1974): 9–10.
Rosselot, Gerald S. *"Clotel*, a Black Romance." *CLAJ* 23 (1980): 296–302.
Takaki, Ronald T. *Violence in the Black Imagination*, 223–225.
Yellin, Jean Fagan. *Intricate Knot*, 172–174.

Clotelle see *Clotel*

BRUCE, CHARLES (1906–1971)

Channel Sore (1954)

Moss, John. *Patterns of Isolation*, 178–188.
Seaman, Andrew Thompson. "Fiction in Atlantic Canada." *CanL* 68–69 (1976): 27–29.

BRUCE, KENILWORTH

Goldie (1933)

Austen, Roger. *Playing the Game*, 69–72.

BRUNNER, JOHN (1934–)

Stand on Zanzibar (1968)

Samuelson, David N. "A Comparative Study of Novels by Brunner and Delany." *Extrapolation* 15 (1973): 77–83, 90–92.

BRYAN, C. D. B. (1936–)

Great Dethriffe (1970)

Long, Robert E. "Image of Gatsby in the Fiction of Louis Auchincloss and C.D.B. Bryan." *F-H Annual* (1972): 326–328.

BUCHANAN, CYNTHIA (1942–)

Maiden (1972)
  Hendin, Josephine. *Vulnerable People*, 173.

BUCK, PEARL S. (1892–1973)

Command the Morning (1959)
  Doyle, Paul A. *Pearl S. Buck*, 124–127.

Dragon Seed (1942)
  Doyle, Paul A. *Pearl S. Buck*, 106–110.

Good Earth (1931)
  Doyle, Paul A. *Pearl S. Buck*, 29–41.

House Divided (1935)
  Doyle, Paul A. *Pearl S. Buck*, 56–61.

Kinfolk (1949)
  Doyle, Paul A. *Pearl S. Buck*, 121–124.

Living Reed (1963)
  Doyle, Paul A. *Pearl S. Buck*, 137–139.

Mother (1934)
  Doyle, Paul A. *Pearl S. Buck*, 62–66.

Other Gods (1940)
  Doyle, Paul A. *Pearl S. Buck*, 98–101.

Patriot (1939)
  Doyle, Paul A. *Pearl S. Buck*, 94–98.

Pavilion of Women (1946)
  Doyle, Paul A. *Pearl S. Buck*, 117–121.

Promise (1943)
  Doyle, Paul A. *Pearl S. Buck*, 110–112.

Proud Heart (1938)
  Doyle, Paul A. *Pearl S. Buck*, 77–80.

Time Is Noon (1967)
  Doyle, Paul A. *Pearl S. Buck*, 139–142.

Townsman (1945)
  Doyle, Paul A. *Pearl S. Buck*, 113–117.

BUCKLER, ERNEST (1908–1984)

Cruelest Month (1963)
  Chambers, Robert D. *Sinclair Ross & Ernest Buckler*, 84–92.
  Spettigue, D. O. "The Way It Was: Ernest Buckler." *Canadian Literature* 32 (Spring 1967): 40–56. Rpt. in Woodcock, George, ed. *Canadian Novel*, 155–160.

Spettigue, D. O. "The Way It Was." *Canadian Literature* 32 (Spring 1967): 40–56. Rpt. in Cook, Gregory M., ed. *Ernest Buckler*, 108–115.

Young, Alan R. *Ernest Buckler*, 37–43.

Mountain and the Valley (1952)

Atwood, Margaret. *Survival*, 186–187.

Chambers, Robert D. *Sinclair Ross & Ernest Buckler*, 66–83.

Dawson, Anthony B. "Coming of Age in Canada." *Mosaic* 11.3 (1978): 52–53.

Dawson, Anthony B. "Coming of Age in Canada," in Wortley, John, ed. *Post-War Canadian Fiction*, 52–53.

Deorksen, L. M. "*Mountain and the Valley:* An Evaluation." *WLWE* 19 (1980): 45–56.

Dooley, D. J. *Moral Vision*, 49–59.

Dooley, D. J. "Style and Communication in *The Mountain and the Valley*." *DR* 57 (1978): 671–683.

Jones, D. G. *Butterfly on Rock*, 23–25.

Moss, John. *Patterns of Isolation*, 232–235.

Moss, John. *Sex and Violence*, 90–94.

Ricou, Laurence. "David Canaan and Buckler's Style in *The Mountain and the Valley*." *DR* 57 (1978): 684–696.

Seaman, Andrew Thompson. "Fiction in Atlantic Canada." *CanL* 68–69 (1976): 30–31.

Spettigue, D. O. "The Way It Was: Ernest Buckler." *Canadian Literature* 32 (Spring 1967): 40–56. Rpt. in Woodcock, George, ed. *Canadian Novel*, 148–155.

Spettigue, D. O. "The Way It Was." *Canadian Literature* 32 (Spring 1967): 40–56. Rpt. in Cook, Gregory M., ed. *Ernest Buckler*, 99–108.

Tallman, Warren. "Wolf in the Snow." *Canadian Literature* 5 (Summer 1960): 7–20 & *Canadian Literature* 6 (Autumn 1960): 41–48. Rpt. in Cook, Gregory M., ed. *Ernest Buckler*, 56, 60–62, 71–74.

Tallman, Warren. "Wolf in the Snow." *Canadian Literature* 5 (Summer 1960): 7–20 & *Canadian Literature* 6 (Autumn 1960): 41–48. Rpt. in Gerson, Carole, comp. *Modern Canadian Fiction*, 101, 105, 106.

Watters, Reginald Eyre. *Essays and Articles*, 103–109.

Watters, R. E. "*Mountain and the Valley*," in Cook, Gregory M., ed. *Ernest Buckler*, 41–48.

Westwater, A. M. "Teufelsdrockh Is Alive and Doing Well in Nova Scotia: Carlylean Strains in *The Mountain and the Valley*." *DR* 56 (1976): 291–298.

Young, Alan R. *Ernest Buckler*, 30–37.

Young, Alan R. "Pastoral Vision of Ernest Buckler in *The Mountain and the Valley*." *DR* 53 (1973): 219–226.

BUDRYS, ALGIS (1931–)

Rogue Moon (1960)

Samuelson, David. *Visions of Tomorrow*, 287–328.

BUELL, JOHN (1927–)

Four Days (1962)

Garebian, Keith. "Real Course of Life." *CanL* 67 (1976): 77–79, 82–83.

Playground (1976)

> Bauer, William. "John Buell's *Playground*." *IFR* 4 (1977): 77–79.

Pyx (1959)

> Garebian, Keith. "Real Course of Life." *CanL* 67 (1976): 74–77.

Shrewsdale Exit (1972)

> Garebian, Keith. "Real Course of Life." *CanL* 67 (1976): 79–82.

BUNTING, JOSIAH (1939–)

Lionheads (1972)

> Beidler, Philip D. "Truth-Telling and Literary Values in the Vietnam Novel." *SAQ* 78 (1979): 143–146.

BURDICK, EUGENE (1918–1965)

Fail Safe (1962)

> Wilkinson, Rupert. "Connections with Toughness: The Novels of Eugene Burdick." *JAmS* 11 (1977): 223–239.

Ugly American (1958)

> Wilkinson, Rupert. "Connections with Toughness: The Novels of Eugene Burdick." *JAmS* 11 (1977): 223–239.

BURKE, FIELDING (1869–1968)

Call Home the Heart (1932)

> Cook, Sylvia Jenkins. *From Tobacco Road to Route 66*, 101–107.

Stone Came Rolling (1935)

> Cook, Sylvia Jenkins. *From Tobacco Road to Route 66*, 107–110.

BURNETT, FRANCES HODGSON (1849–1924)

Little Lord Fauntleroy (1886)

> Downs, Robert B. *Famous American Books*, 172–177.
> Koppes, Phyllis Bixler. "Tradition and the Individual Talent of Frances Hodgson Burnett: A Generic Analysis of *Little Lord Fauntleroy*, *A Little Princess*, and *The Secret Garden*." *ChildL* 7 (1978): 191–205.

Little Princess (1905)

> Koppes, Phyllis Bixler. "Tradition and the Individual Talent of Frances Hodgson Burnett: A Generic Analysis of *Little Lord Fauntleroy*, *A Little Princess*, and *The Secret Garden*." *ChildL* 7 (1978): 191–205.

Secret Garden (1911)

> Koppes, Phyllis Bixler. "Tradition and the Individual Talent of Frances Hodgson Burnett: A Generic Analysis of *Little Lord Fauntleroy*, *A Little Princess*, and *The Secret Garden*." *ChildL* 7 (1978): 191–205.

BURNS, JOHN HORNE (1916–1953)

Gallery (1947)

Austen, Roger. *Playing the Game*, 107–109.
French, Warren. "Fiction: A Handful of Survivors," in French, Warren, ed. *Forties*, 27–31.
Miller, Wayne Charles. *Armed America, Its Face in Fiction*, 162–167.
Waldmeir, Joseph J. *American Novels of the Second World War*, 81–82, 104–107.

Lucifer with a Book (1949)

Austen, Roger. *Playing the Game*, 110–112.

BURROUGHS, EDGAR RICE (1875–1950)

Chessmen of Mars (1922)

Scholes, Robert and Eric S. Rabkin. *Science Fiction*, 13–14.

Princess of Mars (1912)

Attebery, Brian. *Fantasy Tradition in American Literature*, 111–116.

Tarzan of the Apes (1914)

Nesteby, James R. "Tenuous Vine of *Tarzan of the Apes.*" *JPC* 13 (1980): 483–487.

Thuvia, Maid of Mars (1920)

Scholes, Robert and Eric S. Rabkin. *Science Fiction*, 13.

BURROUGHS, WILLIAM S. (1914–1997)

Exterminator (1960)

Tanner, Tony. *City of Words*, 123–125.
Tytell, John. *Naked Angels*, 135–136.

Junkie (1953)

Mottram, Eric. *William Burroughs*, 28–34.
Oxenhandler, Neal. "Listening to Burroughs' Voice," in Federman, Raymond, ed. *Surfiction*, 186–188, 190.
Stull, William L. "Quest and the Question: Cosmology and Myth in the Work of William S. Burroughs, 1953–1960." *TCL* 24 (1978): 228–230, 232–234.
Tanner, Tony. *City of Words*, 113–114.
Tytell, John. *Naked Angels*, 123–126.

Naked Lunch (1959)

Bryant, Jerry H. *Open Decision*, 206–207, 208.
Hilfer, Anthony Channell. "Mariner and Wedding Guest in William Burroughs' *Naked Lunch.*" *Criticism* 22 (1980): 252–265.
Kostelanetz, Richard. "American Fiction in the Sixties," in Kostelanetz, Richard, ed. *On Contemporary Literature*, 642–643.
McCarthy, Mary. *The Writing on the Wall*, 45–53.
Mottram, Eric. *William Burroughs*, 46–63.
Oxenhandler, Neal. "Listening to Burroughs' Voice," in Federman, Raymond, ed. *Surfiction*, 185–197.

Palumbo, Donald. "William Burroughs' Quartet of Science Fiction Novels as Dystopian Social Satire." *Extrapolation* 20 (1979): 321–328.
Pearce, Richard. *Stages of the Clown*, 88–94.
Seltzer, Alvin J. *Chaos in the Novel*, 339–359.
Stull, William L. "Quest and the Question: Cosmology and Myth in the Work of William S. Burroughs, 1953–1960." *TCL* 24 (1978): 235–241.
Tanner, Tony. *City of Words*, 114–123.
Tytell, John. *Naked Angels*, 116, 118–119, 121–123, 127, 133–135.
Vernon, John. *Garden and the Map*, 87, 105–106.

Nova Express (1964)

Bryant, Jerry H. *Open Decision*, 203–204, 207–208.
Mottram, Eric. *William Burroughs*, 102–110.
Palumbo, Donald. "William Burroughs' Quartet of Science Fiction Novels as Dystopian Social Satire." *Extrapolation* 20 (1979): 321–328.
Seltzer, Alvin J. *Chaos in the Novel*, 372–374.
Tanner, Tony. *City of Words*, 111–112, 131–135.
Tytell, John. *Naked Angels*, 128–129.

Soft Machine (1961)

Bryant, Jerry H. *Open Decision*, 204–206.
Mottram, Eric. *William Burroughs*, 64–77.
Oxenhandler, Neal. "Listening to Burroughs' Voice," in Federman, Raymond, ed. *Surfiction*, 193, 194–195, 197–198.
Palumbo, Donald. "William Burroughs' Quartet of Science Fiction Novels as Dystopian Social Satire." *Extrapolation* 20 (1979): 321–328.
Seltzer, Alvin J. *Chaos in the Novel*, 360–364.
Vernon, John. *Garden and the Map*, 102–103.

Ticket That Exploded (1962)

Mottram, Eric. *William Burroughs*, 78–101.
Oxenhandler, Neal. "Listening to Burroughs' Voice," in Federman, Raymond, ed. *Surfiction*, 189,192, 193–194.
Palumbo, Donald. "William Burroughs' Quartet of Science Fiction Novels as Dystopian Social Satire." *Extrapolation* 20 (1979): 321–328.
Seltzer, Alvin J. *Chaos in the Novel*, 364–373.
Tanner, Tony. *City of Words*, 135–138.
Tytell, John. *Naked Angels*, 130–131, 132–133.

Wild Boys (1969)

Tytell, John. *Naked Angels*, 136–138.

CABELL, JAMES BRANCH (1879–1958)

Cords of Vanity (1909)

Flora, Josephy M. "From Virginia to Poictesme: The Early Novels of James Branch Cabell." *MissQ* 32 (1979): 223–227.

Cream of the Jest (1917)

Flora, Josephy M. "From Virginia to Poictesme: The Early Novels of James Branch Cabell." *MissQ* 32 (1979): 232–239.

Godshalk, William L. "Cabell's *Cream of the Jest* and Recent American Fiction." *SLJ* 5.2 (1973): 18–31.

Eagle's Shadow (1904)

Flora, Josephy M. "From Virginia to Poictesme: The Early Novels of James Branch Cabell." *MissQ* 32 (1979): 220–223.

Jurgen (1919)

Attebery, Brian. *Fantasy Tradition in American Literature*, 122–126.

Millett, Fred B. "James Branch Cabell," in Hoyt, Charles Alva, ed. *Minor American Novelists*, 47–50.

Rivet in Grandfather's Neck (1915)

Flora, Joseph M. "From Virginia to Poictesme: The Early Novels of James Branch Cabell." *MissQ* 32 (1979): 228–232.

CABLE, GEORGE WASHINGTON (1844–1925)

Dr. Sevier (1884)

Hearn, Lafcadio. "Mr. Cable's *Dr. Sevier*," in Ichikawa, Sanki, ed. *Essays in American Literature*. Tokyo: Hokuseido Press, 1929. 164–170. Rpt. in Turner, Arlin, ed. *Critical Essays on George W. Cable*, 64–66.

Rubin, Louis D., Jr. *George W. Cable*, 134–151.

Skaggs, Merrill Maguire. *Folk of Southern Fiction*, 158, 160, 163, 164, 166, 167, 168, 172–173.

Grandissimes (1880)

Aaron, Daniel. "George Washington Cable," in Aaron, Daniel. *Unwritten War: American Writers and the Civil War*. New York: Alfred A. Knopf, 1973. 272–282. Rpt. in Turner, Arlin, ed. *Critical Essays on George W. Cable*, 234–237.

Aaron, Daniel. *Unwritten War*, 278–281.

Arvin, Newton. "Introduction to *The Grandissimes*." Cable, George W. *Grandissimes: A Story of Creole Life*. New York: Sagamore Press, 1957. v–xi. Rpt. in Turner, Arlin, ed. *Critical Essays on George W. Cable*, 180–184.

Bendixen, Alfred. "Cable's *The Grandissimes:* A Literary Pioneer Confronts the Southern Tradition." *SoQ* 18.4 (1980): 23–33.

Berkove, Lawrence I. "Free Man of Color in *The Grandissimes* and Works by Harris and Mark Twain." *SoQ* 18.4 (1980): 60–65, 71.

Berzon, Judith R. *Neither White Nor Black*, 106–109.

Brownell, W. C. "Cable's *The Grandissimes*." *Nation* 31 (9 Dec 1880): 415–416. Rpt. in Turner, Arlin, ed. *Critical Essays on George W. Cable*, 17–21.

Campbell, Michael L. "Negro in Cable's *The Grandissimes*." *MissQ* 27 (1974): 165–178.

Clark, William Bedford. "Cable and the Theme of Miscegenation in *Old Creole Days* and *The Grandissimes*." *MissQ* 30 (1977): 602–607.

Clark, William Bedford. "Humor in Cable's *The Grandissimes*." *SoQ* 18.4 (1980): 51–59.

Cleman, John. "Art of Local Color in George W. Cable's *The Grandissimes*." *AL* 47 (1975): 396–410.

Evans, William. "French-English Dialect in *The Grandissimes*." *American Speech* 46 (Fall-Winter 1971): 210–222. Rpt. in Turner, Arlin, ed. *Critical Essays on George W. Cable*, 209–220.

Henderson, Harry B. *Versions of the Past*, 204–209.
Holditch, W. Kenneth and Drayton Hamilton. "*Grandissimes* and the French Quarter." *SoQ* 18.4 (1980): 34–50.
Howell, Elmo. "George Washington Cable's Creoles: Art and Reform in *The Grandissimes*." *MissQ* 26 (1973): 43–53.
Howell, Elmo. "George Washington Cable's Creoles: Art and Reform in *The Grandissimes*." *Mississippi Quarterly* 26 (Winter 1972–73): 42–53. Rpt. in Turner, Arlin, ed. *Critical Essays on George W. Cable*, 221–228.
Jehlen, Myra. *Class and Character in Faulkner's South*, 85–86.
Richardson, Thomas J. "Introduction: Honore Grandissime's Southern Dilemma." *SoQ* 18.4 (1980): 1–12.
Ringe, Donald A. "Narrative Voice in Cable's *The Grandissimes*." *SoQ* 18.4 (1980): 13–22.
Rubin, Louis D., Jr. "Division of the Heart: Cable's *The Grandissimes*." *SLJ* 1.2 (1969): 27–47.
Rubin, Louis D., Jr. "Division of the Heart: Cable's *The Grandissimes*." *Southern Literary Journal* 1 (Spring 1969): 27–47. Rpt. in Turner, Arlin, ed. *Critical Essays on George W. Cable*, 195–208.
Rubin, Louis D., Jr. *George W. Cable*, 79–96.
Skaggs, Merrill Maguire. *Folk of Southern Fiction*, 156, 157, 158, 159, 160, 162, 163, 164, 165–166, 172, 174, 180.
Stephens, Robert O. "Cable's *The Grandissimes* and the Comedy of Manners." *AL* 51 (1980): 507–519.

John March (1894)

Godbold, E. Stanley, Jr. "Battleground Revisited: Reconstruction in Southern Fiction, 1895–1905." *SAQ* 73 (1974): 101–103.
Rubin, Louis D., Jr. *George W. Cable*, 213–238.
Skaggs, Merrill Maguire. *Folk of Southern Fiction*, 107–112.

CAHAN, ABRAHAM (1860–1951)

Rise of David Levinsky (1917)

Chametzky, Jules. "Focus on Abraham Cahan's *The Rise of David Levinsky:* Boats Against the Current," in Madden, David, ed. *American Dreams, American Nightmares*, 87–93.
Guttmann, Allen. *Jewish Writer in America*, 30–33.
Zanger, Jules. "David Levinsky: Master of Pilpul." *PLL* 13 (1977): 283–294.

Yekl (1896)

Fine, David M. "Abraham Cahan, Stephen Crane, and the Romantic Tenement Tale of the Nineties." *AmerS* 14.1 (1974): 102–106.
Marovitz, Sanford E. "*Yekl:* The Ghetto Realism of Abraham Cahan." *ALR* 2 (1969): 271–273.

CAIN, GEORGE (1943–)

Blueschild Baby (1970)

Baker, Houston A., Jr. *Singers of Daybreak*, 81–91.

CAIN, JAMES M. (1892–1977)

Postman Always Rings Twice (1934)

Lehan, Richard. *Dangerous Crossing*, 62–66.
Madden, David. "James M. Cain's *The Postman Always Rings Twice* and Albert Camus's *The Stranger*." *PLL* 6 (1970): 407–419.
Wells, Walter. *Tycoons and Locusts*, 14–35.

CALDWELL, ERSKINE (1903–1987)

Bastard (1929)

Korges, James. *Erskine Caldwell*, 12–13.

Episode in Palmetto (1950)

Korges, James. *Erskine Caldwell*, 40–41.

Georgia Boy (1943)

Korges, James. *Erskine Caldwell*, 36–39.

God's Little Acre (1933)

Cook, Sylvia Jenkins. *From Tobacco Road to Route 66*, 71–76.
Gray, Richard. *Literature of Memory*, 119–124.
Hearn, Charles R. *American Dream in the Great Depression*, 85–86.
Korges, James. *Erskine Caldwell*, 25–32.

House in the Uplands (1946)

Korges, James. *Erskine Caldwell*, 40.

Journeyman (1935)

Korges, James. *Erskine Caldwell*, 32–35.

Miss Mamma Aimee (1967)

Korges, James. *Erskine Caldwell*, 43–44.

Place Called Estherville (1949)

Berzon, Judith R. *Neither White Nor Black*, 73–74.

Poor Fool (1930)

Korges, James. *Erskine Caldwell*, 13.

Tobacco Road (1932)

Cook, Sylvia Jenkins. *From Tobacco Road to Route 66*, 65–71.
Gray, Richard. *Literature of Memory*, 112–113.
Korges, James. *Erskine Caldwell*, 22–24.

Trouble in July (1940)

Korges, James. *Erskine Caldwell*, 35–36.

CALLAGHAN, MORLEY (1903–1990)

Broken Journey (1932)

Hoar, Victor. *Morley Callaghan*, 70–73.
McPherson, Hugo. "Two Worlds of Morley Callaghan," *Queen's Quarterly* 64.3 (Autumn 1957): 350–365. Rpt. in Conron, Brandon, ed. *Morley Callaghan*, 66.

Morley, Patricia. *Morley Callaghan*, 22–25.

Woodcock, George. "Lost Eurydice: The Novels of Callaghan," *Canadian Literature* 21 (Summer 1964): 21–35. Rpt. in Conron, Brandon, ed. *Morley Callaghan*, 95–96.

Woodcock, George. "Lost Eurydice: The Novels of Callaghan," in Woodcock, George, ed. *Canadian Novel*, 78–79.

Woodcock, George. *Odysseus Ever Returning*, 31.

Close to the Sun Again (1977)

Morley, Patricia. *Morley Callaghan*, 59–60.

Fine and Private Place (1975)

Dooley, D. J. *Moral Vision*, 61–62.

Morley, Patricia. *Morley Callaghan*, 55–58.

It's Never Over (1930)

Hoar, Victor. *Morley Callaghan*, 17–19, 57, 67–70, 82–83.

Woodcock, George. "Lost Eurydice: The Novels of Callaghan," *Canadian Literature* 21 (Summer 1964): 21–35. Rpt. in Conron, Brandon, ed. *Morley Callaghan*, 94–95.

Woodcock, George. "Lost Eurydice: The Novels of Callaghan," in Woodcock, George, ed. *Canadian Novel*, 78.

Woodcock, George. *Odysseus Ever Returning*, 30–31.

Loved and the Lost (1951)

Dooley, D. J. *Moral Vision*, 62, 63–77.

Hoar, Victor. *Morley Callaghan*, 38, 57, 107–117.

Jones, D. G. *Butterfly on Rock*, 52–55.

McPherson, Hugo. "Two Worlds of Morley Callaghan," *Queen's Quarterly* 64.3 (Autumn 1957): 350–365. Rpt. in Conron, Brandon, ed. *Morley Callaghan*, 70–73.

Morley, Patricia. *Morley Callaghan*, 41–43.

Walsh, William. *Manifold Voice*, 203–206.

Walsh, William. *Manifold Voice: Studies in Commonwealth Literature*. London: Chatto & Windus, 1970. 185–212. Rpt. in Conron, Brandon, ed. *Morley Callaghan*, 145–148.

Wilson, Edmund. *O Canada: An American's Notes on Canadian Culture*. New York: Farrar, Straus & Giroux, 1965. 9–31. Rpt. in Conron, Brandon, ed. *Morley Callaghan*, 108–109, 112–113, 118–119.

Woodcock, George. "Lost Eurydice: The Novels of Callaghan," *Canadian Literature* 21 (Summer 1964): 21–35. Rpt. in Conron, Brandon, ed. *Morley Callaghan*, 99–100.

Woodcock, George. "Lost Eurydice: The Novels of Callaghan," in Woodcock, George, ed. *Canadian Novel*, 83.

Woodcock, George. *Odysseus Ever Returning*, 35–36.

Many-Colored Coat (1960)

Hoar, Victor. *Morley Callaghan*, 37–38, 46, 57, 88, 103–106.

Morley, Patricia. *Morley Callaghan*, 43–46.

Walsh, William. *Manifold Voice*, 206–212.

Walsh, William. *Manifold Voice: Studies in Commonwealth Literature*. London:

Chatto & Windus, 1970. 185–212. Rpt. in Conron, Brandon, ed. *Morley Callaghan*, 148–154.

Wilson, Edmund. *O Canada: An American's Notes on Canadian Culture*. New York: Farrar, Straus & Giroux, 1965. 9–31. Rpt. in Conron, Brandon, ed. *Morley Callaghan*, 109–114, 118.

Woodcock, George. "Lost Eurydice: The Novels of Callaghan," *Canadian Literature* 21 (Summer 1964): 21–35. Rpt. in Conron, Brandon, ed. *Morley Callaghan*, 100–101.

Woodcock, George. "Lost Eurydice: The Novels of Callaghan," in Woodcock, George, ed. *Canadian Novel*, 83–84.

Woodcock, George. *Odysseus Ever Returning*, 36–37.

More Joy in Heaven (1937)

Dooley, D. J. *Moral Vision*, 63.

Hoar, Victor. *Morley Callaghan*, 54–56, 73–74, 86, 88, 104.

McPherson, Hugo. "Two Worlds of Morley Callaghan," *Queen's Quarterly* 64.3 (Autumn 1957): 350–365. Rpt. in Conron, Brandon, ed. *Morley Callaghan*, 69–70.

Morley, Patricia. *Morley Callaghan*, 34–38.

Walsh, William. *Manifold Voice*, 198–202.

Walsh, William. *Manifold Voice: Studies in Commonwealth Literature*. London: Chatto & Windus, 1970. 185–212. Rpt. in Conron, Brandon, ed. *Morley Callaghan*, 141–145.

Woodcock, George. "Lost Eurydice: The Novels of Callaghan," *Canadian Literature* 21 (Summer 1964): 21–35. Rpt. in Conron, Brandon, ed. *Morley Callaghan*, 96–99.

Woodcock, George. "Lost Eurydice: The Novels of Callaghan," in Woodcock, George, ed. *Canadian Novel*, 80–82.

Woodcock, George. *Odysseus Ever Returning*, 32–34.

Passion in Rome (1961)

Hoar, Victor. *Morley Callaghan*, 14–15, 59–64, 90.

Morley, Patricia. *Morley Callaghan*, 46–47.

Ward, Anthony. "Way of Feeling," *Spectator* 7083 (March 27, 1964): 422–423. Rpt. in Conron, Brandon, ed. *Morley Callaghan*, 104–105.

Watt, Frank W. "Morley Callaghan's *A Passion in Rome*," *Varsity Graduate* (University of Toronto) 9.5 (March 1962): 6, 8, 10, 12. Rpt. in Conron, Brandon, ed. *Morley Callaghan*, 84–87.

Wilson, Milton. "Callaghan's Caviare," *Tamarack Review* 22 (Winter 1962): 88–93. Rpt. in Conron, Brandon, ed. *Morley Callaghan*, 79–83.

Woodcock, George. "Lost Eurydice: The Novels of Callaghan," *Canadian Literature* 21 (Summer 1964): 21–35. Rpt. in Conron, Brandon, ed. *Morley Callaghan*, 101–103.

Woodcock, George. "Lost Eurydice: The Novels of Callaghan," in Woodcock, George, ed. *Canadian Novel*, 84–86.

Woodcock, George. *Odysseus Ever Returning*, 37–39.

Strange Fugitive (1928)

Hoar, Victor. *Morley Callaghan*, 15–17, 29–32, 38, 56–57, 87.

McPherson, Hugo. "Two Worlds of Morley Callaghan," *Queen's Quarterly* 64.3

(Autumn 1957): 350–365. Rpt. in Conron, Brandon, ed. *Morley Callaghan*, 62–65.

Mathews, Robin. *Canadian Literature*, 96–101.

Mathews, Robin D. "Wacousta Factor," in Bessai, Diane and David Jackel, eds. *Figures in a Ground*, 313.

Morley, Patricia. *Morley Callaghan*, 13–15.

Wilson, Edmund. *O Canada: An American's Notes on Canadian Culture*. New York: Farrar, Straus & Giroux, 1965. 9–31. Rpt. in Conron, Brandon, ed. *Morley Callaghan*, 114–115, 118.

Woodcock, George. "Introduction to *Turvey*." Birney, Earle. *Turvey*. Toronto: McClelland and Stewart, 1963. Rpt. in Nesbitt, Bruce, ed. *Earle Birney*, 86–89.

Woodcock, George. "Lost Eurydice: The Novels of Callaghan," *Canadian Literature* 21 (Summer 1964): 21–35. Rpt. in Conron, Brandon, ed. *Morley Callaghan*, 91–94.

Woodcock, George. "Lost Eurydice: The Novels of Callaghan," in Woodcock, George, ed. *Canadian Novel*, 75–77.

Woodcock, George. *Odysseus Ever Returning*, 27–30.

Such Is My Beloved (1934)

Boire, Gary A. "Parable and the Priest." *CanL* 81 (1979): 159–162.

Dooley, D. J. *Moral Vision*, 62–63.

Harrison, Dick. "American Adam and the Canadian Christ." *TCL* 16 (1970): 163–164.

Hoar, Victor. *Morley Callaghan*, 10–12, 79–82, 93–98.

McPherson, Hugo. "Two Worlds of Morley Callaghan," *Queen's Quarterly* 64.3 (Autumn 1957): 350–365. Rpt. in Conron, Brandon, ed. *Morley Callaghan*, 66–68.

Morley, Patricia. *Morley Callaghan*, 27–30.

Sutherland, Ronald. *Second Image*, 76–79.

Walsh, William. *Manifold Voice*, 191–198.

Walsh, William. *Manifold Voice: Studies in Commonwealth Literature*. London: Chatto & Windus, 1970. 185–212. Rpt. in Conron, Brandon, ed. *Morley Callaghan*, 134–140.

Woodcock, George. "Lost Eurydice: The Novels of Callaghan," *Canadian Literature* 21 (Summer 1964): 21–35. Rpt. in Conron, Brandon, ed. *Morley Callaghan*, 96–99.

Woodcock, George. "Lost Eurydice: The Novels of Callaghan," in Woodcock, George, ed. *Canadian Novel*, 79–82.

Woodcock, George. *Odysseus Ever Returning*, 34.

They Shall Inherit the Earth (1935)

Hoar, Victor. *Morley Callaghan*, 12–13, 36–37, 47, 83–86, 88–90, 102–103.

McPherson, Hugo. "Two Worlds of Morley Callaghan," *Queen's Quarterly* 64.3 (Autumn 1957): 350–365. Rpt. in Conron, Brandon, ed. *Morley Callaghan*, 68.

Mathews, Robin. *Canadian Literature*, 96–97, 101–107.

Morley, Patricia. *Morley Callaghan*, 30–33.

Wilson, Edmund. *O Canada: An American's Notes on Canadian Culture*. New York: Farrar, Straus & Giroux, 1965. 9–31. Rpt. in Conron, Brandon, ed. *Morley Callaghan*, 115–116.

Woodcock, George. "Lost Eurydice: The Novels of Callaghan," *Canadian Litera-*

ture 21 (Summer 1964): 21–35. Rpt. in Conron, Brandon, ed. *Morley Callaghan*, 96–99.

Woodcock, George. "Lost Eurydice: The Novels of Callaghan," in Woodcock, George, ed. *Canadian Novel*, 79–82.

Woodcock, George. *Odysseus Ever Returning*, 32–34.

CALMER, EDGAR see CALMER, NED

CALMER, NED (1907–1986)

Beyond the Street (1934)
    Austen, Roger. *Playing the Game*, 76–77.

Strange Land (1950)
    Bryant, Jerry H. *Open Decision*, 122–123, 131, 134–135, 144–145.

CANIZIO, FRANK (1913–)

Man Against Fate (1958)
    Green, Rose Basile. *Italian-American Novel*, 285–288.

CANZONERI, ROBERT (1925–)

Men with Little Hammers (1969)
    Green, Rose Basile. *Italian-American Novel*, 239–243.

CAPE, JUDITH see PAGE, P. K.

CAPOTE, TRUMAN (1924–1984)

In Cold Blood (1965)
    Garson, Helen S. *Truman Capote*, 141–164.
    Gindin, James. *Harvest of a Quiet Eye*, 352–353.
    Hendin, Josephine. *Vulnerable People*, 63–68.
    Hersey, John. "Legend on the License." *YR* 70 (1980): 3–4.
    Hollowell, John. *Fact & Fiction*, 63–86.
    Nance, William L. *Worlds of Truman Capote*, 186–228.
    Tanner, Tony. *City of Words*, 345–346.

Other Voices, Other Rooms (1948)
    Austen, Roger. *Playing the Game*, 114–116.
    Garson, Helen S. *Truman Capote*, 13–25.
    Nance, William L. *Worlds of Truman Capote*, 41–64.
    Perry, J. Douglas, Jr. "Gothic as Vortex: The Form of Horror in Capote, Faulkner, and Styron." *MFS* 19 (1973): 156–159.
    Ruoff, Gene W. "Truman Capote: The Novelist as Commodity," in French, Warren, ed. *Forties*, 266–268.

CARON, LOUIS (1942–)

Le bonhomme sept-heures (1978)
   Poulin, Gabrielle. *Romans du pays*, 285–290.

CARRIER, ROCH (1937–)

Floralie, où es-tu? (1969)
   Hathorn, Ramon. "Imaginary World of Roch Carrier." *CMLR* 31 (1975): 199.
   Poulin, Gabrielle. *Romans du pays*, 104–111.
   Rasporich, Beverly J. "Sacrifice and Death in French-Canadian Fiction: An English
      Reading." *DR* 55 (1975): 462–464.
   Urbas, Jeannette. *From Thirty Acres to Modern Times*, 150–151.

Floralie, where are you? see *Floralie, où es-tu?*

Il est par là, le soleil (1970)
   Atwood, Margaret. *Survival*, 221–222.
   Hathorn, Ramon. "Imaginary World of Roch Carrier." *CMLR* 31 (1975): 199–200.
   Poulin, Gabrielle. *Romans du pays*, 112–123.
   Rasporich, Beverly J. "Sacrifice and Death in French-Canadian Fiction: An English
      Reading." *DR* 55 (1975): 464–465.
   Urbas, Jeannette. *From Thirty Acres to Modern Times*, 151–154.

Is It the Sun, Philibert? see *Il est par là, le soleil*

Jolis deuils (1964)
   Poulin, Gabrielle. *Romans du pays*, 91–95.

Le deux-millième étage (1973)
   Hathorn, Ramon. "Imaginary World of Roch Carrier." *CMLR* 31 (1975): 200.
   Urbas, Jeannette. *From Thirty Acres to Modern Times*, 154.

They won't demolish me! see *Le deux-millième étage*

CATHER, WILLA (1873–1947)

Alexander's Bridge (1912)
   Borgman, Paul. "Dialectic of Willa Cather's Moral Vision." *Renascence* 27
      (1975): 146, 148–149.
   Gerber, Philip. *Willa Cather*, 73–75, 101.
   Giannone, Richard. "Willa Cather and the Human Voice," in Murphy, John J., ed.
      Five Essays on Willa Cather, 33.
   Stouck, David. *Willa Cather's Imagination*, 12–19.

Death Comes for the Archbishop (1927)
   Allen, Walter. *Urgent West*, 202.
   Borgman, Paul. "Dialectic of Willa Cather's Moral Vision." *Renascence* 27
      (1975): 147.
   Curtin, William M. "Willa Cather and *The Varieties of Religious Experience*."
      Renascence 27 (1975): 121–122.
   Dinn, James M. "Novelist's Miracle: Structure and Myth in *Death Comes for the
      Archbishop*." *WAL* 7.1 (1972): 39–46.

Gerber, Philip. *Willa Cather*, 121–123.

Giannone, Richard. "Willa Cather and the Human Voice," in Murphy, John J., ed. *Five Essays on Willa Cather*, 44.

Henderson, Harry B. *Versions of the Past*, 250–253.

McFarland, Dorothy Tuck. *Willa Cather*, 96–110.

McLay, Catherine M. "Religion in the Novels of Willa Cather." *Renascence* 27 (1975): 132–133, 134, 136–137, 138–140, 141, 142, 143.

Murphy, John J. "Willa Cather and Hawthorne: Significant Resemblances." *Renascence* 27 (1975): 172.

Murphy, John J. "Willa Cather's Archbishop: A Western and Classical Perspective." *WAL* 13 (1978): 141–150.

Schneider, Sister Lucy, C. S. J. "Cather's 'Land-Philosophy' in *Death Comes for the Archbishop*." *Renascence* 22 (1970): 78–86.

Shelton, Frank W. "Image of the Rock and the Family in the Novels of Willa Cather." *MarkR* 6 (1976): 12.

Stouck, David. "Willa Cather and the Indian Heritage." *TCL* 22 (1976): 435–436, 441–442.

Stouck, David. *Willa Cather's Imagination*, 129–149.

Stouck, Mary Ann and David Stouck. "Art and Religion in *Death Comes for the Archbishop*." *ArQ* 29 (1973): 293–302.

Stouck, Mary Ann and David Stouck. "Hagiographical Style in *Death Comes to the Archbishop*." *UTQ* 41 (1972): 293–307.

Sullivan, Patrick J. "Willa Cather's Southwest." *WAL* 7.1 (1972): 33–37.

Watkins, Floyd C. *In Time and Place*, 105–130.

Woodress, James. "Genesis of the Prologue of *Death Comes for the Archbishop*." *AL* 50 (1978): 473–478.

Lost Lady (1923)

Allen, Walter. *Urgent West*, 201–202.

Borgman, Paul. "Dialectic of Willa Cather's Moral Vision." *Renascence* 27 (1975): 146.

Brunauer, Dalma H. "Problem of Point of View in *A Lost Lady*." *Renascence* 28 (1975): 47–52.

Gerber, Philip. *Willa Cather*, 109–112.

Giannone, Richard. "Willa Cather and the Human Voice," in Murphy, John J., ed. *Five Essays on Willa Cather*, 44, 45.

Hamner, Eugenie Lambert. "Affirmations in Willa Cather's *A Lost Lady*." *MidQ* 17 (1976): 245–251.

Helmick, Evelyn Thomas. "Broken World: Medievalism in *A Lost Lady*." *Renascence* 28 (1975): 39–46.

Lavender, David. "Petrified West and the Writer." *American Scholar* 37.2 (Spring 1968). Rpt. in Haslam, Gerald W., ed. *Western Writing*, 152.

McFarland, Dorothy Tuck. *Willa Cather*, 62–70.

Moers, Ellen. *Literary Women*, 238–239.

Murphy, John J. "Willa Cather and Hawthorne: Significant Resemblances." *Renascence* 27 (1975): 162–166.

Murphy, John J. "Willa Cather: The Widening Gyre," in Murphy, John J., ed. *Five Essays on Willa Cather*, 63–67.

Randall, John H., III. "Willa Cather and the Pastoral Tradition," in Murphy, John J., ed. *Five Essays on Willa Cather*, 91–94.

Rosowski, Susan J. "Willa Cather's *A Lost Lady:* The Paradoxes of Change." *Novel* 11 (1977): 51–62.

Slote, Bernice. "Willa Cather and the Sense of History," in Lee, L. L. and Merrill Lewis, ed. *Women, Women Writers, and the West*, 168–169.

Stouck, David. *Willa Cather's Imagination*, 58–69.

Lucy Gayheart (1935)

Borgman, Paul. "Dialectic of Willa Cather's Moral Vision." *Renascence* 27 (1975): 147–148.

Giannone, Richard. "Willa Cather and the Human Voice," in Murphy, John J., ed. *Five Essays on Willa Cather*, 44.

McFarland, Dorothy Tuck. *Willa Cather*, 124–127.

Murphy, John J. " 'Lucy's Case': An Interpretation of *Lucy Gayheart*." *MarkR* 9 (1980): 26–29.

Stouck, David. *Willa Cather's Imagination*, 214–225.

My Ántonia (1918)

Allen, Walter. *Urgent West*, 201.

Borgman, Paul. "Dialectic of Willa Cather's Moral Vision." *Renascence* 27 (1975): 152–154.

Curtin, William M. "Willa Cather and *The Varieties of Religious Experience*." *Renascence* 27 (1975): 116–117.

Gelfant, Blanche H. "Forgotten Reaping-Hook: Sex in *My Ántonia*." *AL* 43 (1971): 60–82.

Gerber, Philip. *Willa Cather*, 87–92, 103–104.

Giannone, Richard. "Willa Cather and the Human Voice," in Murphy, John J., ed. *Five Essays on Willa Cather*, 22–23, 40–43.

Harris, Richard C. "Renaissance Pastoral Conventions and the Ending of *My Ántonia*." *MarkR* 8 (1978): 8–11.

Helmick, Evelyn. "Mysteries of Ántonia." *MidQ* 17 (1976): 173–185.

Hinz, Evelyn J. "Willa Cather's Technique and the Ideology of Populism." *WAL* 7.1 (1972): 47–61.

McFarland, Dorothy Tuck. *Willa Cather*, 40–49.

McLay, Catherine M. "Religion in the Novels of Willa Cather." *Renascence* 27 (1975): 129.

Martin, Terence. "Drama of Memory in *My Ántonia*." *PMLA* 84 (1969): 304–311.

Murphy, John J. "Willa Cather and Hawthorne: Significant Resemblances." *Renascence* 27 (1975): 167–168.

Murphy, John J. "Willa Cather: The Widening Gyre," in Murphy, John J., ed. *Five Essays on Willa Cather*, 55–57.

Popken, Randall L. "From Innocence to Experience in *My Ántonia* and *Boy Life on the Prairie*." *NDQ* 46.2 (1978): 73–81.

Randall, John H., III. "Willa Cather and the Pastoral Tradition," in Murphy, John J., ed. *Five Essays on Willa Cather*, 87–91.

Rucker, Mary E. "Prospective Focus in *My Ántonia*." *ArQ* 29 (1973): 303–316.

Slote, Bernice. "Willa Cather and the Sense of History," in Lee, L. L. and Merrill Lewis, ed. *Women, Women Writers, and the West*, 167–168.

Stouck, David. "Perspective as Structure and Theme in *My Ántonia*." *TSLL* 12 (1970): 285–294.

Stouck, David. *Willa Cather's Imagination*, 46–58.

Stuckey, W. J. "*My Ántonia*: A Rose for Miss Cather." *SNNTS* 4 (1972): 473–483.

Sullivan, Patrick J. "Willa Cather's Southwest." *WAL* 7.1 (1972): 26–27.
Watkins, Floyd C. *In Time and Place*, 73–101.

My Mortal Enemy (1926)

Gerber, Philip. *Willa Cather*, 117–120.
McFarland, Dorothy Tuck. *Willa Cather*, 88–94.
McLay, Catherine M. "Religion in the Novels of Willa Cather." *Renascence* 27 (1975): 131–132, 135–136, 140.
Rosowski, S. J. "Narrative Technique in Cather's *My Mortal Enemy*." *JNT* 8 (1978): 141–149.
Stouck, David. *Willa Cather's Imagination*, 120–129.

O Pioneers! (1913)

Bohlke, L. Brent. "Ecstasy of Alexandra Bergson." *CLQ* 11 (1975): 139–149.
Borgman, Paul. "Dialectic of Willa Cather's Moral Vision." *Renascence* 27 (1975): 146, 149–151.
Gerber, Philip. *Willa Cather*, 75–80, 101–102.
Giannone, Richard. "Willa Cather and the Human Voice," in Murphy, John J., ed. *Five Essays on Willa Cather*, 35–37, 39–40.
Hinz, Evelyn J. "Willa Cather's Technique and the Ideology of Populism." *WAL* 7.1 (1972): 47–61.
McFarland, Dorothy Tuck. *Willa Cather*, 20–28.
McLay, Catherine M. "Religion in the Novels of Willa Cather." *Renascence* 27 (1975): 129, 130.
Murphy, John J. "Willa Cather: The Widening Gyre," in Murphy, John J., ed. *Five Essays on Willa Cather*, 52–55.
O'Brien, Sharon. "Unity of Willa Cather's 'Two-Part Pastoral': Passion in *O Pioneers!*" *SAF* 6 (1978): 157–171.
Randall, John H., III. "Willa Cather and the Pastoral Tradition," in Murphy, John J., ed. *Five Essays on Willa Cather*, 81–87.
Shelton, Frank W. "Wild Duck Image in Willa Cather and Henrik Ibsen." *ANQ* 15 (1976): 24–27.
Stouck, David. "Willa Cather and the Indian Heritage." *TCL* 22 (1976): 437–439.
Stouck, David. *Willa Cather's Imagination*, 23–32.

One of Ours (1922)

Arnold, Marilyn. "*One of Ours:* Willa Cather's Losing Battle." *WAL* 13 (1978): 259–266.
Gerber, Philip. *Willa Cather*, 93, 104–109.
McFarland, Dorothy Tuck. *Willa Cather*, 52–60.
McLay, Catherine M. "Religion in the Novels of Willa Cather." *Renascence* 27 (1975): 128–129, 130, 135.
Murphy, John J. "Willa Cather: The Widening Gyre," in Murphy, John J., ed. *Five Essays on Willa Cather*, 57–63.
Stouck, David. *Willa Cather's Imagination*, 82–96.

Professor's House (1925)

Arnold, Marilyn. "Function of Structure in Cather's *The Professor's House*." *CLQ* 11 (1975): 169–178.
Bloom, Lillian D. and Edward A. Bloom. "Poetics of Willa Cather," in Murphy, John J., ed. *Five Essays on Willa Cather*, 105–107.

Borgman, Paul. "Dialectic of Willa Cather's Moral Vision." *Renascence* 27 (1975): 147.

Gerber, Philip. *Willa Cather*, 112–117.

Giannone, Richard. "Willa Cather and the Human Voice," in Murphy, John J., ed. *Five Essays on Willa Cather*, 46–47.

McFarland, Dorothy Tuck. *Willa Cather*, 72–86.

McLay, Catherine M. "Religion in the Novels of Willa Cather." *Renascence* 27 (1975): 131.

Machen, Meredith R. "Carlyle's Presence in *The Professor's House*." *WAL* 14 (1980); 273–286.

Moers, Ellen. *Literary Women*, 235–236.

Morris, Wright. *Earthly Delights, Unearthly Adornments*, 62–66.

Murphy, John J. "Willa Cather and Hawthorne: Significant Resemblances." *Renascence* 27 (1975): 169–172.

Murphy, John J. "Willa Cather: The Widening Gyre," in Murphy, John J., ed. *Five Essays on Willa Cather*, 68–72.

Salo, Alice Bell. "*Professor's House* and *Le Mannequin d'Osier:* A Note on Willa Cather's Narrative Technique." *SAF* 8 (1980): 229–231.

Shelton, Frank W. "Image of the Rock and the Family in the Novels of Willa Cather." *MarkR* 6 (1976): 11–12.

Slote, Bernice. "Willa Cather and the Sense of History," in Lee, L. L. and Merrill Lewis, ed. *Women, Women Writers, and the West*, 169.

Stineback, David C. *Shifting World*, 101–114.

Stineback, David C. "Willa Cather's Ironic Masterpiece." *ArQ* 29 (1973): 317–330.

Stouck, David. "Willa Cather and the Indian Heritage." *TCL* 22 (1976): 435.

Stouck, David. "Willa Cather and *The Professor's House:* 'Letting Go with the Heart'." *WAL* 7.1 (1972): 13–24.

Stouck, David. *Willa Cather's Imagination*, 96–109.

Sullivan, Patrick J. "Willa Cather's Southwest." *WAL* 7.1 (1972): 30–33.

Wild, Barbara. " 'The Thing Not Named' in *The Professor's House*." *WAL* 12 (1978): 263–274.

Yongue, Patricia Lee. "Willa Cather's *The Professor's House* and Dutch Genre Painting." *Renascence* 31 (1979): 155–167.

Sapphira and the Slave Girl (1940)

Berzon, Judith R. *Neither White Nor Black*, 71.

Borgman, Paul. "Dialectic of Willa Cather's Moral Vision." *Renascence* 27 (1975): 145–146, 154–159.

Gerber, Philip. *Willa Cather*, 127–133.

Stouck, David. *Willa Cather's Imagination*, 225–232.

Shadows on the Rock (1931)

Borgman, Paul. "Dialectic of Willa Cather's Moral Vision." *Renascence* 27 (1975): 147.

Gerber, Philip. *Willa Cather*, 123–127.

Hinz, John. "Hand of the Artist in *Shadows on the Rock*." *SAF* 5 (1977): 263–268.

McFarland, Dorothy Tuck. *Willa Cather*, 112–116.

McLay, Catherine M. "Religion in the Novels of Willa Cather." *Renascence* 27 (1975): 133, 137–138, 141, 143–144.

Murphy, John J. "Willa Cather: The Widening Gyre," in Murphy, John J., ed. *Five Essays on Willa Cather*, 72–74.

Shelton, Frank W. "Image of the Rock and the Family in the Novels of Willa Cather." *MarkR* 6 (1976): 12–14.

Stouck, David. *Willa Cather's Imagination*, 149–164.

Song of the Lark (1915)

Borgman, Paul. "Dialectic of Willa Cather's Moral Vision." *Renascence* 27 (1975): 151–152.

Curtin, William M. "Willa Cather and *The Varieties of Religious Experience*." *Renascence* 27 (1975): 117–121.

Gerber, Philip. *Willa Cather*, 80–87, 102–103.

Giannone, Richard. "Willa Cather and the Human Voice," in Murphy, John J., ed. *Five Essays on Willa Cather*, 37–38.

McFarland, Dorothy Tuck. *Willa Cather*, 30–34.

McLay, Catherine M. "Religion in the Novels of Willa Cather." *Renascence* 27 (1975): 127–128.

Moseley, Ann. "Dual Nature of Art in *The Song of the Lark*." *WAL* 14 (1979): 19–32.

Roulston, Robert. "Contrapuntal Complexity of Willa Cather's *The Song of a Lark*." *MidQ* 17 (1976): 350–368.

Shelton, Frank W. "Image of the Rock and the Family in the Novels of Willa Cather." *MarkR* 6 (1976): 10–11.

Slote, Bernice. "Willa Cather and the Sense of History," in Lee, L. L. and Merrill Lewis, ed. *Women, Women Writers, and the West*, 166–167.

Stouck, David. "Willa Cather and the Indian Heritage." *TCL* 22 (1976): 434–435, 439.

Stouck, David. *Willa Cather's Imagination*, 183–198.

Sullivan, Patrick J. "Willa Cather's Southwest." *WAL* 7.1 (1972): 27–30.

CAUTELA, GIUSEPPE (1883–(?))

Moon Harvest (1925)

Green, Rose Basile. *Italian-American Novel*, 68–71.

CENEDELLA, ROBERT (1941–)

Little to the East (1963)

Green, Rose Basile. *Italian-American Novel*, 265–269.

CHAMALES, TOM T. (1924–1960)

Never So Few (1957)

Jones, Peter G. *War and the Novelist*, 178–182.

CHANDLER, RAYMOND (1888–1959)

Big Sleep (1939)

Beekman, E. M. "Raymond Chandler & an American Genre." *MR* 14 (1973): 163–164.

Macdonald, Ross. "Writer as Detective Hero," in Winks, Robin W., ed. *Detective Fiction*, 184.

Rabinowitz, Peter J. "Rats behind the Wainscoting: Politics, Convention, and Chandler's *The Big Sleep*." *TSLL* 22 (1980): 224–245.

Smith, David. "Public Eye of Raymond Chandler." *JAmS* 14 (1980): 426, 427, 439.

Farewell, My Lovely (1940)

Beekman, E. M. "Raymond Chandler & an American Genre." *MR* 14 (1973): 161–162.

Macdonald, Ross. "Writer as Detective Hero," in Winks, Robin W., ed. *Detective Fiction*, 183.

Smith, David. "Public Eye of Raymond Chandler." *JAmS* 14 (1980): 439–440.

Wells, Walter. *Tycoons and Locusts*, 71–85.

High Window (1943)

Beekman, E. M. "Raymond Chandler & an American Genre." *MR* 14 (1973): 163.

Smith, David. "Public Eye of Raymond Chandler." *JAmS* 14 (1980): 425, 427–428.

Long Goodbye (1953)

Beekman, E. M. "Raymond Chandler & an American Genre." *MR* 14 (1973): 164–168.

Macdonald, Ross. "Writer as Detective Hero," in Winks, Robin W., ed. *Detective Fiction*, 184, 185.

Palmer, Jerry. *Thrillers*, 47–50.

Smith, David. "Public Eye of Raymond Chandler." *JAmS* 14 (1980): 428, 429, 439–439.

CHANG, DIANA (1934(?)–)

Frontiers of Love (1956)

Ling, Amy. "Writer in the Hyphenated Condition: Diana Chang." *MELUS* 7.4 (1980): 71–74.

CHAPPELL, FRED (1936–)

Dagon (1968)

Dillard, R. H. W. "Letters from a Distant Lover: The Novels of Fred Chappell." *HC* 10.2 (1973): 10–12.

Gaudy Place (1973)

Dillard, R. H. W. "Letters from a Distant Lover: The Novels of Fred Chappell." *HC* 10.2 (1973): 12–15.

Inkling (1965)

Dillard, R. H. W. "Letters from a Distant Lover: The Novels of Fred Chappell." *HC* 10.2 (1973): 7–10.

It Is Time, Lord (1963)

Dillard, R. H. W. "Letters from a Distant Lover: The Novels of Fred Chappell." *HC* 10.2 (1973): 4–7.

CHAUVEAU, PIERRE J. OLIVER (1820–1890)

Charles Guérin (1853)
Sénécal, André. *"Charles Guérin:* Le récit et la thèse." *V&I* 5 (1980): 333–340.

CHEEVER, JOHN (1912–1982)

Bullet Park (1969)
Coale, Samuel. *John Cheever*, 95–105.
Waldeland, Lynne. *John Cheever*, 104–116.

Falconer (1977)
Coale, Samuel. *John Cheever*, 107–113.
Waldeland, Lynne. *John Cheever*, 127–140.

Wapshot Chronicle (1957)
Coale, Samuel. *John Cheever*, 65–80.
O'Hara, James. "Cheever's *The Wapshot Chronicle:* A Narrative of Exploration."
   Crit 22.2 (1980): 20–30.
Rupp, Richard H. *Celebration in Postwar American Fiction*, 27–33.
Waldeland, Lynne. *John Cheever*, 37–48.

Wapshot Scandal (1964)
Coale, Samuel. *John Cheever*, 81–94.
Rupp, Richard H. *Celebration in Postwar American Fiction*, 33–39.
Waldeland, Lynne. *John Cheever*, 48–62.

CHESEBRO', CAROLINE (1825–1873)

Children of Light (1853)
Baym, Nina. *Woman's Fiction*, 215–217.

Getting Along (1855)
Baym, Nina. *Woman's Fiction*, 217–223.

Isa (1852)
Baym, Nina. *Woman's Fiction*, 211–215.

Peter Carradine (1863)
Baym, Nina. *Woman's Fiction*, 226–230.

Susan, the Fisherman's Daughter see *Getting Along*

Victoria (1856)
Baym, Nina. *Woman's Fiction*, 223–226.

CHESNUTT, CHARLES WADDELL (1858–1932)

Colonel's Dream (1905)
Andrews, William L. *Literary Career of Charles W. Chesnutt*, 222–223, 237–257.
Blake, Susan L. "Better Mousetrap: Washington's Program and *The Colonel's Dream*." *CLAJ* 23 (1979): 45–59.

Elder, Arlene A. *"Hindered Hand"*, 188–195.
Fleming, Robert E. "Humor in the Early Black Novel." *CLAJ* 17 (1973): 260–261.
MacKethan, Lucinda Hardwick. *Dream of Arcady*, 97–103.
Render, Sylvia Lyons. *Charles W. Chesnutt*, 42–43, 72–73, 78–80, 96–100, 101–102, 104–105, 112–113, 139.

House Behind the Cedars (1900)

Andrews, William L. "Chesnutt's Patesville: The Presence and Influence of the Past in *The House Behind the Cedars*." *CLAJ* 15 (1972): 284–294.
Andrews, William L. *Literary Career of Charles W. Chesnutt*, 137–144, 150–152, 157–171.
Berzon, Judith R. *Neither White Nor Black*, 103.
Elder, Arlene A. *"Hindered Hand"*, 174–177.
Gayle, Addison, Jr. *Way of the New World*, 48–50.
Harris, Trudier. "Chesnutt's Frank Fowler: A Failure of Purpose?" *CLAQ* 22 (1979): 215–228.
Render, Sylvia Lyons. *Charles W. Chesnutt*, 38–39, 67, 69–70, 75–78, 90–91, 138–139.

Marrow of Tradition (1901)

Andrews, William L. *Literary Career of Charles W. Chesnutt*, 177–179, 190–208.
Delmar, P. Jay. "Character and Structure in Charles W. Chesnutt's *The Marrow of Tradition* (1901)." *ALR* 13 (1980): 284–289.
Elder, Arlene A. *"Hindered Hand"*, 177–188.
Gayle, Addison, Jr. *Way of the New World*, 50–56.
Reilly, John M. "Dilemma in Chestnutt's *The Marrow of Tradition*." *Phylon* 32 (1971): 31–38.
Render, Sylvia Lyons. *Charles W. Chesnutt*, 39–41, 66–67, 68, 70–73, 96–100, 112–113, 139.
Socken, June. "Charles Waddell Chesnutt and the Solution to the Race Problem." *NALF* 3 (1969): 52–54.

CHIEF EAGLE, DALLAS (1925–1978)

Winter Count (1967)

Larson, Charles R. *American Indian Fiction*, 98–99, 100–112.

CHILD, LYDIA MARIA (1802–1880)

Hobomok (1824)

Osborne, William S. *Lydia Maria Child*, 39–54.

Philothea (1836)

Osborne, William S. *Lydia Maria Child*, 71–90.

Rebels (1825)

Osborne, William S. *Lydia Maria Child*, 55–68.

Romance of the Republic (1867)
   Osborne, William S. *Lydia Maria Child*, 145–158.

CHILD, PHILIP (1898–1978)

God's Sparrows (1937)
   Duffy, Dennis. "Memory = Pain: The Haunted World of Philip Child." *CanL* 84
   (1980): 45–48, 52.

Mr. Ames Against Time (1949)
   Duffy, Dennis. "Memory = Pain: The Haunted World of Philip Child." *CanL* 84
   (1980): 42–43.

Village of Souls (1933)
   Duffy, Dennis. "Memory = Pain: The Haunted World of Philip Child." *CanL* 84
   (1980): 43–45, 48–55.
   Jones, D. G. *Butterfly on Rock*, 45–47.

CHOPIN, KATE (1851–1904)

Awakening (1899)
   Allen, Priscilla. "Old Critics and New: The Treatment of Chopin's *The Awaken-
   ing*," in Diamond, Arlyn and Lee R. Edwards, eds. *Authority of Experience*, 224–
   238.
   Bonner, Thomas, Jr. "Kate Chopin's 'At Fault' and *The Awakening*: A Study in
   Structure." *MarkR* 7 (1977): 10–14.
   Casale, Ottavio Mark. "Beyond Sex: The Dark Romanticism of Kate Chopin's *The
   Awakening*." *BallS* 19.1 (1978): 76–80.
   Fox-Genovese, Elizabeth. "Kate Chopin's *Awakening*." *SoS* 18 (1979): 261–290.
   Fryer, Judith. *Faces of Eve*, 243–258.
   Justus, James H. "Unawakening of Edna Pontellier." *SLJ* 10.2 (1978): 107–122.
   Klinkowitz, Jerome. *Practice of Fiction in America*, 38–48.
   May, John R. "Local Color in *The Awakening*." *SoR* 6 (1970): 1031–1040.
   Moers, Ellen. *Literary Women*, 247.
   Paulsen, Anne Lise Stromness. "Masculine Dilemma in Kate Chopin's *The Awak-
   ening*." *SoS* 18 (1979): 381–424.
   Ringe, Donald A. "Romantic Imagery in Kate Chopin's *The Awakening*." *AL* 43
   (1972): 580–588.
   Rosen, Kenneth M. "Kate Chopin's *The Awakening*: Ambiguity as Art." *JAmS* 5
   (1971): 197–199.
   Seyersted, Per. *Kate Chopin*, 134–163.
   Skaggs, Merrill Maguire. *Folk of Southern Fiction*, 185–188.
   Spacks, Patricia Meyer. *Female Imagination*, 73–77.
   Spangler, George. "Kate Chopin's *The Awakening*: A Partial Dissent." *Novel* 3
   (1970): 249–255.
   Sullivan, Ruth and Stewart Smith. "Narrative Stance in Kate Chopin's *The Awaken-
   ing*." *SAF* 1 (1973): 62–75.
   Thornton, Lawrence. "*Awakening*: A Political Romance." *AL* 52 (1980): 50–66.

Toth, Emily. "Timely and Timeless: The Treatment of Time in *The Awakening* and *Sister Carrie.*" *SoS* 16 (1977): 271–276.
Walker, Nancy. "Feminist or Naturalist: The Social Context of Kate Chopin's *The Awakening.*" *SoQ* 17.2 (1979): 95–103.
Warnken, William P. "Kate Chopin and Henry Ibsen: A Study of *The Awakening* and *A Doll's House.*" *MSE* 4.4 & 5.1 (1974–75): 43–48.
Wolff, Cynthia G. "Thanatos and Eros: Kate Chopin's *The Awakening.*" *AQ* 25 (1973): 449–471.

CHOQUETTE, ADRIENNE (1915–1973)

Le temps des villages (1975)
Poulin, Gabrielle. *Romans du pays*, 327–329.

CHOQUETTE, ERNEST (1862–1941)

La terre (1916)
Hathorn, Ramon. "Soldats, patrons et femmes 'fatales': Figures de l'Anglais' dans le roman québécois des XIXe et XXe siècles." *V&I* 6 (1980): 104–105.

CHOQUETTE, GILBERT (1929–)

L'interrogation (1962)
Belleau, André. *Le romancier fictif*, 95–96.

Un tourment extrême (1979)
Poulin, Gabrielle. *Romans du pays*, 186–191.

Wednesday's Child see *Un tourment extrême*

CLARK, WALTER VAN TILBURG (1909–1971)

City of Trembling Leaves (1945)
Lee, L. L. *Walter Van Tilburg Clark*, 28–36.
Lee, L. L. "Walter Van Tilburg Clark's Ambiguous American Dream." *College English* 26 (1965): 382–387. Rpt. in Pilkington, William T., ed. *Critical Essays on the Western American Novel*, 167–168.
Westbrook, Max. *Walter Van Tilburg Clark*, 69–91.

Ox-Bow Incident (1940)
Flora, Joseph M. "Woman with Parrot in *The Ox-Bow Incident.*" *ANQ* 17 (1979): 74–76.
Lee, L. L. *Walter Van Tilburg Clark*, 18–28.
Lee, L. L. "Walter Van Tilburg Clark's Ambiguous American Dream." *College English* 26 (1965): 382–387. Rpt. in Pilkington, William T., ed. *Critical Essays on the Western American Novel*, 169–171.
Milton, John R. "Novel in the American West." *South Dakota Review* 2.1 (1964): 56–76. Rpt. in Haslam, Gerald W., ed. *Western Writing*, 81–82.
Milton, John R. "Novel in the American West." *South Dakota Review* 2.1 (1964):

56–76. Rpt. in Pilkington, William T., ed. *Critical Essays on the Western American Novel*, 12–13.

Peterson, Levi S. "Tragedy and Western American Literature." *WAL* 6 (1972): 243–249.

Westbrook, Max. "Archetypal Ethic of *The Ox-Bow Incident*." *Western American Literature* 1 (Summer 1966): 105–118. Rpt. in Folsom, James K., ed. *Western*, 73–85.

Westbrook, Max. *Walter Van Tilburg Clark*, 55–67.

Track of the Cat (1949)

Hendricks, George D. "Symbolism in Walter Van Tilburg Clark's *The Track of the Cat*." *SAL* 3 (1973): 77–80.

Lee, L. L. *Walter Van Tilburg Clark*, 36–43.

Lee, L. L. "Walter Van Tilburg Clark's Ambiguous American Dream." *College English* 26 (1965): 382–387. Rpt. in Pilkington, William T., ed. *Critical Essays on the Western American Novel*, 166–167, 169.

Milton, John R. "Novel in the American West." *South Dakota Review* 2.1 (1964): 56–76. Rpt. in Haslam, Gerald W., ed. *Western Writing*, 81, 82.

Milton, John R. "Novel in the American West." *South Dakota Review* 2.1 (1964): 56–76. Rpt. in Pilkington, William T., ed. *Critical Essays on the Western American Novel*, 12–14.

Westbrook, Max. *Walter Van Tilburg Clark*, 93–110.

CLARKE, AUSTIN (1924–)

Meeting Point (1967)

Brown, Lloyd W. "Beneath the North Star: The Canadian Image in Black Literature." *DR* 50 (1970): 324–327.

Survivors of the Crossing (1964)

Brown, Lloyd W. "Beneath the North Star: The Canadian Image in Black Literature." *DR* 50 (1970): 324.

CLEMENS, SAMUEL LANGHORNE see TWAIN, MARK

COBB, HUMPHREY (1899–1944)

Paths of Glory (1935)

Jones, Peter G. *War and the Novelist*, 10–11.

Waldmeir, Joseph J. *American Novels of the Second World War*, 46–47.

COHEN, ALBERT (1895–1981)

Belle du Seigneur (1968)

Bond, David J. "Jewish Destiny in the Novels of Albert Cohen." *StTCL* 1 (1976): 9–22.

Les valeureux (1969)

Bond, David J. "Jewish Destiny in the Novels of Albert Cohen." *StTCL* 1 (1976): 9–22.

Mangeclous (1938)

Bond, David J. "Jewish Destiny in the Novels of Albert Cohen." *StTCL* 1 (1976): 8–22.

Solal (1930)

Bond, David J. "Jewish Destiny in the Novels of Albert Cohen." *StTCL* 1 (1976): 8, 9–22.

COHEN, ARTHUR A. (1928–1986)

In the Days of Simon Stern (1973)

Alexander, Edward. *Resonance of Dust*, 141–145.

COHEN, LEONARD (1934–)

Beautiful Losers (1966)

Atwood, Margaret. *Survival*, 101–102.

Barbour, Douglas. "Down with History: Some Notes Towards and Understanding of *Beautiful Losers*." *Open Letter* 2.3 (Summer 1974): 48–60. Rpt. in Gnarowski, Michael, ed. *Leonard Cohen*, 136–148.

Boyers, Robert. "Attitudes Toward Sex in American 'High Culture.' " *Annals of the American Academy of Political and Social Science* (March 1968). Rpt. in Boyers, Robert. *Excursions*, 127–128.

Harrison, Dick. "American Adam and the Canadian Christ." *TCL* 16 (1970): 165.

Hutcheon, Linda. "*Beautiful Losers:* All the Polarities." *CanL* 59 (1974): 42–55.

Hutcheon, Linda. "*Beautiful Losers:* All the Polarities," in Woodcock, George, ed. *Canadian Novel*, 298–311.

Hutcheon, Linda. "Poet as Novelist." *CanL* 86 (1980): 7–10, 13.

Jones, D. G. *Butterfly on Rock*, 77–82.

Lee, Dennis. *Savage Fields*, 63–103.

Macri, F. M. "*Beautiful Losers* and the Canadian Experience." *JCL* 8.1 (1973): 88–96.

Morley, Patricia A. *Immoral Moralists*, 85–96.

Moss, John. *Sex and Violence*, 94–95, 169–184.

Northey, Margot. *Haunted Wilderness*, 101–107.

Ondaatje, Michael. *Leonard Cohen*, 44–56.

Pacey, Desmond. "Phenomenon of Leonard Cohen." *Canadian Literature* 34 (Autumn 1967): 5–23. Rpt. in Gnarowski, Michael, ed. *Leonard Cohen*, 87–93.

Scobie, Stephen. *Leonard Cohen*, 96–125.

Scobie, Stephen. "Magic, Not Magicians: *Beautiful Losers* and *Story of O.*" *CanL* 45 (1970): 56–60.

Scobie, Stephen. "Magic, Not Magicians: *Beautiful Losers* and *Story of O.*" *Canadian Literature* 45 (Summer 1970): 56–60. Rpt. in Gnarowski, Michael, ed. *Leonard Cohen*, 106–110.

Schulz, Max F. *Black Humor Fiction of the Sixties*, 26–27.

Sutherland, Ronald. *Second Image*, 16–23.

Woodcock, George. *Odysseus Ever Returning*, 106–108.

Woodcock, George. "Song of the Sirens: Reflections on Leonard Cohen," in Woodcock, George. *Odysseus Ever Returning*. Toronto: McClelland and Stewart, 1970. 93–110. Rpt. in Gnarowski, Michael, ed. *Leonard Cohen*, 162, 164–166.

Favourite Game (1963)

Morley, Patricia A. *Immoral Moralists*, 73–83.

Morley, Patricia A. " 'The Knowledge of Strangerhood'; 'Monuments Were Made of Worms.' " *Journal of Canadian Fiction* 1.3 (Summer 1972): 56–60. Rpt. in Gnarowski, Michael, ed. *Leonard Cohen*, 125–134.

Moss, John. *Sex and Violence*, 44–45.

Ondaatje, Michael. *Leonard Cohen*, 23–35.

Pacey, Desmond. "Phenomenon of Leonard Cohen." *Canadian Literature* 34 (Autumn 1967): 5–23. Rpt. in Gnarowski, Michael, ed. *Leonard Cohen*, 78–84.

Scobie, Stephen. *Leonard Cohen*, 74–96.

Woodcock, George. *Odysseus Ever Returning*, 104–106, 107.

Woodcock, George. "Song of the Sirens: Reflections on Leonard Cohen," in Woodcock, George. *Odysseus Ever Returning*. Toronto: McClelland and Stewart, 1970. 93–110. Rpt. in Gnarowski, Michael, ed. *Leonard Cohen*, 161–165.

COHEN, MATT (1942–)

Colours of War (1977)

Kertzer, Jon. "Time and Its Victims: The Writing of Matt Cohen." *ECW* 17 (1980): 98–99.

Woodcock, George. "Armies Moving in the Night: The Fictions of Matt Cohen." *IFR* 6 (1976): 20, 26–30.

Woodcock, George. "To the Past via the Future." *CanL* 75 (1977): 74–77.

Woodcock, George. *World of Canadian Writing*, 140–146.

Disinherited (1974)

Kertzer, Jon. "Time and Its Victims: The Writing of Matt Cohen." *ECW* 17 (1980): 98.

Moss, John. *Sex and Violence*, 185–198.

Woodcock, George. "Armies Moving in the Night: The Fictions of Matt Cohen." *IFR* 6 (1976): 20–24.

Woodcock, George. *World of Canadian Writing*, 133–137.

Sweet Second Summer of Kitty Malone (1979)

Kertzer, Jon. "Time and Its Victims: The Writing of Matt Cohen." *ECW* 17 (1980): 99–100.

Woodcock, George. *World of Canadian Writing*, 146–148.

Wooden Hunters (1975)

Kertzer, Jon. "Time and Its Victims: The Writing of Matt Cohen." *ECW* 17 (1980): 97, 98, 99.

Woodcock, George. "Armies Moving in the Night: The Fictions of Matt Cohen." *IFR* 6 (1976): 24–26.

Woodcock, George. *World of Canadian Writing*, 137–140.

COKER, ELIZABETH BOATWRIGHT (1909–1993)

Daughter of Strangers (1950)

Berzon, Judith R. *Neither White Nor Black*, 194–195.

COLEMAN, LONNIE (1920–1982)

Sam (1959)
   Austen, Roger. *Playing the Game*, 172–174.

COLEMAN, WILLIAM LAURENCE see COLEMAN, LONNIE

COLTER, CYRUS (1910–)

Rivers of Eros (1972)
   Colter, C. "Forms of Determinism in the Fiction of Cyrus Colter." *SIBL* 4.2 (1973): 26–28.

CONAN, LAURE (1845–1924)

Angéline de Montbrun (1881)
   Heidenreich, Rosmarin. "Narrative Strategies in Laure Conan's *Angéline de Montbrun*." *CanL* 81 (1979): 37–46.

CONNELL, EVAN S., JR. (1924–)

Mr. Bridge (1969)
   White, Ray Lewis. "Evan S. Connell Jr.'s *Mrs. Bridge* and *Mr. Bridge:* A Critical Documentary." *Midamerica* 6 (1979): 141–159.

Mrs. Bridge (1959)
   Shepherd, Allen. "Mr. Bridge in *Mrs. Bridge*." *NConL* 3.3 (1973): 7–11.
   White, Ray Lewis. "Evan S. Connell Jr.'s *Mrs. Bridge* and *Mr. Bridge:* A Critical Documentary." *Midamerica* 6 (1979): 141–159.

CONNOR, RALPH (1860–1937)

Corporal Cameron (1912)
   Harrison, Dick. *Unnamed Country*, 77–79.

Foreigner (1909)
   Harrison, Dick. *Unnamed Country*, 81–82, 97–98.

Man from Glengarry (1901)
   Daniells, Roy. "Glengarry Revisited," in Stephens, Donald G., ed. *Writers of the Prairies*, 17–25.

Sky Pilot (1899)
   Harrison, Dick. *Unnamed Country*, 85–86, 95–96.

CONROY, PAT (1945–)

Great Santini (1976)
   Burkholder, Robert E. "Uses of Myth in Pat Conroy's *The Great Santini*." *Crit* 21.1 (1979): 31–37.

COOPER, JAMES FENIMORE (1789–1851)

Afloat and Ashore (1844)

Peck, H. Daniel. *World by Itself*, 42–43.
Stout, Janis P. *Sodoms in Eden*, 79–82.

Bravo (1831)

Henderson, Harry B. *Versions of the Past*, 62–63.
Loveland, Anne C. "James Fenimore Cooper and the American Mission." *AQ* 21 (1969): 245–247.
McCarthy, Harold T. *Expatriate Perspective*, 29–34.
McWilliams, John P., Jr. *Political Justice in a Republic*, 154–166.
Paul, Jay S. "Home as Cherished: The Theme of Family in Fenimore Cooper." *SNNTS* 5 (1973): 47.
Ringe, Donald A. "Light and Shadow in *The Bravo*," in Ringe, Donald A. *Pictorial Mode: Space and Time in the Art of Bryant, Irving, and Cooper*. Lexington, KY: University of Kentucky Press, 1971. 114–121. Rpt. in Fields, Wayne, ed. *James Fenimore Cooper*, 145–152.
Stout, Janis P. *Sodoms in Eden*, 75–77.
Winters, Ivor. "Fenimore Cooper or the Ruins of Time," in Winters, Ivor. *In Defense of Reason*. Chicago: Swallow Press Inc., 1947. Rpt. in Fields, Wayne, ed. *James Fenimore Cooper*, 23–24.

Chainbearer (1845)

Henderson, Harry B. *Versions of the Past*, 78–79.
McWilliams, John P., Jr. *Political Justice in a Republic*, 315–325.
Peck, H. Daniel. *World by Itself*, 151–152.
Stout, Janis P. *Sodoms in Eden*, 84.
Tuttleton, James W. *Novel of Manners in America*, 43–45.

Crater (1847)

McWilliams, John, Jr. "*Crater* and the Constitution.' *TSLL* 12 (1971): 631–645.
McWilliams, John P., Jr. *Political Justice in a Republic*, 346–374.
Peck, H. Daniel. *World by Itself*, 155–159.

Deerslayer (1841)

Baym, Nina. "Women of Cooper's *Leatherstocking Tales*." *AQ* 23 (1971): 705–706.
Baym, Nina. "Women of Cooper's *Leatherstocking Tales*," in Cornillon, Susan Koppelman, ed. *Images of Women in Fiction*, 147–149.
Bewley, Marius. "Moral and Physical Action in *The Deerslayer*," in Bewley, Marius. *Eccentric Design*. New York: Columbia University Press, 1963. 87–100. Rpt. in Fields, Wayne, ed. *James Fenimore Cooper*, 117–128.
Frederick, John T. *Darkened Sky*, 11–12.
Green, Martin. *Dreams of Adventure, Deeds of Empire*, 138–139.
Kolodny, Annette. *Lay of the Land*, 109–114.
Lawrence, D. H. "Fenimore Cooper's Leatherstocking Novels," in Lawrence, D. H. *Studies in Classic American Literature*. New York: Viking Press, 1961. Rpt. in Fields, Wayne, ed. *James Fenimore Cooper*, 49–52.
McWilliams, John P., Jr. *Political Justice in a Republic*, 276–291.
Martin, Terence. "Surviving on the Frontier: The Doubled Consciousness of Natty Bumppo." *SAQ* 75 (1975): 451, 453, 454, 457–458.

Paul, Jay S. "Home as Cherished: The Theme of Family in Fenimore Cooper." *SNNTS* 5 (1973): 48–49.

Peck, H. Daniel. *World by Itself*, 31, 48, 59–61, 65, 68–71, 76, 80, 81–82, 83–85, 159–162.

Porte, Joel. *Romance in America*, 5, 10, 11, 14–19, 22–24, 33–39.

Pratt, Linda Ray. "Abuse of Eve by the New World Adam," in Cornillon, Susan Koppelman, ed. *Images of Women in Fiction*, 158–159.

Sandy, Alan F., Jr. "Voices of Cooper's *The Deerslayer*." *ESQ* 60 (1970): 5–9.

Spengemann, William C. *Adventurous Muse*, 107–116.

Umphlett, Wiley Lee. *Sporting Myth and the American Experience*, 43–46.

Winters, Ivor. "Fenimore Cooper or the Ruins of Time," in Winters, Ivor. *In Defense of Reason*. Chicago: Swallow Press Inc., 1947. Rpt. in Fields, Wayne, ed. *James Fenimore Cooper*, 26–28.

Headsman (1833)

Denne, Constance A. "Cooper's Artistry in *The Headsman*." *NCF* 29 (1974): 77–92.

Henderson, Harry B. *Versions of the Past*, 66–67.

McCarthy, Harold T. *Expatriate Perspective*, 38–46.

McWilliams, John P., Jr. *Political Justice in a Republic*, 173–182.

Heidenmauer (1832)

Frederick, John T. *Darkened Sky*, 19–20.

Henderson, Harry B. *Versions of the Past*, 63–65.

McCarthy, Harold T. *Expatriate Perspective*, 34–37.

McWilliams, John P., Jr. *Political Justice in a Republic*, 166–173.

Home As Found (1838)

Kasson, Joy S. "Templeton Revisited: Social Criticism in *The Pioneers* and *Home as Found*." *SNNTS* 9 (1977): 54–64.

Kligerman, Jack. "Style and Form in James Fenimore Cooper's *Homeward Bound* and *Home as Found*." *JNT* 4 (1974): 45–48, 55–59.

McWilliams, John P., Jr. *Political Justice in a Republic*, 216–237.

Peck, H. Daniel. *World by Itself*, 179–181.

Stout, Janis P. *Sodoms in Eden*, 77–79.

Sundquist, Eric J. *Home as Found*, 1–40.

Sundquist, Eric J. "Incest and Imitation in Cooper's *Home as Found*." *NCF* 32 (1977): 261–284.

Tuttleton, James W. *Novel of Manners in America*, 32, 34–40.

Homeward Bound (1838)

Kligerman, Jack. "Style and Form in James Fenimore Cooper's *Homeward Bound* and *Home as Found*." *JNT* 4 (1974): 45–55.

Tuttleton, James W. *Novel of Manners in America*, 32–34.

Jack Tier (1848)

House, Kay Seymour. "Unstable Element," in House, Kay Seymour. *Cooper's Americans*. Columbus, OH: Ohio State University Press, 1965. Chapter 7. Rpt. in Fields, Wayne, ed. *James Fenimore Cooper*, 136–137.

Last of the Mohicans (1826)

Barnett, Louise K. *Ignoble Savage*, 34–35, 62–64.

Baym, Nina. "Women of Cooper's *Leatherstocking Tales*." *AQ* 23 (1971): 700–701, 704–705.

Baym, Nina. "Women of Cooper's *Leatherstocking Tales*," in Cornillon, Susan Koppelman, ed. *Images of Women in Fiction*, 140–141, 145–147.

Butler, Michael D. "Narrative Structure and Historical Process in *The Last of the Mohicans*." *AL* 48 (1976): 117–139.

Darnell, Donald G. "Cooper, Prescott and the Conquest of Indian America." *ATQ* 30.1 (1976): 10.

Frederick, John T. *Darkened Sky*, 7–9.

Green, Martin. *Dreams of Adventure, Deeds of Empire*, 135–136.

Henderson, Harry B. *Versions of the Past*, 73–77.

Kolodny, Annette. *Lay of the Land*, 96–101.

Lawrence, D. H. "Fenimore Cooper's Leatherstocking Novels," in Lawrence, D. H. *Studies in Classic American Literature*. New York: Viking Press, 1961. Rpt. in Fields, Wayne, ed. *James Fenimore Cooper*, 47–48.

Malin, Irving. "American Gothic Images." *Mosaic* 6.3 (1973): 146, 161–162.

Martin, Terence. "From the Ruins of History: *The Last of the Mohicans*." *Novel* 2 (1969): 221–229.

Martin, Terence. "From the Ruins of History: *The Last of the Mohicans*." *Novel: A Forum on Fiction* (Spring 1969): 221–229. Rpt. in Fields, Wayne, ed. *James Fenimore Cooper*, 80–92.

Martin, Terence. "Surviving on the Frontier: The Doubled Consciousness of Natty Bumppo." *SAQ* 75 (1975): 451–453.

Milder, Robert. "*Last of the Mohicans* and the New World Fall." *AL* 52 (1980): 407–429.

Ousby, Ian. *Reader's Guide to Fifty American Novels*, 35–37.

Paul, Jay S. "Home as Cherished: The Theme of Family in Fenimore Cooper." *SNNTS* 5 (1973): 43–46.

Peck, H. Daniel. *World by Itself*, 91–96, 109–145.

Porte, Joel. *Romance in America*, 18–22, 29–30, 39–41.

Rose, Marilyn O. "Time Discrepancy in *Last of the Mohicans*." *ANQ* 8 (1970): 72–73.

Lionel Lincoln (1825)

Henderson, Harry B. *Versions of the Past*, 59–61.

McWilliams, John P., Jr. *Political Justice in a Republic*, 73–85.

Peck, H. Daniel. *World by Itself*, 75–76, 107–108.

Ringe, Donald A. "Cooper's *Lionel Lincoln:* The Problem of Genre." *ATQ* 24 (1974): 24–30.

Steinbrink, Jeffrey. "Cooper's Romance of the Revolution: *Lionel Lincoln* and the Lessons of Failure." *EAL* 11 (1976–77): 336–343.

Miles Wallingford (1844)

Peck, H. Daniel. *World by Itself*, 182.

Stout, Janis P. *Sodoms in Eden*, 79–82.

Monikins (1835)

McWilliams, John P., Jr. *Political Justice in a Republic*, 341–346.

Winters, Ivor. "Fenimore Cooper or the Ruins of Time," in Winters, Ivor. *In Defense of Reason*. Chicago: Swallow Press Inc., 1947. Rpt. in Fields, Wayne, ed. *James Fenimore Cooper*, 17, 22–23.

Oak Openings (1848)

Darnell, Donald G. "Cooper, Prescott and the Conquest of Indian America." *ATQ* 30.1 (1976): 11–12.

Frederick, John T. *Darkened Sky*, 24–25.
McWilliams, John P., Jr. *Political Justice in a Republic*, 291–297.
Peck, H. Daniel. *World by Itself*, 49–59, 61, 64–65, 72–73, 77–79, 82–83.

Pathfinder (1840)

Baym, Nina. "Women of Cooper's *Leatherstocking Tales.*" *AQ* 23 (1971): 701–703.

Baym, Nina. "Women of Cooper's *Leatherstocking Tales*," in Cornillon, Susan Koppelman, ed. *Images of Women in Fiction*, 141–145.

Frederick, John T. *Darkened Sky*, 11–13.

Green, Martin. *Dreams of Adventure, Deeds of Empire*, 137–138.

Kolodny, Annette. *Lay of the Land*, 105–109.

Kolodny, Annette. *Lay of the Land: Metaphor as Experience and History in American Life and Letters*. Chapel Hill, NC: University of North Carolina Press, 1975. 105–109. Rpt. as "Love and Sexuality in *The Pathfinder*," in Fields, Wayne, ed. *James Fenimore Cooper*, 112–116.

Lawrence, D. H. "Fenimore Cooper's Leatherstocking Novels," in Lawrence, D. H. *Studies in Classic American Literature*. New York: Viking Press, 1961. Rpt. in Fields, Wayne, ed. *James Fenimore Cooper*, 49.

Martin, Terence. "Surviving on the Frontier: The Doubled Consciousness of Natty Bumppo." *SAQ* 75 (1975): 447–448, 453, 454, 458.

Peck, H. Daniel. *World by Itself*, 26–27, 29–31, 43, 44–45, 74, 79–80, 85–86.

Porte, Joel. *Romance in America*, 15–16, 18, 24–28.

Pilot (1823)

House, Kay Seymour. "Unstable Element," in House, Kay Seymour. *Cooper's Americans*. Columbus, OH: Ohio State University Press, 1965. Chapter 7. Rpt. in Fields, Wayne, ed. *James Fenimore Cooper*, 132–136.

McWilliams, John P., Jr. *Political Justice in a Republic*, 66–73.

Miller, Wayne Charles. *Armed America, Its Face in Fiction*, 15–20.

Peck, H. Daniel. *World by Itself*, 22–26, 74–75, 100–102.

Pioneers (1823)

Baym, Nina. "Women of Cooper's *Leatherstocking Tales.*" *AQ* 23 (1971): 699–700.

Baym, Nina. "Women of Cooper's *Leatherstocking Tales*," in Cornillon, Susan Koppelman, ed. *Images of Women in Fiction*, 138–140.

Darnell, Donald G. "Cooper, Prescott and the Conquest of Indian America." *ATQ* 30.1 (1976): 12.

Fiedler, Leslie A. "Natty Bumppo and Chingachgook," in Fiedler, Leslie A. *Love and Death in the American Novel*. New York: Stein and Day, 1960. 192–196. Rpt. in Fields, Wayne, ed. *James Fenimore Cooper*, 54–55.

Green, Martin. *Dreams of Adventure, Deeds of Empire*, 134–135.

Kaplan, Harold. *Democratic Humanism and American Literature*, 107–113.

Kasson, Joy S. "Templeton Revisited: Social Criticism in *The Pioneers* and *Home as Found.*" *SNNTS* 9 (1977): 54–64.

Kehler, Joel R. "Architectural Dialecticism in Cooper's *The Pioneers.*" *TSLL* 18 (1976): 124–134.

Kolodny, Annette. *Lay of the Land*, 90–96.

Lawrence, D. H. "Fenimore Cooper's Leatherstocking Novels," in Lawrence, D.

H. *Studies in Classic American Literature.* New York: Viking Press, 1961. Rpt. in Fields, Wayne, ed. *James Fenimore Cooper*, 44–46.

Lynen, John F. *Design of the Present*, 170–204.

McWilliams, John P., Jr. *Political Justice in a Republic*, 100–129.

Malin, Irving. "American Gothic Images." *Mosaic* 6.3 (1973): 146–147.

Martin, Terence. "Surviving on the Frontier: The Doubled Consciousness of Natty Bumppo." *SAQ* 75 (1975): 451.

Ousby, Ian. *Reader's Guide to Fifty American Novels*, 30–33.

Paul, Jay S. "Education of Elizabeth Temple." *SNNTS* 9 (1977): 187–194.

Paul, Jay S. "Home as Cherished: The Theme of Family in Fenimore Cooper." *SNNTS* 5 (1973): 43.

Peck, H. Daniel. *World by Itself*, 61–62, 102–107.

Person, Leland S. "Cooper's *The Pioneers* and Leatherstocking's Historical Function." *ESQ* 25 (1979): 1–9.

Philbrick, Thomas. "Cooper's *The Pioneers:* Origins and Structure." *PMLA* 79 (Dec 1964): 583–593. Rpt. in Fields, Wayne, ed. *James Fenimore Cooper*, 58–79.

Porte, Joel. *Romance in America*, 4–5, 9–13, 18.

Ross, Morton L. "Cooper's *The Pioneers* and the Ethnographic Impulse." *AS* 16.2 (1975): 29–39.

Stineback, David C. *Shifting World*, 23–42.

Tuttleton, James W. *Novel of Manners in America*, 30–32.

Prairie (1827)

Baym, Nina. "Women of Cooper's *Leatherstocking Tales*." *AQ* 23 (1971): 706–709.

Baym, Nina. "Women of Cooper's *Leatherstocking Tales*," in Cornillon, Susan Koppelman, ed. *Images of Women in Fiction*, 149–152.

Fields, Wayne. "Beyond Definition: A Reading of *The Prairie*," in Fields, Wayne, ed. *James Fenimore Cooper*, 93–111.

Frederick, John T. *Darkened Sky*, 9–11.

Green, Martin. *Dreams of Adventure, Deeds of Empire*, 136–137.

Hirsch, David H. *Reality and Idea in the Early American Novel*, 106–121.

Klotman, Phyllis Rauch. *Another Man Gone*, 40–41, 43–47.

Kolodny, Annette. *Lay of the Land*, 101–105.

Lawrence, D. H. "Fenimore Cooper's Leatherstocking Novels," in Lawrence, D. H. *Studies in Classic American Literature.* New York: Viking Press, 1961. Rpt. in Fields, Wayne, ed. *James Fenimore Cooper*, 46–47.

Lewis, Merrill. "Lost-and-Found in the Wilderness: The Desert Metaphor in Cooper's *The Prairie*." *WAL* 5 (1970): 195–204.

McWilliams, John P., Jr. *Political Justice in a Republic*, 259–276.

Malin, Irving. "American Gothic Images." *Mosaic* 6.3 (1973): 153.

Miller, Edwin Haviland. "James Fenimore Cooper's Elegiac Comedy: *The Prairie*." *Mosaic* 9.4 (1976): 195–205.

Peck, H. Daniel. *World by Itself*, 41–42.

Porte, Joel. *Romance in America*, 5–6, 41–52.

Rucker, Mary E. "Natural, Tribal, and Civil Law in Cooper's *The Prairie*." *WAL* 12 (1977): 215–222.

Precaution (1820)

Petter, Henri. *Early American Novel*, 171–174.

Tuttleton, James W. *Novel of Manners in America*, 29–30.

Red Rover (1828)

House, Kay Seymour. "Unstable Element," in House, Kay Seymour. *Cooper's Americans*. Columbus, OH: Ohio State University Press, 1965. Chapter 7. Rpt. in Fields, Wayne, ed. *James Fenimore Cooper*, 137–143.

Redskins (1846)

McWilliams, John P., Jr. *Political Justice in a Republic*, 325–337.
Tuttleton, James W. *Novel of Manners in America*, 46–47.

Satanstoe (1845)

Henderson, Harry B. *Versions of the Past*, 79–90.
McWilliams, John P., Jr. *Political Justice in a Republic*, 311–315.
Peck, H. Daniel. "*Satanstoe:* The Case for Permanence," in Peck, H. Daniel. *World By Itself: Pastoral Moment in Cooper's Fiction*. New Haven: Yale University Press, 1977. 163–178. Rpt. in Fields, Wayne, ed. *James Fenimore Cooper*, 153–166.
Peck, H. Daniel. *World by Itself*, 75, 163–178.
Stout, Janis P. *Sodoms in Eden*, 82–84.
Tuttleton, James W. *Novel of Manners in America*, 41–43.

Sea Lions (1848)

Frederick, John T. *Darkened Sky*, 25.

Spy (1821)

Berbrich, Joan D. *Three Voices from Paumanok*, 45–55.
Henderson, Harry B. *Versions of the Past*, 54–59.
McWilliams, John P., Jr. *Political Justice in a Republic*, 48–64.
Miller, Wayne Charles. *Armed America, Its Face in Fiction*, 10–15.
Peck, H. Daniel. *World by Itself*, 96–100.
St. Armand, Barton Levi. "Harvey Birch as the Wandering Jew: Literary Calvinism in James Fenimore Cooper's *The Spy*." *AL* 50 (1978): 348–368.
Starke, Catherine Juanita. *Black Portraiture in American Fiction*, 30–35.

Water-Witch (1830)

Peck, H. Daniel. *World by Itself*, 42.
Philbrick, Thomas L. "Language and Meaning in Cooper's *The Water-Witch*." *ESQ* 60 (1970): 10–16.

Ways of the Hour (1850)

Bardes, Barbara Ann and Suzanne Gossett. "Cooper and the 'Cup and Saucer' Law: A New Reading of *The Ways of the Hour*." *AQ* 32 (1980): 499–518.
McWilliams, John P., Jr. *Political Justice in a Republic*, 378–391.
Stout, Janis P. *Sodoms in Eden*, 84–85.

Wept of Wish-ton-Wish (1829)

Darnell, Donald G. "Cooper, Prescott and the Conquest of Indian America." *ATQ* 30.1 (1976): 9–10.
Henderson, Harry B. *Versions of the Past*, 68–71.
McWilliams, John P., Jr. *Political Justice in a Republic*, 246–258.
Paul, Jay S. "Home as Cherished: The Theme of Family in Fenimore Cooper." *SNNTS* 5 (1973): 47.
Peck, H. Daniel. *World by Itself*, 44, 150–151.

Wyandotté (1843)

Henderson, Harry B. *Versions of the Past*, 71–72.
McWilliams, John P., Jr. *Political Justice in a Republic*, 85–99.
Paul, Jay S. "Home as Cherished: The Theme of Family in Fenimore Cooper." *SNNTS* 5 (1973): 47–48.
Peck, H. Daniel. *World by Itself*, 62–63, 151.

COOPER, SUSAN FENIMORE (1813–1894)

Elinor Wyllys (1846)

Baym, Nina. *Woman's Fiction*, 81–82.

COOVER, ROBERT (1932–)

Origin of the Brunists (1967)

Hume, Kathryn. "Robert Coover's Fiction: The Naked and the Mythic." *Novel* 12 (1979): 129–130, 134–136, 138, 141.

Public Burning (1977)

Hume, Kathryn. "Robert Coover's Fiction: The Naked and the Mythic." *Novel* 12 (1979): 131, 139–140, 143–148
Scholes, Robert. *Fabulation and Metafiction*, 206–208.

Universal Baseball Association (1968)

Berman, Neil. "Coover's *Universal Baseball Association:* Play as Personalized Myth." *MFS* 24 (1978): 209–222.
Harris, Charles B. *Contemporary American Novelists of the Absurd*, 131–134.
Heckard, Margaret. "Robert Coover, Metafiction, and Freedom." *TCL* 22 (1976): 224–226.
Hume, Kathryn. "Robert Coover's Fiction: The Naked and the Mythic." *Novel* 12 (1979): 130–131, 136–139, 141.
Shelton, Frank W. "Humor and Balance in Coover's *The Universal Baseball Association, Inc.*" *Crit* 17.1 (1975): 78–90.
Umphlett, Wiley Lee. *Sporting Myth and the American Experience*, 180–184.
Wallace, Ronald. "Great American Game: Robert Coover's *Baseball.*" *ELWIU* 5 (1978): 103–118.
Wallace, Ronald. *Last Laugh*, 115–135.

CORSEL, RALPH (1920–)

Up There the Stars (1968)

Green, Rose Basile. *Italian-American Novel*, 198–202.

COULTER, JOHN (1888–1980)

Turf Smoke (1945)

Anthony, Geraldine, S. C. *John Coulter*, 142–144.

COWAN, JAMES (1870–1943)

Daybreak (1896)

Roemer, Kenneth M. "Sex Roles, Utopia, and Change: The Family in Late Nineteenth-Century Utopian Literature." *AmerS* 13 (1972): 39–40.

COZZENS, JAMES GOULD (1903–1978)

Ask Me Tomorrow (1940)

　　Michel, Pierre. *James Gould Cozzens*, 49–55.

By Love Possessed (1957)

　　Michel, Pierre. *James Gould Cozzens*, 106–127.
　　Milne, Gordon. *Sense of Society*, 225–227.
　　Starke, Catherine Juanita. *Black Portraiture in American Fiction*, 72–74.
　　Tuttleton, James W. *Novel of Manners in America*, 239, 242–243.

Cock Pit (1928)

　　Scholes, Robert. "Moral Realism: The Development of an Attitude," in Bruccoli,
　　Matthew J., ed. *James Gould Cozzens*, 48–50.

Confusion (1924)

　　Scholes, Robert. "Moral Realism: The Development of an Attitude," in Bruccoli,
　　Matthew J., ed. *James Gould Cozzens*, 46–47.

Guard of Honor (1948)

　　Cassill, R. V. "Particularity of *Guard of Honor*," in Bruccoli, Matthew J., ed. *James
　　Gould Cozzens*, 92–98.
　　Coxe, Louis. "Complex World of James Gould Cozzens." *American Literature* 27
　　(May 1955): 157–171. Rpt. in Bruccoli, Matthew J., ed. *James Gould Cozzens*,
　　4–6.
　　Coxe, Louis. *Enabling Acts*, 48–51.
　　Dillard, R. H. W. "*Guard of Honor:* Providential Luck in a Hard-Luck World," in
　　Bruccoli, Matthew J., ed. *James Gould Cozzens*, 81–91.
　　French, Warren. "Fiction: A Handful of Survivors," in French, Warren, ed. *Forties*,
　　10–15.
　　Jones, Peter G. *War and the Novelist*, 4, 79–84.
　　Michel, Pierre. *James Gould Cozzens*, 86–103.
　　Miller, Wayne Charles. *Armed America, Its Face in Fiction*, 188–203.
　　Milne, Gordon. *Sense of Society*, 223–225.
　　Waldmeir, Joseph J. *American Novels of the Second World War*, 124–125, 130–137.

Just and the Unjust (1942)

　　Michel, Pierre. *James Gould Cozzens*, 70–85.
　　Tuttleton, James W. *Novel of Manners in America*, 241.

Last Adam (1933)

　　Cass, Colin S. "Title of *The Last Adam*," in Bruccoli, Matthew J., ed. *James Gould
　　Cozzens*, 63–80.
　　Michel, Pierre. *James Gould Cozzens*, 36–44.
　　Tuttleton, James W. *Novel of Manners in America*, 240.

Men and Brethren (1936)

　　Tuttleton, James W. *Novel of Manners in America*, 242, 244.

Michael Scarlett (1925)

　　Scholes, Robert. "Moral Realism: The Development of an Attitude," in Bruccoli,
　　Matthew J., ed. *James Gould Cozzens*, 47–48.

Morning Noon and Night (1968)

>Cox, Leland H., Jr. "Henry Dodd Worthington: The 'I' in *Morning Noon and Night*," in Bruccoli, Matthew J., ed. *James Gould Cozzens*, 111–126.
>Michel, Pierre. *James Gould Cozzens*, 128–136.

Son of Perdition (1929)

>Scholes, Robert. "Moral Realism: The Development of an Attitude," in Bruccoli, Matthew J., ed. *James Gould Cozzens*, 50–54.

CRANE, STEPHEN (1871–1900)

Active Service (1899)

>Gilkes, Lillian B. "*Third Violet, Active Service*, and *The O'Ruddy:* Stephen Crane's Potboilers," in Katz, Joseph, ed. *Stephen Crane in Transition*, 117–120.
>Nagel, James. *Stephen Crane and Literary Impressionism*, 41, 51–52, 92–93, 101, 160–161.

George's Mother (1896)

>Brennan, Joseph X. "Imagery and Art of *George's Mother*." *CLA Journal* 4 (Dec 1960): 106–115. Rpt. in Wertheim, Stanley, ed. *Merrill Studies in Maggie and George's Mother*, 125–134.
>Cazemajou, Jean. *Stephen Crane*, 16–17.
>Cazemajou, Jean. "Stephen Crane," in Walcutt, Charles Child, ed. *Seven Novelists in the American Naturalist Tradition*, 31–32.
>Cazemajou, Jean. "Stephen Crane," in Wright, George T., ed. *Seven American Stylists, From Poe to Mailer*, 100–101.
>Geismar, Maxwell. *Rebels and Ancestors: The American Novel, 1890–1915*. Boston: Houghton Mifflin Co., 1953. 92–95. Rpt. in Wertheim, Stanley, ed. *Merrill Studies in Maggie and George's Mother*, 121–124.
>Holton, Milne. *Cylinder of Vision*, 55–63.
>Jackson, Agnes M. "Stephen Crane's Imagery of Conflict in *George's Mother*." *ArQ* 25 (1969): 313–318.
>LaFrance, Marston. "*George's Mother* and the Other Half of *Maggie*,' in Katz, Joseph, ed. *Stephen Crane in Transition*, 36–37, 45–51.
>Nagel, James. *Stephen Crane and Literary Impressionism*, 49–50, 65–68, 131–132, 141–143, 150.
>Simoneaux, Katherine G. "Color Imagery in Crane's *George's Mother*." *CLAJ* 14 (1971): 410–419.
>Solomon, Eric. *Stephen Crane: From Parody to Realism*. Cambridge, MA: Harvard University Press, 1966. 50–67. Rpt. in Wertheim, Stanley, ed. *Merrill Studies in Maggie and George's Mother*, 135–146.
>Weinstein, Bernard. "*George's Mother* and the Bowery of Experience." *MarkR* 9 (1980): 45–49.

Maggie (1893)

>Åhnebrink, Lars. *Beginnings of Naturalism in American Fiction*. Upsala, Sweden: A. B. Lundequistska Bokhandeln, 1950. 251–264. Rpt. in Wertheim, Stanley, ed. *Merrill Studies in Maggie and George's Mother*, 31–33.
>Banta, Martha. "They Shall Have Faces, Minds, and (One Day) Flesh: Women in Late Nineteenth-century and Early Twentieth-century American Literature," in Springer, Marlene, ed. *What Manner of Woman*, 260–262.

Begiebing, Robert J. "Stephen Crane's *Maggie:* The Death of the Self." *American Imago* 34 (1977): 50–71.

Bergon, Frank. "Framework of *Maggie*," Bergon, Frank. *Stephen Crane's Artistry.* New York: Columbia University Press, 1975. 71–76. Rpt. in Crane, Stephen. *Maggie*, 230–234.

Bergon, Frank. *Stephen Crane's Artistry*, 66–76.

Berryman, John. "Crane's Art in *Maggie*," Berryman, John. *Stephen Crane*. New York: William Sloane Associates, 1950. 58–61. Rpt. in Crane, Stephen. *Maggie*, 163–165.

Berryman, John. *Stephen Crane*. New York: Willaim Sloane Associates, 1950. 58–61. Rpt. in Wertheim, Stanley, ed. *Merrill Studies in Maggie and George's Mother*, 27–30.

Brennan, Joseph X. "Ironic and Symbolic Structure in Crane's *Maggie*." *Nineteenth-Century Fiction* 16 (March 1962): 303–315. Rpt. in Crane, Stephen. *Maggie*, 173–184.

Brennan, Joseph X. "Ironic and Symbolic Structure in Crane's *Maggie*." *Nineteenth-Century Fiction* 16.4 (March 1962): 304–315. Rpt. in Wertheim, Stanley, ed. *Merrill Studies in Maggie and George's Mother*, 54–64.

Cady, Edwin H. *Light of Common Day*, 176–178.

Cady, Edwin H. *Stephen Crane*, 104–113.

Cady, Edwin H. *Stephen Crane*. New Haven: Twayne Publishers, Inc., 1962. 104–107. Rpt. in Wertheim, Stanley, ed. *Merrill Studies in Maggie and George's Mother*, 50–53.

Cazemajou, Jean. *Stephen Crane*, 14–16.

Cazemajou, Jean. "Stephen Crane," in Walcutt, Charles Child, ed. *Seven Novelists in the American Naturalist Tradition*, 29–31.

Cazemajou, Jean. "Stephen Crane," in Wright, George T., ed. *Seven American Stylists, From Poe to Mailer*, 99–100.

Cunliffe, Marcus. "Stephen Crane and the American Background of *Maggie*." *American Quarterly* 7 (Spring 1955): 31–44. Rpt. in Wertheim, Stanley, ed. *Merrill Studies in Maggie and George's Mother*, 34–44.

Fine, David M. "Abraham Cahan, Stephen Crane, and the Romantic Tenement Tale of the Nineties." *AmerS* 14.1 (1974): 102–106.

Fitelson, David. "Stephen Crane's *Maggie* and Darwinism." *American Quarterly* 16 (Summer 1964): 182–194. Rpt. in Wertheim, Stanley, ed. *Merrill Studies in Maggie and George's Mother*, 68–79.

Ford, Philip H. "Illusion and Reality in Crane's *Maggie*." *ArQ* 25 (1969): 293–303.

Gibson, Donald B. "The Flawed *Maggie*," Gibson, Donald B. *Fiction of Stephen Crane*. Carbondale, IL: Southern Illinois University Press, 1968. 26–34. Rpt. in Crane, Stephen. *Maggie*, 212–218.

Gullason, Thomas A. "Prophetic City in Stephen Crane's 1893 *Maggie*." *MFS* 24 (1978): 129–137.

Gullason, Thomas A. "Tragedy and Melodrama in Stephen Crane's *Maggie*," in Crane, Stephen. *Maggie*, 245–253.

Holton, Milne. *Cylinder of Vision*, 37–54.

Karlen, Arno. "Craft of Stephen Crane." *GR* 28 (1974): 471, 473–477.

Karlen, Arno. "Lapses and Craft in *Maggie*." *Georgia Review* 28 (Fall 1974): 473–477. Rpt. in Crane, Stephen. *Maggie*, 218–222.

Katz, Joseph. "*Maggie* Nobody Knows." *Modern Fiction Studies* 12 (Summer

1966): 200–212. Rpt. in Wertheim, Stanley, ed. *Merrill Studies in Maggie and George's Mother*, 93–107.

LaFrance, Marston. *"George's Mother* and the Other Half of *Maggie*,' in Katz, Joseph, ed. *Stephen Crane in Transition*, 35–36, 37–40, 41–45.

Martin, Jay. "*Maggie* and Satire," Martin, Jay. *Harvests of Change: American Literature 1865–1914*. Englewood Cliffs, NJ: Prentice Hall, 1967. 57–59. Rpt. in Crane, Stephen. *Maggie*, 209–211.

Martin, Jay. *Harvests of Change: American Literature 1865–1914*. Englewood Cliffs, NJ: Prentice Hall, 1967. 57–59. Rpt. in Wertheim, Stanley, ed. *Merrill Studies in Maggie and George's Mother*, 89–92.

Nagel, James. *Stephen Crane and Literary Impressionism*, 48, 62–65, 94–100, 129–131, 140–141.

Overmyer, Janet. "Structure of Crane's *Maggie*." *University of Kansas Review* 29 (Autumn 1962): 71–72. Rpt. in Crane, Stephen. *Maggie*, 184–186.

Overmyer, Janet. "Structure of Crane's *Maggie*." *University of Kansas Review* 29 (October 1962): 71–72. Rpt. in Wertheim, Stanley, ed. *Merrill Studies in Maggie and George's Mother*, 65–67.

Pizer, Donald. "Stephen Crane's *Maggie* and American Naturalism." *Criticism* 7 (Spring 1965): 168–175. Rpt. in Crane, Stephen. *Maggie*, 186–193.

Pizer, Donald. "Stephen Crane's *Maggie* and American Naturalism." *Criticism* 7 (Spring 1965): 168–175. Rpt. in Wertheim, Stanley, ed. *Merrill Studies in Maggie and George's Mother*, 80–88.

Simoneaux, Katherine G. "Color Imagery in Crane's *Maggie: A Girl of the Streets*." *CLAJ* 18 (1974): 91–100.

Simoneaux, Katherine G. "Color Imagery in Crane's *Maggie: A Girl of the Streets*." *CLA Journal* 18 (September 1974): 91–100. Rpt. in Crane, Stephen. *Maggie*, 222–230.

Solomon, Eric. "*Maggie* as a Three-Act Drama," Solomon, Eric. *Stephen Crane: From Parody to Realism*. Cambridge: Harvard University Press, 1966. 35–44. Rpt. in Crane, Stephen. *Maggie*, 203–209.

Stein, William Bysshe. "New Testament Inversions in Crane's *Maggie*." *Modern Language Notes* 73 (April 1958): 268–272. Rpt. in Crane, Stephen. *Maggie*, 170–173.

Stein, William Bysshe. "New Testament Inversions in Crane's *Maggie*." *Modern Language Notes* 73 (April 1958): 268–272. Rpt. in Wertheim, Stanley, ed. *Merrill Studies in Maggie and George's Mother*, 45–49.

Taylor, Gordon O. *Passages of Thought*, 111–119.

Walcutt, Charles Child. "Hallucination and Hysteria in *Maggie*," Walcutt, Charles Child. *American Naturalism: A Divided Stream*. Minneapolis: University of Minnesota Press, 1956. 67–72. Rpt. in Crane, Stephen. *Maggie*, 165–169.

O'Ruddy (1903)

Nagel, James. *Stephen Crane and Literary Impressionism*, 39–40.

Red Badge of Courage (1895)

Aaron, Daniel. *Unwritten War*, 215–218.

Bergon, Frank. *Stephen Crane's Artistry*, 76–86.

Berryman, John. "Stephen Crane: *The Red Badge of Courage*," in Stegner, Wallace, ed. *American Novel: From James Fenimore Cooper to William Faulkner*. New York: Basic Books, 1965. 86–96. Rpt. in Crane, Stephen. *Red Badge of Courage*, 276–285.

Breslin, Paul. "Courage and Convention: *The Red Badge of Courage*." *YR* 66 (1976): 209–222.

Burhans, Clinton S., Jr. "Judging Henry Judging: Point of View in *The Red Badge of Courage*." *BallS* 15.2 (1974): 38–48.

Burhans, Clinton S., Jr. "Twin Lights on Henry Fleming: Structural Parallels in *The Red Badge of Courage*." *ArQ* 30 (1974): 149–159.

Cady, Edwin H. *Light of Common Day*, 178–180.

Cady, Edwin H. "*Red Badge of Courage*," in Cady, Edwin H. *Stephen Crane*. New York: Twayne, 1962. 118–144. Rpt. in Crane, Stephen. *Red Badge of Courage*, 241–264.

Cady, Edwin H. *Stephen Crane*, 115–144.

Cazemajou, Jean. "*Red Badge of Courage:* The 'Religion of Peace' and the War Archetype," in Katz, Joseph, ed. *Stephen Crane in Transition*, 54–64.

Cazemajou, Jean. *Stephen Crane*, 18–22.

Cazemajou, Jean. "Stephen Crane," in Walcutt, Charles Child, ed. *Seven Novelists in the American Naturalist Tradition*, 32–38.

Cazemajou, Jean. "Stephen Crane," in Wright, George T., ed. *Seven American Stylists, From Poe to Mailer*, 101–107.

Colvert, James B. "Stephen Crane: Style as Invention," in Katz, Joseph, ed. *Stephen Crane in Transition*, 137–139.

Colvert, James B. "Stephen Crane's Magic Mountain," in Bassan, Maurice, ed. *Stephen Crane: A Collection of Critical Essays*. Englewood Cliffs, NJ: Prentice-Hall, 1967. 95–105. Rpt. in Crane, Stephen. *Red Badge of Courage*, 301–310.

Dillingham, William B. "Insensibility in *The Red Badge of Courage*." *College English* 25 (Dec 1963): 194–198. Rpt. in Crane, Stephen. *Red Badge of Courage*, 264–269.

Fraser, John. "Crime and Forgiveness: *The Red Badge of Courage* in Time of War." *Criticism* 9 (Summer 1967): 243–256. Rpt. in Crane, Stephen. *Red Badge of Courage*, 311–323.

Frohock, W. M. "*Red Badge* and the Limits of Parody." *SoR* 6 (1970): 137–148.

Gollin, Rita K. " 'Little Souls Who Thirst for Fight' in *The Red Badge of Courage*." *ArQ* 30 (1974): 111–118.

Greenfield, Stanley B. "Unmistakable Stephen Crane." *PMLA* 73 (Dec 1958): 562–563, 568–572. Rpt. in Crane, Stephen. *Red Badge of Courage*, 222–232.

Hart, John E. "*Red Badge of Courage* as Myth and Symbol." *University of Kansas Review* 19 (Summer 1953): 249–256. Rpt. in Crane, Stephen. *Red Badge of Courage*, 206–214.

Henderson, Harry B. *Versions of the Past*, 219–231.

Holton, Milne. *Cylinder of Vision*, 86–118.

Jones, Peter G. *War and the Novelist*, 5–6.

LaFrance, Marston. "Private Fleming: His Various Battles," in LaFrance, Marston. *Reading of Stephen Crane*. New York: Oxford University Press, 1971. 98–99, 104–124. Rpt. in Crane, Stephen. *Red Badge of Courage*, 333–349.

Mangum, A. Bryant. "Latter Days of Henry Fleming." *ANQ* 13 (1975): 136–138.

Marcus, Mordecai. "Unity of *The Red Badge of Courage*," in Lettis, Richard et al., eds. *Red Badge of Courage: Text and Criticism*. New York: Harcourt Brace, 1960. 189–195. Rpt. in Crane, Stephen. *Red Badge of Courage*, 233–241.

Maynard, Reid. "Red as Leitmotiv in *The Red Badge of Courage*." *ArQ* 30 (1974): 135–141.

Miller, Wayne Charles. *Armed America, Its Face in Fiction*, 70–81.

Nagel, James. *Stephen Crane and Literary Impressionism*, 50, 52–61, 80–81, 87–92, 127–129, 146, 150, 152–160.

Ousby, Ian. *Reader's Guide to Fifty American Novels*, 161–163.

Perosa, Sergio. "Naturalism and Impressionism in Stephen Crane's Fiction," in Bassan, Milton, ed. *Stephen Crane: A Collection of Critical Essays*. Englewood Cliffs, NJ: Prentice-Hall, 1967. 80, 87–94. Rpt. in Crane, Stephen. *Red Badge of Courage*, 270–276.

Pizer, Donald. "Late Nineteenth-Century American Naturalism," in Pizer, Donald. *Realism and Naturalism in Nineteenth-Century American Literature*. Carbondale, IL: Southern Illinois University Press, 1966. 11–14, 24–30. Rpt. in Crane, Stephen. *Red Badge of Courage*, 294–301.

Rathbun, John W. "Structure and Meaning in *The Red Badge of Courage*." *BallS* 10.1 (1969): 8–16.

Rathbun, John W. "Structure and Meaning in *The Red Badge of Courage*." *Ball State University Forum* 10 (Winter 1969): 8–16. Rpt. in Crane, Stephen. *Red Badge of Courage*, 323–333.

Rechnitz, Robert M. "Depersonalization and the Dream in *The Red Badge of Courage*." *SNNTS* 6 (1974): 76–87.

Rechnitz, Robert M. "Depersonalization and the Dream in *The Red Badge of Courage*." *Studies in the Novel* 6 (Spring 1974): 76–87. Rpt. in Crane, Stephen. *Red Badge of Courage*, 349–360.

Stallman, R. W. "Stephen Crane: A Revaluation," in Aldridge, John W., ed. *Critiques and Essays on Modern Fiction: 1920–1951*. New York: Ronald Press, 1952. 251–254, 262–269. Rpt. in Crane, Stephen. *Red Badge of Courage*, 195–205.

Starr, Alvin. "Concept of Fear in the Works of Stephen Crane and Richard Wright." *SIBL* 6.2 (1975): 6, 7–9.

Taylor, Gordon O. *Passages of Thought*, 119–134.

Thomas, Donald S. "Crane's *The Red Badge of Courage*." *Expl* 27 (1969): Item 77.

Vanderbilt, Kermit and Daniel Weiss. "From Rifleman to Flagbearer: Henry Fleming's Separate Peace in *The Red Badge of Courage*." *Modern Fiction Studies* 11 (Winter 1965–66): 371–380. Rpt. in Crane, Stephen. *Red Badge of Courage*, 285–294.

Vickery, Olga W. "Inferno of the Moderns," in Friedman, Melvin J. and John B. Vickery, eds. *Shaken Realist*, 152–153.

Walcutt, Charles C. "Stephen Crane: Naturalist and Impressionist," in Walcutt, Charles C. *American Literary Naturalism, A Divided Stream*. Minneapolis: University of Minnesota Press, 1956. vii, viii, 66–67, 74–82. Rpt. in Crane, Stephen. *Red Badge of Courage*, 216–222.

Weeks, Robert P. "Power of the Tacit in Crane and Hemingway." *Modern Fiction Studies* 8 (Winter 1962–63): 415–418. Rpt. in Grebstein, Sheldon Norman, comp. *Merrill Studies*, 102–106.

Wyndham, George. "Remarkable Book." *New Review* 14 (Jan 1896): 32–40. Rpt. in Crane, Stephen. *Red Badge of Courage*, 181–188.

Zambrano, Ana Laura. "Role of Nature in *The Red Badge of Courage*." *ArQ* 30 (1974): 164–166.

Third Violet (1897)

Cazemajou, Jean. *Stephen Crane*, 29.

Cazemajou, Jean. "Stephen Crane," in Walcutt, Charles Child, ed. *Seven Novelists in the American Naturalist Tradition*, 42–43.

Cazemajou, Jean. "Stephen Crane," in Wright, George T., ed. *Seven American Stylists, From Poe to Mailer*, 111–112.

Gilkes, Lillian B. "*Third Violet, Active Service*, and *The O'Ruddy:* Stephen Crane's Potboilers," in Katz, Joseph, ed. *Stephen Crane in Transition*, 109–114.

Holton, Milne. *Cylinder of Vision*, 132–135.

Nagel, James. *Stephen Crane and Literary Impressionism*, 41–42, 150–151.

CREATORE, LUIGI (1921–)

This World Is Mine (1942)

Green, Rose Basile. *Italian-American Novel*, 175–178.

CREWS, HARRY (1935–)

Car (1972)

Seelye, John. "Georgia Boys: The Redclay Satyrs of Erskine Caldwell and Harry Crews." *VQR* 56 (1980): 618–619.

Shepherd, Allen. "Cars in Harry Crews' *Car*." *NConL* 8.1 (1978): 8–9.

Shepherd, Allen. "Matters of Life and Death: The Novels of Harry Crews." *Crit* 20.1 (1978): 55–57.

Feast of Snakes (1976)

Seelye, John. "Georgia Boys: The Redclay Satyrs of Erskine Caldwell and Harry Crews." *VQR* 56 (1980): 622–624.

Shepherd, Allen. "Matters of Life and Death: The Novels of Harry Crews." *Crit* 20.1 (1978): 59–61.

Gospel Singer (1968)

Seelye, John. "Georgia Boys: The Redclay Satyrs of Erskine Caldwell and Harry Crews." *VQR* 56 (1980): 619.

Hawk Is Dying (1973)

Shepherd, Allen. "Matters of Life and Death: The Novels of Harry Crews." *Crit* 20.1 (1978): 57–59.

This Thing Don't Lead to Heaven (1970)

Seelye, John. "Georgia Boys: The Redclay Satyrs of Erskine Caldwell and Harry Crews." *VQR* 56 (1980): 620–621.

CRICHTON, MICHAEL (1942–)

Terminal Man (1972)

Evert, Walter H. "Coadjutors of Oppression: A Romantic and Modern Theory of Evil," in Bornstein, George, ed. *Romantic and Modern*, 48–50.

CROSSEN, KENDELL FOSTER (1910–)

Year of Consent (1954)

Rhodes, Carolyn. "Tyranny by Computer: Automated Data Processing and Oppressive Government in Science Fiction," in Clareson, Thomas D., ed. *Many Futures, Many Worlds*, 74–80.

CROVES, HAL see TRAVEN, B.

CULLEN, COUNTEE (1903–1946)

One Way to Heaven (1932)

Larson, Charles R. "Three Harlem Novels of the Jazz Age." *Crit* 11.3 (1969): 72–77.
Perry, Margaret. *Silence to the Drums*, 80–84.
Singh, Amritjit. *Novels of the Harlem Renaissance*, 80–83.
Starke, Catherine Juanita. *Black Portraiture in American Fiction*, 189–191.
Williams, Sherley Anne. *Give Birth to Brightness*, 83–84

CUMMINGS, E. E. (1894–1962)

Enormous Room (1922)

Engel, Wilson F., III. "Pilgrim as Prisoner: Cummings and Vonnegut." *NConL* 7.1 (1977): 13–14.
McCarthy, Harold T. *Expatriate Perspective*, 131–135.
Peek, George S. "Narrator as Artist and the Artist as Narrator: A Study of E.E. Cummings' *The Enormous Room*." *BallS* 17.4 (1976): 50–60.
Smith, David E. "*Enormous Room* and *The Pilgrim's Progress*." *Twentieth Century Literature* 2 (July 1965): 67–75. Rpt. in Friedman, Norman, ed. *E. E. Cummings*, 121–132.
Walsh, Jeffrey. "Painful Process of Unthinking: E. E. Cummings' Social Vision in *The Enormous Room*," in Klein, Holger, ed. *First World War in Fiction*, 32–42.

CUMMINS, MARIA SUSAN (1827–1866)

El Fureidîs (1860)
Baym, Nina. *Woman's Fiction*, 173.

Haunted Hearts (1864)
Baym, Nina. *Woman's Fiction*, 173–174.

Lamplighter (1854)
Baym, Nina. *Woman's Fiction*, 164–169.

Mabel Vaughan (1857)
Baym, Nina. *Woman's Fiction*, 169–173.

CUOMO, GEORGE (1929–)

Among Thieves (1968)
Green, Rose Basile. *Italian-American Novel*, 301–306.

Bright Day, Dark Runner (1964)
Green, Rose Basile. *Italian-American Novel*, 297–301.

D'AGOSTINO, GUIDO (1910–)

Olives on the Apple Tree (1940)
  Green, Rose Basile. *Italian-American Novel*, 129–131.

DAHLBERG, EDWARD (1900–1977)

Bottom Dogs (1930)
  Chametzky, Jules. "Edward Dahlberg, Early and Late," in Williams, Jonathan, ed. *Edward Dahlberg, A Tribute*, 26–31.
  Moramarco, Fred. *Edward Dahlberg*, 29–37.

From Flushing to Calvary (1932)
  Chametzky, Jules. "Edward Dahlberg, Early and Late," in Williams, Jonathan, ed. *Edward Dahlberg, A Tribute*, 31–32.
  Moramarco, Fred. *Edward Dahlberg*, 37–44.

DANTIN, LOUIS (1865–1945)

Les enfances de Fanny (1951)
  Shek, Ben-Zion. *Social Realism*, 159, 163–164.

DARGAN, OLIVE TILFORD see BURKE, FIELDING

DAVIES, ROBERTSON (1913–)

Fifth Business (1970)
  Baltensperger, Peter. "Battles with the Trolls." *CanL* 71 (1976): 59–67.
  Bjerring, Nancy E. "Deep in the Old Man's Puzzle." *CanL* 62 (1974): 49–60.
  Bjerring, Nancy E. "Deep in the Old Man's Puzzle," in Woodcock, George, ed. *Canadian Novel*, 162–173.
  Boutelle, Ann. "Dorian Gray Phenomenon in Canadian Literature." *DR* 57 (1977): 268–269.
  Brown, Russell M. and Donna A. Bennett. "Magnus Eisengrim: The Shadow of the Trickster in the Novels of Robertson Davies." *MFS* 22 (1976): 350–356.
  Buitenhuis, Elspeth. *Robertson Davies*, 57–66.
  Chapman, Marilyn. "Female Archetypes in *Fifth Business*." *CanL* 80 (1979): 131–138.
  Cude, Wilfred. *Due Sense of Differences*, 206–209.
  Cude, Wilfred. "False as Harlots' Oaths: Dunny Ramsay Looks at Huck Finn," *Studies in Canadian Literature* (Summer, 1977): 164–187. Rpt. in Cude, Wilfred. *Due Sense of Differences*, 85–107.
  Cude, Wilfred. "Historiography and those Damned Saints: Shadow and Light in *Fifth Business*," *Journal of Canadian Studies* (February, 1977): 47–67. Rpt. in Cude, Wilfred. *Due Sense of Differences*, 109–132.
  Cude, Wilfred. "Miracle and Art in *Fifth Business:* or Who the Devil is Liselotte Vitzlipützli?", *Journal of Canadian Studies* (November, 1974): 3–16. Rpt. in Cude, Wilfred. *Due Sense of Differences*, 69–84.

Davy, Paul. "Structure of Davies' Deptford Trilogy." *ECW* 9 (1977–78): 123–133.

Dooley, D. J. *Moral Vision*, 109–122.

Gerson, Carole. "Dunstan Ramsay's Personal Mythology." *ECW* 6 (1977): 100–108.

Goldie, Terry. "Folkloric Background of Robertson Davies' Deptford Trilogy," in Lawrence, Robert G. and Samuel L. Macey, eds. *Studies*, 22–28, 29–30.

Grant, Judith Skelton. *Robertson Davies*, 35–36, 37–40, 46–49.

Hoy, Helen. "Poetry in the Dunghill: The Romance of the Ordinary in Robertson Davies' Fiction." *Ariel* 10.3 (1979): 83–90.

Hutcheon, Linda. "Poet as Novelist." *CanL* 86 (1980): 10–13.

Macey, Samuel L. "Time, Clockwork, and the Devil in Robertson Davies' Deptford Trilogy," in Lawrence, Robert G. and Samuel L. Macey, eds. *Studies*, 32–43.

Merivale, Patricia. "The (Auto)-Biographical Compulsions of Dunstan Ramsay," in Lawrence, Robert G. and Samuel L. Macey, eds. *Studies*, 57–64.

Merivale, Patricia. "Biographical Compulsion: Elegiac Romances in Canadian Fiction." *JML* 8 (1980): 141–148, 151–152.

Monaghan, David. " 'People in Prominent Positions': A Study of the Public Figure in the Deptford Trilogy," in Lawrence, Robert G. and Samuel L. Macey, eds. *Studies*, 45–55.

Monaghan, David M. "Metaphors and Confusions." *CanL* 67 (1976): 64–72.

Moss, John. *Sex and Violence*, 102–104, 107–110, 115–122.

Radford, F. L. "Great Mother and the Boy: Jung, Davies, and *Fifth Business*," in Lawrence, Robert G. and Samuel L. Macey, eds. *Studies*, 66–80.

Roper, Gordon. "Robertson Davies' *Fifth Business* and 'That Old Fantastical Duke of Dark Corners,' C. G. Jung," in Moss, John, ed. *Here and Now*, 53–66.

St. Pierre, Paul M. "Rounding the Ovoid." *Mosaic* 11.3 (1978): 127–135.

St. Pierre, Paul M. "Rounding the Ovoid," in Wortley, John, ed. *Post-War Canadian Fiction*, 127–135.

Sutherland, Ronald. *New Hero*, 75–83.

Warwick, Ellen D. "Transformation of Robertson Davies," in Moss, John, ed. *Here and Now*, 68–71.

Wood, Barry. "In Search of Sainthood: Magic, Myth, and Metaphor in Robertson Davies' *Fifth Business*." *Crit* 19.2 (1977): 23–32.

Leaven of Malice (1954)

Baltensperger, Peter. "Battles with the Trolls." *CanL* 71 (1976): 59–67.

Buitenhuis, Elspeth. *Robertson Davies*, 41–48.

Grant, Judith Skelton. *Robertson Davies*, 27, 29–30, 31–32.

Hoy, Helen. "Poetry in the Dunghill: The Romance of the Ordinary in Robertson Davies' Fiction." *Ariel* 10.3 (1979): 76–78.

Radford, F. L. "Apprentice Sorcerer: Davies' Salerton Trilogy," in Lawrence, Robert G. and Samuel L. Macey, eds. *Studies*, 14–16.

Warwick, Ellen D. "Transformation of Robertson Davies," in Moss, John, ed. *Here and Now*, 71–75.

Manticore (1972)

Baltensperger, Peter. "Battles with the Trolls." *CanL* 71 (1976): 59–67.

Brigg, Peter. "*The Manticore* and the Law," in Lawrence, Robert G. and Samuel L. Macey, eds. *Studies*, 82–99.

Brown, Russell M. "In Search of Lost Causes: The Canadian Novelist as Mystery Writer," in Wortley, John, ed. *Post-War Canadian Fiction*, 8–9.

Brown, Russell M. and Donna A. Bennett. "Magnus Eisengrim: The Shadow of the Trickster in the Novels of Robertson Davies." *MFS* 22 (1976): 356–359.
Davy, Paul. "Structure of Davies' Deptford Trilogy." *ECW* 9 (1977–78): 123–133.
Edinger, Harry G. "Bears in Three Contemporary Fictions." *HAR* 28 (1977): 144–147.
Gerson, Carole. "Dunstan Ramsay's Personal Mythology." *ECW* 6 (1977): 100–108.
Goldie, Terry. "Folkloric Background of Robertson Davies' Deptford Trilogy," in Lawrence, Robert G. and Samuel L. Macey, eds. *Studies*, 25, 27, 28, 29.
Grant, Judith Skelton. *Robertson Davies*, 36, 37, 40–43, 46–49.
Hoy, Helen. "Poetry in the Dunghill: The Romance of the Ordinary in Robertson Davies' Fiction." *Ariel* 10.3 (1979): 90–94.
Macey, Samuel L. "Time, Clockwork, and the Devil in Robertson Davies' Deptford Trilogy," in Lawrence, Robert G. and Samuel L. Macey, eds. *Studies*, 32–43.
Merivale, Patricia. "The (Auto)-Biographical Compulsions of Dunstan Ramsay," in Lawrence, Robert G. and Samuel L. Macey, eds. *Studies*, 63–64.
Monaghan, David. " 'People in Prominent Positions': A Study of the Public Figure in the Deptford Trilogy," in Lawrence, Robert G. and Samuel L. Macey, eds. *Studies*, 45–55.
Monk, Patricia. "Davies and the Drachenloch: A Study of the Archaeological Background of *The Manticore*," in Lawrence, Robert G. and Samuel L. Macey, eds. *Studies*, 100–111.
Moss, John. *Sex and Violence*, 107–110, 113–115.

Mixture of Frailties (1958)

Baltensperger, Peter. "Battles with the Trolls." *CanL* 71 (1976): 59–67.
Buitenhuis, Elspeth. *Robertson Davies*, 49–56.
Grant, Judith Skelton. *Robertson Davies*, 27–28, 30, 32–34.
Hoy, Helen. "Poetry in the Dunghill: The Romance of the Ordinary in Robertson Davies' Fiction." *Ariel* 10.3 (1979): 78–83.
Radford, F. L. "Apprentice Sorcerer: Davies' Salerton Trilogy," in Lawrence, Robert G. and Samuel L. Macey, eds. *Studies*, 14, 15, 16–21.

Tempest-Tost (1951)

Baltensperger, Peter. "Battles with the Trolls." *CanL* 71 (1976): 59–67.
Buitenhuis, Elspeth. *Robertson Davies*, 35–40.
Grant, Judith Skelton. *Robertson Davies*, 27, 28–29, 30–32.
Hoy, Helen. "Poetry in the Dunghill: The Romance of the Ordinary in Robertson Davies' Fiction." *Ariel* 10.3 (1979): 72–76.
Radford, F. L. "Apprentice Sorcerer: Davies' Salerton Trilogy," in Lawrence, Robert G. and Samuel L. Macey, eds. *Studies*, 13–14.

World of Wonders (1975)

Brennan, Anthony. "Robertson Davies: Illusionist." *IFR* 3 (1976): 70–72.
Brown, Russell M. and Donna A. Bennett. "Magnus Eisengrim: The Shadow of the Trickster in the Novels of Robertson Davies." *MFS* 22 (1976): 359–361.
Davy, Paul. "Structure of Davies' Deptford Trilogy." *ECW* 9 (1977–78): 123–133.
Gerson, Carole. "Dunstan Ramsay's Personal Mythology." *ECW* 6 (1977): 102–108.
Goldie, Terry. "Folkloric Background of Robertson Davies' Deptford Trilogy," in Lawrence, Robert G. and Samuel L. Macey, eds. *Studies*, 28–29.

Grant, Judith Skelton. *Robertson Davies*, 36, 43–46, 46–49.

Hoy, Helen. "Poetry in the Dunghill: The Romance of the Ordinary in Robertson Davies' Fiction." *Ariel* 10.3 (1979): 69–70, 94–97.

Lawrence, Robert G. "Canadian Theatre in Robertson Davies' *World of Wonders*," in Lawrence, Robert G. and Samuel L. Macey, eds. *Studies*, 114–123.

Macey, Samuel L. "Time, Clockwork, and the Devil in Robertson Davies' Deptford Trilogy," in Lawrence, Robert G. and Samuel L. Macey, eds. *Studies*, 32–43.

Merivale, Patricia. "The (Auto)-Biographical Compulsions of Dunstan Ramsay," in Lawrence, Robert G. and Samuel L. Macey, eds. *Studies*, 63–64.

Monaghan, David. " 'People in Prominent Positions': A Study of the Public Figure in the Deptford Trilogy," in Lawrence, Robert G. and Samuel L. Macey, eds. *Studies*, 45–55.

Moss, John. *Sex and Violence*, 107–113.

Warwick, Ellen D. "Transformation of Robertson Davies," in Moss, John, ed. *Here and Now*, 75–77.

DAVIS, GEORGE (1939–)

Coming Home (1971)

Klotman, Phyllis Rauch. *Another Man Gone*, 138–141.

DAVIS, H. L. (1896–1960)

Beulah Land (1949)

Bryant, Paul T. *H. L. Davis*, 94–101.

Distant Music (1957)

Bryant, Paul T. *H. L. Davis*, 124–133.

Harp of a Thousand Strings (1947)

Bryant, Paul T. *H. L. Davis*, 83–92.

Honey in the Horn (1934)

Bryant, Paul T. *H. L. Davis*, 73–81.

Etulain, Richard W. "Frontier and Region in Western Literature." *Southwestern American Literature* 1 (1971): 121–128. Rpt. in Pilkington, William T., ed. *Critical Essays on the Western American Novel*, 88–89.

Lavender, David. "Petrified West and the Writer." *American Scholar* 37.2 (Spring 1968). Rpt. in Haslam, Gerald W., ed. *Western Writing*, 150–151.

Winds of Morning (1952)

Bryant, Paul T. *H. L. Davis*, 103–121.

DAVIS, REBECCA HARDING (1831–1910)

Margret Howth (1862)

Duus, Louise. "Neither Saint Nor Sinner: Women in Late Nineteenth-Century Fiction." *ALR* 7 (1974): 276–278.

Waiting for the Verdict (1867)
  Berzon, Judith R. *Neither White Nor Black*, 195–196.

DAVIS, RICHARD HARDING (1864–1916)

Captain Macklin (1902)
  Osborn, Scott Compton and Robert L. Phillips, Jr.. *Richard Harding Davis*, 112–114.

King's Jackal (1898)
  Osborn, Scott Compton and Robert L. Phillips, Jr.. *Richard Harding Davis*, 109–110.

Princess Aline (1895)
  Osborn, Scott Compton and Robert L. Phillips, Jr.. *Richard Harding Davis*, 105–106.

Soldiers of Fortune (1897)
  Osborn, Scott Compton and Robert L. Phillips, Jr.. *Richard Harding Davis*, 106–109.

DE CAPITE, MICHAEL (1915–1958)

Bennett Place (1948)
  Green, Rose Basile. *Italian-American Novel*, 173–174.

No Bright Banner (1944)
  Green, Rose Basile. *Italian-American Novel*, 169–173.

DE CAPITE, RAYMOND (1924–)

Coming of Fabrizze (1960)
  Green, Rose Basile. *Italian-American Novel*, 180–182.

DE FOREST, JOHN WILLIAM (1826–1906)

Miss Ravenel's Conversion from Secession to Loyalty (1867)
  Aaron, Daniel. *Unwritten War*, 172–176.
  Alsen, Eberhard. "Marx and DeForest: The Idea of Class Struggle in *Miss Ravenel's Conversion.*" *AL* 48 (1976): 223–228.
  Hagemann, E. R. "John William De Forest's "Great American Novel," in Hoyt, Charles Alva, ed. *Minor American Novelists*, 17–20.
  Katz, Joseph. "Eroticism in American Literary Realism." *SAF* 5 (1977): 37–38.
  Miller, Wayne Charles. *Armed America, Its Face in Fiction*, 58–66.
  Starke, Catherine Juanita. *Black Portraiture in American Fiction*, 173–175.

Witching Times (1856)
  Hagemann, E. R. "John William De Forest's "Great American Novel," in Hoyt, Charles Alva, ed. *Minor American Novelists*, 15–17.

DE LA ROCHE, MAZO (1879–1961)

Centenary at Jalna (1958)

Fellows, Jo Ann. " 'British Connection' in the Jalna Novels of Mazo de la Roche: The Loyalist Myth Revisited." *DR* 56 (1976): 283–290.

Jalna (1927)

Fellows, Jo Ann. " 'British Connection' in the Jalna Novels of Mazo de la Roche: The Loyalist Myth Revisited." *DR* 56 (1976): 283–290.

Return to Jalna (1929)

Fellows, Jo Ann. " 'British Connection' in the Jalna Novels of Mazo de la Roche: The Loyalist Myth Revisited." *DR* 56 (1976): 283–290.

Variable Winds at Jalna (1954)

Fellows, Jo Ann. " 'British Connection' in the Jalna Novels of Mazo de la Roche: The Loyalist Myth Revisited." *DR* 56 (1976): 283–290.

Wakefield's Course (1941)

Fellows, Jo Ann. " 'British Connection' in the Jalna Novels of Mazo de la Roche: The Loyalist Myth Revisited." *DR* 56 (1976): 283–290.

Whiteoaks of Jalna (1929)

Fellows, Jo Ann. " 'British Connection' in the Jalna Novels of Mazo de la Roche: The Loyalist Myth Revisited." *DR* 56 (1976): 283–290.

DE MARE, GEORGE (1912–)

Empire (1956)

Bryant, Jerry H. *Open Decision*, 187–188.

DE MILLE, JAMES (1833–1880)

Strange Manuscript Found in a Copper Cylinder (1888)

Hughes, Kenneth J. "*Strange Manuscript:* Sources, Satire, A Positive Utopia," in Moss, John, ed. *Beginnings*, 119–123.

Kime, Wayne R. "American Antecedents of James De Mille's *A Strange Manuscript Found in a Copper Cylinder*." *DR* 55 (1975): 280–302.

Watters, Reginald Eyre. *Essays and Articles*, 198–207.

Woodcock, George. "De Mille and the Utopian Vision," in Moss, John, ed. *Beginnings*, 99–110.

DE PEREDA, PRUDENCIO (1912–)

All the Girls We Loved (1948)

Waldmeir, Joseph J. *American Novels of the Second World War*, 23–24, 27–30.

DE VOTO, BERNARD (1897–1955)

Chariot of Fire (1926)

Green, Rose Basile. *Italian-American Novel*, 96–97.

Sawey, Orlan. *Bernard DeVoto*, 23–25.

Crooked Mile (1924)

> Green, Rose Basile. *Italian-American Novel*, 95–96.
> Sawey, Orlan. *Bernard DeVoto*, 19–23.

House of Sun-Goes-Down (1928)

> Green, Rose Basile. *Italian-American Novel*, 97–98.
> Sawey, Orlan. *Bernard DeVoto*, 25–29.

Mountain Time (1947)

> Green, Rose Basile. *Italian-American Novel*, 99–102.
> Sawey, Orlan. *Bernard DeVoto*, 31–32.

We Accept With Pleasure (1934)

> Green, Rose Basile. *Italian-American Novel*, 98–99.
> Sawey, Orlan. *Bernard DeVoto*, 29–31.

DE VRIES, PETER (1910–1993)

Angels Can't Do Better (1944)

> Evans, T. Jeff. "Apprentice Fiction of Peter De Vries." *Crit* 21.3 (1980): 36–40.

Blood of the Lamb (1961)

> Kort, Wesley A. *Shriven Selves*, 36–63.

But Who Wakes the Bugler? (1940)

> Evans, T. Jeff. "Apprentice Fiction of Peter De Vries." *Crit* 21.3 (1980): 29–34.

Handsome Heart (1943)

> Evans, T. Jeff. "Apprentice Fiction of Peter De Vries." *Crit* 21.3 (1980): 34–36.

DELANY, MARTIN R. (1812–1885)

Blake (1859)

> Elder, Arlene A. *"Hindered Hand"*, 61–66.
> Fleming, Robert E. "Humor in the Early Black Novel." *CLAJ* 17 (1973): 253–254.
> Gayle, Addison, Jr. *Way of the New World*, 19–23.
> Takaki, Ronald T. *Violence in the Black Imagination*, 95–99.
> Whitlow, Roger. "Revolutionary Black Novels of Martin R. Delany and Sutton Griggs." *MELUS* 5.3 (1978): 27–31.
> Yellin, Jean Fagan. *Intricate Knot*, 197–208.
> Zeugner, John. "Note on Martin Delany's *Blake*, and Black Militancy." *Phylon* 32 (1971): 98–105.

DELANY, SAMUEL R. (1942–)

Babel-17 (1966)

> Alterman, Peter S. "Surreal Translations of Samuel R. Delany." *SFS* 4 (1977): 31.
> Hardesty, William H., III. "Semiotics, Space Opera and *Babel-17*." *Mosaic* 13.3–4 (1980): 63–69.

Slusser, George Edgar. *Delany Intersection*, 29–42.

Weedman, Jane. "Delany's *Babel-17:* The Powers of Language." *Extrapolation* 19 (1978): 132–137.

Dhalgren (1975)

Alterman, Peter S. "Surreal Translations of Samuel R. Delany." *SFS* 4 (1977): 26, 28–29, 32–33.

Slusser, George Edgar. *Delany Intersection*, 11–12.

Einstein Intersection (1967)

Alterman, Peter S. "Surreal Translations of Samuel R. Delany." *SFS* 4 (1977): 27–28, 33.

Ash, Brian. *Faces of the Future*, 201.

Fredericks, S. C. "Revivals of Ancient Mythologies in Current Science Fiction and Fantasy," in Clareson, Thomas D., ed. *Many Futures, Many Worlds*, 60–61.

Gardiner, H. Jane. "Images of 'The Waste Land' in *The Einstein Intersection*." *Extrapolation* 18 (1977): 116–123.

Samuelson, David N. "A Comparative Study of Novels by Brunner and Delany." *Extrapolation* 15 (1973): 83–92.

Slusser, George Edgar. *Delany Intersection*, 42–53.

Warrick, Patricia. "Images of the Man-Machine Intelligence Relationship in Science Fiction," in Clareson, Thomas D., ed. *Many Futures, Many Worlds*, 215–216.

Warrick, Patricia S. *Cybernetic Imagination in Science Fiction*, 178–179.

Fall of the Towers (1970)

Slusser, George Edgar. *Delany Intersection*, 12–29.

Wolfe, Gary K. *Known and the Unknown*, 105–109.

Nova (1968)

Alterman, Peter S. "Surreal Translations of Samuel R. Delany." *SFS* 4 (1977): 30–31, 32.

Slusser, George Edgar. *Delany Intersection*, 53–60.

Warrick, Patricia. "Images of the Man-Machine Intelligence Relationship in Science Fiction," in Clareson, Thomas D., ed. *Many Futures, Many Worlds*, 216–218.

Warrick, Patricia S. *Cybernetic Imagination in Science Fiction*, 176–178.

Tides of Lust (1973)

Perkins, Michael. *Secret Record*, 181–182.

Slusser, George Edgar. *Delany Intersection*, 11–12.

Triton (1976)

Alterman, Peter S. "Surreal Translations of Samuel R. Delany." *SFS* 4 (1977): 25–26.

Fekete, John. "*Dispossessed* and *Triton:* Act and System in Utopian Science Fiction." *SFS* 6 (1979): 136–141.

Moylan, Tom. "Beyond Negation: The Critical Utopias of Ursula K. Le Guin and Samuel R. Delany." *Extrapolation* 21 (1980): 243–252.

DELILLO, DON (1936–)

Americana (1971)

Oriard, Michael. "Don DeLillo's Search for Walden Pond." *Crit* 20.1 (1978): 5–23.

End Zone (1972)
Oriard, Michael. "Don DeLillo's Search for Walden Pond." *Crit* 20.1 (1978): 5–23.
Taylor, Anya. "Words, War, and Meditation in Don DeLillo's *End Zone*." *IFR* 4 (1977): 68–70.
Great Jones Street (1973)
Oriard, Michael. "Don DeLillo's Search for Walden Pond." *Crit* 20.1 (1978): 5–23.
Ratner's Star (1976)
Oriard, Michael. "Don DeLillo's Search for Walden Pond." *Crit* 20.1 (1978): 5–23.

DELL, FLOYD (1887–1969)

Briary-Bush (1921)
Hart, John E. *Floyd Dell*, 73–80.
Diana Stair (1932)
Hart, John E. *Floyd Dell*, 152–158.
Golden Spike (1934)
Hart, John E. *Floyd Dell*, 159–163.
Homecoming (1933)
Hart, John E. *Floyd Dell*, 158–159.
Janet March (1923)
Hart, John E. *Floyd Dell*, 84–93.
Love without Money (1931)
Hart, John E. *Floyd Dell*, 147–152.
Moon-Calf (1920)
Hart, John E. *Floyd Dell*, 67–73.
Old Man's Folly (1926)
Hart, John E. *Floyd Dell*, 128–134.
Runaway (1925)
Hart, John E. *Floyd Dell*, 98–104.
Souvenir (1929)
Hart, John E. *Floyd Dell*, 80–83.
This Mad Ideal (1925)
Hart, John E. *Floyd Dell*, 93–97.
Unmarried Father (1927)
Hart, John E. *Floyd Dell*, 134–138.

DEMBY, WILLIAM (1922–)

Beetlecreek (1950)
Bigsby, C. W. E., "From Protest to Paradox: The Black Writer at Mid Century," in French, Warren, ed. *Fifties*, 224–226.
Gayle, Addison, Jr. *Way of the New World*, 203–204.

DENKER, HENRY (1912–)

My Son, the Lawyer (1950)
Gelfant, Blanche Housman. *American City Novel*, 243–245.

DI DONATO, PIETRO (1910–1992)

Christ in Concrete (1939)
Green, Rose Basile. *Italian-American Novel*, 151–153.

This Woman (1958)
Green, Rose Basile. *Italian-American Novel*, 153–155.

Three Circles of Light (1960)
Green, Rose Basile. *Italian-American Novel*, 155–157.

DICK, PHILIP K. (1928–1982)

Counter-Clock World (1967)
Pagetti, Carlo. "Dick and Meta-SF." *SFS* 2 (1975): 30.

Do Androids Dream of Electric Sheep? (1968)
Pagetti, Carlo. "Dick and Meta-SF." *SFS* 2 (1975): 28–29.
Warrick, Patricia S. *Cybernetic Imagination in Science Fiction*, 224–228.

Dr. Bloodmoney (1965)
Gillespie, Bruce. "Mad, Mad Worlds: Seven Novels of Philip K. Dick," in Gillespie, Bruce, ed. *Philip K. Dick*, 17–19.
Jameson, Fredric. "After Armageddon: Character Systems in *Dr. Bloodmoney*." *SFS* 2 (1975): 31–42.
Warrick, Patricia S. *Cybernetic Imagination in Science Fiction*, 222–223.

Eye in the Sky (1957)
Scholes, Robert and Eric S. Rabkin. *Science Fiction*, 72.

Flow My Tears, the Policeman Said (1974)
Bray, Mary Kay. "Mandalic Activism: An Approach to Structure, Theme, and Tone in Four Novels by Philip K. Dick." *Extrapolation* 21 (1980): 146–157.
Scholes, Robert and Eric S. Rabkin. *Science Fiction*, 73–74.

Ganymede Takeover (1967)
Gillespie, Bruce. "Mad, Mad Worlds: Seven Novels of Philip K. Dick," in Gillespie, Bruce, ed. *Philip K. Dick*, 21.

Man in the High Castle (1932)
Gillespie, Bruce. "Mad, Mad Worlds: Seven Novels of Philip K. Dick," in Gillespie, Bruce, ed. *Philip K. Dick*, 15–17.
Ketterer, David. *New Worlds for Old*, 242–249.
Malmgre, Carl D. "Philip Dick's *Man in the High Castle* and the Nature of Science-Fictional Worlds," in Slusser, George E., George R. Guffey and Mark Rose, eds. *Bridges to Science Fiction*, 120–130.

Pagetti, Carlo. "Dick and Meta-SF." *SFS* 2 (1975): 26.
Scholes, Robert and Eric S. Rabkin. *Science Fiction*, 74–75.
Warrick, Patricia S. *Cybernetic Imagination in Science Fiction*, 214–215.

Martian Time-Slip (1964)

Aldiss, Brian W. "Dick's Maledictory Web: About and Around *Martian Time-Slip*." *SFS* 2 (1975): 42–47.
Pagetti, Carlo. "Dick and Meta-SF." *SFS* 2 (1975): 26–28.
Warrick, Patricia S. *Cybernetic Imagination in Science Fiction*, 219–220.

Maze of Death (1970)

Bray, Mary Kay. "Mandalic Activism: An Approach to Structure, Theme, and Tone in Four Novels by Philip K. Dick." *Extrapolation* 21 (1980): 146–157.

Now Wait for Last Year (1966)

Bray, Mary Kay. "Mandalic Activism: An Approach to Structure, Theme, and Tone in Four Novels by Philip K. Dick." *Extrapolation* 21 (1980): 146–157.

Penultimate Truth (1964)

Gillespie, Bruce. "Mad, Mad Worlds: Seven Novels of Philip K. Dick," in Gillespie, Bruce, ed. *Philip K. Dick*, 20.
Warrick, Patricia S. *Cybernetic Imagination in Science Fiction*, 220–222.

Simulacra (1964)

Pagetti, Carlo. "Dick and Meta-SF." *SFS* 2 (1975): 28, 29–30.
Warrick, Patricia S. *Cybernetic Imagination in Science Fiction*, 220–222.

Three Stigmata of Palmer Eldritch (1964)

Gillespie, Bruce. "Mad, Mad Worlds: Seven Novels of Philip K. Dick," in Gillespie, Bruce, ed. *Philip K. Dick*, 11–15.

Ubik (1969)

Bray, Mary Kay. "Mandalic Activism: An Approach to Structure, Theme, and Tone in Four Novels by Philip K. Dick." *Extrapolation* 21 (1980): 146–157.
Fitting, Peter. "*Ubik:* The Deconstruction of Bourgeois SF." *SFS* 2 (1975): 47–54.
Keeling, Thomas H. "Science Fiction and the Gothic," in Slusser, George E., George R. Guffey and Mark Rose, eds. *Bridges to Science Fiction*, 108–113.
Lem, Stanislaw. "Philip K. Dick: A Visionary among the Charlatans." Trans. Robert Abernathy. *SFS* 2 (1975): 57–61.
Scholes, Robert and Eric S. Rabkin. *Science Fiction*, 72.

Vulcan's Hammer (1960)

Warrick, Patricia S. *Cybernetic Imagination in Science Fiction*, 213–214.

World Jones Made (1959)

Gillespie, Bruce. "Mad, Mad Worlds: Seven Novels of Philip K. Dick," in Gillespie, Bruce, ed. *Philip K. Dick*, 20–21.

DICKEY, JAMES (1923–1997)

Deliverance (1970)

Beidler, Peter G. " 'The Pride of Thine Heart Hath Deceived Thee': Narrative Distortion in Dickey's *Deliverance*." *SCR* 5.1 (1972): 29–40.

Carnes, Bruce. "Deliverance in James Dickey's 'On the Coosawattee' and *Deliverance.*" *NConL* 7.2 (1977): 2–4.

Coulthard, Ron. "Reflections upon a Golden Eye: A Note on James Dickey's *Deliverance.*" *NConL* 3.2 (1973): 13–15.

Davis, Charles E. "Wilderness Revisited: Irony in James Dickey's *Deliverance.*" *SAF* 4 (1976): 223–230.

Doughtie, Edward. "Art and Nature in *Deliverance.*" *SR* 64 (1979): 167–180.

Edwards, C. Hines, Jr. "Dickey's *Deliverance:* The Owl and the Eye." *Crit* 15.2 (1973): 95–101.

Edwards, C. Hines, Jr. "Foggy Scene in *Deliverance.*" *NConL* 2.5 (1972): 7–9.

Finholt, Richard. *American Visionary Fiction*, 128–143.

Guillory, Daniel L. "Myth and Meaning in James Dickey's *Deliverance.*" *CollL* 3 (1976): 56–62.

Guttenberg, Barnett. "Pattern of Redemption in Dickey's *Deliverance.*" *Crit* 18.3 (1977): 83–91.

Holley, Linda Tarte. "Design and Focus in James Dickey's *Deliverance.*" *SCR* 10.2 (1978): 90–98.

Hughes, Richard E. *Lively Image*, 114–131.

Italia, Paul G. "Love and Lust in James Dickey's *Deliverance.*" *MFS* 21 (1975): 203–213.

Kunz, Don. "Learning the Hard Way in James Dickey's *Deliverance.*" *WAL* 12 (1978): 289–301.

Lennox, John. "Dark Journeys: *Kamouraska* and *Deliverance.*" *ECW* 12 (1978): 84–86, 93–103.

Longen, Eugene M. "Dickey's *Deliverance:* Sex and the Great Outdoors." *SLJ* 9.2 (1977): 137–149.

Marin, Daniel B. "James Dickey's *Deliverance:* Darkness Visible." *SCR* 3 (1970): 49–59.

Marin, Daniel B. "James Dickey's *Deliverance:* Darkness Visible." *South Carolina Review* 3 (Nov 1970): 49–59. Rpt. in Calhoun, Richard J., ed. *James Dickey, The Expansive Imagination*, 105–117.

Markos, Donald W. "Art and Immediacy: James Dickey's *Deliverance.*" *SoR* 7 (1971): 947–953.

Monk, Donald. "Colour Symbolism in James Dickey's *Deliverance.*" *JAmS* 11 (1977): 261–279.

Seelye, John. "Georgia Boys: The Redclay Satyrs of Erskine Caldwell and Harry Crews." *VQR* 56 (1980): 615–616.

Shepherd, Allen. "Counter-Monster Comes Home: The Last Chapter of James Dickey's *Deliverance.*" *NConL* 3.2 (1973): 8–12.

Strong, Paul. "James Dickey's Arrow of Deliverance." *SCR* 11.1 (1978): 108–116.

Sullivan, Rosemary. "*Surfacing* and *Deliverance.*" *CanL* 67 (1976): 6–19.

Wagner, Linda. "*Deliverance:* Initiation and Possibility." *SCR* 10.2 (1978): 49–55.

Wagner, Linda W. *American Modern*, 76–84.

Willig, Charles L. "Ed's Transformation: A Note on *Deliverance.*" *NConL* 3.2 (1973): 4–5.

DICKSON, GORDON R. (1923–)

Dorsai! (1976)

Thompson, Raymond H. "Shai Dorsai!: A Study of the Hero Figure in Gordon R. Dickson's *Dorsai.*" *Extrapolation* 20 (1979): 223–228.

DIDION, JOAN (1934–)

Book of Common Prayer (1977)

Brady, H. Jennifer. "Points West, Then and Now: The Fiction of Joan Didion." *ConL* 20 (1979): 465–469.
Mallon, Thomas. "Limits of History in the Novels of Joan Didion." *Crit* 21.3 (1980): 43–52.
Winchell, Mark Royden. *Joan Didion*, 138–152.

Play It as It Lays (1970)

Brady, H. Jennifer. "Points West, Then and Now: The Fiction of Joan Didion." *ConL* 20 (1979): 463–465.
Chabot, C. Barry. "Joan Didion's *Play It as It Lays* and the Vacuity of the 'Here and Now'." *Crit* 21.3 (1980): 53–60.
Hendin, Josephine. *Vulnerable People*, 182–184.
Mallon, Thomas. "Limits of History in the Novels of Joan Didion." *Crit* 21.3 (1980): 43–52.
Masinton, Martha and Charles G. Masinton. "Second-class Citizenship: The Status of Women in Contemporary American Fiction," in Springer, Marlene, ed. *What Manner of Woman*, 311–312.
Winchell, Mark Royden. *Joan Didion*, 127–137.

Run River (1963)

Brady, H. Jennifer. "Points West, Then and Now: The Fiction of Joan Didion." *ConL* 20 (1979): 456–463.
Hendin, Josephine. *Vulnerable People*, 181–182.
Mallon, Thomas. "Limits of History in the Novels of Joan Didion." *Crit* 21.3 (1980): 43–52.
Winchell, Mark Royden. *Joan Didion*, 101–111.

DIXON, THOMAS (1864–1946)

Clansman (1905)

Baker, Donald G. "Black Images: The Afro-American in Popular Novels, 1900–1945." *JPC* 7 (1973): 330–332.
Cook, Raymond A. *Thomas Dixon*, 63–64, 71–74.
Godbold, E. Stanley, Jr. "Battleground Revisited: Reconstruction in Southern Fiction, 1895–1905." *SAQ* 73 (1974): 107–108.
Starke, Catherine Juanita. *Black Portraiture in American Fiction*, 64–65.

Comrades (1909)

Cook, Raymond A. *Thomas Dixon*, 84–85.

Fall of a Nation (1916)

Cook, Raymond A. *Thomas Dixon*, 92–93.
Davenport, F. Garvin, Jr. *Myth of Southern History*, 41–43.

Flaming Sword (1939)

Cook, Raymond A. *Thomas Dixon*, 88–90.

Foolish Virgin (1915)

    Davenport, F. Garvin, Jr. *Myth of Southern History*, 40–41.

Leopard's Spots (1903)

    Andrews, William L. "Miscegenation in the Late Nineteenth-Century American Novel." *SoHR* 13 (1979): 20–21.
    Cook, Raymond A. *Thomas Dixon*, 59–63, 67–70.
    Davenport, F. Garvin, Jr. *Myth of Southern History*, 24–30, 34–38.
    Godbold, E. Stanley, Jr. "Battleground Revisited: Reconstruction in Southern Fiction, 1895–1905." *SAQ* 73 (1974): 106.
    Starke, Catherine Juanita. *Black Portraiture in American Fiction*, 63–64.

Love Complex (1925)

    Cook, Raymond A. *Thomas Dixon*, 93–94.

One Woman (1903)

    Cook, Raymond A. *Thomas Dixon*, 82–84.
    Davenport, F. Garvin, Jr. *Myth of Southern History*, 39–40.

Root of Evil (1911)

    Cook, Raymond A. *Thomas Dixon*, 85–86.
    Davenport, F. Garvin, Jr. *Myth of Southern History*, 32–34.

Sins of the Father (1912)

    Cook, Raymond A. *Thomas Dixon*, 95–96.
    Davenport, F. Garvin, Jr. *Myth of Southern History*, 30–32.

Sun Virgin (1929)

    Cook, Raymond A. *Thomas Dixon*, 96–98.

Traitor (1907)

    Cook, Raymond A. *Thomas Dixon*, 75–76.

Way of Man (1919)

    Cook, Raymond A. *Thomas Dixon*, 94–95.

DOCTOROW, E. L. (1931–)

Book of Daniel (1971)

    Emblidge, David. "Marching Backward into the Future: Progress as Illusion in Doctorow's Novels." *SR* 62 (1977): 400–404.
    Estrin, Barbara L. "Surviving McCarthyism: E.L. Doctorow's *The Book of Daniel*." *MR* 16 (1975): 577–587.
    Stark, John. "Alienation and Analysis in Doctorow's *The Book of Daniel*." *Crit* 16.3 (1975): 101–110.

Ragtime (1975)

    Emblidge, David. "Marching Backward into the Future: Progress as Illusion in Doctorow's Novels." *SR* 62 (1977): 404–408.
    Foley, Barbara. "From *U.S.A.* to *Ragtime:* Notes on the Forms of Historical Consciousness in Modern Fiction." *AL* 50 (1978): 85–105.

Knorr, Walter L. "Doctorow and Kleist: 'Kohlhaas' in *Ragtime*." *MFS* 22 (1976): 224–227.

Welcome to Hard Times (1960)

Emblidge, David. "Marching Backward into the Future: Progress as Illusion in Doctorow's Novels." *SR* 62 (1977): 398–400.

DONNELLY, IGNATIUS (1831–1901)

Caesar's Column (1891)

Baker, J. Wayne. "Populist Themes in the Fiction of Ignatius Donnelly." *AmerS* 14.2 (1974): 66–72.
Lynn, Kenneth S. *Visions of America*, 194–196.

Dr. Huguet (1891)

Baker, J. Wayne. "Populist Themes in the Fiction of Ignatius Donnelly." *AmerS* 14.2 (1974): 76–80.

Golden Bottle (1892)

Baker, J. Wayne. "Populist Themes in the Fiction of Ignatius Donnelly." *AmerS* 14.2 (1974): 72–76.

DOOLITTLE, HILDA see H. D.

DORR, JULIA CAROLINE RIPLEY (1825–1913)

Farmingdale (1854)

Baym, Nina. *Woman's Fiction*, 237–239.

Lanmere (1856)

Baym, Nina. *Woman's Fiction*, 239.

Mother's Rule see *Farmingdale*

DOS PASSOS, JOHN (1896–1970)

Adventures of a Young Man (1939)

Aldridge, John W. *Devil in the Fire*, 120–121.
Becker, George J. *John Dos Passos*, 83–86.
Blake, Nelson Manfred. *Novelists' America*, 183–193.
Colley, Iain. *Dos Passos & the Fiction of Despair*, 121–126.
Eisinger, Chester E. "Dos Passos and the New Liberalism," in Eisinger, Chester E. *Fiction of the Forties*. Chicago: University of Chicago Press, 1963. 118–125. Rpt. in Belkind, Allen, ed. *Dos Passos, the Critics, and the Writer's Intention*, 140–141.
Gelfant, Blanche H. "Search for Identity in the Novels of John Dos Passos." *PMLA* 74 (March 1961): 133–149. Rpt. in Belkind, Allen, ed. *Dos Passos, the Critics, and the Writer's Intention*, 164, 171–176, 182.

Sanders, David. "The 'Anarchism' of John Dos Passos." *South Atlantic Quarterly* 60 (Winter 1961): 44–55. Rpt. in Belkind, Allen, ed. *Dos Passos, the Critics, and the Writer's Intention*, 131–132.

Wagner, Linda W. *Dos Passos*, 118–120.

Big Money (1936)

Aldridge, John W. *Devil in the Fire*, 118–119.

Becker, George J. *John Dos Passos*, 58–79.

Blake, Nelson Manfred. *Novelists' America*, 174–183.

Colley, Iain. *Dos Passos & the Fiction of Despair*, 101–117.

Foley, Barbara. "Treatment of Time in *The Big Money:* An Examination of Ideology and Literary Form." *MFS* 26 (1980): 447–467.

Hicks, Granville. "Politics of John Dos Passos." *Antioch Review* 10 (March 1950): 85–97. Rpt. in Belkind, Allen, ed. *Dos Passos, the Critics, and the Writer's Intention*, 117.

Kazin, Alfred. "All the Lost Generations," in Kazin, Alfred. *On Native Grounds.* New York: Harcourt, Brace & World, 1942. 341–359. Rpt. as "Dos Passos, Society, and the Individual," in Hook, Andrew, ed. *Dos Passos*, 117–118.

Kazin, Alfred. "Dos Passos and the 'Lost Generation'," in Belkind, Allen, ed. *Dos Passos, the Critics, and the Writer's Intention*, 17–20.

Magny, Claude-Edmonde. "Time in Dos Passos," in Magny, Claude-Edmonde. *Age of the American Novel: The Film Aesthetic of Fiction Between the Two Wars.* Trans. Eleanor Hochman. New York: Frederick Ungar Publishing Co., 1972. Rpt. in Hook, Andrew, ed. *Dos Passos*, 128–130.

Milne, W. Gordon. "John Dos Passos," in Panichas, George A., ed. *Politics of Twentieth-Century Novelists*, 271–272.

Walcutt, Charles C. "Dos Passos and Naturalism," in Walcutt, Charles C. *American Literary Naturalism: A Divided Stream.* Minneapolis, MN: University of Minnesota Press, 1956. 280–289. Rpt. in Belkind, Allen, ed. *Dos Passos, the Critics, and the Writer's Intention*, 86–92.

Ward, John William. "Dos Passos, Fitzgerald, and History," in Ward, John William. *Red, White, and Blue: Men, Books, and Ideas in American Culture.* New York: Oxford University Press, Inc., 1969. 38–47. Rpt. in Hook, Andrew, ed. *Dos Passos*, 121–122, 126–127.

Century's Ebb (1975)

Wagner, Linda W. *Dos Passos*, 159–173.

Chosen Country (1951)

Colley, Iain. *Dos Passos & the Fiction of Despair*, 135–138.

Eisinger, Chester E. "Dos Passos and the New Liberalism," in Eisinger, Chester E. *Fiction of the Forties.* Chicago: University of Chicago Press, 1963. 118–125. Rpt. in Belkind, Allen, ed. *Dos Passos, the Critics, and the Writer's Intention*, 143–144.

Gelfant, Blanche H. "Search for Identity in the Novels of John Dos Passos." *PMLA* 74 (March 1961): 133–149. Rpt. in Belkind, Allen, ed. *Dos Passos, the Critics, and the Writer's Intention*, 160–164, 165, 167, 182, 188–189, 191–193.

Wagner, Linda W. *Dos Passos*, 137–142.

First Encounter (1945)

Miller, Wayne Charles. *Armed America, Its Face in Fiction*, 113–116.

42ⁿᵈ Parallel (1930)

Aldridge, John W. *Devil in the Fire*, 117–118.

Becker, George J. *John Dos Passos*, 58–79.

Colley, Iain. *Dos Passos & the Fiction of Despair*, 66–84.

Donald, Miles. *American Novel in the Twentieth Century*, 48–50.

Kazin, Alfred. "All the Lost Generations," in Kazin, Alfred. *On Native Grounds.* New York: Harcourt, Brace & World, 1942. 341–359. Rpt. as "Dos Passos, Society, and the Individual," in Hook, Andrew, ed. *Dos Passos*, 113–115.

Kazin, Alfred. "Dos Passos and the 'Lost Generation'," in Belkind, Allen, ed. *Dos Passos, the Critics, and the Writer's Intention*, 15–17.

Leavis, F. R. "Serious Artist." *Scrutiny* (1932): 173–179. Rpt. in Hook, Andrew, ed. *Dos Passos*, 70–75.

Milne, W. Gordon. "John Dos Passos," in Panichas, George A., ed. *Politics of Twentieth-Century Novelists*, 269–270.

Walcutt, Charles C. "Dos Passos and Naturalism," in Walcutt, Charles C. *American Literary Naturalism: A Divided Stream.* Minneapolis, MN: University of Minnesota Press, 1956. 280–289. Rpt. in Belkind, Allen, ed. *Dos Passos, the Critics, and the Writer's Intention*, 85–86.

Grand Design (1949)

Aldridge, John W. *Devil in the Fire*, 122.

Becker, George J. *John Dos Passos*, 90–94.

Colley, Iain. *Dos Passos & the Fiction of Despair*, 130–134.

Eisinger, Chester E. "Dos Passos and the New Liberalism," in Eisinger, Chester E. *Fiction of the Forties.* Chicago: University of Chicago Press, 1963. 118–125. Rpt. in Belkind, Allen, ed. *Dos Passos, the Critics, and the Writer's Intention*, 142–143.

Gelfant, Blanche H. "Search for Identity in the Novels of John Dos Passos." *PMLA* 74 (March 1961): 133–149. Rpt. in Belkind, Allen, ed. *Dos Passos, the Critics, and the Writer's Intention*, 189–191.

Sanders, David. "The 'Anarchism' of John Dos Passos." *South Atlantic Quarterly* 60 (Winter 1961): 44–55. Rpt. in Belkind, Allen, ed. *Dos Passos, the Critics, and the Writer's Intention*, 132–134.

Wagner, Linda W. *Dos Passos*, 123–130.

Great Days (1958)

Colley, Iain. *Dos Passos & the Fiction of Despair*, 140–142.

Gelfant, Blanche H. "Search for Identity in the Novels of John Dos Passos." *PMLA* 74 (March 1961): 133–149. Rpt. in Belkind, Allen, ed. *Dos Passos, the Critics, and the Writer's Intention*, 193–196.

Wagner, Linda W. *Dos Passos*, 143–144.

Manhattan Transfer (1925)

Aldridge, John W. *Devil in the Fire*, 114–116.

Beach, Joseph Warren. "*Manhattan Transfer:* Collectivism and Abstract Composition," in Belkind, Allen, ed. *Dos Passos, the Critics, and the Writer's Intention*, 54–69.

Becker, George J. *John Dos Passos*, 38–55.

Carver, Craig. "Newspaper and Other Sources of *Manhattan Transfer*." *SAF* 3 (1975): 167–179.

Colley, Iain. *Dos Passos & the Fiction of Despair*, 47–65.

Cowley, Malcolm. "John Dos Passos: The Poet and the World," in Cowley, Malcolm. *Think Back on Us*. Carbondale, IL: Southern Illinois University Press, 1967. 212–218, 298–301. Rpt. in Belkind, Allen, ed. *Dos Passos, the Critics, and the Writer's Intention*, 32–33.

Festa-McCormick, Diana. *City as Catalyst*, 141–157.

Gelfant, Blanche H. "John Dos Passos: The Synoptic Novel," Gelfant, Blance Housman. *American City Novel*. Norman, OK: University of Oklahoma Press, 1954. 133–151. Rpt. in Hook, Andrew, ed. *Dos Passos*, 43–52.

Gelfant, Blanche H. "Search for Identity in the Novels of John Dos Passos." *PMLA* 74 (March 1961): 133–149. Rpt. in Belkind, Allen, ed. *Dos Passos, the Critics, and the Writer's Intention*, 161, 162–163, 164–165, 171, 183–184.

Gelfant, Blanche Housman. *American City Novel*, 138–152, 153–174.

Hicks, Granville. "Politics of John Dos Passos." *Antioch Review* 10 (March 1950): 85–97. Rpt. in Belkind, Allen, ed. *Dos Passos, the Critics, and the Writer's Intention*, 111.

Hughson, Lois. "Narration in the Making of *Manhattan Transfer*." *SNNTS* 8 (1976): 185–198.

Kazin, Alfred. "All the Lost Generations," Kazin, Alfred. *On Native Grounds*. New York: Harcourt, Brace & World, 1942. 341–359. Rpt. as "Dos Passos, Society, and the Individual," in Hook, Andrew, ed. *Dos Passos*, 109–110

Lane, James B. "*Manhattan Transfer* as a Gateway to the 1920's." *CentR* 16 (1972): 293–311.

Leavis, F. R. "Serious Artist." *Scrutiny* (1932): 173–179. Rpt. in Hook, Andrew, ed. *Dos Passos*, 70–75.

Lee, Brian. "History and John Dos Passos," in Bradbury, Malcolm and David Palmer, eds. *American Novel in the Nineteen Twenties*, 206–209.

Lowry, E. D. "Lively Art of *Manhattan Transfer*." *PMLA* 84 (1969): 1628–1638.

Lowry, E. D. "*Manhattan Transfer:* Dos Passos' Wasteland." *University Review* (1963): 47–52. Rpt. in Hook, Andrew, ed. *Dos Passos*, 53–60.

Lynn, Kenneth S. *Visions of America*, 180–182.

McLuhan, Marshall. *Interior Landscape*, 52–56.

Sanders, David. "*Manhattan Transfer* and "The Service of Things," in Browne, Ray B. and Donald Pizer, eds. *Themes and Directions in American Literature*, 171–183.

Titche, Leon L., Jr. "Döblin and Dos Passos: Aspects of the City Novel." *MFS* 17 (1971): 130–135.

Vanderwerken, David L. "*Manhattan Transfer:* Dos Passos' Babel Story." *AL* 49 (1977): 253–267.

Vickery, Olga W. "Inferno of the Moderns," in Friedman, Melvin J. and John B. Vickery, eds. *Shaken Realist*, 155–156.

Wagner, Linda W. *Dos Passos*, 47–63.

Walcutt, Charles C. "Dos Passos and Naturalism," in Walcutt, Charles C. *American Literary Naturalism: A Divided Stream*. Minneapolis, MN: University of Minnesota Press, 1956. 280–289. Rpt. in Belkind, Allen, ed. *Dos Passos, the Critics, and the Writer's Intention*, 82–85.

Midcentury (1960)

Becker, George J. *John Dos Passos*, 94–98.

Colley, Iain. *Dos Passos & the Fiction of Despair*, 142–144.

Lynn, Kenneth S. *Visions of America*, 184–187.
Moore, Harry T. "Return of John Dos Passos." *New York Times Book Review* (26 Feb 1961). Rpt. in Moore, Harry T. *Age of the Modern*, 37–41.
Wagner, Linda W. *Dos Passos*, 152–159.

Most Likely to Succeed (1954)

Colley, Iain. *Dos Passos & the Fiction of Despair*, 138–140.
Wagner, Linda W. *Dos Passos*, 142–143.

1919 (1932)

Aldridge, John W. *Devil in the Fire*, 118.
Becker, George J. *John Dos Passos*, 58–79.
Blake, Nelson Manfred. *Novelists' America*, 169–174.
Colley, Iain. *Dos Passos & the Fiction of Despair*, 84–101.
Cowley, Malcolm. "John Dos Passos: The Poet and the World," in Cowley, Malcolm. *Think Back on Us*. Carbondale, IL: Southern Illinois University Press, 1967. 212–218, 298–301. Rpt. in Belkind, Allen, ed. *Dos Passos, the Critics, and the Writer's Intention*, 26–30.
Hicks, Granville. "Politics of John Dos Passos." *Antioch Review* 10 (March 1950): 85–97. Rpt. in Belkind, Allen, ed. *Dos Passos, the Critics, and the Writer's Intention*, 115.
Katopes, Peter J. "Wesley Everest in John Dos Passos's *Nineteen Nineteen*." *N&Q* 23 (1976): 22.
Kazin, Alfred. "All the Lost Generations," in Kazin, Alfred. *On Native Grounds*. New York: Harcourt, Brace & World, 1942. 341–359. Rpt. as "Dos Passos, Society, and the Individual," in Hook, Andrew, ed. *Dos Passos*, 116–117.
Leavis, F. R. "Serious Artist." *Scrutiny* (1932): 173–179. Rpt. in Hook, Andrew, ed. *Dos Passos*, 70–75.
Milne, W. Gordon. "John Dos Passos," in Panichas, George A., ed. *Politics of Twentieth-Century Novelists*, 270–271.
Sartre, Jean-Paul. "John Dos Passos and *1919*," in Sartre, Jean-Paul. *Literary and Philosophical Essays*. Trans. Annette Michelson. London: Rider & Company, 1955. 88–96. Rpt. in Hook, Andrew, ed. *Dos Passos*, 61–69.
Sartre, Jean-Paul. "John Dos Passos and *1919*," in Sartre, Jean-Paul. *Literary Essays*. Trans. Annette Michelson. New York: Philosophical Library, 1957. 88–96. Rpt. in Belkind, Allen, ed. *Dos Passos, the Critics, and the Writer's Intention*, 70–80.
Sartre, Jean-Paul. "John Dos Passos and *1919*," in Sartre, Jean-Paul. *Literary Essays*. New York: Philosophical Library, 1957. 88–96. Rpt. in Sanders, David, comp. *Merrill Studies in U.S.A.*, 30–37.
Walcutt, Charles C. "Dos Passos and Naturalism," in Walcutt, Charles C. *American Literary Naturalism: A Divided Stream*. Minneapolis, MN: University of Minnesota Press, 1956. 280–289. Rpt. in Belkind, Allen, ed. *Dos Passos, the Critics, and the Writer's Intention*, 86.

Number One (1943)

Aldridge, John W. *Devil in the Fire*, 121–122.
Colley, Iain. *Dos Passos & the Fiction of Despair*, 126–130.
Eisinger, Chester E. "Dos Passos and the New Liberalism," in Eisinger, Chester E. *Fiction of the Forties*. Chicago: University of Chicago Press, 1963. 118–125.

Rpt. in Belkind, Allen, ed. *Dos Passos, the Critics, and the Writer's Intention*, 141–142.

Sanders, David. "The 'Anarchism' of John Dos Passos." *South Atlantic Quarterly* 60 (Winter 1961): 44–55. Rpt. in Belkind, Allen, ed. *Dos Passos, the Critics, and the Writer's Intention*, 132.

Wagner, Linda W. *Dos Passos*, 120–123.

One Man's Initiation–1917 (1920)

Aldridge, John W. *Devil in the Fire*, 108–112.

Colley, Iain. *Dos Passos & the Fiction of Despair*, 27–33.

Streets of Night (1923)

Colley, Iain. *Dos Passos & the Fiction of Despair*, 18–26.

Gelfant, Blanche H. "Search for Identity in the Novels of John Dos Passos." *PMLA* 74 (March 1961): 133–149. Rpt. in Belkind, Allen, ed. *Dos Passos, the Critics, and the Writer's Intention*, 165, 166–167, 169–171.

Gelfant, Blanche Housman. *American City Novel*, 152–153.

Lee, Brian. "History and John Dos Passos," in Bradbury, Malcolm and David Palmer, eds. *American Novel in the Nineteen Twenties*, 205–206.

Three Soldiers (1921)

Aldridge, John W. *Devil in the Fire*, 112–114.

Becker, George J. *John Dos Passos*, 24–30.

Colley, Iain. *Dos Passos & the Fiction of Despair*, 33–45.

Cooperman, Stanley. "John Dos Passos' *Three Soldiers:* Aesthetics and the Doom of Individualism," in Klein, Holger, ed. *First World War in Fiction*, 23–31.

Gelfant, Blanche H. "Search for Identity in the Novels of John Dos Passos." *PMLA* 74 (March 1961): 133–149. Rpt. in Belkind, Allen, ed. *Dos Passos, the Critics, and the Writer's Intention*, 176–181.

Gilman, Owen W., Jr. "John Dos Passos: *Three Soldiers* and Thoreau." *MFS* 26 (1980): 470–481.

Hicks, Granville. "Politics of John Dos Passos." *Antioch Review* 10 (March 1950): 85–97. Rpt. in Belkind, Allen, ed. *Dos Passos, the Critics, and the Writer's Intention*, 109–110.

Jones, Peter G. *War and the Novelist*, 5–7.

Kazin, Alfred. "All the Lost Generations," in Kazin, Alfred. *On Native Grounds*. New York: Harcourt, Brace & World, 1942. 341–359. Rpt. as "Dos Passos, Society, and the Individual," in Hook, Andrew, ed. *Dos Passos*, 107–108.

Lee, Brian. "History and John Dos Passos," in Bradbury, Malcolm and David Palmer, eds. *American Novel in the Nineteen Twenties*, 202–205.

McIlvaine, Robert. "Dos Passos' *Three Soldiers*." *Expl* 31 (1973): Item 50.

Miller, Wayne Charles. *Armed America, Its Face in Fiction*, 109–113.

U.S.A. (1938)

Aldridge, John W. *After the Lost Generation*. New York: McGraw-Hill, 1951. 71–76. Rpt. in Sanders, David, comp. *Merrill Studies in U.S.A.*, 44–48.

Allen, Walter. *Urgent West*, 208–210.

Becker, George J. *John Dos Passos*, 58–79.

Bradbury, Malcolm. "Denuded Place: War and Form in *Parade's End* and *U.S.A.*," in Klein, Holger, ed. *First World War in Fiction*, 203–209.

Donald, Miles. *American Novel in the Twentieth Century*, 48–59.

Gelfant, Blanche H. "Fulfillment of Form in *U.S.A.*," in Gelfant, Blanche Housman. *American City Novel*. Norman, OK: University of Oklahoma Press, 1954. 166–174. Rpt. in Sanders, David, comp. *Merrill Studies in U.S.A.*, 48–54.

Gelfant, Blanche H. "Search for Identity in the Novels of John Dos Passos." *PMLA* 74 (March 1961): 133–149. Rpt. in Belkind, Allen, ed. *Dos Passos, the Critics, and the Writer's Intention*, 167–169.

Goldman, Arnold. "Dos Passos and His *U.S.A.*" *NLH* 1 (1970): 471–483.

Henderson, Harry B. *Versions of the Past*, 241–246.

Hicks, Granville. "Moods and Tenses of John Dos Passos." *New Masses* 27 (26 April 1938): 22–23. Rpt. in Sanders, David, comp. *Merrill Studies in U.S.A.*, 11–16.

Hughson, Lois. "In Search of the True America: Dos Passos' Debt to Whitman in *U.S.A.*" *MFS* 19 (1973): 179–192.

Kazin, Alfred. "All the Lost Generations," in Kazin, Alfred. *On Native Grounds*. New York: Harcourt, Brace & World, 1942. 341–359. Rpt. as "Dos Passos, Society, and the Individual," in Hook, Andrew, ed. *Dos Passos*, 111–113, 115.

Kazin, Alfred. *On Native Grounds*. New York: Reynal and Hitchcock, 1942. 353–359. Rpt. in Sanders, David, comp. *Merrill Studies in U.S.A.*, 38–43.

Lee, Brian. "History and John Dos Passos," in Bradbury, Malcolm and David Palmer, eds. *American Novel in the Nineteen Twenties*, 209–213.

Lehan, Richard. *Dangerous Crossing*, 40–46.

Ludington, Townsend. "Ordering of the Camera Eye in *U.S.A.*." *AL* 49 (1977): 443–446.

Lydenberg, John. "Dos Passos's *U.S.A.*: The Words of Hollow Men," in Krause, Sidney J., ed. *Essays on Determinism in American Literature*. Kent, OH: Kent State University Press, 1964. 97–107. Rpt. in Belkind, Allen, ed. *Dos Passos, the Critics, and the Writer's Intention*, 93–105.

Lydenberg, John. "Dos Passos's *U.S.A.*: The Words of Hollow Men," in Krause, Sidney J., ed. *Essays on Determinism in American Literature*. Kent, OH: Kent State University Press, 1964. 97–107. Rpt. in Sanders, David, comp. *Merrill Studies in U.S.A.*, 86–95.

Magny, Claude-Edmonde. "Time in Dos Passos," Magny, Claude-Edmonde. *Age of the American Novel: The Film Aesthetic of Fiction Between the Two Wars*. Trans. Eleanor Hochman. New York: Frederick Ungar Publishing Co., 1972. Rpt. in Hook, Andrew, ed. *Dos Passos*, 130–144.

Marz, Charles. "*U.S.A.*: Chronicle and Performance." *MFS* 26 (1980): 398–415.

Milne, W. Gordon. "John Dos Passos," in Panichas, George A., ed. *Politics of Twentieth-Century Novelists*, 269–276.

Morris, Wright. *Earthly Delights, Unearthly Adornments*, 124–129.

Morse, Jonathan. "Dos Passos' *U.S.A.* and the Illusions of Memory." *MFS* 23 (1977–78): 543–555.

Ousby, Ian. *Reader's Guide to Fifty American Novels*, 271–275.

Pizer, Donald. "Camera Eye in *U.S.A.*: The Sexual Center." *MFS* 26 (1980): 417–430.

Rideout, Walter B. "Radicalism of *U.S.A.*," Rideout, Walter B. *Radical Novel in the United States: 1900–1954*. Cambridge, MA: Harvard University Press, 1956. 162–164. Rpt. in Hook, Andrew, ed. *Dos Passos*, 145–147.

Spencer, Sharon. *Space, Time and Structure in the Modern Novel*, 102–106.

Trilling, Lionel. "America of John Dos Passos." *Partisan Review* (April 1938): 26–32. Rpt. in Belkind, Allen, ed. *Dos Passos, the Critics, and the Writer's Intention*, 35–43.

Trilling, Lionel. "America of John Dos Passos." *Partisan Review* (April 1938): 26–32. Rpt. in Hook, Andrew, ed. *Dos Passos*, 93–100.

Trilling, Lionel. "America of John Dos Passos." *Partisan Review* (April 1938): 26–32. Rpt. in Sanders, David, comp. *Merrill Studies in U.S.A.*, 21–28.

Vanderwerken, David L. "*U.S.A.:* Dos Passos and the 'Old Words'." *TCL* 23 (1977): 195–228.

Wagner, Linda W. *Dos Passos*, 85–108.

Walcutt, Charles Child. *American Literary Naturalism: A Divided Stream*. Minneapolis, MN: University of Minnesota Press, 1956. 283–289. Rpt. in Sanders, David, comp. *Merrill Studies in U.S.A.*, 54–59.

Ward, John William. "Dos Passos, Fitzgerald, and History," Ward, John William. *Red, White, and Blue: Men, Books, and Ideas in American Culture*. New York: Oxford University Press, Inc., 1969. 38–47. Rpt. in Hook, Andrew, ed. *Dos Passos*, 123–127.

Westerhoven, James N. "Autobiographical Elements in the Camera Eye." *AL* 48 (1976): 340–364.

Whipple, T. K. "Dos Passos and the U.S.A.." *Nation* (19 February 1938): 210–212. Rpt. in Hook, Andrew, ed. *Dos Passos*, 87–92.

Whipple, T. K. "Dos Passos and the U.S.A.." *Nation* (19 February 1938): 210–212. Rpt. in Sanders, David, comp. *Merrill Studies in U.S.A.*, 17–21.

Widmer, Eleanor. "Lost Girls of *U.S.A.:* Dos Passos' 30s Movie," in French, Warren, ed. *Thirties*, 11–19.

Wrenn, John H. "U.S.A.," in Wreen John H. *John Dos Passos*. New York: Twayne Publishers, 1961. 154–166. Rpt. in Sanders, David, comp. *Merrill Studies in U.S.A.*, 67–78.

DOUGLAS, ELLEN (1921–)

Apostles of Light (1973)

Dean, Michael P. "Ellen Douglas's Small Towns: Fictional Anchors." *SoQ* 19.1 (1980): 169–170.

Family's Affairs (1961)

Dean, Michael P. "Ellen Douglas's Small Towns: Fictional Anchors." *SoQ* 19.1 (1980): 166, 167, 168–169.

Rock Cried Out (1979)

Dean, Michael P. "Ellen Douglas's Small Towns: Fictional Anchors." *SoQ* 19.1 (1980): 161–163, 165, 166–167.

DOWD, HARRISON (1897–1964)

Night Air (1950)

Austen, Roger. *Playing the Game*, 170–172.

DREISER, THEODORE (1871–1945)

American Tragedy (1925)

Bucco, Martin. "East-West Theme in Dreiser's *An American Tragedy*." *WAL* 12 (1977): 177–183.

Campbell, Charles L. "*American Tragedy:* Or, Death in the Woods." *MFS* 15 (1969): 251–259.

Forrey, Roger. "Theodore Dreiser: Oedipus Redivivus." *MFS* 23 (1977): 353–354.

Frohock, W. M. "Theodore Dreiser," in Walcutt, Charles Child, ed. *Seven Novelists in the American Naturalist Tradition*, 116–122.

Gelfant, Blanche Housman. *American City Novel*, 66–67, 69, 75–77, 80–82, 90–91.

Grebstein, Sheldon Norman. "Theodore Dreiser," in Panichas, George A., ed. *Politics of Twentieth-Century Novelists*, 237–238, 239–240, 241 247–249.

Hakutani, Yoshinobu. "*Native Son* and *An American Tragedy:* Two Different Interpretations of Crime and Guilt." *CentR* 23 (1979): 208–226.

Hearn, Charles R. *American Dream in the Great Depression*, 36–40.

Hoffman, Frederick J. "Scene of Violence: Dostoevsky and Dreiser." *Modern Fiction Studies* 6 (Summer 1960): 100–105. Rpt. in Salzman, Jack, comp. *Merrill Studies in An American Tragedy*, 26–31.

Howe, Irving. "*An American Tragedy*," from "Afterword." Dreiser, Theodore. *An American Tragedy*. New York: New American Library, 1964. 815–828. Rpt. in Salzman, Jack, comp. *Merrill Studies in An American Tragedy*, 32–44.

Howe, Irving. "Dreiser and Tragedy: The Stature of Theodore Dreiser." *New Republic* 151 (25 July and 22 Aug 1964): 19–21, 25–28. Rpt. in Lyndenberg, John, ed. *Dreiser*, 146–152.

Lehan, Richard. *Theodore Dreiser*, 142–169.

Lundquist, James. *Theodore Dreiser*, 85–104.

Markels, Julian. "Dreiser and the Plotting of Inarticulate Experience." *Massachusetts Review* 2.3 (Spring 1961): 431–434. Rpt. in Salzman, Jack, comp. *Merrill Studies in An American Tragedy*, 45–55.

Matthiessen, F. O. "Of Crime and Punishment," in Matthiessen, F. O. *Theodore Dreiser*. New York: William Sloane Associates, 1951. 187–211. Rpt. in Salzman, Jack, comp. *Merrill Studies in An American Tragedy*, 56–72.

Moers, Ellen. "Clyde Griffiths: 'The Mechanism Called Man," in Moers, Ellen. *Two Dreisers*. New York: Viking, 1969. 227–239. Rpt. in Salzman, Jack, comp. *Merrill Studies in An American Tragedy*, 73–84.

Orlov, Paul A. "Subversion of the Self: Anti-Naturalistic Crux in *An American Tragedy*." *MFS* 23 (1977): 457–472.

Ousby, Ian. *Reader's Guide to Fifty American Novels*, 180–183.

Phillips, William L. "Imagery of Dreiser's Novels." *PMLA* 78 (Dec 1963): 580–583. Rpt. in Salzman, Jack, comp. *Merrill Studies in An American Tragedy*, 85–92.

Pizer, Donald. *Novels of Theodore Dreiser*, 232–289.

Riggio, Thomas P. "American Gothic: Poe and *An American Tragedy*." *AL* 49 (1978): 515–532.

Samuels, Charles Thomas. "Mr. Trilling, Mr. Warren and *An American Tragedy*." *Yale Review* 53 (Summer 1964): 624–640. Rpt. in Lyndenberg, John, ed. *Dreiser*, 168–170.

Shafer, Robert. "*An American Tragedy*," in Foerster, Norman, ed. *Humanism and*

America. New York: Farrar & Rinehart, 1930. 161–169. Rpt. in Salzman, Jack, comp. *Merrill Studies in An American Tragedy*, 92–98.

Spindler, Michael. "Youth, Class, and Consumerism in Dreiser's *An American Tragedy*." *JAmS* 12 (1978): 63–79.

Vance, William L. "Dreiserian Tragedy." *SNNTS* 4 (1972): 41–42, 44–45, 46.

Walcutt, Charles Child. "Theodore Dreiser and the Divided Stream," in Kazin, Alfred and Charles Shapiro, eds. *Stature of Theodore Dreiser*. Bloomington, IN: University of Indiana Press, 1955. 246–269. Rpt. in Lyndenberg, John, ed. *Dreiser*, 120–122.

Warren, Robert Penn. "*An American Tragedy*." *Yale Review* 52 (Oct 1962): 1–15. Rpt. in Lyndenberg, John, ed. *Dreiser*, 132–140.

Warren, Robert Penn. "*An American Tragedy*." *Yale Review* 52 (Oct 1962): 1–15. Rpt. in Salzman, Jack, comp. *Merrill Studies in An American Tragedy*, 99–111.

Watson, Charles N., Jr. " 'Accidental' Drownings in *Daniel Deronda* and *An American Tragedy*." *ELN* 13 (1976): 288–291.

Bulwark (1946)

Forrey, Roger. "Theodore Dreiser: Oedipus Redivivus." *MFS* 23 (1977): 354.

Grebstein, Sheldon Norman. "Theodore Dreiser," in Panichas, George A., ed. *Politics of Twentieth-Century Novelists*, 242.

Lehan, Richard. *Theodore Dreiser*, 222–235.

Lundquist, James. *Theodore Dreiser*, 73–79.

Pizer, Donald. *Novels of Theodore Dreiser*, 314–331.

Spatz, Jonas. "Dreiser's *Bulwark*: An Archaic Masterpiece," in French, Warren, ed. *Forties*, 155–162.

Trilling, Lionel. "Reality in America: Part II," in Trilling, Lionel. *Liberal Imagination*. New York: Viking Press, Inc., 1968. 21–32. Rpt. in Lyndenberg, John, ed. *Dreiser*, 93–95.

Vance, William L. "Dreiserian Tragedy." *SNNTS* 4 (1972): 47.

Walcutt, Charles Child. "Theodore Dreiser and the Divided Stream," in Kazin, Alfred and Charles Shapiro, eds. *Stature of Theodore Dreiser*. Bloomington, IN: University of Indiana Press, 1955. 246–269. Rpt. in Lyndenberg, John, ed. *Dreiser*, 126–128.

Dawn (1931)

Forrey, Roger. "Theodore Dreiser: Oedipus Redivivus." *MFS* 23 (1977): 350–352.

Financier (1912)

Cohen, Lester H. "Locating One's Self: The Problematics of Dreiser's Social World." *MFS* 23 (1977): 363–365, 368.

Frohock, W. M. "Theodore Dreiser," in Walcutt, Charles Child, ed. *Seven Novelists in the American Naturalist Tradition*, 110.

Gerber, Philip L. "Dreiser's *Financier*: A Genesis." *JML* 1 (1971): 354–374.

Grebstein, Sheldon Norman. "Theodore Dreiser," in Panichas, George A., ed. *Politics of Twentieth-Century Novelists*, 234–235, 240, 246–247.

Lehan, Richard. *Theodore Dreiser*, 97–116.

Lundquist, James. *Theodore Dreiser*, 64–66.

O'Neill, John. "Disproportion of Sadness: Dreiser's *The Financier* and *The Titan*." *MFS* 23 (1977): 409–422.

Pizer, Donald. *Novels of Theodore Dreiser*, 166–182.

Vance, William L. "Dreiserian Tragedy." *SNNTS* 4 (1972): 40–41, 43, 47–49.

Walcutt, Charles Child. "Theodore Dreiser and the Divided Stream," in Kazin, Alfred and Charles Shapiro, eds. *Stature of Theodore Dreiser*. Bloomington, IN: University of Indiana Press, 1955. 246–269. Rpt. in Lyndenberg, John, ed. *Dreiser*, 116–119.

"Genius" (1915)

Forrey, Roger. "Theodore Dreiser: Oedipus Redivivus." *MFS* 23 (1977): 352.

Frohock, W. M. "Theodore Dreiser," in Walcutt, Charles Child, ed. *Seven Novelists in the American Naturalist Tradition*, 114–116.

Gelfant, Blanche Housman. *American City Novel*, 66, 71–72, 82–83.

Grebstein, Sheldon Norman. "Theodore Dreiser," in Panichas, George A., ed. *Politics of Twentieth-Century Novelists*, 241–242.

Klopf, Dorothy. "Theodore Dreiser's *The 'Genius'*: Much Matter and More Art." *MFS* 23 (1977): 441–448.

Lehan, Richard. *Theodore Dreiser*, 117–130.

Lundquist, James. *Theodore Dreiser*, 54–59.

Pizer, Donald. *Novels of Theodore Dreiser*, 140–152.

Riggio, Thomas P. "Another Two Dreisers: The Artist as 'Genius'." *SNNTS* 9 (1977): 119–133.

Vance, William L. "Dreiserian Tragedy." *SNNTS* 4 (1972): 47.

Walcutt, Charles Child. "Theodore Dreiser and the Divided Stream," in Kazin, Alfred and Charles Shapiro, eds. *Stature of Theodore Dreiser*. Bloomington, IN: University of Indiana Press, 1955. 246–269. Rpt. in Lyndenberg, John, ed. *Dreiser*, 119–120.

Jennie Gerhardt (1911)

Cohen, Lester H. "Locating One's Self: The Problematics of Dreiser's Social World." *MFS* 23 (1977): 359–362.

Dance, Daryl C. "Sentimentalism in Dreiser's Heroines, Carrie and Jennie." *CLAJ* 14 (1970): 136–142.

Fiedler, Leslie A. "Dreiser and the Sentimental Novel," in Fiedler, Leslie A. *Love and Death in the American Novel*. New York: Stein and Day Publishers, 1966. 248–255. Rpt. in Lyndenberg, John, ed. *Dreiser*, 49.

Frohock, W. M. "Theodore Dreiser," in Walcutt, Charles Child, ed. *Seven Novelists in the American Naturalist Tradition*, 104–107.

Gelfant, Blanche Housman. *American City Novel*, 75–77, 80–82.

Lehan, Richard. *Theodore Dreiser*, 80–96.

Lundquist, James. *Theodore Dreiser*, 44–49.

Marcus, Mordecai. "Loneliness, Death, and Fulfillment in *Jennie Gerhardt*." *SAF* 7 (1979): 61–73.

Pizer, Donald. "American Literary Naturalism: The Example of Dreiser." *SAF* 5 (1977): 55–62.

Pizer, Donald. *Novels of Theodore Dreiser*, 105–130.

Vance, William L. "Dreiserian Tragedy." *SNNTS* 4 (1972): 40, 43, 46.

Walcutt, Charles Child. "Theodore Dreiser and the Divided Stream," in Kazin, Alfred and Charles Shapiro, eds. *Stature of Theodore Dreiser*. Bloomington, IN: University of Indiana Press, 1955. 246–269. Rpt. in Lyndenberg, John, ed. *Dreiser*, 113–115.

Sister Carrie (1900)

Banta, Martha. "They Shall Have Faces, Minds, and (One Day) Flesh: Women in Late Nineteenth-Century and Early Twentieth-Century American Literature," in Springer, Marlene, ed. *What Manner of Woman*, 254–256.

Bluefarb, Sam. "Middle-Aged Man in Contemporary Literature: Bloom to Herzog." *CLAJ* 20 (1976): 6–7.

Burgan, Mary A. "*Sister Carrie* and the Pathos of Naturalism." *Criticism* 15 (1973): 336–349.

Byers, John R., Jr. "Dreiser's Hurstwood and Jefferson's Rip Van Winkle." *PMLA* 87 (1972): 514–516.

Cohen, Lester H. "Locating One's Self: The Problematics of Dreiser's Social World." *MFS* 23 (1977): 366–368.

Cohn, Jan. "Women as Superfluous Characters in American Realism and Naturalism." *SAF* 1 (1973): 155–156, 157.

Dance, Daryl C. "Sentimentalism in Dreiser's Heroines, Carrie and Jennie." *CLAJ* 14 (1970): 131–136, 138–142.

Davidson, Cathy N. and Arnold E. Davidson. "Carrie's Sisters: The Popular Prototypes for Dreiser's Heroine." *MFS* 23 (1977): 395–407.

Fiedler, Leslie A. "Dreiser and the Sentimental Novel," in Fiedler, Leslie A. *Love and Death in the American Novel.* New York: Stein and Day Publishers, 1966. 248–255. Rpt. in Lyndenberg, John, ed. *Dreiser,* 47–49.

Forrey, Roger. "Theodore Dreiser: Oedipus Redivivus." *MFS* 23 (1977): 345–347.

Frohock, W. M. "Theodore Dreiser," in Walcutt, Charles Child, ed. *Seven Novelists in the American Naturalist Tradition,* 99–103.

Gelfant, Blanche Housman. *American City Novel,* 64–68, 80–87.

Grebstein, Sheldon N. "Dreiser's Victorian Vamp." *Midcontinent American Studies Journal* 4 (Spring 1963): 3–12. Rpt. in Dreiser, Theodore. *Sister Carrie,* 541–551.

Grebstein, Sheldon Norman. "Theodore Dreiser," in Panichas, George A., ed. *Politics of Twentieth-Century Novelists,* 244–246.

Griffith, Clark. "*Sister Carrie:* Dreiser's Wasteland." *AmerS* 16.2 (1975): 41–47.

Handy, William J. "Re-examination of Dreiser's *Sister Carrie.*" *Texas Studies in Literature and Language* 1 (Autumn 1959): 380–389. Rpt. in Dreiser, Theodore. *Sister Carrie,* 518–527.

Katope, Christopher G. "*Sister Carrie* and Spencer's First Principles." *AL* 41 (1969): 64–75.

Lehan, Richard. *Theodore Dreiser,* 54–79.

Lundquist, James. *Theodore Dreiser,* 28–38.

Lynn, Kenneth S. "Introduction to *Sister Carrie.*" Dreiser, Theodore. *Sister Carrie.* New York: Holt, Rinehart and Winston, Inc., 1957. v–xvi. Rpt. in Dreiser, Theodore. *Sister Carrie,* 509–518.

Lynn, Kenneth S. *Visions of America,* 138–148.

Markels, Julian. "Dreiser and the Plotting of Inarticulate Experience." *Massachusetts Review* 2 (Spring 1961): 431–448. Rpt. in Dreiser, Theodore. *Sister Carrie,* 527–541.

Matheson, Terence J. "Two Faces of Sister Carrie: The Characterization of Dreiser's First Heroine." *Ariel* 11.4 (1980): 71–86.

Matthiessen, F. O. "Picture of Conditions," in Matthiessen, F. O. *Theodore Dreiser.* New York: Sloane, 1951. 59–88. Rpt. in Dreiser, Theodore. *Sister Carrie,* 480–495.

Michaels, Walter Benn. "*Sister Carrie's* Popular Economy." *CritI* 7 (1980): 373–390.

Moers, Ellen. "Finesse of Dreiser." *American Scholar* 33 (Winter 1963–64): 109–114. Rpt. in Dreiser, Theodore. *Sister Carrie,* 558–567.

Moers, Ellen. "Finesse of Dreiser." *American Scholar* 33 (Winter 1963): 109–114. Rpt. in Lyndenberg, John, ed. *Dreiser*, 155–162.

Ousby, Ian. *Reader's Guide to Fifty American Novels*, 175–177.

Petrey, Sandy. "Language of Realism, the Language of False Consciousness: A Reading of *Sister Carrie*." *Novel* 10 (1977): 101–113.

Phillips, William L. "Imagery of Dreiser's Novels." *PMLA* 78 (Dec 1963): 572–575. Rpt. in Dreiser, Theodore. *Sister Carrie*, 551–558.

Pizer, Donald. "Late Nineteenth-Century American Naturalism," in Pizer, Donald. *Realism and Naturalism in Nineteenth-Century American Literature*. Carbondale, IL: Southern Illinois University Press, 1966. 11–14, 19–24. Rpt. in Dreiser, Theodore. *Sister Carrie*, 567–573.

Pizer, Donald. *Novels of Theodore Dreiser*, 53–95.

Pizer, Donald. "Problem of Philosophy in the Novel." *Bucknell Review* 18 (March 1970). Rpt. in Dreiser, Theodore. *Sister Carrie*, 583–587.

Poirier, Richard. "Panoramic Environment and the Anonymity of the Self," in Poirier, Richard. *World Elsewhere: The Place of Style in American Literature*. New York: Oxford University Press, 1966. 235–250. Rpt. in Dreiser, Theodore. *Sister Carrie*, 574–583.

Price, Alan. "Lily Bart and Carrie Meeber: Cultural Sisters." *ALR* 13 (1980): 238–244.

Rose, Alan H. "Sin and the City: The Uses of Disorder in the Urban Novel." *CentR* 16 (1972): 212–214.

See, Fred G. "Text as Mirror: *Sister Carrie* and the Lost Language of the Heart." *Criticism* 20 (1978): 144–166.

Seltzer, Leon F. "*Sister Carrie* and the Hidden Longing for Love: Sublimation or Subterfuge?" *TCL* 22 (1976): 192–209.

Szuberla, Guy. "Dreiser at the World's Fair: The City without Limits." *MFS* 23 (1977): 374–377.

Taylor, Gordon O. *Passages of Thought*, 145–157.

Toth, Emily. "Timely and Timeless: The Treatment of Time in *The Awakening* and *Sister Carrie*." *SoS* 16 (1977): 271–276.

Vance, William L. "Dreiserian Tragedy." *SNNTS* 4 (1972): 39–40, 43, 45–46.

Walcutt, Charles Child. "Theodore Dreiser and the Divided Stream," in Kazin, Alfred and Charles Shapiro, eds. *Stature of Theodore Dreiser*. Bloomington, IN: University of Indiana Press, 1955. 246–269. Rpt. in Lyndenberg, John, ed. *Dreiser*, 109–113.

Westbrook, Max. "Dreiser's Defense of Carrie Meeber." *MFS* 23 (1977): 381–393.

Stoic (1947)

Frohock, W. M. "Theodore Dreiser," in Walcutt, Charles Child, ed. *Seven Novelists in the American Naturalist Tradition*, 111–112.

Gelfant, Blanche Housman. *American City Novel*, 86–87.

Grebstein, Sheldon Norman. "Theodore Dreiser," in Panichas, George A., ed. *Politics of Twentieth-Century Novelists*, 236–237.

Lehan, Richard. *Theodore Dreiser*, 97–116, 235–239.

Lundquist, James. *Theodore Dreiser*, 69–71.

Mookerjee, R. N. "Dreiser's Use of Hindu Thought in *The Stoic*." *AL* 43 (1971): 273–278.

Pizer, Donald. *Novels of Theodore Dreiser*, 340–346.

Walcutt, Charles Child. "Theodore Dreiser and the Divided Stream," in Kazin,

Alfred and Charles Shapiro, eds. *Stature of Theodore Dreiser*. Bloomington, IN: University of Indiana Press, 1955. 246–269. Rpt. in Lyndenberg, John, ed. *Dreiser*, 122–126.

Titan (1914)

Cohen, Lester H. "Locating One's Self: The Problematics of Dreiser's Social World." *MFS* 23 (1977): 358–359.

Forrey, Roger. "Theodore Dreiser: Oedipus Redivivus." *MFS* 23 (1977): 350.

Frohock, W. M. "Theodore Dreiser," in Walcutt, Charles Child, ed. *Seven Novelists in the American Naturalist Tradition*, 110–111.

Grebstein, Sheldon Norman. "Theodore Dreiser," in Panichas, George A., ed. *Politics of Twentieth-Century Novelists*, 235–236, 240–241, 242.

Lehan, Richard. *Theodore Dreiser*, 97–116.

Lundquist, James. *Theodore Dreiser*, 67–69.

O'Neill, John. "Disproportion of Sadness: Dreiser's *The Financier* and *The Titan*." *MFS* 23 (1977): 409–422.

Pizer, Donald. *Novels of Theodore Dreiser*, 188–200.

Walcutt, Charles Child. "Theodore Dreiser and the Divided Stream," in Kazin, Alfred and Charles Shapiro, eds. *Stature of Theodore Dreiser*. Bloomington, IN: University of Indiana Press, 1955. 246–269. Rpt. in Lyndenberg, John, ed. *Dreiser*, 116–119.

DREW, WAYLAND (1932–)

Wabeno Feast (1973)

Appenzell, Anthony. "Behind the Avant Garde." *CanL* 58 (1973): 97–98.

Atwood, Margaret. "Canadian Monsters: Some Aspects of the Supernatural in Canadian Fiction," in Staines, David, ed. *Canadian Imagination*, 119–121.

DU BOIS, W.E.B. (1868–1963)

Dark Princess (1928)

Berghahn, Marion. *Images of Africa in Black American Literature*, 101–113.

Davis, Arthur P. *From the Dark Tower*, 23.

Isani, Mukhtar Ali. "Exotic and Protest in Earlier Black Literature: The Use of Alien Setting and Character." *SIBL* 5.2 (1974): 13.

Rampersad, Arnold. *Art and Imagination of W. E. B. Du Bois*, 202–218.

Singh, Amritjit. *Novels of the Harlem Renaissance*, 120–127.

Mansart Builds a School (1959)

Rampersad, Arnold. *Art and Imagination of W. E. B. Du Bois*, 266–287.

Ordeal of Mansart (1957)

Rampersad, Arnold. *Art and Imagination of W. E. B. Du Bois*, 266–287.

Quest of the SilverFleece (1911)

Berghahn, Marion. *Images of Africa in Black American Literature*, 94–101.

Davis, Arthur P. *From the Dark Tower*, 22–23.

Elder, Arlene A. "Swamp Versus Plantation: Symbolic Structure in W.E.B. Du Bois' *The Quest of the Silver Fleece*." *Phylon* 34 (1973): 358–367.

Gayle, Addison, Jr. *Way of the New World*, 71–74.

Rampersad, Arnold. *Art and Imagination of W. E. B. Du Bois*, 116–132.

Schultz, Elizabeth. " 'Free in Fact and at Last': The Image of the Black Woman in Black American Fiction," in Springer, Marlene, ed. *What Manner of Woman*, 339.

Worlds of Color (1961)

Rampersad, Arnold. *Art and Imagination of W. E. B. Du Bois*, 266–287.

DUCHARME, RÉJEAN (1941–)

La fille de Christophe Colomb (1969)

Leduc-Park, Renée. *"La fille de Christophe Colomb:* La Rouerie et les rouages du texte." *V&I* 5 (1980): 319–332.

L'avalée des avalés (1966)

Bond, D. J. "Search for Identity in the Novels of Rejean Ducharme." *Mosaic* 9.2 (1976): 33–44.

Shek, Ben-Zion. *Social Realism*, 293–294.

Sutherland, Ronald. *Second Image*, 89–107.

Vanasse, Andre. "Analyse de textes: Rejean Ducharme et Victor-Levy Beaulieu: Les mots el les choses." *V&I* 3 (1977): 232–238.

Swallower Swallowed see *L'avalée des avalés*

Le nez qui voque (1967)

Bond, D. J. "Search for Identity in the Novels of Rejean Ducharme." *Mosaic* 9.2 (1976): 32–44.

Les enfantômes (1976)

Poulin, Gabrielle. *Romans du pays*, 222–229.

L'hiver de force (1973)

Bond, D. J. "Search for Identity in the Novels of Rejean Ducharme." *Mosaic* 9.2 (1976): 34–44.

Filteau, Claude. *"L'hiver de force* de Réjean Ducharme et la politique du désir." *V&I* 1 (1976): 365–373.

DULEY, MARGARET (1894–1968)

Cold Pastoral (1969)

O'Flaherty, Patrick. "Margaret Duley and Newfoundland." *DR* 57 (1978): 638–340.

Eyes of the Gull (1936)

O'Flaherty, Patrick. "Margaret Duley and Newfoundland." *DR* 57 (1978): 637–638.

Highway to Valour (1941)

O'Flaherty, Patrick. "Margaret Duley and Newfoundland." *DR* 57 (1978): 640–644.

DUNBAR, PAUL LAURENCE (1872–1906)

Fanatics (1901)

Elder, Arlene A. *"Hindered Hand"*, 139–141.
Gayle, Addison, Jr. *Way of the New World*, 43–44.
Revell, Peter. *Paul Laurence Dunbar*, 149–153.

Love of Landry (1900)

Elder, Arlene A. *"Hindered Hand"*, 137–139.
Revell, Peter. *Paul Laurence Dunbar*, 145–148.

Sport of the Gods (1902)

Candela, Gregory L. "We Wear the Mask: Irony in Dunbar's *The Sport of the Gods.*" *AL* 48 (1976): 60–72.
Elder, Arlene A. *"Hindered Hand"*, 141–146.
Gayle, Addison, Jr. *Way of the New World*, 44–46.
Revell, Peter. *Paul Laurence Dunbar*, 153–161.
Turner, Darwin T. "Paul Laurence Dunbar: The Rejected Symbol." *Journal of Negro History* 52 (January 1967) 1–13. Rpt. in Hemenway, Robert, ed. *Black Novelist*, 41–43.

Uncalled (1898)

Elder, Arlene A. *"Hindered Hand"*, 134–137.
Gayle, Addison, Jr. *Way of the New World*, 40–42.
Revell, Peter. *Paul Laurence Dunbar*, 140–145.
Rosenblatt, Roger. *Black Fiction*, 130–142.

DUNCAN, SARA JEANNETTE (1861–1922)

American Girl in London (1891)

Tausky, Thomas E. *Sara Jeanette Duncan*, 90, 94–99.

Burnt Offering (1909)

Nagarajan, S. "Sara Jeannette Duncan's Anglo-Indian Novels." *JCL* 12.1 (1977): 38–44.
Tuasky, T. E. "Duncan's Passage to India." *CanL* 73 (1977): 45–52.
Tausky, Thomas E. *Sara Jeanette Duncan*, 246–257.

Consort (1912)

Tausky, Thomas E. *Sara Jeanette Duncan*, 174–180.

Cousin Cinderella (1908)

Brydon, Diana. "Colonial Heroine: The Novels of Sara Jeannette Duncan & Mrs. Campbell Praed." *CanL* 86 (1980): 45–48.
Tausky, Thomas E. *Sara Jeanette Duncan*, 92–93, 131–145.

Daughter of To-Day (1894)

Cloutier, Pierre. "The First Exile." *CanL* 59 (1974): 30–36.
Tausky, Thomas E. *Sara Jeanette Duncan*, 109–120.

Hilda see *Path of a Star*

His Honour and a Lady (1896)

Tausky, Thomas E. *Sara Jeanette Duncan*, 193–211.

His Royal Happiness (1914)

> Tausky, Thomas E. *Sara Jeanette Duncan*, 145–149.

Imperialist (1904)

> Bailey, Alfred G. "Historical Setting of Sara Duncan's *The Imperialist*," in Moss, John, ed. *Beginnings*, 129–140.
> Dooley, D. J. *Moral Vision*, 25–35.
> Gerson, Carole. "Duncan's Web." *CanL* 63 (1975): 73–80.
> Moss, John. *Patterns of Isolation*, 63–79.
> Slonim, Leon. "Character, Action, and Theme in *The Imperialist*." *ECW* 3 (1975): 15–20.
> Tausky, Thomas E. *Sara Jeanette Duncan*, 153–174.
> Zezulka, Joseph M. "*Imperialist*: Imperialism, Provincialism, and Point of View," in Moss, John, ed. *Beginnings*, 143–156.

Path of a Star (1899)

> Tausky, Thomas E. *Sara Jeanette Duncan*, 211–214.

Set in Authority (1906)

> Nagarajan, S. "Sara Jeannette Duncan's Anglo-Indian Novels." *JCL* 12.1 (1977): 34–38.
> Tausky, Thomas E. *Sara Jeanette Duncan*, 236–241, 242–245.

Simple Adventures of a Memsahib (1893)

> Tuasky, T. E. "Duncan's Passage to India." *CanL* 73 (1977): 41–45.
> Tausky, Thomas E. *Sara Jeanette Duncan*, 184–190.

Those Delightful Americans (1902)

> Tausky, Thomas E. *Sara Jeanette Duncan*, 121–131.

Title Clear (1922)

> Tausky, Thomas E. *Sara Jeanette Duncan*, 149–150.

Two Girls on a Barge (1891)

> Tausky, Thomas E. *Sara Jeanette Duncan*, 100–103.

Voyage of Consolation (1898)

> Tausky, Thomas E. *Sara Jeanette Duncan*, 103–109.

DUPUY, ELIZA (1814–1880)

Planter's Daughter (1857)

> Baym, Nina. *Woman's Fiction*, 241–243.

DURDEN, CHARLES

No Bugles, No Drums (1976)

> Beidler, Philip D. "Truth-Telling and Literary Values in the Vietnam Novel." *SAQ* 78 (1979): 149–156.

DURHAM, ROBERT LEE (1870–1949)

Call of the South (1908)

 Berzon, Judith R. *Neither White Nor Black*, 32–34.

EASTLAKE, WILLIAM (1917–)

Bamboo Bed (1969)

 Beidler, Philip D. "Truth-Telling and Literary Values in the Vietnam Novel." *SAQ*
 78 (1979): 146–149.
 Haslam, Gerald. *William Eastlake*, 36–40.

Bronc People (1958)

 Haslam, Gerald. *William Eastlake*, 17–26.
 McCaffery, Larry. "Absurdity and Oppositions in William Eastlake's Southwestern
 Novels." *Crit* 19.2 (1977): 66–75.
 Wylder, Delbert E. "Novels of William Eastlake." *New Mexico Quarterly* 34
 (1964): 188–203. Rpt. in Pilkington, William T., ed. *Critical Essays on the West-
 ern American Novel*, 199–205, 207–208.

Castle Keep (1965)

 Haslam, Gerald. *William Eastlake*, 33–36.

Dancers in the Scalp House (1975)

 McCaffery, Larry. "Absurdity and Oppositions in William Eastlake's Southwestern
 Novels." *Crit* 19.2 (1977): 65–66, 68–75.

Go in Beauty (1956)

 Haslam, Gerald. *William Eastlake*, 12–17.
 McCaffery, Larry. "Absurdity and Oppositions in William Eastlake's Southwestern
 Novels." *Crit* 19.2 (1977): 68–75.
 Wylder, Delbert E. "Novels of William Eastlake." *New Mexico Quarterly* 34
 (1964): 188–203. Rpt. in Pilkington, William T., ed. *Critical Essays on the West-
 ern American Novel*, 198–199, 207.

Portrait of the Artist with 26 Horses (1963)

 Haslam, Gerald. *William Eastlake*, 26–33.
 McCaffery, Larry. "Absurdity and Oppositions in William Eastlake's Southwestern
 Novels." *Crit* 19.2 (1977): 69–75.
 Wylder, Delbert E. "Novels of William Eastlake." *New Mexico Quarterly* 34
 (1964): 188–203. Rpt. in Pilkington, William T., ed. *Critical Essays on the West-
 ern American Novel*, 205–207.

EDEN, DOROTHY (1912–1982)

Brooding Lake (1953)

 Russ, Joanna. "Somebody's Trying to Kill Me and I Think It's My Husband: The
 Modern Gothic." *JPC* 6 (1973): 666–691.

EFFINGER, GEORGE ALEC (1947–)

What Entropy Means to Me (1972)

Sklepowich, Edward A. "Fictive Quest: Effinger's *What Entropy Means to Me.*" *Extrapolation* 18 (1977): 107–115.

ÉLIE, ROBERT (1915–1973)

Farewell My Dreams see *La fin des songes*

La fin des songes (1950)

Belleau, André. *Le romancier fictif*, 82–84.
Rasporich, Beverly J. "Sacrifice and Death in French-Canadian Fiction: An English Reading." *DR* 55 (1975): 459–460.
Urbas, Jeannette. *From Thirty Acres to Modern Times*, 67–70.

ELKIN, STANLEY (1930–)

Bad Man (1967)

Guttmann, Allen. *Jewish Writer in America*, 84–85.
LeClair, Thomas. "Obsessional Fiction of Stanley Elkin." *ConL* 16 (1975): 150–153.
Olderman, Raymond M. *Beyond the Waste Land*, 52–71.

Boswell (1964)

Guttmann, Allen. *Jewish Writer in America*, 81–84.
LeClair, Thomas. "Obsessional Fiction of Stanley Elkin." *ConL* 16 (1975): 148–150.

Dick Gibson Show (1971)

LeClair, Thomas. "Obsessional Fiction of Stanley Elkin." *ConL* 16 (1975): 153–158.

Franchiser (1976)

Colbert, Robert Edward. "American Salesman as Pitchman and Poet in the Fiction of Stanley Elkin." *Crit* 21.2 (1979): 53–58.
Mcaffery, Larry. "Stanley Elkin's Recovery of the Ordinary." *Crit* 21.2 (1979): 39–50.

ELLISON, RALPH (1914–1994)

Invisible Man (1952)

Abrams, Robert E. "Ambiguities of Dreaming in Ellison's *Invisible Man.*" *AL* 49 (1978): 592–603.
Baker, Houston A., Jr. *Singers of Daybreak*, 25–31.
Bakish, David. *Richard Wright*, 43, 47–48.
Bataille, Robert. "Ellison's *Invisible Man:* The Old Rhetoric and the New." *BALF* 12 (1978): 43–45.
Baumbach, Jonathan. "Nightmare of a Native Son: *Invisible Man*, by Ralph Ellison," in Baumbach, Jonathan. *Landscape of Nightmare*. New York: New York University Press, 1965. 68–86. Cooke, M. G., ed. *Modern Black Novelists*, 64–78.
Baumbach, Jonathan. "Nightmare of a Native Son: *Invisible Man* by Ralph El-

lison," in Baumbach, Jonathan, *Landscape of Nightmare*. New York: New York University Press, 1965. 68–86. Rpt. in Gibson, Donald B., ed. *Five Black Writers*, 73–87.

Bell, J. D. "Ellison's *Invisible Man*." *Expl* 29 (1970): Item 19.

Bellow, Saul. "Man Underground." *Commentary* 13.6 (June 1952): 608–610. Rpt. in Hersey, John, ed. *Ralph Ellison*, 27–30.

Berghahn, Marion. *Images of Africa in Black American Literature*, 168–171.

Berzon, Judith R. *Neither White Nor Black*, 175–176.

Bigsby, C. W. E., "From Protest to Paradox: The Black Writer at Mid Century," in French, Warren, ed. *Fifties*, 229–234.

Blake, Susan L. "Ritual and Rationalization: Black Folklore in the Works of Ralph Ellison." *PMLA* 94 (1979): 126–135.

Bone, Robert. "Ralph Ellison and the Uses of Imagination," in Hill, Herbert, ed. *Anger and Beyond*. New York: Harper & Row Publishers, 1966. 86–111. Rpt. in Reilly, John M., ed. *Twentieth Century Interpretations of Invisible Man*, 22–31.

Bryant, Jerry H. *Open Decision*, 277–281.

Bryant, Jerry H. "Wright, Ellison, Baldwin: Exorcising the Demon." *Phylon* 37 (1976): 180–184.

Bucco, Martin. "Ellison's Invisible West." *WAL* 10 (1975): 237–238.

Butler, Robert J. "Patterns of Movement in Ellison's *Invisible Man*." *AmerS* 21.1 (1980): 5–21.

Callahan, John F. "Chaos, Complexity and Possibility: The Historical Frequencies of Ralph Waldo Ellison." *BALF* 11 (1977): 133–138.

Cash, Earl A. "Narrators in *Invisible Man* and Notes from Underground: Brothers in the Spirit." *CLAJ* 16 (1973): 505–507.

Cheshire, Ardner R., Jr. "*Invisible Man* and the Life of Dialogue." *CLAJ* 20 (1976): 19–34.

Collier, Eugenia W. "Nightmare Truth of an Invisible Man." *BW* 20.2 (1970): 12–19.

Davis, Arthur P. *From the Dark Tower*, 210–213.

Deutsch, Leonard J. "Waste Land in Ellison's *Invisible Man*." *NConL* 7.6 (1977): 5–6.

Donald, Miles. *American Novel in the Twentieth Century*, 146–157.

Ehlers, Leigh A. " 'Give Me the Ocular Proof': *Othello* and Ralph Ellison's *Invisible Man*." *NConL* 6.5 (1976): 10–11.

Emerson, O. B. "Cultural Nationalism in Afro-American Literature," in Lewald, H. Ernest, ed. *Cry of Home*, 222–227.

Finholt, Richard. *American Visionary Fiction*, 98–111.

Fraiberg, Selma. "Two Modern Incest Heroes." *Partisan Review* 28 (Fall/Winter 1961): 646–961. Rpt. in Reilly, John M., ed. *Twentieth Century Interpretations of Invisible Man*, 73–79.

Frohock, W. M. "Edge of Laughter," in Levin, Harry, ed. *Veins of Humor*, 246–250.

Gayle, Addison, Jr. *Way of the New World*, 204–213.

Gibson, Donald B. "Ralph Ellison and James Baldwin," in Panichas, George A., ed. *Politics of Twentieth-Century Novelists*, 309–315.

Glicksberg, Charles I. "Symbolism of Vision." 39 (Summer 1954): 259–265. Rpt. in Reilly, John M., ed. *Twentieth Century Interpretations of Invisible Man*, 48–55.

Goede, William. "On Lower Frequencies: The Buried Men in Wright and Ellison." *MFS* 15 (1969): 489–501.

Greenberg, Alvin. "Choice: Ironic Alternatives in the World of the Contemporary

American Novel," in Madden, David, ed. *American Dreams, American Nightmares*, 177–181, 182.

Griffin, Edward M. "Notes from a Clean, Well-Lighted Place: Ralph Ellison's *Invisible Man*." *TCL* 15 (1969): 129–144.

Griffin, Wilford. "Ellison's *Invisible Man*." *Expl* 36.2 (1978): 28–29.

Guttman, Allen. "Focus on Ralph Ellison's *Invisible Man*: American Nightmare," in Madden, David, ed. *American Dreams, American Nightmares*, 188–196.

Hansen, J. T. "Holistic Approach to *Invisible Man*." *MELUS* 6.1 (1979): 41–54.

Hays, Peter L. *Limping Hero*, 101–102.

Henderson, Harry B. *Versions of the Past*, 285–299.

Horowitz, Ellin. "Rebirth of the Artist," in Kostelanetz, Richard, ed. *On Contemporary Literature*, 330–346.

Horowitz, Ellin. "Rebirth of the Artist," in Kostelanetz, Richard, ed. *On Contemporary Literature*. New York: Avon Books, 1964. 330–346. Rpt. in Reilly, John M., ed. *Twentieth Century Interpretations of Invisible Man*, 80–88.

Horowitz, Floyd R. "Ralph Ellison's Modern Version of Brer Bear and Brer Rabbit in *Invisible Man*." *Midcontinent American Studies Journal* 4.2 (1963): 21–27. Rpt. in Gottesman, Ronald, comp. *Merrill Studies in Invisible Man*, 100–107.

Horowitz, Floyd R. "Ralph Ellison's Modern Version of Brer Bear and Brer Rabbit in *Invisible Man*." Midcontinent American Studies Journal 4.2 (1963): 21–27. Rpt. in Reilly, John M., ed. *Twentieth Century Interpretations of Invisible Man*, 32–38.

Howe, Irving. "Black Boys and Native Sons," in Howe, Irving. *World More Attractive*. New York: Horizon Press, 1963. 98–122. Rpt. in Hersey, John, ed. *Ralph Ellison*, 36–38.

Howe, Irving. *Celebrations and Attacks*, 29–31.

Jackson, Esther Merle. "American Negro and the Image of the Absurd." *Phylon* 23 (Winter 1962): 359–371. Rpt. in Reilly, John M., ed. *Twentieth Century Interpretations of Invisible Man*, 64–72.

Kent, George E. "Ralph Ellison and Afro-American Folk and Cultural Tradition." *CLA* 13.3 (March 1970): 265–276. Rpt. in Hersey, John, ed. *Ralph Ellison*, 162–170.

Kist, E. M. "Langian Analysis of Blackness in Ralph Ellison's *Invisible Man*." *SIBL* 7.2 (1976): 19–23.

Klein, Marcus. "Ralph Ellison's *Invisible Man*," in Klein, Marcus. *After Alienation*. New York: World Publishing Company, 1964. Rpt. in Gibson, Donald B., ed. *Five Black Writers*, 88–101.

Klein, Marcus. "Ralph Ellison's *Invisible Man*," in Klein, Marcus. *After Alienation*. New York: World Publishing Company, 1964. Rpt. in Gottesman, Ronald, comp. *Merrill Studies in Invisible Man*, 74–88.

Klotman, Phyllis Rauch. *Another Man Gone*, 71–84.

Kostelanetz, Richard. "Politics of Ellison's Booker: *Invisible Man* as Symbolic History." *Chicago Review* 19.2 (1967): 5–26. Rpt. in Hemenway, Robert, ed. *Black Novelist*, 90–110.

Lane, James B. "Underground to Manhood: Ralph Ellison's *Invisible Man*." *NALF* 7 (1973): 64–72.

Lee, A. Robert. "Sight and Mask: Ralph Ellison's *Invisible Man*." *NALF* 4 (1970): 22–33.

Lehan, Richard. *Dangerous Crossing*, 150–157.

Lieber, Todd M. "Ralph Ellison and the Metaphor of Invisibility in Black Literary Tradition." *AQ* 24 (1977): 86–100.

Lieberman, Marcia R. "Moral Innocents: Ellison's Invisible Man and Candide."
    CLAJ 15 (1971): 64–79.
Ludington, Charles T., Jr. "Protest and Anti-Protest: Ralph Ellison." *SoHR* 4
    (1970): 36–39.
Lutwack, Leonard. *Heroic Fiction*, 122–141.
May, John R. *Toward a New Earth*, 147–155.
May, John R., "Images of Apocalypse in the Black Novel." *Renascence* 23 (1970):
    33–36.
Neal, Larry. "Ellison's Zoot Suit." 20.2 (Dec. 1970): 31–50. Rpt. in Hersey, John,
    ed. *Ralph Ellison*, 70–79.
O'Daniel, Therman B. "Image of Man as Portrayed by Ralph Ellison." *CLA* 10
    (June 1967): 277–284. Rpt. in Gibson, Donald B., ed. *Five Black Writers*, 102–
    107.
O'Daniel, Therman B. "Image of Man as Portrayed by Ralph Ellison." CLA 10
    (June 1967): 227–284. Rpt. in Reilly, John M., ed. *Twentieth Century Interpreta-
    tions of Invisible Man*, 89–95.
Oliver, M. Celeste. "*Invisible Man* and the Numbers Game." *CLAJ* 22 (1978):
    123–133.
O'Meally, Robert G. *Craft of Ralph Ellison*, 78–104.
Ousby, Ian. *Reader's Guide to Fifty American Novels*, 332–334.
Overmyer, Janet. "*Invisible Man* and White Women." *NConL* 6.3 (1976): 13–15.
Pearce, Richard. *Stages of the Clown*, 118–123.
Pryse, Marjorie. *Mark and the Knowledge*, 143–164.
Radford, Frederick L. "Journey Towards Castration: Interracial Sexual Stereotypes
    in Ellison's *Invisible Man*." *JAmS* 4 (1970): 227–231.
Rodnon, Stewart. "*Adventures of Huckleberry Finn* and *Invisible Man:* Thematic
    and Structural Comparisons." *NALF* 4 (1970): 45–51.
Rodnon, Stewart. "Ralph Ellison's *Invisible Man:* Six Tentative Approaches."
    CLAJ 12 (1969): 244–256.
Rollins, Ronald G. "Ellison's *Invisible Man*." *Expl* 30 (1971): Item 22.
Rosenblatt, Roger. *Black Fiction*, 184–199.
Rovit, Earl H. "Ralph Ellison and the American Comic Tradition." *Wisconsin Stud-
    ies in Contemporary Literature* 1 (Fall 1960): 34–42. Rpt. in Gibson, Donald B.,
    ed. *Five Black Writers*, 108–115.
Rovit, Earl H. "Ralph Ellison and the American Comic Tradition." *Wisconsin Stud-
    ies in Contemporary Literature* 1 (Fall 1960): 34–42. Rpt. in Hersey, John, ed.
    Ralph Ellison, 151–159.
Rovit, Earl H. "Ralph Ellison and the American Comic Tradition." *Wisconsin Stud-
    ies in Contemporary Literature* 1 (Fall 1960): 34–42. Rpt. in Reilly, John M., ed.
    Twentieth Century Interpretations of Invisible Man, 56–63.
Ruotolo, Lucio P. *Six Existential Heroes*, 81–98.
Rupp, Richard H. *Celebration in Postwar American Fiction*, 151–164.
Schafer, William J. "Irony from the Underground—Satiric Elements in *Invisible
    Man*." *Satire Newsletter* 7 (Fall 1969): 22–28. Rpt. in Reilly, John M., ed. *Twenti-
    eth Century Interpretations of Invisible Man*, 39–47.
Schafer, William J. "Ralph Ellison and the Birth of the Anti-Hero." *Critique* 10
    (1968): 81–93. Rpt. in Gottesman, Ronald, comp. *Merrill Studies in Invisible
    Man*, 89–100.
Schafer, William J. "Ralph Ellison and the Birth of the Anti-Hero." *Critique* 10
    (1968): 81–93. Rpt. in Hersey, John, ed. *Ralph Ellison*, 115–126.

Schultz, Elizabeth A. "Heirs of Ralph Ellison: Patterns of Individualism in the Contemporary Afro-American Novel." *CLAJ* 22 (1978): 104–105.
Sequeira, Isaac. "Uncompleted Initiation of the *Invisible Man.*" *SIBL* 6.1 (1975): 9–13.
Singleton, M. K. "Leadership Mirages as Antagonists in *Invisible Man.*" *Arizona Quarterly* 22 (Summer 1966): 157–171. Rpt. in Reilly, John M., ed. *Twentieth Century Interpretations of Invisible Man*, 11–21.
Stark, John. "*Invisible Man:* Ellison's Black Odyssey." *NALF* 7 (1973): 60–63.
Starke, Catherine Juanita. *Black Portraiture in American Fiction*, 197–200.
Steinbrink, Jeffrey. "Toward a Vision of Infinite Possibility: A Reading of *Invisible Man.*" *SIBL* 7.3 (1976): 1–5.
Sylvander, Carolyn W. "Ralph Ellison's *Invisible Man* and Female Stereotypes." *NALF* 9 (1975): 77–79.
Tanner, Tony. *City of Words*, 50–63.
Tanner, Tony. "Music of Invisibility," in Tanner, Tony. *City of Words: American Fiction, 1950–1970.* New York: Harper and Row, Publishers, 1971. 50–64. Rpt. in Hersey, John, ed. *Ralph Ellison*, 80–94.
Thomas, Gillian and Michael Larsen. "Ralph Ellison's Conjure Doctors." *ELN* 17 (1980): 281–288.
Trimmer, Joseph F. "Grandfather's Riddle in Ralph Ellison's *Invisible Man.*" *BALF* 12 (1978): 46–50.
Vogler, Thomas A. "*Invisible Man:* Somebody's Protest Novel." *Iowa Review* 1 (Spring 1970): 64–82. Rpt. in Gottesman, Ronald, comp. *Merrill Studies in Invisible Man*, 51–74.
Vogler, Thomas A. "*Invisible Man:* Somebody's Protest Novel." *Iowa Review* 1 (Spring 1970): 64–82. Rpt. in Hersey, John, ed. *Ralph Ellison*, 127–150.
Wade, Melvin and Margaret Wade. "Black Aesthetic in the Black Novel." *JBS* 2.4 (1972): 395–396.
Walling, William. " 'Art' and 'Protest': Ralph Ellison's *Invisible Man* Twenty Years After." *Phylon* 34 (1973): 120–134.
Walling, William. "Ralph Ellison's *Invisible Man:* 'It Goes a Long Way Back, Some Twenty Years'." *Phylon* 34 (1973): 4–16.
Waniek, Marilyn. "Space Where Sex Should Be: Toward a Definition of the Black American Literary Tradition." *SIBL* 6.3 (1975): 12–13.
Wasserman, Jerry. "Embracing the Negative: *Native Son* and *Invisible Man.*" *SAF* 4 (1976): 100–103.
Weinstein, Sharon R. "Comedy and the Absurd in Ralph Ellison's *Invisible Man.*" *SIBL* 3.3 (1972): 12–16.
Williams, Sherley Anne. *Give Birth to Brightness*, 46–48, 87–96.

ELLSON, HAL (1910–1994)

Golden Spike (1952)
Gelfant, Blanche Housman. *American City Novel*, 257–259.

EPSTEIN, SEYMOUR (1917–)

Successor (1961)
Bryant, Jerry H. *Open Decision*, 191–192.

EVANS, AUGUSTA (1835–1909)

Beulah (1859)
   Baym, Nina. *Woman's Fiction*, 282–286.
Inez (1855)
   Baym, Nina. *Woman's Fiction*, 281–282.
Macaria (1864)
   Baym, Nina. *Woman's Fiction*, 286–290.
St. Elmo (1867)
   Baym, Nina. *Woman's Fiction*, 290–294.
Vashti (1869)
   Baym, Nina. *Woman's Fiction*, 294–296.

EXLEY, FREDERICK (1929–1992)

Fan's Notes (1968)
   Chabot, C. Barry. "Alternative Vision of Frederick Exley's *A Fan's Notes*." *Crit* 19.1 (1977): 87–100.
   Johnson, Donald R. "Hero in Sports Literature and Exley's *A Fan's Notes*." *SoHR* 13 (1979): 233–244.
   Umphlett, Wiley Lee. *Sporting Myth and the American Experience*, 184–188.

FAIR, RONALD L. (1932–)

Hog Butcher (1966)
   Fleming, Robert E. "Novels of Ronald L. Fair." *CLAJ* 15 (1972): 479–483.

FALKNER, WILLIAM C. (1825–1889)

White Rose of Memphis (1881)
   Brown, Calvin S. "Colonel Falkner as General Reader: *The White Rose of Memphis*." *MissQ* 30 (1977): 585–595.

FANTE, JOHN (1911–1983)

Full of Life (1952)
   Green, Rose Basile. *Italian-American Novel*, 161–163.
Wait Until Spring, Bandini (1938)
   Green, Rose Basile. *Italian-American Novel*, 160.

FARIÑA, RICHARD (1937–1966)

Been Down So Long It Looks Like Up to Me (1966)
   Bluestein, Gene. "Laughin' Just to Keep from Cryin': Farina's Blues Novel." *JPC* 9 (1976): 927–934.

FARMER, PHILIP JOSÉ (1918–)

Dare (1965)
   Wymer, Thomas L. "Philip José Farmer: The Trickster as Artist," in Clareson, Thomas, ed. *Voices for the Future* (Vol. 2), 47–48.

Dark Design (1977)

Brizzi, Mary T. *Reader's Guide to Philip José Farmer*, 48–58.

Doc Savage (1973)

Wymer, Thomas L. "Philip José Farmer: The Trickster as Artist," in Clareson, Thomas, ed. *Voices for the Future* (Vol. 2), 38.

Feast Unknown (1969)

Letson, Russell. "Faces of a Thousand Heroes: Philip Jose Farmer." *SFS* 4 (1977): 39–40.

Wymer, Thomas L. "Philip José Farmer: The Trickster as Artist," in Clareson, Thomas, ed. *Voices for the Future* (Vol. 2), 45–47.

Flesh (1968)

Wymer, Thomas L. "Philip José Farmer: The Trickster as Artist," in Clareson, Thomas, ed. *Voices for the Future* (Vol. 2), 44–45.

Image of the Beast (1968)

Perkins, Michael. *Secret Record*, 114–115.

Lord Tyger (1970)

Scholes, Robert and Eric S. Rabkin. *Science Fiction*, 93.

Lovers (1952)

Brizzi, Mary T. *Reader's Guide to Philip José Farmer*, 18–24.

Wymer, Thomas L. "Philip José Farmer: The Trickster as Artist," in Clareson, Thomas, ed. *Voices for the Future* (Vol. 2), 41–42.

Night of Light (1966)

Brizzi, Mary T. *Reader's Guide to Philip José Farmer*, 25–32.

Letson, Russell. "Faces of a Thousand Heroes: Philip Jose Farmer." *SFS* 4 (1977): 37.

Letson, Russell. "Worlds of Philip Jose Farmer." *Extrapolation* 18 (1977): 129–130.

Wymer, Thomas L. "Philip José Farmer: The Trickster as Artist," in Clareson, Thomas, ed. *Voices for the Future* (Vol. 2), 48–49.

Tarzan Alive (1972)

Wymer, Thomas L. "Philip José Farmer: The Trickster as Artist," in Clareson, Thomas, ed. *Voices for the Future* (Vol. 2), 37–39.

To Your Scattered Bodies Go (1971)

Wymer, Thomas L. "Philip José Farmer: The Trickster as Artist," in Clareson, Thomas, ed. *Voices for the Future* (Vol. 2), 51–52.

Venus on the Half-Shell (1975)

Brizzi, Mary T. *Reader's Guide to Philip José Farmer*, 59–62.

FARRELL, JAMES T. (1904–1979)

Bernard Clare (1946)

Branch, Edgar M. "James T. Farrell," in Walcutt, Charles Child, ed. *Seven Novelists in the American Naturalist Tradition*, 267–270.

Gelfant, Blanche Housman. *American City Novel*, 222–226.

Boarding House Blues (1961)

Branch, Edgar M. "James T. Farrell," in Walcutt, Charles Child, ed. *Seven Novelists in the American Naturalist Tradition*, 276–277.

Brand New Life (1968)

Branch, Edgar M. "James T. Farrell," in Walcutt, Charles Child, ed. *Seven Novelists in the American Naturalist Tradition*, 283–284.

Slade, Joseph W. " 'Bare-Assed and Alone': Time and Banality in Farrell's *A Universe of Time*." *TCL* 22 (1976): 74.

Ellen Rogers (1941)

Branch, Edgar M. "James T. Farrell," in Walcutt, Charles Child, ed. *Seven Novelists in the American Naturalist Tradition*, 275–276.

Face of Time (1953)

Branch, Edgar M. "James T. Farrell," in Walcutt, Charles Child, ed. *Seven Novelists in the American Naturalist Tradition*, 261–267.

Father and Son (1940)

Branch, Edgar M. "James T. Farrell," in Walcutt, Charles Child, ed. *Seven Novelists in the American Naturalist Tradition*, 261–267.

Gas-House McGinty (1933)

Branch, Edgar M. "James T. Farrell," in Walcutt, Charles Child, ed. *Seven Novelists in the American Naturalist Tradition*, 273–274.

Invisible Swords (1971)

Branch, Edgar M. "James T. Farrell," in Walcutt, Charles Child, ed. *Seven Novelists in the American Naturalist Tradition*, 284–285.

Slade, Joseph W. " 'Bare-Assed and Alone': Time and Banality in Farrell's *A Universe of Time*." *TCL* 22 (1976): 71–72, 75.

Judgment Day (1935)

Branch, Edgar M. *James T. Farrell*, 36–73.

Branch, Edgar M. "James T. Farrell," in Walcutt, Charles Child, ed. *Seven Novelists in the American Naturalist Tradition*, 256–259.

Craig, David and Michael Egan. *Extreme Situations*, 153–154, 156–158, 160–162.

Gelfant, Blanche Housman. *American City Novel*, 189–202, 207–216.

Hearn, Charles R. *American Dream in the Great Depression*, 100–102.

Lonely for the Future (1966)

Slade, Joseph W. " 'Bare-Assed and Alone': Time and Banality in Farrell's *A Universe of Time*." *TCL* 22 (1976): 71, 73, 77.

My Days of Anger (1934)

Branch, Edgar M. "James T. Farrell," in Walcutt, Charles Child, ed. *Seven Novelists in the American Naturalist Tradition*, 261–267.

Gelfant, Blanche Housman. *American City Novel*, 204–206, 216–220, 228–232.

No Star Is Lost (1938)

Branch, Edgar M. "James T. Farrell," in Walcutt, Charles Child, ed. *Seven Novelists in the American Naturalist Tradition*, 261–267.

Road Between (1949)

Branch, Edgar M. "James T. Farrell," in Walcutt, Charles Child, ed. *Seven Novelists in the American Naturalist Tradition*, 267–270.
Gelfant, Blanche Housman. *American City Novel*, 221–222.

Silence of History (1963)

Slade, Joseph W. " 'Bare-Assed and Alone': Time and Banality in Farrell's *A Universe of Time*." *TCL* 22 (1976): 75.

This Man and This Woman (1951)

Branch, Edgar M. "James T. Farrell," in Walcutt, Charles Child, ed. *Seven Novelists in the American Naturalist Tradition*, 274–275.

What Time Collects (1964)

Branch, Edgar M. "James T. Farrell," in Walcutt, Charles Child, ed. *Seven Novelists in the American Naturalist Tradition*, 283.
Slade, Joseph W. " 'Bare-Assed and Alone': Time and Banality in Farrell's *A Universe of Time*." *TCL* 22 (1976): 72.

World I Never Made (1936)

Branch, Edgar M. "James T. Farrell," in Walcutt, Charles Child, ed. *Seven Novelists in the American Naturalist Tradition*, 261–267.

Yet Other Waters (1952)

Branch, Edgar M. "James T. Farrell," in Walcutt, Charles Child, ed. *Seven Novelists in the American Naturalist Tradition*, 267–268, 271–272.

Young Lonigan (1932)

Branch, Edgar M. *James T. Farrell*, 36–73.
Branch, Edgar M. "James T. Farrell," in Walcutt, Charles Child, ed. *Seven Novelists in the American Naturalist Tradition*, 260–261.
Craig, David and Michael Egan. *Extreme Situations*, 153–155, 160.
Gelfant, Blanche Housman. *American City Novel*, 189–202, 207–216.

Young Manhood of Studs Lonigan (1934)

Branch, Edgar M. *James T. Farrell*, 36–73.
Branch, Edgar M. "James T. Farrell," in Walcutt, Charles Child, ed. *Seven Novelists in the American Naturalist Tradition*, 260–261.
Craig, David and Michael Egan. *Extreme Situations*, 153–154, 158–160.
Gelfant, Blanche Housman. *American City Novel*, 189–202, 207–216.
Hearn, Charles R. *American Dream in the Great Depression*, 99–100.

FAULKNER, WILLIAM (1897–1962)

Absalom, Absalom! (1936)

Aaron, Daniel. *Unwritten War*, 322.
Adamowski, T. H. "Children of the Idea: Heroes and Family Romances in *Absalom, Absalom!*." *Mosaic* 10.1 (1976): 115–131.
Adamowski, Thomas H. "Dombey and Son and Sutpen and Son." *SNNTS* 4 (1972): 384–388.
Allen, Walter. *Urgent West*, 88–91.

Atkins, Anselm. "Matched Halves of *Absalom, Absalom!*" *MFS* 15 (1969): 264–265.

Backman, Melvin. "*Absalom, Absalom!*," in Backman, Melvin. *Faulkner, The Major Years: A Critical Study*. Bloomington, IN: Indiana University Press, 1966. 88–112. Rpt. in Goldman, Arnold, ed. *Twentieth Century Interpretations of Absalom, Absalom!*, 59–75.

Beja, Morris. *Epiphany in the Modern Novel*, 201–208.

Berzon, Judith R. *Neither White Nor Black*, 91–94, 225.

Bradford, M. E. "Brother, Son, and Heir: The Structural Focus of Faulkner's *Absalom, Absalom!*" *SewR* 78 (1970): 76–98.

Brooks, Cleanth. "American 'Innocence': in James, Fitzgerald, and Faulkner." *Shenandoah: The Washington and Lee University Review* 16 (Autumn 1964): 21–37. Rpt. in Stafford, William T., comp. *Merrill Studies in The American*, 111–126.

Brooks, Cleanth. "Narrative Structure of *Absalom, Absalom!*" *GR* 29 (1975): 366–394.

Brooks, Cleanth. "On *Absalom, Absalom!*" *Mosaic* 7.1 (1973): 159–183.

Brooks, Cleanth. *William Faulkner*, 283–328.

Broughton, Panthea Reid. *William Faulkner*, 67–69, 70–72, 85–86, 129–131, 137–138, 177–178.

Carey, Glenn O. "William Faulkner: Man's Fatal Vice." *ArQ* 28 (1972): 294.

Cook, Richard M. "Popeye, Flem, and Sutpen: The Faulknerian Villain as Grotesque." *SAF* 3 (1975): 9–12.

Davenport, F. Garvin, Jr. *Myth of Southern History*, 88–93, 97–106, 118–125.

Davis, Robert Con. "Symbolic Father in Yoknapatawpha County." *JNT* 10 (1980): 39–54.

Dickerson, Lynn. "Possible Source for the Title *Absalom, Absalom!*." *MissQ* 31 (1978): 423–424.

Donald, Miles. *American Novel in the Twentieth Century*, 75–76.

Doody, Terrence. "Shreve McCannon and the Confessions of *Absalom, Absalom!*" *SNNTS* 16 (1974): 454–469.

Doxey, W. S. "Father Time and the Grim Reaper in *Absalom, Absalom!*" *NConL* 8.3 (1978): 6–7.

Edwards, Duane. "Flem Snopes and Thomas Sutpen: Two Versions of Respectability." *DR* 51 (1971–72): 559–570.

Flynn, Peggy. "Sister Figure and 'Little Sister Death' in the Fiction of William Faulkner." *UMSE* 14 (1974): 112–114.

Ford, Daniel G. "Comments on William Faulkner's Temporal Vision in *Sanctuary, The Sound and the Fury, Light in August, Absalom, Absalom!*" *SoQ* 15 (1977): 283–290.

French, Warren. "William Faulkner and the Art of the Detective Story," in French, Warren, ed. *Thirties*, 57–58, 61.

Gallagher, Susan. "To Love and to Honor: Brothers and Sisters in Faulkner's Yoknapatawpha County." *ELWIU* 7 (1980): 219–221.

Garzilli, Enrico. *Circles without Center*, 52–60.

Gidley, Mark. "Elements of the Detective Story in William Faulkner's Fiction." *JPC* 7 (1973): 99–101.

Gidley, Mick. "Elements of the Detective Story in William Faulkner's Fiction," in Landrum, Larry N., Pat Browne and Ray B. Browne, eds. *Dimensions of Detective Fiction*, 237–241.

Goldman, Arnold. "Introduction," in Goldman, Arnold, ed. *Twentieth Century Interpretations of Absalom, Absalom!*, 3–9.

Gray, Richard. *Literature of Memory*, 199–198, 199–201, 207, 238–254.

Guerard, Albert J. *Triumph of the Novel*, 302–339.

Guetti, James. "*Absalom, Absalom!*: The Extended Simile," in Guetti, James. *Limits of Metaphor: A Study of Melville, Conrad, and Faulkner*. Ithaca, NY: Cornell University Press, 1967. 69–108. Rpt. in Goldman, Arnold, ed. *Twentieth Century Interpretations of Absalom, Absalom!*, 76–100.

Hagan, John. "Déjà Vu and the Effect of Timelessness in Faulkner's *Absalom, Absalom*," in Garvin, Harry R., ed. *Makers of the Twentieth-Century Novel*, 192–207.

Hagopian, John V. "*Absalom, Absalom!* and the Negro Question." *MFS* 19 (1973): 207–211.

Hays, Peter L. *Limping Hero*, 163.

Henderson, Harry B. *Versions of the Past*, 254–255, 258–269.

Herndon, Jerry A. "Faulkner: Meteor, Earthquake, and Sword," in Cary, Glenn O., ed. *Faulkner, The Unappeased Imagination*, 174–183, 188.

Hodgson, John A. " 'Logical Sequence and Continuity': Some Observations on the Typographical and Structural Consistency of *Absalom, Absalom!*" *AL* 43 (1971): 97–107.

Holman, C. Hugh. "*Absalom, Absalom!*: The Historian as Detective." *SewR* 79 (1971): 542–553.

Holman, C. Hugh. *Roots of Southern Writing*, 168–176.

Howe, Irving. *William Faulkner*, 71–78, 128–129, 221–232.

Hunter, Edwin R. *William Faulkner*, 65–66, 71–79.

Jehlen, Myra. *Class and Character in Faulkner's South*, 51–73, 75–76, 77–78.

Kartiganer, Donald M. *Fragile Thread*, 69–106.

Kerr, Elizabeth. "Evolution of Yoknapatawpha." *UMSE* 14 (1974): 28–29, 36–37.

Kerr, Elizabeth M. *William Faulkner's Gothic Domain*, 29–52.

King, Richard H. *Southern Renaissance*, 119–129.

Kinney, Arthur F. "Form and Function in *Absalom, Absalom!*" *SoR* 14 (1978): 677–691.

Lawson, Lewis A. "William Faulkner," in Panichas, George A., ed. *Politics of Twentieth-Century Novelists*, 288–291.

Lehan, Richard. *Dangerous Crossing*, 69–71.

Lensing, George S. "Metaphor of Family in *Absalom, Absalom!*" *SoR* 11 (1975): 99–117.

Levins, Lynn G. "Four Narrative Perspectives in *Absalom, Absalom!*" *PMLA* 85 (1970): 35–47.

Lind, Ilse Dusoir. "Design and Meaning of *Absalom! Abasalom!*." *PMLA* (Dec 1955): 887–912. Rpt. in Wagner, Linda Welshimer, ed. *William Faulkner*, 272–297.

MacKethan, Lucinda Hardwick. *Dream of Arcady*, 158–159, 163–168.

Matlack, James H. "Voices of Time: Narrative Structure in *Absalom, Absalom!*" *SoR* 15 (1979): 333–354.

Matthews, John T. "Marriage of Speaking and Hearing in *Absalom, Absalom!*" *ELH* 47 (1980): 575–594.

Millgate, Michael. "*Absalom, Absalom!*," in Millgate, Michael. *Achievement of William Faulkner*. New York: Random House, Inc., 1966. 150–164. Rpt. in Goldman, Arnold, ed. *Twentieth Century Interpretations of Absalom, Absalom!*, 42–58.

Monaghan, David M. "Faulkner's *Absalom, Absalom!*" *Expl* 31 (1972): Item 28.

Newby, Richard L. "Matthew Arnold, the North, and *Absalom, Absalom!*." *ANQ* 16 (1978): 105.

Ousby, Ian. *Reader's Guide to Fifty American Novels*, 300–302.

Parr, Susan Resneck. "Fourteenth Image of the Blackbird: Another Look at Truth in *Absalom, Absalom!*" *ArQ* 35 (1979): 153–164.

Paterson, John. "Hardy, Faulkner, and the Prosaics of Tragedy." *Centennial Review* 5 (1961): 160–163, 166–175. Rpt. in Goldman, Arnold, ed. *Twentieth Century Interpretations of Absalom, Absalom!*, 32–41.

Poirier, Richard. " 'Strange Gods' in Jefferson, Mississippi: Analysis of *Absalom, Absalom!*," in Hoffman, Frederick J. and Olga W. Vickery, eds. *William Faulkner: Two Decades of Criticism*. East Lansing, MI: Michigan State University Press, 1951. 217–243. Rpt. in Goldman, Arnold, ed. *Twentieth Century Interpretations of Absalom, Absalom!*, 12–31.

Polek, Fran. "Tick-tocks, Whirs, and Broken Gears: Time and Identity in Faulkner." *Renascence* 29 (1977): 197–199.

Powers, Lyall H. *Faulkner's Yoknapatawpha Comedy*, 106–124.

Putzel, Max. "What Is Gothic About *Absalom, Absalom!*" *SLJ* 4.1 (1971): 3–19.

Raper, J. R. "Meaning Called to Life: Alogical Structure in *Absalom, Absalom!*" *SoHR* 5 (1971): 9–23.

Rollyson, Carl E., Jr. "Creation of the Past in *Absalom, Absalom!*." *MissQ* 29 (1976): 361–374.

Rollyson, Carle E., Jr. "Faulkner and Historical Fiction: Redgauntlet and *Absalom, Absalom!*" *DR* 56 (1976–77): 671–681.

Rose, Maxine. "From Genesis to Revelation: The Grand Design of William Faulkner's *Absalom, Absalom!*" *SAF* 8 (1980): 219–228.

Rosenman, John B. "Anderson's *Poor White* and Faulkner's *Absalom, Absalom!*" *MissQ* 29 (1976): 437–438.

Rosenzweig, Paul. "Narrative Frames in *Absalom, Absalom!* Faulkner's Involuted Commentary on Art." *ArQ* 35 (1979): 135–152.

Rubin, Louis D., Jr. "Scarlett O'Hara and the Two Quentin Compsons," in Harrington, Evans and Ann J. Abadie, eds. *South and Faulkner's Yoknapatawpha*, 171–191.

Schrank, Bernice. "Patterns of Reversal in *Absalom, Absalom!*" *DR* 54 (1975): 648–666.

Seltzer, Alvin J. *Chaos in the Novel*, 110–111.

Seyppel, Joachim. *William Faulkner*, 62–66.

Skaggs, Merrill Maguire. *Folk of Southern Fiction*, 231–233.

Stafford, William T. "Whale, an Heiress, and a Southern Demigod: Three Symbolic Americas." *CollL* 1 (1974): 108–111.

Strandberg, Victor H. "Between Truth and Fact: Faulkner's Symbols of Identity." *MFS* 21 (1975): 447, 452–453.

Sullivan, Walter. *Death by Melancholy*, 80–81, 83.

Sullivan, Walter. *Requiem for the Renascence*, 9–11.

Tobin, Patricia Dreschel. *Time and the Novel*, 107–132.

Turner, Darwin T. "Faulkner and Slavery," in Harrington, Evans and Ann J. Abadie, eds. *South and Faulkner's Yoknapatawpha*, 81–82, 82–83.

Tuttleton, James W. " 'Combat in the Erogenous Zone': Women in the American

Novel between the Two Wars," in Springer, Marlene, ed. *What Manner of Woman*, 289.

VandeKieft, Ruth M. "Faulkner's Defeat of Time in *Absalom, Absalom!*" *SoR* 6 (1970): 1100–1109.

Waggoner, Hyatt H. "Historical Novel and the Southern Past: The Case of *Absalom, Absalom!*" *SLJ* 2.2 (1970): 69–85.

Wagner, Linda Welshimer. "Faulkner and (Southern) Women," in Harrington, Evans and Ann J. Abadie, eds. *South and Faulkner's Yoknapatawpha*, 137, 207–208.

Wagner, Linda Welshimer. *Hemingway and Faulkner*, 195.

Weinstein, Arnold L. *Vision and Response in Modern Fiction*, 136–153.

Weinstein, Philip M. "Precarious Sanctuaries: Protection and Exposure in Faulkner's Fiction." *SAF* 6 (1978): 183–189.

As I Lay Dying (1930)

Adamowski, T. H. " 'Meet Mrs. Bundren': *As I Lay Dying*—Gentility, Tact, and Psychoanalysis." *UTQ* 49 (1980): 205–227.

Alldredge, Betty. "Spatial Form in Faulkner's *As I Lay Dying*." *SLJ* 11.1 (1978): 3–19.

Annas, Pamela J. "Carpenter of *As I Lay Dying*." *NMW* 8 (1976): 84–99.

Backman, Melvin. "Addie Bundren and William Faulkner," in Cary, Glenn O., ed. *Faulkner, The Unappeased Imagination*, 7–23.

Bleikasten, André. *Faulkner's As I Lay Dying*. Trans. Roger Little. Revised and Enlarged Edition. Bloomington, IN: Indiana University Press, 1973.

Bradford, M. E. "Addie Bundren and the Design of *As I Lay Dying*." *SoR* 6 (1970): 1093–1099.

Brady, Ruth H. "Faulkner's *As I Lay Dying*." *Expl* 33 (1975): Item 60.

Branch, Watson G. "Darl Bundren's 'Cubistic' Vision." *TSLL* 19 (1977): 42–53.

Broughton, Panthea Reid. *William Faulkner*, 125–128, 176–177, 191–193.

Cohn, Dorrit. *Transparent Minds*, 205–206, 207–208.

Cook, Sylvia Jenkins. *From Tobacco Road to Route 66*, 41–47.

Donald, Miles. *American Novel in the Twentieth Century*, 78–82.

Garrison, Joseph M., Jr. "Language, and Reality in *As I Lay Dying*." *ArQ* 32 (1976): 16–30.

Garzilli, Enrico. *Circles without Center*, 60–65.

Gold, Joseph. " 'Sin, Salvation and Bananas': *As I Lay Dying*." *Mosaic* 7.1 (1973): 55–73.

Gray, Richard. *Literature of Memory*, 221–231.

Hauck, Richard Boyd. *Cheerful Nihilism*, 168, 195–200.

Hemenway, Robert. "Enigmas of Being in *As I Lay Dying*." *MFS* 16 (1970): 133–146.

Howe, Irving. *William Faulkner*, 52–56, 175–191.

Hunter, Edwin R. *William Faulkner*, 49–60.

Kartiganer, Donald M. *Fragile Thread*, 23–33.

Kerr, Elizabeth. "Evolution of Yoknapatawpha." *UMSE* 14 (1974): 31–32.

Kerr, Elizabeth M. "*As I Lay Dying* as Ironic Quest." *Wisconsin Studies in Contemporary Literature* 3 (Winter 1962): 5–19. Rpt. in Wagner, Linda Welshimer, ed. *William Faulkner*, 230–242.

Lehan, Richard. *Dangerous Crossing*, 75.

Lyday, Lance. "Jewel Bundren: Faulkner's Achilles." *NConL* 10.2 (1980): 2.

May, John R. *Toward a New Earth*, 93–114.

Middleton, David. "Faulkner's Folklore in *As I Lay Dying:* An Old Motif in a New Manner." *SNNTS* 9 (1977): 46–53.

Milum, Richard A. "Continuity and Change: The Horse, the Automobile, and the Airplane in Faulkner's Fiction," in Cary, Glenn O., ed. *Faulkner, The Unappeased Imagination*, 161–162, 171.

Monaghan, David M. "Single Narrator of *As I Lay Dying*." *MFS* 18 (1972): 213–220.

Nadeau, Robert L. "Morality of Act: A Study of Faulkner's *As I Lay Dying*." *Mosaic* 6.3 (1973): 23–25.

Ousby, Ian. *Reader's Guide to Fifty American Novels*, 290–292.

Palliser, Charles. "Fate and Madness: The Determinist Vision of Darl Bundren." *AL* 49 (1978): 619–633.

Pierce, Constance. "Being, Knowing, and Saying in the 'Addie' Section of Faulkner's *As I Lay Dying*." *TCL* 26 (1980): 294–305.

Polek, Fran. "Tick-tocks, Whirs, and Broken Gears: Time and Identity in Faulkner." *Renascence* 29 (1977): 196–197.

Powers, Lyall H. *Faulkner's Yoknapatawpha Comedy*, 50–72.

Robinson, Fred Miller. *Comedy of Language*, 51–88.

Rooks, George. "Vardaman's Journey in *As I Lay Dying*." *ArQ* 35 (1979): 114–128.

Rosenman, John B. "Another *Othello* Echo in *As I Lay Dying*." *NMW* 8 (1975): 19–21.

Rosenman, John B. "Note on William Faulkner's *As I Lay Dying*." *SAF* 1 (1973): 104–105.

Rosenman, John B. "Physical-Spatial Symbolism in *As I Lay Dying*." *CollL* 4 (1977): 176–177.

Ross, Stephen M. "Shapes of Time and Consciousness in *As I Lay Dying*." *TSLL* 16 (1975): 723–737.

Ross, Stephen M. "Voice in Narrative Texts: The Example of *As I Lay Dying*." *PMLA* 94 (1979): 300–310.

Sanderlin, Robert R. "*As I Lay Dying:* Christian Symbols and Thematic Implications." *SoQ* 7 (1969): 155–166.

Seltzer, Alvin J. *Chaos in the Novel*, 108–110, 111, 118.

Seltzer, Leon F. "Narrative Function vs. Psychopathology: The Problem of Darl in *As I Lay Dying*." *L&P* 25 (1975): 49–64.

Seltzer, Leon F. and Jan Viscomi. "Natural Rhythms and Rebellion: Anse's Role in *As I Lay Dying*." *MFS* 24 (1978–79): 556–564.

Seyppel, Joachim. *William Faulkner*, 47–49.

Shoemaker, Alice. "Wheel within a Wheel: Fusion of Form and Content in Faulkner's *As I Lay Dying*." *ArQ* 35 (1979): 101–113.

Skaggs, Merrill Maguire. *Folk of Southern Fiction*, 224–225.

Slabey, Robert M. "*As I Lay Dying* as an Existential Novel," in Garvin, Harry R., ed. *Makers of the Twentieth-Century Novel*, 208–217.

Stich, K. P. "Note on Ironic Word Formation in *As I Lay Dying*." *NMW* 8 (1976): 100–103.

Stonum, Gary Lee. "Dilemma in *As I Lay Dying*." *Renascence* 28 (1976): 71–81.

Strandberg, Victor H. "Between Truth and Fact: Faulkner's Symbols of Identity." *MFS* 21 (1975): 449, 455.

Wagner, Linda Welshimer. "Faulkner and (Southern) Women," in Harrington, Evans and Ann J. Abadie, eds. *South and Faulkner's Yoknapatawpha*, 135–136.
Wagner, Linda Welshimer. *Hemingway and Faulkner*, 180–190.
Watkins, Floyd C. *In Time and Place*, 175–189.
Watkins, Floyd C. "Word and Deed in Faulkner's First Great Novels," in Watkins, Floyd C. *Flesh and the Word: Eliot, Hemingway, Faulkner*. Vanderbilt University Press, 1971. 181–202. Rpt. in Wagner, Linda Welshimer, ed. *William Faulkner*, 213–229.
Weinstein, Philip M. "Precarious Sanctuaries: Protection and Exposure in Faulkner's Fiction." *SAF* 6 (1978): 174–176.
White, Michael. "Inverse Mimesis in Faulkner's *As I Lay Dying*." *ArQ* 32 (1976): 35–44.
Williams, David. *Faulkner's Women*, 97–126.

Fable (1954)

Brooks, Cleanth. *William Faulkner*, 230–250.
Broughton, Panthea Reid. *William Faulkner*, 103–104, 151–152, 179, 184–185.
Carey, Glenn O. "William Faulkner: Man's Fatal Vice." *ArQ* 28 (1972): 293, 295–300.
Chittick, Kathryn A. "Fables in William Faulkner's *A Fable*." *MissQ* 30 (1977): 403–415.
Howe, Irving. *William Faulkner*, 268–281.
Ilacqua, Alma A. "Faulkner's *A Fable*." *NMW* 10 (1977): 37–46.
Kartiganer, Donald M. *Fragile Thread*, 139–141, 144–146.
Miller, Wayne Charles. *Armed America, Its Face in Fiction*, 126–127.
Millgate, Michael. "Faulkner and History," in Harrington, Evans and Ann J. Abadie, eds. *South and Faulkner's Yoknapatawpha*, 36–38.
Solomon, Eric. "From Christ in Flanders to *Catch-22*: An Approach to War Fiction." *TSLL* 11 (1969): 857–859.
Straumann, Heinrich. "American Interpretation of Existence: Faulkner's *A Fable*." *Anglia* (1955): 484–515. Trans. Grace A. Goodman and Olga W. Vickery. Rpt. in Wagner, Linda Welshimer, ed. *William Faulkner*, 335–357.
Wagner, Linda Welshimer. *Hemingway and Faulkner*, 211–217.
Ziolkowski, Theodore. *Fictional Transfigurations of Jesus*, 171–180.

Flags in the Dust (1973)

Brooks, Cleanth. *William Faulkner*, 165–177.
Broughton, Panthea Reid. *William Faulkner*, 141–142.
Folks, Jeffrey J. "Problem with the Internal Dating of *Flags in the Dust*." *NConL* 9.3 (1979): 8–9.
Hodgin, Katherine C. "Horace Benbow and Bayard Sartoris: Two Romantic Figures in Faulkner's *Flags in the Dust*." *AL* 50 (1979): 647–652.
Kerr, Elizabeth. "Evolution of Yoknapatawpha." *UMSE* 14 (1974): 24–25.
King, Richard H. *Southern Renaissance*, 82–83.
McDaniel, Linda E. "Horace Benbow: Faulkner's Endymion." *MissQ* 33 (1980): 363–370.
Simpson, Lewis P. "Sex & History: Origins of Faulkner's Apocrypha," in Harrington, Evans and Ann J. Abadie, eds. *Maker and the Myth*, 58–62.
Wagner, Linda Welshimer. "Faulkner and (Southern) Women," in Harrington, Evans and Ann J. Abadie, eds. *South and Faulkner's Yoknapatawpha*, 132–133.

Hamlet (1940)

Arpad, Joseph J. "William Faulkner's Legendary Novels: The Snopes Trilogy." *MissQ* 22.3 (1969): 214–215, 216–225.

Broughton, Panthea R. "Masculinity and Menfolk in *The Hamlet.*" *MissQ* 22.3 (1969): 181–189.

Broughton, Panthea Reid. *William Faulkner*, 62–63, 65–66, 118–119, 180, 187–188.

Burch, Beth. "Miltonic Echo in Faulkner's *The Hamlet.*" *NConL* 8.4 (1978): 3–4.

Cook, Richard M. "Popeye, Flem, and Sutpen: The Faulknerian Villain as Grotesque." *SAF* 3 (1975): 6–7.

Cook, Sylvia Jenkins. *From Tobacco Road to Route 66*, 55–59.

Edwards, Duane. "Flem Snopes and Thomas Sutpen: Two Versions of Respectability." *DR* 51 (1971–72): 559–570.

Friedman, Alan W. *Multivalence*, 143–177.

Gallagher, Susan. "To Love and to Honor: Brothers and Sisters in Faulkner's Yoknapatawpha County." *ELWIU* 7 (1980): 214–215.

Gold, Joseph. " 'Normality' of Snopesism: Universal Themes in Faulkner's *The Hamlet.*" *Wisconsin Studies in Contemporary Literature* 3 (Winter 1962): 25–34. Rpt. in Wagner, Linda Welshimer, ed. *William Faulkner*, 318–327.

Gray, Richard. *Literature of Memory*, 215–218.

Greet, T. Y. "Theme and Structure of Faulkner's *The Hamlet.*" *PMLA* (Sept 1957): 775–790. Rpt. in Wagner, Linda Welshimer, ed. *William Faulkner*, 302–317.

Guerard, Albert J. *Triumph of the Novel*, 212–220.

Hauck, Richard Boyd. *Cheerful Nihilism*, 180–187.

Howard, Alan B. "Huck Finn in the House of Usher: The Comic and Grotesque Worlds of *The Hamlet.*" *SoR* 5 (1972): 125–146.

Howe, Irving. *Celebrations and Attacks*, 42–44.

Howe, Irving. *William Faulkner*, 78–81, 85–88, 243–252.

Hunter, Edwin R. *William Faulkner*, 67.

Jehlen, Myra. *Class and Character in Faulkner's South*, 143–150, 154–157.

Kartiganer, Donald M. *Fragile Thread*, 109–129.

Kerr, Elizabeth. "Evolution of Yoknapatawpha." *UMSE* 14 (1974): 38–40.

Kerr, Elizabeth M. *William Faulkner's Gothic Domain*, 186–219.

Leaf, Mark. "William Faulkner's Snopes Trilogy: The South Evolves," in French, Warren, ed. *Fifties*, 53–62.

Lucente, Gregory L. *Narrative of Realism and Myth*, 124–134.

McFarland, Holly. "Mask Not Tragic . . . Just Damned: The Women in Faulkner's Trilogy." *BallS* 18.2 (1977): 27–35.

Milum, Richard A. "Continuity and Change: The Horse, the Automobile, and the Airplane in Faulkner's Fiction," in Cary, Glenn O., ed. *Faulkner, The Unappeased Imagination*, 162–163.

Norris, Nancy. "*Hamlet, The Town*, and *The Mansion:* A Psychological Reading of the Snopes Trilogy." *Mosaic* 7.1 (1973): 213–235.

Payne, Ladell. "Trilogy: Faulkner's Comic Epic in Prose." *SNNTS* 1.1 (1969): 28–36.

Pierle, Robert C. "Snopesism in Faulkner's *The Hamlet.*" *ES* 52 (1971): 246–252.

Powers, Lyall H. *Faulkner's Yoknapatawpha Comedy*, 145–161.

Prior, Linda T. "Themes, Imagery, and Structure in *The Hamlet.*" *MissQ* 22.3 (1969): 237–256.

Rankin, Elizabeth D. "Chasing Spotted Horses: The Quest for Human Dignity in Faulkner's Snopes Trilogy," in Cary, Glenn O., ed. *Faulkner, The Unappeased Imagination*, 139–154.

Seltzer, Alvin J. *Chaos in the Novel*, 102–105, 113.

Simpson, Lewis P. "Sex & History: Origins of Faulkner's Apocrypha," in Harrington, Evans and Ann J. Abadie, eds. *Maker and the Myth*, 56–58.

Skaggs, Merrill Maguire. *Folk of Southern Fiction*, 225–231.

Stineback, David C. *Shifting World*, 142–155.

Stone, Edward. *Certain Morbidness*, 101–120.

Strandberg, Victor H. "Between Truth and Fact: Faulkner's Symbols of Identity." *MFS* 21 (1975): 446–448, 450.

Stroble, Woodrow. "Flem Snopes: A Crazed Mirror," in Cary, Glenn O., ed. *Faulkner, The Unappeased Imagination*, 195–198,198–203, 209–210.

Tuttleton, James W. " 'Combat in the Erogenous Zone': Women in the American Novel between the Two Wars," in Springer, Marlene, ed. *What Manner of Woman*, 288–289.

Wagner, Linda Welshimer. *Hemingway and Faulkner*, 218–224.

Williams, David. *Faulkner's Women*, 197–210.

If I Forget Thee, Jerusalem see *Wild Palms*

Intruder in the Dust (1948)

Alexander, Margaret Walker. "Faulkner & Race," in Harrington, Evans and Ann J. Abadie, eds. *Maker and the Myth*, 114–117.

Berzon, Judith R. *Neither White Nor Black*, 89–91.

Broughton, Panthea Reid. *William Faulkner*, 100.

Davenport, F. Garvin, Jr. *Myth of Southern History*, 127–130.

Gidley, Mick. "Elements of the Detective Story in William Faulkner's Fiction," in Landrum, Larry N., Pat Browne and Ray B. Browne, eds. *Dimensions of Detective Fiction*, 243–246.

Howe, Irving. *William Faulkner*, 98–105, 129–130, 133–134.

Jehlen, Myra. *Class and Character in Faulkner's South*, 124–132.

Kartiganer, Donald M. *Fragile Thread*, 141–144.

Kerr, Elizabeth. "Evolution of Yoknapatawpha." *UMSE* 14 (1974): 44–46.

Kerr, Elizabeth M. *William Faulkner's Gothic Domain*, 162–183.

Monaghan, David M. "Faulkner's Relationship to Gavin Stevens in *Intruder in the Dust*." *DR* 52 (1972): 449–457.

Powers, Lyall H. *Faulkner's Yoknapatawpha Comedy*, 192–203.

Rigsby, Carol R. "Chick Mallison's Expectations and *Intruder in the Dust*." *MissQ* 29 (1976): 389–399.

Samway, Patrick, S. J. "*Intruder in Dust*: A Re-evaluation," in Cary, Glenn O., ed. *Faulkner, The Unappeased Imagination*, 81–108.

Seyppel, Joachim. *William Faulkner*, 80–85.

Skaggs, Merrill Maguire. *Folk of Southern Fiction*, 221–223.

Skerry, Philip J. "*Adventures of Huckleberry Finn* and *Intruder in the Dust*: Two Conflicting Myths of the American Experience." *BallS* 13.1 (1972): 4–13.

Starke, Catherine Juanita. *Black Portraiture in American Fiction*, 192–196.

Tallack, Douglas G. "William Faulkner and the Tradition of the Tough-Guy Detective," in Landrum, Larry N., Pat Browne and Ray B. Browne, eds. *Dimensions of Detective Fiction*, 260–261.

Light in August (1932)

Aaron, Daniel. *Unwritten War*, 318–319.

Able, Darrel. "Frozen Movement in *Light in August*." *Boston University Studies in English* 3 (1957): 32–44. Condensed and rpt. in Minter, David L., ed. *Twentieth Century Interpretations of Light in August*, 42–54.

Able, Darrel. "Frozen Movement in *Light in August*." *Boston University Studies in English* 3 (Spring 1957): 32–44. Rpt. in Inge, M. Thomas, comp. *Merrill Studies in Light in August*, 37–50.

Adamowski, T. H. "Joe Christmas: The Tyranny of Childhood." *Novel* 4 (1971): 240–251.

Beja, Morris. *Epiphany in the Modern Novel*, 194–201.

Benson, Carl. "Thematic Design in *Light in August*." *South Atlantic Quarterly* 53 (1954): 540–555. Rpt. in Wagner, Linda Welshimer, ed. *William Faulkner*, 258–272.

Berzon, Judith R. *Neither White Nor Black*, 225–235.

Blair, Walter. " 'A Man's Voice, Speaking': A Continuum in American Humor," in Levin, Harry, ed. *Veins of Humor*, 203–204.

Bledsoe, Audrey. "Faulkner's Chiaroscuro: Comedy in *Light in August*." *NMW* 11 (1979): 55–63.

Brooks, Cleanth. "Community and the Pariah," in Brooks, Cleanth. *William Faulkner: Yoknapatawpha Country*. New Haven, CT: Yale University Press, 1963. 47–74. Rpt. in Minter, David L., ed. *Twentieth Century Interpretations of Light in August*, 55–70.

Broughton, Panthea Reid. *William Faulkner*, 93–99, 104–105, 131–137, 152–156, 195–198.

Burroughs, Franklin G., Jr. "God the Father and Motherless Children: *Light in August*." *TCL* 19 (1973): 189–202.

Campbell, Jeff H. "Polarity and Paradox: Faulkner's *Light in August*." *CEA* 34.2 (1972): 26–31.

Carey, Glenn O. "William Faulkner: Man's Fatal Vice." *ArQ* 28 (1972): 293–294.

Chase, Richard. *American Novel and Its Tradition*. Garden City, NY: Doubleday & Company, Inc., 1957. 210–219. Rpt. as "Faulkner's *Light in August*," in Minter, David L., ed. *Twentieth Century Interpretations of Light in August*, 17–24.

Chase, Richard. "Stone and Crucifixion." *Kenyon Review* 10 (Autumn 1948): 539–551. Rpt. in Inge, M. Thomas, comp. *Merrill Studies in Light in August*, 27–37.

Clark, William J. "Faulkner's *Light in August*." *Expl* 29 (1969): Item 19.

Coindreau, Maurice Edgar. *Time of William Faulkner*, 30–40.

Collins, R. G. "*Light in August:* Faulkner's Stained Glass Triptych." *Mosaic* 7.1 (1973): 97–157.

Corey, Stephen. "Avengers in *Light in August* and *Native Son*." *CLAJ* 23 (1979): 200–212.

D'Avanso, Mario L. "Allusion in the Percy Grimm Episode of *Light in August*." *NMW* 8 (1975): 63–68.

D'Avanzo, Mario L. "Bobbie Allen and the Ballad Tradition in *Light in August*." *SCR* 8.1 (1975): 22–29.

D'Avanzo, Mario L. "Doc Hines and Euphues in *Light in August*." *NMW* 9 (1976): 101–106.

Davis, Charles E. "William Faulkner's Joe Christmas: A Rage for Order." *ArQ* 32 (1976): 61–73.

Donald, Miles. *American Novel in the Twentieth Century*, 88–89.

Ford, Daniel G. "Comments on William Faulkner's Temporal Vision in *Sanctuary, The Sound and the Fury, Light in August, Absalom, Absalom!*" *SoQ* 15 (1977): 283–290.

Godden, Richard. "Call Me Nigger! Race and Speech in Faulkner's *Light in August.*" *JAmS* 14 (1980): 235–248.

Gray, Richard. *Literature of Memory*, 219–221.

Hays, Peter L. *Limping Hero*, 83–84.

Heimer, Jackson W. "Faulkner's Misogynous Novel: *Light in August.*" *BallS* 14.3 (1973): 11–15.

Henderson, Harry B. *Versions of the Past*, 256–258.

Hirshleifer, Phyllis. "As Whirlwinds in the South: An Analysis of *Light in August.*" *Perspective* 2 (Summer 1949): 225–238. Rpt. in Wagner, Linda Welshimer, ed. *William Faulkner*, 244–257.

Holman, C. Hugh. *Roots of Southern Writing*, 149–167.

Holman, C. Hugh. "Unity of Faulkner's *Light in August.*" *PMLA* 73 (March 1958): 155–166. Rpt. in Inge, M. Thomas, comp. *Merrill Studies in Light in August*, 51–74.

Howe, Irving. *William Faulkner*, 61–70, 125–127, 200–214.

Hunter, Edwin R. *William Faulkner*, 62–65.

Jehlen, Myra. *Class and Character in Faulkner's South*, 78–82, 84–96.

Kartiganer, Donald M. *Fragile Thread*, 37–68.

Kellogg, Jean. *Dark Prophets of Hope*, 137–156.

Kerr, Elizabeth. "Evolution of Yoknapatawpha." *UMSE* 14 (1974): 32–35.

Kerr, Elizabeth M. *William Faulkner's Gothic Domain*, 107–136.

Kimmey, John L. "Good Earth in *Light in August.*" *Mississippi Quarterly* 17 (Winter 1963–64): 1–8. Rpt. in Inge, M. Thomas, comp. *Merrill Studies in Light in August*, 98–107.

King, Richard H. *Southern Renaissance*, 84–85.

Lawson, Lewis A. "William Faulkner," in Panichas, George A., ed. *Politics of Twentieth-Century Novelists*, 286–288.

Lehan, Richard. *Dangerous Crossing*, 75–77.

Lind, Ilse Dusoir. "Apocalyptic Vision as Key to *Light in August.*" *SAF* 3 (1975): 133–141.

Longley, John Lewis, Jr. "Joe Christmas: The Hero in the Modern World," in Longley, John Lewis, Jr. *Tragic Mask: A Study of Faulkner's Heroes*. Chapel Hill: University of North Carolina Press, 1963. 192–205. Rpt. in Inge, M. Thomas, comp. *Merrill Studies in Light in August*, 107–119.

McCormick, John. *Fiction as Knowledge*, 102–108.

McLuhan, Marshall. *Interior Landscape*, 197–198.

Malin, Irving. "American Gothic Images." *Mosaic* 6.3 (1973): 151–152, 161.

Martin, Timothy P. "Art and Rhetoric of Chronology in Faulkner's *Light in August.*" *CollL* 7 (1980): 125–135.

Millgate, Michael. *Achievement of William Faulkner*. New York: Random House, Inc., 1966. 124–137. Rpt. as "Faulkner's *Light in August*," in Minter, David L., ed. *Twentieth Century Interpretations of Light in August*, 71–82.

Milum, Richard A. "Continuity and Change: The Horse, the Automobile, and the Airplane in Faulkner's Fiction," in Cary, Glenn O., ed. *Faulkner, The Unappeased Imagination*, 160.

Minter, David L. "Introduction" to Minter, David L., ed. *Twentieth Century Interpretations of Light in August*, 4–14.

Mulqueen, James E. "*Light in August:* Motion, Eros, and Death." *NMW* 8 (1975): 91–98.

Nash, Harry C. "Faulkner's 'Furniture Repairer and Dealer': Knitting up *Light in August.*" *MFS* 16 (1970): 529–531.

Pearce, Richard. *Stages of the Clown*, 47–66.

Peterson, Richard F. "Faulkner's *Light in August.*" *Expl* 30 (1971): Item 35.

Pitavy, François. *Faulkner's Light in August.* Trans. Gillian E. Cook. Revised and Enlarged Edition. Bloomington, IN: Indiana University Press, 1973.

Polek, Fran. "Tick-tocks, Whirs, and Broken Gears: Time and Identity in Faulkner." *Renascence* 29 (1977): 197.

Powers, Lyall H. *Faulkner's Yoknapatawpha Comedy*, 89–105.

Pryse, Marjorie. *Mark and the Knowledge*, 108–138.

Rose, Alan Henry. *Demonic Vision*, 111–118.

Rosenzweig, Paul J. "Faulkner's Motif of Food in *Light in August.*" *American Imago* 37 (1980): 93–112.

Ruppersburg, Hugh M. "Byron Bunch and Percy Grimm: Strange Twins of *Light in August.*" *MissQ* 30 (1977): 441–443.

Seltzer, Alvin J. *Chaos in the Novel*, 98–100, 105–108, 113, 117.

Seyppel, Joachim. *William Faulkner*, 53–60.

Sichi, Edward, Jr. "Faulkner's Joe Christmas: 'Memory Believes before Knowing Remembers'." *Cithara* 18.2 (1979): 70–77.

Slabey, Robert M. "Myth and Ritual in *Light in August.*" *Texas Studies in Language and Literature* 2 (Autumn 1960): 328–349. Rpt. in Inge, M. Thomas, comp. *Merrill Studies in Light in August*, 75–98.

Sullivan, Walter. *Requiem for the Renascence*, 11–13.

Tallack, Douglas G. "William Faulkner and the Tradition of the Tough-Guy Detective," in Landrum, Larry N., Pat Browne and Ray B. Browne, eds. *Dimensions of Detective Fiction*, 253–255, 256–257.

Tanner, Stephen L. "*Light in August:* The Varieties of Religious Fanaticism." *ELWIU* 7 (1980): 79–90.

Taylor, Carole Anne. "*Light in August:* The Epistemology of Tragic Paradox." *TSLL* 22 (1980): 48–68.

Tuttleton, James W. " 'Combat in the Erogenous Zone': Women in the American Novel between the Two Wars," in Springer, Marlene, ed. *What Manner of Woman*, 289.

Vickery, Olga W. "Shadow and the Mirror: *Light in August*," in Vickery, Olga W. *Novels of William Faulkner: A Critical Interpretation.* Revised Edition. Baton Rouge, LA: Louisiana State University Press, 1959. 66–83. Rpt. in Minter, David L., ed. *Twentieth Century Interpretations of Light in August*, 25–41.

Wagner, Linda Welshimer. "Faulkner and (Southern) Women," in Harrington, Evans and Ann J. Abadie, eds. *South and Faulkner's Yoknapatawpha*, 136, 145–146.

Wagner, Linda Welshimer. *Hemingway and Faulkner*, 138–139, 140, 190–195, 199–200.

Weinstein, Philip M. "Precarious Sanctuaries: Protection and Exposure in Faulkner's Fiction." *SAF* 6 (1978): 181–183.

Williams, David. *Faulkner's Women*, 157–184.

Mansion (1959)

Arpad, Joseph J. "William Faulkner's Legendary Novels: The Snopes Trilogy." *MissQ* 22.3 (1969): 216–225.

Broughton, Panthea Reid. *William Faulkner*, 29–30, 44–45, 66–67, 72–74, 181.

Carey, Glenn O. "William Faulkner: Man's Fatal Vice." *ArQ* 28 (1972): 294–295.

Creighton, Joanne V. "Dilemma of the Human Heart in *The Mansion*." *Renascence* 25 (1972): 35–45.

Edwards, Duane. "Flem Snopes and Thomas Sutpen: Two Versions of Respectability." *DR* 51 (1971–72): 559–570.

Flynn, Peggy. "Sister Figure and 'Little Sister Death' in the Fiction of William Faulkner." *UMSE* 14 (1974): 114–116.

Friedman, Alan W. *Multivalence*, 143–177.

Gregory, Eileen. "Temerity to Revolt: Mink Snopes and the Dispossessed in *The Mansion*." *MissQ* 29 (1976): 401–421.

Hauck, Richard Boyd. *Cheerful Nihilism*, 191–195.

Howe, Irving. *Celebrations and Attacks*, 44–48.

Howe, Irving. *William Faulkner*, 81–85, 110–114, 282–294.

Hunter, Edwin R. *William Faulkner*, 68–69.

Jehlen, Myra. *Class and Character in Faulkner's South*, 133, 134, 136, 137, 140–141, 162–164, 169–174.

Kerr, Elizabeth. "Evolution of Yoknapatawpha." *UMSE* 14 (1974): 51–55.

Kerr, Elizabeth M. *William Faulkner's Gothic Domain*, 186–219.

Leaf, Mark. "William Faulkner's Snopes Trilogy: The South Evolves," in French, Warren, ed. *Fifties*, 53–62.

McFarland, Holly. "Mask Not Tragic . . . Just Damned: The Women in Faulkner's Trilogy." *BallS* 18.2 (1977): 27, 41–50.

Norris, Nancy. "*Hamlet, The Town*, and *The Mansion:* A Psychological Reading of the Snopes Trilogy." *Mosaic* 7.1 (1973): 213–235.

Payne, Ladell. "Trilogy: Faulkner's Comic Epic in Prose." *SNNTS* 1.1 (1969): 30–36.

Powers, Lyall H. *Faulkner's Yoknapatawpha Comedy*, 233–249.

Rankin, Elizabeth D. "Chasing Spotted Horses: The Quest for Human Dignity in Faulkner's Snopes Trilogy," in Cary, Glenn O., ed. *Faulkner, The Unappeased Imagination*, 139–154.

Skaggs, Merrill Maguire. *Folk of Southern Fiction*, 228–231.

Stroble, Woodrow. "Flem Snopes: A Crazed Mirror," in Cary, Glenn O., ed. *Faulkner, The Unappeased Imagination*, 205–209.

Sullivan, Walter. *Death by Melancholy*, 14–18.

Wagner, Linda Welshimer. *Hemingway and Faulkner*, 203, 218–224.

Williams, David. *Faulkner's Women*, 222–226.

Mosquitoes (1927)

Arnold, Edwin T. "Freedom and Stasis in Faulkner's *Mosquitoes*." *MissQ* 28 (1975): 281–297.

Arnold, Edwin T., III. "Faulkner and Huxley: A Note on *Mosquitoes* and *Crome Yellow*." *MissQ* 30 (1977): 433–436.

Bassett, John Earl. "Faulkner's *Mosquitoes:* Toward a Self-Image of the Artist." *SLJ* 12.2 (1980): 49–64.

Brooks, Cleanth. "Faulkner's *Mosquitoes*." *GR* 31 (1977): 213–234.

Brooks, Cleanth. *William Faulkner*, 129–151.

Broughton, Panthea Reid. *William Faulkner*, 26–29, 31, 198.

Dunlap, Mary M. "Sex and the Artist in *Mosquitoes*." *MissQ* 22.3 (1969): 190–206.

Flynn, Peggy. "Sister Figure and 'Little Sister Death' in the Fiction of William Faulkner." *UMSE* 14 (1974): 100–104.

Hepburn, Kenneth W. "Faulkner's *Mosquitoes:* A Poetic Turning Point." *TCL* 17 (1971): 19–28.

Kreiswirth, Martin. "William Faulkner and Siegfried Sassoon: An Allusion in *Mosquitoes*." *MissQ* 29 (1976): 433–434.

Seyppel, Joachim. *William Faulkner*, 27–31.

Simpson, Lewis P. "Sex & History: Origins of Faulkner's Apocrypha," in Harrington, Evans and Ann J. Abadie, eds. *Maker and the Myth*, 51–56.

Wagner, Linda Welshimer. *Hemingway and Faulkner*, 159–161.

Williams, David. *Faulkner's Women*, 32–36.

Pylon (1935)

Brooks, Cleanth. *William Faulkner*, 178–204.

Broughton, Panthea Reid. *William Faulkner*, 74.

Howe, Irving. *William Faulkner*, 215–220.

Milum, Richard A. "Continuity and Change: The Horse, the Automobile, and the Airplane in Faulkner's Fiction," in Cary, Glenn O., ed. *Faulkner, The Unappeased Imagination*, 166–167, 169, 171.

Pearce, Richard. "*Pylon, Awake and Sing!* and the Apocalyptic Imagination of the 30's." *Criticism* 13 (1971): 137–141.

Seyppel, Joachim. *William Faulkner*, 60–62.

Wagner, Linda Welshimer. "Faulkner and (Southern) Women," in Harrington, Evans and Ann J. Abadie, eds. *South and Faulkner's Yoknapatawpha*, 136–137.

Wagner, Linda Welshimer. *Hemingway and Faulkner*, 200–202, 203.

Reivers (1962)

Broughton, Panthea Reid. *William Faulkner*, 166–167.

Devlin, Albert J. "*Reivers:* Readings in Social Psychology." *MissQ* 25 (1972): 327–337.

Howe, Irving. *William Faulkner*, 295–300.

Kerr, Elizabeth. "Evolution of Yoknapatawpha." *UMSE* 14 (1974): 56–57.

Mellard, James M. "Faulkner's 'Golden Book': *The Reivers* as Romantic Comedy," in Garvin, Harry R., ed. *Makers of the Twentieth-Century Novel*, 218–227.

Milum, Richard A. "Continuity and Change: The Horse, the Automobile, and the Airplane in Faulkner's Fiction," in Cary, Glenn O., ed. *Faulkner, The Unappeased Imagination*, 159, 163, 164–165, 167–168, 168–169.

Nelson, Erik C. "Faulkner's Noble Prince." *ArQ* 35 (1979): 129–134.

Rossky, William. "*Reivers:* Faulkner's *Tempest*." *Mississippi Quarterly* (Spring 1965): 82–93. Rpt. in Wagner, Linda Welshimer, ed. *William Faulkner*, 358–368.

Wagner, Linda Welshimer. *Hemingway and Faulkner*, 224–228.

Williams, David. *Faulkner's Women*, 227–241.

Requiem for a Nun (1951)

Beja, Morris. *Epiphany in the Modern Novel*, 208–209.

Broughton, Panthea R. "*Requiem for a Nun:* No Part in Rationality." *SoR* 8 (1972): 749–762.

Broughton, Panthea Reid. *William Faulkner*, 199–201, 205–207.

Carey, Glenn O. "William Faulkner: Man's Fatal Vice." *ArQ* 28 (1972): 294.
Culley, Margaret M. "Judgment in Yoknapatawpha Fiction." *Renascence* 28 (1976): 66–68.
Howe, Irving. *William Faulkner*, 105–107, 132–133.
Kerr, Elizabeth. "Evolution of Yoknapatawpha." *UMSE* 14 (1974): 26.
Millgate, Michael. "Faulkner and History," in Harrington, Evans and Ann J. Abadie, eds. *South and Faulkner's Yoknapatawpha*, 31–34.
Powers, Lyall H. *Faulkner's Yoknapatawpha Comedy*, 204–217.
Ruppersburg, Hugh Michael. "Narrative Structure of Faulkner's *Requiem for a Nun*." *MissQ* 31 (1978): 387–406.
Seyppel, Joachim. *William Faulkner*, 85–87.
Tallack, Douglas G. "William Faulkner and the Tradition of the Tough-Guy Detective," in Landrum, Larry N., Pat Browne and Ray B. Browne, eds. *Dimensions of Detective Fiction*, 260–261.

Sanctuary (1931)

Beja, Morris. *Epiphany in the Modern Novel*, 189–190.
Brown, Calvin S. "*Sanctuary:* From Confrontation to Peaceful Void." *Mosaic* 7.1 (1973): 75–95.
Castille, Philip. " 'There Was a Queen' and Faulkner's Narcissa Sartoris." *MissQ* 28 (1975): 309–311.
Cook, Richard M. "Popeye, Flem, and Sutpen: The Faulknerian Villain as Grotesque." *SAF* 3 (1975): 7–9.
Cook, Sylvia Jenkins. *From Tobacco Road to Route 66*, 47–50.
Creighton, Joanne V. "Self-Destructive Evil in *Sanctuary*." *TCL* 18 (1972): 259–270.
Esslinger, Pat M. "No Spinach in *Sanctuary*." *MFS* 18 (1972–73): 555–558.
Ford, Daniel G. "Comments on William Faulkner's Temporal Vision in *Sanctuary, The Sound and the Fury, Light in August, Absalom, Absalom!*" *SoQ* 15 (1977): 283–290.
Gallagher, Susan. "To Love and to Honor: Brothers and Sisters in Faulkner's Yoknapatawpha County." *ELWIU* 7 (1980): 216–217, 221–222.
Gidley, Mark. "Elements of the Detective Story in William Faulkner's Fiction." *JPC* 7 (1973): 99–101.
Gidley, Mick. "Elements of the Detective Story in William Faulkner's Fiction," in Landrum, Larry N., Pat Browne and Ray B. Browne, eds. *Dimensions of Detective Fiction*, 230–231.
Guerard, Albert J. *Triumph of the Novel*, 120–135.
Hardt, John S. "And Faulkner Nodded: Calvin Coolidge in *Sanctuary*." *NMW* 12 (1979): 30–31.
Howe, Irving. *William Faulkner*, 56–61, 192–199.
Hurd, Myles. "Faulkner's Horace Benbow: The Burden of Characterization and the Confusion of Meaning in *Sanctuary*." *CLAJ* 23 (1980): 416–430.
Kauffman, Linda. "Madam and the Midwife: Reba Rivers and Sairey Gamp." *MissQ* 30 (1977): 395–401.
Kerr, Elizabeth. "Evolution of Yoknapatawpha." *UMSE* 14 (1974): 26–28.
Kerr, Elizabeth M. *William Faulkner's Gothic Domain*, 88–106.
Lawson, Lewis A. "William Faulkner," in Panichas, George A., ed. *Politics of Twentieth-Century Novelists*, 284–286.
Lehan, Richard. *Dangerous Crossing*, 73, 75.

Miller, James E., Jr. *"Sanctuary:* Yoknapatawpha's Waste Land," in Baldwin, Kenneth H. and David R. Kirby, eds. *Individual and Community: Variations on a Theme in American Fiction,* 137–159.

Ousby, Ian. *Reader's Guide to Fifty American Novels,* 295–297.

Perry, J. Douglas, Jr. "Gothic as Vortex: The Form of Horror in Capote, Faulkner, and Styron." *MFS* 19 (1973): 159–162.

Petesch, Donald A. "Temple Drake: Faulkner's Mirror for the Social Order." *SAF* 7 (1979): 38–46.

Powers, Lyall H. *Faulkner's Yoknapatawpha Comedy,* 73–88.

Seyppel, Joachim. *William Faulkner,* 52–54.

Spiegel, Alan. *Fiction and the Camera Eye,* 153–156.

Tallack, Douglas G. "William Faulkner and the Tradition of the Tough-Guy Detective," in Landrum, Larry N., Pat Browne and Ray B. Browne, eds. *Dimensions of Detective Fiction,* 250–252, 253, 258–259, 260, 262–264.

Toles, George. "Space Between: A Study of Faulkner's *Sanctuary." TSLL* 22 (1980): 22–47.

Wagner, Linda Welshimer. "Faulkner and (Southern) Women," in Harrington, Evans and Ann J. Abadie, eds. *South and Faulkner's Yoknapatawpha,* 135, 137–138.

Wagner, Linda Welshimer. *Hemingway and Faulkner,* 199–200, 202.

Watkins, Floyd C. "Word and Deed in Faulkner's First Great Novels," in Watkins, Floyd C. *Flesh and the Word: Eliot, Hemingway, Faulkner.* Vanderbilt University Press, 1971. 181–202. Rpt. in Wagner, Linda Welshimer, ed. *William Faulkner,* 213–229.

Weinstein, Philip M. "Precarious Sanctuaries: Protection and Exposure in Faulkner's Fiction." *SAF* 6 (1978): 177–181.

Williams, David. *Faulkner's Women,* 127–156.

Yonce, Margaret. " 'His True Penelope was Flaubert': *Madame Bovary* and *Sanctuary." MissQ* 29 (1976): 439–442.

Sartoris (1929)

Aaron, Daniel. *Unwritten War,* 319–321.

Adamowski, T. H. "Bayard Sartoris: Mourning and Melancholia." *L&P* 23 (1973): 149–157.

Beja, Morris. *Epiphany in the Modern Novel,* 194.

Blotner, Joseph. "Romantic Elements in Faulkner," in Bornstein, George, ed. *Romantic and Modern,* 215–219.

Gallagher, Susan. "To Love and to Honor: Brothers and Sisters in Faulkner's Yoknapatawpha County." *ELWIU* 7 (1980): 216.

Gray, Richard. *Literature of Memory,* 231–237.

Harley, Marta Powell. "Faulkner's *Sartoris* and the Legend of Rinaldo and Bayard." *ANQ* 18 (1980): 92–93.

Howe, Irving. *William Faulkner,* 33–41, 122–123.

Jehlen, Myra. *Class and Character in Faulkner's South,* 26–41.

Kerr, Elizabeth. "Evolution of Yoknapatawpha." *UMSE* 14 (1974): 24–26.

Kerr, Elizabeth M. *William Faulkner's Gothic Domain,* 74–87.

Lawson, Lewis A. "William Faulkner," in Panichas, George A., ed. *Politics of Twentieth-Century Novelists,* 281–283.

MacKethan, Lucinda Hardwick. *Dream of Arcady,* 157–158, 159–163.

Miller, William. "Hardy, Falls, and Faulkner." *MissQ* 29 (1976): 435–436.

Milum, Richard A. "Continuity and Change: The Horse, the Automobile, and the

Airplane in Faulkner's Fiction," in Cary, Glenn O., ed. *Faulkner, The Unappeased Imagination*, 159, 163, 165–166, 167, 169–170.

Polek, Fran. "Tick-tocks, Whirs, and Broken Gears: Time and Identity in Faulkner." *Renascence* 29 (1977): 195.

Powers, Lyall H. *Faulkner's Yoknapatawpha Comedy*, 9–23.

Seyppel, Joachim. *William Faulkner*, 31–32.

Skaggs, Merrill Maguire. *Folk of Southern Fiction*, 223–224.

Wagner, Linda Welshimer. "Faulkner and (Southern) Women," in Harrington, Evans and Ann J. Abadie, eds. *South and Faulkner's Yoknapatawpha*, 131–132.

Wagner, Linda Welshimer. *Hemingway and Faulkner*, 161–167, 169–172.

Walker, Ronald G. "Death in the Sound of Their Name: Character Motivation in Faulkner's *Sartoris*." *SoHR* 7 (1973): 271–278.

Watson, James Gray. " 'Germ of My Apocrypha': *Sartoris* and the Search for Form." *Mosaic* 7.1 (1973): 15–33.

Williams, David. *Faulkner's Women*, 41–46.

Soldiers' Pay (1926)

Brooks, Cleanth. *William Faulkner*, 67–99.

Carey, Glenn O. "William Faulkner: Man's Fatal Vice." *ArQ* 28 (1972): 294.

Dalgarno, Emily. "*Soldiers' Pay* and Virginia Woolf." *MissQ* 29 (1976): 339–346.

Dalgarno, Emily. "Faulkner and Gibbon: A Note on *Soldiers' Pay*." *NMW* 12 (1979): 36–39.

David, Boyd. "Caddy Compson's Eden." *MissQ* 30 (1977): 383, 386–387.

Flynn, Peggy. "Sister Figure and 'Little Sister Death' in the Fiction of William Faulkner." *UMSE* 14 (1974): 106–108.

Howe, Irving. *William Faulkner*, 120–121.

Hunter, Edwin R. *William Faulkner*, 61–62.

Jehlen, Myra. *Class and Character in Faulkner's South*, 26.

MacMillan, Duane J. " 'Carry on, Cadet': Mores and Morality in *Soldiers' Pay*," in Cary, Glenn O., ed. *Faulkner, The Unappeased Imagination*, 37–55.

Millgate, Michael. "Starting Out in the Twenties: Reflections on *Soldiers' Pay*." *Mosaic* 7.1 (1973): 1–14.

Miller, Wayne Charles. *Armed America, Its Face in Fiction*, 119–121.

Milum, Richard A. "Continuity and Change: The Horse, the Automobile, and the Airplane in Faulkner's Fiction," in Cary, Glenn O., ed. *Faulkner, The Unappeased Imagination*, 170–171.

Seyppel, Joachim. *William Faulkner*, 22–26.

Simpson, Lewis P. "Sex & History: Origins of Faulkner's Apocrypha," in Harrington, Evans and Ann J. Abadie, eds. *Maker and the Myth*, 50–51.

Wagner, Linda Welshimer. "Faulkner and (Southern) Women," in Harrington, Evans and Ann J. Abadie, eds. *South and Faulkner's Yoknapatawpha*, 129–130.

Wagner, Linda Welshimer. *Hemingway and Faulkner*, 154–159.

Williams, David. *Faulkner's Women*, 36–41.

Sound and the Fury (1929)

Beja, Morris. *Epiphany in the Modern Novel*, 184–189, 192–193.

Benson, Jackson J. "Quentin's Responsibility for Caddy's Downfall in Faulkner's *The Sound and the Fury*." *NMW* 5 (1972): 63–64.

Blanchard, Margaret. "Rhetoric of Communion: Voice in *The Sound and the Fury*." *AL* 41 (1970): 555–565.

Bleikasten, André. *Most Splendid Failure: Faulkner's The Sound and the Fury.* Bloomington, IN: Indiana University Press, 1976.

Bridges, Jean Bolen. "Similarities between 'The Waste Land' and *The Sound and the Fury.*" *NConL* 7.1 (1977): 10–13.

Broughton, Panthea Reid. *William Faulkner*, 92–93, 112–117, 188–191.

Brown, May Cameron. "Language of Chaos: Quentin Compson in *The Sound and the Fury.*" *AL* 51 (1980): 544–553.

Caserio, Robert L. *Plot, Story, and the Novel*, 274–279.

Chappell, Fred. "Comic Structure of *The Sound and the Fury.*" *MissQ* 31 (1978): 381–386.

Clark, Edward D., Sr. "Private Truth in *The Sound and the Fury.*" *CLAJ* 19 (1976): 513–523.

Cohn, Dorrit. *Transparent Minds*, 247–255.

Coindreau, Maurice Edgar. *Time of William Faulkner*, 41–50.

Cowley, Malcolm. "Dilsey and the Compsons." *UMSE* 14 (1974): 79–88.

David, Boyd. "Caddy Compson's Eden." *MissQ* 30 (1977): 383, 387–394.

Davis, Thadious M. "Other Family and Luster in *The Sound and the Fury.*" *CLAJ* 20 (1976): 245–261.

Davis, William V. "June 2, 1928: Further Thoughts on Time in *The Sound and the Fury.*" *NMW* 11 (1979): 84–85.

Davis, William V. "Quentin's Death Ritual: Further Christian Allusions in *The Sound and the Fury.*" *NMW* 6 (1973): 27–32.

Donald, Miles. *American Novel in the Twentieth Century*, 83–87.

Dukes, Thomas. "Christianity as Curse and Salvation in *The Sound and the Fury.*" *ArQ* 35 (1979): 170–182.

Flynn, Peggy. "Sister Figure and 'Little Sister Death' in the Fiction of William Faulkner." *UMSE* 14 (1974): 108–112.

Ford, Daniel G. "Comments on William Faulkner's Temporal Vision in *Sanctuary, The Sound and the Fury, Light in August, Absalom, Absalom!*" *SoQ* 15 (1977): 283–290.

Gray, Richard. *Literature of Memory*, 198–199.

Groden, Michael. "Criticism in New Composition: *Ulysses* and *The Sound and the Fury.*" *TCL* 21 (1975): 265–277.

Handy, William J. "*Sound and the Fury:* A Formalist Approach." *NDQ* 44.3 (1976): 71–83.

Hays, Peter L. *Limping Hero*, 82–83.

Howe, Irving. *William Faulkner*, 46–52, 123–125, 134–137, 157–174.

Hunter, Edwin R. *William Faulkner*, 29–47.

Iser, Wolfgang. *Implied Reader*, 136–152.

Jehlen, Myra. *Class and Character in Faulkner's South*, 41–46, 76–77.

Kartiganer, Donald M. *Fragile Thread*, 3–22.

Kellogg, Jean. *Dark Prophets of Hope*, 126–135.

Kerr, Elizabeth. "Evolution of Yoknapatawpha." *UMSE* 14 (1974): 29–31.

Kerr, Elizabeth M. *William Faulkner's Gothic Domain*, 53–73.

King, Richard H. *Southern Renaissance*, 81–82, 113–119.

Lawson, Lewis A. "William Faulkner," in Panichas, George A., ed. *Politics of Twentieth-Century Novelists*, 283–284.

Lehan, Richard. *Dangerous Crossing*, 74–75.

Longley, John L., Jr. " 'Who Never Had a Sister': A Reading of *The Sound and the Fury.*" *Mosaic* 7.1 (1973): 35–53.

McCormick, John. *Fiction as Knowledge*, 97–100.

MacKethan, Lucinda Hardwick. *Dream of Arcady*, 158–159, 168–170.

Malin, Irving. "American Gothic Images." *Mosaic* 6.3 (1973): 161.

Mallard, William. *Reflection of Theology in Literature*, 163–182.

Mellard, James M. "Caliban as Prospero: Benjy and *The Sound and the Fury.*" *Novel* 3 (1970): 233–248.

Mellard, James M. *Exploded Form*, 54–72.

Mellard, James M. "Jason Compson: Humor, Hostility and the Rhetoric of Aggression." *SoHR* 3 (1969): 259–267.

Minter, David. "Faulkner, Childhood, and the Making of *The Sound and the Fury.*" *AL* 51 (1979): 376–393.

Morrison, Gail Moore. " 'Time, Tide, and Twilight': *Mayday* and Faulkner's Quest toward *The Sound and the Fury.*" *MissQ* 31 (1978): 337–357.

Ousby, Ian. *Reader's Guide to Fifty American Novels*, 285–288.

Pinsker, Sanford. "Squaring the Circle in *The Sound and the Fury*," in Cary, Glenn O., ed. *Faulkner, The Unappeased Imagination*, 115–121.

Polek, Fran. "Tick-tocks, Whirs, and Broken Gears: Time and Identity in Faulkner." *Renascence* 29 (1977): 195–196.

Powers, Lyall H. *Faulkner's Yoknapatawpha Comedy*, 24–49.

Ramsey, Roger. "Faulkner's *The Sound and the Fury.*" *Expl* 30 (1972): Item 70.

Ramsey, Roger. "Light Imagery in *The Sound and the Fury:* April 7, 1928." *JNT* 6 (1976): 41–50.

Ross, Stephen M. "Jason Compson and Sut Lovingood: Southwestern Humor as Stream of Consciousness." *SNNTS* 8 (1976): 278–289.

Ross, Stephen M. " 'Loud World' of Quentin Compson." *SNNTS* 7 (1975): 245–246, 247–256.

Seltzer, Alvin J. *Chaos in the Novel*, 100–102, 113, 116–117.

Seymour, Thom. "Faulkner's *The Sound and the Fury.*" *Expl* 39.1 (1980): 24–25.

Seyppel, Joachim. *William Faulkner*, 42–47.

Simpson, Lewis P. "Sex & History: Origins of Faulkner's Apocrypha," in Harrington, Evans and Ann J. Abadie, eds. *Maker and the Myth*, 62–68.

Slater, Judith. "Quentin's Tunnel Vision: Modes of Perception and Their Stylistic Realization in *The Sound and the Fury.*" *L&P* 27 (1977): 4–15.

Thompson, Lawrance. "Mirror Analogues in *The Sound and the Fury*," in *English Institute Essays, 1952.* New York: Columbia University Press, 1953. 83–106. Rpt. in Wagner, Linda Welshimer, ed. *William Faulkner*, 199–212.

Traschen, Isadore. "Tragic Form of *The Sound and the Fury.*" *SoR* 12 (1976): 798–813.

Tuttleton, James W. " 'Combat in the Erogenous Zone': Women in the American Novel between the Two Wars," in Springer, Marlene, ed. *What Manner of Woman*, 291.

Wagner, Linda W. "Jason Compson: The Demands of Honor." *SewR* 79 (1971): 555–575.

Wagner, Linda Welshimer. "Faulkner and (Southern) Women," in Harrington, Evans and Ann J. Abadie, eds. *South and Faulkner's Yoknapatawpha*, 133–134.

Wagner, Linda Welshimer. *Hemingway and Faulkner*, 140, 175–180, 199.

Wall, Carey. "*Sound and the Fury:* The Emotional Center." *MidQ* 11 (1970): 371–387.

Watkins, Floyd C. "Word and Deed in Faulkner's First Great Novels," in Watkins, Floyd C. *Flesh and the Word: Eliot, Hemingway, Faulkner.* Vanderbilt University Press, 1971. 181–202. Rpt. in Wagner, Linda Welshimer, ed. *William Faulkner,* 213–229.

Weinstein, Arnold L. *Vision and Response in Modern Fiction,* 111–135.

Weinstein, Philip M. "Precarious Sanctuaries: Protection and Exposure in Faulkner's Fiction." *SAF* 6 (1978): 177.

Welty, Eudora. "Some Notes on Time in Fiction." *MissQ* 26 (1973): 488–492.

Williams, David. *Faulkner's Women,* 61–95.

Town (1957)

Arpad, Joseph J. "William Faulkner's Legendary Novels: The Snopes Trilogy." *MissQ* 22.3 (1969): 216–225.

Broughton, Panthea Reid. *William Faulkner,* 69–70, 193.

Cook, Richard M. "Popeye, Flem, and Sutpen: The Faulknerian Villain as Grotesque." *SAF* 3 (1975): 6–7.

Edwards, Duane. "Flem Snopes and Thomas Sutpen: Two Versions of Respectability." *DR* 51 (1971–72): 559–570.

Flynn, Peggy. "Sister Figure and 'Little Sister Death' in the Fiction of William Faulkner." *UMSE* 14 (1974): 114–116.

Friedman, Alan W. *Multivalence,* 143–177.

Hauck, Richard Boyd. *Cheerful Nihilism,* 187–191.

Howe, Irving. *William Faulkner,* 107–110, 282–294.

Jehlen, Myra. *Class and Character in Faulkner's South,* 133, 134, 136, 150–151, 157–159, 161, 162, 163.

Kerr, Elizabeth. "Evolution of Yoknapatawpha." *UMSE* 14 (1974): 48–51.

Kerr, Elizabeth M. *William Faulkner's Gothic Domain,* 186–219.

Leaf, Mark. "William Faulkner's Snopes Trilogy: The South Evolves," in French, Warren, ed. *Fifties,* 53–62.

McFarland, Holly. "Mask Not Tragic . . . Just Damned: The Women in Faulkner's Trilogy." *BallS* 18.2 (1977): 35–41,

Moses, Edwin. "Comedy in *The Town,*" in Cary, Glenn O., ed. *Faulkner, The Unappeased Imagination,* 59–71.

Norris, Nancy. "*Hamlet, The Town,* and *The Mansion:* A Psychological Reading of the Snopes Trilogy." *Mosaic* 7.1 (1973): 213–235.

Payne, Ladell. "Trilogy: Faulkner's Comic Epic in Prose." *SNNTS* 1.1 (1969): 31–36.

Powers, Lyall H. *Faulkner's Yoknapatawpha Comedy,* 218–232.

Rankin, Elizabeth D. "Chasing Spotted Horses: The Quest for Human Dignity in Faulkner's Snopes Trilogy," in Cary, Glenn O., ed. *Faulkner, The Unappeased Imagination,* 139–154.

Skaggs, Merrill Maguire. *Folk of Southern Fiction,* 229–231.

Stroble, Woodrow. "Flem Snopes: A Crazed Mirror," in Cary, Glenn O., ed. *Faulkner, The Unappeased Imagination,* 198, 204–205.

Sullivan, Walter. *Death by Melancholy,* 7–9.

Turner, Darwin T. "Faulkner and Slavery," in Harrington, Evans and Ann J. Abadie, eds. *South and Faulkner's Yoknapatawpha,* 82.

Wagner, Linda Welshimer. *Hemingway and Faulkner,* 218–224.

Williams, David. *Faulkner's Women,* 214–221.

Wilson, Raymond J., III. "Imitative Flem Snopes and Faulkner's Causal Sequence in *The Town.*" *TCL* 26 (1980): 432–444.

Unvanquished (1938)

Aaron, Daniel. *Unwritten War*, 317–318, 321–322.

Akin, Warren, IV. " 'Blood and Raising and Background': The Plot of *The Unvanquished.*" *MLS* 11.1 (1980–81): 3–11.

Beauchamp, Gorman. "*Unvanquished:* Faulkner's *Oresteia.*" *MissQ* 23.3 (1970): 273–277.

Beauchamp, Gorman. "*Unvanquished:* Faulkner's *Oresteia.*" *Mississippi Quarterly* 23.3 (Summer 1970): 273–277. Rpt. in Wagner, Linda Welshimer, ed. *William Faulkner*, 298–302.

Bennett, Lee Shaw. "Modern Civil War Novels: The Still Unwritten War?" *SoS* 19 (1980): 118–121.

Bradford, M. E. "Faulkner's *The Unvanquished:* The High Costs of Survival." *SoR* 14 (1978): 428–437.

Gray, Richard. *Literature of Memory*, 208.

Haynes, Jane Isbell. "Faulkner's Verbena." *MissQ* 33 (1980): 355–362.

Howe, Irving. *William Faulkner*, 41–45, 121–122.

Jehlen, Myra. *Class and Character in Faulkner's South*, 47–51.

Memmott, A. James. "Sartoris Ludens: The Play Element in *The Unvanquished.*" *MissQ* 29 (1976): 375–387.

Milum, Richard A. "Continuity and Change: The Horse, the Automobile, and the Airplane in Faulkner's Fiction," in Cary, Glenn O., ed. *Faulkner, The Unappeased Imagination*, 159–161, 162.

Milum, Richard A. "Faulkner, Scott, and Another Source for Drusilla." *MissQ* 31 (1978): 425–428.

Powers, Lyall H. *Faulkner's Yoknapatawpha Comedy*, 125–141.

Pryse, Marjorie. "Miniaturizing Yoknapatawpha: *The Unvanquished* as Faulkner's Theory of Realism." *MissQ* 33 (1980): 343–354.

Roberts, John J. and Scott, R. Leon, Jr. "*Unvanquished.*" *Expl* 34 (1976): Item 49.

Scott, R. Leon, Jr. and John J. Roberts. "Faulkner's *The Unvanquished.*" *Expl* 35.2 (1976): 3–4.

Seyppel, Joachim. *William Faulkner*, 68–70.

Sullivan, Walter. *Death by Melancholy*, 81–83.

Sullivan, Walter. *Requiem for the Renascence*, 37–41.

Trimmer, Joseph F. "*Unvanquished:* The Teller and the Tale." *BallS* 10.1 (1969): 35–42.

Wagner, Linda Welshimer. "Faulkner and (Southern) Women," in Harrington, Evans and Ann J. Abadie, eds. *South and Faulkner's Yoknapatawpha*, 139–141.

Wagner, Linda Welshimer. *Hemingway and Faulkner*, 205–206.

Williams, David. *Faulkner's Women*, 210–214.

Wild Palms (1939)

Brooks, Cleanth. *William Faulkner*, 205–229.

Broughton, Panthea Reid. *William Faulkner*, 141, 168–172, 183–184.

Coindreau, Maurice Edgar. *Time of William Faulkner*, 51–63.

Colson, Theodore. "Analogues of Faulkner's *The Wild Palms* and Hawthorne's 'The Birthmark'." *DR* 56 (1976): 510–518.

Cushman, William Price. "Knowledge and Involvement in Faulkner's *The Wild Palms*," in Cary, Glenn O., ed. *Faulkner, The Unappeased Imagination*, 25–37.

Howe, Irving. *William Faulkner*, 233–242.

McHaney, Thomas L. "Anderson, Hemingway, and Faulkner's *The Wild Palms*." *PMLA* 87 (1972): 465–474.

Monteiro, George. "Limits of Professionalism: A Sociological Approach to Faulkner, Fitzgerald and Hemingway." *Criticism* 15 (1973): 149–151.

Richards, Lewis. "Sex Under *The Wild Palms* and a Moral Question." *ArQ* 28 (1972): 326–332.

Seyppel, Joachim. *William Faulkner*, 70–71.

Wagner, Linda Welshimer. "Faulkner and (Southern) Women," in Harrington, Evans and Ann J. Abadie, eds. *South and Faulkner's Yoknapatawpha*, 141.

Wagner, Linda Welshimer. *Hemingway and Faulkner*, 204–205.

FAUSET, JESSIE (1882–1961)

Chinaberry Tree (1931)

Christian, Barbara. *Black Women Novelists*, 42, 44–46.

Feeney, Joseph J., S. J. "Sardonic, Unconventional Jessie Fauset: The Double Structure and Double Vision of Her Novels." *CLAJ* 22 (1979): 369–370, 372–382.

Gayle, Addison, Jr. *Way of the New World*, 116.

Sato, Hiroko. "Under the Harlem Shadow: A Study of Jessie Fauset and Nella Larsen," in Bontemps, Arna, ed. *Harlem Renaissance Remembered*, 67, 75–77.

Singh, Amritjit. *Novels of the Harlem Renaissance*, 75.

Comedy: American Style (1933)

Feeney, Joseph J., S. J. "Sardonic, Unconventional Jessie Fauset: The Double Structure and Double Vision of Her Novels." *CLAJ* 22 (1979): 370–371, 372–382.

Sato, Hiroko. "Under the Harlem Shadow: A Study of Jessie Fauset and Nella Larsen," in Bontemps, Arna, ed. *Harlem Renaissance Remembered*, 77–79.

Singh, Amritjit. *Novels of the Harlem Renaissance*, 75–76.

Plum Bun (1928)

Feeney, Joseph J., S. J. "Sardonic, Unconventional Jessie Fauset: The Double Structure and Double Vision of Her Novels." *CLAJ* 22 (1979): 368–369, 372–382.

Gayle, Addison, Jr. *Way of the New World*, 120–122.

Sato, Hiroko. "Under the Harlem Shadow: A Study of Jessie Fauset and Nella Larsen," in Bontemps, Arna, ed. *Harlem Renaissance Remembered*, 72–75.

Singh, Amritjit. *Novels of the Harlem Renaissance*, 93–94, 95–98.

There Is Confusion (1924)

Gayle, Addison, Jr. *Way of the New World*, 116–119.

Sato, Hiroko. "Under the Harlem Shadow: A Study of Jessie Fauset and Nella Larsen," in Bontemps, Arna, ed. *Harlem Renaissance Remembered*, 70–72.

Singh, Amritjit. *Novels of the Harlem Renaissance*, 74–75.

FAUST, IRVIN (1924–)

Steagle (1967)

Kostelanetz, Richard. "American Fiction in the Sixties," in Kostelanetz, Richard, ed. *On Contemporary Literature*, 644–646.

FAWCETT, EDGAR (1847–1904)

Ambitious Woman (1884)
 Harrison, Stanley R. *Edgar Fawcett*, 63–66.
American Push (1892)
 Harrison, Stanley R. *Edgar Fawcett*, 85–87.
Confessions of Claud (1887)
 Harrison, Stanley R. *Edgar Fawcett*, 70–73.
Mild Barbarian (1894)
 Harrison, Stanley R. *Edgar Fawcett*, 66–69.

FERGUSSON, HARVEY (1890–1971)

Capitol Hill (1923)
 Pilkington, William T. *Harvey Fergusson*, 46–55.
Conquest of Don Pedro (1954)
 Pilkington, William T. *Harvey Fergusson*, 132–138.
Footloose McGarnigal (1930)
 Pilkington, William T. *Harvey Fergusson*, 87–93.
Grant of Kingdom (1950)
 Pilkington, William T. *Harvey Fergusson*, 124–132.
Life of Riley (1937)
 Pilkington, William T. *Harvey Fergusson*, 93–100.
Wolf Song (1927)
 Pilkington, William T. *Harvey Fergusson*, 111–116.
Women and Wives (1924)
 Pilkington, William T. *Harvey Fergusson*, 55–62.

FERN, FANNY (1811–1872)

Rose Clark (1856)
 Baym, Nina. *Woman's Fiction*, 253–255.
Ruth Hall (1855)
 Baym, Nina. *Woman's Fiction*, 252–253.

FERRON, JACQUES (1921–1985)

Le Saint-Élias (1972)
 Poulin, Gabrielle. *Romans du pays*, 42–44.

FINLEY, MARTHA (1828–1909)

Elsie Dinsmore (1896)
 Jackson, Jacqueline and Philip Kendall. "What Makes a Bad Book Good: *Elsie Dinsmore*." *ChildL* 7 (1978): 45–64.

FISHER, DOROTHY CANFIELD (1879–1958)

Brimming Cup (1919)

Baker, Donald G. "Black Images: The Afro-American in Popular Novels, 1900–1945." *JPC* 7 (1973): 335.

FISHER, RUDOLPH (1897–1934)

Walls of Jericho (1928)

Berzon, Judith R. *Neither White Nor Black*, 65–68.
Davis, Arthur P. *From the Dark Tower*, 101–102.
Gayle, Addison, Jr. *Way of the New World*, 136–138.
Perry, Margaret. *Silence to the Drums*, 64–67.
Singh, Amritjit. *Novels of the Harlem Renaissance*, 83–88.

FISHER, VARDIS (1895–1968)

April (1937)

Chatterton, Wayne. *Vardis Fisher*, 25–29.
Milton, John R. "Primitive World of Vardis Fisher: The Idaho Novels." *MidQ* 17 (1976): 369–384.

Children of God (1939)

Chatterton, Wayne. *Vardis Fisher*, 32–34.

City of Illusion (1941)

Chatterton, Wayne. *Vardis Fisher*, 34–36.

Dark Bridwell (1931)

Chatterton, Wayne. *Vardis Fisher*, 15–19.
Milton, John R. "Primitive World of Vardis Fisher: The Idaho Novels." *MidQ* 17 (1976): 369–384.
Milton, John R. "Primitive World of Vardis Fisher: The Idaho Novels." *Midwest Quarterly* 17 (1976): 369–384. Rpt. in Pilkington, William T., ed. *Critical Essays on the Western American Novel*, 132–135.

In Tragic Life (1932)

Chatterton, Wayne. *Vardis Fisher*, 19–22.

Mothers (1943)

Chatterton, Wayne. *Vardis Fisher*, 36–38.

Mountain Man (1965)

Chatterton, Wayne. *Vardis Fisher*, 42–45.
Flora, Joseph M. "Westering Woman: A Thematic Study of Kesey's *One Flew Over the Cuckoo's Nest* and Fisher's *Mountain Man*," in Lee, L. L. and Merrill Lewis, ed. *Women, Women Writers, and the West*, 139–140.
McAllister, Mick. "You Can't Go Home: Jeremiah Johnson and the Wilderness." *WAL* 13 (1978): 35–49.

Orphans in Gethsemane (1960)

Chatterton, Wayne. *Vardis Fisher*, 22–24.

Pemmican (1956)

Chatterton, Wayne. *Vardis Fisher*, 39–40.

Tale of Valor (1958)

Chatterton, Wayne. *Vardis Fisher*, 40–42.

Milton, John R. "Primitive World of Vardis Fisher: The Idaho Novels." *MidQ* 17 (1976): 369–384.

Toilers of the Hills (1928)

Chatterton, Wayne. *Vardis Fisher*, 12–15.

Milton, John R. "Primitive World of Vardis Fisher: The Idaho Novels." *MidQ* 17 (1976): 369–384.

We Are Betrayed (1935)

Milton, John R. "Primitive World of Vardis Fisher: The Idaho Novels." *MidQ* 17 (1976): 369–384.

FITZGERALD, F. SCOTT (1896–1940)

Beautiful and the Damned (1922)

Arnold, Edwin T. "Motion Picture as Metaphor in the Works of F. Scott Fitzgerald." *F-H Annual* (1977): 46–49.

Bennett, Warren. "Prefigurations of Gatsby, Eckleburg, Owl Eyes, and Klipspringer." *F-H Annual* (1979): 219–220.

Donald, Miles. *American Novel in the Twentieth Century*, 14, 15.

Eble, Kenneth. *F. Scott Fitzgerald*, 70–75.

Fahey, William A. *F. Scott Fitzgerald and the American Dream*, 50–63.

Ferguson, Robert A. "Grotesque in the Novels of F. Scott Fitzgerald." *SAQ* 78 (1979): 461, 464, 465–466.

Gallo, Rose Adrienne. *F. Scott Fitzgerald*, 24–34.

Gindin, James. "Gods and Fathers in F. Scott Fitzgerald's Novels." *MLQ* 30 (1969): 67–71.

Gindin, James. *Harvest of a Quiet Eye*, 241–244.

Hunt, Jan and John M. Suarez. "Evasion of Adult Love in Fitzgerald's Fiction." *CentR* 17 (1973): 161–162, 163–165.

Long, Robert Emmet. *Achieving of The Great Gatsby*, 40–60.

Perosa, Sergio. *"Beautiful and the Damned,"* in Perosa, Sergio. *Art of F. Scott Fitzgerald*. Ann Arbor, MI: University of Michigan Press, 1965. Rpt. in Eble, Kenneth, ed. *F. Scott Fitzgerald: A Collection of Criticism*, 48–59.

Stavola, Thomas J. *Scott Fitzgerald*, 107–123.

Tuttleton, James W. " 'Combat in the Erogenous Zone': Women in the American Novel between the Two Wars," in Springer, Marlene, ed. *What Manner of Woman*, 280.

Wasserstrom, William. "Goad of Guilt: Henry Adams, Scott and Zelda." *JML* 6 (1977): 297–298.

Way, Brian. *F. Scott Fitzgerald and the Art of Social Fiction*, 64–67.

Westbrook, Wayne W. "Portait of a Dandy in *The Beautiful and Damned*." *F-H Annual* (1979): 147–149.

Wilson, Robert N. *Writer as Social Seer*, 20–21, 32.

Great Gatsby (1925)

Alderman, Taylor. "Begetting of Gatsby." *MFS* 19 (1973–74): 563–565.

Aldridge, John W. *Devil in the Fire*, 101–105.

Allen, Walter. *Urgent West*, 9–11.

Barbour, Brian M. "*Great Gatsby* and the American Past." *SoR* 9 (1973): 288–299.

Bennett, Warren. "Prefigurations of Gatsby, Eckleburg, Owl Eyes, and Klip-springer." *F-H Annual* (1979): 207–221.

Bicknell, John W. "Waste Land of F. Scott Fitzgerald." *Virginia Quarterly Review* 30 (Autumn 1954): 556–572. Rpt. in Eble, Kenneth, ed. *F. Scott Fitzgerald: A Collection of Criticism*, 67–73.

Bigsby, C. W. E. "Two Identities of F. Scott Fitzgerald," in Bradbury, Malcolm and David Palmer, eds. *American Novel in the Nineteen Twenties*, 133–137.

Bird, Christine M. and Thomas L. McHaney. "*Great Gatsby* and *The Golden Bough*." *ArQ* 34 (1978): 125–131.

Blake, Nelson Manfred. *Novelists' America*, 66–70.

Bordewyck, Gordon. "Gatsby: The Figure of the Host." *ANQ* 17 (1979): 141–143.

Bremer, Sidney H. "American Dreams and American Cities in Three Post-World War I Novels." *SAQ* 79 (1980): 278–281.

Brooks, Cleanth. "American 'Innocence': in James, Fitzgerald, and Faulkner." *Shenandoah: The Washington and Lee University Review* 16 (Autumn 1964): 21–37. Rpt. in Stafford, William T., comp. *Merrill Studies in The American*, 111–126.

Bufkin, E. C. "Pattern of Parallel and Double: The Function of Myrtle in *The Great Gatsby*." *MFS* 15 (1969): 517–524.

Burhans, Clinton S., Jr. "Jay Gatsby and Dr. Diver: Fitgerald's Songs of Innocence and Experience," in Garvin, Harry R., ed. *Makers of the Twentieth-Century Novel*, 228–234, 243–244.

Cass, Colin S. " 'Pandered in Whispers': Narrative Reliability in *The Great Gatsby*." *CollL* 7 (1980): 113–124.

Cowley, Malcolm. "Romance of Money," in Fitzgerald, F. Scott. *Three Novels of F. Scott Fitzgerald*. Ed. Malcolm Cowley. New York: Charles Scribner's Sons, 1953. Rpt. in Piper, Henry Dan, ed. *Fitzgerald's The Great Gatsby*, 133–140.

Craig, David and Michael Egan. *Extreme Situations*, 128–129, 132.

Dessner, Lawrence Jay. "Photography and *The Great Gatsby*." *ELWIU* 6 (1979): 79–89.

Donald, Miles. *American Novel in the Twentieth Century*, 16–27.

Doyno, Victor A. "Patterns in *The Great Gatsby*." *Modern Fiction Studies* 12 (Winter 1966–67): 415–426. Rpt. in Piper, Henry Dan, ed. *Fitzgerald's The Great Gatsby*, 160–167.

Eble, Kenneth. *F. Scott Fitzgerald*, 88–99.

Ellis, James. "Shadow-Figure behind *The Great Gatsby:* James, Duke of Monmouth ." *F-H Annual* (1978): 171–174.

Elmore, A. E. "Color and Cosmos in *The Great Gatsby*." *SewR* 78 (1970): 427–443.

Fahey, William A. *F. Scott Fitzgerald and the American Dream*, 69–88.

Ferguson, Robert A. "Grotesque in the Novels of F. Scott Fitzgerald." *SAQ* 78 (1979): 462, 466–467, 468, 473–475.

Fetterley, Judith. *Resisting Reader*, 72–100.

Flahiff, F. T. "*The Great Gatsby:* Scott Fitzgerald's Chaucerian Rag," in Bessai, Diane and David Jackel, eds. *Figures in a Ground*, 87–98.

Gallo, Rose Adrienne. *F. Scott Fitzgerald*, 35–56.

Gindin, James. "Gods and Fathers in F. Scott Fitzgerald's Novels." *MLQ* 30 (1969): 71–74.

Gindin, James. *Harvest of a Quiet Eye*, 244–246.

Graham, D. B. "Fitzgerald's Valley of Ashes and Frank Norris' 'Sordid and Grimy Wilderness'." *F-H Annual* (1972): 304–305.

Grant, Mary Kathryn, R.S.M. "Search for Celebration in *The Sun Also Rises* and *The Great Gatsby*." *ArQ* 33 (1977): 190–192.

Gross, Barry. "Back West: Time and Place in *The Great Gatsby*." *WAL* 8 (1973): 3–13.

Gross, Dalton H. "Death of Rosy Rosenthal: A Note on Fitzgerald's Use of Background in *The Great Gatsby*." *N&Q* 23 (1976): 22–23.

Hampton, Riley V. "Owl Eyes in *The Great Gatsby*." *AL* 48 (1976): 229.

Hearn, Charles R. *American Dream in the Great Depression*, 43–46.

Hunt, Jan and John M. Suarez. "Evasion of Adult Love in Fitzgerald's Fiction." *CentR* 17 (1973): 155, 160–161, 163–165.

Johnson, Richard. "Eyes of Dr. T.J. Eckleburg Re-Examined." *ANQ* 9 (1970): 20–21.

Jones, Daryl E. "Fitzgerald and Pulp Fiction: From Diamond Dick to Gatsby." *F-H Annual* (1978): 137–139.

Kenner, Hugh. *Homemade World*, 23–28, 29–31, 35–44.

Klinkowitz, Jerome. *Practice of Fiction in America*, 49–54.

Korenman, Joan S. " 'Only Her Hairdresser . . .': Another Look at Daisy Buchanan." *AL* 46 (1975): 574–578.

Kruse, Horst H. " 'Gatsby' and 'Gadsby'." *MFS* 15 (1969): 539–541.

Kuehl, John. "Scott Fitzgerald: Romantic and Realist." *Texas Studies in Literature and Language* 1 (Autumn 1959). Rpt. in LaHood, Marvin J., ed. *Tender Is the Night*, 2–8.

Kuhnle, John H. "*Great Gatsby* as Pastoral Elegy." *F-H Annual* (1978): 141–154.

LaHurd, Ryan. " 'Absolution': Gatsby's Forgotten Front Door." *CollL* 3 (1976): 113–123.

Laird, David. "Versions of Eden: The Automobile and the American Novel." *MQR* 19–20 (1980–81): 643–648.

Landor, M. "Gift of Hope," in Proffer, Carl R., ed. and trans. *Soviet Criticism of American Literature in the Sixties*, 111–114.

Langman, F. H. "Style and Shape in *The Great Gatsby*." *SoR* 6 (1973): 48–67.

Lawry, J. S. "Green Light or Square of Light in *The Great Gatsby*." *DR* 55 (1975): 114–132.

Lehan, Richard. "F. Scott Fitzgerald and Romantic Destiny." *TCL* 26 (1980): 140–145, 154.

Lehan, Richard. "Focus on F. Scott Fitzgerald's *The Great Gatsby:* The Nowhere Hero," in Madden, David, ed. *American Dreams, American Nightmares*, 106–114.

Lhamon, W. T., Jr. "Essential Houses of The Great Gatsby." *MarkR* 6 (1977): 56–60.

Long, Robert. "Allusion to Gilda Gray in *The Great Gatsby*." *F-H Annual* (1972): 307–309.

Long, Robert Emmet. *Achieving of The Great Gatsby*, 79–184.

MacPhee, Laurence E. "*Great Gatsby*'s 'Romance of Motoring': Nick Carraway and Jordan Baker." *MFS* 18 (1972): 207–212.

Martin, Robert A. "Gatsby's 'Good Night' in Chapter III of *The Great Gatsby*." *CEA* 39.4 (1977): 12–16.

Michelson, Bruce. "Myth of Gatsby." *MFS* 26 (1980–81): 563–577.

Millard, G. C. "F. Scott Fitzgerald: *The Great Gatsby, Tender Is the Night, The Last Tycoon*." *English Studies in Africa* 8 (March 1965). Rpt. in LaHood, Marvin J., ed. *Tender Is the Night*, 20–32.

Milne, Gordon. *Sense of Society*, 215–218.

Mizener, Arthur. "*The Great Gatsby*," in Mizener, Arthur. *Far Side of Paradise: A Biography of F. Scott Fitzgerald*. Revised Edition. New York: Houghton Mifflin Co., 1959. 185–194. Rpt. in Piper, Henry Dan, ed. *Fitzgerald's The Great Gatsby*, 128–132.

Monteiro, George. "James Gatz and John Keats." *F-H Annual* (1972): 291–294.

Moses, Edwin. "Tragic Inevitability in *The Great Gatsby*." *CLAJ* 21 (1977): 51–57.

Moyer, Kermit W., II. "*Great Gatsby:* Fitzgerald's Meditation on American History." *F-H Annual* (1972): 43–57.

Nicholas, Charles A. "G-G-*Great Gatsby*." *CEA* 38.2 (1976): 8–10.

Ornstein, Robert. "Scott Fitzgerald's Fable of East and West." *College English* 18 (Dec 1956): 139–143. Rpt. in Eble, Kenneth, ed. *F. Scott Fitzgerald: A Collection of Criticism*, 60–66.

Ousby, Ian. *Reader's Guide to Fifty American Novels*, 218–221.

Ower, John. "Thematic Reference to *The Rubaiyat of Omar Khayyam* in *The Great Gatsby*." *F-H Annual* (1975): 103–105.

Parker, David. "*Great Gatsby:* Two Versions of the Hero.' *ES* 54 (1973): 37–51.

Person, Leland S., Jr " 'Herstory' and Daisy Buchanan." *AL* 50 (1978): 250–257.

Pinsker, Sanford. "Seeing *The Great Gatsby* Eye to Eye." *CollL* 3 (1976): 69–71.

Piper, Henry Dan. "Untrimmed Christmas Tree: The Religious Background of *The Great Gatsby*," in Piper, Henry Dan, ed. *Fitzgerald's The Great Gatsby*, 93–100.

Podis, Leonard A. "Fitzgerald's *The Great Gatsby*." *Expl* 38.4 (1980): 10–11.

Pottorf, Michael. "*Great Gatsby:* Myrtle's Dog and Its Relation to the Dog-God of Pound and Eliot." *ANQ* 14 (1976): 88–90.

Prigozy, Ruth. "Gatsby's Guest List and Fitzgerald's Technique of Naming." *F-H Annual* (1972): 99–112.

Raleigh, John Henry. "F. Scott Fitzgerald's *The Great Gatsby:* Legendary Bases and Allegorical Significances." *University of Kansas City Review* 24 (October 1957): 55–58. Rpt. in Piper, Henry Dan, ed. *Fitzgerald's The Great Gatsby*, 141–144.

Randall, John H., III. "Jay Gatsby's Hidden Source of Wealth." *Modern Fiction Studies* 13 (Autumn 1967): 247–257. Rpt. in Piper, Henry Dan, ed. *Fitzgerald's The Great Gatsby*, 190–197.

Rose, Alan H. "Sin and the City: The Uses of Disorder in the Urban Novel." *CentR* 16 (1972): 214–217.

Roulston, Robert. "Tom Buchanan: Patrician in Motley." *ArQ* 34 (1978): 101–111.

Roulston, Robert. "Traces of *Tono-Bungay* in *The Great Gatsby*." *JNT* 10 (1980): 68–76.

Samuels, Charles Thomas. "Greatness of 'Gatsby'." *Massachusetts Review* 7 (Autumn 1966): 783–794. Rpt. in Piper, Henry Dan, ed. *Fitzgerald's The Great Gatsby*, 151–159.

Saposnik, Irving S. "Passion and the Life: Technology as Pattern in *The Great Gatsby*." *F-H Annual* (1979): 181–188.

Scanlon, Paul A. "*Great Gatsby:* Romance and Realism." *AntR* 27 (1976): 37–41.

Schneider, Daniel J. "Color Symbolism in *The Great Gatsby.*" *University Review* (formerly *University of Kansas City Review*) 31 (Autumn 1964): 13–18. Rpt. in Piper, Henry Dan, ed. *Fitzgerald's The Great Gatsby*, 145–150.

Schroeder, Chris. "Oculist, the Son, and the Holy Owl Eyes." *ANQ* 18 (1980): 89–90.

Slater, Peter G. "Ethnicity in *The Great Gatsby.*" *TCL* 19 (1973): 53–62.

Spatz, Jonas. "Fitzgerald, Hollywood, and the Myth of Success," in French, Warren, ed. *Thirties*, 33–34.

Stark, Bruce R. "Intricate Pattern in *The Great Gatsby.*" *F-H Annual* (1974): 51–61.

Startsev, A. "Fitzgerald's Bitter Fate," in Proffer, Carl R., ed. and trans. *Soviet Criticism of American Literature in the Sixties*, 102–106.

Stavola, Thomas J. *Scott Fitzgerald*, 125–143.

Steinbrink, Jeffrey. " 'Boats against the Current': Mortality and the Myth of Renewal in *The Great Gatsby.*" *TCL* 26 (1980): 157–170.

Tamke, Alexander R. " 'Gat' in Gatsby: Neglected Aspect of a Novel." *MFS* 14 (1969): 443–445.

Trask, David F. "End of the American Dream." *University Review* (formerly *University of Kansas City Review*) 33 (Spring 1967): 197–202. Rpt. in Piper, Henry Dan, ed. *Fitzgerald's The Great Gatsby*, 213–217.

Trilling, Lionel. "F. Scott Fitzgerald," in Trilling, Lionel. New York: Viking Press, 1950. Rpt. in Rahv, Philip, ed. *Literature in America*, 406–407.

Trouard, Dawn. "Fitzgerald's Missed Moments: Surrealistic Style in His Major Novels." *F-H Annual* (1979): 193, 196–198, 203.

Tuttleton, James W. " 'Combat in the Erogenous Zone': Women in the American Novel between the Two Wars," in Springer, Marlene, ed. *What Manner of Woman*, 281.

Tuttleton, James W. *Novel of Manners in America*, 170–179.

Umphlett, Wiley Lee. *Sporting Myth and the American Experience*, 117.

Wagner, Joseph B. "Gatsby and John Keats: Another Version." *F-H Annual* (1979): 91–98.

Ward, John William. "Dos Passos, Fitzgerald, and History," Ward, John William. *Red, White, and Blue: Men, Books, and Ideas in American Culture*. New York: Oxford University Press, Inc., 1969. 38–47. Rpt. in Hook, Andrew, ed. *Dos Passos*, 120–121.

Wasserstrom, William. "Goad of Guilt: Henry Adams, Scott and Zelda." *JML* 6 (1977): 298–300.

Watkins, Floyd C. "Fitzgerald's Jay Gatz and Young Ben Franklin." *New England Quarterly* 17 (June 1954): 249–252. Rpt. in Piper, Henry Dan, ed. *Fitzgerald's The Great Gatsby*, 201–202.

Way, Brian. *F. Scott Fitzgerald and the Art of Social Fiction*, 98–118.

Whitley, John S. *F. Scott Fitzgerald: The Great Gatsby*. London: Edward Arnold, 1976.

Williams, Harry. "Epistle to Gatsby: On the Use of Riches." *F-H Annual* (1972): 61–65.

Wilson, B. W. "Theatrical Motif in *The Great Gatsby.*" *F-H Annual* (1975): 107–113.

Wilson, Robert N. *Writer as Social Seer*, 18–41.

Last Tycoon (1941)

Arnold, Edwin T. "Motion Picture as Metaphor in the Works of F. Scott Fitzgerald." *F-H Annual* (1977): 57–59.

Bicknell, John W. "Waste Land of F. Scott Fitzgerald." *Virginia Quarterly Review* 30 (Autumn 1954): 556–572. Rpt. in Eble, Kenneth, ed. *F. Scott Fitzgerald: A Collection of Criticism*, 76–79.

Bigsby, C. W. E. "Two Identities of F. Scott Fitzgerald," in Bradbury, Malcolm and David Palmer, eds. *American Novel in the Nineteen Twenties*, 144–147.

Eble, Kenneth. *F. Scott Fitzgerald*, 148–150.

Fahey, William A. *F. Scott Fitzgerald and the American Dream*, 120–134.

Fairey, Wendy. "*Last Tycoon:* The Dilemma of Maturity for F. Scott Fitzgerald." *F-H Annual* (1979): 65–78.

Gallo, Rose Adrienne. *F. Scott Fitzgerald*, 106–124.

Gindin, James. "Gods and Fathers in F. Scott Fitzgerald's Novels." *MLQ* 30 (1969): 80–84.

Gindin, James. *Harvest of a Quiet Eye*, 253–257.

Gross, Barry. "Scott Fitzgerald's *The Last Tycoon:* The Great American Novel?" *ArQ* 26 (1970): 197–216.

Hunt, Jan and John M. Suarez. "Evasion of Adult Love in Fitzgerald's Fiction." *CentR* 17 (1973): 155–156, 163–165.

Kreuter, Kent and Gretchen Kreuter. "Moralism in the Later Fitzgerald." *Modern Fiction Studies* 7 (Spring 1961). Rpt. in LaHood, Marvin J., ed. *Tender Is the Night*, 57–60.

Kuehl, John. "Scott Fitzgerald: Romantic and Realist." *Texas Studies in Literature and Language* 1 (Autumn 1959). Rpt. in LaHood, Marvin J., ed. *Tender Is the Night*, 14–18.

Lehan, Richard. "F. Scott Fitzgerald and Romantic Destiny." *TCL* 26 (1980): 151–153, 155.

Millard, G. C. "F. Scott Fitzgerald: *The Great Gatsby, Tender Is the Night, The Last Tycoon.*" *English Studies in Africa* 8 (March 1965). Rpt. in LaHood, Marvin J., ed. *Tender Is the Night*, 42–46.

Millgate, Michael. "Scott Fitzgerald as Social Novelist: Statement and Technique in *The Last Tycoon.*" *English Studies* 43 (Feb 1962): 29–34. Rpt. as "*Last Tycoon*," in in Eble, Kenneth, ed. *F. Scott Fitzgerald: A Collection of Criticism*, 127–134.

Roulston, Robert. "Whistling 'Dixie' in Encino: *The Last Tycoon* and F. Scott Fitzgerald's Two Souths." *SAQ* 79 (1980): 355–363.

Spatz, Jonas. "Fitzgerald, Hollywood, and the Myth of Success," in French, Warren, ed. *Thirties*, 34–37.

Trouard, Dawn. "Fitzgerald's Missed Moments: Surrealistic Style in His Major Novels." *F-H Annual* (1979): 201–202.

Way, Brian. *F. Scott Fitzgerald and the Art of Social Fiction*, 158–162.

Wells, Walter. *Tycoons and Locusts*, 103–121.

Wilson, Robert N. *Writer as Social Seer*, 18–41.

Tender Is the Night (1934)

Adams, Michael. "Dick Diver and Constance Talmadge." *F-H Annual* (1977): 61.

Arnold, Edwin T. "Motion Picture as Metaphor in the Works of F. Scott Fitzgerald." *F-H Annual* (1977): 53–56.

Bicknell, John W. "Waste Land of F. Scott Fitzgerald." *Virginia Quarterly Review*

30 (Autumn 1954): 556–572. Rpt. in Eble, Kenneth, ed. *F. Scott Fitzgerald: A Collection of Criticism*, 73–75.

Bigsby, C. W. E. "Two Identities of F. Scott Fitzgerald," in Bradbury, Malcolm and David Palmer, eds. *American Novel in the Nineteen Twenties*, 142–144.

Blake, Nelson Manfred. *Novelists' America*, 71–73.

Burhans, Clinton S., Jr. "Jay Gatsby and Dr. Diver: Fitgerald's Songs of Innocence and Experience," in Garvin, Harry R., ed. *Makers of the Twentieth-Century Novel*, 228–229, 234–244.

Deegan, Thomas. "Dick Diver's Childishness in *Tender Is the Night*." *F-H Annual* (1979): 129–133.

DiBattista, Maria. "Aesthetic of Forbearance: Fitzgerald's *Tender Is the Night*." *Novel* 11 (1977): 26–39.

Doherty, William E. "*Tender Is the Night* and The 'Ode to a Nightingale,' " in Reck, Rima Drell, ed. *Explorations of Literature*. Baton Rouge, LA: Louisiana State University Press, 1966. Rpt. in Eble, Kenneth, ed. *F. Scott Fitzgerald: A Collection of Criticism*, 112–126.

Doherty, William E. "*Tender Is the Night* and The 'Ode to a Nightingale,' " in Reck, Rima Drell, ed. *Explorations of Literature*. Baton Rouge, LA: Louisiana State University Press, 1966. Rpt. in LaHood, Marvin J., ed. *Tender Is the Night*, 190–206.

Doughty, Peter. "Seating Arrangement in *Tender Is the Night*." *F-H Annual* (1979): 159–161.

Eble, Kenneth. *F. Scott Fitzgerald*, 137–139.

Ellis, James. "Fitzgerald's Fragmented Hero: Dick Diver." *University Review* 32 (October 1965). Rpt. in LaHood, Marvin J., ed. *Tender Is the Night*, 127–137.

Fahey, William A. *F. Scott Fitzgerald and the American Dream*, 95–114.

Ferguson, Robert A. "Grotesque in the Novels of F. Scott Fitzgerald." *SAQ* 78 (1979): 463–464, 469–473.

Gallo, Rose Adrienne. *F. Scott Fitzgerald*, 57–81.

Gindin, James. "Gods and Fathers in F. Scott Fitzgerald's Novels." *MLQ* 30 (1969): 74–80.

Gindin, James. *Harvest of a Quiet Eye*, 246–253.

Greiff, Louis K. "Perfect Marriage in *Tender Is the Night*: A Study in the Progress of a Symbol." *F-H Annual* (1974): 63–73.

Grenber, Bruce L. "Fitzgerald's 'Figured Curtain': Personality and History in *Tender Is the Night*." *F-H Annual* (1978): 105–136.

Grube, John. "*Tender Is the Night*: Keats and Scott Fitzgerald." *Dalhousie Review* 44 (Winter 1964–65): 179–189. Rpt. in LaHood, Marvin J., ed. *Tender Is the Night*, 179–189.

Hall, William F. "Dialogue and Theme in *Tender Is the Night*." *Modern Language Notes* 76 (November 1961): 144–150. Rpt. in LaHood, Marvin J., ed. *Tender Is the Night*, 144–150.

Horne, Lewis B. "Gesture of Pity in *Jude the Obscure* and *Tender Is the Night*." *Ariel* 11.2 (1980): 53–61.

Hunt, Jan and John M. Suarez. "Evasion of Adult Love in Fitzgerald's Fiction." *CentR* 17 (1973): 158–159, 163–165.

Kenner, Hugh. *Homemade World*, 44–49.

Kinahan, Frank. "Focus on Fitzgerald's *Tender Is the Night*," in Madden, David, ed. *American Dreams, American Nightmares*, 115–128.

Kreuter, Kent and Gretchen Kreuter. "Moralism in the Later Fitzgerald." *Modern*

Fiction Studies 7 (Spring 1961). Rpt. in LaHood, Marvin J., ed. *Tender Is the Night*, 53–55.

Kuehl, John. "Scott Fitzgerald: Romantic and Realist." *Texas Studies in Literature and Language* 1 (Autumn 1959). Rpt. in LaHood, Marvin J., ed. *Tender Is the Night*, 8–14.

LaHood, Marvin J. "Sensuality and Asceticism in *Tender Is the Night*." *English Record* 17 (February 1967). Rpt. in LaHood, Marvin J., ed. *Tender Is the Night*, 151–155.

Lehan, Richard. "F. Scott Fitzgerald and Romantic Destiny." *TCL* 26 (1980): 146–150, 151.

Lehan, Richard D. "*Tender Is the Night*," in LaHood, Marvin J., ed. *Tender Is the Night*, 61–83.

McNicholas, Mary Verity, O.P. "Fitzgerald's Women in *Tender Is the Night*." *CollL* 4 (197): 40–70.

Millard, G. C. "F. Scott Fitzgerald: *The Great Gatsby*, *Tender Is the Night*, *The Last Tycoon*." *English Studies in Africa* 8 (March 1965). Rpt. in LaHood, Marvin J., ed. *Tender Is the Night*, 34–42.

Miller, James E., Jr. "*Tender Is the Night*," in Miller, James E., Jr. *F. Scott Fitzgerald: His Art and His Techinque*. New York: New York University Press, 1964. Rpt. in LaHood, Marvin J., ed *Tender Is the Night*, 86–101.

Milne, Gordon. *Sense of Society*, 218–221.

Mizener, Arthur. "*Tender Is the Night*," in LaHood, Marvin J., ed. *Tender Is the Night*, 102–116.

Monteiro, George. "Limits of Professionalism: A Sociological Approach to Faulkner, Fitzgerald and Hemingway." *Criticism* 15 (1973): 148–149.

Murphy, George D. "Unconscious Dimension of *Tender Is the Night*." *SNNTS* 5 (1973): 314–323.

Nelson, Gerald B. *Ten Versions of America*, 45–60.

Ousby, Ian. *Reader's Guide to Fifty American Novels*, 224–226.

Prigozy, Ruth. "From Griffith's Girls to Daddy's Girl: The Masks of Innocence in *Tender Is the Night*." *TCL* 26 (1980): 189–221.

Qualls, Barry V "Physician in the Counting House: The Religious Motif in *Tender Is the Night*." *ELWIU* 2 (1975): 192–208.

Roulston, Robert. "Dick Diver's Plunge into the Roman Void: The Setting of *Tender Is the Night*." *SAQ* 77 (1978): 85–97.

Roulston, Robert. "Slumbering with the Just: A Maryland Lens for *Tender Is the Night*." *SoQ* 16 (1978): 125–137.

Stanton, Robert. " 'Daddy's Girl': Symbol and Theme in *Tender Is the Night*." *Modern Fiction Studies* 4 (Summer 1958). Rpt. in LaHood, Marvin J., ed. *Tender Is the Night*, 156–163.

Stark, John. "Style of *Tender Is the Night*." *F-H Annual* (1972): 89–95.

Stavola, Thomas J. *Scott Fitzgerald*, 145–164.

Steinberg, A. H. "Fitzgerald's Portrait of a Psychiatrist." *University of Kansas Review* 21 (Spring 1955). Rpt. in LaHood, Marvin J., ed. *Tender Is the Night*, 138–143.

Trouard, Dawn. "Fitzgerald's Missed Moments: Surrealistic Style in His Major Novels." *F-H Annual* (1979): 190, 192, 198–201, 203.

Wasserstrom, William. "Goad of Guilt: Henry Adams, Scott and Zelda." *JML* 6 (1977): 305–307.

Way, Brian. *F. Scott Fitzgerald and the Art of Social Fiction*, 39–40, 119–148.

West, Suzanne. "Nicole's Gardens." *F-H Annual* (1978): 85–94.

White, Eugene. "The 'Intricate Destiny' of Dick Diver." *Modern Fiction Studies* 7 (Spring 1961). Rpt. in LaHood, Marvin J., ed. *Tender Is the Night*, 117–126.

Whitehead, Lee M. "*Tender Is the Night* and George Herbert Mead: an 'Actor's Tragedy." *Literature and Psychology* 15 (Summer 1965). Rpt. in LaHood, Marvin J., ed. *Tender Is the Night*, 165–177.

Wilson, Robert N. *Writer as Social Seer*, 18–41.

This Side of Paradise (1920)

Arnold, Edwin T. "Motion Picture as Metaphor in the Works of F. Scott Fitzgerald." *F-H Annual* (1977): 44–46.

Bennett, Warren. "Prefigurations of Gatsby, Eckleburg, Owl Eyes, and Klipspringer." *F-H Annual* (1979): 213–218.

Blake, Nelson Manfred. *Novelists' America*, 48–52.

Donald, Miles. *American Novel in the Twentieth Century*, 14–15.

Eble, Kenneth. *F. Scott Fitzgerald*, 44–50.

Fahey, William A. *F. Scott Fitzgerald and the American Dream*, 31–43.

Ferguson, Robert A. "Grotesque in the Novels of F. Scott Fitzgerald." *SAQ* 78 (1979): 462–463, 464, 465, 467.

Gallo, Rose Adrienne. *F. Scott Fitzgerald*, 16–23.

Gindin, James. "Gods and Fathers in F. Scott Fitzgerald's Novels." *MLQ* 30 (1969): 65–67.

Gindin, James. *Harvest of a Quiet Eye*, 238–240.

Gross, Barry. "*This Side of Paradise:* The Dominating Intention." *SNNTS* 1.1 (1969): 51–59.

Hoffman, Madelyn. "*This Side of Paradise:* A Study in Pathological Narcissism." *L&P* 28 (1978): 178–185.

Hunt, Jan and John M. Suarez. "Evasion of Adult Love in Fitzgerald's Fiction." *CentR* 17 (1973): 153–154, 156–157, 160, 163–165.

Kahn, Sy. "*This Side of Paradise:* The Pageantry of Disillusion." *Midwest Quarterly* 7 (Jan 1966): 177–194. Rpt. in Eble, Kenneth, ed. *F. Scott Fitzgerald: A Collection of Criticism*, 34–47.

Lehan, Richard. "F. Scott Fitzgerald and Romantic Destiny." *TCL* 26 (1980): 154.

Long, Robert Emmet. *Achieving of The Great Gatsby*, 17–30.

Milne, Gordon. *Sense of Society*, 214–215.

Ousby, Ian. *Reader's Guide to Fifty American Novels*, 212–214.

Roulston, Robert. "*This Side of Paradise:* The Ghost of Rupert Brooke." *F-H Annual* (1975): 117–130.

Stavola, Thomas J. *Scott Fitzgerald*, 73–105.

Trouard, Dawn. "Fitzgerald's Missed Moments: Surrealistic Style in His Major Novels." *F-H Annual* (1979): 194–196.

Tuttleton, James W. " 'Combat in the Erogenous Zone': Women in the American Novel between the Two Wars," in Springer, Marlene, ed. *What Manner of Woman*, 278–279.

Tuttleton, James W. *Novel of Manners in America*, 165–166.

Way, Brian. *F. Scott Fitzgerald and the Art of Social Fiction*, 49–57, 61–62.

FITZGERALD, ZELDA (1899–1948)

Save Me the Waltz (1932)

Going, William T. *Essays on Alabama Literature*, 127–131.

Tavernier-Courbin, Jacqueline. "Art as Woman's Response and Search: Zelda Fitzgerald's *Save Me the Waltz*." *SLJ* 11.2 (1979): 22–42.

FITZHUGH, LOUISE (1928–1974)

Harriet, the Spy (1964)
  Wolf, Virginia L. "*Harriet, the Spy:* Milestone, Masterpiece?" *ChildL* 4 (1975): 120–126.

FOOTE, SHELBY (1916–)

Shiloh (1952)
  Bennett, Lee Shaw. "Modern Civil War Novels: The Still Unwritten War?" *SoS* 19 (1980): 113–115.

FORD, CHARLES HENRI (1913–)

Young and Evil (1933)
  Austen, Roger. *Playing the Game*, 59–62.

FORD, PAUL LEICESTER (1865–1902)

Great K. & A. Train Robbery (1896)
  Kane, Patricia. "Paul Leicester Ford: An Unrealistic 'Realist'." *JPC* 7 (1973): 573–574.

Honorable Peter Stirling (1894)
  Kane, Patricia. "Paul Leicester Ford: An Unrealistic 'Realist'." *JPL* 7 (1973): 571–573.

Janice Meredith (1899)
  Kane, Patricia. "Paul Leicester Ford: An Unrealistic 'Realist'." *JPL* 7 (1973): 575–577.

Story of an Untold Love (1898)
  Kane, Patricia. "Paul Leicester Ford: An Unrealistic 'Realist'." *JPL* 7 (1973): 574–575.

FORGIONE, LOUIS

River Between (1928)
  Green, Rose Basile. *Italian-American Novel*, 81–85.

FORREST, LEON (1937–)

There Is a Tree More Ancient than Eden (1973)
  Schultz, Elizabeth A. "Heirs of Ralph Ellison: Patterns of Individualism in the Contemporary Afro-American Novel." *CLAJ* 22 (1978): 108–112.

FOSTER, HANNAH WEBSTER (1759–1840)

Coquette (1797)
  Petter, Henri. *Early American Novel*, 258–263.

FOX, JOHN, JR. (1862–1919)

Erskine Dale (1920)
  Titus, Warren I. *John Fox, Jr.*, 117–120.

Heart of the Hills (1913)
  Titus, Warren I. *John Fox, Jr.*, 101–106.
Kentuckians (1897)
  Titus, Warren I. *John Fox, Jr.*, 40–44.
Little Shepherd of Kingdom Come (1903)
  Titus, Warren I. *John Fox, Jr.*, 65–73.
Trail of the Lonesome Pine (1908)
  Titus, Warren I. *John Fox, Jr.*, 88–94.

FOX, PAULA (1923–)

Desperate Characters (1970)
  Bassoff, Bruce. "Royalty in a Rainy Country: Two Novels of Paula Fox." *Crit* 20.2
  (1978): 33–47.
Widow's Children (1976)
  Bassoff, Bruce. "Royalty in a Rainy Country: Two Novels of Paula Fox." *Crit* 20.2
  (1978): 33–47.

FRANK, WALDO (1889–1967)

Dark Mother (1920)
  Austen, Roger. *Playing the Game*, 36–37.

FRANKEL, ERNEST

Band of Brothers (1958)
  Jones, Peter G. *War and the Novelist*, 182–185, 197.

FRASER, SYLVIA (1935–)

Candy Factory (1975)
  Moss, John. *Sex and Violence*, 155–160.
Pandora (1972)
  Irvine, Lorna. "Psychological Journey: Mothers and Daughters in English-
  Canadian Fiction," in Davidson, Cathy N. and E. M. Broner, eds. *Lost Tradition*,
  247.

FREDERIC, HAROLD (1856–1898)

Copperhead (1892)
  Aaron, Daniel. *Unwritten War*, 222–223.
  Garner, Stanton. *Harold Frederic*, 21–22.
Damnation of Theron Ware (1896)
  Bredahl, A. Carl, Jr. "Artist in *The Damnation of Theron Ware*." *SNNTS* 4 (1972):
  432–441.

Briggs, Austin, Jr. *Novels of Harold Frederic*, 105–139.

Coale, Samuel. "Frederic and Hawthorne: The Romantic Roots of Naturalism." *AL* 48 (1976): 31–45.

Cohn, Jan. "Women as Superfluous Characters in American Realism and Naturalism." *SAF* 1 (1973): 158–159.

Crowley, John W. "Nude and the Madonna in *The Damnation of Theron Ware*." *AL* 45 (1973): 379–389.

Donaldson, Scott. "Seduction of Theron Ware." *NCF* 29 (1975): 441–452.

Fryer, Judith. *Faces of Eve*, 54–62.

Garner, Stanton. *Harold Frederic*, 33–38.

Katz, Joseph. "Eroticism in American Literary Realism." *SAF* 5 (1977): 42–43.

LeClair, Thomas. "Ascendant Eye: A Reading of *The Damnation of Theron Ware*." *SAF* 3 (1975): 95–102.

Luedtke, Luther S. "Harold Frederic's Satanic Soulsby: Interpretation and Sources." *NCF* 30 (1975): 82–104.

Wilson, Edmund. *Devils and Canon Barham*, 61–66.

Zlotnick, Joan. "*Damnation of Theron Ware*, with a Backward Glance at Hawthorne." *MarkR* 2.5 (1971): 90–92.

Gloria Mundi (1898)

Blackhall, Jean F. "Frederic's *Gloria Mundi* as a Novel of Education." *MarkR* 3 (1972): 41–46.

Briggs, Austin, Jr. *Novels of Harold Frederic*, 161–174.

Illumination see *Damnation of Theron Ware*

In the Valley (1890)

Briggs, Austin, Jr. *Novels of Harold Frederic*, 55–68.

Garner, Stanton. *Harold Frederic*, 18–20.

Lawton Girl (1890)

Briggs, Austin, Jr. *Novels of Harold Frederic*, 74–96.

Garner, Stanton. *Harold Frederic*, 17–18.

March Hares (1896)

Briggs, Austin, Jr. *Novels of Harold Frederic*, 147–156.

Market Place (1899)

Briggs, Austin, Jr. *Novels of Harold Frederic*, 182–200.

Garner, Stanton. *Harold Frederic*, 41–44.

Seth's Brother's Wife (1887)

Briggs, Austin, Jr. *Novels of Harold Frederic*, 24–48.

Garner, Stanton. *Harold Frederic*, 14–17.

Woodward, Robert H. "Illusion and Moral Ambivalence in *Seth's Brother's Wife*." *ALR* 2 (1969): 279–282.

FREEMAN, MARY WILKINS (1852–1930)

Pembroke (1894)

Quina, James H., Jr. "Character Types in the Fiction of Mary Wilkins Freeman." *CLQ* 9 (1971): 433–436, 437, 438.

FRIEDMAN, BRUCE JAY (1930–)

Dick (1970)

> Klein, Marcus. "Further Notes on the Dereliction of Culture: Edward Lewis Wallant and Bruce Jay Friedman," in Malin, Irving, ed. *Contemporary American-Jewish Literature*, 231, 232, 233–234.
> Lewis, Stuart A. "Rootlessness and Alienation in the Novels of Bruce Jay Friedman." *CLAJ* 18 (1975): 424–433.
> Pinsker, Sanford. *Between Two Worlds*, 20–21.
> Schulz, Max F. *Bruce Jay Friedman*, 103–121.

Mother's Kisses (1964)

> Klein, Marcus. "Further Notes on the Dereliction of Culture: Edward Lewis Wallant and Bruce Jay Friedman," in Malin, Irving, ed. *Contemporary American-Jewish Literature*, 241–244.
> Lewis, Stuart A. "Rootlessness and Alienation in the Novels of Bruce Jay Friedman." *CLAJ* 18 (1975): 423–424, 426–433.
> Pinsker, Sanford. *Between Two Worlds*, 17–20.
> Schulz, Max F. *Black Humor Fiction of the Sixties*, 105–108.
> Schulz, Max F. *Bruce Jay Friedman*, 59–77.
> Schulz, Max F. *Radical Sophistication*, 186–189, 191–194.

Stern (1962)

> Klein, Marcus. "Further Notes on the Dereliction of Culture: Edward Lewis Wallant and Bruce Jay Friedman," in Malin, Irving, ed. *Contemporary American-Jewish Literature*, 244–246.
> Lewis, Stuart A. "Rootlessness and Alienation in the Novels of Bruce Jay Friedman." *CLAJ* 18 (1975): 423, 425–433.
> Pinsker, Sanford. *Between Two Worlds*, 12–17.
> Schulz, Max F. *Black Humor Fiction of the Sixties*, 97–99, 100, 107, 111–112, 113–119.
> Schulz, Max F. *Bruce Jay Friedman*, 35–57.
> Schulz, Max F. *Radical Sophistication*, 186, 189–191.

FUCHS, DANIEL (1909–1993)

Homage to Blenholt (1936)

> Guttmann, Allen. *Jewish Writer in America*, 44–46.

Low Company (1937)

> Guttmann, Allen. *Jewish Writer in America*, 47–48.

Summer in Williamsburg (1934)

> Guttmann, Allen. *Jewish Writer in America*, 46–47.

FULLER, HENRY BLAKE (1857–1929)

Bertram Cope's Year (1919)

> Austen, Roger. *Playing the Game*, 27–30.
> Pilkington, John, Jr. *Henry Blake Fuller*, 150–151.

Cliff-Dwellers (1893)

Pilkington, John, Jr. *Henry Blake Fuller*, 86–95.

Scambray, Kenneth. "Romance in Decline: Realism in Henry Blake Fuller's *The Cliff-Dwellers*." *NDQ* 46.2 (1978): 19–28.

Szuberla, Guy. "Making the Sublime Mechanical: Henry Blake Fuller's Chicago." *AmerS* 14.1 (1974): 84–89.

On the Stairs (1918)

Pilkington, John, Jr. *Henry Blake Fuller*, 147–149.

With the Procession (1895)

Cohn, Jan. "Women as Superfluous Characters in American Realism and Naturalism." *SAF* 1 (1973): 157–158.

Couser, G. Thomas. "Art in Chicago: Fuller's *With the Procession*." *ALR* 13 (1980): 31–39.

Pilkington, John, Jr. *Henry Blake Fuller*, 96–109.

Szuberla, Guy. "Making the Sublime Mechanical: Henry Blake Fuller's Chicago." *AmerS* 14.1 (1974): 89–92.

FUMENTO, ROCCO (1923–)

Tree of Dark Reflection (1962)

Green, Rose Basile. *Italian-American Novel*, 183–187.

GADDIS, WILLIAM (1922–1998)

J.R. (1975)

Klemtner, Susan Strehle. " 'For a Very Small Audience': The Fiction of William Gaddis." *Crit* 19.3 (1978): 64–72.

Moore, Steven. "Chronological Difficulties in the Novels of William Gaddis." *Crit* 22.1 (1980): 87–90.

Recognitions (1955)

Klemtner, Susan Strehle. " 'For a Very Small Audience': The Fiction of William Gaddis." *Crit* 19.3 (1978): 61–64.

Moore, Steven. "Chronological Difficulties in the Novels of William Gaddis." *Crit* 22.1 (1980): 79–87.

Salemi, Joseph S. "To Soar in Atonement: Art as Expiation in Gaddis's *The Recognitions*." *Novel* 10 (1977): 127–136.

GAINES, ERNEST (1933–)

Autobiography of Miss Jane Pittman (1971)

Andrews, William L. " 'We Ain't Going Back There': The Idea of Progress in *The Autobiography of Miss Jane Pittman*." *BALF* 11 (1977): 146–149.

Berzon, Judith R. *Neither White Nor Black*, 238–242.

Gayle, Addison, Jr. *Way of the New World*, 294–302.

Hicks, Jack. "To Make These Bones Live: History and Community in Ernest Gaines's Fiction." *BALF* 11 (1977): 16–19.

Catherine Carmier (1964)

> Hicks, Jack. "To Make These Bones Live: History and Community in Ernest Gaines's Fiction." *BALF* 11 (1977): 9–11.

Of Love and Dust (1967)

> Gayle, Addison, Jr. *Way of the New World*, 289–294.
> Hicks, Jack. "To Make These Bones Live: History and Community in Ernest Gaines's Fiction." *BALF* 11 (1977): 11–13.
> Wideman, John. "*Of Love and Dust:* A Reconsideration." *Callaloo* 1.3 (1978): 76–84.
> Williams, Sherley Anne. *Give Birth to Brightness*, 171–208.

GALLANT, MAVIS (1922–)

Fairly Good Time (1970)

> Stevens, Peter. "Perils of Compassion." *CanL* 56 (1973): 61–70.
> Stevens, Peter. "Perils of Compassion," in Woodcock, George, ed. *Canadian Novel*, 202–203, 209–211.

Green Water, Green Sky (1959)

> Stevens, Peter. "Perils of Compassion," in Woodcock, George, ed. *Canadian Novel*, 203–205.

GALLICO, PAUL WILLIAM (1897–1976)

Small Miracle (1952)

> Green, Rose Basile. *Italian-American Novel*, 115–117.

GARDNER, JOHN C. (1933–1982)

Grendel (1971)

> Fitzpatrick, W. P. "Down and Down I Go: A Note on Shelley's 'Prometheus Unbound' and Gardner's *Grendel*." *NConL* 7.1 (1977): 2–5.
> Fredericks, S. C. "Revivals of Ancient Mythologies in Current Science Fiction and Fantasy," in Clareson, Thomas D., ed. *Many Futures, Many Worlds*, 58–59.
> Hendin, Josephine. *Vulnerable People*, 137–138.
> Hutman, Norma L. "Even Monsters Have Mothers: A Study of 'Beowulf' and John Gardner's *Grendel*." *Mosaic* 9.1 (1975): 19–31.
> Milosh, Joseph. "John Gardner's *Grendel:* Sources and Analogues." *ConL* 19 (1978): 48–57.
> Murr, Judy Smith. "John Gardner's Order and Disorder: *Grendel* and *The Sunlight Dialogues*." *Crit* 18.2 (1976): 99–101, 107.
> Strehle, Susan. "John Gardner's Novels: Affirmation and the Alien." *Crit* 18.2 (1976): 92–96.
> Stromme, Craig J. "Twelve Chapters of *Grendel*." *Crit* 20.1 (1978): 83–92.

Nickel Mountain (1973)

> Harris, Richard C. "Ecclesiastical Wisdom and *Nickel Mountain*." *TCL* 26 (1980): 424–431.

Strehle, Susan. "John Gardner's Novels: Affirmation and the Alien." *Crit* 18.2 (1976): 86–87.

October Light (1976)

Butts, Leonard C. "Locking and Unlocking: Nature as Moral Center in John Gardner's *October Light*." *Crit* 22.2 (1980): 47–60.
Hendin, Josephine. *Vulnerable People*, 133–136.

Resurrection (1966)

Strehle, Susan. "John Gardner's Novels: Affirmation and the Alien." *Crit* 18.2 (1976): 86–87.

Sunlight Dialogues (1972)

Murr, Judy Smith. "John Gardner's Order and Disorder: *Grendel* and *The Sunlight Dialogues*." *Crit* 18.2 (1976): 101–107.
Strehle, Susan. "John Gardner's Novels: Affirmation and the Alien." *Crit* 18.2 (1976): 88–92.

Wreckage of Agathon (1970)

Strehle, Susan. "John Gardner's Novels: Affirmation and the Alien." *Crit* 18.2 (1976): 88–92.

GARDNER, LEONARD (1934–)

Fat City (1969)
Umphlett, Wiley Lee. *Sporting Myth and the American Experience*, 176–179.

GARLAND, HAMLIN (1860–1940)

Boy Life on the Prairie (1899)
Popken, Randall L. "From Innocence to Experience in *My Ántonia* and *Boy Life on the Prairie*." *NDQ* 46.2 (1978): 73–81.

Captain of Gray-Horse Troop (1902)
Gish, Robert. *Hamlin Garland: The Far West*, 34–38.

Cavanagh (1910)
Littlefield, Daniel F. and Lonnie E. Underhill. "Emerging New West in Hamlin Garland's Fiction, 1910–1916." *MarkR* 9 (1980): 36–38.

Eagle's Heart (1900)
Gish, Robert. *Hamlin Garland: The Far West*, 22–24.
McCullough, Joseph B. *Hamlin Garland*, 81–84.

Forester's Daughter (1914)
Littlefield, Daniel F. and Lonnie E. Underhill. "Emerging New West in Hamlin Garland's Fiction, 1910–1916." *MarkR* 9 (1980): 38–39.

Her Mountain Lover (1901)
Carp, Roger E. "Hamlin Garland and the Cult of True Womanhood," in Lee, L. L. and Merrill Lewis, ed. *Women, Women Writers, and the West*, 90–91.
Gish, Robert. *Hamlin Garland: The Far West*, 25–26.

Hesper (1903)

>   Gish, Robert. *Hamlin Garland: The Far West*, 26–29.

Money Magic (1907)

>   Gish, Robert. *Hamlin Garland: The Far West*, 29–31.

Rose of Dutcher's Coolly (1895)

>   Carp, Roger E. "Hamlin Garland and the Cult of True Womanhood," in Lee, L. L. and Merrill Lewis, ed. *Women, Women Writers, and the West*, 88–89.
>   McCullough, Joseph B. *Hamlin Garland*, 67–74.
>   Savage, George. " 'The Force That Flowers': Hamlin Garland, Herbert Spencer, and *Rose of Dutcher's Coolly.*" *MarkR* 5 (1976): 41–47.

Spoil of Office (1892)

>   Alsen, Eberhard. "Hamlin Garland's First Novel: *A Spoil of Office.*" *WAL* 4 (1969): 91–105.
>   Carp, Roger E. "Hamlin Garland and the Cult of True Womanhood," in Lee, L. L. and Merrill Lewis, ed. *Women, Women Writers, and the West*, 86–88.

GARNER, HUGH (1913–1979)

Cabbagetown (1950)

>   Edwards, Eileen. "Sense of Place in Hugh Garner's Fiction." *WLWE* 18 (1979): 355–357.
>   Fetherling, Doug. *Hugh Garner*, 16–31.

Intruders (1976)

>   Edwards, Eileen. "Sense of Place in Hugh Garner's Fiction." *WLWE* 18 (1979): 357–359.

Nice Place to Visit (1970)

>   Fetherling, Doug. *Hugh Garner*, 49–58.

Silence on the Shore (1962)

>   Edwards, Eileen. "Sense of Place in Hugh Garner's Fiction." *WLWE* 18 (1979): 359–360.
>   Fetherling, Doug. *Hugh Garner*, 40–48.

Sin Sniper (1970)

>   Fetherling, Doug. *Hugh Garner*, 59–64.

Storm Below (1949)

>   Fetherling, Doug. *Hugh Garner*, 11–15.

GARRETT, GEORGE (1929–)

Death of the Fox (1971)

>   Turner, Joseph W. "History and Imagination in George Garrett's *Death of the Fox.*" *Crit* 22.2 (1980): 31–46.

GASS, WILLIAM (1924–)

Omensetter's Luck (1966)
Schneider, Richard J. "Fortunate Fall in William Gass's *Omensetter's Luck.*" *Crit* 18.1 (1976): 5–20.
Tanner, Tony. *City of Words*, 269–272.

GÉLINAS, PIERRE (1925–)

Les vivants, les morts et les autres (1959)
Shek, Ben-Zion. *Social Realism*, 225–227.

GÉRIN-LAJOIE, ANTOINE (1824–1882)

Jean Rivard (1862)
Servais-Maquoi, Mireille. *Le roman de la terre au Québec*, 33–44.

GESTON, MARK S. (1946–)

Out of the Mouth of the Dragon (1969)
Wollheim, Donald A. *Universe Makers*, 87–89.

GIBSON, GRAEME (1934–)

Five Legs (1969)
Atwood, Margaret. *Survival*, 81–82, 187–189, 208.
Moss, John. *Sex and Violence*, 160–167.

GILMAN, CAROLINE HOWARD (1794–1888)

Love's Progress (1840)
Baym, Nina. *Woman's Fiction*, 70–71.
Recollections of a Housekeeper (1834)
Baym, Nina. *Woman's Fiction*, 67–70.
Recollections of a Southern Matron (1838)
Baym, Nina. *Woman's Fiction*, 70.

GIPSON, FRED (1908–1973)

Old Yeller (1956)
Kelty, Jean McClure. "Cult of Kill in Adolescent Fiction." *EJ* 64.2 (1975): 57–58.

GIROUX, ANDRÉ (1916–1977)

Au-delà des visages (1948)
Shek, Ben-Zion. *Social Realism*, 204–217.

Le gouffre a toujours soif (1953)

   Shek, Ben-Zion. *Social Realism*, 204–217.

GLASGOW, ELLEN (1873–1945)

Ancient Law (1908)

   Kish, Dorothy. "Toward a Perfect Place: Setting in the Early Novels of Ellen Glasgow." *MissQ* 31 (1977–78): 34.

Barren Ground (1925)

   Bond, Tonette L. "Pastoral Transformations in *Barren Ground*." *MissQ* 32 (1979): 565–576.

   Cook, Sylvia Jenkins. *From Tobacco Road to Route 66*, 24–26.

   Lesser, Wayne. "Problematics of Regionalism and the Dilemma of Glasgow's *Barren Ground*." *SLJ* 11.2 (1979): 3–21.

   Murr, Judy Smith. "History in *Barren Ground* and *Vein of Iron:* Theory, Structure, and Symbol." *SLJ* 8.1 (1975): 39–48, 53–54.

   Raper, Julius Rowan. *From the Sunken Garden*, 79–100, 194–195.

   Raper, Julius Rowan. "Landscape of Revenge: Ellen Glasgow's *Barren Ground*." *SoHR* 13 (1979): 63–77.

   Tuttleton, James W. "Hardy and Ellen Glasgow: *Barren Ground*." *MissQ* 32 (1979): 577–590.

   Wagner, Linda W. *American Modern*, 56–66

   Wagner, Linda W. "*Barren Ground*'s Vein of Iron: Dorinda Oakley and Some Concepts of the Heroine in 1925." *MissQ* 32 (1979): 553–564.

   Wagner, Linda W. "Ellen Glasgow: Daughter as Justified," in Davidson, Cathy N. and E. M. Broner, eds. *Lost Tradition*, 142–146.

Battle-Ground (1902)

   Aaron, Daniel. *Unwritten War*, 289–290.

   Kish, Dorothy. "Toward a Perfect Place: Setting in the Early Novels of Ellen Glasgow." *MissQ* 31 (1977–78): 38–39.

   Scura, Dorothy McInnis. "Southern Lady in the Early Novels of Ellen Glasgow." *MissQ* 31 (1977–78): 22–23, 24–25, 26.

Beyond Defeat (1966)

   Raper, Julius Rowan. *From the Sunken Garden*, 187–192.

Builders (1919)

   Raper, Julius Rowan. *From the Sunken Garden*, 37–40, 50–52, 194, 196.

Deliverance (1904)

   Godbold, E. Stanley, Jr. "Battleground Revisited: Reconstruction in Southern Fiction, 1895–1905." *SAQ* 73 (1974): 111–113.

   Kish, Dorothy. "Toward a Perfect Place: Setting in the Early Novels of Ellen Glasgow." *MissQ* 31 (1977–78): 39.

   Scura, Dorothy McInnis. "Southern Lady in the Early Novels of Ellen Glasgow." *MissQ* 31 (1977–78): 19.

Descendant (1897)

   Kish, Dorothy. "Toward a Perfect Place: Setting in the Early Novels of Ellen Glasgow." *MissQ* 31 (1977–78): 35.

Scura, Dorothy McInnis. "Southern Lady in the Early Novels of Ellen Glasgow." *MissQ* 31 (1977–78): 18–19, 20–21.

In This Our Life (1941)

Raper, Julius Rowan. *From the Sunken Garden*, 171–187.
Richmond, Velma Bourgeois. "Sexual Reversals in Thomas Hardy and Ellen Glasgow." *SoHR* 13 (1979): 51–60.

Life and Gabriella (1916)

Milne, Gordon. *Sense of Society*, 153–154.
Raper, Julius Rowan. *From the Sunken Garden*, 15–35, 194, 195–196.
Wagner, Linda W. "Ellen Glasgow: Daughter as Justified," in Davidson, Cathy N. and E. M. Broner, eds. *Lost Tradition*, 141–142.

Miller of Old Church (1911)

Kish, Dorothy. "Toward a Perfect Place: Setting in the Early Novels of Ellen Glasgow." *MissQ* 31 (1977–78): 41–43.

One Man in His Time (1922)

Raper, Julius Rowan. *From the Sunken Garden*, 40–52, 194, 196.

Phases of an Inferior Planet (1898)

Kish, Dorothy. "Toward a Perfect Place: Setting in the Early Novels of Ellen Glasgow." *MissQ* 31 (1977–78): 35–36.

Romance of a Plain Man (1909)

Scura, Dorothy McInnis. "Southern Lady in the Early Novels of Ellen Glasgow." *MissQ* 31 (1977–78): 24, 27–28.

Romantic Comedians (1926)

Kazin, Alfred. "Elegy and Satire: Willa Cather and Ellen Glasgow," in Kazin, Alfred. *On Native Grounds: A Study of American Prose from 1890 to the Present.* New York: Harcourt, Brace & Co., 1942. Rpt. as "Willa Cather and Ellen Glasgow" in Rahv, Philip, ed. *Literature in America*, 321.
Milne, Gordon. *Sense of Society*, 154–158.
Raper, Julius Rowan. *From the Sunken Garden*, 101–117, 195, 196.

Sheltered Life (1932)

Kazin, Alfred. "Elegy and Satire: Willa Cather and Ellen Glasgow," in Kazin, Alfred. *On Native Grounds: A Study of American Prose from 1890 to the Present.* New York: Harcourt, Brace & Co., 1942. Rpt. as "Willa Cather and Ellen Glasgow" in Rahv, Philip, ed. *Literature in America*, 321–322.
Milne, Gordon. *Sense of Society*, 162–165.
Raper, J. R. "Glasgow's Psychology of Deceptions and *The Sheltered Life*." *SLJ* 8.1 (1975): 27–38.
Raper, Julius Rowan. *From the Sunken Garden*, 138–149, 193–194, 198–201.
Stineback, David C. *Shifting World*, 115–127.

They Stooped to Folly (1929)

Kazin, Alfred. "Elegy and Satire: Willa Cather and Ellen Glasgow," in Kazin, Alfred. *On Native Grounds: A Study of American Prose from 1890 to the Present.* New York: Harcourt, Brace & Co., 1942. Rpt. as "Willa Cather and Ellen Glasgow" in Rahv, Philip, ed. *Literature in America*, 320–321.

Milne, Gordon. *Sense of Society*, 158–162.

Raper, Julius Rowan. *From the Sunken Garden*, 118–137, 195, 196–197.

Vein of Iron (1935)

Murr, Judy Smith. "History in *Barren Ground* and *Vein of Iron:* Theory, Structure, and Symbol." *SLJ* 8.1 (1975): 39–42, 48–54.

Raper, Julius Rowan. *From the Sunken Garden*, 150–170, 195, 197.

Spacks, Patricia Meyer. *Female Imagination*, 103–106.

Virginia (1913)

Kazin, Alfred. "Elegy and Satire: Willa Cather and Ellen Glasgow," in Kazin, Alfred. *On Native Grounds: A Study of American Prose from 1890 to the Present.* New York: Harcourt, Brace & Co., 1942. Rpt. as "Willa Cather and Ellen Glasgow" in Rahv, Philip, ed. *Literature in America*, 320.

Kish, Dorothy. "Toward a Perfect Place: Setting in the Early Novels of Ellen Glasgow." *MissQ* 31 (1977–78): 34, 43–44.

Milne, Gordon. *Sense of Society*, 152–153.

Scura, Dorothy McInnis. "Southern Lady in the Early Novels of Ellen Glasgow." *MissQ* 31 (1977–78): 19–20, 23–24, 28–31.

Wagner, Linda W. "Ellen Glasgow: Daughter as Justified," in Davidson, Cathy N. and E. M. Broner, eds. *Lost Tradition*, 140–141.

Voice of the People (1900)

Kish, Dorothy. "Toward a Perfect Place: Setting in the Early Novels of Ellen Glasgow." *MissQ* 31 (1977–78): 36–38.

Scura, Dorothy McInnis. "Southern Lady in the Early Novels of Ellen Glasgow." *MissQ* 31 (1977–78): 21–22.

GLASSCO, JOHN (1909–1981)

Memoirs of Montparnasse (1970)

Moss, John. *Sex and Violence*, 47–49.

GODBOUT, JACQUES (1933–)

D'amour, P.Q. (1972)

Belleau, André. *Le romancier Fictif*, 135–136, 139–147.

Coates, Carrol F. "Le joual comme revendication québécoise: *D'amour, P.Q.* de Jacques Godbout." *FR* 52 (1978): 73–80.

Poulin, Gabrielle. *Romans du pays*, 40–41.

Smith, André. *L'univers romanesque*, 11–14, 19–20, 63–69, 70–90.

Dragon Island see *L'isle au dragon*

Hail Galarneau! see *Salut Galarneau!*

Knife on the Table see *Le couteau sur la table*

L'aquarium (1962)

Falardeau, Jean-Charles. "Evolution of the Hero in the Quebec Novel," in Shouldice, Larry, ed. & trans., *Contemporary Quebec Criticism*, 107.

Smith, André. *L'univers romanesque*, 11–14, 20–37, 70–90.

Urbas, Jeannette. *From Thirty Acres to Modern Times*, 126.

Le couteau sur la table (1965)

Falardeau, Jean-Charles. "Evolution of the Hero in the Quebec Novel," in Should-
ice, Larry, ed. & trans., *Contemporary Quebec Criticism*, 107.

Hathorn, Ramon. "Soldats, patrons et femmes 'fatales': Figures de l'"Anglais' dans
le roman québécois des XIXe et XXe siècles." *V&I* 6 (1980): 101, 111–112.

Pivato, Joseph. "Nouveau roman canadien." *CanL* 58 (1973): 52–60.

Shek, Ben-Zion. *Social Realism*, 273–276.

Smith, André. *L'univers romanesque*, 11–14, 37–56, 70–90.

Sutherland, Ronald. "Fourth Separatism." *CanL* 45 (1970): 13–15.

Sutherland, Ronald. *Second Image*, 16–23, 120–122.

Urbas, Jeannette. *From Thirty Acres to Modern Times*, 136–138, 143.

L'isle au dragon (1976)

Poulin, Gabrielle. *Romans du pays*, 276–279, 419–422.

Salut Galarneau! (1967)

Falardeau, Jean-Charles. "Evolution of the Hero in the Quebec Novel," in Should-
ice, Larry, ed. & trans., *Contemporary Quebec Criticism*, 107–108.

Shek, Ben-Zion. *Social Realism*, 276–278.

Smith, André. *L'univers romanesque*, 15–19, 56–63, 70–90.

Urbas, Jeannette. *From Thirty Acres to Modern Times*, 138.

GODFREY, DAVE (1938–)

New Ancestors (1970)

Monk, Patricia. "Shadow Continent: The Image of Africa in Three Canadian Writers." *Ariel* 8.4 (1977): 4–13.

Moss, John. *Sex and Violence*, 199–231.

Quigley, Theresia. "*New Ancestors:* A Critical Analysis." *AntR* 30 (1977): 65–71.

Smiley, Calvin L. "Godfrey's Progress." *CanL* 75 (1977): 27–39.

GODWIN, GAIL (1937–)

Glass People (1972)

Gaston, Karen C. " 'Beauty and the Beast' in Gail Godwin's *Glass People*." *Crit*
21.3 (1980): 94–102.

Smith, Marilynn J. "Role of the South in the Novels of Gail Godwin." *Crit* 21.3
(1980): 104–105.

Odd Woman (1974)

Lorsch, Susan E. "Gail Godwin's *The Odd Woman:* Literature and the Retreat from
Life." *Crit* 20.2 (1978): 21–32.

Violet Clay (1978)

Smith, Marilynn J. "Role of the South in the Novels of Gail Godwin." *Crit* 21.3
(1980): 106–111.

GOINES, DONALD (1937–1974)

Whoreson (1972)

Graham, D. B. " 'Negative Glamour': The Pimp Hero in the Fiction of Iceberg
Slim." *Obsidian* 1.2 (1975): 7–8.

GOLD, HERBERT (1924–)

Therefore Be Bold (1960)
Bryant, Jerry H. *Open Decision*, 218–219.

GOLDMAN, WILLIAM (1931–)

Boys and Girls Together (1964)
Andersen, Richard. *William Goldman*, 54–62.

Father's Day (1971)
Andersen, Richard. *William Goldman*, 75–80.

Magic (1976)
Andersen, Richard. *William Goldman*, 100–105.

Marathon Man (1974)
Andersen, Richard. *William Goldman*, 94–100.

No Way to Treat a Lady (1964)
Andersen, Richard. *William Goldman*, 62–65.

Princess Bride (1973)
Andersen, Richard. *William Goldman*, 81–93.

Soldier in the Rain (1960)
Andersen, Richard. *William Goldman*, 44–53.

Temple of Gold (1957)
Andersen, Richard. *William Goldman*, 26–34.

Thing of It Is. . . . (1967)
Andersen, Richard. *William Goldman*, 66–72.

Your Turn to Curtsy, My Turn to Bow (1958)
Andersen, Richard. *William Goldman*, 35–43.

GOODMAN, MITCHELL (1923–)

End of It (1961)
Bryant, Jerry H. *Open Decision*, 149–151.
Jones, Peter G. *War and the Novelist*, 145–148.

GOODMAN, PAUL (1911–1972)

Dead of Spring (1950)
Widmer, Kingsley. *Paul Goodman*, 114–116.

Empire City (1959)
Widmer, Kingsley. *Paul Goodman*, 106–118.

Grand Piano (1942)
Widmer, Kingsley. *Paul Goodman*, 109–111.

Making Do (1963)
    Widmer, Kingsley. *Paul Goodman*, 122–126.

Parents' Day (1951)
    Widmer, Kingsley. *Paul Goodman*, 118–122.

State of Nature (1946)
    Widmer, Kingsley. *Paul Goodman*, 111–114.

GORDON, CAROLINE (1895–1981)

Aleck Maury (1934)
    Gray, Richard. *Literature of Memory*, 153–155.
    Stuckey, W. J. *Caroline Gordon*, 33–41.
    Umphlett, Wiley Lee. *Sporting Myth and the American Experience*, 47, 49–57.

Garden of Adonis (1937)
    Stuckey, W. J. *Caroline Gordon*, 55–61.

Glory of Hera (1972)
    Cowan, Bainard. "Serpent's Coils: How to Read Caroline Gordon's Later Fiction." *SoR* 16 (1980): 282–285, 287–298.

Green Centuries (1941)
    Rodenberger, M. Lou. "Folk Narrative in Caroline Gordon's Frontier Fiction," in Lee, L. L. and Merrill Lewis, ed. *Women, Women Writers, and the West*, 199–205.
    Stuckey, W. J. *Caroline Gordon*, 62–66.

Malefactors (1956)
    Stuckey, W. J. *Caroline Gordon*, 94–111.

None Shall Look Back (1937)
    Gray, Richard. *Literature of Memory*, 155–160, 166–174.
    Stuckey, W. J. *Caroline Gordon*, 42–54.
    Sullivan, Walter. *Death by Melancholy*, 75–77.

Penhally (1931)
    Gray, Richard. *Literature of Memory*, 153.
    Stuckey, W. J. *Caroline Gordon*, 24–32.

Strange Children (1951)
    Stuckey, W. J. *Caroline Gordon*, 79–93.

Women on the Porch (1944)
    Cowan, Bainard. "Serpent's Coils: How to Read Caroline Gordon's Later Fiction." *SoR* 16 (1980): 285–286.
    Stuckey, W. J. *Caroline Gordon*, 67–78.

GOULD, LOIS (1937(?)–)

Final Analysis (1974)
    Hendin, Josephine. *Vulnerable People*, 178–179.

Sea Change (1976)
  Hendin, Josephine. *Vulnerable People*, 186–188.

Such Good Friends (1970)
  Crain, Jane L. "Feminist Fiction." *Commentary* 58.6 (1974): 59, 60, 61.
  Hendin, Josephine. *Vulnerable People*, 179–181.

GOYEN, WILLIAM (1915–1983)

Come, the Restorer (1974)
  Phillips, Robert. *William Goyen*, 89–97.

House of Breath (1950)
  Coindreau, Maurice Edgar. *Time of William Faulkner*, 136–140.
  Phillips, Robert. *William Goyen*, 33–45.

In a Farther Country (1955)
  Paul, Jay S. " 'Marvelous Reciprocity': The Fiction of William Goyen." *Crit* 19.2
    (1977): 83–84.
  Phillips, Robert. *William Goyen*, 58–67.

GRAU, SHIRLEY ANN (1929–)

Keepers of the House (1964)
  Going, William T. *Essays on Alabama Literature*, 32–38.

GRAVES, A. J., MRS.

Girlhood and Womanhood (1844)
  Baym, Nina. *Woman's Fiction*, 77–79.

GREENBERG, JOANNE (1932–)

I Never Promised You a Rose Garden (1964)
  Wolfe, Kary K. and Gary K. Wolfe. "Metaphors of Madness: Popular Psychological
    Narratives." *JPC* 9 (1976): 902–906.
  Wolfe, Kary K. and Gary K. Wolfe. "Metaphors of Madness: Popular Psychological
    Narratives." *Journal of Popular Culture* 9 (Spring 1976): 895–907. Rpt. in Lenz,
    Millicent and Ramona M. Mahood, comps. *Young Adult Literature*, 150–152,
    156–160.

GREY, ZANE (1872–1939)

Border Legion (1916)
  Ronald, Ann. *Zane Grey*, 25–26.

Desert Gold (1913)
  Jackson, Carlton. *Zane Grey*, 43–45.

Heritage of the Desert (1910)

    Jackson, Carlton. *Zane Grey*, 33–38.

    Ronald, Ann. *Zane Grey*, 13–17.

Knights of the Range (1939)

    Jackson, Carlton. *Zane Grey*, 101–102.

Lone Star Ranger (1915)

    Jackson, Carlton. *Zane Grey*, 112–113.

    Ronald, Ann. *Zane Grey*, 23–25.

Riders of the Purple Sage (1912)

    Jackson, Carlton. *Zane Grey*, 51–56.

    Ronald, Ann. *Zane Grey*, 17–20.

Shadow on the Trail (1946)

    Jackson, Carlton. *Zane Grey*, 113–114.

Twin Sombreros (1941)

    Jackson, Carlton. *Zane Grey*, 104–105.

U. P. Trail (1918)

    Ronald, Ann. *Zane Grey*, 31–32.

Vanishing American (1925)

    Jackson, Carlton. *Zane Grey*, 78–80.

Wanderer of the Wasteland (1923)

    Jackson, Carlton. *Zane Grey*, 38–40.

Wildfire (1917)

    Jackson, Carlton. *Zane Grey*, 87–89.

GRIGGS, SUTTON E. (1872–1930)

Hindered Hand (1905)

    Andrews, William L. "Miscegenation in the Late Nineteenth-Century American Novel." *SoHR* 13 (1979): 21–22.

    Berzon, Judith R. *Neither White Nor Black*, 205, 207–208, 209–210, 210–211.

    Elder, Arlene A. *"Hindered Hand"*, 88–93, 96, 102.

    Gayle, Addison, Jr. *Way of the New World*, 67–69.

    Gloster, Hugh M. "Sutton E. Griggs: Novelist of the New Negro." *Phylon* 4.4 (1943): 335–345. Rpt. in Hemenway, Robert, ed. *Black Novelist*, 17–19.

    Isani, Mukhtar Ali. "Exotic and Protest in Earlier Black Literature: The Use of Alien Setting and Character." *SIBL* 5.2 (1974): 11.

Imperium in Imperio (1899)

    Berzon, Judith R. *Neither White Nor Black*, 205–207, 210, 211–213.

    Elder, Arlene A. *"Hindered Hand"*, 73–77, 102.

    Fleming, Robert E. "Humor in the Early Black Novel." *CLAJ* 17 (1973): 257–259.

    Fleming, Robert E. "Sutton E. Griggs: Militant Black Novelist." *Phylon* 34 (1973): 73–77.

    Gayle, Addison, Jr. *Way of the New World*, 61–67.

Gloster, Hugh M. "Sutton E. Griggs: Novelist of the New Negro." *Phylon* 4.4 (1943): 335–345. Rpt. in Hemenway, Robert, ed. *Black Novelist*, 13–14.
Isani, Mukhtar Ali. "Exotic and Protest in Earlier Black Literature: The Use of Alien Setting and Character." *SIBL* 5.2 (1974): 11.
Schultz, Elizabeth. " 'Free in Fact and at Last': The Image of the Black Woman in Black American Fiction," in Springer, Marlene, ed. *What Manner of Woman*, 327.
Starke, Catherine Juanita. *Black Portraiture in American Fiction*, 225–228.
Whitlow, Roger. "Revolutionary Black Novels of Martin R. Delany and Sutton Griggs." *MELUS* 5.3 (1978): 31–35.

Overshadowed (1901)

Elder, Arlene A. *"Hindered Hand"*, 72–73, 77–84, 102.
Gloster, Hugh M. "Sutton E. Griggs: Novelist of the New Negro." *Phylon* 4.4 (1943): 335–345. Rpt. in Hemenway, Robert, ed. *Black Novelist*, 14–15.

Pointing the Way (1908)

Berzon, Judith R. *Neither White Nor Black*, 206, 208–209, 210.
Elder, Arlene A. *"Hindered Hand"*, 93–95, 97–99, 102–103.
Gloster, Hugh M. "Sutton E. Griggs: Novelist of the New Negro." *Phylon* 4.4 (1943): 335–345. Rpt. in Hemenway, Robert, ed. *Black Novelist*, 19–21.

Unfettered (1902)

Elder, Arlene A. *"Hindered Hand"*, 84–87, 96–97, 102.
Gloster, Hugh M. "Sutton E. Griggs: Novelist of the New Negro." *Phylon* 4.4 (1943): 335–345. Rpt. in Hemenway, Robert, ed. *Black Novelist*, 15–17.

GRIGNON, CLAUDE-HENRI (1894–1976)

Man and His Sin see *Un homme et son péché*

Un homme et son péché (1933)

Servais-Maquoi, Mireille. *Le roman de la terre au Québec*, 127–147.

Woman and the Miser see *Un homme et son péché*

GROSSMAN, ALFRED (1927–)

Acrobat Admits (1959)

Bryant, Jerry H. *Open Decision*, 212–213.

Many Slippery Errors (1963)

Bryant, Jerry H. *Open Decision*, 210–211.

GROULX, LIONEL (1878–1967)

Call of the Blood see *L'appel de la race*

L'appel de la race (1922)

Cotnam, Jacques. "Cultural Nationalism and its Literary Expression in French-Canadian Fiction." Trans. Noël Corbett. In Lewald, H. Ernest, ed. *Cry of Home*, 276–280.

Hathorn, Ramon. "Soldats, patrons et femmes 'fatales': Figures l'Anglais' dans le roman québécois des XIXe et XXe siècles." *V&I* 6 (1980): 107–109.
Sutherland, Ronald. *Second Image*, 41–46.

GROVE, FREDERICK PHILIP (1879–1948)

Chronicles of Spalding District see *Fruits of the Earth*

Consider Her Ways (1947)
Spettigue, Douglas O. *Frederick Philip Grove*, 126–131, 138.
Sutherland, Ronald. *Frederick Philip Grove*, 33–35.

Fruits of the Earth (1933)
Birbalsingh, Frank. "Grove and Exisentialism," in Stephens, Donald G., ed. *Writers of the Prairies*, 58.
Dooley, D. J. *Moral Vision*, 13–23.
Dudek, Louis. *Selected Essays*, 345, 346–347.
Harrison, Dick. *Unnamed Country*, 101–102, 114, 134.
Jackel. Susan. "House on the Prairies." *CanL* 42 (1969): 50–51.
Jackel, Susan. "House on the Prairies," in Stephens, Donald G., ed. *Writers of the Prairies*, 166, 169–170.
Jones, D. G. *Butterfly on Rock*, 73, 75–76, 89–90..
McCourt, E. A. "Spokesman of Race." McCourt, E. A. *Canadian West in Fiction*. Toronto: Ryerson Press, 1949. 56–70. Rpt. in Pacey, Desmond, ed. *Frederick Philip Grove*, 61–63, 66–69.
McMullin, Stanley E. "Grove and the Promised Land," in Stephens, Donald G., ed. *Writers of the Prairies*, 70–76.
McMullin, Stanley E. "Grove and the Promised Land," in Woodcock, George, ed. *Canadian Novel*, 31–36.
Mathews, Robin. *Canadian Literature*, 66–67, 69–73.
Mathews, Robin D. "Wacousta Factor," in Bessai, Diane and David Jackel, eds. *Figures in a Ground*, 312–313.
Sirois, Antoine. "Grove et Ringuet: Témoins d'une époque." *CanL* 49 (1971): 23–27.
Spettigue, Douglas O. *Frederick Philip Grove*, 109–111, 113–115.
Stobie, Margaret R. *Frederick Philip Grove*, 128–131.
Sutherland, Ronald. *Frederick Philip Grove*, 41, 42–45.

In Search of My Self (1948)
Heidenriech, Rosmarin. "Search for FPG." *CanL* 80 (1979): 63–70.

Master of the Mill (1944)
Birbalsingh, Frank. "Grove and Exisentialism," in Stephens, Donald G., ed. *Writers of the Prairies*, 58, 59, 64.
Cappon, Paul. "General Introduction Part B: Towards a Sociology of English Canadian Literature," in Cappon, Paul, ed. *In Our Own House*, 59.
Jones, D. G. *Butterfly on Rock*, 72–75.
Keith, W. J. "F.P. Grove's 'Difficult' Novel: *The Master of the Mill*." *Ariel* 4.2 (1973): 34–48.
MacDonald, R. D. "Power of F.P. Grove's *The Master of the Mill*." *Mosaic* 7.2 (1974): 89–100.

McMullin, Stanley E. "Grove and the Promised Land," in Stephens, Donald G., ed. *Writers of the Prairies*, 70–76.
McMullin, Stanley E. "Grove and the Promised Land," in Woodcock, George, ed. *Canadian Novel*, 32–36.
Mathews, Robin. *Canadian Literature*, 68–69, 73–74.
Mathews, Robin D. "Wacousta Factor," in Bessai, Diane and David Jackel, eds. *Figures in a Ground*, 315.
Moss, John. *Patterns of Isolation*, 203–207.
Spettigue, Douglas O. *Frederick Philip Grove*, 116–123, 134–135.
Sutherland, Ronald. *Frederick Philip Grove*, 36–39.
Watters, Reginald Eyre. *Essays and Articles*, 141–147.

Our Daily Bread (1928)

Birbalsingh, Frank. "Grove and Exisentialism," in Stephens, Donald G., ed. *Writers of the Prairies*, 58.
Dudek, Louis. *Selected Essays*, 342–343, 345.
Harrison, Dick. *Unnamed Country*, 133.
Jackel. Susan. "House on the Prairies." *CanL* 42 (1969): 50.
Jackel, Susan. "House on the Prairies," in Stephens, Donald G., ed. *Writers of the Prairies*, 169.
Jones, D. G. *Butterfly on Rock*, 73, 74, 76.
McCourt, E. A. "Spokesman of Race." McCourt, E. A. *Canadian West in Fiction.* Toronto: Ryerson Press, 1949. 56–70. Rpt. in Pacey, Desmond, ed. *Frederick Philip Grove*, 61–66.
McMullin, Stanley E. "Grove and the Promised Land," in Stephens, Donald G., ed. *Writers of the Prairies*, 70–76.
McMullin, Stanley E. "Grove and the Promised Land," in Woodcock, George, ed. *Canadian Novel*, 31–36.
Skelton, Isabel. "Frederick Philip Grove." *Dalhousie Review* 19 (July 1939): 147–163. Rpt. as "One Speaking Into a Void," in Pacey, Desmond, ed. *Frederick Philip Grove*, 36–38.
Spettigue, Douglas O. *Frederick Philip Grove*, 108–109, 132–133.
Stobie, Margaret R. *Frederick Philip Grove*, 102–110.
Sutherland, Ronald. *Frederick Philip Grove*, 40–41, 42–45.
Sutherland, Ronald. *Second Image*, 6–10.

Search for America (1927)

Dudek, Louis. *Selected Essays*, 343–344.
Keith, W. J. "Grove's *Search for America*." *CanL* 59 (1974): 57–65.
McMullin, Stanley E. "Grove and the Promised Land," in Stephens, Donald G., ed. *Writers of the Prairies*, 70–76.
McMullin, Stanley E. "Grove and the Promised Land," in Woodcock, George, ed. *Canadian Novel*, 30–31.
Spettigue, Douglas O. *Frederick Philip Grove*, 36–39.
Stobie, Margaret R. *Frederick Philip Grove*, 59–69.

Settlers of the Marsh (1925)

Birbalsingh, Frank. "Grove and Exisentialism," in Stephens, Donald G., ed. *Writers of the Prairies*, 57–58.
Boutelle, Ann. "Dorian Gray Phenomenon in Canadian Literature." *DR* 57 (1977): 272–273.
Dudek, Louis. *Selected Essays*, 345.
Harrison, Dick. *Unnamed Country*, 114–123, 133, 137–142, 144–146.

Jones, D. G. *Butterfly on Rock*, 74, 76–77.

McMullin, Stanley E. "Grove and the Promised Land," in Stephens, Donald G., ed. *Writers of the Prairies*, 70–76.

McMullin, Stanley E. "Grove and the Promised Land," in Woodcock, George, ed. *Canadian Novel*, 31–36.

Skelton, Isabel. "Frederick Philip Grove." *Dalhousie Review* 19 (July 1939): 147–163. Rpt. as "One Speaking Into a Void," in Pacey, Desmond, ed. *Frederick Philip Grove*, 30–36.

Spettigue, Douglas O. *Frederick Philip Grove*, 104–107, 110–111, 112.

Stobie, Margaret R. *Frederick Philip Grove*, 77–84.

Sutherland, Ronald. *Frederick Philip Grove*, 47–51.

Sutherland, Ronald. *Second Image*, 81–82.

Two Generations (1939)

Jackel, Susan. "House on the Prairies," in Stephens, Donald G., ed. *Writers of the Prairies*, 166.

McMullin, Stanley E. "Grove and the Promised Land," in Stephens, Donald G., ed. *Writers of the Prairies*, 70–76.

McMullin, Stanley E. "Grove and the Promised Land," in Woodcock, George, ed. *Canadian Novel*, 31–36.

Skelton, Isabel. "Frederick Philip Grove." *Dalhousie Review* 19 (July 1939): 147–163. Rpt. as "One Speaking Into a Void," in Pacey, Desmond, ed. *Frederick Philip Grove*, 48–49.

Spettigue, Douglas O. *Frederick Philip Grove*, 115–116, 133.

Sutherland, Ronald. *Frederick Philip Grove*, 42–45.

Yoke of Life (1930)

Birbalsingh, Frank. "Grove and Exisentialism," in Stephens, Donald G., ed. *Writers of the Prairies*, 58, 64–65.

Dudek, Louis. *Selected Essays*, 343, 345.

Harrison, Dick. *Unnamed Country*, 148.

McCourt, E. A. "Spokesman of Race." McCourt, E. A. *Canadian West in Fiction*. Toronto: Ryerson Press, 1949. 56–70. Rpt. in Pacey, Desmond, ed. *Frederick Philip Grove*, 69–72.

McMullin, Stanley E. "Grove and the Promised Land," in Stephens, Donald G., ed. *Writers of the Prairies*, 70–76.

McMullin, Stanley E. "Grove and the Promised Land," in Woodcock, George, ed. *Canadian Novel*, 31–36.

Makow, Henry. "Grove's Treatment of Sex: Platonic Love in *The Yoke of Life*." *DR* 58 (1978): 528–540.

Skelton, Isabel. "Frederick Philip Grove." *Dalhousie Review* 19 (July 1939): 147–163. Rpt. as "One Speaking Into a Void," in Pacey, Desmond, ed. *Frederick Philip Grove*, 38–40.

Spettigue, Douglas O. *Frederick Philip Grove*, 104–107.

Stobie, Margaret R. *Frederick Philip Grove*, 84–88.

Sutherland, Ronald. *Frederick Philip Grove*, 52–55.

GUÈVREMONT, GERMAINE (1893–1968)

Le survenant (1945)

Major, Robert. "*Le survenant* et la figure d'Éros dans l'oeuvre de Germaine Guèvremont." *V&I* 2 (1976): 195–203.

Servais-Maquoi, Mireille. *Le roman de la terre au Québec*, 189–238.
Urbas, Jeannette. *From Thirty Acres to Modern Times*, 25–28.

Marie-Didace (1947)

Major, Robert. "*Le survenant* et la figure d'Éros dans l'oeuvre de Germaine Guèvremont." *V&I* 2 (1976): 203–207.
Servais-Maquoi, Mireille. *Le roman de la terre au Québec*, 189–238.
Urbas, Jeannette. *From Thirty Acres to Modern Times*, 25–28.

Outlander see *Le survenant* and *Marie-Didace* (published in single volume as *Outlander*)

GUTHRIE, A. B., JR. (1901–1991)

Big Sky (1947)

Gale, Robert L. "Guthrie's *The Big Sky*." *Expl* 38.4 (1980): 7–8.
Peterson, Levi S. "Tragedy and Western American Literature." *WAL* 6 (1972): 243–249.
Stewart, Donald C. "Functions of Bird and Sky Imagery in Guthrie's *The Big Sky*." *Crit* 19.2 (1977): 53–61.

These Thousand Hills (1956)

Stineback, David C. *Shifting World*, 156–170.

H. D. (1886–1961)

Bid Me to Live (1960)

DuPlessis, Rachel Blau. "Romantic Thralldom in H.D." *ConL* 20 (1979): 182–184.
Weatherhead, A. Kingsley. "Style in H. D.'s Novels." *ConL* 10.4 (1969): 550–555.

Hedylus (1928)

Weatherhead, A. Kingsley. "Style in H. D.'s Novels." *ConL* 10.4 (1969): 546–550.

Palimpsest (1926)

Weatherhead, A. Kingsley. "Style in H. D.'s Novels." *ConL* 10.4 (1969): 540–546.

HAINES, WILLIAM WISTER (1908–1989)

Command Decision (1946)

Miller, Wayne Charles. *Armed America, Its Face in Fiction*, 186–188.

HALBERSTAM, DAVID (1934–)

One Very Hot Day (1967)

Beidler, Philip D. "Truth-Telling and Literary Values in the Vietnam Novel." *SAQ* 78 (1979): 142–143.
Jones, Peter G. *War and the Novelist*, 190–194, 197.

HALDEMAN, JOE (1943–)

All My Sins Remembered (1977)

Gordon, Joan. *Joe Haldeman*, 46–50.

Forever War (1975)
   Gordon, Joan. *Joe Haldeman*, 27–34.
Mindbridge (1976)
   Gordon, Joan. *Joe Haldeman*, 38–41.

HALE, GARTH (1888–1962)

Legacy for Our Sons (1952)
   Bryant, Jerry H. *Open Decision*, 173–174.

HALEY, ALEX (1921–1992)

Roots (1976)
   Skaggs, Merrill Maguire. "*Roots:* A New Black Myth." *SoQ* 17.1 (1978): 42–50.

HAMEL, CHARLES (1914–1961)

Prix David (1962)
   Belleau, André. *Le romancier fictif*, 78–79.
Solitude de la chair (1951)
   Belleau, André. *Le romancier fictif*, 75–78.

HAMELIN, JEAN (1920–1970)

Les occasions profitables (1961)
   Shek, Ben-Zion. *Social Realism*, 227–230.

HAMMETT, DASHIELL (1894–1961)

Dain Curse (1929)
   Whitley, John S. "Stirring Things Up: Dashiell Hammett's Continental Op." *JAmS* 14 (1980): 449–453.
   Wolfe, Peter. *Beams Falling*, 22–23, 30, 36–37, 94–110.
Glass Key (1931)
   Hulley, Kathleen. "From the Crystal Sphere to Edge City: Ideology in the Novels of Dashiell Hammett," in Durand, Régis, ed. *Myth and Ideology in American Culture*, 113–126.
   Palmer, Jerry. *Thrillers*, 43–47.
   Wolfe, Peter. *Beams Falling*, 21–22, 29–30, 40–41.
Maltese Falcon (1930)
   Wolfe, Peter. *Beams Falling*, 19–20, 28, 111–128, 129–147.
Red Harvest (1929)
   Hulley, Kathleen. "From the Crystal Sphere to Edge City: Ideology in the Novels of Dashiell Hammett," in Durand, Régis, ed. *Myth and Ideology in American Culture*, 113–126.

Whitley, John S. "Stirring Things Up: Dashiell Hammett's Continental Op." *JAmS* 14 (1980): 443–448.
Wolfe, Peter. *Beams Falling*, 19, 21–22, 24, 30, 37, 77–93.

Thin Man (1934)
Wolfe, Peter. *Beams Falling*, 41–42, 148–163.

HARBEN, WILL N. (1858–1919)

Abner Daniel (1902)
Murphy, James K. *Will N. Harben*, 87–91.

Almost Persuaded (1891)
Murphy, James K. *Will N. Harben*, 36–39.

Ann Boyd (1906)
Murphy, James K. *Will N. Harben*, 99–102.

Desired Woman (1913)
Murphy, James K. *Will N. Harben*, 118–119.

Dixie Hart (1910)
Murphy, James K. *Will N. Harben*, 110–112.

Georgians (1904)
Murphy, James K. *Will N. Harben*, 94–96.

Gilbert Neal (1908)
Murphy, James K. *Will N. Harben*, 107–109.

Jane Dawson (1911)
Murphy, James K. *Will N. Harben*, 115–117.

Land of the Changing Sun (1894)
Murphy, James K. *Will N. Harben*, 44–46.

Mam' Linda (1907)
Murphy, James K. *Will N. Harben*, 103–106.

Mute Confessor (1892)
Murphy, James K. *Will N. Harben*, 40–42.

Paul Rundel (1912)
Murphy, James K. *Will N. Harben*, 117–118.

Pole Baker (1905)
Murphy, James K. *Will N. Harben*, 97–98.

Substitute (1903)
Murphy, James K. *Will N. Harben*, 92–94.

Triumph (1917)
Murphy, James K. *Will N. Harben*, 124–128.

Westerfelt (1901)
Murphy, James K. *Will N. Harben*, 83–86.

White Marie (1889)
  Murphy, James K. *Will N. Harben*, 30–34.

Woman Who Trusted (1901)
  Murphy, James K. *Will N. Harben*, 81–83.

HARBEN, WILLIAM NATHANIEL see HARBEN, WILL N.

HARINGTON, DONALD (1935–)

Cherry Pit (1965)
  Vonalt, Larry. "Doubling and Duplicity in Donald Harington's *The Cherry Pit*."
    Crit 22.1 (1980): 47–54.

HARLAND, MARION (1830–1922)

Alone (1854)
  Baym, Nina. *Woman's Fiction*, 201–203.

Hidden Path (1855)
  Baym, Nina. *Woman's Fiction*, 203–204.

Moss-Side (1857)
  Baym, Nina. *Woman's Fiction*, 205–206.

HARLOW, ROBERT (1923–)

Scann (1972)
  Moss, John. *Sex and Violence*, 245–254.

HARNESS, CHARLES L. (1915–)

Flight into Yesterday see *Paradox Men*

Paradox Men (1953)
  Hills, Norman L. "Charles L. Harness: The Flowering of Melodrama." *Extrapola-
    tion* 19 (1978): 141–143.

Ring of Ritornel (1968)
  Hills, Norman L. "Charles L. Harness: The Flowering of Melodrama." *Extrapola-
    tion* 19 (1978): 144–146.

HARPER, FRANCES (1825–1911)

Iola Leroy (1892)
  Andrews, William L. "Miscegenation in the Late Nineteenth-Century American
    Novel." *SoHR* 13 (1979): 17.
  Berzon, Judith R. *Neither White Nor Black*, 60.

Christian, Barbara. *Black Women Novelists*, 3–5, 25–30.
Elder, Arlene A. *"Hindered Hand"*, 23, 29, 60.

HARRIS, JOEL CHANDLER (1848–1908)

Chronicles of Aunt Minervy Ann (1899)
Bickley, R. Bruce, Jr. *Joel Chandler Harris*, 134–137.

Gabriel Tolliver (1902)
Bickley, R. Bruce, Jr. *Joel Chandler Harris*, 139–142.
Godbold, E. Stanley, Jr. "Battleground Revisited: Reconstruction in Southern Fiction, 1895–1905." *SAQ* 73 (1974): 108–110.

Sister Jane (1896)
Bickley, R. Bruce, Jr. *Joel Chandler Harris*, 132–134.
Flusche, Michael. "Underlying Despair in the Fiction of Joel Chandler Harris." *MissQ* 29 (1976): 98–102.

HARRIS, MARK (1922–)

Bang the Drum Slowly (1956)
Lavers, Norman. *Mark Harris*, 52–58.
Umphlett, Wiley Lee. *Sporting Myth and the American Experience*, 131, 139–145.

City of Discontent (1952)
Lavers, Norman. *Mark Harris*, 28–33.

Goy (1970)
Lavers, Norman. *Mark Harris*, 87–100.

Killing Everybody (1973)
Lavers, Norman. *Mark Harris*, 101–115.

Something About a Soldier (1957)
Lavers, Norman. *Mark Harris*, 62–73.

Southpaw (1953)
Lavers, Norman. *Mark Harris*, 35–52.

Trumpet to the World (1946)
Lavers, Norman. *Mark Harris*, 24–28.

Wake Up, Stupid (1959)
Lavers, Norman. *Mark Harris*, 74–87.

HARRISON, CHARLES YALE (1898–1954)

Generals Die in Bed (1930)
Moss, John. *Sex and Violence*, 232–234.

HARRISON, HARRY (1925–)

Stainless Steel Rat (1961)
Carter, Steven R. "Harry Harrison's *The Adventures of the Stainless Steel Rat:* A Study in Multiple Interfaces." *Extrapolation* 21 (1980): 139–145.

Stainless Steel Rat Saves the World (1972)

Carter, Steven R. "Harry Harrison's *The Adventures of the Stainless Steel Rat:* A Study in Multiple Interfaces." *Extrapolation* 21 (1980): 139–145.

Stainless Steel Rat's Revenge (1970)

Carter, Steven R. "Harry Harrison's *The Adventures of the Stainless Steel Rat:* A Study in Multiple Interfaces." *Extrapolation* 21 (1980): 139–145.

HARVEY, JEAN-CHARLES (1891–1967)

Fears Folly see *Les demi-civilisés*

Les demi-civilisés (1934)

Belleau, André. *Le romancier fictif*, 73–75.
Cotnam, Jacques. "Cultural Nationalism and its Literary Expression in French-Canadian Fiction." Trans. Noël Corbett. In Lewald, H. Ernest, ed. *Cry of Home*, 281–284.
Rousseau, Guildo. *Jean-Charles Harvey*, 61–63, 70–71, 76–77, 77–79, 82–83, 84–85, 88, 91, 92–94, 104–111, 121–124, 125–139.
Sutherland, Ronald. *Second Image*, 80–81, 82–85.

Les paradis de sable (1953)

Rousseau, Guildo. *Jean-Charles Harvey*, 49–50, 52–54, 63–67, 77, 79–80, 83, 85–87, 89, 91–93, 95–96, 111–116, 121–124, 125–139.

Marcel Faure (1922)

Hathorn, Ramon. "Soldats, patrons et femmes 'fatales': figures de l'Anglais' dans le roman québécois des XIXe et XXe siècles." *V&I* 6 (1980): 105–106.
Rousseau, Guildo. *Jean-Charles Harvey*, 59–61, 67–69, 75–76, 80, 81–82, 83–84, 88, 90, 92, 94, 97–104, 119–121, 125–139.

Sackcloth for Banner see *Les demi-civilisés*

HAWKES, JOHN (1925–1998)

Beetle Leg (1951)

Berry, Eliot. *Poetry of Force and Darkness*, 26–33.
Busch, Frederick. *Hawkes*, 39–60.
Frakes, James R. " 'Undramatized Narrator' in John Hawke's: Who Says?," in Santore, Anthony C. and Michael Pocalyko, eds. *John Hawkes Symposium*, 33–34.
Frost, Lucy. "Drowning of American Adam: Hawkes' *The Beetle Leg*." *Crit* 14.3 (1973): 63–74.
Greiner, Donald J. *Comic Terror*, 97–124.
Guerard, Albert J. "John Hawkes: A Longish View," in Santore, Anthony C. and Michael Pocalyko, eds. *John Hawkes Symposium*, 5.
Klein, Marcus. "John Hawkes' Experimental Compositions," in Federman, Raymond, ed. *Surfiction*, 213.
Kuehl, John. *John Hawkes and the Craft of Conflict*, 23–26, 28–30, 36–40, 59–60, 62, 84–85, 99.
Tanner, Tony. *City of Words*, 209–211.

Blood Oranges (1971)

Abrams, Steven. *"Blood Oranges* as a Visionary Fiction." *JNT* 8 (1978): 97–111.
Allen, C. J. "Desire, Design, and Debris: The Submerged Narrative of John Hawkes' Recent Trilogy." *MFS* 25 (1979–80): 579–583, 592.
Berry, Eliot. *Poetry of Force and Darkness*, 50–56.
Busch, Frederick. *Hawkes*, 139–170.
Busch, Frederick. "Icebergs, Islands, Ships Beneath the Sea," in Santore, Anthony C. and Michael Pocalyko, eds. *John Hawkes Symposium*, 56.
Cuddy, Lois A. "Functional Pastoralism in *The Blood Oranges*." *SAF* 3 (1975): 15–25.
Greiner, Donald J. *Comic Terror*, 201–239.
Knapp, John V. "Hawkes' *The Blood Oranges:* A Sensual New Jerusalem." *Crit* 17.3 (1976): 5–25.
Kuehl, John. *John Hawkes and the Craft of Conflict*, 127–151.
Steiner, Robert. "Form and the Bourgeois Traveler," in Santore, Anthony C. and Michael Pocalyko, eds. *John Hawkes Symposium*, 127–128.
Van Wert, William F. "Narration in John Hawkes' Trilogy." *LR* 24 (1980): 21–29, 37–39.
Veron, Enid. "From Festival to Farce: Design and Meaning in John Hawke's Comic Triad," in Santore, Anthony C. and Michael Pocalyko, eds. *John Hawkes Symposium*, 65–68.

Cannibal (1949)

Armstrong, Thomas W. "Reader, Critic, and the Form of John Hawkes's *The Cannibal*." *BoundaryII* 5 (1977): 829–844.
Berry, Eliot. *Poetry of Force and Darkness*, 18–26.
Bischoff, Joan. "John Hawkes' Horse of the Apocalypse." *NConL* 6.4 (1976): 12–13, 14.
Busch, Frederick. *Hawkes*, 17–37.
Donald, Miles. *American Novel in the Twentieth Century*, 122–124.
Graham, John. "On *The Cannibal*," in Santore, Anthony C. and Michael Pocalyko, eds. *John Hawkes Symposium*, 39–49.
Greiner, Donald J. *Comic Terror*, 67–96.
Guerard, Albert J. "John Hawkes: A Longish View," in Santore, Anthony C. and Michael Pocalyko, eds. *John Hawkes Symposium*, 4–5, 11.
Hendin, Josephine. *Vulnerable People*, 69–70.
Klein, Marcus. "John Hawkes' Experimental Compositions," in Federman, Raymond, ed. *Surfiction*, 209–210, 212, 213.
Kuehl, John. *John Hawkes and the Craft of Conflict*, 4–7, 14–15, 16–18, 42, 60–62, 63–64, 80, 84–85, 110.
Littlejohn, David. *Interruptions*, 25.
Spencer, Sharon. *Space, Time and Structure in the Modern Novel*, 30–32.
Tanner, Tony. *City of Words*, 205–209.
Vickery, Olga W. "Inferno of the Moderns," in Friedman, Melvin J. and John B. Vickery, eds. *Shaken Realist*, 153–155.

Death, Sleep and the Traveler (1974)

Allen, C. J. "Desire, Design, and Debris: The Submerged Narrative of John Hawkes' Recent Trilogy." *MFS* 25 (1979–80): 579–580, 583–589, 592.
Berry, Eliot. *Poetry of Force and Darkness*, 56–59.

Busch, Frederick. "Icebergs, Islands, Ships Beneath the Sea," in Santore, Anthony C. and Michael Pocalyko, eds. *John Hawkes Symposium*, 60–63.

Greiner, Donald J. "*Death, Sleep & the Traveler:* John Hawkes' Return to Terror." *Crit* 17.3 (1976): 26–38.

Kraus, Elisabeth. "Psychic Sores in Search of Compassion: Hawkes' *Death, Sleep & the Traveler.*" *Crit* 17.3 (1976): 39–52.

Steiner, Robert. "Form and the Bourgeois Traveler," in Santore, Anthony C. and Michael Pocalyko, eds. *John Hawkes Symposium*, 119–121, 123–126.

Van Wert, William F. "Narration in John Hawkes' Trilogy." *LR* 24 (1980): 21–22, 29–35, 37–39.

Veron, Enid. "From Festival to Farce: Design and Meaning in John Hawke's Comic Triad," in Santore, Anthony C. and Michael Pocalyko, eds. *John Hawkes Symposium*, 68–73, 74.

Lime Twig (1962)

Berry, Eliot. *Poetry of Force and Darkness*, 38–49.

Bischoff, Joan. "John Hawkes' Horse of the Apocalypse." *NConL* 6.4 (1976):12, 13–14.

Boutrous, Lawrence K. "Parody in Hawkes' *The Lime Twig.*" *Crit* 15.2 (1973): 49–56.

Busch, Frederick. *Hawkes*, 87–106.

Frakes, James R. " 'Undramatized Narrator' in John Hawke's: Who Says?," in Santore, Anthony C. and Michael Pocalyko, eds. *John Hawkes Symposium*, 35–37.

Gault, Pierre. "Genesis and Functions of Hencher in *The Lime Twig*," in Johnson, Ira D. and Christiane Johnson, eds. *Les Américanistes*, 138–155.

Greiner, Donald J. *Comic Terror*, 125–158.

Guerard, Albert J. "John Hawkes: A Longish View," in Santore, Anthony C. and Michael Pocalyko, eds. *John Hawkes Symposium*, 6.

Klein, Marcus. "John Hawkes' Experimental Compositions," in Federman, Raymond, ed. *Surfiction*, 208–209, 212.

Kuehl, John. *John Hawkes and the Craft of Conflict*, 7–8, 13–14, 19–20, 26–27, 30–31, 31–33, 53–54, 69–72, 78–80, 81–82, 82–84, 86–87, 98, 99–100, 101–103, 107, 110–111.

Littlejohn, David. *Interruptions*, 24, 25.

Olderman, Raymond M. *Beyond the Waste Land*, 150–183.

Scholes, Robert. *Fabulation and Metafiction*, 178–189.

Spencer, Sharon. *Space, Time and Structure in the Modern Novel*, 88–90.

Steiner, Robert. "Form and the Bourgeois Traveler," in Santore, Anthony C. and Michael Pocalyko, eds. *John Hawkes Symposium*, 127.

Stubbs, John C. "John Hawkes and the Dream-Work of *The Lime Twig* and *Second Skin.*" *L&P* 21 (1971): 149–156.

Tanner, Tony. *City of Words*, 212–217.

Warner, John M. " 'Internalized Quest Romance' in Hawkes' *The Lime Twig.*" *MFS* 19 (1973): 89–95.

Second Skin (1963)

Berry, Eliot. *Poetry of Force and Darkness*, 33–38.

Brooks, Peter. "Review of *Second Skin.*" *Encounter* 26 (June 1966): 68–72. Rpt. in Graham, John, comp. *Merrill Studies in Second Skin*, 13–18.

Busch, Frederick. *Hawkes*, 107–122.

Busch, Frederick. "Icebergs, Islands, Ships Beneath the Sea," in Santore, Anthony C. and Michael Pocalyko, eds. *John Hawkes Symposium*, 56–57.

Frost, Lucy. "Awakening Paradise," in Graham, John, comp. *Merrill Studies in Second Skin*, 52–63.

Greiner, Donald J. *Comic Terror*, 159–199.

Greiner, Donald J. "Thematic Use of Color in John Hawkes' *Second Skin*." *ConL* 11 (1970): 389–400.

Guerard, Albert J. "John Hawkes: A Longish View," in Santore, Anthony C. and Michael Pocalyko, eds. *John Hawkes Symposium*, 6.

Guerard, Albert J. "*Second Skin:* The Light and the Dark Affirmation," in Graham, John, comp. *Merrill Studies in Second Skin*, 93–102.

Kauffmann, Stanley. "Review of *Second Skin*." *New Republic* 150 (6 June 1964): 19. Rpt. in Graham, John, comp. *Merrill Studies in Second Skin*, 5–8.

Klein, Marcus. "John Hawkes' Experimental Compositions," in Federman, Raymond, ed. *Surfiction*, 213–214.

Kuehl, John. *John Hawkes and the Craft of Conflict*, 15–16, 26, 33–36, 41–42, 46–48, 51–53, 57–58, 72–74, 82, 87, 100, 114–126.

Kuehl, John. "Story into Novel," in Kuehl, John. *Write and Rewrite*. New York: Meredith, 1967. 265, 284–287. Rpt. in Graham, John, comp. *Merrill Studies in Second Skin*, 35–38.

Lavers, Norman. "Structure of *Second Skin*." *Novel* 5 (1972): 208–214.

LeClair, Thomas. "Death and Black Humor." *Crit* 17.1 (1975): 19–21.

LeClair, Thomas. "Unreliability of Innocence: John Hawkes' *Second Skin*." *JNT* 3 (1973): 32–39.

Nichols, Stephen G., Jr. "Vision and Tradition in *Second Skin*," in Graham, John, comp. *Merrill Studies in Second Skin*, 69–82.

O'Donnell, Patrick. "Hero as Artist in John Hawkes's *Second Skin*." *IFR* 4 (1977): 119–127.

Pearce, Richard. *Stages of the Clown*, 103–116.

Ricks, Christopher. "Review of *Second Skin*." *New Statesman* 71 (11 March 1966): 339–340. Rpt. in Graham, John, comp. *Merrill Studies in Second Skin*, 9–12.

Robinson, William R. "John Hawkes' Artificial Inseminator," in Graham, John, comp. *Merrill Studies in Second Skin*, 63–69.

Santore, Anthony C. "Narrative Unreliability and the Structure of *Second Skin*," in Graham, John, comp. *Merrill Studies in Second Skin*, 83–93.

Spencer, Sharon. *Space, Time and Structure in the Modern Novel*, 82–84, 87.

Steiner, Robert. "Form and the Bourgeois Traveler," in Santore, Anthony C. and Michael Pocalyko, eds. *John Hawkes Symposium*, 121–122.

Stubbs, John C. "John Hawkes and the Dream-Work of *The Lime Twig* and *Second Skin*." *L&P* 21 (1971): 149–152, 156–159.

Tanner, Tony. *City of Words*, 218–229.

Wall, Carey. "Solid Ground in John Hawkes's *Second Skin*," in Garvin, Harry R., ed. *Makers of the Twentieth-Century Novel*, 309–319.

Wallace, Ronald. *Last Laugh*, 45–64.

Wallace, Ronald. "Rarer Action: Comedy in John Hawkes's *Second Skin*." *SNNTS* 9 (1977): 169–186.

Travesty (1976)

Allen, C. J. "Desire, Design, and Debris: The Submerged Narrative of John Hawkes' Recent Trilogy." *MFS* 25 (1979–80): 579–580, 589–592.

Baxter, Charles. "In the Suicide Seat: Reading John Hawkes's *Travesty*." *GR* 34 (1980): 871–885.

Berry, Eliot. *Poetry of Force and Darkness*, 60–64.

Greiner, Donald J. "Private Apocalypse: The Visionsf of *Travesty*," in Santore, Anthony C. and Michael Pocalyko, eds. *John Hawkes Symposium*, 142–153.

Klein, Marcus. "Satyr at the Head of the Mob," in Santore, Anthony C. and Michael Pocalyko, eds. *John Hawkes Symposium*, 159–164.

Steiner, Robert. "Form and the Bourgeois Traveler," in Santore, Anthony C. and Michael Pocalyko, eds. *John Hawkes Symposium*, 129–137.

Van Wert, William F. "Narration in John Hawkes' Trilogy." *LR* 24 (1980): 21–22, 35–39.

Veron, Enid. "From Festival to Farce: Design and Meaning in John Hawke's Comic Triad," in Santore, Anthony C. and Michael Pocalyko, eds. *John Hawkes Symposium*, 64–65, 73–75.

HAWLEY, CAMERON (1905–1969)

Executive Suite (1952)

Bryant, Jerry H. *Open Decision*, 174–176.

HAWTHORNE, JULIAN (1846–1934)

Archibald Malmaison (1879)

Park, Martha M. "*Archibald Malmaison:* Julian Hawthorne's Contribution to Gothic Fiction." *Extrapolation* 15 (1974): 103–115.

HAWTHORNE, NATHANIEL (1804–1864)

Blithedale Romance (1852)

Allen, Mary. "Smiles and Laughter in Hawthorne." *PQ* 52 (1973): 121.

Auchincloss, Louis. "*Blithedale Romance:* A Study of Form and Point of View." *NHJ* 2 (1972): 53–58.

Auchincloss, Louis. "*The Blithedale Romance:* A Study of Form and Point of View." *Nathaniel Hawthorne Journal* (1972): 53–58. Rpt. in Hawthorne, Nathaniel. *Blithedale Romance*, 389–395.

Bales, Kent. "Allegory and the Radical Romantic Ethic of *The Blithedale Romance*." *AL* 46 (1974): 41–53.

Bales, Kent. "Allegory and the Radical Romantic Ethic of *The Blithedale Romance*." *American Literature* 46 (1974): 41–53. Rpt. in Hawthorne, Nathaniel. *Blithedale Romance*, 407–413.

Bales, Kent. "*Blithedale Romance:* Coverdale's Mean and Subversive Egotism." *BuR* 21.2 (1973): 60–82.

Baym, Nina. "*Blithedale Romance:* A Radical Reading." *Journal of English and Germanic Philology* 67 (1968): 545–569. Rpt. in Hawthorne, Nathaniel. *Blithedale Romance*, 351–368.

Bell, Michael Davitt. *Development of American Romance*, 185–192.

Brodhead, Richard H. *Hawthorne, Melville, and the Novel*, 11–12, 13, 18–19, 91–115.

Crews, Frederick C. "Turning the Affair into a Ballad," in Crews, Frederick C.

Sins of the Fathers: Hawthorne's Psychological Themes. New York: Oxford University Press, 1966. 194–212. Rpt. in Crowley, J. Donald, ed. *Nathaniel Hawthorne*, 87–100.

Crews, Frederick C. "Turning the Affair into a Ballad," in Crews, Frederick C. *Sins of the Fathers: Hawthorne's Psychological Themes*. New York: Oxford University Press, 1966. 194–212. Rpt. in Hawthorne, Nathaniel. *Blithedale Romance*, 373–380.

Dennis, Carl. "*Blithedale Romance* and the Problem of Self-Integration." *TSLL* 15 (1973): 93–110.

Flint, Allen. " 'essentially a day-dream, and yet a fact': Hawthorne's *Blithedale*." *NHJ* (1972): 75–83.

Flint, Allen. "Saving Grace of Marriage in Hawthorne's Fiction." *ESQ* 71 (1973): 114, 116.

Fogle, Richard H. "Priscilla's Veil: A Study of Hawthorne's Veil-Imagery in *The Blithedale Romance*." *NHJ* 2 (1972): 59–65.

Fossum, Robert H. *Hawthorne's Inviolable Circle*, 140–149.

Frederick, John T. *Darkened Sky*, 54–55, 57–60.

Fryer, Judith. *Faces of Eve*, 89–93, 208–220.

Gollin, Rita K. " 'Dream-Work' in *The Blithedale Romance*." *ESQ* no.71 (1973): 74–83.

Gollin, Rita K. *Nathaniel Hawthorne and the Truth of Dreams*, 164–176.

Griffith, Kelley, Jr. "Form in *The Blithedale Romance*." *American Literature* 40 (1968): 15–26. Rpt. in Hawthorne, Nathaniel. *Blithedale Romance*, 380–389.

Harris, Janet. "Reflections of the Byronic Hero in Hawthorne's Fiction." *NHJ* (1977): 310–311.

Hirsch, David H. *Reality and Idea in the Early American Novel*, 157–163.

Hirsch, John C. "Politics of Blithedale: The Dilemma of the Self." *SIR* 11 (1972): 138–146.

Howe, Irving. "Hawthorne: Pastoral and Politics," in Howe, Irving. *Politics and the Novel*. New York: Horizon Press, 1957. 163–175. Rpt. in Hawthorne, Nathaniel. *Blithedale Romance*, 288–297.

Johnson, Claudia D. "Hawthorne and Nineteenth-Century Perfectionism." *AL* 44 (1973): 593.

Justus, James H. "Hawthorne's Coverdale: Character and Art in *The Blithedale Romance*." *American Literature* 47 (1975): 21–36. Rpt. in Hawthorne, Nathaniel. *Blithedale Romance*, 395–407.

Kaul, A. N. "Community and Society," in Kaul, A. N. *American Vision: Actual and Ideal Society in Nineteenth-Century Fiction*. New Haven: Yale University Press, 1963. 196–213. Rpt. in Hawthorne, Nathaniel. *Blithedale Romance*, 302–311.

Kay, Donald. "Five Acts of *The Blithedale Romance*." *ATQ* 13 (1972): 25–28.

Kerr, Howard. *Mediums, and Spirit-Rappers, and Roaring Radicals*, 58–60.

Klinkowitz, Jerome. "Hawthorne's Sense of an Ending." *ESQ* 70 (1973): 45–46, 47.

Klinkowitz, Jerome. *Practice of Fiction in America*, 14–15.

Koskenlinna, Hazel M. "Setting, Image, and Symbol in Scott and Hawthorne." *ESQ* 70 (1973): 53–54, 55.

Kuhlmann, Susan. *Knave, Fool, and Genius*, 76–79.

Lang, Hans-Joachim. "*Blithedale Romance:* A History of Ideas Approach," in Helmcke, Hans, Klaus Lubbers and Renate Schmidt-von Beardeleben, eds. *Literatur und Sprache der Verinigten Staaten*. Heidelberg, Germany: Carl Winter, 1969. 88–106. Rpt. in Hawthorne, Nathaniel. *Blithedale Romance*, 324–337.

Lefcowitz, Barbara F. and Allan B. Lefcowitz. "Some Rents in the Veil: New Light on Priscilla and Zenobia." *Nineteenth Century Fiction* 21 (1966): 263–275. Rpt. in Hawthorne, Nathaniel. *Blithedale Romance*, 341–350.

Lentz, Vern B. and Allen F. Stein. "Black Flower of Necessity: Structure in *The Blithedale Romance*." *ELWIU* 3 (1976): 86–96.

Levy, Leo B. "*Blithedale Romance:* Hawthorne's 'Voyage Through Chaos.' " *Studies in Romanticism* 8 (1968): 1–15. Rpt. in Hawthorne, Nathaniel. *Blithedale Romance*, 311–324.

McCarthy, Paul. "Extraordinary Man as Idealist in Novels by Hawthorne and Melville." *ESQ* 54 (1969): 45–46, 48, 50.

McGuire, Peter J. "Dante's *Inferno* in The Blithedale Romance." *ELN* 18 (1980): 25–27.

McPherson, Hugo. *Hawthorne as Myth-Maker*, 29–31, 146–158.

Magretta, Joan. "Coverdale Translation: *Blithedale* and the Bible." *NHJ* (1974): 250–256.

Male, Roy R. "Hawthorne's *The Blithedale Romance*." *Expl* 28 (1970): Item 56.

Male, Roy R. "Hawthorne's Fancy, or the Medium of *The Blithedale Romance*." *NHJ* (1972): 67–73.

Male, Roy R. "Pastoral Wasteland: *The Blithedale Romance*," in Male, Roy R. *Hawthorne's Tragic Vision*. Austin, TX: University of Texas Press, 1957. 139–156. Rpt. in Hawthorne, Nathaniel. *Blithedale Romance*, 297–301.

Marks, Alfred H. "Ironic Inversion in *The Blithedale Romance*." *ESQ* 55 (1969): 95–102.

Martin, Robert K. "Hawthorne's *The Blithedale Romance*." *Expl* 28 (1969): Item 11.

May, John R. *Toward a New Earth*, 44–61.

Murphy, John J. "Willa Cather and Hawthorne: Significant Resemblances." *Renascence* 27 (1975): 166–168.

Murray, Peter B. "Mythopoesis in *The Blithedale Romance*." *PMLA* 75 (1960): 591–596. Rpt. in Rountree, Thomas J., ed. *Critics on Hawthorne*, 106–114.

Ousby, Ian. *Reader's Guide to Fifty American Novels*, 61–63.

Pearce, Roy Harvey. "Day-Dream and Fact: The Import of *Blithedale Romance*," in Baldwin, Kenneth H. and David R. Kirby, eds. *Individual and Community: Variations on a Theme in American Fiction*, 49–63.

Porte, Joel. *Romance in America*, 125–137.

Pratt, Linda Ray. "Abuse of Eve by the New World Adam," in Cornillon, Susan Koppelman, ed. *Images of Women in Fiction*, 162–165.

Rahv, Philip. "Dark Lady of Salem." *Partisan Review* 8 (Sept-Oct 1941): 362–381. Rpt. in Hawthorne, Nathaniel. *Blithedale Romance*, 337–340.

Rahv, Philip. "Dark Lady of Salem." *Partisan Review* 8 (Sept-Oct 1941): 362–381. Rpt. in Rahv, Philip. *Essays on Literature and Politics*, 30–33, 34, 37–39.

Rahv, Philip. "Dark Lady of Salem." *Partisan Review* 8 (Sept-Oct 1941): 362–381. Rpt. in Rahv, Philip. *Literature and the Sixth Sense*, 61–64, 66, 69–72.

Rees, John O., Jr. "Shakespeare in *The Blithedale Romance*." *ESQ* no.71 (1973): 84–93.

Rose, Marilyn Gaddis. "Miles Coverdale as Hawthorne's Persona." *ATQ* 1 (1969): 90–91.

Ross, Donald, Jr. "Dreams and Sexual Repression in *The Blithedale Romance*." *PMLA* 86 (1971): 1014–1017.

Spanier, Sandra Whipple. "Two Foursomes in *The Blithedale Romance* and *Women in Love*." *CLS* 16 (1979): 58–68.

Sprague, Claire. "Dream and Disguise in *The Blithedale Romance*." *PMLA* 84 (1969): 596–597.

Stein, Allen F. "Hawthorne's Zenobia and Melville's Urania." *ATQ* 26 supp. (1975): 11–14.

Stock, Irvin. "Hawthorne's Portrait of the Artist: A Defense of *The Blithedale Romance*." *Novel* 11 (1978): 144–156.

Stone, Edward. "Hawthorne's Other Drowning." *NHJ* 2 (1972): 231–236.

Stout, Janis P. *Sodoms in Eden*, 106–112.

Swann, Charles. "Note on *The Blithedale Romance*, or 'Call him Fauntleroy'." *JAmS* 10 (1976): 103–104.

Tatar, Maria M. *Spellbound*, 217–226.

Thomas, W. K. *Fizz Inside*, 87, 97–98.

Van Cromphout, Gustaaf. "Emerson, Hawthorne, and *The Blithedale Romance*." *GR* 25 (1971): 471–480.

Vanderweghe, Richard. "Hawthorne's *The Blithedale Romance:* Miles Coverdale, His Story." *NHJ* (1977): 289–303.

Waggoner, Hyatt H. "Fire and Veils: The Texture of *The Blithedale Romance*," in Waggoner, Hyatt H. *Hawthorne: A Critical Study*. Revised Edition. Cambridge, MA: Harvard University Press, 1963. 188–208. Rpt. in Hawthorne, Nathaniel. *Blithedale Romance*, 368–373.

Waggoner, Hyatt H. *Presence of Hawthorne*, 34–36.

Whelan, Robert E., Jr. "*Blithedale Romance:* The Holy War in Hawthorne's Mansoul." *TSLL* 13 (1971): 91–109.

White, John. " 'Romance' in *The Blithedale Romance*." *ANQ* 9 (1971): 72–73.

Winslow, Joan D. "New Light on Hawthorne's Miles Coverdale." *JNT* 7 (1977): 189–199.

Doctor Grimshawe's Secret (1883)

Autrey, Max L. "Flower Imagery in Hawthorne's Posthumous Narratives." *SNNTS* 7 (1975): 220–226.

Fanshawe (1828)

Ciffelli, E. "Hawthorne as Humorist: A Look at *Fanshawe*." *CEA* 38.4 (1976): 11–17.

Flint, Allen. "Saving Grace of Marriage in Hawthorne's Fiction." *ESQ* 71 (1973): 115.

Harris, Janet. "Reflections of the Byronic Hero in Hawthorne's Fiction." *NHJ* (1977): 311.

Janssen, James G. "*Fanshawe* and Hawthorne's Developing Comic Sense." *ESQ* 22 (1976): 24–27.

Klinkowitz, Jerome. "Hawthorne's Sense of an Ending." *ESQ* 70 (1973): 43.

Sattelmeyer, Robert. "Aesthetic Background of Hawthorne's *Fanshawe*." *NHJ* (1975) 200–209.

House of Seven Gables (1851)

Albertini, Virgil. "Hepzibah and Prayer." *ANQ* 12 (1973): 35.

Arac, Jonathan. "House and the Railroad: *Dombey and Son* and *The House of the Seven Gables*." *NEQ* 51 (1978): 6–11, 15–16, 19.

Bell, Michael Davitt. *Development of American Romance*, 181–185.

Brodhead, Richard H. *Hawthorne, Melville, and the Novel*, 13, 19, 69–90.

Bush, Sargent, Jr. " 'Peter Goldthwaite's Treasure' and *The House of the Seven Gables.*" *ESQ* 62 (1971): 35–38.

Caldwell, Wayne T. "Emblem Tradition and the Symbolic Mode: Clothing Imagery in *The House of the Seven Gables.*" *ESQ* no.70 (1973): 34–42.

Caserio, Robert L. *Plot, Story, and the Novel*, 227–228.

Crews, Frederick C. "Psychoanalytical Interpretation," in Crews, Frederick C. *Sins of the Fathers: Hawthorne's Psychological Themes*. New York: Oxford University Press, 1966. 172–193. Rpt. in Asselineau, Roger, comp. *Merrill Studies in the House of Seven Gables*, 33–49.

Curran, Ronald T. " 'Yankee Gothic': Hawthorne's 'Castle of Pyncheon'." *SNNTS* 8 (1976): 69–80.

Dillingham, William B. "Structure and Theme in *The House of Seven Gables.*" *Nineteenth-Century Fiction* 14.1 (June 1959): 59–70. Rpt. as "Structure and Theme" in Asselineau, Roger, comp. *Merrill Studies in the House of Seven Gables*, 74–85.

Dillingham, William B. "Structure and Theme in *The House of Seven Gables.*" *Nineteenth-Century Fiction* 14.1 (June 1959): 59–70. Rpt. in Rountree, Thomas J., ed. *Critics on Hawthorne*, 96–105.

Dooley, Patrick K. "Genteel Poverty: Hepzibah in *The House of the Seven Gables.*" *MarkR* 9 (1980): 33–35.

Fleck, Richard F. "Industrial Imagery in *The House of the Seven Gables.*" *NHJ* (1974): 273–276.

Flint, Allen. "Saving Grace of Marriage in Hawthorne's Fiction." *ESQ* 71 (1973): 114, 116.

Fossum, Robert H. *Hawthorne's Inviolable Circle*, 128–140.

Frederick, John T. *Darkened Sky*, 54–57.

Gatta, John, Jr. "Progress and Providence in *The House of the Seven Gables.*" *AL* 50 (1978): 37–48.

Gilmore, Michael T. *Middle Way*, 114–130.

Gollin, Rita K. *Nathaniel Hawthorne and the Truth of Dreams*, 151–164.

Hirsch, David H. *Reality and Idea in the Early American Novel*, 151–157.

Humma, John B. " 'Time Passes' in *To the Lighthouse*; 'Governor Pyncheon' in *The House of the Seven Gables.*" *BallS* 20.3 (1979): 54–59.

Jacobs, Edward Craney. "Shakespearean Borrowings in *The House of the Seven Gables.*" *NHJ* (1977): 343–346.

Jarrett. David W. "Hawthorne and Hardy as Modern Romancers." *NCF* 28 (1974): 458–471.

Johnson, Claudia D. "Hawthorne and Nineteenth-Century Perfectionism." *AL* 44 (1973): 591, 592–593.

Kehler, Joel R. "*House of the Seven Gables:* House, Home, and Hawthorne's Psychology of Habitation." *ESQ* 21 (1975): 142–153.

Klinkowitz, Jerome. "Ending the *Seven Gables:* Old Light on a New Problem." *SNNTS* 4 (1972): 396–401.

Klinkowitz, Jerome. "Hawthorne's Sense of an Ending." *ESQ* 70 (1973): 43, 47–48.

Klinkowitz, Jerome. *Practice of Fiction in America*, 17–18.

Lathrop, George Parsons. "On *The House of Seven Gables*," in Lathrop, George

Parsons. *Study of Hawthorne*. Boston: J. R. Osgood and Co., 1876. 235–238. Rpt. in Rountree, Thomas J., ed. *Critics on Hawthorne*, 94–95.

Liebman, Sheldon W. "Point of View in *The House of the Seven Gables*." *ESQ* no.73 (1973): 203–212.

Lubbers, Klaus. "Metaphorical Patterns in *The House of Seven Gables*," in Helmcke, Hans, Klaus Lubbers and Renate Schmidt-v. Bardeleben, eds. *Literatur und Sprache der Vereinigten: Essays in Honor of Hans Galinsky*. Heidelberg: Carl Winter–Universitätsverlag, 1969. 107–116. Rpt. as "Metaphorical Patterns" in Asselineau, Roger, comp. *Merrill Studies in the House of Seven Gables*, 60–73.

MacAndrew, Elizabeth. *Gothic Tradition in Fiction*, 218–219.

McCarthy, Paul. "Extraordinary Man as Idealist in Novels by Hawthorne and Melville." *ESQ* 54 (1969): 45, 50.

McPherson, Hugo. *Hawthorne as Myth-Maker*, 27–29, 132–145.

Malin, Irving. "American Gothic Images." *Mosaic* 6.3 (1973): 148, 155–156., 164–165.

Meikle, Jeffrey. "Hawthorne's Alembic: Alchemical Images in *The House of the Seven Gables*." *ESQ* 26 (1980): 173–183.

Murphy, John J. "Willa Cather and Hawthorne: Significant Resemblances." *Renascence* 27 (1975): 169–172.

Ousby, Ian. *Reader's Guide to Fifty American Novels*, 56–58.

Platizky, Roger S. "Hepzibah's Gingerbread Cakes in *The House of the Seven Gables*." *ANQ* 17 (1979): 106–108.

Porte, Joel. *Romance in America*, 114–125.

Porte, Joel. "Redemption through Art," in Porte, Joel. *Romance in America: Studies in Cooper, Poe, Hawthorne, Melville, and James*. Middletown, CT: Wesleyan University Press, 1969. Rpt. in Crowley, J. Donald, ed. *Nathaniel Hawthorne*, 75–85.

Rahv, Philip. "Dark Lady of Salem." *Partisan Review* (Sept-Oct 1941). Rpt. in Rahv, Philip. *Essays on Literature and Politics*, 29.

Rahv, Philip. "Dark Lady of Salem." *Partisan Review* (Sept-Oct 1941). Rpt. in Rahv, Philip. *Literature and the Sixth Sense*, 59–60.

St. Armand, Barton L. "Golden Stain of Time: Ruskinian Aesthetics and the Ending of Hawthorne's *The House of the Seven Gables*." *NHJ* (1973): 143–153.

Sampson, Edward C. "Some Sights and Sounds," from "Afterword to *House of Seven Gables*." Hawthorne, Nathaniel. *House of Seven Gables*. New York: New American Library, 1961. 281–283, 286. Rpt. in Asselineau, Roger, comp. *Merrill Studies in the House of Seven Gables*, 56–59.

Schoen, Carol. "House of the Seven Deadly Sins." *ESQ* 70 (1973): 26–33.

Smith, Henry Nash. "*The House of Seven Gables* as Social History," in Gohdes, Clarence, ed. *Essays on American Literature in Honor of Jay B. Hubbell*. Durham, NC: Duke University Press, 1967. 92–97. Rpt. in Asselineau, Roger, comp. *Merrill Studies in the House of Seven Gables*, 50–55.

Smith, Julian. "Hawthorne Source for *The House of the Seven Gables*." *ATQ* 1 (1969): 18–19.

Spengemann, William C. *Adventurous Muse*, 172–176.

Steinbrink, Jeffrey. "Hawthorne's Holgravian Temper: The Case against the Past." *ATQ* 31 (1976): 21–23.

Stineback, David C. *Shifting World*, 43–60.

Stone, Edward. "Hawthorne's Other Drowning." *NHJ* 2 (1972): 232–236.

Stout, Janis P. *Sodoms in Eden*, 101–106.

Sundquist, Eric J. *Home as Found*, 86–142.

Swanson, Donald R. "On Building *The House of the Seven Gables*." *BallS* 10.1 (1969): 43–50.

Tatar, Maria M. *Spellbound*, 208–217.

Travis, Mildred K. "Past vs. Present in *The House of the Seven Gables*." *ESQ* 58 (1970): 109–111.

Waggoner, Hyatt H. *Presence of Hawthorne*, 32–34, 76–97.

Waterman, Arthur E. "Dramatic Structure in *The House of the Seven Gables*." *SLitI* 2.1 (1969): 13–19.

Wheeler, Otis B. "Love Among the Ruins: Hawthorne's Surrogate Religion." *SoR* 10 (1974): 554–558.

Whelan, Robert Emmet, Jr. "*House of the Seven Gables:* Allegory of the Heart." *Renascence* 31 (1979): 67–82.

Winner, Viola Hopkins. "American Pictorial Vision: Objects and Ideas in Hawthorne, James, and Hemingway." *SAF* 5 (1977): 146–148.

Yoder, R. A. "Transcendental Conservatism and *The House of the Seven Gables*." *GR* 28 (1974): 33–51.

Young, Philip. *Three Bags Full*, 113–135.

Marble Faun (1860)

Allen, Mary. "Smiles and Laughter in Hawthorne." *PQ* 52 (1973): 121, 122.

Auerbach, Jonathan. "Executing the Model: Painting, Sculpture, and Romance-Writing in Hawthorne's *The Marble Faun*." *ELH* 47 (1980): 103–120.

Baym, Nina. "*Marble Faun:* Hawthorne's Elegy for Art." *NEQ* 44 (1971): 355–376.

Bercovitch, Sacvan. "Of Wise and Foolish Virgins: Hilda *Versus* Miriam in Hawthorne's *Marble Faun*." *New England Quarterly* 41 (June 1968): 281–286. Rpt. in Kesterson, David B., comp. *Merrill Studies in The Marble Faun*, 79–83.

Berthold, Dennis. "Hawthorne, Ruskin, and the Gothic Revival: Transcendent Gothic in *The Marble Faun*." *ESQ* no.74 (1974): 15–32.

Blow, Suzanne. "Pre-Raphaelite Allegory in *The Marble Faun*." *AL* 44 (1972): 122–127.

Coale, Samuel. "*Marble Faun:* 'A Frail Structure of Our Own Reading'." *ELWIU* 7 (1980): 55–65.

Dahl, Curtis. "When the Deity Returns: *The Marble Faun* and *Romola*." *PLL* 5 supp. (1969): 82–99.

Darnell, Donald G. " 'Doctrine by Ensample': The Emblem and *The Marble Faun*." *TSLL* 15 (1973): 301–310.

Dryden, Edgar A. "Limits of Romance: A Reading of *The Marble Faun*," in Baldwin, Kenneth H. and David R. Kirby, eds. *Individual and Community: Variations on a Theme in American Fiction*, 17–48.

Elder, Marjorie J. *Nathaniel Hawthorne, Transcendental Symbolist*, 141–169.

Flint, Allen. "Saving Grace of Marriage in Hawthorne's Fiction." *ESQ* 71 (1973): 114–115, 116.

Fogle, Richard H. "Coleridge, Hilda, and *The Marble Faun*." *ESQ* no.71 (1973): 105–111.

Fossum, Robert H. *Hawthorne's Inviolable Circle*, 151–169.

Frederick, John T. *Darkened Sky*, 65–67.

Fryer, Judith. *Faces of Eve*, 62–71, 93–97.

Goldfarb, Clare R. "*Marble Faun* and Emersonian Self-Reliance." *ATQ* 1 (1969): 19–23.

Gollin, Rita K. *Nathaniel Hawthorne and the Truth of Dreams*, 176–194.

Gollin, Rita K. "Painting and Character in *The Marble Faun*." *ESQ* 21 (1975): 1–10.

Hall, Spencer. "Beatrice Cenci: Symbol and Vision in *The Marble Faun*." *NCF* 25 (1970): 85–95.

Harris, Janet. "Reflections of the Byronic Hero in Hawthorne's Fiction." *NHJ* (1977): 308–309.

Hirsch, David H. *Reality and Idea in the Early American Novel*, 163–164.

James, Henry. *Hawthorne*. New York: Harper & Brothers, 1880. 159–164. Rpt. as "*Marble Faun*," in Kesterson, David B., comp. *Merrill Studies in The Marble Faun*, 7–10.

Johnson, Claudia D. "Hawthorne and Nineteenth-Century Perfectionism." *AL* 44 (1973): 593–594.

Johnson, Claudia D. "Resolution in *The Marble Faun:* A Minority View," in Elliot, Emory, ed. *Puritan Influences in American Literature*, 128–141.

Kesterson, David B. "Journey to Perugia: Dantean Parallels in *The Marble Faun*." *ESQ* no.70 (1973): 94–104.

Klinkowitz, Jerome. "Hawthorne's Sense of an Ending." *ESQ* 70 (1973): 46–47.

Klinkowitz, Jerome. *Practice of Fiction in America*, 15–16.

Koskenlinna, Hazel M. "Setting, Image, and Symbol in Scott and Hawthorne." *ESQ* 70 (1973): 54–55, 56.

Levy, Leo B. "*Marble Faun:* Hawthorne's Landscape of the Fall." *AL* 42 (1970): 139–156.

Liebman, Sheldon W. "Design of *The Marble Faun*." *New England Quarterly* 40 (March 1967): 61–78. Rpt. in Kesterson, David B., comp. *Merrill Studies in The Marble Faun*, 43–58.

McCarthy, Harold T. *Expatriate Perspective*, 62–78.

McCarthy, Paul. "Extraordinary Man as Idealist in Novels by Hawthorne and Melville." *ESQ* 54 (1969): 43–44, 50.

McPherson, Hugo. *Hawthorne as Myth-Maker*, 31–33, 158–170.

Male, Roy R. "Transfiguration of Figures: *The Marble Faun*," in Male, Roy R. *Hawthorne's Tragic Vision*. Austin, TX: University of Texas Press, 1957. 157–177. Rpt. in Kesterson, David B., comp. *Merrill Studies in The Marble Faun*, 103–118.

Malin, Irving. "American Gothic Images." *Mosaic* 6.3 (1973): 148, 165–166.

Matthiessen, F. O. *American Renaissance*. New York: Oxford University Press, 1941. 310–312. Rpt. as "Context of 'The Fortunate Fall,'" in Kesterson, David B., comp. *Merrill Studies in The Marble Faun*, 59–60.

Matthiessen, F. O. *American Renaissance*. New York: Oxford University Press, 1941. 356–361. Rpt. as "Hilda, Kenyon, and 'Cheerless Decay' of America," in Kesterson, David B., comp. *Merrill Studies in The Marble Faun*, 84–88.

Meyers, Jeffrey. *Painting and the Novel*, 6–17.

Mezo, Richard E. "Note on 'Atra Cura' in Hawthorne's *The Marble Faun*." *NHJ* (1977): 347–348.

Mounts, Charles E. "Hawthorne's Echoes of Spenser and Milton." *NHJ* (1973): 169–170.

Murphy, John J. "Willa Cather and Hawthorne: Significant Resemblances." *Renascence* 27 (1975): 172–175.

Ousby, Ian. *Reader's Guide to Fifty American Novels*, 66–69.

Paris, Bernard J. "Optimism and Pessimism in *The Marble Faun*." *Boston University Studies in English* 2 (1956): 95–112. Rpt. in Kesterson, David B., comp. *Merrill Studies in The Marble Faun*, 61–78.

Pattison, Joseph C. "Guilt of the Innocent Donatello." *Emerson Society Quarterly* 31.2 (1963): 66–68. Rpt. in Kesterson, David B., comp. *Merrill Studies in The Marble Faun*, 89–93.

Person, Leland, Jr. "Aesthetic Headaches and European Women in *The Marble Faun* and *The American*." *SAF* 4 (1976): 67–72.

Porte, Joel. *Romance in America*, 137–151.

Pratt, Linda Ray. "Abuse of Eve by the New World Adam," in Cornillon, Susan Koppelman, ed. *Images of Women in Fiction*, 160–162.

Rahv, Philip. "Dark Lady of Salem." *Partisan Review* (Sept-Oct 1941). Rpt. in Rahv, Philip. *Essays on Literature and Politics*, 30–33, 39–41.

Rahv, Philip. "Dark Lady of Salem." *Partisan Review* (Sept-Oct 1941). Rpt. in Rahv, Philip. *Literature and the Sixth Sense*, 61–64, 72–74.

Richardson, Robert D., Jr. *Myth and Literature in the American Renaissance*, 184–194.

Schneider, Daniel J. "Allegory and Symbolism of Hawthorne's *The Marble Faun*." *SNNTS* 1.1 (1969): 38–50.

Scrimgeour, Gary J. "*Marble Faun:* Hawthorne's Faery Land." *American Literature* 36 (Nov 1964): 271–287. Rpt. in Kesterson, David B., comp. *Merrill Studies in The Marble Faun*, 16–31.

Smith, Charles R., Jr. "Structural Principle of *The Marble Faun*." *Thoth* 3 (Winter 1962): 32–38. Rpt. in Kesterson, David B., comp. *Merrill Studies in The Marble Faun*, 36–43.

Stone, Edward. "Hawthorne's Other Drowning." *NHJ* 2 (1972): 235–236.

Stout, Janis P. *Sodoms in Eden*, 112–115.

Strout, Cushing. "Hawthorne's International Novel." *NCF* 24 (1969): 169–181.

Stubbs, John Caldwell. "*Marble Faun:* Hawthorne's Romance of the Adamic Myth," in Stubbs, John Caldwell. *Pursuit of Form: A Study of Hawthorne and Romance*. Urbana, IL: University of Illinois Press, 1970. Rpt. in Crowley, J. Donald, ed. *Nathaniel Hawthorne*, 101–114.

Waggoner, Hyatt H. *Presence of Hawthorne*, 36–37.

Waples, Dorothy. "Suggestions for Interpreting *The Marble Faun*." *American Literature* 13 (1941): 224–239. Rpt. in Rountree, Thomas J., ed. *Critics on Hawthorne*, 115–124.

Wheeler, Otis B. "Love Among the Ruins: Hawthorne's Surrogate Religion." *SoR* 10 (1974): 559–565.

Winner, Viola Hopkins. "American Pictorial Vision: Objects and Ideas in Hawthorne, James, and Hemingway." *SAF* 5 (1977): 148–150.

Yates, Norris. "Ritual and Reality: Mask and Dance Motifs in Hawthorne's Fiction." *Philological Quarterly* 34 (Jan 1955): 66–70. Rpt. as "Mask and Dance Motifs in *The Marble Faun*," in Kesterson, David B., comp. *Merrill Studies in The Marble Faun*, 32–35.

Zivkovic, Peter D. "Evil of the Isolated Intellect: Hilda, in *The Marble Faun*." *Personalist* 43 (Spring 1962): 202–213. Rpt. in Kesterson, David B., comp. *Merrill Studies in The Marble Faun*, 93–103.

Scarlet Letter (1850)

Allen, Mary. "Smiles and Laughter in Hawthorne." *PQ* 52 (1973): 120–121.

Allen, Walter. *Urgent West*, 123–127.

Attebery, Brian. *Fantasy Tradition in American Literature*, 48–51.

Barnett, Louise K. *Ignoble Savage*, 149–150, 154–155, 158–159.

Baumgartner, Alex M. and Michael J. Hoffman. "Illusion and Role in *The Scarlet Letter*." *PLL* 7 (1971): 168–184.

Bayer, John G. "Narrative Techniques and the Oral Tradition in *The Scarlet Letter*." *AL* 52 (1980): 250–263.

Baym, Nina. "Passion and Authority in *The Scarlet Letter*." *NEQ* 43 (1970): 209–230.

Baym, Nina. "Romantic *Malgre Lui:* Hawthorne in the Custom House." *ESQ* 70 (1973): 14–24.

Bell, Michael Davitt. *Development of American Romance*, 176–181.

Benoit, Raymond. "Theology and Literature: *The Scarlet Letter*." *BuR* 20.1 (1972): 83–92.

Brodhead, Richard H. *Hawthorne, Melville, and the Novel*, 10–11, 16–17, 19, 20, 22, 32–36, 38–39, 43–68.

Browning, Preston M. "Hester Prynne as a Secular Saint." *MidQ* 13 (1972): 351–362.

Canaday, Nicholas. "Another Look at Arthur Dimmesdale." *CEA* 41.3 (1979): 13–16.

Canaday, Nicholas, Jr. "Hawthorne's *The Scarlet Letter*." *Expl* 28 (1970): Item 39.

Caruthers, Clifford M. " 'Povera Picciola' and *The Scarlet Letter*." *PLL* 7 (1971): 90–94.

Colacurcio, Michael J. "Footsteps of Ann Hutchinson: The Context of *The Scarlet Letter*." *ELH* 39 (1972): 459–494.

Cox, James M. "*Scarlet Letter:* Through the Old Manse and the Custom House." *VQR* 51 (1975): 432–447.

Dillingham, William B. "Arthur Dimmesdale's Confession." *SLitI* 2.1 (1969): 21–26.

Eakin, Paul J. "Hawthorne's Imagination and the Structure of 'The Custom-House'." *AL* 43 (1971): 346–358.

Eberwein, Jane Donahue. " 'The Scribbler of Bygone Days': Perceptions of Time in Hawthorne's 'Custom-House'." *NHJ* (1977): 239–247.

Elder, Marjorie J. *Nathaniel Hawthorne, Transcendental Symbolist*, 121–141.

Flint, Allen. "Saving Grace of Marriage in Hawthorne's Fiction." *ESQ* 71 (1973): 114.

Fogle, Richard H. "Hawthorne's Variegated Lighting." *BuR* 21.2 (1973): 84–85.

Fogle, Richard Harter. "Poetics of Concealment: *The Scarlet Letter*," in Fogle, Richard Harter. *Hawthorne's Fiction: The Light and the Dark*. Revised Edition. Norman, OK: University of Oklahoma Press, 1964. Rpt. in Crowley, J. Donald, ed. *Nathaniel Hawthorne*, 63–74.

Fossum, Robert H. *Hawthorne's Inviolable Circle*, 105–126.

Franzosa, John. " 'The Custom-House,' *The Scarlet Letter*, and Hawthorne's Separation from Salem." *ESQ* 24 (1978): 57–71.

Frederick, John T. *Darkened Sky*, 50–53.

Fryer, Judith. *Faces of Eve*, 72–84.

Gilmore, Michael T. *Middle Way*, 70–114.

Gollin, Rita K. "Hester, Hetty, and the Two Arthurs." *NHJ* (1977): 319–321.

Gollin, Rita K. *Nathaniel Hawthorne and the Truth of Dreams*, 141–151.

Greenwood, Douglas. "Heraldic Device in *The Scarlet Letter:* Hawthorne's Symbolic Use of the Past." *AL* 46 (1974): 207–210.

Hanse, Elaine Tuttle. "Ambiguity and the Narrator in *The Scarlet Letter.*" *JNT* 5 (1975): 147–163.

Harris, Janet. "Reflections of the Byronic Hero in Hawthorne's Fiction." *NHJ* (1977): 312.

Hart, John E. "*Scarlet Letter* One Hundred Years After." *New England Quarterly* 23 (Sept 1950): 381–395. Rpt. in Turner, Arlin, comp. *Merrill Studies in The Scarlet Letter*, 92–104.

Hays, Peter L. "Why Seven Years in *The Scarlet Letter.*" *NHJ* 2 (1972): 251–253.

Heilbrun, Carolyn G. *Toward a Recognition of Androgyny*, 63–67.

Henderson, Harry B. *Versions of the Past*, 114–126.

Hirsch, David H. *Reality and Idea in the Early American Novel*, 124–151.

Hoffman, Daniel G. "Hester's Double Providence: The Scarlet Letter and the Green," in Hoffman, Daniel G. *Form and Fable in American Fiction*. New York: Oxford University Press, 1961. 169–186. Rpt. in Turner, Arlin, comp. *Merrill Studies in The Scarlet Letter*, 105–119.

Honig, Edwin. *Dark Conceit*, 84–85, 123, 144.

Howells, W. D. "Hawthorne's Hester Prynne," in Howells, W. D. *Heroines of Fiction*. Harper & Brothers, 1901. Vol. 1. 161–174. Rpt. in Turner, Arlin, comp. *Merrill Studies in The Scarlet Letter*, 80–89.

Hutchison, Earl R., Sr. "Antiquity and Mythology in *The Scarlet Letter:* In the Primary Sources." *ArQ* 36 (1980): 197–210.

Isani, Mukhtar A. "Hawthorne and the Branding of William Prynne." *NEQ* 45 (1972): 182–195.

Johnson, Claudia D. "Hawthorne and Nineteenth-Century Perfectionism." *AL* 44 (1973): 591–592.

Jones, Victor H. "Laughter in Hawthorne's Fiction." *CollL* 5 (1978): 60–61.

Josipovici, Gabriel. *World and the Book*, 164–176.

Kaplan, Harold. *Democratic Humanism and American Literature*, 129–139, 150–158.

Kushen, Betty. "Love's Martyrs: *The Scarlet Letter* as Secular Cross." *L&P* 22 (1972): 109–120.

Klinkowitz, Jerome. "Hawthorne's Sense of an Ending." *ESQ* 70 (1973): 46–47.

Klinkowitz, Jerome. *Practice of Fiction in America*, 13–14.

Koskenlinna, Hazel M. "Setting, Image, and Symbol in Scott and Hawthorne." *ESQ* 70 (1973): 53, 56.

Kraft, Quentin G. "Central Problem of James's Fictional Thought: From *The Scarlet Letter* to *Roderick Hudson.*" *ELH* 36 (1969): 418–423.

Kummings, Donald D. "Hawthorne's 'The Custom House' and the Conditions of Fiction in America." *CEA* 33.3 (1971): 15–18.

Lane, Gary. "Structural Dynamics and the Unknowable in *The Scarlet Letter.*" *NHJ* (1977): 323–330.

Lawrence, D. H. "Nathaniel Hawthorne and *The Scarlet Letter*," in Lawrence, D. H. *Studies in Clasic American Literature*. New York: Thomas Seltzer, Inc., 1923. 125–128, 130–133, 137–138, 142–147. Rpt. in Rountree, Thomas J., ed. *Critics on Hawthorne*, 78–81.

Lefcowitz, Allan. "Apologia pro Roger Prynne: A Psychological Study." *L&P* 24 (1974): 34–44.

Lesser, M. X. "Dimmesdale's Wordless Sermon." *ANQ* 12 (1974): 93–94.

Levy, Leo B. "Landscape Modes of *The Scarlet Letter.*" *NCF* 23 (1969): 377–392.

McCarthy, Paul. "Extraordinary Man as Idealist in Novels by Hawthorne and Melville." *ESQ* 54 (1969): 47, 48–49, 50.

McPherson, Hugo. *Hawthorne as Myth-Maker*, 24–27, 170–190.

Manierre, William R. "Some Apparent Confusions in *The Scarlet Letter*." *CEA* 33.3 (1971): 9–13.

Matthiessen, F. O. "*Scarlet Letter*," in Matthiessen, F. O. *American Renaissance: Art and Expression in the Age of Emerson and Whitman*. New York: Oxford University Press, 1941. 275–282. Rpt. in Rountree, Thomas J., ed. *Critics on Hawthorne*, 82–87.

Mayhook, J. Jeffrey. " 'Bearings Unknown to English Heraldry' in *The Scarlet Letter*." *NHJ* (1977): 173–214.

Murphy, John J. "Willa Cather and Hawthorne: Significant Resemblances." *Renascence* 27 (1975): 162–164.

Newberry, Frederick. "Tradition and Disinheritance in *The Scarlet Letter*." *ESQ* 23 (1977): 1–26.

Osborn, Robert and Marijane Osborn. "Another Look at an Old Tombstone." *NEQ* 46 (1973): 278–279.

Ousby, Ian. *Reader's Guide to Fifty American Novels*, 50–53.

Pinsker, Sanford. "Scaffold as Hinge: A Note on the Structure of *The Scarlet Letter*." *CollL* 5 (1978): 144–145.

Porte, Joel. *Romance in America*, 98–114.

Pryse, Marjorie. *Mark and the Knowledge*, 15–42.

Quick, Jonathan R. "*Silas Marner* as Romance: The Example of Hawthorne." *NCF* 29 (1974): 292–297.

Quilligan, Maureen. *Language of Allegory*, 51–58, 249–252.

Rahv, Philip. "Dark Lady of Salem." *Partisan Review* (Sept-Oct 1941). Rpt. in Rahv, Philip. *Essays on Literature and Politics*, 30–33, 35–37.

Rahv, Philip. "Dark Lady of Salem." *Partisan Review* (Sept-Oct 1941). Rpt. in Rahv, Philip. *Literature and the Sixth Sense*, 61–64, 66–69.

Ringe, Donald. "Hawthorne's Psychology of the Head and Heart." *PMLA* 65 (1950): 120–132. Rpt. in Rountree, Thomas J., ed. *Critics on Hawthorne*, 89–95.

Rovit, Earl H. "Ambiguity in Hawthorne's *Scarlet Letter*." *Archiv für das Studium der Neuren Sprachen und Literaturen* 198 (June 1961): 76–88. Rpt. in Turner, Arlin, comp. *Merrill Studies in The Scarlet Letter*, 120–132.

Ryskamp, Charles. "New England Sources of *The Scarlet Letter*." *American Literature* 31 (Nov 1959): 257–272. Rpt. in Turner, Arlin, comp. *Merrill Studies in The Scarlet Letter*, 26–41.

Sanderlin, R. Reed. "Hawthorne's *Scarlet Letter:* A Study of the Meaning of Meaning." *SoHR* 9 (1975): 145–157.

Shear, Walter. "Characterization in *The Scarlet Letter*." *MidQ* 12 (1971): 437–454.

Simpson, Lewis P. "Southern Spiritual Nationalism: Notes on the Background of Modern Southern Fiction," in Lewald, H. Ernest, ed. *Cry of Home*, 193–194.

Small, Michel. "Hawthorne's *The Scarlet Letter:* Arthur Dimmesdale's Manipulation of Language." *American Imago* 37 (1980): 113–123.

Spengemann, William C. *Adventurous Muse*, 162–172.

Stein, William Bysshe. "Rhetoric of 'P.P.' in *The Scarlet Letter*." *ATQ* 39 (1978): 281–299.

Stephens, Rosemary. " 'A' is for 'Art' in *The Scarlet Letter*." *ATQ* 1 (1969): 23–27.

Stone, Edward. "Chillingworth and His 'Dark Necessity'." *CollL* 4 (1977): 136–143.

Stone, Edward. " 'Many Morals' of *The Scarlet Letter.*" *NHJ* (1977): 215–238.

Stout, Janis P. *Sodoms in Eden*, 96–101.

Todd, Robert E. "Magna Mater Archetype in *The Scarlet Letter.*" *NEQ* 45 (1972): 421–429.

Trollope, Anthony. "Genius of Nathaniel Hawthorne." *North American Review* 129 (Sept 1978): 204–213. Rpt. in Turner, Arlin, comp. *Merrill Studies in The Scarlet Letter*, 70–79.

Van Deusen, Marshall. "Narrative Tone in "The Custom House" and *The Scarlet Letter.*" *Nineteeth-Century Fiction* 21.1 (June 1966): 61–71. Rpt. in Crowley, J. Donald, ed. *Nathaniel Hawthorne*, 53–62.

Vogel, Dan. "Hawthorne's Concept of Tragedy in *The Scarlet Letter.*" *NHJ* (1972): 183–193.

Waggoner, Hyatt H. *Presence of Hawthorne*, 30–32, 67–75.

Warren, Austin. "*Scarlet Letter:* A Literary Exercise in Moral Theology." *Southern Review* 1 n.s. (Winter 1965): 22–45. Rpt. in Turner, Arlin, comp. *Merrill Studies in The Scarlet Letter*, 133–153.

Wheeler, Otis B. "Love Among the Ruins: Hawthorne's Surrogate Religion." *SoR* 10 (1974): 548–554.

Septimius Felton (1872)

Autrey, Max L. "Flower Imagery in Hawthorne's Posthumous Narratives." *SNNTS* 7 (1975): 217–220.

Barnett, Louise K. *Ignoble Savage*, 159–160, 163–164.

Frederick, John T. *Darkened Sky*, 70–72.

HAY, JOHN (1838–1905)

Bread-Winners (1884)

Gale, Robert L. *John Hay*, 87–94.

Vandersee, Charles. "Great Literary Mystery of the Gilded Age." *ALR* 7 (1974): 245–272.

HAYES, ALFRED (1911–1985)

All Thy Conquests (1946)

Waldmeir, Joseph J. *American Novels of the Second World War*, 83–88.

HÉBERT, ANNE (1916–2000)

Children of the Black Sabbath see *Les enfants du sabbat*

Kamouraska (1970)

Blodgett, E. D. "Prisms and Structures in Hébert and Munro," in Bessai, Diane and David Jackel, eds. *Figures in a Ground*, 101, 107, 108–109, 112.

Boutelle, Ann. "Dorian Gray Phenomenon in Canadian Literature." *DR* 57 (1977): 274.

Lennox, John. "Dark Journeys: *Kamouraska* and *Deliverance.*" *ECW* 12 (1978): 84–93, 102–103.

Maccabée-Iqbal, Françoise. "Kamouraska: 'la fausse représentation démasquée'."
    V&I 4 (1979): 460–478.
Northey, Margot. *Haunted Wilderness*, 53–61.
Ouellette, Gabriel Pierre. "Espace et délire dans *Kamouraska* d'Anne Hebert."
    V&I 1 (1975): 241–264.
Pascal-Smith, Gabrielle. "La condition féminine dans *Kamouraska* d'Anne Hé-
    bert." *FR* 54 (1980): 85–92.
Thériault, Serge A. *La quête*, 83–142, 181–194.
Urbas, Jeannette. *From Thirty Acres to Modern Times*, 104–108.

Le torrent (1950)

Roy-Hewitson, Lucille. "Anne Hébert: *Le torrent* ou l'intégration au cosmos." *FR*
    53 (1980): 826–833.

Les chambres de bois (1958)

Blodgett, E. D. "Prisms and Structures in Hébert and Munro," in Bessai, Diane
    and David Jackel, eds. *Figures in a Ground*, 101, 107, 109, 110, 112.
Thériault, Serge A. *La quête*, 33–80, 181–194.
Urbas, Jeannette. *From Thirty Acres to Modern Times*, 102–104, 107–108.

Les enfants du sabbat (1975)

Bouchard, Denis. "*Les enfants du sabbat* d'Anne Hébert: L'Enveloppe des
    mythes." *V&I* 1 (1976): 374–385.
Poulin, Gabrielle. *Romans du pays*, 299–313.
Thériault, Serge A. *La quête*, 145–177, 181–194.

Silent Rooms see *Les chambres de bois*

HECHT, BEN (1893–1964)

Humpty Dumpty (1924)

Fincke, Gary. "Polarity in Ben Hecht's Winkelbergs." *Crit* 15.2 (1973): 103–108.

HEGGEN, THOMAS (1919–1949)

Mister Roberts (1946)

French, Warren. "Fiction: A Handful of Survivors," in French, Warren, ed. *Forties*,
    25–27.

HEINLEIN, ROBERT A. (1907–1988)

Between Planets (1951)

Franklin, H. Bruce. *Robert A. Heinlein*, 80–82.
Williamson, Jack. "Youth Against Space: Heinlein's Juveniles Revisited," in
    Olander, Joseph D. and Martin Harry Greenberg, eds. *Robert A. Heinlein*, 21–22.

Beyond This Horizon (1942)

Franklin, H. Bruce. *Robert A. Heinlein*, 57–60.
Lehman-Wilzig, Sam N. "Science Fiction as Futurist Prediction: Alternative Vi-
    sions of Heinlein and Clarke." *LR* 20 (1976): 140–141.
Samuelson, David N. "Major Frontier Worlds of Robert A. Heinlein: The Future

and Fantasy," in Clareson, Thomas, ed. *Voices for the Future*. Bowling Green, OH: Bowling Green University Popular Press, 1976. Rpt. in Olander, Joseph D. and Martin Harry Greenberg, eds. *Robert A. Heinlein*, 43–44.

Smith, Philip E., II. "Evolution of Politics and the Politics of Evolution: Social Darwinism in Heinlein's Fiction," in Olander, Joseph D. and Martin Harry Greenberg, eds. *Robert A. Heinlein*, 138–142.

Citizen of the Galaxy (1957)

Franklin, H. Bruce. *Robert A. Heinlein*, 90–91.

Williamson, Jack. "Youth Against Space: Heinlein's Juveniles Revisited," in Olander, Joseph D. and Martin Harry Greenberg, eds. *Robert A. Heinlein*, 28–29.

Door into Summer (1956)

Franklin, H. Bruce. *Robert A. Heinlein*, 105–109.

Samuelson, David N. "Frontier Worlds of Robert A. Heinlein," in Clareson, Thomas D., ed. *Voices for the Future* (Vol. 1), 137–139.

Samuelson, David N. "Major Frontier Worlds of Robert A. Heinlein: The Future and Fantasy," in Clareson, Thomas, ed. *Voices for the Future*. Bowling Green, OH: Bowling Green University Popular Press, 1976. Rpt. in Olander, Joseph D. and Martin Harry Greenberg, eds. *Robert A. Heinlein*, 50–51.

Smith, Philip E., II. "Evolution of Politics and the Politics of Evolution: Social Darwinism in Heinlein's Fiction," in Olander, Joseph D. and Martin Harry Greenberg, eds. *Robert A. Heinlein*, 151–152.

Speer, Diane P. "Heinlein's *The Door into Summer* and *Roderick Random*." *Extrapolation* 12 (1970): 30–34.

Double Star (1956)

Franklin, H. Bruce. *Robert A. Heinlein*, 103–105.

Hull, Elizabeth Anne. "Justifying the Ways of God to Man: The Novels of Robert A. Heinlein." *Extrapolation* 20 (1979): 45.

Samuelson, David N. "Frontier Worlds of Robert A. Heinlein," in Clareson, Thomas D., ed. *Voices for the Future* (Vol. 1), 137.

Samuelson, David N. "Major Frontier Worlds of Robert A. Heinlein: The Future and Fantasy," in Clareson, Thomas, ed. *Voices for the Future*. Bowling Green, OH: Bowling Green University Popular Press, 1976. Rpt. in Olander, Joseph D. and Martin Harry Greenberg, eds. *Robert A. Heinlein*, 50.

Slusser, George Edgar. *Robert A. Heinlein*, 15–22.

Smith, Philip E., II. "Evolution of Politics and the Politics of Evolution: Social Darwinism in Heinlein's Fiction," in Olander, Joseph D. and Martin Harry Greenberg, eds. *Robert A. Heinlein*, 150–151.

Farmer in the Sky (1950)

Franklin, H. Bruce. *Robert A. Heinlein*, 79–80.

Williamson, Jack. "Youth Against Space: Heinlein's Juveniles Revisited," in Olander, Joseph D. and Martin Harry Greenberg, eds. *Robert A. Heinlein*, 20–21.

Farnham's Freehold (1964)

Franklin, H. Bruce. *Robert A. Heinlein*, 151–159.

Hull, Elizabeth Anne. "Justifying the Ways of God to Man: The Novels of Robert A. Heinlein." *Extrapolation* 20 (1979): 42.

Samuelson, David N. "Frontier Worlds of Robert A. Heinlein," in Clareson, Thomas D., ed. *Voices for the Future* (Vol. 1), 141–142.

Samuelson, David N. "Major Frontier Worlds of Robert A. Heinlein: The Future and Fantasy," in Clareson, Thomas, ed. *Voices for the Future*. Bowling Green, OH: Bowling Green University Popular Press, 1976. Rpt. in Olander, Joseph D. and Martin Harry Greenberg, eds. *Robert A. Heinlein*, 54–55.

Smith, Philip E., II. "Evolution of Politics and the Politics of Evolution: Social Darwinism in Heinlein's Fiction," in Olander, Joseph D. and Martin Harry Greenberg, eds. *Robert A. Heinlein*, 163–164.

Glory Road (1963)

Franklin, H. Bruce. *Robert A. Heinlein*, 146–151.

Samuelson, David N. "Frontier Worlds of Robert A. Heinlein," in Clareson, Thomas D., ed. *Voices for the Future* (Vol. 1), 140–141.

Samuelson, David N. "Major Frontier Worlds of Robert A. Heinlein: The Future and Fantasy," in Clareson, Thomas, ed. *Voices for the Future*. Bowling Green, OH: Bowling Green University Popular Press, 1976. Rpt. in Olander, Joseph D. and Martin Harry Greenberg, eds. *Robert A. Heinlein*, 53.

Have Space Suit—Will Travel (1958)

Franklin, H. Bruce. *Robert A. Heinlein*, 92–93.

Slusser, George Edgar. *Classic Years of Robert A. Heinlein*, 51–57.

Williamson, Jack. "Youth Against Space: Heinlein's Juveniles Revisited," in Olander, Joseph D. and Martin Harry Greenberg, eds. *Robert A. Heinlein*, 29–30.

I Will Fear No Evil (1970)

Franklin, H. Bruce. *Robert A. Heinlein*, 172–180.

Gaar, Alice Carol. "Human as Machine Analog: The Big Daddy of Interchangeable Parts in the Fiction of Robert A. Heinlein," in Olander, Joseph D. and Martin Harry Greenberg, eds. *Robert A. Heinlein*, 79–80.

Hull, Elizabeth Anne. "Justifying the Ways of God to Man: The Novels of Robert A. Heinlein." *Extrapolation* 20 (1979): 47–48.

Samuelson, David N. "Major Frontier Worlds of Robert A. Heinlein: The Future and Fantasy," in Clareson, Thomas, ed. *Voices for the Future*. Bowling Green, OH: Bowling Green University Popular Press, 1976. Rpt. in Olander, Joseph D. and Martin Harry Greenberg, eds. *Robert A. Heinlein*, 56.

Sarti, Ronald. "Variations on a Theme: Human Sexuality in the Work of Robert A. Heinlein," in Olander, Joseph D. and Martin Harry Greenberg, eds. *Robert A. Heinlein*, 127–130.

Slusser, George Edgar. *Robert A. Heinlein*, 23–24, 42–48.

Methuselah's Children (1941)

Franklin, H. Bruce. *Robert A. Heinlein*, 38–43.

Gaar, Alice Carol. "Human as Machine Analog: The Big Daddy of Interchangeable Parts in the Fiction of Robert A. Heinlein," in Olander, Joseph D. and Martin Harry Greenberg, eds. *Robert A. Heinlein*, 68–73.

Letson, Russell. "Returns of Lazarus Long," in Olander, Joseph D. and Martin Harry Greenberg, eds. *Robert A. Heinlein*, 218–219.

Samuelson, David N. "Major Frontier Worlds of Robert A. Heinlein: The Future and Fantasy," in Clareson, Thomas, ed. *Voices for the Future*. Bowling Green, OH: Bowling Green University Popular Press, 1976. Rpt. in Olander, Joseph D. and Martin Harry Greenberg, eds. *Robert A. Heinlein*, 40–41.

Smith, Philip E., II. "Evolution of Politics and the Politics of Evolution: Social

Darwinism in Heinlein's Fiction," in Olander, Joseph D. and Martin Harry Greenberg, eds. *Robert A. Heinlein*, 152–154.

Moon Is a Harsh Mistress (1966)

Franklin, H. Bruce. *Robert A. Heinlein*, 162–170.

Gaar, Alice Carol. "Human as Machine Analog: The Big Daddy of Interchangeable Parts in the Fiction of Robert A. Heinlein," in Olander, Joseph D. and Martin Harry Greenberg, eds. *Robert A. Heinlein*, 78–79.

Hull, Elizabeth Anne. "Justifying the Ways of God to Man: The Novels of Robert A. Heinlein." *Extrapolation* 20 (1979): 46.

Ketterer, David. *New Worlds for Old*, 149–156.

Lehman-Wilzig, Sam N. "Science Fiction as Futurist Prediction: Alternative Visions of Heinlein and Clarke." *LR* 20 (1976): 141–142.

Perkins, James Ashbrook. "MYCROFTXX is Alive and Well: The Ambiguous Ending of *The Moon is a Harsh Mistress*." *NConL* 5.1 (1975): 13–15.

Samuelson, David N. "Frontier Worlds of Robert A. Heinlein," in Clareson, Thomas D., ed. *Voices for the Future* (Vol. 1), 142–144.

Samuelson, David N. "Major Frontier Worlds of Robert A. Heinlein: The Future and Fantasy," in Clareson, Thomas, ed. *Voices for the Future*. Bowling Green, OH: Bowling Green University Popular Press, 1976. Rpt. in Olander, Joseph D. and Martin Harry Greenberg, eds. *Robert A. Heinlein*, 55–56.

Smith, Philip E., II. "Evolution of Politics and the Politics of Evolution: Social Darwinism in Heinlein's Fiction," in Olander, Joseph D. and Martin Harry Greenberg, eds. *Robert A. Heinlein*, 164–166.

Tucker, Frank H. "Major Political and Social Elements in Heinlein's Fiction," in Olander, Joseph D. and Martin Harry Greenberg, eds. *Robert A. Heinlein*, 181–184.

Warrick, Patricia S. *Cybernetic Imagination in Science Fiction*, 175–176.

Number of the Beast (1980)

Franklin, H. Bruce. *Robert A. Heinlein*, 198–212.

Planets in Combat see *Between Planets*

Podkayne of Mars (1963)

Franklin, H. Bruce. *Robert A. Heinlein*, 140–146.

Puppet Masters (1951)

Franklin, H. Bruce. *Robert A. Heinlein*, 98–101.

Hull, Elizabeth Anne. "Justifying the Ways of God to Man: The Novels of Robert A. Heinlein." *Extrapolation* 20 (1979): 42, 45.

Samuelson, David N. "Frontier Worlds of Robert A. Heinlein," in Clareson, Thomas D., ed. *Voices for the Future* (Vol. 1), 136–137.

Samuelson, David N. "Major Frontier Worlds of Robert A. Heinlein: The Future and Fantasy," in Clareson, Thomas, ed. *Voices for the Future*. Bowling Green, OH: Bowling Green University Popular Press, 1976. Rpt. in Olander, Joseph D. and Martin Harry Greenberg, eds. *Robert A. Heinlein*, 49–50.

Slusser, George Edgar. *Classic Years of Robert A. Heinlein*, 42–43, 46–49..

Smith, Philip E., II. "Evolution of Politics and the Politics of Evolution: Social Darwinism in Heinlein's Fiction," in Olander, Joseph D. and Martin Harry Greenberg, eds. *Robert A. Heinlein*, 149–150.

Red Planet (1949)

Franklin, H. Bruce. *Robert A. Heinlein*, 78–79.
Samuelson, David N. "Frontier Worlds of Robert A. Heinlein," in Clareson,
Thomas D., ed. *Voices for the Future* (Vol. 1), 123.
Slusser, George Edgar. *Classic Years of Robert A. Heinlein*, 43.
Williamson, Jack. "Youth Against Space: Heinlein's Juveniles Revisited," in
Olander, Joseph D. and Martin Harry Greenberg, eds. *Robert A. Heinlein*, 19–20.

Rocket Ship Galileo (1947)

Franklin, H. Bruce. *Robert A. Heinlein*, 75–76.
Slusser, George Edgar. *Classic Years of Robert A. Heinlein*, 42–43, 44–46.

Rolling Stones (1952)

Franklin, H. Bruce. *Robert A. Heinlein*, 82–83.
Williamson, Jack. "Youth Against Space: Heinlein's Juveniles Revisited," in
Olander, Joseph D. and Martin Harry Greenberg, eds. *Robert A. Heinlein*, 22–23.

Satellite Scout see *Farmer in the Sky*

Sixth Column (1941)

Franklin, H. Bruce. *Robert A. Heinlein*, 49–52.

Space Cadet (1948)

Franklin, H. Bruce. *Robert A. Heinlein*, 76–78.
Samuelson, David N. "Frontier Worlds of Robert A. Heinlein," in Clareson,
Thomas D., ed. *Voices for the Future* (Vol. 1), 122–123.

Star Beast (1954)

Franklin, H. Bruce. *Robert A. Heinlein*, 84–86.
Williamson, Jack. "Youth Against Space: Heinlein's Juveniles Revisited," in
Olander, Joseph D. and Martin Harry Greenberg, eds. *Robert A. Heinlein*, 24–26.

Star Lummox see *Star Beast*

Starman Jones (1953)

Franklin, H. Bruce. *Robert A. Heinlein*, 83–84.
Samuelson, David N. "Frontier Worlds of Robert A. Heinlein," in Clareson,
Thomas D., ed. *Voices for the Future* (Vol. 1), 125.
Slusser, George Edgar. *Classic Years of Robert A. Heinlein*, 50–51.
Williamson, Jack. "Youth Against Space: Heinlein's Juveniles Revisited," in
Olander, Joseph D. and Martin Harry Greenberg, eds. *Robert A. Heinlein*, 23–24.

Starship Troopers (1959)

Franklin, H. Bruce. *Robert A. Heinlein*, 110–120.
Gaar, Alice Carol. "Human as Machine Analog: The Big Daddy of Interchangeable
Parts in the Fiction of Robert A. Heinlein," in Olander, Joseph D. and Martin
Harry Greenberg, eds. *Robert A. Heinlein*, 75–76.
Hull, Elizabeth Anne. "Justifying the Ways of God to Man: The Novels of Robert
A. Heinlein." *Extrapolation* 20 (1979): 43–45.
Samuelson, David N. "Frontier Worlds of Robert A. Heinlein," in Clareson,
Thomas D., ed. *Voices for the Future* (Vol. 1), 129–130.
Slusser, George Edgar. *Classic Years of Robert A. Heinlein*, 43.
Smith, Philip E., II. "Evolution of Politics and the Politics of Evolution: Social

Darwinism in Heinlein's Fiction," in Olander, Joseph D. and Martin Harry Greenberg, eds. *Robert A. Heinlein*, 155–159.

Tucker, Frank H. "Major Political and Social Elements in Heinlein's Fiction," in Olander, Joseph D. and Martin Harry Greenberg, eds. *Robert A. Heinlein*, 187–189, 190–191.

Stranger in a Strange Land (1961)

Ash, Brian. *Faces of the Future*, 135–136.

Blish, James. "Cathedrals in Space," in Knight, Damon, ed. *Turning Points*, 154–162.

Donald, Miles. *American Novel in the Twentieth Century*, 182–185.

Franklin, H. Bruce. *Robert A. Heinlein*, 126–140.

Gaar, Alice Carol. "Human as Machine Analog: The Big Daddy of Interchangeable Parts in the Fiction of Robert A. Heinlein," in Olander, Joseph D. and Martin Harry Greenberg, eds. *Robert A. Heinlein*, 76–78.

Hendin, Josephine. *Vulnerable People*, 40–41.

Hull, Elizabeth Anne. "Justifying the Ways of God to Man: The Novels of Robert A. Heinlein." *Extrapolation* 20 (1979): 46–47.

Lehman-Wilzig, Sam N. "Science Fiction as Futurist Prediction: Alternative Visions of Heinlein and Clarke." *LR* 20 (1976): 139–140.

Plank, Robert. "Omnipotent Cannibals in *Stranger in a Strange Land*," in Olander, Joseph D. and Martin Harry Greenberg, eds. *Robert A. Heinlein*, 83–106.

Plank, Robert. "Omnipotent Cannibals: Thoughts on Reading Robert Heinlein's *Stranger in a Strange Land*." *RQ* 5 (1971): 30–37.

Samuelson, David N. "Frontier Worlds of Robert A. Heinlein," in Clareson, Thomas D., ed. *Voices for the Future* (Vol. 1), 139–140.

Samuelson, David N. "Major Frontier Worlds of Robert A. Heinlein: The Future and Fantasy," in Clareson, Thomas, ed. *Voices for the Future*. Bowling Green, OH: Bowling Green University Popular Press, 1976. Rpt. in Olander, Joseph D. and Martin Harry Greenberg, eds. *Robert A. Heinlein*, 51–53.

Samuelson, David N. "*Stranger* in the Sixties: Model or Mirror?", in Riley, Dick, ed. *Critical Encounters*, 145–172.

Sarti, Ronald. "Variations on a Theme: Human Sexuality in the Work of Robert A. Heinlein," in Olander, Joseph D. and Martin Harry Greenberg, eds. *Robert A. Heinlein*, 124–126.

Scholes, Robert and Eric S. Rabkin. *Science Fiction*, 57–58.

Slusser, George Edgar. *Robert A. Heinlein*, 23–42.

Smith, Philip E., II. "Evolution of Politics and the Politics of Evolution: Social Darwinism in Heinlein's Fiction," in Olander, Joseph D. and Martin Harry Greenberg, eds. *Robert A. Heinlein*, 159–163.

Time Enough for Love (1973)

Christopher, Joe R. "Lazarus, Come Forth from That Tomb!" *RQ* 6 (1975): 190–197.

Franklin, H. Bruce. *Robert A. Heinlein*, 180–196.

Gaar, Alice Carol. "Human as Machine Analog: The Big Daddy of Interchangeable Parts in the Fiction of Robert A. Heinlein," in Olander, Joseph D. and Martin Harry Greenberg, eds. *Robert A. Heinlein*, 80–82.

Hull, Elizabeth Anne. "Justifying the Ways of God to Man: The Novels of Robert A. Heinlein." *Extrapolation* 20 (1979): 48.

Letson, Russell. "Returns of Lazarus Long," in Olander, Joseph D. and Martin Harry Greenberg, eds. *Robert A. Heinlein*, 195–218, 219–221.

Rogers, Ivor A. "Robert Heinlein: Folklorist of Outer Space," in Olander, Joseph D. and Martin Harry Greenberg, eds. *Robert A. Heinlein*, 223–239.

Samuelson, David N. "Frontier Worlds of Robert A. Heinlein," in Clareson, Thomas D., ed. *Voices for the Future* (Vol. 1), 144–147.

Samuelson, David N. "Major Frontier Worlds of Robert A. Heinlein: The Future and Fantasy," in Clareson, Thomas, ed. *Voices for the Future*. Bowling Green, OH: Bowling Green University Popular Press, 1976. Rpt. in Olander, Joseph D. and Martin Harry Greenberg, eds. *Robert A. Heinlein*, 56–59.

Sarti, Ronald. "Variations on a Theme: Human Sexuality in the Work of Robert A. Heinlein," in Olander, Joseph D. and Martin Harry Greenberg, eds. *Robert A. Heinlein*, 130–133.

Slusser, George Edgar. *Robert A. Heinlein*, 48–62.

Smith, Philip E., II. "Evolution of Politics and the Politics of Evolution: Social Darwinism in Heinlein's Fiction," in Olander, Joseph D. and Martin Harry Greenberg, eds. *Robert A. Heinlein*, 167–169.

Time for the Stars (1956)

Franklin, H. Bruce. *Robert A. Heinlein*, 88–90.

Slusser, George Edgar. *Robert A. Heinlein*, 10–15.

Williamson, Jack. "Youth Against Space: Heinlein's Juveniles Revisited," in Olander, Joseph D. and Martin Harry Greenberg, eds. *Robert A. Heinlein*, 27–28.

Tramp Space Ship see *Rolling Stones*

Tunnel in the Sky (1955)

Franklin, H. Bruce. *Robert A. Heinlein*, 86–88.

Samuelson, David N. "Frontier Worlds of Robert A. Heinlein," in Clareson, Thomas D., ed. *Voices for the Future* (Vol. 1), 126–127.

Slusser, George Edgar. *Classic Years of Robert A. Heinlein*, 43–44.

Williamson, Jack. "Youth Against Space: Heinlein's Juveniles Revisited," in Olander, Joseph D. and Martin Harry Greenberg, eds. *Robert A. Heinlein*, 26–27.

HELLER, JOSEPH (1923–1999)

Catch-22 (1961)

Anonymous. "Review of *Catch-22*." *Daedalus* 92 (Winter 1963): 155–165. Rpt. in Kiley, Frederick and Walter McDonald, eds. *Catch-22 Casebook*, 27–39.

Billson, Marcus K., III. "Un-Minderbinding of Yossarian: Genesis Inverted in *Catch-22*." *ArQ* 36 (1980): 315–329.

Blues, Thomas. "Moral Structure of *Catch-22*." *SNNTS* 3 (1971): 64–79.

Bronson, Daniel Ross. "Man on a String: *Catch 22*." *NConL* 7.2 (1977): 8–9.

Brustein, Robert. "Logic of Survival in a Lunatic World." *New Republic* 145 (13 Nov 1961): 11–13. Rpt. in Kiley, Frederick and Walter McDonald, eds. *Catch-22 Casebook*, 6–13.

Bryant, Jerry H. *Open Decision*, 156–164.

Burhans, Clinton S., Jr. "Spindrift and the Sea: Structural Patterns and Unifying Elements in *Catch-22*." *TCL* 19 (1973): 239–249.

Castelli, Jim. "*Catch-22* and the New Hero." *Catholic World* 211 (Aug 1970):

199–202. Rpt. in Kiley, Frederick and Walter McDonald, eds. *Catch-22 Casebook*, 174–181.

Cheuse, Alan. "Laughing on the Outside." *Studies on the Left* 3 (Fall 1963): 81–87. Rpt. in Kiley, Frederick and Walter McDonald, eds. *Catch-22 Casebook*, 86–93.

Colmer, John. *Coleridge to Catch-22*, 210–221.

Craig, David and Michael Egan. *Extreme Situations*, 52–53.

David, Gary W. "*Catch-22* and the Language of Discontinuity." *Novel* 12 (1978): 66–77.

Day, Douglas. "*Catch-22:* A Manifesto for Anarchists." *Carolina Quarterly* 15 (Summer 1963): 86–92. Rpt. in Kiley, Frederick and Walter McDonald, eds. *Catch-22 Casebook*, 181–187.

Denniston, Constance. "*Catch-22:* A Romance-Parody," in Kiley, Frederick and Walter McDonald, eds. *Catch-22 Casebook*, 51–57.

Doskow, Minna. "Night Journey in *Catch-22*." *Twentieth-Century Literature* 12 (Jan 1967): 186–193. Rpt. in Kiley, Frederick and Walter McDonald, eds. *Catch-22 Casebook*, 166–174.

Gaukroger, Doug. "Time Structure in *Catch-22*." *Crit* 12.2 (1970): 70–85.

Gaukroger, Doug. "Time Structure in *Catch-22*." *Critique* 12.2 (1970): 70–85. Rpt. in Kiley, Frederick and Walter McDonald, eds. *Catch-22 Casebook*, 132–144.

Glass, Peyton, III. "Heller's *Catch-22*." *Expl* 36.2 (1978): 25–26.

Greenberg, Alvin. "Choice: Ironic Alternatives in the World of the Contemporary American Novel," in Madden, David, ed. *American Dreams, American Nightmares*, 181, 185–186.

Harris, Charles B. *Contemporary American Novelists of the Absurd*, 33–50.

Hartshorne, Thomas L. "From *Catch-22* to *Slaughterhouse V:* The Decline of the Political Mode." *SAQ* 78 (1979): 17–24.

Hendin, Josephine. *Vulnerable People*, 110–111.

Henry, G. B. Mck. "Significant Corn: *Catch-22*." *Critical Review* 9 (1966): 133–144. Rpt. in Kiley, Frederick and Walter McDonald, eds. *Catch-22 Casebook*, 187–201.

Hunt, John W. "Comic Escape and Anti-Vision: Joseph Heller's *Catch-22*," in Scott, Nathan A., Jr., ed. *Adversity and Grace: Studies in Recent American Literature*. Chicago: University of Chicago Press, 1968. Rpt. in Kiley, Frederick and Walter McDonald, eds. *Catch-22 Casebook*, 242–247.

Jones, Peter G. *War and the Novelist*, 44–52, 62–63.

Karl, Frederick R. "Joseph Heller's *Catch-22:* Only Fools Walk in Darkness," in Moore, Harry T., ed. *Contemporary American Novelists*. Carbondale, IL: Southern Illinois University Press, 1965. 134–142. Rpt. in Kiley, Frederick and Walter McDonald, eds. *Catch-22 Casebook*, 159–165.

Kennard, Jean. "Joseph Heller: At War with Absurdity." *Mosaic* 4.3 (Spring 1971): 75–87. Rpt. in Kiley, Frederick and Walter McDonald, eds. *Catch-22 Casebook*, 255–269.

Kennard, Jean E. "Joseph Heller: At War with Absurdity." *Mosaic* 4.3 (1971): 75–87.

Kennard, Jean E. *Number and Nightmare*, 41–56.

Klinkowitz, Jerome. *American 1960's*, 26–31.

Kostelanetz, Richard. "American Fiction in the Sixties," in Kostelanetz, Richard, ed. *On Contemporary Literature*, 639–640.

Larsen, Michael J. "Shakespearean Echoes in *Catch-22*." *ANQ* 17 (1979): 76–78.

LeClair, Thomas. "Death and Black Humor." *Crit* 17.1 (1975): 14–16.

Lehan, Richard. *Dangerous Crossing*, 163–172.

Littlejohn, David. *Interruptions*, 26–27.

MacDonald, James L. "I See Everything Twice!: The Structure of Joseph Heller's *Catch-22*." *University Review* 34 (Spring 1968): 175–180. Rpt. in Kiley, Frederick and Walter McDonald, eds. *Catch-22 Casebook*, 102–108.

McDonald, Walter R. "He Took Off: Yossarian and the Different Drummer." *CEA* 36.1 (1973): 14–16.

McDonald, Walter R. "Look Back in Horror: The Functional Comedy of *Catch-22*." *CEA* 35.2 (1973): 18–21.

Meeker, Joseph W. *Comedy of Survival*, 34–35, 98–101, 115–116.

Mellard, James M. "*Catch-22: Déjà vu* and the Labyrinth of Memory." *Bucknell Review* 16.2 (1966): 29–44. Rpt. in Kiley, Frederick and Walter McDonald, eds. *Catch-22 Casebook*, 109–121.

Mellard, James M. *Exploded Form*, 108–121.

Merrill, Robert. "Rhetorical Structure of *Catch-22*." *NConL* 8.3 (1978): 9–11.

Miller, Wayne Charles. *Armed America, Its Face in Fiction*, 205–243.

Mills, Russell. "Multiple Characterization in *Catch-22*." *NConL* 9.4 (1979): 6–7.

Milne, Victor J. "Heller's 'Bologniad': A Theological Perspective on *Catch-22*." *Critique* 12.2 (1970): 50–69. Rpt. in Kiley, Frederick and Walter McDonald, eds. *Catch-22 Casebook*, 58–73.

Monk, Donald. "Experiment in Therapy: A Study of *Catch-22*." *London Review* 2 (Autumn 1967): 12–19. Rpt. in Kiley, Frederick and Walter McDonald, eds. *Catch-22 Casebook*, 212–220.

Nelson, Gerald B. *Ten Versions of America*, 165–182.

Nelson, Thomas A. "Theme and Structure in *Catch-22*." *Renascence* 23 (1971): 173–182.

Oetgen, George R. "Twenty-Two of Heller's Catch." *ANQ* 18 (1980): 160.

Olderman, Raymond M. *Beyond the Waste Land*, 94–116.

Orr, Richard W. "Flat Characters in *Catch-22*." *NConL* 1.1 (1971): 4.

Pearson, Carol. "*Catch-22* and the Debasement of Language." *CEA* 38.4 (1976): 30–35.

Pinsker, Sanford. *Between Two Worlds*, 22–24.

Podhoretz, Norman. "Best Catch There Is," in Podhoretz, Norman. *Doings and Undoings*. New York: Farrar, Straus & Giroux, Inc., 1964. Rpt. in Kiley, Frederick and Walter McDonald, eds. *Catch-22 Casebook*, 237–241.

Protherough, Robert. "Sanity of *Catch-22*." *Human World* 3 (May 1971): 59–70. Rpt. in Kiley, Frederick and Walter McDonald, eds. *Catch-22 Casebook*, 201–212.

Ramsey, Vance. "From Here to Absurdity: Heller's *Catch-22*," in Whitbread, Thomas B., ed. *Seven Contemporary Authors: Essays on Cozzens, Miller, West, Golding, Heller, and Powers*. Austin, TX: University of Texas Press, 1968. Rpt. in Kiley, Frederick and Walter McDonald, eds. *Catch-22 Casebook*, 221–236.

Richter, David H. *Fable's End*, 136–165.

Ritter, Jesse. "Fearful Comedy: *Catch-22* as Avatar of the Social Surrealist Novel," in Kiley, Frederick and Walter McDonald, eds. *Catch-22 Casebook*, 73–86.

Schulz, Max F. *Black Humor Fiction of the Sixties*, 91–93, 95.

Seltzer, Leon F. "Milo's 'Culpable Innocence': Absurdity as Moral Insanity in *Catch-22*." *PLL* 15 (1979): 290–310.

Sniderman, Stephen L. " 'It Was All Yossarian's Fault': Power and Responsibility in *Catch-22*." *TCL* 19 (1973): 251–258.

Solomon, Eric. "From Christ in Flanders to *Catch-22*: An Approach to War Fiction." *TSLL* 11 (1969): 851–866.

Solomon, Eric. "From Christ in Flanders to *Catch-22:* An Approach to War Fiction." *Texas Studies in Literature and Language* 11.1 (Spring 1969): 851–866. Rpt. in Kiley, Frederick and Walter McDonald, eds. *Catch-22 Casebook*, 94–101.

Solomon, Jan. "Structure of Joseph Heller's *Catch-22*." *Critique* 9.2 (1967): 46–57. Rpt. in Kiley, Frederick and Walter McDonald, eds. *Catch-22 Casebook*, 122–132.

Stark, Howard J. "Anatomy of *Catch-22*," in Kiley, Frederick and Walter McDonald, eds. *Catch-22 Casebook*, 145–158.

Tanner, Tony. *City of Words*, 72–84.

Thomas, W. K. "Mythic Dimension of *Catch-22*." *TSSL* 15 (1973): 189–198.

Thomas, W. K. " 'What Difference Does It Make?': Logic in *Catch-22*." *DR* 50 (1971): 488–495.

Thomas, W. K. " 'What Difference Does It Make?': Logic in *Catch-22*," *Dalhousie Review* (Winter, 1970–71), Rpt. in Thomas, W. K. *Fizz Inside*, 27–34.

Torrance, Robert M. *Comic Hero*, 268–269.

Toynbee, Philip. "Here's Greatness – in Satire." *Observer* (London) 17 June 1962. Rpt. in Kiley, Frederick and Walter McDonald, eds. *Catch-22 Casebook*, 12–15.

Vos, Nelvin. "Angel, the Beast, and the Machine," in Vos, Nelvin. *For God's Sake Laugh!* Richmond, VA: John Knox Press, 1967. 53–58. Rpt. in Kiley, Frederick and Walter McDonald, eds. *Catch-22 Casebook*, 247–250.

Wain, John. "New Novel about Old Troubles." *Critical Quarterly* 5 (Summer 1963): 168–173. Rpt. in Kiley, Frederick and Walter McDonald, eds. *Catch-22 Casebook*, 43–49.

Widmer, Kingsley. "Post-Modernist Art of Protest: Kesey and Mailer as American Expressions of Rebellion." *CentR* 19.3 (1975): 125–126.

Wincelberg, Shimon. "Deadly Serious Lunacy." *New Leader* 65 (14 May 1962): 26–27. Rpt. in Kiley, Frederick and Walter McDonald, eds. *Catch-22 Casebook*, 16–18.

Good as Gold (1979)

Miller, Wayne C. "Ethnic Identity as Moral Focus: A Reading of Joseph Heller's *Good as Gold*." *MELUS* 6.3 (1979): 3–17.

Something Happened (1974)

Hendin, Josephine. *Vulnerable People*, 111–113.

Hoeber, Daniel R. "Joseph Heller's Corporate Catcher." *NConL* 8.2 (1978): 10–11.

Klemtner, Susan Strehle. " 'A Permanent Game of Excuses': Determinism in Heller's *Something Happened*." *MFS* 24 (1978–79): 550–556.

LeClair, Thomas. "Death and Black Humor." *Crit* 17.1 (1975): 16–17.

Proffitt, Edward. "Slocum's Accident: An American Tragedy." *NConL* 7.3 (1977): 7–8.

Searles, George J. "*Something Happened:* A New Direction for Joseph Heller." *Crit* 18.3 (1977): 74–82.

HEMINGWAY, ERNEST (1899–1961)

Across the River and into the Trees (1950)

Adair, William. "Death the Hunter: A Note on *Across the River and into the Trees*." *NConL* 7.1 (1977): 6–8.

Baker, Carlos. *Ernest Hemingway*, 266–288.

Benson, Jackson J. *Hemingway*, 50–54.

Bluefarb, Sam. "Middle-Aged Man in Contemporary Literature: Bloom to Herzog." *CLAJ* 20 (1976): 10–11.

Gordon, David J. *Literary Art and the Unconscious*, 190–192.

Grebstein, Sheldon Norman. *Hemingway's Craft*, 31–32, 129–130, 159.

Hassan, Ihab. *Dismemberment of Orpheus*, 106.

Hipkiss, Robert A. "Ernest Hemingway's *The Things that I Know.*" *TCL* 19 (1973): 275–281.

Knowles, A. Sidney, Jr. "Hemingway's *Across the River and into the Trees:* Adversity and Art." *ELWIU* 5 (1978): 195–208.

Kort, Wesley A. "Human Time in Hemingway's Fiction." *MFS* 26 (1980–81): 593–595.

Lisca, Peter. "Structure of Hemingway's *Across the River and into the Trees.*" *Modern Fiction Studies* 12 (Summer 1966): 232–250. Rpt. in Wagner, Linda Welshimer, ed. *Ernest Hemingway*, 290–305.

Meyer, William E., Jr. "Hemingway's Novels: The Shift in Orthodoxy and Symbolism." *ArQ* 33 (1977): 143, 145, 151–152.

Miller, Wayne Charles. *Armed America, Its Face in Fiction*, 168–174.

Nahal, Chaman. *Narrative Pattern in Ernest Hemingway's Fiction*, 150–169.

Oldsey, Bern. "Snows of Ernest Hemingway," in Waldhorn, Arthur, ed. *Ernest Hemingway*, 58–59.

Shaw, Samuel. *Ernest Hemingway*, 106–111.

Wagner, Linda Welshimer. *Hemingway and Faulkner*, 107–111.

Waldhorn, Arthur. *Reader's Guide to Ernest Hemingway*, 178–188.

Williams, Wirt. "Tragic Patterns and Rhythms in *Across the River and into the Trees.*" *F-H Annual* (1979): 389–405.

Wylder, Delbert E. *Hemingway's Heroes*, 165–198.

Farewell to Arms (1929)

Adair, William. "Ernest Hemingway and the Poetics of Loss." *CollL* 5 (1978): 14–17.

Adair, William L. "*Farewell to Arms:* A Dream Book." *JNT* 5 (1975): 40–56.

Baker, Carlos. *Ernest Hemingway*, 94–116.

Baker, Carlos. "Ernest Hemingway: *A Farewell to Arms,*" in Stegner, Wallace. *American Novel from Cooper to Faulkner.* New York: Basic Books, Inc., 1965. 192–205. Rpt. in Graham, John, comp. *Merrill Studies in A Farewell to Arms*, 27–38.

Baker, Carlos. "Mountain and the Plain," in Baker, Carlos. *Hemingway: The Writer as Artist.* Revised Edition. Princeton, NJ: Princeton University Press, 1963. 94–96. Rpt. in Gellens, Jay, ed. *Twentieth Century Interpretations of A Farewell to Arms*, 56–64.

Benson, Jackson J. *Hemingway*, 81–112, 114–116.

Burhans, Clinton S., Jr. "Hemingway and Vonnegut: Diminishing Vision in a Dying Age." *MFS* 21 (1975): 177.

Cantelupe, Eugene B. "Statues and Lovers in *A Farewell to Arms.*" *F-H Annual* (1977): 203–205.

Carson, David L. "Symbolism in *A Farewell to Arms.*" *ES* 53 (1972): 518–522.

Cowley, Malcolm. "Introduction to *Portable Hemingway.*" Hemingway, Ernest. *Portable Hemingway.* Ed. Malcolm Cowley. New York: Viking Press, Inc., 1944.

16. Rpt. as "Rain as Disaster," in Gellens, Jay, ed. *Twentieth Century Interpretations of A Farewell to Arms*, 54–55.

D'Avanzo, Mario L. "Hemingway's *A Farewell to Arms*, Chapter XXV." *Expl* 27 (1969): Item 39.

Davis, Robert M. " 'If You Did Not Go Forward': Process and Stasis in *A Farewell to Arms*." *SNNTS* 2 (1970): 305–311.

Davison, Richard A. "Hemingway's *A Farewell to Arms*." *Expl* 29 (1971): Item 46.

Donald, Miles. *American Novel in the Twentieth Century*, 36–39.

Fetterley, Judith. "*A Farewell to Arms:* Ernest Hemingway's 'Resentful Cryptogram'," in Diamond, Arlyn and Lee R. Edwards, eds. *Authority of Experience*, 257–273.

Fetterley, Judith. "*Farewell to Arms:* Hemingway's 'Resentful Cryptogram'." *JPC* 10 (1976): 203–214.

Fetterley, Judith. *Resisting Reader*, 46–71.

Fiedler, Leslie. "Love and Death," in Fiedler, Leslie. *Love and Death in the American Novel*. New York: Stein and Day Publishers, 1966. 317–318. Rpt. in Gellens, Jay, ed. *Twentieth Century Interpretations of A Farewell to Arms*, 111–112.

Friedman, Norman. "Criticism and the Novel: Hardy, Hemingway, Crane, Woolf, Conrad." *Antioch Review* 17 (1958): 352–355. Rpt. as "Small Hips, Not War," in Gellens, Jay, ed. *Twentieth Century Interpretations of A Farewell to Arms*, 105–107.

Friedrich, Otto. "Ernest Hemingway: Joy Through Strength," excerpted from *American Scholar* 26 (Autumn 1957): 519–524. Rpt. in Graham, John, comp. *Merrill Studies in A Farewell to Arms*, 46–54.

Ganzel, Dewey. "*Farewell to Arms:* The Danger of Imagination." *SewR* 79 (1971): 576–597.

Garrety, Michael. "Love and War: R. H. Mottram, *The Spanish Farm Trilogy* and Ernest Hemingway *A Farewell to Arms*," in Klein, Holger, ed. *First World War in Fiction*, 18–22.

Geismar, Maxwell. *Writers in Crisis: The American Novel Between Two Wars*. Boston: Houghton Mifflin Company, 1942. 46–47. Rpt. as "Human Will," in Gellens, Jay, ed. *Twentieth Century Interpretations of A Farewell to Arms*, 114–115.

Gelfant, Blanche. "Language as a Moral Code in *A Farewell to Arms*." *Modern Fiction Studies* 9 (1963): 173–176. Rpt. in Graham, John, comp. *Merrill Studies in A Farewell to Arms*, 83–87.

Gellens, Jay. "Introduction," in Gellens, Jay, ed. *Twentieth Century Interpretations of A Farewell to Arms*, 5–14.

Gordon, David J. *Literary Art and the Unconscious*, 179–181.

Graham, John. "Ernest Hemingway: The Meaning of Style," in Waldhorn, Arthur, ed. *Ernest Hemingway*, 26–27, 32.

Graham, John. "Ernest Hemingway: The Meaning of Style." *Modern Fiction Studies* 6 (1960–61): 298–313. Rpt. in Graham, John, comp. *Merrill Studies in A Farewell to Arms*, 88–105.

Grebstein, Sheldon Norman. *Hemingway's Craft*, 30–31, 32–35, 41–42, 73–76, 119–121, 122–124, 149–150, 153–156, 182–183, 188, 189–190, 191.

Halliday, E. M. "Hemingway's Ambiguity: Symbolism and Irony," in Waldhorn, Arthur, ed. *Ernest Hemingway*, 41–51.

Halliday, E. M. "Hemingway's Ambiguity: Symbolism and Irony." *American Literature* 27 (1956): 57–63. Rpt. in Gellens, Jay, ed. *Twentieth Century Interpretations of A Farewell to Arms*, 64–71.

Hassan, Ihab. *Dismemberment of Orpheus*, 98–100.

Hassan, Ihab. "Silence of Ernest Hemingway," in Friedman, Melvin J. and John B. Vickery, eds. *Shaken Realist*, 16–18.

Hoffman, Frederick J. *Twenties: American Writing in the Postwar Decade*. New York: Viking Press, Inc., 1955. Rpt. as "Secret Wound," in Gellens, Jay, ed. *Twentieth Century Interpretations of A Farewell to Arms*, 108–111.

Johnson, Edgar. "Farewell the Separate Peace." *Sewanee Review* 48 (1940): 289–290. Rpt. in Gellens, Jay, ed. *Twentieth Century Interpretations of A Farewell to Arms*, 112–114.

Johnston, Kenneth G. "Hemingway and Mantegna: The Bitter Nail Holes." *JNT* 1 (1971): 91–92.

Jones, Peter G. *War and the Novelist*, 7–9.

Killinger, John. "Existential Hero," in Killinger, John. *Hemingway and the Dead Gods*. Lexington, KY: University of Kentucky Press, 1960. 46–48. Rpt. in Gellens, Jay, ed. *Twentieth Century Interpretations of A Farewell to Arms*, 103–105.

Kobler, J. F. "Why Does Catherine Barkley Die?" *F-H Annual* (1978): 313–319.

Kort, Wesley A. "Human Time in Hemingway's Fiction." *MFS* 26 (1980–81): 583–585.

Lehan, Richard. *Dangerous Crossing*, 48–50.

Lewis, Robert W., Jr. "Tough Romance," in Lewis, Robert W., Jr. *Hemingway on Love*. Austin, TX: University of Texas Press, 1965. Rpt. in Gellens, Jay, ed. *Twentieth Century Interpretations of A Farewell to Arms*, 41–53.

Lewis, Wyndham. "Dumb Ox," in Lewis, Wyndam. *Men Without Art*. New York: Russell & Russell, 1964. 17–41. Rpt. as " 'Dumb Ox' in Love and War," in Gellens, Jay, ed. *Twentieth Century Interpretations of A Farewell to Arms*, 72–90.

Light, James F. "Religion of Death in *A Farewell to Arms*." *Modern Fiction Studies* 7 (Summer 1961): 169–173. Revised and rpt. in Graham, John, comp. *Merrill Studies in A Farewell to Arms*, 39–45.

McCarthy, Paul. "Chapter Beginnings in *A Farewell to Arms*." *BallS* 10.2 (1969): 21–30.

McCormick, John. *Fiction as Knowledge*, 117–119.

Martz, Louis L. "Saint as Tragic Hero," in Brooks, Cleanth, ed. *Tragic Themes is Western Literature*. New Haven:, CT: Yale University Press, 1955. Rpt. as "Unreferable Rain," in Gellens, Jay, ed. *Twentieth Century Interpretations of A Farewell to Arms*, 55–56.

Meyer, William E., Jr. "Hemingway's Novels: The Shift in Orthodoxy and Symbolism." *ArQ* 33 (1977): 142, 144, 146–147, 149–150.

Miller, Wayne Charles. *Armed America, Its Face in Fiction*, 105–108.

Nahal, Chaman. *Narrative Pattern in Ernest Hemingway's Fiction*, 49–79.

Oldsey, Bern. "Snows of Ernest Hemingway," in Waldhorn, Arthur, ed. *Ernest Hemingway*, 57, 60–61.

Oldsey, Bernard. "Genesis of *A Farewell to Arms*." *SAF* 5 (1977): 175–183.

Oldsey, Bernard. "Sense of an Ending in *A Farewell to Arms*." *MFS* 23 (1977–78): 491–510.

Ousby, Ian. *Reader's Guide to Fifty American Novels*, 237–240.

Parton, Linda C. "Time: The Novelistic Cohesive in *A Farewell to Arms*." *F-H Annual* (1979): 355–362.

Reynolds, Michale S. *Hemingway's First War*, 238–274.

Robinson, Forrest D. "Frederick Henry: The Hemingway Hero as Storyteller." *CEA* 34.4 (1972): 13–16.

Rovit, Earl. *Ernest Hemingway*. New York: Twayne Publishers, Inc., 1963. 98–106. Rpt. as "Learning to Care," in Gellens, Jay, ed. *Twentieth Century Interpretations of A Farewell to Arms*, 33–40.

Savage, D. S. *Withered Branch*. London: Eyre & Spottiswoode, Ltd., 1950. 23–36. Rpt. as "Ciphers at the Front," in Gellens, Jay, ed. *Twentieth Century Interpretations of A Farewell to Arms*, 91–102.

Schneider, Daniel J. "Hemingway's *A Farewell to Arms:* The Novel as Pure Poetry." *Modern Fiction Studies* 14 (Autumn 1968): 283–296. Rpt. in Graham, John, comp. *Merrill Studies in A Farewell to Arms*, 66–82.

Schneider, Daniel J. "Hemingway's *A Farewell to Arms:* The Novel as Pure Poetry." *Modern Fiction Studies* 14 (Autumn 1968): 283–296. Rpt. in Wagner, Linda Welshimer, ed. *Ernest Hemingway*, 252–266.

Seelye, John. "Hyperion to a Satyr: *Farewell to Arms* and *Love Story*." *CollL* 6 (1979): 130–135.

Sharrock, Roger. "Singles and Couples: Hemingway's *A Farewell to Arms* and Updike's *Couples*." *Ariel* 4.4 (1973): 21–43.

Shaw, Samuel. *Ernest Hemingway*, 54–65.

Spofford, William K. "Beyond the Feminist Perspective: Love in *A Farewell to Arms*." *F-H Annual* (1978): 307–312.

Stephens, Robert O. "Hemingway and Stendhal: The Matrix of *A Farewell to Arms*." *PMLA* 88 (1973): 271–280.

Tuttleton, James W. " 'Combat in the Erogenous Zone': Women in the American Novel between the Two Wars," in Springer, Marlene, ed. *What Manner of Woman*, 284–286.

Unfried, Sarah P. *Man's Place in the Natural Order*, 61–78, 95.

Unrue, John. "Valley of Baca and *A Farewell to Arms*." *F-H Annual* (1974): 229–234.

Vandersee, Charles. "Stopped Worlds of Frederic Henry," in Graham, John, comp. *Merrill Studies in A Farewell to Arms*, 55–65.

Wagner, Linda Welshimer. *Hemingway and Faulkner*, 80–83.

Waldhorn, Arthur. *Reader's Guide to Ernest Hemingway*, 113–130.

Warren, Robert Penn. "Ernest Hemingway," in Warren, Robert Penn. *Selected Essays*. New York: Random House, 1951. 80–118. Rpt. in Wagner, Linda Welshimer, ed. *Ernest Hemingway*, 86–87, 89, 94–99.

West, Ray B., Jr. "Ernest Hemingway: *A Farewell to Arms*," in West, Ray B., Jr. *Art of Modern Fiction*. New York: Holt, Rinehart & Winston, Inc., 1949. 139–151. Rpt. as "Unadulterated Sensibility," in Gellens, Jay, ed. *Twentieth Century Interpretations of A Farewell to Arms*, 15–27.

Whitlow, Roger. "Destruction/Prevention of the Family Relationship in Hemingway's Fiction." *LR* 20 (1976): 10–12.

Whitlow, Roger. "Mission or Love, Frederick Henry? You Can't Have It Both Ways." *MarkR* 8 (1979): 33–36.

Wilson, Edmund. "Hemingway: The Gauge of Morale," in Wilson, Edmund. *Wound and the Bow: Seven Studies in Literature*. Boston: Houghton, Mifflin Co., 1941. Rpt. in Rahv, Philip, ed. *Literature in America*, 377–378.

Wilson, Robert N. *Writer as Social Seer*, 47–48.

Wylder, Delbert E. *Hemingway's Heroes*, 66–95.

Young, Philip. *Ernest Hemingway: A Reconsideration.* University Park, PA: Pennsylvania State University Press, 1966. 89–95. Rpt. as "Loser Take Nothing," in Gellens, Jay, ed. *Twentieth Century Interpretations of A Farewell to Arms*, 28–32.

For Whom the Bell Tolls (1940)

Adair, William. "Ernest Hemingway and the Poetics of Loss." *CollL* 5 (1978): 14–17.

Allen, John J. "English of Heminway's Spaniards." *South Atlantic Bulletin* 27 (November 1961): 6–7. Rpt. in Grebstein, Sheldon Norman, comp. *Merrill Studies in For Whom the Bell Tolls*, 91–93.

Allen, Michael J. B. "Unspanish War in *For Whom the Bell Tolls.*" *ConL* 13 (1972): 204–212.

Baker, Carlos. *Ernest Hemingway*, 237–259.

Barea, Arturo. "Not Spain but Hemingway." *Horizon* 3 (May 1941): 350–361. Rpt. in Grebstein, Sheldon Norman, comp. *Merrill Studies in For Whom the Bell Tolls*, 80–90.

Benson, Jackson J. *Hemingway*, 153–168.

Brenner, Gerry. "Epic Machinery in Hemingway's *For Whom the Bell Tolls.*" *MFS* 16 (1970): 491–504.

Burhans, Clinton S., Jr. "Hemingway and Vonnegut: Diminishing Vision in a Dying Age." *MFS* 21 (1975): 178, 182, 183.

Carpenter, F. I. "Hemingway Achieves the Fifth Dimension," in Carpenter, F. I. *American Literature and the Dream.* New York: Philosophical Library, 1955. Rpt. in Wagner, Linda Welshimer, ed. *Ernest Hemingway*, 283–285.

Carpenter, F. I. "Hemingway Achieves the Fifth Dimension," in Waldhorn, Arthur, ed. *Ernest Hemingway*, 87–90.

Cass, Colin S. "Love Story in *For Whom the Bell Tolls.*" *F-H Annual* (1972): 225–235.

Delaney, Paul. "Robert Jordan's 'Real Absinthe' in *For Whom the Bell Tolls.*" *F-H Annual* (1972): 317–320.

Eby, Cecil D. "Real Robert Jordan." *American Literature* 38 (November 1966): 380–386. Rpt. in Grebstein, Sheldon Norman, comp. *Merrill Studies in For Whom the Bell Tolls*, 43–49.

Elliott, Gary D. "*For Whom the Bell Tolls:* Regeneration of the Hemingway Hero." *CEA* 38.4 (1976): 24–29.

Evans, Robert. "Hemingway and the Pale Cast of Thought," in Waldhorn, Arthur, ed. *Ernest Hemingway*, 119–123.

Fleming, Robert E. "Hemingway's Treatment of Suicide: 'Fathers and Sons' and *For Whom the Bell Tolls.*" *ArQ* 33 (1977): 124–132.

French, Warren. "Troubled World—'You'd Like Malindi,' " in French, Warren. *Social Novel at the End of an Era.* Carbondale, IL: Southern Illinois University Press, 1966. 87–91, 109–124. Rpt. as "From *Social Novel at the End of an Era*," in Grebstein, Sheldon Norman, comp. *Merrill Studies in For Whom the Bell Tolls*, 56–70.

Gordon, David J. *Literary Art and the Unconscious*, 186–189.

Graham, John. "Ernest Hemingway: The Meaning of Style," in Waldhorn, Arthur, ed. *Ernest Hemingway*, 21–22, 24–26, 29–31, 32–33.

Graham, John. "Ernest Hemingway: The Meaning of Style." *Modern Fiction Studies* 6 (1960–61): 298–313. Rpt. in Graham, John, comp. *Merrill Studies in A Farewell to Arms*, 88–105.

Grebstein, Sheldon Norman. *Hemingway's Craft*, 31, 42–52, 88–89, 125–129, 147–149, 151–152, 171, 183–186, 200.

Guttman, Allen. "Mechanized Doom: Ernest Hemingway and the Spanish Civil War." *Massachusetts Review* 1 (May 1960): 541–547, 557–561. Rpt. in Grebstein, Sheldon Norman, comp. *Merrill Studies in For Whom the Bell Tolls*, 71–79.

Halliday, E. M. "Hemingway's Ambiguity: Symbolism and Irony," in Waldhorn, Arthur, ed. *Ernest Hemingway*, 51–54.

Kinnamon, Keneth. "Hemingway, the *Corrida*, and Spain." *Texas Studies in Literature and Language* 1 (Spring 1959): 44–61. Rpt. in Wagner, Linda Welshimer, ed. *Ernest Hemingway*, 70–72.

Kort, Wesley A. "Human Time in Hemingway's Fiction." *MFS* 26 (1980–81): 586–588.

Krzyzanowski, Jerzy R. "*For Whom the Bell Tolls:* The Origin of General Golz." *Polish Review* 7 (1962): 69–74. Rpt. in Grebstein, Sheldon Norman, comp. *Merrill Studies in For Whom the Bell Tolls*, 50–55.

Lehan, Richard. *Dangerous Crossing*, 52–53.

Lutwack, Leonard. *Heroic Fiction*, 64–87.

McClellan, David. "Is Custer a Model for the Fascist Captain in *For Whom the Bell Tolls*?" *F-H Annual* (1974): 239–241.

May, Keith M. *Out of the Maelstrom*, 90.

Meyer, William E., Jr. "Hemingway's Novels: The Shift in Orthodoxy and Symbolism." *ArQ* 33 (1977): 142–143, 144–145, 147–149, 150–151.

Moses, Carole. "Language as Theme in *For Whom the Bell Tolls*." *F-H Annual* (1978): 215–223.

Moynihan, William T. "Martyrdom of Robert Jordan." *College English* 21 (December 1959): 127–132. Rpt. in Grebstein, Sheldon Norman, comp. *Merrill Studies in For Whom the Bell Tolls*, 94–101.

Nahal, Chaman. *Narrative Pattern in Ernest Hemingway's Fiction*, 120–149.

Nibbelink, Herman. "Meaning of Nature in *For Whom the Bell Tolls*." *ArQ* 33 (1977): 165–172.

Oldsey, Bern. "Snows of Ernest Hemingway," in Waldhorn, Arthur, ed. *Ernest Hemingway*, 57, 62–64.

Orlova, R. "*For Whom the Bell Tolls*," in Proffer, Carl R., ed. and trans. *Soviet Criticism of American Literature in the Sixties*, 117–148.

Orr, John. *Tragic Realism and Modern Society*, 150–159.

Ousby, Ian. *Reader's Guide to Fifty American Novels*, 243–245.

Parsons, Thornton H. "Hemingway's Tyrannous Plot." *University of Kansas City Review* 27 (Summer 1961): 261–266. Rpt. in Grebstein, Sheldon Norman, comp. *Merrill Studies in For Whom the Bell Tolls*, 107–112.

Rovit, Earl. *Ernest Hemingway*. New York: Twayne Publishers, 1963. 136–146. Rpt. in Grebstein, Sheldon Norman, comp. *Merrill Studies in For Whom the Bell Tolls*, 113–122.

Sanders, David. "Ernest Hemingway's Spanish Civil War Experience." *American Quarterly* 12 (Summer 1960): 133–143. Rpt. in Grebstein, Sheldon Norman, comp. *Merrill Studies in For Whom the Bell Tolls*, 39–42.

Shaw, Samuel. *Ernest Hemingway*, 97–103.

Slatoff, Walter J. " 'Great Sin' in *For Whom the Bell Tolls*." *JNT* 7 (1977): 142–148.

Stephens, Robert O. "Language Magic and Reality in *For Whom the Bell Tolls*." *Criticism* 14 (1972): 151–164.

Stephens, Robert O. "Language Magic and Reality in *For Whom the Bell Tolls*." *Criticism* 14 (Fall 1972): 151–164. Rpt. in Wagner, Linda Welshimer, ed. *Ernest Hemingway*, 266–278.

Thorne, Creath S. "Shape of Equivocation in Ernest Hemingway's *For Whom the Bell Tolls*." *AL* 51 (1980): 520–535.

Tuttleton, James W. " 'Combat in the Erogenous Zone': Women in the American Novel between the Two Wars," in Springer, Marlene, ed. *What Manner of Woman*, 284–286.

Unfried, Sarah P. *Man's Place in the Natural Order*, 79–93, 95–96.

Wagner, Linda W. "Marinating of *For Whom the Bell Tolls*." *JML* 2 (1972): 533–546.

Wagner, Linda Welshimer. *Hemingway and Faulkner*, 86–106.

Waldhorn, Arthur. *Reader's Guide to Ernest Hemingway*, 163–177.

Walker, Robert G. "Anselmo, Atonement and Hemingway's *For Whom the Bell Tolls*." *NConL* 7.2 (1977): 7–8.

Warren, Robert Penn. "Ernest Hemingway," in Warren, Robert Penn. *Selected Essays*. New York: Random House, 1951. 80–118. Rpt. in Wagner, Linda Welshimer, ed. *Ernest Hemingway*, 91–94.

Weeks, Robert P. "Power of the Tacit in Crane and Hemingway." *Modern Fiction Studies* 8 (Winter 1962–63): 415–418. Rpt. in Grebstein, Sheldon Norman, comp. *Merrill Studies in For Whom the Bell Tolls*, 102–106.

Whitlow, Roger. "Adoptive Territoriality in *For Whom the Bell Tolls*." *CEA* 41.2 (1979): 2–8.

Whitlow, Roger. "Destruction/Prevention of the Family Relationship in Hemingway's Fiction." *LR* 20 (1976): 12–13.

Wylder, Delbert E. *Hemingway's Heroes*, 127–164.

Yu, Beongcheon. "Still Center of Hemingway's World." *Phoenix* (Korea) 12 (Spring 1968): 15–44. Rpt. in Wagner, Linda Welshimer, ed. *Ernest Hemingway*, 126–127.

Zehr, David E. "Bourgeois Politics: Hemingway's Case in *For Whom the Bell Tolls*." *MidQ* 17 (1976): 268–278.

Islands in the Stream (1970)

Gordon, David J. *Literary Art and the Unconscious*, 189–190.

Grebstein, Sheldon Norman. *Hemingway's Craft*, 32, 37–38, 130, 163–164.

Lehan, Richard. *Dangerous Crossing*, 53–55.

Shepherd, Allen. "Hudson's Cats in Hemingway's *Islands in the Stream*." *NConL* 2.4 (1972): 3–6.

Shepherd, Allen. " 'Other Things,' Unanswerable Questions: Hemingway's *Islands in the Stream*." *AntR* 9 (1972): 37–39.

Waldhorn, Arthur. *Reader's Guide to Ernest Hemingway*, 200–211.

Winner, Viola Hopkins. "American Pictorial Vision: Objects and Ideas in Hawthorne, James, and Hemingway." *SAF* 5 (1977): 143–145.

Sun Also Rises (1926)

Adair, William. "Ernest Hemingway and the Poetics of Loss." *CollL* 5 (1978): 13–17.

Adams, Richard P. "Sunrise Out of the Waste Land." *Tulane Studies in English*

9 (1959): 119–131. Rpt. in Wagner, Linda Welshimer, ed. *Ernest Hemingway*, 246–251.

Baker, Carlos. *Ernest Hemingway*, 82–93.

Baker, Carlos. "Way It Was," in Baker, Carlos. *Hemingway: The Writer as Artist*. Princeton, NJ: Princeton University Press, 1956. 48–59. Rpt. in White, William, comp. *Merrill Studies in The Sun Also Rises*, 26–36.

Baker, Sheridan. "Jake Barnes and Spring Torrents," in Baker, Sheridan. *Ernest Hemingway: An Introduction and Interpretation*. New York: Holt, Rinehart and Winston, Inc., 1967. 40–55. Rpt. in White, William, comp. *Merrill Studies in The Sun Also Rises*, 37–52.

Bass, Eben. "Hemingway's Women of Another Country." *MarkR* 6 (1977): 37–38.

Benson, Jackson J. *Hemingway*, 30–43, 63–66, 141–142.

Bier, Jesse. "Liquor and Caffeine in *The Sun Also Rises*." *ANQ* 18 (1980): 143–144.

Brenner, Gerry. "Hemingway's 'Vulgar' Ethic: *The Sun Also Rises*." *ArQ* 33 (1977): 101–115.

Burhans, Clinton S., Jr. "Hemingway and Vonnegut: Diminishing Vision in a Dying Age." *MFS* 21 (1975): 177, 178, 182–183.

Comley, Nancy. "Hemingway: The Economics of Survival." *Novel* 12 (1979): 244–253.

Daiker, Donald A. "Pied Piper in *The Sun Also Rises*." *F-H Annual* (1975): 235–237.

Donald, Miles. *American Novel in the Twentieth Century*, 31–35.

Donaldson, Scott. "Hemingway's Morality of Compensation." *AL* 43 (1971): 399–420.

Ellis, James. "Hemingway's *The Sun Also Rises*." *Expl* 36.3 (1978): 24.

Farrell, James T. "*Sun Also Rises*," *New York Times* (1 Aug 1943). Rpt. in White, William, comp. *Merrill Studies in The Sun Also Rises*, 53–57.

Goldknopf, David. "Tourism in *The Sun Also Rises*." *CEA* 41.3 (1979): 2–8.

Gordon, David J. *Literary Art and the Unconscious*, 175–177.

Gordon, Gerald T. "Hemingway's Wilson-Harris: The Search for Value in *The Sun Also Rises*." *F-H Annual* (1972): 237–244.

Graham, John. "Ernest Hemingway: The Meaning of Style," in Waldhorn, Arthur, ed. *Ernest Hemingway*, 22–23, 25, 27–29, 30, 31–32, 34.

Graham, John. "Ernest Hemingway: The Meaning of Style." *Modern Fiction Studies* 6 (1960–61): 298–313. Rpt. in Graham, John, comp. *Merrill Studies in A Farewell to Arms*, 88–105.

Grant, Mary Kathryn, R.S.M. "Search for Celebration in *The Sun Also Rises* and *The Great Gatsby*." *ArQ* 33 (1977): 185–190.

Grebstein, Sheldon Norman. *Hemingway's Craft*, 29–30, 36–37, 40, 67–73, 116–119, 121–122, 151, 176, 179–180, 192–193.

Hassan, Ihab. *Dismemberment of Orpheus*, 96–98.

Hassan, Ihab. "Silence of Ernest Hemingway," in Friedman, Melvin J. and John B. Vickery, eds. *Shaken Realist*, 14–16.

Hays, Peter L. *Limping Hero*, 68–70, 155–158.

Jungman, Robert E. "Note on the Ending of *The Sun Also Rises*." *F-H Annual* (1977): 214.

Kinnamon, Keneth. "Hemingway, the *Corrida*, and Spain." *Texas Studies in Literature and Language* 1 (Spring 1959): 44–61. Rpt. in Wagner, Linda Welshimer, ed. *Ernest Hemingway*, 59–61.

Kort, Wesley A. "Human Time in Hemingway's Fiction." *MFS* 26 (1980–81): 590–593.

Lehan, Richard. *Dangerous Crossing*, 47–48.

Light, Martin. "Sweeping Out Chivalric Silliness: The Example of Huck Finn and *The Sun Also Rises*." *MTJ* 17.3 (1974): 19–21.

Linebarger, J. M. "Symbolic Hats in *The Sun Also Rises*." *F-H Annual* (1972): 323–324.

Meyer, William E., Jr. "Hemingway's Novels: The Shift in Orthodoxy and Symbolism." *ArQ* 33 (1977): 141–142, 143–144, 149.

Murphy, George D. "Hemingway's *The Sun Also Rises*." *Expl* 28 (1969): Item 23.

Nahal, Chaman. *Narrative Pattern in Ernest Hemingway's Fiction*, 28–48.

Nelson, Gerald B. *Ten Versions of America*, 25–42.

Nichols, Kathleen L. "Morality of Asceticism in *The Sun Also Rises:* A Structural Reinterpretation." *F-H Annual* (1978): 321–330.

Oldsey, Bern. "Snows of Ernest Hemingway," in Waldhorn, Arthur, ed. *Ernest Hemingway*, 60.

Ousby, Ian. *Reader's Guide to Fifty American Novels*, 232–234.

Phillips, Steven R. "Hemingway and the Bullfight: The Archetypes of Tragedy." *ArQ* 29 (1973): 41, 46–47.

Reardon, John. "Hemingway's Esthetic and Ethical Sportsmen." *University Review* 34 (October 1967): 13–23. Rpt. in Wagner, Linda Welshimer, ed. *Ernest Hemingway*, 133–134, 135–136.

Ross, Morton L. "Bill Gorton, the Preacher in *The Sun Also Rises*." *MFS* 18 (1972–73): 517–527.

Rovit, Earl. "*Sun Also Rises:* An Essay in Applied Principles," in Rovit, Earl. *Ernest Hemingway*. New York: Twayne, 1963. 147–162. Rpt. in White, William, comp. *Merrill Studies in The Sun Also Rises*, 58–72.

Schonhorn, Manuel. "*Sun Also Rises:* I. The Jacob Allusion II. Parody as Meaning." *BallS* 16.2 (1975): 49–55.

Shaw, Samuel. *Ernest Hemingway*, 40–50.

Spilka, Mark. "Death of Love in *The Sun Also Rises*," in Shapiro, Charles. *Twelve Original Essays on Great American Novels*. Detroit: Wayne State University Press, 1958. 238–256. Rpt. in White, William, comp. *Merrill Studies in The Sun Also Rises*, 73–85.

Sprague, Claire. "*Sun Also Rises:* Its 'Clear Financial Basis'." *AQ* 21 (1969): 259–266.

Stuckey, W. J. "*Sun Also Rises* on Its Own Ground." *JNT* 6 (1976): 224–232.

Sugg, Richard P. "Hemingway, Money and *The Sun Also Rises*." *F-H Annual* (1972): 257–267.

Torchiana, Donald T. "*Sun Also Rises:* A Reconsideration." *F-H Annual* (1969): 77–103.

Tuttleton, James W. " 'Combat in the Erogenous Zone': Women in the American Novel between the Two Wars," in Springer, Marlene, ed. *What Manner of Woman*, 283.

Twitchell, James. "Hemingway's *The Sun Also Rises*." *Expl* 31 (1972): Item 24.

Unfried, Sarah P. *Man's Place in the Natural Order*, 45–60, 95.

Vanderbilt, Kermit. "*Sun Also Rises:* Time Uncertain." *TCL* 15 (1969): 153–154.

Vanderwerken, David L. "One More River to Cross: The Bridge Motif in *The Sun Also Rises*." *CEA* 37.2 (1975): 21–22.

Vopat, Carole G. "End of *The Sun Also Rises:* A New Beginning." *F-H Annual* (1972): 245–255.

Wagner, Linda W. " 'Proud and Friendly and Gently': Women in Hemingway's Early Fiction." *CollL* 7 (1980): 242–244.

Wagner, Linda W. "*Sun Also Rises:* One Debt to Imagism." *JNT* 2 (1972): 88–98.

Wagner, Linda Welshimer. *Hemingway and Faulkner,* 41–51.

Waldhorn, Arthur. *Reader's Guide to Ernest Hemingway,* 93–112.

Warren, Robert Penn. "Ernest Hemingway," in Warren, Robert Penn. *Selected Essays.* New York: Random House, 1951. 80–118. Rpt. in Wagner, Linda Welshimer, ed. *Ernest Hemingway,* 80, 86.

Weber, Brom. "Ernest Hemingway's Genteel Bullfight," in Bradbury, Malcolm and David Palmer, eds. *American Novel in the Nineteen Twenties,* 160–163.

Whitlow, Roger. "Destruction/Prevention of the Family Relationship in Hemingway's Fiction." *LR* 20 (1976): 9–10.

Wilson, Edmund. "Hemingway: The Gauge of Morale," in Wilson, Edmund. *Wound and the Bow: Seven Studies in Literature.* Boston: Houghton, Mifflin Co., 1941. Rpt. in Rahv, Philip, ed. *Literature in America,* 375–376.

Wilson, Robert N. *Writer as Social Seer,* 45–49.

Wylder, Delbert E. *Hemingway's Heroes,* 31–65.

Young, Philip. "[*Sun Also Rises:* A Commentary]", in Young, Philip. *Ernest Hemingway.* New York: Holt, Rinehart and Winston, Inc., 1952. 54–60. Rpt. in White, William, comp. *Merrill Studies in The Sun Also Rises,* 86–90.

Yu, Beongcheon. "Still Center of Hemingway's World." *Phoenix* (Korea) 12 (Spring 1968): 15–44. Rpt. in Wagner, Linda Welshimer, ed. *Ernest Hemingway,* 110–113.

Zehr, David Morgan. "Paris and the Expatriate Mystique: Hemingway's *The Sun Also Rises.*" *ArQ* 33 (1977): 156–164.

Things That I Know see *Across the River and into the Trees*

To Have and Have Not (1937)

Adair, William. "Ernest Hemingway and the Poetics of Loss." *CollL* 5 (1978): 16–17.

Baker, Carlos. *Ernest Hemingway,* 207–222.

Benson, Jackson J. *Hemingway,* 150–151.

Burhans, Clinton S., Jr. "Hemingway and Vonnegut: Diminishing Vision in a Dying Age." *MFS* 21 (1975): 184.

Gordon, David J. *Literary Art and the Unconscious,* 184–186.

Grebstein, Sheldon Norman. *Hemingway's Craft,* 31, 35–36, 77–78, 124–125, 181–182.

Hearn, Charles R. *American Dream in the Great Depression,* 124–125.

Lehan, Richard. *Dangerous Crossing,* 50–52.

May, Keith M. *Out of the Maelstrom,* 90.

Meyer, William E., Jr. "Hemingway's Novels: The Shift in Orthodoxy and Symbolism." *ArQ* 33 (1977): 152–153.

Shaw, Samuel. *Ernest Hemingway,* 92–95.

Wagner, Linda Welshimer. *Hemingway and Faulkner,* 73–76.

Waldhorn, Arthur. *Reader's Guide to Ernest Hemingway,* 152–162.

Warren, Robert Penn. "Ernest Hemingway," in Warren, Robert Penn. *Selected Essays.* New York: Random House, 1951. 80–118. Rpt. in Wagner, Linda Welshimer, ed. *Ernest Hemingway,* 91–94.

Wylder, Delbert E. *Hemingway's Heroes,* 96–126.

HÉMON, LOUIS (1880–1913)

Maria Chapdelaine (1916)

Deschamps, Nicole, Raymonde Héroux, and Normand Villeneuve. *Le mythe de Maria Chapdelaine.* Montréal: Les Presses de l'Université de Montréal, 1980.

Paré, François. "*Maria Chapdelaine* au Canada anglais: Reflexions sur notre extravagance." *V&I* 2 (1976): 265–278.

Rasporich, Beverly J. "Sacrifice and Death in French-Canadian Fiction: An English Reading." *DR* 55 (1975): 451–455.

Servais-Maquoi, Mireille. *Le roman de la terre au Québec,* 47–68.

Sutherland, Ronald. *Second Image,* 4–6.

Urbas, Jeannette. *From Thirty Acres to Modern Times,* 9–13.

HENTZ, CAROLINE LEE (1800–1856)

Eoline (1852)

Baym, Nina. *Woman's Fiction,* 132–133.

Ernest Linwood (1856)

Baym, Nina. *Woman's Fiction,* 136–138.

Helen and Arthur (1853)

Baym, Nina. *Woman's Fiction,* 133–136.

Linda (1850)

Baym, Nina. *Woman's Fiction,* 128–130.

Planter's Northern Bride (1854)

Baym, Nina. *Woman's Fiction,* 136.

Rena (1850)

Baym, Nina. *Woman's Fiction,* 130–132.

HERBERT, FRANK (1920–1986)

Children of Dune (1976)

Brigg, Peter. "Frank Herbert: On Getting Our Heads Together." *Mosaic* 13.3–4 (1980): 195, 200–201.

Miller, David M. *Frank Herbert,* 29–31.

Redekop, Ernest H. "Labyrinths in Space and Time." *Mosaic* 13.3–4 (1980): 109–111.

Destination: Void (1966)

Miller, David M. *Frank Herbert,* 35–38.

Warrick, Patricia. "Images of the Man-Machine Intelligence Relationship in Science Fiction," in Clareson, Thomas D., ed. *Many Futures, Many Worlds,* 211–212.

Warrick, Patricia S. *Cybernetic Imagination in Science Fiction,* 181–188.

Dosadi Experiment (1978)

Miller, David M. *Frank Herbert,* 52–53.

Dragon in the Sea (1956)

Miller, David M. *Frank Herbert,* 14–15.

Dune (1965)

 Brigg, Peter. "Frank Herbert: On Getting Our Heads Together." *Mosaic* 13.3–4
 (1980): 195, 200.

 Miller, David M. *Frank Herbert*, 15–24.

 O'Reilly, Timothy. "From Concept to Fable: The Evolution of Frank Herbert's
 Dune," in Riley, Dick, ed. *Critical Encounters*, 41–55.

 Scholes, Robert. *Structural Fabulation*, 67–70.

Dune Messiah (1972)

 Miller, David M. *Frank Herbert*, 26–28.

Eyes of Heisenberg (1966)

 Miller, David M. *Frank Herbert*, 31–33.

Godmakers (1971)

 Miller, David M. *Frank Herbert*, 48–49.

Green Brain (1966)

 Brigg, Peter. "Frank Herbert: On Getting Our Heads Together." *Mosaic* 13.3–4
 (1980): 195, 197.

 Miller, David M. *Frank Herbert*, 33–35.

Heaven Makers (1968)

 Miller, David M. *Frank Herbert*, 39–40.

Hellstrom's Hive (1973)

 Brigg, Peter. "Frank Herbert: On Getting Our Heads Together." *Mosaic* 13.3–4
 (1980): 195–197.

 Miller, David M. *Frank Herbert*, 45–47.

Jesus Incident (1979)

 Miller, David M. *Frank Herbert*, 54–56.

Santaroga Barrier (1968)

 Brigg, Peter. "Frank Herbert: On Getting Our Heads Together." *Mosaic* 13.3–4
 (1980): 194–195, 197–200.

 Miller, David M. *Frank Herbert*, 41–43.

Soul Catcher (1972)

 Miller, David M. *Frank Herbert*, 50–52.

Under Pressure see *Dragon in the Sea*

Whipping Star (1970)

 Miller, David M. *Frank Herbert*, 43–45.

HERNTON, CALVIN C. (1934–)

Scarecrow (1974)

 Klotman, Phyllis Rauch. *Another Man Gone*, 136–137.

HERR, MICHAEL (1940(?)–)

Dispatches (1977)

 Hellmann, John. "New Journalism and Vietnam: Memory as Structure in Michael
 Herr's *Dispatches*." *SAQ* 79 (1980): 141–151.

HERRICK, ROBERT (1868–1938)

Chimes (1926)
  Budd, L. J. *Robert Herrick*, 105–109.

Clark's Field (1914)
  Budd, L. J. *Robert Herrick*, 87–90.

Common Lot (1904)
  Budd, L. J. *Robert Herrick*, 50–55.

End of Desire (1932)
  Budd, L. J. *Robert Herrick*, 109–113.

Gospel of Freedom (1898)
  Budd, L. J. *Robert Herrick*, 34–38.

Healer (1911)
  Budd, L. J. *Robert Herrick*, 78–80.

Homely Lilla (1923)
  Budd, L. J. *Robert Herrick*, 93–97.

Life for a Life (1910)
  Budd, L. J. *Robert Herrick*, 74–78.

Memoirs of an American Citizen (1905)
  Budd, L. J. *Robert Herrick*, 55–59.

One Woman's Life (1913)
  Budd, L. J. *Robert Herrick*, 83–87.

Real World (1901)
  Budd, L. J. *Robert Herrick*, 45–49.

Together (1908)
  Budd, L. J. *Robert Herrick*, 63–70.

Waste (1924)
  Budd, L. J. *Robert Herrick*, 97–100.

Web of Life (1900)
  Budd, L. J. *Robert Herrick*, 41–45.

HERSEY, JOHN (1914–1993)

War Lover (1959)
  Jones, Peter G. *War and the Novelist*, 148–152.
  Waldmeir, Joseph J. *American Novels of the Second World War*, 30–32.

White Lotus (1965)
  Haltresht, Michael. "Dreams as a Characterization Device in Hersey's *White Lotus*." *NConL* 1.3 (1971): 4–5.

HEYWARD, DUBOSE (1885–1940)

Mamba's Daughters (1929)

Baker, Donald G. "Black Images: The Afro-American in Popular Novels, 1900–1945." *JPC* 7 (1973): 336–337.

Berzon, Judith R. *Neither White Nor Black*, 175, 177–178.

HIGGINSON, THOMAS WENTWORTH (1823–1911)

Malbone (1869)

Tuttleton, James W. *Thomas Wentworth Higginson*, 82–88.

HILDRETH, RICHARD (1807–1865)

Archy Moore see *Slave*

Slave (1836)

Berzon, Judith R. *Neither White Nor Black*, 192–193.

Brandstadter, Evan. "Uncle Tom and Archy Moore: The Antislavery Novel as Ideological Symbol." *AQ* 26 (1974): 160–175.

Canaday, Nicholas, Jr. "Antislavery Novel Prior to 1852 and Holdreth's *The Slave* (1836)." *CLAJ* 17 (1973): 178–191.

Yellin, Jean Fagan. *Intricate Knot*, 91–116.

White Slave see *Slave*

HILL, RUTH BEEBE (1913–)

Hanta Yo (1979)

Laubin, Reginald and Gladys Laubin. "Comments on *Hanta Yo*." *WAL* 15 (1980): 143–144.

HIMES, CHESTER (1909–1984)

All Shot Up (1960)

Nelson, Raymond. "Domestic Harlem: The Detective Fiction of Chester Himes." *VQR* 48 (1972): 262–263, 264–276.

Reilly, John M. "Chester Himes' Harlem Tough Guys." *JPC* 9 (1976): 941–942.

Big Gold Dream (1960)

Nelson, Raymond. "Domestic Harlem: The Detective Fiction of Chester Himes." *VQR* 48 (1972): 262–263, 264–276.

Reilly, John M. "Chester Himes' Harlem Tough Guys." *JPC* 9 (1976): 941.

Blind Man with a Pistol (1969)

Franklin, H. Bruce. *Victim as Criminal and Artist*, 227–229.

Lundquist, James. *Chester Himes*, 116–133.

Nelson, Raymond. "Domestic Harlem: The Detective Fiction of Chester Himes." *VQR* 48 (1972): 262–263, 264–276.

Reilly, John M. "Chester Himes' Harlem Tough Guys." *JPC* 9 (1976): 943–946.

Cast the First Stone (1952)

Davis, Arthur P. *From the Dark Tower*, 165.
Franklin, H. Bruce. *Victim as Criminal and Artist*, 211–212.
Lundquist, James. *Chester Himes*, 74–81.
Milliken, Stephen F. *Chester Himes*, 43–44, 45–46, 159–180.

Cotton Comes to Harlem (1965)

Lundquist, James. *Chester Himes*, 109–112.
Nelson, Raymond. "Domestic Harlem: The Detective Fiction of Chester Himes."
  VQR 48 (1972): 262–263, 264–276.
Reilly, John M. "Chester Himes' Harlem Tough Guys." *JPC* 9 (1976): 942–943.

Crazy Kill (1959)

Lundquist, James. *Chester Himes*, 112–116.
Nelson, Raymond. "Domestic Harlem: The Detective Fiction of Chester Himes."
  VQR 48 (1972): 262–263, 264–276.
Reilly, John M. "Chester Himes' Harlem Tough Guys." *JPC* 9 (1976): 939–940.

Don't Play with Death see *All Shot Up*

For Love of Imabelle see *Rage in Harlem*

Heats On (1961)

Reilly, John M. "Chester Himes' Harlem Tough Guys." *JPC* 9 (1976): 942.

If He Hollers Let Him Go (1945)

Berzon, Judith R. *Neither White Nor Black*, 172–174.
Davis, Arthur P. *From the Dark Tower*, 163.
Gayle, Addison, Jr. *Way of the New World*, 181–185.
Klotman, Phyllis Rauch. *Another Man Gone*, 132–133.
Lundquist, James. *Chester Himes*, 27–47.
Milliken, Stephen F. *Chester Himes*, 70–96.
Rosenblatt, Roger. *Black Fiction*, 164–173.

Lonely Crusade (1947)

Davis, Arthur P. *From the Dark Tower*, 163–164.
Gayle, Addison, Jr. *Way of the New World*, 185–191.
Lundquist, James. *Chester Himes*, 47–72.
Milliken, Stephen F. *Chester Himes*, 96–134.
Reckley, Ralph. "Use of the Doppelganger or Double in Chester Himes' *Lonely
  Crusade*." *CLAJ* 20 (1977): 448–458.

Pinktoes (1965)

Davis, Arthur P. *From the Dark Tower*, 165–166.
Lundquist, James. *Chester Himes*, 135–140.
Milliken, Stephen F. *Chester Himes*, 258–268.

Primitive (1955)

Davis, Arthur P. *From the Dark Tower*, 164–165.
Lundquist, James. *Chester Himes*, 93–105.
Milliken, Stephen F. *Chester Himes*, 180–206.
Wade, Melvin and Margaret Wade. "Black Aesthetic in the Black Novel." *JBS* 2.4
  (1972): 402–403.

Rage in Harlem (1957)

Nelson, Raymond. "Domestic Harlem: The Detective Fiction of Chester Himes." *VQR* 48 (1972): 263–264.

Reilly, John M. "Chester Himes' Harlem Tough Guys." *JPC* 9 (1976): 937–939.

Real Cool Killers (1959)

Nelson, Raymond. "Domestic Harlem: The Detective Fiction of Chester Himes." *VQR* 48 (1972): 262–263, 264–276.

Reilly, John M. "Chester Himes' Harlem Tough Guys." *JPC* 9 (1976): 939.

Run Man Run (1959)

Reilly, John M. "Chester Himes' Harlem Tough Guys." *JPC* 9 (1976): 940–941.

Third Generation (1954)

Berzon, Judith R. *Neither White Nor Black*, 77–78.

Davis, Arthur P. *From the Dark Tower*, 164.

Lundquist, James. *Chester Himes*, 81–93.

Milliken, Stephen F. *Chester Himes*, 138–159.

Reckley, Ralph. "Oedipal Complex and Intraracial Conflict in Chester Himes' *The Third Generation*." *CLAJ* 21 (1977): 275–281.

Schultz, Elizabeth. " 'Free in Fact and at Last': The Image of the Black Woman in Black American Fiction," in Springer, Marlene, ed. *What Manner of Woman*, 324.

HODGINS, JACK (1938–)

Invention of the World (1977)

Lecker, Robert. "Haunted by a Glut of Ghosts: *The Invention of the World*," in Gerson, Carole, comp. *Modern Canadian Fiction*, 185–194.

HOFFMAN, WILLIAM (1925–)

Trumpet Unblown (1957)

Waldmeir, Joseph J. *American Novels of the Second World War*, 23–27.

HOLMAN, JESSE (1784–1842)

Prisoners of Niagara (1810)

Barnett, Louise K. *Ignoble Savage*, 59–60.

HOLMES, JOHN CLELLON (1926–1988)

Get Home Free (1964)

Bryant, Jerry H. *Open Decision*, 215–218.

HOLMES, MARY JANE (1825–1907)

Dora Dean (1859)

Baym, Nina. *Woman's Fiction*, 194–195.

English Orphans (1855)
Baym, Nina. *Woman's Fiction*, 191–192.
Lena Rivers (1856)
Baym, Nina. *Woman's Fiction*, 192–193.
Marian Grey (1863)
Baym, Nina. *Woman's Fiction*, 195–196.
Meadow-brook (1857)
Baym, Nina. *Woman's Fiction*, 193–194.
Tempest and Sunshine (1854)
Baym, Nina. *Woman's Fiction*, 189–191.

HOLMES, OLIVER WENDELL (1809–1894)

Elsie Venner (1861)
Fryer, Judith. *Faces of Eve*, 29–40.

Guardian Angel (1867)
Parker, Gail T. "Sex, Sentiment, and Oliver Wendell Holmes." *WS* 1 (1972): 52–53, 56.

Mortal Antipathy (1885)
Faderman, Lillian. "Female Same-Sex Relationships in Novels by Longfellow, Holmes, and James." *NEQ* 51 (1978): 318–323.
Parker, Gail T. "Sex, Sentiment, and Oliver Wendell Holmes." *WS* 1 (1972): 53–55.

HOLT, JOHN DOMINIS (1919–1993)

Waimea Summer (1976)
Hershinow, Sheldon J. "John Dominis Holt: Hawaiian-American Traditionalist." *MELUS* 7.2 (1980): 71.

HOOD, HUGH (1928–)

Camera Always Lies (1967)
Blandford, Patrick. "Hood *à la mode:* Bicultural Tension in the Works of Hugh Hood," in Struthers, J. R., ed. *Before the Flood*, 147, 149–150.
Duffy, Dennis. "Grace: The Novels of Hugh Hood." *CanL* 47 (1971): 12–17.
Duffy, Dennis. "Grace: The Novels of Hugh Hood," in Woodcock, George, ed. *Canadian Novel*, 244–248.
Morley, Patricia A. *Comedians*, 27–37.
Woodcock, George. "Taming the Tiger of Power: Notes on Certain Fictions by Hugh Hood." *ECW* 13–14 (1978–79): 171–176.
Woodcock, George. "Taming the Tiger of Power: Notes on Certain Fictions by Hugh Hood," in Struthers, J. R., ed. *Before the Flood*, 171, 173–176.
Woodcock, George. *World of Canadian Writing*, 80–83.

Game of Touch (1970)

Blandford, Patrick. "Hood *à la mode:* Bicultural Tension in the Works of Hugh Hood," in Struthers, J. R., ed. *Before the Flood*, 148, 149, 158–168.

Duffy, Dennis. "Grace: The Novels of Hugh Hood." *CanL* 47 (1971): 20–24.

Duffy, Dennis. "Grace: The Novels of Hugh Hood," in Woodcock, George, ed. *Canadian Novel*, 252–256.

Morley, Patricia A. *Comedians*, 39–48.

Woodcock, George. "Taming the Tiger of Power: Notes on Certain Fictions by Hugh Hood." *ECW* 13–14 (1978–79): 176–180.

Woodcock, George. "Taming the Tiger of Power: Notes on Certain Fictions by Hugh Hood," in Struthers, J. R., ed. *Before the Flood*, 172, 173, 176–180.

Woodcock, George. *World of Canadian Writing*, 83–87.

New Athens (1977)

Mathews, Lawrence. "Secular and the Sacral: Notes on *A New Athens* and Three Stories by Hugh Hood." *ECW* 13–14 (1978–79): 211–213, 223–228.

Mathews, Lawrence. "The Secular and the Sacred: Notes on *A New Athens* and Three Stories by Hugh Hood," in Struthers, J. R., ed. *Before the Flood*, 222–228.

Mills, John. "Hugh Hood and the Anagogical Method." *ECW* 13–14 (1978–79): 104–111.

Mills, John. "Hugh Hood and the Anagogical Method," in Struthers, J. R., ed. *Before the Flood*, 104–111.

Swing in the Garden (1975)

Lecker, Robert. "Spirit of Communion: *The Swing in the Garden*." *ECW* 13–14 (1978–79): 187–209.

Lecker, Robert. "A Spirit of Communion: *The Swing in the Garden*," in Struthers, J. R., ed. *Before the Flood*, 187–209.

White Figure, White Ground (1964)

Blandford, Patrick. "Hood *à la mode:* Bicultural Tension in the Works of Hugh Hood," in Struthers, J. R., ed. *Before the Flood*, 147, 149.

Duffy, Dennis. "Grace: The Novels of Hugh Hood." *CanL* 47 (1971): 17–20.

Duffy, Dennis. "Grace: The Novels of Hugh Hood," in Woodcock, George, ed. *Canadian Novel*, 248–252.

Mills, John. "Hugh Hood and the Anagogical Method," in Struthers, J. R., ed. *Before the Flood*, 101–104.

Morley, Patricia A. *Comedians*, 14–25.

Moss, John. *Sex and Violence*, 101–102.

You Can't Get There from Here (1972)

Blandford, Patrick. "Hood *à la mode:* Bicultural Tension in the Works of Hugh Hood," in Struthers, J. R., ed. *Before the Flood*, 147–148, 168–169.

Morley, Patricia A. *Comedians*, 50–60.

Moss, John. *Sex and Violence*, 236–245.

Woodcock, George. "Taming the Tiger of Power: Notes on Certain Fictions by Hugh Hood." *ECW* 13–14 (1978–79): 180–185.

Woodcock, George. "Taming the Tiger of Power: Notes on Certain Fictions by Hugh Hood," in Struthers, J. R., ed. *Before the Flood*, 173, 180–185.

Woodcock, George. *World of Canadian Writing*, 88–92.

HOPKINS, PAULINE E. (1859–1930)

Contending Forces (1900)
  Berzon, Judith R. *Neither White Nor Black*, 202.

HOUGH, EMERSON (1857–1923)

North of 36 (1923)
  Downey, Linda K. "Woman on the Trail: Hough's *North of 36*." *WAL* 14 (1979): 217–220.

HOWARD, JAMES H. W.

Bond and Free (1886)
  Elder, Arlene A. *"Hindered Hand,"* 18–19, 20, 46–47, 49–50, 55–56, 60.
  Fleming, Robert E. "Humor in the Early Black Novel." *CLAJ* 17 (1973): 252.

HOWATCH, SUSAN (1940–)

Dark Shore (1965)
  Russ, Joanna. "Somebody's Trying to Kill Me and I Think It's My Husband: The Modern Gothic." *JPC* 6 (1973): 666–691.

HOWE, E. W. (1853–1937)

Story of a Country Town (1883)
  Sackett, S. J. *E. W. Howe*, 41–68.

HOWELLS, WILLIAM DEAN (1837–1920)

Annie Kilburn (1888)
  Bennett, George N. *Realism of William Dean Howells*, 28–35.
  Habegger, Alfred. "Autistic Tyrant: Howells' Self-Sacrificial Woman and Jamesian Renunciation." *Novel* 10 (1976): 27.
  Taylor, Walter F. "William Dean Howells and the Economic Novel." *American Literature* 4 (May 1932): 103–113. Rpt. in Eschholz, Paul A., ed. *Critics on William Dean Howells*, 95, 97.

April Hopes (1887)
  Bremer, Sidney H. "William Dean Howells' Ingenues and the Road to Marriage." *ALR* 12 (1979): 146.
  Habegger, Alfred. "Autistic Tyrant: Howells' Self-Sacrificial Woman and Jamesian Renunciation." *Novel* 10 (1976): 31, 33, 36–39.
  Wilson, Jack H. "Howells' Use of George Eliot's *Romola* in *April Hopes*." *PMLA* 84 (1969): 1620–1627.

Boy's Town (1890)
  Towers, Tom H. "Savagery and Civilization: The Moral Dimensions of Howells's *A Boy's Town*." *AL* 40 (1969): 499–509.

Chance Acquaintance (1873)

Milne, Gordon. *Sense of Society*, 75–77.
Taylor, Gordon O. *Passages of Thought*, 34–41.
Tuttleton, James W. *Novel of Manners in America*, 92–97.

Coast of Bohemia (1893)

Bennett, George N. *Realism of William Dean Howells*, 105–114.

Day of Their Wedding (1896)

Bennett, George N. *Realism of William Dean Howells*, 123–125.

Dr. Breen's Practice (1881)

Fryer, Judith. *Faces of Eve*, 234–240.
Habegger, Alfred. "Autistic Tyrant: Howells' Self-Sacrificial Woman and Jamesian Renunciation." *Novel* 10 (1976): 33.
Stein, Allen F. "Marriage in Howells's Novels." *AL* 48 (1977): 505, 508–510.

Fennel and Rue (1908)

Bennett, George N. *Realism of William Dean Howells*, 219–224.
Crowley, John W. "Oedipal Theme in Howells's *Fennel and Rue*." *SNNTS* 5 (1973): 104–109.

Foregone Conclusion (1875)

Crowley, John W. " 'A Completer Verity': The Ending of W.D. Howells' *A Foregone Conclusion*." *ELN* 14 (1977): 192–197.
Habegger, Alfred. "Autistic Tyrant: Howells' Self-Sacrificial Woman and Jamesian Renunciation." *Novel* 10 (1976): 32.

Hazard of New Fortunes (1890)

Arms, George. "Howells' New York Novel: Comedy and Belief." *New England Quarterly* 16 (September 1948): 313–325. Rpt. in Eschholz, Paul A., ed. *Critics on William Dean Howells*, 102–110.
Bennett, George N. *Realism of William Dean Howells*, 35–44.
Bremer, Sidney H. "William Dean Howells' Ingenues and the Road to Marriage." *ALR* 12 (1979): 146.
Cohn, Jan. "Women as Superfluous Characters in American Realism and Naturalism." *SAF* 1 (1973): 160.
Fischer, William C., Jr. "William Dean Howells: Reverie and the Nonsymbolic Aesthetic." *NCF* 25 (1970): 23–29.
Frazier, David L. "Howells' Symbolic Houses: The Plutocrats and Palaces." *ALR* 10 (1977): 268–271.
Frederick, John T. *Darkened Sky*, 204–206.
Gindin, James. *Harvest of a Quiet Eye*, 106–109.
Klinkowitz, Jerome. *Practice of Fiction in America*, 26–30.
McMurray, William. "Moral Law and Justice in Howells' Fiction." *ALR* 10 (1977): 282–284.
Stein, Allen F. "Marriage in Howells's Novels." *AL* 48 (1977): 519–523.
Taylor, Gordon O. *Passages of Thought*, 102–109.
Taylor, Walter F. "William Dean Howells and the Economic Novel." *American Literature* 4 (May 1932): 103–113. Rpt. in Eschholz, Paul A., ed. *Critics on William Dean Howells*, 93–94.

Imperative Duty (1891)

Andrews, William L. "Miscegenation in the Late Nineteenth-Century American Novel." *SoHR* 13 (1979): 18–19.

Bennett, George N. *Realism of William Dean Howells*, 94–105.

Berzon, Judith R. *Neither White Nor Black*, 109–115.

Cady, Edwin H. *Light of Common Day*, 147–150.

Indian Summer (1886)

Habegger, Alfred. "Autistic Tyrant: Howells' Self-Sacrificial Woman and Jamesian Renunciation." *Novel* 10 (1976): 33–36.

Milne, Gordon. *Sense of Society*, 85–90.

Kentons (1902)

Bennett, George N. *Realism of William Dean Howells*, 180–191.

Cady, Edwin H. *Light of Common Day*, 163–166.

Habegger, Alfred. "Autistic Tyrant: Howells' Self-Sacrificial Woman and Jamesian Renunciation." *Novel* 10 (1976): 27.

Milne, Gordon. *Sense of Society*, 91–93.

Lady of the Aroostook (1879)

Crowley, John W. "Interoceanic Episode: *The Lady of the Aroostook*." *AL* 49 (1977): 180–191.

Habegger, Alfred. "Autistic Tyrant: Howells' Self-Sacrificial Woman and Jamesian Renunciation." *Novel* 10 (1976): 32.

Milne, Gordon. *Sense of Society*, 77–80.

Nettels, Elsa. "William Dean Howells and the American Language." *NEQ* 53 (1980): 318–319.

Landlord of Lion's Head (1897)

Bennett, George N. *Realism of William Dean Howells*, 129–153.

Cady, Edwin H. *Light of Common Day*, 150–152.

Frazier, David L. "Howells' Symbolic Houses: The Plutocrats and Palaces." *ALR* 10 (1977): 275–277.

Frederick, John T. *Darkened Sky*, 211.

Gindin, James. *Harvest of a Quiet Eye*, 110–111.

McMurray, William. "Moral Law and Justice in Howells' Fiction." *ALR* 10 (1977): 286–288.

McMurray, William. "Point of View in Howells's *The Landlord of Lion's Head*." *American Literature* 34 (May 1962): 207–214. Rpt. in Eschholz, Paul A., ed. *Critics on William Dean Howells*, 112–117.

Storhoff, Gary P. "Ironic Technique in *The Landlord at Lion's Head*." *NDQ* 46.2 (1978): 55–64.

Toth, Susan Allen. "Character and Focus in *The Landlord at Lion's Head*." *CLQ* 11 (1975): 116–128.

Leatherwood God (1916)

Bennett, George N. *Realism of William Dean Howells*, 224–233.

Bennett, George N. "Religion and Life: *The Leatherwood God*," in Bennett, George N. *Realism of William Dean Howells, 1889–1920*. Nashville, TN: Vanderbilt Unversity Press, 1973. 224–233. Rpt. in Eschholz, Paul A., ed. *Critics on William Dean Howells*, 118–124.

Cady, Edwin H. *Light of Common Day*, 156–160.

Dean, James L. "Wests of Howells and Crane." *ALR* 10 (1977): 262–264.

Frederick, John T. *Darkened Sky*, 222–225.

Kuhlmann, Susan. *Knave, Fool, and Genius*, 83–87.

Letters Home (1903)

Bennett, George N. *Realism of William Dean Howells*, 191–196.

Minister's Charge (1887)

Boardman, Arthur. "Howellsian Sex." *SNNTS* 2.1 (1970): 56–57, 58.

Goldfarb, Clare R. "William Dean Howells' *The Minister's Charge:* A Study of Psychological Perception." *MarkR* 2.1 (1969): 1–4.

Goldfarb, Clare R. "William Dean Howells' *The Minister's Charge:* A Study of Psychological Perception." *Markham Review* 2 (September 1969): 1–4. Rpt. in Eschholz, Paul A., ed. *Critics on William Dean Howells*, 85–90.

Habegger, Alfred. "Autistic Tyrant: Howells' Self-Sacrificial Woman and Jamesian Renunciation." *Novel* 10 (1976): 28–29.

Nettels, Elsa. "William Dean Howells and the American Language." *NEQ* 53 (1980): 320–328.

Stein, Allen F. "Marriage in Howells's Novels." *AL* 48 (1977): 517–519.

Miss Bellard's Inspiration (1905)

Bennett, George N. *Realism of William Dean Howells*, 212–219.

Modern Instance (1882)

Boardman, Arthur. "Howellsian Sex." *SNNTS* 2.1 (1970): 56, 57, 58.

Bogardus, Ralph F. "Literary Realist and the Camera: W.D. Howells and the Uses of Photography." *ALR* 10 (1977): 235.

Bremer, Sidney H. "William Dean Howells' Ingenues and the Road to Marriage." *ALR* 12 (1979): 146–147.

Budd, Louis J. "Hungry Bear of American Realism." *ALR* 5 (1972): 486–487.

Eschholz, Paul A. "Howells' *A Modern Instance:* A Realist's Moralistic Vision of America." *South Dakota Review* 10 (Spring 1972): 91–102. Rpt. in Eschholz, Paul A., ed. *Critics on William Dean Howells*, 71–79.

Frederick, John T. *Darkened Sky*, 196–199.

Gindin, James. *Harvest of a Quiet Eye*, 105–106.

Gross, Seymour and Rosalie Murphy. "Commonplace Reality and the Romantic Phantoms: Howells' *A Modern Instance* and *The Rise of Silas Lapham.*" *SAF* 4 (1976): 4–8.

Habegger, Alfred. "Autistic Tyrant: Howells' Self-Sacrificial Woman and Jamesian Renunciation." *Novel* 10 (1976): 28, 33.

McMurray, William. "Moral Law and Justice in Howells' Fiction." *ALR* 10 (1977): 280–281.

Ousby, Ian. *Reader's Guide to Fifty American Novels*, 142–144.

Perkins, George. "*Modern Instance:* Howells' Transition to Artistic Maturity." *NEQ* 47 (1974): 427–439.

See, Fred G. "Demystification of Style: Metaphoric and Metonymic Language in *A Modern Instance.*" *NCF* 28 (1974): 379–403.

Smith, Geoffrey D. "Bartley Hubbard and Behavioral Art in William Dean Howells' *A Modern Instance.*" *SAF* 7 (1979): 83–91.

Stein, Allen F. "Marriage in Howells's Novels." *AL* 48 (1977): 510–515.

Tavernier-Courbin, Jacqueline. "Towards the City: Howells' Characterization in *A Modern Instance.*" *MFS* 24 (1978): 111–127.

Tavernier-Courbin, Jacqueline. "Village and After: Social Evolution through Character in *A Modern Instance*." *ALR* 12 (1979): 127–142.

Taylor, Gordon O. *Passages of Thought*, 86–95.

Tuttleton, James W. *Novel of Manners in America*, 98–109.

Open-Eyed Conspiracy (1897)

Bennett, George N. *Realism of William Dean Howells*, 125–129.

Bremer, Sidney H. "William Dean Howells' Ingenues and the Road to Marriage." *ALR* 12 (1979): 145–146.

Klinkowitz, Jerome. *Practice of Fiction in America*, 33–35.

Quality of Mercy (1892)

Bennett, George N. *Realism of William Dean Howells*, 44–49.

Frazier, David L. "Howells' Symbolic Houses: The Plutocrats and Palaces." *ALR* 10 (1977): 273–275.

Frederick, John T. *Darkened Sky*, 209–210.

Taylor, Walter F. "William Dean Howells and the Economic Novel." *American Literature* 4 (May 1932): 103–113. Rpt. in Eschholz, Paul A., ed. *Critics on William Dean Howells*, 94, 97–98.

Ragged Lady (1899)

Bennett, George N. *Realism of William Dean Howells*, 153–162.

Rise of Silas Lapham (1885)

Berces, Francis A. "Mimesis, Morality and *The Rise of Silas Lapham*." *AQ* 22 (1970): 190–202.

Boardman, Arthur. "Howellsian Sex." *SNNTS* 2.1 (1970): 57.

Bogardus, Ralph F. "Literary Realist and the Camera: W.D. Howells and the Uses of Photography." *ALR* 10 (1977): 234–235.

Bremer, Sidney H. "William Dean Howells' Ingenues and the Road to Marriage." *ALR* 12 (1979): 145.

Cohn, Jan. "House of Fiction: Domestic Architecture in Howells and Edith Wharton." *TSLL* 15 (1973): 541–544.

Dooley, Patrick. "Nineteenth Century Business Ethics and *The Rise of Silas Lapham*." *AmerS* 21.2 (1980): 79–93.

Fischer, William C., Jr. "William Dean Howells: Reverie and the Nonsymbolic Aesthetic." *NCF* 25 (1970): 18–23.

Frazier, David L. "Howells' Symbolic Houses: The Plutocrats and Palaces." *ALR* 10 (1977): 271–273.

Gindin, James. *Harvest of a Quiet Eye*, 103–105.

Gross, Seymour and Rosalie Murphy. "Commonplace Reality and the Romantic Phantoms: Howells' *A Modern Instance* and *The Rise of Silas Lapham*." *SAF* 4 (1976): 8–13.

Habegger, Alfred. "Autistic Tyrant: Howells' Self-Sacrificial Woman and Jamesian Renunciation." *Novel* 10 (1976): 28.

Jenkins, R. B. "Howells' *The Rise of Silas Lapham*." *Expl* 36.3 (1978): 37–40.

McMurray, William. "Moral Law and Justice in Howells' Fiction." *ALR* 10 (1977): 281–282.

MacNaughton, W. R. " 'Englishmen' in *The Rise of Silas Lapham*." *MTJ* 18.2 (1976): 11–12.

Milne, Gordon. *Sense of Society*, 80–85.

Moore, Harry T. "Afterword." Howells, William Dean. *Rise of Silas Lapham*. New

York: New American Library, 1963. Rpt. in Moore, Harry T. *Age of the Modern*, 53–58.

Nettels, Elsa. "William Dean Howells and the American Language." *NEQ* 53 (1980): 319–320.

Ousby, Ian. *Reader's Guide to Fifty American Novels*, 148–149.

Pizer, Donald. "Ethical Unity of *The Rise of Silas Lapham*." *American Literature* 32 (November 1960): 322–327. Rpt. in Eschholz, Paul A., ed. *Critics on William Dean Howells*, 80–83.

Stein, Allen F. "Marriage in Howells's Novels." *AL* 48 (1977): 515–517.

Tanselle, G. Thomas. "Boston Seasons of *Silas Lapham*." *SNNTS* 1.1 (1969): 60–66.

Taylor, Gordon O. *Passages of Thought*, 95–102.

Tuttleton, James W. *Novel of Manners in America*, 110–120.

Shadow of a Dream (1890)

Bennett, George N. *Realism of William Dean Howells*, 79–94.

Cady, Edwin H. *Light of Common Day*, 144–147.

Crowley, John W. "Length of Howells' *Shadow of a Dream*." *NCF* 27 (1972): 182–196.

Habegger, Alfred. "Autistic Tyrant: Howells' Self-Sacrificial Woman and Jamesian Renunciation." *Novel* 10 (1976): 28.

Hilton, Earl. "Howells's *The Shadow of a Dream* and Shakespeare." *AL* 46 (1974): 220–222.

Klinkowitz, Jerome. *Practice of Fiction in America*, 30–32.

McMurray, William. "Moral Law and Justice in Howells' Fiction." *ALR* 10 (1977): 284–286.

Parker, Barbara L. "Howells's *Oresteia:* The Union of Theme and Structure in *The Shadow of a Dream*." *AL* 49 (1977): 57–69.

Stein, Allen F. "Marriage in Howells's Novels." *AL* 48 (1977): 523–524.

Son of Royal Langbrith (1904)

Bennett, George N. *Realism of William Dean Howells*, 66–68, 197–212.

Cady, Edwin H. *Light of Common Day*, 152–156.

Nettels, Elsa. "Howells and Ibsen." *TSLL* 20 (1978): 160–166.

Story of a Play (1898)

Bennett, George N. *Realism of William Dean Howells*, 114–121.

Their Wedding Journey (1872)

Boardman, Arthur. "Howellsian Sex." *SNNTS* 2.1 (1970): 52–56.

Cumpiano, Marion W. "Dark Side of *Their Wedding Journey*." *AL* 40 (1969): 472–486.

Frazier, David L. "*Their Wedding Journey:* Howells' Fictional Craft." *NEQ* 42 (1969): 323–349.

Hunt, Gary A. " 'A Reality That Can't Be Quite Definitely Spoken': Sexuality in Their Wedding Journey." *SNNTS* 9 (1977): 17–32.

Klinkowitz, Jerome. *Practice of Fiction in America*, 20–26.

Milne, Gordon. *Sense of Society*, 74–75.

Nettels, Elsa. "William Dean Howells and the American Language." *NEQ* 53 (1980): 317–318.

Seib, Kenneth. "Uneasiness at Niagara: Howells' *Their Wedding Journey*." *SAF* 4 (1976): 15–25.

Stein, Allen F. "Marriage in Howells's Novels." *AL* 48 (1977): 505–508.
Tuttleton, James W. *Novel of Manners in America*, 88–92.

Their Silver Wedding Journey (1899)

Bennett, George N. *Realism of William Dean Howells*, 176–179.

Undiscovered Country (1880)

Baldwin, Marilyn. "Transcendental Phase of William Dean Howells." *ESQ* 57 (1969): 59–60.
Banta, Martha. *Henry James and the Occult*, 94–96.
Frederick, John T. *Darkened Sky*, 192–195.
Habegger, Alfred. "Autistic Tyrant: Howells' Self-Sacrificial Woman and Jamesian Renunciation." *Novel* 10 (1976): 32.
Kerr, Howard. *Mediums, and Spirit-Rappers, and Roaring Radicals*, 121–154.
Kuhlmann, Susan. *Knave, Fool, and Genius*, 79–81.
Long, Robert Emmet. "Transformations: *The Blithedale Romance* to Howells and James." *AL* 47 (1976): 554–559.

Vacation of the Kelwyns (1920)

Bennett, George N. *Realism of William Dean Howells*, 234–243.
Gindin, James. *Harvest of a Quiet Eye*, 111–112.
Habegger, Alfred. "Autistic Tyrant: Howells' Self-Sacrificial Woman and Jamesian Renunciation." *Novel* 10 (1976): 32.
Milne, Gordon. *Sense of Society*, 93–96.
Stein, Allen F. "Marriage in Howells's Novels." *AL* 48 (1977): 524.

Woman's Reason (1882)

Habegger, Alfred. "Autistic Tyrant: Howells' Self-Sacrificial Woman and Jamesian Renunciation." *Novel* 10 (1976): 28, 29.

World of Chance (1892)

Bennett, George N. *Realism of William Dean Howells*, 49–61.
Dennis, Scott A. "*World of Chance:* Howells' Hawthornian Self-Parody." *AL* 52 (1980): 279–293.
Taylor, Walter F. "William Dean Howells and the Economic Novel." *American Literature* 4 (May 1932): 103–113. Rpt. in Eschholz, Paul A., ed. *Critics on William Dean Howells*, 94, 95–97, 98.

HUGHES, LANGSTON (1902–1967)

Not without Laughter (1930)

Davis, Arthur P. *From the Dark Tower*, 71–72.
Farrison, William Edward. "*Not without Laughter but without Tears*," in O'Daniel, Therman B., ed. *Langston Hughes Black Genius*, 96–109.
Miller, R. Baxter. " 'Done Made Us Leave Our Home': Langston Hughes's *Not without Laughter*—Unifying Image and Three Dimensions." *Phylon* 37 (1976): 362–369.
Perry, Margaret. *Silence to the Drums*, 54–87.
Rosenblatt, Roger. *Black Fiction*, 76–84.
Singh, Amritjit. *Novels of the Harlem Renaissance*, 77–80.
Starke, Catherine Juanita. *Black Portraiture in American Fiction*, 187–189.
Williams, Sherley Anne. *Give Birth to Brightness*, 137–140.

HUNTER, KRISTIN (1931–)

God Bless the Child (1964)

> Williams, Gladys Margaret. "Blind and Seeing Eyes in the Novel *God Bless the Child*." *Obsidian* 1.2 (1975): 18–26.

HUNTER, ROBERT (1941–)

Erebus (1968)

> Ricou, Laurence R. "Empty as Nightmare: Man and Landscape in Recent Canadian Prairie Fiction." *Mosaic* 6.2 (1973): 155–156.

HURSTON, ZORA NEALE (1891–1960)

Jonah's Gourd Vine (1934)

> Bone, Robert. "Zora Neale Hurston," in Hemenway, Robert, ed. *Black Novelist*, 57–58.
> Davis, Arthur P. *From the Dark Tower*, 115–116.
> Gayle, Addison, Jr. *Way of the New World*, 140–144.
> Howard, Lillie P. "Marriage: Zora Neale Hurston's System of Values." *CLAJ* 21 (1977): 262–263.
> Love, Theresa R. "Zora Neale Hurston's America." *PLL* 12 (1976): 464.
> Rambeau, James. "Fiction of Zora Neale Hurston." *MarkR* 5 (1976): 62–64.
> Southerland, Ellease. "Influence of Voodoo on the Fiction of Zora Neale Hurston," in Bell, Roseann P., Bettye J. Parker and Beverly Guy-Sheftall, eds. *Study Black Bridges*, 181.

Moses, Man of the Mountain (1939)

> Davis, Arthur P. *From the Dark Tower*, 117–118.
> Southerland, Ellease. "Influence of Voodoo on the Fiction of Zora Neale Hurston," in Bell, Roseann P., Bettye J. Parker and Beverly Guy-Sheftall, eds. *Study Black Bridges*, 180–181.

Seraph on the Suwanee (1948)

> Davis, Arthur P. *From the Dark Tower*, 118–119.
> Howard, Lillie P. "Marriage: Zora Neale Hurston's System of Values." *CLAJ* 21 (1977): 266–268.

Their Eyes Were Watching God (1937)

> Berzon, Judith R. *Neither White Nor Black*, 75–76.
> Bone, Robert. "Zora Neale Hurston," in Hemenway, Robert, ed. *Black Novelist*, 58–61.
> Brown, Lloyd W. "Zora Neale Hurston and the Nature of Female Perception." *Obsidian* 4.3 (1978): 39–45.
> Christian, Barbara. *Black Women Novelists*, 57–60.
> Davis, Arthur P. *From the Dark Tower*, 116–117.
> Gayle, Addison, Jr. *Way of the New World*, 144–148.
> Howard, Lillie P. "Marriage: Zora Neale Hurston's System of Values." *CLAJ* 21 (1977): 264–266.
> Jordon, June. "On Richard Wright and Zora Neale Hurston: Notes Toward a Balancing of Love and Hatred." *BW* 23.10 (1974): 4–8.

Lee, Valerie Gray. "Use of Folktalk in Novels by Black Women Writers." *CLAJ* 23 (1980): 266–268.
Rosenblatt, Roger. *Black Fiction*, 84–90.
Schultz, Elizabeth. " 'Free in Fact and at Last': The Image of the Black Woman in Black American Fiction," in Springer, Marlene, ed. *What Manner of Woman*, 321–322, 337–338.
Southerland, Ellease. "Influence of Voodoo on the Fiction of Zora Neale Hurston," in Bell, Roseann P., Bettye J. Parker and Beverly Guy-Sheftall, eds. *Study Black Bridges*, 172–177, 179–180, 181–183.
Starke, Catherine Juanita. *Black Portraiture in American Fiction*, 186–187.

JACKSON, CHARLES (1903–1968)

Fall of Valor (1946)
Austen, Roger. *Playing the Game*, 103–106.

JACKSON, HELEN HUNT (1830–1885)

Ramona (1884)
Byers, John R., Jr. "Indian Matter of Helen Hunt Jackson's *Ramona:* From Fact to Fiction." *AIQ* 2 (1975): 331–346.

JACKSON, SHIRLEY (1919–1965)

Bird's Nest (1954)
Friedman, Lenemaja. *Shirley Jackson*, 95–103.

Hangsaman (1951)
Friedman, Lenemaja. *Shirley Jackson*, 86–95.

Haunting of Hill House (1959)
Friedman, Lenemaja. *Shirley Jackson*, 121–135.
Kahane, Claire. "Gothic Mirrors and Feminine Identity." *CentR* 24 (1980): 53–55.

Road through the Wall (1948)
Friedman, Lenemaja. *Shirley Jackson*, 78–85.

Sundial (1958)
Friedman, Lenemaja. *Shirley Jackson*, 104–119.

We Have Always Lived in the Castle (1962)
Friedman, Lenemaja. *Shirley Jackson*, 135–144.

JAMES, HENRY (1843–1916)

Ambassadors (1903)
Anderson, Charles R. *Person, Place, and Thing in Henry James's Novels*, 220–276.
Auchincloss, Louis. *Reading Henry James*, 133–138.
Bailery, N. I. "Pragmatism in *The Ambassadors*." *DR* 53 (1973): 143–148.
Barnett, Louise K. "Displacement of Kin in the Fiction of Henry James." *Criticism* 22 (1980): 153–155.

Beach, Joseph Warren. "Full Prime," in Beach, Joseph Warren. *Method of Henry James*. New Haven, CT: Yale University Press, 1918. 255–256, 258–259, 260–262, 266–270. Rpt. in Stone, Albert E., ed. *Twentieth Century Interpretations of The Ambassadors*, 38–42.

Bennett, Joan. "Art of Henry James: *The Ambassadors.*" *Chicago Review* 9 (Winter 1956): 16–26. Rpt. in Stone, Albert E., ed. *Twentieth Century Interpretations of The Ambassadors*, 57–65.

Blackmur, R. P. "Dramas of the Soul in Action," from "Introduction to *Wings of the Dove.*" James, Henry. *Golden Bowl*. New York: Grove Press, 1952. Rpt. in James, Henry. *Wings of the Dove*, 504–507.

Blackmur, Richard P. "Loose and Baggy Monsters of Henry James," in Blackmur, Richard P. *Lion and the Honeycomb: Essays in Solicitude and Critique*. New York: Harcourt, Brace & World, Inc., 1955. 276–277, 279–283, 284–288. Rpt. in Stone, Albert E., ed. *Twentieth Century Interpretations of The Ambassadors*, 49–56.

Bluefarb, Sam. "Middle-Aged Man in Contemporary Literature: Bloom to Herzog." *CLAJ* 20 (1976): 5–6.

Bradbury, Nicola. *Henry James*, 36–71.

Brennan, Joseph G. "Three Novels of Depaysement." *CL* 22 (1970): 223–236.

Burde, Edgar J. "*Ambassadors* and the Double Vision of Henry James." *ELWIU* 4 (1977): 59–77.

Cosgrove, William and Irene Mathees. " 'To See Life Reflected': Seeing as Living in *The Ambassadors.*" *HJR* 1 (1980): 204–210.

Deans, Thomas R. "Henry James' *The Ambassadors:* The Primal Scene Revisited." *American Imago* 29 (1972): 233–256.

Fogel, Daniel Mark. "Jamesian Dialectic in *The Ambassadors.*" *SoR* 13 (1977): 468–491.

Frederick, John T. *Darkened Sky*, 246.

Geismar, Maxwell. "Achieved Life à la Henry James," in Geismar, Maxwell. *Henry James and the Jacobites*. Boston: Houghton Mifflin Company, 1963. 279–290. Rpt. in Stone, Albert E., ed. *Twentieth Century Interpretations of The Ambassadors*, 96–105.

Gindin, James. *Harvest of a Quiet Eye*, 119–121, 126–127.

Greenstein, Susan M. "*Ambassadors:* The Man of Imagination Encaged and Provided For." *SNNTS* 9 (1977): 137–153.

Grigg, Quay. "Novel in John Gabriel Borkman: Henry James's *The Ambassadors.*" *HJR* 1 (1980): 211–218.

Hartsock, Mildred E. "Time for Comedy: The Late Novels of Henry James." *ES* 56 (1975): 114–128.

Higgins, Joanna A. "Ambassadorial Motif in *The Ambassadors.*" *JNT* 8 (1978): 165–175.

Jones, Granville H. *Henry James's Psychology of Experience*, 261–273.

Kaplan, Harold. *Democratic Humanism and American Literature*, 271–287.

Knoepflmacher, U. C. " 'O Rare for Strether!' *Antony and Cleopatra* and *The Ambassadors.*" *Nineteenth-Century Fiction* 19 (1964–65): 333–344. Rpt. in Stone, Albert E., ed. *Twentieth Century Interpretations of The Ambassadors*, 106–116.

Kraft, Quentin G. "Central Problem of James's Fictional Thought: From *The Scarlet Letter* to *Roderick Hudson.*" *ELH* 36 (1969): 418.

Lee, Brian. *Novels of Henry James*, 68–98.

Levy, Leo B. "Henry James and the Image of Franklin." *SoR* 16 (1980): 555–556.

Lohmann, Christoph K. "Jamesian Irony and the American Sense of Mission." *TSLL* 16 (1974): 338–347.

Long, Robert E. "*Ambassadors* and the Genteel Tradition: James's Correction of Hawthorne and Howells." *NEQ* 42 (1969): 44–64.

McCarthy, Harold T. *Expatriate Perspective*, 111–112.

McFee, Michael. "Church Scenes in *The Ambassadors, The American,* and *The Wings of the Dove.*" *PLL* 16 (1980): 325–328.

Matthiessen, F. O. "*Ambassadors,*" in Matthiessen, F. O. *Henry James: The Major Phase.* New York: Oxford University Press, 1944. 18–23, 38–41. Rpt. in Stone, Albert E., ed. *Twentieth Century Interpretations of The Ambassadors*, 43–48.

Maves, Carl. *Sensuous Pessimism*, 105–107.

Milne, Gordon. *Sense of Society*, 65–66.

Nash, Cristopher. "Henry James, Puppetmaster: The Narrative Status of Maria Gostrey, Susan Stringham, and Fanny Assingham as Ficelles." *SNNTS* 9 (1977): 297–307.

Nettels, Elsa. *James & Conrad*, 46–57, 99–100.

Oates, Joyce Carol. *New Heaven, New Earth*, 15–16.

Ousby, Ian. *Reader's Guide to Fifty American Novels*, 134–137.

Richards, Bernard. "*Ambassadors* and *The Sacred Fount:* The Artist Manqué," in Goode, John, ed. *Air of Reality*, 219–243.

Robinson, David. "James and Emerson: The Ethical Context of *The Ambassadors.*" *SNNTS* 10 (1978): 431–446.

Rogers, Robert. *Psychoanalytic Study of the Double in Literature*, 113–114.

Samuels, Charles Thomas. *Ambiguity of Henry James*, 194–209.

Schneider, Daniel J. *Crystal Cage*, 76–77, 78–83, 112–113, 136–138.

Schneider, Daniel J. *Symbolism*, 92–112.

Shucard, Alan R. "Diplomacy in Henry James's *The Ambassadors.*" *ArQ* 29 (1973): 123–129.

Spengemann, William C. *Adventurous Muse*, 254–262.

Stowell, H. Peter. *Literary Impressionism*, 208–220.

Taylor, Gordon O. *Passages of Thought*, 71–84.

Tilford, John E., Jr. "James The Old Intruder." *Modern Fiction Studies* 4 (Summer 1958): 157–164. Rpt. in Stone, Albert E., ed. *Twentieth Century Interpretations of The Ambassadors*, 66–74.

Tintner, Adeline R. "Balzac's 'Madame Firmiani' and James's *The Ambassadors.*" *CL* 25 (1973): 128–135.

Vernon, John. *Garden and the Map*, 123–124.

Wallace, Ronald. *Henry James and the Comic Form*, 42–43, 60–61, 119–136.

Ward, J. A. "*Ambassadors* as a Conversion Experience." *SoR* 5 (1969): 350–374.

Warner, John M. " 'In View of Other Matters': The Religious Dimension of *The Ambassadors.*" *ELWIU* 4 (1977): 78–94.

Watt, Ian. "First Paragraph of *The Ambassadors:* An Explication." *Essays in Criticism* 10 (July 1960): 254–268. Rpt. in Stone, Albert E., ed. *Twentieth Century Interpretations of The Ambassadors*, 75–87.

Weinstein, Arnold L. *Vision and Response in Modern Fiction*, 70–72.

Weinstein, Philip M. *Henry James and the Requirements of the Imagination*, 121–164.

Winner, Viola Hopkins. "American Pictorial Vision: Objects and Ideas in Hawthorne, James, and Hemingway." *SAF* 5 (1977): 150–155.

Winner, Viola Hopkins. *Henry James and the Visual Arts*, 74–78, 112–115.

Wolf, H. R. "Psychology and Aesthetics of Abandonment in *The Ambassadors.*" *L&P* 21 (1971): 133–147.

Yeazell, Ruth Bernard. *Language and Knowledge in the Late Novels of Henry James*, 16, 21–25, 28–32, 51–54, 60–62, 65–76.

American (1877)

Anderson, Charles R. *Person, Place, and Thing in Henry James's Novels*, 41–79.

Auchincloss, Louis. *Reading Henry James*, 43–46.

Banta, Martha. "Rebirth or Revenge: The Endings of *Huckleberry Finn* and *The American.*" *MFS* 15 (1969): 191–207.

Beach, Joseph Warren. *Method of Henry James*. New Haven, CT: Yale Unversity Press, 1918. 199–205. Rpt. in Stafford, William T., comp. *Merrill Studies in The American*, 33–37.

Blasing, Mutlu. "Double Focus in *The American.*" *NCF* 28 (1973): 74–84.

Brooks, Cleanth. "American 'Innocence': in James, Fitzgerald, and Faulkner." *Shenandoah: The Washington and Lee University Review* 16 (Autumn 1964): 21–37. Rpt. in Stafford, William T., comp. *Merrill Studies in The American*, 111–126.

Butterfield, R. W. "*American,*" in Goode, John, ed. *Air of Reality*, 5–32.

Cargill, Oscar. *Novels of Henry James*. New York: Macmillan Co., 1961. 41–61 Rpt. in Stafford, William T., comp. *Merrill Studies in The American*, 45–62.

Cargill, Oscar. "Surge of Patriotic Indignation," Cargill, Oscar. *Novels of Henry James*. New York: Macmillan, 1961. 41–61. Rpt. in James, Henry. *American*, 426–441.

Caserio, Robert L. *Plot, Story, and the Novel*, 205–207.

Clair, John A. "*American:* A Reinterpretation." *PMLA* 74 (Dec 1959): 613–618. Rpt. in Stafford, William T., comp. *Merrill Studies in The American*, 80–91.

Deakin, Motley F. " Real and Fictive Quest of Henry James," in Garvin, Harry R., ed. *Makers of the Twentieth-Century Novel*, 186–187.

Edel, Leon. "Portrait Rich in National Ambiguities," Edel, Leon. *Henry James: The Conquest of London, 1870–1881*. Philadelphia: J. B. Lippincott Company, 1962. 245–260. Rpt. in James, Henry. *American*, 417–426.

Frederick, John T. *Darkened Sky*, 243.

Fryer, Judith. *Faces of Eve*, 165–168, 189–195.

Gargano, James W. "Foreshadowing in *The American.*" *Modern Language Notes* 74 (Dec 1959): 600–601. Rpt. in Stafford, William T., comp. *Merrill Studies in The American*, 95–97.

Gindin, James. *Harvest of a Quiet Eye*, 118–119.

Howe, Irving. "Henry James and the Millionaire." *Tomorrow* 9 (January 1950): 53–55. Rpt. in James, Henry. *American*, 442–445.

Jefferson, D. W. *Henry James and the Modern Reader*. New York: St. Martin's Press, 1964. 89–90. Rpt. as "Mrs. Tristram and 'A Sense of Type'," in Stafford, William T., comp. *Merrill Studies in The American*, 98–99.

Jones, Granville H. *Henry James's Psychology of Experience*, 207–217.

Knox, George. "Romance and Fable in James's *The American.*" *Anglia* 83 (1965): 308–322. Rpt. in Stafford, William T., comp. *Merrill Studies in The American*, 65–79.

Lee, Brian. *Novels of Henry James*, 33–35.

Levy, Leo B. "Henry James and the Image of Franklin." *SoR* 16 (1980): 554–555.

Lohmann, Christoph K. "Jamesian Irony and the American Sense of Mission." *TSLL* 16 (1974): 332–337.

McCarthy, Harold T. "Henry James and the American Aristocracy." *ALR* 4 (1971): 67–68.

McFee, Michael. "Church Scenes in *The Ambassadors, The American,* and *The Wings of the Dove.*" *PLL* 16 (1980): 325–328.

Milne, Gordon. *Sense of Society,* 50–55.

Moore, Harry T. *Age of the Modern,* 151–154.

Morgan, Alice. "Henry James: Money and Morality." *TSLL* 12 (1970): 78–80.

Mull, Donald L. *Henry James's "Sublime Economy",* 39–44.

Nettels, Elsa. *James & Conrad,* 88–93.

Person, Leland, Jr. "Aesthetic Headaches and European Women in *The Marble Faun* and *The American.*" *SAF* 4 (1976): 72–77.

Poirier, Richard. "Comedy of Fixed and Free Characters," Poirier, Richard. *Comic Sense of Henry James: A Study of the Early Novels.* New York: Oxford University Press, 1960. 44–50. Rpt. in James, Henry. *American,* 457–462.

Porte, Joel. *Romance in America,* 193–209.

Rourke, Constance. *American Humor: A Study of the National Character.* New York: Harcourt, Brace & World, 1931. 194–201. Rpt. in Stafford, William T., comp. *Merrill Studies in The American,* 38–44.

Samuels, Charles Thomas. *Ambiguity of Henry James,* 41–50.

Schneider, Daniel J. *Crystal Cage,* 42–45, 102–104, 119–120, 123–124.

Schneider, Daniel J. *Symbolism,* 64–74.

Spengemann, William C. *Adventurous Muse,* 247–254.

Stafford, William T. "Ending of James's *The American:* A Defense of the Early Version." *Nineteenth Century Fiction* 18 (June 1963): 86–89. Rpt. in Stafford, William T., comp. *Merrill Studies in The American,* 104–107.

Tuttleton, James W. "Henry James: The Superstitious Valuation of Europe," Tuttleton, James W. *Novel of Manners in America.* New York: W. W. Norton & Co., 1974. 48–50, 59–70. Rpt. in James, Henry. *American,* 445–457.

Tuttleton, James W. *Novel of Manners in America,* 60–70.

Tuttleton, James W. "Rereading *The American:* A Century Since." *HJR* 1 (1980): 139–153.

Veeder, William. *Henry James—The Lessons of the Master,* 34–35, 48–49, 69, 78–80, 117–119.

Wallace, Ronald. *Henry James and the Comic Form,* 17–24, 39–40, 61, 72–76, 105.

Watkins, Floyd C. "Christopher Newman's Final Instinct." *Nineteenth Century Fiction* 12 (June 1957): 85–88. Rpt. in Stafford, William T., comp. *Merrill Studies in The American,* 100–103.

Winner, Viola Hopkins. *Henry James and the Visual Arts,* 128–133.

Awkward Age (1899)

Auchincloss, Louis. *Reading Henry James,* 110–114.

Barnett, Louise K. "Displacement of Kin in the Fiction of Henry James." *Criticism* 22 (1980): 147–148.

Blackall, Jean Frantz. "Literary Allusion as Imaginative Event in *The Awkward Age.*" *MFS* 26 (1980): 179–197.

Bradbury, Nicola. *Henry James,* 24–27.

Caserio, Robert L. *Plot, Story, and the Novel,* 207–210.

Davidson, Arnold E. "James's Dramatic Method in *The Awkward Age*." *NCF* 29 (1974): 320–335.

Donoghue, Denis. "James's *The Awkward Age* and Pound's 'Mauberley'." *N&Q* 17 (1970): 49–50.

Fergusson, Francis. *Literary Landmarks*, 54–55.

Gillen, Francis. "Dramatist in His Drama: Theory vs. Effect in *The Awkward Age*." *TSLL* 12 (1971): 663–674.

Jacobson, Marcia. "Literary Convention and Social Criticism in Henry James's *The Awkward Age*." *PQ* 54 (1975): 633–646.

Jones, Granville H. *Henry James's Psychology of Experience*, 28–33, 193–194.

Lee, Brian. *Novels of Henry James*, 62–65.

Nelson, Carl. "James's Social Criticism: The Voice of the Ringmaster in *The Awkward Age*." *ArQ* 29 (1973): 151–168.

Perosa, Sergio. *Henry James and the Experimental Novel*, 68–74.

Purdy, Strother B. *Hole in the Fabric*, 137–149.

Samuels, Charles Thomas. *Ambiguity of Henry James*, 161–174.

Schneider, Daniel J. *Crystal Cage*, 56–58.

Schneider, Daniel J. "James's *The Awkward Age:* A Reading and an Evaluation." *HJR* 1 (1980): 219–227.

Sicker, Philip. *Love and the Quest for Identity*, 85–100.

Sklepowich, E. A. "Gilded Bondage: Games and Gamesplaying in *The Awkward Age*." *ELWIU* 5 (1978): 187–193.

Todorov, Tzvetan. "Verbal Age." Trans. Patricia Martin Gibby. *CritI* 4 (1977): 351–371.

Wallace, Ronald. *Henry James and the Comic Form*, 58–60, 65–67, 93–99, 106–107.

Walters, Margaret. "Keeping the Place Tidy for the Female Mind: *The Awkward Age*," in Goode, John, ed. *Air of Reality*, 190–218.

Yeazell, Ruth Bernard. *Language and Knowledge in the Late Novels of Henry James*, 64.

Bostonians (1886)

Auchincloss, Louis. *Reading Henry James*, 75–85.

Auerbach, Nina. *Communities of Women*, 119–141.

Banta, Martha. *Henry James and the Occult*, 96–100, 178–183.

Buitenhuis, Peter. *Grasping Imagination*, 141–159.

Colmer, John. *Coleridge to Catch-22*, 117–121.

Davis, Sara deSaussure. "Feminist Sources in *The Bostonians*." *AL* 50 (1979): 570–587.

Faderman, Lillian. "Female Same-Sex Relationships in Novels by Longfellow, Holmes, and James." *NEQ* 51 (1978): 323–331.

Fetterley, Judith. *Resisting Reader*, 101–153.

Fryer, Judith. *Faces of Eve*, 143–152, 220–234.

Gindin, James. *Harvest of a Quiet Eye*, 115–116.

Habegger, Alfred. "Disunity of *The Bostonians*." *NCF* 24 (1969): 193–209.

Heaton, Daniel H. "Altered Characterization of Miss Birdseye in Henry James's *The Bostonians*." *AL* 50 (1979): 588–603.

Howard, David. "*Bostonians*," in Goode, John, ed. *Air of Reality*, 60–80.

Jacobson, Marcia. "Popular Fiction and Henry James's Unpopular *Bostonians*." *MP* 73 (1976): 264–275.

Johnson, Lee Ann. "Psychology of Characterization: James's Portraits of Verena Tarrant and Olive Chancellor." *SNNTS* 6 (1974): 295–303.

Jones, Granville H. *Henry James's Psychology of Experience*, 136–144.

Kerr, Howard. *Mediums, and Spirit-Rappers, and Roaring Radicals*, 190–222.

Kimmey, John L. "*Tragic Muse* and Its Forerunners." *AL* 41 (1970): 519–524.

Kuhlmann, Susan. *Knave, Fool, and Genius*, 81–83.

LaBrie, Ross. "Power of Consciousness in Henry James." *ArQ* 29 (1973): 101–104.

Lee, Brian. *Novels of Henry James*, 19–26.

Long, Robert Emmet. *Great Succession*, 117–157.

Long, Robert Emmet. "Transformations: *The Blithedale Romance* to Howells and James." *AL* 47 (1976): 561–571.

McLean, Robert C. "*Bostonians:* New England Pastoral." *PLL* 7 (1971): 374–381.

McMahan, Elizabeth. "Sexual Desire and Illusion in *The Bostonians*." *MFS* 25 (1979): 241–251.

Maglin, Nan Bauer. "Fictional Feminists in *The Bostonians* and *The Odd Woman*," in Cornillon, Susan Koppelman, ed. *Images of Women in Fiction*, 218–225.

Menikoff, Barry. "House Divided: A New Reading of *The Bostonians*." *CLAJ* 20 (1977): 459–474.

Morris, R. A. "Classical Vision and the American City: Henry James's *The Bostonians*." *NEQ* 46 (1973): 543–557.

Nettels, Elsa. *James & Conrad*, 142–144.

Page, Philip. "Curious Narration of *The Bostonians*." *AL* 46 (1974): 374–383.

Pearce, Howard D. "Witchcraft Imagery and Allusion in James's *Bostonians*." *SNNTS* 6 (1974): 236–247.

Perosa, Sergio. *Henry James and the Experimental Novel*, 20–27.

Pirie, Gordon. *Henry James*, 81–100.

Powers, Lyall H. *Henry James and the Naturalist Movement*, 52–87.

Rihoit, Catherine. "*Bostonians:* An Investigation of the Female Feature in James's Cosmogony," in Durand, Régis, ed. *Myth and Ideology in American Culture*, 83–108.

Samuels, Charles Thomas. *Ambiguity of Henry James*, 91–107.

Schneider, Daniel J. *Crystal Cage*, 46, 125.

Stineback, David C. *Shifting World*, 75–86.

Tatar, Maria M. *Spellbound*, 235–243.

Tintner, Adeline R. "James and Balzac: *The Bostonians* and 'La fille aux yeux d'or'." *CL* 29 (1977): 241–254.

Trilling, Lionel. *Opposing Self*, 92–101.

Wallace, Ronald. *Henry James and the Comic Form*, 35–38, 103.

Wolstenholme, Susan. "Possession and Personality: Spiritualism in *The Bostonians*." *AL* 49 (1978): 580–591.

Europeans (1878)

Buitenhuis, Peter. *Grasping Imagination*, 89–102.

Henderson, Harry B. *Versions of the Past*, 209–212.

Jones, Granville H. *Henry James's Psychology of Experience*, 164–169.

Lee, Brian. *Novels of Henry James*, 12–16.

Long, Robert Emmet. *Great Succession*, 54–63.

Mull, Donald L. *Henry James's "Sublime Economy"*, 44–47.

Pirie, Gordon. *Henry James*, 32–45.

Samuels, Charles Thomas. *Ambiguity of Henry James*, 133–138.
Wallace, Ronald. *Henry James and the Comic Form*, 42, 53–55, 64–65, 76–79, 107.
Way, Brian. *F. Scott Fitzgerald and the Art of Social Fiction*, 27–28.
Winner, Viola Hopkins. *Henry James and the Visual Arts*, 133–135.

Golden Bowl (1904)

Antush, John V. "Money as Myth and Reality in the World of Henry James." *ArQ* 25 (1969): 131–133.
Auchincloss, Louis. *Reading Henry James*, 124–126,128–132.
Blackmur, R. P. "Dramas of the Soul in Action," from "Introduction to *Wings of the Dove*." James, Henry. *Golden Bowl*. New York: Grove Press, 1952. Rpt. in James, Henry. *Wings of the Dove*, 504–507.
Bradbury, Nicola. *Henry James*, 15, 16, 123–196.
Byrd, Scott. "Fractured Crystal in *Middlemarch* and *The Golden Bowl*." *MFS* 18 (1972–73): 551–554.
Deakin, Motley F. " Real and Fictive Quest of Henry James," in Garvin, Harry R., ed. *Makers of the Twentieth-Century Novel*, 188.
Dean, Sharon. "James' *The Golden Bowl*." *Expl* 35.4 (1977): 8–9.
Dean, Sharon. "Principino and the Ending of James's *The Golden Bowl*." *ANQ* 16 (1977): 43–44.
Fergusson, Francis. *Literary Landmarks*, 56–57.
Frederick, John T. *Darkened Sky*, 247.
Fryer, Judith. *Faces of Eve*, 112–126.
Gilmore, Michael T. *Middle Way*, 195–208.
Gindin, James. *Harvest of a Quiet Eye*, 124–125, 126.
Greene, Mildred S. "Les liaisons dangereuses and *The Golden Bowl:* Maggie's 'Loving Reason'." *MFS* 19 (1973–74): 531–540.
Hartsock, Mildred E. "Time for Comedy: The Late Novels of Henry James." *ES* 56 (1975): 114–128.
Jones, Granville H. *Henry James's Psychology of Experience*, 179–191.
Krupnick, Mark L. "*Golden Bowl:* Henry James's Novel about Nothing." *ES* 57 (1976): 533–540.
Kummings, Donald D. "Issue of Morality in James's *The Golden Bowl*." *ArQ* 32 (1976): 381–391.
LaBrie, Ross. "Power of Consciousness in Henry James." *ArQ* 29 (1973): 111–112.
Lee, Brian. *Novels of Henry James*, 102–107.
Levy, Leo B. "*Golden Bowl* and 'the Voice of Blood'." *HJR* 1 (1980): 154–163.
Ling, Amy. "Pagoda Image in Henry James's *The Golden Bowl*." *AL* 46 (1974): 383–388.
McCarthy, Harold T. *Expatriate Perspective*, 115–119.
Maves, Carl. *Sensuous Pessimism*, 125–149.
Milne, Gordon. *Sense of Society*, 66–69.
Moore, Harry T. *Age of the Modern*, 154–158.
Morgan, Alice. "Henry James: Money and Morality." *TSLL* 12 (1970): 81–82.
Moss, Howard. *Writing Against Time*, 148–153.
Mull, Donald L. *Henry James's "Sublime Economy"*, 116–163.
Nash, Cristopher. "Henry James, Puppetmaster: The Narrative Status of Maria Gos-

trey, Susan Stringham, and Fanny Assingham as Ficelles." *SNNTS* 9 (1977): 298–307.

Nettels, Elsa. "Henry James and the Idea of Race." *ES* 59 (1978): 45–47.

Nettels, Elsa. *James & Conrad*, 67–68, 175–180.

Norrman, Ralf. "End-Linking as an Intensity-Creating Device in the Dialogue of Henry James's *The Golden Bowl*." *ES* 61 (1980): 236–251.

Oates, Joyce Carol. *New Heaven, New Earth*, 19–23.

Pearson, Gabriel. "Novel to End All Novels: *The Golden Bowl*," in Goode, John, ed. *Air of Reality*, 301–360.

Porte, Joel. *Romance in America*, 215–226.

Rowe, John Carlos. *Henry Adams and Henry James*, 198–225.

Samuels, Charles Thomas. *Ambiguity of Henry James*, 210–225.

Schneider, Daniel J. *Crystal Cage*, 89–93, 113–116, 134–136, 140–147.

Sicker, Philip. *Love and the Quest for Identity*, 146–168.

Stowell, H. Peter. *Literary Impressionism*, 221–239.

Tintner, Adeline R. "James Corrects Poe: The Appropriation of Pym in *The Golden Bowl*." *ATQ* 37 (1978): 87–91.

Tintner, Adeline R. "Maggie's Pagoda: Architectural Follies in *The Golden Bowl*." *MarkR* 3 (1973): 113–115.

Torgovnick, Marianne. "Gestural Pattern and Meaning in *The Golden Bowl*." *TCL* 26 (1980): 445–457.

Wallace, Ronald. *Henry James and the Comic Form*, 49–51, 67–68, 136–147.

Weinstein, Philip M. *Henry James and the Requirements of the Imagination*, 165–194.

Winner, Viola Hopkins. *Henry James and the Visual Arts*, 153–169.

Yeazell, Ruth Bernard. *Language and Knowledge in the Late Novels of Henry James*, 2–15, 16–17, 18–21, 25–28, 41–49,84–99, 100–130.

In the Cage (1879)

Jones, Granville H. *Henry James's Psychology of Experience*, 131–133.

Norrman, Ralf. "Intercepted Telegram Plot in Henry James's *In the Cage*." *N&Q* 24 (1977): 425–427.

Samuels, Charles Thomas. *Ambiguity of Henry James*, 151–154.

Sicker, Philip. *Love and the Quest for Identity*, 78–83.

Stone, William B. "On the Background of James's *In the Cage*." *ALR* 6 (1973): 243–247.

Ivory Tower (1917)

Buitenhuis, Peter. *Grasping Imagination*, 240–260.

Jones, Granville H. *Henry James's Psychology of Experience*, 88–92.

Mull, Donald L. *Henry James's "Sublime Economy"*, 164–176.

Perosa, Sergio. *Henry James and the Experimental Novel*, 161–198.

Other House (1896)

Fryer, Judith. *Faces of Eve*, 184–189.

Jones, Granville H. *Henry James's Psychology of Experience*, 96–97.

Portrait of a Lady (1881)

Anderson, Charles R. *Person, Place, and Thing in Henry James's Novels*, 80–123.

Anderson, Quentin. *American Henry James*. New Brunswick, NJ: Rutgers University Press, 1957. 183, 184–198. Rpt. in Powers, Lyall H., comp. *Merrill Studies in The Portrait of a Lady*, 67–79.

Antush, John V. "Money as Myth and Reality in the World of Henry James." *ArQ* 25 (1969): 130–131, 133.

Auchincloss, Louis. *Reading Henry James*, 60–70.

Banta, Martha. *Henry James and the Occult*, 169–178.

Barnett, Louise K. "Displacement of Kin in the Fiction of Henry James." *Criticism* 22 (1980): 151–153.

Bazzanella, Dominic J. "Conclusion to *The Portrait of a Lady* Re-Examined." *AL* 41 (1969): 55–63.

Black, Michael. *Literature of Fidelity*, 153–168.

Blodgett, Harriet. "Verbal Clues in *The Portrait of a Lady:* A Note in Defense of Isabel Archer." *SAF* 7 (1979): 27–36.

Bradbury, Nicola. *Henry James*, 14–15, 15–16.

Buitenhuis, Peter. *Grasping Imagination*, 103–112.

Caserio, Robert L. *Plot, Story, and the Novel*, 201–202.

Collins, Martha. "Narrator, the Satellites, and Isabel Archer: Point of View in *The Portrait of a Lady*." *SNNTS* 8 (1976): 142–157.

Davis, Sara deSaussure. "Two Portraits of a Lady: Henry James and T.S. Eliot." *ArQ* 32 (1976): 370–375.

Deakin, Motley F. "Real and Fictive Quest of Henry James," in Garvin, Harry R., ed. *Makers of the Twentieth-Century Novel*, 187–188.

Edel, Leon. "Portrait of a Lady," in Edel, Leon. *Henry James: The Conquest of London, 1870–1881*. Philadelphia : J.B. Lippincott Company, 1962. Rpt. in Powers, Lyall H., comp. *Merrill Studies in The Portrait of a Lady*, 94–105.

Fiedelson, Charles. "Moment of *The Portrait of a Lady*." *Ventures* 8.2 (1968): 47–55. Rpt. in James, Henry. *Portrait of a Lady*, 741–751.

Frederick, John T. *Darkened Sky*, 244.

Frederick, John T. "Patterns of Imagery in Chapter XLII of Henry James's *The Portrait of a Lady*." *ArQ* 25 (1969): 150–156.

Fryer, Judith. *Faces of Eve*, 126–142, 177–182, 195–202.

Galloway, David. *Henry James: The Portrait of a Lady*. London: Edward Arnold, 1976.

Gass, William H. "High Brutality of Good Intentions." *Accent* 18 (Winter 1958): 62–71. Rpt. in James, Henry. *Portrait of a Lady*, 704–713.

Gervais, David. *Flaubert and Henry James*, 147–197.

Gindin, James. *Harvest of a Quiet Eye*, 114–115.

Greene, Graham. "*Portrait of a Lady*," in Greene, Graham. *Collected Essays*. New York: Viking Press, 1951. Rpt. in James, Henry. *Portrait of a Lady*, 667–671.

Holland, Laurence B. "Marriage," in Holland, Laurence B. *Expense of Vision: Essays on the Craft of Henry James*. Princeton, NJ: Princeton University Press, 1964. 28–42. Rpt. in James, Henry. *Portrait of a Lady*, 730–741.

Johnson, Courtney. "Adam and Eve and Isabel Archer." *Renascence* 21 (1969): 134–144, 167.

Jones, Granville H. *Henry James's Psychology of Experience*, 25–28, 40–51.

Kettle, Arnold. "Henry James: *The Portrait of a Lady*," in Kettle, Arnold. *Introduction to the English Novel*. London: Hutchinson's University Library, 1953. Vol. 2. 13–34. Rpt. in James, Henry. *Portrait of a Lady*, 671–689.

Kettle, Arnold. "Henry James: *The Portrait of a Lady*," in Kettle, Arnold. *Introduction to the English Novel*. London: Hutchinson's University Library, 1953. Vol. 2. 13–34. Rpt. in Powers, Lyall H., comp. *Merrill Studies in The Portrait of a Lady*, 46–66.

King, Mary J. "Touch of the Earth: A Word and a Theme in *The Portrait of a Lady*." *NCF* 29 (1974): 345–347.

Kleinberg, Seymour. "Ambiguity and Ambivalence: The Psychology of Sexuality in Henry James' *The Portrait of a Lady*." *MarkR* (5 May 1969): 2–7.

Korenman, Joan S. "Henry James and the Murderous Mind." *ELWIU* 4 (1977): 209–210.

Krier, William J. " 'Latent Extravagance' of *The Portrait of a Lady*." *Mosaic* 9.3 (1976): 57–65.

Krook, Dorothea. "*Portrait of a Lady*," in Krook, Dorothea. *Ordeal of Consciousness in Henry James*. New York: Cambridge University Press, 1962. 39–60. Rpt. in James, Henry. *Portrait of a Lady*, 713–729.

Kuhlmann, Susan. *Knave, Fool, and Genius*, 96–97.

Lay, Mary M. "Parallels: Henry James's *The Portrait of a Lady* and Nella Larsen's *Quicksand*." *CLAJ* 20 (1977): 476–486.

Lee, Brian. *Novels of Henry James*, 35–40.

Liebman, Sheldon W. "Light and the Dark: Character Design in *The Portrait of a Lady*." *PLL* 6 (1970): 163–179.

Liebman, Sheldon W. "Point of View in *The Portrait of A Lady*." *ES* 52 (1971): 136–147.

Lindberg, Gary H. *Edith Wharton and the Novel of Manners*, 27–33.

Long, Robert Emmet. *Great Succession*, 98–116.

McCarthy, Harold T. "Henry James and the American Aristocracy." *ALR* 4 (1971): 69–71.

McMaster, Juliet. "Portrait of Isabel Archer." *AL* 45 (1973): 50–66.

Maves, Carl. *Sensuous Pessimism*, 72–80.

Mazzella, Anthony J. "James' *The Portrait of a Lady*." *Expl* 30 (1972): Item 37.

Milne, Gordon. *Sense of Society*, 56–60.

Morgan, Alice. "Henry James: Money and Morality." *TSLL* 12 (1970): 84–90.

Mull, Donald L. "Freedom and Judgment: The Antinomy of Action in *The Portrait of a Lady*." *ArQ* 27 (1971): 124–132.

Mull, Donald L. *Henry James's "Sublime Economy"*, 48–115.

Nettels, Elsa. *James & Conrad*, 100–107, 115–118.

O'Connor, Dennis L. "Intimacy and Spectatorship in *The Portrait of a Lady*." *HJR* 2 (1980): 25–35.

Ousby, Ian. *Reader's Guide to Fifty American Novels*, 128–130.

Perloff, Marjorie. "Cinderella Becomes the Wicked Stepmother: *The Portrait of a Lady* as Ironic Fairy Tale" *NCF* 23 (1969): 413–433.

Peterson, Carla L. "Dialogue and Characterization in *The Portrait of a Lady*." *SAF* 8 (1980): 13–22.

Pirie, Gordon. *Henry James*, 59–80.

Pratt, Linda Ray. "Abuse of Eve by the New World Adam," in Cornillon, Susan Koppelman, ed. *Images of Women in Fiction*, 165–170.

Rahv, Philip. "Heiress of All Ages." *Partisan Review* (May-June 1943). Rpt. in Rahv, Philip. *Essays on Literature and Politics*, 51–57.

Rahv, Philip. "Heiress of All Ages." *Partisan Review* (May-June 1943). Rpt. in Rahv, Philip. *Literature and the Sixth Sense*, 113–120.

Rahv, Philip. "Heiress of All Ages," in Powers, Lyall H., comp. *Merrill Studies in The Portrait of a Lady*, 19–27.

Rogers, Robert. *Psychoanalytic Study of the Double in Literature*, 101–108.

Roman, Christine M. "Henry James and the Surrogate Mother." *ATQ* 38 (1978): 194, 195–204.

Routh, Michael. "Isabel Archer's Double Exposure: A Repeated Scene in *The Portrait of a Lady*." *HJR* 1 (1980): 262–263.

Routh, Michael. "Isabel Archer's 'Inconsequence': A Motif Analysis of *The Portrait of a Lady*." *JNT* 7 (1977): 128–141.

Sabiston, E. "Prison of Womanhood." *CL* 25 (1973): 336–351.

Samuels, Charles Thomas. *Ambiguity of Henry James*, 108–128.

Scharnhorst, Gary. "*Wuthering Heights* and *The Portrait of a Lady:* A Dynamic Parallel." *BallS* 19.1 (1978): 17–22.

Schneider, Daniel J. *Crystal Cage*, 45–46, 104, 107, 120–123.

Schneider, Daniel J. *Symbolism*, 75–91.

Schriber, Mary S. "Isabel Archer and Victorian Manners." *SNNTS* 8 (1976): 441–457.

Sebouhian, George. "Henry James's Transcendental Imagination." *ELWIU* 3 (1976): 219–221.

Sicker, Philip. *Love and the Quest for Identity*, 53–63.

Snow, Lotus. "Discerning Poetry of Mary Temple: A Comparison of the Imagery of *The Portrait of a Lady* and *The Wings of a Dove*." *New England Quarterly* 31 (Sept 1958): 312–323, 336–339. Rpt. in Powers, Lyall H., comp. *Merrill Studies in The Portrait of a Lady*, 80–93.

Spacks, Patricia Meyer. *Female Imagination*, 251–253.

Stambaugh, Sara. "Aesthetic Movement and *The Portrait of a Lady*." *NCF* 30 (1976): 495–510.

Stelzig, Eugene L. "Henry James and the 'Immensities of Perception': Actors and Victims in *The Portrait of a Lady* and *The Wings of the Dove*." *SoHR* 11 (1977): 253–258, 259–260, 263–265.

Stowell, H. Peter. *Literary Impressionism*, 177–186.

Tanner, Tony. "Fearful Self: Henry James's *The Portrait of a Lady*." *Critical Quarterly* 7 (Autumn 1965): 205–219. Rpt. in Powers, Lyall H., comp. *Merrill Studies in The Portrait of a Lady*, 106–122.

Taylor, Gordon O. *Passages of Thought*, 56–71.

Tintner, Adeline R. "Isabel's Carriage-Image and Emma's Day Dream." *MFS* 22 (1976): 227–231.

Treadwell, J. M. "Mrs. Touchett's Three Questions." *AL* 50 (1979): 641–644.

Tuttleton, James W. *Novel of Manners in America*, 82–84.

Van Ghent, Dorothy. "On *The Portrait of a Lady*," in Van Ghent, Dorothy. *English Novel: Form and Function*. New York: Holt, Rinehart & Winston, Inc., 1953. Rpt. in James, Henry. *Portrait of a Lady*, 689–704.

Van Ghent, Dorothy. "On *The Portrait of a Lady*," in Van Ghent, Dorothy. *English Novel: Form and Function*. New York: Holt, Rinehart and Winston, Inc., 1953. Rpt. in Powers, Lyall H., comp. *Merrill Studies in The Portrait of a Lady*, 28–45.

Veeder, William. *Henry James—The Lessons of the Master*, 35–38, 40–41, 45–46, 50–53, 68–72, 80–86, 100–105, 119–150, 160–183.

Wallace, Ronald. *Henry James and the Comic Form*, 24–30, 43–47, 61–63, 101–102.

Way, Brian. *F. Scott Fitzgerald and the Art of Social Fiction*, 39–40.

Weinstein, Philip M. *Henry James and the Requirements of the Imagination*, 31–71.

Winner, Viola Hopkins. *Henry James and the Visual Arts*, 135–143.

Princess Casamassima (1886)

Anderson, Charles R. *Person, Place, and Thing in Henry James's Novels*, 124–172.
Auchincloss, Louis. *Reading Henry James*, 71–75.
Badger, Reid. "Character and Myth of Hyacinth: A Key to *The Princess Casamassima*." *ArQ* 32 (1976): 316–326.
Buitenhuis, Peter. *Grasping Imagination*, 160–161.
Colmer, John. *Coleridge to Catch-22*, 92–104.
Deakin, Motley F. "Real and Fictive Quest of Henry James," in Garvin, Harry R., ed. *Makers of the Twentieth-Century Novel*, 188.
Dolan, Paul J. *Of War and War's Alarms*, 70–95.
Faber, M. D. "Henry James: Revolutionary Involvement, the Princess, and the Hero." *American Imago* 37 (1980): 245–277.
Gindin, James. *Harvest of a Quiet Eye*, 116–118.
Harsock, Mildred. "Most Valuable Thing: James on Death." *MFS* 22 (1976–77): 517–518.
Hartsock, Mildred E. "*Princess Casamassima:* The Politics of Power." *SNNTS* 1 (1969): 297–309.
Hubert, Thomas. "*Princess Casamassima:* Ideas against Persons." *ArQ* 32 (1976): 341–352.
Jones, Granville H. *Henry James's Psychology of Experience*, 75–85.
Kimmey, John L. "*Tragic Muse* and Its Forerunners." *AL* 41 (1970): 524–531.
Lay, Mary M. "Real Beasts: Surrogate Brothers in James's 'The Pupil' and *The Princess Casamassima*." *ALR* 13 (1980): 75–83.
Lee, Brian. *Novels of Henry James*, 42–48.
Maves, Carl. *Sensuous Pessimism*, 83–87.
Nettels, Elsa. "Henry James and the Idea of Race." *ES* 59 (1978): 36–37, 44–45.
Nettels, Elsa. *James & Conrad*, 207–214.
Perosa, Sergio. *Henry James and the Experimental Novel*, 20, 27–34.
Powers, Lyall H. *Henry James and the Naturalist Movement*, 90–123.
Samuels, Charles Thomas. *Ambiguity of Henry James*, 50–60.
Schneider, Daniel J. *Crystal Cage*, 47–48, 109–110, 125–128.
Sicker, Philip. *Love and the Quest for Identity*, 64–72.
Tintner, Adeline R. "Elgin Marbles and Titian's 'Bacchus and Ariadne': A Cluster of Keatsian Associations in Henry James." *N&Q* 20 (1973): 250–252.
Tintner, Adeline R. "Hyacinth at the Play: The Play Within the Play as a Novelistic Device in James." *JNT* 2 (1972): 171–184.
Tintner, Adeline R. "Keats and James and *The Princess Casamassima*." *NCF* 28 (1973): 179–193.
Tuttleton, James W. *Novel of Manners in America*, 79–80.
Winner, Viola Hopkins. *Henry James and the Visual Arts*, 144–148.

Reverberator (1888)

Jones, Granville H. *Henry James's Psychology of Experience*, 56–58.
Perosa, Sergio. *Henry James and the Experimental Novel*, 20, 34–38.
Wallace, Ronald. *Henry James and the Comic Form*, 40, 48, 106.

Roderick Hudson (1876)

Anderson, Charles R. *Person, Place, and Thing in Henry James's Novels*, 9–40.
Auchincloss, Louis. *Reading Henry James*, 40–43.
Buitenhuis, Peter. *Grasping Imagination*, 78–84.

Deakin, Motley F. "Real and Fictive Quest of Henry James," in Garvin, Harry R., ed. *Makers of the Twentieth-Century Novel*, 185–186.

Goodman, Charlotte. "Henry James's *Roderick Hudson* and Nathaniel Parker Willis's *Paul Fane.*" *AL* 43 (1972): 642–645.

Graham, Kenneth. *Henry James, The Drama of Fulfilment*, 29–57.

Jones, Granville H. *Henry James's Psychology of Experience*, 64–74.

Kraft, Quentin G. "Central Problem of James's Fictional Thought: From *The Scarlet Letter* to *Roderick Hudson.*" *ELH* 36 (1969): 423–439.

Lee, Brian. *Novels of Henry James*, 28–33.

Levy, Leo B. "Henry James and the Image of Franklin." *SoR* 16 (1980): 555.

Long, Robert Emmet. *Great Succession*, 38–53.

McCarthy, Harold T. "Henry James and the American Aristocracy." *ALR* 4 (1971): 65–66.

McMaster, R. D. " 'An Honorable Emulation of the Author of *The Newcomes*': James and Thackeray." *NCF* 32 (1978): 404–419.

Marovitz, Sanford E. "*Roderick Hudson:* James's *Marble Faun.*" *TSLL* 11 (1970): 1427–1443.

Martin, Robert K. " 'High Felicity' of Comradeship: A New Reading of *Roderick Hudson.*" *ALR* 11 (1978): 100–108.

Maves, Carl. *Sensuous Pessimism*, 47–56.

Morgan, Alice. "Henry James: Money and Morality." *TSLL* 12 (1970): 77–78.

Mull, Donald L. *Henry James's "Sublime Economy"*, 30–39.

Nettels, Elsa. "Action and Point of View in *Roderick Hudson.*" *ES* 53 (1972): 238–247.

Nettels, Elsa. *James & Conrad*, 97–98, 196–200.

Rahv, Philip. "Heiress of All Ages." *Partisan Review* (May-June 1943). Rpt. in Rahv, Philip. *Essays on Literature and Politics*, 49–50.

Rahv, Philip. "Heiress of All Ages." *Partisan Review* (May-June 1943). Rpt. in Rahv, Philip. *Literature and the Sixth Sense*, 111–112.

Scherting, John. "*Roderick Hudson:* A Re-Evaluation." *ArQ* 25 (1969): 101–119.

Schneider, Daniel J. *Crystal Cage*, 39–42.

Sicker, Philip. *Love and the Quest for Identity*, 26–27, 43–45.

Taylor, Gordon O. *Passages of Thought*, 45–56.

Tuttleton, James W. *Novel of Manners in America*, 50–59.

Unrue, Darlene. "Henry James and the Grotesque." *ArQ* 32 (1976): 294–295.

Veeder, William. *Henry James—The Lessons of the Master*, 32–33, 38–40, 43–45, 113–117.

Way, Brian. *F. Scott Fitzgerald and the Art of Social Fiction*, 25–26.

Weinstein, Philip M. *Henry James and the Requirements of the Imagination*, 8–30.

Winner, Viola Hopkins. *Henry James and the Visual Arts*, 97–108, 116–117, 129.

Sacred Fount (1901)

Banta, Martha. *Henry James and the Occult*, 47–49, 100–103.

Bellringer, Alan W. "*Sacred Fount:* The Scientific Method." *EIC* 22 (1972): 244–264.

Bouraoui, H. A. "Henry James's *The Sacred Fount:* Nouveau roman avant la lettre?" *IFR* 1 (1974): 96–105.

Bradbury, Nicola. *Henry James*, 27–35.

Diehl, Joanne Feit. " 'One Life within Us and Abroad': The Subverted Realist in *The Sacred Fount.*" *JNT* 6 (1976): 92–100.

Gargano, James W. "James's *The Sacred Fount:* The Phantasmagorical Made Evidential." *HJR* 2 (1980): 49–60.

Hall, William F. "Meaning of *The Sacred Fount:* 'Its Own Little Law of Composition' " *MLQ* 37 (1976): 168–178.

Harris, Josephine. "*Sacred Fount:* The Geometry in the Jungle." *MQR* 13 (1974): 57–73.

Jones, Granville H. *Henry James's Psychology of Experience*, 224–230.

LaBrie, Ross. "Power of Consciousness in Henry James." *ArQ* 29 (1973): 105–110.

Perosa, Sergio. *Henry James and the Experimental Novel*, 77–93, 103–104.

Richards, Bernard. "*Ambassadors and The Sacred Fount:* The Artist Manqué," in Goode, John, ed. *Air of Reality*, 219–243.

Rimmon, Shlomith. *Concept of Ambiguity*, 167–226.

Rowe, John C. "Authority of the Sign in Henry James's *The Sacred Fount.*" *Criticism* 19 (1977): 223–240.

Samuels, Charles Thomas. *Ambiguity of Henry James*, 25–39.

Schero, Elliot M. "Narrator's Palace of Thought in *The Sacred Fount.*" *MP* 68 (1971): 269–288.

Sicker, Philip. *Love and the Quest for Identity*, 109–115.

Stowell, H. Peter. *Literary Impressionism*, 196–208.

Wallace, Ronald. *Henry James and the Comic Form*, 30–35.

Weinstein, Arnold L. *Vision and Response in Modern Fiction*, 73–74.

Weinstein, Philip M. *Henry James and the Requirements of the Imagination*, 97–120.

Sense of the Past (1917)

Banta, Martha. *Henry James and the Occult*, 138–139, 142–152.

Briggs, Julia. *Night Visitors*, 115–117.

Caserio, Robert L. *Plot, Story, and the Novel*, 210–211.

Jones, Granville H. *Henry James's Psychology of Experience*, 85–88.

LaBrie, Ross. "Power of Consciousness in Henry James." *ArQ* 29 (1973): 113–114.

Perosa, Sergio. *Henry James and the Experimental Novel*, 131–160.

Purdy, Strother B. *Hole in the Fabric*, 88–93.

Sicker, Philip. *Love and the Quest for Identity*, 107–108.

Spoils of Poynton (1897)

Auchincloss, Louis. *Reading Henry James*, 119–121.

Baym, Nina. "Fleda Vetch and the Plot of *The Spoils of Poynton.*" *PMLA* 84 (1969): 102–111.

Graham, Kenneth. *Henry James, The Drama of Fulfilment*, 127–159.

Jones, Granville H. *Henry James's Psychology of Experience*, 126–131.

Kaston, Carren O. "Emersonian Consciousness and *The Spoils of Poynton.*" *ESQ* 26 (1980): 88–99.

Kaufman, Jule S. "*Spoils of Poynton:* In Defense of Fleda Vetch." *ArQ* 35 (1979): 342–356.

Lee, Brian. *Novels of Henry James*, 57–62.

Morgan, Alice. "Henry James: Money and Morality." *TSLL* 12 (1970): 90–92.

Nettels, Elsa. *James & Conrad*, 161–162.

Palliser, Charles. " 'A Conscious Prize': Moral and Aesthetic Value in the *Spoils of Poynton.*" *MLQ* 40 (1979): 37–52.

Perosa, Sergio. *Henry James and the Experimental Novel*, 56–60.
Roman, Christine M. "Henry James and the Surrogate Mother." *ATQ* 38 (1978): 195.
Samuels, Charles Thomas. *Ambiguity of Henry James*, 75–85.
Schneider, Daniel J. *Crystal Cage*, 53–55, 83–88, 131–133.
Sebouhian, George. "Henry James's Transcendental Imagination." *ELWIU* 3 (1976): 221–222.
Tintner, Adeline R. " 'The Old Things': Balzac's *Le curé de Tours* and James's *The Spoils of Poynton*." *NCF* 26 (1971): 436–455.
Wallace, Ronald. *Henry James and the Comic Form*, 41–42, 80–88, 107.
Winner, Viola Hopkins. *Henry James and the Visual Arts*, 148–153.

Tragic Muse (1890)

Auchincloss, Louis. *Reading Henry James*, 87–92.
Baker, Robert S. "Gabriel Nash's 'House of Strange Idols': Aestheticism in *The Tragic Muse*." *TSLL* 15 (1973): 149–166.
Bellringer, Alan W. "*Tragic Muse:* The Objective Centre." *JAmS* 4 (1970): 73–89.
Falk, Robert. "*Tragic Muse:* Henry James's Loosest, Baggiest Novel?," in Browne, Ray B. and Donald Pizer, eds. *Themes and Directions in American Literature*, 148–160.
Frederick, John T. *Darkened Sky*, 245.
Goetz, William R. "Allegory of Representation in *The Tragic Muse*." *JNT* 8 (1978): 151–164.
Gordon, D. J. and John Stokes. "Reference of *The Tragic Muse*," in Goode, John, ed. *Air of Reality*, 81–163.
Graham, Kenneth. *Henry James, The Drama of Fulfilment*, 79–126.
Jones, Granville H. *Henry James's Psychology of Experience*, 148–154, 194–195.
Kimmey, John L. "*Tragic Muse* and Its Forerunners." *AL* 41 (1970): 518–531.
Lee, Brian. *Novels of Henry James*, 53–56.
Perosa, Sergio. *Henry James and the Experimental Novel*, 20, 38–43.
Powers, Lyall H. *Henry James and the Naturalist Movement*, 129–163.
Schneider, Daniel J. *Crystal Cage*, 51–52, 104–106, 128–131.
Wallace, Ronald. "Gabriel Nash: Henry James's Comic Spirit." *NCF* 29 (1973): 220–224.
Wallace, Ronald. *Henry James and the Comic Form*, 104–105.
Winner, Viola Hopkins. *Henry James and the Visual Arts*, 118–126.

Washington Square (1881)

Auchincloss, Louis. *Reading Henry James*, 48–53.
Barnett, Louise K. "Displacement of Kin in the Fiction of Henry James." *Criticism* 22 (1980): 150–151.
Johannsen, Robert R. "Two Sides of *Washington Square*." *SCR* 6.2 (1974): 60–65.
Kronenberger, Louis. *Polished Surface*, 233–245.
Lee, Brian. *Novels of Henry James*, 16–19.
Long, Robert E. "James's *Washington Square:* The Hawthorne Relation." *NEQ* 46 (1973): 573–590.
Long, Robert Emmet. *Great Succession*, 83–97.
Lucas, John. "*Washington Square*," in Goode, John, ed. *Air of Reality*, 36–59.
Maini, Darshan Singh. "*Washington Square:* A Centennial Essay." *HJR* 1 (1979): 89–101.
Nettels, Elsa. *James & Conrad*, 94–97.

Ousby, Ian. *Reader's Guide to Fifty American Novels*, 121–124.

Pirie, Gordon. *Henry James*, 46–58.

Roman, Christine M. "Henry James and the Surrogate Mother." *ATQ* 38 (1978): 195.

Samuels, Charles Thomas. *Ambiguity of Henry James*, 142–149.

Springer, Mary Doyle. *Rhetoric of Literary Character*, 77–89.

Veeder, William. *Henry James—The Lessons of the Master*, 49–50, 187–205.

Watch and Ward (1878)

Buitenhuis, Peter. *Grasping Imagination*, 57–66.

Johnson, Lee Ann. " 'A Dog in the Manger': James's Depiction of Roger Lawrence in *Watch and Ward*." *ArQ* 29 (1973): 169–176.

Jones, Granville H. *Henry James's Psychology of Experience*, 20–22.

Morgan, Alice. "Henry James: Money and Morality." *TSLL* 12 (1970): 76–77.

Mull, Donald L. *Henry James's "Sublime Economy"*, 27–30.

Taylor, Gordon O. *Passages of Thought*, 27–34.

Veeder, William. *Henry James—The Lessons of the Master*, 59–65, 80, 106–112.

What Maisie Knew (1897)

Armstrong, Paul B. "How Maisie Knows: The Phenomenology of James's Moral Vision." *TSLL* 20 (1978): 517–537.

Auchincloss, Louis. *Reading Henry James*, 114–116.

Barnett, Louise K. "Displacement of Kin in the Fiction of Henry James." *Criticism* 22 (1980): 145–146.

Blackall, Jean Frantz. "Moral Geography in *What Maisie Knew*." *UTQ* 48 (1978): 130–148.

Bradbury, Nicola. *Henry James*, 17–24.

Cohn, Dorrit. *Transparent Minds*, 46–48.

Fryer, Judith. *Faces of Eve*, 168–174.

Gindin, James. *Harvest of a Quiet Eye*, 115.

Girgus, Sam B. "Other Maisie: Inner Death and Fatalism in *What Maisie Knew*." *ArQ* 29 (1973): 115–122.

Habegger, Alfred. "Reciprocity and the Market Place in *The Wings of the Dove* and *What Maisie Knew*." *NCF* 25 (1971): 464–473.

Hall, William F. "Caricature in Dickens and James." *UTQ* 39 (1970): 243–244, 250–256.

Jeffers, Thomas L. "Maisie's Moral Sense: Finding Out for Herself." *NCF* 34 (1979): 154–172.

Johnson, Lee Ann. "James's Mrs. Wix: The 'Dim, Crooked Reflector'." *NCF* 29 (1974): 164–172.

Jones, Granville H. *Henry James's Psychology of Experience*, 5–10.

Kaston, Carren Osna. "Houses of Fiction in *What Maisie Knew*." *Criticism* 18 (1976): 27–42.

Lee, Brian. *Novels of Henry James*, 65–66.

Marotta, Kenny. "*What Maisie Knew*: The Question of Our Speech." *ELH* 46 (1979): 495–508.

Mitchell, Juliet. "*What Maisie Knew*: Portrait of the Artist as a Young Girl," in Goode, John, ed. *Air of Reality*, 168–189.

Nance, William L. "*What Maisie Knew*: The Myth of the Artist." *SNNTS* 8 (1976): 88–102.

Nettels, Elsa. *James & Conrad*, 94–95, 172–175.

Oates, Joyce Carol. *New Heaven, New Earth*, 23.
Perosa, Sergio. *Henry James and the Experimental Novel*, 61–68.
Pirie, Gordon. *Henry James*, 101–120.
Samuels, Charles Thomas. *Ambiguity of Henry James*, 184–194.
Schneider, Daniel J. *Crystal Cage*, 107–108, 133.
Snyder, John. "James's Girl Huck *What Maisie Knew*." *ALR* 11 (1978): 109–123.
Stowell, H. Peter. *Literary Impressionism*, 186–196.
Wallace, Ronald. *Henry James and the Comic Form*, 40–41, 48–49, 55–58, 89–93.
Way, Brian. *F. Scott Fitzgerald and the Art of Social Fiction*, 40–42.
Weinstein, Philip M. *Henry James and the Requirements of the Imagination*, 72–96.
Williams, M.A. "Drama of Maisie's Vision." *HJR* 2 (1980): 36–48.

Whole Family (1907)

Perosa, Sergio. *Henry James and the Experimental Novel*, 107–130.

Wings of the Dove (1902)

Anderson, Charles R. *Person, Place, and Thing in Henry James's Novels*, 173–219.
Antush, John V. "Money as Myth and Reality in the World of Henry James." *ArQ* 25 (1969): 131, 133.
Auchincloss, Louis. *Reading Henry James*, 124–128.
Banta, Martha. *Henry James and the Occult*, 183–194.
Banta, Martha. "They Shall Have Faces, Minds, and (One Day) Flesh: Women in Late Nineteenth-century and Early Twentieth-century American Literature," in Springer, Marlene, ed. *What Manner of Woman*, 240–242, 244.
Beach, Joseph Warren. "Full Prime," in Beach, Joseph Warren. *Method of Henry James*. New Haven, CT: Yale University Press, 1918. 255–256, 258–259, 260–262, 266–270. Rpt. in Stone, Albert E., ed. *Twentieth Century Interpretations of The Ambassadors*, 38.
Bell, Millicent. "Dream of Being Possessed and Possessing: Henry James's *The Wings of the Dove*." *MR* 10 (1969): 97–114.
Blackmur, R. P. "Dramas of the Soul in Action," from "Introduction to *Wings of the Dove*." James, Henry. *Golden Bowl*. New York: Grove Press, 1952. Rpt. in James, Henry. *Wings of the Dove*, 504–507.
Bradbury, Nicola. *Henry James*, 72–122.
Caserio, Robert L. *Plot, Story, and the Novel*, 211–224.
Conger, Syndy M. "Admirable Villains in Henry James's *The Wings of the Dove*." *ArQ* 27 (1971): 151–160.
Deakin, Motley F. "Real and Fictive Quest of Henry James," in Garvin, Harry R., ed. *Makers of the Twentieth-Century Novel*, 188–190.
Fowler, Virginia C. "Milly Theale's Malady of Self." *Novel* 14 (1980): 57–74.
Frederick, John T. *Darkened Sky*, 246–247.
Fryer, Judith. *Faces of Eve*, 101–112.
Gindin, James. *Harvest of a Quiet Eye*, 121–123.
Goode, John. "Pervasive Mystery of Style: *The Wings of the Dove*," in Goode, John, ed. *Air of Reality*, 244–299.
Graham, Kenneth. *Henry James, The Drama of Fulfilment*, 160–232.
Grove, James. "Neglected Dinner in James's *The Wings of the Dove*." *ANQ* 18 (1979): 5–6.
Habegger, Alfred. "Reciprocity and the Market Place in *The Wings of the Dove* and *What Maisie Knew*." *NCF* 25 (1971): 459–464.

Hartsock, Mildred. "Most Valuable Thing: James on Death." *MFS* 22 (1976–77): 521–523.

Hartsock, Mildred E. "Time for Comedy: The Late Novels of Henry James." *ES* 56 (1975): 114–128.

Holland, Laurence B. "Language as Fate," Holland, Laurence B. *Expense of Vision: Essays on the Craft of Henry James.* Princeton: Princeton University Press, 1964. 285–291, 298–301, 306–310. Rpt. in James, Henry. *Wings of the Dove,* 563–573.

Hutchinson, Stuart. "James's Medal: Optimism in *The Wings of the Dove.*" *EIC* 27 (1977): 315–335.

Jones, Granville H. *Henry James's Psychology of Experience,* 170–179.

Korenman, Joan S. "Henry James and the Murderous Mind." *ELWIU* 4 (1977): 203.

Kornfeld, Milton. "Villainy and Responsibility in *The Wings of the Dove.*" *TSLL* 14 (1972): 337–346.

Krook, Dorothea. "Milly's and Densher's Ordeal of Consciousness," Krook, Dorothea. *Ordeal of Consciousness in Henry James.* Cambridge: Cambridge University Press, 1962. 203–215, 221–229. Rpt. in James, Henry. *Wings of the Dove,* 535–550.

Kuhlmann, Susan. *Knave, Fool, and Genius,* 97–103.

Lee, Brian. *Novels of Henry James,* 98–102.

McCarthy, Harold T. *Expatriate Perspective,* 112–115.

McFee, Michael. "Church Scenes in *The Ambassadors, The American,* and *The Wings of the Dove.*" *PLL* 16 (1980): 325–328.

Matthiessen, F. O. "James's Masterpiece," Matthiessen, F. O. *Henry James: The Major Phase.* New York: Oxford University Press, 1944. 42–43, 50–52, 55–60, 62–80. Rpt. in James, Henry. *Wings of the Dove,* 488–504.

Maves, Carl. *Sensuous Pessimism,* 108–117.

Meyers, Jeffrey. *Painting and the Novel,* 19–29.

Milne, Gordon. *Sense of Society,* 61–65.

Moore, Harry T. *Age of the Modern,* 146–150.

Morgan, Alice. "Henry James: Money and Morality." *TSLL* 12 (1970): 80–81.

Nettels, Elsa. *James & Conrad,* 217–225.

Oates, Joyce Carol. *New Heaven, New Earth,* 16–19.

Rowe, John C. "Symbolization of Milly Theale: Henry James's *The Wings of the Dove.*" *ELH* 40 (1973): 131–164.

Rowe, John Carlos. *Henry Adams and Henry James,* 166–197.

Samuels, Charles Thomas. *Ambiguity of Henry James,* 61–72.

Samuels, Charles Thomas. "Flawed Hymn to Renunciation," Samuels, Charles Thomas. *Ambiguity of Henry James.* Urbana: University of Illinois Press, 1971. 61–65, 66–68, 69–72. Rpt. in James, Henry. *Wings of the Dove,* 574–580.

Sandeen, Ernest. "*The Wings of the Dove* and *The Portrait of a Lady:* A Study of Henry James's Later Phase." *PMLA* 69 (December 1954): 1060–1061, 1064–1075. Rpt. in James, Henry. *Wings of the Dove,* 507–520.

Schneider, Daniel J. *Crystal Cage,* 60–63, 110–112, 138–140.

Sears, Sallie. "Kate Croy and Merton Densher," Sears, Sallie. *Negative Imagination: Form and Perspective in the Novels of Henry James.* Ithaca: Cornell University Press, 1968. 63–74, 90–98. Rpt. in James, Henry. *Wings of the Dove,* 551–563.

Sebouhian, George. "Henry James's Transcendental Imagination." *ELWIU* 3 (1976): 222–224.

Sicker, Philip. *Love and the Quest for Identity*, 116–145.

Snow, Lotus. "Discerning Poetry of Mary Temple: A Comparison of the Imagery of *The Portrait of a Lady* and *The Wings of a Dove.*" *New England Quarterly* 31 (Sept 1958): 312–323, 336–339. Rpt. in Powers, Lyall H., comp. *Merrill Studies in The Portrait of a Lady*, 80–93.

Stafford, William T. "Whale, an Heiress, and a Southern Demigod: Three Symbolic Americas." *CollL* 1 (1974): 106–108.

Stein, William Bysshe. "*Wings of the Dove:* James's Eucharist of Punch." *CenR* 21 (1977): 236–260.

Stelzig, Eugene L. "Henry James and the 'Immensities of Perception': Actors and Victims in *The Portrait of a Lady* and *The Wings of the Dove.*" *SoHR* 11 (1977): 253–254, 258, 259–265.

Unrue, Darlene. "Henry James and the Grotesque." *ArQ* 32 (1976): 295–296.

Vernon, John. *Garden and the Map*, 124–125.

Ward, J. A. "Social Disintegration in *The Wings of the Dove.*" *Criticism* 2 (Spring 1960): 190–195, 195–199, 200–201, 202–203. Rpt. in James, Henry. *Wings of the Dove*, 529–535.

Wegelin, Christof. "Lesson of Spiritual Beauty." Wegelin, Christof. *Image of Europe in Henry James*. Dallas: Southern Methodist University Press, 1958. 106–109, 112–115, 117–121. Rpt. in James, Henry. *Wings of the Dove*, 520–529.

Winner, Viola Hopkins. *Henry James and the Visual Arts*, 81–85.

Yeazell, Ruth Bernard. *Language and Knowledge in the Late Novels of Henry James*, 16, 32–33, 54–59, 76–84.

JASMIN, CLAUDE (1930–)

Délivrez-nous du mal (1961)

Bond, David J. "Claude Jasmin's Fictional World." *IFR* 3 (1976): 113–118.

Et puis tout est silence (1960)

Bond, David J. "Claude Jasmin's Fictional World." *IFR* 3 (1976): 113–118.
Shek, Ben-Zion. *Social Realism*, 246–247.

Ethel et le terroriste (1964)

Bond, David J. "Claude Jasmin's Fictional World." *IFR* 3 (1976): 113–118.
Shek, Ben-Zion. *Social Realism*, 251–257.
Sutherland, Ronald. "Fourth Separatism." *CanL* 45 (1970): 11–13.
Sutherland, Ronald. *Second Image*, 116–120.
Urbas, Jeannette. *From Thirty Acres to Modern Times*, 141–143.

La corde au cou (1961)

Bond, David J. "Claude Jasmin's Fictional World." *IFR* 3 (1976): 113–118.
Shek, Ben-Zion. *Social Realism*, 247–251, 257.

Pleure pas, Germaine (1965)

Bond, David J. "Claude Jasmin's Fictional World." *IFR* 3 (1976): 113–118.

JEWETT, SARAH ORNE (1849–1909)

Country Doctor (1884)

Donovan, Josephine. *Sarah Orne Jewett*, 64–69.

Country of Pointed Firs (1896)

Berthoff, Warner. "Art of Jewett's *Pointed Firs.*" *New England Quarterly* 32 (March 1959): 31–53. Rpt. in Berthoff, Warner. *Fictions and Events*, 243–263.

Berthoff, Warner. "Art of Jewett's *Pointed Firs.*" *New England Quarterly* 32 (March 1959): 31–53. Rpt. in Cary, Richard, ed. *Appreciation of Sarah Orne Jewett*, 144–160.

Boggio-Sola, Jean. "Poetic Realism of Sarah Orne Jewett." *Colby Library Quarterly* 7 (June 1965): 74–81. Rpt. in Cary, Richard, ed. *Appreciation of Sarah Orne Jewett*, 197–198.

Donovan, Josephine. *Sarah Orne Jewett*, 99–100, 101–112.

Donovan, Josephine. "Woman's Vision of Transcendence: A New Interpretation of the Works of Sarah Orne Jewett." *MR* 21 (1980): 376–380.

Eakin, Paul John. "Sarah Orne Jewett and the Meaning of Country Life." *American Literature* 38 (Jan 1967): 508–531. Rpt. in Cary, Richard, ed. *Appreciation of Sarah Orne Jewett*, 216–221.

Fike, Francis. "An Interpretation of *Pointed Firs.*" *New England Quarterly* 34 (Dec 1961): 478–491. Rpt. in Cary, Richard, ed. *Appreciation of Sarah Orne Jewett*, 170–179.

Howe, Irving. *Celebrations and Attacks*, 132–134.

Magowan, Robin. "Pastoral and the Art of Landscape in *The Country of Pointed Firs.*" *New England Quarterly* 36 (June 1963): 229–240. Rpt. in Cary, Richard, ed. *Appreciation of Sarah Orne Jewett*, 187–195.

Stouck, David. "*Country of Pointed Firs:* A Pastoral of Innocence." *Colby Library Quarterly* 9 (Dec 1970): 213–220. Rpt. in Cary, Richard, ed. *Appreciation of Sarah Orne Jewett*, 249–254.

Vella, Michael W. "Sarah Orne Jewett: A Reading of *The Country of the Pointed Firs.*" *ESQ* no.73 (1973): 275–282.

Voelker, Paul D. "*Country of Pointed Firs:* A Novel by Sarah Orne Jewett." *Colby Library Quarterly* 9 (Dec 1970): 238–247.

Waggoner, Hyatt H. "Unity of *The Country of Pointed Firs.*" *Twentieth-Century Literature* 5 (July 1959): 67–73. Rpt. in Cary, Richard, ed. *Appreciation of Sarah Orne Jewett*, 162–169.

Marsh Island (1885)

Donovan, Josephine. *Sarah Orne Jewett*, 60–64.

Mawer, Randall R. "Classical Myth in Jewett's *A Marsh Island.*" *ANQ* 14 (1976): 85–87.

JOHNSON, CHARLES (1948–)

Faith and the Good Thing (1974)

Schultz, Elizabeth A. "Heirs of Ralph Ellison: Patterns of Individualism in the Contemporary Afro-American Novel." *CLAJ* 22 (1978): 106–108.

JOHNSON, JAMES WELDON (1871–1938)

Autobiography of an Ex-Colored Man (1912)

Baker, Houston A., Jr. *Singers of Daybreak*, 19–30.

Berzon, Judith R. *Neither White Nor Black*, 150–159.

Collier, Eugenia W. "Endless Journey of an Ex-Coloured Man." *Phylon* 32 (1971): 365–373.

Davis, Arthur P. *From the Dark Tower*, 30–31.

Fleming, Robert E. "Contemporary Themes in Johnson's *Autobiography of an Ex-Colored Man.*" *NALF* 4 (1970): 120–124, 141.

Gayle, Addison, Jr. *Way of the New World*, 91–96.

Isani, Mukhtar Ali. "Exotic and Protest in Earlier Black Literature: The Use of Alien Setting and Character." *SIBL* 5.2 (1974): 10.

Kostelanetz, Richard. "Politics of Passing: The Fiction of James Weldon Johnson." *NALF* 3 (1969): 22–24.

O'Sullivan, Maurice J., Jr. "Of Souls and Pottage: James Weldon Johnson's *The Autobiography of an Ex-Coloured Man.*" *CLAJ* 23 (1979): 60–70.

Payne, Ladell. "Themes and Cadences: James Weldon Johnson's Novel." *SLJ* 11.2 (1979): 43–55.

Perry, Margaret. *Silence to the Drums*, 77–80.

Rosenblatt, Roger. *Black Fiction*, 173–184.

Skerrett, Joseph T., Jr. "Irony and Symbolic Action in James Weldon Johnson's *The Autobiography of an Ex-Coloured Man.*" *AQ* 32 (1980): 540–558.

Starke, Catherine Juanita. *Black Portraiture in American Fiction*, 100–101.

Wade, Melvin and Margaret Wade. "Black Aesthetic in the Black Novel." *JBS* 2.4 (1972): 403–404.

Waniek, Marilyn. "Space Where Sex Should Be: Toward a Definition of the Black American Literary Tradition." *SIBL* 6.3 (1975): 9–10, 13.

JONES, GAYL (1949–)

Corregidora (1975)

Lee, Valerie Gray. "Use of Folktalk in Novels by Black Women Writers." *CLAJ* 23 (1980): 270–271.

Tate, Claudia C. "*Corregidora:* Ursa's Blues Medley." *BALF* 13 (1979): 139–141.

Eva's Man (1976)

Byerman, Keith. "Black Vortex: The Gothic Structure of *Eva's Man.*" *MELUS* 7.4 (1980): 93–101.

JONES, J. MCHENRY (1859–1909)

Hearts of Gold (1896)

Elder, Arlene A. *"Hindered Hand"*, 13–14, 15, 20, 26–27, 28, 44–45, 47, 50, 51–52, 58, 60.

JONES, JAMES (1921–1977)

From Here to Eternity (1951)

Bryant, Jerry H. *Open Decision*, 123–125, 128–129, 130, 138–139.

Jones, Peter G. *War and the Novelist*, 32–44, 61–62, 97–99, 118–120.

Miller, Wayne Charles. *Armed America, Its Face in Fiction*, 138–142.

Umphlett, Wiley Lee. *Sporting Myth and the American Experience*, 102–103, 110–116.

Thin Red Line (1962)
  Bryant, Jerry H. *Open Decision*, 154–156.
  Jones, Peter G. *War and the Novelist*, 117–118, 139–140, 171–177, 197.

JONES, LEROI see BARAKA, AMIRI

JONES, MADISON (1925–)

Exile (1967)
  Sullivan, Walter. *Death by Melancholy*, 97–98, 99–100.

JONG, ERICA (1942–)

Fear of Flying (1973)
  Avery, Evelyn Gross. "Tradition and Independence in Jewish Feminist Novels."
    MELUS 7.4 (1980): 52–53.
  Cohen, Sarah Blacher. "Jewish Literary Comediennes," in Cohen, Sara Blacher,
    ed. *Comic Relief*, 177–179.
  Crain, Jane L. "Feminist Fiction." *Commentary* 58.6 (1974): 59–60, 61.
  Regan, Nancy. "Home of One's Own: Women's Bodies in Recent Women's Fic-
    tion." *JPC* 11 (1978): 777–779.

JUDD, SYLVESTER (1813–1853)

Margaret (1845)
  Ronda, Bruce A. "Sylvester Judd's *Margaret:* Open Spirits and Hidden Hearts."
    ATQ 39 (1978): 217–229.

KAFKA, JOHN (1905–)

Sicilian Street (1949)
  Gelfant, Blanche Housman. *American City Novel*, 247–248.

KANTOR, MACKINLAY (1904–1977)

Andersonville (1955)
  Bennett, Lee Shaw. "Modern Civil War Novels: The Still Unwritten War?" *SoS* 19
    (1980): 115–116.

KAUFFMANN, STANLEY (1916–)

Change of Climate (1954)
  Bryant, Jerry H. *Open Decision*, 184–187.

KAUFMAN, SUE (1926–1977)

Diary of a Mad Housewife (1967)
  Crain, Jane L. "Feminist Fiction." *Commentary* 58.6 (1974): 59, 60, 61,
  Masinton, Martha and Charles G. Masinton. "Second-class Citizenship: The Status

of Women in Contemporary American Fiction," in Springer, Marlene, ed. *What Manner of Woman*, 309.

KAUFMANN, MYRON (1921–)

Remember Me to God (1957)

Guttmann, Allen. *Jewish Writer in America*, 60–62.

KELLEY, EDITH SUMMER (1884–1956)

Weeds (1923)

Cook, Sylvia Jenkins. *From Tobacco Road to Route 66*, 21–23.

KELLEY, WILLIAM MELVIN (1937–)

dem (1967)

Baker, Houston A., Jr. "View of William Melvin Kelley's *dem*." *Obsidian* 3.2 (1977): 12–16.
Klotman, Phyllis Rauch. *Another Man Gone*, 118–125.
Rosenblatt, Roger. *Black Fiction*, 142–150.

Different Drummer (1962)

Faulkner, Howard J. "Uses of Tradition: William Melvin Kelley's *A Different Drummer*." *MFS* 21 (1975): 535–542.
Gayle, Addison, Jr. *Way of the New World*, 302–305, 308–309.
Ingrasci, Hugh J. "Strategic Withdrawal or Retreat: Deliverance from Racial Oppression in Kelley's *A Different Drummer* and Faulkner's *Go Down, Moses*." *SIBL* 6.3 (1975): 1–6.
Klotman, Phyllis Rauch. *Another Man Gone*, 85–90.
Nadeau, Robert L. "Black Jesus: A Study of Kelley's *A Different Drummer*." *SIBL* 2.2 (1971): 13–15.
Starke, Catherine Juanita. *Black Portraiture in American Fiction*, 228–230.
Weyant, N. Jill. "Kelley Saga: Violence in America." *CLAJ* 19 (1975): 211–213.
Williams, Gladys M. "Technique as Evaluation of Subject in *A Different Drummer*." *CLAJ* 19 (1975): 221–237.

Drop of Patience (1965)

Weyant, N. Jill. "Kelley Saga: Violence in America." *CLAJ* 19 (1975): 217–218.

Dunsfords Travels Everywheres (1970)

Eckley, Grace. "Awakening of Mr. Afrinnegan: Kelley's Dunfords Travels Everywheres and Joyce's Finnegans Wake." *Obsidian* 1.2 (1975): 27–40.
Gayle, Addison, Jr. *Way of the New World*, 305–309.
Weyant, N. Jill. "Kelley Saga: Violence in America." *CLAJ* 19 (1975): 218–219.

KENNEDY, JOHN PENDLETON (1795–1870)

Swallow Barn (1832)

Rose, Alan Henry. *Demonic Vision*, 56–62.
Yellin, Jean Fagan. *Intricate Knot*, 51–60.

KENT, NIAL (1908–)

Divided Path (1949)
  Austen, Roger. *Playing the Game*, 125–128.

KENTFIELD, CALVIN (1924–)

Alchemist's Voyage (1955)
  Burns, Landon C. "Man as Mariner: Kentfield's *The Alchemist's Voyage.*" *Crit* 18.1 (1976): 92–104.

KEROUAC, JACK (1922–1969)

Big Sur (1962)
  Hipkiss, Robert A. *Jack Kerouac, Prophet of the New Romanticism*, 11, 26, 42–43, 50–51, 53–54, 55–56, 58–59, 66, 68, 96, 135.
  Tytell, John. *Naked Angels*, 206–208.

Desolation Angels (1965)
  Hipkiss, Robert A. *Jack Kerouac, Prophet of the New Romanticism*, 6, 19–20, 24, 26, 34, 41, 66, 67, 71–72.
  Tytell, John. *Naked Angels*, 173–175.

Dharma Bums (1958)
  Hart, John E. "Future Hero in Paradise: Kerouac's *The Dharma Bums.*" *Crit* 14.3 (1973): 52–62.
  Hipkiss, Robert A. *Jack Kerouac, Prophet of the New Romanticism*, 10, 56, 63–66, 92, 96, 100, 104.
  Hull, Keith N. "Dharma Bum Goes West to Meet the East." *WAL* 11 (1977): 321–329.
  Tytell, John. *Naked Angels*, 171–173.

Doctor Sax (1959)
  Hipkiss, Robert A. *Jack Kerouac, Prophet of the New Romanticism*, 11, 17, 19, 29–30, 91, 101–102.
  Tytell, John. *Naked Angels*, 187–190.

Maggie Cassidy (1959)
  Hipkiss, Robert A. *Jack Kerouac, Prophet of the New Romanticism*, 16–17, 18, 19, 26.
  Tytell, John. *Naked Angels*, 191–196.

On the Road (1957)
  Bryant, Jerry H. *Open Decision*, 215, 216.
  Donald, Miles. *American Novel in the Twentieth Century*, 117–121.
  Glicksberg, Charles I. *Literature of Commitment*, 172–173.
  Hipkiss, Robert A. *Jack Kerouac, Prophet of the New Romanticism*, 4, 6, 7, 11, 12, 23, 30–37, 39, 48, 49, 53, 59–60.
  Tytell, John. *Naked Angels*, 158–171.
  Vopat, Carole G. "Jack Kerouac's *On the Road:* A Re-evaluation." *MidQ* 14 (1973): 385–407.

Subterraneans (1958)

> Bryant, Jerry H. *Open Decision*, 224–225.
>
> Hipkiss, Robert A. *Jack Kerouac, Prophet of the New Romanticism*, 8–9, 21–22, 78, 84–85, 101, 104, 116.
>
> Tytell, John. *Naked Angels*, 196–201.

Town and the City (1950)

> Hipkiss, Robert A. *Jack Kerouac, Prophet of the New Romanticism*, 4–5, 16, 18, 29, 34, 45, 54, 93.
>
> Tytell, John. *Naked Angels*, 149–157.

Visions of Cody (1973)

> Hipkiss, Robert A. *Jack Kerouac, Prophet of the New Romanticism*, 18, 30, 31–34, 36–37, 41–44, 49, 51, 53, 77, 83–84, 89–90.
>
> Tytell, John. *Naked Angels*, 175–187.

KESEY, KEN (1935–)

One Flew Over the Cuckoo's Nest (1962)

> Allen, Mary. *Necessary Blankness*, 63–69.
>
> Boyers, Robert. "Attitudes Toward Sex in American 'High Culture'." *Annals of the American Academy of Political and Social Science* (March 1968). Rpt. in Boyers, Robert. *Excursions*, 118–122.
>
> Brady, Ruth H. "Kesey's *One Flew Over the Cuckoo's Nest*." *Expl* 31 (1973): Item 41.
>
> Bryant, Jerry H. *Open Decision*, 268–273.
>
> Donald, Miles. *American Novel in the Twentieth Century*, 129–132.
>
> Doxey, William S. "Kesey's *One Flew Over the Cuckoo's Nest*." *Expl* 32 (1973): Item 32.
>
> Evert, Walter H. "Coadjutors of Oppression: A Romantic and Modern Theory of Evil," in Bornstein, George, ed. *Romantic and Modern*, 47–48.
>
> Flora, Joseph M. "Westering Woman: A Thematic Study of Kesey's *One Flew Over the Cuckoo's Nest* and Fisher's *Mountain Man*," in Lee, L. L. and Merrill Lewis, ed. *Women, Women Writers, and the West*, 134–136.
>
> Forrey, Robert. "Ken Kesey's Psychopathic Savior: A Rejoinder." *MFS* 21 (1975): 222–230.
>
> Glicksberg, Charles I. *Literature of Commitment*, 173–174.
>
> Hendin, Josephine. *Vulnerable People*, 132–133.
>
> Horton, Andrew S. "Ken Kesey, John Updike and the Lone Ranger." *JPC* 8 (1974): 572–574.
>
> Huffman, James R. "Cuckoo Clocks in Kesey's Nest." *MLS* 7.1 (1977): 62–73.
>
> Klinkowitz, Jerome. *American 1960's*, 21–25.
>
> Knapp, James F. "Tangled in the Language of the Past: Ken Kesey and Cultural Revolution." *MidQ* 19 (1978): 398–401, 408, 409–412.
>
> Kunz, Don R. "Mechanistic and Totemistic Symbolization in Kesey's *One Flew Over the Cuckoo's Nest*." *SAF* 3 (1975): 65–82.
>
> McMahan, Elizabeth E. "Big Nurse as Ratchet: Sexism in Kesey's *Cuckoo's Nest*." *CEA* 37.4 (1975): 25–27.
>
> Martin, Terence. "*One Flew Over the Cuckoo's Nest* and the High Cost of Living." *MFS* 19 (1973): 43–55.

Olderman, Raymond M. *Beyond the Waste Land*, 35–51.

Pinsker, Sanford. *Between Two Worlds*, 24–26.

Roberts, William H. "Narrative Technique in *One Flew over the Cuckoo's Nest.*" *NConL* 9.4 (1979): 11–12.

Rose, Alan Henry. *Demonic Vision*, 134–136.

Rosenman, John B. "Kesey's *One Flew over the Cuckoo's Nest.*" *Expl* 36.1 (1977): 23.

Sherman, W. D. "Novels of Ken Kesey." *JAmS* 5 (1971): 185–191.

Sherwood, Terry G. "*One Flew Over the Cuckoo's Nest* and the Comic Strip." *Crit* 13.1 (1971): 96–109.

Spiegel, Alan. *Fiction and the Camera Eye*, 159–160.

Stone, Edward. "Straws for the Cuckoo's Nest." *JPC* 10 (1976): 199–202.

Sullivan, Ruth. "Big Mama, Big Papa, and Little Sons in Ken Kesey's *One Flew Over the Cuckoo's Nest.*" *L&P* 25 (1975): 34–44.

Tanner, Stephen L. "Salvation Through Laughter: Ken Kesey & the *Cuckoo's Nest.*" *SR* 58 (1973): 125–137.

Tanner, Tony. *City of Words*, 373–376.

Torrance, Robert M. *Comic Hero*, 270–272.

Vickery, Olga W. "Inferno of the Moderns," in Friedman, Melvin J. and John B. Vickery, eds. *Shaken Realist*, 159–164.

Wallace, Ronald. *Last Laugh*, 90–114.

Widmer, Kingsley. "Post-Modernist Art of Protest: Kesey and Mailer as American Expressions of Rebellion." *CentR* 19.3 (1975): 124–130.

Wiener, Gary A. "From Huck to Holden to Bromden: The Nonconformist in *One Flew over the Cuckoo's Nest.*" *Studies in the Humanities* 7.2 (1979): 21–26.

Wills, Arthur. "Doctor and the Flounder: Psychoanalysis and *One Flew over the Cuckoo's Nest.*" *Studies in the Humanities* 5.1 (1976): 19–25.

Sometimes a Great Notion (1964)

Knapp, James F. "Tangled in the Language of the Past: Ken Kesey and Cultural Revolution." *MidQ* 19 (1978): 402, 408.

Sherman, W. D. "Novels of Ken Kesey." *JAmS* 5 (1971): 191–196.

Tanner, Tony. *City of Words*, 376–380.

KILLENS, JOHN OLIVER (1916–1987)

And Then We Heard the Thunder (1962)

Couch, William, Jr. "Image of the Black Soldier in Selected American Novels." *CLAJ* 20 (1976): 182–183.

Gayle, Addison, Jr. *Way of the New World*, 262–268.

Klotman, Phyllis Rauch. *Another Man Gone*, 133–134.

Waldmeir, Joseph J. *American Novels of the Second World War*, 109–110, 118–123.

Cotillion (1971)

Berzon, Judith R. *Neither White Nor Black*, 245–252.

Gayle, Addison, Jr. *Way of the New World*, 268–276.

Youngblood (1954)

Bigsby, C. W. E., "From Protest to Paradox: The Black Writer at Mid Century," in French, Warren, ed. *Fifties*, 220–221.

KIM, RICHARD E. (1932–)

Innocent (1968)
  Goar, Robert J. "Humanism of Richard Kim." *MidQ* 21 (1980): 460–463.
Martyred (1964)
  Goar, Robert J. "Humanism of Richard Kim." *MidQ* 21 (1980): 450–460.

KING, GRACE (1852–1932)

La dame de Sainte Hermine (1924)
  Kirby, David. *Grace King*, 76–79.
Pleasant Ways of St. Médard (1916)
  Kirby, David. *Grace King*, 53–75.

KING, STEPHEN (1947–)

Carrie (1975)
  Alexander, Alex E. "Stephen King's *Carrie:* A Universal Fairytale." *JPC* 13 (1979): 282–288.

KIRBY, WILLIAM (1817–1906)

Golden Dog (*Le chien d'or*) (1877)
  Early, L. R. "Myth and Prejudice in Kirby, Richardson, and Parker." *CanL* 81 (1979): 24–31.
  Early, L. R. "Myth and Prejudice in Kirby, Richardson, and Parker," in Moss, John, ed. *Beginnings*, 198–207.
  Northey, Margot. *Haunted Wilderness*, 27–32.

KLEIN, A. M. (1909–1972)

Second Scroll (1951)
  Fischer, G. K. *In Search of Jerusalem*, 161–210.
  Greenstein, Michael. "History in *The Second Scroll*." *CanL* 76 (1978): 37–45.
  Kertzer, J. M. "A.M. Klein's Meditation on Life" *JCL* 13.1 (1978): 10–18.
  Marshall, Tom. "Theorems Made Flesh: Klein's Poetic Universe." *Canadian Literature* 25. Rpt. in Marshall, Tom, ed. *A.M. Klein*, 152,159, 161–162.
  Matthews, John. "Abraham Klein and the Problem of Synthesis." *Journal of Commonwealth Literature* 1 (1965). Rpt. in Marshall, Tom, ed. *A.M. Klein*, 135–137, 138–139, 147–150.
  Mendelbaum, Allen. "Everyman on Babylon's Shore." *Commentary* 12 (1951): 602–604. Rpt. in Marshall, Tom, ed. *A.M. Klein*, 75–78.
  Merivale, Patricia. "Biographical Compulsion: Elegiac Romances in Canadian Fiction." *JML* 8 (1980): 141–148, 151–152.
  Ross, Malcolm. "Review of *The Second Scroll*." *Canadian Forum* 31 (1952): 234. Rpt. in Marshall, Tom, ed. *A.M. Klein*, 90–91.
  Samuel, Maurice. "Book of the Miracle." *Jewish Frontier* (November 1951): 11–15. Rpt. in Marshall, Tom, ed. *A.M. Klein*, 79–88.

Waddington, Miriam. *A. M. Klein*, 117–131.
Woodcock, George. *World of Canadian Writing*, 273–274.

KNOWLES, JOHN (1926–)

Separate Peace (1959)
Umphlett, Wiley Lee. *Sporting Myth and the American Experience*, 131–139.

KORNBLUTH, C. M. (1924–1958)

Space Merchants (1953)
Donald, Miles. *American Novel in the Twentieth Century*, 178–182.

KOSINSKI, JERZY (1933–1991)

Being There (1971)
Brown, Earl B., Jr. "Kosinski's Modern Proposal: The Problem of Satire in the Mid-Twentieth Century." *Crit* 22.2 (1980): 84–87.
Coale, Samuel. "Quest for the Elusive Self: The Fiction of Jerzy Kosinski." *Crit* 14.3 (1973): 30, 35–37.
Gogal, John M. "Kosinski's Chance: McLuhan Age Narcissus." *NConL* 1.4 (1971): 8–10.
Lilly, Paul R., Jr. "Jerzy Kosinski: Words in Search of Victims." *Crit* 22.2 (1980): 74–75.
Prendowska, Krystyna. "Jerzy Kosinski: A Literature of Contortions." *JNT* 8 (1978): 19–20.
Weales, Gerald. "Jerzy Kosinski: The Painted Bird and Other Disguises." *HC* 9.3 (1972): 11–12.

Blind Date (1977)
Lilly, Paul R., Jr. "Jerzy Kosinski: Words in Search of Victims." *Crit* 22.2 (1980): 77–78.

Cockpit (1975)
Lilly, Paul R., Jr. "Jerzy Kosinski: Words in Search of Victims." *Crit* 22.2 (1980): 76–77.
Prendowska, Krystyna. "Jerzy Kosinski: A Literature of Contortions." *JNT* 8 (1978): 21–24.

Devil Tree (1973)
Lilly, Paul R., Jr. "Jerzy Kosinski: Words in Search of Victims." *Crit* 22.2 (1980): 75–76.
Prendowska, Krystyna. "Jerzy Kosinski: A Literature of Contortions." *JNT* 8 (1978): 20–21.

Painted Bird (1965)
Cahill, Daniel J. "Jerzy Kosinski: Retreat from Violence." *TCL* 18 (1972): 123–126.
Coale, Samuel. "Quest for the Elusive Self: The Fiction of Jerzy Kosinski." *Crit* 14.3 (1973): 27–33.

Corngold, Stanley. "Jerzy Kosinski's *The Painted Bird:* Language Lost and Regained." *Mosaic* 6.4 (1973): 153–167.

Klinkowitz, Jerome. "Two Bibliographical Questions in Kosinski's *The Painted Bird.*" *ConL* 16 (1975): 126–128.

Lale, Meta and John S. Williams. "Narrator of *The Painted Bird:* A Case Study." *Renascence* 24 (1972): 198–206.

Langer, Lawrence L. *Holocaust and the Literary Imagination,* 167–191.

Lilly, Paul R., Jr. "Jerzy Kosinski: Words in Search of Victims." *Crit* 22.2 (1980): 69–72.

McGinnis, Wayne D. "Transcendence and Primitive Sympathy in Kosinski's *The Painted Bird.*" *Studies in the Humanities* 8.1 (1980): 22–27.

Prendowska, Krystyna. "Jerzy Kosinski: A Literature of Contortions." *JNT* 8 (1978): 13–16.

Spendal, R. J. "Structure of *The Painted Bird.*" *JNT* 6 (1976): 132–136.

Weales, Gerald. "Jerzy Kosinski: The Painted Bird and Other Disguises." *HC* 9.3 (1972): 7–10.

Passion Play (1979)

Lilly, Paul R., Jr. "Jerzy Kosinski: Words in Search of Victims." *Crit* 22.2 (1980): 78–80.

KREY, LAURA (1890–1985)

And Tell of Time (1938)

Baker, Donald G. "Black Images: The Afro-American in Popular Novels, 1900–1945." *JPC* 7 (1973): 338–340.

KROETSCH, ROBERT (1927–)

Badlands (1975)

Harvey, Connie. "Tear-Glazed Vision of Laughter." *ECW* 11 (1978): 28–53.

Nicolaisen, W. F. H. "Ordering the Chaos: Name Strategies in Robert Kroetsch's Novels." *ECW* 11 (1978): 55–64.

Sullivan, Rosemary. "Fascinating Place Between: The Fiction of Robert Kroetsch." *Mosaic* 11.3 (1978): 174–175.

Sullivan, Rosemary. "Fascinating Place Between: The Fiction of Robert Kroetsch," Wortley, John, ed. *Post-War Canadian Fiction,* 174–175.

Thomas, Peter. *Robert Kroetsch,* 80–96.

But We Are Exiles (1965)

Brown, Russell M. "In Search of Lost Causes: The Canadian Novelist as Mystery Writer," in Wortley, John, ed. *Post-War Canadian Fiction,* 5–6.

Moss, John. *Patterns of Isolation,* 39–42.

Moss, John. *Sex and Violence,* 104–105.

Nicolaisen, W. F. H. "Ordering the Chaos: Name Strategies in Robert Kroetsch's Novels." *ECW* 11 (1978): 55–64.

Ross, Morton L. "Robert Kroetsch and His Novels," in Stephens, Donald G., ed. *Writers of the Prairies,* 102–107.

Thomas, Peter. "Priapus in the Danse Macabre." *CanL* 61 (1974): 55–57.

Thomas, Peter. "Priapus in the Danse Macabre: The Novels of Robert Kroetsch," in Woodcock, George, ed. *Canadian Novel*, 286–288.

Thomas, Peter. *Robert Kroetsch*, 33–38.

Gone Indian (1973)

Harvey, Roderick W. "Limitations of Media." *CanL* 77 (1978): 22–27.

MacKendrick, Louis K. "Robert Kroetsch and the Modern Canadian Novel of Exhaustion." *ECW* 11 (1978): 22–25.

Mathews, Robin. *Canadian Literature*, 23–24.

Mathews, Robin D. "Wacousta Factor," in Bessai, Diane and David Jackel, eds. *Figures in a Ground*, 309–310.

Moss, John. *Sex and Violence*, 38–39, 289–292.

Surrette, P. L. "Fabular Fiction of Robert Kroetsch." *CanL* 77 (1978): 6–18.

Thomas, Peter. *Robert Kroetsch*, 68–80.

Studhorse Man (1969)

Harrison, Dick. *Unnamed Country*, 206–208, 210–212.

Harvey, Roderick W. "Limitations of Media." *CanL* 77 (1978): 20–21, 27.

MacKendrick, Louis K. "Robert Kroetsch and the Modern Canadian Novel of Exhaustion." *ECW* 11 (1978): 18–22.

Moss, John. *Sex and Violence*, 292–298.

New, W. H. *Articulating West*, 179–186.

Nicolaisen, W. F. H. "Ordering the Chaos: Name Strategies in Robert Kroetsch's Novels." *ECW* 11 (1978): 55–64.

Ricou, Laurence R. "Empty as Nightmare: Man and Landscape in Recent Canadian Prairie Fiction." *Mosaic* 6.2 (1973): 158–160.

Ross, Morton L. "Robert Kroetsch and His Novels," in Stephens, Donald G., ed. *Writers of the Prairies*, 110–114.

Sullivan, Rosemary. "Fascinating Place Between: The Fiction of Robert Kroetsch." *Mosaic* 11.3 (1978): 172–174.

Sullivan, Rosemary. "Fascinating Place Between: The Fiction of Robert Kroetsch," Wortley, John, ed. *Post-War Canadian Fiction*, 172–174.

Surrette, P. L. "Fabular Fiction of Robert Kroetsch." *CanL* 77 (1978): 6–18.

Thomas, Peter. "Priapus in the Danse Macabre." *CanL* 61 (1974): 58–64.

Thomas, Peter. "Priapus in the Danse Macabre: The Novels of Robert Kroetsch," in Woodcock, George, ed. *Canadian Novel*, 291–296.

Thomas, Peter. *Robert Kroetsch*, 51–67.

What the Crow Said (1978)

Thomas, Peter. *Robert Kroetsch*, 100–115.

Words of My Roaring (1966)

Harrison, Dick. "American Adam and the Canadian Christ." *TCL* 16 (1970): 166.

Harrison, Dick. *Unnamed Country*, 205–206.

Moss, John. *Sex and Violence*, 287–289.

Nicolaisen, W. F. H. "Ordering the Chaos: Name Strategies in Robert Kroetsch's Novels." *ECW* 11 (1978): 55–64.

Ricou, Laurence R. "Empty as Nightmare: Man and Landscape in Recent Canadian Prairie Fiction." *Mosaic* 6.2 (1973): 157–158.

Ross, Morton L. "Robert Kroetsch and His Novels," in Stephens, Donald G., ed. *Writers of the Prairies*, 107–110.

Sullivan, Rosemary. "Fascinating Place Between: The Fiction of Robert Kroetsch." *Mosaic* 11.3 (1978): 168–171.

Sullivan, Rosemary. "Fascinating Place Between: The Fiction of Robert Kroetsch," Wortley, John, ed. *Post-War Canadian Fiction*, 168–171.

Surrette, P. L. "Fabular Fiction of Robert Kroetsch." *CanL* 77 (1978): 6–18.

Thomas, Peter. "Priapus in the Danse Macabre." *CanL* 61 (1974): 57–58.

Thomas, Peter. "Priapus in the Danse Macabre: The Novels of Robert Kroetsch," in Woodcock, George, ed. *Canadian Novel*, 288–291.

Thomas, Peter. *Robert Kroetsch*, 38–50.

LABERGE, ALBERT (1871–1960)

La scouine (1918)

Vuong-Riddick, Thuong. "Une Relecture de *La scouine*." *V&I* 3 (1977): 116–126.

LACASSE, LISE (1938–)

Au défaut de la cuirasse (1977)

Poulin, Gabrielle. *Romans du pays*, 157–159.

LANGEVIN, ANDRÉ (1927–)

Dust Over the City see *Poussière sur la ville*

Evadé de la nuit (1951)

Bessette, Gérard. *Trois romanciers québécois*, 144–145.

Falardeau, Jean-Charles. "Evolution of the Hero in the Quebec Novel," in Should-ice, Larry, ed. & trans., *Contemporary Quebec Criticism*, 104–105.

Pascal, Gabrielle. *La quête*, 9–13, 15–16, 21–22, 24–25, 29, 31, 32, 36–37, 39, 41, 42, 43, 45, 47, 50–59, 60–61, 67, 68–69, 75–76, 77–78, 81, 82, 84–87.

Le temps des hommes (1956)

Bessette, Gérard. *Trois romanciers québécois*, 146–147.

Falardeau, Jean-Charles. "Evolution of the Hero in the Quebec Novel," in Should-ice, Larry, ed. & trans., *Contemporary Quebec Criticism*, 104–105.

Gallays, François. "*Le temps des hommes* d'André Langevin: Une Relecture." *V&I* 1 (1976): 406–416.

Pascal, Gabrielle. *La quête*, 9–13, 14–15, 19–20, 21–22, 23–24, 26–29, 32, 37, 39–40, 42, 43, 44, 45–46, 47, 49–50, 50–59, 61–62, 66–67, 70, 76, 77, 79–80, 84–87.

Sutherland, Ronald. *Second Image*, 75.

L'élan d'Amérique (1972)

Bessette, Gérard. *Trois romanciers québécois*, 133–144, 147–177.

Pascal, Gabrielle. *La quête*, 9–13, 20–22, 28, 30–31, 33–35, 40, 41–42, 43, 46, 47, 50–59, 62–66, 70–71, 80–81, 81–82, 84–89.

Poulin, Gabrielle. *Romans du pays*, 47–51.

Poussière sur la ville (1953)

Bessette, Gérard. *Trois romanciers québécois*, 145–146.

Falardeau, Jean-Charles. "Evolution of the Hero in the Quebec Novel," in Should-ice, Larry, ed. & trans., *Contemporary Quebec Criticism*, 104–105.

Hébert, Pierre. "Forme et signification du temps et du discours immediat dans *Poussière sur la ville:* Le récit d'une victoire." *V&I* 2 (1976): 209–229.

Pascal, Gabrielle. *La quête,* 9–13, 20, 21–22, 26, 31, 32, 39, 42, 43, 45, 47–49, 50–59, 69–70, 77, 78, 84–87.

Rasporich, Beverly J. "Sacrifice and Death in French-Canadian Fiction: An English Reading." *DR* 55 (1975): 460–462.

Socken, Paul. "Alain Dubois's Commitment: A Reading of *Poussière sur la ville.*" *IFR* 4 (1977): 174–177.

Sutherland, Ronald. *New Hero,* 51–56.

Urbas, Jeannette. *From Thirty Acres to Modern Times,* 70–74.

Une chaîne dans le parc (1974)

Pascal, Gabrielle. *La quête,* 9–13, 16–19, 21–22, 24, 25, 29–30, 33, 35, 37–39, 40, 42, 44–45, 46, 47, 50–59, 68, 71–75, 76–77, 79, 82, 84–87.

Sutherland, Ronald. *New Hero,* 13–16.

LANGUIRAND, JACQUES (1930–)

All Things Considered see *Tout compte fait*

Tout compte fait (1963)

Shek, Ben-Zion. *Social Realism,* 204–217.

Urbas, Jeannette. *From Thirty Acres to Modern Times,* 126–127.

LAPOLLA, GARIBALDI (1888–1954)

Grand Gennaro (1935)

Green, Rose Basile. *Italian-American Novel,* 74–78.

LARNER, JEREMY (1937–)

Drive, He Said (1964)

Umphlett, Wiley Lee. *Sporting Myth and the American Experience,* 173–176.

LARSEN, NELLA (1891–1964)

Passing (1929)

Davis, Arthur P. *From the Dark Tower,* 97–98.

Gayle, Addison, Jr. *Way of the New World,* 111–114.

Sato, Hiroko. "Under the Harlem Shadow: A Study of Jessie Fauset and Nella Larsen," in Bontemps, Arna, ed. *Harlem Renaissance Remembered,* 88–89.

Singh, Amritjit. *Novels of the Harlem Renaissance,* 98–100.

Tate, Claudia. "Nella Larsen's *Passing:* A Problem of Interpretation." *BALF* 14 (1980): 142–146.

Quicksand (1933)

Berzon, Judith R. *Neither White Nor Black,* 174–175, 222–225.

Christian, Barbara. *Black Women Novelists,* 48–53.

Davis, Arthur P. *From the Dark Tower,* 96–97.

Gayle, Addison, Jr. *Way of the New World*, 108–111.

Lay, Mary M. "Parallels: Henry James's *The Portrait of a Lady* and Nella Larsen's *Quicksand*." *CLAJ* 20 (1977): 475–486.

Perry, Margaret. *Silence to the Drums*, 74–77.

Sato, Hiroko. "Under the Harlem Shadow: A Study of Jessie Fauset and Nella Larsen," in Bontemps, Arna, ed. *Harlem Renaissance Remembered*, 83–88.

Schultz, Elizabeth. " 'Free in Fact and at Last': The Image of the Black Woman in Black American Fiction," in Springer, Marlene, ed. *What Manner of Woman*, 333–334.

Singh, Amritjit. *Novels of the Harlem Renaissance*, 100–103.

Thornton, Hortense E. "Sexism as Quagmire: Nella Larsen's *Quicksand*." *CLAJ* 16 (1973): 285–301.

Wade, Melvin and Margaret Wade. "Black Aesthetic in the Black Novel." *JBS* 2.4 (1972): 405.

LAURENCE, MARGARET (1926–1987)

Diviners (1974)

Atherton, Stan. "Margaret Laurence's Progress." *IFR* 2 (1975): 62–64.

Brown, Russell M. "In Search of Lost Causes: The Canadian Novelist as Mystery Writer," in Wortley, John, ed. *Post-War Canadian Fiction*, 5.

Carrington, Ildiko de Papp. " 'Tales in the Telling': *The Diviners* as Fiction about Fiction." *ECW* 9 (1977–78): 154–169.

Cooper, Cheryl. "Images of Closure in *The Diviners*," in Moss, John, ed. *Here and Now*, 93–101.

Dombrowski, Theo Quayle. "Word and Fact: Laurence and the Problem of Language." *CanL* 80 (1979): 50–61.

Gom, Leona M. "Laurence and the Use of Memory." *CanL* 71 (1976): 50–52, 56–57.

Gom, Leona M. "Margaret Laurence and The First Person." *DR* 55 (1975): 236–250.

Grace, Sherrill E. "Crossing Jordan: Time and Memory in the Fiction of Margaret Laurence." *WLWE* 16 (1977): 328–329, 335–337.

Hehner, Barbara. "River of Now and Then: Margaret Laurence's Narratives." *CanL* 74 (1977): 40–42, 46–47, 48–56.

Johnston, Eleanor. "Quest of the Diviners." *Mosaic* 11.3 (1978): 112–117.

Johnston, Eleanor. "Quest of the Diviners," in Wortley, John, ed. *Post-War Canadian Fiction*, 107, 112–117.

Labonte, Ronald N. "Disclosing and Touching: Reevaluating the Manawaka World," in Sorfleet, John R., ed. *Work of Margaret Laurence*, 178–180.

Maeser, Angelika. "Finding the Mother: The Individuation of Laurence's Heroines," in Sorfleet, John R., ed. *Work of Margaret Laurence*, 159–164.

Monk, Patricia. "Shadow Continent: The Image of Africa in Three Canadian Writers." *Ariel* 8.4 (1977): 20–21.

Monkman, Leslie. "Tonnerre Family: Mirrors of Suffering," in Sorfleet, John R., ed. *Work of Margaret Laurence*, 148–150.

Mortlock, Melanie. "Religion of Heritage: *The Diviners* as a Thematic Conclusion to the Manawaka Series," in Sorfleet, John R., ed. *Work of Margaret Laurence*, 132–141.

Moss, John. *Sex and Violence*, 69–83.

Thomas, Clara. *Manawaka World*, 130–172.

Thomas, Clara. "Myth and Manitoba in *The Diviners*," in Moss, John, ed. *Here and Now*, 103–117.

Thomas, Clara. "Wild Garden and the Manawaka World." *MFS* 22 (1976): 401–411.

Williams, David. "Indian Our Ancestor: Three Modes of Vision in Recent Canadian Fiction." *DR* 58 (1978): 309–311, 321–325.

Woodcock, George. *World of Canadian Writing*, 56, 59–62.

Fire-Dwellers (1969)

Atwood, Margaret. *Survival*, 98–99.

Forman, Denyse and Uma Parameswaran. "Echoes and Refrains in the Canadian Novels of Margaret Laurence." *CentR* 16 (1972): 233–239.

Forman, Denyse and Uma Parameswaran. "Echoes and Refrains in the Canadian Novels of Margaret Laurence." *Centennial Review* 16.3 (1972): 233–253. Rpt. in New, William, ed. *Margaret Laurence*, 85–100.

Gom, Leona. "Margaret Laurence: The Importance of Place." *WCR* 10.2 (1975): 26–29.

Gom, Leona M. "Laurence and the Use of Memory." *CanL* 71 (1976): 53.

Gom, Leona M. "Margaret Laurence and The First Person." *DR* 55 (1975): 236–250.

Hehner, Barbara. "River of Now and Then: Margaret Laurence's Narratives." *CanL* 74 (1977): 44–45, 48.

Irvine, Lorna. "Psychological Journey: Mothers and Daughters in English-Canadian Fiction," in Davidson, Cathy N. and E. M. Broner, eds. *Lost Tradition*, 248–249.

Johnston, Eleanor. "Quest of the Diviners." *Mosaic* 11.3 (1978): 110–112.

Johnston, Eleanor. "Quest of the Diviners," in Wortley, John, ed. *Post-War Canadian Fiction*, 110–112.

Labonte, Ronald N. "Disclosing and Touching: Reevaluating the Manawaka World," in Sorfleet, John R., ed. *Work of Margaret Laurence*, 177–178.

Maeser, Angelika. "Finding the Mother: The Individuation of Laurence's Heroines," in Sorfleet, John R., ed. *Work of Margaret Laurence*, 157–159.

Monk, Patricia. "Shadow Continent: The Image of Africa in Three Canadian Writers." *Ariel* 8.4 (1977): 21–23.

Monkman, Leslie. "Tonnerre Family: Mirrors of Suffering," in Sorfleet, John R., ed. *Work of Margaret Laurence*, 146–148.

Packer, Miriam. "Dance of Life: *The Fire-Dwellers*," in Sorfleet, John R., ed. *Work of Margaret Laurence*, 124–130.

Pesando, Frank. "In a Nameless Land: Apocalyptic Mythology in the Writings of Margaret Laurence," in Moss, John, ed. *Here and Now*, 83, 85–86, 87–88, 89–90.

Thomas, Clara. *Manawaka World*, 114–129.

Thomas, Clara. "Novels of Margaret Laurence." *SNNTS* 4 (1972): 158–159, 161–163.

Thomas, Clara. "Novels of Margaret Laurence." *Studies in the Novel* 4.2 (1972): 154–164. Rpt. in New, William, ed. *Margaret Laurence*, 57, 59–60, 63–65.

Jason's Quest (1970)

Johnston, Eleanor. "Quest of the Diviners." *Mosaic* 11.3 (1978): 107–108.

Johnston, Eleanor. "Quest of the Diviners," in Wortley, John, ed. *Post-War Canadian Fiction*, 107–108.

Thomas, Clara. *Manawaka World*, 108–113.

Jest of God (1966)

Bowering, George. "That Fool of a Fear: Notes on *A Jest of God*." *CanL* 50 (1971): 41–56.

Bowering, George. "That Fool of a Fear: Notes on *A Jest of God*," in Stephens, Donald G., ed. *Writers of the Prairies*, 149–164.

Bowering, George. "That Fool of a Fear: Notes on *A Jest of God*," in Woodcock, George, ed. *Canadian Novel*, 219–234.

Djwa, Sandra. "False Gods and the True Covenant: Thematic Continuity Between Margaret Laurence and Sinclair Ross." *Journal of Canadian Fiction* 1.4 , 43–50. Rpt. in New, William, ed. *Margaret Laurence*, 70–71, 77–79.

Forman, Denyse and Uma Parameswaran. "Echoes and Refrains in the Canadian Novels of Margaret Laurence." *CentR* 16 (1972): 233–253.

Forman, Denyse and Uma Parameswaran. "Echoes and Refrains in the Canadian Novels of Margaret Laurence." *Centennial Review* 16.3 (1972): 233–253. Rpt. in New, William, ed. *Margaret Laurence*, 85–100.

Gom, Leona. "Margaret Laurence: The Importance of Place." *WCR* 10.2 (1975): 26–29.

Gom, Leona M. "Laurence and the Use of Memory." *CanL* 71 (1976): 52–53.

Gom, Leona M. "Margaret Laurence and The First Person." *DR* 55 (1975): 236–250.

Hehner, Barbara. "River of Now and Then: Margaret Laurence's Narratives." *CanL* 74 (1977): 43–44, 48.

Irvine, Lorna. "Psychological Journey: Mothers and Daughters in English-Canadian Fiction," in Davidson, Cathy N. and E. M. Broner, eds. *Lost Tradition*, 245–246, 248.

Johnston, Eleanor. "Quest of the Diviners." *Mosaic* 11.3 (1978): 109–110.

Johnston, Eleanor. "Quest of the Diviners," in Wortley, John, ed. *Post-War Canadian Fiction*, 109–110.

Kearns, Judy. "Rachel and Social Determinism: A Feminist Reading of *A Jest of God*," in Sorfleet, John R., ed. *Work of Margaret Laurence*, 101–120.

Labonte, Ronald N. "Disclosing and Touching: Reevaluating the Manawaka World," in Sorfleet, John R., ed. *Work of Margaret Laurence*, 175–177.

McLay, C. M. "Every Man Is an Island: Isolation in *A Jest of God*." *CanL* 50 (1971): 57–68.

Maeser, Angelika. "Finding the Mother: The Individuation of Laurence's Heroines," in Sorfleet, John R., ed. *Work of Margaret Laurence*, 155–157.

Monk, Patricia. "Shadow Continent: The Image of Africa in Three Canadian Writers." *Ariel* 8.4 (1977): 19–20.

Monkman, Leslie. "Tonnerre Family: Mirrors of Suffering," in Sorfleet, John R., ed. *Work of Margaret Laurence*, 146.

Pesando, Frank. "In a Nameless Land: Apocalyptic Mythology in the Writings of Margaret Laurence," in Moss, John, ed. *Here and Now*, 88–89.

Ricou, Laurence R. "Empty as Nightmare: Man and Landscape in Recent Canadian Prairie Fiction." *Mosaic* 6.2 (1973): 147–148.

Thomas, Clara. *Manawaka World*, 78–95.

Thomas, Clara. *Margaret Laurence*, 45–54.

Thomas, Clara. "Novels of Margaret Laurence." *SNNTS* 4 (1972): 157–158, 160–161.

Thomas, Clara. "Novels of Margaret Laurence." *Studies in the Novel* 4.2 (1972): 154–164. Rpt. in New, William, ed. *Margaret Laurence*, 57, 58–59, 60, 61–63.

Woodcock, George. *World of Canadian Writing*, 56–57.

Rachel, Rachel see *Jest of God*

Stone Angel (1964)

Atwood, Margaret. *Survival*, 205–206.

Coldwell, Joan. "Hagar as Meg Merrilies, The Homeless Gypsy," in Sorfleet, John R., ed. *Work of Margaret Laurence*, 92–100.

Cooley, Dennis. "Antimacassared in the Wilderness: Art and Nature in *The Stone Angel*." *Mosaic* 11.3 (1978): 29–46.

Cooley, Dennis. "Antimacassared in the Wilderness: Art and Nature in *The Stone Angel*." *Mosaic* 11.3, Spring 1978. Rpt. in Gerson, Carole, comp. *Modern Canadian Fiction*, 119–129.

Cooley, Dennis. "Antimacassared in the Wilderness: Art and Nature in *The Stone Angel*," in Wortley, John, ed. *Post-War Canadian Fiction*, 29–46.

Djwa, Sandra. "False Gods and the True Covenant: Thematic Continuity Between Margaret Laurence and Sinclair Ross." *Journal of Canadian Fiction* 1.4 , 43–50. Rpt. in New, William, ed. *Margaret Laurence*, 74–76.

Dooley, D. J. *Moral Vision*, 123–136.

Endres, Robin. "Marxist Literary Criticism and English Canadian Literature," in Cappon, Paul, ed. *In Our Own House*, 115–116, 119–121, 122.

Forman, Denyse and Uma Parameswaran. "Echoes and Refrains in the Canadian Novels of Margaret Laurence." *CentR* 16 (1972): 233–253.

Forman, Denyse and Uma Parameswaran. "Echoes and Refrains in the Canadian Novels of Margaret Laurence." *Centennial Review* 16.3 (1972): 233–253. Rpt. in New, William, ed. *Margaret Laurence*, 85–100.

Gom, Leona. "Margaret Laurence: The Importance of Place." *WCR* 10.2 (1975): 26–29.

Gom, Leona M. "Laurence and the Use of Memory." *CanL* 71 (1976): 48–50, 55–56.

Gom, Leona M. "Laurence and the Use of Memory." *Canadian Literature* 71 (Winter 1976). Rpt. in Gerson, Carole, comp. *Modern Canadian Fiction*, 141–142.

Gom, Leona M. "Margaret Laurence and The First Person." *DR* 55 (1975): 236–250.

Grace, Sherrill E. "Crossing Jordan: Time and Memory in the Fiction of Margaret Laurence." *WLWE* 16 (1977): 328.

Harrison, Dick. *Unnamed Country*, 194–197.

Hehner, Barbara. "River of Now and Then: Margaret Laurence's Narratives." *CanL* 74 (1977): 42–43.

Irvine, Lorna. "Psychological Journey: Mothers and Daughters in English-Canadian Fiction," in Davidson, Cathy N. and E. M. Broner, eds. *Lost Tradition*, 251.

Jackel. Susan. "House on the Prairies." *CanL* 42 (1969): 54.

Jackel, Susan. "House on the Prairies," in Stephens, Donald G., ed. *Writers of the Prairies*, 173.

Jeffrey, David L. "Biblical Hermeneutic and Family History in Contemporary Canadian Fiction: Wiebe and Laurence," in Wortley, John, ed. *Post-War Canadian Fiction*, 91–97.

Jeffrey, David Lyle. "Biblical Hermeneutic and Family History in Contemporary Canadian Fiction: Wiebe and Laurence." *Mosaic* 11.3 (1978): 91–99.

Johnston, Eleanor. "Quest of the Diviners." *Mosaic* 11.3 (1978): 108–109.

Johnston, Eleanor. "Quest of the Diviners," in Wortley, John, ed. *Post-War Canadian Fiction*, 108–109.

Jones, D. G. *Butterfly on Rock*, 43–44, 54–55.

Kertzer, Jon M. "*Stone Angel:* Time and Responsibility." *DR* 54 (1973): 499–509.

Labonte, Ronald N. "Disclosing and Touching: Reevaluating the Manawaka World," in Sorfleet, John R., ed. *Work of Margaret Laurence*, 173–175.

Maeser, Angelika. "Finding the Mother: The Individuation of Laurence's Heroines," in Sorfleet, John R., ed. *Work of Margaret Laurence*, 152–155.

Monk, Patricia. "Shadow Continent: The Image of Africa in Three Canadian Writers." *Ariel* 8.4 (1977): 19.

Monkman, Leslie. "Tonnerre Family: Mirrors of Suffering," in Sorfleet, John R., ed. *Work of Margaret Laurence*, 143–144.

Moss, John. *Patterns of Isolation*, 230–232.

New, W. H. *Articulating West*, 207–215.

New, William. "Introduction to *The Stone Angel*." Laurence, Margaret. *The Stone Angel*. Toronto: McClelland and Stewart Limited, 1968. Rpt. in New, William, ed. *Margaret Laurence*, 135–142.

Osachoff, Margaret Gail. "Moral Vision in *The Stone Angel*." *Studies in Canadian Literature* 4.1, Winter 1979. Rpt. in Gerson, Carole, comp. *Modern Canadian Fiction*, 131–138.

Pesando, Frank. "In a Nameless Land: Apocalyptic Mythology in the Writings of Margaret Laurence," in Moss, John, ed. *Here and Now*, 82, 83–84, 85, 87.

Pollack, Claudette. "Paradox of *The Stone Angel*." *HAR* 27 (1969): 267–275.

Read, S. E. "Maze of Life: The Work of Margaret Laurence." *Canadian Literature* 27 (1966): 5–14. Rpt. in New, William, ed. *Margaret Laurence*, 50–54.

Read, S. E. "Maze of Life: The Work of Margaret Laurence," in Stephens, Donald G., ed. *Writers of the Prairies*, 137–139, 140–141.

Ricou, Laurence R. "Empty as Nightmare: Man and Landscape in Recent Canadian Prairie Fiction." *Mosaic* 6.2 (1973): 146–147.

Thomas, Clara. *Manawaka World*, 61–76.

Thomas, Clara. *Margaret Laurence*, 35–44.

Thomas, Clara. "Novels of Margaret Laurence." *SNNTS* 4 (1972): 155–157, 159–160.

Thomas, Clara. "Novels of Margaret Laurence." *Studies in the Novel* 4.2 (1972): 154–164. Rpt. in New, William, ed. *Margaret Laurence*, 56–58, 60–61.

Woodcock, George. *World of Canadian Writing*, 57–59.

This Side Jordan (1960)

Djwa, Sandra. "False Gods and the True Covenant: Thematic Continuity Between Margaret Laurence and Sinclair Ross." *Journal of Canadian Fiction* 1.4 , 43–50. Rpt. in New, William, ed. *Margaret Laurence*, 73–74.

Grace, Sherrill E. "Crossing Jordan: Time and Memory in the Fiction of Margaret Laurence." *WLWE* 16 (1977): 328, 329.

Leney, Jane. "Prospero and Caliban in Laurence's African Fiction," in Sorfleet, John R., ed. *Work of Margaret Laurence*, 65–73.

Pesando, Frank. "In a Nameless Land: Apocalyptic Mythology in the Writings of Margaret Laurence," in Moss, John, ed. *Here and Now*, 84, 88.

Read, S. E. "Maze of Life: The Work of Margaret Laurence." *Canadian Literature* 27 (1966): 5–14. Rpt. in New, William, ed. *Margaret Laurence*, 49–50.

Read, S. E. "Maze of Life: The Work of Margaret Laurence," in Stephens, Donald G., ed. *Writers of the Prairies*, 136–137.

Thomas, Clara. *Manawaka World*, 49–58.

Thomas, Clara. *Margaret Laurence*, 28–34.

LE GUIN, URSULA K. (1929–)

City of Illusions (1967)

Bain, Dena C. "Tao Te Ching as Background to the Novels of Ursula K. Le Guin." *Extrapolation* 21 (1980): 209–214, 217.

Crow, John H. and Richard D. Erlich. "Words of Binding: Patterns of Integration in the Earthsea Trilogy," in Olander, Joseph D. and Martin Harry Greenberg, eds. *Ursula K. Le Guin*, 218, 221–222, 223.

Gunew, Sneja. "Mythic Reversals: The Evolution of the Shadow Motif," in Olander, Joseph D. and Martin Harry Greenberg, eds. *Ursula K. Le Guin*, 180–181, 182, 186, 187–188.

Koper, Peter T. "Science and Rhetoric in the Fiction of Ursula Le Guin," in DeBolt, Joe, ed. *Ursula K. Le Guin*, 78–80.

Nudelman, Rafail and Alan G. Myers. "Approach to the Structure of Le Guin's SF." *SFS* 2 (1975): 210–220.

Remington, Thomas J. "Other Side of Suffering: Touch as Theme and Metaphor in Le Guin's Science Fiction Novels," in Olander, Joseph D. and Martin Harry Greenberg, eds. *Ursula K. Le Guin*, 158–161.

Sinclair, Karen. "Solitary Being: The Hero as Anthropologist," in DeBolt, Joe, ed. *Ursula K. Le Guin*, 53–55.

Slusser, George Edgar. *Farthest Shores of Ursula K. Le Guin*, 6–7, 8, 9–10, 15–16.

Wood, Susan. "Discovering Worlds: The Fiction of Ursula K. Le Guin," in Clareson, Thomas, ed. *Voices for the Future* (Vol. 2), 160, 162.

Dispossessed (1974)

Annas, Pamela J. "New Worlds, New Words: Androgyny in Feminist Science Fiction." *SFS* 5 (1978): 152–153.

Bain, Dena C. "Tao Te Ching as Background to the Novels of Ursula K. Le Guin." *Extrapolation* 21 (1980): 209–211, 218–221.

Bierman, Judah. "Ambiguity in Utopia: *The Dispossessed*." *SFS* 2 (1975): 249–255.

Brennan, John P. and Michael C. Downs. "Anarchism and Utopian Tradition in *The Dispossessed*," in Olander, Joseph D. and Martin Harry Greenberg, eds. *Ursula K. Le Guin*, 116–152.

Brigg, Peter. "Archetype of the Journey in Ursula K. Le Guin's Fiction," in Olander, Joseph D. and Martin Harry Greenberg, eds. *Ursula K. Le Guin*, 36–63.

Cogell, Elizabeth Cummins. "Taoist Configuations: *Dispossessed*," in DeBolt, Joe, ed. *Ursula K. Le Guin*, 153–179.

Fekete, John. "*Dispossessed* and *Triton*: Act and System in Utopian Science Fiction." *SFS* 6 (1979): 131–136, 139–141.

Jameson, Fredric, "World-Reduction in Le Guin: The Emergence of Utopian Narrative." *SFS* 2 (1975): 224–230.

Klein, Gerard and Richard Astle. "Le Guin's 'Aberrant' Opus: Escaping the Trap of Discontent." *SFS* 4 (1977): 288–292.

Koper, Peter T. "Science and Rhetoric in the Fiction of Ursula Le Guin," in DeBolt, Joe, ed. *Ursula K. Le Guin*, 81–83.

Meyers, Walter E. *Aliens and Linguists*, 203–208.

Moylan, Tom. "Beyond Negation: The Critical Utopias of Ursula K. Le Guin and Samuel R. Delany." *Extrapolation* 21 (1980): 238–243, 249–252.

Remington, Thomas J. "Other Side of Suffering: Touch as Theme and Metaphor in Le Guin's Science Fiction Novels," in Olander, Joseph D. and Martin Harry Greenberg, eds. *Ursula K. Le Guin*, 170, 171–173, 174–177.

Scholes, Robert and Eric S. Rabkin. *Science Fiction*, 80.

Sinclair, Karen. "Solitary Being: The Hero as Anthropologist," in DeBolt, Joe, ed. *Ursula K. Le Guin*, 60–62.

Slusser, George Edgar. *Farthest Shores of Ursula K. Le Guin*, 34, 46–56.

Smith, Philip E, II. "Unbuilding Walls: Human Nature and the Nature of Evolutionary and Political Theory in *The Dispossessed*," in Olander, Joseph D. and Martin Harry Greenberg, eds. *Ursula K. Le Guin*, 77–96.

Tayormina, M. Teresa. "Physics as Metaphor: The General Temporal Theory in *The Dispossessed*." *Mosaic* 13.3–4 (1980): 51–62.

Theall, Donald F. "Art of Social-Science Fiction: The Ambiguous Utopian Dialectics of Ursula K. Le Guin." *SFS* 2 (1975): 260–264.

Tifft, Larry L. and Dennis C. Sullivan. "Possessed Sociology and Le Guin's *Dispossessed*: From Exile to Anarchism," in DeBolt, Joe, ed. *Ursula K. Le Guin*, 180–197.

Urbanowicz, Victor. "Personal and Political in *The Dispossessed*." *SFS* 5 (1978): 110–117.

Watson, Ian. "Le Guin's *Lathe of Heaven* and the Role of Dick: The False Reality as Mediator." *SFS* 2 (1975): 72–73.

Wolfe, Gary K. "Known and the Unknown: Structure and Image in Science Fiction," in Clareson, Thomas D., ed. *Many Futures, Many Worlds*, 102–103.

Wood, Susan. "Discovering Worlds: The Fiction of Ursula K. Le Guin," in Clareson, Thomas, ed. *Voices for the Future* (Vol. 2), 161–162, 171–175.

Farthest Shore (1972)

Attebery, Brian. *Fantasy Tradition in American Literature*, 176, 177–179, 181, 182.

Attebery, Brian. "On a Far Shore: The Myth of Earthsea." *Extrapolation* 21 (1980): 269–277.

Crow, John H. and Richard D. Erlich. "Words of Binding: Patterns of Integration in the Earthsea Trilogy," in Olander, Joseph D. and Martin Harry Greenberg, eds. *Ursula K. Le Guin*, 200–216.

Dooley, Patricia. "Magic and Art in Ursula Le Guin's Earthsea Trilogy." *ChildL* 8 (1979): 103–109.

Esmonde, Margaret P. "Master Pattern: The Psychological Journey in the Earthsea Trilogy," in Olander, Joseph D. and Martin Harry Greenberg, eds. *Ursula K. Le Guin*, 27–31, 32–34.

Galbreath, Robert. "Taoist Magic in the Earthsea Trilogy." *Extrapolation* 21 (1980): 263–266.

Gunew, Sneja. "Mythic Reversals: The Evolution of the Shadow Motif," in Olander, Joseph D. and Martin Harry Greenberg, eds. *Ursula K. Le Guin*, 183–184, 190–193, 195–196.

Lasseter, Rollin A. "Four Letters About Le Guin," in DeBolt, Joe, ed. *Ursula K. Le Guin*, 89–91, 105–114.

Manlove, C. N. "Conservatism in the Fantasy of Le Guin." *Extrapolation* 21 (1980): 287–297.

Molson, Francis J. "Earthsea Trilogy: Ethical Fantasy for Children," in DeBolt, Joe, ed. *Ursula K. Le Guin*, 145–148.

Pfeiffer, John R. " 'But Dragons Have Keen Ears': On Hearing 'Earthsea' with Recollections of 'Beowulf,' " in DeBolt, Joe, ed. *Ursula K. Le Guin*, 115–127.

Remington, Thomas J. "Time to Live and a Time to Die: Cyclical Renewal in the Earthsea Trilogy." *Extrapolation* 21 (1980): 283–285.

Shippey, T. A. "Magic Art and the Evolution of Words: Ursula Le Guin's Earthsea Trilogy." *Mosaic* 10.2 (1977): 159–162.

Slusser, George Edgar. *Farthest Shores of Ursula K. Le Guin*, 34, 35, 42–46.

White, Virginia L. "Bright the Hawk's Flight: The Journey of the Hero in Ursula Le Guin's Earthsea Trilogy." *BallS* 20.4 (1979): 34–35., 42–45.

Wood, Susan. "Discovering Worlds: The Fiction of Ursula K. Le Guin," in Clareson, Thomas, ed. *Voices for the Future* (Vol. 2), 175–179.

Lathe of Heaven (1971)

Annas, Pamela J. "New Worlds, New Words: Androgyny in Feminist Science Fiction." *SFS* 5 (1978): 151–152.

Cogell, Elizabeth Cummins. "Middle-Landscape Myth in Science Fiction." *SFS* 5 (1978): 136–138.

Crow, John H. and Richard D. Erlich. "Words of Binding: Patterns of Integration in the Earthsea Trilogy," in Olander, Joseph D. and Martin Harry Greenberg, eds. *Ursula K. Le Guin*, 218–219.

Gunew, Sneja. "Mythic Reversals: The Evolution of the Shadow Motif," in Olander, Joseph D. and Martin Harry Greenberg, eds. *Ursula K. Le Guin*, 181, 193.

Klein, Gerard and Richard Astle. "Le Guin's 'Aberrant' Opus: Escaping the Trap of Discontent." *SFS* 4 (1977): 292–293.

Koper, Peter T. "Science and Rhetoric in the Fiction of Ursula Le Guin," in DeBolt, Joe, ed. *Ursula K. Le Guin*, 80–81.

Plank, Robert. "Ursula K. Le Guin and the Decline of Romantic Love." *SFS* 3 (1976): 37–38.

Remington, Thomas J. "Other Side of Suffering: Touch as Theme and Metaphor in Le Guin's Science Fiction Novels," in Olander, Joseph D. and Martin Harry Greenberg, eds. *Ursula K. Le Guin*, 168–170.

Scholes, Robert and Eric S. Rabkin. *Science Fiction*, 79–80.

Watson, Ian. "Le Guin's *Lathe of Heaven* and the Role of Dick: The False Reality as Mediator." *SFS* 2 (1975): 67–72.

Wood, Susan. "Discovering Worlds: The Fiction of Ursula K. Le Guin," in Clareson, Thomas, ed. *Voices for the Future* (Vol. 2), 169–171.

Left Hand of Darkness (1969)

Annas, Pamela J. "New Worlds, New Words: Androgyny in Feminist Science Fiction." *SFS* 5 (1978): 150–151.

Bain, Dena C. "Tao Te Ching as Background to the Novels of Ursula K. Le Guin." *Extrapolation* 21 (1980): 209–211, 214–218, 221.

Bickman, Martin. "Le Guin's *The Left Hand of Darkness:* Form and Content." *SFS* 4 (1977): 42–47.

Brigg, Peter. "Archetype of the Journey in Ursula K. Le Guin's Fiction," in Olander, Joseph D. and Martin Harry Greenberg, eds. *Ursula K. Le Guin*, 36–63.

Brown, Barbara. "*Left Hand of Darkness:* Androgyny, Future, Present, and Past." *Extrapolation* 21 (1980): 227–235.

Bucknall, Barbara J. "Androgynes in Outer Space," in Riley, Dick, ed. *Critical Encounters*, 56–69.

Cogell, Elizabeth Cummins. "Setting as Analogue to Characterization in Ursula Le Guin." *Extrapolation* 18 (1977): 135–140.

Friend, Beverly. "Virgin Territory: The Bonds and Boundaries of Women in Science Fiction," in Clareson, Thomas D., ed. *Many Futures, Many Worlds*, 157–160.

Gunew, Sneja. "Mythic Reversals: The Evolution of the Shadow Motif," in Olander, Joseph D. and Martin Harry Greenberg, eds. *Ursula K. Le Guin*, 182, 185–186, 193–194, 196–197.

Hayles, N. B. "Androgyny, Ambivalence, and Assimilation in *The Left Hand of Darkness*," in Olander, Joseph D. and Martin Harry Greenberg, eds. *Ursula K. Le Guin*, 97–115.

Huntington, John. "Public and Private Imperatives in Le Guin's Novels." *SFS* 2 (1975): 238–242.

Jameson, Fredric, "World-Reduction in Le Guin: The Emergence of Utopian Narrative." *SFS* 2 (1975): 221–230.

Ketterer, David. "*Left Hand of Darkness:* Ursula K. LeGuin's Archetypal 'Winter-Journey'." *RQ* 5 (1973): 288–297.

Ketterer, David. *New Worlds for Old*, 76–90.

Klein, Gerard and Richard Astle. "Le Guin's 'Aberrant' Opus: Escaping the Trap of Discontent." *SFS* 4 (1977): 288–292.

Koper, Peter T. "Science and Rhetoric in the Fiction of Ursula Le Guin," in DeBolt, Joe, ed. *Ursula K. Le Guin*, 70–73.

Nudelman, Rafail and Alan G. Myers. "Approach to the Structure of Le Guin's SF." *SFS* 2 (1975): 210–220.

Rabkin, Eric S. "Determinism, Free Will, and Point of View in Le Guin's *The Left Hand of Darkness*." *Extrapolation* 20 (1979): 5–19.

Redekop, Ernest H. "Labyrinths in Space and Time." *Mosaic* 13.3–4 (1980): 111.

Remington, Thomas J. "Other Side of Suffering: Touch as Theme and Metaphor in Le Guin's Science Fiction Novels," in Olander, Joseph D. and Martin Harry Greenberg, eds. *Ursula K. Le Guin*, 161–168, 170, 171, 173.

Russ, Joanna. "Image of Women in Science Fiction," in Cornillon, Susan Koppelman, ed. *Images of Women in Fiction*, 89–91.

Scholes, Robert and Eric S. Rabkin. *Science Fiction*, 226–230.

Scholes, Robert. *Structural Fabulation*, 87–98.

Sinclair, Karen. "Solitary Being: The Hero as Anthropologist," in DeBolt, Joe, ed. *Ursula K. Le Guin*, 55–60.

Slusser, George Edgar. *Farthest Shores of Ursula K. Le Guin*, 10, 17–31.

Theall, Donald F. "Art of Social-Science Fiction: The Ambiguous Utopian Dialectics of Ursula K. Le Guin." *SFS* 2 (1975): 256–260, 263–264.

Walker, Jeanne Murray. "Myth, Exchange and History in *The Left Hand of Darkness*." *SFS* 6 (1979): 180–189.

Wood, Susan. "Discovering Worlds: The Fiction of Ursula K. Le Guin," in Clareson, Thomas, ed. *Voices for the Future* (Vol. 2), 162–1633, 164–169.

Planet of Exile (1966)

Cogell, Elizabeth Cummins. "Setting as Analogue to Characterization in Ursula Le Guin." *Extrapolation* 18 (1977): 132–135.

Gunew, Sneja. "Mythic Reversals: The Evolution of the Shadow Motif," in Olander, Joseph D. and Martin Harry Greenberg, eds. *Ursula K. Le Guin*, 182, 187, 193.

Koper, Peter T. "Science and Rhetoric in the Fiction of Ursula Le Guin," in DeBolt, Joe, ed. *Ursula K. Le Guin*, 78.

Nudelman, Rafail and Alan G. Myers. "Approach to the Structure of Le Guin's SF." *SFS* 2 (1975): 210–220.

Remington, Thomas J. "Other Side of Suffering: Touch as Theme and Metaphor in Le Guin's Science Fiction Novels," in Olander, Joseph D. and Martin Harry Greenberg, eds. *Ursula K. Le Guin*, 155–158, 171, 173.

Slusser, George Edgar. *Farthest Shores of Ursula K. Le Guin*, 7, 13–15.

Wood, Susan. "Discovering Worlds: The Fiction of Ursula K. Le Guin," in Clareson, Thomas, ed. *Voices for the Future* (Vol. 2), 160, 162, 163–164.

Rocannon's World (1966)

Brigg, Peter. "Archetype of the Journey in Ursula K. Le Guin's Fiction," in Olander, Joseph D. and Martin Harry Greenberg, eds. *Ursula K. Le Guin*, 36–63.

Cogell, Elizabeth Cummins. "Setting as Analogue to Characterization in Ursula Le Guin." *Extrapolation* 18 (1977): 131–132.

Crow, John H. and Richard D. Erlich. "Words of Binding: Patterns of Integration in the Earthsea Trilogy," in Olander, Joseph D. and Martin Harry Greenberg, eds. *Ursula K. Le Guin*, 222–223, 224.

Gunew, Sneja. "Mythic Reversals: The Evolution of the Shadow Motif," in Olander, Joseph D. and Martin Harry Greenberg, eds. *Ursula K. Le Guin*, 181–182, 183, 187, 195, 196.

Huntington, John. "Public and Private Imperatives in Le Guin's Novels." *SFS* 2 (1975): 238–242.

Klein, Gerard and Richard Astle. "Le Guin's 'Aberrant' Opus: Escaping the Trap of Discontent." *SFS* 4 (1977): 288–292.

Koper, Peter T. "Science and Rhetoric in the Fiction of Ursula Le Guin," in DeBolt, Joe, ed. *Ursula K. Le Guin*, 77–78.

Nudelman, Rafail and Alan G. Myers. "Approach to the Structure of Le Guin's SF." *SFS* 2 (1975): 210–220.

Remington, Thomas J. "Other Side of Suffering: Touch as Theme and Metaphor in Le Guin's Science Fiction Novels," in Olander, Joseph D. and Martin Harry Greenberg, eds. *Ursula K. Le Guin*, 154–155, 171, 173.

Sinclair, Karen. "Solitary Being: The Hero as Anthropologist," in DeBolt, Joe, ed. *Ursula K. Le Guin*, 52–53.

Slusser, George Edgar. *Farthest Shores of Ursula K. Le Guin*, 8–9, 12–13.

Wood, Susan. "Discovering Worlds: The Fiction of Ursula K. Le Guin," in Clareson, Thomas, ed. *Voices for the Future* (Vol. 2), 158–160, 162.

Tombs of Atuan (1971)

Attebery, Brian. *Fantasy Tradition in American Literature*, 171–173, 176–177.

Crow, John H. and Richard D. Erlich. "Words of Binding: Patterns of Integration in the Earthsea Trilogy," in Olander, Joseph D. and Martin Harry Greenberg, eds. *Ursula K. Le Guin*, 200–216.

Dooley, Patricia. "Magic and Art in Ursula Le Guin's Earthsea Trilogy." *ChildL* 8 (1979): 103–109.

Esmonde, Margaret P. "Master Pattern: The Psychological Journey in the Earthsea

Trilogy," in Olander, Joseph D. and Martin Harry Greenberg, eds. *Ursula K. Le Guin*, 20–27, 32.

Gunew, Sneja. "Mythic Reversals: The Evolution of the Shadow Motif," in Olander, Joseph D. and Martin Harry Greenberg, eds. *Ursula K. Le Guin*, 184–185, 189–190, 195.

Lasseter, Rollin A. "Four Letters About Le Guin," in DeBolt, Joe, ed. *Ursula K. Le Guin*, 98–105.

Manlove, C. N. "Conservatism in the Fantasy of Le Guin." *Extrapolation* 21 (1980): 289–297.

Molson, Francis J. "Earthsea Trilogy: Ethical Fantasy for Children," in DeBolt, Joe, ed. *Ursula K. Le Guin*, 140–145.

Pfeiffer, John R. " 'But Dragons Have Keen Ears': On Hearing 'Earthsea' with Recollections of 'Beowulf,' " in DeBolt, Joe, ed. *Ursula K. Le Guin*, 115–127.

Remington, Thomas J. "Time to Live and a Time to Die: Cyclical Renewal in the Earthsea Trilogy." *Extrapolation* 21 (1980): 279–283, 285.

Shippey, T. A. "Magic Art and the Evolution of Words: Ursula Le Guin's Earthsea Trilogy." *Mosaic* 10.2 (1977): 155–158.

Slusser, George Edgar. *Farthest Shores of Ursula K. Le Guin*, 38–42.

White, Virginia L. "Bright the Hawk's Flight: The Journey of the Hero in Ursula Le Guin's Earthsea Trilogy." *BallS* 20.4 (1979): 34–35, 39–42.

Wood, Susan. "Discovering Worlds: The Fiction of Ursula K. Le Guin," in Clareson, Thomas, ed. *Voices for the Future* (Vol. 2), 175–179.

Wizard of Earthsea (1968)

Attebery, Brian. *Fantasy Tradition in American Literature*, 168–169, 173–175, 182–183.

Bailey, Edgar C. "Shadows in Earthsea: Le Guin's Use of a Jungian Archetype." *Extrapolation* 21 (1980): 256–261.

Crow, John H. and Richard D. Erlich. "Words of Binding: Patterns of Integration in the Earthsea Trilogy," in Olander, Joseph D. and Martin Harry Greenberg, eds. *Ursula K. Le Guin*, 200–217.

Dooley, Patricia. "Magic and Art in Ursula Le Guin's Earthsea Trilogy." *ChildL* 8 (1979): 103–109.

Esmonde, Margaret P. "Master Pattern: The Psychological Journey in the Earthsea Trilogy," in Olander, Joseph D. and Martin Harry Greenberg, eds. *Ursula K. Le Guin*, 17–20, 31–32.

Galbreath, Robert. "Taoist Magic in the Earthsea Trilogy." *Extrapolation* 21 (1980): 263–266.

Gunew, Sneja. "Mythic Reversals: The Evolution of the Shadow Motif," in Olander, Joseph D. and Martin Harry Greenberg, eds. *Ursula K. Le Guin*, 183, 188–189.

Koper, Peter T. "Science and Rhetoric in the Fiction of Ursula Le Guin," in DeBolt, Joe, ed. *Ursula K. Le Guin*, 83–84.

Lasseter, Rollin A. "Four Letters About Le Guin," in DeBolt, Joe, ed. *Ursula K. Le Guin*, 91–98.

Manlove, C. N. "Conservatism in the Fantasy of Le Guin." *Extrapolation* 21 (1980): 287–297.

Molson, Francis J. "Earthsea Trilogy: Ethical Fantasy for Children," in DeBolt, Joe, ed. *Ursula K. Le Guin*, 133–140.

Pfeiffer, John R. " 'But Dragons Have Keen Ears': On Hearing 'Earthsea' with Recollections of 'Beowulf,' " in DeBolt, Joe, ed. *Ursula K. Le Guin*, 115–127.

Remington, Thomas J. "Time to Live and a Time to Die: Cyclical Renewal in the Earthsea Trilogy." *Extrapolation* 21 (1980): 278–279, 282–283, 285.

Scholes, Robert and Eric S. Rabkin. *Science Fiction*, 76–78.

Scholes, Robert. *Structural Fabulation*, 83–86.

Shippey, T. A. "Magic Art and the Evolution of Words: Ursula Le Guin's Earthsea Trilogy." *Mosaic* 10.2 (1977): 149–155.

Slusser, George Edgar. *Farthest Shores of Ursula K. Le Guin*, 34, 35–38.

Walker, Jeanne Murray. "Rites of Passage Today: The Cultural Significance of *The Wizard of Earthsea*." *Mosaic* 13.3–4 (1980): 179–191.

White, Virginia L. "Bright the Hawk's Flight: The Journey of the Hero in Ursula Le Guin's Earthsea Trilogy." *BallS* 20.4 (1979): 34–39.

Wood, Susan. "Discovering Worlds: The Fiction of Ursula K. Le Guin," in Clareson, Thomas, ed. *Voices for the Future* (Vol. 2), 175–179.

Word for World Is Forest (1972)

Alterman, Peter S. "Ursula K. Le Guin: Damsel with a Dulcimer," in Olander, Joseph D. and Martin Harry Greenberg, eds. *Ursula K. Le Guin*, 64–76.

Annas, Pamela J. "New Worlds, New Words: Androgyny in Feminist Science Fiction." *SFS* 5 (1978): 152.

Crow, John H. and Richard D. Erlich. "Words of Binding: Patterns of Integration in the Earthsea Trilogy," in Olander, Joseph D. and Martin Harry Greenberg, eds. *Ursula K. Le Guin*, 219.

Gunew, Sneja. "Mythic Reversals: The Evolution of the Shadow Motif," in Olander, Joseph D. and Martin Harry Greenberg, eds. *Ursula K. Le Guin*, 198–199.

Huntington, John. "Public and Private Imperatives in Le Guin's Novels." *SFS* 2 (1975): 240–242.

Sinclair, Karen. "Solitary Being: The Hero as Anthropologist," in DeBolt, Joe, ed. *Ursula K. Le Guin*, 62–64.

Yoke, Carl. "Precious Metal in White Clay." *Extrapolation* 21 (1980): 197–208.

LE PAN, DOUGLAS (1914–)

Deserter (1964)

Jones, D. G. *Butterfly on Rock*, 153–157.

Sutherland, Ronald. *Second Image*, 16–23.

LEACOCK, STEPHEN (1869–1944)

Arcadian Adventures with the Idle Rich (1959)

Davies, Robertson. *Stephen Leacock*, 28–31.

Dooley, D. J. *Moral Vision*, 5–10.

Kushner, J. and R. D. MacDonald. "Leacock: Economist/Satirist in *Arcadian Adventures* and *Sunshine Sketches*." *DR* 56 (1976): 495–505, 509.

Magee, W. H. "Stephen Leacock: Local Colourist." *CanL* 39 (1969): 41–42.

Sunshine Sketches of a Little Town (1912)

Cameron, D. A. "Enchanted Houses: Leacock's Irony," in Woodcock, George, ed. *Canadian Novel*, 1–13.

Davies, Robertson. *Stephen Leacock*, 21–25.
Dooley, D. J. *Moral Vision*, 3–5.
Jones, D. G. *Butterfly on Rock*, 59–60.
Kushner, J. and R. D. MacDonald. "Leacock: Economist/Satirist in *Arcadian Adventures* and *Sunshine Sketches*." *DR* 56 (1976): 505–509.
Magee, W. H. "Stephen Leacock: Local Colourist." *CanL* 39 (1969): 37–41.
Magee, William H. "Genial Humor in Stephen Leacock." *DR* 56 (1976): 272–279.
Mantz, Douglas. "Preposterous and the Profound: A New Look at the Envoi of *Sunshine Sketches*," in Moss, John, ed. *Beginnings*, 161–174.
Marshall, Tom. "Balance and Perspective in *Sunshine Sketches*," in Moss, John, ed. *Beginnings*, 176–187.

LEDERER, WILLIAM J. (1912–)

Ugly American (1958)
   Wilkinson, Rupert. "Connections with Toughness: The Novels of Eugene Burdick." *JAmS* 11 (1977): 223–239.

LEE, HARPER (1926–)

To Kill a Mockingbird (1960)
   Going, William T. *Essays on Alabama Literature*, 9–16, 23–31.

LEGGETT, JOHN (1917–)

Gloucester Branch (1964)
   Milne, Gordon. *Sense of Society*, 262–265.

Who Took the Gold Away (1969)
   Milne, Gordon. *Sense of Society*, 265–271.

LEIBER, FRITZ (1910–)

Conjure Wife (1952)
   Frane, Jeff. *Fritz Leiber*, 15–19.

Gather, Darkness (1950)
   Frane, Jeff. *Fritz Leiber*, 20–23.

Specter Is Haunting Texas (1969)
   Frane, Jeff. *Fritz Leiber*, 36–37.

Wanderer (1964)
   Frane, Jeff. *Fritz Leiber*, 33–36.

LEMELIN, ROGER (1919–1992)

Au pied de la pente douce (1944)
   Belleau, André. *Le romancier fictif*, 19–38, 57–72.
   Shek, Ben-Zion. *Social Realism*, 112–129, 147–156.
   Urbas, Jeannette. *From Thirty Acres to Modern Times*, 35–39.

In Quest of Splendour see *Pierre le magnifique*

Les Plouffe (1948)

Belleau, André. *Le romancier fictif*, 57–72.

Shek, Ben-Zion. *Social Realism*, 129–141, 147–156.

Urbas, Jeannette. *From Thirty Acres to Modern Times*, 39–41.

Pierre le magnifique (1952)

Belleau, André. *Le romancier fictif*, 57–72

Shek, Ben-Zion. *Social Realism*, 141–156.

Urbas, Jeannette. *From Thirty Acres to Modern Times*, 41–42.

Plouffe Family see *Les Plouffe*

Town Below see *Au pied de la pente douce*

LEMOINE, WILFRED (1927–)

Le déroulement (1976)

Poulin, Gabrielle. *Romans du pays*, 230–239.

LENTZ, PERRY (1943–)

Falling Hills (1967)

Bennett, Lee Shaw. "Modern Civil War Novels: The Still Unwritten War?" *SoS* 19 (1980): 116–118.

LEPAN, DOUGLAS see LE PAN, DOUGLAS

LESLIE, ELIZA (1787–1858)

Amelia (1848)

Baym, Nina. *Woman's Fiction*, 84–85.

LEVERIDGE, RALPH (1922(?)–)

Walk on the Water (1951)

Jones, Peter G. *War and the Novelist*, 121–123.

LEVIN, DAN (1914–)

Mask of Glory (1948)

Bryant, Jerry H. *Open Decision*, 135, 144, 145.

LEVIN, IRA (1929–)

Perfect Day (1970)

Rhodes, Carolyn. "Tyranny by Computer: Automated Data Processing and Oppressive Government in Science Fiction," in Clareson, Thomas D., ed. *Many Futures, Many Worlds*, 87–90.

LEVIN, MEYER (1905–1981)

Old Bunch (1937)
   Guttmann, Allen. *Jewish Writer in America*, 39–44.

LEWIS, JANET (1899–)

Against a Darkening Sky (1943)
   Crow, Charles L. *Janet Lewis*, 17–23.

Ghost of Monsieur Scarron (1959)
   Crow, Charles L. *Janet Lewis*, 35–38.

Invasion (1932)
   Crow, Charles L. *Janet Lewis*, 12–17.

Trial of Sören Qvist (1947)
   Crow, Charles L. *Janet Lewis*, 31–34.

LEWIS, SINCLAIR (1885–1951)

Ann Vickers (1933)
   Light, Martin. *Quixotic Vision of Sinclair Lewis*, 119–120.

Arrowsmith (1925)
   Blake, Nelson Manfred. *Novelists' America*, 35–36.
   Helleberg, Marilyn M. "Paper-Doll Characters of Sinclair Lewis' *Arrowsmith*."
      MTJ 14.1 (1969): 17–21.
   Light, Martin. *Quixotic Vision of Sinclair Lewis*, 85–97.
   Lundquist, James. *Sinclair Lewis*, 44–46, 74–76.

Babbitt (1922)
   Allen, Walter. *Urgent West*, 199–200.
   Blake, Nelson Manfred. *Novelists' America*, 24–32, 37–38.
   Brown, Daniel R. "Lewis's Satire– A Negative Emphasis." *Renascence* 18 (Win-
      ter 1966): 63–72. Rpt. in Light, Martin, comp. *Merrill Studies in Babbitt*, 51–63.
   Coard, Robert L. "Mark Twain's *The Gilded Age* and Sinclair Lewis's *Babbitt*."
      MidQ 13 (1972): 319–333.
   Daniels, Howell. "Sinclair Lewis and the Drama of Dissociation," in Bradbury,
      Malcolm and David Palmer, eds. *American Novel in the Nineteen Twenties*, 93–
      100.
   Friedman, Philip Allan. "*Babbitt:* Satiric Realism in Form and Content." *Satire
      Newsletter* 4 (Fall 1966): 20–29. Rpt. in Light, Martin, comp. *Merrill Studies in
      Babbitt*, 64–75.
   Geismar, Maxwell. "On *Babbitt*," in Geismar, Maxwell. *Last of the Provincials:
      The American Novel, 1915–1925*. Boston: Houghton, Mifflin and Co., 1947. 89–
      97. Rpt. in Light, Martin, comp. *Merrill Studies in Babbitt*, 91–97.
   Grebstein, Sheldon Norman. "*Babbitt:* Synonym for a State of Mind," in
      Grebstein, Sheldon Norman. *Sinclair Lewis*. New York: Twayne Publishers, Inc.,
      1962. 73–85. Rpt. in Light, Martin, comp. *Merrill Studies in Babbitt*, 32–44.
   Hilfer, Anthony Charles. "Lost in a World of Machines," in Hilfer, Anthony

Charles. *Revolt from the Village: 1915–1930*. Chapel Hill, NC: University of North Carolina Press, 1969. 167–176. Rpt. in Light, Martin, comp. *Merrill Studies in Babbitt*, 83–91.

Hoffman, Frederick J. "Critique of the Middle Class: Sinclair Lewis's *Babbitt*," in Hoffman, Frederick J. *Twenties: American Writing in the Postwar Decade*. New York: Viking Press, Inc., 1955. 364–370. Rpt. in Light, Martin, comp. *Merrill Studies in Babbitt*, 45–51.

Kazin, Alfred. "New Realism: Sinclair Lewis," in Kazin, Alfred. *On Native Grounds*. New York: Harcourt Brace Jovanovich, Inc., 1942. 217–226. Rpt. in Light, Martin, comp. *Merrill Studies in Babbitt*, 97–105.

Light, Martin. *Quixotic Vision of Sinclair Lewis*, 73–84.

Lundquist, James. *Sinclair Lewis*, 40–44, 70–74.

Ousby, Ian. *Reader's Guide to Fifty American Novels*, 201–203.

Quivey, James R. "George Babbitt's Quest for Masculinity." *BallS* 10.2 (1969): 4–7.

Schorer, Mark. "Sinclair Lewis: *Babbitt*," in Cohen, Hennig, ed. *Landmarks of American Writing*. New York: Basic Books, Inc., Publishers, 1969. 315–327. Rpt. in Light, Martin, comp. *Merrill Studies in Babbitt*, 105–116.

Wagenaar, Dick. "Knight and the Pioneer: Europe and America in the Fiction of Sinclair Lewis." *AL* 50 (1978): 235–238.

Whipple, T. K. "Sinclair Lewis," in Whipple, T. K. *Spokesman*. New York: D. Appleton and Co., 1928, 208–220. Rpt. in Light, Martin, comp. *Merrill Studies in Babbitt*, 75–83.

Dodsworth (1929)

Barry, James D. "*Dodsworth:* Sinclair Lewis' Novel of Character." *BallS* 10.2 (1969): 8–14.

Blake, Nelson Manfred. *Novelists' America*, 33–35.

Daniels, Howell. "Sinclair Lewis and the Drama of Dissociation," in Bradbury, Malcolm and David Palmer, eds. *American Novel in the Nineteen Twenties*, 100–103.

Hearn, Charles R. *American Dream in the Great Depression*, 50–52.

Light, Martin. *Quixotic Vision of Sinclair Lewis*, 108–116.

Lundquist, James. *Sinclair Lewis*, 55–60, 81–84.

Milne, Gordon. *Sense of Society*, 208–210.

Wagenaar, Dick. "Knight and the Pioneer: Europe and America in the Fiction of Sinclair Lewis." *AL* 50 (1978): 240–246.

Elmer Gantry (1927)

Blake, Nelson Manfred. *Novelists' America*, 39–43.

Light, Martin. *Quixotic Vision of Sinclair Lewis*, 99–107.

Lundquist, James. *Sinclair Lewis*, 49–53, 77–80.

Free Air (1919)

Light, Martin. *Quixotic Vision of Sinclair Lewis*, 58.

Tuttleton, James W. *Novel of Manners in America*, 143–145.

Gideon Planish (1943)

Light, Martin. *Quixotic Vision of Sinclair Lewis*, 127–128.

God-Seeker (1949)

Light, Martin. *Quixotic Vision of Sinclair Lewis*, 130–132.

It Can Happen Here (1935)
   Light, Martin. *Quixotic Vision of Sinclair Lewis*, 122–126.

Job (1917)
   Light, Martin. *Quixotic Vision of Sinclair Lewis*, 56–57.

Kingsblood Royal (1947)
   Berzon, Judith R. *Neither White Nor Black*, 123–127.
   Light, Martin. *Quixotic Vision of Sinclair Lewis*, 129–130.

Main Street (1920)
   Blake, Nelson Manfred. *Novelists' America*, 11–22.
   Daniels, Howell. "Sinclair Lewis and the Drama of Dissociation," in Bradbury,
      Malcolm and David Palmer, eds. *American Novel in the Nineteen Twenties*,
      91–93.
   Downs, Robert B. *Famous American Books*, 257–265.
   Light, Martin. *Quixotic Vision of Sinclair Lewis*, 60–72.
   Lundquist, James. *Sinclair Lewis*, 35–40, 68–70.
   Milne, Gordon. *Sense of Society*, 206–208.
   Ousby, Ian. *Reader's Guide to Fifty American Novels*, 195–198.
   Tuttleton, James W. *Novel of Manners in America*, 145–159.
   Watkins, Floyd C. *In Time and Place*, 193–213.

Man Who Knew Coolidge (1928)
   Lundquist, James. *Sinclair Lewis*, 53–54.

Mantrap (1926)
   Lundquist, James. *Sinclair Lewis*, 47–49.

Our Mr. Wrenn (1914)
   Light, Martin. *Quixotic Vision of Sinclair Lewis*, 48–49.
   Wagenaar, Dick. "Knight and the Pioneer: Europe and America in the Fiction of
      Sinclair Lewis." *AL* 50 (1978): 238–240.

Prodigal Parents (1938)
   Light, Martin. *Quixotic Vision of Sinclair Lewis*, 126–127.

Trail of the Hawk (1915)
   Light, Martin. *Quixotic Vision of Sinclair Lewis*, 49–53.

World So Wide (1951)
   Wagenaar, Dick. "Knight and the Pioneer: Europe and America in the Fiction of
      Sinclair Lewis." *AL* 50 (1978): 232–234, 246–249.

LINAKIS, STEPHEN (1923–)

Spring the War Ended (1965)
   Bryant, Jerry H. *Open Decision*, 153–154.

LIPPARD, GEORGE (1822–1854)

Empire City (1850)
   Stout, Janis P. *Sodoms in Eden*, 50–54.

Nazarene (1846)

Stout, Janis P. *Sodoms in Eden*, 50–54.

Quaker City (1844)

Stout, Janis P. *Sodoms in Eden*, 50–54.

LIPSYTE, ROBERT (1938–)

Contender (1967)

Bachner, Saul. "Junior Novel and Identity: Robert Lipsyte's *The Contender*." *NALF* 9 (1975): 62–63.

LOCKRIDGE, ROSS, JR. (1914–1948)

Raintree County (1948)

Erisman, Fred. "*Raintree County* and the Power of Place." *MarkR* 8 (1979): 36–40.
Greiner, Donald J. "Ross Lockridge and the Tragedy of *Raintree County*." *Crit* 20.3 (1978): 51–62.
Lutwack, Leonard. "*Raintree County* and the Epicising Poet in American Fiction." *BallS* 13.1 (1972): 14–28.
Nemanic, Gerald C. "Ross Lockridge, *Raintree County*, and the Epic of Irony." *Midamerica* 2 (1975): 35–46.

LONDON, JACK (1876–1916)

Adventure (1911)

Stasz, Clarice. "Androgyny in the Novels of Jack London." *WAL* 11 (1976): 126–127.

Before Adam (1907)

Labor, Earle. *Jack London*, 106–109.
Pankake, Jon. "Jack London's Wild Man: The Broken Myths of *Before Adam*." *MFS* 22 (1976): 37–49.

Burning Daylight (1910)

Labor, Earle. *Jack London*, 138–142.
Stasz, Clarice. "Androgyny in the Novels of Jack London." *WAL* 11 (1976): 125–126.
Walcutt, Charles Child. "Jack London," in Walcutt, Charles Child, ed. *Seven Novelists in the American Naturalist Tradition*, 151–152.

Call of the Wild (1903)

Labor, Earle. *Jack London*, 72–78.
Mann, John S. "Theme of the Double in *The Call of the Wild*." *MarkR* 8 (1978): 1–5.
Walcutt, Charles Child. "Jack London," in Walcutt, Charles Child, ed. *Seven Novelists in the American Naturalist Tradition*, 144–147.

Daughter of the Snows (1902)

Giles, James R. "Beneficial Atavism in Frank Norris and Jack London." *WAL* 4 (1969): 21–23.

Stasz, Clarice. "Androgyny in the Novels of Jack London." *WAL* 11 (1976): 122–123.

Iron Heel (1908)

Beauchamp, Gorman. "*Iron Heel* and *Looking Backward:* Two Paths to Utopia." *ALR* 9 (1976): 307–313.

Ketterer, David. *New Worlds for Old*, 126–133.

Labor, Earle. *Jack London*, 101–105.

Lynn, Kenneth S. *Visions of America*, 196–198.

Stasz, Clarice. "Androgyny in the Novels of Jack London." *WAL* 11 (1976): 124.

Stein, Paul. "Jack London's *The Iron Heel:* Art as Manifesto." *SAF* 6 (1978): 77–92.

Teich, Nathaniel. "Marxist Dialectics in Content, Form, Point of View: Structures in Jack London's *The Iron Heel*." *MFS* 22 (1976): 85–99.

Little Lady of the Big House (1916)

Forrey, Robert. "Three Modes of Sexuality in London's *The Little Lady of the Big House*." *L&P* 26 (1976): 52–60.

Labor, Earle. *Jack London*, 143–145.

Stasz, Clarice. "Androgyny in the Novels of Jack London." *WAL* 11 (1976): 128–131.

Martin Eden (1909)

Baskett, Sam S. "*Martin Eden:* Jack London's Poem of the Mind." *MFS* 22 (1976): 23–36.

Cohn, Jan. "Women as Superfluous Characters in American Realism and Naturalism." *SAF* 1 (1973): 159–160.

Labor, Earle. *Jack London*, 116–123.

Mills, Gordon. "Transformation of Material in a Mimetic Fiction." *MFS* 22 (1976): 9–22.

Ousby, Ian. *Reader's Guide to Fifty American Novels*, 188–190.

Stasz, Clarice. "Androgyny in the Novels of Jack London." *WAL* 11 (1976): 125.

Walcutt, Charles Child. "Jack London," in Walcutt, Charles Child, ed. *Seven Novelists in the American Naturalist Tradition*, 158–164.

Scarlet Plague (1912)

Labor, Earle. *Jack London*, 109–112.

Sea Wolf (1904)

Labor, Earle. *Jack London*, 94–99.

Stasz, Clarice. "Androgyny in the Novels of Jack London." *WAL* 11 (1976): 123–124.

Walcutt, Charles Child. "Jack London," in Walcutt, Charles Child, ed. *Seven Novelists in the American Naturalist Tradition*, 149–151.

Watson, Charles N., Jr. "Sexual Conflict in *The Sea-Wolf:* Further Notes on London's Reading of Kipling and Norris." *WAL* 11 (1976): 239–248.

Star Rover (1915)

Labor, Earle. *Jack London*, 113–115.

Valley of the Moon (1913)

Labor, Earle. *Jack London*, 142–143.

Stasz, Clarice. "Androgyny in the Novels of Jack London." *WAL* 11 (1976): 127.

White Fang (1906)

> Labor, Earle. *Jack London*, 79–81, 137–138.
> Walcutt, Charles Child. "Jack London," in Walcutt, Charles Child, ed. *Seven Novelists in the American Naturalist Tradition*, 147–149.

LONGBAUGH, HARRY see GOLDMAN, WILLIAM

LONGFELLOW, HENRY WADSWORTH (1807–1882)

Kavanagh (1849)

> Faderman, Lillian. "Female Same-Sex Relationships in Novels by Longfellow, Holmes, and James." *NEQ* 51 (1978): 315–318.

LONGO, LUCAS (1919–)

Family on Vendetta Street (1968)

> Green, Rose Basile. *Italian-American Novel*, 207–210.

LOOMIS, EDWARD (1924–)

End of a War (1958)

> Jones, Peter G. *War and the Novelist*, 169–171.
> Waldmeir, Joseph J. *American Novels of the Second World War*, 91–92.

LOWRY, MALCOLM (1909–1957)

Dark as the Grave Wherein My Friend Is Laid (1968)

> Bareham, Terence. "After the Volcano: An Assessment of Malcolm Lowry's Posthumous Fiction." *SNNTS* 6 (1974): 357–358.
> Corrigan, Matthew. "Masks and the Man: The Writer as Actor." *Shenandoah* 19.4 (Summer 1968): 89–93. Rpt. in Wood, Barry, ed. *Malcolm Lowry*, 210–215.
> Costa, Richard Hauer. *Malcolm Lowry*, 115–123.
> Cross, Richard K. *Malcolm Lowry*, 69–75.
> New, William H. *Malcolm Lowry*, 44–51.

October Ferry to Gabriola (1971)

> Bareham, Terence. "After the Volcano: An Assessment of Malcolm Lowry's Posthumous Fiction." *SNNTS* 6 (1974): 351–361.
> Bareham, Terence. "After the Volcano: An Assessment of Malcolm Lowry's Posthumous Fiction." *Studies in the Novel* 6.3 (Fall 1974): 349–362. Rpt. in Wood, Barry, ed. *Malcolm Lowry*, 241–248.
> Bradbrook, M. C. "Intention and Design in *October Ferry to Gabriola*," in Smith, Anne, ed. *Art of Malcolm Lowry*, 144–150.
> Bradbrook, M. C. *Malcolm Lowry, His Art and Early Life*, 85–106.
> Costa, Richard Hauer. *Malcolm Lowry*, 146–154.
> Cross, Richard K. *Malcolm Lowry*, 75–83.

Grace, Sherrill E. "Malcolm Lowry and Expressionist Vision," in Smith, Anne, ed. *Art of Malcolm Lowry*, 103, 107, 108–109.

Kilgallin, Anthony R. "Long Voyage Home: *October Ferry to Gabriola*." Woodcock, George. *Malcolm Lowry: The Man and His Work*. Vancouver: University of British Columbia Press, 1971. 78–87. Rpt. in Wood, Barry, ed. *Malcolm Lowry*, 215–225.

New, William H. "Gabriola: Malcolm Lowry's Floating Island." *Literary Half-Yearly* 13.1 (1972): 115–125. Rpt. in Wood, Barry, ed. *Malcolm Lowry*, 226–234.

New, William H. *Malcolm Lowry*, 42–44.

Ultramarine (1933)

Bradbrook, M. C. *Malcolm Lowry, His Art and Early Life*, 40–53.

Cross, Richard K. *Malcolm Lowry*, 3–13.

Grace, Sherrill E. "Malcolm Lowry and Expressionist Vision," in Smith, Anne, ed. *Art of Malcolm Lowry*, 100.

Grace, Sherrill E. "Outward Bound." *Canadian Literature* 71 (Winter 1976): 73–79. Rpt. in Wood, Barry, ed. *Malcolm Lowry*, 6–14.

New, William H. *Malcolm Lowry*, 20–25.

Woodcock, George. *Odysseus Ever Returning*, 63–65.

Woodcock, George. "Own Place on the Mind: An Essay in Lowrian Topography," in Smith, Anne, ed. *Art of Malcolm Lowry*, 115–116.

Under the Volcano (1947)

Allen, Walter. "Masterpiece of the Forties," in Kostelanetz, Richard, ed. *On Contemporary Literature*, 419–421.

Anderson, David. *Tragic Protest*, 133–134.

Bareham, Terence. "Paradigms of Hell: Symbolic Patterning in *Under the Volcano*." Benedikz, B S., ed. *On the Novel: A Present for Walter Allen on His Birthday from His Friends and Colleagues*. London: J.M. Dent, 1971. 113–127. Rpt. in Wood, Barry, ed. *Malcolm Lowry*, 101–113.

Bradbrook, M. C. "Lowry's Tartarus." Bradbrook, M.C. *Malcolm Lowry: His Art and Early Life: A Study in Transformation*. 54–68. Rpt. in Wood, Barry, ed. *Malcolm Lowry*, 114–124.

Bradbrook, M. C. *Malcolm Lowry, His Art and Early Life*, 54–68.

Costa, Richard Hauer. *Malcolm Lowry*, 61–105, 169–175.

Cross, Richard K. *Malcolm Lowry*, 26–64.

Cross, Richard K. "*Moby-Dick* and *Under the Volcano*: Poetry from the Abyss." *MFS* 20 (1974): 149–156.

Dodson, Daniel B. *Malcolm Lowry*, 10–34.

Edmonds, Dale. "*Under the Volcano*: A Reading of the 'Immediate Level'." *Tulane Studies in English* 16 (1968): 63–105. Rpt. in Wood, Barry, ed. *Malcolm Lowry*, 57–97.

Epstein, Perle. *Private Labyrinth of Malcolm Lowry: Under the Volcano and The Cabbala*. New York: Holt, Rinehart and Winston, 1969.

Grace, Sherrill E. "Malcolm Lowry and Expressionist Vision," in Smith, Anne, ed. *Art of Malcolm Lowry*, 97, 98–100, 103, 105–108, 109.

Gunn, Drewey Wayne. *American and British Writers in Mexico*, 168–172.

Heilman, Robert B. "Possessed Artist of the Lost Soul." *Canadian Literature* 8 (Spring 1961): 7–16. Rpt. in Wood, Barry, ed. *Malcolm Lowry*, 48–57.

Hill, Art. "Alcoholic on Alcoholism." *CanL* 62 (1974): 33–48.

Hill, Art. "Alcoholic on Alcoholism." *Canadian Literature* 62 (Autumn 1974): 33–48. Rpt. in Wood, Barry, ed. *Malcolm Lowry*, 126–141.

Hill, Arthur N. "Alcoholic Novelist on Alcoholism: Lowry's Unique Achievement in *Under the Volcano*," in Woodcock, George, ed. *Canadian Novel*, 87–102.

Littlejohn, David. *Interruptions*, 28–29.

Markson, David. *Malcolm Lowry's Volcano: Myth, Symbol, Meaning.* New York: Times Books, 1978.

New, William H. *Malcolm Lowry*, 29–41.

O'Kill, Brian. "Aspects of Language in *Under the Volcano*," in Smith, Anne, ed. *Art of Malcolm Lowry*, 72–90.

Orr, John. *Tragic Realism and Modern Society*, 45–76.

Schorer, Mark. "Downward Flight of a Soul." *New York Herald Tribune Weekly Book Review* (23 February 1947). Rpt. in Wood, Barry, ed. *Malcolm Lowry*, 46–48.

Slade, Carole. "*Under the Volcano* and Dante's *Inferno I*." *University of Windsor Review* 10.2 (1975): 44–52. Rpt. in Wood, Barry, ed. *Malcolm Lowry*, 143–150.

Tifft, Stephen. "Tragedy as Meditation on Itself: Reflexiveness in *Under the Volcano*," in Smith, Anne, ed. *Art of Malcolm Lowry*, 46–69.

Widmer, Eleanor. "Drunken Wheel: Malcolm Lowry and *Under the Volcano*," in French, Warren, ed. *Forties*, 217–226.

Woodcock, George. *Odysseus Ever Returning*, 56–62, 65–67.

Woodcock, George. "Own Place on the Mind: An Essay in Lowrian Topography," in Smith, Anne, ed. *Art of Malcolm Lowry*, 115, 116–124.

LUDWIG, JACK (1922–)

Above Ground (1968)

Moss, John. *Sex and Violence*, 43–44.

Confusions (1963)

James, Esther. "Ludwig's *Confusions*." *CanL* 40 (1969): 49–53.

LUMPKIN, GRACE (1892(?)–1980)

Sign for Cain (1935)

Cook, Sylvia Jenkins. *From Tobacco Road to Route 66*, 115–117.

To Make My Bread (1932)

Cook, Sylvia Jenkins. *From Tobacco Road to Route 66*, 110–115.

LYTLE, ANDREW (1902–1995)

At the Moon's Inn (1941)

Benson, Robert G. "Progress of Hernando de Soto in Andrew Lytle's *At the Moon's Inn*." *Georgia Review* 27 (1973): 232–244. Modified slightly and published as "Yankee's of the Race: The Decline and Fall of Hernando de Soto," in Bradford, M. E., ed. *Form Discovered*, 84–96.

Ghilselin, Brewster. "Andrew Lytle's Selva Obscura," in Bradford, M. E., ed. *Form Discovered*, 74–76.

Long Night (1936)

Sullivan, Walter. *Death by Melancholy*, 72–75.

Sullivan, Walter. *Requiem for the Renascence*, 26–31.

Weatherby, H. L. "Quality of Richness: Observations on Andrew Lytle," in Bradford, M. E., ed. *Form Discovered*, 35–41.

Name for Evil (1947)

Clark, Charles C. *"Name for Evil: A Search for Order,"* in Bradford, M. E., ed. *Form Discovered*, 24–34.

Velvet Horn (1957)

Ghilselin, Brewster. "Andrew Lytle's Selva Obscura," in Bradford, M. E., ed. *Form Discovered*, 76–78.

Landess, Thomas H. "Unity of Action in *The Velvet Horn*," in Bradford, M. E., ed. *Form Discovered*, 3–15.

MCCARTHY, CORMAC (1933–)

Child of God (1974)

Sullivan, Walter. *Requiem for the Renascence*, 70–72.

MCCARTHY, MARY (1912–1989)

Birds of America (1965)

Martin, Wendy. "Satire and Moral Vision of Mary McCarthy," in Cohen, Sara Blacher, ed. *Comic Relief*, 202–203

Charmed Life (1955)

Martin, Wendy. "Satire and Moral Vision of Mary McCarthy," in Cohen, Sara Blacher, ed. *Comic Relief*, 196–199.

Widmer, Eleanor. "Finally a Lady: Mary McCarthy," in French, Warren, ed. *Fifties*, 99–101.

Company She Keeps (1942)

Martin, Wendy. "Satire and Moral Vision of Mary McCarthy," in Cohen, Sara Blacher, ed. *Comic Relief*, 189–192.

Spacks, Patricia Meyer. *Female Imagination*, 254–260.

Spacks, Patricia Meyer. "Mary McCarthy: Society's Demands," in Spacks, Patrica Meyer. *Female Imagination*. New York: Alfred A. Knopf, Inc., 1975. 254–260. Rpt. in Spacks, Patricia Meyer, ed. *Contemporary Women Novelists*, 85–91.

Group (1963)

Martin, Wendy. "Satire and Moral Vision of Mary McCarthy," in Cohen, Sara Blacher, ed. *Comic Relief*, 199–202.

Groves of Academe (1952)

Martin, Wendy. "Satire and Moral Vision of Mary McCarthy," in Cohen, Sara Blacher, ed. *Comic Relief*, 195–196.

Widmer, Eleanor. "Finally a Lady: Mary McCarthy," in French, Warren, ed. *Fifties*, 98–99.

MCCLUNG, NELLIE (1873–1951)

Painted Firs (1921)

Harrison, Dick. *Unnamed Country*, 94.

Sowing Seeds in Danny (1908)

Jackel. Susan. "House on the Prairies." *CanL* 42 (1969): 48–49.
Jackel, Susan. "House on the Prairies," in Stephens, Donald G., ed. *Writers of the Prairies*, 167–168.

MCCLUSKEY, JOHN (1944–)

Look What They Done to My Song (1974)

Schultz, Elizabeth A. "Heirs of Ralph Ellison: Patterns of Individualism in the Contemporary Afro-American Novel." *CLAJ* 22 (1978): 119–122.

MCCOURT, EDWARD (1907–1972)

Fasting Friar (1963)

Ricou, Laurence R. "Empty as Nightmare: Man and Landscape in Recent Canadian Prairie Fiction." *Mosaic* 6.2 (1973): 153–155.

Home Is the Stranger (1950)

Harrison, Dick. *Unnamed Country*, 146–147.
Jackel. Susan. "House on the Prairies." *CanL* 42 (1969): 52–53.
Jackel, Susan. "House on the Prairies," in Stephens, Donald G., ed. *Writers of the Prairies*, 171–172.
Ricou, Laurence R. "Empty as Nightmare: Man and Landscape in Recent Canadian Prairie Fiction." *Mosaic* 6.2 (1973): 145–146.

Music at the Close (1947)

Harrison, Dick. *Unnamed Country*, 127–128.

Wooden Sword (1956)

Ricou, Laurence R. "Empty as Nightmare: Man and Landscape in Recent Canadian Prairie Fiction." *Mosaic* 6.2 (1973): 152–153.

MCCOY, HORACE (1897–1955)

They Shoot Horses, Don't They? (1935)

Wells, Walter. *Tycoons and Locusts*, 14–35.

MCCULLERS, CARSON (1917–1967)

Clock without Hands (1961)

Cook, Richard M. *Carson McCullers*, 106–120.
Graver, Lawrence. *Carson McCullers*, 42–45.
Levidova, Inna M. "Carson McCullers and Her Last Book," in Proffer, Carl R., ed. and trans. *Soviet Criticism of American Literature in the Sixties*, 89–96.
McDowell, Margaret B. *Carson McCullers*, 98–116.

Heart Is a Lonely Hunter (1940)

Box, Patricia S. "Androgyny and the Musical Vision: A Study of Two Novels by Carson McCullers." *SoQ* 16 (1978): 117–123.

Buchen, Irving H. "Carson McCullers, a Case of Convergence." *BuR* 21.1 (1973): 21–22.

Cook, Richard M. *Carson McCullers*, 20–45.

Edmonds, Dale. "Hunting the Lonely Hunter." *SoR* 12 (1976): 442–444.

Graver, Lawrence. *Carson McCullers*, 10–20.

Knowles, A. S., Jr. "Six Bronze Petals and Two Red: Carson McCullers and the Forties," in French, Warren, ed. *Forties*, 87–94.

Korenman, Joan S. "Carson McCullers' 'Proletarian Novel'." *Studies in the Humanities* 5.1 (1976): 8–13.

McDowell, Margaret B. *Carson McCullers*, 31–43.

Rich, Nancy B. " 'Ironic Parable of Fascism' in *The Heart Is a Lonely Hunter*." *SLJ* 9.2 (1977): 108–123.

Rose, Alan Henry. *Demonic Vision*, 121–122.

Smith, C. Michael. " 'A Voice in a Fugue': Characters and Musical Structure in *The Heart Is a Lonely Hunter*." *MFS* 25 (1979): 258–263.

Westling, Louise. "Carson McCullers's Tomboys." *SoHR* 14 (1980): 341–344.

Member of the Wedding (1946)

Box, Patricia S. "Androgyny and the Musical Vision: A Study of Two Novels by Carson McCullers." *SoQ* 16 (1978): 117–123.

Bryant, Jerry H. *Open Decision*, 245–249.

Buchen, Irving H. "Carson McCullers, a Case of Convergence." *BuR* 21.1 (1973): 22, 23–25.

Cook, Richard M. *Carson McCullers*, 60–81.

Graver, Lawrence. *Carson McCullers*, 33–41.

McDowell, Margaret B. *Carson McCullers*, 80–95.

Walker, Sue B. "Link in the Chain Called Love: A New Look at Carson McCullers' Novels." *MTJ* 18.3 (1976): 8–11.

Westling, Louise. "Carson McCullers's Tomboys." *SoHR* 14 (1980): 344–350.

Reflections in a Golden Eye (1940)

Cook, Richard M. *Carson McCullers*, 48–58.

Graver, Lawrence. *Carson McCullers*, 20–24.

Knowles, A. S., Jr. "Six Bronze Petals and Two Red: Carson McCullers and the Forties," in French, Warren, ed. *Forties*, 94.

McDowell, Margaret B. *Carson McCullers*, 44–64.

MACDONALD, ANSON see HEINLEIN, ROBERT A.

MACDONALD, JOHN D. (1916–1986)

Bright Orange for the Shroud (1965)

Campbell, Frank D., Jr. *John D. MacDonald and The Colorful World of Travis McGee*, 20–23.

Darker than Amber (1966)

Campbell, Frank D., Jr. *John D. MacDonald and The Colorful World of Travis McGee*, 23–27.

Deadly Shade of Gold (1965)

Campbell, Frank D., Jr. *John D. MacDonald and The Colorful World of Travis McGee*, 16–20.

Dreadful Lemon Sky (1975)

Campbell, Frank D., Jr. *John D. MacDonald and The Colorful World of Travis McGee*, 57–62.

Dress Her in Indigo (1969)

Campbell, Frank D., Jr. *John D. MacDonald and The Colorful World of Travis McGee*, 38–41.

Executioners (1957)

Kelly, R. Gordon. "Precarious World of John D. MacDonald," in Landrum, Larry N., Pat Browne and Ray B. Browne, eds. *Dimensions of Detective Fiction*, 150–161.

Girl in the Plain Brown Wrapper (1968)

Campbell, Frank D., Jr. *John D. MacDonald and The Colorful World of Travis McGee*, 34–38.

Long Lavender Look (1970)

Campbell, Frank D., Jr. *John D. MacDonald and The Colorful World of Travis McGee*, 41–45.

One Fearful Yellow Eye (1966)

Campbell, Frank D., Jr. *John D. MacDonald and The Colorful World of Travis McGee*, 27–30.

Pale Gray for Guilt (1968)

Campbell, Frank D., Jr. *John D. MacDonald and The Colorful World of Travis McGee*, 30–34.

Purple Place forDying (1964)

Campbell, Frank D., Jr. *John D. MacDonald and The Colorful World of Travis McGee*, 9–12.

Quick Red Fox (1964)

Campbell, Frank D., Jr. *John D. MacDonald and The Colorful World of Travis McGee*, 12–16.

Scarlet Ruse (1973)

Campbell, Frank D., Jr. *John D. MacDonald and The Colorful World of Travis McGee*, 49–52.

Tan and Sandy Silence (1971)

Campbell, Frank D., Jr. *John D. MacDonald and The Colorful World of Travis McGee*, 45–49.

Turquoise Lament (1973)

Campbell, Frank D., Jr. *John D. MacDonald and The Colorful World of Travis McGee*, 52–56.

MACDONALD, JOHN ROSS see MACDONALD, ROSS

MACDONALD, ROSS (1915–1983)

Black Money (1966)
> Speir, Jerry. *Ross Macdonald*, 80–85, 132, 133.
> Wolfe, Peter. *Dreamers Who Live Their Dreams*, 259–273.

Blue City (1947)
> Speir, Jerry. *Ross Macdonald*, 17–20, 135.
> Wolfe, Peter. *Dreamers Who Live Their Dreams*, 86–92.

Blue Hammer (1976)
> Speir, Jerry. *Ross Macdonald*, 104–108, 134–135, 136–137, 140, 147–149.

Chill (1964)
> Speir, Jerry. *Ross Macdonald*, 67–78, 129, 133, 134, 135.
> Wolfe, Peter. *Dreamers Who Live Their Dreams*, 232–246.

Dark Tunnel (1944)
> Speir, Jerry. *Ross Macdonald*, 13–16, 135.
> Wolfe, Peter. *Dreamers Who Live Their Dreams*, 69–77.

Doomsters (1958)
> Speir, Jerry. *Ross Macdonald*, 40–47, 129, 131, 132, 135, 145, 150.
> Wolfe, Peter. *Dreamers Who Live Their Dreams*, 167–178.

Drowning Pool (1950)
> Speir, Jerry. *Ross Macdonald*, 27–29, 130, 135.
> Wolfe, Peter. *Dreamers Who Live Their Dreams*, 112–121.

Far Side of the Dollar (1965)
> Speir, Jerry. *Ross Macdonald*, 78–79.
> Wolfe, Peter. *Dreamers Who Live Their Dreams*, 246–259.

Ferguson Affair (1960)
> Speir, Jerry. *Ross Macdonald*, 55–58.
> Wolfe, Peter. *Dreamers Who Live Their Dreams*, 191–205.

Find a Victim (1954)
> Speir, Jerry. *Ross Macdonald*, 36–37, 129, 139–140.
> Wolfe, Peter. *Dreamers Who Live Their Dreams*, 146–155.

Galton Case (1959)
> Speir, Jerry. *Ross Macdonald*, 48–54, 131, 133, 135, 151–152.
> Wolfe, Peter. *Dreamers Who Live Their Dreams*, 178–191.

Goodbye Look (1969)
> Speir, Jerry. *Ross Macdonald*, 87–95, 128.
> Wolfe, Peter. *Dreamers Who Live Their Dreams*, 290–305.

Instant Enemy (1968)
> Speir, Jerry. *Ross Macdonald*, 85–87, 137.
> Wolfe, Peter. *Dreamers Who Live Their Dreams*, 276–289.

Ivory Grin (1952)
> Speir, Jerry. *Ross Macdonald*, 32–34, 129.
> Wolfe, Peter. *Dreamers Who Live Their Dreams*, 128–136.

Meet Me at the Morgue (1953)

Speir, Jerry. *Ross Macdonald*, 34–36, 131.
Wolfe, Peter. *Dreamers Who Live Their Dreams*, 136–146.

Moving Target (1949)

Speir, Jerry. *Ross Macdonald*, 24–27, 132, 135–136.
Wolfe, Peter. *Dreamers Who Live Their Dreams*, 104–112.

Sleeping Beauty (1973)

Speir, Jerry. *Ross Macdonald*, 102–104.
Wolfe, Peter. *Dreamers Who Live Their Dreams*, 321–337.

Three Roads (1948)

Speir, Jerry. *Ross Macdonald*, 20–24, 130–131, 132, 147.
Wolfe, Peter. *Dreamers Who Live Their Dreams*, 92–102.

Trouble Follows Me (1946)

Speir, Jerry. *Ross Macdonald*, 16–17.
Wolfe, Peter. *Dreamers Who Live Their Dreams*, 77–86.

Underground Man (1971)

Speir, Jerry. *Ross Macdonald*, 95–102, 129, 132, 143–145.
Wolfe, Peter. *Dreamers Who Live Their Dreams*, 306–321.

Way Some People Die (1951)

Speir, Jerry. *Ross Macdonald*, 29–32.
Wolfe, Peter. *Dreamers Who Live Their Dreams*, 121–1128.

Wycherly Woman (1961)

Speir, Jerry. *Ross Macdonald*, 58–60, 136.
Wolfe, Peter. *Dreamers Who Live Their Dreams*, 207–218.

Zebra-Striped Hearse (1962)

Speir, Jerry. *Ross Macdonald*, 60–67, 128, 131, 133, 140–141, 145–147, 158.
Wolfe, Peter. *Dreamers Who Live Their Dreams*, 218–232.

MCDOUGALL, COLIN (1917–1984)

Execution (1958)

Jones, D. G. *Butterfly on Rock*, 141–143.
Sutherland, Ronald. *New Hero*, 33–34, 35, 36–37.
Sutherland, Ronald. *Second Image*, 139–142.

MCDOWELL, CATHERINE see BONNER, SHERWOOD

MACEWEN, GWENDOLYN (1941–1987)

Julian the Magician (1963)

Gose, E. B. "They Shall Have Arcana," in Woodcock, George, ed. *Canadian Novel*, 328–336.

MCGUANE, THOMAS (1939–)

Bushwhacked Piano (1971)
  Carter, Albert Howard, III. "McGuane's First Three Novels: Games, Fun, Nemesis." *Crit* 17.1 (1975): 95–99.

Ninety-two in the Shade (1973)
  Carter, Albert Howard, III. "McGuane's First Three Novels: Games, Fun, Nemesis." *Crit* 17.1 (1975): 99–102.

Sporting Club (1968)
  Carter, Albert Howard, III. "McGuane's First Three Novels: Games, Fun, Nemesis." *Crit* 17.1 (1975): 91–95.

MCINTOSH, MARIA (1803–1878)

Charms and Counter-Charms (1848)
  Baym, Nina. *Woman's Fiction*, 93–96.

Lofty and the Lowly (1853)
  Baym, Nina. *Woman's Fiction*, 97–101.

Two Lives (1846)
  Baym, Nina. *Woman's Fiction*, 91–93.

Two Pictures (1863)
  Baym, Nina. *Woman's Fiction*, 104–109.

Violet (1856)
  Baym, Nina. *Woman's Fiction*, 101–103.

Woman an Enigma (1843)
  Baym, Nina. *Woman's Fiction*, 87–91.

MCKAY, CLAUDE (1890–1948)

Banana Bottom (1933)
  Davis, Arthur P. *From the Dark Tower*, 42.
  Gayle, Addison, Jr. *Way of the New World*, 133–134.
  Giles, James R. *Claude McKay*, 94–108.
  Priebe, Richard. "Search for Community in the Novels of Claude McKay." *SIBL* 3.2 (1972): 22, 27–29.
  Ramchand, Kenneth. "Claude McKay and *Banana Bottom*." *SoR* 4 (1970): 53–66.
  Singh, Amritjit. *Novels of the Harlem Renaissance*, 53–55, 57.
  Stoff, Michael B. "Claude McKay and the Cult of Primitivism," in Bontemps, Arna, ed. *Harlem Renaissance Remembered*, 139–142.

Banjo (1929)
  Berghahn, Marion. *Images of Africa in Black American Literature*, 149–150.
  Davis, Arthur P. *From the Dark Tower*, 41–42.
  Fabre, Michel. "Aesthetics and Ideology in *Banjo*," in Durand, Régis, ed. *Myth and Ideology in American Culture*, 197–208.

Giles, James R. *Claude McKay*, 84–94.

Perry, Margaret. *Silence to the Drums*, 71–72.

Priebe, Richard. "Search for Community in the Novels of Claude McKay." *SIBL* 3.2 (1972): 25–27.

Singh, Amritjit. *Novels of the Harlem Renaissance*, 47–53, 57–58, 59.

Stoff, Michael B. "Claude McKay and the Cult of Primitivism," in Bontemps, Arna, ed. *Harlem Renaissance Remembered*, 134–139.

Home to Harlem (1928)

Barksdale, Richard K. "Symbolism and Irony in McKay's *Home to Harlem*." *CLAJ* 15 (1972): 338–344.

Berghahn, Marion. *Images of Africa in Black American Literature*, 146–147.

Couch, William, Jr. "Image of the Black Soldier in Selected American Novels." *CLAJ* 20 (1976): 181.

Davis, Arthur P. *From the Dark Tower*, 39–41.

Gayle, Addison, Jr. *Way of the New World*, 130–132.

Giles, James R. *Claude McKay*, 73–84.

Klotman, Phyllis Rauch. *Another Man Gone*, 130.

Larson, Charles R. "Three Harlem Novels of the Jazz Age." *Crit* 11.3 (1969): 66–70.

Perry, Margaret. *Silence to the Drums*, 70–71.

Priebe, Richard. "Search for Community in the Novels of Claude McKay." *SIBL* 3.2 (1972): 23–25.

Rosenblatt, Roger. *Black Fiction*, 90–97.

Singh, Amritjit. *Novels of the Harlem Renaissance*, 43–44, 47, 48, 50, 51, 56, 57, 58–59.

Starke, Catherine Juanita. *Black Portraiture in American Fiction*, 149–151.

Stoff, Michael B. "Claude McKay and the Cult of Primitivism," in Bontemps, Arna, ed. *Harlem Renaissance Remembered*, 130–134.

MACLENNAN, HUGH (1907–1990)

Barometer Rising (1941)

Boeschenstein, Hermann. "Hugh MacLennan, a Canadian Novelist," in Goetsch, Paul, ed. *Hugh MacLennan*, 36–38.

Buitenhuis, Peter. *Hugh MacLennan*, 19–29.

Cockburn, Robert H. *Novels of Hugh MacLennan*, 29–45.

Goetsch, Paul. "Too Long to the Courtly Muses: Hugh MacLennan as a Contemporary Writer," in Woodcock, George, ed. *Canadian Novel*, 103–105.

Lucas, Alec. *Hugh MacLennan*, 47–48.

Lucas, Alec. "Hugh MacLennan," in Lucas, Alec. *Hugh MacLennan*. Toronto: McClelland and Stewart, 1970. Rpt. in Gerson, Carole, comp. *Modern Canadian Fiction*, 68.

MacLulich, T. D. "Oedipus and Eve: The Novels of Hugh MacLennan." *DR* 59 (1979): 505–507, 517–518.

McPherson, Hugo. "Novels of Hugh MacLennan." *Queens Quarterly* 60 (Summer 1953): 186–198. Rpt. in Goetsch, Paul, ed. *Hugh MacLennan*, 24–26.

Mathews, Robin. *Canadian Literature*, 78–87.

Morley, Patricia A. *Immoral Moralists*, 38–51, 53–61, 131.

New, W. H. *Articulating West*, 95–107.

New, William H. "Storm and After: Imagery and Symbolism in Hugh MacLennan's *Barometer Rising.*" *Queens Quarterly* 74 (Summer 1967): 302–312. Rpt. in Goetsch, Paul, ed. *Hugh MacLennan*, 75–86.

O'Donnell, Kathleen. "Wanderer in *Barometer Rising.*" *University of Windsor Review* 3 (Spring 1968): 12–18. Rpt. in Goetsch, Paul, ed. *Hugh MacLennan*, 89–96.

Staines, David. "Mapping the Terrain." *Mosaic* 11.3 (1978): 141–143.

Staines, David. "Mapping the Terrain," in Wortley, John, ed. *Post-War Canadian Fiction*, 141–143.

Woodcock, George. *Hugh MacLennan*, 55–68.

Woodcock, George. "Hugh MacLennan." *Northern Review* 3 (April-May 1950): 2–10. Rpt. in Goetsch, Paul, ed. *Hugh MacLennan*, 11–16.

Woodcock, George. "A Nation's Odyssey: the Novels of Hugh MacLennan," in Smith, A. J. N., ed. *Masks of Fiction*. Toronto: McClelland and Stewart, 1961. Rpt. in Gerson, Carole, comp. *Modern Canadian Fiction*, 60–62.

Woodcock, George. *Odysseus Ever Returning*, 12–16.

Each Man's Son (1951)

Boeschenstein, Hermann. "Hugh MacLennan, a Canadian Novelist," in Goetsch, Paul, ed. *Hugh MacLennan*, 47–49.

Buitenhuis, Peter. *Hugh MacLennan*, 46–55.

Cockburn, Robert H. *Novels of Hugh MacLennan*, 89–108.

Davis, Marilyn J. "Fathers and Sons." *CanL* 58 (1973): 41–49.

Goetsch, Paul. "Too Long to the Courtly Muses: Hugh MacLennan as a Contemporary Writer," in Woodcock, George, ed. *Canadian Novel*, 107–109.

Jones, D. G. *Butterfly on Rock*, 62–65.

Lucas, Alec. *Hugh MacLennan*, 21, 22, 24–25, 48.

Lucas, Alec. "Hugh MacLennan," in Lucas, Alec. *Hugh MacLennan*. Toronto: McClelland and Stewart, 1970. Rpt. in Gerson, Carole, comp. *Modern Canadian Fiction*, 68–69.

MacLulich, T. D. "Oedipus and Eve: The Novels of Hugh MacLennan." *DR* 59 (1979): 508–511, 517–518.

McPherson, Hugo. "Novels of Hugh MacLennan." *Queens Quarterly* 60 (Summer 1953): 186–198. Rpt. in Goetsch, Paul, ed. *Hugh MacLennan*, 30–33.

Marshall, Joyce. "*Each Man's Son.*" *Canadian Forum* 31, Sept. 1951. Rpt. in Gerson, Carole, comp. *Modern Canadian Fiction*, 59.

Morley, Patricia A. *Immoral Moralists*, 4–6, 63–71, 132.

Morley, Patricia A. "Need and the Allness of Love," in Morley, Patricia A. *Immoral Moralists*. Toronto: Clarke Irwin and Company, 1972. Rpt. in Gerson, Carole, comp. *Modern Canadian Fiction*, 70–74.

Seaman, Andrew Thompson. "Fiction in Atlantic Canada." *CanL* 68–69 (1976): 33–35.

Staines, David. "Mapping the Terrain." *Mosaic* 11.3 (1978): 148–149.

Staines, David. "Mapping the Terrain," in Wortley, John, ed. *Post-War Canadian Fiction*, 148–149.

Tallman, Warren. "Wolf in the Snow." *Canadian Literature* 5 (Summer 1960): 7–20 & *Canadian Literature* 6 (Autumn 1960): 41–48. Rpt. in Cook, Gregory M., ed. *Ernest Buckler*, 67–71, 72–74.

Tallman, Warren. "Wolf in the Snow." *Canadian Literature* 5 (Summer 1960): 7–20 & *Canadian Literature* 6 (Autumn 1960): 41–48. Rpt. in Gerson, Carole, comp. *Modern Canadian Fiction*, 101–102, 103–105, 106.

Woodcock, George. *Hugh MacLennan*, 90–99.
Woodcock, George. "A Nation's Odyssey: the Novels of Hugh MacLennan," in Smith, A. J. N., ed. *Masks of Fiction*. Toronto: McClelland and Stewart, 1961. Rpt. in Gerson, Carole, comp. *Modern Canadian Fiction*, 64.
Woodcock, George. *Odysseus Ever Returning*, 19–21.

Man Should Rejoice (unpublished novel completed in 1937)

Staines, David. "Mapping the Terrain." *Mosaic* 11.3 (1978): 139–141.
Staines, David. "Mapping the Terrain," in Wortley, John, ed. *Post-War Canadian Fiction*, 139–140.

Precipice (1948)

Boeschenstein, Hermann. "Hugh MacLennan, a Canadian Novelist," in Goetsch, Paul, ed. *Hugh MacLennan*, 45–47.
Buitenhuis, Peter. *Hugh MacLennan*, 40–46.
Cameron, Elspeth. "Ordeal by Fire: The Genesis of MacLennan's *The Precipice*." *CanL* 82 (1979): 35–46.
Cockburn, Robert H. *Novels of Hugh MacLennan*, 71–88.
Goetsch, Paul. "Too Long to the Courtly Muses: Hugh MacLennan as a Contemporary Writer," in Woodcock, George, ed. *Canadian Novel*, 106–107.
Lucas, Alec. *Hugh MacLennan*, 52–53.
MacLulich, T. D. "Oedipus and Eve: The Novels of Hugh MacLennan." *DR* 59 (1979): 507–508, 517–518.
McPherson, Hugo. "Novels of Hugh MacLennan." *Queens Quarterly* 60 (Summer 1953): 186–198. Rpt. in Goetsch, Paul, ed. *Hugh MacLennan*, 28–30.
Morley, Patricia A. *Immoral Moralists*, 5–6, 38–51, 53–61, 132.
Spettigue, Douglas. "Beauty and the Beast." *Queen's Quarterly* 74 (1967): 762–765. Rpt. in Goetsch, Paul, ed. *Hugh MacLennan*, 158.
Staines, David. "Mapping the Terrain." *Mosaic* 11.3 (1978): 145–148.
Staines, David. "Mapping the Terrain," in Wortley, John, ed. *Post-War Canadian Fiction*, 145–148.
Woodcock, George. *Hugh MacLennan*, 81–89.
Woodcock, George. "Hugh MacLennan." *Northern Review* 3 (April-May 1950): 2–10. Rpt. in Goetsch, Paul, ed. *Hugh MacLennan*, 19–20.
Woodcock, George. "A Nation's Odyssey: the Novels of Hugh MacLennan," in Smith, A. J. N., ed. *Masks of Fiction*. Toronto: McClelland and Stewart, 1961. Rpt. in Gerson, Carole, comp. *Modern Canadian Fiction*, 63–64.
Woodcock, George. *Odysseus Ever Returning*, 18–19.

Return of the Sphinx (1967)

Buitenhuis, Peter. *Hugh MacLennan*, 64–72.
Cockburn, Robert H. *Novels of Hugh MacLennan*, 127–144.
Jones, D. G. *Butterfly on Rock*, 84–85.
Lucas, Alec. *Hugh MacLennan*, 26–28, 48, 50, 51, 53–54.
MacLulich, T. D. "Oedipus and Eve: The Novels of Hugh MacLennan." *DR* 59 (1979): 515–518.
Mathews, Robin. *Canadian Literature*, 87–90.
Morley, Patricia A. *Immoral Moralists*, 110–124, 132, 133, 136.
Moss, John. *Sex and Violence*, 105.
New, W. H. *Articulating West*, 128–138.

New, William H. "Winter and the Night-People." *Canadian Literature* 36 (Spring 1968): 26–33. Rpt. in Goetsch, Paul, ed. *Hugh MacLennan*, 166–172.

Spettigue, Douglas. "Beauty and the Beast." *Queen's Quarterly* 74 (1967): 762–765. Rpt. in Goetsch, Paul, ed. *Hugh MacLennan*, 159–160.

Staines, David. "Mapping the Terrain." *Mosaic* 11.3 (1978): 149–150.

Sutherland, Ronald. "Fourth Separatism." *CanL* 45 (1970): 15–21.

Sutherland, Ronald. *Second Image*, 123–134.

Woodcock, George. *Hugh MacLennan*, 111–118.

So All Their Praises (unpublished novel completed in 1934)

Staines, David. "Mapping the Terrain." *Mosaic* 11.3 (1978): 138–139.

Staines, David. "Mapping the Terrain," in Wortley, John, ed. *Post-War Canadian Fiction*, 138–139.

Two Solitudes (1945)

Boeschenstein, Hermann. "Hugh MacLennan, a Canadian Novelist," in Goetsch, Paul, ed. *Hugh MacLennan*, 39–44.

Buitenhuis, Peter. *Hugh MacLennan*, 29–39.

Chambers, Robert. "Novels of Hugh MacLennan." *Journal of Canadian Studies* 2 (August 1967): 3–11. Rpt. in Goetsch, Paul, ed. *Hugh MacLennan*, 63–65.

Cockburn, Robert H. *Novels of Hugh MacLennan*, 47–69.

Goetsch, Paul. "Too Long to the Courtly Muses: Hugh MacLennan as a Contemporary Writer," in Woodcock, George, ed. *Canadian Novel*, 105–106.

Kelly, Sister Catherine. "Unity of *Two Solitudes*." *Ariel* 6.2 (1975): 38–61.

MacLulich, T. D. "Oedipus and Eve: The Novels of Hugh MacLennan." *DR* 59 (1979): 507–508, 517–518.

McPherson, Hugo. "Novels of Hugh MacLennan." *Queens Quarterly* 60 (Summer 1953): 186–198. Rpt. in Goetsch, Paul, ed. *Hugh MacLennan*, 26–28.

Mathews, Robin D. "Wacousta Factor," in Bessai, Diane and David Jackel, eds. *Figures in a Ground*, 314.

Morley, Patricia A. *Immoral Moralists*, 38–51, 53–61, 131–132, 136.

Staines, David. "Mapping the Terrain." *Mosaic* 11.3 (1978): 143–145.

Staines, David. "Mapping the Terrain," in Wortley, John, ed. *Post-War Canadian Fiction*, 143–145.

Stevenson, Warren. "Neglected Theme in *Two Solitudes*." *CanL* 75 (1977): 53–60.

Sutherland, Ronald. *Second Image*, 55–56.

Woodcock, George. *Hugh MacLennan*, 69–80.

Woodcock, George. "Hugh MacLennan." *Northern Review* 3 (April–May 1950): 2–10. Rpt. in Goetsch, Paul, ed. *Hugh MacLennan*, 17–19.

Woodcock, George. "A Nation's Odyssey: the Novels of Hugh MacLennan," in Smith, A. J. N., ed. *Masks of Fiction*. Toronto: McClelland and Stewart, 1961. Rpt. in Gerson, Carole, comp. *Modern Canadian Fiction*, 62–63.

Woodcock, George. *Odysseus Ever Returning*, 17–18.

Watch That Ends the Night (1959)

Boeschenstein, Hermann. "Hugh MacLennan, a Canadian Novelist," in Goetsch, Paul, ed. *Hugh MacLennan*, 50–56.

Buitenhuis, Peter. *Hugh MacLennan*, 55–64.

Chambers, Robert. "Novels of Hugh MacLennan." *Journal of Canadian Studies* 2 (August 1967): 3–11. Rpt. in Goetsch, Paul, ed. *Hugh MacLennan*, 67–72.

Cockburn, Robert H. *Novels of Hugh MacLennan*, 109–126.

Dooley, D. J. *Moral Vision*, 80–92.

Farmiloe, Dorothy. "Hugh MacLennan and the Canadian Myth." *Mosaic* 2.3 (1969): 1–9.

Farmiloe, Dorothy. "Hugh MacLennan and the Canadian Myth." *Mosaic* 2–3 (Spring 1969): 1–9. Rpt. in Goetsch, Paul, ed. *Hugh MacLennan*, 145–154.

Goetsch, Paul. "Too Long to the Courtly Muses: Hugh MacLennan as a Contemporary Writer," in Woodcock, George, ed. *Canadian Novel*, 109–111.

Harrison, Dick. "American Adam and the Canadian Christ." *TCL* 16 (1970): 162.

Jones, D. G. *Butterfly on Rock*, 140, 157–162.

Lucas, Alec. *Hugh MacLennan*, 21–23, 25–26, 54–55.

MacLulich, T. D. "Oedipus and Eve: The Novels of Hugh MacLennan." *DR* 59 (1979): 512–515, 517–518.

Merivale, Patricia. "Biographical Compulsion: Elegiac Romances in Canadian Fiction." *JML* 8 (1980): 141–148, 151–152.

Morley, Patricia A. *Immoral Moralists*, 98–108, 133–134, 135–136.

Moss, John. *Sex and Violence*, 95–101.

New, W. H. *Articulating West*, 116–127.

Ross, Catherine Sheldrick. "Hugh MacLennan's Two Worlds." *CanL* 80 (1979): 5–12.

Spettigue, Douglas. "Beauty and the Beast." *Queen's Quarterly* 74 (1967): 762–765. Rpt. in Goetsch, Paul, ed. *Hugh MacLennan*, 159.

Staines, David. "Mapping the Terrain." *Mosaic* 11.3 (1978): 149.

Sutherland, Ronald. *Second Image*, 11–16, 151–153.

Thorne, W. B. "Relation of Structure to Theme in *The Watch That Ends the Night*." *Humanities Association Bulletin* 20 (1969): 42–45. Rpt. in Goetsch, Paul, ed. *Hugh MacLennan*, 139–143.

Thorne, William B. "Relation of Structure to Theme in *The Watch That Ends the Night*." *HAR* 20.2 (1969): 42–45.

Woodcock, George. *Hugh MacLennan*, 100–110.

Woodcock, George. "A Nation's Odyssey: the Novels of Hugh MacLennan," in Smith, A. J. N., ed. *Masks of Fiction*. Toronto: McClelland and Stewart, 1961. Rpt. in Gerson, Carole, comp. *Modern Canadian Fiction*, 64–66.

Woodcock, George. *Odysseus Ever Returning*, 21–23.

MCMURTRY, LARRY (1936–)

All My Friends Are Going to Be Strangers (1972)

Neinstein, Raymond L. *Ghost Country*, 39–47.

Peavy, Charles D. *Larry McMurtry*, 41–44, 68–69, 73–74.

Stout, Janis P. "Journeying as a Metaphor for Cultural Loss in the Novels of Larry McMurtry." *WAL* 11 (1976): 38, 47–48.

Horseman, Pass By (1958)

Ahearn, Kerry. "More D'Urban: The Texas Novels of Larry McMurtry." *Texas Quarterly* 19.3 (1976): 109–129. Rpt. in Pilkington, William T., ed. *Critical Essays on the Western American Novel*, 224–227.

Landess, Thomas. *Larry McMurtry*, 5–14.

Neinstein, Raymond L. *Ghost Country*, 1–10.

Peavy, Charles D. *Larry McMurtry*, 28–31, 46–48, 57–60, 66, 79–80.

Stout, Janis P. "Journeying as a Metaphor for Cultural Loss in the Novels of Larry McMurtry." *WAL* 11 (1976): 38, 39–40.

Hud see *Horseman, Pass By*

Last Picture Show (1966)

Ahearn, Kerry. "More D'Urban: The Texas Novels of Larry McMurtry." *Texas Quarterly* 19.3 (1976): 109–129. Rpt. in Pilkington, William T., ed. *Critical Essays on the Western American Novel*, 229–233.

Landess, Thomas. *Larry McMurtry*, 22–30.

Neinstein, Raymond L. *Ghost Country*, 17–25.

Peavy, Charles D. *Larry McMurtry*, 34–36, 52–57, 60–63, 67, 72–73, 75–76, 78, 80, 102–105.

Stout, Janis P. "Journeying as a Metaphor for Cultural Loss in the Novels of Larry McMurtry." *WAL* 11 (1976): 38, 42–44, 48.

Leaving Cheyenne (1962)

Ahearn, Kerry. "More D'Urban: The Texas Novels of Larry McMurtry." *Texas Quarterly* 19.3 (1976): 109–129. Rpt. in Pilkington, William T., ed. *Critical Essays on the Western American Novel*, 227–229.

Landess, Thomas. *Larry McMurtry*, 14–22.

Neinstein, Raymond L. *Ghost Country*, 11–16.

Peavy, Charles D. *Larry McMurtry*, 31–34, 48–52, 66–67, 78.

Stout, Janis P. "Journeying as a Metaphor for Cultural Loss in the Novels of Larry McMurtry." *WAL* 11 (1976): 38, 40–42, 48.

Moving On (1970)

Ahearn, Kerry. "More D'Urban: The Texas Novels of Larry McMurtry." *Texas Quarterly* 19.3 (1976): 109–129. Rpt. in Pilkington, William T., ed. *Critical Essays on the Western American Novel*, 233–237.

Neinstein, Raymond L. *Ghost Country*, 27–39.

Peavy, Charles D. *Larry McMurtry*, 38–41, 67–68, 76–77, 78, 80, 80–83.

Stout, Janis P. "Journeying as a Metaphor for Cultural Loss in the Novels of Larry McMurtry." *WAL* 11 (1976): 38, 44–47.

Terms of Endearment (1975)

Peavy, Charles D. *Larry McMurtry*, 44–45, 69, 74–75.

MCNICKLE, D'ARCY (1904–1977)

Surrounded (1936)

Larson, Charles R. *American Indian Fiction*, 66–78, 95–96.

Oaks, Priscilla. "First Generation of Native American Novelists." *MELUS* 5.1 (1978): 60–63.

MADDEN, DAVID (1933–)

Cassandra Singing (1969)

Pinsker, Sanford. *Between Two Worlds*, 103–114.

Pinsker, Sanford. "Mixed Cords of David Madden's *Cassandra Singing*." *Crit* 15.2 (1973): 15–26.

MAHEUX-FORCIER, LOUISE (1929–)

Appassionata (1978)

Poulin, Gabrielle. *Romans du pays*, 357–363.

MAILER, NORMAN (1923–)

American Dream (1965)

Adams, Laura. *Existential Battles*, 70–97.

Alter, Robert. "Norman Mailer," in Panichas, George A., ed. *Politics of Twentieth-Century Novelists*, 329–331.

Bailey, Jennifer. *Norman Mailer*, 54–67.

Begiebing, Robert J. *Acts of Regeneration*, 58–88.

Bersani, Leo. "Interpretation of Dreams." (Review of *An American Dream*) *Partisan Review* 32.4 (Fall 1965): 603–608. Rpt. in Braudy, Leo, ed. *Norman Mailer: A Collection of Critical Essays*, 120–126.

Boyers, Robert. "Attitudes Toward Sex in American 'High Culture.' " *Annals of the American Academy of Political and Social Science* (March 1968). Rpt. in Boyers, Robert. *Excursions*, 111–115.

Braudy, Leo. "Introduction, Norman Mailer: The Pride and the Vulnerability," in Braudy, Leo, ed. *Norman Mailer: A Collection of Critical Essays*, 5–6.

Bryant, Jerry H. *Open Decision*, 371–373, 383–388.

Bufithis, Philip H. *Norman Mailer*, 65–74.

Fetterley, Judith. *Resisting Reader*, 154–189.

Finholt, Richard. *American Visionary Fiction*, 112–127.

Gindin, James. *Harvest of a Quiet Eye*, 355.

Gindin, James. "Megalotopia and the WASP Backlash: The Fiction of Mailer and Updike." *CentR* 15 (1971): 41–42.

Gordon, Andrew. *American Dreamer*, 129–169.

Guttmann, Allen. *Jewish Writer in America*, 163–165.

Hendin, Josephine. *Vulnerable People*, 124–126.

Kaufmann, Donald L. *Norman Mailer*, 35–50, 51, 76–83, 91–97, 123–128, 132–142, 144–148.

Leeds, Barry H. *Structured Vision of Norman Mailer*, 125–176.

Lehan, Richard. *Dangerous Crossing*, 89–93.

McConnell, Frank D. *Four Postwar American Novelists*, 94–100.

Masinton, Martha and Charles G. Masinton. "Second-class Citizenship: The Status of Women in Contemporary American Fiction," in Springer, Marlene, ed. *What Manner of Woman*, 300–302.

May, Keith M. *Out of the Maelstrom*, 117.

Merrill, Robert. *Norman Mailer*, 67–78.

Nikolyukin, A. N. "Realism and Modernism in the Works of Norman Mailer," in Proffer, Carl R., ed. and trans. *Soviet Criticism of American Literature in the Sixties*, 75–79.

Radford, Jean. *Norman Mailer*, 33–37, 101–110, 148–155.

Rahv, Philip. *Essays on Literature and Politics*, 67–74.

Rahv, Philip. *Literature and the Sixth Sense*, 409–416.

Rose, Alan Henry. *Demonic Vision*, 132.

Schulz, Max F. *Radical Sophistication*, 90–99.

Scott, Nathan A., Jr. *Three American Moralists*, 56–70.

Sheridan, James J. "Mailer's *An American Dream*." *Expl* 34 (1975): Item 8.

Tanner, Tony. *City of Words*, 356–366.

Tanner, Tony. "On the Parapet: A Study of the Novels of Norman Mailer." *CritQ* 12 (1970): 161–171.

Weinberg, Helen A. "Activist Norman Mailer," in Malin, Irving, ed. *Contemporary American-Jewish Literature*, 84

Armies of the Night (1968)

Adams, Laura. *Existential Battles*, 99–100, 121–136.

Alter, Robert. "Norman Mailer," in Panichas, George A., ed. *Politics of Twentieth-Century Novelists*, 333–334.

Bailey, Jennifer. *Norman Mailer*, 81–94.

Begiebing, Robert J. *Acts of Regeneration*, 141–165.

Berthoff, Warner. "Witness and Testament: Two Contemporary Classics," in Miller, J. Hillis, ed. *Aspects of Narrative*, 192–197.

Berthoff, Warner. "Witness and Testament: Two Contemporary Classics." *New Literary History* (Winter 1971). Rpt. in Bertfhoff, Warner. *Fictions and Events*, 301–308.

Bufithis, Philip H. *Norman Mailer*, 86–94.

Cowan, Michael. "Americanness of Norman Mailer," in Braudy, Leo, ed. *Norman Mailer: A Collection of Critical Essays*, 149–150, 151, 152.

Gindin, James. *Harvest of a Quiet Eye*, 353–354.

Gindin, James. "Megalotopia and the WASP Backlash: The Fiction of Mailer and Updike." *CentR* 15 (1971): 42–43, 50.

Gordon, Andrew. *American Dreamer*, 186–205.

Guttmann, Allen. *Jewish Writer in America*, 168–170.

Henderson, Harry B. *Versions of the Past*, 300–304.

Hollowell, John. *Fact & Fiction*, 90–101.

Leeds, Barry H. *Structured Vision of Norman Mailer*, 247–254, 258–262.

McConnell, Frank D. *Four Postwar American Novelists*, 105–106.

Merrill, Robert. *Norman Mailer*, 110–128.

Radford, Jean. *Norman Mailer*, 72–74, 117–120.

Widmer, Kingsley. "Post-Modernist Art of Protest: Kesey and Mailer as American Expressions of Rebellion." *CentR* 19.3 (1975): 131–135.

Barbary Shore (1951)

Adams, Laura. *Existential Battles*, 39–42.

Alter, Robert. "Norman Mailer," in Panichas, George A., ed. *Politics of Twentieth-Century Novelists*, 323–325.

Bailey, Jennifer. *Norman Mailer*, 16–20.

Begiebing, Robert J. *Acts of Regeneration*, 13–32.

Braudy, Leo. "Introduction, Norman Mailer: The Pride and the Vulnerability," in Braudy, Leo, ed. *Norman Mailer: A Collection of Critical Essays*, 3–4.

Bryant, Jerry H. *Open Decision*, 370, 374–376.

Bufithis, Philip H. *Norman Mailer*, 31–38.

Dienstfrey, Harris. "Fiction of Norman Mailer," in Kostelanetz, Richard, ed. *On Contemporary Literature*, 425–429.

Gindin, James. "Megalotopia and the WASP Backlash: The Fiction of Mailer and Updike." *CentR* 15 (1971): 39–40.

Gordon, Andrew. *American Dreamer*, 73–85.

Guttmann, Allen. *Jewish Writer in America*, 157–159.
Hoffa, William. "Norman Mailer: *Advertisements for Myself*, or, A Portrait of the Artist as a Disgruntled Counter-Puncher," in French, Warren, ed. *Fifties*, 75–77.
Howe, Irving. *Celebrations and Attacks*, 39–40.
Kaufmann, Donald L. *Norman Mailer*, 12–23, 53–57, 72–73, 115–117.
Leeds, Barry H. *Structured Vision of Norman Mailer*, 53–100.
Lehan, Richard. *Dangerous Crossing*, 84–86.
McConnell, Frank D. *Four Postwar American Novelists*, 80–87.
Radford, Jean. *Norman Mailer*, 16–19, 50–54, 82–85, 130–132.
Schulz, Max F. *Radical Sophistication*, 73–81.
Scott, Nathan A., Jr. *Three American Moralists*, 30–39.
Tanner, Tony. *City of Words*, 351–352.
Tanner, Tony. "On the Parapet: A Study of the Novels of Norman Mailer." *CritQ* 12 (1970): 155–156.
Trilling, Diana. "Radical Moralism of Norman Mailer," in Trilling, Diana. *Claremont Essays*. New York: Harcourt Brace Jovanovich, Inc., 1962. 175–202. Rpt. in Braudy, Leo, ed. *Norman Mailer: A Collection of Critical Essays*, 50–52, 53.
Weinberg, Helen A. "Activist Norman Mailer," in Malin, Irving, ed. *Contemporary American-Jewish Literature*, 83.

Deer Park (1955)

Alter, Robert. "Norman Mailer," in Panichas, George A., ed. *Politics of Twentieth-Century Novelists*, 325–329.
Bailey, Jennifer. *Norman Mailer*, 23–29.
Begiebing, Robert J. *Acts of Regeneration*, 33–57.
Bryant, Jerry H. *Open Decision*, 370–371, 376–383.
Bufithis, Philip H. *Norman Mailer*, 39–51.
Dienstfrey, Harris. "Fiction of Norman Mailer," in Kostelanetz, Richard, ed. *On Contemporary Literature*, 431–435.
Foster, Richard. "Norman Mailer," in Wright, George T., ed. *Seven American Stylists, From Poe to Mailer*, 246–250.
Gindin, James. "Megalotopia and the WASP Backlash: The Fiction of Mailer and Updike." *CentR* 15 (1971): 40.
Gordon, Andrew. *American Dreamer*, 95–111.
Guttmann, Allen. *Jewish Writer in America*, 159–160.
Hendin, Josephine. *Vulnerable People*, 121–124.
Hoffa, William. "Norman Mailer: *Advertisements for Myself*, or, A Portrait of the Artist as a Disgruntled Counter-Puncher," in French, Warren, ed. *Fifties*, 77–79.
Kaufmann, Donald L. *Norman Mailer*, 24–34, 58–59, 73–74, 117–120.
Leeds, Barry H. *Structured Vision of Norman Mailer*, 105–122.
Lehan, Richard. *Dangerous Crossing*, 86–89.
McConnell, Frank D. *Four Postwar American Novelists*, 87–94.
Merrill, Robert. *Norman Mailer*, 43–65.
Radford, Jean. *Norman Mailer*, 19–27, 55–57, 85–88, 132–140.
Schulz, Max F. *Radical Sophistication*, 81–90.
Scott, Nathan A., Jr. *Three American Moralists*, 39–46.
Tanner, Tony. *City of Words*, 352–355.
Tanner, Tony. "On the Parapet: A Study of the Novels of Norman Mailer." *CritQ* 12 (1970): 156–160.

Taylor, Robert, Jr. "Sounding the Trumpets of Defiance: Mark Twain and Norman Mailer." *MTJ* 16.3 (1972): 13.

Trilling, Diana. "Radical Moralism of Norman Mailer," in Trilling, Diana. *Claremont Essays*. New York: Harcourt Brace Jovanovich, Inc., 1962. 175–202. Rpt. in Braudy, Leo, ed. *Norman Mailer: A Collection of Critical Essays*, 54–57

Weinberg, Helen A. "Activist Norman Mailer," in Malin, Irving, ed. *Contemporary American-Jewish Literature*, 83–84.

Executioner's Song (1979)

Begiebing, Robert J. *Acts of Regeneration*, 186–191.

Hersey, John. "Legend on the License." *YR* 70 (1980): 13–22.

Naked and the Dead (1948)

Alter, Robert. "Norman Mailer," in Panichas, George A., ed. *Politics of Twentieth-Century Novelists*, 322–323.

Bailey, Jennifer. *Norman Mailer*, 9–16.

Bryant, Jerry H. *Open Decision*, 123–127, 130, 136–138, 373–374, 379.

Bufithis, Philip H. *Norman Mailer*, 15–29.

Cowan, Michael. "Americanness of Norman Mailer," in Braudy, Leo, ed. *Norman Mailer: A Collection of Critical Essays*, 147–148.

Craig, David and Michael Egan. *Extreme Situations*, 38–52.

Dienstfrey, Harris. "Fiction of Norman Mailer," in Kostelanetz, Richard, ed. *On Contemporary Literature*, 422–425.

Foster, Richard. "Norman Mailer," in Wright, George T., ed. *Seven American Stylists, From Poe to Mailer*, 240–246.

Gordon, Andrew. *American Dreamer*, 55–71.

Gordon, Andrew. "*Naked and the Dead:* The Triumph of Impotence." *L&P* 19.3 (1969): 3–13.

Guttmann, Allen. *Jewish Writer in America*, 154–157.

Hendin, Josephine. *Vulnerable People*, 118–121.

Jones, Peter G. *War and the Novelist*, 87–95.

Kaufmann, Donald L. *Norman Mailer*, 1–12, 51–53, 70–72, 112–115, 142–143.

Leeds, Barry H. *Structured Vision of Norman Mailer*, 9–51.

Lehan, Richard. *Dangerous Crossing*, 81–84.

McConnell, Frank D. *Four Postwar American Novelists*, 65–80.

May, Keith M. *Out of the Maelstrom*, 90–92.

Merrill, Robert. *Norman Mailer*, 25–42.

Miller, Wayne Charles. *Armed America, Its Face in Fiction*, 158–162.

Mudrick, Marvin. *On Culture and Literature*, 177–180.

Nikolyukin, A. N. "Realism and Modernism in the Works of Norman Mailer," in Proffer, Carl R., ed. and trans. *Soviet Criticism of American Literature in the Sixties*, 72–74.

Ousby, Ian. *Reader's Guide to Fifty American Novels*, 320–322.

Radford, Jean. *Norman Mailer*, 7–16, 44–50, 77–82, 124–130.

Scott, Nathan A., Jr. *Three American Moralists*, 23–30.

Tanner, Tony. *City of Words*, 349–351.

Tanner, Tony. "On the Parapet: A Study of the Novels of Norman Mailer." *CritQ* 12 (1970): 153–155.

Taylor, Robert, Jr. "Sounding the Trumpets of Defiance: Mark Twain and Norman Mailer." *MTJ* 16.3 (1972): 12–13.

Trilling, Diana. "Radical Moralism of Norman Mailer," in Trilling, Diana. *Clare-*

mont Essays. New York: Harcourt Brace Jovanovich, Inc., 1962. 175–202. Rpt. in Braudy, Leo, ed. *Norman Mailer: A Collection of Critical Essays*, 47–50, 53–54.
Waldmeir, Joseph J. *American Novels of the Second World War*, 109–118, 147–148.
Waldron, Randall H. "The Naked, the Dead, and the Machine: A New Look at Norman Mailer's First Novel." *PMLA* 87 (1972): 271–277.

Why Are We in Vietnam? (1967)

Adams, Laura. *Existential Battles*, 113–120.
Alter, Robert. "Norman Mailer," in Panichas, George A., ed. *Politics of Twentieth-Century Novelists*, 331–333.
Bailey, Jennifer. *Norman Mailer*, 71–81.
Begiebing, Robert J. *Acts of Regeneration*, 89–112.
Begiebing, Robert J. "Norman Mailer's *Why Are We in Vietnam?* The Ritual of Regeneration." *American Imago* 37 (1980): 12–37.
Bryant, Jerry H. *Open Decision*, 388–394.
Bufithis, Philip H. *Norman Mailer*, 75–84.
Cowan, Michael. "Americanness of Norman Mailer," in Braudy, Leo, ed. *Norman Mailer: A Collection of Critical Essays*, 148.
Edinger, Harry G. "Bears in Three Contemporary Fictions." *HAR* 28 (1977): 147–150.
Finholt, Richard. *American Visionary Fiction*, 112–127.
Foster, Richard. "Norman Mailer," in Wright, George T., ed. *Seven American Stylists, From Poe to Mailer*, 251–253.
Gindin, James. *Harvest of a Quiet Eye*, 355–356.
Gindin, James. "Megalotopia and the WASP Backlash: The Fiction of Mailer and Updike." *CentR* 15 (1971): 42, 50.
Gordon, Andrew. *American Dreamer*, 172–184.
Guttmann, Allen. *Jewish Writer in America*, 167–168.
Hassan, Ihab. "Focus on Norman Mailer's *Why Are We in Vietnam?*," in Madden, David, ed. *American Dreams, American Nightmares*, 197–203.
Jones, Peter G. *War and the Novelist*, 53–64, 152–157, 161.
Kelty, Jean McClure. "Cult of Kill in Adolescent Fiction." *EJ* 64.2 (1975): 60–61.
Leeds, Barry H. *Structured Vision of Norman Mailer*, 179–206.
Lehan, Richard. *Dangerous Crossing*, 93–95.
McConnell, Frank D. *Four Postwar American Novelists*, 100–105.
May, Keith M. *Out of the Maelstrom*, 117.
Merrill, Robert. *Norman Mailer*, 79–84.
Nikolyukin, A. N. "Realism and Modernism in the Works of Norman Mailer," in Proffer, Carl R., ed. and trans. *Soviet Criticism of American Literature in the Sixties*, 80–82.
Oates, Joyce Carol. *New Heaven, New Earth*, 188–203.
Radford, Jean. *Norman Mailer*, 37–41, 99–100, 115–116.
Scott, Nathan A., Jr. *Three American Moralists*, 70–81.
Tanner, Tony. *City of Words*, 366–370.
Tanner, Tony. "On the Parapet: A Study of the Novels of Norman Mailer." *CritQ* 12 (1970): 171–176.

MAILLET, ANDRÉE (1921–1995)

À la mémoire d'un héros (1975)

Poulin, Gabrielle. *Romans du pays*, 160–162.

Le miroir de Salomé (1977)

    Poulin, Gabrielle. *Romans du pays*, 167–173.

Lettres au surhomme (1976)

    Poulin, Gabrielle. *Romans du pays*, 163–166.

MAILLET, ANTONINE (1929–)

Don l'original (1972)

    Drolet, Bruno. *Entre dune et aboiteaux*, 63–72, 96, 109–118, 131–137, 151–152.

La sagouine (1973)

    Shek, Ben Z. "Thèmes et structures de la contestation dans *La sagouine* d'Antonine Maillet." *V&I* 1 (1975): 206–219.

Les cordes-de-bois (1977)

    Poulin, Gabrielle. *Romans du pays*, 182–184.

Mariaagélas (1973)

    Drolet, Bruno. *Entre dune et aboiteaux*, 73–81, 96, 109–118, 121–129, 152–154.

On a mangé la dune (1962)

    Drolet, Bruno. *Entre dune et aboiteaux*, 25–37, 96, 100–101, 101–102, 121–129, 151.

Pélagie-la-charette (1979)

    Shek, Ben Z. "Antonine Maillet and the Prix Goncourt." *CMLR* 36 (1980): 392–395.

Pointe-aux-Coques (1972)

    Drolet, Bruno. *Entre dune et aboiteaux*, 15–23, 95–100, 101–102, 121–129, 143–144, 150–151.
    Poulin, Gabrielle. *Romans du pays*, 176–178.

Tale of Don L'Original see *Don l'original*

MAJOR, ANDRÉ (1942–)

Inspector Therrien see *L'épidémie*

L'épidémie (1975)

    Poulin, Gabrielle. *Romans du pays*, 62–67, 75–77, 81–87.

L'épouvantail (1974)

    Poulin, Gabrielle. *Romans du pays*, 58–60, 62–67, 78–79, 81–87.

Les rescapés (1976)

    Poulin, Gabrielle. *Romans du pays*, 62–67, 79–80, 81–87.

Man on the Run see *Les rescapés*

Scarecrows of Saint-Emmanuel see *L'épouvantail*

MAJOR, CLARENCE (1936–)

All-Night Visitors (1969)
Perkins, Michael. *Secret Record*, 106–107.

MALAMUD, BERNARD (1914–1986)

Assistant (1957)
Alter, Robert. *After the Tradition*, 120–121.
Bluefarb, Sam. "Scope of Caricature," in Field, Leslie A. and Joyce W. Field, eds. *Bernard Malamud and the Critics*, 152–154.
Bluefarb, Sam. "Syncretism of Bernard Malamud," in Field, Leslie A. and Joyce W. Field, eds. *Bernard Malamud*, 73, 77.
Bryant, Jerry H. *Open Decision*, 329–332.
Donald, Miles. *American Novel in the Twentieth Century*, 168–169.
Ducharme, Robert. *Art and Idea in the Novels of Bernard Malamud*, 13–19, 36–42, 59–64, 77, 82–86, 104–106.
Eigner, Edwin M. "Loathly Ladies," in Field, Leslie A. and Joyce W. Field, eds. *Bernard Malamud and the Critics*, 86–87, 91, 95–97.
Freedman, William. "From Bernard Malamud, with Discipline and with Love," in French, Warren, ed. *Fifties*, 138–143.
Freedman, William. "From Bernard Malamud, with Discipline and with Love," in French, Warren, ed. *Fifties: Fiction, Poetry, Drama*. Deland, FL: Everett/Edwards, 1970. 133–143. Rpt. in Field, Leslie A. and Joyce W. Field, eds. *Bernard Malamud*, 160–165.
Goldsmith, Arnold L. "Nature in Bernard Malamud's *The Assistant*." *Renascence* 29 (1977): 211–223.
Grebstein, Sheldon Norman. "Bernard Malamud and the Jewish Movement," in Malin, Irving, ed. *Contemporary American-Jewish Literature*, 181–182, 189–191, 199–200, 205–207.
Grebstein, Sheldon Norman. "Bernard Malamud and the Jewish Movement," in Malin, Irving, ed. *Contemporary American-Jewish Literature*. Bloomington, IN: Indiana University Press, 1973. 175–212. Rpt. in Field, Leslie A. and Joyce W. Field, eds. *Bernard Malamud*, 22–23, 28–30, 35, 36, 39–41.
Griffith, John. "Malamud's *The Assistant*." *Expl* 31 (1972): Item 1.
Guttmann, Allen. *Jewish Writer in America*, 116–118.
Handy, W. J. "Malamud Hero: A Quest for Existence," in Astro, Richard and Jackson J. Benson, eds. *Fiction of Bernard Malamud*, 74–80.
Hassan, Ihab. "Qualified Encounter," in Field, Leslie A. and Joyce W. Field, eds. *Bernard Malamud and the Critics*, 199–206.
Hays, Peter L. "Complex Pattern of Redemption," in Field, Leslie A. and Joyce W. Field, eds. *Bernard Malamud and the Critics*, 219–232.
Hays, Peter L. "Complex Pattern of Redemption in *The Assistant*." *CentR* 13 (1969): 200–214.
Hays, Peter L. *Limping Hero*, 48–55.
Hershinow, Sheldon J. *Bernard Malamud*, 29–47.
Hoyt, Charles Alva. "New Romanticism," in Field, Leslie A. and Joyce W. Field, eds. *Bernard Malamud and the Critics*, 174–177.
Leer, Norman. "Double Theme in Malamud's *Assistant:* Dostoevsky with Irony." *Mosaic* 4.3 (1971): 89–102.

Mellard, James M. "Four Versions of Pastoral," in Field, Leslie A. and Joyce W. Field, eds. *Bernard Malamud and the Critics*, 67–81.

Ozick, Cynthia. "Literary Blacks and Jews." *Midstream* 18.6 (June/July 1972): 10–24. Rpt. in Field, Leslie A. and Joyce W. Field, eds. *Bernard Malamud*, 82.

Pinsker, Sanford. "Bernard Malamud's Ironic Heroes," in Pinsker, Sanford. *Schlemiel as Metaphor: Studies in the Yiddish and American Jewish Novel*. Carbondale, IL: Southern Illinois University Press, 1971. Rpt. in Field, Leslie A. and Joyce W. Field, eds. *Bernard Malamud*, 49–54.

Rupp, Richard H. *Celebration in Postwar American Fiction*, 171–175.

Schulz, Max F. "Mythic Proletarians," in Field, Leslie A. and Joyce W. Field, eds. *Bernard Malamud and the Critics*, 185–194.

Schulz, Max F. *Radical Sophistication*, 56–67.

Shear, Walter. "Culture Conflict," in Field, Leslie A. and Joyce W. Field, eds. *Bernard Malamud and the Critics*, 208–218.

Siegel, Ben. "Through a Glass Darkly: Bernard Malamud's Painful Views of the Self," in Astro, Richard and Jackson J. Benson, eds. *Fiction of Bernard Malamud*, 121–125.

Siegel, Ben. "Victims in Motion: The Sad and Bitter Clowns," in Field, Leslie A. and Joyce W. Field, eds. *Bernard Malamud and the Critics*, 125–127.

Stinson, John J. "Non-Jewish Dialogue in *The Assistant*: Stilted, Runyonesque, or Both?" *NConL* 9.1 (1979): 6–7.

Tanner, Tony. *City of Words*, 327–329.

Waniek, Marilyn Nelson. "Schizoid Implied Authors of Two Jewish-American Novels." *MELUS* 7.1 (1980): 26–30.

Dubin's Lives (1979)

Hershinow, Sheldon J. *Bernard Malamud*, 101–118.

Fixer (1966)

Alter, Robert. *After the Tradition*, 122–130.

Bryant, Jerry H. *Open Decision*, 336–341.

Ducharme, Robert. *Art and Idea in the Novels of Bernard Malamud*, 23–29, 47–52, 69–75, 77–78, 92–97, 99–100, 113–122.

Eigner, Edwin M. "Loathly Ladies," in Field, Leslie A. and Joyce W. Field, eds. *Bernard Malamud and the Critics*, 91–92, 94, 100–107.

Friedberg, Maurice. "History and Imagination— Two Voices of the Beiliss Case," in Field, Leslie A. and Joyce W. Field, eds. *Bernard Malamud and the Critics*, 275–284.

Friedman, Alan Warren. "Hero as Schnook," in Field, Leslie A. and Joyce W. Field, eds. *Bernard Malamud and the Critics*, 285–303.

Grebstein, Sheldon Norman. "Bernard Malamud and the Jewish Movement," in Malin, Irving, ed. *Contemporary American-Jewish Literature*, 183–184, 191–192, 208–209.

Grebstein, Sheldon Norman. "Bernard Malamud and the Jewish Movement," in Malin, Irving, ed. *Contemporary American-Jewish Literature*. Bloomington, IN: Indiana University Press, 1973. 175–212. Rpt. in Field, Leslie A. and Joyce W. Field, eds. *Bernard Malamud*, 21, 24, 30, 35, 37, 42.

Guttmann, Allen. *Jewish Writer in America*, 119.

Handy, W. J. "Malamud Hero: A Quest for Existence," in Astro, Richard and Jackson J. Benson, eds. *Fiction of Bernard Malamud*, 80–86.

Hays, Peter L. *Limping Hero*, 113–117.

Henderson, Harry B. *Versions of the Past*, 273–277.

Hershinow, Sheldon J. *Bernard Malamud*, 63–75.

Hoag, Gerald. "Malamud's Trial: *The Fixer* and the Critics." *Western Humanities Review* 24.1 (Winter 1970): 1–12. Rpt. in Field, Leslie A. and Joyce W. Field, eds. *Bernard Malamud*, 132–142.

Kort, Wesley A. *Shriven Selves*, 90–115.

Mellard, James M. "Four Versions of Pastoral," in Field, Leslie A. and Joyce W. Field, eds. *Bernard Malamud and the Critics*, 67–81.

Ozick, Cynthia. "Literary Blacks and Jews." *Midstream* 18.6 (June/July 1972): 10–24. Rpt. in Field, Leslie A. and Joyce W. Field, eds. *Bernard Malamud*, 82.

Pinsker, Sanford. "Bernard Malamud's Ironic Heroes," in Pinsker, Sanford. *Schlemiel as Metaphor: Studies in the Yiddish and American Jewish Novel*. Carbondale, IL: Southern Illinois University Press, 1971. Rpt. in Field, Leslie A. and Joyce W. Field, eds. *Bernard Malamud*, 65–71.

Pinsker, Sanford. *Between Two Worlds*, 61–66.

Ruotolo, Lucio P. *Six Existential Heroes*, 121–139.

Rupp, Richard H. *Celebration in Postwar American Fiction*, 181–185.

Scholes, Robert. *Fabulation and Metafiction*, 201–203.

Schulz, Max F. "Mythic Proletarians," in Field, Leslie A. and Joyce W. Field, eds. *Bernard Malamud and the Critics*, 185–194.

Schulz, Max F. *Radical Sophistication*, 56–67.

Tanner, Tony. *City of Words*, 333–338.

Natural (1952)

Bluefarb, Sam. "Syncretism of Bernard Malamud," in Field, Leslie A. and Joyce W. Field, eds. *Bernard Malamud*, 77.

Bryant, Jerry H. *Open Decision*, 326–329.

Ducharme, Robert. *Art and Idea in the Novels of Bernard Malamud*, 9–13, 33–36, 55–58, 77, 78–81, 101–104.

Eigner, Edwin M. "Loathly Ladies," in Field, Leslie A. and Joyce W. Field, eds. *Bernard Malamud and the Critics*, 85–86, 89–91, 95.

Freedman, William. "From Bernard Malamud, with Discipline and with Love," in French, Warren, ed. *Fifties*, 136–138.

Freedman, William. "From Bernard Malamud, with Discipline and with Love," in French, Warren, ed. *Fifties: Fiction, Poetry, Drama*. Deland, FL: Everett/Edwards, 1970. 133–143. Rpt. in Field, Leslie A. and Joyce W. Field, eds. *Bernard Malamud*, 158–160.

Goldman, Mark. "Comic Vision and the Theme of Identity," in Field, Leslie A. and Joyce W. Field, eds. *Bernard Malamud and the Critics*, 163–165.

Grebstein, Sheldon Norman. "Bernard Malamud and the Jewish Movement," in Malin, Irving, ed. *Contemporary American-Jewish Literature*, 181, 188–189.

Grebstein, Sheldon Norman. "Bernard Malamud and the Jewish Movement," in Malin, Irving, ed. *Contemporary American-Jewish Literature*. Bloomington, IN: Indiana University Press, 1973. 175–212. Rpt. in Field, Leslie A. and Joyce W. Field, eds. *Bernard Malamud*, 22, 27–28, 41.

Guttmann, Allen. *Jewish Writer in America*, 112–113.

Hays, Peter L. *Limping Hero*, 98–101.

Hershinow, Sheldon J. *Bernard Malamud*, 16–28.

Hoyt, Charles Alva. "New Romanticism," in Field, Leslie A. and Joyce W. Field, eds. *Bernard Malamud and the Critics*, 183–184.

Laird, David. "Versions of Eden: The Automobile and the American Novel." *MQR* 19–20 (1980–81): 648–649.

Mellard, James M. "Four Versions of Pastoral," in Field, Leslie A. and Joyce W. Field, eds. *Bernard Malamud and the Critics*, 67–81.

Rupp, Richard H. *Celebration in Postwar American Fiction*, 166–171.

Schulz, Max F. "Mythic Proletarians," in Field, Leslie A. and Joyce W. Field, eds. *Bernard Malamud and the Critics*, 185–194.

Schulz, Max F. *Radical Sophistication*, 56–67.

Siegel, Ben. "Through a Glass Darkly: Bernard Malamud's Painful Views of the Self," in Astro, Richard and Jackson J. Benson, eds. *Fiction of Bernard Malamud*, 119–121.

Siegel, Ben. "Victims in Motion: The Sad and Bitter Clowns," in Field, Leslie A. and Joyce W. Field, eds. *Bernard Malamud and the Critics*, 124–125.

Tanner, Tony. *City of Words*, 323–327.

Turner, Frederick W., III. "Myth Inside and Out: *The Natural*," 109–118.

Umphlett, Wiley Lee. *Sporting Myth and the American Experience*, 156–168.

Wasserman, Earl R. "*The Natural:* World Ceres," in Field, Leslie A. and Joyce W. Field, eds. *Bernard Malamud and the Critics*, 45–65.

New Life (1961)

Alter, Robert. *After the Tradition*, 120, 121.

Astro, Richard. "In the Heart of the Valley: Bernard Malamud's *A New Life*," in Field, Leslie A. and Joyce W. Field, eds. *Bernard Malamud*, 143–155.

Barsness, John A. "*New Life:* The Frontier Myth in Perspective." *WAL* 3 (1969): 297–302.

Bluefarb, Sam. "Syncretism of Bernard Malamud," in Field, Leslie A. and Joyce W. Field, eds. *Bernard Malamud*, 76.

Bryant, Jerry H. *Open Decision*, 332–336.

Ducharme, Robert. *Art and Idea in the Novels of Bernard Malamud*, 19–23, 42–47, 64–69, 77, 87–92, 99, 106–112.

Eigner, Edwin M. "Loathly Ladies," in Field, Leslie A. and Joyce W. Field, eds. *Bernard Malamud and the Critics*, 86, 87–89, 91–95, 97–100.

Fiedler, Leslie. "Malamud's Travesty Western." *Novel* 10 (1977): 212–219.

Fiedler, Leslie. "Many Names of S. Levin: An Essay in Genre Criticism," in Astro, Richard and Jackson J. Benson, eds. *Fiction of Bernard Malamud*, 149–161.

Goldman, Mark. "Comic Vision and the Theme of Identity," in Field, Leslie A. and Joyce W. Field, eds. *Bernard Malamud and the Critics*, 165–167.

Grebstein, Sheldon Norman. "Bernard Malamud and the Jewish Movement," in Malin, Irving, ed. *Contemporary American-Jewish Literature*, 182–183, 192–194, 197–198.

Grebstein, Sheldon Norman. "Bernard Malamud and the Jewish Movement," in Malin, Irving, ed. *Contemporary American-Jewish Literature*. Bloomington, IN: Indiana University Press, 1973. 175–212. Rpt. in Field, Leslie A. and Joyce W. Field, eds. *Bernard Malamud*, 23–24, 31–32, 34–35, 41–42.

Handy, W. J. "Malamud Hero: A Quest for Existence," in Astro, Richard and Jackson J. Benson, eds. *Fiction of Bernard Malamud*, 68–74.

Hays, Peter L. *Limping Hero*, 44–48.

Hershinow, Sheldon J. *Bernard Malamud*, 48–62.

Hoyt, Charles Alva. "New Romanticism," in Field, Leslie A. and Joyce W. Field, eds. *Bernard Malamud and the Critics*, 180–182.

Hyman, Stanley Edgar. "New Life for a Good Man." *New Leader* (2 Oct 1961). Rpt. in Kostelanetz, Richard, ed. *On Contemporary Literature*, 442–446.

Klein, Marcus. "Sadness of Goodness," in Field, Leslie A. and Joyce W. Field, eds. *Bernard Malamud and the Critics*, 249–259.

Mandel, Ruth B. "Ironic Affirmation," in Field, Leslie A. and Joyce W. Field, eds. *Bernard Malamud and the Critics*, 261–273.

Mellard, James M. "Four Versions of Pastoral," in Field, Leslie A. and Joyce W. Field, eds. *Bernard Malamud and the Critics*, 67–81.

Pinsker, Sanford. "Bernard Malamud's Ironic Heroes," in Pinsker, Sanford. *Schlemiel as Metaphor: Studies in the Yiddish and American Jewish Novel*. Carbondale, IL: Southern Illinois University Press, 1971. Rpt. in Field, Leslie A. and Joyce W. Field, eds. *Bernard Malamud*, 54–65.

Rupp, Richard H. *Celebration in Postwar American Fiction*, 175–181.

Schulz, Max F. "Mythic Proletarians," in Field, Leslie A. and Joyce W. Field, eds. *Bernard Malamud and the Critics*, 185–194.

Schulz, Max F. *Radical Sophistication*, 56–67.

Siegel, Ben. "Through a Glass Darkly: Bernard Malamud's Painful Views of the Self," in Astro, Richard and Jackson J. Benson, eds. *Fiction of Bernard Malamud*, 128–132.

Siegel, Ben. "Victims in Motion: The Sad and Bitter Clowns," in Field, Leslie A. and Joyce W. Field, eds. *Bernard Malamud and the Critics*, 134–136.

Solotaroff, Theodore. "Old Life and the New," in Field, Leslie A. and Joyce W. Field, eds. *Bernard Malamud and the Critics*, 235–248.

Tanner, Tony. *City of Words*, 329–332.

Tenants (1971)

Allen, John A. "Promised End: Bernard Malamud's *The Tenants*." *HC* 8.5 (1971): 1–15.

Allen, John A. "Promised End: Bernard Malamud's *The Tenants*." *Hollins Critic* 8.5 (1971): 1–15. Rpt. in Field, Leslie A. and Joyce W. Field, eds. *Bernard Malamud*, 104–116.

Alter, Robert. "Updike, Malamud, and the Fire This Time," in Thorburn, David and Howard Eiland, eds. *John Updike*, 39–49.

Bluefarb, Sam. "Syncretism of Bernard Malamud," in Field, Leslie A. and Joyce W. Field, eds. *Bernard Malamud*, 73.

Hershinow, Sheldon J. *Bernard Malamud*, 89–100.

Kellman, Steven G. "*The Tenants* in the House of Fiction." *SNNTS* 8 (1976): 458–467.

Lindberg-Seyersted, Brita. "Reading of Bernard Malamud's *The Tenants*." *JAmS* 9 (1975): 85–102.

Ozick, Cynthia. "Literary Blacks and Jews." *Midstream* 18.6 (June/July 1972): 10–24. Rpt. in Field, Leslie A. and Joyce W. Field, eds. *Bernard Malamud*, 81–82, 83–85, 89–98.

Siegel, Ben. "Through a Glass Darkly: Bernard Malamud's Painful Views of the Self," in Astro, Richard and Jackson J. Benson, eds. *Fiction of Bernard Malamud*, 137–141.

MALONEY, RALPH (1927–1973)

Daily Bread (1960)

Bryant, Jerry H. *Open Decision*, 193–194.

MALTZ, ALBERT (1908–1985)

Cross and the Arrow (1944)
Salzman, Jack. *Albert Maltz*, 74–84.

Journey of Simon McKeever (1949)
Salzman, Jack. *Albert Maltz*, 106–114.

Long Day in a Short Life (1957)
Salzman, Jack. *Albert Maltz*, 120–126.

Underground Stream (1940)
Salzman, Jack. *Albert Maltz*, 54–69.

MANDEL, GEORGE (1920–)

Wax Boom (1962)
Bryant, Jerry H. *Open Decision*, 151–152.

MANFRED, FREDERICK FEIKEMA (1912–1994)

Lord Grizzly (1954)
Milton, John R. "Novel in the American West." *South Dakota Review* 2.1 (1964): 56–76. Rpt. in Haslam, Gerald W., ed. *Western Writing*, 84–86.
Milton, John R. "Novel in the American West." *South Dakota Review* 2.1 (1964): 56–76. Rpt. in Pilkington, William T., ed. *Critical Essays on the Western American Novel*, 15–16.

Riders of Judgment (1957)
Westbrook, Max. "*Riders of Judgment:* An Exercise in Ontological Criticism." *WAL* 12 (1977): 41–51.

MANGIONE, GERALDO see MANGIONE, JERRE

MANGIONE, JERRE (1909–1998)

Mount Allegro (1942)
Green, Rose Basile. *Italian-American Novel*, 138–141.

Night Search (1965)
Green, Rose Basile. *Italian-American Novel*, 143–145.

Ship and the Flame (1948)
Green, Rose Basile. *Italian-American Novel*, 141–143.

MARCH, WILLIAM (1893–1954)

Bad Seed (1954)
Going, William T. *Essays on Alabama Literature*, 111–112.

Come In at the Door (1934)

Going, William T. *Essays on Alabama Literature*, 98–101, 111.

Company K (1931)

Medlicott, Alexander, Jr. " 'Soldiers Are Citizens of Death's Gray Land': William March's *Company K.*" *ArQ* 28 (1972): 209–224.

Looking-Glass (1943)

Going, William T. *Essays on Alabama Literature*, 105–110, 112–113.

Tallons (1936)

Going, William T. *Essays on Alabama Literature*, 101–105.

MARCOTTE, GILLES (1925–)

Le poids de Dieu (1961)

Sutherland, Ronald. *Second Image*, 76–79.

MARLYN, JOHN (1912–)

Under the Ribs of Death (1957)

Atwood, Margaret. *Survival*, 152–154.
Sutherland, Ronald. *Second Image*, 11–16.

MARQUAND, JOHN P. (1893–1960)

Late George Apley (1937)

Milne, Gordon. *Sense of Society*, 171–178.
Tuttleton, James W. *Novel of Manners in America*, 212–220.

Point of No Return (1949)

Bryant, Jerry H. *Open Decision*, 188–190.
Milne, Gordon. *Sense of Society*, 180–190.
Tuttleton, James W. *Novel of Manners in America*, 220–231.

Sincerely, Willis Wade (1954)

Bryant, Jerry H. *Open Decision*, 190.

Women and Thomas Harrow (1958)

Milne, Gordon. *Sense of Society*, 192–200.
Tuttleton, James W. *Novel of Manners in America*, 231–234.

MARSHALL, PAULE (1929–)

Brown Girl, Brownstones (1959)

Benston, Kimberly W. "Architectural Imagery and Unity in Paule Marshall's *Brown Girl, Brownstones.*" *NALF* 9 (1975): 67–70.
Christian, Barbara. *Black Women Novelists*, 81–104, 242–246.
Kapai, Leela. "Dominant Themes and Technique in Paule Marshall's Fiction." *CLAJ* 16 (1972): 50, 53, 55, 56, 57.

Keizs, Marcia. "Themes and Style in the Works of Paule Marshall." *NALF* 9 (1975):71–72.

Schultz, Elizabeth. " 'Free in Fact and at Last': The Image of the Black Woman in Black American Fiction," in Springer, Marlene, ed. *What Manner of Woman*, 320, 335.

Chosen Place, Timeless People (1969)

Brown, Lloyd W. "Beneath the North Star: The Canadian Image in Black Literature." *DR* 50 (1970): 322–323.

Christian, Barbara. *Black Women Novelists*, 104–133, 247–252.

Kapai, Leela. "Dominant Themes and Technique in Paule Marshall's Fiction." *CLAJ* 16 (1972): 52–53, 54–55, 56, 57.

Keizs, Marcia. "Themes and Style in the Works of Paule Marshall." *NALF* 9 (1975): 73–74.

Starke, Catherine Juanita. *Black Portraiture in American Fiction*, 241–243.

MARTIN, CLAIRE (1914–)

Doux-amer (1960)

Belleau, André. *Le romancier fictif*, 130–132.

MATHESON, RICHARD (1926–)

Beardless Warriors (1960)

Jones, Peter G. *War and the Novelist*, 23–27.

MATHEWS, CORNELIUS (1817–1889)

Behemoth (1839)

Stein, Allen F. *Cornelius Mathews*, 38–45.

Career of Puffer Hopkins (1842)

Stein, Allen F. *Cornelius Mathews*, 124–128, 139–140.

Moneypenny (1849)

Stein, Allen F. *Cornelius Mathews*, 89–104.

MATHEWS, JOHN J. (1895–1979)

Sundown (1934)

Larson, Charles R. *American Indian Fiction*, 56–64.

MATTHEWS, JACK (1925–)

Beyond the Bridge (1970)

Suderman, Elmer F. "Jack Matthews and the Shape of Human Feelings." *Crit* 21.1 (1979): 45–46.

Charisma Campaigns (1972)

Suderman, Elmer F. "Jack Matthews and the Shape of Human Feelings." *Crit* 21.1 (1979): 43–45.

Pictures of the Journey Back (1973)

> Suderman, Elmer F. "Jack Matthews and the Shape of Human Feelings." *Crit* 21.1 (1979): 38–43.

Tale of Asa Bean (1971)

> Suderman, Elmer F. "Jack Matthews and the Shape of Human Feelings." *Crit* 21.1 (1979): 46–47.

MATTHEWS, JOHN H. see MATTHEWS, JACK

MATTHIESSEN, PETER (1927–)

At Play in the Fields of the Lord (1965)

> Patteson, Richard F. "*At Play in the Fields of the Lord:* The Imperialist Idea and the Discovery of Self." *Crit* 21.2 (1979): 5–14.

Far Tortuga (1975)

> Grove, James P. "Pastoralism and Anti-Pastoralism in Peter Matthiessen's *Far Tortuga.*" *Crit* 21.2 (1979): 15–29.

MAXWELL, WILLIAM (1908–)

Folded Leaf (1945)

> Austen, Roger. *Playing the Game*, 100–103.

MAYBURY, ANNE

I Am Gabriella! (1962)

> Russ, Joanna. "Somebody's Trying to Kill Me and I Think It's My Husband: The Modern Gothic." *JPC* 6 (1973): 666–691.

MAYFIELD, JULIAN (1928–1984)

Hit (1957)

> Davis, Arthur P. *From the Dark Tower*, 199–200, 201.

MAYNE, XAVIER (1868–1942)

Imre (1906)

> Austen, Roger. *Playing the Game*, 20–27.

MEAD, SHEPHERD (1914–)

Big Ball of Wax (1954)

> Rhodes, Carolyn. "Tyranny by Computer: Automated Data Processing and Oppressive Government in Science Fiction," in Clareson, Thomas D., ed. *Many Futures, Many Worlds*, 81–82.

MEEKER, RICHARD (1901–)
Better Angel (1933)
Austen, Roger. *Playing the Game*, 68–69.

MELVILLE, HERMAN (1819–1891)
Confidence-Man (1857)
Alter, Robert. *Partial Magic*, 127–137.
Attebery, Brian. *Fantasy Tradition in American Literature*, 56–57.
Baim, Joseph. "Confidence-Man as 'Trickster'." *ATQ* 1 (1969): 81–83.
Barnett, Louise K. *Ignoble Savage*, 181–182, 183.
Bell, Michael Davitt. *Development of American Romance*, 211–212, 236–242.
Berthoff, Warner. *Fictions and Events*, 229–242.
Blair, John G. *Confidence Man in Modern Fiction*, 33–50.
Blair, John G. "Puns and Equivocation in Melville's *The Confidence-Man*." *ATQ* 22 (1974): 91–95.
Bowen, Merlin. "Tactics of Indirection in Melville's *The Confidence-Man*." *SNNTS* 1.4 (1969): 401–420.
Branch, Watson G. "Mute as 'Metaphysical Scamp'," in Melville, Herman. *Confidence Man, His Masquerade*, 316–319.
Bredahl, A. Carl, Jr. *Melville's Angles of Vision*, 56–62.
Brodhead, Richard H. *Hawthorne, Melville, and the Novel*, 127, 132.
Brodtkorb, Paul, Jr. "*Confidence-Man:* The Con Man as Hero." *SNNTS* 1.4 (1969): 421–435.
Brouwer, Fred E. "Melville's *The Confidence-Man* as Ship of Philosophers." *SoHR* 3 (1969): 158–165.
Caraber, Andrew J., Jr. "Melville's *The Confidence-Man*." *Expl* 29 (1970): Item 9.
Cook, Richard M. "Evolving the Inscrutable: The Grotesque in Melville's Fiction." *AL* 49 (1978): 556–559.
Foster, Elizabeth S. "Introduction to *The Confidence-Man*." Melville, Herman. *The Confidence-Man*. New York: Hendricks House, 1954. xxiii–xxix, xxxi, xxxii. Rpt. as "Emerson in *The Confidence-Man*," in Melville, Herman. *Confidence Man, His Masquerade*, 333–339.
Franklin, H. Bruce. *Victim as Criminal and Artist*, 63–66.
Frederick, John T. *Darkened Sky*, 104–106.
Haberstroh, Charles J., Jr. *Melville and Male Identity*, 113–114.
Hauck, Richard Boyd. *Cheerful Nihilism*, 78, 112–130.
Hayford, Harrison. "Poe in *The Confidence-Man*." *Nineteenth-Century Fiction* 14 (Dec 1959): 207–218. Rpt. in Melville, Herman. *Confidence Man, His Masquerade*, 344–353.
Hays, Peter L. *Limping Hero*, 134–135.
Hillway, Tyrus. *Herman Melville*, 119–122.
Honig, Edwin. *Dark Conceit*, 82–84.
Karcher, Carolyn L. *Shadow over the Promised Land*, 186–257.
Karcher, Carolyn L. "Spiritualism and Philanthropy in Brownson's The Spirit-Rapper and Melville's *The Confidence-Man*." *ESQ* 25 (1979): 28–35.
Kemper, Steven E. "*Confidence-Man:* A Knavishly-Packed Deck." *SAF* 8 (1980): 23–35.
Ketterer, David. *New Worlds for Old*, 267–295.

Keyser, Elizabeth. " 'Quite an Original': The Cosmopolitan in *The Confidence-Man*." *TSLL* 15 (1973): 279–300.

Klotman, Phyllis Rauch. *Another Man Gone*, 47–49.

Korkowski, Eugene. "Melville and Des Periers: An Analogue for *The Confidence-Man*." *ATQ* 31 (1976): 14–19.

Kuhlmann, Susan. *Knave, Fool, and Genius*, 108–122.

Lenz, William E. "Melville's *The Confidence-Man:* His Masquerade." *Expl* 39.1 (1980): 20–21.

McCarthy, Paul. "Affirmative Elements in *The Confidence-Man*." *ATQ* 7 (1970): 56–61.

McCarthy, Paul. "Elements of Anatomy in Melville's Fiction." *SNNTS* 6 (1974): 53–58.

McCarthy, Paul. "Melville's Rascals on Land, Sea, and in the Air." *SoQ* 16 (1978): 317–320, 332–336.

McCarthy, Paul. " 'Soldier of Fortune' in Melville's *The Confidence-Man*." *Emerson Society Quarterly* 33 (1963): 21–24. Rpt. in Rountree, Thomas J., ed. *Critics on Melville*, 113–116.

McHaney, Thomas. "*Confidence-Man* and Satan's Disguises in *Paradise Lost*." *NCF* 30 (1975): 200–206.

Malin, Irving. "American Gothic Images." *Mosaic* 6.3 (1973): 166–167.

May, John R. *Toward a New Earth*, 61–74.

Oates, Joyce Carol. *Edge of Impossibility*, 71–80.

Parker, Hershel. "Metaphysics of Indian-hating." *Nineteenth-Century Fiction* 18 (Sept 1963): 165–173. Rpt. in Melville, Herman. *Confidence Man, His Masquerade*, 323–331.

Polk, James. "Melville and the Idea of the City." *UTQ* 41 (1972): 287.

Pops, Martin Leonard. *Melville Archetype*, 162–171.

Porte, Joel. *Romance in America*, 155–170.

Ramsey, William M. "Moot Points of Melville's Indian-Hating." *AL* 52 (1980): 224–235.

Quilligan, Maureen. *Language of Allegory*, 86–96, 197, 198–203, 263–265.

Quirk, Tom. "Saint Paul's Types of the Faithful and Melville's *Confidence-Man*." *NCF* 28 (1974): 472–477.

Ramsey, William M. "Melville's and Barnum's Man with a Weed." *AL* 51 (1979): 101–104.

Ramsey, William M. " 'Touching' Scenes in *The Confidence-Man*." *ESQ* 25 (1979): 37–42.

Reynolds, Michael. "Prototype for Melville's Confidence-Man." *PMLA* 86 (1971): 1009–1013.

Rosenberry, Edward H. *Melville*, 51–53.

Seelye, John D. " 'Ungraspable Phantom': Reflections of Hawthorne in *Pierre* and *The Confidence-Man*." *SNNTS* 1.4 (1969): 439.

Seltzer, Alvin J. *Chaos in the Novel*, 52–79.

Shroeder, John W. "Sources and Symbols for Melville's *Confidence Man*." *PMLA* 66 (June 1951): 364–380. Rpt. in Melville, Herman. *Confidence Man, His Masquerade*, 298–316.

Stein, William Bysshe. "Melville's *The Confidence-Man:* Quicksands of the Word." *ATQ* 24 (1974): 38–50.

Sten, Christopher W. "Dialogue of Crisis in *The Confidence-Man:* Melville's 'New Novel'." *SNNTS* 6 (1974): 165–185.

Tichi, Cecelia. "Melville's Craft and Theme of Language Debased in *The Confidence-Man*." *ELH* 39 (1972): 639–658.

Trimpi, Helen P. "Harlequin-Confidence-Man: The Satirical Tradition of Commedia Dell'Arte and Pantomime in Melville's *The Confidence Man*." *TSLL* 16 (1974): 147–193.

Trimpi, Helen P. "Three of Melville's Confidence Men: William Cullen Bryant, Theodore Parker, and Horace Greeley." *TSLL* 21 (1979): 368–391.

Wadlington, Warwick. *Confidence Game in American Literature*, 137–170.

Watson, Charles N., Jr. "Melville and the Theme of Timonism: From *Pierre* to *The Confidence Man*." *AL* 44 (1972): 406–413.

Watters, Reginald Eyre. *Essays and Articles*, 35–36.

Yannella, Donald. "Source for the Diddling of William Cream in *The Confidence-Man*." *ATQ* 17 (1973): 22–24.

Israel Potter (1855)

Bredahl, A. Carl, Jr. *Melville's Angles of Vision*, 51–56.

Carlson, Thomas C. "Twin Parables of Melville's *Israel Potter*." *ATQ* 41 (1979): 85–92.

Farnsworth, Robert M. "*Israel Potter:* Pathetic Comedy." *Bulletin of the New York Public Library* 65 (Feb 1961): 125–132. Rpt. in Rountree, Thomas J., ed. *Critics on Melville*, 101–107.

George, J. L. "*Israel Potter:* The Height of Patriotism." *ATQ* 7 (1970): 53–56.

Gilmore, Michael T. *Middle Way*, 151–165.

Henderson, Harry B. *Versions of the Past*, 138–147.

Karcher, Carolyn L. *Shadow over the Promised Land*, 102–108.

Miller, Wayne Charles. *Armed America, Its Face in Fiction*, 29–32.

Neff, Winifred. "Satirical Use of a 'Silly Reference' in *Israel Potter*." *ATQ* 7 (1970): 51–53.

Polk, James. "Melville and the Idea of the City." *UTQ* 41 (1972): 286.

Pops, Martin Leonard. *Melville Archetype*, 157–162.

Rosenberry, Edward H. *Melville*, 102–108.

Stout, Janis P. "Encroaching Sodom: Melville's Urban Fiction." *TSLL* 17 (1975): 169–170.

Stout, Janis P. *Sodoms in Eden*, 134–136.

Turner, Frederick W., III. "Melville and Thomas Berger: The Novelist as Cultural Anthropologist." *CentR* 13 (1969): 103–107.

Watson, Charles N., Jr. "Melville's *Israel Potter:* Fathers and Sons." *SNNTS* 7 (1975): 563–568.

Watson, Charles N., Jr. "Premature Burial in "Arthur Gordon Pym" and *Israel Potter*." *AL* 47 (1975): 105–107.

Mardi (1849)

Attebery, Brian. *Fantasy Tradition in American Literature*, 52–53.

Babin, James L. "Melville and the Deformation of Being: From *Typee* to *Leviathan*." *SoR* 7 (1971): 105–108.

Barnett, Louise K. *Ignoble Savage*, 181.

Baym, Nina. "Portrayal of Women in American Literature, 1790–1870," in Springer, Marlene, ed. *What Manner of Woman*, 223.

Bell, Michael Davitt. *Development of American Romance*, 143–145, 204–206.

Brodhead, Richard H. *Hawthorne, Melville, and the Novel*, 125–126.

Chaffee, Patricia. "Paradox in *Mardi*." *ATQ* 29 (1976): 80–83.

Cook, Richard M. "Evolving the Inscrutable: The Grotesque in Melville's Fiction." *AL* 49 (1978): 550–551.

Cook, Richard M. "Grotesque and Melville's *Mardi*." *ESQ* 21 (1975): 103–110.

Dew, Marjorie. "Black-Hearted Melville: 'Geniality' Reconsidered," in DeMott, Robert J. and Sanford E. Marovitz, eds. *Artful Thunder*, 179–185.

Dillingham, William B. *Artist in the Rigging*, 105–130, 135–136, 143.

Frederick, John T. *Darkened Sky*, 87–90.

Garrison, Daniel H. "Melville's Doubloon and the Shield of Achilles." *NCF* 26 (1971): 172.

Haberstroh, Charles, Jr. "Melville, Marriage, and *Mardi*." *SNNTS* 9 (1977): 247–260.

Haberstroh, Charles J., Jr. *Melville and Male Identity*, 53–66.

Hauck, Richard Boyd. *Cheerful Nihilism*, 93–100.

Henderson, Harry B. *Versions of the Past*, 129–131.

Hillway, Tyrus. *Herman Melville*, 78–83.

Lucas, Thomas E. "Herman Melville: The Purpose of the Novel." *TSLL* 13 (1972): 645, 648, 652–653, 654.

McCarthy, Paul. "Elements of Anatomy in Melville's Fiction." *SNNTS* 6 (1974): 40–43.

McCarthy, Paul. "Extraordinary Man as Idealist in Novels by Hawthorne and Melville." *ESQ* 54 (1969): 44–45, 47, 50.

McCarthy, Paul. "Melville's Rascals on Land, Sea, and in the Air." *SoQ* 16 (1978): 328–331, 334–336.

Mason, Ronald. *Spirit Above the Dust*, 38–66.

Meldrum, Barbara. "Artist in Melville's *Mardi*." *SNNTS* 1.4 (1969): 459–467.

Miller, James E., Jr. "Many Masks of *Mardi*." *Journal of English and Germanic Philology* 58 (July 1959): 400–413. Rpt. in Rountree, Thomas J., ed. *Critics on Melville*, 63–69.

Packard, Hyland. "*Mardi:* The Role of Hyperbole in Melville's Search for Expression." *AL* 49 (1977): 241–253.

Polk, James. "Melville and the Idea of the City." *UTQ* 41 (1972): 279–280.

Pops, Martin Leonard. *Melville Archetype*, 39–50, 60–63.

Richardson, Robert D., Jr. *Myth and Literature in the American Renaissance*, 201–210.

Rosenberry, Edward H. *Melville*, 44–51.

Sears, J. Michael. "Melville's *Mardi:* One Book or Three?" *SNNTS* 10 (1978): 411–419.

Simpson, Eleanor E. "Melville and the Negro: From *Typee* to 'Benito Cereno'." *AL* 41 (1969): 21–23.

Thomas, Joel J. "Melville's Use of Mysticism." *PQ* 53 (1974): 415–417.

Wadlington, Warwick. *Confidence Game in American Literature*, 68–72, 106–110.

Watters, Reginald Eyre. *Essays and Articles*, 2–4, 5–11, 13, 28–29, 38.

Moby-Dick (1851)

Alexis, Gerhard T. "Two Footnotes on a Faceless Whale." *ANQ* 11 (1973): 99–100.

Allen, Walter. *Urgent West*, 130–134.

Andrews, William L. "*Moby-Dick* and the Legend of Mahuika." *ATQ* 42 (1979): 123–127.

Arbur, Rosemarie. "Melville's *Moby-Dick*." *Expl* 36.1 (1977): 28–29.

Arvin, Newton. *Herman Melville*. New York: William Sloane Associates, Inc.,

1950. 160–165. Rpt. as "Metaphor and Language in *Moby-Dick*," in Gilmore, Michael T. *Twentieth Century Interpretations of Moby-Dick*, 82–86.

Arvin, Newton. "The Whale," in Arvin, Newton. *Herman Melville*. New York: William Sloane Associates, 1950. 165–193. Rpt. in Rahv, Philip, ed. *Literature in America*, 168–188

Attebery, Brian. *Fantasy Tradition in American Literature*, 53–55.

Auden, W. H. "Ishmael-Melville," in Auden, W. H. *Enchafèd Flood*. New York: Random House, 1950. 115–124. Rpt. in Vincent, Howard P., comp. *Merrill Studies in Moby-Dick*, 146–151.

Auden, W. H. "Romantic Use of Symbols," in Auden, W. H. *Enchafèd Flood*. New York: Random House, 1950. 58–63. Rpt. in Gilmore, Michael T. *Twentieth Century Interpretations of Moby-Dick*, 9–12.

Ausband, Stephen C. "Whale and the Machine: An Approach to *Moby-Dick*." *AL* 47 (1975): 197–211.

Babin, James L. "Melville and the Deformation of Being: From *Typee* to *Leviathan*." *SoR* 7 (1971): 108–114.

Barbour, James and Leon Howard. "Carlyle and the Conclusion of *Moby-Dick*." *NEQ* 49 (1976): 214–224.

Barnett, Louise K. *Ignoble Savage*, 171–173, 175–176, 178–180.

Bell, Michael Davitt. *Development of American Romance*, 196, 197–198, 217–226.

Bender, Bert. "*Moby-Dick*, an American Lyrical Novel." *SNNTS* 10 (1978): 346–356.

Bergstrom, Robert F. "Topmost Grief: Rejection of Ahab's Faith." *ELWIU* 2 (1975): 171–180.

Berkeley, David S. "Figurae Futurarum in *Moby-Dick*." *BuR* 21.2 (1973): 108–123.

Bewley, Marius. *Eccentric Design*. New York: Columbia University Press, 1959. 206–210. Rpt. as "*Moby-Dick* and Creative Force," in Vincent, Howard P., comp. *Merrill Studies in Moby-Dick*, 152–157.

Bezanson, Walter. "*Moby-Dick*: Work of Art," in Hillway, Tyrus and Luther S. Mansfield, eds. *Moby-Dick Centennial Essays*. Dallas: Southern Methodist University Press, 1953. 35–57. Rpt. as "Dynamic and Structure in *Moby-Dick*," in Vincent, Howard P., comp. *Merrill Studies in Moby-Dick*, 87–103.

Bickman, Martin. *Unsounded Centre*, 56–57.

Booth, Thornton Y. "*Moby-Dick*: Standing up to God." *Nineteenth-Century Fiction* 17 (June 1962): 33–43. Rpt. in Rountree, Thomas J., ed. *Critics on Melville*, 87–93.

Boudreau, Gordon V. "Of Pale Ushers and Gothic Piles: Melville's Architectural Symbology." *ESQ* no.67 (1972): 67–82.

Brodhead, Richard H. *Hawthorne, Melville, and the Novel*, 19, 22, 126–127, 129, 130, 134–162.

Carothers, Robert L. and John L. Marsh. "Whale and the Panorama." *NCF* 26 (1971): 319–328.

Caserio, Robert L. *Plot, Story, and the Novel*, 134–159.

Cecchi, Emilio. "[A Note] on Melville," excerpted from "Two Notes on Melville." *Sewanee Review* 68 (July–Sept 1960): 398–406. Rpt. in Vincent, Howard P., comp. *Merrill Studies in Moby-Dick*, 138–140.

Clark, Marden J. "Blending Cadences: Rhythm and Structure in *Moby-Dick*." *SNNTS* 8 (1976): 158–171.

Cohen, Hennig. "Melville's Tomahawk Pipe: Artifact and Symbol." *SNNTS* 1.4 (1969): 397–399.

Colcord, Lincoln. "Notes on *Moby-Dick*." *Freeman* 5 (23 Aug and 30 Aug, 1922): 559–562. Rpt. in Vincent, Howard P., comp. *Merrill Studies in Moby-Dick*, 32–43.

Cook, Richard M. "Evolving the Inscrutable: The Grotesque in Melville's Fiction." *AL* 49 (1978): 546–548, 552–556.

Cromphout, Gustaaf van. "*Moby-Dick:* The Transformations of the Faustian Ethos." *AL* 51 (1979): 17–32.

Cross, Richard K. "*Moby-Dick* and *Under the Volcano:* Poetry from the Abyss." *MFS* 20 (1974): 149–156.

Donaldson, Scott. "Damned Dollars and a Blessed Company: Financial Imagery in *Moby-Dick*." *NEQ* 46 (1973): 279–283.

Donoghue, Denis. *Thieves of Fire*, 88–96, 101–105.

Douglas, Ann. *Feminization of American Culture*, 304–308.

Downs, Robert B. *Famous American Books*, 107–114.

Edinger, Edward F. *Melville's Moby-Dick: A Jungian Commentary, An American Nekyia*. New York: New Directions Publishing Company, 1975.

Evans, William A. "Boy and the Shadow: The Role of Pip and Fedallah in *Moby-Dick*." *SLitI* 2.1 (1969): 77–81.

Feidelson, Charles, Jr. "Symbolism in *Moby-Dick*," in Feidelson, Charles, Jr. *Symbolism and American Literature*. Chicago: University of Chicago Press, 1953. 27–35. Rpt. in Rountree, Thomas J., ed. *Critics on Melville*, 81–86.

Finholt, Richard. *American Visionary Fiction*, 61–82.

Fabricant, Carole. "*Tristam Shandy* and *Moby-Dick:* A Cock and Bull Story and a Tale of a Tub." *JNT* 7 (1977): 57–67.

Franklin, H. Bruce. *Victim as Criminal and Artist*, 44–51.

Franklin, H. Bruce. *Wake of the Gods: Melville's Mythology*. Stanford, CA: Stanford University Press, 1963. 54–61. Rpt. as "*Moby-Dick* as Myth," in Vincent, Howard P., comp. *Merrill Studies in Moby-Dick*, 130–136.

Frederick, John T. *Darkened Sky*, 91–96.

Garrison, Daniel H. "Melville's Doubloon and the Shield of Achilles." *NCF* 26 (1971): 171–184.

Gibbs, Robert J. "Living Contour: The Whale Symbol in Melville and Pratt." *CanL* 40 (1969): 17–25.

Gilmore, Michael T. "Introduction," in Gilmore, Michael T. *Twentieth Century Interpretations of Moby-Dick*, 1–8.

Gilmore, Michael T. "Melville's Apocalypse: American Millennialism and *Moby-Dick*." *ESQ* 21 (1975): 154–161.

Gilmore, Michael T. *Middle Way*, 136–151.

Glasser, William. "*Moby-Dick*." *SewR* 77 (1969): 462–486.

Glenn, Barbara. "Melville and the Sublime in *Moby-Dick*." *AL* 48 (1976): 165–182.

Golemba, Henry L. "Shape of *Moby-Dick*." *SNNTS* 5 (1973): 197–210.

Grove, James P. "Melville's Vision of Death in *Moby-Dick:* Stepping Away from the 'Snug Sofa'." *NEQ* 52 (1979): 177–196.

Haberstroh, Charles J., Jr. *Melville and Male Identity*, 92–102.

Hands, Charles B. "Comic Entrance to *Moby-Dick*." *CollL* 2 (1975): 182–191.

Hauck, Richard Boyd. *Cheerful Nihilism*, 78–79, 100–106.

Hayford, Harrison. " 'Loomings': Yarns and Figures in the Fabric," in DeMott, Robert J. and Sanford E. Marovitz, eds. *Artful Thunder*, 119–137.

Hays, Peter L. *Limping Hero*, 129–132.

Henderson, Harry B. *Versions of the Past*, 134–138.

Hennelly, Mark. "Ishmael's Nightmare and the American Eve." *American Imago* 30 (1974): 274–293.

Herbert, T. Walter, Jr. "Calvinism and Cosmic Evil in *Moby-Dick*." *PMLA* 84 (1969): 1613–1619.

Herbert, T. Walter, Jr. *Moby-Dick and Calvinism: A World Dismantled*. New Brunswick, NJ: Rutgers University Press, 1977.

Hillway, Tyrus. *Herman Melville*, 83–106.

Hirsch, David H. *Reality and Idea in the Early American Novel*, 166–219.

Hoffman, Daniel. "*Moby-Dick:* Jonah's Whale or Job's?", in Hoffman, Daniel. *Form and Fable in American Fiction*. New York: Oxford University Press, 1961. 233–236, 256–262, 269–278. Rpt. in Gilmore, Michael T. *Twentieth Century Interpretations of Moby-Dick*, 59–75.

Honig, Edwin. *Dark Conceit*, 113–114, 117, 131, 132, 133, 140–144.

Horsford, Howard C. "Design of the Argument in *Moby-Dick*." *Modern Fiction Studies* 8 (Autumn 1962): 233–251. Rpt. in Vincent, Howard P., comp. *Merrill Studies in Moby-Dick*, 67–86.

Howard, Leon. "Creation of *Moby-Dick*," in Howard, Leon. *Herman Melville*. Minneapolis, MN: University of Minnesota Press, 1961. 18–25. Rpt. in Vincent, Howard P., comp. *Merrill Studies in Moby-Dick*, 104–109.

Isani, Mukhtar A. "Zoroastrianism and the Fire Symbolism in *Moby-Dick*." *AL* 44 (1972): 385–397.

Jeske, Jeffrey M. "Macbeth, Ahab, and the Unconscious." *ATQ* 31 (1976): 8–12.

Kaplan, Harold. *Democratic Humanism and American Literature*, 159–184.

Karcher, Carolyn L. "Melville and Racial Prejudice: A Re-Evaluation." *SoR* 12 (1976): 291–296.

Karcher, Carolyn L. *Shadow over the Promised Land*, 55–61, 62–91.

Kearns, Edward A. "Omniscient Ambiguity: The Narrators of *Moby-Dick* and 'Billy Budd'." *ESQ* 58 (1970): 117–120.

Kirk, Carey H. "*Moby-Dick:* The Challenge of Response." *PLL* 13 (1977): 383–390.

Kirkham, E. Bruce. "Iron Crown of Lombardy in *Moby-Dick*." *ESQ* 58 (1970): 127–129.

Kirkham, E. Bruce. "Melville and the Iron Crown of Lombardy." *ANQ* 10 (1972): 133–134.

Klotman, Phyllis Rauch. *Another Man Gone*, 36–39.

Lauber, John. "Sultan of the Pequod: Ahab as Hero." *DR* 58 (1978): 30–45.

Lawrence, D. H. "Herman Melville's *Moby-Dick*," in Lawrence, D. H. *Studies in Classic American Literature*. New York: Viking Press, 1923. Rpt. in Vincent, Howard P., comp. *Merrill Studies in Moby-Dick*, 44–50.

Leonard, David Charles. "Cartesian Vortex in *Moby-Dick*." *AL* 51 (1979): 105–109.

Levin, Michael E. "Ahab as Socratic Philosopher: The Myth of the Cave Inverted." *ATQ* 41 (1979): 61–73.

Lewis, R. W. B. *American Adam*. Chicago: University of Chicago Press, 1955. 139–145. Rpt. as "*Moby-Dick* and Homer," in Vincent, Howard P., comp. *Merrill Studies in Moby-Dick*, 123–129.

Lieber, Todd M. *Endless Experiments*, 113–163.

Lloyd, Francis V., Jr. "Melville's *Moby-Dick.*" *Expl* 29 (1971): Item 72.

Loving, Jerome M. "Melville's Pardonable Sin." *NEQ* 47 (1974): 262–278.

Lucas, Thomas E. "Herman Melville: The Purpose of the Novel." *TSLL* 13 (1972): 648, 651–652, 653, 654–658, 660, 661.

McCarthy, Paul. "Elements of Anatomy in Melville's Fiction." *SNNTS* 6 (1974): 47–53.

McCarthy, Paul. "Extraordinary Man as Idealist in Novels by Hawthorne and Melville." *ESQ* 54 (1969): 46, 48–50.

McDonald, Walter R. "Ishmael: The Function of a Comic Mask." *CEA* 37.2 (1975): 8–11.

MacMechan, Archibald. "Best Sea Story Ever Written." *Queen's Quarterly* 7 (Oct 1899): 181–197. Rpt. in Vincent, Howard P., comp. *Merrill Studies in Moby-Dick*, 22–31.

McMillan, Grant. "Ishmael's Dilemma—The Significance of the Fiery Hunt." *CentR* 15 (1971): 204–217.

Marovitz, Sanford E. "Old Man Ahab," in DeMott, Robert J. and Sanford E. Marovitz, eds. *Artful Thunder*, 139–161.

Mason, Ronald. *Spirit Above the Dust*, 111–157.

Meldrum, Barbara. "Structure in *Moby-Dick:* The Whale Killings and Ishmael's Quest." *ESQ* 21 (1975): 162–168.

Millhauser, Milton. "Form of *Moby-Dick.*" *Journal of Aesthetics and Art Criticism* 13 (June 1955): 527–532. Rpt. in Rountree, Thomas J., ed. *Critics on Melville*, 76–80.

Mowder, William. "Volition in *Moby-Dick.*" *ELWIU* 1.3 (1973): 18–30.

Mulqueen, James E. "Ishmael's Voyage: The Cycle of Everyman's Faith." *AQ* 31 (1975): 57–68.

Mumford, Lewis. "*Moby-Dick* as Poetic Epic," in Mumford, Lewis. *Herman Melville: A Study of His Life and Vision*. Revised Edition. New York: Harcourt Brace Jovanovich, Inc., 1929. 123–127. Rpt. in Gilmore, Michael T. *Twentieth Century Interpretations of Moby-Dick*, 76–81.

Murray, Henry A. "In Nomine Diaboli." *New England Quarterly* 24 (Dec 1951): 435–452. Rpt. in Vincent, Howard P., comp. *Merrill Studies in Moby-Dick*, 52–66.

Nechas, James W. "Ambiguity of Word and Whale: The Negative Affix in *Moby-Dick.*" *CollL* 2 (1975): 198–225.

Oates, Joyce Carol. *Edge of Impossibility*, 64–66.

Oglesby, Carl. "Melville, or water consciousness & its madness: a fragment from a work in progress," in White, George Abbot and Charles Newman, eds. *Literature in Revolution*, 123–141.

Olson, Charles. "Ahab and His Fool," in Olson, Charles. *Call Me Ishmael*. San Francisco: City Lights Books, 1947. 59–63. Rpt. in Gilmore, Michael T. *Twentieth Century Interpretations of Moby-Dick*, 55–58.

Ousby, Ian. *Reader's Guide to Fifty American Novels*, 79–82.

Pavese, Cesare. "Literary Whaler (1923)." *Sewanee Review* 68 (Summer 1960): 407–418. Rpt. in Vincent, Howard P., comp. *Merrill Studies in Moby-Dick*, 141–145.

Percival, M. O. *Reading of Moby-Dick*. Chicago: Unversity of Chicago Press, 1950. 14–23. Rpt. as "Captain Ahab and Moby Dick," in Vincent, Howard P., comp. *Merrill Studies in Moby-Dick*, 116–122.

Polk, James. "Melville and the Idea of the City." *UTQ* 41 (1972): 280–281.

Pops, Martin Leonard. *Melville Archetype*, 65–87.

Pryse, Marjorie. *Mark and the Knowledge*, 49–88.

Rees, John O., Jr. "Spenserian Analogues in *Moby-Dick*." *ESQ* no.68 (1972): 174–178.

Reid, B. L. *Tragic Occasions*, 97–134.

Rice, Julian C. "Male Sexuality in *Moby-Dick*." *ATQ* 39 (1978): 237–244.

Rice, Julian C. "Ship as Cosmic Symbol in *Moby-Dick* and 'Benito Cereno'." *CentR* 16 (1972): 144–149.

Richardson, Robert D., Jr. *Myth and Literature in the American Renaissance*, 210–226.

Rose, Edward J. "Annihilation and Ambiguity: *Moby-Dick* and 'The Town-ho's Story'." *NEQ* 45 (1972): 541–558.

Rosenberry, Edward H. *Melville*, 71–86.

Ross, Morton L. "*Moby-Dick* as an Education." *SNNTS* 6 (1974): 62–75.

Rothfork, John. "Sailing of the Pequod: An Existential Voyage." *ArQ* 28 (1972): 55–60.

Samson, Joan P. "Ambiguity of Ambergris in *Moby-Dick*." *CollL* 2 (1975): 226–228.

Sartre, Jean-Paul. "Herman Melville's *Moby-Dick*," excerpted from Sartre, Jean Paul. *Writings of Jean Paul Sartre*. Vol. 2. Ed. Michel Contat and Michel Rybalka. Trans. Richard McCleary. Evanston, IL: Northwestern University Press, 1974. 138–140. Rpt. in Gilmore, Michael T. *Twentieth Century Interpretations of Moby-Dick*, 94–97.

Sewall, Richard B. "*Moby-Dick*," in Sewall, Richard B. *Vision of Tragedy*. New Haven, CT: Yale University Press, 1959. Rpt. in Gilmore, Michael T. *Twentieth Century Interpretations of Moby-Dick*, 42–54.

Sherrill, Rowland A. *Prophetic Melville*, 85–107, 121–163, 167–188.

Simpson, Eleanor E. "Melville and the Negro: From *Typee* to 'Benito Cereno'." *AL* 41 (1969): 25–32.

Slochower, Harry. *Mythopoesis*, 223–241.

Slotkin, Richard. "*Moby-Dick*: The American National Epic," in Slotkin, Richard. *Regeneration Through Violence: The Mythology of the American Frontier, 1600–1860*. Middletown, CT: Wesleyan University Press, 1973. Rpt. in Gilmore, Michael T. *Twentieth Century Interpretations of Moby-Dick*, 13–26.

Smith, Henry Nash. "Image of Society in *Moby-Dick*," in Hillway, Tyrus and Luther S. Mansfield, eds. *Moby-Dick: Centennial Essays*. Dallas: Southern Methodist University Press, 1953. 59–75. Rpt. in Gilmore, Michael T. *Twentieth Century Interpretations of Moby-Dick*, 27–41.

Smith, Henry Nash. "Madness of Ahab." *YR* 66 (1976): 14–32.

Spengemann, William C. *Adventurous Muse*, 188–198.

Stafford, William T. "Whale, an Heiress, and a Southern Demigod: Three Symbolic Americas." *CollL* 1 (1974): 102–106.

Stark, John. " 'The Cassock' Chapter in *Moby-Dick* and the Theme of Literary Creativity." *SAF* 1 (1973): 105–111.

Starke, Catherine Juanita. *Black Portraiture in American Fiction*, 42–44, 155–158.

Stein, Allen F. "Ahab's Turbid Wake and Job's Leviathan." *ATQ* 17 (1973): 13–14.

Stelzig, Eugene L. "Romantic Paradoxes of *Moby-Dick*." *ATQ* 26 supp. (1975): 41–44.

Stern, Milton R. *"Moby-Dick*, Millennial Attitudes, and Politics." *ESQ* 54 (1969): 51–60.

Sternlicht, Sanford. "Sermons in *Moby-Dick*." *BallS* 10.1 (1969): 51–52.

Stone, Edward. *Certain Morbidness*, 16–42.

Stone, Edward. "Function of the Gams in *Moby-Dick*." *CollL* 2 (1975): 171–181.

Stone, Edward. "Whiteness of 'The Whale'." *CLAJ* 18 (1975): 348–363.

Strauch, Carl F. "Ishmael: Time and Personality in *Moby-Dick*." *SNNTS* 1.4 (1969): 468–483.

Thomas, Joel J. "Melville's Use of Mysticism." *PQ* 53 (1974): 417–422.

Vincent, Howard P. "Ishmael, Writer and Art Critic," in Browne, Ray B. and Donald Pizer, eds. *Themes and Directions in American Literature*, 69–79.

Wadlington, Warwick. *Confidence Game in American Literature*, 73–103.

Wadlington, Warwick. "Ishmael's Godly Gamesomeness: Selftaste and Rhetoric in *Moby-Dick*." *ELH* 39 (1972): 309–331.

Watters, Reginald Eyre. *Essays and Articles*, 5–11, 15–20, 21–22, 31, 32–33, 34, 36–37, 70–83.

Way, Brian. *Herman Melville: Moby-Dick*. London: Edward Arnold, 1977.

Weintraub, Rodelle and Stanley Weintraub. *"Moby-Dick* and Seven Pillars of Wisdom." *SAF* 2 (1974): 238–240.

Werge, Thomas. *"Moby-Dick* and the Calvinist Tradition." *SNNTS* 1.4 (1969): 484–506.

Werge, Thomas. *"Moby-Dick:* Scriptural Source of 'Blackness and Darkness'." *ANQ* 9 (1970): 6.

Wright, Nathalia. *"Mosses from an Old Manse* and *Moby-Dick:* The Shock of Discovery." *Modern Language Notes* (June 1952): 387–392. Rpt. in Vincent, Howard P., comp. *Merrill Studies in Moby-Dick*, 110–115.

Zoellner, Robert. "Queequeg: The Well-Governed Shark," in Zoellner, Robert. *Salt-Sea Mastodon: A Reading of Moby-Dick*. Berkeley, CA: University of California Press, 1973. 219–225. Rpt. in Gilmore, Michael T. *Twentieth Century Interpretations of Moby-Dick*, 87–93.

Zoellner, Robert. *Salt-Sea Mastodon: A Reading of Moby-Dick*. Berkeley, CA: University of California Press, 1973.

Omoo (1847)

Abrams, Robert E. *"Typee* and *Omoo:* Herman Melville and the Ungraspable Phantom of Identity." *ArQ* 31 (1975): 33–36, 45–50.

Barnett, Louise K. *Ignoble Savage*, 171, 175.

Dillingham, William B. *Artist in the Rigging*, 79–102, 134–135.

Gollin, Rita K. "Quondam Sailor and Melville's *Omoo*." *AL* 48 (1976): 75–79.

Haberstroh, Charles J., Jr. *Melville and Male Identity*, 41–51.

Hauck, Richard Boyd. *Cheerful Nihilism*, 83–85.

Hillway, Tyrus. *Herman Melville*, 70–72.

Kemper, Steven E. *"Omoo:* Germinal Melville." *SNNTS* 10 (1978): 420–430.

McCarthy, Paul. "Melville's Rascals on Land, Sea, and in the Air." *SoQ* 16 (1978): 320–322, 334–336.

Mason, Ronald. *Spirit Above the Dust*, 31–37.

Pops, Martin Leonard. *Melville Archetype*, 37–39.

Rosenberry, Edward H. *Melville*, 34–42.

Wadlington, Warwick. *Confidence Game in American Literature*, 42–56.

Pierre (1852)

Arvin, Newton. "Melville and the Gothic Novel." *New England Quarterly* 22 (March 1949): 41–44. Rpt. in Willett, Ralph, comp. *Merrill Studies in Pierre*, 12–15.

Bach, Bert C. "Narrative Technique and Structure in *Pierre*." *ATQ* 7 (1970): 5–8.

Baym, Nina. "Portrayal of Women in American Literature, 1790–1870," in Springer, Marlene, ed. *What Manner of Woman*, 223.

Bell, Michael D. "Glendinning Heritage: Melville's Literary Borrowings in *Pierre*." *SIR* 12 (1973): 741–762.

Bell, Michael Davitt. *Development of American Romance*, 226–231.

Berthoff, Warner. *Example of Melville*. Princeton, NJ: Princeton University Press, 1962. Rpt. in Willett, Ralph, comp. *Merrill Studies in Pierre*, 81–85.

Bowan, Merlin. *Long Encounter: Self and Experience in the Writings of Herman Melville*. Chicago: University of Chicago Press, 1960. 157–161. Rpt. in Willett, Ralph, comp. *Merrill Studies in Pierre*, 70–73.

Braswell, William. "Early Love Scenes in Melville's *Pierre*." *American Literature* 22 (November 1950): 285–289. Rpt. in Willett, Ralph, comp. *Merrill Studies in Pierre*, 20–23.

Bredahl, A. Carl, Jr. *Melville's Angles of Vision*, 39–48.

Brodhead, Richard H. *Hawthorne, Melville, and the Novel*, 12, 13, 17–18, 19, 127–128, 129, 163–193.

Canaday, Nicholas, Jr. "Melville's *Pierre*: At War with Social Convention." *PLL* 5 (1969): 51–62.

Cook, Richard M. "Evolving the Inscrutable: The Grotesque in Melville's Fiction." *AL* 49 (1978): 548–549.

Dichmann, Mary E. "Absolutism in Melville's *Pierre*." *PMLA* 67 (September 1952): 707–710. Rpt. in Willett, Ralph, comp. *Merrill Studies in Pierre*, 24–26.

Douglas, Ann. *Feminization of American Culture*, 294–296, 300, 309–313.

Dryden, Edgar A. "Entangled Text: Melville's *Pierre* and the Problem of Reading." *BoundaryII* 7.3 (1979): 145–173.

Duban, James. "Spenserian Maze of Melville's *Pierre*." *ESQ* 23 (1977): 217–225.

Fiedelson, Charles, Jr. *Symbolism and American Literature*. Chicago: University of Chicago Press, 1953. 191–201. Rpt. in Willett, Ralph, comp. *Merrill Studies in Pierre*, 47–55.

Franklin, H. Bruce. *Victim as Criminal and Artist*, 51–52.

Franklin, H. Bruce. *Wake of the Gods: Melville's Mythology*. Stanford, CA: Stanford University Press, 1963. 100–105, 110. Rpt. in Willett, Ralph, comp. *Merrill Studies in Pierre*, 88–92.

Frederick, John T. *Darkened Sky*, 98–101.

Fryer, Judith. *Faces of Eve*, 47–54, 87–89.

Furrow, Sharon. "Terrible Made Visible: Melville, Salvator Rosa, and Piranesi." *ESQ* 73 (1973): 244–251.

Gamble, Richard H. "Reflections of the Hawthorne-Melville Relationship in *Pierre*." *AL* 47 (1976): 629–632.

Giovannini, G. "Melville's *Pierre* and Dante's *Inferno*." *PMLA* 64 (March 1949): 74–78. Rpt. in Willett, Ralph, comp. *Merrill Studies in Pierre*, 15–19.

Haberstroh, Charles J., Jr. *Melville and Male Identity*, 66–70, 107–111.

Hauck, Richard Boyd. *Cheerful Nihilism*, 106–111.

Hauser, Helen A. "Spinozan Philosophy in *Pierre*." *AL* 49 (1977): 49–56.

Higgins, Brian. "Plinlimmon and the Pamphlet Again." *SNNTS* 4 (1972): 27–38.

Hillway, Tyrus. *Herman Melville*, 106–111.

Humphreys, A. R. *Herman Melville*. New York: Grove Press, 1960. 85–87, 90–92. Rpt. in Willett, Ralph, comp. *Merrill Studies in Pierre*, 85–87.

Karcher, Carolyn L. *Shadow over the Promised Land*, 94–102.

Kellner, R. Scott. "Sex, Toads, and Scorpions: A Study of the Psychological Themes in Melville's *Pierre*." *AQ* 31 (1975): 5–20.

Litman, Vicki H. "Cottage and the Temple: Melville's Symbolic Use of Architecture." *AQ* 21 (1969): 631, 632, 633, 634–637.

Lucas, Thomas E. "Herman Melville: The Purpose of the Novel." *TSLL* 13 (1972): 648–649, 651, 659, 660–661.

McCarthy, Paul. "Extraordinary Man as Idealist in Novels by Hawthorne and Melville." *ESQ* 54 (1969): 48, 50.

McCarthy, Paul. "Melville's Rascals on Land, Sea, and in the Air." *SoQ* 16 (1978): 315–317, 334–336.

Magretta, Joan. "Radical Disunities: Models of Mind and Madness in *Pierre* and *The Idiot*." *SNNTS* 10 (1978): 235–248.

Malin, Irving. "American Gothic Images." *Mosaic* 6.3 (1973): 149.

Mason, Ronald. *Spirit Above the Dust*, 158–178.

Matthiessen, F. O. *American Renaissance*. New York: Oxford University Press, 1941. 468–469. Rpt. in Willett, Ralph, comp. *Merrill Studies in Pierre*, 11–12.

Milder, Robert. "Melville's 'Intentions' in *Pierre*." *SNNTS* 6 (1974): 186–199.

Miller, Perry. "Melville and Transcendentalism." *Virginia Quarterly Review* 29.4 (August 1953): 571–575. Rpt. in Willett, Ralph, comp. *Merrill Studies in Pierre*, 45–46.

Miller, Perry. *Raven and the Whale*. New York: Harcourt Brace Jovanovich, 1956. 306–308. Rpt. in Willett, Ralph, comp. *Merrill Studies in Pierre*, 59–60.

Moorman, Charles. "Melville's *Pierre* and the Fortunate Fall." *American Literature* 25 (March 1953): 13–30. Rpt. in Willett, Ralph, comp. *Merrill Studies in Pierre*, 30–44.

Moorman, Charles. "Melville's Pierre in the City." *American Literature* 27 (January 1956): 571–572, 573–577. Rpt. in Willett, Ralph, comp. *Merrill Studies in Pierre*, 55–58.

Nelson, Raymond J. "Art of Herman Melville: the Author of *Pierre*." *Yale Review* 54 (Winter 1970): 197–214. Rpt. in Willett, Ralph, comp. *Merrill Studies in Pierre*, 97–110.

Oates, Joyce Carol. *Edge of Impossibility*, 66–71.

O'Connor, William Van. "Plotinus Plinlimmon and the Principle of Name Giving," in O'Connor, William Van. *Grotesque: An American Genre and Other Essays*. Carbondale, IL: Southern Illinois University Press, 1962. 94–96. Rpt. in Willett, Ralph, comp. *Merrill Studies in Pierre*, 79–80.

Parker, Hershel. "Why Pierre Went Wrong." *SNNTS* 8 (1976): 7–23.

Polk, James. "Melville and the Idea of the City." *UTQ* 41 (1972): 283–286.

Pops, Martin Leonard. *Melville Archetype*, 28–32, 88–120.

Porte, Joel. *Romance in America*, 170–184.

Rosenberry, Edward H. *Melville*, 87–100.

Rogers, Robert. *Psychoanalytic Study of the Double in Literature*, 133–137.

Seelye, John D. " 'Ungraspable Phantom': Reflections of Hawthorne in *Pierre* and *The Confidence-Man*." *SNNTS* 1.4 (1969): 438–439, 442.

Sherrill, Rowland A. *Prophetic Melville*, 188–199.

Spengemann, William C. *Adventurous Muse*, 201–209.

Stern, Milton R. *Fine Hammered Steel of Herman Melville*. Urbana, IL: University of Illinois Press, 1957. 151–161. Rpt. in Willett, Ralph, comp. *Merrill Studies in Pierre*, 60–70.

Stout, Janis P. "Encroaching Sodom: Melville's Urban Fiction." *TSLL* 17 (1975): 164–169.

Stout, Janis P. *Sodoms in Eden*, 129–134.

Strickland, Carol Colclough. "Coherence and Ambivalence in Melville's *Pierre*." *AL* 48 (1976): 302–311.

Sundquist, Eric J. *Home as Found*, 143–185.

Thomas, Joel J. "Melville's Use of Mysticism." *PQ* 53 (1974): 422–424.

Thompson, Lawrance. *Melville's Quarrel with God*. Princeton, NJ: Princeton University Press, 1967. 272–276. Rpt. in Willett, Ralph, comp. *Merrill Studies in Pierre*, 27–30.

Tobin, Patricia Dreschel. *Time and the Novel*, 42–46.

Travis, Mildred K. "Melville's 'Furies' Continued in *Pierre*." *ESQ* no.62 (1971): 33–35.

Travis, Mildred K. "Relevant Digressions in *Pierre*." *ATQ* 24 supp. 1 (1974): 7–8.

Wadlington, Warwick. *Confidence Game in American Literature*, 110–113, 116–120.

Watkins, Floyd. "Melville's Plotinus Plinlimmon and Pierre," in Walker, William E. and Robert L. Welker, eds. *Reality and Myth: Essays in American Literature in memory of Richard Croom Beatty*. Nashville, TN: Vanderbilt University Press, 1964. Rpt. in Willett, Ralph, comp. *Merrill Studies in Pierre*, 93–97.

Watson, E. L. Grant. "Melville's *Pierre*." *New England Quarterly* 3 (April 1930): 195–234. Rpt. in Rountree, Thomas J., ed. *Critics on Melville*, 94–100.

Watters, Reginald Eyre. *Essays and Articles*, 4, 5, 9–10, 14, 15–19, 31, 33, 37–38.

Wilson, James D. "Incest and American Romantic Fiction." *SLitI* 7.1 (1974): 46–49.

Wright, Nathalia. "*Pierre:* Herman Melville's *Inferno*." *American Literature* 32 (May 1960): 173–179. Rpt. in Willett, Ralph, comp. *Merrill Studies in Pierre*, 74–78.

Redburn (1849)

Andersen, Marilyn. "Melville's Jackets: *Redburn* and *White-Jacket*." *ArQ* 26 (1970): 173–175.

Barnett, Louise K. *Ignoble Savage*, 170, 173, 181.

Bell, Michael D. "Melville's *Redburn:* Initiation and Authority." *NEQ* 46 (1973): 558–572.

Bell, Michael Davitt. *Development of American Romance*, 202–203, 207–208, 209.

Bredahl, A. Carl, Jr. *Melville's Angles of Vision*, 16–26.

Canaday, Nicolas, Jr. "Harry Bolton and Redburn: The Old World and the New," in Kirby, Thomas Austin and William John Olive, eds. *Essays in Honor of Esmond Linworth Marilla*, 291–298.

Cook, Richard M. "Evolving the Inscrutable: The Grotesque in Melville's Fiction." *AL* 49 (1978): 545–546.

Dillingham, William B. *Artist in the Rigging*, 31–54, 133.

Douglas, Ann. *Feminization of American Culture*, 300–301.

Haberstoh, Charles. "*Redburn:* The Psychological Pattern." *SAF* 2 (1974): 133–144.

Haberstroh, Charles J., Jr. *Melville and Male Identity*, 73–84.

Hauck, Richard Boyd. *Cheerful Nihilism*, 90–92.

Henderson, Harry B. *Versions of the Past*, 131, 133–134.

Hillway, Tyrus. *Herman Melville*, 72–74.

Karcher, Carolyn L. "Melville and Racial Prejudice: A Re-Evaluation." *SoR* 12 (1976): 289–291.

Karcher, Carolyn L. *Shadow over the Promised Land*, 28–39.

Lewis, R. W. B. "Adamic Experience in *Redburn*," in Lewis, R. W. B. *American Adam: Innocence, Tragedy and Tradition in the Nineteenth Century*. Chicago: University of Chicago Press, 1955. 136–138. Rpt. in Rountree, Thomas J., ed. *Critics on Melville*, 70–71.

Litman, Vicki H. "Cottage and the Temple: Melville's Symbolic Use of Architecture." *AQ* 21 (1969): 630.

McCarthy, Harold T. *Expatriate Perspective*, 47–61.

McCarthy, Harold T. "Melville's *Redburn* and the City." *MidQ* 12 (1971): 395–410.

McCarthy, Paul. "Melville's Rascals on Land, Sea, and in the Air." *SoQ* 16 (1978): 313–315, 323–325, 334–336.

Malin, Irving. "American Gothic Images." *Mosaic* 6.3 (1973): 157–158, 167.

Mason, Ronald. *Spirit Above the Dust*, 67–79.

Polk, James. "Melville and the Idea of the City." *UTQ* 41 (1972): 281–283.

Pops, Martin Leonard. *Melville Archetype*, 50–57.

Rosenberry, Edward H. *Melville*, 61–66.

Sattelmeyer, Robert. "Origin of Harry Bolton in *Redburn*." *ATQ* 31 (1976): 23–25.

Sherrill, Rowland A. *Prophetic Melville*, 33–61, 111–112, 116–121.

Simpson, Eleanor E. "Melville and the Negro: From *Typee* to 'Benito Cereno'." *AL* 41 (1969): 24–25.

Stout, Janis P. "Encroaching Sodom: Melville's Urban Fiction." *TSLL* 17 (1975): 159–162.

Stout, Janis P. *Sodoms in Eden*, 122–127.

Watson, Charles N., Jr. "Melville's Jackson: *Redburn*'s Heroic 'Double'." *ESQ* no.62 (1971): 8–10.

Watters, Reginald Eyre. *Essays and Articles*, 29.

Typee (1846)

Abrams, Robert E. "*Typee* and *Omoo*: Herman Melville and the Ungraspable Phantom of Identity." *ArQ* 31 (1975): 33–45.

Babin, James L. "Melville and the Deformation of Being: From *Typee* to *Leviathan*." *SoR* 7 (1971): 91–105.

Barnett, Louise K. *Ignoble Savage*, 167–168, 169–170, 171, 173–175.

Bell, Michael Davitt. *Development of American Romance*, 203–204.

Bredahl, A. Carl, Jr. *Melville's Angles of Vision*, 7–15.

Clark, Michael. "Melville's *Typee*: Fact, Fiction, and Esthetics." *ArQ* 34 (1978): 351–370.

Cook, Richard M. "Evolving the Inscrutable: The Grotesque in Melville's Fiction." *AL* 49 (1978): 545.

Dillingham, William B. *Artist in the Rigging*, 9–30, 132–133.

Firebaugh, Joseph J. "Humorist as Rebel: The Melville of *Typee*." *Nineteenth-Century Fiction* 9 (Sept 1954): 108–120. Rpt. in Rountree, Thomas J., ed. *Critics on Melville*, 55–61.

Giltrow, Janet. "Speaking Out: Travel and Structure in Herman Melville's Early Narratives." *AL* 52 (1980): 18–31.

Haberstroh, Charles J., Jr. *Melville and Male Identity*, 33–41.

Hauck, Richard Boyd. *Cheerful Nihilism*, 79–82.

Hays, Peter L. *Limping Hero*, 132–134.

Henderson, Harry B. *Versions of the Past*, 128–129.

Hillway, Tyrus. *Herman Melville*, 68–70.

Joswick, Thomas P. "*Typee:* The Quest for Origin." *Criticism* 17 (1975): 335–354.

McCarthy, Paul. "Elements of Anatomy in Melville's Fiction." *SNNTS* 6 (1974): 39–40.

McCarthy, Paul. "Melville's Rascals on Land, Sea, and in the Air." *SoQ* 16 (1978): 320–323, 334–336.

Mason, Ronald. *Spirit Above the Dust*, 21–30.

Ousby, Ian. *Reader's Guide to Fifty American Novels*, 74–76.

Pops, Martin Leonard. *Melville Archetype*, 33–37.

Rosenberry, Edward H. *Melville*, 34–42.

Sattelmeyer, Robert. "Thoreau and Melville's *Typee*." *AL* 52 (1980): 462–468.

Sherrill, Rowland A. *Prophetic Melville*, 7–32, 112–116.

Spengemann, William C. *Adventurous Muse*, 178–188.

Sweeney, Gerard M. "Melville's Smoky Humor: Fire-Lighting in *Typee*." *ArQ* 34 (1978): 371–376.

Wadlington, Warwick. *Confidence Game in American Literature*, 56–68.

Watters, Reginald Eyre. *Essays and Articles*, 13, 20, 29, 31, 38.

Witherington, Paul. "Art of Melville's *Typee*." *ArQ* 26 (1970): 136–150.

Young, Philip. *Three Bags Full*, 99–112.

White-Jacket (1850)

Albrecht, Robert C. "White Jacket's Intentional Fall." *SNNTS* 4 (1972): 17–26.

Allen, Priscilla. "*White-Jacket* and the Man-of-War Microcosm." *AQ* 25 (1973): 32–47.

Andersen, Marilyn. "Melville's Jackets: *Redburn* and *White-Jacket*." *ArQ* 26 (1970): 175–181.

Barnett, Louise K. *Ignoble Savage*, 170, 171, 176–178.

Bell, Michael Davitt. *Development of American Romance*, 200–202, 208–210, 210–211.

Bredahl, A. Carl, Jr. *Melville's Angles of Vision*, 27–38.

Caserio, Robert L. *Plot, Story, and the Novel*, 134, 159–166.

Cook, Richard M. "Evolving the Inscrutable: The Grotesque in Melville's Fiction." *AL* 49 (1978): 551–552.

Dillingham, William B. *Artist in the Rigging*, 57–78, 133–134.

Douglas, Ann. *Feminization of American Culture*, 297–298, 303–304.

Frederick, John T. *Darkened Sky*, 91.

Giantvalley, Scott and Christina C. Stough. " 'Precedents Are Against It': An Examination of *White-Jacket* as a Corrective for the 'Two Moby-Dicks' Theory." *SAF* 8 (1980): 165–181.

Haberstroh, Charles J., Jr. *Melville and Male Identity*, 73–76, 84–92.

Hauck, Richard Boyd. *Cheerful Nihilism*, 85–90.

Henderson, Harry B. *Versions of the Past*, 134.

Hillway, Tyrus. *Herman Melville*, 74–77.

Huntress, Keith. " 'Guinea' of *White-Jacket* and Chief Justice Shaw." *AL* 43 (1972): 639–641.

Karcher, Carolyn L. *Shadow Over the Promised Land*, 39–55.

McCarthy, Paul. "Elements of Anatomy in Melville's Fiction." *SNNTS* 6 (1974): 43–47.

McCarthy, Paul. "Melville's Rascals on Land, Sea, and in the Air." *SoQ* 16 (1978): 325–327, 331–332, 334–336.

Mason, Ronald. *Spirit Above the Dust*, 80–95.

Miller, Wayne Charles. *Armed America, Its Face in Fiction*, 33–42.

Oates, Joyce Carol. *Edge of Impossibility*, 63–64.

Polk, James. "Melville and the Idea of the City." *UTQ* 41 (1972): 280.

Pops, Martin Leonard. *Melville Archetype*, 57–59.

Reynolds, Larry J. "Antidemocratic Emphasis in *White-Jacket*." *AL* 48 (1976): 13–28.

Rosenberry, Edward H. *Melville*, 66–70.

Sherrill, Rowland A. *Prophetic Melville*, 62–81.

Simpson, Eleanor E. "Melville and the Negro: From *Typee* to 'Benito Cereno'." *AL* 41 (1969): 25.

Stout, Janis P. "Encroaching Sodom: Melville's Urban Fiction." *TSLL* 17 (1975): 162–164.

Stout, Janis P. *Sodoms in Eden*, 127–129.

Vincent, Howard P. "*White-Jacket:* An Essay in Interpretation." *New England Quarterly* 22 (Sept 1949): 304–315. Rpt. in Rountree, Thomas J., ed. *Critics on Melville*, 72–75.

Watters, Reginald Eyre. *Essays and Articles*, 14, 33.

MÉNDEZ, MIGUEL (1930–)

Peregrinos de Aztlán (1974)

Robinson, Cecil. *Mexico and the Hispanic Southwest in American Literature*, 328–330.

Pilgrims of Aztán see *Peregrinos de Aztlán*

MERIWETHER, LOUISE (1923–)

Daddy Was a Number Runner (1970)

Schultz, Elizabeth. " 'Free in Fact and at Last': The Image of the Black Woman in Black American Fiction," in Springer, Marlene, ed. *What Manner of Woman*, 330, 332, 334–335.

MICELI, FRANK (1932–)

Seventh Month (1969)

Green, Rose Basile. *Italian-American Novel*, 243–250.

MILLAR, KENNETH see MACDONALD, ROSS

MILLEN, GILMORE (1897–(?))

Sweet Man (1930)

    Berzon, Judith R. *Neither White Nor Black*, 64.

MILLER, CAROLINE (1903–)

Lamb in His Bosom (1933)

    Baker, Donald G. "Black Images: The Afro-American in Popular Novels, 1900–1945." *JPC* 7 (1973): 338.

MILLER, HENRY (1891–1980)

Tropic of Cancer (1934)

    Donald, Miles. *American Novel in the Twentieth Century*, 109–113.
    Friedman, Alan W. *Multivalence*, 39–46.
    Gutierrez, Donald. " 'Hypocrite lecteur': *Tropic of Cancer* as Sexual Comedy." *Mosaic* 11.2 (1978): 21–33.
    Jackson, Paul R. "Caterwauling and Harmony: Music in *Tropic of Cancer*." *Crit* 20.3 (1978): 40–50.
    Jackson, Paul R. "Henry Miller's Literary Pregnancies." *L&P* 19 (1969): 41–42.
    Littlejohn, David. *Interruptions*, 37–44.
    Rahv, Philip. *Literature and the Sixth Sense*, 90–94.

Tropic of Capricorn (1939)

    Friedman, Alan W. *Multivalence*, 39–46.
    Jackson, Paul R. "Henry Miller's Literary Pregnancies." *L&P* 19 (1969): 38–39, 43–45.
    Littlejohn, David. *Interruptions*, 37–44.
    Rahv, Philip. *Literature and the Sixth Sense*, 90–94.

MILLER, WALTER M. JR., (1923–)

Canticle for Leibowitz (1959)

    Ash, Brian. *Faces of the Future*, 194–196.
    Griffin, Russell M. "Medievalism in *A Canticle for Leibowitz*." *Extrapolation* 14 (1973): 112–125.
    Ketterer, David. *New Worlds for Old*, 140–148.
    Ketterer, David. "Take-Off to Cosmic Irony: Science-Fiction Humor and the Absurd," in Cohen, Sara Blacher, ed. *Comic Relief*, 79–81, 82.
    Percy, Walker. "Walter M. Miller, Jr.'s *A Canticle for Leibowitz:* A Rediscovery." *SoR* 7 (1971): 572–578.
    Samuelson, David. *Visions of Tomorrow*, 228–279.
    Scholes, Robert and Eric S. Rabkin. *Science Fiction*, 50–51, 221–226.
    Wolfe, Gary K. *Known and the Unknown*, 137–145.

MIRABELLI, EUGENE (1931–)

Way In (1968)

Green, Rose Basile. *Italian-American Novel*, 233–236.

MITCHELL, MARGARET (1900–1949)

Gone with the Wind (1936)

Baker, Donald G. "Black Images: The Afro-American in Popular Novels, 1900–1945." *JPC* 7 (1973): 340.

Gelfant, Blanche H. "*Gone with the Wind* and the Impossibilities of Fiction." *SLJ* 13.1 (1980): 3–31.

May, Robert E. "*Gone with the Wind* as Southern History: A Reappraisal." *SoQ* 17.1 (1978): 51–64.

Rubin, Louis D., Jr. "Scarlett O'Hara and the Two Quentin Compsons," in Harrington, Evans and Ann J. Abadie, eds. *South and Faulkner's Yoknapatawpha*, 171–191.

Schefski, Harold K. "Margaret Mitchell: *Gone with the Wind* and *War and Peace*." *SoS* 19 (1980): 243–260.

Watkins, Floyd C. *In Time and Place*, 33–48.

MITCHELL, S. WEIR (1829–1914)

Adventures of François (1898)

Lovering, Joseph P. *S. Weir Mitchell*, 143–148.

Characteristics (1891)

Lovering, Joseph P. *S. Weir Mitchell*, 114–118.

Circumstance (1901)

Lovering, Joseph P. *S. Weir Mitchell*, 76–82.

Constance Trescot (1905)

Lovering, Joseph P. *S. Weir Mitchell*, 82–93.

Dr. North and His Friends (1909)

Lovering, Joseph P. *S. Weir Mitchell*, 118–133.

Far in the Forest (1889)

Lovering, Joseph P. *S. Weir Mitchell*, 101–106.

Hugh Wynne (1896)

Lovering, Joseph P. *S. Weir Mitchell*, 134–139.

In War Time (1884)

Lovering, Joseph P. *S. Weir Mitchell*, 52–64.

John Sherwood (1911)

Lovering, Joseph P. *S. Weir Mitchell*, 109–113.

Red City (1907)

Lovering, Joseph P. *S. Weir Mitchell*, 148–154.

Roland Blake (1886)

    Lovering, Joseph P. *S. Weir Mitchell*, 64–75.

Westways (1913)

    Lovering, Joseph P. *S. Weir Mitchell*, 93–98.

When All the Woods Are Green (1894)

    Lovering, Joseph P. *S. Weir Mitchell*, 106–109.

MITCHELL, W. O. (1914–)

Kite (1962)

    New, W. H. *Articulating West*, 45, 50–52, 56–59.

    New, W. H. "Feeling of Completion: Aspects of W. O. Mitchell," in Stephens, Donald G., ed. *Writers of the Prairies*, 89, 93–95, 97–100.

    New, W. H. "Feeling of Completion: Aspects of W. O. Mitchell," in Woodcock, George, ed. *Canadian Novel*, 178–180, 182–185.

Vanishing Point (1973)

    Bartlett, Donald R. "Dumplings and Dignity." *CanL* 77 (1978): 73–80.

    Harrison, Dick. *Unnamed Country*, 197–199.

    Williams, David. "Indian Our Ancestor: Three Modes of Vision in Recent Canadian Fiction." *DR* 58 (1978): 316–321.

Who Has Seen the Wind (1947)

    Dawson, Anthony B. "Coming of Age in Canada." *Mosaic* 11.3 (1978): 50–52.

    Harrison, Dick. *Unnamed Country*, 172–180.

    Jones, D. G. *Butterfly on Rock*, 37–38.

    Kreisel, Henry. "Prairie: A State of Mind." *Transactions of the Royal Society of Canada* 6.4 (June 1968). Rpt. in Gerson, Carole, comp. *Modern Canadian Fiction*, 6.

    Mathews, Robin. *Canadian Literature*, 22, 109–118.

    Mathews, Robin D. "Wacousta Factor," in Bessai, Diane and David Jackel, eds. *Figures in a Ground*, 311.

    New, W. H. *Articulating West*, 45–50, 52–56.

    New, W. H. "Feeling of Completion: Aspects of W. O. Mitchell," in Stephens, Donald G., ed. *Writers of the Prairies*, 89–93, 95–97, 99, 100.

    New, W. H. "Feeling of Completion: Aspects of W. O. Mitchell," in Woodcock, George, ed. *Canadian Novel*, 174–178, 180–182, 184–185.

    Sutherland, Ronald. *Second Image*, 11–16, 89–107.

    Tallman, Warren. "Wolf in the Snow." *Canadian Literature* 5 (Summer 1960): 7–20 & *Canadian Literature* 6 (Autumn 1960): 41–48. Rpt. in Cook, Gregory M., ed. *Ernest Buckler*, 56, 57–60, 72–74.

    Tallman, Warren. "Wolf in the Snow." *Canadian Literature* 5 (Summer 1960): 7–20 & *Canadian Literature* 6 (Autumn 1960): 41–48. Rpt. in Gerson, Carole, comp. *Modern Canadian Fiction*, 101, 106.

MOCKINGBIRD, JON (1903(?)–)

Wokosani Road (1962)

    Larson, Charles R. *American Indian Fiction*, 181–189.

MOJTABAI, A. G. (1938–)

Mundome (1974)

Olson, Carol Booth. "Mirrors and Madness: A.G. Mojtabai's *Mundome.*" *Crit* 20.2 (1978): 71–82.

MOMADAY, N. SCOTT (1934–)

House Made of Dawn (1969)

Allen, Paula Gunn. "Stranger in My Own Life: Alienation in American Indian Prose and Poetry." *MELUS* 7.2 (1980): 11–13.

Barry, Nora Baker. "Bear's Son Folk Tale in *When the Legends Die* and *House Made of Dawn.*" *WAL* 12 (1978): 281–287.

Beidler, Peter. "Animals and Human Development in the Contemporary American Indian Novel." *WAL* 14 (1979): 134–139.

Dickinson-Brown, Roger. "Art and Importance of N. Scott Momaday." *SoR* 14 (1978): 30–33.

Espey, David B. "Endings in Contemporary American Indian Fiction." *WAL* 13 (1978): 137–139.

Evers, Lawrence J. "Words and Place: A Reading of *House Made of Dawn.*" *WAL* 11 (1977): 297–320.

Evers, Lawrence J. "Words and Place: A Reading of [N. Scott Momaday's] *House Made of Dawn.*" *Western American Literature* 11 (1977): 297–320. Rpt. in Pilkington, William T., ed. *Critical Essays on the Western American Novel*, 243–259.

Hylton, Marion W. "On a Trail of Pollen: Momaday's *House Made of Dawn.*" *Crit* 14.2 (1972): 60–69.

Kerr, Baine. "The Novel as Sacred Text: N. Scott Momaday's Myth-Making Ethic." *SR* 63 (1978): 172–179.

Larson, Charles R. *American Indian Fiction*, 66–68, 78–96.

Lattin, Vernon E. "Quest for Mythic Vision in Contemporary Native American and Chicano Fiction." *AL* 50 (1979): 632–637.

McAllister, H. S. "Be a Man, Be a Woman: Androgyny in *House Made of Dawn.*" *AIQ* 2 (1975): 14–22.

Trimble, Martha Scott. *N. Scott Momaday*, 20–27.

Watkins, Floyd C. *In Time and Place*, 133–171.

Woodward, Charles L. "Momaday's *House Made of Dawn.*" *Expl* 36.2 (1978): 27–28.

MONTGOMERY, L. M. (1874–1942)

Anne of Green Gables (1908)

Fredeman, Jane Cowan. "Land of Lost Content: The Use of Fantasy in L. M. Montgomery's Novels," in Sorfleet, John Robert, ed. *L.M. Montgomery*, 65, 66.

Rubio, Mary. "Satire, Realism, and Imagination in *Anne of Green Gables,*" in Sorfleet, John Robert, ed. *L.M. Montgomery*, 27–35.

Whitaker, Muriel A. " 'Queer Children': L. M. Montgomery's Heroines," in Sorfleet, John Robert, ed. *L.M. Montgomery*, 51–53, 55–56, 57.

Willis, Leslie. "Bogus Ugly Duckling: Anne Shirley Unmasked." *DR* 56 (1976): 247–251.

Anne of Ingleside (1939)

    Thomas, Gillian. "Decline of Anne: Matron vs. Child," in Sorfleet, John Robert, ed. *L.M. Montgomery*, 37–41.

Blue Castle (1926)

    Fredeman, Jane Cowan. "Land of Lost Content: The Use of Fantasy in L. M. Montgomery's Novels," in Sorfleet, John Robert, ed. *L.M. Montgomery*, 61–64.

    Whitaker, Muriel A. " 'Queer Children': L. M. Montgomery's Heroines," in Sorfleet, John Robert, ed. *L.M. Montgomery*, 53–54, 56, 57.

Emily of New Moon (1923)

    Fredeman, Jane Cowan. "Land of Lost Content: The Use of Fantasy in L. M. Montgomery's Novels," in Sorfleet, John Robert, ed. *L.M. Montgomery*, 67–69.

    Whitaker, Muriel A. " 'Queer Children': L. M. Montgomery's Heroines," in Sorfleet, John Robert, ed. *L.M. Montgomery*, 51–53, 55–56, 57.

Magic for Marigold (1929)

    Fredeman, Jane Cowan. "Land of Lost Content: The Use of Fantasy in L. M. Montgomery's Novels," in Sorfleet, John Robert, ed. *L.M. Montgomery*, 61–62, 64.

Pat of Silver Bush (1933)

    Fredeman, Jane Cowan. "Land of Lost Content: The Use of Fantasy in L. M. Montgomery's Novels," in Sorfleet, John Robert, ed. *L.M. Montgomery*, 66.

    Whitaker, Muriel A. " 'Queer Children': L. M. Montgomery's Heroines," in Sorfleet, John Robert, ed. *L.M. Montgomery*, 55, 56, 57.

Story Girl (1911)

    Fredeman, Jane Cowan. "Land of Lost Content: The Use of Fantasy in L. M. Montgomery's Novels," in Sorfleet, John Robert, ed. *L.M. Montgomery*, 64–66.

MOON, BUCKLIN (1911–)

Without Magnolias (1949)

    Starke, Catherine Juanita. *Black Portraiture in American Fiction*, 196–197.

MOORE, BRIAN (1921– 1999)

Answer from Limbo (1962)

    Dahlie, Hallvard. *Brian Moore*, 65–84.

    Woodcock, George. *Odysseus Ever Returning*, 42, 43, 47–48.

Emperor of Ice Cream (1965)

    Dahlie, Hallvard. *Brian Moore*, 85–103.

    Woodcock, George. *Odysseus Ever Returning*, 42, 44.

Feast of Lupercal (1957)

    Dahlie, Hallvard. *Brian Moore*, 32–47.

    Ludwig, Jack. "Mirror of Moore," in Woodcock, George, ed. *Canadian Novel*, 212–213.

    Woodcock, George. *Odysseus Ever Returning*, 42, 43, 44–45.

I Am Mary Dunne (1968)
Dahlie, Hallvard. *Brian Moore*, 104–119.
Moss, John. *Sex and Violence*, 41–42.
Woodcock, George. *Odysseus Ever Returning*, 41–42, 43, 48–49.

Judith Hearne (1955)
Dahlie, Hallvard. *Brian Moore*, 12–31.
Ludwig, Jack. "Mirror of Moore," in Woodcock, George, ed. *Canadian Novel*, 212.
Woodcock, George. *Odysseus Ever Returning*, 41, 42, 43, 44, 47.

Lonely Passion of Judith Hearne see *Judith Hearne*

Luck of Ginger Coffey (1960)
Atwood, Margaret. *Survival*, 157–158.
Dahlie, Hallvard. *Brian Moore*, 48–64.
Ludwig, Jack. "Mirror of Moore," in Woodcock, George, ed. *Canadian Novel*, 213–218.
Woodcock, George. *Odysseus Ever Returning*, 42, 45–47.

MORGAN, JOE (1912–)

Expense Account (1958)
Bryant, Jerry H. *Open Decision*, 183–184.

MORRIS, WRIGHT (1910–)

Ceremony in a Lone Tree (1960)
Harper, Robert D. "Wright Morris's *Ceremony in Lone Tree:* A Picture of Life in Middle America." *WAL* 11 (1976): 199–213.

MORRISON, TONI (1931–)

Bluest Eye (1970)
Bischoff, Joan. "Novels of Toni Morrison: Studies in Thwarted Sensitivity." *SIBL* 6.3 (1975): 21–22, 23.
Christian, Barbara. *Black Women Novelists*, 138–153 176–179, 242–246.
Ogunyemi, Chikwenye Okonjo. "Order and Disorder in Toni Morrison's *The Bluest Eye.*" *Crit* 19.1 (1977): 112–120.
Schultz, Elizabeth. " 'Free in Fact and at Last': The Image of the Black Woman in Black American Fiction," in Springer, Marlene, ed. *What Manner of Woman*, 324.
Weever, Jacqueline de. "Inverted World of Toni Morrison's *The Bluest Eye* and *Sula.*" *CLAJ* 22 (1979): 402–407.

Song of Solomon (1978)
Blake, Susan L. "Folklore and Community in *Song of Solomon.*" *MELUS* 7.3 (1980): 77–82.
Harris, A. Leslie. "Myth as Structure in Toni Morrison's *Song of Solomon.*" *MELUS* 7.3 (1980): 69–76.

Sula (1974)
Bischoff, Joan. "Novels of Toni Morrison: Studies in Thwarted Sensitivity." *SIBL* 6.3 (1975): 22–23.

Christian, Barbara. *Black Women Novelists*, 153–175, 176–179, 246–252.
Lee, Valerie Gray. "Use of Folktalk in Novels by Black Women Writers." *CLAJ* 23 (1980): 269–270.
Schultz, Elizabeth. " 'Free in Fact and at Last': The Image of the Black Woman in Black American Fiction," in Springer, Marlene, ed. *What Manner of Woman*, 336–337.
Weever, Jacqueline de. "Inverted World of Toni Morrison's *The Bluest Eye* and *Sula*." *CLAJ* 22 (1979): 408–414.

MORTON, FREDERIC (1924–)

Asphalt and Desire (1952)
  Gelfant, Blanche Housman. *American City Novel*, 245–246.

MOTLEY, WILLARD (1909–1965)

Knock on Any Door (1947)
  Bayliss, John F. "Nick Romano: Father and Son." *NALF* 3 (1969): 18–20.
  Gelfant, Blanche Housman. *American City Novel*, 248–252.
  Grenander, M. E. "Criminal Responsibility in *Native Son* and *Knock on Any Door*." *AL* 49 (1977): 221–233.
Let No Man Write My Epitaph (1958)
  Bayliss, John F. "Nick Romano: Father and Son." *NALF* 3 (1969): 20–21.
  Weyant, N. Jill. "Willard Motley's Pivotal Novel: *Let No Man Write My Epitaph*." *BALF* 11 (1977): 56–60.
We Fished All Night (1951)
  Bigsby, C. W. E., "From Protest to Paradox: The Black Writer at Mid Century," in French, Warren, ed. *Fifties*, 221–222.

MOURNING DOVE (1888(?)–1933)

Co-ge-we-a (1927)
  Larson, Charles R. *American Indian Fiction*, 173–180.

MOWAT, FARLEY (1921–)

Whale for the Killing (1972)
  Polk, James. "(Farley) Mowat's Leviathan." *CanL* 57 (1973): 120–124.

MURPHY, DENNIS

Sergeant (1958)
  Jones, Peter G. *War and the Novelist*, 123–128.

MURRAY, ALBERT (1916–)

Train, Whistle, Guitar (1974)
  Schultz, Elizabeth A. "Heirs of Ralph Ellison: Patterns of Individualism in the Contemporary Afro-American Novel." *CLAJ* 22 (1978): 114–117.

MYRER, ANTON (1922–)

Big War (1957)

Jones, Peter G. *War and the Novelist*, 27–32.
Waldmeir, Joseph J. *American Novels of the Second World War*, 103–104.

Once an Eagle (1968)

Jones, Peter G. *War and the Novelist*, 99–105, 199–200.

NABOKOV, VLADIMIR (1899–1977)

Ada (1969)

Bader, Julia. *Crystal Land*, 123–162.
Bok, Sissela. "Redemption Through Art in Nabokov's *Ada*." *Crit* 12.3 (1971): 110–120.
Ciancio, Ralph A. "Nabokov and the Verbal Mode of the Grotesque." *ConL* 18 (1977): 519.
Couturier, Maurice. "Nabokov's Performative Writing," in Johnson, Ira D. and Christiane Johnson, eds. *Les Américanistes*, 158, 160, 162, 163, 164–165, 166–167, 169, 170, 171–173, 174, 175–176, 177, 178–179.
Godshalk, William L. "Nabokov's Byronic *Ada:* A Note." *NConL* 2.2 (1972): 2–4.
Lee, L. L. *Vladimir Nabokov*, 144–152.
Morton, Donald E. *Vladimir Nabokov*, 131–142.
Pifer, Ellen. "Dark Paradise: Shades of Heaven and Hell in *Ada*." *MFS* 25 (1979): 481–497.
Pifer, Ellen. *Nabokov and the Novel*, 132–157.
Purdy, Strother B. *Hole in the Fabric*, 93–131, 165–167.
Rivers, J. E. and William Walker. "Nabokov's *Ada*." *Expl* 36.2 (1978): 7–8.
Stark, John. *Literature of Exhaustion*, 62–117.
Swanson, Roy Arthur. "Nabokov's *Ada* as Science Fiction." *SFS* 2 (1975): 76–87.
Tobin, Patricia Dreschel. *Time and the Novel*, 133–163.

Bend Sinister (1947)

Bader, Julia. *Crystal Land*, 95–122.
Baxter, Charles. "Nabokov, Idolatry, and the Police State." *BoundaryII* 5 (1977): 818–821.
Green, Geoffrey. "Nabokov's Signs of Reference, Symbols of Design." *CollL* 7 (1980): 109–110.
Lee, L. L. *Vladimir Nabokov*, 104–114.
Mead, David G. "Nabokovian Borrowing." *ANQ* 13 (1974): 23–24.
Morton, Donald E. *Vladimir Nabokov*, 43–44, 53–61.
Moynahan, Julian. "Vladimir Nabokov," in Wright, George T., ed. *Seven American Stylists, From Poe to Mailer*, 178–179.
Patteson, Richard F. " Nabokov's *Bend Sinister:* The Narrator as God." *SAF* 5 (1977): 241–253.
Pifer, Ellen. *Nabokov and the Novel*, 68–96, 105–106.
Schaeffer, Susan F. "*Bend Sinister* and the Novelist as Anthropomorphic Deity." *CentR* 17 (1973): 115–151.
Sheidlower, David I. "Reading between the Lines and the Squares." *MFS* 25 (1979): 413–424.

Defense (1930)

Lee, L. L. *Vladimir Nabokov*, 46–50.
Morton, Donald E. *Vladimir Nabokov*, 34–35.
Moynahan, Julian. "Vladimir Nabokov," in Wright, George T., ed. *Seven American Stylists, From Poe to Mailer*, 175–176.

Despair (1936)

Lee, L. L. *Vladimir Nabokov*, 62–70.
Morton, Donald E. *Vladimir Nabokov*, 35–36.
Pifer, Ellen. *Nabokov and the Novel*, 98–105.
Stuart, Dabney. *Nabokov*, 115–132.

Eye (1938)

Morton, Donald E. *Vladimir Nabokov*, 33–34.
Moynahan, Julian. "Vladimir Nabokov," in Wright, George T., ed. *Seven American Stylists, From Poe to Mailer*, 175.

Gift (1937)

Begnal, Michael H. "Fiction, Biography, History: Nabokov's *The Gift*." *JNT* 10 (1980): 138–143.
Lee, L. L. *Vladimir Nabokov*, 80–94.
Morton, Donald E. *Vladimir Nabokov*, 38–39.
Moynahan, Julian. *Vladimir Nabokov*, 37–40.
Moynahan, Julian. "Vladimir Nabokov," in Wright, George T., ed. *Seven American Stylists, From Poe to Mailer*, 191–195.

Glory (1932)

Lee, L. L. *Vladimir Nabokov*, 50–55.
Morton, Donald E. *Vladimir Nabokov*, 37–38.

Invitation to a Beheading (1938)

Klemter, Susan Strehle. "To 'Special Space': Transformotion in *Invitation to a Beheading*." *MFS* 25 (1979): 427–438.
Lee, L. L. *Vladimir Nabokov*, 70–79.
Morton, Donald E. *Vladimir Nabokov*, 39–40.
Moynahan, Julian. "Vladimir Nabokov," in Wright, George T., ed. *Seven American Stylists, From Poe to Mailer*, 177–178.
Penner, Dick. "*Invitation to a Beheading:* Nabokov's Absurdist Initiation." *Crit* 20.3 (1978): 27–38.
Pifer, Ellen. *Nabokov and the Novel*, 49–67.
Schuman, Samuel. "Vladimir Nabokov's *Invitation to a Beheading* and Robert Heinlein's 'They'." *TCL* 19 (1973): 99–101.
Stuart, Dabney. *Nabokov*, 56–85.

King, Queen, Knave (1928)

Lee, L. L. *Vladimir Nabokov*, 38–45.
Morton, Donald E. *Vladimir Nabokov*, 28–29, 31.
Moynahan, Julian. "Vladimir Nabokov," in Wright, George T., ed. *Seven American Stylists, From Poe to Mailer*, 174–175.
Pifer, Ellen. *Nabokov and the Novel*, 14–48.

Laughter in the Dark (1933)

Lee, L. L. *Vladimir Nabokov*, 56–62.
Morton, Donald E. *Vladimir Nabokov*, 29–30, 31.
Moynahan, Julian. *Vladimir Nabokov*, 25–31.
Moynahan, Julian. "Vladimir Nabokov," in Wright, George T., ed. *Seven American Stylists, From Poe to Mailer*, 181–186.
Pifer, Ellen. *Nabokov and the Novel*, 159–163.
Stuart, Dabney. *Nabokov*, 87–113.

Lolita (1955)

Anderson, William. "Time and Memory in Nabokov's *Lolita*." *CentR* 24 (1980): 360–383.
Bader, Julia. *Crystal Land*, 57–81.
Ciancio, Ralph A. "Nabokov and the Verbal Mode of the Grotesque." *ConL* 18 (1977): 520, 521–522, 523–530, 531–532.
Donald, Miles. *American Novel in the Twentieth Century*, 137–140.
Green, Geoffrey. "Nabokov's Signs of Reference, Symbols of Design." *CollL* 7 (1980): 110.
Harold, Brent. "*Lolita:* Nabokov's Critique of Aloofness." *PLL* 11 (1975): 71–82.
Josipovici, Gabriel. *World and the Book*, 201–220.
Lee, L. L. *Vladimir Nabokov*, 115–124.
Levine, Robert T. "*Lolita* and the Originality of Style." *ELWIU* 4 (1977): 110–121.
Levine, Robert T. " 'My Ultraviolet Darling': The Loss of Lolita's Childhood." *MFS* 25 (1979): 471–479.
Merrill, Robert. "Nabokov and Fictional Artifice." *MFS* 25 (1979): 446–454.
Miles, Thomas H. "Lolita: Humbert's Playful Goddess." *NConL* 6.4 (1976): 5–7.
Morton, Donald E. *Vladimir Nabokov*, 64–81.
Moynahan, Julian. *Vladimir Nabokov*, 31–36.
Moynahan, Julian. "Vladimir Nabokov," in Wright, George T., ed. *Seven American Stylists, From Poe to Mailer*, 181–182, 186–191.
Nelson, Gerald B. *Ten Versions of America*, 185–201.
Pearce, Richard. "Nabokov's Black (Hole) Humor: *Lolita* and *Pale Fire*," in Cohen, Sara Blacher, ed. *Comic Relief*, 32–38, 43–44.
Pearce, Richard. *Stages of the Clown*, 94–101.
Pifer, Ellen. *Nabokov and the Novel*, 106–110, 164–170.
Prioleau, Elizabeth. "Humbert Humbert Through the Looking Glass." *TCL* 21 (1975): 428–437.
Purdy, Strother B. *Hole in the Fabric*, 136–149.
Roth, Phyllis A. "In Search of Aesthetic Bliss: A Rereading of *Lolita*." *CollL* 2 (1975): 28–49.
Rubman, Lewis H. "Creatures and Creators in *Lolita* and 'Death and the Compass'." *MFS* 19 (1973): 433–444.
Schuman, Samuel. "Tempest in a Fleshpot." *Mosaic* 10.1 (1976): 1–5.
Spiegel, Alan. *Fiction and the Camera Eye*, 120–124.
Stark, John. *Literature of Exhaustion*, 62–117.
Tekiner, Christina. "Time in *Lolita*." *MFS* 25 (1979): 463–469.
Trilling, Lionel. *Speaking of Literature and Society*, 322–342.
Veeder, William. "Technique and Recovery: *Lolita* and *Mother Night*," in Klinkowitz, Jerome and Donald L. Lawler, eds. *Vonnegut in America*, 97–132.
Vesterman, William. "Why Humbert Shoots Quilty." *ELWIU* 5 (1978): 85–93.

Wallace, Ronald. *Last Laugh*, 65–89.

Winston, Mathew. "*Lolita* and the Dangers of Fiction." *TCL* 21 (1975): 421–427.

Mary (1925)

Lee, L. L. *Vladimir Nabokov*, 34–38.

Morton, Donald E. *Vladimir Nabokov*, 27–28, 30–31.

Pale Fire (1962)

Alter, Robert. *Partial Magic*, 183–217.

Bader, Julia. *Crystal Land*, 31–36.

Baxter, Charles. "Nabokov, Idolatry, and the Police State." *BoundaryII* 5 (1977): 821–824.

Ciancio, Ralph A. "Nabokov and the Verbal Mode of the Grotesque." *ConL* 18 (1977): 522–523, 531, 533.

Couturier, Maurice. "Nabokov's Performative Writing," in Johnson, Ira D. and Christiane Johnson, eds. *Les Américanistes*, 161–162, 165–166, 168–169, 171, 175, 177–178, 179.

Donald, Miles. *American Novel in the Twentieth Century*, 134–136.

Flower, Timothy F. "Scientific Art of Nabokov's *Pale Fire*." *Criticism* 17 (1975): 223–233.

Green, Geoffrey. "Nabokov's Signs of Reference, Symbols of Design." *CollL* 7 (1980): 110–111.

Kostelanetz, Richard. "American Fiction in the Sixties," in Kostelanetz, Richard, ed. *On Contemporary Literature*, 641–642.

Kostelanetz, Richard. "Nabokov's Obtuse Fool," in Kostelanetz, Richard, ed. *On Contemporary Literature*, 481–485.

LeClair, Thomas. "Poe's 'Pym' and Nabokov's *Pale Fire*." *NConL* 3.2 (1973): 2–3.

Lee, L. L. *Vladimir Nabokov*, 132–144.

Merrill, Robert. "Nabokov and Fictional Artifice." *MFS* 25 (1979): 454–462.

Moynahan, Julian. *Vladimir Nabokov*, 40–45.

Moynahan, Julian. "Vladimir Nabokov," in Wright, George T., ed. *Seven American Stylists, From Poe to Mailer*, 176–177, 195–199.

Pearce, Richard. "Nabokov's Black (Hole) Humor: *Lolita* and *Pale Fire*," in Cohen, Sara Blacher, ed. *Comic Relief*, 38–44.

Pifer, Ellen. *Nabokov and the Novel*, 110–118.

Renaker, David. "*Pale Fire*." *Expl* 36.3 (1978): 22–24.

Roth, Phyllis A. "Psychology of the Double in Nabokov's *Pale Fire*." *ELWIU* 2 (1975): 209–229.

Quilligan, Maureen. *Language of Allegory*, 145–154.

Spencer, Sharon. *Space, Time and Structure in the Modern Novel*, 90–92.

Stark, John. "Borges' Tlon, Uqbar, Orbis Tertius' and Nabokov's *Pale Fire*: Literature of Exhaustion." *TSLL* 14 (1972): 141–145.

Stark, John. *Literature of Exhaustion*, 62–117.

Walker, David. " 'The Viewer and the View': Chance and Choice in *Pale Fire*." *SAF* 4 (1976): 203–221.

Pnin (1957)

Bader, Julia. *Crystal Land*, 82–94.

Lee, L. L. *Vladimir Nabokov*, 124–131.

Nicol, Charles D. "Pnin's History." *Novel* 4 (1971): 197–208.

Stuart, Dabney. *Nabokov*, 133–161.
Stuart, Dabney. "Nabokov's *Pnin:* Floating and Singing," in Garvin, Harry R., ed.
    Makers of the Twentieth-Century Novel, 259–275.

Real Life of Sebastian Knight (1941)

Bader, Julia. *Crystal Land*, 13–30.
Bruffee, K. A. "Form and Meaning in Nabokov's *Real Life of Sebastian Knight:*
    An Example of Elegiac Romance." *MLQ* 34 (1973): 180–190.
Lee, L. L. *Vladimir Nabokov*, 95–104.
Merivale, Patricia. "Biographical Compulsion: Elegiac Romances in Canadian Fic-
    tion." *JML* 8 (1980): 148–152.
Morton, Donald E. *Vladimir Nabokov*, 43–53.
Stuart, Dabney. *Nabokov*, 1–63.

NASNAGA (1941–)

Indians' Summer (1975)

Larson, Charles R. *American Indian Fiction*, 161–163.

NEAL, JOHN (1793–1876)

Authorship (1830)

Lease, Bejamin. *That Wild Fellow John Neal and the American Literary Revolution*,
    146–151.
Sears, Donald A. *John Neal*, 84–87.

Brother Jonathan (1825)

Lease, Bejamin. *That Wild Fellow John Neal and the American Literary Revolution*,
    107–120.
Sears, Donald A. *John Neal*, 72–76.

Errata (1823)

Lease, Bejamin. *That Wild Fellow John Neal and the American Literary Revolution*,
    101–106.

Keep Cool (1817)

Lease, Bejamin. *That Wild Fellow John Neal and the American Literary Revolution*,
    81–84.
Petter, Henri. *Early American Novel*, 177–180.
Sears, Donald A. *John Neal*. 35–39.

Logan (1822)

Lease, Bejamin. *That Wild Fellow John Neal and the American Literary Revolution*,
    89–94.
Sears, Donald A. *John Neal*, 39–45.

Rachel Dyer (1828)

Lease, Bejamin. *That Wild Fellow John Neal and the American Literary Revolution*,
    137–145.
Scheick, William J. "Power, Authority, and Revolutionary Impulse in John Neal's
    Rachel Dyer." *SAF* 4 (1976): 143–155.
Sears, Donald A. *John Neal*, 79–84.

Randolph (1823)
> Lease, Bejamin. *That Wild Fellow John Neal and the American Literary Revolution*, 97–101.
> Sears, Donald A. *John Neal*, 53–56.

Seventy-six (1823)
> Lease, Bejamin. *That Wild Fellow John Neal and the American Literary Revolution*, 92–96.
> Sears, Donald A. *John Neal*, 45–52.

NEUGEBOREN, JAY (1938–)

Big Man (1966)
> Umphlett, Wiley Lee. *Sporting Myth and the American Experience*, 171–173.

NICHOLS, JOHN (1940–)

Sterile Cuckoo (1965)
> Blessing, Richard A. "For Pookie, with Love and Good Riddance: John Nichols' *The Sterile Cuckoo*." *JPC* 7 (1973): 124–135.

NICHOLS, MARY SARGEANT (1810–1884)

Mary Lyndon (1855)
> Baym, Nina. *Woman's Fiction*, 255–258.

NILES, BLAIR (1880(?)–1959)

Strange Brother (1931)
> Austen, Roger. *Playing the Game*, 64–67.

NIN, ANAÏS (1903–1977)

Children of the Albatross (1947)
> Franklin, Benjamin, V and Duane Schneider. *Anaïs Nin*, 83–98.
> Knapp, Bettina. *Anaïs Nin*, 111–122.
> Spencer, Sharon. *Collage of Dreams*, 29–31, 42–43, 77–78.

Four-Chambered Heart (1950)
> Demetrakopoulos, Stephanie A. "Anaïs Nin and the Feminine Quest for Consciousness: The Quelling of the Devouring Mother and the Ascension of the Sophia," in Garvin, Harry R., ed. *Women, Literature, Criticism*, 125–128.
> Franklin, Benjamin, V and Duane Schneider. *Anaïs Nin*, 99–112.
> Knapp, Bettina. *Anaïs Nin*, 122–130.
> Spencer, Sharon. *Collage of Dreams*, 31, 34–35, 42, 78–80.

Ladders to Fire (1946)
> Franklin, Benjamin, V and Duane Schneider. *Anaïs Nin*, 62–82.
> Knapp, Bettina. *Anaïs Nin*, 98–111.

Spencer, Sharon. *Collage of Dreams*, 31, 35–36, 75, 82–84.
Spencer, Sharon. *Space, Time and Structure in the Modern Novel*, 16–18.

Seduction of the Minotaur (1961)

Franklin, Benjamin, V and Duane Schneider. *Anaïs Nin*, 130–146.
Knapp, Bettina. *Anaïs Nin*, 139, 140, 145–148.
Spencer, Sharon. *Collage of Dreams*, 34, 62–65, 75–77.
Spencer, Sharon. *Space, Time and Structure in the Modern Novel*, 16.

NIVEN, FREDERICK (1878–1944)

Mine Inheritance (1940)

Mathews, Robin D. "Wacousta Factor," in Bessai, Diane and David Jackel, eds.
Figures in a Ground, 303–304.

NORRIS, FRANK (1870–1902)

Blix (1899)

Dillingham, William B. *Frank Norris*, 80.
McElrath, Joseph R., Jr. "Allegory in Frank Norris's *Blix:* Its Relevance to *Vandover*." *MarkR* 8 (1979): 8, 25–27.
Pizer, Donald. "Masculine-Feminine Ethic in Frank Norris's Popular Novels." *Texas Studies in Literature and Language* 6.1 (Spring 1964): 84–91. Rpt. in Graham, Don, ed. *Critical Essays on Frank Norris*, 47–48, 50–52.

McTeague (1899)

Banta, Martha. "They Shall Have Faces, Minds, and (One Day) Flesh: Women in Late Nineteenth-century and Early Twentieth-century American Literature," in Springer, Marlene, ed. *What Manner of Woman*, 251–254.
Chase, Richard. "*McTeague*," Chase, Richard. *American Novel and Its Tradition*. Garden City, NY: Doubleday, 1957. 188–192. Rpt. in Pizer, Donald, ed. *McTeague*, 341–344.
Dillingham, William B. *Frank Norris*, 74–75, 82–83, 91–92, 116–119, 138–139.
Dillingham, William B. "Norris's Prose Style and the Gold Symbolism in *McTeague*," Dillingham, William B. *Frank Norris: Instinct and Art*. Boston: Houghton Mifflin Co., 1969. 104–109; 115–119. Rpt. in Pizer, Donald, ed. *McTeague*, 354–361.
Dillingham, William B. "Old Folks of *McTeague*." *Nineteenth-Century Fiction* 16 (September 1961): 169–173. Rpt. in Pizer, Donald, ed. *McTeague*, 344–348.
Freedman, William. "Oral Passivity and Oral Sadism in Norris's *McTeague*." *L&P* 30 (1980): 52–61.
Frohock, W. M. "Frank Norris," in Walcutt, Charles Child, ed. *Seven Novelists in the American Naturalist Tradition*, 58, 59–65, 83–84.
Gardner, Joseph H. "Dickens, Romance, and *McTeague:* A Study in Mutual Interpretation." *Essays in Literature* 1 (Spring 1974): 69–82. Rpt. in Pizer, Donald, ed. *McTeague*, 361–377.
Geismar, Maxwell. "Frank Norris: And the Brute," in Geismar, Maxwell. *American Novel, 1890–1915*. Boston: Houghton Mifflin, 1953. 14–21. Rpt. in Pizer, Donald, ed. *McTeague*, 332–337.
Goldman, Suzy B. "*McTeague:* The Imagistic Network." *WAL* 7 (1972): 83–99.

Graham, D. B. "Aesthetic Experience in Realism." *ALR* 8 (1975): 289–290.

Graham, D. B. "Art in *McTeague*." *SAF* 3 (1975): 143–155.

Graham, Don. "Art in *McTeague*." *Studies in American Fiction* 3 (1975): 143–155. Rpt. in Graham, Don, ed. *Critical Essays on Frank Norris*, 74–85.

Graham, Don. *Fiction of Frank Norris*, 43–65.

Isani, Mukhtar A. "Frank Norris on the Purpose of *McTeague*." *ANQ* 10 (1972): 118.

Love, Glen A. "Frank Norris's Western Metropolitans." *WAL* 11 (1976): 7–14.

Love, Glen A. "Frank Norris's Western Metropolitans." *Western American Literature* 11 (May 1976): 3–22. Rpt. in Graham, Don, ed. *Critical Essays on Frank Norris*, 209–213.

Marchand, Ernest. "Norris and Zola," in Marchand, Ernest. *Frank Norris: A Study*. Stanford, CA: Stanford University Press, 1942. 90–96. Rpt. in Pizer, Donald, ed. *McTeague*, 276–279.

Miller, Edwin Haviland. "Art of Frank Norris in *McTeague*." *MarkR* 8 (1979): 61–66.

Ousby, Ian. *Reader's Guide to Fifty American Novels*, 168–170.

Pizer, Donald. "Late Nineteenth-Century American Naturalism," in Pizer, Donald. *Realism and Naturalism in Nineteenth-Century American Literature*. Carbondale, IL: Southern Illinois University Press, 1966. Rpt. in Pizer, Donald, ed. *McTeague*, 348–353.

Pizer, Donald. "Life, Not Literature," in Norris, Frank. *Literary Criticism of Frank Norris*. Austin: University of Texas Press, 1964. xiii–xvi. Rpt. in Pizer, Donald, ed. *McTeague*, 305–308.

Sheppard, Keith S. "New Note for *McTeague*'s Canary." *WAL* 9 (1974): 217–218.

Spangler, George M. "Structure of *McTeague*." *ES* 59 (1978): 48–56.

Spangler, George M. "Structure of *McTeague*." *English Studies* 59 (Feb 1978): 48–56. Rpt. in Graham, Don, ed. *Critical Essays on Frank Norris*, 88–97.

Taylor, Gordon O. *Passages of Thought*, 137–145.

Walcutt, Charles C. "Frank Norris and the Search for Form." Walcutt, Charles C. *American Literary Naturalism, A Divided Stream*. Minneapolis: University of Minnesota Press, 1956. 125, 128–132. Rpt. in Pizer, Donald, ed. *McTeague*, 337–341.

Man's Woman (1900)

Pizer, Donald. "Masculine-Feminine Ethic in Frank Norris's Popular Novels." *Texas Studies in Literature and Language* 6.1 (Spring 1964): 84–91. Rpt. in Graham, Don, ed. *Critical Essays on Frank Norris*, 48–52.

Moran of the Lady Letty (1898)

Dillingham, William B. *Frank Norris*, 79, 80, 88–90.

Love, Glen A. "Frank Norris's Western Metropolitans." *WAL* 11 (1976): 5–8.

Love, Glen A. "Frank Norris's Western Metropolitans." *Western American Literature* 11 (May 1976): 3–22. Rpt. in Graham, Don, ed. *Critical Essays on Frank Norris*, 206–209.

Pizer, Donald. "Masculine-Feminine Ethic in Frank Norris's Popular Novels." *Texas Studies in Literature and Language* 6.1 (Spring 1964): 84–91. Rpt. in Graham, Don, ed. *Critical Essays on Frank Norris*, 46–47, 50–52.

Octopus (1901)

Burns, Stuart L. "Rapist in Frank Norris's *The Octopus*." *AL* 42 (1971): 567–569.

Chase, Richard. *American Novel and Its Tradition*. Garden City, NY: Doubleday &

Company, 1957. 193–204. Rpt. in Davison, Richard Allan, comp. *Merrill Studies in The Octopus*, 101–104.

Crow, Charles L. "Real Vanamee and His Influence on Frank Norris' *The Octopus*." *WAL* 9 (1974): 131–139.

Davis, Richard Allan. "Frank Norris's *The Octopus:* Some Observations on Vanamee, Shelgrim and St. Paul," in Falk, Robert, ed. *Literature and Ideas in America*. Columbus, OH: Ohio University Press, 1976. 182–203. Rpt. in Graham, Don, ed. *Critical Essays on Frank Norris*, 99–111.

Dillingham, William B. *Frank Norris*, 60–65, 78–79, 80–81, 93–96, 119–121, 140.

Folsom, James K. "Social Darwinism or Social Protest? The 'Philosophy' of *The Octopus*." *Modern Fiction Studies* 8 (Winter 1962–63): 393–400. Rpt. in Davison, Richard Allan, comp. *Merrill Studies in The Octopus*, 132–140.

French, Warren. *Frank Norris*. New York: Twayne Publishers, Inc., 1962. 89–106. Rpt. in Davison, Richard Allan, comp. *Merrill Studies in The Octopus*, 114–131.

Frohock, W. M. "Frank Norris," in Walcutt, Charles Child, ed. *Seven Novelists in the American Naturalist Tradition*, 70–75, 84–87.

Geismar, Maxwell. *Rebels and Ancestors: The American Novel, 1890–1915*. New York: Hill and Wang, 1963. Rpt. in Davison, Richard Allan, comp. *Merrill Studies in The Octopus*, 84–87.

Giles, James R. "Beneficial Atavism in Frank Norris and Jack London." *WAL* 4 (1969): 15–21.

Graham, D. B. "Frank Norris's *Afternoon of a Faun*." *PLL* 10 (1974): 307–312.

Graham, D. B. "Studio Art in *The Octopus*." *AL* 44 (1973): 657–666.

Graham, Don. *Fiction of Frank Norris*, 66–122.

Hicks, Granville. *Great Tradition*. New York: Macmillan Company, 1933. 168–175. Rpt. in Davison, Richard Allan, comp. *Merrill Studies in The Octopus*, 38–40.

Love, Glen A. "Frank Norris's Western Metropolitans." *WAL* 11 (1976): 15–19.

Love, Glen A. "Frank Norris's Western Metropolitans." *Western American Literature* 11 (May 1976): 3–22. Rpt. in Graham, Don, ed. *Critical Essays on Frank Norris*, 214–218.

Lutwack, Leonard. *Heroic Fiction*, 23–46.

Lynn, Kenneth S. *Visions of America*, 129–136.

McElrath, Joseph R., Jr. "Frank Norris's *The Octopus:* The Christian Ethic as Pragmatic Response," in Graham, Don, ed. *Critical Essays on Frank Norris*, 138–151.

Marchand, Ernest. *Frank Norris: A Study*. Stanford, CA: Stanford University Press, 1942. 130–173. Rpt. in Davison, Richard Allan, comp. *Merrill Studies in The Octopus*, 52–63.

Meyer, George Wilbur. "New Interpretation of *The Octopus*." *College English* 4 (March 1943): 351–359. Rpt. in Davison, Richard Allan, comp. *Merrill Studies in The Octopus*, 68–81.

Pizer, Donald. "Another Look at *The Octopus*." *Nineteenth-Century Fiction* 10 (1955): 217–224. Rpt. in Davison, Richard Allan, comp. *Merrill Studies in The Octopus*, 88–95.

Pizer, Donald. "Concept of Nature in Frank Norris' *The Octopus*." *American Quarterly* 14 (Spring 1962): 73–80. Rpt. in Davison, Richard Allan, comp. *Merrill Studies in The Octopus*, 105–113.

Taylor, Walter Fuller. *Economical Novel in America*. Chapel Hill, NC: University of North Carolina Press, 1942. 282–306. Rpt. in Davison, Richard Allan, comp. *Merrill Studies in The Octopus*, 64–67.

Vance, William L. "Romance in *The Octopus*." *Genre* 3 (June 1970): 111–136. Rpt. in Graham, Don, ed. *Critical Essays on Frank Norris*, 116–134.

Vernon, John. *Garden and the Map*, 60–62.

Walcutt, Charles Child. *American Literary Naturalism, A Divided Stream*. Minneapolis, MN: University of Minneapolis Press, 1966. Rpt. in Davison, Richard Allan, comp. *Merrill Studies in The Octopus*, 96–100.

Pit (1903)

Cohn, Jan. "Women as Superfluous Characters in American Realism and Naturalism." *SAF* 1 (1973): 156–157.

Dillingham, William B. *Frank Norris*, 81, 96–97, 121–125.

French, Warren. "It's When You Are Quiet That You Are At Your Best," in French, Warren. *Frank Norris*. New York: Twayne Publishers, Inc., 1962. Rpt. in Graham, Don, ed. *Critical Essays on Frank Norris*, 153–162.

Frohock, W. M. "Frank Norris," in Walcutt, Charles Child, ed. *Seven Novelists in the American Naturalist Tradition*, 75–77.

Graham, Don. *Fiction of Frank Norris*, 123–156.

Katz, Joseph. "Eroticism in American Literary Realism." *SAF* 5 (1977): 44–49.

Katz, Joseph. "Eroticism in American Literary Realism." *Studies in American Fiction* 5 (Spring 1977): 35–50. Rpt. as "Eroticism in *The Pit*," in Graham, Don, ed. *Critical Essays on Frank Norris*, 163–167.

Love, Glen A. "Frank Norris's Western Metropolitans." *WAL* 11 (1976): 19–22.

Love, Glen A. "Frank Norris's Western Metropolitans." *Western American Literature* 11 (May 1976): 3–22. Rpt. in Graham, Don, ed. *Critical Essays on Frank Norris*, 218–220.

Vandover and the Brute (1914)

Dillingham, William B. *Frank Norris*, 69–74, 80, 91, 139–140.

Frohock, W. M. "Frank Norris," in Walcutt, Charles Child, ed. *Seven Novelists in the American Naturalist Tradition*, 65–69.

Graham, D. B. "Fitzgerald's Valley of Ashes and Frank Norris' 'Sordid and Grimy Wilderness'." *F-H Annual* (1972): 304–305.

Graham, Don. *Fiction of Frank Norris*, 16–42.

McElrath, Joseph R., Jr. "Allegory in Frank Norris's *Blix:* Its Relevance to *Vandover*." *MarkR* 8 (1979): 8, 25–27.

McElrath, Joseph R., Jr. "Frank Norris' *Vandover and the Brute:* Narrative Technique and the Socio-Critical Viewpoint." *SAF* 4 (1976): 24–43.

McElrath, Joseph R., Jr. "Frank Norris's *Vandover and the Brute:* Narrative Technique and the Socio-Critical Viewpoint." *Studies in American Fiction* 4 (Spring 1976): 27–43. Rpt. in Graham, Don, ed. *Critical Essays on Frank Norris*, 177–192.

Walcutt, Charles Child. "Naturalism of *Vandover and the Brute*," in O'Connor, William Van. *Forms of Modern Fiction*. Minneapolis, MN: University of Minnesota Press, 1948. 254–268. Rpt. in Graham, Don, ed. *Critical Essays on Frank Norris*, 169–176.

NOWLAN, ALDEN (1933–1983)

Various Persons Named Kevin O'Brien (1973)

Moss, John. *Sex and Violence*, 40–41.

OAKES SMITH, ELIZABETH (1806–1893)

Bertha and Lily (1854)

Baym, Nina. *Woman's Fiction*, 260–261.

OATES, JOYCE CAROL (1938–)

Assassins (1975)

Creighton, Joanne V. *Joyce Carol Oates*, 94–106.
Friedman, Ellen G. *Joyce Carol Oates*, 135–161.
Waller, G. F. *Dreaming America*, 183–198.
Waller, G. F. "Through Obsession to Transcendence: The Lawrentian Mode of Oates's Recent Fiction," in Wagner, Linda W., ed. *Critical Essays on Joyce Carol Oates*, 164–167.

Childwold (1976)

Bender, Eileen T. " 'Paedomorphic' Art: Joyce Carol Oates' *Childwold*," in Wagner, Linda W., ed. *Critical Essays on Joyce Carol Oates*, 117–122.
Creighton, Joanne V. *Joyce Carol Oates*, 106–112.
Friedman, Ellen G. *Joyce Carol Oates*, 163–185.
Hendin, Josephine. *Vulnerable People*, 157–159.
Waller, G. F. *Dreaming America*, 198–212.
Waller, G. F. "Through Obsession to Transcendence: The Lawrentian Mode of Oates's Recent Fiction," in Wagner, Linda W., ed. *Critical Essays on Joyce Carol Oates*, 169–170.
Waller, G. F. "Through Obsession to Transcendence: The Recent Work of Joyce Carol Oates." *WLWE* 17 (1978): 178–179.

Do with Me What You Will (1973)

Burwell, Rose Marie. "Process of Individuation as Narrative Structure: Joyce Carol Oates' *Do with Me What You Will*." *Crit* 17.2 (1975): 93–106.
Creighton, Joanne V. *Joyce Carol Oates*, 87–93.
Creighton, Joanne V. "Unliberated Women in Joyce Carol Oates' Fiction." *WLWE* 17 (1978): 166–168.
Creighton, Joanne V. "Unliberated Women in Joyce Carol Oates' Fiction." *World Literature Written in English* 17 (April 1978): 165–175. Rpt. in Wagner, Linda W., ed. *Critical Essays on Joyce Carol Oates*, 148–150.
Friedman, Ellen G. *Joyce Carol Oates*, 117–134.
Grant, Mary Kathryn. "Language of Tragedy and Violence," in Grant, Mary Kathryn. *Tragic Vision of Joyce Carol Oates*. Durham, NC: Duke University Press, 1978. 93–116. Rpt. in Wagner, Linda W., ed. *Critical Essays on Joyce Carol Oates*, 63–64, 67–68, 75.
Grant, Mary Kathryn. *Tragic Vision of Joyce Carol Oates*, 37–38, 59, 71–73, 75, 97, 102–103, 114.
Masinton, Martha and Charles G. Masinton. "Second-class Citizenship: The Status of Women in Contemporary American Fiction," in Springer, Marlene, ed. *What Manner of Woman*, 312.
Waller, G. F. *Dreaming America*, 37, 45, 53, 157–182.

Expensive People (1968)

Allen, Mary. *Necessary Blankness*, 137.
Creighton, Joanne V. *Joyce Carol Oates*, 55–63.

Fossum, Robert H. "Only Control: The Novels of Joyce Carol Oates." *SNNTS* 7 (1975): 289–291.

Fossum, Robert H. "Only Control: The Novels of Joyce Carol Oates." *Studies in the Novel* 7 (1975): 285–297. Rpt. in Wagner, Linda W., ed. *Critical Essays on Joyce Carol Oates*, 52–54.

Friedman, Ellen G. *Joyce Carol Oates*, 55–72.

Grant, Mary Kathryn. "Language of Tragedy and Violence," in Grant, Mary Kathryn. *Tragic Vision of Joyce Carol Oates*. Durham, NC: Duke University Press, 1978. 93–116. Rpt. in Wagner, Linda W., ed. *Critical Essays on Joyce Carol Oates*, 66, 68–69, 71–72, 73–74.

Grant, Mary Kathryn. *Tragic Vision of Joyce Carol Oates*, 40–41, 48–51, 75–77, 81–82, 90, 100–101, 104–105, 108–109, 111–112.

Pinsker, Sanford. "Suburban Molesters: Joyce Carol Oates' *Expensive People*." *MidQ* 19 (1977): 89–103.

Pinsker, Sanford. "Suburban Molesters: Joyce Carol Oates' *Expensive People*." *Midwest Quarterly* 19 (Autumn 1977): 89–103. Rpt. in Wagner, Linda W., ed. *Critical Essays on Joyce Carol Oates*, 93–101.

Sullivan, Walter. "Artificial Demon: Joyce Carol Oates and the Dimensions of the Real." *Hollins Critic* 9 (Dec 1972): 1–12. Rpt. in Wagner, Linda W., ed. *Critical Essays on Joyce Carol Oates*, 80.

Waller, G. F. *Dreaming America*, 114–123.

Garden of Earthly Delights (1967)

Allen, Mary. *Necessary Blankness*, 134–136.

Burwell, Rose M. "Joyce Carol Oates and an Old Master." *Crit* 15.1 (1973): 48–57.

Creighton, Joanne V. *Joyce Carol Oates*, 49–55.

Fossum, Robert H. "Only Control: The Novels of Joyce Carol Oates." *SNNTS* 7 (1975): 287–289.

Fossum, Robert H. "Only Control: The Novels of Joyce Carol Oates." *Studies in the Novel* 7 (1975): 285–297. Rpt. in Wagner, Linda W., ed. *Critical Essays on Joyce Carol Oates*, 51–52.

Friedman, Ellen G. *Joyce Carol Oates*, 36–53.

Grant, Mary Kathryn. "Language of Tragedy and Violence," in Grant, Mary Kathryn. *Tragic Vision of Joyce Carol Oates*. Durham, NC: Duke University Press, 1978. 93–116. Rpt. in Wagner, Linda W., ed. *Critical Essays on Joyce Carol Oates*, 66–67, 74, 75.

Grant, Mary Kathryn. *Tragic Vision of Joyce Carol Oates*, 40, 45–48, 81, 82–83, 89, 89–90, 101–102, 112–113, 114–115, 127–128.

Sullivan, Walter. "Artificial Demon: Joyce Carol Oates and the Dimensions of the Real." *Hollins Critic* 9 (Dec 1972): 1–12. Rpt. in Wagner, Linda W., ed. *Critical Essays on Joyce Carol Oates*, 81–82.

Waller, G. F. *Dreaming America*, 102–112.

them (1969)

Allen, Mary. *Necessary Blankness*, 151–159.

Creighton, Joanne V. *Joyce Carol Oates*, 63–73.

Creighton, Joanne V. "Unliberated Women in Joyce Carol Oates' Fiction." *World Literature Written in English* 17 (April 1978): 165–175. Rpt. in Wagner, Linda W., ed. *Critical Essays on Joyce Carol Oates*, 148–149.

DeCurtis, Anthony. "Process of Fictionalization in Joyce Carol Oates's *them*." *IFR* 6 (1979): 121–128.

OATES

Fossum, Robert H. "Only Control: The Novels of Joyce Carol Oates." *SNNTS* 7 (1975): 291–293.
Fossum, Robert H. "Only Control: The Novels of Joyce Carol Oates." *Studies in the Novel* 7 (1975): 285–297. Rpt. in Wagner, Linda W., ed. *Critical Essays on Joyce Carol Oates*, 54–56.
Friedman, Ellen G. *Joyce Carol Oates*, 73–93.
Giles, James R. "Suffering, Transcendence, and Artistic 'Form': Joyce Carol Oates's *them.*" *ArQ* 32 (1976): 231–226.
Grant, Mary Kathryn. "Language of Tragedy and Violence," in Grant, Mary Kathryn. *Tragic Vision of Joyce Carol Oates*. Durham, NC: Duke University Press, 1978. 93–116. Rpt. in Wagner, Linda W., ed. *Critical Essays on Joyce Carol Oates*, 63, 66, 67, 68, 69, 71, 74–75.
Grant, Mary Kathryn. *Tragic Vision of Joyce Carol Oates*, 40, 52–55, 70–71, 83–84, 91, 96–97, 100, 102, 104, 105, 107–108, 113, 128.
Hendin, Josephine. *Vulnerable People*, 155–157.
Sullivan, Walter. "Artificial Demon: Joyce Carol Oates and the Dimensions of the Real." *Hollins Critic* 9 (Dec 1972): 1–12. Rpt. in Wagner, Linda W., ed. *Critical Essays on Joyce Carol Oates*, 83–85.
Waller, G. F. *Dreaming America*, 34–35, 37, 38–39, 54–55, 123–142.

With Shuddering Fall (1964)

Allen, Mary. *Necessary Blankness*, 140–141.
Burwell, Rose Marie. "Joyce Carol Oates' First Novel." *CanL* 73 (1977): 54–66.
Creighton, Joanne V. "Unliberated Women in Joyce Carol Oates' Fiction." *World Literature Written in English* 17 (April 1978): 165–175. Rpt. in Wagner, Linda W., ed. *Critical Essays on Joyce Carol Oates*, 148–149.
Fossum, Robert H. "Only Control: The Novels of Joyce Carol Oates." *SNNTS* 7 (1975): 286–287.
Fossum, Robert H. "Only Control: The Novels of Joyce Carol Oates." *Studies in the Novel* 7 (1975): 285–297. Rpt. in Wagner, Linda W., ed. *Critical Essays on Joyce Carol Oates*, 50–51.
Friedman, Ellen G. *Joyce Carol Oates*, 21–34.
Grant, Mary Kathryn. "Language of Tragedy and Violence," in Grant, Mary Kathryn. *Tragic Vision of Joyce Carol Oates*. Durham, NC: Duke University Press, 1978. 93–116. Rpt. in Wagner, Linda W., ed. *Critical Essays on Joyce Carol Oates*, 62–63, 67, 72–73, 75.
Grant, Mary Kathryn. *Tragic Vision of Joyce Carol Oates*, 41–45, 87, 95–96, 102, 107, 109–111, 114, 129.
Waller, G. F. *Dreaming America*, 38, 90–102.

Wonderland (1971)

Allen, Mary. *Necessary Blankness*, 137–138.
Creighton, Joanne V. *Joyce Carol Oates*, 75–87.
Creighton, Joanne V. "Unliberated Women in Joyce Carol Oates' Fiction." *World Literature Written in English* 17 (April 1978): 165–175. Rpt. in Wagner, Linda W., ed. *Critical Essays on Joyce Carol Oates*, 148–149.
Fossum, Robert H. "Only Control: The Novels of Joyce Carol Oates." *SNNTS* 7 (1975): 293–297.
Fossum, Robert H. "Only Control: The Novels of Joyce Carol Oates." *Studies in the Novel* 7 (1975): 285–297. Rpt. in Wagner, Linda W., ed. *Critical Essays on Joyce Carol Oates*, 56–59.

Friedman, Ellen. "Journey from the 'I' to the 'Eye': *Wonderland*," in Wagner, Linda W., ed. *Critical Essays on Joyce Carol Oates*, 102–115.

Friedman, Ellen G. "Journey from the 'I' to the 'Eye': Joyce Carol Oates' *Wonderland*." *SAF* 8 (1980): 37–50.

Friedman, Ellen G. *Joyce Carol Oates*, 95–115.

Giles, James R. " 'Marivaudian Being' Drowns His Children: Dehumanization in Donald Barthelme's 'Robert Kennedy Saved from Drowning' and Joyce Carol Oates' *Wonderland*." *SoHR* 9 (1975): 64–75.

Grant, Mary Kathryn. "Language of Tragedy and Violence," in Grant, Mary Kathryn. *Tragic Vision of Joyce Carol Oates*. Durham, NC: Duke University Press, 1978. 93–116. Rpt. in Wagner, Linda W., ed. *Critical Essays on Joyce Carol Oates*, 75–76.

Grant, Mary Kathryn. *Tragic Vision of Joyce Carol Oates*, 37, 55–59, 77–80, 88–89, 91–92, 105, 115, 128.

Higdon, David Leon. " 'Suitable Conclusions': The Two Endings of Oates's *Wonderland*." *SNNTS* 10 (1978): 447–453.

Pinsker, Sanford. "Joyce Carol Oates's *Wonderland:* A Hungering for Personality." *Crit* 20.2 (1978): 59–70.

Sullivan, Walter. "Artificial Demon: Joyce Carol Oates and the Dimensions of the Real." *Hollins Critic* 9 (Dec 1972): 1–12. Rpt. in Wagner, Linda W., ed. *Critical Essays on Joyce Carol Oates*, 80–81.

Waller, G. F. *Dreaming America*, 51, 144–157.

O'BRIEN, TIM (1946–)

Going After Cacciato (1975)

Saltzman, Arthur M. "Betrayal of the Imagination: Paul Brodeur's *The Stunt Man* and Tim O'Brien's *Going after Cacciato*." *Crit* 22.1 (1980): 35–37.

O'CONNOR, EDWIN (1918–1968)

All in the Family (1966)

Rank, Hugh. *Edwin O'Connor*, 155–170.

Edge of Sadness (1961)

Rank, Hugh. *Edwin O'Connor*, 105–128.

I Was Dancing (1964)

Rank, Hugh. *Edwin O'Connor*, 131–144.

Last Hurrah (1956)

Rank, Hugh. *Edwin O'Connor*, 60–95.

O'CONNOR, FLANNERY (1925–1965)

Violent Bear It Away (1960)

Bleikasten, André. "Heresy of Flannery O'Connor," in Johnson, Ira D. and Christiane Johnson, eds. *Les Américanistes*, 55, 58–65, 67–68.

Brinkmeyer, Robert H., Jr. "Borne Away by Violence: The Reader and Flannery O'Connor." *SoR* 15 (1979): 316–321.

Browning, Preston M., Jr. *Flannery O'Connor*, 72–98.

Browning, Preston M., Jr. "Flannery O'Connor and the Demonic." *MFS* 19 (1973): 34–35.

Casper, Leonard. "Unspeakable Peacock: Apocalypse in Flannery, O'Connor," in Friedman, Melvin J. and John B. Vickery, eds. *Shaken Realist*, 288–289, 291, 296, 297.

Eggenschwiler, David. *Christian Humanism of Flannery O'Connor*, 114–139.

Eggenschwiler, David. "Flannery O'Connor's True and False Prophets." *Renascence* 21 (1969): 151–160.

Feeley, Kathleen. *Flannery O'Connor*, 154–171.

Friedman, Melvin J. "Flannery O'Connor's Sacred Objects," in Friedman, Melvin J., ed. *Vision Obscured*, 71–73.

Levine, Paul. "Flannery O'Connor: The Soul of the Grotesque," in Hoyt, Charles Alva, ed. *Minor American Novelists*, 111–116.

McFarland, Dorothy Tuck. *Flannery O'Connor*, 91–111.

May, John R. *Pruning Word*, 137–150.

May, John R. *Toward a New Earth*, 126–144.

Mayer, David R. "*Violent Bear It Away:* Flannery O'Connor's Shaman." *SLJ* 4.2 (1972): 41–54.

Montgomery, Marion. "Flannery O'Connor's Territorial Center." *Crit* 11.3 (1969): 6–8.

Muller, Gilbert H. *Nightmares and Visions*, 24–25, 60–67, 93–95.

Muller, Gilbert H. "*Violent Bear It Away:* Moral and Dramatic Sense." *Renascence* 22 (1969): 17–25.

Oates, Joyce Carol. *New Heaven, New Earth*, 153–160.

Orvell, Miles. *Invisible Parade*, 96–125.

Pearce, Richard. *Stages of the Clown*, 79–83.

Rupp, Richard H. *Celebration in Postwar American Fiction*, 85–87.

Shloss, Carol. *Flannery O'Connor's Dark Comedies*, 81–101.

Sonnenfeld, Albert. "Flannery O'Connor: The Catholic Writer as Baptist." *ConL* 13 (1972): 447–454.

Tate, J. O. "Flannery O'Connor's Counterplot." *SoR* 16 (1980): 877.

Walters, Dorothy. *Flannery O'Connor*, 90–101.

Wasserman, Renata R. Mautner. "Backwards to Ninevah." *Renascence* 32 (1979): 27–29.

Wise Blood (1949)

Bleikasten, André. "Heresy of Flannery O'Connor," in Johnson, Ira D. and Christiane Johnson, eds. *Les Américanistes*, 55, 58–65, 67.

Browning, Preston M., Jr. *Flannery O'Connor*, 25–39.

Browning, Preston M., Jr. "Flannery O'Connor and the Demonic." *MFS* 19 (1973): 36.

Bryant, Jerry H. *Open Decision*, 258–264, 267–268.

Burns, Stuart L. "Evolution of *Wise Blood*." *MFS* 16 (1970): 147–162.

Casper, Leonard. "Unspeakable Peacock: Apocalypse in Flannery, O'Connor," in Friedman, Melvin J. and John B. Vickery, eds. *Shaken Realist*, 289, 291, 295–296.

Eggenschwiler, David. *Christian Humanism of Flannery O'Connor*, 102–114.

Eggenschwiler, David. "Flannery O'Connor's True and False Prophets." *Renascence* 21 (1969): 160–166.

Feeley, Kathleen. *Flannery O'Connor*, 56–69.

Feeley, Margaret Peller. "Flannery O'Connor's *Wise Blood:* The Negative Way." *SoQ* 17.2 (1979): 104–122.

Friedman, Melvin J. "Flannery O'Connor's Sacred Objects," in Friedman, Melvin J., ed. *Vision Obscured*, 71.

Gray, Richard. *Literature of Memory*, 277–284.

Hughes, Richard E. *Lively Image*, 185–195.

Kahane, Claire. "Gothic Mirrors and Feminine Identity." *CentR* 24 (1980): 56–57.

LeClair, Thomas. "Flannery O'Connor's *Wise Blood:* The Oedipal Theme." *MissQ* 29 (1976): 197–205.

Levine, Paul. "Flannery O'Connor: The Soul of the Grotesque," in Hoyt, Charles Alva, ed. *Minor American Novelists*, 107–111.

Littlefield, Daniel F., Jr. "Flannery O'Connor's *Wise Blood:* 'Unparalleled Prosperity' and Spiritual Chaos." *MissQ* 23 (1970): 121–133.

McFarland, Dorothy Tuck. *Flannery O'Connor*, 73–89.

May, John R. *Pruning Word*, 125–137.

Muller, Gilbert H. *Nightmares and Visions*, 23–24, 28–30, 36–37, 68, 92–93.

Nelson, Gerald B. *Ten Versions of America*, 111–125.

Oates, Joyce Carol. *New Heaven, New Earth*, 149–152.

Orvell, Miles. *Invisible Parade*, 66–95.

Pearce, Richard. *Stages of the Clown*, 73–78, 83.

Rose, Alan Henry. *Demonic Vision*, 122–124.

Rupp, Richard H. *Celebration in Postwar American Fiction*, 83–85.

Sonnenfeld, Albert. "Flannery O'Connor: The Catholic Writer as Baptist." *ConL* 13 (1972): 447, 455–456.

Tate, J. O. "Flannery O'Connor's Counterplot." *SoR* 16 (1980): 872–873, 878.

Walters, Dorothy. *Flannery O'Connor*, 42–62.

Wasserman, Renata R. Mautner. "Backwards to Ninevah." *Renascence* 32 (1979): 23–27.

O'HAGAN, HOWARD (1902–1982)

Tay John (1939)

Atwood, Margaret. "Canadian Monsters: Some Aspects of the Supernatural in Canadian Fiction," in Staines, David, ed. *Canadian Imagination*, 104–106.

Jones, D. G. *Butterfly on Rock*, 49–50, 66–68, 70–71.

Ondaatje, Michael. "Howard O'Hagan and 'The Rough-Edged Chronicle," in Woodcock, George, ed. *Canadian Novel*, 276–284.

Ondaatje, Michael. "O'Hagan's Rough-Edged Chronicle." *CanL* 61 (1974): 24–31.

O'HARA, JOHN (1905–1970)

Appointment in Samarra (1934)

Milne, Gordon. *Sense of Society*, 228–230.

Tuttleton, James W. *Novel of Manners in America*, 193–194, 195–197, 198–200, 203–204, 205.

Walcutt, Charles Child. *John O'Hara*, 13–17.

Big Laugh (1962)

Walcutt, Charles Child. *John O'Hara*, 29–32.

Elizabeth Appleton (1963)

Milne, Gordon. *Sense of Society*, 230–231.
Walcutt, Charles Child. *John O'Hara*, 32–36.

From the Terrace (1958)

Tuttleton, James W. *Novel of Manners in America*, 195, 200–202.

Hope of Heaven (1938)

Wells, Walter. *Tycoons and Locusts*, 36–48.

Lockwood Concern (1965)

Tuttleton, James W. *Novel of Manners in America*, 202–203, 205.
Walcutt, Charles Child. *John O'Hara*, 37–45.

Rage to Live (1949)

Tuttleton, James W. *Novel of Manners in America*, 204–205.

Ten North Frederick (1955)

Tuttleton, James W. *Novel of Manners in America*, 197–198.

OKADA, JOHN (1923–)

No-No Boy (1957)

McDonald, Dorothy Ritsuko. "After Imprisonment: Ichiro's Search for Redemption in *No-No Boy*." *MELUS* 6.3 (1979): 19–26.

OLERICH, HENRY (1851–(?))

Cityless and Countryless World (1893)

Roemer, Kenneth M. "Sex Roles, Utopia, and Change: The Family in Late Nineteenth-Century Utopian Literature." *AmerS* 13 (1972): 41–42, 43.

ONDAATJE, MICHAEL (1943–)

Collected Works of Billy the Kid (1970)

Lee, Dennis. *Savage Fields*, 15–44.
Nodelman, Perry M. "Collected Photographs of Billy the Kid." *CanL* 87 (1980): 68–79.
Sarkar, Eileen. "Michael Ondaatje's *Billy the Kid:* The Esthetics of Violence." *WLWE* 12 (1973): 230–239.
Scobie, Stephen A. C. "Two Authors in Search of a Character." *CanL* 54 (1972): 37–55.

Coming Through the Slaughter (1976)

MacSkimming, Roy. "Good Jazz." *CanL* 73 (1977): 92–94.
Scobie, Stephen. "*Coming Through Slaughter:* Fictional Magnets and Spider's Webbs." *ECW* 12 (1978): 5–22.
Solecki, Sam. "Making and Destroying: Michael Ondaatje's *Coming through Slaughter* and Extremist Art." *ECW* 12 (1978): 24–47.

OSKISON, JOHN M. (1874–1947)

Black Jack Davy (1926)
  Larson, Charles R. *American Indian Fiction*, 49–51.

Brother's Three (1935)
  Larson, Charles R. *American Indian Fiction*, 51–55.

Wild Harvest (1925)
  Larson, Charles R. *American Indian Fiction*, 46–49.

OSTENSO, MARTHA (1900–1963)

Wild Geese (1925)
  Harrison, Dick. *Unnamed Country*, 107–114, 132–133, 149.
  Jackel. Susan. "House on the Prairies." *CanL* 42 (1969): 50.
  Jackel, Susan. "House on the Prairies," in Stephens, Donald G., ed. *Writers of the Prairies*, 166, 169.
  Kreisel, Henry. "Prairie: A State of Mind." *Transactions of the Royal Society of Canada* 6.4, June 1968. Rpt. in Gerson, Carole, comp. *Modern Canadian Fiction*, 4–6.
  Moss, John. *Patterns of Isolation*, 36–38.
  Northey, Margot. *Haunted Wilderness*, 62–65, 69.
  Thomas, Clara. "Martha Ostenso's Trial of Strength," in Stephens, Donald G., ed. *Writers of the Prairies*, 41–42, 43.

Young May Moon (1929)
  Thomas, Clara. "Martha Ostenso's Trial of Strength," in Stephens, Donald G., ed. *Writers of the Prairies*, 43–49.

OULLETTE, FERNAND (1930–)

Tu regardais intensément Geneviève (1978)
  Poulin, Gabrielle. *Romans du pays*, 246–249.

OXENHANDLER, NEAL (1926–)

Change of Gods (1962)
  Guttmann, Allen. *Jewish Writer in America*, 63–64.

PAGANO, JO (1906–)

Condemned (1947)
  Green, Rose Basile. *Italian-American Novel*, 132–133.

Golden Wedding (1943)
  Green, Rose Basile. *Italian-American Novel*, 131–132.

PAGE, MYRA (1897–1993)

Gathering Storm (1932)
  Cook, Sylvia Jenkins. *From Tobacco Road to Route 66*, 118–122.

PAGE, P. K. (1916–)

Sun and the Moon (1944)

Atwood, Margaret. "Canadian Monsters: Some Aspects of the Supernatural in Canadian Fiction," in Staines, David, ed. *Canadian Imagination*, 106–109.

PAGE, THOMAS NELSON (1853–1922)

Gordon Keith (1903)

MacKethan, Lucinda Hardwick. *Dream of Arcady*, 47–48, 51–52.

Red Rock (1900)

Berzon, Judith R. *Neither White Nor Black*, 59–60.
Godbold, E. Stanley, Jr. "Battleground Revisited: Reconstruction in Southern Fiction, 1895–1905." *SAQ* 73 (1974): 104–105.
MacKethan, Lucinda Hardwick. *Dream of Arcady*, 46–47, 50–51.
Starke, Catherine Juanita. *Black Portraiture in American Fiction*, 62–63.

PANNETON, PHILIPPE see RINGUET

PAPALEO, JOSEPH (1925–)

All the Comforts (1967)

Green, Rose Basile. *Italian-American Novel*, 269–272.

Out of Place (1970)

Green, Rose Basile. *Italian-American Novel*, 272–276.

PARENT, GAIL (1940–)

Sheila Levine Is Dead and Living in New York (1972)

Cohen, Sarah Blacher. "Jewish Literary Comediennes," in Cohen, Sara Blacher, ed. *Comic Relief*, 175–177.

PARKER, GILBERT (1862–1932)

Seats of the Mighty (1894)

Waterson, Elizabeth. "Politics of Conquest in Canadian Historical Fiction." *Mosaic* 3.1 (1969): 116–124.

PARKER, ROBERT B. (1932–)

God Save the Child (1974)

Geherin, David. *Sons of Sam Spade*, 23–39.

Godwulf Manuscript (1974)

Geherin, David. *Sons of Sam Spade*, 9–23.

Judas Goat (1978)

Geherin, David. *Sons of Sam Spade*, 69–82.

Mortal Stakes (1975)
  Geherin, David. *Sons of Sam Spade*, 39–54.
Promised Land (1976)
  Geherin, David. *Sons of Sam Spade*, 54–69.

PARTON, SARA PAYSON WILLIS see FERN, FANNY

PASINETTI, P. M. (1913–)

From the Academy Bridge (1970)
  Green, Rose Basile. *Italian-American Novel*, 219–223.
Il ponte dell'Accademia see *From the Academy Bridge*

PAULDING, JAMES KIRKE (1778–1860)

Westward Ho! (1832)
  Yellin, Jean Fagan. *Intricate Knot*, 37–41.

PECK, ROBERT (1928–)

Day No Pigs Would Die (1972)
  Kelty, Jean McClure. "Cult of Kill in Adolescent Fiction." *EJ* 64.2 (1975): 58, 60.

PEI, MARIO ANDREW (1901–1978)

Swords of Anjou (1953)
  Green, Rose Basile. *Italian-American Novel*, 251–257.

PELLERIN, JEAN (1917–)

Le diable par la queue (1957)
  Shek, Ben-Zion. *Social Realism*, 158–159, 160, 161, 163, 165.

PENNELL, JOSEPH STANLEY (1908–1963)

History of Rome Hanks and Kindred Matters (1944)
  Bennett, Lee Shaw. "Modern Civil War Novels: The Still Unwritten War?" *SoS* 19 (1980): 121–123.

PERCY, WALKER (1916–1990)

Lancelot (1977)
  Brinkmeyer, Robert H., Jr. "Percy's Bludgeon: Message and Narrative Strategy." *SoQ* 18.3 (1980): 83–89.

Brooks, Cleanth. "Walker Percy and Modern Gnosticism," in Broughton, Panthea Reid, ed. *Art of Walker Percy*, 270–271.

Cashin, Edward J. "History as Mores: Walker Percy's *Lancelot.*" *GR* 31 (1977): 875–880.

Christensen, Jerome C. "*Lancelot:* Sign for the Times." *SoQ* 18.3 (1980): 107–120.

Coles, Robert. *Walker Percy*, 212–233.

Dale, Corinne. "*Lancelot* and the Medieval Quests of Sir Lancelot and Dante." *SoQ* 18.3 (1980): 99–106.

Daniel, Robert D. "Walker Percy's *Lancelot:* Secular Raving and Religious Silence." *SoR* 14 (1978): 186–194.

Dowie, William J. "*Lancelot* and the Search for Sin," in Broughton, Panthea Reid, ed. *Art of Walker Percy*, 245–259.

Eubanks, Cecil L. "Walker Percy: Eschatology and the Politics of Grace." *SoQ* 18.3 (1980): 134.

Holley, Joe. "Walker Percy and the Novel of Ultimate Concern." *SR* 65 (1980): 225, 232–233.

Kreyling, Michael. "Crime and Punishment: The Pattern beneath the Surface of Percy's *Lancelot.*" *NMW* 11 (1978): 36–44.

Lawson, Lewis A. "Fall of the House of Lamar," in Broughton, Panthea Reid, ed. *Art of Walker Percy*, 219–244.

Lawson, Lewis A. "Gnostic Vision in *Lancelot.*" *Renascence* 32 (1979): 52–64.

Lawson, Lewis A. "Walker Percy's Silent Character." *MissQ* 33 (1980): 123–140.

Pearson, Michael. "Art as Symbolic Action: Walker Percy's Aesthetic." *SoQ* 18.3 (1980): 61–64.

Spivey, Ted R. "Walker Percy and the Archetypes," in Broughton, Panthea Reid, ed. *Art of Walker Percy*, 290–292.

Tellote, J. P. "Symbolic Structure for Walker Percy's Fiction." *MFS* 26 (1980): 232–233.

Telotte, J. P. "Walker Percy's Language of Creation." *SoQ* 16 (1978): 105–116.

Last Gentleman (1969)

Brinkmeyer, Robert H., Jr. "Percy's Bludgeon: Message and Narrative Strategy." *SoQ* 18.3 (1980): 82–83.

Broughton, Pantheia Reid. "Gentlemen and Fornicators: *The Last Gentleman* and a Bisected Reality," in Broughton, Panthea Reid, ed. *Art of Walker Percy*, 96–114.

Chesnick, Eugene. "Novel's Ending and World's End: The Fiction of Walker Percy." *HC* 10.5 (1973): 6–8.

Coles, Robert. *Walker Percy*, 172–191.

Dowie, William, S. J. "Walker Percy: Sensualist-Thinker." *Novel* 6 (1972): 53–55, 60–62.

Eubanks, Cecil L. "Walker Percy: Eschatology and the Politics of Grace." *SoQ* 18.3 (1980): 124–125, 130.

Hall, Constance. "Ladies in *The Last Gentleman.*" *NMW* 11 (1978): 26–35.

Holley, Joe. "Walker Percy and the Novel of Ultimate Concern." *SR* 65 (1980): 227, 228–229.

Johnson, Mark. "Search for Place in Walker Percy's Novels." *SLJ* 8.1 (1975): 59–62, 64–69, 79–81.

Laird, David. "Versions of Eden: The Automobile and the American Novel." *MQR* 19–20 (1980–81): 643.

Lawson, Lewis A. "Walker Percy's Indirect Communications." *TSLL* 11 (1969): 892–900.

Lawson, Lewis A. "Walker Percy's Southern Stoic." *SLJ* 3.1 (1970): 20–31.

LeClair, Thomas. "Death and Black Humor." *Crit* 17.1 (1975): 21–22.

Lehan, Richard. *Dangerous Crossing*, 140–143.

Luschei, Martin. *Sovereign Wayfarer*, 30, 41, 52, 111–168, 234.

Pearson, Michael. "Art as Symbolic Action: Walker Percy's Aesthetic." *SoQ* 18.3 (1980): 61.

Pindell, Richard. "Toward Home: Place, Language, and Death in *The Last Gentleman*," in Broughton, Panthea Reid, ed. *Art of Walker Percy*, 50–68.

Spivey, Ted R. "Walker Percy and the Archetypes," in Broughton, Panthea Reid, ed. *Art of Walker Percy*, 282–290.

Sullivan, Walter. *Requiem for the Renascence*, 65–66.

Tanner, Tony. *City of Words*, 260–262.

Telotte, J. P. "Butting Heads with Faulkner's Soldier." *NConL* 9.3 (1979): 7–8.

Telotte, J. P. "Walker Percy's Language of Creation." *SoQ* 16 (1978): 105–116.

Vauthier, Simone. "Narrative Triangulation in *The Last Gentleman*," in Broughton, Panthea Reid, ed. *Art of Walker Percy*, 69–95.

Love in the Ruins (1971)

Brinkmeyer, Robert H., Jr. "Percy's Bludgeon: Message and Narrative Strategy." *SoQ* 18.3 (1980): 83–84.

Brooks, Cleanth. "Walker Percy and Modern Gnosticism," in Broughton, Panthea Reid, ed. *Art of Walker Percy*, 267–270.

Chesnick, Eugene. "Novel's Ending and World's End: The Fiction of Walker Percy." *HC* 10.5 (1973): 3–5, 9–11.

Cogell, Elizabeth Cummins. "Middle-Landscape Myth in Science Fiction." *SFS* 5 (1978): 138.

Coles, Robert. *Walker Percy*, 191–208.

Dowie, William, S. J. "Walker Percy: Sensualist-Thinker." *Novel* 6 (1972): 53–56, 62–65.

Eubanks, Cecil L. "Walker Percy: Eschatology and the Politics of Grace." *SoQ* 18.3 (1980): 123–124, 125, 128, 130.

Godshalk, William Leigh. "*Love in the Ruins:* Thomas More's Distorted Vision," in Broughton, Panthea Reid, ed. *Art of Walker Percy*, 137–156.

Holley, Joe. "Walker Percy and the Novel of Ultimate Concern." *SR* 65 (1980): 226–227, 230–231.

Johnson, Mark. "Search for Place in Walker Percy's Novels." *SLJ* 8.1 (1975): 69–76.

Kennedy, J. Gerald. "Sundered Self and the Riven World: *Love in the Ruins*," in Broughton, Panthea Reid, ed. *Art of Walker Percy*, 115–136.

Leclair, Thomas. "Walker Percy's Devil." *SLJ* 10.1 (1977): 3–13.

Leclair, Thomas. "Walker Percy's Devil," in Broughton, Panthea Reid, ed. *Art of Walker Percy*, 157–168.

Lehan, Richard. *Dangerous Crossing*, 143–145.

Luschei, Martin. *Sovereign Wayfarer*, 29, 169–232.

Pearson, Michael. "Art as Symbolic Action: Walker Percy's Aesthetic." *SoQ* 18.3 (1980): 57–58.

Sivley, Sherry. "Percy's Down Home Version of More's *Utopia*." *NConL* 7.4 (1977): 3–5.

Spivey, Ted R. "Walker Percy and the Archetypes," in Broughton, Panthea Reid, ed. *Art of Walker Percy*, 290.

Sullivan, Walter. *Requiem for the Renascence*, 66–69, 72–73.

Tellote, J. P. "Symbolic Structure for Walker Percy's Fiction." *MFS* 26 (1980): 233–240.

Telotte, J. P. "Walker Percy's Language of Creation." *SoQ* 16 (1978): 105–116.

Moviegoer (1961)

Brinkmeyer, Robert H., Jr. "Percy's Bludgeon: Message and Narrative Strategy." *SoQ* 18.3 (1980): 82–83.

Bryant, Jerry H. *Open Decision*, 273–277.

Chesnick, Eugene. "Novel's Ending and World's End: The Fiction of Walker Percy." *HC* 10.5 (1973): 5–6.

Coles, Robert. *Walker Percy*, 146–172.

Dowie, William, S. J. "Walker Percy: Sensualist-Thinker." *Novel* 6 (1972): 53–55, 56–60.

Filippidis, Barbara. "Vision and the Journey to Selfhood in Walker Percy's *The Moviegoer*." *Renascence* 32 (1980): 10–23.

Hobbs, Janet. "Binx Bolling and the Stages on Life's Way," in Broughton, Panthea Reid, ed. *Art of Walker Percy*, 37–49.

Holley, Joe. "Walker Percy and the Novel of Ultimate Concern." *SR* 65 (1980): 227–228, 229–230, 231–232.

Johnson, Mark. "Search for Place in Walker Percy's Novels." *SLJ* 8.1 (1975): 58–59, 62–64, 77–79.

Kostelanetz, Richard. "American Fiction in the Sixties," in Kostelanetz, Richard, ed. *On Contemporary Literature*, 642.

Lawson, Lewis A. "Moviegoing in *The Moviegoer*." *SoQ* 18.3 (1980): 26–42.

Lawson, Lewis A. "Walker Percy's Indirect Communications." *TSLL* 11 (1969): 869–889.

Lawson, Lewis A. "Walker Percy's Southern Stoic." *SLJ* 3.1 (1970): 15–20.

Lehan, Richard. *Dangerous Crossing*, 136–140.

Luschei, Martin. "*Moviegoer* as Dissolve," in Broughton, Panthea Reid, ed. *Art of Walker Percy*, 24–36.

Luschei, Martin. *Sovereign Wayfarer*, 21, 24, 26, 35, 48–49, 64–110.

Pearson, Michael. "Art as Symbolic Action: Walker Percy's Aesthetic." *SoQ* 18.3 (1980): 61.

Pindell, Richard. "Basking in the Eye of the Storm: The Esthetics of Loss in Walker Percy's *The Moviegoer*." *BoundaryII* 4 (1975): 219–230.

Spivey, Ted R. "Walker Percy and the Archetypes," in Broughton, Panthea Reid, ed. *Art of Walker Percy*, 278–281, 282–283.

Sullivan, Walter. *Requiem for the Renascence*, 64–65.

Telotte, J. P. "Walker Percy's Language of Creation." *SoQ* 16 (1978): 105–116.

Van Cleave, Jim. "Versions of Percy." *SoR* 6 (1970): 991–992, 994–1010.

Vanderwerken, David L. "Americanness of *The Moviegoer*." *NMW* 12 (1979): 40–53.

Vauthier, Simone. "Narrative Triangle and Triple Alliance: A Look at *The Moviegoer*," in Johnson, Ira D. and Christiane Johnson, eds. *Les Américanistes*, 71–93.

Vauthier, Simone. "Title as Microtext: The Example of *The Moviegoer*." *JNT* 5 (1975): 219–229.

Walter, James. "Spinning and Spieling: A Trick and a Kick in Walker Percy's *The Moviegoer*." *SoR* 16 (1980): 574–590.

Webb, Max. "Binx Bolling's New Orleans: Moviegoing, Southern Writing, and Father Abraham," in Broughton, Panthea Reid, ed. *Art of Walker Percy*, 1–23.

PERRY, GEORGE SESSIONS (1910–1956)

Hold Autumn in Your Hand (1941)

Hairston, Maxine Cousins. *George Sessions Perry*, 121–133.

Southerner see *Hold Autumn in Your Hand*

Walls Rise Up (1939)

Hairston, Maxine Cousins. *George Sessions Perry*, 110–120.

PETER, JOHN (1921–)

Take Hands at Winter (1967)

Ricou, Laurence R. "Empty as Nightmare: Man and Landscape in Recent Canadian Prairie Fiction." *Mosaic* 6.2 (1973): 155.

PETERKIN, JULIA (1880–1961)

Black April (1927)

Landess, Thomas H. *Julia Peterkin*, 61–80.

Bright Skin (1932)

Landess, Thomas H. *Julia Peterkin*, 107–121.

Scarlet Sister Mary (1928)

Baker, Donald G. "Black Images: The Afro-American in Popular Novels, 1900–1945." *JPC* 7 (1973): 337–338.

Landess, Thomas H. *Julia Peterkin*, 81–106.

Starke, Catherine Juanita. *Black Portraiture in American Fiction*, 147–148.

PETESCH, NATALIE L. M. (1924–)

Odyssey of Katinou Kalokovich (1974)

Rosinsky, Natalie M. "Mothers and Daughters: Another Minority Group," in Davidson, Cathy N. and E. M. Broner, eds. *Lost Tradition*, 286.

PETRY, ANN (1912–1997)

Country Place (1947)

Davis, Arthur P. *From the Dark Tower*, 194–195.

Lattin, Vernon E. "Ann Petry and the American Dream." *BALF* 12 (1978): 69–72.

Shinn, Thelma J. "Women in the Novels of Ann Petry." *Critique* 16.1 (1974): 110–120. Rpt. in Spacks, Patricia Meyer, ed. *Contemporary Women Novelists*, 112–116.

Narrows (1953)

Davis, Arthur P. *From the Dark Tower*, 195–196.
McDowell, Margaret B. *"The Narrows:* A Fuller View of Ann Petry." *BALF* 14 (1980): 135–141.
Shinn, Thelma J. "Women in the Novels of Ann Petry." *Critique* 16.1 (1974): 110–120. Rpt. in Spacks, Patricia Meyer, ed. *Contemporary Women Novelists*, 116–117.

Street (1946)

Christian, Barbara. *Black Women Novelists*, 64–67.
Davis, Arthur P. *From the Dark Tower*, 194.
Gayle, Addison, Jr. *Way of the New World*, 192–197.
Schultz, Elizabeth. " 'Free in Fact and at Last': The Image of the Black Woman in Black American Fiction," in Springer, Marlene, ed. *What Manner of Woman*, 332–333.
Shinn, Thelma J. "Women in the Novels of Ann Petry." *Critique* 16.1 (1974): 110–120. Rpt. in Spacks, Patricia Meyer, ed. *Contemporary Women Novelists*, 108–112.

PHARR, ROBERT DEANE (1916–1992)

Book of Numbers (1969)

Epps, Garrett. "To Know the Truth: The Novels of Robert Deane Pharr." *HC* 13.5 (1976): 3–6.

S. R. O. (1971)

Epps, Garrett. "To Know the Truth: The Novels of Robert Deane Pharr." *HC* 13.5 (1976): 6–8.

Soul Murder Case (1975)

Epps, Garrett. "To Know the Truth: The Novels of Robert Deane Pharr." *HC* 13.5 (1976): 8–10.

PHELPS, ALMIRA HART (1793–1884)

Ida Norman (1848)

Baym, Nina. *Woman's Fiction*, 82–84.

PHELPS, ELIZABETH STUART (1815–1852)

Doctor Zay (1882)

Stansell, Christine. "Elizabeth Stuart Phelps: A Study in Female Rebellion." *MR* 13 (1972): 250–252.

Gates Ajar (1869)

Rees, Robert A. " 'Captain Stormfield's Visit to Heaven' and *The Gates Ajar*." *ELN* 7 (1970): 197–202.
Stansell, Christine. "Elizabeth Stuart Phelps: A Study in Female Rebellion." *MR* 13 (1972): 243–246.

Peep at Number Five (1852)
  Baym, Nina. *Woman's Fiction*, 246–247.

Story of Avis (1877)
  Stansell, Christine. "Elizabeth Stuart Phelps: A Study in Female Rebellion." *MR* 13 (1972): 246–249.

Sunny Side (1851)
  Baym, Nina. *Woman's Fiction*, 246–247.

PHILIPSON, MORRIS H. (1926–)

Wallpaper Fox (1976)
  Heilbrun, Carolyn G. "Marriage and Contemporary Fiction." *CritI* 5 (1978): 314–316.

PHILLIPS, THOMAS HAL (1922–)

Bitterweed Path (1949)
  Austen, Roger. *Playing the Game*, 129–131.

PIAZZA, BEN (1934–)

Exact and Very Strange Truth (1964)
  Green, Rose Basile. *Italian-American Novel*, 225–229.

PIERCY, MARGE (1936–)

Small Changes (1973)
  Masinton, Martha and Charles G. Masinton. "Second-class Citizenship: The Status of Women in Contemporary American Fiction," in Springer, Marlene, ed. *What Manner of Woman*, 311.

Woman on the Edge of Time (1976)
  Annas, Pamela J. "New Worlds, New Words: Androgyny in Feminist Science Fiction." *SFS* 5 (1978): 153–155.

PIERRE, GEORGE (1926–)

Autumn's Bounty (1972)
  Larson, Charles R. *American Indian Fiction*, 136–140.

PLAGEMANN, BENTZ (1913– 1991)

Steel Cocoon (1958)
  Jones, Peter G. *War and the Novelist*, 128–132.

PLATH, SYLVIA (1932–1963)

Bell Jar (1963)
  Aird, Eileen M. *Sylvia Plath*, 88–100.
  Allen, Mary. *Necessary Blankness*, 160–178.

Barnard, Caroline King. *Sylvia Plath*, 24–33.

Ellmann, Mary. "*Bell Jar:* An American Girlhood," in Newman, Charles, ed. *Art of Sylvia Plath*, 221–226.

Lameyer, Gordon. "Double in Sylvia Plath's *The Bell Jar*," in Butscher, Edward, ed. *Sylvia Plath*, 143–165.

Newman, Charles. "Candor Is the Only Wile: The Art of Sylvia Plath," in Newman, Charles, ed. *Art of Sylvia Plath*, 35–43.

Oates, Joyce Carol. "Death Throes of Romanticism: The Poetry of Sylvia Plath," in Butscher, Edward, ed. *Sylvia Plath*, 222.

Perloff, Marjorie G. " 'A Ritual for Being Born Twice': Sylvia Plath's *The Bell Jar.*" *ConL* 13 (1972): 507–522.

Smith, Stan. "Attitudes Counterfeiting Life: The Irony of Artifice in Sylvia Plath's *Bell Jar.*" *CritQ* 17 (1975): 247–260.

Spacks, Patricia Meyer. *Female Imagination*, 144–150.

Tanner, Tony. *City of Words*, 262–264.

POHL, FREDERIK (1919–)

Space Merchants (1953)

Donald, Miles. *American Novel in the Twentieth Century*, 178–182.

POIRIER, JEAN-MARIE (1922–)

Le prix du souvenir (1957)

Belleau, André. *Le romancier fictif*, 108–113.

POKAGON, CHIEF SIMON (1830(?)–1899)

Queen of the Woods (1899)

Larson, Charles R. *American Indian Fiction*, 37–46.

POLLINI, FRANCIS (1930–)

Crown (1967)

Green, Rose Basile. *Italian-American Novel*, 323–329.

Excursion (1965)

Green, Rose Basile. *Italian-American Novel*, 318–323.

Glover (1965)

Green, Rose Basile. *Italian-American Novel*, 312–318.

Night (1961)

Green, Rose Basile. *Italian-American Novel*, 308–312.

Pretty Maids All in a Row (1968)

Green, Rose Basile. *Italian-American Novel*, 329–335.

PORTER, GENE STRATTON (1863(?)–1924)

Her Father's Daughter (1921)

Baker, Donald G. "Black Images: The Afro-American in Popular Novels, 1900–1945." *JPC* 7 (1973): 334–335.

PORTER, KATHERINE ANNE (1890–1980)

Ship of Fools (1962)

Auchincloss, Louis. "Bound for Bremerhaven – and Eternity." [Book Review of *Ship of Fools*] *New York Herald Tribune* (1 April 1962). Rpt. in Warren, Robert Penn, ed. *Katherine Anne Porter*, 162–164.

Bedford, Sybille. "Voyage to Everywhere." [Book Review of *Ship of Fools*] *Spectator* (16 Nov 1962): 763–764. Rpt. in Warren, Robert Penn, ed. *Katherine Anne Porter*, 150–154.

Givner, Joan. "Genesis of *Ship of Fools*." *SLJ* 10.1 (1977): 14–30.

Hardy, John Edward. *Katherine Anne Porter*, 110–140.

Hartley, Lodwick. "Dark Voyagers," in Hartley, Lodwick and George Core, eds. *Katherine Anne Porter*, 215–226.

Heilman, Robert B. "*Ship of Fools:* Notes on Style," in Hartley, Lodwick and George Core, eds. *Katherine Anne Porter*, 197–210.

Kirkpatrick, Smith. "*Ship of Fools*." *Sewanee Review* (Winter 1963). Rpt. in Warren, Robert Penn, ed. *Katherine Anne Porter*, 165–169.

Liberman, M. M. *Katherine Anne Porter's Fiction*, 27–36.

Liberman, M. M. "Responsibility of the Novelist," in Hartley, Lodwick and George Core, eds. *Katherine Anne Porter*, 191–196.

Moss, Howard. "No Safe Harbor," in Moss, Howard. *Writing Against Time: Critical Essays and Reviews*. New York: William Morrow & Co., Inc., 1969. Rpt. in Warren, Robert Penn, ed. *Katherine Anne Porter*, 155–161.

Moss, Howard. *Writing Against Time*, 44–54.

Schorer, Mark. "We're All on the Passenger List." [Book Review of *Ship of Fools*] *New York Times* (1 April 1962). Rpt. in Warren, Robert Penn, ed. *Katherine Anne Porter*, 130–133.

West, Ray B., Jr. "*Ship of Fools*," excerpted from West, Ray B., Jr. *Katherine Anne Porter*. Minneapolis, MN: University of Minnestoa Press, 1963. 32–43. Rpt. in Warren, Robert Penn, ed. *Katherine Anne Porter*, 170–178.

Wiesenfarth, Joseph. "Negatives of Hope: A Reading of Katherine Anne Porter." *Renascence* 25 (1973): 90–92.

POST, MELVILLE DAVISSON (1871–1930)

Dwellers in the Hills (1901)

Norton, Charles A. *Melville Davisson Post*, 87–94.

Gilded Chair (1910)

Norton, Charles A. *Melville Davisson Post*, 94–101.

Mountain School-Teacher (1922)

Norton, Charles A. *Melville Davisson Post*, 175–186.

POTOK, CHAIM (1929–)

Chosen (1967)

Bluefarb, Sam. "Head, the Heart and the Conflict of Generations in Chaim Potok's *The Chosen*." *CLAJ* 14 (1971): 402–409.

Guttmann, Allen. *Jewish Writer in America*, 125–126.

Promise (1969)
  Guttmann, Allen. *Jewish Writer in America*, 126–127.

POULIN, JACQUES (1937–)

Le coeur de la baleine bleue (1970)
  Poulin, Gabrielle. *Romans du pays*, 263–270.

Les grandes marées (1978)
  Poulin, Gabrielle. *Romans du pays*, 271–275.

Spring Tides see *Les grandes marées*

POUPART, JEAN-MARIE (1946–)

Ma tite vache mal au pattes (1970)
  Poulin, Gabrielle. *Romans du pays*, 198–204.

POWERS, J. F. (1917–)

Morte D'Urban (1962)
  Kort, Wesley A. *Shriven Selves*, 15–35.

PRICE, REYNOLDS (1933–)

Generous Man (1966)
  Kreyling, Michael. "Motion and Rest in the Novels of Reynolds Price." *SoR* 16 (1980): 855–856.
  Shepherd, Allen. "Notes on Nature in the Fiction of Reynolds Price." *Crit* 15.2 (1973): 86–88.

Long and Happy Life (1962)
  Kreyling, Michael. "Motion and Rest in the Novels of Reynolds Price." *SoR* 16 (1980): 854–855.
  Shepherd, Allen. "Notes on Nature in the Fiction of Reynolds Price." *Crit* 15.2 (1973): 84–86.

Surface of the Earth (1975)
  Kreyling, Michael. "Motion and Rest in the Novels of Reynolds Price." *SoR* 16 (1980): 853–854, 858–868.

PRICE, RICHARD (1949–)

Bloodbrothers (1976)
  Shelton, Frank W. "Family, Community, and Masculinity in the Urban Novels of Richard Price." *Crit* 21.1 (1979): 10–13.

Ladies' Man (1978)
  Shelton, Frank W. "Family, Community, and Masculinity in the Urban Novels of Richard Price." *Crit* 21.1 (1979): 13–14.

Wanderers (1974)

    Shelton, Frank W. "Family, Community, and Masculinity in the Urban Novels of Richard Price." *Crit* 21.1 (1979): 7–10, 12–13.

PRIME-STEVENSON, EDWARD see MAYNE, XAVIER

PRYOR, GEORGE LANGHORNE (1857–(?))

Neither Bond nor Free (1902)

    Berzon, Judith R. *Neither White Nor Black*, 200–202.
    Isani, Mukhtar Ali. "Exotic and Protest in Earlier Black Literature: The Use of Alien Setting and Character." *SIBL* 5.2 (1974): 10–11.

PURDY, JAMES (1923–)

Cabot Wright Begins (1964)

    Adams, Stephen D. *James Purdy*, 75–94.
    Allen, Mary. *Necessary Blankness*, 56–63.
    Baldanza, Frank. "Playing House for Keeps with James Purdy." *ConL* 11 (1970): 500–504, 509.
    Boyers, Robert. "Attitudes Toward Sex in American 'High Culture.' " *Annals of the American Academy of Political and Social Science* (March 1968). Rpt. in Boyers, Robert. *Excursions*, 124–125.
    Chupack, Henry. *James Purdy*, 78–94.
    Kennard, Jean E. *Number and Nightmare*, 94–97.
    Tanner, Tony. *City of Words*, 95–105.

Eustace Chisholm and the Works (1967)

    Adams, Stephen D. *James Purdy*, 94–108.
    Baldanza, Frank. "Playing House for Keeps with James Purdy." *ConL* 11 (1970): 504–509.
    Chupack, Henry. *James Purdy*, 94–106.
    Kennard, Jean E. *Number and Nightmare*, 97–99.
    Tanner, Tony. *City of Words*, 105–108.

House of the Solitary Maggot (1974)

    Adams, Stephen D. *James Purdy*, 109–128.

Jeremy's Version (1970)

    Adams, Stephen D. *James Purdy*, 109–128.
    Chupack, Henry. *James Purdy*, 109–124.
    Kennard, Jean E. *Number and Nightmare*, 99–100.

Malcolm (1959)

    Adams, Stephen D. *James Purdy*, 26–41.
    Baldanza, Frank. "Playing House for Keeps with James Purdy." *ConL* 11 (1970): 491–496, 509–510.
    Chupack, Henry. *James Purdy*, 43–53.
    Harris, Charles B. *Contemporary American Novelists of the Absurd*, 127–128.
    Kennard, Jean E. *Number and Nightmare*, 87–92.

Pease, Donald. "James Purdy: Shaman in Nowhere Land," in French, Warren, ed. *Fifties*, 150–153.

Stetler, Charles. "Purdy's *Malcolm:* Allegory of No Man." *Crit* 14.3 (1973): 91–99.

Nephew (1960)

Adams, Stephen D. *James Purdy*, 43–73.

Allen, Mary. *Necessary Blankness*, 55–56.

Baldanza, Frank. "Playing House for Keeps with James Purdy." *ConL* 11 (1970): 496–500.

Bryant, Jerry H. *Open Decision*, 249–252.

Chupack, Henry. *James Purdy*, 53–60.

Kennard, Jean E. *Number and Nightmare*, 92–94.

PUZO, MARIO (1920–1999)

Dark Arena (1953)

Green, Rose Basile. *Italian-American Novel*, 337–342.

Fortunate Pilgrim (1964)

Green, Rose Basile. *Italian-American Novel*, 342–351.

Godfather (1969)

Carlisle, Charles R. "Strangers Within, Enemies Without: Alienation in Popular Mafia Fiction," in Landrum, Larry N., Pat Browne and Ray B. Browne, eds. *Dimensions of Detective Fiction*, 195–200.

Chiampi, James Thomas. "Resurrecting *The Godfather*." *MELUS* 5.4 (1978): 18–31.

Green, Rose Basile. *Italian-American Novel*, 352–367.

PYNCHON, THOMAS (1937–)

Crying of Lot 49 (1966)

Abernethy, Peter L. "Entropy in Pynchon's *The Crying of Lot 49*." *Crit* 14.2 (1972): 18–33.

Allen, Mary. *Necessary Blankness*, 46–51.

Cowart, David. *Thomas Pynchon*, 23–30, 78–82, 85, 101–107, 109–111, 112–113, 127–128.

Cox, Stephen D. "Berkeley, Blake, and the Apocalypse of Pynchon's *The Crying of Lot 49*." *ELWIU* 7 (1980): 91–99.

Davidson, Cathy N. "Oedipa as Androgyne in Thomas Pynchon's *The Crying of Lot 49*." *ConL* 18 (1977): 38–50.

Fowler, Douglas. "Pynchon's Magic World." *SAQ* 79 (1980): 53, 54, 56–57.

Harris, Charles B. *Contemporary American Novelists of the Absurd*, 93–99.

Henkle, Roger B. "Pynchon's Tapestries on the Western Wall." *MFS* (1971): 213–220.

Henkle, Roger B. "Pynchon's Tapestries on the Western Wall." *Modern Fiction Studies* 17 (1971): 207–220. Rpt. in Mendelson, Edward, ed. *Pynchon*, 97–111.

Kermode, Frank. "Use of the Codes," in Chatman, Seymour, ed. *Approaches to Poetics*. New York: Columiba University Press, 1973. Rpt. as "Decoding the Trystero," in Mendelson, Edward, ed. *Pynchon*, 162–166.

Kolodny, Annette and Daniel J. Peters. "Pynchon's *The Crying of Lot 49:* The Novel as Subversive Experience." *MFS* 19 (1973): 79–87.

Kostelanetz, Richard. "American Fiction in the Sixties," in Kostelanetz, Richard, ed. *On Contemporary Literature*, 650–651.

Laird, David. "Versions of Eden: The Automobile and the American Novel." *MQR* 19–20 (1980–81): 649–650.

LeClair, Thomas. "Death and Black Humor." *Crit* 17.1 (1975): 25–26.

Levine, George. "Risking the Moment: Anarchy and Possibility in Pynchon's Fiction," in Levine, George and David Leverenz, eds. *Mindful Pleasures*, 124–126.

Loofbourow, John W. "Realism in the Anglo-American Novel," in Halperin, John, ed. *Theory of the Novel*, 267–269.

McConnell, Frank D. *Four Postwar American Novelists*, 169–174.

Mackey, Douglas A. *Rainbow Quest of Thomas Pynchon*, 26–36.

Mangel, Anne. "Maxwell's Demon, Entropy, Information: *The Crying of Lot 49.*" *TriQuarterly* 20 (Winter 1971): 194–208. Rpt. in Levine, George and David Leverenz, eds. *Mindful Pleasures*, 87–99.

May, John R. *Toward a New Earth*, 180–191.

Mendelson, Edward. "The Sacred, the Profane, and *The Crying of Lot 49*," in Baldwin, Kenneth H. and David R. Kirby, eds. *Individual and Community: Variations on a Theme in American Fiction*, 182–222.

Mendelson, Edward. "The Sacred, the Profane, and *The Crying of Lot 49*," in Baldwin, Kenneth H. and David R. Kirby, eds. *Individual and Community: Variations on a Theme in American Fiction.* Durham, NC: Duke University Press, 1975. 182–222. Revised slightly and rpt. in Mendelson, Edward, ed. *Pynchon*, 112–146.

Merrill, Robert. "Form and Meaning of Pynchon's *The Crying of Lot 49.*" *Ariel* 8.1 (1977): 53–71.

Nohrnberg, James. "Pynchon's Paraclete," Mendelson, Edward. "The Sacred, the Profane, and *The Crying of Lot 49*," in Mendelson, Edward, ed. *Pynchon*, 147–158.

Pearce, Richard. "Thomas Pynchon and the Novel of Motion: Where're They At, Where're They Going?" *MR* 21 (1980): 185–190.

Pearson, C. S. "Puritans, Literary Critics, and Thomas Pynchon's *The Crying of Lot 49.*" *NConL* 8.2 (1978): 8–9.

Plater, William M. *Grim Phoenix*, 14, 16–17, 18–19, 26–28, 34–35, 39, 43, 48–49, 56–57, 59–60, 81–87, 115–117, 120, 149–154, 180–181, 193–195, 202–205, 211–212, 213, 228–233.

Puetz, Manfred. "Thomas Pychon's *The Crying of Lot 49:* The World Is a Tristero System." *Mosaic* 7.4 (1974): 125–137.

Quilligan, Maureen. *Language of Allegory*, 42–46, 261–263.

Seed, David. "Fictional Labyrinths of Thomas Pynchon." *CritQ* 18.4 (1976): 76–78.

Sklar, Robert. "New Novel, USA: Thomas Pynchon." *Nation* 205 (25 Sept 1967): 277–280. Rpt. as "An Anarchist Miracle: The Novels of Thomas Pynchon," in Mendelson, Edward, ed. *Pynchon*, 92–96.

Slade, Joseph W. *Thomas Pynchon*, 125–175.

Stimpson, Catharine R. "Pre-Apocalyptic Atavism: Thomas Pynchon's Early Fiction," in Levine, George and David Leverenz, eds. *Mindful Pleasures*, 42–45.

Tanner, Tony. "*V.* and V-2," in Mendelson, Edward, ed. *Pynchon*, 39–47.

Vernon, John. *Garden and the Map*, 65.

Wagner, Linda W. *American Modern*, 85–92.

Gravity's Rainbow (1973)

Black, Joel D. "Probing a Post-Romantic Paleontology: Thomas Pynchon's *Gravity's Rainbow.*" *BoundaryII* 8.2 (1980): 229–254.

Cocks, Geoffrey. "War, Man, and Gravity: Thomas Pynchon and Science Fiction." *Extrapolation* 20 (1979): 368–375.

Cowart, David. "Pynchon's Use of the Tannhauser-Legend in *Gravity's Rainbow.*" *NConL* 9.3 (1979): 2–3.

Cowart, David. " 'Sacrificial Ape': King Kong and His Antitypes in *Gravity's Rainbow.*" *L&P* 29 (1978): 112–118.

Cowart, David. *Thomas Pynchon*, 31–62, 82–94, 100–101, 120–127, 128–130.

Doody, Terence A. "Updike's Idea of Reification." *ConL* 20 (1979): 212–214.

Fowler, Douglas. "Pynchon's Magic World." *SAQ* 79 (1980): 53, 54–55, 57–60.

Fussell, Paul. *Great War and Modern Memory*. New York: Oxford University Press, 1975. Rpt. as "Brigadier Remembers," in Mendelson, Edward, ed. *Pynchon*, 213–219.

Hendin, Josephine. *Vulnerable People*, 198–209.

Kappel, Lawrence. "Psychic Geography in *Gravity's Rainbow.*" *ConL* 21 (1980): 225–251.

Kaufman, Marjorie. "Brünnhilde and the Chemists: Women in *Gravity's Rainbow*," in Levine, George and David Leverenz, eds. *Mindful Pleasures*, 197–226.

Krafft, John M. " 'And How Far-Fallen': Puritan Themes in *Gravity's Rainbow.*" *Crit* 18.3 (1977): 55–73.

LeClair, Thomas. "Death and Black Humor." *Crit* 17.1 (1975): 26–28.

Leverenz, David. "On Trying to Read *Gravity's Rainbow*," in Levine, George and David Leverenz, eds. *Mindful Pleasures*, 229–249.

Levine, George. "Risking the Moment: Anarchy and Possibility in Pynchon's Fiction," in Levine, George and David Leverenz, eds. *Mindful Pleasures*, 126–135.

McClintock, James I. "United State Revisited: Pynchon and Zamiatin." *ConL* 18 (1977): 475–490.

McConnell, Frank D. *Four Postwar American Novelists*, 174–197.

Mackey, Douglas A. *Rainbow Quest of Thomas Pynchon*, 36–61.

Mendelson, Edward. "Gravity's Encyclopedia," in Levine, George and David Leverenz, eds. *Mindful Pleasures*, 161–192.

Morgan, Speer. "*Gravity's Rainbow:* What's the Big Idea?" *MFS* 23 (1977): 199–216.

Pearce, Richard. "Thomas Pynchon and the Novel of Motion: Where're They At, Where're They Going?" *MR* 21 (1980): 190–195.

Plater, William M. *Grim Phoenix*, 14–15, 17–18, 28–30, 35–36, 37–41, 43–45, 49–53, 57–63, 64–65, 87–102, 109–114, 117–127, 131–134, 136–137, 154–176, 181–186, 195–201, 205–211, 213–219, 234–241.

Quilligan, Maureen. *Language of Allegory*, 204–220, 222, 265–277.

Rose, Alan Henry. *Demonic Vision*, 132–134.

Safer, Elaine B. "Allusive Mode and Black Humor in Barth's *Giles Goat-Boy* and Pynchon's *Gravity's Rainbow.*" *Renascence* 32 (1980): 93–100.

Sanders, Scott. "Pychon's Paranoid History," in Levine, George and David Leverenz, eds. *Mindful Pleasures*, 139–159.

Seed, David. "Fictional Labyrinths of Thomas Pynchon." *CritQ* 18.4 (1976): 78–81.

Seidel, Michael. "Satiric Plots of *Gravity's Rainbow*," in Mendelson, Edward, ed. *Pynchon*, 193–212.

Siegel, Mark R. "Creative Paranoia: Understanding the System of *Gravity's Rainbow*." *Crit* 18.3 (1977): 39–54.

Siegel, Mark Richard. *Pynchon: Creative Paranoia in Gravity's Rainbow*. Port Washington, NY: Kennikat Press, 1978.

Slade, Joseph W. "Escaping Rationalization: Options for the Self in *Gravity's Rainbow*." *Crit* 18.3 (1977): 27–38.

Slade, Joseph W. *Thomas Pynchon*, 176–248.

Tanner, Tony. *City of Words*, 173–180.

Tanner, Tony. "*V.* and V-2," in Mendelson, Edward, ed. *Pynchon*, 47–55.

Westervelt, Linda A. " 'A Place Dependent on Ourselves': The Reader as System-Builder in *Gravity's Rainbow*." *TSLL* 22 (1980): 69–90.

Wolfley, Lawrence C. "Repression's Rainbow: The Presence of Norman O. Brown in Pynchon's Big Novel." *PMLA* 92 (1977): 873–887.

V. (1963)

Allen, Mary. *Necessary Blankness*, 37–46.

Bryant, Jerry H. *Open Decision*, 252–257.

Cowart, David. "Love and Death: Variations on a Theme in Pynchon's Early Fiction." *JNT* 7 (1977): 157–169.

Cowart, David. "Pynchon's *The Crying of Lot 49* and the Paintings of Remedios Varo." *Crit* 18.3 (1977): 19–26.

Cowart, David. *Thomas Pynchon*, 13–22, 65–78, 107–109, 45–46.

Fahy, Joseph. "Thomas Pynchon's *V.* and Mythology." *Crit* 18.3 (1977): 5–18.

Fowler, Douglas. "Pynchon's Magic World." *SAQ* 79 (1980): 54.

Golden, Robert E. "Mass Man and Modernism: Violence in Pynchon's *V.*" *Crit* 14.2 (1972): 5–17.

Greiner, Donald J. "Fiction as History, History as Fiction: The Reader and Thomas Pynchon's *V.*" *SCR* 10.1 (1977): 4–18.

Harris, Charles B. *Contemporary American Novelists of the Absurd*, 79–93.

Henderson, Harry B. *Versions of the Past*, 277–285.

Hendin, Josephine. *Vulnerable People*, 192–197, 204.

Henkle, Roger B. "Pynchon's Tapestries on the Western Wall." *MFS* (1971): 207–212, 217–220.

Henkle, Roger B. "Pynchon's Tapestries on the Western Wall." *Modern Fiction Studies* 17 (1971): 207–220. Rpt. in Mendelson, Edward, ed. *Pynchon*, 97–111.

Hyman, Stanley Edgar. "Goddess and the Schlemihl." *New Leader* (18 March 1963). Rpt. in Kostelanetz, Richard, ed. *On Contemporary Literature*, 507–510.

Kostelanetz, Richard. "American Fiction in the Sixties," in Kostelanetz, Richard, ed. *On Contemporary Literature*, 640.

LeClair, Thomas. "Death and Black Humor." *Crit* 17.1 (1975): 25.

Lehan, Richard. *Dangerous Crossing*, 157–162.

Levine, George. "Risking the Moment: Anarchy and Possibility in Pynchon's Fiction," in Levine, George and David Leverenz, eds. *Mindful Pleasures*, 119–123.

Lhamon, W. T., Jr. "Pentecost, Promiscuity and Pynchon's *V.*: From the Scaffold to the Impulsive." *TCL* 21 (1975): 163–176.

Lhamon, W. T., Jr. "Pentecost, Promiscuity, and Pynchon's *V.*: From the Scaffold to the Impulsive," in Levine, George and David Leverenz, eds. *Mindful Pleasures*, 69–85.

McConnell, Frank D. *Four Postwar American Novelists*, 164–169.

Mackey, Douglas A. *Rainbow Quest of Thomas Pynchon*, 12–26.

New, Melvyn. "Profaned and Stenciled Texts: In Search of Pynchon's *V.*" *GR* 33 (1979): 395–412.

O'Connor, Peter. "Wasteland of Thomas Pynchon's *V.*" *CollL* 3 (1976): 49–55.

Olderman, Raymond M. *Beyond the Waste Land*, 123–149.

Pearce, Richard. "Thomas Pynchon and the Novel of Motion: Where're They At, Where're They Going?" *MR* 21 (1980): 181–185.

Plater, William M. *Grim Phoenix*, 13–14, 19–26, 30–34, 36–37, 39, 41–43, 45–48, 67–81, 113–115, 129–130, 140–149, 177–180, 191–193, 201–202, 211, 212–213, 225–228.

Richter, David H. *Fable's End*, 101–135.

Schulz, Max F. *Black Humor Fiction of the Sixties*, 61–64, 77–82.

Seed, David. "Fictional Labyrinths of Thomas Pynchon." *CritQ* 18.4 (1976): 73–76.

Sklar, Robert. "New Novel, USA: Thomas Pynchon." *Nation* 205 (25 Sept 1967): 277–280. Rpt. as "An Anarchist Miracle: The Novels of Thomas Pynchon," in Mendelson, Edward, ed. *Pynchon*, 89–92.

Slade, Joseph W. *Thomas Pynchon*, 48–124.

Stimpson, Catharine R. "Pre-Apocalyptic Atavism: Thomas Pynchon's Early Fiction," in Levine, George and David Leverenz, eds. *Mindful Pleasures*, 32–42.

Tanner, Tony. "Caries and Cabals," in Tanner, Tony. *City of Words: American Fiction: 1950–1970*. New York: Harper and Row, 1971. 153–173. Rpt. in Levine, George and David Leverenz, eds. *Mindful Pleasures*, 52–67.

Tanner, Tony. *City of Words*, 156–173.

Tanner, Tony. "*V.* and V-2," in Mendelson, Edward, ed. *Pynchon*, 16–39.

RADDALL, THOMAS (1903–)

Hangman's Beach (1966)

Seaman, Andrew Thompson. "Fiction in Atlantic Canada." *CanL* 68–69 (1976): 31–32.

Nymph and the Lamp (1950)

Moss, John. *Patterns of Isolation*, 129–138.
Moss, John. *Sex and Violence*, 105.

RAND, AYN (1905–1982)

Atlas Shrugged (1957)

Bryant, Jerry H. *Open Decision*, 169–173.

RAWLINGS, MARJORIE KINNAN (1896–1953)

Golden Apples (1935)

Bellman, Samuel I. *Marjorie Kinnan Rawlings*, 42–53.
York, Lamar. "Marjorie Kinnan Rawlings's Rivers." *SLJ* 9.2 (1977): 99–101.

Sojourner (1953)
  Bellman, Samuel I. *Marjorie Kinnan Rawlings*, 119–132.

South Moon Under (1933)
  Bellman, Samuel I. *Marjorie Kinnan Rawlings*, 27–41.
  York, Lamar. "Marjorie Kinnan Rawlings's Rivers." *SLJ* 9.2 (1977): 95–99.

Yearling (1938)
  Bellman, Samuel I. *Marjorie Kinnan Rawlings*, 54–84.
  Kelty, Jean McClure. "Cult of Kill in Adolescent Fiction." *EJ* 64.2 (1975): 57.
  York, Lamar. "Marjorie Kinnan Rawlings's Rivers." *SLJ* 9.2 (1977): 101–104.

READ, MARTHA

Monima (1802)
  Petter, Henri. *Early American Novel*, 231–233.

RECHY, JOHN (1934–)

City of Night (1963)
  Austen, Roger. *Playing the Game*, 205–207.

REDDING, J. SAUNDERS (1906–1988)

Stranger and Alone (1950)
  Berzon, Judith R. *Neither White Nor Black*, 203.

REED, ISHMAEL (1938–)

Flight to Canada (1976)
  Harris, Norman. "Politics as an Innovative Aspect of Literary Folklore: A Study of Ishmael Reed." *Obsidian* 5.1–2 (1979): 47–48.

Free-Lance Pallbearers (1967)
  Emerson, O. B. "Cultural Nationalism in Afro-American Literature," in Lewald, H. Ernest, ed. *Cry of Home*, 236–238.
  Fabre, Michel. "Ishmael Reed's *Free-Lance Pallbearers* on The Dialectics of Shit." *Obsidian* 3.3 (1977): 5–19.
  Musgrave, Marian E. "Sexual Excess and Deviation as Structural Devices in Gunter Grass's *Blechtrommel* and Ishmael Reed's *Free-Lance Pallbearers*." *CLAJ* 2 (1979): 229–239.
  Nichols, Charles H. "Comic Modes in Black America (A Ramble through Afro-American Humor)," in Cohen, Sara Blacher, ed. *Comic Relief*, 120–122.
  Wade, Melvin and Margaret Wade. "Black Aesthetic in the Black Novel." *JBS* 2.4 (1972): 402.

Last Days of Louisiana Red (1974)
  Carter, Steven R. "Ishmael Reed's Neo-Hoodoo Detection," in Landrum, Larry N., Pat Browne and Ray B. Browne, eds. *Dimensions of Detective Fiction*, 270–273.
  Harris, Norman. "Politics as an Innovative Aspect of Literary Folklore: A Study of Ishmael Reed." *Obsidian* 5.1–2 (1979): 45–47.

Nichols, Charles H. "Comic Modes in Black America (A Ramble through Afro-American Humor)," in Cohen, Sara Blacher, ed. *Comic Relief,* 124–125.

Scholes, Robert. *Fabulation and Metafiction,* 193–196.

Mumbo Jumbo (1972)

Carter, Steven R. "Ishmael Reed's Neo-Hoodoo Detection," in Landrum, Larry N., Pat Browne and Ray B. Browne, eds. *Dimensions of Detective Fiction,* 265–270.

Harris, Norman. "Politics as an Innovative Aspect of Literary Folklore: A Study of Ishmael Reed." *Obsidian* 5.1–2 (1979): 43–44.

Nichols, Charles H. "Comic Modes in Black America (A Ramble through Afro-American Humor)," in Cohen, Sara Blacher, ed. *Comic Relief,* 122–123.

Yellow Back Radio Broke-Down (1969)

Ambler, Madge. "Ishmael Reed: Whose Radio Broke Down?" *NALF* 6 (1972): 125–131.

Jones, Robert W. "Language and Structure in Ishmael Reed's *Yellow Back Radio Broke-Down.*" *NConL* 8.2 (1978): 2–3.

RELF, SAMUEL (1776–1823)

Infidelity (1797)

Petter, Henri. *Early American Novel,* 267–271.

REMINGTON, FREDERIC (1861–1909)

John Ermine of the Yellowstone (1902)

Alter, Judith. "Frederic Remington's Major Novel: *John Ermine.*" *SAL* 2 (1972): 42–46.

RENAUD, JACQUES (1943–)

Le cassé (1964)

Filteau, Claude. "*Le cassé* de Jacques Renaud: un certain parti pris sur le vernaculaire français québécois." *V&I* 5 (1980): 271–289.

Shek, Ben-Zion. *Social Realism,* 257–266.

REYNOLDS, DALLAS MCCORD see REYNOLDS, MACK

REYNOLDS, MACK (1917–)

Earth War (1963)

Warrick, Patricia. "Mack Reynolds: The Future as Socio-economic Possibility," in Clareson, Thomas, ed. *Voices for the Future* (Vol. 2), 142–145.

Five Way Secret Agent (1969)

Warrick, Patricia. "Mack Reynolds: The Future as Socio-economic Possibility," in Clareson, Thomas, ed. *Voices for the Future* (Vol. 2), 145–146.

Looking Backward from the Year 2000 (1973)

Warrick, Patricia. "Mack Reynolds: The Future as Socio-economic Possibility," in Clareson, Thomas, ed. *Voices for the Future* (Vol. 2), 146–149.

Mercenary from Tomorrow (1968)

Warrick, Patricia. "Mack Reynolds: The Future as Socio-economic Possibility," in Clareson, Thomas, ed. *Voices for the Future* (Vol. 2), 142–145.

Time Gladiator (1969)

Warrick, Patricia. "Mack Reynolds: The Future as Socio-economic Possibility," in Clareson, Thomas, ed. *Voices for the Future* (Vol. 2), 142–145.

Space Barbarians (1960)

Warrick, Patricia. "Mack Reynolds: The Future as Socio-economic Possibility," in Clareson, Thomas, ed. *Voices for the Future* (Vol. 2), 139–141.

RICHARD, JEAN-JULES (1911–1975)

Le feu dans l'amiante (1956)

Shek, Ben-Zion. *Social Realism*, 222–225.

RICHARDSON, JOHN (1796–1852)

Wacousta (1832)

Early, L. R. "Myth and Prejudice in Kirby, Richardson, and Parker." *CanL* 81 (1979): 24–31.

Early, L. R. "Myth and Prejudice in Kirby, Richardson, and Parker," in Moss, John, ed. *Beginnings*, 198–207.

Hurley, Michael. "*Wacousta:* The Borders of Nightmare," in Moss, John, ed. *Beginnings*, 60–68.

Lecker, Robert. "Patterns of Deception in *Wacousta*," in Moss, John, ed. *Beginnings*, 47–58.

Mathews, Robin. *Canadian Literature*, 13–22.

Mathews, Robin D. "Wacousta Factor," in Bessai, Diane and David Jackel, eds. *Figures in a Ground*, 295–303, 304–309.

Moss, John. *Patterns of Isolation*, 42–52.

Moss, John. *Sex and Violence*, 88–90.

Northey, Margot. *Haunted Wilderness*, 18–26.

RICHLER, MORDECAI (1931–)

Acrobats (1954)

Birbalsingh, Frank M. "Mordecai Richler and the Jewish-Canadian Novel." *JCL* 7.1 (1972): 72–73.

Bowering, George. "And the Sun Goes Down: Richler's First Novel." *Canadian Literature* 29 (Summer 1966): 7–17. Rpt. in Sheps, G. David, ed. *Mordecai Richler*, 1–14.

Woodcock, George. *Mordecai Richler*, 13–19.

Apprenticeship of Duddy Kravitz (1959)

Bevan, A. R. "*Apprenticeship of Duddy Kravitz*," from "Introduction to *Apprenticeship of Duddy Kravitz*." Richler, Mordecai. *Duddy Kravitz*. Toronto: McClelland and Stewart Limited, 1969. Rpt. in Sheps, G. David, ed. *Mordecai Richler*, 84–91.

Birbalsingh, Frank M. "Mordecai Richler and the Jewish-Canadian Novel." *JCL* 7.1 (1972): 75–76.

Boutelle, Ann. "Dorian Gray Phenomenon in Canadian Literature." *DR* 57 (1977): 268–269.

Dooley, D. J. *Moral Vision*, 93–107.

Marshall, Tom. "Third Solitude: Canadian as Jew," in Moss, John, ed. *Here and Now*, 147–153.

Marshall, Tom. "Third Solitude: Canadian as Jew," in Moss, John, ed. *Here and Now*. Toronto: NC Press, 1978. Rpt. in Gerson, Carole, comp. *Modern Canadian Fiction*, 113–116.

Mathews, Robin D. "Wacousta Factor," in Bessai, Diane and David Jackel, eds. *Figures in a Ground*, 314.

Myers, David. "Mordecai Richler as Satirist." *Ariel* 4.1 (1973): 50–51, 52.

New, W. H. *Articulating West*, 108–116, 126–127.

New, William H. "Apprenticeship of Discovery." *Canadian Literature* 29 (Summer 1966): 18–33. Rpt. in Sheps, G. David, ed. *Mordecai Richler*, 69–77.

Ower, John. "Sociology, Psychology, and Satire in *The Apprenticeship of Duddy Kravitz*." *MFS* 22 (1976): 413–428.

Pache, Walter. "English-Canadian Fiction & the Pastoral Tradition." *CanL* 86 (1980): 20–22.

Tallman, Warren. "Richler and the Faithless City." *Canadian Literature* 3, Winter 1960. Rpt. in Gerson, Carole, comp. *Modern Canadian Fiction*, 117–118.

Tallman, Warren. "Wolf in the Snow." *Canadian Literature* 5 (Summer 1960): 7–20 & *Canadian Literature* 6 (Autumn 1960): 41–48. Rpt. in Cook, Gregory M., ed. *Ernest Buckler*, 74–79.

Tallman, Warren. "Wolf in the Snow." *Canadian Literature* 5 (Summer 1960): 7–20 & *Canadian Literature* 6 (Autumn 1960): 41–48. Rpt. in Gerson, Carole, comp. *Modern Canadian Fiction*, 107–109.

Tallman, Warren. "Wolf in the Snow." *Canadian Literature* 6 (Autumn 1960): 41–48. Rpt. in Sheps, G. David, ed. *Mordecai Richler*, 79–83.

Woodcock, George. *Mordecai Richler*, 35–43.

Woodcock, George. "Mordecai Richler," in Woodcock, George. *Mordecai Richler*. Toronto: McClelland and Stewart, 1971. Rpt. in Gerson, Carole, comp. *Modern Canadian Fiction*, 110–112.

Choice of Enemies (1957)

Birbalsingh, Frank M. "Mordecai Richler and the Jewish-Canadian Novel." *JCL* 7.1 (1972): 74–75.

Scott, Peter Dale. "Choice of Certainties." *Tamarack Review* 8 (1958): 73–82. Rpt. in Sheps, G. David, ed. *Mordecai Richler*, 59–68.

Woodcock, George. *Mordecai Richler*, 28–34.

Cocksure (1968)

Birbalsingh, Frank M. "Mordecai Richler and the Jewish-Canadian Novel." *JCL* 7.1 (1972): 77–78.

Myers, David. "Mordecai Richler as Satirist." *Ariel* 4.1 (1973): 51–56.

Northey, Margot. *Haunted Wilderness*, 95–100.

Woodcock, George. *Mordecai Richler*, 47–54.

Incomparable Atuk (1963)

Birbalsingh, Frank M. "Mordecai Richler and the Jewish-Canadian Novel." *JCL* 7.1 (1972): 76–77.

Woodcock, George. *Mordecai Richler*, 44–46.

St. Urbain's Horseman (1971)

Cohn-Sfetcu, Ofelia. "Of Self, Temporal Cubism, and Metaphor: Mordecai Richler's *St. Urbain's Horseman*." *IFR* 3 (1976): 30–34.

Cohn-Sfetcu, Ofelia. "To Live in Abundance of Life: Time in Canadian Literature." *CanL* 76 (1978): 33–35.

Cude, Wilfred. *Due Sense of Differences*, 199–203.

Cude, Wilfred. "The Golem as Metaphor for Art: The Monster Takes Meaning in *St. Urbain's Horseman*," *Journal of Canadian Studies* (Spring, 1977): 50–69. Rpt. in Cude, Wilfred. *Due Sense of Differences*, 172–196.

Marshall, Tom. "Third Solitude: Canadian as Jew," in Moss, John, ed. *Here and Now*, 153–154.

Moss, John. "Richler's Horseman," in Moss, John, ed. *Here and Now*, 156–165.Moss, John. *Sex and Violence*, 123–139, 144–145.

Myers, David. "Mordecai Richler as Satirist." *Ariel* 4.1 (1973): 51–52, 56–60.

Tallman, Warren. "Need for Laughter." *CanL* 56 (1973): 71–83.

Tallman, Warren. "Need for Laughter," in Woodcock, George, ed. *Canadian Novel*, 258–270.

Son of a Smaller Hero (1955)

Atwood, Margaret. *Survival*, 156–157.

Birbalsingh, Frank M. "Mordecai Richler and the Jewish-Canadian Novel." *JCL* 7.1 (1972): 73–74.

Greenstein, Michael. "Apprenticeship of Noah Adler." *CanL* 78 (1978): 43–51.

Moss, John. *Patterns of Isolation*, 227–230, 235–237.

Myers, David. "Mordecai Richler as Satirist." *Ariel* 4.1 (1973): 48–50.

Woodcock, George. *Mordecai Richler*, 20–27.

Woodcock, George. *"Son of a Smaller Hero*," from "Introduction to *Sun of a Smaller Hero*." Richler, Mordecai. *Son of a Smaller Hero*. Toronto: McClelland and Stewart Limited, 1966. Rpt. in Sheps, G. David, ed. *Mordecai Richler*, 15–21.

RICHTER, CONRAD (1890–1968)

Fields (1946)

Edwards, Clifford D. *Conrad Richter's Ohio Trilogy.* The Hague, Netherlands: Mouton, 1970.

Lady (1957)

Meldrum, Barbara. "Conrad Richter's Southwestern Ladies," in Lee, L. L. and Merrill Lewis, ed. *Women, Women Writers, and the West*, 126–127.

Sea of Grass (1937)

Meldrum, Barbara. "Conrad Richter's Southwestern Ladies," in Lee, L. L. and Merrill Lewis, ed. *Women, Women Writers, and the West*, 121–123.

Tacey Cromwell (1942)

Meldrum, Barbara. "Conrad Richter's Southwestern Ladies," in Lee, L. L. and Merrill Lewis, ed. *Women, Women Writers, and the West*, 123–126.

Town (1950)

Edwards, Clifford D. *Conrad Richter's Ohio Trilogy*. The Hague, Netherlands: Mouton, 1970.

Trees (1940)

Edwards, Clifford D. *Conrad Richter's Ohio Trilogy*. The Hague, Netherlands: Mouton, 1970.

RINGUET (1895–1960)

Le poids du jour (1949)

Panneton, Jean. *Ringuet*, 77–89.
Shek, Ben-Zion. *Social Realism*, 158, 159, 160–163, 165.

Thirty Acres see *Trente arpents*

Trente arpents (1938)

Cotnam, Jacques. "Cultural Nationalism and Its Literary Expression in French-Canadian Fiction." Trans. Noël Corbett. In Lewald, H. Ernest, ed. *Cry of Home*, 286–287.
Hathorn, Ramon. "Soldats, patrons et femmes 'fatales': Figures de l'Anglais' dans le roman québécois des XIXe et XXe siècles." *V&I* 6 (1980): 109–110.
Hoekema, H. "Illusion of Realism in *Thirty Acres*." *ECW* 17 (1980): 102–112.
Legris, Maurice R. "Modern French-Canadian Novel." *TCL* 16 (1970): 170.
Mathews, Robin D. "Wacousta Factor," in Bessai, Diane and David Jackel, eds. *Figures in a Ground*, 313–314.
Panneton, Jean. *Ringuet*, 42–51.
Rasporich, Beverly J. "Sacrifice and Death in French-Canadian Fiction: An English Reading." *DR* 55 (1975): 455–459.
Servais-Maquoi, Mireille. *Le roman de la terre au Québec*, 151–188.
Sirois, Antoine. "Grove et Ringuet: Témoins d'une époque." *CanL* 49 (1971): 22–27.
Sutherland, Ronald. *Second Image*, 6–10.
Urbas, Jeannette. *From Thirty Acres to Modern Times*, 19–25.
Viens, Jacques. *La terre de Zola et Trente arpents de Ringuet: étude comparée*. Montréal: Editions Cosmos, 1970.

RIVES, AMÉLIE (1863–1945)

Barbara Dering (1892)

Lojek, Helen. "Southern Lady Gets a Divorce: 'Saner Feminism' in the Novels of Amélie Rives." *SLJ* 12.1 (1979): 56–60.
Taylor, Welford Dunaway. *Amélie Rives*, 58–64.

Golden Rose (1908)

Taylor, Welford Dunaway. *Amélie Rives*, 82–87.

Queerness of Celia (1926)

Taylor, Welford Dunaway. *Amélie Rives*, 123–127.

Quick or the Dead? (1888)

    Taylor, Welford Dunaway. *Amélie Rives*, 35–39.

Shadows of Flames (1914)

    Lojek, Helen. "Southern Lady Gets a Divorce: 'Saner Feminism' in the Novels of Amélie Rives." *SLJ* 12.1 (1979): 62–64.

Trix and Over the Moon (1906)

    Lojek, Helen. "Southern Lady Gets a Divorce: 'Saner Feminism' in the Novels of Amélie Rives." *SLJ* 12.1 (1979): 60–61.

Witness of the Sun (1889)

    Taylor, Welford Dunaway. *Amélie Rives*, 49–54.

World's End (1914)

    Taylor, Welford Dunaway. *Amélie Rives*, 96–101.

ROBBINS, TOM (1936–)

Another Roadside Attraction (1971)

    Nadeau, Robert L. "Physics and Cosmology in the Fiction of Tom Robbins." *Crit* 20.1 (1978): 63–70.
    Siegel, Mark. *Tom Robbins*, 12–21, 31–42.

Even Cowgirls Get the Blues (1976)

    Nadeau, Robert L. "Physics and Cosmology in the Fiction of Tom Robbins." *Crit* 20.1 (1978): 63–65, 70–74.
    Siegel, Mark. *Tom Robbins*, 21–42.

Still Life with Woodpecker (1980)

    Siegel, Mark. *Tom Robbins*, 42–48.

ROBERTS, CHARLES G. D. (1860–1943)

Barbara Ladd (1902)

    Keith, W. J. *Charles G. D. Roberts*, 73–76.

Heart of the Ancient Wood (1900)

    Mallinson, Jean. "Maiden Archetype in *The Heart of the Ancient Wood*." *ECW* 3 (1975): 47–51.
    Morley, Patricia. " 'We and the Beasts Are Kin': Attitudes towards Nature in Nineteenth and Early Twentieth-Century Canadian Literature." *WLWE* 16 (1977): 347–349.

Heart that Knows (1906)

    Keith, W. J. *Charles G. D. Roberts*, 76–80.

In the Morning of Time (1919)

    Keith, W. J. *Charles G. D. Roberts*, 80–83.

ROBERTS, ELIZABETH MADOX (1886–1941)

Great Meadow (1930)

    Tyree, Wade. "Time's Own River: The Three Major Novels of Elizabeth Madox Roberts." *MQR* 16 (1977): 38–41.

My Heart and My Flesh (1927)

Tyree, Wade. "Time's Own River: The Three Major Novels of Elizabeth Madox Roberts." *MQR* 16 (1977): 41–45.

Time of Man (1926)

Cook, Sylvia Jenkins. *From Tobacco Road to Route 66*, 23–24.

Gray, Richard. *Literature of Memory*, 108–111.

Tyree, Wade. "Time's Own River: The Three Major Novels of Elizabeth Madox Roberts." *MQR* 16 (1977): 35–38.

ROIPHE, ANNE RICHARDSON (1935–)

Long Division (1972)

Avery, Evelyn Gross. "Tradition and Independence in Jewish Feminist Novels." *MELUS* 7.4 (1980): 50–52.

ROLLINS, WILLIAM, JR. (1897–1971)

Shadow Before (1934)

Cook, Sylvia Jenkins. *From Tobacco Road to Route 66*, 135–140.

RÖLVAAG, OLE E. (1876–1931)

Boat of Longing (1933)

Paulson, Kristoffer. "What Was Lost: Ole Rolvaag's *The Boat of Longing*." *MELUS* 7.1 (1980): 51–60.

Giants in the Earth (1927)

Grider, Sylvia. "Madness and Personification in *Giants in the Earth*," in Lee, L. L. and Merrill Lewis, ed. *Women, Women Writers, and the West*, 111–117.

McKnight, Jeannie. "American Dream, Nightmare Underside: Diaries, Letters, and Fiction of Women on the American Frontier," in Lee, L. L. and Merrill Lewis, ed. *Women, Women Writers, and the West*, 28–29.

Moseley, Ann. "Land as Metaphor in Two Scandinavian Immigrant Novels." *MELUS* 5.2 (1978): 35–38.

ROSEN, GERALD (1938–)

Carmen Miranda Memorial Flagpole (1977)

Friedman, Edward H. "Gerald Rosen's *The Carmen Miranda Memorial Flagpole: Variations on an Unamunian Theme*." *NConL* 10.4 (1980): 5–6.

ROSENFELD, ISAAC (1918–1956)

Passage from Home (1946)

Guttmann, Allen. *Jewish Writer in America*, 55–57.

ROSS, JAMES E.

Dead Are Mine (1963)

Bryant, Jerry H. *Open Decision*, 152–153.

ROSS, SAM (1912–)

Sidewalks Are Free (1950)
Gelfant, Blanche Housman. *American City Novel*, 241–243.

ROSS, SINCLAIR (1908–)

As For Me and My House (1941)
Atwood, Margaret. *Survival*, 185–186.
Chambers, Robert D. *Sinclair Ross & Ernest Buckler*, 25–39.
Cude, Wilfred. "Beyond Mrs. Bentley: A Study of *As For Me and My House*," *Journal of Canadian Studies* (February, 1973): 3–18. Rpt. in Cude, Wilfred. *Due Sense of Differences*, 31–48.
Cude, Wilfred. "Beyond Mrs. Bentley: A Study of *As For Me and My House*," *Journal of Canadian Studies* (February, 1973): 3–18. Rpt. in Gerson, Carole, comp. *Modern Canadian Fiction*, 33–46.
Cude, Wilfred. *Due Sense of Differences*, 209–213.
Cude, Wilfred. "Turn it Upside Down: The Right Perspective on *As For Me and My House*," *English Studies in Canada* (Winter, 1979): 469–488. Rpt. in Cude, Wilfred. *Due Sense of Differences*, 50–67.
Djwa, Sandra. "False Gods and the True Covenant: Thematic Continuity Between Margaret Laurence and Sinclair Ross." *Journal of Canadian Fiction* 1.4 , 43–50. Rpt. in New, William, ed. *Margaret Laurence*, 67–69.
Djwa, Sandra. "No Other Way: Sinclair Ross's Stories and Novels." *CanL* 47 (1971): 54–62.
Djwa, Sandra. "No Other Way: Sinclair Ross's Stories and Novels," in Stephens, Donald G., ed. *Writers of the Prairies*, 190, 193, 194–203.
Djwa, Sandra. "No Other Way: Sinclair Ross's Stories and Novels," in Stephens, Donald G., ed. *Writers of the Prairies*. Vancouver: University of British Columbia Press, 1973. 189–205. Rpt. in Gerson, Carole, comp. *Modern Canadian Fiction*, 8–9, 11–16.
Djwa, Sandra. "No Other Way: Sinclair Ross's Stories and Novels," in Woodcock, George, ed. *Canadian Novel*, 128, 131–142.
Dooley, D. J. *Moral Vision*, 37–47.
Endres, Robin. "Marxist Literary Criticism and English Canadian Literature," in Cappon, Paul, ed. *In Our Own House*, 123–126.
Harrison, Dick. *Unnamed Country*, 126, 128–130, 134–136, 148–153.
Jackel, Susan. "House on the Prairies." *CanL* 42 (1969): 51–52.
Jackel, Susan. "House on the Prairies," in Stephens, Donald G., ed. *Writers of the Prairies*, 170–171.
Jones, D. G. *Butterfly on Rock*, 38–43.
MacDonald, Bruce. "*As For Me and My House*." *Literary Criterion* 13.1 (1978). Rpt. in Gerson, Carole, comp. *Modern Canadian Fiction*, 51–58.
McMullen, Lorraine. *Sinclair Ross*, 56–87.
Mathews, Robin D. "Wacousta Factor," in Bessai, Diane and David Jackel, eds. *Figures in a Ground*, 315.
Moss, John. *Patterns of Isolation*, 149–165.
New, W. H. *Articulating West*, 60–67.
New, W. H. "Sinclair Ross's Ambivalent World," in Stephens, Donald G., ed. *Writers of the Prairies*, 183–188.

New, W. H. "Sinclair Ross's Ambivalent World," in Stephens, Donald G., ed. *Writers of the Prairies*. Vancouver: University of British Columbia Press, 1973. 183–188. Rpt. in Gerson, Carole, comp. *Modern Canadian Fiction*, 47–50.

New , William H. "Sinclair Ross's Ambivalent World." *CanL* 40 (1969): 26–32.

Stephens, Donald G. "Wind, Sun and Dust," in Stephens, Donald G., ed. *Writers of the Prairies*, 175–182.

Stephens, Donald G. "Wind, Sun and Dust," in Stephens, Donald G., ed. *Writers of the Prairies*. Vancouver: University of British Columbia Press, 1973. 175–182. Rpt. in Gerson, Carole, comp. *Modern Canadian Fiction*, 28–32.

Stouck, David. "Mirror and the Lamp in Sinclair Ross's *As for Me and My House*." *Mosaic* 7.2 (1974): 141–150.

Sutherland, Ronald. *New Hero*, 8.

Sutherland, Ronald. *Second Image*, 74–75.

Tallman, Warren. "Wolf in the Snow." *Canadian Literature* 5 (Summer 1960): 7–20 & *Canadian Literature* 6 (Autumn 1960): 41–48. Rpt. in Cook, Gregory M., ed. *Ernest Buckler*, 55–56, 62–66, 72–74.

Tallman, Warren. "Wolf in the Snow." *Canadian Literature* 5 (Summer 1960): 7–20 & *Canadian Literature* 6 (Autumn 1960): 41–48. Rpt. in Gerson, Carole, comp. *Modern Canadian Fiction*, 101, 102–103, 106.

Sawbones Memorial (1974)

Bowen, Gail. "Fiction of Sinclair Ross." *CanL* 80 (1979): 37–48.

McMullen, Lorraine. *Sinclair Ross*, 118–133.

Sutherland, Ronald. *New Hero*, 8–10, 13.

Well (1958)

Chambers, Robert D. *Sinclair Ross & Ernest Buckler*, 40–46.

Djwa, Sandra. "No Other Way: Sinclair Ross's Stories and Novels," in Stephens, Donald G., ed. *Writers of the Prairies*, 190–191.

Djwa, Sandra. "No Other Way: Sinclair Ross's Stories and Novels," in Stephens, Donald G., ed. *Writers of the Prairies*. Vancouver: University of British Columbia Press, 1973. 189–205. Rpt. in Gerson, Carole, comp. *Modern Canadian Fiction*, 15–16.

Djwa, Sandra. "No Other Way: Sinclair Ross's Stories and Novels," in Woodcock, George, ed. *Canadian Novel*, 128–129.

McMullen, Lorraine. *Sinclair Ross*, 88–100.

Whir of Gold (1970)

Chambers, Robert D. *Sinclair Ross & Ernest Buckler*, 47–52.

McMullen, Lorraine. *Sinclair Ross*, 101–117.

ROSSNER, JUDITH (1935–)

Looking for Mr. Goodbar (1975)

Hendin, Josephine. *Vulnerable People*, 184–186.

Regan, Nancy. "Home of One's Own: Women's Bodies in Recent Women's Fiction." *JPC* 11 (1978): 779–780.

ROTH, HENRY (1906–)

Call It Sleep (1934)

Allen, Walter. *Urgent West*, 101–102.

Donald, Miles. *American Novel in the Twentieth Century*, 161–162.

Freedman, William. "Henry Roth and the Redemptive Imagination," in French, Warren, ed. *Thirties*, 107–114.
Guttmann, Allen. *Jewish Writer in America*, 49–55.
Lyons, Bonnie. *Henry Roth*, 39–133.
Lyons, Bonnie. "Symbolic Structure of Henry Roth's *Call It Sleep.*" *ConL* 13 (1972): 186–203.
Pearce, Richard. "*Pylon, Awake and Sing!* and the Apocalyptic Imagination of the 30's." *Criticism* 13 (1971): 134.
Samet, Tom. "Henry Roth's Bull Story: Guilt and Betrayal in *Call It Sleep.*" *SNNTS* 7 (1976): 569–583.
Sheres, Ita. "Exile and Redemption in Henry Roth's *Call It Sleep.*" *MarkR* 6 (1977): 72–77.
Walden, Daniel. "Henry Roth's *Call It Sleep:* Ethnicity, 'The Sign,' and the Power." *MFS* 25 (1979): 268–272.
Wirth-Nesher, Hana. "Modern Jewish Novel and the City: Franz Kafka, Henry Roth, and Amos Oz." *MFS* 24 (1978): 94–99.

ROTH, PHILIP (1933–)

Great American Novel (1973)

McDaniel, John N. *Fiction of Philip Roth*, 161–168.
Pinsker, Sanford. *Comedy that "Hoits"*, 85–101.
Rodgers, Bernard F., Jr. *Philip Roth*, 109–122.
Siegel, Ben. "Myths of Summer: Philip Roth's *The Great American Novel.*" *ConL* 17 (1976): 171–190.

Letting Go (1962)

Allen, Mary. *Necessary Blankness*, 73, 76–87.
Guttmann, Allen. *Jewish Writer in America*, 67–73.
Hyman, Stanley Edgar. "Novelist of Great Promise." *New Leader* (11 June 1962). Rpt. in Kostelanetz, Richard, ed. *On Contemporary Literature*, 534–536.
McDaniel, John N. *Fiction of Philip Roth*, 76–89, 116–120.
Michel, Pierre. "What Price Misanthropy? Philip Roth's Fiction." *ES* 58 (1977): 234, 238.
Pinsker, Sanford. *Comedy that "Hoits"*, 28–42.
Rodgers, Bernard F., Jr. *Philip Roth*, 47–59.

My Life as a Man (1974)

McDaniel, John N. *Fiction of Philip Roth*, 177–198.
Michel, Pierre. "What Price Misanthropy? Philip Roth's Fiction." *ES* 58 (1977): 237–239.
Pinsker, Sanford. *Comedy that "Hoits"*, 101–121.
Rodgers, Bernard F., Jr. *Philip Roth*, 141–156.

Our Gang (1971)

McDaniel, John N. *Fiction of Philip Roth*, 157–161.
Pinsker, Sanford. *Comedy that "Hoits"*, 71–84.
Rodgers, Bernard F., Jr. *Philip Roth*, 97–108.

Portnoy's Complaint (1969)

Adair, William. "*Portnoy's Complaint:* A Camp Version of *Notes from Underground.*" *NConL* 7.3 (1977): 9–10.

Allen, Mary. *Necessary Blankness*, 70–75.
Friedman, Melvin J. "Jewish Mothers and Sons: The Expense of *Chutzpah*," in Malin, Irving, ed. *Contemporary American-Jewish Literature*, 167–172.
Gindin, James. *Harvest of a Quiet Eye*, 357–358.
Gordon, Lois G. *"Portnoy's Complaint:* Coming of Age in Jersey City." *L&P* 19.3–4 (1969): 57–60.
Grebstein, Sheldon. "Comic Anatomy of *Portnoy's Complaint*," in Cohen, Sara Blacher, ed. *Comic Relief*, 152–171.
Guttmann, Allen. *Jewish Writer in America*, 74–76.
McDaniel, John N. *Fiction of Philip Roth*, 132–148.
Michel, Pierre. "What Price Misanthropy? Philip Roth's Fiction." *ES* 58 (1977): 234–236, 238.
Pinsker, Sanford. *Between Two Worlds*, 44–56.
Pinsker, Sanford. *Comedy that "Hoits"*, 55–71.
Rodgers, Bernard F., Jr. *Philip Roth*, 80–96.
Tanner, Tony. *City of Words*, 310–316.
Waniek, Marilyn Nelson. "Schizoid Implied Authors of Two Jewish-American Novels." *MELUS* 7.1 (1980): 30–37.

Professor of Desire (1977)

Rodgers, Bernard F., Jr. *Philip Roth*, 157–169.

When She Was Good (1967)

Allen, Mary. *Necessary Blankness*, 87–95.
Gindin, James. *Harvest of a Quiet Eye*, 356–357.
McDaniel, John N. *Fiction of Philip Roth*, 120–132.
Pinsker, Sanford. *Comedy that "Hoits"*, 42–55.
Raban, Jonathan. "New Philip Roth." *Novel* 2 (1969): 153–163.
Rodgers, Bernard F., Jr. *Philip Roth*, 60–74.

ROWSON, SUSANNA (1762(?)–1824)

Charlotte Temple (1791)

McGrath, Kathleen Conway. "Popular Literature as Social Reinforcement: The Case of *Charlotte Temple*," in Cornillon, Susan Koppelman, ed. *Images of Women in Fiction*, 21–27.
Petter, Henri. *Early American Novel*, 36–38.
Spengemann, William C. *Adventurous Muse*, 88–93.
Stein, Roger B. "Pulled Out of the Bay: American Fiction in the Eighteenth Century." *SAF* 2 (1974): 17–19, 30–31.

Fille de chambre (1794)

Petter, Henri. *Early American Novel*, 30–34.

Reuben and Rachel (1798)

Barnett, Louise K. *Ignoble Savage*, 58–59.

ROY, GABRIELLE (1909–1983)

Alexandre Chenevert (1954)

Bessette, Gérard. *Trois romanciers québécois*, 203–237.
Grosskurth, Phylllis. *Gabrielle Roy*, 26–37.

Grosskurth, Phyllis. "Gabrielle Roy," in Grosskurth, Phyllis. *Gabrielle Roy*. Toronto: Forum House, 1972. Rpt. in Gerson, Carole, comp. *Modern Canadian Fiction*, 85–86.

Grosskurth, Phyllis. "Gabrielle Roy and the Silken Noose." *CanL* 42 (1969): 9–10.

Grosskurth, Phyllis. "Gabrielle Roy and the Silken Noose." *Canadian Literature* 42 (Autumn 1969). Rpt. in Gerson, Carole, comp. *Modern Canadian Fiction*, 95.

Jones, D. G. *Butterfly on Rock*, 143–145.

Lewis, Paula Gilbert. "Incessant Call of the Open Road: Gabrielle Roy's Incorrigible Nomads." *FR* 53 (1980): 816–825.

McPherson, Hugo. "Garden and the Cage: The Acheivement of Gabrielle Roy." *Canadian Literature* 1, Spring 1959. Rpt. in Gerson, Carole, comp. *Modern Canadian Fiction*, 90–92.

Mitcham, Allison. "Northern Innocent in the Fiction of Gabrielle Roy." *HAR* 24 (1973): 26.

Murphy, John J. "Alexandre Chenevert: Gabrielle Roy's Crucified Canadian." *Queen's Quarterly* 2 (1965). Rpt. in Gerson, Carole, comp. *Modern Canadian Fiction*, 76–82.

Primeau, Marguerite A. "Gabrielle Roy et la prairie Canadienne," in Stephens, Donald G., ed. *Writers of the Prairies*, 126–127.

Randall, Julia. "Gabrielle Roy: Granddaughter of Quebec." *HC* 14.5 (1977): 3–6.

Ricard, François. *Gabrielle Roy*, 75–87.

Saint-Pierre, Annette. *Gabrielle Roy: sous le signe du rêve*, 53–69.

Shek, Ben-Zion. *Social Realism*, 173–203.

Shek, Ben-Zion. "Social Realism in the French-Canadian Novel: *Alexandre Chenevert*," in Shek, Ben-Zion. *Social Realism in the French Canadian Novel*. Montreal: Harvest House Limited Publishers, 1977. Rpt. in Gerson, Carole, comp. *Modern Canadian Fiction*, 83–84.

Urbas, Jeannette. *From Thirty Acres to Modern Times*, 49–52.

Bonheur d'occasion (1945)

Atwood, Margaret. *Survival*, 219–220.

Boutelle, Ann. "Dorian Gray Phenomenon in Canadian Literature." *DR* 57 (1977): 274.

Grosskurth, Phylllis. *Gabrielle Roy*, 9–21.

Grosskurth, Phyllis. "Gabrielle Roy and the Silken Noose." *CanL* 42 (1969): 7–9.

Grosskurth, Phyllis. "Gabrielle Roy and the Silken Noose." *Canadian Literature* 42 (Autumn 1969). Rpt. in Gerson, Carole, comp. *Modern Canadian Fiction*, 94–95.

Laflèche, Guy. "Les Bonheurs d'occasion du roman québécois." *V&I* 3 (1977): 96–114.

Lewis, Paula Gilbert. "Incessant Call of the Open Road: Gabrielle Roy's Incorrigible Nomads." *FR* 53 (1980): 816–825.

McPherson, Hugo. "Garden and the Cage: The Acheivement of Gabrielle Roy." *Canadian Literature* 1, Spring 1959. Rpt. in Gerson, Carole, comp. *Modern Canadian Fiction*, 89–90.

Mitcham, Allison. "Gabrielle Roy's Children." *AntR* 36 (1979): 95.

Primeau, Marguerite A. "Gabrielle Roy et la prairie Canadienne," in Stephens, Donald G., ed. *Writers of the Prairies*, 117–122, 125–126.

Ricard, François. *Gabrielle Roy*, 52–64, 74–75, 86–87.

Saint-Pierre, Annette. *Gabrielle Roy: sous le signe du rêve*, 13–37.

Shek, Ben-Zion. *Social Realism*, 65–111.

Socken, Paul. "Use of Language in *Bonheur d'occasion:* A Case in Point." *ECW* 11 (1978): 66–71.

Sutherland, Ronald. *Second Image*, 11–16.

Urbas, Jeannette. *From Thirty Acres to Modern Times*, 45–49.

Cashier see *Alexandre Chenevert*

Ces enfants de ma vie (1977)

Poulin, Gabrielle. *Romans du pays*, 351–356.

Children of My Heart see *Ces enfants de ma vie*

Garden in the Wind see *Un jardin au bout du monde*

Hidden Mountain see *La montagne secrète*

La montagne secrète (1961)

Bessette, Gérard. *Trois romanciers québécois*, 185–199.

Grenier-Francoeur, Marie. "Étude de la structure anaphorique dans *la montagne secrète* de Gabrielle Roy." *V&I* 1 (1976): 387–404.

Grosskurth, Phylllis. *Gabrielle Roy*, 44–50.

Grosskurth, Phyllis. "Gabrielle Roy and the Silken Noose." *CanL* 42 (1969): 11–12.

Grosskurth, Phyllis. "Gabrielle Roy and the Silken Noose." *Canadian Literature* 42, Autumn 1969. Rpt. in Gerson, Carole, comp. *Modern Canadian Fiction*, 96.

Jones, D. G. *Butterfly on Rock*, 25–26, 141, 145–147.

Lewis, Paula Gilbert. "Incessant Call of the Open Road: Gabrielle Roy's Incorrigible Nomads." *FR* 53 (1980): 816–825.

Mitcham, Allison. "Northern Innocent in the Fiction of Gabrielle Roy." *HAR* 24 (1973): 26–27.

Primeau, Marguerite A. "Gabrielle Roy et la prairie Canadienne," in Stephens, Donald G., ed. *Writers of the Prairies*, 127–128.

Randall, Julia. "Gabrielle Roy: Granddaughter of Quebec." *HC* 14.5 (1977): 6–9.

Ricard, François. *Gabrielle Roy*, 100–112.

Saint-Pierre, Annette. *Gabrielle Roy: sous le signe du rêve*, 71–87.

Urbas, Jeannette. *From Thirty Acres to Modern Times*, 56–57.

La petite poule d'eau (1950)

Davidson, Arnold E. "Gabrielle Roy's *Where Nests the Water Hen:* An Island beyond the Waste Land." *NDQ* 47.4 (1979): 4–10.

Grosskurth, Phylllis. *Gabrielle Roy*, 21–26.

Grosskurth, Phyllis. "Gabrielle Roy and the Silken Noose." *CanL* 42 (1969): 10–11.

Grosskurth, Phyllis. "Gabrielle Roy and the Silken Noose." *Canadian Literature* 42, Autumn 1969. Rpt. in Gerson, Carole, comp. *Modern Canadian Fiction*, 95–96.

Lewis, Paula Gilbert. "Incessant Call of the Open Road: Gabrielle Roy's Incorrigible Nomads." *FR* 53 (1980): 816–825.

Mitcham, Allison. "Gabrielle Roy's Children." *AntR* 36 (1979): 95–96.

Mitcham, Allison. "Northern Innocent in the Fiction of Gabrielle Roy." *HAR* 24 (1973): 26.

Primeau, Marguerite A. "Gabrielle Roy et la prairie Canadienne," in Stephens, Donald G., ed. *Writers of the Prairies*, 117–118, 122–125.

Ricard, François. *Gabrielle Roy*, 64–75, 86–87.

Saint-Pierre, Annette. *Gabrielle Roy: sous le signe du rêve*, 39–50.

Urbas, Jeannette. *From Thirty Acres to Modern Times*, 52–53.

La rivière sans repos (1970)

Mitcham, Allison. "Gabrielle Roy's Children." *AntR* 36 (1979): 96.

Mitcham, Allison. "Northern Innocent in the Fiction of Gabrielle Roy." *HAR* 24 (1973): 25–26, 27–29.

Urbas, Jeannette. *From Thirty Acres to Modern Times*, 57–59.

La route d'Altamont (1966)

Belleau, André. *Le romancier fictif*, 39–55.

Bessette, Gérard. *Trois romanciers québécois*, 185–199.

Blodgett, E. D. "Gardens at the World's End or Gone West in French." *ECW* 17 (1980): 118–119, 121–122.

Grosskurth, Phylllis. *Gabrielle Roy*, 50–56.

Lewis, Paula Gilbert. "Themes of Memory and Death in Gabrielle Roy's *La route d'Altamont*." *MFS* 22 (1976): 457–466.

Ricard, François. *Gabrielle Roy*, 113–124.

Saint-Pierre, Annette. *Gabrielle Roy: sous le signe du rêve*, 111–129.

Urbas, Jeannette. *From Thirty Acres to Modern Times*, 54–56.

Tin Flute see *Bonheur d'occasion*

Un jardin au bout du monde (1975)

Poulin, Gabrielle. *Romans du pays*, 329–331.

Where Nests the Water Hen see *La petite poule d'eau*

Wildflower see *La rivière sans repos*

Windflower see *La rivière san repos*

RUSH, REBECCA (1779–(?))

Kelroy (1812)

Meserole, Harrison T. "Some Notes on Early American Fiction: Kelroy Was There." *SAF* 5 (1977): 5–12.

Petter, Henri. *Early American Novel*, 201–205.

RUSS, JOANNA (1937–)

Female Man (1975)

Annas, Pamela J. "New Worlds, New Words: Androgyny in Feminist Science Fiction." *SFS* 5 (1978): 148–150.

RUSSELL, ROGER see NASNAGA

RYGA, GEORGE (1932–1987)

Ballad of a Stone-Picker (1966)

Ricou, Laurence R. "Empty as Nightmare: Man and Landscape in Recent Canadian Prairie Fiction." *Mosaic* 6.2 (1973): 150–151.

Hungry Hills (1963)

Ricou, Laurence R. "Empty as Nightmare: Man and Landscape in Recent Canadian Prairie Fiction." *Mosaic* 6.2 (1973): 149–150.

SACK, JOHN (1930–)

M (1967)

Jones, Peter G. *War and the Novelist*, 194–197, 197–198.

SALINGER, J. D. (1919–)

Catcher in the Rye (1951)

Anderson, David. *Tragic Protest*, 50.

Bellman, Samuel I. "Peripheral (?) Characters in *Huckleberry Finn* and *Catcher in the Rye*." *MTJ* 19.1 (1977–78): 4–6.

Bryant, Jerry H. *Open Decision*, 236–240.

Cohn, Dorrit. *Transparent Minds*, 186–187.

Edwards, Duane. "Holden Caulfield: 'Don't Ever Tell Anybody Anything'." *ELH* 44 (1977): 554–565.

French, Warren. "Age of Salinger," in French, Warren, ed. *Fifties*, 25–30.

French, Warren. *J. D. Salinger*, 107–129.

Galloway, David D. *Absurd Hero in American Fiction*, 140–145.

Gross, Theodore L. "J. D. Salinger: Suicide and Survival in the Modern World." *SAQ* 68 (1969): 455.

Hendin, Josephine. *Vulnerable People*, 113–114.

Luedtke, Luther S. "J.D. Salinger and Robert Burns: *The Catcher in the Rye*." *MFS* 16 (1970): 198–201.

Lundquist, James. *J. D. Salinger*, 37–68.

McCarthy, Mary. *The Writing on the Wall*, 35–36.

McSweeney, Kerry. "Salinger Revisited." *CritQ* 20.1 (1978): 66–68.

May, Keith M. *Out of the Maelstrom*, 94.

Ousby, Ian. *Reader's Guide to Fifty American Novels*, 326–329.

Panova, Vera. "On J. D. Salinger's Novel," in Proffer, Carl R., ed. and trans. *Soviet Criticism of American Literature in the Sixties*, 4–10.

Roper, Pamela E. "Holden's Hat." *NConL* 7.3 (1977): 8–9.

Rose, Alan H. "Sin and the City: The Uses of Disorder in the Urban Novel." *CentR* 16 (1972): 217–220.

Rosen, Gerald. "Retrospective Look at *The Catcher in the Rye*." *AQ* 29 (1977): 547–562.

Rosen, Gerald. "A Retrospective Look at *The Catcher in the Rye*." *American Quarterly* 29 (Winter 1977): 547–562. Rpt. in Lenz, Millicent and Ramona M. Mahood, comps. *Young Adult Literature*, 86–100.

Rupp, Richard H. *Celebration in Postwar American Fiction*, 114–118.

Franny and Zooey (1961)

Gross, Theodore L. "J. D. Salinger: Suicide and Survival in the Modern World." *SAQ* 68 (1969):456–462.

Lundquist, James. *J. D. Salinger*, 119–136.

McCarthy, Mary. *The Writing on the Wall*, 36–41.

May, Keith M. *Out of the Maelstrom*, 94–95.

Panichas, George A. *Reverent Discipline*, 292–305.
Schulz, Max F. *Radical Sophistication*, 198–202.

SANCHEZ, THOMAS (1944–)

Rabbit Boss (1973)
Sanchez, Thomas. "Visionary Imagination." *MELUS* 3.2 (1976): 2–5.

SANDA (pseudonym of William H. Anderson and Walter Stowers)

Appointed (1894)
Elder, Arlene A. *"Hindered Hand"*, 4–5, 14, 22.

SANDOZ, MARI (1896–1966)

Capital City (1939)
Greenwell, Scott L. "Fascists in Fiction: Two Early Novels of Mari Sandoz." *WAL* 12 (1977): 141–143.

Slogum House (1937)
Greenwell, Scott L. "Fascists in Fiction: Two Early Novels of Mari Sandoz." *WAL* 12 (1977): 136–137, 139.

SARTON, MAY (1912–1995)

Birth of a Grandfather (1957)
Bakerman, Jane S. " 'Kinds of Love': Love and Friendship in Novels of May Sarton." *Crit* 20.2 (1978): 84–85, 90.

Kinds of Love (1970)
Bakerman, Jane S. " 'Kinds of Love': Love and Friendship in Novels of May Sarton." *Crit* 20.2 (1978): 85, 86–87, 90.

Mrs. Stevens Hears the Mermaids Singing (1965)
Anderson, Dawn Holt. "May Sarton's Women," in Cornillon, Susan Koppelman, ed. *Images of Women in Fiction*, 244–246.
Bakerman, Jane S. " 'Kinds of Love': Love and Friendship in Novels of May Sarton." *Crit* 20.2 (1978): 85, 87, 88–89.

Small Room (1961)
Anderson, Dawn Holt. "May Sarton's Women," in Cornillon, Susan Koppelman, ed. *Images of Women in Fiction*, 244, 247–250.
Bakerman, Jane S. " 'Kinds of Love': Love and Friendship in Novels of May Sarton." *Crit* 20.2 (1978): 85, 87.

SAVARD, FÉLIX-ANTOINE (1896–1982)

Boss of the River see *Menaud*

Master of the River see *Menaud*

Menaud (1937)

Cotnam, Jacques. "Cultural Nationalism and its Literary Expression in French-Canadian Fiction." Trans. Noël Corbett. In Lewald, H. Ernest, ed. *Cry of Home*, 284–286.

Hathorn, Ramon. "Soldats, patrons et femmes 'fatales': Figures de l'Anglais' dans le roman québécois des XIXe et XXe siècles." *V&I* 6 (1980): 106.

Servais-Maquoi, Mireille. *Le roman de la terre au Québec*, 71–95.

Urbas, Jeannette. *From Thirty Acres to Modern Times*, 13–16.

Weinmann, Heinz. "Menaud, fils de Perrault ou de Savard?" *V&I* 3 (1978): 396–407.

SAXON, LYLE (1891–1946)

Children of Strangers (1937)

Thomas, James W. "Lyle Saxon's Struggle with *Children of Strangers*." *SoS* 16 (1977): 27–40.

SCARBOROUGH, DOROTHY (1878–1935)

Can't Get a Red Bird (1929)

Cook, Sylvia Jenkins. *From Tobacco Road to Route 66*, 26, 27–28.

In the Land of Cotton (1923)

Cook, Sylvia Jenkins. *From Tobacco Road to Route 66*, 26–27.

Wind (1925)

Quissel, Barbara. "Dorothy Scarborough's Critique of the Frontier Experience in *The Wind*," in Lee, L. L. and Merrill Lewis, ed. *Women, Women Writers, and the West*, 173–190.

SCHAEFFER, SUSAN FROMBERG (1941–)

Anya (1974)

Alexander, Edward. *Resonance of Dust*, 133–137.

Falling (1973)

Avery, Evelyn Gross. "Tradition and Independence in Jewish Feminist Novels." *MELUS* 7.4 (1980): 53–55.

SCHINDLER, SOLOMON (1842–1915)

Young West (1894)

Segal, Howard P. "*Young West:* The Psyche of Technological Utopianism." *Extrapolation* 19 (1977): 50–58.

SCHNECK, STEPHEN (1933–)

Nightclerk (1966)
Tanner, Tony. *City of Words*, 347–348.

SCHULBERG, BUDD (1914–)

What Makes Sammy Run? (1941)
Hearn, Charles R. *American Dream in the Great Depression*, 184–189.
Wells, Walter. *Tycoons and Locusts*, 86–102.

SCHUYLER, GEORGE S. (1895–1977)

Black No More (1931)
Davis, Arthur P. *From the Dark Tower*, 105–106.
Gayle, Addison, Jr. *Way of the New World*, 105–107.
Perry, Margaret. *Silence to the Drums*, 100–102.
Singh, Amritjit. *Novels of the Harlem Renaissance*, 59–61.
Williams, Sherley Anne. *Give Birth to Brightness*, 81–83.

Slaves Today (1931)
Davis, Arthur P. *From the Dark Tower*, 106–107.
Gayle, Addison, Jr. *Way of the New World*, 104–105.
Isani, Mukhtar Ali. "Exotic and Protest in Earlier Black Literature: The Use of Alien Setting and Character." *SIBL* 5.2 (1974): 12.
Singh, Amritjit. *Novels of the Harlem Renaissance*, 113–119.

SEARS, DENNIS T. PATRICK (1925–)

Lark in the Clear Air (1974)
Moss, John. *Sex and Violence*, 39–40.

SEDGES, JOHN see BUCK, PEARL S.

SEDGWICK, CATHERINE MARIA (1789–1867)

Clarence (1830)
Baym, Nina. *Woman's Fiction*, 59–61.
Foster, Edward Halsey. *Catherine Maria Sedgwick*, 99–105.

Hope Leslie (1827)
Foster, Edward Halsey. *Catherine Maria Sedgwick*, 73–90.

Linwoods (1935)
Foster, Edward Halsey. *Catherine Maria Sedgwick*, 107–112.

Married or Single? (1857)
Baym, Nina. *Woman's Fiction*, 61–63.

New England Tale (1822)
Baym, Nina. *Woman's Fiction*, 54–56.
Foster, Edward Halsey. *Catherine Maria Sedgwick*, 45–55.

Redwood (1824)
Baym, Nina. *Woman's Fiction*, 56–58.
Foster, Edward Halsey. *Catherine Maria Sedgwick*, 56–69.

SERVICE, ROBERT W. (1874–1958)

Trail of '98 (1910)
Atherton, Stanley S. "Klondike Muse." *CanL* 47 (1971): 70–72.

SHAINBERG, LAWRENCE (1936–)

One on One (1970)
Berman, Neil. "Zen and the Art of Basketball in Lawrence Shainberg's *One on One*." *Crit* 22.1 (1980): 5–20.

SHAW, IRWIN (1913–1984)

Young Lions (1948)
Bryant, Jerry H. *Open Decision*, 140–142.
Jones, Peter G. *War and the Novelist*, 140–144.
Waldmeir, Joseph J. *American Novels of the Second World War*, 92–101, 107–108, 149–152.

SHIELDS, CAROL (1935–)

Small Ceremonies (1976)
Irvine, Lorna. "Psychological Journey: Mothers and Daughters in English-Canadian Fiction," in Davidson, Cathy N. and E. M. Broner, eds. *Lost Tradition*, 249–250.
MacDonald, Bruce F. "Quiet Manifesto: Carol Shield's *Small Ceremonies*." *IFR* 3 (1976): 147–150.

SHULMAN, ALIX KATES (1932–)

Memoirs of an Ex-Prom Queen (1972)
Hendin, Josephine. *Vulnerable People*, 176–177.
Masinton, Martha and Charles G. Masinton. "Second-class Citizenship: The Status of Women in Contemporary American Fiction," in Springer, Marlene, ed. *What Manner of Woman*, 309–310.
Morgan, Ellen. "Humanbecoming: Form & Focus in the Neo-Feminist Novel," in Cornillon, Susan Koppelman, ed. *Images of Women in Fiction*, 197–204.

SICILIANO, VINCENT (1911–)

Unless They Kill Me First (1970)
Green, Rose Basile. *Italian-American Novel*, 288–292.

SILKO, LESLIE MARMON (1948–)

Ceremony (1977)
Allen, Paula Gunn. "Psychological Landscape of *Ceremony*." *AIQ* 5 (1979): 7–12.
Allen, Paula Gunn. "Stranger in My Own Life: Alienation in American Indian Prose and Poetry." *MELUS* 7.2 (1980): 13–15.
Beidler, Peter. "Animals and Human Development in the Contemporary American Indian Novel." *WAL* 14 (1979): 143–148.
Beidler, Peter G. "Animals and Theme in *Ceremony*." *AIQ* 5 (1979): 13–18.
Bell, Robert C. "Circular Design in *Ceremony*." *AIQ* 5 (1979): 47–62.
Evers, Larry. "A Response: Going Along with the Story." *AIQ* 5 (1979): 71–75.
Jahner, Elaine. "Act of Attention: Event Structure in *Ceremony*." *AIQ* 5 (1979): 37–46.
Larson, Charles R. *American Indian Fiction*, 150–161.
Mitchell, Carol. "*Ceremony* as Ritual." *AIQ* 5 (1979): 27–35.
Sands, Kathleen M., et al. "Discussion of *Ceremony*." *AIQ* 5 (1979): 63–70.
Scarberry, Susan J. "Memory as Medicine: The Power of Recollection in *Ceremony*." *AIQ* 5 (1979): 19–26.

SILVERBERG, ROBERT (1935–)

Book of Skulls (1972)
Clareson, Thomas D. "Fictions of Robert Silverberg," in Clareson, Thomas D., ed. *Voices for the Future* (Vol. 2), 26–27.

Downward to the Earth (1970)
Clareson, Thomas D. "Fictions of Robert Silverberg," in Clareson, Thomas D., ed. *Voices for the Future* (Vol. 2), 20–23.
Hunt, Robert. "Visionary States and the Search for Transcendence in Science Fiction," in Slusser, George E., George R. Guffey and Mark Rose, eds. *Bridges to Science Fiction*, 75–76.

Dying Inside (1972)
Clareson, Thomas D. "Fictions of Robert Silverberg," in Clareson, Thomas D., ed. *Voices for the Future* (Vol. 2), 24–25.

Invaders from Earth (1957)
Clareson, Thomas D. "Fictions of Robert Silverberg," in Clareson, Thomas D., ed. *Voices for the Future* (Vol. 2), 13–14.

Man in the Maze (1969)
Clareson, Thomas D. "Fictions of Robert Silverberg," in Clareson, Thomas D., ed. *Voices for the Future* (Vol. 2), 9–12.
Dean, John. "Sick Hero Reborn: Two Versions of the Philoctetes Myth." *CLS* 17 (1980): 334–339.

Nightwings (1969)

Clareson, Thomas D. "Fictions of Robert Silverberg," in Clareson, Thomas D., ed. *Voices for the Future* (Vol. 2), 17–19.

Recalled to Life (1957)

Clareson, Thomas D. "Fictions of Robert Silverberg," in Clareson, Thomas D., ed. *Voices for the Future* (Vol. 2), 23.

Shadrach in the Furnace (1977)

Clareson, Thomas D. "Fictions of Robert Silverberg," in Clareson, Thomas D., ed. *Voices for the Future* (Vol. 2), 30–33.

Silent Invaders (1957)

Clareson, Thomas D. "Fictions of Robert Silverberg," in Clareson, Thomas D., ed. *Voices for the Future* (Vol. 2), 14.

Stochastic Man (1975)

Clareson, Thomas D. "Fictions of Robert Silverberg," in Clareson, Thomas D., ed. *Voices for the Future* (Vol. 2), 11.

Thorns (1967)

Clareson, Thomas D. "Fictions of Robert Silverberg," in Clareson, Thomas D., ed. *Voices for the Future* (Vol. 2), 8–9.

Time of Changes (1971)

Hunt, Robert. "Visionary States and the Search for Transcendence in Science Fiction," in Slusser, George E., George R. Guffey and Mark Rose, eds. *Bridges to Science Fiction*, 73–75.

Tower of Glass (1970)

Clareson, Thomas D. "Fictions of Robert Silverberg," in Clareson, Thomas D., ed. *Voices for the Future* (Vol. 2), 28–30.

World Inside (1971)

Dunn, Thomas P. and Richard D. Erlich. "Mechanical Hive: Urbmon 116 as the Villain-Hero of Silverberg's *The World Inside*." *Extrapolation* 21 (1980): 338–347.

SIMAK, CLIFFORD D. (1904–1988)

All Flesh Is Grass (1965)

Clareson, Thomas D. "Clifford D. Simak: The Inhabited Universe," in Clareson, Thomas D., ed. *Voices for the Future* (Vol. 1), 81–82

All the Traps of Earth (1960)

Clareson, Thomas D. "Clifford D. Simak: The Inhabited Universe," in Clareson, Thomas D., ed. *Voices for the Future* (Vol. 1), 80.

Choice of Gods (1972)

Clareson, Thomas D. "Clifford D. Simak: The Inhabited Universe," in Clareson, Thomas D., ed. *Voices for the Future* (Vol. 1), 83–88.

Cosmic Engineers (1950)

Clareson, Thomas D. "Clifford D. Simak: The Inhabited Universe," in Clareson, Thomas D., ed. *Voices for the Future* (Vol. 1), 67–68.

Destiny Doll (1971)

Clareson, Thomas D. "Clifford D. Simak: The Inhabited Universe," in Clareson, Thomas, ed. *Voices for the Future* (Vol. 1), 80–81

Goblin Reservation (1968)

Clareson, Thomas D. "Clifford D. Simak: The Inhabited Universe," in Clareson, Thomas, ed. *Voices for the Future* (Vol. 1), 77.

Out of Their Minds (1970)

Clareson, Thomas D. "Clifford D. Simak: The Inhabited Universe," in Clareson, Thomas, ed. *Voices for the Future* (Vol. 1), 77.

Time Is the Simplest Thing (1961)

Clareson, Thomas D. "Clifford D. Simak: The Inhabited Universe," in Clareson, Thomas, ed. *Voices for the Future* (Vol. 1), 81.

Werewolf Principle (1967)

Clareson, Thomas D. "Clifford D. Simak: The Inhabited Universe," in Clareson, Thomas, ed. *Voices for the Future* (Vol. 1), 82.

Why Call Them Back from Heaven (1967)

Clareson, Thomas D. "Clifford D. Simak: The Inhabited Universe," in Clareson, Thomas, ed. *Voices for the Future* (Vol. 1), 82.

SIMARD, JEAN (1916–)

Les sentiers de la nuit (1959)

Hathorn, Ramon. "Soldats, patrons et femmes 'fatales': Figures de l'Anglais' dans le roman québécois des XIXe et XXe siècles." *V&I* 6 (1980): 110–111.
Shek, Ben-Zion. *Social Realism*, 204–217.

Mon fils pourtant heureux (1956)

Belleau, André. *Le romancier fictif*, 96–103.
Sutherland, Ronald. *Second Image*, 149–151.

SIMMS, WILLIAM GILMORE (1806–1870)

Cassique of Kiawah (1859)

Howell, Elmo. "William Gilmore Simms and the American Indian." *SCR* 5.2 (1973): 60–62.
Wimsatt, Mary Ann. "Realism and Romance in Simms's Midcentury Fiction." *SLJ* 12.2 (1980): 41–48.

Eutaw (1856)

Vauthier, Simone. "Of Time and the South: The Fiction of William Gilmore Simms." *SLJ* 5.1 (1972): 28–31.
Wimsatt, Mary Ann. "Realism and Romance in Simms's Midcentury Fiction." *SLJ* 12.2 (1980): 40–41.
Wimsatt, Mary Ann. "Simms's Porgy, the Romance, and the Southern Revolutionary Militia." *SoHR* 13 (1979): 7–8.

Forayers (1855)

Dale, Corinne. "William Gilmore Simms's Porgy as Domestic Hero." *SLJ* 13.1 (1980): 57–58.

Kolodny, Annette. *Lay of the Land*, 117–131.

Kolodny, Annette. "Unchanging Landscape: The Pastoral Impulse in Simm's Revolutionary War Romances." *SLJ* 5.1 (1972): 48–67.

Vauthier, Simone. "Of Time and the South: The Fiction of William Gilmore Simms." *SLJ* 5.1 (1972): 28–31.

Wimsatt, Mary Ann. "Simms's Porgy, the Romance, and the Southern Revolutionary Militia." *SoHR* 13 (1979): 6.

Guy Rivers (1834)

Vauthier, Simone. "Of Time and the South: The Fiction of William Gilmore Simms." *SLJ* 5.1 (1972): 20–21.

Katharine Woodson (1850)

Kolodny, Annette. *Lay of the Land*, 117–131.

Kolodny, Annette. "Unchanging Landscape: The Pastoral Impulse in Simm's Revolutionary War Romances." *SLJ* 5.1 (1972): 48–67.

Wimsatt, Mary Ann. "Realism and Romance in Simms's Midcentury Fiction." *SLJ* 12.2 (1980): 40, 41.

Wimsatt, Mary Ann. "Simms as Novelist of Manners: *Katharine Walton*." *SLJ* 5.1 (1972): 68–88.

Wimsatt, Mary Ann. "Simms's Porgy, the Romance, and the Southern Revolutionary Militia." *SoHR* 13 (1979): 6.

Mellichampe (1836)

Kolodny, Annette. *Lay of the Land*, 117–131.

Kolodny, Annette. "Unchanging Landscape: The Pastoral Impulse in Simm's Revolutionary War Romances." *SLJ* 5.1 (1972): 48–67.

Partisan (1835)

Dale, Corinne. "William Gilmore Simms's Porgy as Domestic Hero." *SLJ* 13.1 (1980): 56–57.

Kolodny, Annette. *Lay of the Land*, 117–131.

Kolodny, Annette. "Unchanging Landscape: The Pastoral Impulse in Simm's Revolutionary War Romances." *SLJ* 5.1 (1972): 48–67.

Wimsatt, Mary Ann. "Simms's Porgy, the Romance, and the Southern Revolutionary Militia." *SoHR* 13 (1979): 3–6.

Richard Hurdis (1838)

Vauthier, Simone. "Of Time and the South: The Fiction of William Gilmore Simms." *SLJ* 5.1 (1972): 21–25.

Scout (1854)

Kolodny, Annette. *Lay of the Land*, 117–131.

Kolodny, Annette. "Unchanging Landscape: The Pastoral Impulse in Simm's Revolutionary War Romances." *SLJ* 5.1 (1972): 48–67.

Woodcraft (1854)

Dale, Corinne. "William Gilmore Simms's Porgy as Domestic Hero." *SLJ* 13.1 (1980): 58–61, 63–66, 67, 68–71.

Kolodny, Annette. *Lay of the Land*, 117–131.

Kolodny, Annette. "Unchanging Landscape: The Pastoral Impulse in Simm's Revolutionary War Romances." *SLJ* 5.1 (1972): 48–67.

Rose, Alan Henry. *Demonic Vision*, 43.

Vauthier, Simone. "Of Time and the South: The Fiction of William Gilmore Simms." *SLJ* 5.1 (1972): 25–28, 31–32, 36–37, 41–43.

Watson, Charles S. "Simms's Answer to *Uncle Tom's Cabin:* Criticism of the South in *Woodcraft*" *SLJ* 9.1 (1976): 78–90.

Wimsatt, Mary Ann. "Simms's Porgy, the Romance, and the Southern Revolutionary Militia." *SoHR* 13 (1979): 8–10.

Yellin, Jean Fagan. *Intricate Knot*, 71–77.

Yemassee (1835)

Howell, Elmo. "William Gilmore Simms and the American Indian." *SCR* 5.2 (1973): 59–60.

Hubert, Thomas. "Simms's Use of Milton and Wordsworth in *The Yemassee:* An Aspect of Symbolism in the Novel." *SCR* 6.1 (1973): 58–65.

Martin, Terence. "Surviving on the Frontier: The Doubled Consciousness of Natty Bumppo." *SAQ* 75 (1975): 456–457.

Rose, Alan Henry. *Demonic Vision*, 43–47.

Watson, Charles S. "New Approach to Simms: Imagery and Meaning in *The Yemassee*." *MissQ* 26 (1973): 155–163.

Yellin, Jean Fagan. *Intricate Knot*, 64–67.

SIMON, ROGER L. (1943–)

Big Fix (1973)

Geherin, David. *Sons of Sam Spade*, 86–101.

Peking Duck (1979)

Geherin, David. *Sons of Sam Spade*, 115–127.

Wild Turkey (1975)

Geherin, David. *Sons of Sam Spade*, 101–115.

SIMPSON, LEO (1934–)

Arkwright (1971)

Moss, John. *Sex and Violence*, 282–287.

Peacock Papers (1973)

Moss, John. *Sex and Violence*, 275, 278–282.

SINCLAIR, UPTON (1878–1968)

Boston (1928)

Bloodworth, William A., Jr. *Upton Sinclair*, 112–123.

Yoder, Jon A. *Upton Sinclair*, 78–85.

Jimmie Higgins (1919)

Bloodworth, William A., Jr. *Upton Sinclair*, 95–97.

Yoder, Jon A. *Upton Sinclair*, 61–63.

Jungle (1906)

Bloodworth, William A., Jr. *Upton Sinclair*, 49–64.
Downs, Robert. *Books That Changed America*. New York: Macmillan, 1970. 144–145, 147–148, 150. Rpt. in Blinderman, Abraham, ed. *Critics on Upton Sinclair*, 120–122.
Rideout, Walter. *Radical Novel in the United States*. Cambridge: Harvard University Press, 1956. 33–36. Rpt. in Blinderman, Abraham, ed. *Critics on Upton Sinclair*, 113–115.
Yoder, Jon A. *Upton Sinclair*, 30–48.

King Coal (1917)

Bloodworth, William A., Jr. *Upton Sinclair*, 85–91.
Yoder, Jon A. *Upton Sinclair*, 56–60.

Love's Pilgrimage (1911)

Bloodworth, William A., Jr. *Upton Sinclair*, 72–74.

Oil! (1927)

Bloodworth, William A., Jr. *Upton Sinclair*, 104–111.
Yoder, Jon A. *Upton Sinclair*, 70–78.

World's End (1940)

Bloodworth, William A., Jr. *Upton Sinclair*, 140–143.
Yoder, Jon A. *Upton Sinclair*, 97–100.

SINGER, ISAAC BASHEVIS (1904–1991)

Enemies (1972)

Alexander, Edward. *Isaac Bashevis Singer*, 99–112.
Alexander, Edward. *Resonance of Dust*, 153–154, 158.
Siegel, Ben. "Jew as Underground/Confidence Man: I.B. Singer's *Enemies, A Love Story*." *SNNTS* 10 (1978): 397–410.

Estate (1969)

Alexander, Edward. *Isaac Bashevis Singer*, 83–98.
Alexander, Edward. *Resonance of Dust*, 155.
Malin, Irving. *Isaac Bashevis Singer*, 31–39.

Family Moskat (1950)

Alexander, Edward. *Isaac Bashevis Singer*, 39–59.
Alexander, Edward. *Resonance of Dust*, 149–150, 159–166.
Chametzky, Jules. "History in I. B. Singer's Novels," in Malin, Irving, ed. *Critical Views of Isaac Bashevis Singer*, 169, 170, 174–176.
Fixler, Michael. "Redeemers: Themes in the Fiction of Isaac Bashevis Singer," in Malin, Irving, ed. *Critical Views of Isaac Bashevis Singer*, 77–78, 80–81.
Malin, Irving. *Isaac Bashevis Singer*, 12–21.
Novak, Maximillian E. "Moral Grotesque and Decorative Grotesque in Singer's Fiction," in Allentuck, Marcia, ed. *Achievement of Isaac Bashevis Singer*, 55.
Schulz, Max F. "Family Chronicle as Paradigm of History: *The Brothers Ashkenazi* and *Family Moskat*," in Allentuck, Marcia, ed. *Achievement of Isaac Bashevis Singer*, 81–91.

Schulz, Max F. "Isaac Bashevis Singer, Radical Sophistication, and the Jewish Novel," in Malin, Irving, ed. *Critical Views of Isaac Bashevis Singer*, 138–139.

Siegel, Ben. *Isaac Bashevis Singer*, 11–14.

Magician of Lublin (1960)

Alexander, Edward. *Isaac Bashevis Singer*, 60–70.

Bezanker, Abraham. "I.B. Singer's Crises of Identity." *Crit* 14.2 (1972): 80–81.

Chametzky, Jules. "History in I. B. Singer's Novels," in Malin, Irving, ed. *Critical Views of Isaac Bashevis Singer*, 172–173.

Fixler, Michael. "Redeemers: Themes in the Fiction of Isaac Bashevis Singer," in Malin, Irving, ed. *Critical Views of Isaac Bashevis Singer*, 77–78, 81–82.

Friedman, Melvin J. "Isaac Bashevis Singer: The Appeal of Numbers," in Malin, Irving, ed. *Critical Views of Isaac Bashevis Singer*, 185–188.

Howe, Irving. "Demonic Fiction of a Yiddish 'Modernist." *Commentary* (October 1960). Rpt. in Kostelanetz, Richard, ed. *On Contemporary Literature*, 579–585.

Malin, Irving. *Isaac Bashevis Singer*, 51–59.

Malkoff, Karl. "Demonology and Dualism: The Supernatural in Isaac Singer and Muriel Spark," in Malin, Irving, ed. *Critical Views of Isaac Bashevis Singer*, 152.

Novak, Maximillian E. "Moral Grotesque and Decorative Grotesque in Singer's Fiction," in Allentuck, Marcia, ed. *Achievement of Isaac Bashevis Singer*, 52–55.

Pinsker, Sanford. "Fictive Worlds of Isaac Bashevis Singer." *Crit* 11.2 (1969): 34–38.

Pondrom, Cyrena N. "Conjuring Reality: I. B. Singer's *The Magician of Lublin*," in Allentuck, Marcia, ed. *Achievement of Isaac Bashevis Singer*, 93–111.

Schulz, Max F. "Isaac Bashevis Singer, Radical Sophistication, and the Jewish Novel," in Malin, Irving, ed. *Critical Views of Isaac Bashevis Singer*, 137–138, 141.

Siegel, Ben. *Isaac Bashevis Singer*, 21–25.

Wolkenfeld, J. S. "Isaac Bashevis Singer: The Faith of His Devils and Magicians," in Malin, Irving, ed. *Critical Views of Isaac Bashevis Singer*, 94–98.

Manor (1967)

Alexander, Edward. *Isaac Bashevis Singer*, 83–98.

Alexander, Edward. *Resonance of Dust*, 154–155.

Chametzky, Jules. "History in I. B. Singer's Novels," in Malin, Irving, ed. *Critical Views of Isaac Bashevis Singer*, 169–170, 174–176.

Ellmann, Mary. "Piety of Things in *The Manor*," in Allentuck, Marcia, ed. *Achievement of Isaac Bashevis Singer*, 124–144.

Malin, Irving. *Isaac Bashevis Singer*, 21–31.

Novak, Maximillian E. "Moral Grotesque and Decorative Grotesque in Singer's Fiction," in Allentuck, Marcia, ed. *Achievement of Isaac Bashevis Singer*, 55–56.

Siegel, Ben. *Isaac Bashevis Singer*, 36–39.

Satan in Goray (1955)

Alexander, Edward. *Isaac Bashevis Singer*, 22–38.

Alexander, Edward. *Resonance of Dust*, 156.

Bezanker, Abraham. "I.B. Singer's Crises of Identity." *Crit* 14.2 (1972): 78–79.

Chametzky, Jules. "History in I. B. Singer's Novels," in Malin, Irving, ed. *Critical Views of Isaac Bashevis Singer*, 170–171.

Fixler, Michael. "Redeemers: Themes in the Fiction of Isaac Bashevis Singer," in Malin, Irving, ed. *Critical Views of Isaac Bashevis Singer*, 77–78.

Friedman, Melvin J. "Isaac Bashevis Singer: The Appeal of Numbers," in Malin, Irving, ed. *Critical Views of Isaac Bashevis Singer*, 188–190.

Gittleman, Edwin. "Singer's Apocalyptic Town: *Satan in Goray*," in Allentuck, Marcia, ed. *Achievement of Isaac Bashevis Singer*, 64–76.

Malin, Irving. *Isaac Bashevis Singer*, 43–51.

Malkoff, Karl. "Demonology and Dualism: The Supernatural in Isaac Singer and Muriel Spark," in Malin, Irving, ed. *Critical Views of Isaac Bashevis Singer*, 152, 154–157.

Novak, Maximillian E. "Moral Grotesque and Decorative Grotesque in Singer's Fiction," in Allentuck, Marcia, ed. *Achievement of Isaac Bashevis Singer*, 58–62.

Siegel, Ben. *Isaac Bashevis Singer*, 14–16.

Wolkenfeld, J. S. "Isaac Bashevis Singer: The Faith of His Devils and Magicians," in Malin, Irving, ed. *Critical Views of Isaac Bashevis Singer*, 88–94.

Shosha (1978)

Alexander, Edward. *Isaac Bashevis Singer*, 113–123.

Slave (1962)

Alexander, Edward. *Isaac Bashevis Singer*, 71–82.

Alexander, Edward. *Resonance of Dust*, 150–151.

Bezanker, Abraham. "I.B. Singer's Crises of Identity." *Crit* 14.2 (1972): 79–80.

Chametzky, Jules. "History in I. B. Singer's Novels," in Malin, Irving, ed. *Critical Views of Isaac Bashevis Singer*, 171–172.

Fixler, Michael. "Redeemers: Themes in the Fiction of Isaac Bashevis Singer," in Malin, Irving, ed. *Critical Views of Isaac Bashevis Singer*, 77–78, 82–85.

Friedman, Melvin J. "Isaac Bashevis Singer: The Appeal of Numbers," in Malin, Irving, ed. *Critical Views of Isaac Bashevis Singer*, 183–185.

Karl, Frederick R. " Jacob Reborn, Zion Regained: I. B. Singer's *The Slave*," in Allentuck, Marcia, ed. *Achievement of Isaac Bashevis Singer*, 112–123.

Malin, Irving. *Isaac Bashevis Singer*, 59–68.

Malkoff, Karl. "Demonology and Dualism: The Supernatural in Isaac Singer and Muriel Spark," in Malin, Irving, ed. *Critical Views of Isaac Bashevis Singer*, 150, 152, 161–164.

Novak, Maximillian E. "Moral Grotesque and Decorative Grotesque in Singer's Fiction," in Allentuck, Marcia, ed. *Achievement of Isaac Bashevis Singer*, 57–58.

Pinsker, Sanford. "Fictive Worlds of Isaac Bashevis Singer." *Crit* 11.2 (1969): 38–39.

Schulz, Max F. "Isaac Bashevis Singer, Radical Sophistication, and the Jewish Novel," in Malin, Irving, ed. *Critical Views of Isaac Bashevis Singer*, 136–137, 141.

Siegel, Ben. *Isaac Bashevis Singer*, 28–30.

SIRE, GLEN

Deathmakers (1960)

Jones, Peter G. *War and the Novelist*, 133–138, 165–167.

SKINNER, B. F. (1904–1990)

Walden Two (1948)

Glicksberg, Charles I. *Modern Literary Perspectivism*, 107–111.

Meyers, Walter E. *Aliens and Linguists*, 201–203.

Thomas, W. K. *Fizz Inside*, 90–93.
Wolfe, Peter. "*Walden Two* Twenty-five Years Later: A Retrospective Look.." *SLitI*
6.2 (1973): 11–26.

SLIM, ICEBERG (1918–)

Mama Black Widow (1969)
Graham, D. B. " 'Negative Glamour': The Pimp Hero in the Fiction of Iceberg
Slim." *Obsidian* 1.2 (1975): 9–10.

Trick Baby (1967)
Graham, D. B. " 'Negative Glamour': The Pimp Hero in the Fiction of Iceberg
Slim." *Obsidian* 1.2 (1975): 9.

SMEDLEY, AGNES (1892–1950)

Daughter of Earth (1929)
Rosinsky, Natalie M. "Mothers and Daughters: Another Minority Group," in Davidson, Cathy N. and E. M. Broner, eds. *Lost Tradition*, 288–289.

SMITH, BETTY (1896–1972)

Tree Grows in Brooklyn (1942)
Gelfant, Blanche Housman. *American City Novel*, 237–240.

SMITH, LILLIAN EUGENIA (1897–1966)

Strange Fruit (1944)
Baker, Donald G. "Black Images: The Afro-American in Popular Novels, 1900–
1945." *JPC* 7 (1973): 341–342.

SMITH, MARGARET BAYARD (1778–1844)

Winter in Washington (1824)
Baym, Nina. *Woman's Fiction*, 64–65.

What Is Gentility? (1828)
Baym, Nina. *Woman's Fiction*, 65–67.

SMITH, RAY (1941–)

Lord Nelson Tavern (1971)
Moss, John. *Sex and Violence*, 149, 150–154.

SMITH, WILLIAM GARDNER (1926–1974)

Anger at Innocence (1950)
Bryant, Jerry H. "Individuality and Fraternity: The Novels of William Gardner
Smith." *SIBL* 3.2 (1972): 4–8.

Last of the Conquerors (1948)

Bryant, Jerry H. "Individuality and Fraternity: The Novels of William Gardner Smith." *SIBL* 3.2 (1972): 4–8.

South Street (1954)

Bryant, Jerry H. "Individuality and Fraternity: The Novels of William Gardner Smith." *SIBL* 3.2 (1972): 4–8.

Stone Face (1963)

Bryant, Jerry H. "Individuality and Fraternity: The Novels of William Gardner Smith." *SIBL* 3.2 (1972): 4–8.
Gayle, Addison, Jr. *Way of the New World*, 197–202.

SOLOMON, BARBARA PROBST (1928–)

Beat of Life (1960)

Guttmann, Allen. *Jewish Writer in America*, 62–63.

SONTAG, SUSAN (1933–)

Death Kit (1967)

Tanner, Tony. *City of Words*, 265–269.

SORENSEN, VIRGINIA (1912–1991)

Evening and the Morning (1949)

Lee, L. L. and Sylvia B. Lee. *Virginia Sorensen*, 29–34.
Lee, Sylvia B. "Mormon Novel: Virginia Sorensen's *The Evening and the Morning*," in Lee, L. L. and Merrill Lewis, ed. *Women, Women Writers, and the West*, 209–217.

Kingdom Come (1960)

Lee, L. L. and Sylvia B. Lee. *Virginia Sorensen*, 42–45.

Little Lower than the Angels (1942)

Lee, L. L. and Sylvia B. Lee. *Virginia Sorensen*, 14–20.

Man with the Key (1974)

Lee, L. L. and Sylvia B. Lee. *Virginia Sorensen*, 45–48.

Many Heavens (1954)

Lee, L. L. and Sylvia B. Lee. *Virginia Sorensen*, 38–42.

Neighbors (1947)

Lee, L. L. and Sylvia B. Lee. *Virginia Sorensen*, 27–29.

On This Star (1946)

Lee, L. L. and Sylvia B. Lee. *Virginia Sorensen*, 21–27.

Proper Gods (1951)

Lee, L. L. and Sylvia B. Lee. *Virginia Sorensen*, 34–38.

SOUCY, JEAN-YVES (1945–)

Creatures of the Chase see *Un dieu chasseur*

Un dieu chasseur (1976)
  Poulin, Gabrielle. *Romans du pays*, 332–339.

SOUTHERN, TERRY (1924–1995)

Magic Christian (1959)
  Scholes, Robert. *Fabulation and Metafiction*, 165–168.

SOUTHWORTH, E.D.E.N. (1819–1899)

Curse of Clifton (1853)
  Baym, Nina. *Woman's Fiction*, 122–123.
Discarded Daughter (1852)
  Baym, Nina. *Woman's Fiction*, 121–122.
Fallen Pride see *Curse of Clifton*
India (1855)
  Baym, Nina. *Woman's Fiction*, 123.
Lost Heiress (1854)
  Baym, Nina. *Woman's Fiction*, 123–124.
Mother-in-Law (1850)
  Baym, Nina. *Woman's Fiction*, 120–121.
Mountain Girl's Love see *Curse of Clifton*
Pearl of Pearl Island see *India*
Retribution (1849)
  Baym, Nina. *Woman's Fiction*, 118–120.
Shannondale (1851)
  Baym, Nina. *Woman's Fiction*, 121.

SPENCER, ELIZABETH (1921–)

Voice at the Back Door (1956)
  Pugh, David G. *"Voice at the Back Door:* Elizabeth Spencer Looks into Mississippi," in French, Warren, ed. *Fifties*, 103–110.

SPILLANE, FRANK MORRISON see SPILLANE, MICKEY

SPILLANE, MICKEY (1918–)

Bloody Sunrise (1965)
  Palmer, Jerry. *Thrillers*, 65.
By-Pass Control (1967)
  Banks, R. Jeff. "Spillane's Anti-Establishment Heroes," in Landrum, Larry N., Pat Browne and Ray B. Browne, eds. *Dimensions of Detective Fiction*, 131, 132.

Day of the Guns (1964)

Banks, R. Jeff. "Spillane's Anti-Establishment Heroes," in Landrum, Larry N., Pat Browne and Ray B. Browne, eds. *Dimensions of Detective Fiction*, 130, 131.

Death Dealers (1965)

Banks, R. Jeff. "Spillane's Anti-Establishment Heroes," in Landrum, Larry N., Pat Browne and Ray B. Browne, eds. *Dimensions of Detective Fiction*, 130–132.

Deep (1961)

Banks, R. Jeff. "Spillane's Anti-Establishment Heroes," in Landrum, Larry N., Pat Browne and Ray B. Browne, eds. *Dimensions of Detective Fiction*, 129.
Palmer, Jerry. *Thrillers*, 36–38.

I, the Jury (1947)

Banks, R. Jeff. "Anti-Professionalism in the Works of Mickey Spillane." *NConL* 3.2 (1973): 7.

Kiss Me, Deadly (1952)

Banks, R. Jeff. "Spillane's Anti-Establishment Heroes," in Landrum, Larry N., Pat Browne and Ray B. Browne, eds. *Dimensions of Detective Fiction*, 126–127.

Long Wait (1951)

Banks, R. Jeff. "Spillane's Anti-Establishment Heroes," in Landrum, Larry N., Pat Browne and Ray B. Browne, eds. *Dimensions of Detective Fiction*, 128.

My Gun Is Quick (1951)

Palmer, Jerry. *Thrillers*, 63–64.

One Lonely Night (1951)

Banks, R. Jeff. "Spillane's Anti-Establishment Heroes," in Landrum, Larry N., Pat Browne and Ray B. Browne, eds. *Dimensions of Detective Fiction*, 126, 127–128.

Survival Zero (1970)

Banks, R. Jeff. "Spillane's Anti-Establishment Heroes," in Landrum, Larry N., Pat Browne and Ray B. Browne, eds. *Dimensions of Detective Fiction*, 127.

SPINRAD, NORMAN (1940–)

Bug Jack Baron (1969)

Scholes, Robert and Eric S. Rabkin. *Science Fiction*, 92–93.

STAFFORD, JEAN (1915–1979)

Boston Adventure (1944)

Mann, Jeanette W. "Toward New Archetypal Forms: *Boston Adventure*." *SNNTS* 8 (1976): 291–303.

Mountain Lion (1947)

Jensen, Sidney L. "Noble Wicked West of Jean Stafford." *WAL* 7 (1973): 267–268.
Pilkington, William T. "Introduction to *Mountain Lion*." Stafford, Jean. *Mountain Lion*. Alburquerque, NM: University of New Mexico Press, 1977. Rpt. in Pilkington, William T., ed. *Critical Essays on the Western American Novel*, 182–186.

STAPLEDON, OLAF (1886–1950)

Last and First Men (1930)

Ash, Brian. *Faces of the Future*, 139–140.
Smith, Curtis C. "Olaf Stapledon's Dispassionate Objectivity," in Clareson, Thomas, ed. *Voices for the Future* (Vol. 1), 46–49.
Wollheim, Donald A. *Universe Makers*, 32–35.

Odd John (1935)

Smith, Curtis C. "Olaf Stapledon's Dispassionate Objectivity," in Clareson, Thomas, ed. *Voices for the Future* (Vol. 1), 54–58.

Sirius (1944)

Smith, Curtis C. "Olaf Stapledon's Dispassionate Objectivity," in Clareson, Thomas, ed. *Voices for the Future* (Vol. 1), 58–62.

Star Maker (1937)

Ash, Brian. *Faces of the Future*, 189–190.
Scholes, Robert. *Structural Fabulation*, 64–67.
Smith, Curtis C. "Olaf Stapledon's Dispassionate Objectivity," in Clareson, Thomas, ed. *Voices for the Future* (Vol. 1), 49–53.
Wollheim, Donald A. *Universe Makers*, 35–36.

STARK, RICHARD (1933–)

Plunder Squad (1974)

Palmer, Jerry. *Thrillers*, 212–215.

STEAD, ROBERT J. C. (1880–1959)

Bail Jumper (1914)

Elder, A. T. "Western Panorama: Settings and Themes in Robert J. C. Stead," in Stephens, Donald G., ed. *Writers of the Prairies*, 26, 29, 31, 32, 34.
Elder, A. T. "Western Panorama: Settings and Themes in Robert J. C. Stead," in Woodcock, George, ed. *Canadian Novel*, 41, 43, 45, 46.

Cowpuncher (1918)

Elder, A. T. "Western Panorama: Settings and Themes in Robert J. C. Stead," in Stephens, Donald G., ed. *Writers of the Prairies*, 29, 30, 32, 34–35, 37.
Elder, A. T. "Western Panorama: Settings and Themes in Robert J. C. Stead," in Woodcock, George, ed. *Canadian Novel*, 41–42, 43, 46–47, 49, 50.
Jackel, Susan. "House on the Prairies," in Stephens, Donald G., ed. *Writers of the Prairies*, 166.

Dennison Grant (1920)

Elder, A. T. "Western Panorama: Settings and Themes in Robert J. C. Stead," in Stephens, Donald G., ed. *Writers of the Prairies*, 32, 34, 35–37.
Elder, A. T. "Western Panorama: Settings and Themes in Robert J. C. Stead," in Woodcock, George, ed. *Canadian Novel*, 43, 46, 47–49, 50.
Jackel, Susan. "House on the Prairies," in Stephens, Donald G., ed. *Writers of the Prairies*, 168.

Grain (1926)

Elder, A. T. "Western Panorama: Settings and Themes in Robert J. C. Stead," in Stephens, Donald G., ed. *Writers of the Prairies*, 27–28, 32, 32–33, 34, 38.

Elder, A. T. "Western Panorama: Settings and Themes in Robert J. C. Stead," in Woodcock, George, ed. *Canadian Novel*, 39–40, 44, 46, 49, 50.

Harrison, Dick. *Unnamed Country*, 102–107, 132.

Jackel, Susan. "House on the Prairies," in Stephens, Donald G., ed. *Writers of the Prairies*, 168–169.

Homesteaders (1916)

Elder, A. T. "Western Panorama: Settings and Themes in Robert J. C. Stead," in Stephens, Donald G., ed. *Writers of the Prairies*, 26–27, 29–30, 32, 33, 34, 38.

Elder, A. T. "Western Panorama: Settings and Themes in Robert J. C. Stead," in Woodcock, George, ed. *Canadian Novel*, 41, 44, 45, 46, 50.

Harrison, Dick. *Unnamed Country*, 75–76, 89–90.

Jackel. Susan. "House on the Prairies." *CanL* 42 (1969): 49–50.

Jackel, Susan. "House on the Prairies," in Stephens, Donald G., ed. *Writers of the Prairies*, 166, 168.

Neighbors (1922)

Elder, A. T. "Western Panorama: Settings and Themes in Robert J. C. Stead," in Stephens, Donald G., ed. *Writers of the Prairies*, 30–31, 33.

Elder, A. T. "Western Panorama: Settings and Themes in Robert J. C. Stead," in Woodcock, George, ed. *Canadian Novel*, 42–43, 45.

Smoking Flax (1924)

Elder, A. T. "Western Panorama: Settings and Themes in Robert J. C. Stead," in Stephens, Donald G., ed. *Writers of the Prairies*, 28–29, 32–33, 33–34, 37–38.

Elder, A. T. "Western Panorama: Settings and Themes in Robert J. C. Stead," in Woodcock, George, ed. *Canadian Novel*, 40, 43, 44, 45–46, 49.

STEADMAN, MARK (1930–)

Lion's Share (1975)

Greiner, Donald J. "Southern Fiction of Mark Steadman." *SCR* 9 (1976): 8–11.

STEGNER, WALLACE (1909–1993)

All the Little Live Things (1967)

Ahearn, Kerry. "Heroes vs. Women: Conflict and Duplicity in Stegner," in Lee, L. L. and Merrill Lewis, ed. *Women, Women Writers, and the West*, 151.

Canzoneri, Robert. "Wallace Stegner: Trial by Existence." *SoR* 9 (1973): 804, 820–824.

Moseley, Richard. "First-Person Narration in Wallace Stegner's *All the Little Live Things*." *NConL* 3.2 (1973): 12–13.

Angle of Repose (1971)

Ahearn, Kerry. "Heroes vs. Women: Conflict and Duplicity in Stegner," in Lee, L. L. and Merrill Lewis, ed. *Women, Women Writers, and the West*, 151–155.

Canzoneri, Robert. "Wallace Stegner: Trial by Existence." *SoR* 9 (1973): 798, 805, 824–826.

Etulain, Richard W. "Frontier and Region in Western Literature." *Southwestern American Literature* 1 (1971): 121–128. Rpt. in Pilkington, William T., ed. *Critical Essays on the Western American Novel*, 90–92.
Lewis, Merrill and Lorene Lewis. *Wallace Stegner*, 34–37.

Big Rock Candy Mountain (1943)

Ahearn, Kerry. "Heroes vs. Women: Conflict and Duplicity in Stegner," in Lee, L. L. and Merrill Lewis, ed. *Women, Women Writers, and the West*, 147–148.
Canzoneri, Robert. "Wallace Stegner: Trial by Existence." *SoR* 9 (1973): 802–804, 805–806, 808–812.
Lewis, Merrill and Lorene Lewis. *Wallace Stegner*, 14–20.

On a Darkling Plain (1939)

Harrison, Dick. *Unnamed Country*, 125–126.

Preacher and the Slave (1950)

Lewis, Merrill and Lorene Lewis. *Wallace Stegner*, 24–25.

Shooting Star (1961)

Ahearn, Kerry. "Heroes vs. Women: Conflict and Duplicity in Stegner," in Lee, L. L. and Merrill Lewis, ed. *Women, Women Writers, and the West*, 148–151.

Spectator Bird (1976)

Ahearn, Kerry. "Heroes vs. Women: Conflict and Duplicity in Stegner," in Lee, L. L. and Merrill Lewis, ed. *Women, Women Writers, and the West*, 155–157.

STEIN, GERTRUDE (1874–1946)

Ida (1941)

Secor, Cynthia. "*Ida*, a Great American Novel." *TCL* 24 (1978): 96–107.

Making of Americans (1925)

Bush, Clive. "Toward the Outside: The Quest for Discontinuity in Gertrude Stein's *The Making of Americans:* Being a History of a Family's Progress." *TCL* 24 (1978): 27–55.
Hoffman, Frederick J. "Gertrude Stein," in Wright, George T., ed. *Seven American Stylists, From Poe to Mailer*, 151–153.
Katz, Leon. "Weininger and *The Making of Americans*." *TCL* 24 (1978): 8–26.
Spencer, Sharon. *Space, Time and Structure in the Modern Novel*, 119–121.
Weinstein, Norman. *Gertrude Stein and the Literature of the Modern Consciousness*, 28–46.

STEINBECK, JOHN (1902–1968)

Acts of King Arthur and His Noble Knights (1976)

Hodges, Laura F. "Arthur, Lancelot, and the Psychodrama of Steinbeck." *StQ* 13 (1980): 71–79.

Cannery Row (1945)

Alexander, Stanley. "*Cannery Row:* Steinbeck's Pastoral Poem." *Western American Literature* 2 (1968): 281–295. Rpt. in Davis, Robert Murray, ed. *Steinbeck*, 135–148.

Astro, Richard. "Steinbeck's Post-War Trilogy: A Return to Nature and the Natural Man." *TCL* 16 (1970): 109–114.

Bedford, Richard C. "Steinbeck's Uses of the Oriental." *StQ* 13 (1980): 9–11.

Benson, Jackson J. "John Steinbeck's *Cannery Row:* A Reconsideration." *WAL* 12 (1977): 11–40.

Benton, Robert M. "Ecological Nature of *Cannery Row*," in Astro, Richard and Tetsumaro Hayashi, eds. *Steinbeck*, 131–139.

French, Warren. *John Steinbeck*, 112–124.

Levant, Howard. *Novels of John Steinbeck*, 164–184.

Lisca, Peter. *John Steinbeck*, 112–123.

McCarthy, Paul. *John Steinbeck*, 97–105.

Metzger, Charles R. "Steinbeck's *Cannery Row*," in Hayashi, Tetsumaro, ed. *Study Guide to Steinbeck*, 21–26.

Cup of Gold (1929)

French, Warren. *John Steinbeck*, 45–48, 49–52.

Gray, James. *John Steinbeck*, 32–33.

Gray, James. "John Steinbeck," in Walcutt, Charles Child, ed. *Seven Novelists in the American Naturalist Tradition*, 231–232.

Levant, Howard. *Novels of John Steinbeck*, 10–22.

Lisca, Peter. "Escape and Commitment: Two Poles of the Steinbeck Hero," in Astro, Richard and Tetsumaro Hayashi, eds. *Steinbeck*, 75–76.

Lisca, Peter. *John Steinbeck*, 26–35.

East of Eden (1952)

Bedford, Richard C. "Steinbeck's Uses of the Oriental." *StQ* 13 (1980): 11–16.

Benson, Jackson J. "John Steinbeck: Novelist as Scientist." *Novel* 10 (1977): 256, 263.

Covici, Pascal, Jr. "From Commitment to Choice: Double Vision and the Problem of Vitality for John Steinbeck," in French, Warren, ed. *Fifties*, 64–71.

French, Warren. *John Steinbeck*, 141–152.

Gray, James. *John Steinbeck*, 18–20.

Gray, James. "John Steinbeck," in Walcutt, Charles Child, ed. *Seven Novelists in the American Naturalist Tradition*, 218–221.

Levant, Howard. *Novels of John Steinbeck*, 234–258.

Lisca, Peter. *John Steinbeck*, 161–176.

McCarthy, Paul. *John Steinbeck*, 116–124.

Grapes of Wrath (1939)

Allen, Walter. *Urgent West*, 216–217.

Benson, Jackson J. "John Steinbeck: Novelist as Scientist." *Novel* 10 (1977): 255–256, 257, 262.

Blake, Nelson Manfred. *Novelists' America*, 140–159.

Caldwell, Mary Ellen. "New Consideration of the Intercalary Chapters in *The Grapes of Wrath*." *MarkR* 3 (1973): 115–119.

Cook, Sylvia Jenkins. *From Tobacco Road to Route 66*, 171–183.

Craig, David and Michael Egan. *Extreme Situations*, 162–166, 168.

Ditsky, John. "*Grapes of Wrath:* A Reconsideration." *SoHR* 13 (1979): 215–220.

Donald, Miles. *American Novel in the Twentieth Century*, 60–72.

Downs, Robert B. *Famous American Books*, 311–319.

French, Warren. *John Steinbeck*, 92–102.

French, Warren. "Steinbeck's *The Grapes of Wrath*," in Hayashi, Tetsumaro, ed. *Study Guide to Steinbeck*, 35–41.

Gray, James. *John Steinbeck*, 13–16.

Gray, James. "John Steinbeck," in Walcutt, Charles Child, ed. *Seven Novelists in the American Naturalist Tradition*, 213–216, 237–240.

Hearn, Charles R. *American Dream in the Great Depression*, 86–88.

Levant, Howard. *Novels of John Steinbeck*, 93–129.

Lisca, Peter. "Escape and Commitment: Two Poles of the Steinbeck Hero," in Astro, Richard and Tetsumaro Hayashi, eds. *Steinbeck*, 83.

Lisca, Peter. "*Grapes of Wrath*," in Lisca, Peter. *Wide World of John Steinbeck*. New Brunswick, NJ: Rutgers University Press, 1958. 144–177. Rpt. in Davis, Robert Murray, ed. *Steinbeck*, 75–101.

Lisca, Peter. *John Steinbeck*, 87–110.

Lutwack, Leonard. *Heroic Fiction*, 47–63.

McCarthy, Paul. *John Steinbeck*, 67–86.

Mullen, Patrick B. "American Folklife and *The Grapes of Wrath*." *JACult* 1 (1978): 742–753.

Ousby, Ian. *Reader's Guide to Fifty American Novels*, 312–315.

Vassilowitch, John, Jr. "Bing Crosby and *The Grapes of Wrath*: Bad History, Good Art." *StQ* 13 (1980): 97–98.

Watkins, Floyd C. *In Time and Place*, 19–29.

White, Ray Lewis and Robert J. Robbins. "Steinbeck and Maupassant: A Parallel Occurrence." *StQ* 12 (1979): 27–28.

Ziolkowski, Theodore. *Fictional Transfigurations of Jesus*, 182–190.

In Dubious Battle (1936)

Allen, Walter. *Urgent West*, 216.

Benson, Jackson J. and Anne Loftis. "John Steinbeck and Farm Labor Unionization: The Background of *In Dubious Battle*." *AL* 52 (1980): 194–223.

Benson, Jackson J. "John Steinbeck: Novelist as Scientist." *Novel* 10 (1977): 254, 255, 256, 257.

Cook, Sylvia Jenkins. *From Tobacco Road to Route 66*, 161–167.

French, Warren. *John Steinbeck*, 76–81.

Gray, James. *John Steinbeck*, 16–18.

Gray, James. "John Steinbeck," in Walcutt, Charles Child, ed. *Seven Novelists in the American Naturalist Tradition*, 216–218.

Levant, Howard. *Novels of John Steinbeck*, 74–92.

Levant, Howard. "Unity of *In Dubious Battle*: Violence and Dehumanization." *Modern Fiction Studies* 11.1 (Spring 1965): 21–33. Rpt. in Davis, Robert Murray, ed. *Steinbeck*, 49–62.

Lisca, Peter. "Escape and Commitment: Two Poles of the Steinbeck Hero," in Astro, Richard and Tetsumaro Hayashi, eds. *Steinbeck*, 80–82.

Lisca, Peter. *John Steinbeck*, 63–76.

McCarthy, Paul. *John Steinbeck*, 47–56.

Perez, Betty L. "Steinbeck's *In Dubious Battle*," in Hayashi, Tetsumaro, ed. *Study Guide to Steinbeck*, 54–62.

Sarchett, Barry W. "*In Dubious Battle*: A Revaluation." *StQ* 13 (1980): 87–97.

Wilson, Jerry W. "*In Dubious Battle*: Engagement in Collectivity." *StQ* 13 (1980): 31–42.

Pastures of Heaven (1932)

Bedford, Richard C. "Steinbeck's Uses of the Oriental." *StQ* 13 (1980): 5.

French, Warren. *John Steinbeck*, 54–62.

Levant, Howard. *Novels of John Steinbeck*, 34–51.

Lisca, Peter. *John Steinbeck*, 46–54.

Lisca, Peter. "Escape and Commitment: Two Poles of the Steinbeck Hero," in Astro, Richard and Tetsumaro Hayashi, eds. *Steinbeck*, 76–78.

McCarthy, Paul. *John Steinbeck*, 32–38.

Mawer, Randall R. "Takashi Kato, 'Good American': The Central Episode in Steinbeck's *The Pastures of Haaven*." *StQ* 13 (1980): 23–31.

Peterson, Richard. "Turning Point: *The Pastures of Heaven* (1932)," in Hayashi, Tetsumaro, ed. *Study Guide to Steinbeck*, 93–102.

Short Reign of Pippin IV (1957)

French, Warren. *John Steinbeck*, 157–158.

Levant, Howard. *Novels of John Steinbeck*, 273–287.

Lisca, Peter. *John Steinbeck*, 208–212.

Sweet Thursday (1954)

Bedford, Richard C. "Steinbeck's Uses of the Oriental." *StQ* 13 (1980): 6, 16–17.

French, Warren. *John Steinbeck*, 154–157.

Levant, Howard. *Novels of John Steinbeck*, 259–272.

Metzger, Charles R. "Steinbeck's Mexican Americans," in Astro, Richard and Tetsumaro Hayashi, eds. *Steinbeck*, 153–155.

To a God Unknown (1933)

Covici, Pascal, Jr. "John Steinbeck and the Language of Awareness," in French, Warren, ed. *Thirties*, 50–52.

DeMott, Robert. "Steinbeck's *To a God Unknown*," in Hayashi, Tetsumaro, ed. *Study Guide to Steinbeck*, 188–207.

French, Warren. *John Steinbeck*, 48–49, 50–52.

Gray, James. *John Steinbeck*, 24–26.

Gray, James. "John Steinbeck," in Walcutt, Charles Child, ed. *Seven Novelists in the American Naturalist Tradition*, 224–226.

Levant, Howard. *Novels of John Steinbeck*, 22–34.

Lisca, Peter. *John Steinbeck*, 35–45.

Metzger, Charles R. "Steinbeck's Mexican Americans," in Astro, Richard and Tetsumaro Hayashi, eds. *Steinbeck*, 151–152.

Tortilla Flat (1935)

Bedford, Richard C. "Steinbeck's Uses of the Oriental." *StQ* 13 (1980): 5–6.

Covici, Pascal, Jr. "John Steinbeck and the Language of Awareness," in French, Warren, ed. *Thirties*, 52.

French, Warren. *John Steinbeck*, 70–75.

Gray, James. *John Steinbeck*, 27–28.

Gray, James. "John Steinbeck," in Walcutt, Charles Child, ed. *Seven Novelists in the American Naturalist Tradition*, 226–228.

Kinney, Arthur F. "Arthurian Cycle in *Tortilla Flat*." *Modern Fiction Studies* 11.1 (Spring 1965): 11–20. Rpt. in Davis, Robert Murray, ed. *Steinbeck*, 36–46.

Levant, Howard. *Novels of John Steinbeck*, 52–73.

Lisca, Peter. "Escape and Commitment: Two Poles of the Steinbeck Hero," in Astro, Richard and Tetsumaro Hayashi, eds. *Steinbeck*, 78–80.

Lisca, Peter. *John Steinbeck*, 54–62.

McCarthy, Paul. *John Steinbeck*, 38–45.

Simpson, Arthur L., Jr. "Steinbeck's *Tortilla Flat*," in Hayashi, Tetsumaro, ed. *Study Guide to Steinbeck*, 222–235.

Wayward Bus (1947)

Astro, Richard. "Steinbeck's Post-War Trilogy: A Return to Nature and the Natural Man." *TCL* 16 (1970): 114–118.

Bedford, Richard C. "Steinbeck's Uses of the Oriental." *StQ* 13 (1980): 11.

French, Warren. *John Steinbeck*, 131–137.

Levant, Howard. *Novels of John Steinbeck*, 207–233.

Lisca, Peter. *John Steinbeck*, 141–153.

McCarthy, Paul. *John Steinbeck*, 110–116.

Metzger, Charles R. "Steinbeck's Mexican Americans," in Astro, Richard and Tetsumaro Hayashi, eds. *Steinbeck*, 152–153.

Winter of Our Discontent (1961)

Bedford, Richard C. "Steinbeck's Uses of the Oriental." *StQ* 13 (1980): 17–18.

Bedford, Richard C. "Genesis and Consolation of *Our Discontent*." *Criticism* 14 (1972): 277–294.

French, Warren. *John Steinbeck*, 159–165.

Garcia, Reloy. "Steinbeck's *The Winter of Our Discontent*," in Hayashi, Tetsumaro, ed. *Study Guide to Steinbeck*, 248–254.

Gray, James. *John Steinbeck*, 35–37.

Gray, James. "John Steinbeck," in Walcutt, Charles Child, ed. *Seven Novelists in the American Naturalist Tradition*, 235–236.

Levant, Howard. *Novels of John Steinbeck*, 288–300.

Lisca, Peter. *John Steinbeck*, 176–188.

McCarthy, Paul. *John Steinbeck*, 128–133.

STEPHENS, ANN SOPHIA (1810–1886)

Fashion and Famine (1854)

Baym, Nina. *Woman's Fiction*, 184–185.

Heiress of Greenhurst (1857)

Baym, Nina. *Woman's Fiction*, 182–184.

Mary Derwent (1858)

Baym, Nina. *Woman's Fiction*, 181–182.

Old Homestead (1855)

Baym, Nina. *Woman's Fiction*, 185–188.

Zana see *Heiress of Greenhurst*

STEWART, GEORGE (1895–1980)

Earth Abides (1949)

Cogell, Elizabeth Cummins. "Middle-Landscape Myth in Science Fiction." *SFS* 5 (1978): 135–136.

STODDARD, CHARLES WARREN (1843–1909)

For the Pleasure of His Company (1903)
Austen, Roger. *Playing the Game*, 13–15.

STODDARD, ELIZABETH (1843–1902)

Morgesons (1862)
Weir, Sybil. "*Morgesons:* A Neglected Feminist Bildungsroman." *NEQ* 49 (1976): 427–439.

STONE, ROBERT (1937–)

Dog Soldiers (1974)
Hendin, Josephine. *Vulnerable People*, 131–132.

Hall of Mirrors (1967)
Hendin, Josephine. *Vulnerable People*, 128–131.

STORM, HYEMEYOHSTS (1933–)

Seven Arrows (1972)
Larson, Charles R. *American Indian Fiction*, 99, 112–126.

STOWE, HARRIET BEECHER (1811–1896)

Dred (1856)
Berzon, Judith R. *Neither White Nor Black*, 34–35.
Crozier, Alice C. *Novels of Harriet Beecher Stowe*, 34–54, 74–84.
Hovet, Theodore R. "Christian Revolution: Harriet Beecher Stowe's Response to Slavery and the Civil War." *NEQ* 47 (1974): 541–545.
Yellin, Jean Fagan. *Intricate Knot*, 143–146.

Minister's Wooing (1859)
Buell, Lawrence. "Calvinism Romanticized: Harriet Beecher Stowe, Samuel Hopkins, and *The Minister's Wooing*." *ESQ* 24 (1978): 119–132.
Crozier, Alice C. *Novels of Harriet Beecher Stowe*, 97–98, 100–102, 110–111, 136.

My Wife and I (1871)
Baym, Nina. *Woman's Fiction*, 236.
Crozier, Alice C. *Novels of Harriet Beecher Stowe*, 181–186.

Oldtown Folks (1869)
Crozier, Alice C. *Novels of Harriet Beecher Stowe*, 102–103, 108–109, 111–114, 116.

Pearl of Orr's Island (1862)
Crozier, Alice C. *Novels of Harriet Beecher Stowe*, 98–100, 102, 136–141.

Pink and White Tyranny (1871)
Baym, Nina. *Woman's Fiction*, 235.

Poganuc People (1878)

Crozier, Alice C. *Novels of Harriet Beecher Stowe*, 144–150.

Uncle Tom's Cabin (1852)

Ammons, Elizabeth. "Heroines in *Uncle Tom's Cabin*." *AL* 49 (1977): 161–179.

Baldwin, James. "Everybody's Protest Novel," in *Notes of a Native Son*. Boston: Beacon Press, 1955. 13–23. Rpt. in Hemenway, Robert, ed. *Black Novelist*, 220–223.

Berzon, Judith R. *Neither White Nor Black*, 55–57, 101.

Brandstadter, Evan. "Uncle Tom and Archy Moore: The Antislavery Novel as Ideological Symbol." *AQ* 26 (1974): 164–175.

Cassara, Ernest. "Rehabilitation of Uncle Tom: Significant Themes in Mrs. Stowe's Antislavery Novel." *CLAJ* 17 (1973): 230–240.

Crozier, Alice C. *Novels of Harriet Beecher Stowe*, 3–33, 55–73.

Graham, Thomas. "Harriet Beecher Stowe and the Question of Race." *NEQ* 46 (1973): 614–622.

Lynn, Kenneth S. *Visions of America*, 30–48.

Miller, Randall M. "Stowe's Black Sources in *Uncle Tom's Cabin*." *ANQ* 14 (1975): 38–39.

Moers, Ellen. *Harriet Beecher Stowe and American Literature*, 1–26.

Moers, Ellen. *Literary Women*, 37–38, 85–86.

Prior, Moody E. "Mrs. Stowes's Uncle Tom." *CritI* 7 (1979): 645–650.

Rexroth, Kenneth. *Elastic Retort*, 103–107.

Starke, Catherine Juanita. *Black Portraiture in American Fiction*, 107–111.

Steele, Thomas J., S. J. "Tom and Eva: Mrs. Stowe's Two Dying Christs." *NALF* 6 (1972): 85–90.

Taylor, Gordon O. *Passages of Thought*, 18–26.

Van Hoy, Milton S. "Two Allusions to Hungary in *Uncle Tom's Cabin*." *Phylon* 34 (1973): 433–435.

Yellin, Jean Fagan. *Intricate Knot*, 130–137.

STRAIGHT, MICHAEL WHITNEY (1916–)

Very Small Remnant (1963)

Graham, Don. "Tragedy and Western American Literature: The Example of Michael Straight's *A Very Small Remant*," in Pilkington, William T., ed. *Critical Essays on the Western American Novel*, 187–194.

STREET, JAMES H. (1903–1954)

Good-bye, My Lady (1941)

Kelty, Jean McClure. "Cult of Kill in Adolescent Fiction." *EJ* 64.2 (1975): 58.

STRIBLING, T. S. (1881–1965)

Backwater (1930)

Eckley, Wilton. *T. S. Stribling*, 61–62.

Birthright (1922)

Cook, Sylvia Jenkins. *From Tobacco Road to Route 66*, 31.

Eckley, Wilton. *T. S. Stribling*, 25–31.

Bright Metal (1928)

Cook, Sylvia Jenkins. *From Tobacco Road to Route 66*, 33–34.
Eckley, Wilton. *T. S. Stribling*, 54–61.

Fombombo (1923)

Eckley, Wilton. *T. S. Stribling*, 33–39.

Forge (1931)

Eckley, Wilton. *T. S. Stribling*, 64–73.
Rocks, James E. "T.S. Stribling's Burden of Southern History: The Vaiden Trilogy." *SoHR* 6 (1972): 225–228.

Red Sand (1924)

Eckley, Wilton. *T. S. Stribling*, 40–44.

Sound Wagon (1935)

Eckley, Wilton. *T. S. Stribling*, 96–101.

Store (1933)

Eckley, Wilton. *T. S. Stribling*, 74–83.
Going, William T. *Essays on Alabama Literature*, 9–22, 30–31.
Rocks, James E. "T.S. Stribling's Burden of Southern History: The Vaiden Trilogy." *SoHR* 6 (1972): 228–230.

Teeftallow (1926)

Cook, Sylvia Jenkins. *From Tobacco Road to Route 66*, 31–33.
Eckley, Wilton. *T. S. Stribling*, 45–53.

These Bars of Flesh (1938)

Eckley, Wilton. *T. S. Stribling*, 101–107.

Unfinished Cathedral (1934)

Eckley, Wilton. *T. S. Stribling*, 84–95.
Rocks, James E. "T.S. Stribling's Burden of Southern History: The Vaiden Trilogy." *SoHR* 6 (1972): 230–232.

STRINGER, ARTHUR (1874–1950)

Mud Lark (1931)

Harrison, Dick. *Unnamed Country*, 96–97.

Prairie Wife (1915)

Harrison, Dick. *Unnamed Country*, 93–94.

STUART, JESSE (1906–1984)

Daughter of the Legend (1965)

Flanagan, John T. "Jesse Stuart, Regional Novelist," in LeMaster, J. R. and Mary Washington Clark, eds. *Jesse Stuart*, 75, 80, 91–82, 84–85.
Pennington, Lee. "Symbolism and Vision in *Daughter of the Legend*," in LeMaster, J. R., ed. *Jesse Stuart*, 169–186.

Foretaste of Glory (1946)

Flanagan, John T. "Jesse Stuart, Regional Novelist," in LeMaster, J. R. and Mary Washington Clark, eds. *Jesse Stuart*, 79–80, 85, 86.

Hall, Wade. "Humor in Jesse Stuart's Fiction," in LeMaster, J. R. and Mary Washington Clark, eds. *Jesse Stuart*, 99–100.

Good Spirit of Laurel Ridge (1953)

Clarke, Kenneth. "Jesse Stuart's Use of Folklore," in LeMaster, J. R. and Mary Washington Clark, eds. *Jesse Stuart*, 120–122.

Flanagan, John T. "Jesse Stuart, Regional Novelist," in LeMaster, J. R. and Mary Washington Clark, eds. *Jesse Stuart*, 73, 77–78, 81, 84.

Hall, Wade. "Humor in Jesse Stuart's Fiction," in LeMaster, J. R. and Mary Washington Clark, eds. *Jesse Stuart*, 97–98.

Hie to the Hunters (1950)

Flanagan, John T. "Jesse Stuart, Regional Novelist," in LeMaster, J. R. and Mary Washington Clark, eds. *Jesse Stuart*, 72–73, 74, 80–81.

Hall, Wade. "Humor in Jesse Stuart's Fiction," in LeMaster, J. R. and Mary Washington Clark, eds. *Jesse Stuart*, 91.

Mr. Gallion's School (1967)

Flanagan, John T. "Jesse Stuart, Regional Novelist," in LeMaster, J. R. and Mary Washington Clark, eds. *Jesse Stuart*, 76–77, 80.

Taps for Private Tussie (1943)

Clarke, Kenneth. "Jesse Stuart's Use of Folklore," in LeMaster, J. R. and Mary Washington Clark, eds. *Jesse Stuart*, 122–123.

Clarke, Mary Washington. "Jesse Stuart's Educational Saga as Humanistic Affirmation," in LeMaster, J. R. and Mary Washington Clark, eds. *Jesse Stuart*, 143–145.

Flanagan, John T. "Jesse Stuart, Regional Novelist," in LeMaster, J. R. and Mary Washington Clark, eds. *Jesse Stuart*, 73–74, 82–84, 85.

Hall, Wade. "Humor in Jesse Stuart's Fiction," in LeMaster, J. R. and Mary Washington Clark, eds. *Jesse Stuart*, 92

Trees of Heaven (1940)

Flanagan, John T. "Jesse Stuart, Regional Novelist," in LeMaster, J. R. and Mary Washington Clark, eds. *Jesse Stuart*, 72, 79, 80.

Hall, Wade. "Humor in Jesse Stuart's Fiction," in LeMaster, J. R. and Mary Washington Clark, eds. *Jesse Stuart*, 97.

Leavell, Frank H. "Dualism in Stuart's *Trees of Heaven*," in LeMaster, J. R. and Mary Washington Clark, eds. *Jesse Stuart*, 54–69.

STURGEON, THEODORE (1918–1985)

Cosmic Rape (1958)

Hassler, Donald M. "Images for an Ethos, Images for Change and Style." *Extrapolation* 20 (1979): 182–184.

More Than Human (1953)

Hassler, Donald M. "Images for an Ethos, Images for Change and Style." *Extrapolation* 20 (1979): 179–182.

Rabkin, Eric S. *Fantastic in Literature*, 122–127.

Rabkin, Eric S. "Genre Criticism: Science Fiction and the Fantastic," in Rose, Mark, ed. *Science Fiction*, 93–96.

Sackmary, Regina. "Ideal of Three: The Art of Theodore Sturgeon," in Riley, Dick, ed. *Critical Encounters*, 141–142.

Samuelson, David. *Visions of Tomorrow*, 171–220.

Wolfe, Gary K. *Known and the Unknown*, 217–221.

Venus Plus X (1960)

Ash, Brian. *Faces of the Future*, 136–137.

Friend, Beverly. "Virgin Territory: The Bonds and Boundaries of Women in Science Fiction," in Clareson, Thomas D., ed. *Many Futures, Many Worlds*, 155–157.

Ketterer, David. *New Worlds for Old*, 118–122.

STYRON, WILLIAM (1925–)

Confessions of Nat Turner (1968)

Amis, Harry D. "History as Self-Serving Myth: Another Look at Styron's *The Confessions of Nat Turner*." *CLAJ* 22 (1978): 134–146.

Cheshire, Ardner R., Jr. "Recollective Structure of *The Confessions of Nat Turner*." *SoR* 12 (1976): 110–121.

Cobbs, John L. "Baring the Unbearable: William Styron and the Problem of Pain." *MissQ* 34 (1980–81): 16–17, 20–21.

Friedman, Melvin J. *William Styron*, 12–18.

Gayle, Addison, Jr. *Way of the New World*, 234–237.

Gindin, James. *Harvest of a Quiet Eye*, 349–350.

Gray, Richard. *Literature of Memory*, 291–300, 301–305.

Hays, Peter L. *Limping Hero*, 92–95.

Henderson, Harry B. *Versions of the Past*, 273–277.

Holder, Alan. "Styron's Slave: *The Confessions of Nat Turner*." *SAQ* 68 (1969): 167–180.

Kort, Wesley A. *Shriven Selves*, 116–140.

McGill, William J. "William Styron's Nat Turner and Religion." *SAQ* 79 (1980): 75–81.

Mackin, Cooper R. *William Styron*, 22–36.

Pearce, Richard. *William Styron*, 6, 9, 39–45.

Pinsker, Sanford. *Between Two Worlds*, 66–73.

Ratner, Marc L. "Styron's Reble." *AQ* 21 (1969): 595–608.

Ratner, Marc L. *William Styron*, 91–119, 122, 123–125.

Sullivan, Walter. *Death by Melancholy*, 98–99, 100–102.

Watkins, Floyd C. *In Time and Place*, 51–70.

White, John. "Novelist as Historian: William Styron and American Negro Slavery." *JAmS* 4 (1970): 233–245.

Lie Down in Darkness (1951)

Cobbs, John L. "Baring the Unbearable: William Styron and the Problem of Pain." *MissQ* 34 (1980–81): 15, 19.

Friedman, Melvin J. "William Styron," in Panichas, George A., ed. *Politics of Twentieth-Century Novelists*, 337–338.

Galloway, David D. *Absurd Hero in American Fiction*, 53–61.
Friedman, Melvin J. *William Styron*, 27–35.
Gray, Richard. *Literature of Memory*, 285–291.
Hassan, Ihab H. "Ecounter with Necessity," in Hassan, Ihab. *Radical Innocence*.
  Princeton, NJ: Princeton University Press, 1961. Rpt. in Kostelanetz, Richard, ed.
  On Contemporary Literature, 598–606.
Hays, Peter L. *Limping Hero*, 89–92.
Leon, Philip W. "Lost Boy and a Lost Girl." *SLJ* 9.1 (1976): 62–69.
Mackin, Cooper R. *William Styron*, 4–12.
Pearce, Richard. *William Styron*, 6–7, 9, 11–19.
Ratner, Marc L. *William Styron*, 35–56, 122–123.
Rose, Alan Henry. *Demonic Vision*, 128.
Scheick, William J. "Discarded Watermelon Rinds: The Rainbow Aesthetic of Styr-
  on's *Lie Down in Darkness*." *MFS* 24 (1978): 247–254.

Set This House on Fire (1960)

Bryant, Jerry H. *Open Decision*, 264–268.
Cobbs, John L. "Baring the Unbearable: William Styron and the Problem of Pain."
  MissQ 34 (1980–81): 16, 19–20.
Friedman, Melvin J. *William Styron*, 8–11, 23–27.
Friedman, Melvin J. "William Styron," in Panichas, George A., ed. *Politics of
  Twentieth-Century Novelists*, 339.
Galloway, David D. *Absurd Hero in American Fiction*, 65–81.
Landor, Mikhail. "Centaur-Novels," in Proffer, Carl R., ed. and trans. *Soviet Criti-
  cism of American Literature in the Sixties*, 37–43.
Mackin, Cooper R. *William Styron*, 14–22.
Pearce, Richard. *William Styron*, 6, 7, 24–39.
Perry, J. Douglas, Jr. "Gothic as Vortex: The Form of Horror in Capote, Faulkner,
  and Styron." *MFS* 19 (1973): 162–166.
Ratner, Marc L. *William Styron*, 71–90, 121–122, 123.

Sophie's Choice (1980)

Cobbs, John L. "Baring the Unbearable: William Styron and the Problem of Pain."
  MissQ 34 (1980–81): 17–19, 21, 23–24.

SUCH, PETER (1939–)

Riverrun (1973)

Moss, John. *Sex and Violence*, 260–261, 269–273.

SUCKOW, RUTH (1892–1960)

Bonney Family (1926)

Hamblen, Abigail Ann. *Ruth Suckow*, 11–16.
Kissane, Leedice McAnelly. *Ruth Suckow*, 67–72.
Omranin, Margaret Stewart. *Ruth Suckow*, 44–46, 77–80, 110–113, 126–128, 133–
  135, 143–145.

Cora (1929)

> Hamblen, Abigail Ann. *Ruth Suckow*, 20–27.
> Kissane, Leedice McAnelly. *Ruth Suckow*, 72–78.
> Omranin, Margaret Stewart. *Ruth Suckow*, 46–47, 56–57, 60, 80–83, 148–149.

Country People (1924)

> Hamblen, Abigail Ann. *Ruth Suckow*, 18–19.
> Kissane, Leedice McAnelly. *Ruth Suckow*, 52–58.
> Omranin, Margaret Stewart. *Ruth Suckow*, 18–27, 67–70, 75, 143, 146–147.

Folks (1934)

> Hamblen, Abigail Ann. *Ruth Suckow*, 17–18, 30–38.
> Kissane, Leedice McAnelly. *Ruth Suckow*, 93–114.
> Omranin, Margaret Stewart. *Ruth Suckow*, 27–28, 47–48, 72, 83–88, 115–126, 128–133, 135–138, 145–146, 149.

John Wood Case (1959)

> Hamblen, Abigail Ann. *Ruth Suckow*, 40–42.
> Kissane, Leedice McAnelly. *Ruth Suckow*, 139–152.
> Omranin, Margaret Stewart. *Ruth Suckow*, 54–55, 60, 138–143.

Kramer Girls (1930)

> Kissane, Leedice McAnelly. *Ruth Suckow*, 78–83, 44.
> Omranin, Margaret Stewart. *Ruth Suckow*, 113–115.

New Hope (1942)

> Kissane, Leedice McAnelly. *Ruth Suckow*, 119–126.
> Omranin, Margaret Stewart. *Ruth Suckow*, 28, 48–54, 88–92, 97, 98–103.

Odyssey of a Nice Girl (1925)

> Kissane, Leedice McAnelly. *Ruth Suckow*, 58–65.
> Omranin, Margaret Stewart. *Ruth Suckow*, 27, 42–44, 70–72, 75–76, 103–109, 126.

SUMMERTON, MARGARET

Nightingale at Noon (1962)

> Russ, Joanna. "Somebody's Trying to Kill Me and I Think It's My Husband: The Modern Gothic." *JPC* 6 (1973): 666–691.

SWIGGETT, HOWARD (1891–1957)

Durable Fire (1957)

> Bryant, Jerry H. *Open Decision*, 179–180.

Power and the Prize (1954)

> Bryant, Jerry H. *Open Decision*, 178–179.

SYMONS, SCOTT (1933–)

Place d'armes (1967)

> Brigg, Peter. "Insite: *Place d'armes*." *CanL* 73 (1977): 79–85.

TALSMAN, WILLIAM

Gaudy Image (1958)
    Austen, Roger. *Playing the Game*, 152–158.

TARDIVEL, J. P. (1851–1905)

Pour la patrie (1895)
    Northey, Margot. *Haunted Wilderness*, 42–46.

TARKINGTON, BOOTH (1869–1946)

Alice Adams (1921)
    Fennimore, Keith J. *Booth Tarkington*, 85–92.

Penrod (1914)
    Baker, Donald G. "Black Images: The Afro-American in Popular Novels, 1900–1945." *JPC* 7 (1973): 333–334.

Plutocrat (1927)
    Fennimore, Keith J. *Booth Tarkington*, 72–75.

Turmoil (1915)
    Fennimore, Keith J. *Booth Tarkington*, 60–72.

TATE, ALLEN (1899–1979)

Fathers (1938)
    Aaron, Daniel. *Unwritten War*, 302–304.
    Allen, Walter. *Urgent West*, 85–87.
    Anonymous. "Southern Style." *London Times Literary Supplement* 59 (5 Aug 1960): 496. Rpt. in Squires, Radcliffe, ed. *Allen Tate and His Works*, 134–139.
    Bennett, Lee Shaw. "Modern Civil War Novels: The Still Unwritten War?" *SoS* 19 (1980): 112–113.
    Carpenter, Lynette. "Battle Within: The Beleaguered Consciousness in Allen Tate's *The Fathers*." *SLJ* 8.2 (1976): 3–23.
    Donoghue, Denis. "American Style of Failure." *SewR* 82 (1974): 420–424.
    Gray, Richard. *Literature of Memory*, 82–94.
    Kermode, Frank. "Old Orders Changing (Tate and Lampedusa)," in Kermode, Frank. *Puzzles and Epiphanies*. New York: Chilmark Press, 1962. 131–139. Rpt. in Squires, Radcliffe, ed. *Allen Tate and His Works*, 140–148.
    King, Richard H. *Southern Renaissance*, 105–111.
    MacKethan, Lucinda Hardwick. *Dream of Arcady*, 147–152, 153–155.
    McMillen, William. "Memory in Allen Tate's *The Fathers*." *NConL* 8.1 (1978): 10.
    Mizener, Arthur. "*The Fathers*." *Sewannee Review* 67 (Autumn 1959): 604–613. Rpt. in Squires, Radcliffe, ed. *Allen Tate and His Works*, 121–129.
    Smith, Janet Adam. "End of the Old Dominion." *New Statesman* 59 (14 May 1960): 718–719. Rpt. in Squires, Radcliffe, ed. *Allen Tate and His Works*, 129–134.

Stineback, David C. *Shifting World*, 128–141.
Sullivan, Walter. *Death by Melancholy*, 70–72.
Sullivan, Walter. "*Fathers* and the Failures of Tradition." *SoR* 12 (1976): 758–766.
Sullivan, Walter. *Requiem for the Renascence*, 31–37.
Young, Thomas Daniel. "Allen Tate's Double Focus: The Past in the Present." *MissQ* 30 (1977): 521–525.

TAYLOR, BAYARD (1825–1878)

Hannah Thurston (1863)
Wermuth, Paul C. *Bayard Taylor*, 77–82.

John Godfrey's Fortunes (1864)
Rose, Alan H. "Sin and the City: The Uses of Disorder in the Urban Novel." *CentR* 16 (1972): 207–212.
Wermuth, Paul C. *Bayard Taylor*, 82–87.

Joseph and His Friend (1870)
Austen, Roger. *Playing the Game*, 9–11.
Wermuth, Paul C. *Bayard Taylor*, 94–99.

Story of Kennett (1866)
Wermuth, Paul C. *Bayard Taylor*, 87–94.

TAYLOR, PETER (1917–1994)

Woman of Means (1950)
Griffith, Albert J. *Peter Taylor*, 57–71.

TELLIER, ANDRÉ (1902–)

Twilight Men (1931)
Austen, Roger. *Playing the Game*, 67–68.

TENNEY, TABITHA (1762–1837)

Female Quixotism (1801)
Petter, Henri. *Early American Novel*, 46–55.

TERHUNE, MARY VIRGINIA see HARLAND, MARION

TESCH, GERALD

Never the Same Again (1956)
Austen, Roger. *Playing the Game*, 175–176.

THÉRIAULT, YVES (1915–1983)

Aaron (1954)
Shek, Ben-Zion. *Social Realism*, 159–160, 162–168.
Sutherland, Ronald. *Second Image*, 50–55.

Agaguk (1958)
 Lacroix, Yves. "Lecture d'*Agaguk*." *V&I* 5 (1980): 245–269.
 Mathews, Robin D. "Wacousta Factor," in Bessai, Diane and David Jackel, eds.
  Figures in a Ground, 311.
 Urbas, Jeannette. *From Thirty Acres to Modern Times*, 76–81.

Agoak (1975)
 Nelson, Louise Vanhee. "Theriault's *Agoak*." *CanL* 82 (1979): 128–130.

Ashini (1960)
 Urbas, Jeannette. *From Thirty Acres to Modern Times*, 81–83.

Tayaout (1969)
 Nelson-Vanhee, Louise E. "*Tayaout*, une quete mystique." *CanL* 71 (1976): 35–38.

THÉRIO, ADRIEN (1925–)

C'est ici que le monde a commencé (1978)
 Poulin, Gabrielle. *Romans du pays*, 291–296.

THOMAS, AUDREY CALLAHAN (1935–)

Blown Figures (1974)
 Diotte, Robert. "Romance of Penelope: Audrey Thomas's Isobel Carpenter Trilogy." *CanL* 86 (1980): 66–68.
 Monk, Patricia. "Shadow Continent: The Image of Africa in Three Canadian Writers." *Ariel* 8.4 (1977): 15–17.

Mrs. Blood (1970)
 Diotte, Robert. "Romance of Penelope: Audrey Thomas's Isobel Carpenter Trilogy." *CanL* 86 (1980): 62–63, 65–66.
 Monk, Patricia. "Shadow Continent: The Image of Africa in Three Canadian Writers." *Ariel* 8.4 (1977): 13–15.

Songs My Mother Taught Me (1973)
 Diotte, Robert. "Romance of Penelope: Audrey Thomas's Isobel Carpenter Trilogy." *CanL* 86 (1980): 63–65.
 Stevens, Peter. "Audrey Thomas' *Songs My Mother Taught Me*." *WLWE* 13 (1974):
  259–260.

THOMAS, WARD

Stranger in the Land (1949)
 Austen, Roger. *Playing the Game*, 131–133.

THOMPSON, DANIEL (1795–1868)

Doomed Chief (1860)
 Barnett, Louise K. *Ignoble Savage*, 36–37.

THOMPSON, HUNTER S. (1939–)

Fear and Loathing in Las Vegas (1971)
 Hendin, Josephine. *Vulnerable People*, 68–69.

Fear and Loathing: On the Campaign Trail '72 (1973)

Hellman, John. "Corporate Fiction, Private Fable, and Hunter S. Thompson's *Fear and Loathing: On the Campaign Trail '72.*" *Crit* 21.1 (1979): 16–30.

THURMAN, WALLACE (1902–1934)

Blacker the Berry (1929)

Davis, Arthur P. *From the Dark Tower*, 109–111.
Gayle, Addison, Jr. *Way of the New World*, 123–126.
Schultz, Elizabeth. " 'Free in Fact and at Last': The Image of the Black Woman in Black American Fiction," in Springer, Marlene, ed. *What Manner of Woman*, 323–324.
Singh, Amritjit. *Novels of the Harlem Renaissance*, 105–111.

Infants of Spring (1932)

Davis, Arthur P. *From the Dark Tower*, 111–113.
Gayle, Addison, Jr. *Way of the New World*, 126.
Henderson, Mae Gwendolyn. "Portrait of Wallace Thurman," in Bontemps, Arna, ed. *Harlem Renaissance Remembered*, 165–169.
Perry, Margaret. *Silence to the Drums*, 90–93.
Singh, Amritjit. *Novels of the Harlem Renaissance*, 33–36.

TOMASI, MARI (1895–1965)

Like Lesser Gods (1949)

Green, Rose Basile. *Italian-American Novel*, 134–138.

TRAVEN, B. (1890(?)–1969)

Bridge in the Jungle (1929)

Chankin, Donald O. *Anonymity and Death*, 64–78.

Death Ship (1926)

Chankin, Donald O. *Anonymity and Death*, 16–41.
Fraser, John. "Rereading Traven's *The Death Ship.*" *SoR* 9 (1973): 69–92.

Government (1931)

Chankin, Donald O. *Anonymity and Death*, 88–96.

March to the Montería (1933)

Chankin, Donald O. *Anonymity and Death*, 85–88.

Rebellion of the Hanged (1936)

Chankin, Donald O. *Anonymity and Death*, 79–86.

Treasure of Sierra Madre (1927)

Chankin, Donald O. *Anonymity and Death*, 42–63.

TRILLING, LIONEL (1905–1975)

Middle of the Journey (1947)

Chace, William M. "*Middle of the Journey:* Death and Politics." *Novel* 10 (1977): 137–144.

Freedman, William. *"Middle of the Journey:* Lionel Trilling and the Novel of Ideas," in French, Warren, ed. *Forties,* 239–248.

TROCCHI, ALEXANDER (1925–1984)

Cain's Book (1960)
 Bryant, Jerry H. *Open Decision,* 200–202, 225–227.
 Green, Rose Basile. *Italian-American Novel,* 292–295.

TROUBETZKOY, PRINCESS see RIVES, AMÉLIE

TRUMBO, DALTON (1905–1976)

Johnny Got His Gun (1939)
 Waldmeir, Joseph J. *American Novels of the Second World War,* 47–49.

TUCCI, NICCOLÒ (1908–)

Unfinished Funeral (1964)
 Green, Rose Basile. *Italian-American Novel,* 218–219.

TUCKER, BEVERLEY (1784–1851)

Partisan Leader (1836)
 Starke, Catherine Juanita. *Black Portraiture in American Fiction,* 37–40.

TUCKER, GEORGE (1775–1861)

Valley of Shenandoah (1824)
 Yellin, Jean Fagan. *Intricate Knot,* 24–30.

TURPIN, WATERS E. (1910–1968)

O Canaan! (1939)
 Fleming, Robert E. "Overshadowed by Richard Wright: Three Black Chicago Novelists." *NALF* 7 (1973): 75–76, 79.

TUTHILL, LOUISA C. (1799–1879)

Belle, the Blue, and the Bigot (1844)
 Baym, Nina. *Woman's Fiction,* 79–80.
My Wife (1846)
 Baym, Nina. *Woman's Fiction,* 80.

Reality (1856)
Baym, Nina. *Woman's Fiction*, 80–81.

TWAIN, MARK (1835–1910)

Adventures of Huckleberry Finn (1885)

Allen, Walter. *Urgent West*, 172–179.

Banta, Martha. "Rebirth or Revenge: The Endings of *Huckleberry Finn* and *The American*." *MFS* 15 (1969): 191–207.

Barchilon, José and Joel S. Kovel. "*Huckleberry Finn:* A Psychoanalytic Study." *Journal of the American Psychoanalytic Association* 14 (Oct 1966): 799–808. Rpt. as "Last Section: A Psychoanalytic Study," in Gerber, John C., comp. *Merrill Studies in Huckleberry Finn*, 113–120.

Beaver, Harold. "Run, Nigger, Run: *Adventures of Huckleberry Finn* as a Fugitive Slave Narrative." *JAmS* 8 (1974): 339–361.

Beidler, Peter G. "Raft Episode in *Huckleberry Finn*." *Modern Fiction Studies* 14 (Spring 1968): 11–20. Rpt. in Gerber, John C., comp. *Merrill Studies in Huckleberry Finn*, 101–112.

Bellman, Samuel I. "Peripheral (?) Characters in *Huckleberry Finn* and *Catcher in the Rye*." *MTJ* 19.1 (1977–78): 4–6.

Bendixen, Alfred. "Huck Finn and *Pilgrim's Progress*." *MTJ* 18.3 (1976): 21.

Berger, Arthur Asa. "Huck Finn as an Existential Hero: Making Sense of Absurdity." *MTJ* 18.2 (1976): 12–17.

Berkove, Lawrence I. "Free Man of Color in *The Grandissimes* and Works by Harris and Mark Twain." *SoQ* 18.4 (1980): 69–71.

Blair, Walter. *Mark Twain and Huck Finn*. Berkeley, CA: University of California Press, 1960. 334–346. Rpt. as "Raft and Shore: Wish and Belief," in Gerber, John C., comp. *Merrill Studies in Huckleberry Finn*, 90–101.

Blair, Walter. "Tom and Huck," Blair, Walter. *Mark Twain and Huck Finn*. Berkeley, CA: University of California Press, 1960. 71–76. Rpt. in Twain, Mark. *Adventures of Huckleberry Finn*, 436–440.

Branch, Edgar M. "Two Providences: Thematic Form in *Huckleberry Finn*." *College English* 11 (Jan 1950): 188–195. Rpt. in Gerber, John C., comp. *Merrill Studies in Huckleberry Finn*, 67–77.

Briden, Earl F. "Huck's Island Adventure and the Selkirk Legend." *MTJ* 18.3 (1976): 12–14.

Burg, David F. "Another View of *Huckleberry Finn*." *NCF* 29 (1974): 299–319.

Byers, John R., Jr. "Pokeville Preacher's Invitation in *Huckleberry Finn*." *MTJ* 18.4 (1977): 15–16.

Cady, Edwin H. "*Huckleberry Finn* by Common Day," Cady, Edwin H. *Light of Common Day: Realism in American Fiction*. Bloomington, IN: Indiana University Press, 1971. 88–89, 101–119. Rpt. in Twain, Mark. *Adventures of Huckleberry Finn*, 385–398.

Cady, Edwin H. *Light of Common Day*, 101–119.

Carkeet, David. "Dialects in *Huckleberry Finn*." *AL* 51 (1979): 315–332.

Carrington, George C., Jr. *Dramatic Unity of Huckleberry Finn*. Columbus, OH: Ohio State University Press, 1976.

Cecil, L. Moffitt. "Historical Ending of *Adventures of Huckleberry Finn:* How Nigger Jim Was Set Free." *ALR* 13 (1980): 280–283.

Collins, Billy G. "Huckleberry Finn: A Mississippi Moses." *JNT* 5 (1975): 86–104.

Colwell, James L. "Huckleberries and Humans: On the Naming of Huckleberry Finn." *PMLA* 86 (1971): 70–74.

Cox, James M. "Uncomfortable Ending of *Huckleberry Finn*," Cox, James M. *Mark Twain: The Fate of Humor*. Princeton, NJ: Princeton University Press, 1966. 172–184. Rpt. in Twain, Mark. *Adventures of Huckleberry Finn*, 350–358.

Cude, Wilfred. "False as Harlots' Oaths: Dunny Ramsay Looks at Huck Finn," *Studies in Canadian Literature* (Summer, 1977): 164–187. Rpt. in Cude, Wilfred. *Due Sense of Differences*, 85–107.

De Voto, Bernard. "Mark Twain: The Artist as American," De Voto, Bernard. *Mark Twain's America*. New York: Houghton Mifflin Company, 1932. 308, 310–320. Rpt. in Twain, Mark. *Adventures of Huckleberry Finn*, 300–309.

De Voto, Bernard. *Mark Twain's America*. New York: Little, Brown, 1920. 310–321. Rpt. as "Breadth of *Huckleberry Finn*," in Gerber, John C., comp. *Merrill Studies in Huckleberry Finn*, 32–41.

Downs, Robert B. *Famous American Books*, 163–171.

Duncan, Jeffrey L. "Empirical and the Ideal in Mark Twain." *PMLA* 95 (1980): 203–204, 206–208.

Dyson, A. E. "*Huckleberry Finn* and the Whole Truth," in Dyson, A. E. *Crazy Fabric: Essays in Irony*. New York: St. Martins Press, 1965. Rpt. in Schmitter, Dean Morgan, ed. *Mark Twain*, 95–107.

Eliot, T. S. "Introduction to *Huckleberry Finn*." Twain, Mark. *Adventures of Huckleberry Finn*. London: Cresset Press, 1950. vii–xvi. Rpt. in Twain, Mark. *Adventures of Huckleberry Finn*, 328–335.

Eliot, T. S. "Introduction to *Huckleberry Finn*." Twain, Mark. *Adventures of Huckleberry Finn*. New York: Chanticleer, 1950. vii–xvi. Rpt. in Kesterson, David B. ed. *Critics on Mark Twain*, 62–69.

Ellison, Ralph. "Change the Joke and Slip the Yoke." *Partisan Review* 25.2 (Spring 1958): 212–222. Rpt. in Twain, Mark. *Adventures of Huckleberry Finn*, 421–422.

Eschholz, Paul A. "Mark Twain and the Language of Gesture." *MTJ* 17.1 (1973–74): 6–7.

Ferguson, DeLancey. "Huck Finn Aborning." *Colophon* 3 New Series (Spring 1938): 171–180. Rpt. in Twain, Mark. *Adventures of Huckleberry Finn*, 309–317.

Fetterley, Judith. "Disenchantment: Tom Sawyer in *Huckleberry Finn*." *PMLA* 87 (1972): 69–74.

Fetterley, Judith. "Disenchantment: Tom Sawyer in *Huckleberry Finn*." *PMLA* 87.1 (January 1972): 69–74. Rpt. in Twain, Mark. *Adventures of Huckleberry Finn*, 440–450.

Fiedler, Leslie. "Accommodation and Transcendence," in Fiedler, Leslie. *Love and Death in the American Novel*. New York: Stein and Day, 1960. 575–591. Rpt. in Gerber, John C., comp. *Merrill Studies in Huckleberry Finn*, 78–90.

Fiedler, Leslie. "Come Back to the Raft Ag'in, Huck Honey," Fiedler, Leslie. *Collected Essays of Leslie Fiedler*. Volume One. New York: Stein and Day, 1971. 142–151. Rpt. in Twain, Mark. *Adventures of Huckleberry Finn*, 413–420.

Fite, Montgomery. "Mark Twain's Naming of Huckleberry Finn." *ANQ* 13 (1975): 140–141.

Foner, Philip S. *Mark Twain Social Critic*, 266–272.

Frank, Albert J. von . "Huck Finn and the Flight from Maturity." *SAF* 7 (1979): 1–15.

Frederick, John T. *Darkened Sky*, 153.

Galligan, Edward L. "True Comedians and False: *Don Quixote* and *Huckleberry Finn.*" *SewR* 86 (1978): 76–83.

Gaston, Georg Meri Akri. "Function of Tom Sawyer in *Huckleberry Finn.*" *MissQ* 27 (1973–74): 33–39.

Gibson, William M. *Art of Mark Twain*, 101–131.

Goede, William. "On Lower Frequencies: The Buried Men in Wright and Ellison." *MFS* 15 (1969): 483–484.

Goodyear, Russell H. "Huck Finn's Anachronistic Double Eagles." *ANQ* 10 (1971): 39.

Harris, Susan K. " 'This Peace, This Deep Contentment': Images of Temporal Freedom in the Writings of Mark Twain." *ELWIU* 7 (1980): 205–206.

Harrison, Stanley R. "Mark Twain's Requiem for the Past." *MTJ* 16.2 (1972): 8–10.

Harwood, C. Edwin. "Twain's *Huckleberry Finn*, Chapter XIV." *Expl* 28 (1969): Item 36.

Hauck, Richard Boyd. *Cheerful Nihilism*, 147–151.

Hoffman, Daniel G. "Black Magic—and White—in *Huckleberry Finn.*" Hoffman, Daniel G. *Form and Fable in American Fiction*. New York: Oxford University Press, 1961. 317–342. Rpt. in Twain, Mark. *Adventures of Huckleberry Finn*, 423–436.

Hoy, James F. "Grangerford-Shepherdson Feud in *Huckleberry Finn.*" *MTJ* 18.1 (1975–76): 19–20.

Kaplan, Harold. *Democratic Humanism and American Literature*, 225–252.

Kerr, Howard. *Mediums, and Spirit-Rappers, and Roaring Radicals*, 171–177.

King, Bruce. "*Huckleberry Finn.*" *Ariel* 2.4 (1971): 69–77.

King, Bruce. "*Huckleberry Finn.*" *Ariel* 2 (Oct 1971): 69–77. Rpt. in Schmitter, Dean Morgan, ed. *Mark Twain*, 109–116.

Klotman, Phyllis Rauch. *Another Man Gone*, 39–40.

Kravec, Maureen T. "Huckleberry Finn's Aristocratic Ancestry." *MTJ* 18.2 (1976): 19–20.

Kuhlmann, Susan. *Knave, Fool, and Genius*, 63–68.

Lewis, Stuart. "Twain's *Huckleberry Finn*, Chapter XIV." *Expl* 30 (1972): Item 61.

Lynn, Kenneth S. *Visions of America*, 53–59.

Lynn, Kenneth S. "You Can't Go Home Again," Lynn, Kenneth S. *Mark Twain and Southwestern Humor*. Boston: Little, Brown & Co., 1959. Sections 3, 7, and 8 of Chapter 9. Rpt. in Twain, Mark. *Adventures of Huckleberry Finn*, 398–413.

McCullough, Joseph B. "Uses of the Bible in *Huckleberry Finn.*" *MTJ* 19.3 (1978–79): 2–3.

McMahan, Elizabeth E. "Money Motif: Economic Implications in *Huckleberry Finn.*" *MTJ* 15.4 (1971): 5–10.

McNamara, Eugene. "*Adventures of Huckleberry Finn:* Chapter One as Microcosm." *MTJ* 18.4 (1977): 17–18.

Malin, Irving. "American Gothic Images." *Mosaic* 6.3 (1973): 169–170.

Marks, Barry A. "Huck Finn Swindle." *WAL* 14 (1979): 121–132.

Marx, Leo. "Mr. Eliot, Mr. Trilling, and *Huckleberry Finn.*" *American Scholar* 22.4 (Autumn 1953): 423–440. Rpt. in Twain, Mark. *Adventures of Huckleberry Finn*, 336–349.

Michelson, Bruce. "Huck and the Games of the World." *ALR* 13 (1980): 108–119.

Miller, Lee. "Huckleberries and Humans." *PMLA* 87 (1972): 314.

Mulqueen, James E. "Huck Finn, Imagist Poet." *CEA* 37.3 (1975): 14–15.

Oriard, Michael. "From Tom Sawyer to Huckleberry Finn: Toward Godly Play." *SAF* 8 (1980): 187–200.

Ousby, Ian. *Reader's Guide to Fifty American Novels*, 99–101.

Pearce, Roy Harvey. " 'The End. Yours Truly, Huck Finn': Postscript." *Modern Language Quarterly* 24.3 (September 1963): 253–256. Rpt. in Twain, Mark. *Adventures of Huckleberry Finn*, 358–362.

Pettit, Arthur G. *Mark Twain & the South*, 83–92, 109–122.

Piacentino, Edward J. "Significance of Pap's Drunken Diatribe against the Government in *Huckleberry Finn*." *MTJ* 19.4 (1979): 19–21.

Raban, Jonathan. *Mark Twain: Huckleberry Finn*. London: Edward Arnold, 1979.

Rodnon, Stewart. "*Adventures of Huckleberry Finn* and *Invisible Man:* Thematic and Structural Comparisons." *NALF* 4 (1970): 45–51.

Rose, Alan Henry. *Demonic Vision*, 87–96.

Rulon, Curt M. "Geographical Delimitation of the Dialect Areas in *The Adventures Huckleberry Finn*." *MTJ* 14.1 (1969): 9–12.

Scheick, William J. "Spunk of a Rabbit: An Allusion in *The Adventures of Huckleberry Finn*." *MTJ* 15.4 (1971): 14–16.

Schmitz, Neil. "Paradox of Liberation in *Huckleberry Finn*." *TSLL* 13 (1971): 125–136.

Schmitz, Neil. "Twain, *Huckleberry Finn*, and the Reconstruction." *AmerS* 12.1 (1971): 59–67.

Shear, Walter. "Games People Play in *Huckleberry Finn*." *MidQ* 20 (1979): 378–393.

Shockley, Martin Staples. "Structure of *Huckleberry Finn*." *South-Central Bulletin* 20 (Winter 1960): 3–10. Rpt. in Kesterson, David B. ed. *Critics on Mark Twain*, 70–80.

Skerry, Philip J. "*Adventures of Huckleberry Finn* and *Intruder in the Dust:* Two Conflicting Myths of the American Experience." *BallS* 13.1 (1972): 4–13.

Sloane, David E. E. *Mark Twain as Literary Comedian*, 128–145.

Smith, Henry Nash. "Sound Heart and a Deformed Conscience," Smith, Henry Nash. *Mark Twain: Development of a Writer*. Cambridge, MA: Belknap Press, 1962. 113–137. Rpt in Gerber, John C., comp. *Merrill Studies in Huckleberry Finn*, 43–67.

Smith, Henry Nash. "Sound Heart and a Deformed Conscience," Smith, Henry Nash. *Mark Twain: Development of a Writer*. Cambridge, MA: Belknap Press, 1962. 113–114, 118–122. Rpt. in Kesterson, David B. ed. *Critics on Mark Twain*, 82–86.

Smith, Henry Nash. "Sound Heart and a Deformed Conscience," Smith, Henry Nash. *Mark Twain: Development of a Writer*. Cambridge, MA: Belknap Press, 1962. 113–137. Rpt. in Twain, Mark. *Adventures of Huckleberry Finn*, 363–385.

Spengemann, William C. *Adventurous Muse*, 228–233.

Starke, Catherine Juanita. *Black Portraiture in American Fiction*, 175–180.

Stein, Allen F. "Return to Phelps Farm: *Huckleberry Finn* and the Old Southwestern Framing Device." *MissQ* 24 (1971): 111–116.

Taylor, Robert, Jr. "Sounding the Trumpets of Defiance: Mark Twain and Norman Mailer." *MTJ* 16.3 (1972): 6–8.

Trachtenberg, Alan. "Form of Freedom in *Adventures of Huckleberry Finn*." *SoR* 6 (1970): 954–971.

Trensky, Anne. "Bad Boy in Nineteenth-Century American Fiction." *GR* 27 (1973): 509–510.

Trilling, Lionel. "Form and Symbol: The River and the Shore," from "Introduction to *Adventures of Huckleberry Finn*." Twain, Mark. *Adventures of Huckleberry Finn*. Rinehart Editions. New York: Holt, Rinehart and Winston, Inc., 1948. Also collected in Trilling, Lionel. *Liberal Imagination: Essays on Literature and Society*. Garden City, NY: Doubleday, 1950. Rpt. in Twain, Mark. *Adventures of Huckleberry Finn*, 318–328.

Wadlington, Warwick. *Confidence Game in American Literature*, 241–284.

Walters, Thomas N. "Twain's Finn and Alger's Gilman: Picaresque Counter-Directions." *MarkR* 3 (1972): 53–58.

Weaver, Thomas and Merline A. Williams. "Mark Twain's Jim: Identity as an Index to Cultural Attitudes." *ALR* 13 (1980): 19–30.

Wells, Anna M. and Judith Fetterley. "Huck Finn, Tom Sawyer, and Samuel Clemens." *PMLA* 87 (1972): 1130–1131.

Werge, Thomas. "Mark Twain and the Fall of Adam." *MTJ* 15.2 (1970): 8–13.

Wexman, Virginia. "Role of Structure in *Tom Sawyer* and *Huckleberry Finn*." *ALR* 6 (1973): 3–9.

Wilson, James D. "*Adventures of Huckleberry Finn:* From Abstraction to Humanity." *SoR* 10 (1974): 80–93.

Young, Philip. *Three Bags Full*, 136–153.

Adventures of Tom Sawyer (1876)

Byers, John R., Jr. "Hannibal Summer: The Framework of *The Adventures of Tom Sawyer*." *SAF* 8 (1980): 81–88.

Dillingham, William B. "Setting and Theme in *Tom Sawyer*." *Mark Twain Journal* 12 (Spring 1964): 6–8. Rpt. in Kesterson, David B. ed. *Critics on Mark Twain*, 87–91.

Feeney, Joseph J., S.J. "Darkness at Morning: The Bitterness in Mark Twain's Early Novel *Tom Sawyer*." *MTJ* 19.3 (1978–79): 4–5.

Fetterley, Judith. "Sanctioned Rebel." *Studies in the Novel* 3 (Fall 1971): 293–304. Rpt. in Kesterson, David B. ed. *Critics on Mark Twain*, 92–102.

Gibson, William M. *Art of Mark Twain*, 98–101.

Howell, Elmo. "In Defense of Tom Sawyer." *MTJ* 15.1 (1970): 17–21.

Howell, Elmo. "Tom Sawyer's Mock Funeral: A Note on Mark Twain's Religion." *MTJ* 16.3 (1972): 15–16.

Karpowitz, Steven. "Tom Sawyer and Mark Twain: Fictional Women and Real in the Play of Conscience with the Imagination." *L&P* 23 (1973): 5–11.

Oriard, Michael. "From Tom Sawyer to Huckleberry Finn: Toward Godly Play." *SAF* 8 (1980): 184–187.

Ousby, Ian. *Reader's Guide to Fifty American Novels*, 94–96.

Powers, Lyall H. "Sweet Success of Twain's Tom." *DR* 53 (1973): 310–323.

Rose, Alan Henry. *Demonic Vision*, 72–85.

Sloane, David E. E. *Mark Twain as Literary Comedian*, 114–117.

Smith, Henry Nash. "*Tom Sawyer*," in Smith, Henry Nash. *Mark Twain: The Development of a Writer*. Cambridge, MA: Belknap Press, 1962. Rpt. in Schmitter, Dean Morgan, ed. *Mark Twain*, 85–94.

Towers, Tom H. " 'I Never Thought We Might Want to Come Back': Strategies of Transcendence in *Tom Sawyer*." *MFS* 21 (1975): 509–520.

Wexman, Virginia. "Role of Structure in *Tom Sawyer* and *Huckleberry Finn*." *ALR* 6 (1973): 1–3.

Wolff, Cynthia Griffin. "*Adventures of Tom Sawyer:* A Nightmare Vision of American Boyhood." *MR* 21 (1980): 637–652.

American Claimant (1892)
Sloane, David E. E. *Mark Twain as Literary Comedian*, 169–177.

Connecticut Yankee in King Arthur's Court (1889)
Aaron, Daniel. *Unwritten War*, 140–145.

Attebery, Brian. *Fantasy Tradition in American Literature*, 79–81.

Baldanza, Frank. "*Connecticut Yankee*," in Baldanza, Frank. *Mark Twain: An Introduction and Interpretation.* New York: Barnes and Noble, 1961. Rpt. in Schmitter, Dean Morgan, ed. *Mark Twain*, 117–121.

Berzon, Judith R. *Neither White Nor Black*, 40.

Butcher, Philip. " 'The Godfathership' of *A Connecticut Yankee*." *CLAJ* 12 (1969): 189–198.

Carter, Everett. "Meaning of *A Connecticut Yankee*." *AL* 50 (1978): 418–440.

Duncan, Jeffrey L. "Empirical and the Ideal in Mark Twain." *PMLA* 95 (1980): 204–206, 208–209.

Eschholz, Paul A. "Mark Twain and the Language of Gesture." *MTJ* 17.1 (1973–74): 6, 7.

Fetterley, Judith. "Yankee Showman and Reformer: The Character of Mark Twain's Hank Morgan." *TSLL* 14 (1972): 667–680.

Foner, Philip S. *Mark Twain Social Critic*, 136–152.

Frederick, John T. *Darkened Sky*, 156–160.

Girgus, Sam B. "Conscience in Connecticut: Civilization and Its Discontents in Twain's Camelot." *NEQ* 51 (1978): 547–560.

Green, Martin. *Dreams of Adventure, Deeds of Empire*, 236–244.

Griffith, Clark. "Merlin's Grin: From 'Tom' to 'Huck' in *A Connecticut Yankee*." *NEQ* 48 (1975): 28–46.

Guttmann, Allen. "Mark Twain's *Connecticut Yankee:* Affirmation of the Vernacular Tradition?" *New England Quarterly* 33 (June 1960): 232–237. Rpt. in Kesterson, David B. ed. *Critics on Mark Twain*, 103–106.

Hansen, Chadwick. "Once and Future Boss: Mark Twain's Yankee." *NCF* 28 (1973): 62–73.

Hauck, Richard Boyd. *Cheerful Nihilism*, 133–135, 137–138, 151–156.

Henderson, Harry B. *Versions of the Past*, 175–197.

Kegel, Paul L. "Henry Adams and Mark Twain: Two Views of Medievalism." *MTJ* 15.3 (1970): 11–21.

Ketterer, David. *New Worlds for Old*, 213–232.

Klass, Philip. "Innocent in Time: Mark Twain in King Arthur's Court." *Extrapolation* 16 (1974): 17–31.

Kuhlmann, Susan. *Knave, Fool, and Genius*, 68–71.

Ousby, Ian. *Reader's Guide to Fifty American Novels*, 104–106.

Rogers, Rodney O. "Twain, Taine, and Lecky: The Genesis of a Passage in *A Connecticut Yankee*." *MLQ* 34 (1973): 436–447.

Schroth, Evelyn. "Mark Twain's Literary Dialect in *A Connecticut Yankee*." *MTJ* 19.2 (1978): 26–29.

Sloane, David E. E. *Mark Twain as Literary Comedian*, 146–167.

Spengemann, William C. *Adventurous Muse*, 235–239.

Spofford, William K. "Mark Twain's Connecticut Yankee: An Ignoramus Nevertheless." *MTJ* 15.2 (1970): 15–18.

Taylor, Robert, Jr. "Sounding the Trumpets of Defiance: Mark Twain and Norman Mailer." *MTJ* 16.3 (1972): 8–9.

Turnbull, Deborah Berger. "Hank Morgan as American Individualist." *MTJ* 20.2 (1980): 19–21.

Wilson, James D. "Hank Morgan, Philip Traum and Milton's Satan." *MTJ* 16.4 (1973): 20–21.

Winters, Donald E. "Utopianism of Survival: Bellamy's *Looking Backward* and Twain's *A Connecticut Yankee*." *AmerS* 21.1. (1980): 28–30, 31–33, 34–35, 36–37.

Gilded Age (1873)

Coard, Robert L. "Mark Twain's *The Gilded Age* and Sinclair Lewis's *Babbitt*." *MidQ* 13 (1972): 319–333.

Cohn, Jan. "Women as Superfluous Characters in American Realism and Naturalism." *SAF* 1 (1973): 158.

Crowley, John W. "Note on *The Gilded Age*." *ELN* 10 (1972): 116–118.

Foner, Philip S. *Mark Twain Social Critic*, 91–113.

French, Bryant M. "James Hammond Trumbull's Alternative Chapter: Mottoes for *The Gilded Age*." *PQ* 50 (1971): 271–280.

Krauth, Leland. "Mark Twain: At Home in the Gilded Age." *GR* 28 (1974): 105–113.

Kuhlmann, Susan. *Knave, Fool, and Genius*, 54–55.

Mixon, Wayne. "Mark Twain, *The Gilded Age*, and the New South Movement." *SoHR* 7 (1973): 403–408.

Schleiner, Louise. "Romance Motifs in Three Novels of Mark Twain." *CLS* 13 (1976): 335–338.

Sloane, David E. E. *Mark Twain as Literary Comedian*, 104–114.

Taylor, Robert, Jr. "Sounding the Trumpets of Defiance: Mark Twain and Norman Mailer," *MTJ* 16.3 (1972): 5–6.

Prince and the Pauper (1881)

Berzon, Judith R. *Neither White Nor Black*, 37–38.

Foner, Philip S. *Mark Twain Social Critic*, 134–136.

Kegel, Paul L. "Henry Adams and Mark Twain: Two Views of Medievalism." *MTJ* 15.3 (1970): 11–21.

Schleiner, Louise. "Romance Motifs in Three Novels of Mark Twain." *CLS* 13 (1976): 338–342.

Sloane, David E. E. *Mark Twain as Literary Comedian*, 117–127.

Taylor, Robert, Jr. "Sounding the Trumpets of Defiance: Mark Twain and Norman Mailer." *MTJ* 16.3 (1972): 5–6.

Towers, Tom H. "*Prince and the Pauper:* Mark Twain's Once and Future King." *SAF* 6 (1978): 193–202.

Tragedy of Pudd'nhead Wilson (1894)

Alsen, Eberhard. "Pudd'nhead Wilson's Fight for Popularity and Power." *WAL* 7 (1972): 135–143.

Andrews, William L. "Miscegenation in the Late Nineteenth-Century American Novel." *SoHR* 13 (1979): 19–20.

Aspiz, Harold. "Other Half of Pudd'nhead's Dog." *MTJ* 17.4 (1975): 10–11.

Berzon, Judith R. *Neither White Nor Black*, 40–48, 119, 121–122.

Brand, John M. "Incipient Wilderness: A Study of *Pudd'nhead Wilson*." *WAL* 7 (1972): 125–134.

Brand, John M. "Incipient Wilderness: A Study of *Pudd'nhead Wilson.*" *Western American Literature* 8 (Summer 1972): 125–134. Rpt. in Twain, Mark. *Pudd'nhead Wilson and Those Extraordinary Twins*, 315–324.

Briden, Earl F. "Idiots First, Then Juries: Legal Metaphors in Mark Twain's *Pudd'nhead Wilson.*" *TSLL* 20 (1978): 169–180.

Briden, Earl F. "*Pudd'nhead Wilson* and the Bandit's Tale in *Gil Blas.*" *MTJ* 19.1 (1977–78): 16–17.

Brodwin, Stanley. "Blackness and the Adamic Myth in Mark Twain's *Pudd'nhead Wilson.*" *TSLL* 15 (1973): 167–176.

Brodwin, Stanley. "Blackness and the Adamic Myth in Mark Twain's *Pudd'nhead Wilson.*" *Texas Studies in Literature and Language* 15 (1973–74): 167–176. Rpt. in Twain, Mark. *Pudd'nhead Wilson and Those Extraordinary Twins*, 332–342.

Cox, James M. "Ironic Stranger," Cox, James M. *Mark Twain: The Fate of Humor.* Princeton, NJ: Princeton University Press, 1966. 222–246. Rpt. in Twain, Mark. *Pudd'nhead Wilson and Those Extraordinary Twins*, 259–267.

Cronin, Frank C. "Ultimate Perspective in *Pudd'nhead Wilson.*" *MTJ* 16.1 (1972): 14–16.

De Voto, Bernard. "Mark Twain's Presentation of Slavery," De Voto, Bernard. *Mark Twain's America.* Boston: Little, Brown and Company, 1932. 293–294. Rpt. in Twain, Mark. *Pudd'nhead Wilson and Those Extraordinary Twins*, 219–220.

Eschholz, Paul A. "Mark Twain and the Language of Gesture." *MTJ* 17.1 (1973–74): 7–8.

Eschholz, Paul A. "Twain's *The Tragedy of Pudd'nhead Wilson.*" *Expl* 31 (1973): Item 67.

Fiedler, Leslie. " 'As Free as Any Cretur . . .'." *New Republic* 133.7–8 (Aug 15 and 22, 1955): 130–139. Rpt. in Twain, Mark. *Pudd'nhead Wilson and Those Extraordinary Twins*, 220–229.

Fisher, Marvin and Michael Elliott. "*Pudd'nhead Wilson:* Half a Dog Is Worse Than None." *SoR* 8 (1972): 533–547.

Fisher, Marvin and Michael Elliott. "*Pudd'nhead Wilson:* Half a Dog Is Worse than None." *Southern Review* 8 n.s. (Summer 1972): 3, 533–547. Rpt. in Twain, Mark. *Pudd'nhead Wilson and Those Extraordinary Twins*, 304–315.

Foner, Philip S. *Mark Twain Social Critic*, 273–277.

Ford, Thomas W. "*Pudd'nhead Wilson*'s Calendar." *MTJ* 19.2 (1978): 15–19.

Gargano, James W. "*Pudd'nhead Wilson:* Mark Twain as Genial Satan." *SAQ* 74 (1975): 365–375.

Gerber, John C. "*Pudd'nhead Wilson* as Fabulation." *Studies in American Humor* 2.1 (April 1975): 21–31. Rpt. in Twain, Mark. *Pudd'nhead Wilson and Those Extraordinary Twins*, 360–370.

Gibson, William M. *Art of Mark Twain*, 158–176.

Haines, James B. "Of Dogs and Men: A Symbolic Variation on the Twin Motif in *Pudd'nhead Wilson.*" *MTJ* 18.3 (1976): 14–17.

Hogan, Jerry B. "*Pudd'nhead Wilson:* Whose Tragedy Is It?" *MTJ* 20.2 (1980): 9–12.

Jehlen, Myra. *Class and Character in Faulkner's South*, 82–83.

Kolin, Philip C. "Mark Twain, Aristotle, and *Pudd'nhead Wilson.*" *MTJ* 15.2 (1970): 1–4.

Leavis, F. R. "Mark Twain's Neglected Classic: The Moral Astringency of *Pudd'n-*

head Wilson." *Commentary* 21 (Feb 1956): 133–136. Rpt. in Kesterson, David B. ed. *Critics on Mark Twain*, 108–112.

Leavis, F. R. "Mark Twain's Neglected Classic: The Moral Astringency of *Pudd'n-head Wilson*." *Commentary* 21 (Feb 1956): 128–136. Rpt. in Twain, Mark. *Pudd-'nhead Wilson and Those Extraordinary Twins*, 229–242.

Lynn, Kenneth S. *Visions of America*, 204–205.

McCullough, Joseph B. "*Pudd'nhead Wilson:* A Search for Identity." *MTJ* 18.4 (1977): 1–6.

Malin, Irving. "American Gothic Images." *Mosaic* 6.3 (1973): 170–171.

Morsberger, Robert E. "*Pudd'nhead Wilson* and the Iron Mask." *MarkR* 7 (1978): 25–27.

Ousby, Ian. *Reader's Guide to Fifty American Novels*, 109–112.

Pettit, Arthur G. "Black and White Curse: *Pudd'nhead Wilson* and Miscegenation," Pettit, Arthur G. *Mark Twain and the South*. Lexington, KY: University Press of Kentucky, 1974. 139–155, 207–210. Rpt. in Twain, Mark. *Pudd'nhead Wilson and Those Extraordinary Twins*, 346–360.

Pettit, Arthur G. *Mark Twain & the South*, 141–155.

Regan, Robert. "Unpromising Hero," Regan, Robert. *Unpromising Heroes: Mark Twain and His Characters*. Berkeley: University of California Press, 1966. 207–219. 240–241. Rpt. in Twain, Mark. *Pudd'nhead Wilson and Those Extraordinary Twins*, 268–274.

Rose, Alan Henry. *Demonic Vision*, 97–100.

Ross, Michael L. "Mark Twain's *Pudd'nhead Wilson:* Dawson's Landing and the Ladder of Nobility." *Novel* 6 (1973): 244–256.

Schleiner, Louise. "Romance Motifs in Three Novels of Mark Twain." *CLS* 13 (1976): 342–344.

Sloane, David E. E. *Mark Twain as Literary Comedian*, 177–188.

Smith, Henry Nash. "*Pudd'nhead Wilson* as Criticism of the Dominant Culture," Smith, Henry Nash. *Mark Twain: The Development of a Writer*. Cambridge, MA: Belknap Press, 1962. 173–183, 207. Rpt. in Twain, Mark. *Pudd'nhead Wilson and Those Extraordinary Twins*, 247–254.

Spangler, George M. "*Pudd'nhead Wilson:* A Parable of Property." *American Literature* 42 (March 1970): 1, 28–37. Rpt. in Twain, Mark. *Pudd'nhead Wilson and Those Extraordinary Twins*, 295–303.

Turner, Arlin. "Mark Twain and the South: *Pudd'nhead Wilson*." From "Mark Twain and the South: An Affair of Love and Anger." *Southern Review* 4 n.s. (April 1968): 493–519. Rpt. in Schmitter, Dean Morgan, ed. *Mark Twain*, 123–132.

Turner, Arlin. "Mark Twain and the South: *Pudd'nhead Wilson*." From "Mark Twain and the South: An Affair of Love and Anger." *Southern Review* 4 n.s. (April 1968): 493–519. Rpt. in Twain, Mark. *Pudd'nhead Wilson and Those Extraordinary Twins*, 274–282.

Vanderwerken, David L. "Triumph of Medievalism in *Pudd'nhead Wilson*." *MTJ* 18.4 (1977): 7–11.

Wheelock, C. Webster. "Point of Pudd'nhead's Half-A-Dog Joke." *ANQ* 8 (1970): 150–151.

Wiggins, Robert A. "Flawed Structure of *Pudd'nhead Wilson*," Wiggins, Robert A. *Mark Twain: Jackleg Novelist*. Seattle: University of Washington Press, 1964. 105–112, 128. Rpt. in Twain, Mark. *Pudd'nhead Wilson and Those Extraordinary Twins*, 255–259.

Williams, Murial B. "Unmasking of Meaning: A Study of the Twins in *Pudd'nhead Wilson*." *MissQ* 33 (1979–80): 39–53.

Wood, Barry. "Narrative Action and Structural Symmetry in *Pudd'nhead Wilson*," in Twain, Mark. *Pudd'nhead Wilson and Those Extraordinary Twins*, 370–381.

TYLER, ANNE (1941–)

Earthly Possessions (1977)

Nesanovich, Stella. "Individual in the Family: Anne Tyler's *Searching for Caleb* and *Earthly Possessions*." *SoR* 14 (1978): 173–176.

Searching for Caleb (1976)

Nesanovich, Stella. "Individual in the Family: Anne Tyler's *Searching for Caleb* and *Earthly Possessions*." *SoR* 14 (1978): 170–173.

TYLER, PARKER (1907–1974)

Young and Evil (1933)

Austen, Roger. *Playing the Game*, 59–62.

TYLER, ROYALL (1757–1826)

Algerine Captive (1797)

Spengemann, William C. *Adventurous Muse*, 120–138.
Stein, Roger B. "Pulled Out of the Bay: American Fiction in the Eighteenth Century." *SAF* 2 (1974): 28–30.

UPCHURCH, BOYD see BOYD, JOHN

UPDIKE, JOHN (1932–)

Centaur (1963)

Burchard, Rachael C. *John Updike, Yea Sayings*, 53–70.
Detweiler, Robert. *John Updike*, 80–97.
Galloway, David D. *Absurd Hero in American Fiction*, 40–49.
Gindin, James. *Harvest of a Quiet Eye*, 343–344.
Hamilton, Alice and Kenneth. *Elements of John Updike*, 156–180.
Hendin, Josephine. *Vulnerable People*, 92–93.
Hill, John S. "Quest for Belief: Theme in the Novels of John Updike." *SoHR* 3 (1969): 168–171.
Hoag, Ronald Wesley. "*Centaur:* What Cures George Caldwell?" *SAF* 8 (1980): 88–98.
Hunt, George. *John Updike and the three great secret things*, 49–80.
Kort, Wesley A. *Shriven Selves*, 64–89.
Landor, Mikhail. "Centaur-Novels," in Proffer, Carl R., ed. and trans. *Soviet Criticism of American Literature in the Sixties*, 47–48.
LeClair, Thomas. "Death and Black Humor." *Crit* 17.1 (1975): 7–9.
Levidova, Inna. "John Updike's *The Centaur* in Russian," in Proffer, Carl R., ed. and trans. *Soviet Criticism of American Literature in the Sixties*, 190–196.
Markle, Joyce B. *Fighters and Lovers*, 61–83.
Mellard, James M. "Novel as Lyric Elegy: The Mode of Updike's *The Centaur*." *TSLL* 21 (1979): 112–127.

Myers, David. "Questing Fear: Christian Allegory in John Updike's *The Centaur*." *TCL* 17 (1971): 73–82.

Oates, Joyce Carol. "Updike's American Comedies." *MFS* 21 (1975): 462–464, 466, 470–471.

Oates, Joyce Carol. "Updike's American Comedies." *Modern Fiction Studies* 21.3 (Fall 1975): 459–472. Rpt. in Thorburn, David and Howard Eiland, eds. *John Updike*, 56–59, 61–62, 65–68.

Petter, H. "John Updike's Metaphoric Novels." *ES* 50 (1969): 199, 200, 202–206.

Price, Martin. "A Note on Character in *The Centaur*," in Thorburn, David and Howard Eiland, eds. *John Updike*, 132–133.

Rupp, Richard H. *Celebration in Postwar American Fiction*, 51–54.

Samuels, Charles Thomas. *John Updike*, 15–19.

Schopen, Bernard A. "Faith, Morality, and the Novels of John Updike." *TCL* 24 (1978): 528, 529–530.

Strandberg, Victory. "John Updike and the Changing of the Gods." *Mosaic* 12.1 (1978): 164, 166, 167–169, 172, 174–175.

Tanner, Tony. *City of Words*, 284–287.

Taylor, Larry E. "*Centaur:* Epic Paean and Pastoral Lament," in Taylor, Larry E. *Pastoral and Anti-Pastoral Patterns in John Updike's Fiction*. Carbondale, IL: Southern Illinois University Press, 1971. 86–101. Rpt. in Thorburn, David and Howard Eiland, eds. *John Updike*, 117–131.

Taylor, Larry E. *Pastoral and Anti-Pastoral Patterns in John Updike's Fiction*, 86–101.

Uphaus, Suzanne. "*Centaur:* Updike's Mock Epic." *JNT* 7 (1977): 24–36.

Uphaus, Suzanne Henning. *John Updike*, 32–43.

Vargo, Edward P. "Necessity of Myth in Updike's *The Centaur*." *PMLA* 88 (1973): 452–460.

Vargo, Edward P. *Rainstorms and Fire*, 81–103.

Vickery, John B. "*Centaur:* Myth, History, and Narrative." *MFS* 20 (1974): 29–43.

Coup (1978)

Hunt, George. *John Updike and the three great secret things*, 195–206.

McGill, Deborah. "Boy's Life." *Harpers* (Jan 1979): 87–89. Rpt. in Thorburn, David and Howard Eiland, eds. *John Updike*, 162–166.

Towers, Robert. "Updike in Africa." *New York Times Book Review* (10 Dec 1978): 1, 55. Rpt. in Thorburn, David and Howard Eiland, eds. *John Updike*, 157–161.

Uphaus, Suzanne Henning. *John Updike*, 110–120.

Couples (1968)

Backscheider, Paula and Nick Backscheider. "Updike's *Couples:* Squeak in the Night." *MFS* 20 (1974): 45–52.

Burchard, Rachael C. *John Updike, Yea Sayings*, 89–132.

Detweiler, Robert. *John Updike*, 130–142.

Donald, Miles. *American Novel in the Twentieth Century*, 91–106.

Doody, Terence A. "Updike's Idea of Reification." *ConL* 20 (1979): 215–217.

Eiland, Howard. "Play in *Couples*," in Thorburn, David and Howard Eiland, eds. *John Updike*, 69–83.

Gindin, James. *Harvest of a Quiet Eye*, 344–346.

Gindin, James. "Megalotopia and the WASP Backlash: The Fiction of Mailer and Updike." *CentR* 15 (1971): 46–50, 51–52.

Hamilton, Alice and Kenneth. *Elements of John Updike*, 215–242.

Hill, John S. "Quest for Belief: Theme in the Novels of John Updike." *SoHR* 3 (1969): 172–174.

Hunt, George. *John Updike and the three great secret things*, 117–138, 147–152.

Lodge, David. *Novelist at the Crossroads*, 237–244.

Lodge, David. "Post-Pill Paradise Lost: *Couples*," in Lodge, David. *Novelist at the Crossroads*. Ithaca, NY: Cornell University Press, 1971. 237–244. Rpt. in Thorburn, David and Howard Eiland, eds. *John Updike*, 84–92.

McKenzie, Alan T. " 'A Craftsman's Intimate Satisfactions': The Parlor Games in *Couples*." *MFS* 20 (1974): 53–58.

Markle, Joyce B. *Fighters and Lovers*, 106–145.

Masinton, Martha and Charles G. Masinton. "Second-class Citizenship: The Status of Women in Contemporary American Fiction," in Springer, Marlene, ed. *What Manner of Woman*, 300, 304–306.

Mendelson, M. O. "Social Criticism in the Works of Bellow, Updike, and Cheever," in Proffer, Carl R., ed. and trans. *Soviet Criticism of American Literature in the Sixties*, 67–70.

Oates, Joyce Carol. "Updike's American Comedies." *MFS* 21 (1975): 461, 467–468.

Oates, Joyce Carol. "Updike's American Comedies." *Modern Fiction Studies* 21.3 (Fall 1975): 459–472. Rpt. in Thorburn, David and Howard Eiland, eds. *John Updike*, 55, 62–64.

Petter, H. "John Updike's Metaphoric Novels." *ES* 50 (1969): 199, 200–201, 202, 203–206.

Plagman, Linda M. "Eros and Agape: The Opposition in Updike's *Couples*." *Renascence* 28 (1976): 83–93.

Samuels, Charles Thomas. *John Updike*, 34–37.

Schopen, Bernard A. "Faith, Morality, and the Novels of John Updike." *TCL* 24 (1978): 533.

Sharrock, Roger. "Singles and Couples: Hemingway's *A Farewell to Arms* and Updike's *Couples*." *Ariel* 4.4 (1973): 21–43.

Strandberg, Victory. "John Updike and the Changing of the Gods." *Mosaic* 12.1 (1978): 159, 163–164, 166–167, 172.

Tanner, Tony. *City of Words*, 288–294.

Taylor, Larry E. *Pastoral and Anti-Pastoral Patterns in John Updike's Fiction*, 122–128.

Uphaus, Suzanne Henning. *John Updike*, 55–68.

Vargo, Edward P. *Rainstorms and Fire*, 124–148.

Marry Me (1976)

Hendin, Josephine. "Updike as Matchmaker." *Nation* 223.14 (30 Oct 1976): 437–439. Rpt. as "Updike as Matchmaker: *Marry Me*," in Thorburn, David and Howard Eiland, eds. *John Updike*, 99–106.

Hendin, Josephine. *Vulnerable People*, 98–99.

Hunt, George. *John Updike and the three great secret things*, 117–130, 139–152.

Strandberg, Victory. "John Updike and the Changing of the Gods." *Mosaic* 12.1 (1978): 170–172.

Uphaus, Suzanne Henning. *John Updike*, 102–109.

Month of Sundays (1974)

Doody, Terence A. "Updike's Idea of Reification." *ConL* 20 (1979): 204–212.

Hendin, Josephine. *Vulnerable People*, 96–98.

Hunt, George. *John Updike and the three great secret things*, 181–194.

Hunt, George W., S. J. "Updike's Omega-Shaped Shelter: Structure and Psyche in *A Month of Sundays.*" *Crit* 19.3 (1978): 47–60.

Schopen, Bernard A. "Faith, Morality, and the Novels of John Updike." *TCL* 24 (1978): 534.

Steiner, George. "Scarlet Letters." *New Yorker* 51 (10 March 1975): 116–118. Rpt. as "*Month of Sundays:* Scarlet Letters," in Thorburn, David and Howard Eiland, eds. *John Updike*, 93–98.

Strandberg, Victory. "John Updike and the Changing of the Gods." *Mosaic* 12.1 (1978): 170.

Uphaus, Suzanne Henning. *John Updike*, 91–101.

Of the Farm (1965)

Allen, Mary. *Necessary Blankness*, 99–102.

Burchard, Rachael C. *John Updike, Yea Sayings*, 71–88.

Detweiler, Robert. *John Updike*, 98–110.

Gindin, James. "Megalotopia and the WASP Backlash: The Fiction of Mailer and Updike." *CentR* 15 (1971): 45–46.

Hamilton, Alice and Kenneth. *Elements of John Updike*, 181–199.

Hendin, Josephine. *Vulnerable People*, 91–92.

Hill, John S. "Quest for Belief: Theme in the Novels of John Updike." *SoHR* 3 (1969): 171–172.

Hunt, George. *John Updike and the three great secret things*, 81–101.

Markle, Joyce B. *Fighters and Lovers*, 84–105.

Petter, H. "John Updike's Metaphoric Novels." *ES* 50 (1969): 199, 202, 203–206.

Rupp, Richard H. *Celebration in Postwar American Fiction*, 54–57.

Samuels, Charles Thomas. *John Updike*, 22–27.

Samuels, Charles Thomas. *John Updike*. Minneapolis: University of Minnesota, 1969. 22–27. Rpt as "Family Quarrels in *Of the Farm*," in Thorburn, David and Howard Eiland, eds. *John Updike*, 151–154.

Schopen, Bernard A. "Faith, Morality, and the Novels of John Updike." *TCL* 24 (1978): 532, 533.

Taylor, Larry E. *Pastoral and Anti-Pastoral Patterns in John Updike's Fiction*, 102–111.

Uphaus, Suzanne Henning. *John Updike*, 44–54.

Vargo, Edward P. *Rainstorms and Fire*, 104–123.

Vargo, Edward P. "Shrine and Sanctuary: *Of the Farm*," in Vargo, Edward P. *Rainstorms and Fire: Ritual in the Novels of John Updike*. Port Washington, NY: Kennikat Press, 1973. 104–123. Rpt. in Thorburn, David and Howard Eiland, eds. *John Updike*, 134–150.

Poorhouse Fair (1959)

Burchard, Rachael C. *John Updike, Yea Sayings*, 30–41.

Detweiler, Robert. *John Updike*, 31–44.

Doner, Dean. "Rabbit Angstrom's Unseen World," in Doner, Dean. *New World Writing 20*. Philadelphia: J. B. Lippincott Co., 1962. 63–75. Rpt. in Thorburn, David and Howard Eiland, eds. *John Updike*, 19–22.

Doody, Terence A. "Updike's Idea of Reification." *ConL* 20 (1979): 214.

Galloway, David D. *Absurd Hero in American Fiction*, 21–27.

Grummond, W. W. de. "Classical Influence in *The Poorhouse Fair*." *ANQ* 13 (1974): 21–23.

Hamilton, Alice and Kenneth. *Elements of John Updike*, 119–136.

Hill, John S. "Quest for Belief: Theme in the Novels of John Updike." *SoHR* 3 (1969): 166–167.

Hunt, George. *John Updike and the three great secret things*, 38–48.

Markle, Joyce B. *Fighters and Lovers*, 13–36.

Markle, Joyce B. "*Poorhouse Fair:* A Fragile Vision of Specialness," in Thorburn, David and Howard Eiland, eds. *John Updike*, 109–116.

Petter, H. "John Updike's Metaphoric Novels." *ES* 50 (1969): 198–199, 200, 202, 203–206.

Samuels, Charles Thomas. *John Updike*, 31–35.

Schopen, Bernard A. "Faith, Morality, and the Novels of John Updike." *TCL* 24 (1978): 527–529.

Tanner, Tony. *City of Words*, 276–279.

Taylor, Larry E. *Pastoral and Anti-Pastoral Patterns in John Updike's Fiction*, 50–55.

Uphaus, Suzanne Henning. *John Updike*, 10–18.

Vargo, Edward P. *Rainstorms and Fire*, 28–50.

Rabbit Redux (1971)

Allen, Mary. *Necessary Blankness*, 121–130.

Alter, Robert. "Updike, Malamud, and the Fire This Time," in Thorburn, David and Howard Eiland, eds. *John Updike*, 39–49.

Detweiler, Robert. *John Updike*, 152–166.

Donald, Miles. *American Novel in the Twentieth Century*, 91–106.

Doody, Terence A. "Updike's Idea of Reification." *ConL* 20 (1979): 217.

Falke, Wayne. "*Rabbit Redux:* Time/Order/God." *MFS* 20 (1974): 59–75.

Hendin, Josephine. *Vulnerable People*, 89–91.

Horton, Andrew S. "Ken Kesey, John Updike and the Lone Ranger." *JPC* 8 (1974): 574–577.

Hunt, George. *John Updike and the three great secret things*, 165–179.

Le Pellec, Yves. "Rabbit Underground," in Johnson, Ira D. and Christiane Johnson, eds. *Les Américanistes*, 95–109.

Locke, Richard. "*Rabbit Redux.*" *New York Times Book Review* 76 (7 Nov 1971): 1–2ff. Rpt. as "Rabbit's Progress," in Thorburn, David and Howard Eiland, eds. *John Updike*, 35–38.

Lyons, Eugene. "John Updike: The Beginning and the End." *Crit* 14.2 (1972): 44–58.

Markle, Joyce B. *Fighters and Lovers*, 146–167.

Oates, Joyce Carol. "Updike's American Comedies." *Modern Fiction Studies* 21.3 (Fall 1975): 459–472. Rpt. in Thorburn, David and Howard Eiland, eds. *John Updike*, 59.

Rose, Alan Henry. *Demonic Vision*, 131–132.

Turner, Kermit S. "Rabbit Brought Nowhere: John Updike's *Rabbit Redux.*" *SCR* 8.1 (1975): 35–42.

Umphlett, Wiley Lee. *Sporting Myth and the American Experience*, 188–191.

Uphaus, Suzanne Henning. *John Updike*, 76–90.

Vanderwerken, David L. "Rabbit 'Re-docks': Updike's Inner Space Odyssey." *CollL* 2 (1975): 73–77.

Vargo, Edward P. *Rainstorms and Fire*, 149–171.

Rabbit, Run (1960)

Allen, Mary. *Necessary Blankness*, 114–121.

Borgman, Paul. "Tragic Hero of Updike's *Rabbit, Run.*" *Renascence* 29 (1977): 106–112.

Bryant, Jerry H. *Open Decision*, 240–245.

Burchard, Rachael C. *John Updike, Yea Sayings*, 42–52.

Burhans, Clinton S., Jr. "Things Falling Apart: Structure and Theme in *Rabbit, Run.*" *SNNTS* 5 (1973): 336–351.

Detweiler, Robert. *John Updike*, 45–59.

Donald, Miles. *American Novel in the Twentieth Century*, 91–106.

Doner, Dean. "Rabbit Angstrom's Unseen World," in Doner, Dean. *New World Writing 20.* Philadelphia: J. B. Lippincott Co., 1962. 63–75. Rpt. in Thorburn, David and Howard Eiland, eds. *John Updike*, 17–18, 22–34.

Doody, Terence A. "Updike's Idea of Reification." *ConL* 20 (1979): 215.

Ellis, James. "Karl Barth and Socrates as Mouseketeers in *Rabbit, Run.*" *NConL* 7.5 (1977): 3.

Galloway, David D. *Absurd Hero in American Fiction*, 27–40.

Gilman, Richard. "Distinguised Image of Precarious Life." *Commonweal* 73 (28 Oct 1960): 128–129. Rpt. as "Image of a Precarious Life," in Thorburn, David and Howard Eiland, eds. *John Updike*, 13–16.

Gindin, James. "Megalotopia and the WASP Backlash: The Fiction of Mailer and Updike." *CentR* 15 (1971): 44–45.

Hamilton, Alice and Kenneth. *Elements of John Updike*, 137–155.

Hendin, Josephine. *Vulnerable People*, 89.

Hill, John S. "Quest for Belief: Theme in the Novels of John Updike." *SoHR* 3 (1969): 167–168.

Hogan, Robert E. "Catharism and John Updike's *Rabbit, Run.*" *Renascence* 33 (1980): 229–239.

Hunt, George. *John Updike and the three great secret things*, 38–48.

Landor, Mikhail. "Centaur-Novels," in Proffer, Carl R., ed. and trans. *Soviet Criticism of American Literature in the Sixties*, 43–47.

Le Pellec, Yves. "Rabbit Underground," in Johnson, Ira D. and Christiane Johnson, eds. *Les Américanistes*, 95–109.

McGinnis, Wayne D. "Salvation by Death in *Rabbit, Run.*" *NConL* 8.2 (1978): 7–8.

Markle, Joyce B. *Fighters and Lovers*, 37–60.

May, Keith M. *Out of the Maelstrom*, 95.

Petter, H. "John Updike's Metaphoric Novels." *ES* 50 (1969): 199, 200, 201, 202, 203–206.

Rupp, Richard H. *Celebration in Postwar American Fiction*, 48–51.

Samuels, Charles Thomas. *John Updike*, 37–43.

Schopen, Bernard A. "Faith, Morality, and the Novels of John Updike." *TCL* 24 (1978): 530–532.

Tanner, Tony. *City of Words*, 279–284.

Taylor, Larry E. *Pastoral and Anti-Pastoral Patterns in John Updike's Fiction*, 70–85.

Umphlett, Wiley Lee. *Sporting Myth and the American Experience*, 147–156.

Uphaus, Suzanne Henning. *John Updike*, 19–31.

Vargo, Edward P. *Rainstorms and Fire*, 51–80.

Waldmeir, Joseph. "It's the Going That's Important, Not the Getting There: Rabbit's Questing Non-Quest." *MFS* 20 (1974): 18–27.

VAILLANCOURT, JEAN (1923–1961)

Les Canadiens errants (1954)
  Sutherland, Ronald. *New Hero*, 35–36.
  Sutherland, Ronald. *Second Image*, 139–142.

VAN DER MARK, CHRISTINE (1917–)

In Due Season (1947)
  Harrison, Dick. *Unnamed Country*, 124.

VAN DYKE, HENRY (1928–)

Blood of Strawberries (1968)
  Starke, Catherine Juanita. *Black Portraiture in American Fiction*, 211–214.

Ladies of the Rachmaninoff Eyes (1965)
  Starke, Catherine Juanita. *Black Portraiture in American Fiction*, 209–211.

VAN VECTEN, CARL (1880–1964)

Blind Bow-Boy (1923)
  Austen, Roger. *Playing the Game*, 39–40.

Nigger Heaven (1926)
  Gayle, Addison, Jr. *Way of the New World*, 86–90, 122.
  Larson, Charles R. "Three Harlem Novels of the Jazz Age." *Crit* 11.3 (1969): 70–72.

VAN VOGT, A.E. (1912–)

Slan (1940)
  Scholes, Robert and Eric S. Rabkin. *Science Fiction*, 51–52.

VÁSQUEZ, RICHARD (1928–)

Chicano (1970)
  Robinson, Cecil. *Mexico and the Hispanic Southwest in American Literature*, 322.

VERGARA, JOSEPH R. (1915–)

Love E Pasta (1968)
  Green, Rose Basile. *Italian-American Novel*, 202–206.

VICKERY, SUKEY (1779–1821)

Emily Hamilton (1803)
  Petter, Henri. *Early American Novel*, 180–182.

VIAU, ROGER (1906–1986)

Au milieu, la montagne (1951)
  Shek, Ben-Zion. *Social Realism*, 160–161, 164–165, 168.

VIDAL, GORE (1925–)

City and the Pillar (1948)
  Austen, Roger. *Playing the Game*, 118–125.
  Dick, Bernard F. *Apostate Angel*, 26–39.

Dark Green, Bright Red (1950)
  Dick, Bernard F. *Apostate Angel*, 60–64.

1876 (1976)
  Schlereth, Thomas J. "Fiction and Facts: Henry Adams's *Democracy* and Gore
  Vidal's *1876*." *SoQ* 16 (1978): 209–222.

In a Yellow Wood (1947)
  Dick, Bernard F. *Apostate Angel*, 18–25.

Judgment of Paris (1952)
  Dick, Bernard F. *Apostate Angel*, 66–77.

Julian (1964)
  Dick, Bernard F. *Apostate Angel*, 103–117.

Kalki (1978)
  Berryman, Charles. "Satire in Gore Vidal's *Kalki*." *Crit* 22.2 (1980): 88–96.

Messiah (1954)
  Dick, Bernard F. *Apostate Angel*, 95–103.
  Ziolkowski, Theodore. *Fictional Transfigurations of Jesus*, 250–256.

Myra Breckinridge (1968)
  Dick, Bernard F. *Apostate Angel*, 141–170.

Search for the King (1950)
  Dick, Bernard F. *Apostate Angel*, 54–60.

Season of Comfort (1949)
  Dick, Bernard F. *Apostate Angel*, 40–52.

Washington D.C. (1967)
  Dick, Bernard F. *Apostate Angel*, 125–134.

Williwaw (1946)
   Dick, Bernard F. *Apostate Angel*, 13–17.

VILLARREAL, JOSÉ ANTONIO (1924–)

Pocho (1959)
   Robinson, Cecil. *Mexico and the Hispanic Southwest in American Literature*, 318–319.

VINCIGUERRA, FRANCES see WINWAR, FRANCES

VIVANTE, ARTURO (1923–)

Doctor Giovanni (1969)
   Green, Rose Basile. *Italian-American Novel*, 214–216.

Goodly Babe (1966)
   Green, Rose Basile. *Italian-American Novel*, 212–214.

VONNEGUT, KURT JR., (1922–)

Breakfast of Champions (1973)
   Buck, Lynn. "Vonnegut's World of Comic Futility." *SAF* 3 (1975): 181–184, 189–190, 191, 192–196.
   Burhans, Clinton S., Jr. "Hemingway and Vonnegut: Diminishing Vision in a Dying Age." *MFS* 21 (1975): 185.
   Giannone, Richard. *Vonnegut: A Preface to His Novels*, 101–112.
   Jones, Peter G. *War and the Novelist*, 222.
   Kennard, Jean E. *Number and Nightmare*, 125–128.
   LeClair, Thomas. "Death and Black Humor." *Crit* 17.1 (1975): 24–25.
   Lundquist, James. *Kurt Vonnegut*, 55–62.
   Merrill, Robert. "Vonnegut's *Breakfast of Champions:* The Conversion of Heliogabalus." *Crit* 18.3 (1977): 99–109.
   Messent, Peter B. "*Breakfast of Champions:* The Direction of Kurt Vonnegut's Fiction." *JAmS* 8 (1974): 101–114.
   Myers, David. "Kurt Vonnegut, Jr.: Morality-Myth in the Antinovel." *IFR* 3 (1976): 52–56.
   Nadeau, Robert L. "Physics and Metaphysics in the Novels of Kurt Vonnegut, Jr." *Mosaic* 13.2 (1980): 43–44.
   Reed, Peter J. "Later Vonnegut," in Klinkowitz, Jerome and Donald L. Lawler, eds. *Vonnegut in America*, 153–169.
   Schatt, Stanley. *Kurt Vonnegut, Jr.*, 97–109.
   Uphaus, Robert W. "Expected Meaning in Vonnegut's Dead-End Fiction." *Novel* 8 (1975): 171–174.

Cat's Cradle (1963)
   Ash, Brian. *Faces of the Future*, 196–198.
   Blair, John G. *Confidence Man in Modern Fiction*, 100–110.

Bryant, Jerry H. *Open Decision*, 315–319.

Buck, Lynn. "Vonnegut's World of Comic Futility." *SAF* 3 (1975): 189, 191, 192.

Burhans, Clinton S., Jr. "Hemingway and Vonnegut: Diminishing Vision in a Dying Age." *MFS* 21 (1975): 178–179, 181, 185, 186, 187, 189.

Festa, Conrad. "Vonnegut's Satire," in Klinkowitz, Jerome and Donald L. Lawler, eds. *Vonnegut in America*, 143.

Giannone, Richard. *Vonnegut: A Preface to His Novels*, 53–68.

Hansen, Arlen J. "Celebration of Solipsism: A New Trend in American Fiction." *MFS* 19 (1973): 6–7.

Harris, Charles B. *Contemporary American Novelists of the Absurd*, 62–64, 66, 68–69.

Hendin, Josephine. *Vulnerable People*, 34–36.

Jones, Peter G. *War and the Novelist*, 204, 205, 206, 207, 209, 210, 213–217, 221.

Kennard, Jean E. *Number and Nightmare*, 114–119.

Klinkowitz, Jerome. *American 1960's*, 49–53.

Klinkowitz, Jerome. "Kurt Vonnegut, Jr. and the Crime of His Times." *Crit* 12.3 (1971): 46–52.

Klinkowitz, Jerome. "*Mother Night, Cat's Cradle*, and the Crimes of Our Times," in Klinkowitz, Jerome and John Somer, eds. *Vonnegut Statement*, 169–176.

Leverence, W. John. "*Cat's Cradle* and Traditional American Humor." *JPC* 5 (1972): 955–963.

Lundquist, James. *Kurt Vonnegut*, 33–39.

McGinnis, Wayne D. "Source and Implications of Ice-Nine in Vonnegut's *Cat's Cradle*." *ANQ* 13 (1974): 40–41.

Mangum, Bryant. "*Cat's Cradle*'s Jonah-John and the Garden of Ice-Nine." *NConL* 9.3 (1979): 9–11.

May, John R. *Toward a New Earth*, 191–199.

May, John R. "Vonnegut's Humor and the Limits of Hope." *TCL* 18 (1972): 25–26, 30–32.

Meeter, Glenn. "Vonnegut's Formal and Moral Otherworldliness: *Cat's Cradle* and *Slaughterhouse Five*," in Klinkowitz, Jerome and John Somer, eds. *Vonnegut Statement*, 204–219.

Morrow, Patrick D. "Womb Image in Vonnegut's *Cat's Cradle*." *NConL* 6.5 (1976): 11–13.

Myers, David. "Kurt Vonnegut, Jr.: Morality-Myth in the Antinovel." *IFR* 3 (1976): 52–56.

Nadeau, Robert L. "Physics and Metaphysics in the Novels of Kurt Vonnegut, Jr." *Mosaic* 13.2 (1980): 40–42.

Olderman, Raymond M. *Beyond the Waste Land*, 190, 201–202, 204–205, 215–216, 218–219.

Pinsker, Sanford. *Between Two Worlds*, 92–94.

Reed, Peter J. *Kurt Vonnegut, Jr.*, 119–145.

Rubens, Philip M. "Names in Vonnegut's *Cat's Cradle*." *NConL* 8.1 (1978): 7.

Schatt, Stanley. *Kurt Vonnegut, Jr.*, 56–68.

Schatt, Stanley. "Whale and the Cross: Vonnegut's Jonah and Christ Figures." *SR* 56 (1971): 35–38.

Schatt, Stanley. "World of Kurt Vonnegut, Jr." *Crit* 12.3 (1971): 57–61.

Scholes, Robert. *Fabulation and Metafiction*, 145–147, 157–159.

Schulz, Max F. *Black Humor Fiction of the Sixties*, 55–57.

Schulz, Max F. "Unconfirmed Thesis: Kurt Vonnegut, Black Humor, and Contemporary Art." *Crit* 12.3 (1971): 18–20.

Somer, John. "Geodesic Vonnegut; or, If Buckminster Fuller Wrote Novels," in Klinkowitz, Jerome and John Somer, eds. *Vonnegut Statement*, 226–227, 252.

Tanner, Tony. *City of Words*, 188–191.

Trachtenberg, Stanley. "Vonnegut's *Cradle:* The Erosion of Comedy." *MQR* 12 (1973): 66–71.

Uphaus, Robert W. "Expected Meaning in Vonnegut's Dead-End Fiction." *Novel* 8 (1975): 165, 168, 170–171.

Vasbinder, Sam. "Meaning of Foma in *Cat's Cradle.*" *RQ* 5 (1973): 300–302.

Wood, Karen and Charles Wood. "Vonnegut Effect: Science Fiction and Beyond," in Klinkowitz, Jerome and John Somer, eds. *Vonnegut Statement*, 146–148, 153.

Wymer, Thomas L. "Swiftian Satire of Kurt Vonnegut, Jr.," in Clareson, Thomas D., ed. *Voices for the Future* (Vol. 1), 254–259.

God Bless You, Mr. Rosewater (1965)

Bryant, Jerry H. *Open Decision*, 303–305, 310–312.

Buck, Lynn. "Vonnegut's World of Comic Futility." *SAF* 3 (1975): 188–189.

Burhans, Clinton S., Jr. "Hemingway and Vonnegut: Diminishing Vision in a Dying Age." *MFS* 21 (1975): 186, 188–189.

Giannone, Richard. *Vonnegut: A Preface to His Novels*, 69–81.

Godshalk, William L. "Vonnegut and Shakespeare: Rosewater at Elsinore." *Crit* 15.2 (1973): 37–48.

Harris, Charles B. *Contemporary American Novelists of the Absurd*, 57–60, 66.

Jones, Peter G. *War and the Novelist*, 207, 209, 210–213, 221–222.

Kennard, Jean E. *Number and Nightmare*, 119–122.

Klinkowitz, Jerome. *American 1960's*, 53–54.

Lundquist, James. *Kurt Vonnegut*, 39–46.

May, John R. "Vonnegut's Humor and the Limits of Hope." *TCL* 18 (1972): 26–28.

Myers, David. "Kurt Vonnegut, Jr.: Morality-Myth in the Antinovel." *IFR* 3 (1976): 52–56.

Nelson, Gerald B. *Ten Versions of America*, 63–76.

Olderman, Raymond M. *Beyond the Waste Land*, 205–208, 217–219.

Pinsker, Sanford. *Between Two Worlds*, 94–95.

Reed, Peter J. *Kurt Vonnegut, Jr.*, 146–171.

Schatt, Stanley. *Kurt Vonnegut, Jr.*, 69–80.

Schatt, Stanley. "Whale and the Cross: Vonnegut's Jonah and Christ Figures." *SR* 56 (1971): 38–42.

Schatt, Stanley. "World of Kurt Vonnegut, Jr." *Crit* 12.3 (1971): 61–65.

Schulz, Max F. *Black Humor Fiction of the Sixties*, 45–51.

Schulz, Max F. "Unconfirmed Thesis: Kurt Vonnegut, Black Humor, and Contemporary Art." *Crit* 12.3 (1971): 8–14.

Somer, John. "Geodesic Vonnegut; or, If Buckminster Fuller Wrote Novels," in Klinkowitz, Jerome and John Somer, eds. *Vonnegut Statement*, 227–228.

Tanner, Tony. *City of Words*, 192–194.

Uphaus, Robert W. "Expected Meaning in Vonnegut's Dead-End Fiction." *Novel* 8 (1975): 165, 168–169.

Wood, Karen and Charles Wood. "Vonnegut Effect: Science Fiction and Beyond," in Klinkowitz, Jerome and John Somer, eds. *Vonnegut Statement*, 151–153.

Mother Night (1961)

Bryant, Jerry H. *Open Decision*, 312–315.

Buck, Lynn. "Vonnegut's World of Comic Futility." *SAF* 3 (1975): 187–188, 190, 192, 193.

Burhans, Clinton S., Jr. "Hemingway and Vonnegut: Diminishing Vision in a Dying Age." *MFS* 21 (1975): 188.

Giannone, Richard. *Vonnegut: A Preface to His Novels*, 39–52.

Harris, Charles B. *Contemporary American Novelists of the Absurd*, 54–56, 67.

Hendin, Josephine. *Vulnerable People*, 36–37.

Jones, Peter G. *War and the Novelist*, 207, 208–210.

Kennard, Jean E. *Number and Nightmare*, 112–114.

Klinkowitz, Jerome. "Kurt Vonnegut, Jr. and the Crime of His Times." *Crit* 12.3 (1971): 39–46.

Klinkowitz, Jerome. *"Mother Night, Cat's Cradle*, and the Crimes of Our Times," in Klinkowitz, Jerome and John Somer, eds. *Vonnegut Statement*, 160–169.

Lundquist, James. *Kurt Vonnegut*, 30–33.

May, John R. "Vonnegut's Humor and the Limits of Hope." *TCL* 18 (1972): 34–35.

Myers, David. "Kurt Vonnegut, Jr.: Morality-Myth in the Antinovel." *IFR* 3 (1976): 52–56.

Nadeau, Robert L. "Physics and Metaphysics in the Novels of Kurt Vonnegut, Jr." *Mosaic* 13.2 (1980): 45–46.

Olderman, Raymond M. *Beyond the Waste Land*, 196–197, 200, 208–212.

Pinsker, Sanford. *Between Two Worlds*, 88–91.

Reed, Peter J. *Kurt Vonnegut, Jr.*, 88–118.

Schatt, Stanley. *Kurt Vonnegut, Jr.*, 43–55.

Schatt, Stanley. "World of Kurt Vonnegut, Jr." *Crit* 12.3 (1971): 54–57.

Scholes, Robert. *Fabulation and Metafiction*, 159–161.

Schulz, Max F. *Black Humor Fiction of the Sixties*, 58–59.

Schulz, Max F. "Unconfirmed Thesis: Kurt Vonnegut, Black Humor, and Contemporary Art." *Crit* 12.3 (1971): 21–23.

Somer, John. "Geodesic Vonnegut; or, If Buckminster Fuller Wrote Novels," in Klinkowitz, Jerome and John Somer, eds. *Vonnegut Statement*, 225–226.

Tanner, Tony. *City of Words*, 185–188.

Uphaus, Robert W. "Expected Meaning in Vonnegut's Dead-End Fiction." *Novel* 8 (1975): 165, 167–168.

Veeder, William. "Technique and Recovery: *Lolita* and *Mother Night*," in Klinkowitz, Jerome and Donald L. Lawler, eds. *Vonnegut in America*, 97–132.

Player Piano (1952)

Bryant, Jerry H. *Open Decision*, 303–305, 309–310.

Buck, Lynn. "Vonnegut's World of Comic Futility." *SAF* 3 (1975): 186.

Burhans, Clinton S., Jr. "Hemingway and Vonnegut: Diminishing Vision in a Dying Age." *MFS* 21 (1975): 185–186.

Giannone, Richard. *Vonnegut: A Preface to His Novels*, 12–24.

Harris, Charles B. *Contemporary American Novelists of the Absurd*, 65–66.

Jones, Peter G. *War and the Novelist*, 203–204, 221.

Kennard, Jean E. *Number and Nightmare*, 104–107.

Lundquist, James. *Kurt Vonnegut*, 22–26.

May, John R. "Vonnegut's Humor and the Limits of Hope." *TCL* 18 (1972): 32–33.

Mellard, James M. "Modes of Vonnegut's Fiction: or, *Player Piano* Ousts *Mechan-*

ical Bride and *The Sirens of Titan* Invade *The Gutenberg Galaxy*," in Klinkowitz, Jerome and John Somer, eds. *Vonnegut Statement*, 179–191.

Myers, David. "Kurt Vonnegut, Jr.: Morality-Myth in the Antinovel." *IFR* 3 (1976): 52–56.

Nadeau, Robert L. "Physics and Metaphysics in the Novels of Kurt Vonnegut, Jr." *Mosaic* 13.2 (1980): 45.

Reed, Peter J. *Kurt Vonnegut, Jr.*, 24–56.

Rhodes, Carolyn. "Tyranny by Computer: Automated Data Processing and Oppressive Government in Science Fiction," in Clareson, Thomas D., ed. *Many Futures, Many Worlds*, 67–73.

Schatt, Stanley. *Kurt Vonnegut, Jr.*, 16–30.

Schatt, Stanley. "Whale and the Cross: Vonnegut's Jonah and Christ Figures." *SR* 56 (1971): 30–31.

Schulz, Max F. *Black Humor Fiction of the Sixties*, 57–58.

Schulz, Max F. "Unconfirmed Thesis: Kurt Vonnegut, Black Humor, and Contemporary Art." *Crit* 12.3 (1971): 21.

Somer, John. "Geodesic Vonnegut; or, If Buckminster Fuller Wrote Novels," in Klinkowitz, Jerome and John Somer, eds. *Vonnegut Statement*, 224.

Tanner, Tony. *City of Words*, 181–182.

Uphaus, Robert W. "Expected Meaning in Vonnegut's Dead-End Fiction." *Novel* 8 (1975): 164, 166–167.

Warrick, Patricia S. *Cybernetic Imagination in Science Fiction*, 135–139.

Wood, Karen and Charles Wood. "Vonnegut Effect: Science Fiction and Beyond," in Klinkowitz, Jerome and John Somer, eds. *Vonnegut Statement*, 142–146.

Sirens of Titan (1959)

Ash, Brian. *Faces of the Future*, 146–148.

Bryant, Jerry H. *Open Decision*, 305–308.

Buck, Lynn. "Vonnegut's World of Comic Futility." *SAF* 3 (1975): 186–187, 190, 193.

Burhans, Clinton S., Jr. "Hemingway and Vonnegut: Diminishing Vision in a Dying Age." *MFS* 21 (1975): 178, 179, 180, 181, 188, 189–190.

Donald, Miles. *American Novel in the Twentieth Century*, 185–186.

Giannone, Richard. *Vonnegut: A Preface to His Novels*, 25–38.

Harris, Charles B. *Contemporary American Novelists of the Absurd*, 61–62.

Jones, Peter G. *War and the Novelist*, 204–207.

Kennard, Jean E. *Number and Nightmare*, 107–112.

Ketterer, David. *New Worlds for Old*, 303–333.

Lawler, Donald L. "*Sirens of Titan*: Vonnegut's Metaphysical Shaggy-Dog Story," in Klinkowitz, Jerome and Donald L. Lawler, eds. *Vonnegut in America*, 61–84.

Lundquist, James. *Kurt Vonnegut*, 26–30.

May, John R. "Vonnegut's Humor and the Limits of Hope." *TCL* 18 (1972): 35–36.

Mellard, James M. "Modes of Vonnegut's Fiction: or, *Player Piano* Ousts *Mechanical Bride* and *The Sirens of Titan* Invade *The Gutenberg Galaxy*," in Klinkowitz, Jerome and John Somer, eds. *Vonnegut Statement*, 191–201.

Myers, David. "Kurt Vonnegut, Jr.: Morality-Myth in the Antinovel." *IFR* 3 (1976): 52–56.

Nadeau, Robert L. "Physics and Metaphysics in the Novels of Kurt Vonnegut, Jr." *Mosaic* 13.2 (1980): 38–40.

Reed, Peter J. *Kurt Vonnegut, Jr.*, 57–87.

Rose, Ellen Cronan. "It's All a Joke: Science Fiction in Kurt Vonnegut's *The Sirens of Titan.*" *L&P* 29 (1979): 160–168.

Rubens, Philip M. " 'Nothing's Ever Final': Vonnegut's Concept of Time." *CollL* 6 (1979): 65–67.

Schatt, Stanley. *Kurt Vonnegut, Jr.*, 30–42.

Schatt, Stanley. "Whale and the Cross: Vonnegut's Jonah and Christ Figures." *SR* 56 (1971): 31–35.

Schulz, Max F. "Unconfirmed Thesis: Kurt Vonnegut, Black Humor, and Contemporary Art." *Crit* 12.3 (1971): 21.

Somer, John. "Geodesic Vonnegut; or, If Buckminster Fuller Wrote Novels," in Klinkowitz, Jerome and John Somer, eds. *Vonnegut Statement*, 224–225.

Tanner, Tony. *City of Words*, 182–185.

Uphaus, Robert W. "Expected Meaning in Vonnegut's Dead-End Fiction." *Novel* 8 (1975): 164–165, 167.

Wolfe, G. K. "Vonnegut and the Metaphor of Science Fiction: *The Sirens of Titan.*" *JPC* 5 (1972): 964–969.

Wollheim, Donald A. *Universe Makers*, 70–73.

Wood, Karen and Charles Wood. "Vonnegut Effect: Science Fiction and Beyond," in Klinkowitz, Jerome and John Somer, eds. *Vonnegut Statement*, 148–151.

Wymer, Thomas L. "Swiftian Satire of Kurt Vonnegut, Jr.," in Clareson, Thomas D., ed. *Voices for the Future* (Vol. 1), 251–253.

Slapstick (1976)

Giannone, Richard. *Vonnegut: A Preface to His Novels*, 113–121.

Lundquist, James. *Kurt Vonnegut*, 62–67.

Reed, Peter J. "Later Vonnegut," in Klinkowitz, Jerome and Donald L. Lawler, eds. *Vonnegut in America*, 169–185.

Schatt, Stanley. *Kurt Vonnegut, Jr.*, 110–118.

Slaughterhouse-Five (1969)

Ash, Brian. *Faces of the Future*, 145–146, 158.

Bryant, Jerry H. *Open Decision*, 319–324.

Buck, Lynn. "Vonnegut's World of Comic Futility." *SAF* 3 (1975): 187, 191.

Burhans, Clinton S., Jr. "Hemingway and Vonnegut: Diminishing Vision in a Dying Age." *MFS* 21 (1975): 179, 180, 185, 187.

Colmer, John. *Coleridge to Catch-22*, 207–208.

Craig, David and Michael Egan. *Extreme Situations*, 53–64.

Donald, Miles. *American Novel in the Twentieth Century*, 186–189.

Edelstein, Arnold. "*Slaughterhouse-Five:* Time Out of Joint." *CollL* 1 (1974): 128–139.

Engel, Wilson F., III. "Pilgrim as Prisoner: Cummings and Vonnegut." *NConL* 7.1 (1977): 13–14.

Festa, Conrad. "Vonnegut's Satire," in Klinkowitz, Jerome and Donald L. Lawler, eds. *Vonnegut in America*, 143–147.

Giannone, Richard. *Vonnegut: A Preface to His Novels*, 82–97.

Greiner, Donald J. "Vonnegut's *Slaughterhouse-Five* and the Fiction of Atrocity." *Crit* 14.3 (1973): 38–51.

Gros-Louis, Dolores K. "*Slaughterhouse-Five:* Pacifism vs. Passiveness." *BallS* 18.2 (1977): 3–8.

Harris, Charles B. *Contemporary American Novelists of the Absurd*, 68, 69–74.

Harris, Charles B. "Time, Uncertainty, and Kurt Vonnegut, Jr.: A Reading of *Slaughterhouse-Five.*" *CentR* 20 (1976): 228–243.

Hartshorne, Thomas L. "From *Catch-22* to *Slaughterhouse V:* The Decline of the Political Mode." *SAQ* 78 (1979): 17–20, 24–27.

Hendin, Josephine. *Vulnerable People*, 37–40.

Jones, Peter G. *War and the Novelist*, 207–208, 217–221, 222.

Kennard, Jean E. *Number and Nightmare*, 122–125.

Ketterer, David. *New Worlds for Old*, 299–303.

Klinkowitz, Jerome. *American 1960's*, 54–58.

Kopper, Edward A., Jr. "Operation Gomorrah in *Slaughterhouse-Five.*" *NConL* 8.4 (1978): 6.

LeClair, Thomas. "Death and Black Humor." *Crit* 17.1 (1975): 23–24.

Lundquist, James. *Kurt Vonnegut*, 46–55, 69–83.

McGinnis, Wayne D. "Arbitrary Cycle of *Slaughterhouse-Five:* A Relation of Form to Theme." *Crit* 17.1 (1975): 55–68.

McNelly, Willis E. "Science Fiction and the Modern Mythology [Vonnegut's *Slaughterhouse-Five*]," in Clareson, Thomas D., ed. *SF: The Other Side of Realism*, 193–198.

May, John R. "Vonnegut's Humor and the Limits of Hope." *TCL* 18 (1972): 28–30.

Meeter, Glenn. "Vonnegut's Formal and Moral Otherworldliness: *Cat's Cradle* and *Slaughterhouse Five*," in Klinkowitz, Jerome and John Somer, eds. *Vonnegut Statement*, 204–219.

Merrill, Robert and Peter A. Scholl. "Vonnegut's *Slaughterhouse-Five:* The Requirements of Chaos." *SAF* 6 (1978): 65–76.

Myers, David. "Kurt Vonnegut, Jr.: Morality-Myth in the Antinovel." *IFR* 3 (1976): 52–56.

Nadeau, Robert L. "Physics and Metaphysics in the Novels of Kurt Vonnegut, Jr." *Mosaic* 13.2 (1980): 42–43.

O'Connor, Gerard W. "Function of Time Travel in Vonnegut's *Slaughterhouse-Five.*" *RQ* 5 (1972): 206–207.

Olderman, Raymond M. *Beyond the Waste Land*, 191–195, 196–200, 203–204, 212–214, 216–217.

O'Sullivan, Maurice J., Jr. "*Slaughterhouse-Five:* Kurt Vonnegut's Anti-Memoirs." *ELWIU* 3 (1976): 244–250.

Pinsker, Sanford. *Between Two Worlds*, 95–100.

Reed, Peter J. *Kurt Vonnegut, Jr.*, 172–203.

Rubens, Philip M. " 'Nothing's Ever Final': Vonnegut's Concept of Time." *CollL* 6 (1979): 67–70.

Schatt, Stanley. *Kurt Vonnegut, Jr.*, 81–96.

Schatt, Stanley. "World of Kurt Vonnegut, Jr." *Crit* 12.3 (1971): 65–68.

Scholes, Robert. *Fabulation and Metafiction*, 203–205.

Schulz, Max F. *Black Humor Fiction of the Sixties*, 59–60.

Schulz, Max F. "Unconfirmed Thesis: Kurt Vonnegut, Black Humor, and Contemporary Art." *Crit* 12.3 (1971): 23.

Somer, John. "Geodesic Vonnegut; or, If Buckminster Fuller Wrote Novels," in Klinkowitz, Jerome and John Somer, eds. *Vonnegut Statement*, 228–231, 242–251.

Tanner, Tony. *City of Words*, 194–201.

Tilton, John W. *Cosmic Satire in the Contemporary Novel*, 69–102.

Uphaus, Robert W. "Expected Meaning in Vonnegut's Dead-End Fiction." *Novel* 8 (1975): 165, 169–170.

Wood, Karen and Charles Wood. "Vonnegut Effect: Science Fiction and Beyond," in Klinkowitz, Jerome and John Somer, eds. *Vonnegut Statement*, 153–156.

Wymer, Thomas L. "Swiftian Satire of Kurt Vonnegut, Jr.," in Clareson, Thomas D., ed. *Voices for the Future* (Vol. 1), 241–251, 259–262.

VORSE, MARY HEATON (1874–1966)

Strike! (1930)

Cook, Sylvia Jenkins. *From Tobacco Road to Route 66*, 93–97.

WAKEMAN, FREDERIC (1909–)

Hucksters (1946)

Pugh, David G. "Reading an Old Best-Seller: The Obvious and the Unobtrusive," in French, Warren, ed. *Forties*, 181–187.

WALDEN, AMELIA ELIZABETH (1909–)

Bradford Story (1956)

Bryant, Jerry H. *Open Decision*, 180–182.

WALDO, EDWARD HAMILTON see STURGEON, THEODORE

WALKER, ALICE (1944–)

Meridian (1976)

Christian, Barbara. *Black Women Novelists*, 204–234, 234–238, 249–252.

Third Life of Grange Copeland (1970)

Christian, Barbara. *Black Women Novelists*, 183–204, 234–238.

Harris, Trudier. "Folklore in the Fiction of Alice Walker: A Perpetuation of Historical and Literary Traditions." *BALF* 11 (1977): 7–8.

Harris, Trudier. "Violence in *The Third Life of Grange Copeland*." *CLAJ* 19 (1975): 238–247.

Schultz, Elizabeth. " 'Free in Fact and at Last': The Image of the Black Woman in Black American Fiction," in Springer, Marlene, ed. *What Manner of Woman*, 335–336.

WALKER, MARGARET (1915–1998)

Jubilee (1966)

Christian, Barbara. *Black Women Novelists*, 71–72.

Davis, Arthur P. *From the Dark Tower*, 184.

Klotman, Phyllis Rauch. " 'Oh Freedom': Women and History in Margaret Walker's *Jubilee*." *BALF* 11 (1977): 139–145.

Powell, Bertie J. "Black Experience in Margaret Walker's *Jubilee* and Lorraine Hansberry's *The Drinking Gourd*." *CLAJ* 21 (1977): 304–308.

Schultz, Elizabeth. " 'Free in Fact and at Last': The Image of the Black Woman in Black American Fiction," in Springer, Marlene, ed. *What Manner of Woman*, 326–327.

WALLACE, HORACE BINNEY (1817–1852)

Henry Pulteney (1987)

Hatvary, George Egon. *Horace Binney Wallace*, 55–57.

Stanley (1838)

Hatvary, George Egon. *Horace Binney Wallace*, 39–54.

WALLACE, IRVING (1916–)

Man (1964)

Starke, Catherine Juanita. *Black Portraiture in American Fiction*, 217–220.

WALLANT, EDWARD LEWIS (1926–1962)

Children at the Gate (1964)

Beja, Morris. *Epiphany in the Modern Novel*, 214–215.

Galloway, David. *Edward Lewis Wallant*, 91–112.

Klein, Marcus. "Further Notes on the Dereliction of Culture: Edward Lewis Wallant and Bruce Jay Friedman," in Malin, Irving, ed. *Contemporary American-Jewish Literature*, 236, 237–238.

Levine, Paul. "Flannery O'Connor: The Soul of the Grotesque," in Hoyt, Charles Alva, ed. *Minor American Novelists*, 130–134.

Schulz, Max F. *Radical Sophistication*, 174–185.

Human Season (1960)

Beja, Morris. *Epiphany in the Modern Novel*, 214.

Davis, William V. "Renewal of Dialogical Immediacy in Edward Lewis Wallant." *Renascence* 24 (1972): 59–69.

Galloway, David. *Edward Lewis Wallant*, 40–60.

Hoyt, Charles Alva. "Sudden Hunger: An Essay on the Novels of Edward Lewis Wallant," in Hoyt, Charles Alva, ed. *Minor American Novelists*, 124–127.

Klein, Marcus. "Further Notes on the Dereliction of Culture: Edward Lewis Wallant and Bruce Jay Friedman," in Malin, Irving, ed. *Contemporary American-Jewish Literature*, 230–231, 231–233, 234, 239–240.

Lewis, Robert W. "Hung-up Heroes of Edward Lewis Wallant." *Renascence* 24 (1972): 71, 74.

Schulz, Max F. *Radical Sophistication*, 174–185.

Pawnbroker (1961)

Alexander, Edward. *Resonance of Dust*, 128–131.

Beja, Morris. *Epiphany in the Modern Novel*, 214.

Galloway, David. *Edward Lewis Wallant*, 70–90.

Klein, Marcus. "Further Notes on the Dereliction of Culture: Edward Lewis Wallant and Bruce Jay Friedman," in Malin, Irving, ed. *Contemporary American-Jewish Literature*, 236, 237.

Levine, Paul. "Flannery O'Connor: The Soul of the Grotesque," in Hoyt, Charles Alva, ed. *Minor American Novelists*, 127–130.

Lewis, Robert W. "Hung-up Heroes of Edward Lewis Wallant." *Renascence* 24 (1972): 71–74.

Schulz, Max F. *Radical Sophistication*, 174–185.

Tenants of Moonbloom (1963)

Beja, Morris. *Epiphany in the Modern Novel*, 215–216.

Galloway, David. *Edward Lewis Wallant*, 113–139.

Klein, Marcus. "Further Notes on the Dereliction of Culture: Edward Lewis Wallant and Bruce Jay Friedman," in Malin, Irving, ed. *Contemporary American-Jewish Literature*, 236, 237.

Levine, Paul. "Flannery O'Connor: The Soul of the Grotesque," in Hoyt, Charles Alva, ed. *Minor American Novelists*, 134–137.

Lewis, Robert W. "Hung-up Heroes of Edward Lewis Wallant." *Renascence* 24 (1972): 74–84.

Schulz, Max F. *Radical Sophistication*, 174–185.

WALTON, BRYCE (1918–)

Harpoon Gunner (1964)

Kelty, Jean McClure. "Cult of Kill in Adolescent Fiction." *EJ* 64.2 (1975): 59–60.

WAMBAUGH, JOSEPH (1937–)

Black Marble (1978)

Jeffrey, David K. "Wambaugh's Police Stories." *MidQ* 21 (1980): 480–482.

Blue Knight (1972)

Jeffrey, David K. "Wambaugh's Police Stories." *MidQ* 21 (1980): 475–477.

Choirboys (1975)

Jeffrey, David K. "Wambaugh's Police Stories." *MidQ* 21 (1980): 479–480.

New Centurions (1970)

Jeffrey, David K. "Wambaugh's Police Stories." *MidQ* 21 (1980): 471–474.

WARD, ELIZABETH STUART PHELPS (1844–1911)

Singular Life (1894)

Ziolkowski, Theodore. *Fictional Transfigurations of Jesus*, 64–68.

WARING, ROBERT LEWIS (1863–(?))

As We See It (1910)

Fleming, Robert E. "Humor in the Early Black Novel." *CLAJ* 17 (1973): 253.

WARNER, ANNA (1827–1915)

Dollars and Cents (1852)

Baym, Nina. *Woman's Fiction*, 157–160.

Foster, Edward Halsey. *Susan and Anna Warner*, 76–81.

My Brother's Keeper (1855)

Baym, Nina. *Woman's Fiction*, 160.
Foster, Edward Halsey. *Susan and Anna Warner*, 81–82.

Say and Seal (1860)

Baym, Nina. *Woman's Fiction*, 160–163.
Foster, Edward Halsey. *Susan and Anna Warner*, 82–85.

WARNER, CHARLES DUDLEY (1829–1900)

Gilded Age (1873)

Coard, Robert L. "Mark Twain's *The Gilded Age* and Sinclair Lewis's *Babbitt*." *MidQ* 13 (1972): 319–333.
Cohn, Jan. "Women as Superfluous Characters in American Realism and Naturalism." *SAF* 1 (1973): 158.
Crowley, John W. "Note on *The Gilded Age*." *ELN* 10 (1972): 116–118.
Foner, Philip S. *Mark Twain Social Critic*, 91–113.
French, Bryant M. "James Hammond Trumbull's Alternative Chapter: Mottoes for *The Gilded Age*." *PQ* 50 (1971): 271–280.
Krauth, Leland. "Mark Twain: At Home in the Gilded Age." *GR* 28 (1974): 105–113.
Kuhlmann, Susan. *Knave, Fool, and Genius*, 54–55.
Mixon, Wayne. "Mark Twain, *The Gilded Age*, and the New South Movement." *SoHR* 7 (1973): 403–408.
Schleiner, Louise. "Romance Motifs in Three Novels of Mark Twain." *CLS* 13 (1976): 335–338.
Sloane, David E. E. *Mark Twain as Literary Comedian*, 104–114.
Taylor, Robert, Jr. "Sounding the Trumpets of Defiance: Mark Twain and Norman Mailer." *MTJ* 16.3 (1972): 5–6.

WARNER, SUSAN (1819–1885)

Hills of the Shatemuc (1856)

Baym, Nina. *Woman's Fiction*, 156–157.
Foster, Edward Halsey. *Susan and Anna Warner*, 69–72.

Queechy (1852)

Baym, Nina. *Woman's Fiction*, 150–156.
Foster, Edward Halsey. *Susan and Anna Warner*, 60–67.

Say and Seal (1860)

Baym, Nina. *Woman's Fiction*, 160–163.
Foster, Edward Halsey. *Susan and Anna Warner*, 82–85.

Wide, Wide World (1850)

Baym, Nina. *Woman's Fiction*, 143–150.
Foster, Edward Halsey. *Susan and Anna Warner*, 34–53.

WARREN, ROBERT PENN (1905–1989)

All the King's Men (1946)

Baumbach, Jonathan. "Metaphysics of Demagoguery: *All the King's Men* by Robert Penn Warren," in Baumbach, Jonathan. *Landscape of Nightmare*. New York:

New York University Press, 1965. Rpt. in Chambers, Robert H., ed. *Twentieth Century Interpretations of All the King's Men*, 126–142.

Bentley, Eric. "Meaning of Robert Penn Warren's Novels." *Kenyon Review* (Summer 1948). Rpt. in Kostelanetz, Richard, ed. *On Contemporary Literature*, 621–629.

Brooks, Cleanth. "Experience Redeemed in Knowledge," in Brooks, Cleanth. *Hidden God: Studies in Hemingway, Faulkner, Yeats, Eliot, and Warren*. New Haven: Yale University Press, 1963. 98–111, 118–127. Rpt. in Gray, Richard, ed. *Robert Penn Warren*, 20–25.

Chambers, Robert H. "Introduction," in Chambers, Robert H., ed. *Twentieth Century Interpretations of All the King's Men*, 6–15.

Cottrell, Beekman W. "Cass Mastern and the Awful Responsibility of Time," in Sochatoff, A. Fred, et. al., eds. *All the King's Men: A Symposium*. Pittsburgh: Carnegie Institute of Technology, 1957. 39–49. Rpt. in Chambers, Robert H., ed. *Twentieth Century Interpretations of All the King's Men*, 116–125.

Davenport, F. Garvin, Jr. *Myth of Southern History*, 144–149, 155–161.

Girault, Norton R. "Narrator's Mind as Symbol: An Analysis of *All the King's Men*." *Accent* 7 : 220–234. Rpt. in Chambers, Robert H., ed. *Twentieth Century Interpretations of All the King's Men*, 29–47.

Gray, Richard. *Literature of Memory*, 70–80.

Gray, Richard J. "American Novelist and American History: A Revaluation of *All the King's Men*." *JAmS* 6 (1972): 297–307.

Guttenberg, Barnett. *Web of Being*, 34–55.

Hannaford, Richard. "Sugar-Boy and Violence in *All the King's Men*." *NConL* 6.3 (1976): 10–13.

Heilman, Robert B. "Melpomene as Wallflower; or, the Reading of Tragedy." *Sewanee Review* 55 (1947): 154–166. Rpt. in Chambers, Robert H., ed. *Twentieth Century Interpretations of All the King's Men*, 16–28.

Henderson, Harry B. *Versions of the Past*, 271–273.

Johnson, Glen M. "Pastness of *All the King's Men*." *AL* 51 (1980): 553–557.

Justus, James H. "All the Burdens of Warren's *All the King's Men*," in French, Warren, ed. *Forties*, 193–201.

King, Richard H. *Southern Renaissance*, 231–241.

Law, Richard G. " 'The Case of the Upright Judge': The Nature of Truth in *All the King's Men*." *SAF* 6 (1978): 1–19.

McCarron, William E. "Tennyson, Donne, and *All the King's Men*." *ANQ* 17 (1979): 140–141.

McCarthy, Paul. 'Sports and Recreation in *All the King's Men*." *MissQ* 22 (1969): 113–130.

Mansfield, Luther Stearns. "History and the Historical Process in *All the King's Men*." *CentR* 22 (1978): 214–230.

Meckier, Jerome. "Burden's Complaint: The Disintegrated Personality as Theme and Style in Robert Penn Warren's *All the King's Men*." *Studies in the Novel* 2.1, 7–21. Rpt. in Chambers, Robert H., ed. *Twentieth Century Interpretations of All the King's Men*, 57–72.

Mizener, Arthur. "Robert Penn Warren: *All the King's Men*." *Southern Review* 3 (1967): 874–894. Rpt. in Gray, Richard, ed. *Robert Penn Warren*, 51–66.

Olson, David B. "Jack Burden and the Ending of *All The King's Men*." *MissQ* 26 (1973): 165–176.

Payne, Ladell. "Willie Stark and Huey Long: Atmosphere, Myth, or Suggestion?"

American Quarterly 20 (Fall 1968): 580–595. Rpt. in Chambers, Robert H., ed. *Twentieth Century Interpretations of All the King's Men*, 98–115.

Ruoff, James. "Humpty Dumpty and *All the King's Men:* A Note on Robert Penn Warren's Teleology." *Twentieth-Century Literature* 3 (1957): 128–134. Rpt. in Chambers, Robert H., ed. *Twentieth Century Interpretations of All the King's Men*, 84–92.

Shepherd, Allen. "Sugar-Boy as Foil in *All the King's Men.*" *NConL* 1.2 (1971): 15.

Shepherd, Allen. "Toward an Analysis of the Prose Style of Robert Penn Warren." *SAF* 1 (1973): 191–192, 194, 198, 200.

Simmons, James C. "Adam's Lobectomy Operation and the Meaning of *All the King's Men.*" *PMLA* 86 (1971): 84–89. Rpt. in Chambers, Robert H., ed. *Twentieth Century Interpretations of All the King's Men*, 73–83.

Slack, Robert C. "Telemachus Theme in *All the King's Men*," in Sochatoff, A. Fred, et al., eds. *All the King's Men: A Symposium*. Pittsburgh: Carnegie Institute of Technology, 1957. 29–38. Rpt. in Chambers, Robert H., ed. *Twentieth Century Interpretations of All the King's Men*, 48–56.

Strout, Cushing. "*All the King's Men* and the Shadow of William James." *SoR* 6 (1970): 920–934.

Sullivan, Walter. *Requiem for the Renascence*, 19–21.

Vauthier, Simone. "Case of the Vanishing Narratee: An Inquiry into *All the King's Men.*" *SLJ* 6.2 (1974): 42–69.

Walker, Marshall. *Robert Penn Warren*, 97–106.

West, Paul. "Robert Penn Warren," in Wright, George T., ed. *Seven American Stylists, From Poe to Mailer*, 221–226.

Wilcox, Earl J. " 'A Cause for Laughter, a Thing for Tears': Humor in *All the King's Men.*" *SLJ* 12.1 (1979): 27–35.

Winchell, Mark Royden. "O Happy Sin! Felix Culpa in *All the King's Men.*" *MissQ* 31 (1978): 570–585.

At Heaven's Gate (1943)

Bentley, Eric. "Meaning of Robert Penn Warren's Novels." *Kenyon Review* (Summer 1948). Rpt. in Kostelanetz, Richard, ed. *On Contemporary Literature*, 619–621.

Davenport, F. Garvin, Jr. *Myth of Southern History*, 143–144.

Guttenberg, Barnett. *Web of Being*, 17–33.

Justus, James H. "On the Politics of the Self-Created: *At Heaven's Gate.*" *SewR* 82 (1974): 284–299.

Justus, James H. "On the Politics of the Self-Created: *At Heaven's Gate.*" *Sewanee Review* 82 (1974): 284–299. Rpt. in Gray, Richard, ed. *Robert Penn Warren*, 40–50.

Shepherd, Allen. "Toward an Analysis of the Prose Style of Robert Penn Warren." *SAF* 1 (1973): 197–200.

Walker, Marshall. *Robert Penn Warren*, 92–97.

West, Paul. "Robert Penn Warren," in Wright, George T., ed. *Seven American Stylists, From Poe to Mailer*, 220–221.

Band of Angels (1955)

Berzon, Judith R. *Neither White Nor Black*, 127–137.

Guttenberg, Barnett. *Web of Being*, 71–84.

Shepherd, Allen. "Carrying Manty Home: Robert Penn Warren's *Band of Angels.*"

Four Quarters 21.4 (1972): 101–109. Rpt. in Gray, Richard, ed. *Robert Penn Warren*, 76–84.

Shepherd, Allen. "Toward an Analysis of the Prose Style of Robert Penn Warren." *SAF* 1 (1973): 192–193.

Sullivan, Walter. *Death by Melancholy*, 36–51.

Sullivan, Walter. "Historical Novelist and the Existential Peril: Robert Penn Warren's *Band of Angels*." *SLJ* 2.2 (1970): 104–116.

Walker, Marshall. *Robert Penn Warren*, 125–130.

West, Paul. "Robert Penn Warren," in Wright, George T., ed. *Seven American Stylists, From Poe to Mailer*, 232–233.

Cave (1959)

Guttenberg, Barnett. *Web of Being*, 85–103.

Justus, James H. "Uses of Gesture in Warren's *The Cave*." *Modern Language Quarterly* 26 (1965): 448–461. Rpt. in Gray, Richard, ed. *Robert Penn Warren*, 85–96.

Walker, Marshall. *Robert Penn Warren*, 185–191.

West, Paul. "Robert Penn Warren," in Wright, George T., ed. *Seven American Stylists, From Poe to Mailer*, 233–234.

Flood (1964)

Burt, David J. "Robert Penn Warren's Debt to Homer in *Flood*." *NConL* 3.1 (1973): 12–14.

Guttenberg, Barnett. *Web of Being*, 119–138.

Mizener, Arthur. "Uncorrupted Consciouness." *Sewanee Review* 72 (1964): 690–698. Rpt. in Gray, Richard, ed. *Robert Penn Warren*, 105–111.

Walker, Marshall. *Robert Penn Warren*, 191–200.

West, Paul. "Robert Penn Warren," in Wright, George T., ed. *Seven American Stylists, From Poe to Mailer*, 235–237.

Meet Me in Green Glen (1971)

Guttenberg, Barnett. *"Meet Me in the Green Glen,"* in Guttenberg, Barnett. *Web of Being: The Novels of Robert Penn Warren*. Nashville, TN: Vanderbilt University Press, 1975. 139–155. Rpt. in Gray, Richard, ed. *Robert Penn Warren*, 112–124.

Guttenberg, Barnett. *Web of Being*, 139–155.

Walker, Marshall. *Robert Penn Warren*, 201–213.

Night Rider (1939)

Bentley, Eric. "Meaning of Robert Penn Warren's Novels." *Kenyon Review* (Summer 1948). Rpt. in Kostelanetz, Richard, ed. *On Contemporary Literature*, 617–619.

Burt, David J. and Annette C. Burt. "Robert Penn Warren's Debt to Ibsen in *Night Rider*." *MissQ* 22 (1969): 359–361.

Davenport, F. Garvin, Jr. *Myth of Southern History*, 141–143.

Guttenberg, Barnett. *Web of Being*, 3–16.

Law, Richard. "Warren's *Night Rider* and the Issue of Naturalism: The 'Nightmare' of Our Age." *SLJ* 8.2 (1976): 41–61.

Ryan, Alvan S. "Robert Penn Warren's *Night Rider:* The Nihilism of the Isolated Temperament." *Modern Fiction Studies* 7.4 (Winter 1961–62): 338–346. Rpt. in Gray, Richard, ed. *Robert Penn Warren*, 32–39.

Walker, Marshall. *Robert Penn Warren*, 89–92.

West, Paul. "Robert Penn Warren," in Wright, George T., ed. *Seven American Stylists, From Poe to Mailer*, 218–220.

Place to Come To (1977)

Bonds, Diane S. "Vision and Being in *A Place to Come To*." *SoR* 16 (1980): 816–828.

Casper, Leonard. "Circle with a Center Outside: Robert Penn Warren's *A Place to Come To*." *SR* 65 (1980): 399–410.

Shepherd, Allen. "Dick Diver in Nashville: A Note on Robert Penn Warren's *A Place to Come To*." *F-H Annual* (1979): 173–175.

Walker, Marshall. *Robert Penn Warren*, 216–229.

Westendorp, Tjebbe. "*Place to Come To*," in Gray, Richard, ed. *Robert Penn Warren*, 125–131.

Wilderness (1961)

Bennett, Lee Shaw. "Modern Civil War Novels: The Still Unwritten War?" *SoS* 19 (1980): 123–125.

Brooks, Cleanth. "Experience Redeemed in Knowledge," in Brooks, Cleanth. *Hidden God: Studies in Hemingway, Faulkner, Yeats, Eliot, and Warren*. New Haven: Yale University Press, 1963. 98–111, 118–127. Rpt. in Gray, Richard, ed. *Robert Penn Warren*, 27–30.

Casper, Leonard. "Trial by Wilderness: Warren's Exemplum." *Studies in Contemporary Literature* 3 (1962): 45–53. Rpt. in Gray, Richard, ed. *Robert Penn Warren*, 97–104.

Guttenberg, Barnett. *Web of Being*, 104–118.

Walker, Marshall. *Robert Penn Warren*, 130–132.

West, Paul. "Robert Penn Warren," in Wright, George T., ed. *Seven American Stylists, From Poe to Mailer*, 234–235.

Witte, Flo. "Adam's Rebirth in Robert Penn Warren's *Wilderness*." *SoQ* 12 (1974): 365–377.

World Enough and Time (1950)

Berner, Robert. "Required Past: *World Enough and Time*." *Modern Fiction Studies* 6.1 (Spring 1960): 55–64. Rpt. in Gray, Richard, ed. *Robert Penn Warren*, 67–75.

Guttenberg, Barnett. *Web of Being*, 56–70.

Shepherd, Allen. "Toward an Analysis of the Prose Style of Robert Penn Warren." *SAF* 1 (1973): 197.

Walker, Marshall. *Robert Penn Warren*, 110–116.

West, Paul. "Robert Penn Warren," in Wright, George T., ed. *Seven American Stylists, From Poe to Mailer*, 230–232.

WATERS, FRANK (1902–1995)

Below Grass Roots (1937)

Bucco, Martin. *Frank Waters*, 13–14.

Lyon, Thomas J. *Frank Waters*, 86–91.

Dust Within the Rock (1940)

Bucco, Martin. *Frank Waters*, 14–17.

Lyon, Thomas J. *Frank Waters*, 91–95.

Fever Pitch (1930)
  Bucco, Martin. *Frank Waters*, 10–12.
  Lyon, Thomas J. *Frank Waters*, 69–77.

Man Who Killed the Deer (1942)
  Bucco, Martin. *Frank Waters*, 21–24.
  Davis, Jack L. and June H. Davis. "Frank Waters and the Native American Con-
  sciousness." *WAL* 9 (1974): 35–37.
  Lyon, Thomas J. *Frank Waters*, 104–113.

People of the Valley (1941)
  Bucco, Martin. *Frank Waters*, 18–21.
  Lyon, Thomas J. *Frank Waters*, 95–104.

Pike's Peak (1971)
  Lyon, Thomas J. *Frank Waters*, 131–133.

River Lady (1942)
  Bucco, Martin. *Frank Waters*, 25–26.

Wild Earth's Nobility (1935)
  Bucco, Martin. *Frank Waters*, 12–13.
  Lyon, Thomas J. *Frank Waters*, 78–86.

Woman of Otowi Crossing (1966)
  Bucco, Martin. *Frank Waters*, 38–40.
  Davis, Jack L. and June H. Davis. "Frank Waters and the Native American Con-
  sciousness." *WAL* 9 (1974): 41–43.
  Lyon, Thomas J. *Frank Waters*, 122–131.

Yogi of Cockroach Court (1947)
  Bucco, Martin. *Frank Waters*, 28–30.
  Lyon, Thomas J. *Frank Waters*, 113–122.

WATMOUGH, DAVID (1926–)

No More into the Garden (1978)
  Woodcock, George. *World of Canadian Writing*, 213, 219–221.

WEBB, CHRISTOPHER (1915–1983)

Quest of the Otter (1963)
  Kelty, Jean McClure. "Cult of Kill in Adolescent Fiction." *EJ* 64.2 (1975): 58–59.

WEBB, FRANK J. (ca.1830–ca. 1870)

Garies and Their Friends (1857)
  Berzon, Judith R. *Neither White Nor Black*, 102.
  Bogardus, R. F. "Frank J. Webb's *The Garies and Their Friends:* An Early Black
  Novelist's Venture into Realism." *SIBL* 5.2 (1974): 15–20.
  DeVries, James H. "Tradition of the Sentimental Novel in *The Garies and Their
  Friends.*" *CLAJ* 17 (1973): 241–249.

Elder, Arlene A. *"Hindered Hand"*, 11–12, 14, 19–20, 21, 27–28, 47–48, 49, 50, 52–53, 54–55, 60–61.

Fleming, Robert E. "Humor in the Early Black Novel." *CLAJ* 17 (1973): 256–257, 259–260.

Gayle, Addison, Jr. *Way of the New World*, 11–15.

WEIDMAN, JEROME (1913–1998)

I Can Get It for You Wholesale (1937)

Hearn, Charles R. *American Dream in the Great Depression*, 181–184.

WELCH, JAMES (1940–)

Death of Jim Loney (1979)

Allen, Paula Gunn. "Stranger in My Own Life: Alienation in American Indian Prose and Poetry." *MELUS* 7.2 (1980): 16–18.

Winter in the Blood (1974)

Allen, Paula Gunn. "Stranger in My Own Life: Alienation in American Indian Prose and Poetry." *MELUS* 7.2 (1980): 15–46.

Barnett, Louise K. "Alienation and Ritual in *Winter in the Blood*." *AIQ* 4 (1978): 123–130.

Barry, Nora Baker. "*Winter in the Blood* as Elegy." *AIQ* 4 (1978): 149–157.

Beidler, Peter. "Animals and Human Development in the Contemporary American Indian Novel." *WAL* 14 (1979): 139–143.

Espey, David B. "Endings in Contemporary American Indian Fiction." *WAL* 13 (1978): 136–137.

Horton, Andrew. "Bitter Humor of *Winter in the Blood*." *AIQ* 4 (1978): 131–139.

Kunz, Don. "Lost in the Distance of Winter: James Welch's *Winter in the Blood*." *Crit* 20.1 (1978): 93–99.

Larson, Charles R. *American Indian Fiction*, 140–149.

Lattin, Vernon E. "Quest for Mythic Vision in Contemporary Native American and Chicano Fiction." *AL* 50 (1979): 627–628.

Ruoff, A. LaVonne. "Alienation and the Female Principle in *Winter in the Blood*." *AIQ* 4 (1978): 107–122.

Sands, Kathleen M. "Alienation and Broken Narrative in *Winter in the Blood*." *AIQ* 4 (1978): 97–105.

Thackeray, William W. " 'Crying for Pity' in *Winter in the Blood*." *MELUS* 7.1 (1980): 61–78.

Velie, Alan R. "*Winter in the Blood* as Comic Novel." *AIQ* 4 (1978): 141–147.

WELTY, EUDORA (1909–)

Delta Wedding (1946)

Allen, John A. "Eudora Welty: The Three Moments." *Virginia Quarterly Review* 51.4 (Autumn 1975): 605–627. Rpt. in Desmond, John F., ed. *Still Moment*, 16–22.

Allen, John Alexander. "Other Ways to Live: Demigods in Eudora Welty's Fiction," in Prenshaw, Peggy Whitman, ed. *Eudora Welty*, 28–30, 35–45.

Bolsterli, Margaret. " 'Bound' Characters in Porter, Welty, McCullers: The Prerevolutionary Status of Women in American Fiction," in Garvin, Harry R., ed. *Women, Literature, Criticism*, 100–103.

Bolsterli, Margaret Jones. "Woman's Vision: The Worlds of Women in *Delta Wedding*, *Losing Battles* and *The Optimist's Daughter*," in Prenshaw, Peggy Whitman, ed. *Eudora Welty*, 149–152, 155–156.

Bradford, M. E. "Fairchild as Composite Protagonist in *Delta Wedding*," in Prenshaw, Peggy Whitman, ed. *Eudora Welty*, 201–207.

Eisinger, Chester E. "Traditionalism and Modernism in Eudora Welty," in Prenshaw, Peggy Whitman, ed. *Eudora Welty*, 15–17.

Gray, Richard. *Literature of Memory*, 177–184.

Hardy, John Edward. "*Delta Wedding* as Region and Symbol." *Sewanee Review* 60 (Summer 1952): 397–417. Rpt. in Spacks, Patricia Meyer, ed. *Contemporary Women Novelists*, 150–166.

Hardy, John Edward. "Marrying Down in Eudora Welty's Novels," in Prenshaw, Peggy Whitman, ed. *Eudora Welty*, 93–100.

Hinton, Jane L. "Role of Family in *Delta Wedding*, *Losing Battles* and *The Optimist's Daughter*," in Prenshaw, Peggy Whitman, ed. *Eudora Welty*, 120–124.

Howell, Elmo. "Eudora Welty and the City of Man." *GR* 33 (1979): 777, 780–781.

Howell, Elmo. "Eudora Welty and the Use of Place in Southern Fiction." *ArQ* 28 (1972): 249.

Isaacs, Neil D. *Eudora Welty*, 33–36.

Kerr, Elizabeth M. "World of Eudora Welty's Women," in Prenshaw, Peggy Whitman, ed. *Eudora Welty*, 133–134, 135–138.

Landess, Thomas H. "Function of Taste in the Fiction of Eudora Welty." *MissQ* 26 (1973): 551–554.

MacKethan, Lucinda H. "To See Things in Their Time: The Act of Focus in Eudora Welty's Fiction." *AL* 50 (1978): 259–275.

MacKethan, Lucinda Hardwick. *Dream of Arcady*, 184–189, 191–195.

Messerli, Douglas. "The Problem of Time in Welty's *Delta Wedding*." *SAF* 5 (1977): 227–240.

Neault, D. James. "Time in the Fiction of Eudora Welty," in Desmond, John F., ed. *Still Moment*, 38, 40–41.

Rupp, Richard H. *Celebration in Postwar American Fiction*, 61–64.

Skaggs, Merrill Maguire. *Folk of Southern Fiction*, 240–241.

Vande-Kieft, Ruth M. "Vision of Eudora Welty." *MissQ* 26 (1973):529–530.

Losing Battles (1970)

Allen, John A. "Eudora Welty: The Three Moments." *Virginia Quarterly Review* 51.4 (Autumn 1975): 605–627. Rpt. in Desmond, John F., ed. *Still Moment*, 13, 14, 27–31.

Allen, John Alexander. "Other Ways to Live: Demigods in Eudora Welty's Fiction," in Prenshaw, Peggy Whitman, ed. *Eudora Welty*, 47–55.

Bolsterli, Margaret Jones. "Woman's Vision: The Worlds of Women in *Delta Wedding*, *Losing Battles* and *The Optimist's Daughter*," in Prenshaw, Peggy Whitman, ed. *Eudora Welty*, 149–150, 153–155.

Bradford, M. E. "Looking Down from a High Place: The Serenity of Miss Welty's *Losing Battles*." *Recherches Anglaises et Américaines* 4 (1971): 92–97. Rpt. in Desmond, John F., ed. *Still Moment*, 103–107.

Bryant, J. A., Jr. "Recovery of the Confident Narrator: *A Curtain of Green* to

Losing Battles," in Prenshaw, Peggy Whitman, ed. *Eudora Welty*, 70–71, 72–75, 77–82.

Eisinger, Chester E. "Traditionalism and Modernism in Eudora Welty," in Prenshaw, Peggy Whitman, ed. *Eudora Welty*, 21–23.

Ferguson, Mary Anne. "*Losing Battles* as a Comic Epic in Prose," in Prenshaw, Peggy Whitman, ed. *Eudora Welty*, 305–324.

Gossett, Louise Y. "Eudora Welty's New Novel: The Comedy of Loss." *SLJ* 3.1 (1970): 122–137.

Gossett, Louise Y. "*Losing Battles:* Festival and Celebration," in Prenshaw, Peggy Whitman, ed. *Eudora Welty*, 341–350.

Gross, Seymour. "Long Day's Living: The Angelic Ingenuities of *Losing Battles*," in Prenshaw, Peggy Whitman, ed. *Eudora Welty*, 325–340.

Hardy, John Edward. "Marrying Down in Eudora Welty's Novels," in Prenshaw, Peggy Whitman, ed. *Eudora Welty*, 103–107.

Heilman, Robert B. "*Losing Battles* and Winning the War," in Prenshaw, Peggy Whitman, ed. *Eudora Welty*, 269–304.

Hinton, Jane L. "Role of Family in *Delta Wedding*, *Losing Battles* and *The Optimist's Daughter*," in Prenshaw, Peggy Whitman, ed. *Eudora Welty*, 124–128.

Howell, Elmo. "Eudora Welty and the City of Man." *GR* 33 (1979): 773–774.

Howell, Elmo. "Eudora Welty and the Use of Place in Southern Fiction." *ArQ* 28 (1972): 255–256.

Kerr, Elizabeth M. "World of Eudora Welty's Women," in Prenshaw, Peggy Whitman, ed. *Eudora Welty*, 133–134, 134–135, 140–143.

Kreyling, Michael. "Myth and History: The Foes of *Losing Battles*." *MissQ* 26 (1973): 639–649.

Landess, Thomas H. "More Trouble in Mississippi: Family vs. Antifamily in Miss Welty's *Losing Battles*." *SewR* 79 (1971): 626–634.

MacKethan, Lucinda H. "To See Things in Their Time: The Act of Focus in Eudora Welty's Fiction." *AL* 50 (1978): 259–275.

MacKethan, Lucinda Hardwick. *Dream of Arcady*, 184–186, 189–190, 195–199.

McMillen, William. "Circling-In: The Concept of the Home in Eudora Welty's *Losing Battles* and *The Optimist's Daughter*," in Desmond, John F., ed. *Still Moment*, 110–116.

McMillen, William E. "Conflict and Resolution in Welty's *Losing Battles*." *Crit* 15.1 (1973): 110–124.

Messerli, Douglas. " 'A Battle with Both Sides Using the Same Tactics': The Language of Time in *Losing Battles*," in Prenshaw, Peggy Whitman, ed. *Eudora Welty*, 351–366.

Moore, Carol A. "Insulation of Illusion and *Losing Battles*." *MissQ* 26 (1973): 651–658.

Neault, D. James. "Time in the Fiction of Eudora Welty," in Desmond, John F., ed. *Still Moment*, 41–43, 46.

Oates, Joyce Carol. "Eudora's Web." *Atlantic Monthly* 225.4 (April 1970). Rpt. in Spacks, Patricia Meyer, ed. *Contemporary Women Novelists*, 167–172.

Reynolds, Larry J. "Enlightening Darkness: Theme and Structure in Eudora Welty's *Losing Battles*." *JNT* 8 (1978): 133–140.

Tarbox, Raymond. "Eudora Welty's Fiction: The Salvation Theme." *American Imago* 29 (1972): 74–75.

Vande-Kieft, Ruth M. "Vision of Eudora Welty." *MissQ* 26 (1973): 534–537.

Optimist's Daughter (1972)

Allen, John A. "Eudora Welty: The Three Moments." *Virginia Quarterly Review* 51.4 (Autumn 1975): 605–627. Rpt. in Desmond, John F., ed. *Still Moment*, 14, 26–27.

Allen, John Alexander. "Other Ways to Live: Demigods in Eudora Welty's Fiction," in Prenshaw, Peggy Whitman, ed. *Eudora Welty*, 45–46.

Bolsterli, Margaret Jones. "Woman's Vision: The Worlds of Women in *Delta Wedding, Losing Battles* and *The Optimist's Daughter*," in Prenshaw, Peggy Whitman, ed. *Eudora Welty*, 149–150, 152–153.

Desmond, John F. "Pattern and Vision in *The Optimist's Daughter*," in Desmond, John F., ed. *Still Moment*, 118–137.

Eisinger, Chester E. "Traditionalism and Modernism in Eudora Welty," in Prenshaw, Peggy Whitman, ed. *Eudora Welty*, 23–25.

Hardy, John Edward. "Marrying Down in Eudora Welty's Novels," in Prenshaw, Peggy Whitman, ed. *Eudora Welty*, 107–119.

Hinton, Jane L. "Role of Family in *Delta Wedding, Losing Battles* and *The Optimist's Daughter*," in Prenshaw, Peggy Whitman, ed. *Eudora Welty*, 128–131.

Howell, Elmo. "Eudora Welty and the City of Man." *GR* 33 (1979): 777–780.

Kerr, Elizabeth M. "World of Eudora Welty's Women," in Prenshaw, Peggy Whitman, ed. *Eudora Welty*, 134, 138–140.

Kreyling, Michael. "Life with People: Virginia Woolf, Eudora Welty, and *The Optimist's Daughter*." *SoR* 13 (1977): 250–271.

Landess, Thomas H. "Function of Taste in the Fiction of Eudora Welty." *MissQ* 26 (1973): 550–551.

MacKethan, Lucinda H. "To See Things in Their Time: The Act of Focus in Eudora Welty's Fiction." *AL* 50 (1978): 259–275.

MacKethan, Lucinda Hardwick. *Dream of Arcady*, 184–187, 190–191, 203–206.

McMillen, William. "Circling-In: The Concept of the Home in Eudora Welty's *Losing Battles* and *The Optimist's Daughter*," in Desmond, John F., ed. *Still Moment*, 110–116.

Neault, D. James. "Time in the Fiction of Eudora Welty," in Desmond, John F., ed. *Still Moment*, 46–47.

Spacks, Patricia Meyer. *Female Imagination*, 264–266, 269–271.

Sullivan, Walter. *Requiem for the Renascence*, 52–58.

Vande-Kieft, Ruth M. "Vision of Eudora Welty." *MissQ* 26 (1973): 537–542.

Young, Thomas Daniel. "Social Form and Social Order: An Examination of *The Optimist's Daughter*," in Prenshaw, Peggy Whitman, ed. *Eudora Welty*, 367–385.

Ponder Heart (1954)

Allen, John A. "Eudora Welty: The Three Moments." *Virginia Quarterly Review* 51.4 (Autumn 1975): 605–627. Rpt. in Desmond, John F., ed. *Still Moment*, 22–26.

Cornell, Brenda G. "Ambiguous Necessity: A Study of *The Ponder Heart*," in Prenshaw, Peggy Whitman, ed. *Eudora Welty*, 208–219.

Hardy, John Edward. "Marrying Down in Eudora Welty's Novels," in Prenshaw, Peggy Whitman, ed. *Eudora Welty*, 100–103.

Isaacs, Neil D. *Eudora Welty*, 12–14.

Weiner, Rachel V. "Eudora Welty's *The Ponder Heart:* The Judgment of Art." *SoS* 19 (1980): 261–273.

Robber Bridegroom (1942)

Allen, John A. "Eudora Welty: The Three Moments." *Virginia Quarterly Review* 51.4 (Autumn 1975): 605–627. Rpt. in Desmond, John F., ed. *Still Moment*, 13–14.

Allen, John Alexander. "Other Ways to Live: Demigods in Eudora Welty's Fiction," in Prenshaw, Peggy Whitman, ed. *Eudora Welty*, 45.

Arnold, Marilyn. "Eudora Welty's Parody." *NMW* 11 (1978): 15–22.

Bryant, J. A., Jr. "Recovery of the Confident Narrator: *A Curtain of Green* to *Losing Battles*," in Prenshaw, Peggy Whitman, ed. *Eudora Welty*, 75–77.

Clark, Charles C. "*Robber Bridegroom:* Realism and Fantasy on the Natchez Trace." *MissQ* 26 (1973): 625–638.

Davis, Charles E. "Eudora Welty's *Robber Bridegroom* and Old Southwest Humor: A Doubleness of Vision," in Desmond, John F., ed. *Still Moment*, 71–80.

Devlin, Albert J. "Eudora Welty's Mississippi," in Prenshaw, Peggy Whitman, ed. *Eudora Welty*, 169–173.

Eisinger, Chester E. "Traditionalism and Modernism in Eudora Welty," in Prenshaw, Peggy Whitman, ed. *Eudora Welty*, 11–12.

French, Warren. " 'All Things Are Double': Eudora Welty as a Civilized Writer," in Prenshaw, Peggy Whitman, ed. *Eudora Welty*, 179–188.

Isaacs, Neil D. *Eudora Welty*, 16–20.

Moore, Carol A. "Aunt Studney's Sack." *SoR* 16 (1980): 591–596.

Neault, D. James. "Time in the Fiction of Eudora Welty," in Desmond, John F., ed. *Still Moment*, 45–46.

Phillips, Robert L., Jr. "Structural Approach to Myth in the Fiction of Eudora Welty," in Prenshaw, Peggy Whitman, ed. *Eudora Welty*, 62–64.

Pickett, Nell A. "Colloquialism as a Style in the First-Person-Narrator Fiction of Eudora Welty." *MissQ* 26 (1973): 559–572.

Rupp, Richard H. *Celebration in Postwar American Fiction*, 60–61.

WESCOTT, GLENWAY (1901–1987)

Apartment in Athens (1945)

Johnson, Ira. *Glenway Wescott*, 143–165.

Apple of the Eye (1924)

Johnson, Ira. *Glenway Wescott*, 7–40.

Grandmothers (1927)

Johnson, Ira. *Glenway Wescott*, 41–82.

WEST, DOROTHY (1907–1998)

Living Is Easy (1948)

Berzon, Judith R. *Neither White Nor Black*, 178–187.

WEST, JESSAMYN (1902–1984)

Leafy Rivers (1967)

Shivers, Alfred S. *Jessamyn West*, 77–83.

Matter of Time (1966)

Shivers, Alfred S. *Jessamyn West*, 115–123.

South of the Angels (1960)

Shivers, Alfred S. *Jessamyn West*, 106–115.

Witch Diggers (1951)

Shivers, Alfred S. *Jessamyn West*, 65–73.

WESTLAKE, DONALD E. see STARK, RICHARD

WHARTON, EDITH (1862–1937)

Age of Innocence (1920)

Ammons, Elizabeth. *Edith Wharton's Argument with America*, 143–153.

Bremer, Sidney H. "American Dreams and American Cities in Three Post-World War I Novels." *SAQ* 79 (1980): 276–278.

Coxe, Louis. *Enabling Acts*, 62–69.

Evans, Elizabeth. "Musical Allusions in *The Age of Innocence*." *NConL* 4.3 (1974): 4–7.

Gelfant, Blanche Housman. *American City Novel*, 110–119.

Henderson, Harry B. *Versions of the Past*, 238–241.

Kronenberger, Louis. *Polished Surface*, 247–255.

Lawson, Richard H. *Edith Wharton*, 15–27.

Lindberg, Gary H. *Edith Wharton and the Novel of Manners*, 48–49, 52–53, 56, 57, 59–60, 76–86, 100–108, 112–114, 128–137, 147–148, 152–157, 162, 164, 166–168, 169–170.

McDowell, Margaret B. *Edith Wharton*, 92–104.

McDowell, Margaret B. "Viewing the Custom of Her Country: Edith Wharton's Feminism." *ConL* 15 (1974): 535.

Milne, Gordon. *Sense of Society*, 118–129.

Spacks, Patricia Meyer. *Female Imagination*, 243–244, 248–249.

Tintner, Adeline R. "Jamesian Structures in *The Age of Innocence* and Related Stories." *TCL* 26 (1980): 337–346.

Tuttleton, James W. " 'Combat in the Erogenous Zone': Women in the American Novel between the Two Wars," in Springer, Marlene, ed. *What Manner of Woman*, 274–276.

Tuttleton, James W. "Edith Wharton: The Archeological Motive." *YR* 61 (1972): 569–570.

Tuttleton, James W. *Novel of Manners in America*, 128–133.

Walton, Geoffrey. *Edith Wharton*, 130–139.

Wolff, Cynthia Griffin. "*Age of Innocence:* Wharton's 'Portrait of a Gentleman'." *SoR* 12 (1976): 640–658.

Wolff, Cynthia Griffin. *Feast of Words*, 312–334.

Backward Glance (1934)

Tuttleton, James W. "Edith Wharton: The Archeological Motive." *YR* 61 (1972): 571–572.

Buccaneers (1938)

McDowell, Margaret B. *Edith Wharton*, 137–141.
Milne, Gordon. *Sense of Society*, 137–142.
Spacks, Patricia Meyer. *Female Imagination*, 246, 249, 253–254.
Tuttleton, James W. "Edith Wharton: The Archeological Motive." *YR* 61 (1972): 572–574.
Walton, Geoffrey. *Edith Wharton*, 176–196.
Wolff, Cynthia Griffin. *Feast of Words*, 399–406.

Children (1928)

Ammons, Elizabeth. *Edith Wharton's Argument with America*, 173–181.
McDowell, Margaret B. *Edith Wharton*, 119–122.
Walton, Geoffrey. *Edith Wharton*, 151–158.
Wolff, Cynthia Griffin. *Feast of Words*, 383–391.

Custom of the Country (1913)

Ammons, Elizabeth. "Business of Marriage in Edith Wharton's *The Custom of the Country*." *Criticism* 16 (1974): 326–338.
Ammons, Elizabeth. *Edith Wharton's Argument with America*, 97–124.
Lawson, Richard H. *Edith Wharton*, 41–53.
Lindberg, Gary H. *Edith Wharton and the Novel of Manners*, 48, 50–51, 59–60, 67–76, 93–100, 111–112, 115–122, 146–147, 162–163, 166, 167.
McDowell, Margaret B. *Edith Wharton*, 73–83.
Milne, Gordon. *Sense of Society*, 134–135.
Tuttleton, James W. "Edith Wharton: The Archeological Motive." *YR* 61 (1972): 570–571.
Walton, Geoffrey. *Edith Wharton*, 107–129.
Way, Brian. *F. Scott Fitzgerald and the Art of Social Fiction*, 46–47.
Wolff, Cynthia Griffin. *Feast of Words*, 231–258.

Fruit of the Tree (1907)

Ammons, Elizabeth. *Edith Wharton's Argument with America*, 43–55.
McDowell, Margaret B. *Edith Wharton*, 53–56.
McDowell, Margaret B. "Viewing the Custom of Her Country: Edith Wharton's Feminism." *ConL* 15 (1974): 530–533.
Stein, Allen F. "Wharton's *Blithedale:* A New Reading of *The Fruit of the Tree*." *ALR* 12 (1979): 330–337.
Walton, Geoffrey. *Edith Wharton*, 93–99.
Wolff, Cynthia Griffin. *Feast of Words*, 140–143.

Glimpses of the Moon (1922)

Ammons, Elizabeth. *Edith Wharton's Argument with America*, 160–162.
Wolff, Cynthia Griffin. *Feast of Words*, 346–348.

Gods Arrive (1932)

McDowell, Margaret B. *Edith Wharton*, 124–132.
Tuttleton, James W. "Edith Wharton: The Archeological Motive." *YR* 61 (1972): 568.
Tuttleton, James W. *Novel of Manners in America*, 136–139.
Walton, Geoffrey. *Edith Wharton*, 171–174.
Wolff, Cynthia Griffin. *Feast of Words*, 391–395.

House of Mirth (1905)

Ammons, Elizabeth. *Edith Wharton's Argument with America*, 25–43.
Benoit, Raymond. "Wharton's *House of Mirth*." *Expl* 29 (1971): Item 59.
Cohn, Jan. "House of Fiction: Domestic Architecture in Howells and Edith Wharton." *TSLL* 15 (1973): 544–547.
Cohn, Jan. "Women as Superfluous Characters in American Realism and Naturalism." *SAF* 1 (1973): 161.
Dahl, Curtis. "Edith Wharton's *The House of Mirth:* Sermon on a Text.." *MFS* 21 (1975): 572–576.
Davidson, Cathy N. "Kept Women in *The House of Mirth*." *MarkR* 9 (1979): 10–13.
Fetterley, Judith. " 'The Temptation to Be a Beautiful Object': Double Standard and Double Bind in *The House of Mirth*." *SAF* 5 (1977): 199–211.
Gargano, James W. "*The House of Mirth:* Social Futility and Faith." *AL* 44 (1972): 137–143.
Gelfant, Blanche Housman. *American City Novel*, 107–110, 112–114, 116, 118–119.
Hays, Peter L. "Bearding the Lily: Wharton's Names." *ANQ* 18 (1980): 75–76.
Kronenberger, Louis. *Polished Surface*, 255–270.
Lawson, Richard H. *Edith Wharton*, 29–39.
Lidoff, Joan. "Another Sleeping Beauty: Narcissism in *The House of Mirth*." *AQ* 32 (1980): 519–539.
Lindberg, Gary H. *Edith Wharton and the Novel of Manners*, 48, 54–55, 56–57, 61–71, 87–93, 112, 122–128, 142–145, 167, 168–169.
McDowell, Margaret B. *Edith Wharton*, 43–52.
McIlvaine, Robert. "Edith Wharton's American Beauty Rose." *JAmS* 7 (1973): 183–185.
Milne, Gordon. *Sense of Society*, 132–134.
Price, Alan. "Lily Bart and Carrie Meeber: Cultural Sisters." *ALR* 13 (1980): 239–244.
Spacks, Patricia Meyer. *Female Imagination*, 241–242, 245.
Stineback, David C. *Shifting World*, 87–100.
Tuttleton, James W. "Edith Wharton: The Archeological Motive." *YR* 61 (1972): 566–567.
Tuttleton, James W. *Novel of Manners in America*, 124–128.
Vella, Michael W. "Technique and Theme in *The House of Mirth*." *MarkR* 2.3 (1970): 17–20.
Walton, Geoffrey. *Edith Wharton*, 44–62.
Westbrook, Wayne W. "*House of Mirth* and the Insurance Scandal of 1905." *ANQ* 14 (1976): 134–137.
Wolff, Cynthia G. "Lily Bart and the Beautiful Death." *AL* 46 (1974): 16–40.
Wolff, Cynthia Griffin. *Feast of Words*, 109–133.

Hudson River Bracketed (1929)

Cohn, Jan. "House of Fiction: Domestic Architecture in Howells and Edith Wharton." *TSLL* 15 (1973): 547–549.
McDowell, Margaret B. *Edith Wharton*, 124–136.
Tuttleton, James W. "Edith Wharton: The Archeological Motive." *YR* 61 (1972): 567–568.
Tuttleton, James W. *Novel of Manners in America*, 134–136, 138.

Walton, Geoffrey. *Edith Wharton*, 166–171.
Wolff, Cynthia Griffin. *Feast of Words*, 391–395.

Mother's Recompense (1925)

Ammons, Elizabeth. *Edith Wharton's Argument with America*, 162–164.
Milne, Gordon. *Sense of Society*, 131, 136–137.
Spacks, Patricia Meyer. *Female Imagination*, 244–245, 250–251.
Tintner, Adeline R. "Mothers, Daughters, and Incest in the Late Novels of Edith Wharton," in Davidson, Cathy N. and E. M. Broner, eds. *Lost Tradition*, 149–153.
Wolff, Cynthia Griffin. *Feast of Words*, 357–372.

Old Maid (1924)

Tintner, Adeline R. "Mothers, Daughters, and Incest in the Late Novels of Edith Wharton," in Davidson, Cathy N. and E. M. Broner, eds. *Lost Tradition*, 148–149.
Wolff, Cynthia Griffin. *Feast of Words*, 352–357.

Reef (1912)

Ammons, Elizabeth. *Edith Wharton's Argument with America*, 78–96.
Ammons, Elizabeth. "Fairy-Tale Love and *The Reef*." *AL* 47 (1976): 615–628.
Gargano, James W. "Edith Wharton's *The Reef:* The Genteel Woman's Quest for Knowledge." *Novel* 10 (1976): 40–48.
Lawson, Richard H. *Edith Wharton*, 55–65.
McDowell, Margaret B. *Edith Wharton*, 58–63.
McDowell, Margaret B. "Viewing the Custom of Her Country: Edith Wharton's Feminism." *ConL* 15 (1974): 533–534.
Wolff, Cynthia Griffin. *Feast of Words*, 207–219.

Son at the Front (1922)

McDowell, Margaret B. *Edith Wharton*, 109–114.
Wolff, Cynthia Griffin. *Feast of Words*, 348–351.

Summer (1918)

Ammons, Elizabeth. *Edith Wharton's Argument with America*, 130–141.
McDowell, Margaret B. *Edith Wharton*, 69–71.
Walton, Geoffrey. *Edith Wharton*, 83–92.
Wolff, Cynthia Griffin. *Feast of Words*, 270–295, 305–307.

Touchstone (1900)

Walton, Geoffrey. *Edith Wharton*, 34–36.

Twilight Sleep (1927)

Ammons, Elizabeth. *Edith Wharton's Argument with America*, 164–165.
McDowell, Margaret B. *Edith Wharton*, 114–119.
Tintner, Adeline R. "Mothers, Daughters, and Incest in the Late Novels of Edith Wharton," in Davidson, Cathy N. and E. M. Broner, eds. *Lost Tradition*, 153–155.
Walton, Geoffrey. *Edith Wharton*, 141–151.
Wolff, Cynthia Griffin. *Feast of Words*, 374–376.

Valley of Decision (1902)

Lindberg, Gary H. *Edith Wharton and the Novel of Manners*, 15–16, 41–42, 53–54, 59–60.

Tuttleton, James W. "Edith Wharton: The Archeological Motive." *YR* 61 (1972): 565–566.

Walton, Geoffrey. *Edith Wharton*, 36–39.

WHEELER, HARVEY (1918–)

Fail Safe (1962)

Wilkinson, Rupert. "Connections with Toughness: The Novels of Eugene Burdick." *JAmS* 11 (1977): 223–239.

WHITE, E. B. (1899–1985)

Charlotte's Web (1952)

Griffith, John. "*Charlotte's Web:* A Lonely Fantasy of Love. *ChildL* 8 (1979): 111–117.

WHITE, WALTER (1893–1955)

Flight (1926)

Singh, Amritjit. *Novels of the Harlem Renaissance*, 93–95.

WHITNEY, PHYLLIS (1903–)

Columbella (1966)

Russ, Joanna. "Somebody's Trying to Kill Me and I Think It's My Husband: The Modern Gothic." *JPC* 6 (1973): 666–691.

WIBBERLEY, LEONARD see WEBB, CHRISTOPHER

WIDEMAN, JOHN EDGAR (1941–)

Hurry Home (1970)

Schultz, Elizabeth A. "Heirs of Ralph Ellison: Patterns of Individualism in the Contemporary Afro-American Novel." *CLAJ* 22 (1978): 112–114.

WIEBE, RUDY (1934–)

Blue Mountains of China (1970)

Bilan, R. P. "Wiebe & Religious Struggle." *CanL* 77 (1978): 50–63.

Ferris, Ina. "Religious Vision and Fictional Form: Rudy Wiebe's *The Blue Mountains of China*." *Mosaic* 11.3 (1978): 79–85.

Ferris, Ina. "Religious Vision and Fictional Form: Rudy Wiebe's *The Blue Mountains of China*," in Wortley, John, ed. *Post-War Canadian Fiction*, 79–85.

Jeffrey, David L. "Biblical Hermeneutic and Family History in Contemporary Canadian Fiction: Wiebe and Laurence," in Wortley, John, ed. *Post-War Canadian Fiction*, 99–105.

Jeffrey, David Lyle. "Biblical Hermeneutic and Family History in Contemporary Canadian Fiction: Wiebe and Laurence." *Mosaic* 11.3 (1978): 99–105.

Morley, Patricia A. *Comedians*, 74–82.

Tiessen, Hildegard E. " Mighty Inner River: 'Peace' in the Early Fiction of Rudy Wiebe," in Moss, John, ed. *Here and Now*, 169–180.

First and Vital Candle (1966)

Morley, Patricia A. *Comedians*, 85–95.

Peace Shall Destroy Many (1962)

Mansbridge, Francis. "Wiebe's Sense of Community." *CanL* 77 (1978): 42–49.

Morley, Patricia A. *Comedians*, 62–73.

Tiessen, Hildegard E. " Mighty Inner River: 'Peace' in the Early Fiction of Rudy Wiebe," in Moss, John, ed. *Here and Now*, 169–180.

Scorched-Wood People (1977)

Dueck, Allan. "Rudy Wiebe's Approach to Historical Fiction: A Study of *The Temptations of Big Bear* and *The Scorched-Wood People*," in Moss, John, ed. *Here and Now*, 189–199.

Tefs, Wayne A. "Rudy Wiebe: Mystery and Reality." *Mosaic* 11.4 (1978): 156–158.

Temptations of Big Bear (1973)

Dueck, Allan. "Rudy Wiebe's Approach to Historical Fiction: A Study of *The Temptations of Big Bear* and *The Scorched-Wood People*," in Moss, John, ed. *Here and Now*, 183–189.

Harrison, Dick. *Unnamed Country*, 199–204.

Morley, Patricia A. *Comedians*, 97–106.

Moss, John. *Sex and Violence*, 258–259, 261–269, 272–273.

Roemer, Kenneth M. "Ruth M. Buck's *Voices of the Plains Cree*; Rudy Wiebe's *The Temptations of Big Bear*." *WLWE* 13 (1974): 263–265.

Taylor, Lauralyn. "*Temptations of Big Bear*: A Filmic Novel?" *ECW* 9 (1977–78): 134–138.

Tefs, Wayne A. "Rudy Wiebe: Mystery and Reality." *Mosaic* 11.4 (1978): 156.

Williams, David. "Indian Our Ancestor: Three Modes of Vision in Recent Canadian Fiction." *DR* 58 (1978): 311–316.

WIER, ESTER (1910–)

Loner (1963)

Kelty, Jean McClure. "Cult of Kill in Adolescent Fiction." *EJ* 64.2 (1975): 58.

WIESEL, ELIE (1928–)

Accident see *Le jour*

Beggar in Jerusalem see *Le mendiant de Jérusalem*

Dawn see *L'aube*

Gates of the Forest see *Les portes de la forêt*

La ville de la chance (1962)

Alter, Robert. "Elie Wiesel: Between Hangman and Victim," in Cargas, Harry James, ed. *Responses to Elie Wiesel*, 85, 88–89.

Berenbaum, Michael. *Vision of the Void*, 31–51.

Des Pres, Terrence. "Authority of Silence in Elie Wiesel's Art," in Rosenfeld, Alvin and Irving Greenberg, eds. *Confronting the Holocaust*, 67–68.

Estess, Ted L. *Elie Wiesel*, 51–56, 64.

Estess, Ted L. "Elie Wiesel and the Drama of Interrogation," in Cargas, Harry James, ed. *Responses to Elie Wiesel*, 182–186, 193–194.

Fine, Ellen. "Journey Homeward: The Theme of the Town in the Works of Elie Wiesel," in Cargas, Harry James, ed. *Responses to Elie Wiesel*, 235, 237–238, 240, 241, 242, 243–244, 246–256.

Friedman, Maurice. "Elie Wiesel: The Job of Auschwitz," in Cargas, Harry James, ed. *Responses to Elie Wiesel*, 210–212.

Halperin, Irving. "From *Night* to *The Gates of the Forest:* The Novels of Elie Wiesel," in Cargas, Harry James, ed. *Responses to Elie Wiesel*, 60–61, 64–71.

Halperin, Irving. *Messengers from the Dead*, 86–93.

Indinopulos, Thomas A. "Holocaust in the Stories of Elie Wiesel," in Cargas, Harry James, ed. *Responses to Elie Wiesel*, 119–121.

Joseloff, Samuel. "Link and Promise: The Works of Elie Wiesel." *SoHR* 8 (1974): 168–164, 167–168.

Kahn, Lothar. "Elie Wiesel: Neo-Hasidism," in Cargas, Harry James, ed. *Responses to Elie Wiesel*, 106–107, 113.

Knopp, Josephine. "Wiesel and the Absurd.." *ConL* 15 (1974): 217–218.

Knopp, Josephine. "Wiesel and the Absurd," in Cargas, Harry James, ed. *Responses to Elie Wiesel*, 97–98.

L'aube (1960)

Alter, Robert. "Elie Wiesel: Between Hangman and Victim," in Cargas, Harry James, ed. *Responses to Elie Wiesel*, 85.

Berenbaum, Michael. *Vision of the Void*, 21–25.

Des Pres, Terrence. "Authority of Silence in Elie Wiesel's Art," in Rosenfeld, Alvin and Irving Greenberg, eds. *Confronting the Holocaust*, 62–64.

Estess, Ted L. *Elie Wiesel*, 37–44.

Estess, Ted L. "Elie Wiesel and the Drama of Interrogation," in Cargas, Harry James, ed. *Responses to Elie Wiesel*, 179–180.

Friedman, Maurice. "Elie Wiesel: The Job of Auschwitz," in Cargas, Harry James, ed. *Responses to Elie Wiesel*, 207–208.

Halperin, Irving. "From *Night* to *The Gates of the Forest:* The Novels of Elie Wiesel," in Cargas, Harry James, ed. *Responses to Elie Wiesel*, 56–59.

Halperin, Irving. *Messengers from the Dead*, 77–81.

Indinopulos, Thomas A. "Holocaust in the Stories of Elie Wiesel," in Cargas, Harry James, ed. *Responses to Elie Wiesel*, 119.

Joseloff, Samuel. "Link and Promise: The Works of Elie Wiesel." *SoHR* 8 (1974): 164.

Kahn, Lothar. "Elie Wiesel: Neo-Hasidism," in Cargas, Harry James, ed. *Responses to Elie Wiesel*, 105–106.

Le jour (1961)

Alter, Robert. "Elie Wiesel: Between Hangman and Victim," in Cargas, Harry James, ed. *Responses to Elie Wiesel*, 85.

Berenbaum, Michael. *Vision of the Void*, 25–29.

Des Pres, Terrence. "Authority of Silence in Elie Wiesel's Art," in Rosenfeld, Alvin and Irving Greenberg, eds. *Confronting the Holocaust*, 64–65.

Estess, Ted L. *Elie Wiesel*, 44–51.

Estess, Ted L. "Elie Wiesel and the Drama of Interrogation," in Cargas, Harry James, ed. *Responses to Elie Wiesel*, 180, 192–193.

Friedman, Maurice. "Elie Wiesel: The Job of Auschwitz," in Cargas, Harry James, ed. *Responses to Elie Wiesel*, 208–210.

Halperin, Irving. "From *Night* to *The Gates of the Forest:* The Novels of Elie Wiesel," in Cargas, Harry James, ed. *Responses to Elie Wiesel*, 59–60, 61–64.

Halperin, Irving. *Messengers from the Dead*, 81–86.

Indinopulos, Thomas A. "Holocaust in the Stories of Elie Wiesel," in Cargas, Harry James, ed. *Responses to Elie Wiesel*, 121.

Joseloff, Samuel. "Link and Promise: The Works of Elie Wiesel." *SoHR* 8 (1974): 166.

Knopp, Josephine. "Wiesel and the Absurd.." *ConL* 15 (1974): 215–217.

Knopp, Josephine. "Wiesel and the Absurd," in Cargas, Harry James, ed. *Responses to Elie Wiesel*, 94–97.

Lamont, Rosette C. "Elie Wiesel: In Search of a Tongue," in Rosenfeld, Alvin and Irving Greenberg, eds. *Confronting the Holocaust*, 93–96.

Le mendiant de Jérusalem (1968)

Berenbaum, Michael. *Vision of the Void*, 69–80.

Des Pres, Terrence. "Authority of Silence in Elie Wiesel's Art," in Rosenfeld, Alvin and Irving Greenberg, eds. *Confronting the Holocaust*, 69.

Estess, Ted L. *Elie Wiesel*, 93, 99–100.

Fine, Ellen. "Journey Homeward: The Theme of the Town in the Works of Elie Wiesel," in Cargas, Harry James, ed. *Responses to Elie Wiesel*, 238, 239, 240–241, 242, 243.

Friedman, Maurice. "Elie Wiesel: The Job of Auschwitz," in Cargas, Harry James, ed. *Responses to Elie Wiesel*, 217–219, 220–221.

Joseloff, Samuel. "Link and Promise: The Works of Elie Wiesel." *SoHR* 8 (1974): 167, 169.

Le serment de Kolvillàg (1973)

Berenbaum, Michael. *Vision of the Void*, 91–102.

Des Pres, Terrence. "Authority of Silence in Elie Wiesel's Art," in Rosenfeld, Alvin and Irving Greenberg, eds. *Confronting the Holocaust*, 69–70.

Estess, Ted L. *Elie Wiesel*, 90–112.

Estess, Ted L. "Elie Wiesel and the Drama of Interrogation," in Cargas, Harry James, ed. *Responses to Elie Wiesel*, 189–191.

Fine, Ellen. "Journey Homeward: The Theme of the Town in the Works of Elie Wiesel," in Cargas, Harry James, ed. *Responses to Elie Wiesel*, 239, 241.

Friedman, Maurice. "Elie Wiesel: The Job of Auschwitz," in Cargas, Harry James, ed. *Responses to Elie Wiesel*, 223–228.

Les portes de la forêt (1964)

Alter, Robert. *After the Tradition*, 158–160.

Alter, Robert. "Elie Wiesel: Between Hangman and Victim," in Cargas, Harry James, ed. *Responses to Elie Wiesel*, 85, 89–91.

Berenbaum, Michael. *Vision of the Void*, 52–68, 89.

Des Pres, Terrence. "Authority of Silence in Elie Wiesel's Art," in Rosenfeld, Alvin and Irving Greenberg, eds. *Confronting the Holocaust*, 65–67.

Estess, Ted L. *Elie Wiesel*, 59, 64–88, 93, 99.

Estess, Ted L. "Elie Wiesel and the Drama of Interrogation," in Cargas, Harry James, ed. *Responses to Elie Wiesel*, 186–189, 193.

Fine, Ellen. "Journey Homeward: The Theme of the Town in the Works of Elie Wiesel," in Cargas, Harry James, ed. *Responses to Elie Wiesel*, 240.

Friedman, Maurice. "Elie Wiesel: The Job of Auschwitz," in Cargas, Harry James, ed. *Responses to Elie Wiesel*, 212–215.

Halperin, Irving. "From *Night* to *The Gates of the Forest:* The Novels of Elie Wiesel," in Cargas, Harry James, ed. *Responses to Elie Wiesel*, 50, 51, 71–80.

Halperin, Irving. *Messengers from the Dead*, 93–104.

Indinopulos, Thomas A. "Holocaust in the Stories of Elie Wiesel," in Cargas, Harry James, ed. *Responses to Elie Wiesel*, 121–130.

Joseloff, Samuel. "Link and Promise: The Works of Elie Wiesel." *SoHR* 8 (1974): 166–167..

Kahn, Lothar. "Elie Wiesel: Neo-Hasidism," in Cargas, Harry James, ed. *Responses to Elie Wiesel*, 107–113.

Knopp, Josephine. "Wiesel and the Absurd.." *ConL* 15 (1974): 218–220.

Knopp, Josephine. "Wiesel and the Absurd," in Cargas, Harry James, ed. *Responses to Elie Wiesel*, 98–100.

Oath see *Le serment de Kolvillàg*

Town Beyond the Wall see *La ville de la chance*

WILDER, THORNTON (1897–1975)

Bridge of San Luis Rey (1927)

Burbank, Rex. *Thornton Wilder*, 39–49.
Kuner, M. C. *Thornton Wilder*, 62–79.
Stresau, Hermann. *Thornton Wilder*, 20–26.

Cabala (1926)

Burbank, Rex. *Thornton Wilder*, 31–38.
Kuner, M. C. *Thornton Wilder*, 52–62.
Stresau, Hermann. *Thornton Wilder*, 14–18.

Eighth Day (1967)

Burbank, Rex. *Thornton Wilder*, 116–123.
Kuner, M. C. *Thornton Wilder*, 191–208.
Stresau, Hermann. *Thornton Wilder*, 105–114.

Heaven's My Destination (1935)

Burbank, Rex. *Thornton Wilder*, 63–69.
Kuner, M. C. *Thornton Wilder*, 112–124.
Stresau, Hermann. *Thornton Wilder*, 50–54.

Ides of March (1948)

Burbank, Rex. *Thornton Wilder*, 97–106.
Kuner, M. C. *Thornton Wilder*, 160–178.
Stresau, Hermann. *Thornton Wilder*, 74–83.

Theophilus North (1973)
  Burbank, Rex. *Thornton Wilder*, 123–126.

Woman of Andros (1930)
  Kuner, M. C. *Thornton Wilder*, 79–90.
  Stresau, Hermann. *Thornton Wilder*, 36–44.

WILLIAMS, BEN AMES (1889–1953)

House Divided (1947)
  Bennett, Lee Shaw. "Modern Civil War Novels: The Still Unwritten War?" *SoS* 19 (1980): 108–110.

WILLIAMS, JOHN (1922–1994)

Augustus (1971)
  Stark, John. "Novels of John Williams." *HC* 17.4 (1980): 5–9.

Butcher's Crossing (1960)
  Stark, John. "Novels of John Williams." *HC* 17.4 (1980): 2–4.

Stoner (1965)
  Howe, Irving. *Celebrations and Attacks*, 109–111.
  Stark, John. "Novels of John Williams." *HC* 17.4 (1980): 4–5.

WILLIAMS, JOHN A. (1925–)

Angry Ones (1960)
  Munro, C. Lynn. "Culture and Quest in the Fiction of John A. Williams." *CLAJ* 22 (1978): 74–76, 79.
  Walcott, Ronald. "Man Who Cried I Am: Crying in the Dark." *SIBL* 3.1 (1972): 24.

Captain Blackman (1973)
  Couch, William, Jr. "Image of the Black Soldier in Selected American Novels." *CLAJ* 20 (1976): 183–184.
  Gayle, Addison, Jr. *Way of the New World*, 280–286.
  Klotman, Phyllis Rauch. *Another Man Gone*, 128–129, 136.
  Munro, C. Lynn. "Culture and Quest in the Fiction of John A. Williams." *CLAJ* 22 (1978): 92–94.

Junior Bachelor Society (1976)
  Berzon, Judith R. *Neither White Nor Black*, 242–244.
  Munro, C. Lynn. "Culture and Quest in the Fiction of John A. Williams." *CLAJ* 22 (1978): 97–99.

Man Who Cried I Am (1967)
  Bryant, Jerry H. "John A. Williams: The Political Use of the Novel." *Crit* 16.3 (1975): 92–100.
  Emerson, O. B. "Cultural Nationalism in Afro-American Literature," in Lewald, H. Ernest, ed. *Cry of Home*, 230–235, 285–286.

Gayle, Addison, Jr. *Way of the New World*, 277–280.

Klotman, Phyllis Rauch. *Another Man Gone*, 111–117.

Munro, C. Lynn. "Culture and Quest in the Fiction of John A. Williams." *CLAJ* 22 (1978): 85–89.

Smith, Anneliese H. "Pain in the Ass: Metaphor in John A. Williams' *The Man Who Cried I Am*." *SIBL* 3.3 (1972): 25–27.

Starke, Catherine Juanita. *Black Portraiture in American Fiction*, 231–236.

Walcott, Ronald. "Man Who Cried I Am: Crying in the Dark." *SIBL* 3.1 (1972): 25–32.

Mothersill and the Foxes (1975)

Munro, C. Lynn. "Culture and Quest in the Fiction of John A. Williams." *CLAJ* 22 (1978): 94–96.

Night Song (1961)

Bryant, Jerry H. "John A. Williams: The Political Use of the Novel." *Crit* 16.3 (1975): 86–88.

Munro, C. Lynn. "Culture and Quest in the Fiction of John A. Williams." *CLAJ* 22 (1978): 76–78, 79.

Sissie (1963)

Bryant, Jerry H. "John A. Williams: The Political Use of the Novel." *Crit* 16.3 (1975): 88–92.

Munro, C. Lynn. "Culture and Quest in the Fiction of John A. Williams." *CLAJ* 22 (1978): 80–83.

Sons of Darkness, Sons of Light (1969)

Bryant, Jerry H. "John A. Williams: The Political Use of the Novel." *Crit* 16.3 (1975): 83–85.

Emerson, O. B. "Cultural Nationalism in Afro-American Literature," in Lewald, H. Ernest, ed. *Cry of Home*, 235–236.

Munro, C. Lynn. "Culture and Quest in the Fiction of John A. Williams." *CLAJ* 22 (1978): 90–92.

WILLIAMS, WILLIAM (1727–1791)

Mr. Penrose (1815)

Stein, Roger B. "Pulled Out of the Bay: American Fiction in the Eighteenth Century." *SAF* 2 (1974): 26–28.

WILLIAMS, WILLIAM CARLOS (1883–1963)

Build Up (1952)

Coles, Robert. *William Carlos Williams*, 141–153, 163–178.

Wagner, Linda Welshimer. *Prose of William Carlos Williams*, 130–133.

In the Money (1940)

Coles, Robert. *William Carlos Williams*, 141–163.

Wagner, Linda Welshimer. *Prose of William Carlos Williams*, 128–130.

Voyage to Pagany (1927)
> Breslin, James E. *William Carlos Williams*, 133–138.
> Levin, Harry. "William Carlos Williams and the Old World." *YR* 59 (1970): 521–531.
> Wagner, Linda Welshimer. *Prose of William Carlos Williams*, 78–85.

White Mule (1937)
> Breslin, James E. *William Carlos Williams*, 163–167.
> Coles, Robert. *William Carlos Williams*, 64–121.
> Wagner, Linda Welshimer. *Prose of William Carlos Williams*, 123–127.

WILLIAMSON, JACK (1908–)

Bright New Universe (1967)
> Stewart, Alfred D. "Jack Williamson: The Comedy of Cosmic Evolution," in Clareson, Thomas D., ed. *Voices for the Future* (Vol. 1), 29, 30, 32, 34–43.

Cometeers (1936)
> Stewart, Alfred D. "Jack Williamson: The Comedy of Cosmic Evolution," in Clareson, Thomas D., ed. *Voices for the Future* (Vol. 1), 29.

Darker than You Think (1938)
> Aldiss, Brian. *Billion Year Spree*, 221–223.
> Stewart, Alfred D. "Jack Williamson: The Comedy of Cosmic Evolution," in Clareson, Thomas D., ed. *Voices for the Future* (Vol. 1), 24–25.

Dragon's Island (1951)
> Stewart, Alfred D. "Jack Williamson: The Comedy of Cosmic Evolution," in Clareson, Thomas D., ed. *Voices for the Future* (Vol. 1), 25–26, 32.

Humanoids (1948)
> Stewart, Alfred D. "Jack Williamson: The Comedy of Cosmic Evolution," in Clareson, Thomas D., ed. *Voices for the Future* (Vol. 1), 26–29, 30–31.
> Wolfe, Gary K. *Known and the Unknown*, 164, 166–174.

Legion of Time (1938)
> Stewart, Alfred D. "Jack Williamson: The Comedy of Cosmic Evolution," in Clareson, Thomas D., ed. *Voices for the Future* (Vol. 1), 26, 29.

WILLIAMSON, JOHN STUART see WILLIAMSON, JACK

WILLINGHAM, CALDER (1922–1995)

Eternal Fire (1963)
> Parr, J. L. "Calder Willingham: The Forgotten Novelist." *Crit* 11.3 (1969): 62–64.

Reach to the Stars (1951)
> Parr, J. L. "Calder Willingham: The Forgotten Novelist." *Crit* 11.3 (1969):58–60.

WILLIS, NATHANIEL PARKER (1806–1867)

Paul Fane (1857)
> Goodman, Charlotte. "Henry James's *Roderick Hudson* and Nathaniel Parker Willis's *Paul Fane*." *AL* 43 (1972): 642–645.

WILSON, AUGUSTA see EVANS, AUGUSTA

WILSON, ETHEL (1888–1980)

Hetty Dorval (1947)

 Birbalsingh, Frank. "Ethel Wilson: Innocent Traveller." *CanL* 49 (1971): 36.
 McDonald, R. D. "Serious Whimsy." *CanL* 63 (1975): 40–50.
 New, W. H. *Articulating West*, 68–70.
 Stouck, David. "Ethel Wilson's Novels." *CanL* 74 (1977): 74–77.
 Urbas, Jeannette. "Perquisites of Love." *CanL* 59 (1974): 6–9, 15.
 Urbas, Jeannette. "Perquisites of Love," in Woodcock, George, ed. *Canadian Novel*, 57–60.

Innocent Traveller (1949)

 Birbalsingh, Frank. "Ethel Wilson: Innocent Traveller." *CanL* 49 (1971): 36–37.
 Mitchell, Beverley. " 'On The *Other* Side of the Mountains': The Westering Experience in the Fiction of Ethel Wilson," in Lee, L. L. and Merrill Lewis, ed. *Women, Women Writers, and the West*, 221–223.
 New, W. H. *Articulating West*, 70–74, 83–92.
 Stouck, David. "Ethel Wilson's Novels." *CanL* 74 (1977): 77–79.
 Urbas, Jeannette. "Perquisites of Love." *CanL* 59 (1974): 9–11.
 Urbas, Jeannette. "Perquisites of Love," in Woodcock, George, ed. *Canadian Novel*, 60–62.

Lilly's Story (1952)

 Birbalsingh, Frank. "Ethel Wilson: Innocent Traveller." *CanL* 49 (1971): 38–39.

Love and Salt Water (1956)

 Birbalsingh, Frank. "Ethel Wilson: Innocent Traveller." *CanL* 49 (1971): 40–41.
 Stouck, David. "Ethel Wilson's Novels." *CanL* 74 (1977): 85–87.
 Urbas, Jeannette. "Perquisites of Love," in Woodcock, George, ed. *Canadian Novel*, 64–65.

Swamp Angel (1954)

 Birbalsingh, Frank. "Ethel Wilson: Innocent Traveller." *CanL* 49 (1971): 39–40.
 Moss, John. *Patterns of Isolation*, 139–147.
 New, W. H. *Articulating West*, 76–78.
 Stouck, David. "Ethel Wilson's Novels." *CanL* 74 (1977): 82–85.
 Urbas, Jeannette. "Perquisites of Love." *CanL* 59 (1974): 12–14.
 Urbas, Jeannette. "Perquisites of Love," in Woodcock, George, ed. *Canadian Novel*, 59, 63–64.

WILSON, SLOAN (1920–)

Man in the Gray Flannel Suit (1956)

 Bryant, Jerry H. *Open Decision*, 167–169.

WINTHER, SOPHUS KEITH (1893–1983)

Take All to Nebraska (1936)

 Moseley, Ann. "Land as Metaphor in Two Scandinavian Immigrant Novels." *MELUS* 5.2 (1978): 35–38.

WINWAR, FRANCES (1900–)

Eagle and the Rock (1953)
> Green, Rose Basile. *Italian-American Novel*, 105–110.

Last Love of Camille (1955)
> Green, Rose Basile. *Italian-American Novel*, 110–114.

WISE, JOHN S. (1846–1913)

Lion's Skin (1905)
> Godbold, E. Stanley, Jr. "Battleground Revisited: Reconstruction in Southern Fiction, 1895–1905." *SAQ* 73 (1974): 113–115.

WISEMAN, ADELE (1928–)

Crackpot (1974)
> Moss, John. *Sex and Violence*, 46–47.
> Sutherland, Ronald. *New Hero*, 11–13.

Sacrifice (1956)
> Atwood, Margaret. *Survival*, 154–155.
> Greenstein, Michael. "Movement and Vision in *The Sacrifice*." *CanL* 80 (1979): 23–36.
> Jones, D. G. *Butterfly on Rock*, 147–153.
> Mathews, Robin. *Canadian Literature*, 22–23.
> Mathews, Robin D. "Wacousta Factor," in Bessai, Diane and David Jackel, eds. *Figures in a Ground*, 310, 312.
> Moss, John. *Patterns of Isolation*, 95–103.
> Ricou, Laurence R. "Empty as Nightmare: Man and Landscape in Recent Canadian Prairie Fiction." *Mosaic* 6.2 (1973): 152.
> Rosenthal, Hélène. "Spiritual Ecology: Adele Wiseman's *The Sacrifice*," in Stephens, Donald G., ed. *Writers of the Prairies*, 77–88.
> Sutherland, Ronald. *Second Image*, 145–147.

WISTER, OWEN (1860–1938)

Lady Baltimore (1906)
> Baker, Donald G. "Black Images: The Afro-American in Popular Novels, 1900–1945." *JPC* 7 (1973): 332–333.
> Cobbs, John L. "Charleston: The Image of Aristocracy in Owen Wister's *Lady Baltimore*." *SCR* 9.1 (1976): 44–51.

Lin McLean (1897)
> Etulain, Richard W. *Owen Wister*, 28–30.
> Lambert, Neal. "Owen Wister's *Lin McLean:* The Failure of the Vernacular Hero." *WAL* 5 (1970): 219–232.
> Mogen, David. "Owen Wister's Cowboy Heroes." *Southwestern American Literature* 5 (1977): 47–61. Rpt. in Folsom, James K., ed. *Western*, 57–66.

Virginian (1902)

Cady, Edwin H. *Light of Common Day*, 172–173, 182–192.
DeVoto, Bernard. "Birth of an Art," in Haslam, Gerald W., ed. *Western Writing*, 11–15.
Downs, Robert B. *Famous American Books*, 213–219.
Etulain, Richard W. *Owen Wister*, 33–37.
Harrison, Dick. *Unnamed Country*, 75–78.
Houghton, Donald E. "Two Heroes in One: Reflections on the Popularity of [Owen Wister's] *The Virginian*." *Journal of Popular Culture* 4 (1970): 497–506. Rpt. in Pilkington, William T., ed. *Critical Essays on the Western American Novel*, 118–124.
Lambert, Neal. "Owen Wister's *Virginian:* The Genesis of a Cultural Hero." *WAL* 6 (1971): 99–107.
Lavender, David. "Petrified West and the Writer." *American Scholar* 37.2 (Spring 1968). Rpt. in Haslam, Gerald W., ed. *Western Writing*, 152–153.
Marovitz, Sanford E. "Testament of a Patriot: The Virginian, the Tenderfoot, and Owen Wister." *TSLL* 15 (1973): 560–575.
Mogen, David. "Owen Wister's Cowboy Heroes." *Southwestern American Literature* 5 (1977): 47–61. Rpt. in Folsom, James K., ed. *Western*, 66–72.

WOJCIECHOWSKA, MAIA (1927–)

Shadow of a Bull (1964)

Kelty, Jean McClure. "Cult of Kill in Adolescent Fiction." *EJ* 64.2 (1975): 59.

WOLFE, BERNARD (1915–1985)

Come on Out, Daddy (1963)

Geduld, Carolyn. *Bernard Wolfe*, 126–138.

Everything Happens at Night see *Late Risers*

Great Prince Died (1959)

Geduld, Carolyn. *Bernard Wolfe*, 84–109.

In Deep (1957)

Geduld, Carolyn. *Bernard Wolfe*, 76–83.

Late Risers (1954)

Geduld, Carolyn. *Bernard Wolfe*, 112–119.

Limbo (1952)

Geduld, Carolyn. *Bernard Wolfe*, 35–74.
Samuelson, David N. "*Limbo:* The Great American Dystopia." *Extrapolation* 19 (1977): 76–87.
Warrick, Patricia. "Images of the Man-Machine Intelligence Relationship in Science Fiction," in Clareson, Thomas D., ed. *Many Futures, Many Worlds*, 203–205.
Warrick, Patricia S. *Cybernetic Imagination in Science Fiction*, 147–150.

Magic of Their Singing (1961)

Geduld, Carolyn. *Bernard Wolfe*, 119–125.

WOLFE, THOMAS (1900–1938)

Hills Beyond (1941)

Boyle, Thomas E. "Frederick Jackson Turner and Thomas Wolfe: The Frontier as History and Literature." *WAL* 4 (1970): 277–279.

Foster, Ruel E. "Thomas Wolfe's Mountain Gloom and Glory." *AL* 44 (1973): 643–647.

Gray, Richard. *Literature of Memory*, 143–149.

Howell, Elmo. "Thomas Wolfe and the Sense of Place." *SCR* 11.1 (1978): 102–104.

Look Homeward, Angel (1929)

Albrecht, W. P. "Titles of *Look Homeward, Angel: A Story of the Buried Life.*" *Modern Language Quarterly* 11 (March 1950): 50–57. Rpt. in Reeves, Paschal, comp. *Merrill Studies in Look Homeward, Angel*, 97–106.

Beja, Morris. *Epiphany in the Modern Novel*, 150, 152, 155, 159–162.

Boyle, Thomas E. "Frederick Jackson Turner and Thomas Wolfe: The Frontier as History and Literature." *WAL* 4 (1970): 276–277.

Bredahl, A. Carl, Jr. "*Look Homeward, Angel:* Individuation and Articulation." *SLJ* 6.1 (1973): 47–58.

Budd, Louis J. "Grotesques of Anderson and Wolfe." *Modern Fiction Studies* 5 (Winter 1959–60): 304–310. Rpt. in Reeves, Paschal, comp. *Merrill Studies in Look Homeward, Angel*, 126–133.

Donald, Miles. *American Novel in the Twentieth Century*, 44–46.

Evans, Elizabeth. "Music in *Look Homeward, Angel*." *SLJ* 8.2 (1976): 62–73.

Foster, Ruel E. "Thomas Wolfe's Mountain Gloom and Glory." *AL* 44 (1973): 640–642, 647.

Geismar, Maxwell. "Diary of a Provincial," in Geismar, Maxwell. *Writers in Crisis: The American Novel Between Two Wars*. New York: Houghton Mifflin Company, 1942. Rpt. in Reeves, Paschal, comp. *Merrill Studies in Look Homeward, Angel*, 56–65.

Gray, Richard. *Literature of Memory*, 133, 134, 135–136, 139–143.

Gurko, Leo. *Thomas Wolfe*, 49–78.

Hill, John S. "Eugene Gant and the Ghost of Ben." *Modern Fiction Studies* 11 (Autumn 1965): 245–249. Rpt. in Reeves, Paschal, comp. *Merrill Studies in Look Homeward, Angel*, 134–139.

Holman, C. Hugh. "Loneliness at the Core." *New Republic* 133 (10 Oct 1955): 16–17. Rpt. in Reeves, Paschal, comp. *Merrill Studies in Look Homeward, Angel*, 38–43.

Holman, C. Hugh. *Roots of Southern Writing*, 134–138.

Howell, Elmo. "Thomas Wolfe and the Sense of Place." *SCR* 11.1 (1978): 99–101.

Johnson, Pamela Hansford. "Incommunicable Prison," in Johnson, Pamela Hansford. *Hungry Gulliver: A English Critical Appraisal of Thomas Wolfe*. New York: Charles Scribner's Sons, 1948. Rpt. in Reeves, Paschal, comp. *Merrill Studies in Look Homeward, Angel*, 147–154.

Johnson, Pamela Hansford. "Thomas Wolfe and the Kicking Season." *Encounter* 12 (April 1959): 87–90. Rpt. in Rubin, Louis D., Jr., ed., *Thomas Wolfe*, 108–113.

Kennedy, Richard S. "Wolfe's *Look Homeward, Angel* as a Novel of Development." *South Atlantic Quarterly* 63 (Spring 1964): 218–226. Rpt. in Reeves, Paschal, comp. *Merrill Studies in Look Homeward, Angel*, 82–90.

McElderry, B. R., Jr. "Durable Humor of *Look Homeward, Angel*." *Arizona Quarterly* 11 (Summer 1955): 123–128. Rpt. in Reeves, Paschal, comp. *Merrill Studies in Look Homeward, Angel*, 91–96.

Millichap, Joseph R. "Narrative Structure and Symbolic Imagery in *Look Homeward, Angel*." *SoHR* 7 (1973): 295–303.

Moser, Thomas C. "Thomas Wolfe: *Look Homeward, Angel*," Stegner, Wallace, ed. *American Novel: From James Fenimore Cooper to William Faulkner*. New York: Basic Books, Inc., 1965. Rpt. in Rubin, Louis D., Jr., ed., *Thomas Wolfe*, 116–127.

Ousby, Ian. *Reader's Guide to Fifty American Novels*, 255–257.

Payne, Ladell. *Thomas Wolfe*, 8–18.

Reaver, J. Russell and Robert I. Strozier. "Thomas Wolfe and Death." *Georgia Review* 16 (Fall 1962): 330–337, 350. Rpt. in Reeves, Paschal, comp. *Merrill Studies in Look Homeward, Angel*, 125.

Reck, Rima D. "Céline and Wolfe: Toward a Theory of the Autobiographical Novel." *MissQ* 22 (1969): 19–27.

Rubin, Larry. "Thomas Wolfe and the Lost Paradise." *Modern Fiction Studies* 11 (Autumn 1965): 250–258. Rpt. in Reeves, Paschal, comp. *Merrill Studies in Look Homeward, Angel*, 107–116.

Rubin, Louis D., Jr. *Faraway Country: Writers of the Modern South*. Seattle: University of Washington Press, 1963. Rpt. in Reeves, Paschal, comp. *Merrill Studies in Look Homeward, Angel*, 140–146.

Ryssel, Fritz Heinrich. *Thomas Wolfe*, 26–38.

Walser, Richard. "Look Homeward, Angel," in Walser, Richard. *Thomas Wolfe: An Introduction and Interpretation*. New York: Holt, Rinehart, Winston, Inc., 1961. Rpt. in Reeves, Paschal, comp. *Merrill Studies in Look Homeward, Angel*, 66–79.

Of Time and the River (1935)

Beja, Morris. *Epiphany in the Modern Novel*, 151–154, 155, 156, 162–165.

Beja, Morris. "You Can't Go Home Again: Thomas Wolfe and 'The Escapes of Time and Memory.' " *Modern Fiction Studies* 11.3 (Autumn 1965): 297–314. Rpt. in Rubin, Louis D., Jr., ed., *Thomas Wolfe*, 128–137.

Frohock, W. M. "Thomas Wolfe: Of Time and Neurosis," in Frohock, W. M. *Novel of Violence in America*. Dallas: Southern Methodist University Press, 1950. 47–66. Rpt. in Rubin, Louis D., Jr., ed. *Thomas Wolfe*, 37–46.

Gelfant, Blanche Housman. *American City Novel*, 120–132.

Gray, Richard. *Literature of Memory*, 134–135.

Gurko, Leo. *Thomas Wolfe*, 79–107.

Payne, Ladell. *Thomas Wolfe*, 18–28.

Ryssel, Fritz Heinrich. *Thomas Wolfe*, 40–49.

Portrait of Bascom Hawke (1932)

Domnarski, William. "Thomas Wolfe's Success as Short Novelist: Structure and Theme in *A Portrait of Bascom Hawke*." *SLJ* 13.1 (1980): 32–41.

Web and the Rock (1939)

Beja, Morris. *Epiphany in the Modern Novel*, 153–154, 155, 156–157, 169–173.

Beja, Morris. "You Can't Go Home Again: Thomas Wolfe and 'The Escapes of

Time and Memory.' " *Modern Fiction Studies* 11.3 (Autumn 1965): 297–314.
Rpt. in Rubin, Louis D., Jr., ed., *Thomas Wolfe*, 138–142.
Gelfant, Blanche Housman. *American City Novel*, 120–132.
Gray, Richard. *Literature of Memory*, 134, 135, 137–143.
Gurko, Leo. *Thomas Wolfe*, 108–136.
Payne, Ladell. *Thomas Wolfe*, 28–40.
Rose, Alan Henry. *Demonic Vision*, 120–121.
Ryssel, Fritz Heinrich. *Thomas Wolfe*, 62–71.

You Can't Go Home Again (1940)

Beja, Morris. *Epiphany in the Modern Novel*, 154, 173–175, 179–180.
Beja, Morris. "You Can't Go Home Again: Thomas Wolfe and 'The Escapes of Time and Memory.' " *Modern Fiction Studies* 11.3 (Autumn 1965): 297–314. Rpt. in Rubin, Louis D., Jr., ed., *Thomas Wolfe*, 142–147.
Boyle, Thomas E. "Frederick Jackson Turner and Thomas Wolfe: The Frontier as History and Literature." *WAL* 4 (1970): 279–285.
Cracroft, Richard H. "Pebble in the Pool: Organic Theme and Structure in Thomas Wolfe's *You Can't Go Home Again*." *MFS* 17 (1971–72): 533–553.
Gurko, Leo. *Thomas Wolfe*, 137–158.
Holman, C. Hugh. "Focus on Thomas Wolfe's *You Can't Go Home Again:* Agrarian Dream and Industrial Nightmare," in Madden, David, ed. *American Dreams, American Nightmares*, 149–157.
Holman, C. Hugh. *Loneliness at the Core*, 89–106.
Ryssel, Fritz Heinrich. *Thomas Wolfe*, 74–91.

WOLFE, TOM (1931–)

Electric Kool-Aid Acid Test (1968)

Hollowell, John. *Fact & Fiction*, 131–144.
Tanner, Tony. *City of Words*, 380–387.

WOUK, HERMAN (1915–)

Caine Mutiny (1951)

Bryant, Jerry H. *Open Decision*, 132–133, 139–140.
Jones, Peter G. *War and the Novelist*, 73–79.
Miller, Wayne Charles. *Armed America, Its Face in Fiction*, 151–154.
Waldmeir, Joseph J. *American Novels of the Second World War*, 124–130.

Marjorie Morningstar (1955)

Guttmann, Allen. *Jewish Writer in America*, 121–123.

Winds of War (1971)

Bolton, Richard R. "*Winds of War* and Wouk's Wish for the World." *MidQ* 16 (1975): 389–408.

WRIGHT, CHARLES (1932–)

Wig (1966)

Schulz, Max F. *Black Humor Fiction of the Sixties*, 97–98, 99, 100–101, 108–111, 112–113, 119–122.

WRIGHT, RICHARD (1908–1960)

Lawd Today (1963)

Bakish, David. *Richard Wright*, 13–16.
Berghahn, Marion. *Images of Africa in Black American Literature*, 162–163.
Brady, Owen. "Wright's *Lawd Today:* The American Dream Festering in the Sun."
   CLAJ 22 (1978): 167–172.
Brignano, Russell Carl. *Richard Wright*, 22–28, 71–77, 129–131.
Cauley, Anne O. "Definition of Freedom in the Fiction of Richard Wright." *CLAJ*
   19 (1976): 330–331.
Felgar, Robert. *Richard Wright*, 55–62.
Graham, Don B. "*Lawd Today* and the Example of 'The Waste Land'." *CLAJ* 17
   (1974): 327–332.
Hoeveler, Diane Long. "Oedipus Agonistes: Mothers and Sons in Richard Wright's
   Fiction." *BALF* 12 (1978): 65–66.
Keady, Sylvia H. "Richard Wright's Women Characters and Inequality." *BALF* 10
   (1976): 125.
Kinnamon, Keneth. *Emergence of Richard Wright*, 75–80.
Kinnamon, Keneth. "*Lawd Today:* Richard Wright's Apprentice Novel." *SIBL* 2.2
   (1971): 16–18.
McCall, Dan. *Example of Richard Wright*, 18–23.
Margolies, Edward. *Art of Richard Wright*, 90–103.
Reilly, John M. "Richard Wright's Experiment in Naturalism." *SIBL* 2.3 (1971):
   14–17.
Rickels, Milton and Patricia Rickels. *Richard Wright*, 38–42.

Long Dream (1958)

Bakish, David. *Richard Wright*, 90–94.
Berghahn, Marion. *Images of Africa in Black American Literature*, 155–158.
Brignano, Russell Carl. *Richard Wright*, 42–48.
Davis, Arthur P. *From the Dark Tower*, 154–155.
Felgar, Robert. *Richard Wright*, 126–136.
Gayle, Addison, Jr. *Way of the New World*, 173–178.
Hamalian, Linda Bearman. "Richard Wright's Use of Epigraphs in *The Long
   Dream*." *BALF* 10 (1976): 120–123.
Keady, Sylvia H. "Richard Wright's Women Characters and Inequality." *BALF* 10
   (1976): 124–125.
Klotman, Phyllis Rauch. *Another Man Gone*, 63–64.
Lehan, Richard. *Dangerous Crossing*, 104.
McCall, Dan. *Example of Richard Wright*, 155–160.
Margolies, Edward. *Art of Richard Wright*, 149–167.
Rickels, Milton and Patricia Rickels. *Richard Wright*, 27–31.
Sprandel, Katherine. "*Long Dream*," in Ray, David and Robert M. Farnsworth,
   eds. *Richard Wright*, 174–182.

Native Son (1940)

Bakish, David. *Richard Wright*, 31–40.
Baldwin, James. "Everybody's Protest Novel," in Baldwin, James. *Notes of a Na-
   tive Son*. Boston: Beacon Press, 1955. 13–23. Rpt. in Hemenway, Robert, ed.
   Black Novelist, 225–226.
Baldwin, James. "Many Thousands Gone," in Baldwin, James. *Notes of a Native*

Son. Boston: Beacon Press, 1955. 24–45. Rpt. in Baker, Houston A., Jr., ed. *Twentieth Century Interpretations of Native Son,* 52–62.

Baldwin, Richard E. "Creative Vision of *Native Son.*" *MR* 14 (1973): 378–390.

Bigsby, C. W. E., "From Protest to Paradox: The Black Writer at Mid Century," in French, Warren, ed. *Fifties,* 226–227.

Blake, Nelson Manfred. *Novelists' America,* 234–253.

Bone, Robert A. "Aspects of the Racial Past," in Bone Robert. *Negro Novel in America.* New Haven, CT: Yale University Press, 1968. Rpt. as "Richard Wright," in Baker, Houston A., Jr., ed. *Twentieth Century Interpretations of Native Son,* 71–81.

Bone, Robert. *Richard Wright,* 20–25.

Brignano, Russell Carl. *Richard Wright,* 28–39, 77–82, 143–148.

Brivic, Sheldon. "Conflict of Values: Richard Wright's *Native Son.*" *Novel* 7 (1974): 231–245.

Bryant, Jerry H. "Wright, Ellison, Baldwin: Exorcising the Demon." *Phylon* 37 (1976): 175–179.

Cauley, Anne O. "Definition of Freedom in the Fiction of Richard Wright." *CLAJ* 19 (1976): 333–337.

Corey, Stephen. "Avengers in *Light in August* and *Native Son.*" *CLAJ* 23 (1979): 200–212.

Cowley, Malcolm. "Richard Wright: The Case of Bigger Thomas," in Cowley, Malcolm. *Think Back on Us . . . A Contemporary Chronicle of the 1930s.* Carbondale, IL: Southern Illinois University Press, 1967. Rpt. in Baker, Houston A., Jr., ed. *Twentieth Century Interpretations of Native Son,* 112–114.

Davis, Arthur P. *From the Dark Tower,* 152–153.

De Arman, Charles. "Bigger Thomas: The Symbolic Negro and the Discrete Human Entity." *BALF* 12 (1978): 61–64.

Donald, Miles. *American Novel in the Twentieth Century,* 143–146.

Emerson, O. B. "Cultural Nationalism in Afro-American Literature," in Lewald, H. Ernest, ed. *Cry of Home,* 219–222.

Felgar, Robert. *Richard Wright,* 78–108.

Felgar, Robert. " 'The Kingdom of the Beast': The Landscape of *Native Son.*" *CLAJ* 17 (1974): 333–337.

Ford, Nick Aaron. "Ordeal of Richard Wright." *College English* 15 (1953): 87–94. Rpt. in Gibson, Donald B., ed. *Five Black Writers,* 27–29.

Gayle, Addison, Jr. *Way of the New World,* 168–173, 179–181.

Gibson, Donald B. 'Wright's Invisible Native Son." *AQ* 21 (1969): 728–738.

Gibson, Donald B. "Wright's Invisible Native Son." *American Quarterly* 21.4 (1969): 728–738. Rpt. in Baker, Houston A., Jr., ed. *Twentieth Century Interpretations of Native Son,* 96–108.

Graham, Louis. "White Self-Image Conflict in *Native Son.*" *SIBL* 3.2 (1972): 19–21.

Grenander, M. E. "Criminal Responsibility in *Native Son* and *Knock on Any Door.*" *AL* 49 (1977): 221–233.

Gross, Seymour L. " 'Dalton' and Color-Blindness in *Native Son.*" *MissQ* 27 (1973–74): 75–77.

Hakutani, Yoshinobu. "*Native Son* and *An American Tragedy:* Two Different Interpretations of Crime and Guilt." *CentR* 23 (1979): 208–226.

Hearn, Charles R. *American Dream in the Great Depression,* 126–127.

Hoeveler, Diane Long. "Oedipus Agonistes: Mothers and Sons in Richard Wright's Fiction." *BALF* 12 (1978): 66–67.

Howe, Irving. "Black Boys and Native Sons," in Howe, Irving. *World More Attractive*. New York: Horizon Press, 1963. 100–110. Rpt. in Baker, Houston A., Jr., ed. *Twentieth Century Interpretations of Native Son*, 63–70.

Jordon, June. "On Richard Wright and Zora Neale Hurston: Notes Toward a Balancing of Love and Hatred." *BW* 23.10 (1974): 4–8.

Keady, Sylvia H. "Richard Wright's Women Characters and Inequality." *BALF* 10 (1976): 125–126.

Kent, George E. "Richard Wright: Blackness and the Adventure of Western Culture." *CLA Journal* 12 (June 1969): 339–343. Rpt. in Baker, Houston A., Jr., ed. *Twentieth Century Interpretations of Native Son*, 91–95.

Kim, Kichung. "Wright, the Protest Novel, and Baldwin's Faith." *CLAJ* 17 (1974): 388–394.

Kinnamon, Keneth. *Emergence of Richard Wright*, 118–143.

Kinnamon, Keneth. "Richard Wright's Use of *Othello* in *Native Son*." *CLAJ* 12.4 (1969): 358–359.

Klotman, Phyllis R. "Moral Distancing as a Rhetorical Technique in *Native Son:* A Note on 'Fate'." *CLAJ* 18 (1974): 284–291.

Klotman, Phyllis Rauch. *Another Man Gone*, 57–60.

Larsen, R. B. V. "Four Voices of Richard Wright's *Native Son*." *NALF* 6 (1972): 105–109.

Lehan, Richard. *Dangerous Crossing*, 96–100.

McCall, Dan. "Bad Nigger," in McCall, Dan. *Example of Richard Wright*. New York: Harcourt Brace Jovanovich, Inc., 1969. 74–85. Rpt. in Baker, Houston A., Jr., ed. *Twentieth Century Interpretations of Native Son*, 82–90.

McCall, Dan. *Example of Richard Wright*, 64–102.

Margolies, Edward. *Art of Richard Wright*, 104–120.

May, John R. *Toward a New Earth*, 161–169.

May, John R., S. J. "Images of Apocalypse in the Black Novel." *Renascence* 23 (1970): 40–44.

Miller, Eugene E. "Voodoo Parallels in *Native Son*." *CLAJ* 16 (1972): 81–95.

Redden, Dorothy S. "Richard Wright and *Native Son:* Not Guilty." *BALF* 10 (1976): 111–116.

Reed, Kenneth T. "*Native Son:* An American Crime and Punishment." *SIBL* 1.2 (1970): 33–34.

Rickels, Milton and Patricia Rickels. *Richard Wright*, 9–13.

Rosenblatt, Roger. *Black Fiction*, 19–36.

Sadler, Jeffrey. "Split Consciousness in Richard Wright's *Native Son*." *SCR* 8.2 (1976): 11–24.

Savory, Jerold J. "Bigger Thomas and the Book of Job: The Epigraph to *Native Son*." *NALF* 9 (1975): 55–56.

Scott, Nathan A, Jr. "Dark and Haunted Tower of Richard Wright," in Gayle, Addison, Jr., ed. *Black Expression*. New York: Weybright and Talley, 1969. 296–311. Rpt. in Hemenway, Robert, ed. *Black Novelist*, 75–78.

Scott, Nathan A, Jr. "Dark and Haunted Tower of Richard Wright," in Gibson, Donald B., ed. *Five Black Writers*, 13–18.

Scruggs, Charles W. "Importance of the City in *Native Son*." *Ariel* 9.3 (1978): 37–47.

Siegel, Paul N. "Conclusion of Richard Wright's *Native Son.*" *PMLA* 89 (1974): 517–523.

Singh, Amritjit. "Misdirected Responses to Bigger Thomas." *SIBL* 5.2 (1974): 5–8.

Singh, Raman K. "Christian Heroes and Anti-Heroes in Richard Wright's Fiction." *NALF* 6 (1972): 101–102.

Singh, Raman K. "Some Basic Ideas and Ideals in Richard Wright's Fiction." *CLAJ* 13 (1969): 79–83.

Starr, Alvin. "Concept of Fear in the Works of Stephen Crane and Richard Wright." *SIBL* 6.2 (1975): 6–9.

Waniek, Marilyn. "Space Where Sex Should Be: Toward a Definition of the Black American Literary Tradition." *SIBL* 6.3 (1975): 10–12, 13.

Wasserman, Jerry. "Embracing the Negative: *Native Son* and *Invisible Man.*" *SAF* 4 (1976): 94–100.

Watson, Edward A. "Bessie's Blues," in Ray, David and Robert M. Farnsworth, eds. *Richard Wright*, 167–173.

Williams, Sherley Anne. *Give Birth to Brightness*, 74–77.

Wright, Richard. "How Bigger Was Born," in Wright, Richard. *Native Son.* New York: Harper and Brothers, 1940. xiii–li. Rpt. in Hemenway, Robert, ed. *Black Novelist*, 167–190.

Outsider (1953)

Bakish, David. *Richard Wright*, 64–72.

Berghahn, Marion. *Images of Africa in Black American Literature*, 159–160.

Bigsby, C. W. E., "From Protest to Paradox: The Black Writer at Mid Century," in French, Warren, ed. *Fifties*, 228.

Bone, Robert. *Richard Wright*, 37–43.

Brignano, Russell Carl. *Richard Wright*, 82–85, 155–163.

Cauley, Anne O. "Definition of Freedom in the Fiction of Richard Wright." *CLAJ* 19 (1976): 340–345.

Davis, Arthur P. *From the Dark Tower*, 153–154.

Felgar, Robert. *Richard Wright*, 109–121.

Ferguson, Alfred R. "Black Men, White Cities: The Quest for Humanity by Black Protagonists in James Baldwin's *Another Country* and Richard Wright's *The Outsider.*" *BallS* 18.2 (1977): 54–58.

Ford, Nick Aaron. "Ordeal of Richard Wright." *College English* 15 (1953): 87–94. Rpt. in Gibson, Donald B., ed. *Five Black Writers*, 30–35.

Keady, Sylvia H. "Richard Wright's Women Characters and Inequality." *BALF* 10 (1976): 126–128.

Klotman, Phyllis Rauch. *Another Man Gone*, 60–62.

McCarthy, Harold T. *Expatriate Perspective*, 186–187.

McCall, Dan. *Example of Richard Wright*, 149–155.

Margolies, Edward. *Art of Richard Wright*, 121–138.

Rickels, Milton and Patricia Rickels. *Richard Wright*, 18–20.

Scott, Nathan A, Jr. "Dark and Haunted Tower of Richard Wright," in Gayle, Addison, Jr., ed. *Black Expression.* New York: Weybright and Talley, 1969. 296–311. Rpt. in Hemenway, Robert, ed. *Black Novelist*, 75, 81–84.

Scott, Nathan A, Jr. "Dark and Haunted Tower of Richard Wright," in Gibson, Donald B., ed. *Five Black Writers*, 19–23.

Singh, Raman K. "Christian Heroes and Anti-Heroes in Richard Wright's Fiction." *NALF* 6 (1972): 102–104.

Singh, Raman K. "Some Basic Ideas and Ideals in Richard Wright's Fiction." *CLAJ* 13 (1969): 83–84.

Starke, Catherine Juanita. *Black Portraiture in American Fiction*, 200–204.

Turner, Darwin T. *"Outsider:* Revision of an Idea." *CLAJ* 12.4 (1969): 310–321.

Widmer, Kingsley. "Black Existentialism: Richard Wright," in Cooke, M. G., ed. *Modern Black Novelists*, 80–87.

Widmer, Kingsley. "Existential Darkness: Richard Wright's *The Outsider.*" *Wisconsin Studies in Contemporary Literature* 1 (1960): 13–21. Rpt. in Gibson, Donald B., ed. *Five Black Writers*, 50–57.

Savage Holiday (1954)

Bakish, David. *Richard Wright*, 72–74.

Brignano, Russell Carl. *Richard Wright*, 133–143.

Felgar, Robert. *Richard Wright*, 121–126.

Gounard, J. F. and Beverley Roberts Gounard. "Richard Wright's *Savage Holiday:* Use or Abuse of Psychoanalysis?" *CLAJ* 22 (1979): 344–349.

Hoeveler, Diane Long. "Oedipus Agonistes: Mothers and Sons in Richard Wright's Fiction." *BALF* 12 (1978): 67–68.

Margolies, Edward. *Art of Richard Wright*, 138–148.

Reilly, John M. "Richard Wright's Curious Thriller, *Savage Holiday.*" *CLAJ* 21 (1977): 218–223.

WURLITZER, RUDOLPH (1938(?)–)

Flats (1970)

Bolling, Douglass. "Rudolph Wurlitzer's *Nog* and *Flats.*" *Crit* 14.3 (1973): 11–15.

Nog (1968)

Bolling, Douglass. "Rudolph Wurlitzer's *Nog* and *Flats.*" *Crit* 14.3 (1973): 5–11, 14–15.

Quake (1972)

Bolling, Douglass T. "Waking Nightmare: American Society in Rudolph Wurlitzer's *Quake.*" *Crit* 16.3 (1975): 70–80.

WYLIE, ELINOR (1885–1928)

Jennifer Lorn (1923)

Pizer, Donald. " 'Symbolic Romances of the Mind': The Novels of Elinor Wylie." *CentR* 24 (1980): 285–301.

Mr. Hodge and Mr. Hazard (1928)

Pizer, Donald. " 'Symbolic Romances of the Mind': The Novels of Elinor Wylie." *CentR* 24 (1980): 285–301.

Orphan Angel (1926)

Pizer, Donald. " 'Symbolic Romances of the Mind': The Novels of Elinor Wylie." *CentR* 24 (1980): 285–301.

Venetian Glass Nephew (1925)
Pizer, Donald. " 'Symbolic Romances of the Mind': The Novels of Elinor Wylie."
CentR 24 (1980): 285–301.

WYLIE, PHILIP (1902–1971)

After Worlds Collide (1934)
Bendau, Clifford P. *Philip Wylie*, 16.

April Afternoon (1938)
Bendau, Clifford P. *Philip Wylie*, 22–23.
Keefer, Truman Frederick. *Philip Wylie*, 91–94.

Babes and Sucklings (1929)
Bendau, Clifford P. *Philip Wylie*, 9–10.
Keefer, Truman Frederick. *Philip Wylie*, 40–46.

Disappearance (1951)
Bendau, Clifford P. *Philip Wylie*, 44–47.
Keefer, Truman Frederick. *Philip Wylie*, 121–124.

End of the Dream (1972)
Bendau, Clifford P. *Philip Wylie*, 59.
Keefer, Truman Frederick. *Philip Wylie*, 153–154.

Finnley Wren (1934)
Bendau, Clifford P. *Philip Wylie*, 19–21.
Keefer, Truman Frederick. *Philip Wylie*, 66–75.

Footprint of Cinderella (1931)
Keefer, Truman Frederick. *Philip Wylie*, 57–61.

Gladiator (1930)
Bendau, Clifford P. *Philip Wylie*, 10–12.
Keefer, Truman Frederick. *Philip Wylie*, 46–49.

Heavy Laden (1928)
Bendau, Clifford P. *Philip Wylie*, 8–9.
Keefer, Truman Frederick. *Philip Wylie*, 36–40.

Los Angeles: A.D. 2017 (1970)
Bendau, Clifford P. *Philip Wylie*, 59.
Keefer, Truman Frederick. *Philip Wylie*, 151–152.

Murderer Invisible (1931)
Bendau, Clifford P. *Philip Wylie*, 12–13.
Keefer, Truman Frederick. *Philip Wylie*, 54–56.

9 Rittenhouse Square see *Footprint of Cinderella*

Night Unto Night (1944)
Keefer, Truman Frederick. *Philip Wylie*, 104–108.

Savage Gentleman (1932)
Bendau, Clifford P. *Philip Wylie*, 16–17.

Spy Who Spoke Porpoise (1969)
Bendau, Clifford P. *Philip Wylie*, 55.
Keefer, Truman Frederick. *Philip Wylie*, 145–148.

They Both Were Naked (1965)
Bendau, Clifford P. *Philip Wylie*, 54–55.
Keefer, Truman Frederick. *Philip Wylie*, 136–140

Tomorrow! (1954)
Bendau, Clifford P. *Philip Wylie*, 47–50.
Keefer, Truman Frederick. *Philip Wylie*, 124–128.

Too Much of Everything (1936)
Bendau, Clifford P. *Philip Wylie*, 22.
Keefer, Truman Frederick. *Philip Wylie*, 81–83.

Triumph (1963)
Bendau, Clifford P. *Philip Wylie*, 52–54.
Keefer, Truman Frederick. *Philip Wylie*, 134–136.

When Worlds Collide (1932)
Bendau, Clifford P. *Philip Wylie*, 13–16.

YERBY, FRANK (1916–1991)

Foxes of Harrow (1946)
Berzon, Judith R. *Neither White Nor Black*, 71–72.

Vixens (1947)
Berzon, Judith R. *Neither White Nor Black*, 73.

YEZIERSKA, ANZIA (1885–1970)

Bread Givers (1925)
Rosinsky, Natalie M. "Mothers and Daughters: Another Minority Group," in Davidson, Cathy N. and E. M. Broner, eds. *Lost Tradition*, 287–288.

YOUNG, AL (1939–)

Who Is Angelina? (1975)
Schultz, Elizabeth A. "Heirs of Ralph Ellison: Patterns of Individualism in the Contemporary Afro-American Novel." *CLAJ* 22 (1978): 117–119.

YOUNG, STARK (1881–1963)

Heaven Trees (1926)
Stovell, Floyd. "Stark Young: Critic and Creative Artist." *SLJ* 9.1 (1976): 95.

River House (1929)
Stovell, Floyd. "Stark Young: Critic and Creative Artist." *SLJ* 9.1 (1976): 96–97.

So Red the Rose (1934)

Stovell, Floyd. "Stark Young: Critic and Creative Artist." *SLJ* 9.1 (1976): 97–99.
Sullivan, Walter. *Death by Melancholy*, 77–80.

Torches Flare (1928)

McAlexander, Hubert, Jr. "William Faulkner—The Young Poet in Stark Young's *The Torches Flare*." *AL* 43 (1972): 647–649.

YURICK, SOL (1925–)

Warriors (1965)

Graham, D. B. "Naturalism and the Revolutionary Imperative: Yurick's *The Warriors*." *Crit* 18.1 (1976): 119–128.

ZELAZNY, ROGER (1937–1995)

Creatures of Light and Darkness (1969)

Fredericks, S. C. "Revivals of Ancient Mythologies in Current Science Fiction and Fantasy," in Clareson, Thomas D., ed. *Many Futures, Many Worlds*, 55–56.

Damnation Alley (1969)

Yoke, Carl B. "Zelazny's *Damnation Alley:* Hell Noh." *Extrapolation* 15 (1973): 6–16.

Doorways in the Sand (1976)

Sanders, Joe. "Zelazny: Unfinished Business," in Clareson, Thomas, ed. *Voices for the Future* (Vol. 2), 195.

Immortal (1966)

Fredericks, S. C. "Revivals of Ancient Mythologies in Current Science Fiction and Fantasy," in Clareson, Thomas D., ed. *Many Futures, Many Worlds*, 52–53.
Sanders, Joe. "Zelazny: Unfinished Business," in Clareson, Thomas, ed. *Voices for the Future* (Vol. 2), 190.

Jack of Shadows (1971)

Sanders, Joe. "Zelazny: Unfinished Business," in Clareson, Thomas, ed. *Voices for the Future* (Vol. 2), 182–183.

Lord of Light (1967)

Fredericks, S. C. "Revivals of Ancient Mythologies in Current Science Fiction and Fantasy," in Clareson, Thomas D., ed. *Many Futures, Many Worlds*, 53–54.
Sanders, Joe. "Zelazny: Unfinished Business," in Clareson, Thomas, ed. *Voices for the Future* (Vol. 2), 190–194.

ZINDEL, PAUL (1936–)

I Never Loved Your Mind (1970)

Henke, James T. "Six Characters in Search of the Family: The Novels of Paul Zindel." *ChildL* 5 (1976): 134–136, 138–139.

My Darling, My Hamburger (1969)

Henke, James T. "Six Characters in Search of the Family: The Novels of Paul Zindel." *ChildL* 5 (1976): 133–134, 138.

Pigman (1968)

Clarke, Loretta. "*Pigman:* A Novel of Adolescence." *EJ* 61 (1972): 1163–1169, 1175.

Henke, James T. "Six Characters in Search of the Family: The Novels of Paul Zindel." *ChildL* 5 (1976): 130–133, 137–138.

Henke, James T. "Six Characters in Search of the Family: The Novels of Paul Zindel." *Children's Literature* 5 (1976): 130–140. Rpt. in Lenz, Millicent and Ramona M. Mahood, comps. *Young Adult Literature*, 133–135, 139.

ZUGSMITH, LEANE (1903–1969)

Never Enough (1932)

Josephson, Matthew. "Leane Zugsmith: The Social Novel of the Thirties." *SoR* 11 (1975): 542.

Reckoning (1934)

Josephson, Matthew. "Leane Zugsmith: The Social Novel of the Thirties." *SoR* 11 (1975): 542–543.

Summer Soldier (1938)

Josephson, Matthew. "Leane Zugsmith: The Social Novel of the Thirties." *SoR* 11 (1975): 545–547.

Time to Remember (1936)

Josephson, Matthew. "Leane Zugsmith: The Social Novel of the Thirties." *SoR* 11 (1975): 544–545.

List of Books Indexed

Aaron, Daniel. *Unwritten War: American Writers and the Civil War*. New York: Alfred A. Knopf, 1973.

Adams, Laura. *Existential Battles: The Growth of Norman Mailer*. Athens, OH: Ohio University Press, 1976.

Adams, Stephen D. *James Purdy*. New York: Barnes & Noble Books, 1976.

Aichinger, Peter. *Earle Birney*. Boston: Twayne Publishers, 1979.

Aird, Eileen M. *Sylvia Plath: Her Life and Work*. New York: Harper and Row, 1973.

Aldiss, Brian. *Billion Year Spree: The True History of Science Fiction*. New York: Schocken Books, 1973.

Aldridge, John W. *Devil in the Fire: Retrospective Essays on American Literature and Culture 1951–1971*. New York: Harper's Magazine Press Book, 1972.

Alexander, Edward. *Isaac Bashevis Singer*. Boston: Twayne Publishers, 1980.

Alexander, Edward. *Resonance of Dust: Essays on Holocaust Literature and Jewish Fate*. Columbus, OH: Ohio State University Press, 1979.

Allen, Mary. *Necessary Blankness: Women in Major American Fiction of the Sixties*. Chicago: University of Illinois Press, 1976.

Allen, Walter. *Urgent West: The American Dream and Modern Man*. New York: E. P. Dutton & Co., Inc., 1969.

Allentuck, Marcia, ed. *Achievement of Isaac Bashevis Singer*. Carbondale, IL: Southern Illinois University Press, 1969.

Alter, Robert. *After the Tradition: Essays on Modern Jewish Writing*. New York: E. P. Dutton & Co., Inc., 1969.

Alter, Robert. *Partial Magic: The Novel as a Self-Conscious Genre*. Berkeley, CA: University of California Press, 1975.

Ammons, Elizabeth. *Edith Wharton's Argument with America*. Athens, GA: University of Georgia Press, 1980.

Andersen, Richard. *William Goldman*. Boston: Twayne Publishers, 1979.

Anderson, Charles R. *Person, Place, and Thing in Henry James's Novels*. Durham, NC: Duke University Press, 1977.

Anderson, David. *Tragic Protest: A Christian Study of Some Modern Literature*. Richmond, VA: John Knox Press, 1969.

Anderson, David D., ed. *Sherwood Anderson, Dimensions of His Literary Art: A Collection of Critical Essays*. East Lansing, MI: Michigan State University Press, 1976.

Bloodworth, William A., Jr. *Upton Sinclair.* Boston: Twayne Publishers, 1977.

Bone, Robert. *Richard Wright.* Minneapolis, MN: University of Minnesota Press, 1969.

Bontemps, Arna, ed. *Harlem Renaissance Remembered.* New York: Dodd, Mead & Company, 1972.

Bornstein, George, ed. *Romantic and Modern: Revaluations of Literary Tradition.* Pittsburgh: University of Pittsburgh Press, 1977.

Boucher, Yvon, ed. *Hubert Aquin.* Montréal: Guérin, 1976.

Boyers, Robert. *Excursions: Selected Literary Essays.* Port Washington, NY: Kennikat Press, 1977.

Bradbrook, M. C. *Malcolm Lowry, His Art and Early Life: A Study in Transformation.* Cambridge: Cambridge University Press, 1974.

Bradbury, Malcolm and David Palmer, eds. *American Novel in the Nineteen Twenties.* New York: Crane, Russak, 1971.

Bradbury, Nicola. *Henry James: The Later Novels.* Oxford, England: Clarendon Press, 1979.

Bradford, M. E., ed. *Form Discovered: Essays on the Achievement of Andrew Lytle.* Jackson, MS: University and College Press of Mississippi, 1973.

Branch, Edgar M. *James T. Farrell.* New York: Twayne Publishers, Inc., 1971.

Braudy, Leo, ed. *Norman Mailer: A Collection of Critical Essays.* Englewood Cliffs, NJ: Prentice-Hall, Inc., 1972.

Bredahl, A. Carl, Jr. *Melville's Angles of Vision.* Gainesville, FL: University of Florida Press, 1972.

Breslin, James E. *William Carlos Williams: An American Artist.* New York: Oxford University Press, 1970.

Briggs, Austin, Jr. *Novels of Harold Frederic.* Ithaca, NY: Cornell University Press, 1969.

Briggs, Julia. *Night Visitors: The Rise and Fall of the English Ghost Story.* London: Faber and Faber Limited, 1977.

Brignano, Russell Carl. *Richard Wright: An Introduction to the Man and His Work.* Pittsburgh: University of Pittsburgh Press, 1970.

Brizzi, Mary T. *Reader's Guide to Philip José Farmer.* Mercer Island, WA: Starmont House, 1980.

Brodhead, Richard H. *Hawthorne, Melville, and the Novel.* Chicago: University of Chicago Press, 1976.

Brooks, Cleanth. *William Faulkner: Toward Yoknapatawhpha and Beyond.* New Haven, CT: Yale University Press, 1978.

Broughton, Panthea Reid, ed. *Art of Walker Percy: Stratagems for Being.* Baton Rouge, LA: Louisiana State University Press, 1979.

Broughton, Panthea Reid. *William Faulkner: The Abstract and the Actual.* Baton Rouge, LA: Louisiana State University Press, 1974.

Brown, Lloyd W. *Amiri Baraka.* Boston: Twayne Publishers, 1980.

Browne, Ray B. and Donald Pizer, eds. *Themes and Directions in American Literature: Essays in Honor of Leon Howard.* Lafayette, IN: Purdue University Studies, 1969.

Browning, Preston M., Jr. *Flannery O'Connor.* Carbondale, IL: Southern Illinois University Press, 1974.

Bruccoli, Matthew J., ed. *James Gould Cozzens: New Acquist of True Experience.* Carbondale, IL: Southern Illinois University Press, 1979.

Christian, Barbara. *Black Women Novelists: The Development of a Tradition, 1892–
    1976*. Westport, CT: Greenwood Press, 1980.
Chupack, Henry. *James Purdy*. Boston: Twayne Publishers, 1975.
Clareson, Thomas, ed. *Voices for the Future: Essays on Major Science Fiction Writers*.
    Vol. 2. Bowling Green, OH: Bowling Green University Popular Press, 1979.
Clareson, Thomas D., ed. *Many Futures, Many Worlds: Theme and Form in Science
    Fiction*. Kent, OH: Kent State University Press, 1977.
Clareson, Thomas D., ed. *SF: The Other Side of Realism, Essays on Modern Fantasy
    and Science Fiction*. Bowling Green, OH: Bowling Green University Popular
    Press, 1971.
Clareson, Thomas D., ed. *Voices for the Future: Essays on Major Science Fiction
    Writers*. Vol. 1. Bowling Green, OH: Bowling Green University Popular Press,
    1976.
Clayton, John Jacob. *Saul Bellow: In Defense of Man*. Second Edition. Bloomington,
    IN: Indiana University Press, 1979.
Coale, Samuel. *John Cheever*. New York: Frederick Ungar Publishing Co., 1977.
Cockburn, Robert H. *Novels of Hugh MacLennan*. Montreal: Harvest House Ltd.,
    1969.
Cohen, Sara Blacher, ed. *Comic Relief: Humor in Contemporary American Literature*.
    Urbana: University of Illinois Press, 1978.
Cohen, Sarah Blacher. *Saul Bellow's Enigmatic Laughter*. Chicago: University of Illi-
    nois Press, 1974.
Cohn, Dorrit. *Transparent Minds: Narrative Modes for Presenting Consciousness in
    Fiction*. Princeton, NJ: Princeton University Press, 1978.
Coindreau, Maurice Edgar. *Time of William Faulkner: A French View of Modern
    American Fiction*. Ed. and trans. George McMillan Reeves. Columbia, SC: Uni-
    versity of South Carolina Press, 1971.
Coles, Robert. *Irony in the Mind's Life: Essays on Novels by James Agee, Elizabeth
    Bowen, and George Eliot*. Charlottesville, VA: University of Virginia Press, 1974.
Coles, Robert. *Walker Percy: An American Search*. Boston: Little, Brown and Com-
    pany, 1978.
Coles, Robert. *William Carlos Williams: The Knack of Survival in America*. New
    Brunswick, NJ: Rutgers University Press, 1975.
Colley, Iain. *Dos Passos & the Fiction of Despair*. Totowa, NJ: Rowman and Little-
    field, 1978.
Colmer, John. *Coleridge to Catch-22: Images of Society*. New York: St. Martins Press,
    1978.
Conron, Brandon, ed. *Morley Callaghan*. Toronto: McGraw-Hill Ryerson Limited,
    1975.
Cook, Gregory M., ed. *Ernest Buckler*. Toronto: McGraw-Hill Ryerston Limited, 1972.
Cook, Raymond A. *Thomas Dixon*. New York: Twayne Publishers, Inc., 1974.
Cook, Richard M. *Carson McCullers*. New York: Frederick Ungar Publishing Co.,
    1975.
Cook, Sylvia Jenkins. *From Tobacco Road to Route 66: The Southern Poor White in
    Fiction*. Chapel Hill, NC: University of North Carolina Press, 1976.
Cooke, M. G., ed. *Modern Black Novelists: A Collection of Critical Essays*. Englewood
    Cliffs, NJ: Prentice-Hall, Inc., 1971.
Cornillon, Susan Koppelman, ed. *Images of Women in Fiction: Feminist Perspectives*.
    Bowling Green, OH: Bowling Green University Popular Press, 1972.
Costa, Richard Hauer. *Malcolm Lowry*. New York: Twayne Publishers, Inc., 1972.

Diamond, Arlyn and Lee R. Edwards, eds. *Authority of Experience: Essays on Feminist Criticism*. Amherst, MA: University of Massachusetts Press, 1977.

Dick, Bernard F. *Apostate Angel: A Critical Study of Gore Vidal*. New York: Random House, 1974.

Dillingham, William B. *Artist in the Rigging: The Early Work of Herman Melville*. Athens, GA: University of Georgia Press, 1972.

Dillingham, William B. *Frank Norris: Instinct and Art*. Boston: Houghton Mifflin Company, 1969.

Dodson, Daniel B. *Malcolm Lowry*. New York: Columbia University Press, 1970.

Dolan, Paul J. *Of War and War's Alarms: Fiction and Politics in the Modern World*. New York: Free Press, 1976.

Donald, Miles. *American Novel in the Twentieth Century*. New York: Barnes & Noble Books, 1978.

Donoghue, Denis. *Thieves of Fire*. New York: Oxford University Press, 1974.

Donovan, Josephine. *Sarah Orne Jewett*. New York: Frederick Ungar Publishing Co., 1980.

Dooley, D. J. *Moral Vision in the Canadian Novel*. Toronto: Clarke, Irwin & Company Limited, 1979.

Douglas, Ann. *Feminization of American Culture*. New York: Alfred A. Knopf, 1977.

Downs, Robert B. *Famous American Books*. New York: McGraw-Hill Book Company, 1971.

Doyle, Paul A. *Pearl S. Buck*. Revised Edition. Boston: Twayne Publishers, 1980.

Dreiser, Theodore. *Sister Carrie: An Authoritative Text, Backgrounds and Sources, Criticism*. Ed. Donald Pizer. New York: W. W. Norton & Company, Inc., 1970.

Drolet, Bruno. *Entre dune et aboiteaux . . . un peuple: étude critique des oeuvres d'Antonine Maillet*. Montréal: Éditions Pleins Bords, 1975.

Ducharme, Robert. *Art and Idea in the Novels of Bernard Malamud: Toward The Fixer*. The Hague: Mouton, 1974.

Dudek, Louis. *Selected Essays and Criticism*. Ottawa: Tecumseh Press, 1978.

Durand, Régis, ed. *Myth and Ideology in American Culture*. Lille, France: Université de Lille, 1976.

Eble, Kenneth. *F. Scott Fitzgerald*. New York: Twayne Publishers, Inc., 1977.

Eble, Kenneth, ed. *F. Scott Fitzgerald: A Collection of Criticism*. New York: McGraw-Hill Book Company, 1973.

Eckley, Wilton. *Harriette Arnow*. New York: Twayne Publishers, Inc., 1974.

Eckley, Wilton. *T. S. Stribling*. Boston: Twayne Publishers, 1975.

Edinger, Edward F. *Melville's Moby-Dick: A Jungian Commentary, An American Nekyia*. New York: New Directions Publishing Company, 1975.

Edwards, Clifford D. *Conrad Richter's Ohio Trilogy*. The Hague, Netherlands: Mouton, 1970.

Eggenschwiler, David. *Christian Humanism of Flannery O'Connor*. Detroit: Wayne State University Press, 1972.

Elder, Arlene A. *"Hindered Hand": Cultural Implications of Early African-American Fiction*. Westport, CT: Greenwood Press, 1978.

Elder, Marjorie J. *Nathaniel Hawthorne, Transcendental Symbolist*. Athens, OH: Ohio University Press, 1969.

Elliot, Emory, ed. *Puritan Influences in American Literature*. Urbana, IL: University of Illinois Press, 1979.

Emerson, Everett, ed. *Major Writers of Early American Literature*. Madison, WI: University of Wisconsin Press, 1972.

Epstein, Perle. *Private Labyrinth of Malcolm Lowry: Under the Volcano and The Cabbala*. New York: Holt, Rinehart and Winston, 1969.

Eschholz, Paul A., ed. *Critics on William Dean Howells: Readings in Literary Criticism*. Coral Gables, FL: University of Miami Press, 1975.

Estess, Ted L. *Elie Wiesel*. New York: Frederick Ungar Publishing Co., 1980.

Etulain, Richard W. *Owen Wister*. Boise, ID: Boise State College, 1973.

Fabi, Thérèse. *Le monde perturbé des jeunes dans l'oeuvre de Marie-Claire Blais: sa vie, son oeuvre, la critique*. Montréal: Éditions Agence d'ARC Inc., 1973.

Fahey, William A. *F. Scott Fitzgerald and the American Dream*. New York: Thomas Y. Crowell Company, 1973.

Farrison, William Edward. *William Wells Brown: Author & Reformer*. Chicago: University of Chicago Press, 1969.

Feder, Lillian. *Madness in Literature*. Princeton, NJ: Princeton University Press, 1980.

Federman, Raymond, ed. *Surfiction: Fiction Now . . . and Tomorrow*. Chicago: Swallow Press, Inc., 1975.

Feeley, Kathleen. *Flannery O'Connor: Voice of the Peacock*. Brunswick, NJ: Rutgers University Press, 1972.

Felgar, Robert. *Richard Wright*. Boston: Twayne Publishers, 1980.

Fennimore, Keith J. *Booth Tarkington*. New York: Twayne Publishers, Inc., 1974.

Fergusson, Francis. *Literary Landmarks: Essays on the Theory and Practice of Literature*. New Brunswick, NJ: Rutgers University Press, 1975.

Festa-McCormick, Diana. *City as Catalyst: A Study of Ten Novels*. Rutherford, NJ: Fairleigh Dickinson University Press, 1979.

Fetherling, Doug. *Hugh Garner*. Toronto: Forum House Publishing Company, 1972.

Fetterley, Judith. *Resisting Reader: A Feminist Approach to American Fiction*. Bloomington, IN: Indiana University Press, 1978.

Field, Leslie A. and Joyce W. Field, eds. *Bernard Malamud: A Collection of Critical Essays*. Englewood Cliffs, NJ: Prentice-Hall, Inc., 1975.

Field, Leslie A. and Joyce W. Field, eds. *Bernard Malamud and the Critics*. New York: New York University Press, 1970.

Fields, Wayne, ed. *James Fenimore Cooper: A Collection of Critical Essays*. Englewood Cliffs, NJ: Prentice-Hall, Inc., 1979.

Finholt, Richard. *American Visionary Fiction: Mad Metaphysics as Salvation Psychology*. Port Washington, NY: Kennikat Press, 1978.

Fischer, G. K. *In Search of Jerusalem: Religion and Ethics in the Writings of A.M. Klein*. Montreal: McGill-Queen's University Press, 1975.

Folsom, James K., ed. *Western: A Collection of Critical Essays*. Englewood Cliffs, NJ: Prentice-Hall, Inc., 1979.

Foner, Philip S. *Mark Twain Social Critic*. Third Edition. New York: International Publishers, 1972.

Fossum, Robert H. *Hawthorne's Inviolable Circle: The Problem of Time*. Deland, FL: Everett/Edwards, Inc., 1972.

Foster, Edward Halsey. *Catherine Maria Sedgwick*. New York: Twayne Publishers, Inc., 1974.

Foster, Edward Halsey. *Susan and Anna Warner*. Boston: Twayne Publishers, 1978.

Frane, Jeff. *Fritz Leiber*. Mercer Island, WA: Starmont House, 1980.

Frank, William L. *Sherwood Bonner (Catherine McDowell)*. Boston: Twayne Publishers, 1976.

Franklin, Benjamin, V and Duane Schneider. *Anaïs Nin: An Introduction*. Athens, OH: Ohio University Press, 1979.

Franklin, H. Bruce. *Robert A. Heinlein: America as Science Fiction*. New York: Oxford University Press, 1980.

Franklin, H. Bruce. *Victim as Criminal and Artist: Literature from the American Prison*. New York: Oxford University Press, 1978.

Frederick, John T. *Darkened Sky: Nineteenth-Century American Novelists and Religion*. Notre Dame, IN: University of Notre Dame Press, 1969.

Fredrickson, Robert S. *Hjalmar Hjorth Boyesen*. Boston: Twayne Publishers, 1980.

French, Warren, ed. *Fifties: Fiction, Poetry, Drama*. DeLand, FL: Everett/Edwards, Inc., 1970.

French, Warren, ed. *Forties: Fiction, Poetry, Drama*. DeLand, FL: Everett/Edwards, Inc., 1969.

French, Warren. *J. D. Salinger*. Revised Edition. Boston: Twayne Publishers, 1976.

French, Warren. *John Steinbeck*. Second Edition, Revised. Boston: Twayne Publishers, 1975.

French, Warren, ed. *Thirties: Fiction, Poetry, Drama*. Second Edition, Revised. DeLand, FL: Everett/Edwards, Inc., 1976.

Friedman, Alan W. *Multivalence: The Moral Quality of Form in the Modern Novel*. Baton Rouge: Louisiana State University Press, 1978.

Friedman, Ellen G. *Joyce Carol Oates*. New York: Frederick Ungar Publishing Co., 1980.

Friedman, Lenemaja. *Shirley Jackson*. Boston: Twayne Publishers, 1975.

Friedman, Melvin J., ed. *Vision Obscured: Perceptions of Some Twentieth-Century Catholic Novelists*. New York: Forham University Press, 1970.

Friedman, Melvin J. *William Styron*. Bowling Green, OH: Bowling Green University Popular Press, 1974.

Friedman, Melvin J. and John B. Vickery, eds. *Shaken Realist: Essays in Honor of Frederick J. Hoffman*. Baton Rouge, LA: Louisiana State University Press, 1970.

Friedman, Norman, ed. *E. E. Cummings: A Collection of Critical Essays*. Englewood Cliffs, NJ: Prentice-Hall, Inc., 1972.

Frohock, W. M. *Theodore Dreiser*. Minneapolis: University of Minnesota Press, 1972.

Fryer, Judith. *Faces of Eve: Women in the Nineteenth-Century American Novel*. New York: Oxford University Press, 1976.

Gale, Robert L. *John Hay*. Boston: Twayne Publishers, 1978.

Gallo, Rose Adrienne. *F. Scott Fitzgerald*. New York: Frederick Ungar Publishing Co.,1978.

Galloway, David. *Edward Lewis Wallant*. Boston: Twayne Publishers, 1979.

Galloway, David. *Henry James: The Portrait of a Lady*. London: Edward Arnold, 1976.

Galloway, David D. *Absurd Hero in American Fiction: Updike, Styron, Bellow, Salinger*. Revised Edition. Austin, TX: University of Texas Press, 1970.

Garner, Stanton. *Harold Frederic*. Minneapolis, MN: University of Minnesota Press, 1969.

Garson, Helen S. *Truman Capote*. New York: Frederick Ungar Publishing Co., 1980.

Garvin, Harry R., ed. *Makers of the Twentieth-Century Novel*. Lewisburg, PA: Bucknell University Press, 1977.

Garvin, Harry R., ed. *Women, Literature, Criticism*. Lewisburg, PA: Bucknell University Press, 1978. (Reprint of *Bucknell Review* 24.1, Spring 1978)

Garzilli, Enrico. *Circles without Center: Paths to the Discovery and Creation of Self in Modern Literature*. Cambridge, MA: Harvard University Press, 1972.

Gordon, David J. *Literary Art and the Unconscious*. Baton Rouge, LA: Louisiana State University Press, 1976.

Gordon, Joan. *Joe Haldeman*. Mercer Island, WA: Starmont House, 1980.

Gottesman, Ronald, comp. *Merrill Studies in Invisible Man*. Columbus, OH: Charles E. Merrill Publishing Company, 1971.

Grace, Sherrill. *Violent Duality: A Study of Margaret Atwood*. Montreal: Véhicule Press, 1980.

Graham, Don, ed. *Critical Essays on Frank Norris*. Boston: G. K. Hall & Co., 1980.

Graham, Don. *Fiction of Frank Norris: The Aesthetic Context*. Columbia, MO: University of Missouri Press, 1978.

Graham, John, comp. *Merrill Studies in A Farewell to Arms*. Columbus, OH: Charles E. Merrill Publishing Company, 1971.

Graham, John, comp. *Merrill Studies in Second Skin*. Columbus, OH: Charles E. Merrill Publishing Company, 1971.

Graham, Kenneth. *Henry James, The Drama of Fulfilment: An Approach to the Novels*. Oxford, England: Clarendon Press, 1975.

Grant, Judith Skelton. *Robertson Davies*. Toronto: McClelland and Stewart Limited, 1978.

Grant, Mary Kathryn. *Tragic Vision of Joyce Carol Oates*. Durham, NC: Duke University Press, 1978.

Graver, Lawrence. *Carson McCullers*. Minneapolis, MN: University of Minnesota Press, 1969.

Gray, James. *John Steinbeck*. Minneapolis, MN: University of Minnesota Press, 1971.

Gray, Richard. *Literature of Memory: Modern Writers of the American South*. Baltimore, MD: Johns Hopkins University Press, 1977.

Gray, Richard, ed. *Robert Penn Warren: A Collection of Critical Essays*. Englewood Cliffs, NJ: Prentice-Hall, Inc., 1980.

Grebstein, Sheldon Norman. *Hemingway's Craft*. Carbondale, IL: Southern Illinois University Press, 1973.

Grebstein, Sheldon Norman, comp. *Merrill Studies in For Whom the Bell Tolls*. Columbus, OH: Charles E. Merrill Publishing Company, 1971.

Green, Martin. *Dreams of Adventure, Deeds of Empire*. New York: Basic Books, Inc., 1979.

Green, Rose Basile. *Italian-American Novel: A Document of the Interaction of Two Cultures*. Rutherford, NJ: Fairleigh Dickinson University Press, 1974.

Greenberg, Martin Harry and Joseph D. Olander, eds. *Ray Bradbury*. New York: Taplinger Publishing Company, 1980.

Greiner, Donald J. *Comic Terror: The Novels of John Hawkes*. Memphis, TN: Memphis State University Press, 1973.

Griffith, Albert J. *Peter Taylor*. New York: Twayne Publishers, Inc., 1970.

Grosskurth, Phylllis. *Gabrielle Roy*. Toronto: Forum House Publishing Company, 1969.

Guerard, Albert J. *Triumph of the Novel: Dickens, Dostoevsky, Faulkner*. New York: Oxford University Press, 1976.

Gunn, Drewey Wayne. *American and British Writers in Mexico, 1556–1973*. Austin, TX: University of Texas Press, 1974.

Gurko, Leo. *Thomas Wolfe: Beyond the Romantic Ego*. New York: Thomas Y. Crowell Company, 1975.

Guttenberg, Barnett. *Web of Being: The Novels of Robert Penn Warren*. Nashville, TN: Vanderbilt University Press, 1975.

Guttmann, Allen. *Jewish Writer in America: Assimilation and the Crisis of Identity.* New York: Oxford University Press, 1971.

Haberstroh, Charles J., Jr. *Melville and Male Identity.* Rutherford, NJ: Fairleigh Dickinson, 1980.

Hairston, Maxine Cousins. *George Sessions Perry: His Life and Works.* Austin, TX: Jenkins Publishing Company, 1973.

Halperin, Irving. *Messengers from the Dead: Literature of the Holocaust.* Philadelphia, PA: Westminster Press, 1970.

Halperin, John, ed. *Theory of the Novel: New Essays.* New York: Oxford University Press, 1974.

Hamblen, Abigail Ann. *Ruth Suckow.* Boise, ID: Boise State Univesity, 1978.

Hamilton, Alice and Kenneth. *Elements of John Updike.* Grand Rapids, MI: William B. Eerdmans Publishing Co., 1970.

Hardy, John Edward. *Katherine Anne Porter.* New York: Frederick Ungar Publishing Co., Inc., 1973.

Harrington, Evans and Ann J. Abadie, eds. *Maker and the Myth: Faulkner and Yoknapatawpha, 1977.* Jackson, MS: University Press of Mississippi, 1978.

Harrington, Evans and Ann J. Abadie, eds. *South and Faulkner's Yoknapatawpha: The Actual and the Apocryphal.* Jackson, MS: University Press of Mississippi, 1977.

Harris, Charles B. *Contemporary American Novelists of the Absurd.* New Haven, CT: College & University Press, 1971.

Harrison, Dick. *Unnamed Country: The Struggle for a Canadian Prairie Fiction.* Edmonton, AL: University of Alberta Press, 1977.

Harrison, Stanley R. *Edgar Fawcett.* New York: Twayne Publishers, Inc., 1972.

Hart, John E. *Floyd Dell.* New York: Twayne Publishers, Inc., 1971.

Hartley, Lodwick and George Core, eds. *Katherine Anne Porter: A Critical Symposium.* Athens, GA: University of Georgia Press, 1969.

Haslam, Gerald. *William Eastlake.* Austin, TX: Steck-Vaughn Company, 1970.

Haslam, Gerald W., ed. *Western Writing.* Albuquerque, NM: University of New Mexico Press, 1974.

Hassan, Ihab. *Dismemberment of Orpheus: Toward a Postmodern Literature.* New York: Oxford University Press, 1971.

Hatvary, George Egon. *Horace Binney Wallace.* Boston: Twayne Publishers, 1977.

Hauck, Richard Boyd. *Cheerful Nihilism: Confidence & "The Absurd" in American Humorous Fiction.* Bloomington, IN: Indiana University Press, 1971.

Hawthorne, Nathaniel. *Blithedale Romance: An Authoritative Text, Backgrounds and Sources, Criticism.* Eds. Seymour Gross and Rosalie Murphy. New York: W. W. Norton & Company, 1978.

Hayashi, Tetsumaro, ed. *Study Guide to Steinbeck: a Handbook to His Major Works.* Metuchen, NJ: Scarecrow Press, Inc., 1974.

Hays, Peter L. *Limping Hero: Grotesques in Literature.* New York: New York University Press, 1971.

Hearn, Charles R. *American Dream in the Great Depression.* Westport, CT: Greenwood Press, 1977.

Heilbrun, Carolyn G. *Toward a Recognition of Androgyny.* New York: Harper and Row, Publishers, 1973.

Hemenway, Robert, ed. *Black Novelist.* Columbus, OH: Charles E. Merrill Publishing Company, 1970.

Henderson, Harry B. *Versions of the Past: The Historical Imagination in American Fiction.* New York: Oxford University Press, 1974.

Hendin, Josephine. *Vulnerable People: A View of American Fiction Since 1945*. New York: Oxford University Press, 1978.

Herbert, T. Walter, Jr. *Moby-Dick and Calvinism: A World Dismantled*. New Brunswick, NJ: Rutgers University Press, 1977.

Hersey, John, ed. *Ralph Ellison: A Collection of Critical Essays*. Englewood Cliffs, NJ: Prentice Hall, Inc., 1974.

Hershinow, Sheldon J. *Bernard Malamud*. New York: Frederick Ungar Publishing Co., 1980.

Hillway, Tyrus. *Herman Melville*. Rev. ed. Boston: Twayne Publishers, 1979.

Hipkiss, Robert A. *Jack Kerouac, Prophet of the New Romanticism: A Critical Study of the Published Works of Kerouac and a Comparison of Them to Those of J. D. Salinger, James Purdy, John Knowles, and Ken Kesey*. Lawrence, KS: Regents Press of Kansas, 1976.

Hirsch, David H. *Reality and Idea in the Early American Novel*. The Hague: Mouton, 1971.

Hoar, Victor. *Morley Callaghan*. Toronto: Copp Clark Publishing Company, 1969.

Hollowell, John. *Fact & Fiction: The New Journalism and the Nonfiction Novel*. Chapel Hill, NC: University of North Carolina, 1977.

Holman, C. Hugh. *Loneliness at the Core: Studies in Thomas Wolfe*. Baton Rouge: Louisiana State University Press, 1975.

Holman, C. Hugh. *Roots of Southern Writing: Essays of the Literature of the American South*. Athens, GA: University of Georgia Press, 1972.

Holton, Milne. *Cylinder of Vision: The Fiction and Journalistic Writings of Stephen Crane*. Baton Rouge, LA: Louisiana State University Press, 1972.

Honig, Edwin. *Dark Conceit: The Making of Allegory*. Providence, RI: Brown University Press, 1972.

Hook, Andrew, ed. *Dos Passos: A Collection of Critical Essays*. Englewood Cliffs, NJ: Prentice-Hall, Inc., 1974.

Howe, Irving. *Celebrations and Attacks: Thirty Years of Literary and Cultural Commentary*. New York: Horizon Press, 1979.

Howe, Irving. *William Faulkner: A Critical Study*. Third Edition, Revised and Expanded. Chicago: University of Chicago Press, 1975.

Hoyt, Charles Alva, ed. *Minor American Novelists*. Carbondale, IL: Southern Illinois University Press, 1970.

Hudson, Theodore R. *From LeRoi Jones to Amiri Baraka: The Literary Works*. Durham, NC: Duke University Press, 1973.

Hughes, Richard E. *Lively Image: 4 Myths in Literature*. Cambridge, MA: Winthrop Publishers, Inc., 1975.

Hunt, George. *John Updike and the three great secret things: Sex, Religion, and Art*. Grand Rapids, MI: William B. Eerdmans Publishing Company, 1980.

Hunter, Edwin R. *William Faulkner: Narrative Practice and Prose Style*. Washington, DC: Windhover Press, 1973.

Inge, M. Thomas, comp. *Merrill Studies in Light in August*. Columbus, OH: Charles E. Merrill Publishing Company, 1971.

Isaacs, Neil D. *Eudora Welty*. Austin, TX: Steck-Vaughn Company, 1969.

Iser, Wolfgang. *Implied Reader: Patterns of Communication in Prose Fiction From Bunyan to Beckett*. Baltimore: Johns Hopkins University Press, 1974.

Jackson, Carlton. *Zane Grey*. New York: Twayne Publishers, Inc., 1973.

James, Henry. *American: An Authoritative Text, Backgrounds and Sources, Criticism*. Ed. James W. Tuttleton. New York: W. W. Norton, 1978.

James, Henry. *Portrait of a Lady: An Authoritative Text, Henry James and the Novel, Reviews and Criticism.* Ed. Robert D. Bamberg. New York: W. W. Norton, 1975.

James, Henry. *Wings of the Dove: An Authoritative Text, the Author and the Novel, Criticism.* Eds. J. Donald Crowley and Richard A. Hocks. New York: W. W. Norton, 1978.

Jehlen, Myra. *Class and Character in Faulkner's South.* New York: Columbia University Press, 1976.

Johnson, Ira. *Glenway Wescott: The Paradox of Voice.* Port Washington, NY: Kennikat Press, 1971.

Johnson, Ira D. and Christiane Johnson, eds. *Les Américanistes: New French Criticism on Modern American Fiction.* Port Washington, NY: Kennikat Press, 1978.

Johnson, Wayne L. *Ray Bradbury.* New York: Frederick Ungar Publishing Co., 1980.

Jones, D. G. *Butterfly on Rock: A Study of Themes and Images in Canadian Literature.* Toronto: University of Toronto Press, 1970.

Jones, Granville H. *Henry James's Psychology of Experience: Innocence, Responsibility, and Renunciation in the Fiction of Henry James.* The Hague, Netherlands: Mouton & Co., 1975.

Jones, Peter G. *War and the Novelist: Appraising the American War Novel.* Columbia, MO: University of Missouri Press, 1976.

Joseph, Gerhard. *John Barth.* Minneapolis, MN: University of Minnesota Press, 1970.

Josipovici, Gabriel. *World and the Book: a Study of Modern Fiction.* Stanford, CA: Stanford University Press, 1971.

Kannenstine, Louis F. *Art of Djuna Barnes: Duality and Damnation.* New York: New York University Press, 1977.

Kaplan, Harold. *Democratic Humanism and American Literature.* Chicago: University of Chicago Press, 1972.

Karcher, Carolyn L. *Shadow over the Promised Land: Slavery, Race, and Violence in Melville's America.* Baton Rouge, LA: Louisiana State University Press, 1980.

Kartiganer, Donald M. *Fragile Thread: The Meaning of Form in Faulkner's Novels.* Amherst, PA: University of Massachusetts Press, 1979.

Katz, Joseph, ed. *Stephen Crane in Transition: Centenary Essays.* Dekalb, IL: Northern Illinois University Press, 1972.

Kaufmann, Donald L. *Norman Mailer: The Countdown (The First Twenty Years).* Carbondale, IL: Southern Illinois University Press, 1969.

Kazin, Alfred. "Elegy and Satire: Willa Cather and Ellen Glasgow," in Kazin, Alfred. *On Native Grounds: A Study of American Prose from 1890 to the Present.* New York: Harcourt, Brace & Co., 1942. Rpt. as "Willa Cather and Ellen Glasgow" in Rahv, Philip, ed. *Literature in America*, 314–316.

Keefer, Truman Frederick. *Philip Wylie.* Boston: Twayne Publishers, 1977.

Kellogg, Jean. *Dark Prophets of Hope: Dostoevsky, Sartre, Camus, Faulkner.* Chicago: Loyola University Press, 1975.

Kennard, Jean E. *Number and Nightmare: Forms of Fantasy in Contemporary Fiction.* Hamden, CT: Archon Books, 1975.

Kenner, Hugh. *Homemade World: The American Modernist Writers.* New York: Alfred A. Knopf, 1975.

Kerr, Elizabeth M. *William Faulkner's Gothic Domain.* Port Washington, NY: Kennikat Press, 1979.

Kerr, Howard. *Mediums, and Spirit-Rappers, and Roaring Radicals: Spiritualism in American Literature, 1850–1900.* Urbana: University of Illinois Press, 1972.

Kesterson, David B. ed. *Critics on Mark Twain*. Coral Gables, FL: University of Miami Press, 1973.

Kesterson, David B., comp. *Merrill Studies in The Marble Faun*. Columbus, OH: Charles E. Merrill Publishing Company, 1971.

Ketterer, David. *New Worlds for Old: The Apocalyptic Imagination, Science Fiction, and American Literature*. Garden City, NY: Anchor Press/Doubleday, 1974.

Keith, W. J. *Charles G. D. Roberts*. Toronto: Copp Clark Publishing Company, 1969.

Kiley, Frederick and Walter McDonald, eds. *Catch-22 Casebook*. New York: Thomas Y. Crowell Company, 1973.

King, Richard H. *Southern Renaissance: The Cultural Awakening of the American South, 1930–1955*. New York: Oxford University Press, 1980.

Kinnamon, Keneth. *Emergence of Richard Wright: A Study of the Literature and Society*. Urbana, IL: University of Illinois Press, 1972.

Kinnamon, Keneth, ed. *James Baldwin: A Collection of Critical Essays*. Englewood Cliffs, NJ: Prentice-Hall, Inc., 1974.

Kirby, David. *Grace King*. Boston: Twayne Publishers, 1980.

Kirby, Thomas Austin and William John Olive, eds. *Essays in Honor of Esmond Linworth Marilla*. Baton Rouge, LA: Louisiana State University Press, 1970.

Kissane, Leedice McAnelly. *Ruth Suckow*. New York: Twayne Publishers, Inc., 1969.

Klein, Holger, ed. *First World War in Fiction: A Collection of Critical Essays*. New York: Macmillan Press Ltd., 1976.

Klinkowitz, Jerome. *American 1960's: Imaginative Acts in a Decade of Change*. Ames, IA: Iowa State University Press, 1980.

Klinkowitz, Jerome. *Practice of Fiction in America: Writers from Hawthorne to the Present*. Ames, IA: Iowa State University Press, 1980.

Klinkowitz, Jerome and Donald L. Lawler, eds. *Vonnegut in America: an Introduction to the Life and Work of Kurt Vonnegut*. New York: Delacorte Press, 1977.

Klinkowitz, Jerome and John Somer, eds. *Vonnegut Statement*. New York: Dell Publishing Co., 1973.

Klotman, Phyllis Rauch. *Another Man Gone: The Black Runner in Contemporary Afro-American Literature*. Port Washington, NY: Kennikat Press, 1977.

Knapp, Bettina. *Anaïs Nin*. New York: Frederick Ungar Publishing Co.,1978.

Knight, Damon, ed. *Turning Points: Essays on the Art of Science Fiction*. New York: Harper &Row, Publishers, 1977.

Kolodny, Annette. *Lay of the Land: Metaphor as Experience and History in American Life and Letters*. Chapel Hill, NC: University of North Carolina Press, 1975.

Korges, James. *Erskine Caldwell*. Minneapolis, MN: University of Minnesota Press, 1969.

Kort, Wesley A. *Shriven Selves: Religious Problems in Recent American Fiction*. Philadelphia: Fortress Press, 1972.

Kostelanetz, Richard, ed. *On Contemporary Literature*. Expanded ed. New York: Avon Books, 1969.

Kramer, Victor A. *James Agee*. Boston: Twayne Publishers, 1975.

Kronenberger, Louis. *Polished Surface: Essays in the Literature of Worldliness*. New York: Alfred A. Knopf, 1969.

Kuehl, John. *John Hawkes and the Craft of Conflict*. New Brunswick, NJ: Rutgers University Press, 1975.

Kuhlmann, Susan. *Knave, Fool, and Genius: The Confidence Man as He Appears in Nineteenth-Century American Fiction*. Chapel Hill, NC: University of North Carolina Press, 1973.

Malin, Irving. *Saul Bellow's Fiction*. Carbondale, IL: Southern Illinois University Press, 1969.

Mallard, William. *Reflection of Theology in Literature: A Case Study in Theology and Culture*. San Antonio, TX: Trinity University Press, 1977.

Malley, Terence. *Richard Brautigan*. New York: Warner Paperback Library, 1972.

Margolies, Edward. *Art of Richard Wright*. Carbondale, IL: Southern Illinois University Press, 1969.

Markle, Joyce B. *Fighters and Lovers: Theme in the Novels of John Updike*. New York: New York University Press, 1973.

Markson, David. *Malcolm Lowry's Volcano: Myth, Symbol, Meaning*. New York: Times Books, 1978.

Marshall, Tom, ed. *A.M. Klein*. Toronto: Ryerson Press, 1970.

Mason, Ronald. *Spirit Above the Dust: A Study of Herman Melville*. Second Edition. Mamaroneck, NY: Paul P. Appel, 1972.

Mathews, Robin. *Canadian Literature: Surrender or Revolution*. Toronto: Steel Rail Educational Publishing, 1978.

Maves, Carl. *Sensuous Pessimism: Italy in the Works of Henry James*. Bloomington, IN: Indiana University Press, 1973.

May, John R. *Pruning Word: The Parables of Flannery O'Connor*. Notre Dame, IN: University of Notre Dame Press, 1976.

May, John R. *Toward a New Earth: Apocalypse in the American Novel*. Notre Dame, IN: University of Notre Dame Press, 1972.

May, Keith M. *Out of the Maelstrom: Psychology and the Novel in the Twentieth Century*. New York: St. Martin's Press, 1977.

Meeker, Joseph W. *Comedy of Survival: Studies in Literary Ecology*. New York: Charles Scribner's Sons, 1974.

Mellard, James M. *Exploded Form: The Modernist Novel in America*. Urbana, IL: University of Illinois Press, 1980.

Melville, Herman. *Confidence Man, His Masquerade: An Authoritative Text, Backgrounds and Sources, Reviews, Criticism, An Annotated Bibliography*. Ed. Hershel Parker. New York: W. W. Norton & Company, Inc., 1971.

Mendelson, Edward, ed. *Pynchon: A Collection of Critical Essays*. Englewood Cliffs, NJ: Prentice-Hall, Inc., 1978.

Merrill, Robert. *Norman Mailer*. Boston: Twayne Publishers, 1978.

Meyers, Jeffrey. *Painting and the Novel*. Manchester: Manchester University Press, 1975.

Meyers, Walter E. *Aliens and Linguists: Language Study and Science Fiction*. Athens, GA: University of Georgia Press, 1980.

Michel, Pierre. *James Gould Cozzens*. New York: Twayne Publishers, Inc., 1974.

Miesel, Sandra. *Against Time's Arrow: The High Crusade of Poul Anderson*. San Bernardino, CA: Borgo Press, 1978.

Miller, David M. *Frank Herbert*. Mercer Island, WA: Starmont House, 1980.

Miller, J. Hillis, ed. *Aspects of Narrative: Selected Papers from the English Institute*. New York: Columbia University Press, 1971.

Miller, Wayne Charles. *Armed America, Its Face in Fiction: A History of the American Military Novel*. New York: New York University Press, 1970.

Millichap, Joseph R. *Hamilton Basso*. Boston: Twayne Publishers, 1979.

Milliken, Stephen F. *Chester Himes: A Critical Appraisal*. Columbia, MO: University of Missouri Press, 1976.

Nagel, James. *Stephen Crane and Literary Impressionism*. University Park, PA: Pennsylvania State University Press, 1980.

Nahal, Chaman. *Narrative Pattern in Ernest Hemingway's Fiction*. Rutherford, NJ: Fairleigh Dickinson University Press, 1971.

Nance, William L. *Worlds of Truman Capote*. New York: Stein and Day, 1970.

Neinstein, Raymond L. *Ghost Country: A Study of the Novels of Larry McMurtry*. Berkeley, CA: Creative Arts Book Company, 1976.

Nelson, Gerald B. *Ten Versions of America*. New York: Alfred A. Knopf, 1972.

Nesbitt, Bruce, ed. *Earle Birney*. Toronto: McGraw-Hill Ryerson Limited, 1974.

Nettels, Elsa. *James & Conrad*. Athens, GA: University of Georgia Press, 1977.

New, W. H. *Articulating West: Essays on Purpose and Form in Modern Canadian Literature*. Toronto: New Press, 1972.

New, William, ed. *Margaret Laurence*. Toronto: McGraw-Hill Ryerson Limited, 1977.

New, William H. *Malcolm Lowry*. Toronto: McClelland and Stewart Limited, 1971.

Newman, Charles, ed. *Art of Sylvia Plath: A Symposium*. Bloomington, IN: Indiana University Press, 1970.

Norris, Frank. *McTeague: An Authoritative Text, Backgrounds and Sources, Criticism*. Ed. Donald Pizer. New York: W. W. Norton & Company, 1977.

Northey, Margot. *Haunted Wilderness: The Gothic and Grotesque in Canadian Fiction*. Toronto: University of Toronto Press, 1976.

Norton, Charles A. *Melville Davisson Post: Man of Many Mysteries*. Bowling Green, OH: Bowling Green University Popular Press, 1973.

Oates, Joyce Carol. *Edge of Impossibility: Tragic Forms in Literature*. New York: Vanguard Press, Inc., 1972.

Oates, Joyce Carol. *New Heaven, New Earth: the Visionary Experience in Literature*. New York: Vanguard Press, Inc., 1974.

O'Daniel, Therman B., ed. *James Baldwin: A Critical Evaluation*. Washington, DC: Howard University Press, 1977.

O'Daniel, Therman B., ed. *Langston Hughes Black Genius: A Critical Evaluation*. New York: William Morrow & Company, Inc., 1971.

Olander, Joseph D. and Martin Harry Greenberg, eds. *Isaac Asimov*. New York: Taplinger Publishing Company, 1977.

Olander, Joseph D. and Martin Harry Greenberg, eds. *Robert A. Heinlein*. New York: Taplinger Publishing Company, 1978.

Olander, Joseph D. and Martin Harry Greenberg, eds. *Ursula K. Le Guin*. New York: Taplinger Publishing Company, 1979.

Olderman, Raymond M. *Beyond the Waste Land: A Study of the American Novel in the Nineteen-Sixties*. New Haven, CT: Yale University Press, 1972.

O'Meally, Robert G. *Craft of Ralph Ellison*. Cambridge, MA: Harvard University Press, 1980.

Omranin, Margaret Stewart. *Ruth Suckow: A Critical Study of Her Fiction*. Philadelphia: Dorrance & Company, 1972.

Ondaatje, Michael. *Leonard Cohen*. Toronto: McClelland and Stewart Limited, 1970.

Orr, John. *Tragic Realism and Modern Society: Studies in the Sociology of the Modern Novel*. Pittsburgh: University of Pittsburgh Press, 1978.

Orvell, Miles. *Invisible Parade: The Fiction of Flannery O'Connor*. Philadelphia: Temple University Press, 1972.

Osborn, Scott Compton and Robert L. Phillips, Jr.. *Richard Harding Davis*. Boston: Twayne Publishers, 1978.

Osborne, William S. *Lydia Maria Child*. Boston: Twayne Publishers, 1980.

Pops, Martin Leonard. *Melville Archetype*. Kent, OH: Kent State University Press, 1970.

Porte, Joel. *Romance in America: Studies in Cooper, Poe, Hawthorne, Melville, and James*. Middletown, CT: Wesleyan University Press, 1969.

Porter, M. Gilbert. *Whence the Power?: The Artistry and Humanity of Saul Bellow*. Columbia, MO: University of Missouri Press, 1974.

Poulin, Gabrielle. *Romans du pays: 1968–1979*. Montréal: Les Éditions Bellarmin, 1980.

Powers, Lyall H. *Faulkner's Yoknapatawpha Comedy*. Ann Arbor, MI: University of Michigan Press, 1980.

Powers, Lyall H. *Henry James and the Naturalist Movement*. East Lansing, MI: Michigan State University Press, 1971.

Powers, Lyall H., comp. *Merrill Studies in The Portrait of a Lady*. Columbus, OH: Charles E. Merrill Publishing Company, 1970.

Pratt, Louis H. *James Baldwin*. Boston: Twayne Publishers, 1978.

Prenshaw, Peggy Whitman, ed. *Eudora Welty: Critical Essays*. Jackson, MS: University Press of Mississippi, 1979.

Proffer, Carl R., ed. and trans. *Soviet Criticism of American Literature in the Sixties: An Anthology*. Ann Arbor, MI: Ardis Publishers, 1972.

Pryse, Marjorie. *Mark and the Knowledge: Social Stigma in Classic American Fiction*. Columbus, OH: Ohio State University Press, 1979.

Purdy, Strother B. *Hole in the Fabric: Science, Contemporary Literature, and Henry James*. Pittsburgh, PA: University of Pittsburgh Press, 1977.

Quilligan, Maureen. *Language of Allegory: Defining the Genre*. Ithaca, NY: Cornell University Press, 1979.

Raban, Jonathan. *Mark Twain: Huckleberry Finn*. London: Edward Arnold, 1979.

Rabkin, Eric S. *Fantastic in Literature*. Princeton, NJ: Princeton University Press, 1976.

Radford, Jean. *Norman Mailer: A Critical Study*. New York: Barnes & Noble Books, 1975.

Rahv, Philip. *Essays on Literature and Politics: 1932–1972*. Boston: Houghton Mifflin Company, 1978.

Rahv, Philip. *Literature and the Sixth Sense*. Boston: Houghton Mifflin Company, 1969.

Rahv, Philip, ed. *Literature in America*. Gloucester, MA: Peter Smith, 1973.

Rampersad, Arnold. *Art and Imagination of W. E. B. Du Bois*. Cambridge, MA: Harvard University Press, 1976.

Rank, Hugh. *Edwin O'Connor*. New York: Twayne Publishers, Inc., 1974.

Raper, Julius Rowan. *From the Sunken Garden: The Fiction of Ellen Glasgow, 1916–1945*. Baton Rouge, LA: Louisiana State University Press, 1980.

Ratner, Marc L. *William Styron*. New York: Twayne Publishers, Inc.: 1972.

Ray, David and Robert M. Farnsworth, eds. *Richard Wright: Impressions and Perspectives*. Ann Arbor, MI: University of Michigan Press, 1971.

Reed, Peter J. *Kurt Vonnegut, Jr.* New York: Warner Paperback Library, 1972.

Reeves, Paschal, comp. *Merrill Studies in Look Homeward, Angel*. Columbus, OH: Charles E. Merrill Publishing Company, 1970.

Reid, B. L. *Tragic Occasions: Essays on Several Forms*. Port Washington, NY: Kennikat Press, 1971.

Reilly, John M., ed. *Twentieth Century Interpretations of Invisible Man: A Collection of Critical Essays*. Englewood Cliffs, NJ: Prentice-Hall, Inc., 1970.

Smith, Anne, ed. *Art of Malcolm Lowry*. London: Vision Press Limited, 1978.

Sorfleet, John R. *Work of Margaret Laurence*. Montreal: JCF Press, 1980.

Sorfleet, John Robert, ed. *L.M. Montgomery: An Assessment*. Guelph, ON: Canadian Children's Press, 1976. (Articles contained in this book were published in part in *Canadian Children's Literature*, No. 3, 1975)

Spacks, Patricia Meyer, ed. *Contemporary Women Novelists: A Collection of Critical Essays*. Englewood Cliffs, NJ: Prentice-Hall, Inc., 1977.

Spacks, Patricia Meyer. *Female Imagination*. New York: Alfred A. Knopf, 1975.

Speir, Jerry. *Ross Macdonald*. New York: Frederick Ungar Publishing Co., 1978.

Spencer, Sharon. *Collage of Dreams: The Writings of Anaïs Nin*. Chicago: Swallow Press, 1977.

Spencer, Sharon. *Space, Time and Structure in the Modern Novel*. New York: New York University Press, 1971.

Spengemann, William C. *Adventurous Muse: The Poetics of American Fiction, 1789–1900*. New Haven, CT: Yale University Press, 1977

Spettigue, Douglas O. *Frederick Philip Grove*. Toronto: Copp Clark Publishing Company, 1969.

Spiegel, Alan. *Fiction and the Camera Eye: Visual Consciousness in Film and the Modern Novel*. Charlottesville, VA: University Press of Virginia, 1976.

Spilka, Mark, ed. *Towards a Poetics of Fiction*. Bloomington, IN: Indiana University Press, 1977.

Springer, Marlene, ed. *What Manner of Woman: Essays on English and American Life and Literature*. New York: New York University Press, 1977.

Springer, Mary Doyle. *Rhetoric of Literary Character: Some Women of Henry James*. Chicago: University of Chicago Press, 1978.

Squires, Radcliffe, ed. *Allen Tate and His Works: Critical Evaluations*. Minneapolis: University of Minnesota Press, 1972.

Stafford, William T., comp. *Merrill Studies in The American*. Columbus, OH: Charles E. Merrill Publishing Company, 1971.

Staines, David, ed. *Canadian Imagination: Dimensions of a Literary Culture*. Cambridge, MA: Harvard University Press, 1977.

Stark, John. *Literature of Exhaustion: Borges, Nabokov, Barth*. Durham, NC: Duke University Press, 1974.

Starke, Catherine Juanita. *Black Portraiture in American Fiction: Stock Characters, Archetypes and Individuals*. New York: Basic Books, Inc., Publishers, 1971.

Stavola, Thomas J. *Scott Fitzgerald: Crisis in an American Identity*. London: Vision Press Limited, 1979.

Stein, Allen F. *Cornelius Mathews*. New York: Twayne Publishers, Inc., 1974.

Stephens, Donald G., ed. *Writers of the Prairies*. Vancouver: University of British Columbia Press, 1973.

Stewart, Lawrence D. *Paul Bowles: The Illumination of North Africa*. Carbondale, IL: Southern Illinois University Press, 1974.

Stineback, David C. *Shifting World: Social Change and Nostalgia in the American Novel*. Lewisburg, PA: Bucknell University Press, 1976.

Stobie, Margaret R. *Frederick Philip Grove*. New York: Twayne Publishers, Inc.: 1973.

Stone, Albert E., ed. *Twentieth Century Interpretations of The Ambassadors: A Collection of Critical Essays*. Englewood Cliffs, NJ: Prentice-Hall, Inc., 1969.

Stone, Edward. *Certain Morbidness: A View of American Literature*. Carbondale, IL: Southern Illinois University Press, 1969.

Stouck, David. *Willa Cather's Imagination.* Lincoln, NE: University of Nebraska Press, 1975.

Stout, Janis P. *Sodoms in Eden: The City in American Fiction Before 1860.* Westport, CT: Greenwood Press, 1976.

Stowell, H. Peter. *Literary Impressionism, James and Chekov.* Athens, GA: University of Georgia Press, 1980.

Stratford, Philip. *Marie-Claire Blais.* Toronto: Coles Publishing Company Limited, 1971.

Stresau, Hermann. *Thornton Wilder.* Trans. Frieda Schutze. New York: Frederick Ungar Publishing Co., 1971.

Struthers, J. R., ed. *Before the Flood: Our Exagmination round His Factification for Incamination of Hugh Hood's Work in Progress.* Toronto: ECW Press, 1979. (Rpt. of *Essays on Canadian Writing,* Nos. 13/14, Winter/Spring 1978–79)

Stuart, Dabney. *Nabokov: The Dimensions of Parody.* Baton Rouge, LA: Louisiana State University Press, 1978.

Stuckey, W. J. *Caroline Gordon.* New York: Twayne Publishers, Inc., 1972.

Sullivan, Walter. *Death by Melancholy: Essays on Modern Southern Fiction.* Baton Rouge, LA: Louisiana State University Press, 1972.

Sullivan, Walter. *Requiem for the Renascence: The State of Fiction in the South.* Athens, GA: University of Georgia Press, 1976.

Sundquist, Eric J. *Home as Found: Authority Genealogy in Nineteenth-Century American Literature.* Baltimore, MD: Johns Hopkins University Press, 1979.

Sutherland, Ronald. *Frederick Philip Grove.* Toronto: McClelland and Stewart Limited, 1969.

Sutherland, Ronald. *New Hero: Essays in Comparative Quebec/Canadian Literature.* Toronto: Macmillan of Canada, 1977.

Sutherland, Ronald. *Second Image: Comparative Studies in Québec/Canadian Literature.* Don Mills, ON: New Press, 1971.

Sylvander, Carolyn Wedin. *James Baldwin.* New York: Frederick Ungar Publishing Company, 1980.

Takaki, Ronald T. *Violence in the Black Imagination: Essays and Documents.* New York: G. P. Putnam's Sons, 1972.

Tanner, Tony. *City of Words: American Fiction 1950–1970.* New York: Harper & Row, Publishers, 1971.

Tatar, Maria M. *Spellbound: Studies on Mesmerism and Literature.* Princeton, NJ: Princeton University Press, 1978.

Tausky, Thomas E. *Sara Jeanette Duncan: Novelist of Empire.* Port Credit, ON: P. D. Meany Publishers, 1980.

Taylor, Gordon O. *Passages of Thought: Psychological Representation in the American Novel 1870–1900.* New York: Oxford University Press, 1969.

Taylor, Larry E. *Pastoral and Anti-Pastoral Patterns in John Updike's Fiction.* Carbondale, IL: Southern Illinois University Press, 1971.

Taylor, Lloyd C., Jr. *Margaret Ayer Barnes.* New York: Twayne Publishers, Inc., 1974.

Taylor, Welford Dunaway. *Amélie Rives (Princess Troubetzkoy).* New York: Twayne Publishers, Inc., 1973.

Taylor, Welford Dunaway. *Sherwood Anderson.* New York: Frederick Ungar Publishing Co., 1977.

Tharpe, Jac. *John Barth: The Comic Sublimity of Paradox.* Carbondale, IL: Southern Illinois University Press, 1974.

Thériault, Serge A. *La quête d'équilibre dans l'oeuvre romanesque d'Anne Hébert.* Hull, PQ: Les éditions Asticou enrg., 1980.

Thomas, Clara. *Manawaka World of Margaret Laurence.* Toronto: McClelland and Stewart Limited, 1975.

Thomas, Clara. *Margaret Laurence.* Toronto: McClelland and Stewart Limited, 1969.

Thomas, Peter. *Robert Kroetsch.* Vancouver: Douglas and McIntyre Limited, 1980.

Thomas, W. K. *Fizz Inside: Critical Essays of a Lighter Kind.* Waterloo, ON: University of Waterloo Press, 1980.

Thorburn, David and Howard Eiland, eds. *John Updike: A Collection of Critical Essays.* Englewood Cliffs, NJ: Prentice-Hall, Inc., 1979.

Tilton, John W. *Cosmic Satire in the Contemporary Novel.* Lewisburg, PA: Bucknell University Press, 1977.

Titus, Warren I. *John Fox, Jr.* New York: Twayne Publishers, Inc., 1971.

Tobin, Patricia Dreschel. *Time and the Novel: The Genealogical Imperative.* Princeton, NJ: Princeton University Press, 1978.

Torrance, Robert M. *Comic Hero.* Cambridge, MA: Harvard University Press, 1978.

Trachtenberg, Stanley, ed. *Critical Essays on Saul Bellow.* Boston: G. K. Hall & Co., 1979.

Trilling, Lionel. *Opposing Self: Nine Essays in Criticism.* New York: Harcourt Brace Jovanovich, 1978.

Trilling, Lionel. *Speaking of Literature and Society.* Ed. Diana Trilling. New York: Harcourt Brace Jovanovich, 1980.

Trimble, Martha Scott. *N. Scott Momaday.* Boise, ID: Boise State College, 1973.

Turner, Arlin, ed. *Critical Essays on George W. Cable.* Boston: G. K. Hall & Co., 1980.

Turner, Arlin, comp. *Merrill Studies in The Scarlet Letter.* Columbus, OH: Charles E. Merrill Publishing Company, 1970.

Tuttleton, James W. *Novel of Manners in America.* Chapel Hill, NC: University of North Carolina Press, 1972.

Tuttleton, James W. *Thomas Wentworth Higginson.* Boston: Twayne Publishers, 1978.

Twain, Mark. *Adventures of Huckleberry Finn: An Authoritative Text, Backgrounds and Sources, Criticism.* Ed. Sculley Bradley, et. al. 2nd ed. New York: W. W. Norton & Company, 1977.

Twain, Mark. *Pudd'nhead Wilson and Those Extraordinary Twins: Authoritative Texts, Textual Introduction and Tables of Variants, Criticism.* Ed. Sidney E. Berger. W. W. Norton & Company, 1980.

Tytell, John. *Naked Angels: The Lives & Literature of the Beat Generation.* New York: McGraw-Hill Book Company, 1976.

Umphlett, Wiley Lee. *Sporting Myth and the American Experience: Studies in Contemporary Fiction.* Lewisburg, PA: Bucknell University Press, 1975.

Unfried, Sarah P. *Man's Place in the Natural Order: A Study of Hemingway's Major Works.* New York: Gordon Press, 1976.

Uphaus, Suzanne Henning. *John Updike.* New York: Frederick Ungar Publishing Co., 1980.

Urbas, Jeannette. *From Thirty Acres to Modern Times: The Story of French Canadian Literature.* Toronto: McGraw-Hill Ryerson Limited, 1976.

Vargo, Edward P. *Rainstorms and Fire: Ritual in the Novels of John Updike.* Port Washington, NY: Kennikat Press, 1973.

Veeder, William. *Henry James—The Lessons of the Master: Popular Fiction and Per-*

sonal Style in the Nineteenth Century. Chicago: University of Chicago Press, 1975.

Vernon, John. *Garden and the Map: Schizophrenia in Twentieth-Century Literature and Culture.* Urbana, IL: University of Illinois Press, 1973.

Viens, Jacques. *La terre de Zola et Trentes arpents de Ringuet: étude comparée.* Montréal: Editions Cosmos, 1970.

Vincent, Howard P., comp. *Merrill Studies in Moby-Dick.* Columbus, OH: Charles E. Merrill Publishing Company, 1969.

Waddington, Miriam. *A. M. Klein.* Toronto: Copp Clark Publishing Company, 1970.

Wadlington, Warwick. *Confidence Game in American Literature.* Princeton, NJ: Princeton University Press, 1975.

Waggoner, Hyatt H. *Presence of Hawthorne.* Baton Rouge, LA: Louisiana State University Press, 1979.

Wagner, Linda W. *American Modern: Essays in Fiction and Poetry.* Port Washington, NY: Kennikat Press, 1980.

Wagner, Linda W., ed. *Critical Essays on Joyce Carol Oates.* Boston: G. K. Hall & Co., 1979.

Wagner, Linda W. *Dos Passos: Artist as American.* Austin, TX: University of Texas Press, 1979.

Wagner, Linda Welshimer, ed. *Ernest Hemingway: Five Decades of Criticism.* East Lansing, MI: Michigan State University Press, 1974.

Wagner, Linda Welshimer. *Hemingway and Faulkner: inventors/masters.* Metuchen, NJ: Scarecrow Press, Inc., 1975.

Wagner, Linda Welshimer, ed. *William Faulkner: Four Decades of Criticism.* East Lansing, MI: Michigan State University Press, 1973.

Wagner, Linda Welshimer. *Prose of William Carlos Williams.* Middleton, CT: Wesleyan University Press, 1970.

Walcutt, Charles Child. *John O'Hara.* Minneapolis, MN: University of Minnesota Press, 1969.

Walcutt, Charles Child, ed. *Seven Novelists in the American Naturalist Tradition: An Introduction.* Minneapolis, MN: University of Minnesota Press, 1974.

Waldeland, Lynne. *John Cheever.* Boston: Twayne Publishers, 1979.

Waldhorn, Arthur, ed. *Ernest Hemingway: A Collection of Criticism.* New York: McGraw-Hill Book Company, 1973.

Waldhorn, Arthur. *Reader's Guide to Ernest Hemingway.* New York: Farrar, Straus and Giroux, 1972.

Waldmeir, Joseph J. *American Novels of the Second World War.* Hague, Netherlands: Mouton, 1969.

Waldmeir, Joseph J., ed. *Critical Essays on John Barth.* Boston: G. K. Hall & Co., 1980.

Walker, Dorothea. *Alice Brown.* New York: Twayne Publishers, Inc., 1974.

Walker, Marshall. *Robert Penn Warren: A Vision Earned.* New York: Barnes and Noble, 1979.

Wallace, Ronald. *Henry James and the Comic Form.* Ann Arbor, MI: University of Michigan Press, 1975.

Wallace, Ronald. *Last Laugh: Form and Affirmation in the Contemporary American Novel.* Columbia, MO: University of Missouri Press, 1979.

Waller, G. F. *Dreaming America: Obsession and Transcendence in the Fiction of Joyce Carol Oates.* Baton Rouge, LA: Louisian State University Press, 1979.

Walsh, William. *Manifold Voice: Studies in Commonwealth Literature*. London: Chatto & Windus, 1970

Walters, Dorothy. *Flannery O'Connor*. Boston: Twayne Publishers, 1973.

Walton, Geoffrey. *Edith Wharton: A Critical Interpretation*. Rutherford, NJ: Fairleigh Dickinson University Press, 1970.

Warren, Robert Penn, ed. *Katherine Anne Porter: A Collection of Critical Essays*. Englewood Cliffs, NJ: Prentice Hall, Inc., 1979.

Warrick, Patricia S. *Cybernetic Imagination in Science Fiction*. Cambridge, MA: MIT Press, 1980.

Watkins, Floyd C. *In Time and Place: Some Origins of American Fiction*. Athens, GA: University of Georgia Press, 1977.

Watters, Reginald Eyre. *Essays and Articles on Canadian and American Literature*. Kingston, ON: Royal Military College of Canada, 1980.

Way, Brian. *F. Scott Fitzgerald and the Art of Social Fiction*. New York: St. Martin's Press, 1980.

Way, Brian. *Herman Melville: Moby-Dick*. London: Edward Arnold, 1977.

Weinstein, Arnold L. *Vision and Response in Modern Fiction*. Ithaca, NY: Cornell University Press, 1974.

Weinstein, Norman. *Gertrude Stein and the Literature of the Modern Consciousness*. New York: Frederick Ungar Publishing Co., 1970.

Weinstein, Philip M. *Henry James and the Requirements of the Imagination*. Cambridge, MA: Harvard University Press, 1971.

Wells, Walter. *Tycoons and Locusts: A Regional Look at Hollywood Fiction of the 1930's*. Carbondale, IL: Southern Illinois University Press, 1973.

Wermuth, Paul C. *Bayard Taylor*. New York: Twayne Publishers, Inc., 1973.

Wertheim, Stanley, ed. *Merrill Studies in Maggie and George's Mother*. Columbus, OH: Charles E. Merrill Publishing Company, 1970.

Westbrook, Max. *Walter Van Tilburg Clark*. New York: Twayne Publishers, Inc., 1969.

White, George Abbot and Charles Newman, eds. *Literature in Revolution*. New York: Holt, Rinehart and Winston, 1972.

White, William, comp. *Merrill Studies in The Sun Also Rises*. Columbus, OH: Charles E. Merrill Publishing Company, 1969.

Whitley, John S. *F. Scott Fitzgerald: The Great Gatsby*. London: Edward Arnold, 1976.

Widmer, Kingsley. *Paul Goodman*. Boston: Twayne Publishers, 1980.

Willett, Ralph, comp. *Merrill Studies in Pierre*. Columbus, OH: Charles E. Merrill Publishing Company, 1971.

Williams, David. *Faulkner's Women: The Myth and the Muse*. Montreal: McGill-Queen's University Press, 1977.

Williams, Jonathan, ed. *Edward Dahlberg, A Tribute: Essays, Reminiscences, Correspondence, Tributes*. New York: David Lewis, Inc., 1970.

Williams, Sherley Anne. *Give Birth to Brightness: A Thematic Study in Neo-Black Literature*. New York: Dial Press, 1972.

Wilson, Edmund. *Devils and Canon Barham: Ten Essays on Poets, Novelists and Monsters*. New York: Farrar, Straus and Giroux, 1973.

Wilson, Robert N. *Writer as Social Seer*. Chapel Hill, NC: University of North Carolina Press, 1979.

Winchell, Mark Royden. *Joan Didion*. Boston: Twayne Publishers, 1980.

Winks, Robin W., ed. *Detective Fiction: A Collection of Critical Essays*. Englewood Cliffs, NJ: Prentice-Hall, Inc., 1980.

Winner, Viola Hopkins. *Henry James and the Visual Arts*. Charlottesville, VA: University Press of Virginia, 1970.

Wolfe, Gary K. *Known and the Unknown: The Iconography of Science Fiction*. Kent, OH: Kent State University Press, 1979.

Wolfe, Peter. *Beams Falling: The Art of Dashiell Hammett*. Bowling Green, OH: Bowling Green University Popular Press, 1980.

Wolfe, Peter. *Dreamers Who Live Their Dreams: The World of Ross Macdonald's Novels*. Bowling Green, OH: Bowling Green University Popular Press, 1976.

Wolff, Cynthia Griffin. *Feast of Words: The Triumph of Edith Wharton*. New York: Oxford University Press, 1977.

Wollheim, Donald A. *Universe Makers: Science Fiction Today*. New York: Harper & Row, Publishers, 1971.

Wood, Barry, ed. *Malcolm Lowry: The Writer and His Critics*. Ottawa: Tecumseh Press, 1980.

Woodcock, George, ed. *Canadian Novel in the Twentieth Century: Essays from Canadian Literature*. Toronto: McClelland and Stewart Limited, 1975.

Woodcock, George. *Hugh MacLennan*. Toronto: Copp Clark Publishing Company, 1969.

Woodcock, George. *Mordecai Richler*. Toronto: McClelland and Stewart Limited, 1971.

Woodcock, George. *Odysseus Ever Returning*. Toronto: McClelland and Stewart Limited, 1970.

Woodcock, George. *World of Canadian Writing: Critiques and Recollections*. Seattle: University of Washington Press, 1980.

Wortley, John, ed. *Post-War Canadian Fiction*. Winnipeg, MB: University of Manitoba Press, 1978. (Reprint of *Mosaic* 11.3, Spring 1978).

Wright, George T., ed. *Seven American Stylists, From Poe to Mailer: An Introduction*. Minneapolis, MN: University of Minnesota Press, 1973.

Wylder, Delbert E. *Hemingway's Heroes*. Albuquerque, NM: University of New Mexico Press, 1969.

Yeazell, Ruth Bernard. *Language and Knowledge in the Late Novels of Henry James*. Chicago: University of Chicago Press, 1976.

Yellin, Jean Fagan. *Intricate Knot: Black Figures in American Literature 1776–1863*. New York: New York University Press, 1972.

Yoder, Jon A. *Upton Sinclair*. New York: Frederick Ungar Publishing Co., 1975.

Young, Alan R. *Ernest Buckler*. Toronto: McClelland and Stewart Limited, 1976.

Young, Philip. *Three Bags Full: Essays in American Fiction*. New York: Harcourt Brace Jovanovich, Inc., 1972.

Ziolkowski, Theodore. *Fictional Transfigurations of Jesus*. Princeton, NJ: Princeton University Press, 1972.

Zoellner, Robert. *Salt-Sea Mastodon: A Reading of Moby-Dick*. Berkeley, CA: University of California Press, 1973.

Index

STRAIGHT, MICHAEL WHITNEY, 433
Strange Brother, 363
Strange Children, 187
Strange Fruit, 421
Strange Fugitive, 67
Strange Land, 69
Strange Manuscript Found in a Copper Cyl-
inder, 105
Stranger and Alone, 393
Stranger in a Strange Land, 221
Stranger in the Land, 441
Street, 382
STREET, JAMES H., 433
Streets of Night, 119
STRIBLING, T. S., 433–434
Strike!, 468
STRINGER, ARTHUR, 434
STUART, JESSE, 434–435
Studhorse Man, 282
Stunt Man, 51
STURGEON, THEODORE, 435–436
STYRON, WILLIAM, 436–437
Substitute, 196
Subterraneans, 277
Successor, 136
Such Good Friends, 188
Such Is My Beloved, 68
SUCH, PETER, 437
SUCKOW, RUTH, 437–438
Sula, 356–357
Summer, 485
Summer in Williamsburg, 176
Summer Soldier, 508
SUMMERTON, MARGARET, 438
Sun Also Rises, 232–235
Sun and the Moon, 376
Sun in Capricorn, 31
Sun Virgin, 113
Sundial, 252
Sundown, 333
Sunlight Dialogues, 179
Sunny Side, 383
Sunshine Sketches of a Little Town,
296–297
Surface of the Earth, 386
Surfacing, 18–19
Surrounded, 319
Survival Zero, 424
Survivors of the Crossing, 81
Susan, the Fisherman's Daughter see Get-
ting Along
Swallow Barn, 275
Swallower Swallowed see L'avalée des
avalés
Swamp Angel, 494

Sweet Man, 351
Sweet Second Summer of Kitty Malone, 83
Sweet Thursday, 430
SWIGGETT, HOWARD, 438
Swing in the Garden, 243
Swords of Anjou, 377
Sybil, 20
SYMONS, SCOTT, 438
System of Dante's Hell, 24–25

Tacey Cromwell, 398
Take All to Nebraska, 494
Take Hands at Winter, 381
Tale of Asa Bean, 334
Tale of Don L'Original see Don l'original
Tale of Valor, 164
Tallons, 332
TALSMAN, WILLIAM, 439
Tan and Sandy Silence, 310
Taps for Private Tussie, 435
TARDIVEL, J. P., 439
TARKINGTON, BOOTH, 439
Tarzan Alive, 138
Tarzan of the Apes, 61
TATE, ALLEN, 439–440
Tau Zero, 10
Tay John, 373
Tayaout, 441
TAYLOR, BAYARD, 440
TAYLOR, PETER, 440
Teeftallow, 434
Tell Me How Long the Train's Been Gone,
24
TELLIER, ANDRÉ, 440
Tempest and Sunshine, 242
Tempest-Tost, 102
Temple of Gold, 186
Temptations of Big Bear, 487
Ten North Frederick, 374
Tenants of Moonbloom, 470
Tenants, 330
Tender Is the Night, 169–172
TENNEY, TABITHA, 440
TERHUNE, MARY VIRGINIA see HAR-
LAND, MARION
Terminal Man, 98
Terms of Endearment, 319
TESCH, GERALD, 440
Tête blanche, 45
Their Eyes Were Watching God, 251–252
Their Silver Wedding Journey, 250
Their Wedding Journey, 249–250
them, 369–370
Theophilus North, 491

DATE			

American Naval History

American Naval History

AN ILLUSTRATED CHRONOLOGY OF THE U.S. NAVY AND MARINE CORPS 1775–PRESENT

By Jack Sweetman

Naval Institute Press
Annapolis, Maryland

Library of Congress Cataloging in Publication Data

Sweetman, Jack, 1940–
  American naval history.
  Bibliography: p.
  Includes indexes.
  1. United States. Navy—History—Chronology.
2. United States. Marine Corps—History—Chronology.
3. United States—History, Naval—Chronology. I. Title.
VA58.4.S94   1984   359′.00973   84-16689
ISBN 0-87021-290-7

Printed in the United States of America

To Gee

Contents

List of Maps

Preface

This book is a chronology of significant events in the history of the United States Navy and Marine Corps from their foundation to the present day. "Significant" is the key word; obviously, every event cannot be so classified. Upon learning that I had undertaken such a chronology, friends often asked what basis I was using to determine which events to include. My answer was the basis of ten years' teaching American naval history. That remains a fair summation, but the user of the book may benefit from a more substantial explanation of the ideas that guided it.

In the first place, it seemed to me that the work should do more than simply catalogue events. Contrary to the old saying, "the facts" do not necessarily speak for themselves. The significance of the fact that a ship has been commissioned, assuming there is nothing distinctive about said vessel, is to an extent self-evident; but the fact that the Battle of the Sunda Strait took place on the night of February 28, 1942, is not in itself particularly enlightening. Wherever it appeared appropriate, therefore, I have given a brief description of the event and a summary of its effect on those that followed.

I have also attempted, when dealing with events of great importance, to provide earlier entries that give the background to and highlight the stages of development of these events. A chronology is by its nature strongly oriented towards the specific event, but history does not happen in freeze-frames. I hope that these background entries will help to supply a sense of context and continuity.

Overall, the entries can be divided into two broad categories. The first consists of events of obvious, intrinsic significance. Those in this category include:
- battles, landings, and campaigns
- the capture or destruction of major enemy warships
- the loss of important American naval vessels in war and peace, particularly the former
- explorations and expeditions
- the introduction of new ship types
- technological firsts
- the commissioning of all modern capital ships
- significant administrative innovations
- the appointment of all secretaries of the navy, commandants of the marine corps, superintendents of the naval academy, chiefs of naval operations, and secretaries of defense
- and a number of events, external to the sea services—the Roosevelt Corollary to the Monroe Doctrine, for instance—that influenced their activities as instruments of national policy

In the second category are events, relatively minor in themselves, chosen as examples of operations typical of their period.

To facilitate ease of reference, key entries have been given titles set in bold-faced type.

Especially up to around 1825, there is often considerable disagreement between authorities as to the exact date and details of lesser naval engagements and the characteristics of the ships involved. The number of guns credited to units of the sailing navy should be regarded as nominal, in any case, since enterprising captains often crowded on more than their ships had been designed to carry. To cite a single example, the frigate *Constellation* was officially a 36, but when she fought the *Vengeance* she actually had 50 pieces of ordnance on board.

Every effort has been made, in sometimes perplexing circumstances, to ensure the accuracy of the data given here. Much as I would like to believe that this effort has achieved 100 percent success, that is probably too much to expect. I will, therefore, be grateful to readers who suspect that they have identified errors if they would notify me, *citing the source of their information*, c/o the Naval Institute Press, so that these can be corrected in any future editions.

Acknowledgments

One of the pleasures of completing a book is the opportunity it affords to record the thanks due to the people who helped along the way.

For their assistance in pinning down elusive dates, I am indebted to: Ms. Cathie Hall and Ms. Barbara A. Parker and their colleagues in the reference section of the Nimitz Library at the U.S. Naval Academy; Ms. Alice Creighton, Head of the library's Special Collections, and to Ms. Pamela J. Sherbert and Ms. Mary Jane Catalfamo of her department; Dr. Dean Allard of the Naval History Division and Mr. Jack Shulimson of the U.S. Marine Corps History and Museums Division, and the members of their staffs; and Dr. Robert L. Scheina, the Historian of the U.S. Coast Guard. Mr. Fred H. Rainbow, managing editor of the Naval Institute *Proceedings*, also contributed useful information. Of course, the responsibility for any errors of fact or interpretation is mine, not theirs.

The selection of illustrations was aided by the friendly cooperation and expert counsel of Ms. Patty Maddocks, Director of the Naval Institute Library and Photographic Service, ably seconded by Ms. Mary Sprawls; Mr. James W. Cheevers, Curator of the Naval Academy Museum; Ms. Sigrid Trumpy, Curator of the museum's Beverley R. Robinson Collection of naval prints; and Colonel John Miller and Mr. Benis Frank of the U.S. Marine Corps History and Museums Division.

Ms. Carol Swartz of the Naval Institute Press greatly improved the quality of the manuscript by her meticulous copy editing, and Ms. Beverly Baum met the challenge of producing a design that would be both attractive and accessible with what appears to me to be great success. Ms. Marjorie Whittington typed many long years overnight, and Mr. W. M. Shannon transformed my rough sketches into handsome maps.

I am especially grateful to Mr. Thomas F. Epley, director of the Naval Institute Press, who suggested the work and encouraged its progress with his customary editorial acumen.

And I am most grateful to Gisela, *eine wahre Wunderfrau*, whose support could not have been excelled, and to my parents, whose interest is an inspiration.

American Naval History

1775

April 19. **Beginning of the American Revolution.** The first shots of the war are fired in Massachusetts at the Battle of Lexington and Concord.

June 12. **First naval action of the revolution.** Citizens of Machias, Maine, led by Jeremiah O'Brien, board and capture the British armed schooner *Margaretta*, Midshipman James Moore, in Machias Bay.

June 15. **First "official" naval action.** Two armed vessels chartered by the government of Rhode Island, sailing under the command of Captain Abraham Whipple, capture a tender belonging to the British frigate *Rose* in Narragansett Bay.

August 26. The Rhode Island legislature instructs its delegates to the Continental Congress to propose the foundation of a continental navy. They do so on October 3.

September 2. **Birth of "Washington's Navy."** General George Washington, commanding the American forces at Boston, charters the *Hannah*, a schooner of 78 tons, to attack British transports and supply ships. In the following months other ships are similarly engaged. Before the squadron is disbanded in 1777, it has included 11 vessels and taken 55 prizes, many containing provisions much needed by Washington's army.

October 13. **Foundation of the Continental Navy.** Acting on the Rhode Island proposal, Congress authorizes the outfitting of two vessels "of ten carriage guns . . . for a cruise of three months" against British supply ships. A Naval Committee of three members—Silas Deane, Christopher Gadsden, and John Langdon—is appointed to supervise the work.

October 16. **Attack on Falmouth.** A British squadron of five vessels under Lieutenant Henry Mouatt shells Falmouth (present-day Portland), Maine. A landing party is repulsed, but much of the town is destroyed. American opinion is outraged.

October 30. Congress approves the outfitting of another two vessels and adds four members to the Naval Committee: John Adams, Joseph Hewes, Stephen Hopkins and Richard Henry Lee.

November 2. **First Continental Fleet.** The Naval Committee is voted $100,000 to obtain and equip ships of war. It purchases and renames eight merchant vessels: the *Alfred*, 24 guns; *Columbus*, 18–20; *Andrew Doria*, 14; *Cabot*, 14; *Providence*, 12; *Hornet*, 10; *Wasp*, 8; and *Fly*, 8.

November 10. **Foundation of the Continental Marines.** A resolution providing for the organization of two battalions of "American Marines" is passed by Congress. The senior officer is Captain Samuel Nicholas, now considered first commandant of the U.S. Marine Corps.

November 25. **Privateering.** Congress authorizes privateering against all vessels in British government service and urges the individual colonies to establish prize courts. In the course of the conflict, Congress will issue letters of marque to 1,697 vessels, which take 600 prizes—triple the captures made by ships of the Continental Navy.

November 28. Off Cape Anne, Massachusetts, Washington's Navy makes its most valuable capture when the schooner *Lee*, 4, Captain John Manly, takes the brig *Nancy*, whose cargo includes 2,000 stands of arms, a number of artillery pieces, and 30 tons of shot.

November 28. **First naval regulations.** Congress issues "Rules for the Regulation of the Navy of the United Colonies." They were written by John Adams.

December 3. At Philadelphia, Lieutenant John Paul Jones raises the Grand Union flag (having 13 stripes, with the British jack in the field) aboard the *Alfred*. This is the first time an American flag has been unfurled over a Continental warship.

December 11–14.   A permanent Marine Committee, consisting of one member from each of the 13 colonies, is established by Congress "to devise ways and means for furnishing these colonies with a naval armament."

December 22.   **First naval construction.** The Marine Committee submits a report, approved by Congress, calling for the construction of 13 frigates: five of 32 guns, five of 28, and three of 24. It is specified that four of these vessels will be built in Pennsylvania, two each in Massachusetts, New York, and Rhode Island, and one each in Connecticut, Maryland, and New Hampshire. Only seven will ever be completed, and all will be lost during the war.

December 22.   **First officers are commissioned.** Congress appoints the first eighteen officers of the Continental Navy. The senior is Commodore Esek Hopkins, "commander in chief of the fleet." Below him are four captains: Dudley Saltonstall (*Alfred*); Abraham Whipple (*Columbus*); Nicholas Biddle (*Andrew Doria*); and the commodore's son John Burroughs Hopkins (*Cabot*). The list of five first lieutenants is headed by a 28-year-old Scotsman, John Paul Jones.

1776

January 5.   Commodore Hopkins is ordered by Congress to take the fleet to sea to clear the Chesapeake Bay and the coasts of Virginia and the Carolinas of British raiders.

February 17.   **First operation of the Continental Navy.** In accordance with the above orders, Hopkins sails from the Delaware with a squadron consisting of the eight vessels purchased in November 1775. On the evening of February 19, the *Hornet* and the *Fly* lose contact with the squadron and go their separate ways. Hopkins takes advantage of a discretionary clause in his orders and instead of operating off the American coast, sets course for the Bahamas.

March 3.   **Capture of New Providence Is-** land. Hopkins lands a force of 300 men under Captain Samuel Nicholas, Continental Marines, which, covered by the guns of the *Providence* and the *Wasp*, storms Forts Nassau and Montagu and occupies New Providence Island in the Bahamas. Some 73 cannons and mortars and a large quantity of munitions are captured and loaded aboard ship to be carried back to the Continental Army. This is the first amphibious operation involving American marines.

March 17.   Hopkins's squadron sails from New Providence, bound for home.

March 17.   The British evacuate Boston.

March 23.   Congress authorizes privateering against all ships "belonging to any inhabitant or inhabitants of Great Britain," whether or not in government service.

April 4.   **First engagement with an enemy warship.** On the voyage from the Bahamas, one of Hopkins's ships, the *Columbus*, 20, Captain Abraham Whipple, captures the British schooner *Hawk*, 6, Lieutenant Wallace, off Block Island, Rhode Island.

April 5.   Hopkins's flagship, the *Alfred*, 24, captures the British brig *Bolton*, 8, Lieutenant Edward Sneyd.

April 6.   **Action with HMS Glasgow.** Shortly past midnight, Hopkins's fleet encounters the British sloop-of-war *Glasgow*, 20, Captain Tyringham Howe, and her tender, which crowd on sail for Newport. The pursuit is not well managed. Her tender is taken, but the *Glasgow* escapes after disabling the *Cabot*. American losses are 10 men killed and 14 wounded; British, 1 killed and 3 wounded.

April 7.   The Continental brig *Lexington*, 16, Captain John Barry, captures the British sloop *Edward*, 6, Lieutenant Boucher, after an hour's action off the Virginia Capes.

April 8.   Hopkins's squadron arrives at New London, Connecticut. It never again sails as a unit, for the profits of privateering lure seamen from the navy, and Hopkins is unable to keep his crews up to strength. All that he can do is send out single ships to attack enemy commerce.

May 10.   John Paul Jones receives his first independent command, the sloop *Providence*, 12.

May 16.   **Cruise of the Andrew Doria.** The Continental brig *Andrew Doria*, 14, Captain Nicholas Biddle, is ordered to sea. During a cruise of four months between the Delaware Capes and Maine, she takes 10 prizes, including two British transports with 400 men embarked.

June 28. **Unsuccessful attack on Charleston.** A British fleet of 10 ships commanded by Admiral Sir Peter Parker with 30 transports carrying 2,500 troops under General Sir Henry Clinton is driven off by the earthwork fortifications on Sullivan's Island, defending Charleston, South Carolina. Parker's flagship, HMS *Bristol*, is hulled 70 times. Two years will pass before the British undertake another operation in the South.

June 29. **Beginning of the campaign for New York.** Following the British evacuation of Boston, Washington began concentrating his forces at New York, where he arrived in April, correctly anticipating that the city was the most likely site for a British landing. On this day a fleet commanded by Admiral Richard Howe and the transports of an invasion force under his brother, Major General Sir William Howe, more than 100 sail altogether, anchor in New York harbor. They are soon joined by the expedition that has been repulsed at Charleston. The strategic problem Washington faces is insoluble: how to defend Long Island and Manhattan Island when the British can use their command of the sea to land troops wherever they please.

July 4. **Congress issues the Declaration of Independence.** Henceforth the colonies are fighting, not to improve their status within the British Empire, but to withdraw from it.

July 27. **Reprisal vs. Shark.** The Continental brig *Reprisal*, 18, Captain Lambert Wickes, is detailed to carry a colonial commercial and naval agent, William Bingham, to Martinique. En route, three prizes are captured and manned. At the entrance to the harbor of St. Pierre, the *Reprisal* is challenged by the British sloop-of-war *Shark*, 16, Captain Chapman. Although shorthanded, the *Reprisal* shows such fight the *Shark* soon withdraws.

August 8. John Paul Jones is promoted to the rank of captain in the Continental Navy.

August 21–October 8. **Cruise of the Providence.** On her first war cruise under the command of John Paul Jones, the Continental sloop *Providence*, 12, captures 16 prizes between the Delaware Capes and Nova Scotia, narrowly escaping the British frigate *Solebay*, 28, by Jones's superb shiphandling.

August 27. **Battle of Long Island.** At New York, General Howe lands 20,000 men who turn the flank of the American defenders.

August 28–29. Washington evacuates Long Island.

September 5. The first uniforms are prescribed for the navy and the marine corps.

September 7. **First submarine operation.** At New York a 34-year-old Yale graduate, David Bushnell, has built a one-man submarine, the *American Turtle*. Propulsion is by means of a screw on a hand-crank. On

The British attack on Charleston, South Carolina: an aquatint published in London in 1815. Courtesy Beverley R. Robinson Collection, U.S. Naval Academy Museum.

this evening Sergeant Ezra Lee of the Continental Army takes the *Turtle* out to attack HMS *Eagle*, 64, off Staten Island. His plan is to bore a hole in her hull and attach a time-bomb. Unfortunately, his drill is unable to penetrate the ship's copper sheathing.

September 12.   Washington concludes that he must evacuate New York.

September 16.   **Battle of Harlem Heights.** Washington checks Howe's pursuit, but is forced to fall back when the British advance up the East River.

October 3.   Congress authorizes a frigate and two cutters to be procured in Europe.

October 11–13.   **Battle of Valcour Island.** In 1775 American forces under General Philip Schuyler and (later) Richard Montgomery invaded Canada via the avenue through the wilderness formed by the almost uninterrupted waterway (the Hudson River, Lake George, Lake Champlain, the Richelieu River) from New York to Montreal. Defeated before the gates of Quebec on December 31, 1775, they held Montreal until the summer of 1776, when the arrival of 8,000 British reinforcements enabled the Governor General of Canada, Major General Sir Guy Carleton, to launch a counteroffensive south along the same route. At Lake Champlain, Brigadier General Benedict Arnold (not yet turned traitor) began a furious ship-building program to

dispute command of the lake. Carleton, dependent on water-borne supplies, was compelled to halt and build a fleet of his own. This consumed the remainder of the summer and most of the fall. By the time the British are ready to fight they have achieved a marked superiority, and Arnold's force, consisting of the sloop *Enterprise*, 12; the schooners *Royal Savage*, 12, *Liberty*, 8, *Revenge*, 8; eight gundalows, and five galleys, is destroyed in a running battle on October 11–13. The season is so far advanced, however, that Carleton falls back to Canada to go into winter quarters, postponing the continuation of the offensive until the following spring. The delay is decisive. When a British army under Major General John Burgoyne pushes south in 1777, it is captured at the Battle of Saratoga, prompting France to enter the war on the American side. Although tactically a defeat, strategically Valcour Island is by far the greatest victory won by American naval forces during the War of the Revolution.

October 16.   Commodore Hopkins is censured by Congress for having departed from his instructions in failing to clear the American coast of raiders during his cruise earlier in the year.

November 1–December 18.   **Cruise of the Alfred and the Providence.** The Continental sloop-of-war *Alfred*, 24, Captain

The Battle of Valcour Island: an engraving published in London in December 1776. Official U.S. Navy photograph.

John Paul Jones, and *Providence*, 12, Captain Hoysted Hacker, sail from Providence, Rhode Island, with orders from Commodore Hopkins to raid British shipping off Cape Breton, Nova Scotia. The *Providence* develops leaks and turns back on November 13. Jones continues the cruise in the *Alfred*, taking or destroying nine ships. One of his prizes, the *John*, 10, is recaptured during a brush with the British frigate *Milford*, 28, Captain John Burr, on December 8–9.

November 15. Congress establishes a new pay scale for naval officers and relative ranks for officers of the army and navy.

November 16. **First salute to the flag.** Entering port at St. Eustatius, Dutch West Indies, to purchase supplies for the Continental Army, the brig *Andrew Doria*, 14, Captain Isaiah Robinson, exchanges salutes with the shore fortifications. Subsequently, the British government protests so strongly that the Dutch dismiss the governor of the port and disavow the salute.

November 20. Congress authorizes the construction of three 74-gun ships-of-the-line, five frigates of 36 guns, and two smaller vessels. Of the ships of the line only the *America*, and of the frigates, only the *Alliance* will be completed.

November 29. **First Continental ship in European waters.** The brig *Reprisal*, 18, Captain Lambert Wickes, enters Quiberon Bay, France, carrying three diplomatic commissioners—Benjamin Franklin, Silas Deane, and Arthur Lee—sent by the Continental Congress to treat with the French government.

December (late) **Andrew Doria vs. Racehorse.** Returning from St. Eustatius, the Continental brig *Andrew Doria*, 14, Captain Isaiah Robinson, captures the British sloop *Racehorse*, 12, Lieutenant James Jones, in a hard-fought action lasting two hours off the west coast of Puerto Rico.

December 20. **Adventures of the Lexington.** The Continental brig *Lexington*, 16, Captain William Hallock, is captured by the frigate *Pearl*, 32, while returning from the West Indies with a cargo of military stores. That evening the *Lexington*'s company overpower the British prize crew and sail on to Baltimore. Among the leaders in the

recapture of the vessel is Master's Mate Richard Dale, later John Paul Jones's executive officer in the *Bonhomme Richard*.

1777

January 15 (?)–February 14. **Cruise of the Reprisal.** The Continental brig *Reprisal*, 18, Captain Lambert Wickes, takes five prizes off the Atlantic coasts of France and Spain.

January 23. Congress approves the construction of two more frigates, one of 36 guns and one of 28.

February 7. The British government authorizes privateering against the United States.

March 3. **Loss of the Cabot.** The Continental brig *Cabot*, 14, Captain Joseph Olney, runs aground and is captured by the British frigate *Milford*, 28, Captain John Burr, during an engagement off the coast of Nova Scotia. The *Cabot*'s crew escape ashore, seize a schooner and sail home.

April 19. Congress establishes a Navy Board of the Eastern Department at Boston to supervise "all naval and maritime affairs" in Massachusetts, Connecticut, New Hampshire, and Rhode Island under the direction of the Marine Committee. The activities and initiative of this board, composed of James Warren, William Vernon, and James Deshon, make a major contribution to the Continental war effort.

April 19. Two British transports are captured by the frigate *Trumbull*, 28, Captain Dudley Saltonstall, off New York.

May 1. **Cruise of the Surprise.** The lugger *Surprize*, 10, Captain Gustavus Connyngham, sails from Dunkirk, France, to attack enemy commerce in European waters. She captures the mail packet *Prince of Orange* in the English Channel (May 3) and the brig *Joseph* off the Dutch coast (May 4). The British reaction is so strong that when the *Surprize* returns to port, the French, still officially neutral and undecided whether to enter the war, seize the ship and arrest Connyngham. For a time it appears they may hand him over to the British, but in the end the American commissioners arrange his release.

May 21. The Continental frigates *Boston*, 24, Captain Hector McNeill, and *Hancock*, 32,

Captain John Manly, sail from Boston for a North Atlantic cruise.

May 28. **First squadron in European waters.** The brig *Reprisal*, 18, Captain Lambert Wickes, brig *Lexington*, 16, Captain Henry Johnson, and cutter *Dolphin*, 10, Lieutenant Samuel Nicholson, sail from Nantes, France, under the overall command of Wickes to attack shipping in British waters. They return to France late in June, having taken 18 prizes and narrowly escaped the British ship-of-the-line *Burford*, 74.

June 7. In the North Atlantic, the British frigate *Fox*, 28, Captain Patrick Fotheringham, is captured by the frigates *Boston*, 24, Captain Hector McNeill, and *Hancock*, 32, Captain John Manly, which have previously taken two British merchantmen.

June 14. **Adoption of the American flag.** Congress approves the design of a national flag to consist of 13 red-and-white stripes, representing the 13 states, with a blue field containing one star for each state.

June 14. John Paul Jones is appointed to command the ship sloop *Ranger*, 18.

July 4. The first Stars-and-Stripes flag to fly over an American warship is hoisted by John Paul Jones in the *Ranger* in Portsmouth, New Hampshire.

July 7. **Loss of the Hancock.** The Continental frigate *Hancock*, 32, Captain John Manly, is captured and the prize frigate *Fox* retaken by HMS *Rainbow*, 44, Captain Sir George Collier, *Flora*, 32, and *Victor*, 18, off Halifax, Nova Scotia. The *Boston* makes away, for which Captain McNeill is dismissed from the navy.

July 17. **Cruises of the Revenge.** The Continental cutter *Revenge*, 14, Captain Gustavus Connyngham, sails from Dunkirk, France, on a raid in British coastal waters, during which she will take at least 20 prizes. During the following months Connyngham operates out of Spanish ports. Eventually British diplomatic pressure on Spain wears out Connyngham's welcome, and he sails for America. By the time he reaches Martinique, on September 1, 1778, he has captured a total of 60 British merchantmen.

September 2–4. **Action in the North Atlantic.** The new Continental frigate *Raleigh*, 32, Captain Thomas Thompson, and ship

Alfred, 24, Captain Elisha Hinman, capture the *Nancy*, a straggler from a British convoy of 60 ships homeward bound from the West Indies. The next morning the *Raleigh* infiltrates the convoy, and the following day disables the sloop-of-war *Druid*, 14, Commander Peter Cartaret, before the approach of other British escorts forces her to break off the action. The two Continental ships shadow the convoy for several days.

September 14. **Loss of the Reprisal.** The brig *Reprisal*, 18, Captain Lambert Wickes, sails for home from France. Off the coast of Newfoundland she goes down in a gale, with the loss of all hands except the ship's cook. Wickes's death deprives the Continental Navy of one of its most aggressive officers.

September 20. **Lexington vs. Alert.** The Continental brig *Lexington*, 16, Captain Henry Johnson, is captured off Ushant, France, by the British cutter *Alert*, 10, Lieutenant John Bazely, after a sharp action during which she runs out of ammunition.

September 26. **Fall of Philadelphia.** A British army of 18,500 men under Major General Sir William Howe, embarking at New York on July 23, lands at the head of the Chesapeake Bay on August 25, defeats Washington's 10,500 men at the Battle of Brandywine on September 11, and proceeds to occupy the Continental capital. For Howe to hold Philadelphia, however, it will be necessary for him to gain control of the Delaware River, which is defended by a system of forts and obstructions and a sizable force of Continental and Pennsylvania state vessels, all under the command of Commodore J. Hazlewood of the Pennsylvania State Marine.

September 27. **Loss of the Delaware.** The new Continental frigate *Delaware*, 24, Captain Charles Alexander, the most powerful of the American vessels in the Delaware, runs aground and surrenders while engaging British shore batteries.

October 1–November 22. **Defense of the Delaware River.** To open river communications between Howe's army at Philadelphia and the sea, a British task force commanded by Admiral Richard Howe, consisting of the ships-of-the-line *Augusta*, 64, and *Somerset*, 64, the 44-gun ship *Roe-*

buck, the frigates *Liverpool*, 32, and *Pearl*, 32, the sloop-of-war *Merlin*, 18, and several smaller vessels, begins to push up the Delaware against obstinate American resistance. The *Augusta*, Captain Francis Reynolds, and *Merlin*, Commander Samuel Reeve, ground on obstructions, where they are attacked and burned on October 22. Eventually, however, the British break through, overcoming Forts Mifflin and Mercer and forcing the Americans to destroy their ships to keep them from being captured. Lost on November 21 are the Continental brig *Andrew Doria*, 14, the sloops-of-war *Hornet*, 10, *Racehorse*, 10, *Wasp*, 8, and *Fly*, 8, and the entire Pennsylvania state navy.

October 6. **Loss of the Congress and the Montgomery.** On the Hudson River, the *Congress*, 28, and the *Montgomery*, 24, 2 of the 13 frigates authorized by Congress in December 1775, are burned to prevent their capture.

October 17. **Saratoga: turning point of the Revolution.** A British army under Major General John Burgoyne, initially of 7,200 men, attempts to renew the offensive down the Hudson valley invasion highway that had been blocked by Arnold's defense of Lake Champlain in 1776. After many misadventures, Burgoyne is compelled to surrender to the Continental army of Major General Horatio Gates at Saratoga, in upper New York state. This victory gives Benjamin Franklin the leverage necessary to persuade the French government to intervene in the conflict.

November 1. John Paul Jones sails from Portsmouth, New Hampshire, for France in command of the ship sloop *Ranger*, 18. He anchors at Nantes on December 2, having taken two prizes en route, the brigs *George* and *Mary*.

December 31. In the course of the year, American ships have captured a total of 464 British vessels.

1778

January 2. Commodore Hopkins is dismissed from the Continental Navy. No other naval commander-in-chief is appointed.

January 27. **Second capture of New Providence Island.** The brig *Providence*, 12, Captain John P. Rathbun, repeats Hopkins's exploit by landing a party that captures the seat of British government in the Bahamas. An attack by the British sloop-of-war *Grayton* is beaten off; a privateer, five other vessels, and a quantity of munitions are captured, and 20 American prisoners are released.

February 6. **Treaties of commerce and alliance are signed with France.** The secret treaty of alliance is to enter effect should Great Britain go to war with France, an event that now becomes inevitable. When this occurs, the War of the Revolution expands into a worldwide conflict.

February 14. **First official salute to the American flag.** In Quiberon Bay, on the Atlantic coast of France, the Continental sloop-of-war *Ranger*, 18, Captain John Paul Jones, exchanges salutes with the *Robuste*, flagship of the French Admiral Lamotte-Picquet.

February 26. At Fort Penn, on the Delaware River, an American boat party of 27 men under Captain John Barry board and capture four transports and the schooner *Alert*, 10, whose crew of 116 is locked below deck.

March 7. **Randolph vs. Yarmouth.** While escorting a merchant convoy, the Continental frigate *Randolph*, 32, Captain Nicholas Biddle, engages the British ship-of-the-line *Yarmouth*, 64, Captain Nicholas Vincent. After a sharp action of 15 minutes, the *Randolph* blows up. Of her crew of 315, there are only 4 survivors. This is the greatest loss of life suffered by an American vessel in action prior to the sinking of the battleship *Arizona* at Pearl Harbor. Biddle is among those lost. He was the Continental Navy's only professionally trained officer, having served as a midshipman in the Royal Navy.

March 9. **Loss of the Alfred.** Returning from France, the Continental ship *Alfred*, 24, Captain Elisha Hinman, is captured by the British sloop-of-war *Ariadne*, 24, Captain Thomas Pringle, and *Ceres*, 18, Commander James R. Dacres.

March 27. **Loss of the Columbus.** The Continental ship *Columbus*, 20, Captain Abraham Whipple, is driven ashore and burned by a British squadron at Point Judith, Rhode Island.

March 31.   **Loss of the Virginia.** The Continental frigate *Virginia*, 28, Captain James Nicholson, runs aground in the Chesapeake Bay and surrenders to HMS *Emerald*, 32, and *Conqueror*.

April 10.   **John Paul Jones's first cruise in British waters.** Jones sails from Brest, France, in the ship sloop *Ranger*, 18, to attack enemy commerce.

April 13.   In anticipation of the outbreak of war with Britain, the French Toulon squadron, 12 ships-of-the-line commanded by Vice Admiral Charles Henri Comte d'Estaing, sails for North America.

April 22–23.   **Whitehaven Raid.** Around midnight, John Paul Jones leads a boat expedition of 40 men from the *Ranger* ashore at Whitehaven, on the west coast of England, to burn the ships in harbor. One of his men deserts and alarms the inhabitants, who extinguish the fire, but the news of the raid causes a sensation. It is the first time since 1667 that an enemy landing party has set foot on English soil.

John Paul Jones, as depicted on the obverse of his congressional gold medal. The engraver, Augustin Dupré, modelled the profile on the bust for which Jones posed for the sculptor Jean-Antoine Houdon. Courtesy U.S. Naval Academy Museum.

April 23.   **Raid on St. Mary's Isle.** Jones lands a party on St. Mary's Isle, off Kirkcudbright in the Irish Sea, with the aim of seizing the Earl of Selkirk, whom he believes would be valuable as a political prisoner. The earl is absent, but greatly to Jones's chagrin, his men insist on seizing the Selkirk family silver. He later buys it from them and restores it to the Selkirks at his own expense.

April 24.   **Ranger vs. Drake.** Jones captures the British sloop-of-war *Drake*, 20, Commander George Burdon, in an hour's action off Carrickfergus, Ireland. The *Drake* losses are 4 men killed (including her captain) and 19 wounded; the *Ranger*, 3 killed (including Lieutenant Samuel Wallingford, Continental Marines) and 5 wounded.

April 24.   **Loss of the Independence.** The Continental sloop *Independence*, 10, Captain John Young, runs aground while attempting to enter Ocracoke Inlet, North Carolina.

April 27.   Congress authorizes the acquisition of another 12 vessels.

May 7.   **Loss of the Effingham and Washington.** The Continental frigates *Effingham*, 28, and *Washington*, 32, are burned in the Delaware River by a British raiding party without ever having gotten to sea.

June 17.   **France officially enters the war.** In the English Channel four French naval vessels are pursued by a British fleet under Admiral Augustus Lord Keppel. The frigate *Licorne*, 32, Lieutenant de Belizal, and the lugger *Coureur*, 10, are captured.

July 6.   **First French fleet.** For France, North America is only one theater of an almostglobal war with Britain. The movements of the fleets she sends to the Western Hemisphere follow a seasonal rhythm. These forces spend much of the year in the West Indies, fighting for control of the "sugar islands," whose exports are more valuable than those of all the Thirteen Colonies combined. Only during the Caribbean hurricane season, from July through October, are they available for operations in North America. The first French fleet, sailing from Toulon under the command of Vice Admiral Charles Henri Comte d'Estaing, reaches the Delaware Capes on July 6. The hopes raised by its arrival are soon disappointed. A concerted land-sea attack on New York, where Admiral Richard Howe has only 4 ships-of-the-line to d'Estaing's 12, must be abandoned when, on July 16, it is learned that the French ships draw too much water to cross the bar into the harbor. D'Estaing then proposes to act against the British position at Newport, Rhode Island. Washington concurs, and the fleet proceeds to Narragansett Bay. Preparations are being made for the land attack when Admiral Howe, who has been reinforced, appears off Newport on August 9 with 8 ships-of-the-line. D'Estaing sails to meet him. Before an engagement can take place, however, both fleets are badly damaged in a storm. D'Estaing withdraws to Boston to refit and sails for the West Indies in November.

September 24–27. **Loss of the Raleigh.** The Continental frigate *Raleigh*, 32, Captain John Barry, is pursued by the British ships *Experiment*, 50, Captain Sir James Wallace, and *Unicorn*, 28, Commander Matthew Squire. After losing part of her masts in action with the *Unicorn*, the *Raleigh* is run aground on an island off the coast of Maine. Barry and about half his men escape.

1779

January 5.   Stephen Decatur is born at Sinepuxent on the Eastern Shore of Maryland.

January 14.   The Continental frigate *Alliance*, 36, Captain Pierre Landais, sails from Boston to carry the 20-year-old Marquis de Lafayette, who has been serving as a volunteer on Washington's staff, back to France to concert arrangements for the dispatch of a French expeditionary force.

February 7.   **The Bonhomme Richard.** The French government purchases an old East Indiaman, *Le Duc de Duras,* of 850 to 900 tons burthen and places her at the disposal of John Paul Jones. Jones renames the ship *Bonhomme Richard,* in honor of Benjamin Franklin, the French translation of whose famous *Poor Richard's Almanac* is entitled *Les Maxims du Bonhomme Richard.* It will take Jones six months to arm and outfit his new command.

March 13.   The Continental frigates *Warren*, 32, Captain John B. Hopkins, and *Queen of*

France, 28, Captain Joseph Olney, and ship sloop *Ranger,* 18, Captain Thomas Simpson, sail from Boston for a month's cruise along the eastern seaboard, during which they capture the privateer *Hibernia,* 8, and 7 of 9 vessels in a British merchant convoy, including the ship *Jason,* 20.

May 7.   **Providence vs. Diligent.** The Continental sloop *Providence,* 12, Captain Hoysted Hacker, captures the British brig *Diligent,* 12, Lieutenant Thomas Walbeoff, in the Atlantic.

June 6.   On a cruise from the Delaware the Continental frigates *Confederacy,* 32, Captain Seth Harding, and *Boston,* 24, Captain Samuel Tucker, capture the privateer *Pole,* 24, Captain J. Maddock, and two other vessels.

June 21.   **Spanish intervention.** Spain declares war on Great Britain. Unlike France, however, she does not recognize the independence of the United States.

July 15.   A Continental squadron consisting of the frigates *Providence,* 28, Captain Abraham Whipple, and *Queen of France,* 28, Captain J. P. Rathbun, and ship sloop *Ranger,* 18, Captain Thomas Simpson, encounter a homeward-bound British West Indian convoy of some 60 sail off Newfoundland. Operating under cover of a dense fog, they succeed in cutting out 11 vessels in one of the most successful attacks of the war.

July 19–August 17.   **Disaster at Penobscot.** The largest American amphibious operation of the war is undertaken to eliminate a British force that has fortified a base at Castine on the Penobscot River in Maine. The naval component, under the command of Captain Dudley Saltonstall, consists of the Continental frigate *Warren,* 32, brig *Diligent,* 12, and sloop *Providence,* 12; three vessels from the Massachusetts and New Hampshire state navies; and 13 privateers temporarily in Massachusetts state service. The landing force, commanded by Brigadier General Solomon Lovell, is made up of 3,000 Massachusetts militia embarked in 20 transports. Siege operations begin on July 25, but the British are still holding out on August 14, on which day the Continental forces have scheduled a concerted attack by land and sea. Just before it is to begin, a British squadron arrives on the scene from New York. Commanded by Commodore Sir George Collier, it consists of the ship-of-the-line *Raisonable,* 64, frigates *Blonde,* 32, and *Virginia,* 32, and sloops *Greyhound,* 20, *Camilla,* 20, *Galatea,* 20, and *Otter,* 14. Saltonstall has little choice but to order his ships to scatter. Not one escapes. Most flee up the river, where they are either captured or burned by their crews, who take to the woods. British casualties number 14; American, 474. Saltonstall is courtmartialed and dismissed from the service.

August 2–24. The French-built Continental frigate *Deane,* 32, Captain Samuel Nicholson, and *Boston,* 24, Captain Samuel Tucker, capture 8 prizes, including the sloop-of-war *Thorn,* 16, Lieutenant William Wardlaw, in a cruise from the Chesapeake Bay.

August 14. **Cruise of the Bonhomme Richard.** A squadron of seven ships sails under the command of John Paul Jones from the Ile de Groix, France, to raid British coastal waters. It consists of Jones's own ship, the frigate *Bonhomme Richard,* 40, the Continental frigate *Alliance,* 36, Captain Pierre Landais, the French frigate *Pallas,* 32, Captain Denis-Nicolas Cottineau, the French corvette *La Vengeance,* 12, Captain Philippe-Nicholas Ricot, the French cutter *Cerf,* 18, Captain Joseph Varage, and two French privateers, the *Monsieur,* 38, and *Granville,* 10. The latter three vessels soon leave the squadron.

August 31–October 9. **Second French fleet.** At the end of the Caribbean campaigning season, a French fleet commanded by Vice Admiral Charles Henri Comte d'Estaing appears to answer an appeal, received on July 31, to assist American forces in the recapture of Savannah, Georgia. Washington, who would have much preferred a combined operation against New York, does not learn of d'Estaing's arrival until mid-September. As d'Estaing had already disregarded orders to return to Toulon, however, there could be no question of prolonging his stay in American waters. At Savannah the troops landed from the French squadron and patriot forces led by Brigadier General Benjamin Lincoln are

stoutly opposed by a British garrison of 3,500 under General Augustine Prevost. Anxious to bring the operation to a conclusion, d'Estaing insists on an assault in which the storming columns are repulsed with heavy losses and he himself is wounded. On October 18 the siege is lifted and the French fleet sails for home.

September. **Action on Lake Pontchartrain.** The Spanish colonial government of Louisiana provides an armed schooner, renamed the *Morris,* with which Captain William Pickles captures the British sloop-of-war *West Florida,* 14, Lieutenant John W. Payne.

September 23. **Battle off Flamborough Head: Bonhomme Richard vs. Serapis.** Sailing south along the east coast of England, John Paul Jones's squadron (see August 14), now consisting of the frigates *Bonhomme Richard,* 40, and *Alliance,* 36, Captain Pierre Landais, and *Pallas,* 32, Captain Denis-Nicholas Cottineau, encounter a British convoy of 41 sail homeward-bound from the Baltic off Flamborough Head, Yorkshire. Escorting the convoy are two British warships, the frigate *Serapis,* 50, Captain Richard Pearson, and the sloop-of-war *Countess of Scarborough,* 20, Commander Thomas Piercy, which place themselves between the merchantmen and Jones's squadron. Jones engages the *Serapis,* a faster ship with a much heavier broadside, in the *Bonhomme Richard,* while the *Pallas* takes on the *Countess of Scarborough.* The *Alliance,* whose captain was probably mentally deranged, keeps clear of both actions at first, eventually intervenes to pour three destructive broadsides into the *Bonhomme Richard,* and then withdraws. Realizing that his only hope of victory is to close, Jones succeeds in making his ship fast to the *Serapis.* It is at this early stage of the action that he replies to Captain Pearson's demand to surrender with the defiant promise, "I have not yet begun to fight!" After a gruelling combat of around three hours, during which both ships are reduced to little more than wrecks, the *Serapis* strikes her colors. The *Countess of Scarborough* has already surrendered to the *Pallas.* The *Bonhomme Richard* has lost 150 men killed and wounded out of a crew of 322; the *Serapis,*

The *Bonhomme Richard* vs. the *Serapis*. This contemporary painting by a British naval officer, Lieutenant William Elliott, is among the most accurate representations of the engagement. Courtesy U.S. Naval Academy Museum.

170 of 325 (both figures approximate). Pearson's action has, however, allowed his convoy to escape. The battered *Bonhomme Richard* sinks on September 25 and Jones transfers his captives and crew to the *Serapis,* in which he enters the Texel on October 3. Both captains receive heroes' welcomes. Jones is made a Chevalier of the French Order of Military Merit and presented with a magnificent court-sword by Louis XVI; Pearson is knighted by George III.

October 28.   The Continental Marine Committee is replaced by a Board of Admiralty consisting of two members of Congress and three commissioners.

November 20.   In anticipation of a British attack on Charleston, South Carolina, a Continental squadron consisting of the frigates *Boston,* 24, *Providence,* 28, and *Queen of France,* 28, and the ship sloop *Ranger,* 18, is formed under the command of Captain Abraham Whipple and sent to assist in the defense of the port.

1780

February 11.   **Second Attack on Charleston.** The British have adopted a "southern strategy" designed to roll the revolution up from the south. As the Americans had expected, the blow falls on Charleston, South Carolina, where a British army of 14,000 men under Major General Sir Henry Clinton is supported by a powerful naval squadron commanded by Vice Admiral Marriot Arbuthnot. Despite an energetic defense conducted by Brigadier General Benjamin Lincoln, the investment of the city is completed on April 11. The four vessels of Whipple's squadron (see November 20, 1779) serve as floating batteries.

March 14.   **Capture of Mobile.** The prize sloop *West Florida*, Captain William Pickles, co-operates with Spanish colonial forces in the campaign leading to the capture of Mobile, then capital of British West Florida.

May 4.   Congress adopts the first official Navy seal.

May 12.   **Fall of Charleston.** The greatest American defeat of the war occurs when the city's 5,400 defenders are compelled to surrender to the British forces. Of the Continental ships present, the frigates *Boston*, 24, and *Providence*, 28, and ship sloop *Ranger*, 18, are captured and the *Queen of France* is scuttled. Their loss reduces the strength of the Continental Navy to seven vessels (two on loan from France): the frigates *Alliance, Confederacy, Deane, Pallas,* and *Trumbull,* and the sloops *Ariel* and *Saratoga.* Following the occupation of the city, a British army under General Charles Lord Cornwallis moves north in an attempt to pacify the Carolinas.

June 1.   **Trumbull vs. Watt.** On a cruise along the American coast the Continental frigate *Trumbull*, 28, Captain James Nicholson, encounters the British privateer *Watt*, 32, Captain John Coulthard. After an exceptionally fierce engagement of two-and-one-half hours, the *Trumbull* loses her main and mizzen masts and the badly battered privateer breaks off the action.

July 12.   **The French arrive.** An expeditionary force of 6,000 troops led by Lieutenant General Jean Baptiste Comte de Rochambeau lands at Newport, Rhode Island. It has crossed the Atlantic in 30 transports escorted by a squadron of seven ships-of-the-line and two frigates commanded by the Chevalier de Ternay. The French fortify Newport, where the squadron is blockaded and de Ternay dies on December 15.

December 18.   John Paul Jones sails from France for America in command of the sloop-of-war *Ariel*, 14. Near the West Indies he engages the British privateer *Triumph*, 20, Captain John Pindar, which strikes her colors, but then escapes. This is the last action Jones fights in the Continental Navy.

1781

February 7.   Congress creates the office of Secretary of Marine to take over the management of naval affairs from the Board of Admiralty, but cannot agree on a man to fill it.

March 1.   Congress adopts the Articles of Confederation, by which the country will be governed until the adoption of the Constitution in 1788.

March 14.   John Paul Jones and his men receive a congressional vote of thanks.

March 18.   **Loss of the *Saratoga*.** The Continental ship sloop *Saratoga*, 18, Captain John Young, goes down with all hands in a sudden gale three days after sailing from Cap Français, Haiti, as part of the escort force of a France-American merchant convoy. Her loss is witnessed by the prize crew of an English merchantman she had left the convoy to capture.

April 2.   Off the coast of France, the Continental frigate *Alliance*, 36, Captain John Barry, captures the British privateer sloops *Mars*, 26, Captain J. Privo, and *Minerva*, 10, Captain J. Lecoster.

April 14.   **Loss of the Confederacy.** The Continental frigate *Confederacy*, 32, Captain Seth Harding, is captured by the British two-decker *Roebuck*, 44, Captain John Orde, and frigate *Orpheus*, 32, Captain John Colpoys, off the Virginia Capes.

May 21.   **Origins of the Yorktown Campaign.** Washington and de Rochambeau meet at Wethersfield, Connecticut, to plan strategy for the coming year. De Rochambeau has been informed that a French fleet commanded by Vice Admiral François Comte de Grasse is to arrive late in the summer to free the squadron blockaded at Newport, but is under orders not to reveal this to Washington. In the discussion Washington revives the idea of a concerted land-sea offensive against the British forces at New York. De Rochambeau is not enthusiastic about attacking New York, and in writing de Grasse, suggests that the Chesapeake Bay might be a more promising theater for joint operations. The decision is left to de Grasse.

May 29.   **Alliance vs. Trepassy and Atalanta.** The Continental frigate *Alliance*, 36, Captain John Barry, is attacked by the British brigs *Atalanta*, 16, Commander Sampson Edwards, and *Trepassy*, 14, Commander James Smyth. Both enemy ships are compelled to strike after a spirited action in which Barry is seriously wounded.

June 13. The American privateers *Pilgrim* and *Rambler* capture the British sloop *Snake*, 12, Lieutenant William Jackson, in the Atlantic.

August 4. **Cornwallis reaches Yorktown.** The British army of Lord Cornwallis, some 7,000 strong, establishes itself at Yorktown, Virginia, where it can maintain sea communications with Clinton in New York. Lafayette, following at a distance with a force of 4,500, informs Washington.

August 5. **De Grasse starts north.** De Grasse sails from Cap Français, Hispaniola, sending a fast frigate ahead to America with the

information that he is bound for the Chesapeake Bay.

August 9. **Trumbull vs. Iris and General Monk.** The Continental frigate *Trumbull*, 28, Captain James Nicholson, strikes her colors after an hour's action off the Delaware Capes with the British frigate *Iris*, 32, (formerly the Continental frigate *Hancock*), and brig *General Monk*, 18.

August 14. Washington receives de Grasse's communication (see August 5).

August 21. Washington marches south, having prepared an elaborate and successful deception that convinces the British that he is preparing to attack Staten Island, New York.

August 29. Unable to find a Secretary of Ma-

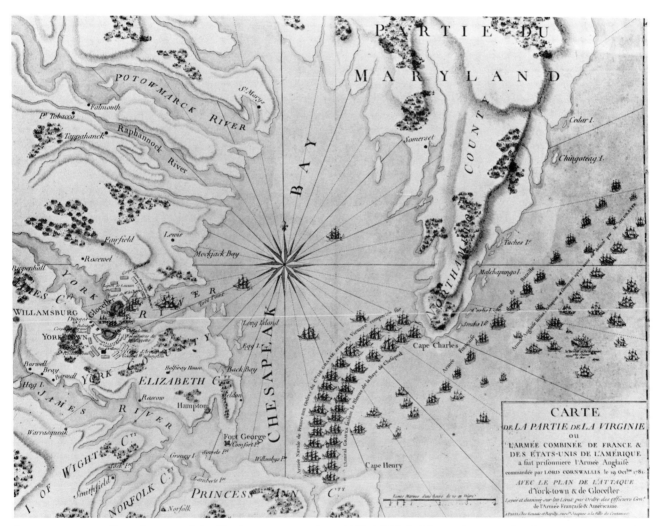

A contemporary French map of the Yorktown campaign. Official U.S. Navy photograph of an engraving in the Library of Congress.

rine, as a temporary expedient Congress establishes the office of Agent of Marine.

August 30. **De Grasse reaches Yorktown.** There he begins to land 3,000 French troops under the Marquis de Saint-Simon to strengthen Lafayette's little army.

September 5. **Battle of the Virginia Capes.** A British fleet of 19 ships-of-the-line, one 50-gun ship and six frigates commanded by Admiral Thomas Lord Graves appears at the mouth of the Chesapeake, having hurried from New York to evacuate Cornwallis's army. De Grasse, who has detached four ships-of-the-line to blockade the York and James rivers, goes out to fight with his other 24 ships, fearing that to remain in the bay would allow the British to intercept the French squadron that has been ordered down from Newport. The French fleet mounts considerably more guns than the British, 1,794 to 1,410, but many of them cannot be manned as almost 2,000 of its crewmen have been caught ashore, unloading provisions and troops. The opposing lines meet at an angle and only their van and center divisions become engaged. The fighting dies out at dusk. No ships are sunk on either side, but the British suffer much more damage than the French. Casualties are 336 for Graves and 240 for de Grasse. The two fleets maneuver in close proximity for several days, but the action is not renewed.

September 5. The armies of Washington and de Rochambeau unite at Chesterfield, Pennsylvania, the same day on which Washington learns that de Grasse's fleet has entered the Chesapeake.

September 6. Off Charleston, South Carolina, the privateer *Congress*, 24, captures the British sloop *Savage*, 16, Commander Charles Stirling.

September 7. Congress appoints Robert Morris Agent of Marine.

September 10. The French Newport squadron, eight ships, now commanded by Admiral Comte de Barras de Saint Laurent, slips past the British fleet and enters the Chesapeake Bay. Under its escort are 18 transports carrying munitions and de Rochambeau's siege artillery. The squadron's arrival raises de Grasse's strength to 36 ships-of-the-line against Grave's 19.

September 11. De Grasse reenters the Chesapeake Bay.

September 13. Finding the French forces united inside the bay, Graves sails to New York to gather reinforcements.

September 14–26. **Washington's and Rochambeau's forces reach Yorktown.** Most of the troops are transported down the bay from Head of Elk (Elkton), Baltimore, and Annapolis, Maryland, in French ships.

September 28. **The siege of Yorktown begins.** Cornwallis's 8,000 men are faced by 9,500 Americans and 7,000 French regulars.

October 19. **Cornwallis surrenders.** For practical purposes, the War of the Revolution is over. Independence has been won.

October 24. Admiral Graves returns to the Chesapeake with a stronger fleet and 7,000 troops under Major General Sir Henry Clinton, to discover that he is too late.

December 31. At year's end, the Continental Navy retains only two vessels in commission, the frigates *Alliance* and *Deane*, plus two others, the *Ariel* and *Pallas*, on loan from France.

1782

April 8. **Hyder Ally vs. General Monk.** The Pennsylvania state sloop-of-war *Hyder Ally*, 16, Captain Joshua Barney, captures the British brig *General Monk*, 18, Commander Josiah Rogers, after a fierce, 30-minute action in Delaware Bay.

September 2. The only Continental ship-of-the-line to be completed, the *America*, 74, is presented to France in compensation for the loss of the *Magnifique*, which had grounded in Boston harbor on August 9. She was to have been commanded by John Paul Jones.

November 30. A preliminary peace treaty is signed by representatives of the United States and Great Britain. It is to become effective upon the conclusion of peace between Great Britain and France, the terms of the Franco-American Treaty of Alliance having stipulated that neither nation would make a separate peace.

1783

January 30.   France and Spain sign preliminary peace treaties with Britain, clearing the way for a final settlement.

March 10.   **Last naval action of the American Revolution.** The frigate *Alliance*, 36, Captain John Barry, one of the two Continental ships still in commission, engages the British frigate *Sybil*, 28, Captain James Vashon, off the Atlantic coast of Florida. The *Sybil* is heavily damaged, but the *Alliance* is forced to break off the action upon the appearance of two other British warships.

March 24.   Congress orders all Continental naval vessels and privateers home.

April 11.   The cessation of hostilities with Great Britain is proclaimed by Congress.

September 3.   **Official end of the War of the Revolution.** In Paris, the American and British commissioners sign the definitive treaty of peace.

November 1.   Robert Morris resigns the office of Agent of Marine. No successor is appointed.

1785

June 3.   **End of the Continental Navy.** Congress authorizes the sale of the one remaining American naval vessel, the frigate *Alliance*. For the next nine years, the nation will have no navy.

1787

September 17.   The Constitutional Convention, called to organize a stronger federal government for the United States, approves the Constitution, which is then submitted to the individual states for ratification. Among the powers to be specifically vested in the new government is "to provide and maintain a Navy." The process of ratification is completed in the summer of 1788, but years will pass before a navy is actually established.

October 16.   Congress votes unanimously to award a gold medal to John Paul Jones.

1788

April 15.   **John Paul Jones in Russia.** The Empress Catherine the Great decides to offer Jones a commission as rear admiral in the Imperial Russian Navy. He accepts.

June 17.   **First Battle of the Liman.** Jones commands one of the two Russian squadrons engaged against the Turks in an action in the estuary (Liman) of the Dnieper on the Black Sea coast. His dispositions are responsible for the repulse of the Turkish fleet.

June 28–29.   **Second Battle of the Liman.** The Turkish fleet is badly defeated, losing 15 vessels, in a battle planned and dominated by Jones. Another foreign officer in Russian service, the German Prince Nassau-Siegen, manages to steal most of the credit, and Jones leaves Russia in August 1789 without having obtained another command.

1789

August 7.   The War Department is established. Its responsibilities include naval affairs, of which there are none.

1790

August 4.   **Foundation of the U.S. Coast Guard.** Congress creates the Revenue Marine, which evolves into the U.S. Coast Guard.

1791

January 6.   **The Barbary pirates.** For centuries the four Barbary powers on the coast of North Africa—from west to east, Morocco, Algiers, Tunis, and Tripoli—have operated a maritime protection racket, demanding tribute from foreign nations not to attack their ships. As long as the thirteen states were British colonies, they could rely on the protection of the Royal Navy, but after the revolution they are on their own, and they begin to be seized as early as October 1783. The United States concludes a treaty involving the payment of tribute with Morocco in 1787, but Algiers, in particular, continues to prey on American vessels. On this date the Senate Committee on Mediterranean Trade reports that only a naval force can assure the safety of American shipping in that area.

1792

April 20. **Beginning of the wars of the French Revolution and Empire.** The French Legislative Assembly declares war on Austria, initiating a titanic struggle that will keep Europe in turmoil for the next 23 years. When in 1793 Great Britain enters the conflict, President George Washington proclaims American neutrality and calls upon his countrymen to display a "friendly and impartial" attitude towards the warring powers. But it is not that easy. At sea, the efforts of each antagonist to prevent trade with the other will result in a consistent disregard of neutral rights and grave injury to the American merchant marine. Before a lasting peace is concluded in 1815, the United States will have been drawn into wars with both Britain and France.

July 18. **John Paul Jones dies in Paris at the age of 45.** Upon its discovery in 1905 his body is so well preserved that it is possible to perform an autopsy, revealing the cause of death to be a combination of jaundice, nephritis, and bronchial pneumonia.

1793

April 22. President George Washington recommends the construction of six frigates to protect American commerce from Algerine corsairs.

July 8–25. During this period, no fewer than eight American merchantmen are captured by the Algerines.

1794

January 2. A Congressional resolution calls for the establishment of a navy to protect American shipping from the Algerines. Supported by Alexander Hamilton's Federalist Party, which speaks for the northeastern mercantile and maritime community, the bill is bitterly opposed by Thomas Jefferson's Republicans, who represent the agrarian South and inland areas. The latter fear that a navy will be a ruinously expensive, aristocratic institution, subversive of democratic ideals, whose glory-hungry officers will drag the country into unwanted adventures overseas.

March 27. **Foundation of the U.S. Navy.** A compromise is achieved. Congress authorizes the construction or purchase of six frigates, three of 44 guns and three of 36, but it is stipulated that they will be canceled in the event peace is made with Algiers prior to their completion.

June 28. **Humphrey's frigates.** Joshua Humphreys, a prominent Philadelphia shipbuilder, is engaged to design the two classes of frigates authorized by the Navy Act of March 27, 1794. His plans, developed in collaboration with William Doughty, a draftman in his employ, and Josiah Fox, an English emigrant, produce the largest and most powerful frigates afloat, at no sacrifice of speed. These well-nigh revolutionary vessels will prove their worth in the Quasi-War with France and even more in the War of 1812.

On this same date, the first officers of the new navy are appointed. There are six captains: Joshua Barney, John Barry, Richard Dale, Samuel Nicholson, Silas Talbot, and Thomas Truxtun.

1795

February 23. **Foundation of the Supply Corps.** Congress establishes the Office of Purveyor of Supplies.

September 5. **Peace with Algiers.** A treaty is negotiated with the Dey of Algiers, according to which attacks on American merchantmen will cease in exchange for the payment of a $525,000 ransom for the seamen already captured, the gift of a 36-gun frigate, and an annual tribute of $21,000 in naval stores.

1796

March 2.   Congress ratifies the treaty with Algiers. According to the provision of the Navy Act of March 27, 1794, construction of the six frigates is to cease.

March 15.   President Washington urges Congress to complete the frigates.

April 20.   **Three frigates instead.** Once again, a compromise is reached. Despite the conclusion of peace with Algiers, Congress authorizes the completion of the *Constitution*, 44, the *United States*, 44, and the *Constellation*, 36. The three unfinished frigates will be put "in ordinary" (mothballed).

November 4.   **Peace with Tripoli.** A treaty of peace is concluded between the United States and the Pasha of Tripoli.

December 6.   In a message to Congress, President Washington recommends that the strength of the navy should be increased.

1797

February 27.   Secretary of State Timothy Pickering presents a report detailing French attacks upon, and injuries to, the American merchant marine.

May 10.   The frigate *United States*, 44, is launched at Philadelphia.

May 16.   The new president, John Adams, repeats Washington's recommendation to Congress to increase the strength of the navy.

July 1.   The first "Navy Regulations" are approved by Congress.

August 14.   **Peace with Tunis.** In Paris, U.S. commissioner David Humphreys approves a treaty of peace his agents have negotiated with Tunis. By the terms of this treaty, confirmed by the Senate in 1799, the United States agrees to pay the Barbary power $107,000 not to attack its shipping.

September 7.   The frigate *Constellation*, 36, is launched at Baltimore.

October 4.   **XYZ Affair.** An American delegation consisting of Charles C. Pinckney, John Marshall, and Elbridge Gerry is sent to France in an attempt to repair relations between the two countries and bring an end to French harassment of American merchant shipping. In Paris they are met by three French agents—"X, Y, and Z"—who inform them that they must pay a substantial bribe to so much as see the foreign minister. The Americans indignantly refuse. News of the incident provokes a storm of outrage in the United States and sets the stage for the Quasi-War with France.

October 21.   The frigate *Constitution*, 44, is launched at Boston, Massachusetts.

1798

January 27.   France declares that all vessels trading with Britain will be liable to seizure and sale.

March 27.   Congress directs that the three frigates launched in 1797 are to be equipped for active operations.

April 27.   Congress authorizes President Adams to procure another 12 ships mounting up to 22 guns each.

April 30.   **Foundation of the Navy Department.** An Act of Congress creates the new department and the office of secretary of the navy.

May 4.   President Adams is authorized by Congress to build or purchase 10 small vessels for the defense of the American coast.

May 18.   Benjamin Stoddert is nominated by President Adams to be the first secretary

The frigate *Constitution*: a contemporary engraving (undated) published in Boston. Courtesy Beverley R. Robinson Collection, U.S. Naval Academy Museum.

of the navy. The Senate confirms his appointment three days later.

May 24.   **First naval vessel to sail.** The ship *Ganges*, 26, Captain Richard Dale, leaves Philadelphia to become the first ship in America's new navy to actually get underway.

May 28.   **Quasi-War with France.** An undeclared naval war begins when Congress instructs U.S. warships "to capture any French vessel found near the coast preying upon American commerce." In the course of the conflict the number of American fighting ships in service, including revenue cutters, will reach a total of 54.

June 25.   American merchant vessels are authorized to resist interference by French ships.

June 28.   Congress approves the sale of lawful captures, part of the proceeds from which are to be used to pay prize money to American crews.

July 7.   The United States abrogates all existing treaties with France.

July 7.   **First capture of the Quasi-War.** The sloop-of-war *Delaware*, 20, Captain Stephen Decatur (Sr.), captures the French privateer *Le Croyable*, 14, off the Delaware. She is taken into U.S. service under the name *Retaliation*.

July 9.   Privateering against French vessels is authorized by Congress. Some 365 letters of marque and reprisal are issued in the next nine months.

July 11.   **Birthday of the U.S. Marine Corps.** President John Adams approves an act "for Establishing and Organizing a Marine Corps." The bill had been introduced by Samuel Sewall, chairman of the House Naval Committee. William Ward Burrows is appointed major commandant. The strength of the corps is set at 33 officers and 848 men.

July 16.   Congress authorizes the completion of the three unfinished frigates (*Congress*, 36, *Chesapeake*, 36, and *President*, 44).

November 16.   Escorting a convoy from Charleston to Havana, the ship sloop *Baltimore*, 20, Captain Isaac Philips, meets a British squadron, including three ships-of-the-line, which impresses five of his seamen. Upon his return the unfortunate Philips is dismissed from the service.

November 20.   **Loss of the Retaliation.** The schooner *Retaliation*, 14, Lieutenant William Bainbridge, is overtaken by two French frigates, surrendering to *L'Insurgente*, 40, Captain M.P. Barreaut.

December 31.   **Progress of the Quasi-War.** Including *Le Croyable*, to date three French privateers have been captured.

1799

February 9.   **First victory over an enemy warship: Constellation vs. L'Insurgente.** Between the Caribbean islands of Nevis and St. Kitts, the frigate *Constellation*, 48, Captain Thomas Truxtun, overtakes the French frigate *L'Insurgente*, 40, Captain M.P. Barreaut. The *Constellation* enjoys a slight superiority in the weight of her broadside, but *L'Insurgente* has the larger crew, more than 400 to the *Constellation*'s 309 men. Skillfully avoiding the enemy's attempt to close, Truxtun crosses her bow twice to deliver a deadly raking fire. When he is in position to rake a third time, *L'Insurgente* hauls down her colors. French losses are 29 men killed and 41 wounded; American, 2 killed and 3 wounded. The captured vessel is commissioned into the U.S. Navy as the *Insurgent*.

February 25.   Congress authorizes the construction of six ships-of-the-line and six sloops-of-war, but they are never built.

March 2.   Congress approves the establishment

The *Constellation* vs. *L'Insurgente*: an engraving published in Philadelphia in 1799. Courtesy Beverley R. Robinson Collection, U.S. Naval Academy Museum.

of naval pensions and an increase in the strength of the Marine Corps.

August 15.   The *Congress,* 36, fourth of the six frigates authorized by the Navy Act of 1794, is launched in Portsmouth, New Hampshire.

October 2.   The Washington Navy Yard is established.

December 2.   The frigate *Chesapeake,* 36, fifth of the original six, is launched in Norfolk, Virginia.

1800

February 1.   **Constellation vs. Vengeance.** After a full day's chase, the frigate *Constellation,* 50, Captain Thomas Truxtun, overtakes the French frigate *Vengeance,* 56, Captain A.M. Pitot, southwest of Guadeloupe. The ensuing night action lasts five hours. Although the *Vengeance* is considerably superior in weight of broadside, she receives much the worst of the action and strikes her colors twice, but resumes resistance when her surrender is unobserved. Eventually the *Constellation* loses her mainmast and the *Vengeance* sheers away, limping into Curaçao to report that she has been attacked by a ship-of-the-line. French casualties are approximately 50 killed and 110 wounded of a crew of 330; American, 14 killed and 25 wounded of a crew of 310.

February 7.   **First across the equator.** En route to the East Indies, the frigate *Essex,* 32, Captain Edward Preble, becomes the first U.S. naval vessel to cross the equator.

April 1.   The *President,* 44, last of the original six frigates, is launched at New York.

July 1.   **First convoy.** The frigate *Essex,* 32, Captain Edward Preble, sails from the Sunda Strait, escorting 14 American merchantmen home from the Dutch East Indies.

August 8.   **Loss of the Insurgent.** The U.S. (late French) frigate *Insurgent,* Captain Patrick Fletcher, sails from Norfolk, Virginia, bound for the West Indies. Somewhere en route she is lost with her entire company (340 men).

August 20.   **Loss of the Pickering.** The revenue cutter *Pickering,* 14, Lieutenant B. Hillar, sails from New Castle, Delaware, for the West Indies, and disappears at sea.

September 30.   **Preliminary peace.** In Paris, American and French representatives sign the Convention of 1800, winding down the Quasi-War. France agrees to the abrogation of the treaties of 1778, in return for which the United States government assumes the liability for the losses to American citizens caused by French actions since 1793. President Adams regarded the settlement of this conflict as his greatest achievement.

October 12.   **Boston vs. Le Berceau.** The frigate *Boston,* 28, Captain George Little, captures the French frigate *Le Berceau,* 24, Captain André Senez, after a severe engagement 600 miles northwest of Guadeloupe. *Le Berceau* loses 34 men killed and 18 wounded.

October 20.   **Seizure of the George Washington.** The frigate *George Washington,* 32, Captain William Bainbridge, is ordered to carry American tribute to the Dey of Algiers. Upon her arrival, the Dey demands that the ship be placed in his service to transport an Algerine embassy and tribute to the Sultan of Turkey. Bainbridge and American consul Richard O'Brien protest strongly, but finally conclude that if they refuse to humor him the Dey will resume attacks on American merchantmen. On this day, the chagrined Bainbridge sets sail for Constantinople, Algerines aboard. His frustration is partially allayed by the respectful welcome he receives from the Turks.

December 31.   In the course of the year the navy has captured 49 French privateers or merchantmen and the frigate *Le Berceau* and recaptured numerous prizes without losing a ship to enemy action.

1801

February 3.   **End of the Quasi-War with France.** The Senate ratifies the Convention of 1800 without serious debate. During the conflict, in which the *Retaliation* was the only American warship lost, the navy has taken 85 French ships, including two frigates.

March 3.   Congress passes the Peace Establishment Act, reducing the strength of the navy from 33 to 13 ships.

March 4. **Thomas Jefferson assumes the presidency.** The new chief executive's attitude towards the navy has not changed much since the days when he opposed its foundation. Apprehensive that ocean-going warships may involve the young republic in foreign wars, he sponsors the creation of a "gunboat navy" of small vessels of one or two guns meant to complement the army's coastal fortifications in defending the country against invasion.

May 14. **War with Tripoli.** Declaring that the amount of tribute being paid him by the United States to be insufficient, the Pasha of Tripoli, Yusuf Karamanli, declares war.

May 20. **The first American squadron is sent to the Mediterranean.** Although the news of the Tripolitan declaration of war has not yet been received, prior reports of the pasha's discontent have led President Jefferson to the decision to dispatch a naval force to protect American commerce in the Mediterranean. Commanded by Commodore Richard Dale, the squadron consists of the frigates *President,* 44 (flag), Captain James Barron, *Philadelphia,* 36, Captain Samuel Barron, and *Essex,* 32, Captain William Bainbridge, and the schooner *Enterprise,* 12, Lieutenant Andrew Sterrett.

July 5. Future admiral David Glasgow Farragut is born in Knoxville, Tennessee.

July 27. Robert Smith is appointed second secretary of the navy.

August 1. **First action of the War with Tripoli.** The *Enterprise,* 12, Lieutenant Andrew Sterrett, captures the Tripolitan polacre *Tripoli,* 14, off Malta after a three-hour fight during which the enemy feigns surrender twice. The Tripolitan losses are 20 killed and 30 wounded; the *Enterprise* suffers not a single casualty. As the American squadron's orders exclude the taking of prizes, Sterrett jettisons the *Tripoli*'s cannons and leaves her with one mast to limp back home. Congress awards Sterrett a sword of honor.

1802

March 3. **Truxtun resigns.** Commodore Thomas Truxtun, the leading American naval officer in the Quasi-War with France, is offered command of the second squadron to be sent to the Mediterranean. Angered by Secretary of the Navy Smith's refusal to authorize him to have a flag captain, he resigns his commission.

March 10. **Second Mediterranean Squadron.** Commodore Dale sails from Gibraltar for home on this date. He has been unable to accomplish a great deal during his nine months in the Mediterranean, his squadron being too weak to enforce an effective blockade of Tripoli or to attack its fortifications. His replacement is Commodore Richard V. Morris, who arrives in the Mediterranean in the frigate *Chesapeake,* 36, in May. The ships of his squadron, which reach their station between March and November, are the frigates *Constellation,* 36, *New York,* 36, *Adams,* 28, and *John Adams,* 28, and the schooner *Enterprise,* 12. The frigate *Boston,* 28, is nominally assigned to this force, but leaves for home.

July 22. The frigate *Constellation,* 36, Captain Alexander Murray, engages a Tripolitan galley and eight gunboats, sinking two.

1803

May 12. Blockading off Tripoli, the frigate *John Adams,* 28, Captain John Rodgers, captures the Tripolitan ship *Meshuda,* 20, without resistance as she attempts to slip into port under the Moroccan flag.

May 23. Lieutenant David Porter leads a party of 50 men from the frigate *New York,* 36, ashore to destroy a dozen Tripolitan feluccas drawn up on the beach 35 miles west of the city. A sharp action is fought with the feluccas' crews, who manage to extinguish the fires set in half of their vessels, and Porter retires, having suffered 15 casualties.

June 22. The frigate *John Adams,* 28, engages a Tripolitan polacre of 22 guns anchored near shore several miles west of Tripoli. After an action of 45 minutes the Tripolitans abandon their ship, which blows up before Rodgers's men reach her.

June 26. Apprehensive of trouble with Morocco, Commodore Morris lifts the blockade of Tripoli.

August 26. Only two days after entering the Mediterranean, the frigate *Philadelphia,* 36, Captain William Bainbridge, captures the Moroccan ship *Mirboha,* 22, Ibrahim Lubarez, with an American prize (the brig *Celia*) in tow near Cape de Gata, Spain.

September 13. **Preble reaches the Mediterranean.** Commodore Edward Preble, a flinty, 42-year-old native of Maine, reaches Tangiers in the frigate *Constitution,* 44, to command the third American Mediterranean Squadron. Orders directing Commodore Morris to return home had been written on June 21. In the spring of 1804 he will be censured by a court of inquiry for "inactive and dilatory conduct" while in command in the Mediterranean and, shortly thereafter, dismissed from the navy. Preble's squadron, the last of which arrives in November, consists of the frigates *Constitution* (flag) and *Philadelphia,* 36, Captain William Bainbridge; the brigs *Argus,* 16, Lieutenant Stephen Decatur, and *Syren.* 16,

Lieutenant Charles Stewart; and the schooners *Enterprise,* 12, Lieutenant Isaac Hull, *Nautilus,* 12, Lieutenant Richard Somers, and *Vixen,* 12, Lieutenant John Smith. These officers, none of whom is over 30 years old, will become known to history as "Preble's Boys."

October 12. **Peace with Morocco.** In a meeting with Commodore Preble and James Simpson, U.S. consul at Tangiers, the Sultan of Morocco, Mulai Suleiman, ratifies the treaty of peace originally concluded in 1787.

October 31. **Capture of the Philadelphia.** On patrol off Tripoli the frigate *Philadelphia,* 36, Captain William Bainbridge, sights a ship trying to slip into harbor. Having earlier dispatched the schooner *Vixen,* 12, on an independent search, Bainbridge pursues the enemy into shallow water with his frigate and runs hard aground on an uncharted reef. Every means of refloating the ship, including cutting away her foremast and jettisoning most of her cannon, is tried, without success. Soon Tripolitan gunboats appear and open fire, which the *Philadelphia* cannot return. After consulting his officers, Bainbridge surrenders to avoid useless loss of life; 307 officers and men enter captivity. A few days later a storm frees the ship and the Tripolitans bring her into the harbor.

November 25. A British warship informs Commodore Preble of the capture of the *Philadelphia.* Once the shock has passed, he begins to consider how she can be destroyed.

December 23. The schooner *Enterprise,* 12, Lieutenant Stephen Decatur, captures the Tripolitan ketch *Mastico.* The ship is taken into the U.S. Navy under the name *Intrepid.*

1804

February 16. **Decatur destroys the Philadelphia.** At nightfall, Lieutenant Stephen Decatur sails into Tripoli harbor with 80 volunteers in the *Intrepid* (ex-*Mastico*) to burn the frigate *Philadelphia.* The *Intrepid*'s Mediterranean rig leads the Tripolitans to assume that she is a local trader, a misimpression reinforced by the fact that the

Commodore Edward Preble: the obverse of his congressional gold medal, engraved by John Reich from a drawing by Rembrandt Peale. Courtesy U.S. Naval Academy Museum.

men on her deck—Decatur, Italian pilot Salvador Catalano, and a few others—are dressed in Maltese costume. The seven or eight guards in the *Philadelphia* see through the ruse at the last moment, but it is too late. Decatur leads a boarding party that quickly overcomes them and sets the frigate ablaze. Only one of his men is wounded. Britain's Lord Nelson calls the exploit "the most daring act of the age." Decatur is promoted to captain, aged twenty-five. To this day he remains the youngest man ever to hold that rank.

March 7.   Lieutenant Colonel Franklin Wharton is appointed third commandant of the marine corps.

May 13.   After months of negotiation with the kingdom of Naples, Preble is informed that six gunboats and two bomb ketches will be placed at his disposal for use against Tripoli. A lack of ships, aggravated by the loss of the *Philadelphia*, has hampered Preble ever since his arrival in the Mediterranean, and he has repeatedly requested reinforcements, in vain. By the summer of 1804, the effects of the blockade he has maintained are beginning to be felt in Tripoli, but he is anxious to take more forceful action.

July 25.   The eight Neapolitan ships join Preble's squadron.

August 3.   **First bombardment of Tripoli.** Covered by the frigate *Constitution*, which

Captain Stephen Decatur. This charming portrait was painted by the Italian miniaturist Olivio Sozzi before Decatur's return from the Mediterranean in 1805. Courtesy U.S. Naval Academy Museum.

engages the enemy shore batteries, Preble's borrowed gunboats and bomb ketches (with American captains and crews) stand in towards Tripoli. The two ketches deliver a desultory bombardment of the city while the six gunboats engage a flotilla of 18 Tripolitan gunboats. Three of the latter are captured in savage, hand-to-hand fighting by boarding parties, two led by Lieutenant Stephen Decatur, the other by Sailing Master John Trippe, and the remainder are driven into the harbor.

August 7.   **Second bombardment of Tripoli.** Preble renews the attack on Tripoli from a new location, the bay east of the city. The prizes taken on August 3 raise the number of his gunboats to nine. In the midst of the action, one of these prizes, *Gunboat No. 9*, blows up. Her commander, Lieutenant James R. Caldwell, and 9 of the 28 men aboard are killed; 6 others are wounded.

August 7.   A few hours after breaking off the bombardment of Tripoli, Preble is joined by the frigate *John Adams*, 28, Master Commandant Isaac Chauncey, from the United States. She carries dispatches informing Preble that, galvanized by the loss of the *Philadelphia*, the government is sending four more frigates to the Mediterranean, one under Captain Samuel Barron, who, as Preble's senior, will assume command of the squadron.

August 11–24.   Determined to do everything in his power to wind up the war before his relief can arrive, Preble makes six attempts to bombard Tripoli by night. Wind and currents foil the first five and the sixth, delivered on the night of August 23–24, is ineffective.

August 27.   **Fourth bombardment of Tripoli.** Preble tries again. Beginning around 3:00 A.M., the frigate *Constitution* and the gunboats shell Tripoli for four hours. Afterwards, the French consul, Bonaventure Beaussier, who is acting as Preble's diplomatic intermediary to the Tripolitans, informs him that Pasha Yusuf Karamanli has not been impressed.

September 2.   **Fifth bombardment of Tripoli.** Preble shells the city for the last time, but no serious damage is done.

September 3.   **The Intrepid.** Meanwhile, realizing that the bombardments of Tripoli have

The destruction of the *Philadelphia* in Tripoli harbor: an engraving by J. B. Guerrazzi sold in Leghorn, Italy, in 1805. Courtesy Beverley R. Robinson Collection, U.S. Naval Academy Museum.

The bombardment of Tripoli: a painting done for Commodore Preble by Michel F. Corné. From left to right, foreground, the *Enterprise, Nautilus, Argus, Syren, Vixen,* and *Constitution.* Courtesy U.S. Naval Academy Museum.

not moved the Pasha closer to peace, Preble has reverted to an idea that occurred to him in March. It is to destroy the Tripolitan flotilla by sailing a ship filled with explosives into the harbor under cover of darkness. Once the vessel comes within range of the flotilla, a fire will be set some ways from the powder, giving the crew time to escape in small boats and deterring the Tripolitans from boarding her. The vessel chosen is the ketch *Intrepid*. Volunteers for the mission are numerous. Preble selects those who have missed an opportunity to distinguish themselves in previous actions: Lieutenant Richard Somers, Midshipmen Henry Wadsworth and Joseph Israel, and 10 seamen. The first attempt to enter the harbor on September 1 is defeated when the wind fails. On September 3, the *Intrepid* gets under way at 8:00 P.M. At 9:47 P.M., there is a terrific explosion. Later it is learned that the *Intrepid* blew up at the entrance to the harbor, well short of any target, with the loss of everyone aboard. The reason for her premature detonation remains a mystery, but her officers had declared that they would never allow the five tons of powder she carried to fall into enemy hands.

September 9.   Commodore Samuel Barron, flying his pennant in the frigate *President*, 44, relieves Commodore Preble as commander of the Mediterranean Squadron. In the following months he maintains the blockade of Tripoli.

1805

February 25.   Commodore Edward Preble reaches the United States and discovers that his energetic prosecution of the War with Tripoli has made him a national hero. On March 3, he is awarded a Congressional gold medal.

March 2.   Congress authorizes the construction of 25 gunboats for coast defense.

March 8.   **March on Tripoli.** Since 1801, William Eaton, then U.S. consul at Tunis, has advocated putting pressure on Tripolitan Pasha Yusuf Karamanli by supporting the pretensions of his elder brother, Hamet, from whom Yusuf had seized the throne

in 1795. Commodore Preble had seriously considered the idea, but finally decided against it. In the meanwhile, Eaton has been to the United States and returned with the title of "Navy Agent to the Barbary States" and authority to put his project into execution. On this date he and Hamet begin a march from Alexandria, Egypt, Hamet's home in exile, with an army of 400 Arabs and seven marines commanded by First Lieutenant Presley O'Bannon.

April 27.   **Capture of Derna.** After an almost 600-mile desert march during which Hamet Karamanli often indicates his readiness to forget the whole thing, Eaton's forces arrive outside Derna, on the Tripolitan frontier, on April 26. Supported by fire from the brig *Argus*, 16, Master Commandant Isaac Hull, the schooner *Nautilus*, 12, Master Commandant J.H. Dent, and the sloop *Hornet*, 10, Lieutenant S. Evans, the little army captures the city the next day. The American flag raised by Lieutenant O'Bannon is the first to fly over an enemy fortress outside the Western Hemisphere.

May 26.   **Negotiations with Tripoli.** Colonel Tobias Lear, U.S. consul general at Algiers, arrives off Tripoli in the frigate *Essex* and opens negotiations with Pasha Yusuf Karamanli, who has tired of the war.

June 3.   **Peace with Tripoli.** The preliminary treaty is signed. The United States agrees to pay $60,000 for the release of the American prisoners and to evacuate Derna; Tripoli waives all claims to future tribute.

June 4.   Tripoli releases Captain Bainbridge and the crew of the *Philadelphia*.

June 10.   The final treaty of peace between the United States and Tripoli is signed.

June 12.   A British squadron impresses three sailors from *Gunboat No. 6*, Lieutenant James Lawrence, off Cadiz, Spain.

1806

April 23.   **Nonimportation Act.** Congress declares that unless Britain agrees to abandon maritime policies injurious to American interests—most especially, the impressment of American seamen—a ban on specified British imports will go into effect on No-

The explosion of the *Intrepid*: an unsigned contemporary engraving. Courtesy Beverley R. Robinson Collection, U.S. Naval Academy Museum.

vember 15, 1806. President Jefferson later extends the deadline in hopes that negotiations will be successful, but no agreement is reached.

May 16. **Fox's Blockade.** The British government imposes a blockade, named after Foreign Secretary Charles James Fox, on the coast of Europe from Brest to the mouth of the Elbe. By the end of 1807 the blockade will have been extended to every port under French control.

November 21. **Berlin Decree.** Napoleon counters the British blockade by a decree prohibiting all trade with the British Isles. This marks the birth of Napoleon's "Continental System" of economic warfare against England.

1807

June 22. **Chesapeake-Leopard Affair.** The frigate *Chesapeake*, 36, Captain Charles Gordon, sails from Hampton Roads, Virginia, carrying Commodore James Barron to assume command in the Mediterranean. Just outside the mouth of the Chesapeake Bay she is intercepted by the British frigate *Leopard*, 56, Captain S.P. Humphreys, who demands to search the ship for British deserters presumed aboard. When Barron refuses to allow this, the *Leopard* opens fire. The *Chesapeake* is completely unprepared for action; after 15 minutes of confusion, Lieutenant William Howard Allen saves the ship's honor by carrying a burning coal from the galley to fire a single gun in her defense. Barron then strikes his colors. Four of the *Chesapeake*'s company have been killed or mortally wounded and twenty, including the commodore, wounded. A British boarding party seizes four crewmen, one of whom is really a British deserter. He is taken to Halifax, Nova Scotia, and hanged. After four years of diplomatic protests, the United States secures the release of the two surviving sailors, the third having died in British service. Commodore Barron is court-martialed, found guilty of negligence in not clearing for action before the attack, and suspended from the navy for five years. News of the incident provokes a furious outcry throughout the United States.

July 2. President Jefferson expresses his indignation over the *Chesapeake-Leopard* affair by ordering all British naval vessels to leave American ports.

August 11. **First steamship.** Robert Fulton's *Clermont* makes her maiden voyage up the Hudson from New York to Albany.

August 25. Commodore Edward Preble dies of a stomach ailment in Portland, Maine.

November 11. **British Orders in Council.** Beginning to feel the pinch of the Berlin Decree, Britain responds by declaring that all neutral ships trading with the Continent must obtain a license in a British port; those which do not will be subject to lawful capture.

December 11. **Milan Decree.** Napoleon counters the British Orders in Council by decreeing that neutral ships that submit to them will be treated as enemy vessels. The United States, being the largest neutral carrier, is caught squarely in the middle of the rival systems of economic warfare.

December 14. The Nonimportation Act goes into force.

December 18. **More gunboats.** Congress approves the construction of another 188 gunboats for coast defense.

December 22. **Embargo Act.** Hoping to persuade Britain to mend her maritime ways by economic coercion, President Jefferson sponsors an act that prohibits American ships from trading with any foreign country. This does not work. The British economy is scarcely affected, but the American economy is nearly ruined.

1808

April 17. **Bayonne Decree.** Napoleon responds to the Embargo Act by declaring that the claim to American nationality of any vessels entering French-controlled ports will be considered fraudulent and the ships and their cargoes seized. His Rambouillet Decree of March 23, 1810, orders these vessels sold. Nearly 140 American merchantmen with cargoes valued at $10,000,000 are victimized by these rulings.

1809

March 1. **Non-intercourse Act.** Three days before President James Madison enters office the highly unpopular Embargo Act is repealed and, with his blessing, replaced by the Non-intercourse Act, which reopens American commerce with all nations except Great Britain and France and stipulates that trade with either or both of them will resume as soon as they abandon policies inimical to the American merchant marine.

May 15. Paul Hamilton enters office as third secretary of the navy.

1810

February. In the course of the month, the ketch *Vesuvius*, 11, Lieutenant Benjamin F. Reed, and a boat party under Midshipman Francis H. Gregory capture the pirate ships *Duke of Montebello*, 5, *Diomede*, 1, and *Alexandria*, 4, off the mouth of the Mississippi.

May 1. **Macon's Bill Number 2.** Following the expiration of the Non-intercourse Act, Congress passes a bill that authorizes the resumption of trade with both Great Britain and France, but states that should one revoke policies injurious to American shipping, a prohibition will be placed on trade with the other.

1811

January 9. The schooner *Revenge,* 12, Lieutenant Oliver Hazard Perry, grounds and is lost off Newport, Rhode Island. Her crew is saved.

May 1.   HMS *Guerrière* stops the American merchant ship *Spitfire* and impresses several seamen off Sandy Hook, New Jersey.

May 6.   The U.S. frigate *President,* 44, Commodore John Rodgers, is sent to patrol off Sandy Hook.

May 16.   **President and Little Belt.** Around 12:30 P.M., the *President* encounters the British sloop-of-war *Little Belt,* 20, Captain Arthur B. Bingham, approximately 45 miles northeast of Cape Henry, Virginia. After a long chase, during which Rodgers is unable to identify the other vessel as anything more than a man-of-war, the *President* overtakes the *Little Belt* at about 8:30 P.M., and firing breaks out. Later, both sides accuse the other of having fired the first shot. The *Little Belt* is heavily damaged, losing 13 killed and 19 wounded; the *President* has 1 boy wounded. At daybreak Rodgers sends a boat to the *Little Belt* to express his regrets and offer to help her with repairs. Rodgers is commended by President Madison and Secretary Hamilton.

August 7.   Off Pensacola, Florida, *Gunboat No. 162,* 5, Midshipman F.H. Gregory, attacks and cripples the pirate schooner *La Franchise,* 5.

August 10.   *Gunboat No. 162* captures the pirate schooner *Santa Maria,* 4, off Mobile, Alabama.

September 11.   *Gunboat No. 162,* still commanded by the redoubtable Midshipman Gregory, captures the pirate ship *La Divina Pastora,* 14, and the schooners *La Sophie,* 6, and *Le Vengeance,* 4, between Brassa and Barataria, Louisiana.

1812

June 1.   President James Madison asks Congress to declare war on Great Britain.

The *President* attacks the *Little Belt*: an aquatint published in London in October 1811. Courtesy Beverley R. Robinson Collection, U.S. Naval Academy Museum.

June 17.   Hoping to head off war with the United States, the British cabinet revokes the Orders in Council to which Americans so object.

June 18.   **War of 1812.** It is too late. Congress votes for war with Britain. As of this date, the U.S. fleet (excluding gunboats) consists of 17 seaworthy ships: 9 frigates and 8 smaller vessels. The Royal Navy numbers more than 1,048, including approximately 120 ships-of-the-line and 116 frigates. These odds ensure that American ships will be used, as they had in the Revolution, for coast defense and commerce raiding. (In the course of the conflict, naval vessels and privateers will capture approximately 1,800 British merchantmen.) On land, the United States appears to enjoy an immense advantage, with a regular army of 6,700 men and state militias numbering, in the aggregate, several hundred thousands to oppose the British garrison of Canada— 4,500 regular troops, and a modest Canadian militia. But many American militia units exist only on paper; most of those that take the field are undisciplined and ill-trained, and the caliber of American military leadership at the beginning of the war leaves much to be desired.

June 21–August 29.   **Cruise of Rodgers's squadron.** Commodore John Rodgers, the senior-ranking American naval officer, sails from Boston with a squadron consisting of the frigates *President,* 44 (flag), *United States,* 44, *Congress,* 36, sloop *Hornet,* 18, and brig *Argus,* 16, to raid British commerce in the North Atlantic. On June 23, the squadron encounters, but cannot overtake, the British frigate *Belvidere,* 36. Altogether, it captures only seven merchantmen, a meager showing. Hereafter, the strategy of squadron operations is abandoned, and American warships cruise singly or, infrequently, in groups of two or three.

July 3–September 7.   **First Cruise of the Essex.** Master Commandant David Porter sails from New York in the small frigate *Essex,* 32, on a cruise in which he captures seven merchantmen, a transport, and the first British warship taken in the War of 1812 (see August 13).

July 17.   **Loss of the Nautilus.** The brig *Nau-* *tilus,* 12, Lieutenant William M. Crane, is captured off New York by the ship-of-the-line *Africa,* 64, and the frigates *Aeolus,* 32, and *Shannon,* 38. She is the first U.S. naval vessel lost in the War of 1812.

July 17–20.   **Escape of the Constitution.** Off the coast of New Jersey the frigate *Constitution,* 44, Captain Issac Hull, is becalmed in the presence of seven British ships. She escapes through brilliant seamanship after an epic chase lasting 66 hours.

July–August.   **Defeats on land.** American plans for an invasion of Canada quickly come to grief. The British capture Fort Mackinac, on Lake Huron, on July 17. Fort Dearborn (modern-day Chicago) falls on August 15, and the next day, at Detroit, General William Hull surrenders his 2,500 men to a force of 1,300 Canadians and Indians under Brigadier General Sir Isaac Brock.

August 9.   A British squadron bombards Stonington, Connecticut.

August 13.   **Essex vs. Alert.** The frigate *Essex,* 32, Master Commandant David Porter, captures the sloop *Alert,* 20, Captain Thomas L.P. Laugharne, after an eight-minute action in the Atlantic. The *Alert* is the first British warship taken in the War of 1812

August 19.   **Constitution vs. Guerrière.** The war's first battle between frigates results in an American victory when the *Constitution,* 44, Captain Isaac Hull, dismasts and captures the *Guerrière,* 38, Captain James R. Dacres, in a 40-minute action 700 miles east of Boston. The *Guerrière,* which is so

The *Constitution* vs. the *Guerrière*: "Dropping Astern," the third of a series of four paintings of the action done for Captain Hull by Michel F. Corné. Courtesy U.S. Naval Academy Museum.

badly damaged that she must be sunk, loses 23 men killed and 56 wounded; the *Constitution,* 7 and 7, respectively. The news of this victory, following the dreary succession of defeats on land, sends a wave of jubilation throughout the country.

September 3.   **War on the Great Lakes.** Commodore Isaac Chauncey, commandant of the New York Navy Yard, is ordered to take command on Lake Erie and Lake Ontario. British control of the lakes had played a crucial role in General Brock's victories in July and August. Establishing his headquarters at Sacket's Harbor, New York, on the eastern shore of Lake Ontario, Chauncey begins a building race that will continue throughout the war.

October 8.   **Action on Lake Erie.** Before daybreak, the British brigs *Detroit,* 6, and *Caledonia,* 2, are captured at anchor off Fort Erie by two boat parties under the command of Lieutenant Jesse D. Elliott.

October 8.   On Lake Ontario, the brig *Oneida,* 16, and four schooners under Commodore Chauncey pursue the British sloop *Royal George,* 22, into Kingston Harbor, where she runs aground under cover of the shore batteries.

October 18.   **Wasp vs. Frolic.** Five days out of Philadelphia, the sloop *Wasp,* 18, Master Commandant Jacob Jones, encounters a British merchant convoy of six ships escorted by the sloop *Frolic,* 18, Captain T. Whinyates, which she attacks. The *Frolic* surrenders to a boarding party led by Lieutenant James Biddle after a spirited action of 43 minutes. American losses are 5 men killed and the same number wounded out of a crew of 135; British losses, approximately 30 killed and 45 wounded of a crew of 110. A few hours later the *Wasp* and her prize, both more-or-less crippled, are captured by the British 74-gun ship-of-the-line *Poictiers,* Captain John Poer Beresford.

October 25.   **United States vs. Macedonian.** The British frigate *Macedonian,* 38, Captain John S. Carden, surrenders to the frigate *United States,* 44, Captain Stephen Decatur, after an action lasting one hour and 50 minutes in the central Atlantic. British casualties are 36 killed and 48 wounded; American, 5 killed and 7 wounded. A prize crew sails the *Macedonian* to Newport, Rhode Island, where she is repaired and taken into the U.S. Navy.

October 28–March 28, 1814.   **Second cruise of the Essex.** The frigate *Essex,* 32, Captain David Porter, sails from Chester, Pennsylvania, to join the frigate *Constitution* and sloop *Hornet* on a raid on British commerce extending as far as the Indian Ocean. Failing to make contact with these vessels at the prearranged rendezvous in the South Atlantic, Porter decides to proceed into the Pacific on a voyage in which the *Essex* will become the first American warship to round Cape Horn, destroy the British whaling industry, and annex America's first overseas territory.

November 9.   On Lake Ontario, a squadron of seven American ships under Commodore Isaac Chauncey shells the forts guarding Kingston, on the Canadian shore, but withdraws when the weather becomes threatening.

November 19.   An attempted invasion of Canada along the Lake Champlain route by an army of 5,000 men under Major General Henry Dearborn is stymied when his militia units refuse to leave American soil.

November 22.   The schooner *Vixen,* 12, Lieutenant George W. Read, is captured by the British frigate *Southampton,* 32, Captain Sir James L. Yeo, in the West Indies.

November 29.   **Constitution vs. Java.** The U.S. Navy wins its third consecutive frigate action when the *Constitution,* 44, Captain William Bainbridge, meets the *Java,* 44, Captain Henry Lambert, 30 miles off the coast of Brazil. The two vessels are rela-

The *Constitution* vs. the *Java*: a preliminary study by Michel F. Corné. Official U.S. Navy photograph.

tively well matched and the engagement, which lasts almost two hours, is the hardest fought of the frigate actions to date. In the end, the Americans' superior gunnery and slightly heavier broadside are decisive. British casualties number 122 of the crew of 426; American, 34 of 475.

December 26. **British blockade.** Britain proclaims a blockade of the Chesapeake and Delaware Bays. Leaving New York and the New England states open to trade is intended to divide American opinion and strengthen antiwar sentiment in New England.

1813

January 2. **Naval build-up.** Congress authorizes the construction of two 74-gun ships-of-the-line (the navy's first) and six 44-gun frigates.

January 13. The British blockade of the Chesapeake and Delaware Bays, announced in December, is made real by the arrival on the American coast of a squadron commanded by Rear Admiral Sir George Cockburn.

January 17. The brig *Viper*, 10, Lieutenant John D. Henley, is captured by the British frigate *Narcissus*, 38, Captain John Richard Lumley, off Belize, British Honduras.

January 19. William Jones becomes the fourth secretary of the navy.

February 14. **The Essex in the Pacific.** The frigate *Essex*, 32, Captain David Porter, rounds Cape Horn into the Pacific, where she will virtually destroy the British whaling fleet, taking 12 prizes around the Galápagos Islands from April through July. She also recaptures the American whaler *Barclay* and disarms the Peruvian privateer *Nereyda*.

February 17. Master Commandant Oliver Hazard Perry is ordered to assume command of American naval forces on Lake Erie.

February 24. **Hornet vs. Peacock.** The sloop *Hornet*, 18, Master Commandant James Lawrence, defeats the British brig *Peacock*, 18, Captain William Peake, in a brief action off British Guiana. The *Hornet* has four men killed and four wounded; the *Peacock*,

Commodore Oliver Hazard Perry, by an unknown artist. Courtesy U.S. Naval Academy Museum.

which sinks immediately after the action, has five killed and thirty-three wounded.

March 4. **British on the Chesapeake.** Rear Admiral Sir George Cockburn enters the bay with the ship-of-the-line *Marlborough*, 74, several frigates, and a number of smaller vessels. Joined later by Vice Admiral Sir John B. Warren, commander of the North American Station, with additional ships of all classes, Cockburn remains on the Chesapeake until the end of June, sending expeditions up the navigable rivers of tidewater Maryland and Virginia to destroy shipping, supplies, and stores. Personal property is generally respected, but where resistance is offered (as it is at Havre-de-Grace, Fredericktown, and Georgetown) unoccupied dwellings are put to the torch.

April 9. The British privateer *Caledonia*, 8, is captured by the schooner *Nonsuch*, 14, Sailing Master James Mork, off the southern Atlantic coast.

April 27–May 8. **Capture of York.** On Lake Ontario, Commodore Isaac Chauncey's squadron, now grown to number 12 vessels, lands an expedition of 1,700 men under Major General Henry Dearborn, which briefly occupies York (now Toronto), the capital of Upper Canada. The British schooner *Duke of Gloucester*, 10, is captured, and the nearly completed 24-gun sloop *Sir Isaac Brock* is destroyed on the stocks. Contrary to orders, the troops burn the government buildings at York.

May 27.   Nine of Commodore Chauncey's ships cooperate with 4,000 troops under Colonel Winfield Scott in an amphibious operation that captures Fort George at the mouth of the Niagara River.

May 28–29.   A British amphibious assault on Sacket's Harbor, the American naval base on Lake Ontario, is repulsed by New York militia.

June 1.   **Chesapeake vs. Shannon.** The succession of American frigate victories comes to an end when Captain James Lawrence, newly appointed to command the *Chesapeake*, 36, at Boston, takes his ship out with an untrained and disaffected crew to engage the *Shannon*, 38, Captain Philip B.V. Broke, probably the best-drilled frigate in the Royal Navy. Lawrence is mortally wounded at the opening of the action and carried below, calling, "Don't give up the ship!" The *Shannon*'s raking broadsides quickly clear the *Chesapeake*'s spardeck, and Broke leads a boarding party that secures the ship after a short, sharp fight, during which he is badly wounded by a cutlass blow to the skull. From start to finish, the engagement lasts only 15 minutes. American casualties are 148 men killed and wounded, British, 83. Captain Broke is made a knight baronet.

June 3.   The sloops *Growler* and *Eagle* are captured by British gunboats in the Sorel River, at the northern end of Lake Champlain.

June 13.   Future admiral David Dixon Porter is born in Chester, Pennsylvania.

June 18–August 14.   **Cruise of the Argus.** The brig *Argus*, 16, Lieutenant William Henry Allen, carries U.S. Minister W.H. Crawford to France and then captures 20 British merchant ships in a daring raid in the English Channel.

July 14.   **Gamble of the Greenwich.** In the South Pacific the armed whaler *Greenwich*, 10, a prize of the frigate *Essex*, engages and cap-

The *Chesapeake* vs. the *Shannon*: a contemporary engraving (undated) published in London under the supervision of a British officer who had served in the *Shannon*. Courtesy Beverley R. Robinson Collection, U.S. Naval Academy Museum.

Lieutenant James Marshall Gamble, USMC, shown as a brevet lieutenant colonel in a painting by A. de Rose, *circa* 1830. Defense Department photo (Marine Corps).

tures the British privateer *Seringapatam*, 22. What makes this event unusual is that the *Greenwich*'s captain is Lieutenant James Marshall Gamble, USMC, who remains today the only marine officer ever to have commanded a ship. He was given the *Greenwich* when the *Essex* ran out of naval officers to use as prize captains.

July 30.   York, the capital of Upper Canada, is captured for a second time by an amphibious expedition consisting of 12 ships of Commodore Chauncey's squadron and 300 regulars under Colonel Winfield Scott. The landing is unopposed and the expedition withdraws the next day, having captured various military material.

August 7–11.   On Lake Ontario, Commodore Chauncey's squadron of 13 vessels (128 guns) spars with Captain Sir James L. Yeo's British squadron of 6 vessels (99 guns) without ever coming to close quarters. Two American ships, the schooners *Scourge*, 12, and *Hamilton*, 9, sink in a storm on August 8, and the gunboats *Growler*, 2, and *Julia*, 2, are captured on August 10.

August 14.   **Argus vs. Pelican.** The brig *Argus*,

16, Lieutenant William Henry Allen, is captured by the British brig *Pelican*, 18, Captain John F. Maples, off the coast of Ireland. American casualties are 10 killed, including Allen, and 14 wounded; British, 2 killed and 5 wounded.

September 5.   **Enterprise vs. Boxer.** The *Enterprise*, 16, Lieutenant William Burrows, captures the British brig *Boxer*, 14, Lieutenant Samuel Blythe, in an action fought off Portland, Maine. Burrows is the only man killed on the American side.

September 10.   **Battle of Lake Erie.** The most important naval action of the war to date is fought hundreds of miles from the sea, when a squadron of nine ships mounting 54 guns under 28-year-old Commodore Oliver Hazard Perry meets a British squadron of six ships mounting 64 guns under Commodore Robert H. Barclay, a one-armed veteran of the Battle of Trafalgar. Closing the British line in his flagship, the brig *Lawrence*, 20, behind the schooners *Ariel*, 4, and *Scorpion*, 2, Perry is left to fight alone for two hours, the remainder of his squadron inexplicably failing to come to his support. When the *Lawrence* is completely disabled, he rows back to the brig *Niagara*, 20, and returns to break the British line. Every ship in the enemy squadron is taken. This victory gives the Americans control of Lake Erie and enables General William Henry Harrison, who has assembled an army of 7,000 men on its southern shore, to launch an offensive to recover Detroit.

September 11.   Commodore Chauncey's squadron engages in another inconclusive, long-range action with the British on Lake Ontario.

September 22.   The British schooner *High Flyer*, 5, Lieutenant William Hutchinson, a tender to the ship-of-the-line *St. Domingo*, is captured in the Atlantic by the frigate *President*, 44, Commodore John Rodgers.

September 28.   Still another indecisive action is fought on Lake Ontario by Commodore Chauncey's squadron against a smaller British force under Captain Sir James L. Yeo.

September 29.   The American army of General William Henry Harrison, most of which is transported across Lake Erie in Perry's ships,

The Battle of Lake Erie: a contemporary engraving (undated) published in Philadelphia. Courtesy Beverley R. Robinson Collection, U.S. Naval Academy Museum.

recaptures Detroit and pursues the British up the Thames River.

October 4.   The British privateer *Dart*, 6, Captain Ross, is boarded and captured by the revenue cutter *Vigilant*, Captain John Cahoone, off Newport, Rhode Island.

October 5.   **Battle of the Thames.** With 3,500 men, General Harrison overtakes and effectively destroys Brigadier General Henry A. Proctor's army of 1,800 British regulars and Indian warriors. This action leaves the Americans in lasting control of the northwestern theater.

October 5.   On Lake Ontario, the small British schooners *Drummond*, *Lady Gore*, *Mary*, *Hamilton* (ex-USS *Growler*), and *Confiance* (ex-USS *Julia*) are captured by the corvette *General Pike*, 24, Lieutenant Arthur Sinclair, schooners *Sylph*, 16, *Governor Tomkins*, 6, and *Lady of the Lake*, 5.

October 25.   **Battle of Chateauguay.** Another American advance on Canada up Lake Champlain, this time by an army of 4,000 men under Brigadier General Wade Hampton, is repulsed by 1,000 Canadians and Indians.

November 19.   In the South Pacific, Captain David Porter of the frigate *Essex* annexes Nukahiva Island, in the Marquesas, to the United States. Informed months later, the U.S. government ignores his initiative.

December 18–31.   **Defeats on the Niagara frontier.** Following the surrender of Fort Niagara, at the mouth of the Niagara River on the southern shore of Lake Ontario, British and Indian forces advance into New York, capturing and burning Buffalo, Black Rock, and several villages. The American schooners *Chippewa*, 3, and *Little Belt*, 3, and sloop *Trippe*, 1, are destroyed in Buffalo Creek.

December 25.   The brig *Vixen* (II), 14, Captain Thomas Hall, is captured by the British frigate *Belvidera*, 36, Captain Richard Byron, off the middle Atlantic seaboard.

1814

February 2.   The schooner *Ferret*, 8, Lieutenant Lawrence Kearny, wrecks without loss of life at Stono Inlet, North Carolina.

February 28.   **Capture of the Essex.** The frigate *Essex*, 32, Captain David Porter, is forced to strike her colors after a gruelling action of two-and-a-half hours off Valparaiso, Chile, with the frigate *Phoebe*, 36, Captain James Hillyar, and sloop *Cherub*, 28, Captain Thomas J. Tucker. All except 6 of the 46 guns the *Essex* actually carried are short-range carronades. The two British ships keep out of range of the carronades, skillfully avoiding Porter's attempts to close, and pound the *Essex* to pieces. By the time of the surrender, the *Essex* has lost 58 men killed, 65 wounded, and 31 missing—60 percent of her crew. British losses are 5 dead and 10 wounded.

April. **British offensive.** With the defeat of Napoleon, whose first abdication is signed on April 6, the British government is able to apply more of its resources to the war in North America. Its plans include a series of raids on the eastern seaboard, principally in the Chesapeake Bay area; a major invasion of the northeastern United States down the Lake Champlain corridor; and the capture of New Orleans.

April 7. A British landing party raids Pettipaug, Connecticut, destroying 20 boats.

April 20. **Loss of the Frolic.** The ship sloop *Frolic,* 18, Master Commandant Joseph Bainbridge, is captured by the British frigate *Orpheus,* 36, Captain Hugh Pigot, in the Florida Straits.

April 23. The British blockade is extended to cover the entire coastline of the United States.

April 29. **Peacock vs. Epervier.** The British brig *Epervier,* 18, Captain Richard W. Wales, is captured by the ship sloop *Peacock,* 18, Master Commandant Lewis Warrington, after an action lasting 45 minutes off Cape Canaveral, Florida.

May 6. A British amphibious expedition commanded by Captain Sir James L. Yeo captures Fort Oswego, on the southern shore of Lake Ontario, and the schooner *Growler,* 2. This is the third time that vessel has changed hands.

May–December. **British return to the Chesapeake.** Establishing an advanced base at Tangier Island, at the mouth of the bay, powerful British amphibious forces under Rear Admiral Sir George Cockburn appear in the Chesapeake for the second consecutive summer. Once again, they will sweep the Tidewater, but this time they will also attack Washington and Baltimore.

June 8–10. In St. Leonard's Creek off the Patuxent River, Maryland, the 13 gunboats

of Commodore Joshua Barney's Chesapeake Bay Flotilla repulse repeated attacks by British boat parties.

June 19. On Lake Ontario, three boats commanded by Lieutenant Francis H. Gregory capture and scuttle the British gunboat *Blacksnake,* 1, Lieutenant H. Landon.

June 22. The brig *Rattlesnake,* 14, Lieutenant James Renshaw, is captured by the British frigate *Leander,* 50, Captain Sir George R. Collier, off Cape Sable, Nova Scotia.

June 26. The British frigates *Loire,* Captain T. Brown, and *Narcissus,* Captain John R. Lumley, retire down the Patuxent River, Maryland, after being shelled by Commodore Joshua Barney's Chesapeake Bay Flotilla.

June 28. **Wasp vs. Reindeer.** The new sloop *Wasp,* 18, Master Commandant Johnston Blakeley, captures the British brig *Reindeer,* 18, Captain William Manners, after a 29 minute action in the North Atlantic. Captain Manners is killed leading a gallant attempt to board the *Wasp.* American losses are 11 dead and 15 wounded from a crew of 173; the British, 33 dead and 34 wounded from a crew of 118.

July 1. At Presqu'ile, Lake Ontario, a boat party commanded by Lieutenant Francis H. Gregory burns a 10-gun British schooner on the stocks ready for launching.

July 14. Off the coast of New England, *Gunboat No. 88,* Sailing Master G. Clement, captures the British schooner *Chebacque,* Lieutenant C.L. Baker.

July 20. **Operations on Lake Huron.** Captain Arthur Sinclair enters Lake Huron in command of an amphibious expedition composed of the brigs *Niagara,* 20, *Lawrence,* 20, and *Caledonia,* 3, and the schooners *Scorpion,* 2, and *Tigress,* 1, with 750 troops embarked. His mission is to disrupt the British fur trade and recapture Fort Mackinac. Operations begin on this date with the destruction of the trading post and fort at St. Joseph's. The post at Sault-St.-Marie suffers the same fate, but an attack on Fort Mackinac on August 4 is repulsed. Sinclair then destroys the blockhouse at the mouth of the Nautawassaga River, through which Mackinac is supplied, and leaves the *Scorpion* and *Tigress* to blockade the river mouth.

July 25.   An American invasion of Canada across the Niagara River is checked at the Battle of Lundy's Lane, near Niagara Falls.

July 31.   On Lake Ontario, the British brig *Magnet,* 14, is chased ashore and burned by the schooner *Sylph,* 16, Master Commandant Jesse D. Elliott.

August 12.   British parties led by Captain Alexander Dobbs of the brig *Charwell* carry six boats 28 miles overland from Lake Ontario to Lake Erie to surprise and capture the American schooners *Somers,* 2, and *Ohio,* 1, Lieutenant Conkling.

August 14–17.   The British forces already operating in the Chesapeake Bay are joined by a squadron under Vice Admiral Sir Alexander Cochrane with transports carrying 5,400 veteran troops under Major General Robert Ross for the attack on Washington.

August 19.   **March on Washington.** General Ross's army lands unopposed at Benedict, on the Patuxent River, Maryland, to begin its advance on the U.S. capital.

August 22.   Commodore Joshua Barney burns the boats of his Chesapeake flotilla on the upper Patuxent and takes his crews—approximately 400 seamen and marines—to join the land forces assembling to defend Washington.

August 24.   **Battle of Bladensburg.** An American force of 6,500 men, mostly militia, is routed by the advance guard of General Ross's army in a brief action east of the capital. Only Commodore Barney's naval brigade and a handful of U.S. regulars stand by their guns. Barney and marine Captain Samuel Miller are wounded and captured covering the retreat.

August 24–25.   **Burning of Washington.** The British army occupies Washington, setting fire to the White House and other public buildings in retaliation for the burning of York (see April 22, 1813). At the Navy Yard, the old frigates *Boston, General Green,* and *New York* and two ships under construction, the frigate *Columbia* and sloop *Argus* (II), are destroyed to prevent their capture.

August 28.   A second British force, advancing up the Potomac, occupies Alexandria, Virginia.

August 30.   General Ross's British army reembarks at Benedict on the Patuxent and proceeds up the Chesapeake Bay to Baltimore.

September 1.   Castine and Belfast, Maine, are captured by a British amphibious expedition under Captain Hyde Parker.

September 1.   **Wasp vs. Avon.** The sloop *Wasp,* 18, Master Commandant Johnston Blakeley, sinks the British brig *Avon,* 18, Captain the Honourable James Arbuthnot, in a night action in the eastern Atlantic.

September 1, 4.   On Lake Huron, the schooners *Tigress,* 1, Sailing Master Champlin, and *Scorpion,* 2, Midshipman Henry B. Turner, are captured in boarding actions led by Lieutenant A.H. Bulger, Royal Newfoundland Regiment, and Lieutenant Worseley, RN.

September 3.   The frigate *Adams,* 28, Captain Charles Morris, is burned to prevent her capture at Hampden, Maine.

September 11.   **Battle of Lake Champlain.** The major British military effort of the war begins in August, when an army of 11,000 men under Major General Sir George Prevost, Governor General of Canada, moves down the Richelieu River towards Lake Champlain and the Hudson River Valley—the same route taken by Carlton in 1777 and Burgoyne in 1778. To oppose him on land, the Americans muster only

Commodore Thomas Macdonough, by Gilbert Stuart. Courtesy National Gallery of Art, Mellon Collection.

1,500 regulars and perhaps 3,000 militia, with which Brigadier General Alexander Macomb fortifies a position below Plattsburg, on the western shore of Lake Champlain; but Prevost believes, as had Carleton, that to continue his advance he must hold command of the lake, which is contested by Commodore Thomas Macdonough's American Squadron, composed of the corvette *Saratoga,* 24 (flag), brig *Eagle,* 20, schooner *Ticonderoga,* 17, sloop *Preble,* 7, and 10 gunboats. On this date Macdonough's ships, anchored bow to stern in Plattsburg Bay, await the attack of a British squadron consisting of the frigate *Confiance,* 37 (flag), brig *Linnet,* 18, sloop *Chub,* 11, and *Finch,* 11, and 13 gunboats under Commodore George Downie. In an action of two hours and 20 minutes, all four of the principal British vessels are forced to surrender, 3 gunboats are sunk, and the others are put to flight. General Prevost begins a precipitate retreat to Canada that evening. This event, more than any other, convinces the British government to seek peace.

September 11–October 1. **Action against Lafitte.** The pirate stronghold of Jean Lafitte on Barataria Island, near the mouth of the Mississippi, is attacked by an expedition under Commodore Daniel T. Patterson, consisting of the schooners *Carolina,* 14, and *Seahorse,* 1, and six gunboats, supported by 70 men of the 44th Infantry. The settlement is burned, and 11 vessels, mounting up to 20 guns, are captured.

September 12–14. **Attack on Baltimore.** The British army of Major General Robert Ross, fresh from the scorching of Washington, lands at North Point, on the Patapsco River, while Vice Admiral Sir Alexander Cochrane's ships continue upstream and begin to bombard Fort McHenry, commanding Baltimore harbor. Ross is mortally wounded in an action with militia who do not run away, and Fort McHenry, the defense of which eyewitness Francis Scott Key immortalizes in "The Star-Spangled Banner," is not silenced. The British reembark.

September 24. *Gunboat No. 23,* 5, Lieutenant Isaac McKeever, captures a pirate craft off Southwest Pass, Mississippi.

September 26–27. **Defense of the General Armstrong.** The American privateer *General Armstrong,* 8, Captain Samuel C. Reid, is attacked after nightfall in the neutral port of Fayal, in the Azores, by boat parties from the ship-of-the-line *Plantagenet,* 74, frigate *Rota,* 38, and brig *Carnation,* 18. The boats are beaten off with heavy losses, those of the *Rota* alone having 34 men killed and 85 wounded, against American casualties of 2 dead and 7 wounded. At dawn the *Carnation* stands in to engage, whereupon Reid sets fire to his ship and leads his men ashore.

October 9. The sloop *Wasp,* 18, Master Commandant, Johnston Blakeley, vanishes at sea, being last sighted on this date.

October 29. **The Demologos (Fulton I).** The world's first steam-powered warship is launched in New York. Designed by Robert Fulton for harbor defense, it is propelled by a central paddle wheel and carries 32 cannon.

December 8. **Beginning of the campaign for New Orleans.** The leading elements of a major British amphibious expedition that includes 7,500 battle-hardened Peninsula veterans under Major General Sir Edward M. Pakenham anchor at Chandeleur Island off the mouth of the Mississippi. Vice Admiral Sir Alexander Cochrane decides that in view of the difficulty of contending with the Mississippi currents, the advance on New Orleans will be made by way of Lake Borgne.

December 13. The British passage through Lake Borgne is barred by a tiny American squadron of five gunboats and two tenders under Lieutenant Thomas ap Catesby Jones. On this date one of the tenders, the schooner *Seahorse,* 1, Sailing Master William Johnson, is burned to prevent her capture, after first repelling an attack by seven British launches.

December 14. Jones's other tender, the sloop *Alligator,* 1, Sailing Master Richard S. Shepperd, is captured while attempting to join his gunboats.

December 14. **Battle of Lake Borgne.** Lieutenant Thomas ap Catesby Jones's five gunboats, anchored in line of battle, are overwhelmed by 42 British barges commanded by Captain Nicholas Lockyer, RN,

The Battle of Lake Borgne: a painting by T. L. Hornbrook. Courtesy U.S. Naval Academy Museum.

after an action lasting an hour and 40 minutes. American casualties are 6 men killed and 35 wounded, including Lieutenant Jones; British, 17 killed and 77 wounded, including Captain Lockyer.

December 23. The schooner *Carolina,* 14, Master Commandant John D. Henley, drops down the Mississippi from New Orleans and shells the British forces encamped at Villeré's plantation.

December 24. **Treaty of Ghent.** At Ghent, Belgium, where peace negotiations began in August, American and British commissioners agree on a simple return to the prewar *status quo.* Britain refuses to relinquish the right of impressment, but having vanquished Napoleon, no longer needs to practice it. The treaty does not reach the United States until February 15, 1815, and hostilities continue for some months.

December 27. On the Mississippi River below New Orleans, the schooner *Carolina,* 14, Master Commandant John D. Henley, is destroyed by red-hot shot from British land batteries.

December 29–31. **Naval battery at New Orleans.** Commodore Daniel T. Patterson lands guns from his remaining vessel, the sloop *Louisiana,* 16, to establish a naval battery on the west bank of the Mississippi, where its fire can cover the front of the fortifications General Andrew Jackson has built on the opposite bank.

1815

January 6. On Lake Borgne, Louisiana, the British brig *Cyprus,* 4, carrying clothing for Pakenham's army, is boarded and captured by a boat party of 38 men under Sailing Master William Johnson.

January 8. **Battle of New Orleans.** General Pakenham launches his troops against the American lines on both sides of the Mississippi. The naval battery on the west bank is overrun, but not before its flanking fire has contributed to the bloody repulse of the main attack on Jackson's position on the east bank. By midafternoon, when the fighting ends, the British have lost 2,036 men killed, wounded, and missing, including General Pakenham, who is picked off while leading an assault; the American losses are only 71. The attack is not renewed.

January 13–15. **Capture of the President.** Attempting to run the blockade out of New York, the frigate *President*, 44, Captain Stephen Decatur, encounters the British frigates *Majestic*, 54, *Endymion*, 24, *Pomone*, and *Tenedos*. After a long chase, Decatur turns and disables the *Endymion*, but this allows the *Pomone* and *Tenedos* to overtake him. With almost 20 percent of his crew already dead or wounded, Decatur deems the situation hopeless and strikes his flag.

January 16. Benjamin Crowninshield becomes the fifth secretary of the navy.

January 19–21. Six boats carrying 50 men under the command of Purser Thomas Shields capture two British schooners, a launch and six boats on Lake Borgne, Louisiana.

January 29. Off North Edisto, South Carolina, Lieutenant Lawrence Kearny leads 25 men in three barges to board and capture the tender and launch of the British frigate *Hebrus*.

February 7. **Board of Navy Commissioners.** A permanent board of three senior captains is established to supervise all matters relating to naval construction, equipment, and repair. Its first members are Commodores John Rodgers, David Porter, and Isaac Hull (soon replaced by Stephen Decatur).

February 17. **Official end of the War of 1812.** Congress ratifies the Treaty of Ghent.

February 20. **Constitution vs. Levant and Cyane.** Some 180 miles east of Madeira, the frigate *Constitution*, 44, Captain Charles Stewart, encounters the British frigate *Cyane*, 34, Captain Thomas G. Falcon, and sloop *Levant*, 18, Captain the Honourable George Douglas. Although the two British ships together are superior to his own, by skillful seamanship Stewart engages and captures each in turn.

March 2. **War with Algiers.** The Dey of Algiers, dissatisfied with the tribute being paid him, has expelled the U.S. consul and renewed the attack on American merchant shipping, capturing the brig *Edwin* of Salem and enslaving her crew. Eight days after the conclusion of peace with Great Britain, President Madison urges Congress to declare war on Algiers. It does so on this date.

March 23. **Hornet vs. Penguin.** The sloop *Hornet*, 18, Master Commandant James Biddle, takes the British sloop *Penguin*, 19, Commander James Dickenson, off the island of Tristan de Cunha in the South Atlantic.

May 20. **Decatur sails for the Mediterranean.** An American squadron of three frigates— the *Guerrière*, 44, *Constellation*, 36, and *Macedonian*, 38—and seven smaller vessels leaves New York under the command of Commodore Stephen Decatur to prosecute the war with Algiers.

June 17. The Algerine flagship *Mashouda*, 46, Rais Hamida, is captured by the *Guerrière*, 44, *Constellation*, 36, *Ontario*, 18, and *Epervier*, 18. Thirty of her crewmen are killed and 406 made prisoner.

June 19. A second Algerine vessel, the brig *Estedio*, 22, is run aground by four of Decatur's smaller ships off Cape de Gata.

June 30. **Peace with Algiers.** The Dey of Algiers accepts a treaty of peace, dictated in Decatur's words, "at the mouths of our cannons." According to its terms, Algiers releases the American prisoners, pays a $10,000 indemnity for the attack on the *Edwin*, and relinquishes her claim to tribute from the United States.

June 30. **Peacock vs. Nautilus.** The final naval action of the War of 1812 is fought in the Sunda Strait by the sloop *Peacock*, 18, Master Commandant Lewis Warrington, and the East India Company brig *Nautilus*, 14, Lieutenant Charles Boyce. Boyce first hailed the *Peacock*, reporting that the war was over, but Warrington would not take his word for it. The *Nautilus* surrenders after a brief action in which she has six men killed and eight wounded.

July 3. A second American squadron of nine ships under Commodore William Bainbridge sails for the Mediterranean to reinforce Decatur.

July 14. **Loss of the Epervier.** The sloop-of-war *Epervier*, 18, Lieutenant John T. Shubrick, sails from Gibraltar for the United States and disappears en route.

July 26. **Settling with Tunis.** Proceeding from Algiers to Tunis, Decatur learns that during the War of 1812 the Bey violated the terms of his treaty with the United States by allowing the British to repossess prizes an American privateer had sent into port. As compensation for this misbehavior, De-

The *Constitution* captures the *Levant* and *Cyane*: a contemporary lithograph from *U.S. Military Magazine*. Courtesy Beverley R. Robinson Collection, U.S. Naval Academy Museum.

catur demands $46,000. It is duly, albeit reluctantly, paid.

August 5.   Continuing to Tripoli, whose Pasha also had turned American prizes over to the British, Decatur demands and collects a $25,000 indemnity.

1816

April 29.   **Naval build-up.** Taking the lessons of the War of 1812 to heart, Congress appropriates $8,000,000 to be spent over an eight-year period to complete or begin construction of nine 74-gun ships-of-the-line and twelve frigates of 44 guns.

December 23.   **End of the Barbary Wars.** A final treaty of peace is signed by the United States and Algiers.

1818

August 19.   The Oregon Territory is claimed for the United States by Captain James Biddle of the sloop *Ontario*, who lands at Cape Disappointment on the Columbia River. According to the terms of the Anglo-American Convention of 1818, the territory will be jointly occupied by the United States and Great Britain.

1819

January 1.   Smith Thompson enters office as sixth secretary of the navy.

February 26.   **War against pirates.** The Caribbean swarms with pirates, many outfitted with meaningless letters of marque issued by the governments of Spain and her rebellious South American colonies. Hundreds of merchantmen are plundered annually. On this date, Congress passes an act, signed by President James Monroe on March 3, "to protect the commerce of the United States, and to punish the crime of piracy." Navy vessels are authorized to convoy American merchant ships and to recapture those unlawfully seized at sea.

March 3.   **Slave patrol.** Congress passes an act authorizing the president to use the navy to suppress American participation in the West African slave trade. To carry out the prerequisite patrols and also to support the colonization of Liberia by American blacks, an African Squadron is established in 1820. Deactivated three years later, after which only individual ships are intermittently on station, it is reestablished following the conclusion of the Webster-Ashburton Treaty with Britain in 1842.

March 3.   Major Anthony Gale becomes fourth commandant of the marine corps.

August 13.   Commodore Oliver Hazard Perry dies of yellow fever aboard the schooner *Nonsuch* at Trinidad after a diplomatic mission to Venezuela. He was thirty-four.

1820

March 22.   **Decatur-Barron duel.** Commodore Stephen Decatur is mortally wounded in a duel with Commodore James Barron at Bladensburg, Maryland, a short distance outside the District of Columbia. Once close friends, they had become estranged when Decatur, despite his request to be excused, was ordered to sit on the court-martial that found Barron guilty of negligence in the *Chesapeake-Leopard* affair. During his suspension from duty Barron entered the merchant marine. Caught in Europe at the outbreak of the War of 1812, he did not return home to reenter the service until the conclusion of peace. Although Barron claimed that it had been impossible for him to arrange passage during the conflict, many officers ascribed his absence to cowardice. Hearing that Decatur was among this number, Barron challenged him, hoping in this manner to demonstrate his courage. There is something very close to a reconciliation between the two men on the duelling field, and had their seconds (Commodore William Bainbridge for Decatur and Captain Jesse D. Elliot for Barron) shown proper initiative, the quarrel could probably have been resolved without bloodshed. As it is, neither of them shoots to kill. Barron is hit in the thigh. Decatur is struck in the hip by a ball that ricochets up into his groin. He dies, aged forty, after 12 hours of extreme agony. Barron recovers and lives on eventually to become the most senior officer in the navy, but he is never given command at sea.

April 5–12.   Five slave ships are captured by the frigate *Cyane*, 34, Captain Edward Tren-

chard, between Cape Mount and the mouth of the River Gallinas (now the Moa) off present-day Liberia.

May 16.   The frigate *Congress*, 36, Captain J.D. Henley, sails from Hampton Roads, Virginia, to become the first U.S. naval vessel to visit China. She arrives there in December.

October 17.   Brevet Major Archibald Henderson is appointed fifth commandant of the marine corps, which post he will hold for almost 40 years.

1821

January 21.   The schooner *Lynx*, 6, Lieutenant J.R. Madison, sails from St. Mary's, Georgia, for the West Indies and disappears en route. She probably wrecked on Carysfort Reef, Florida.

May 17–25.   Four French slavers are captured off the mouth of the River Gallinas (now the Moa) on the west coast of Africa by the schooner *Alligator*, 12, Lieutenant Robert F. Stockton.

October 16.   The brig *Enterprise*, 16, Lieutenant Lawrence Kearny, discovers four pirate schooners and a sloop in the act of plundering three American merchantmen off Cape San Antonio, Cuba. The pirates set fire to two of their vessels and attempt to escape in the others, but all are captured.

October 29.   The pirate schooner *Moscow* is captured off the coast of Santo Domingo by the sloop *Hornet*, 18, Captain Robert Henley.

November 5.   **Alligator vs. Marianno Flora.** The schooner *Alligator*, 12, Lieutenant Robert F. Stockton, is fired on by the Portuguese warship *Marianno Flora*, 12, in the central Atlantic. The latter is then captured after an action of one hour and twenty minutes.

November 8.   The schooner *Porpoise*, 12, Lieutenant James Ramage, destroys a private vessel off Cape San Antonio, Cuba.

December 21.   A pirate schooner is burned by the brig *Enterprise*, 16, Lieutenant Lawrence Kearny, near Cape San Antonio, Cuba. The *Enterprise* also lands a party that destroys the pirate base ashore.

1822

January 7.   In the West Indies, the brig *Spark*, 12, Lieutenant John H. Elton, recaptures a Dutch merchantman taken by pirates and lands a party that destroys a pirate base.

January 7.   A boat expedition from the schooner *Porpoise*, 12, Lieutenant James Ramage, destroys a pirate base and six vessels near Bahia Honda, Cuba.

March 7.   The schooner *Revenge*, (formerly *Gunboat No. 158*), 1, Lieutenant G.W. Hamersley, captures a pirate barge in the West Indies.

March 8.   Seven small pirate vessels are destroyed off Cape San Antonio, Cuba, by the brig *Enterprise*, 16, Lieutenant Lawrence Kearny.

March 26.   **Foundation of the West India Squadron.** Commodore James Biddle is given command and charged with protecting American shipping and suppressing piracy off the coast of Cuba, Puerto Rico, and Central America. The force assigned him consists of the frigates *Congress*, 36, *John Adams*, 28, *Macedonian*, 38, and *Cyane*, 34; the sloops *Hornet*, 18, and *Peacock*, 18; the brigs *Enterprise*, 16, and *Spark*, 12; the schooners *Alligator*, 12, *Grampus*, 12, *Porpoise*, 12, *Shark*, 12, *Revenge*, 1; and *Gunboat No. 168*.

April 30.   The Colombian privateer *Cienega*, 5, is taken near the Windward Islands by the schooner *Alligator*, 12, Lieutenant W.W. McKean.

May 1.   Near Sugar Key, Cuba, boat parties from the *Alligator*, 12, *Grampus*, 12, and the chartered ship *Jane* commanded by Sailing Master Barney capture four pirate schooners and release a pirate prize.

June.   The schooners *Shark*, 12, Lieutenant Matthew C. Perry, and *Grampus*, 12, Lieutenant Francis H. Gregory, capture the pirate schooner *Bandera de Sangre* ("Bloody Banner") off the northern coast of Cuba.

August 16.   The privateer *Palmyra* (ex-*Pancheta*), 9, surrenders to the schooner *Grampus*, 12, Lieutenant Francis H. Gregory, after a brief action off Puerto Rico.

September 28–30.   Five pirate ships are captured, and the pirate settlement at Bahia Honda, Cuba, is destroyed by the sloop *Peacock*, 18, Captain Stephen Cassin, and revenue cutter *Louisiana*, 8.

November 9.   Three pirate schooners in possession of five American merchantmen are attacked in shoal water 45 miles east of Matanzas, Cuba, by boat parties led by Lieutenant William Howard Allen of the schooner *Alligator*. The merchant ships are freed, and one of the pirate schooners is captured. Allen is mortally wounded. The bodies of 14 pirates are counted.

November 19.   The *Alligator*, Lieutenant W.W. McKean, wrecks without loss of life on Carysfort Reef, Florida.

December 21.   Commodore David Porter is appointed commander of the West India Squadron.

1823

February 14.   **First steamer to see action.** Commodore Porter sails from New York to assume command of the West India Squadron. For inshore operations in the shallow waters of the Cuban and Puerto Rican coasts, he has ordered the construction of five 20-oared barges, the *Gallinipper, Gnat, Midge, Mosquito,* and *Sandfly*, and purchased eight small schooners (Chesapeake "bay boats"), each mounting three guns, the *Beagle, Ferret, Fox, Greyhound, Jackall, Terrier, Weasel,* and *Wild Cat*; the schooner *Decoy*, 6; and the former Hudson River ferryboat, *Sea Gull*, 3, a paddlewheeler that becomes the first steamship in the world to enter combat.

March 6.   Lieutenant William H. Cocke, commanding the schooner *Fox*, is mortally wounded when his ship is fired on while entering San Juan, Puerto Rico. The Spanish governor apologizes for the error.

April 8.   Supported by the sloop *Peacock*, 18, Captain Stephen Cassin, the 20-oar barges *Gallinipper*, Lieutenant William H. Watson, and *Mosquito*, Lieutenant Cornelius K. Stribling, capture the pirate schooner *Pilot* near Havana, Cuba, and land marines to pursue the pirates ashore.

April 16.   The *Peacock* captures two pirate ships off Colorados, Cuba.

May 22.   Off Campeche, Mexico, two pirate

Commodore David Porter, by an unknown artist. Courtesy U.S. Naval Academy Museum.

vessels are captured by the schooner *Grampus*, 12, Lieutenant Francis H. Gregory.

July.   The pirate schooner *Catalina* and a launch under the pirate leader Diaboleto are captured near Sigaumpa Bay, Cuba, by the barges *Gallinipper*, Lieutenant William H. Watson, and *Mosquito*, Lieutenant W.T. Inman. Approximately 75 pirates are killed or captured. Diaboleto is among the former.

July 9.   The brig *Enterprise*, 16, Lieutenant Lawrence Kearny, is wrecked without loss of life on Little Curaço Island in the West Indies.

July 22.   **Action at Cape Cruz, Cuba.** The schooners *Beagle*, 3, Lieutenant J.T. Newton, and *Greyhound*, 3, Lieutenant Lawrence Kearny, shell the pirate stronghold at Cape Cruz from the sea while a landing party of sailors and marines under Lieutenant David Glasgow Farragut circles around to attack from the rear. Eight armed boats are captured with the village.

August 3. The Spanish schooner *Gallago Se-*

gunda, 1, fires on and then surrenders to the schooner *Weasel*, 3, Lieutenant Beverley Kennon, off Colorados, Cuba. After adjudication, the vessel is returned to her owners.

September 16.   Samuel Southard enters office as seventh secretary of the navy.

December 2.   **Monroe Doctrine.** In his seventh annual message to Congress, President Monroe declares that the Americas "are henceforth not to be considered as subjects for the future colonization by any European powers. . . . [and] that we should consider any attempt on their part to extend their system to any portion of this hemisphere as dangerous to our peace and safety." At this time the doctrine is supported principally by the ships of the Royal Navy, for Britain does not want to see Spanish authority and exclusionary trade policies reasserted in that country's former colonies in South and Central America.

1824

August 17.   A pirate launch is captured off Havana, Cuba, by the schooner *Terrier*, 3, Lieutenant Thomas Paine, Jr.

August 26.   The *Terrier* captures a pirate schooner in Bahia Honda, Cuba.

October 20.   Near Matanzas, Cuba, the schooner *Porpoise*, 12, Lieutenant Charles W. Skinner, supported by five boats under Lieutenant William M. Hunter, captures a pirate schooner and three boats.

October 27.   Accompanied by Midshipman Robert Ritchie, Lieutenant Charles Platt, commanding officer of the schooner *Beagle*, 3, lands at Fajardo, on the east coast of Puerto Rico, to confer with Spanish officials regarding the rumored presence in the town of property stolen from the American consul on St. Thomas. The local authorities pretend to disbelieve that he is an American officer, and he and Ritchie are detained most of the day.

October 28.   The schooner *Wild Cat*, 3, Midshipman L.M. Booth, is lost with all hands between Cuba and Thompson's Island, West Indies.

November 14.   **"Foxhardo" Affair.** Outraged by the treatment Lieutenant Platt received at Fajardo (see October 27), Commodore David Porter goes ashore with 200 seamen and marines from the frigate *John Adams* and sends a message to the town demanding an apology to the lieutenant. "If any resistance is made," he warns, "the total destruction of Foxhardo will be the certain and immediate consequence." The apology is promptly tendered. Upon returning to the United States in the spring of 1825, Porter is court-martialed for exceeding his instructions and suspended from duty for six months, albeit at full pay. Outraged again, he begins to investigate the possibility of obtaining a commission in the Mexican Navy.

December 27.   Captain Lewis Warrington succeeds David Porter as commodore of the West India Squadron.

1825

February 4.   The schooner *Ferret*, 3, Lieutenant C.H. Bell, capsizes in a storm off the Cuban coast with the loss of nine lives.

March 4.   The schooner *Grampus*, 12, Lieutenant John D. Sloat, captures a pirate sloop after an action of 45 minutes off Ponce, Puerto Rico. Sloat receives the thanks of the governor of Puerto Rico.

March 4.   A prize sloop with a crew of 26 men under Lieutenant G. Pendergast captures a pirate sloop near Boca del Inferno, West Indies, after a sharp action lasting 40 minutes.

March 25.   An Anglo-American expedition under Lieutenant Isaac McKeever of the barge *Gallinipper*, supported by boat parties from HMS *Dartmouth, Lion,* and *Union,* destroys a pirate lair at Rio Sagua la Grande, east of Matanzas, Cuba.

September 7.   The Marquis de Lafayette, "Hero of Two Worlds," ends a triumphant American tour by boarding the frigate *Brandywine* to return to France.

1826

July 1.   **Porter resigns.** Smarting under the censure he received for the "Foxhardo" Affair, Commodore David Porter resigns his

commission after 28 years' service to accept the appointment of commander-in-chief of the Mexican Navy.

September 3.   **First U.S. Navy circumnavigation.** The new ship sloop *Vincennes*, 18, Captain W.B. Finch, sails for the Pacific to become the first U.S. naval vessel to sail around the world. She returns home in June 1830.

1827

October 4.   **Anti-pirate operations in the Mediterranean.** During the Greek war of independence from Turkey, now nearing its conclusion, the revolutionary government has licensed many privateers. Especially after the destruction of the Turkish fleet by an allied British, French, and Russian force at the Battle of Navarino in April 1827, these privateers swarm throughout the eastern Mediterranean, often crossing the line into piracy. On this date the sloop *Warren*, 18, Master Commandant Lawrence J. Kearny, captures a pirate brig of 16 guns and a pirate boat off the village of Carabusa in the Greek Cyclades Islands.

October 16.   The schooner *Porpoise*, 12, Lieutenant Benjamin Cooper, is convoying merchant ships from Smyrna, Turkey, to Port Mahon, Minorca. After nightfall one of her charges, an English brig, is attacked and captured by several Greek caiques in Doro Passage. Cooper lowers four boats carrying 40 men under Lieutenants Louis M. Goldsborough, John A. Carr, and Thomas J. Manning and Midshipman Alexander W. Wilson, who drive off the pirates, killing around 40, and recapture the brig. There are no American casualties.

October 25.   The sloop *Warren*, 18, Master Commandant Lawrence Kearny, pursues a Carabusan pirate brig of 10 guns, which grounds herself and sinks off Argenteira Island. The crew escapes ashore.

October 28.   The *Warren* recovers the captured American brig *Cherub* at Syra, Greece.

October 30–31.   Cruising off Miconi (Mikonos) in the Cyclades Islands, the *Warren* captures a pirate galley of 40 oars.

November 1.   The *Warren* sends a party ashore at Mikonos. The detachment recovers equipment and stores from three captured merchant vessels and burns a pirate boat.

November 7.   A boat party from the *Warren* under Lieutenant William L. Hudson captures a pirate boat and burns another during a cruise around Andros Island in the Aegean Sea.

1829

March 9.   John Branch enters office as eighth secretary of the navy.

June 4.   **Loss of the Fulton (Demologos).** The navy's first steamship, built during the War of 1812, blows up at Brooklyn, killing 24 persons and injuring 19.

August 16.   **Loss of the Hornet.** The ship sloop *Hornet*, 18 (another veteran of the War of 1812), Lieutenant O. Norris, sails from Pensacola, Florida, and disappears. She probably went down in a storm off Tampico, Mexico, on September 10.

1830

December 6.   **Naval Observatory.** The Depot of Charts and Instruments, later renamed the Naval Observatory, is established at Washington, D.C., under the command of Lieutenant Louis M. Goldsborough.

1831

May 23.   Levi Woodbury assumes office as ninth secretary of the navy.

August 28.   The frigate *Potomac*, 44, Captain John Downes, sails from Sandy Hook for the East Indies to protect American commerce from the Sumatran pirates.

1832

January 1.   **Landing in the Falklands.** The sloop *Lexington*, 18, Master Commandant Silas Duncan, lands a party of sailors and marines to obtain redress for the seizure of two American whalers in the Falkland Islands, then nominally under Argentine administration.

February 6.   **Battle of Kuala Batu (Quallah Battoo).** The frigate *Potomac*, 44, Captain John Downes, has been sent to chastise Kuala Batu, a town on the western coast of Sumatra, whose inhabitants had plundered the American trader *Friendship* and killed three of her crew. Disguised as a Danish merchantman, the *Potomac* anchors off Kuala Batu at dawn and lands a detachment of 282 sailors and marines divided into four parties commanded by First Lieutenant Alvin Edson, USMC, and Lieutenants Irvine Shubrick, Henry Hoff, and Jonathan Ingersoll, USN. Four forts defending the town are taken after two hours' hard fighting, and Kuala Batu is captured and burned. Some 150 Sumatrans are killed, including their leader, Rajah Po Mahomet. American casualties are two dead and eleven wounded.

1833

March 20.   **First Far Eastern Treaty.** A treaty of commerce between the United States and Siam is concluded by Captain David Geisinger of the sloop *Peacock*.

June 17.   **First dry dock.** The navy's first dry dock opens to receive the ship-of-the-line *Delaware*, at the Charleston Navy Yard at Boston, Massachusetts.

October 31.   A detachment of 43 seamen and marines lands from the sloop *Lexington*, 18, to protect foreign interests at Buenos Aires, Argentina.

1834

June 30.   Congress appropriates the sum of $5,000 for research on shipboard steam engines, and passes an Act "For the Better Organization of the United States Marine Corps." Commandant Archibald Henderson is promoted to the rank of colonel; the authorized strength of the corps is increased to 63 officers and 1,271 NCOs and men; and it is clearly established that the marine corps is part of the naval service.

July 1.   Mahlon Dickerson assumes office as tenth secretary of the navy.

1835

November 19. **First U.S. naval vessel visits Guam.** The sloop *Vincennes*, 18, Commander John H. Aulick, anchors at Apra.

December 17. The marine detachment of the frigate *Brandywine*, 44, is landed to protect the U.S. consulate at Lima, Peru. The marines are withdrawn on January 24, 1836.

December 28. **Dade Massacre: outbreak of the Second Seminole War.** Plans to move them west of the Mississippi have aroused the ire of the Florida Seminoles. Two companies of U.S. regulars under Major Francis L. Dade are ordered from Fort Brooke, inland of Tampa Bay, to reinforce the garrison of Fort King, near Silver Springs, where increasingly acrimonious negotiations are being held. En route, the column is ambushed by a considerably larger force of Seminoles incited by Osceola; 3 of its 110 men escape. The ensuing conflict is the largest Indian War fought by the United States east of the Mississippi and the only one in which the navy will play a significant role.

1836

January 21. **Blockade of Florida.** Commodore Alexander J. Dallas, commander of the West India Squadron, is directed to institute a blockade of southern Florida, whose settlers are certain that the Seminoles are receiving arms from Cuba and the Bahamas. Although not a single gunrunner is ever apprehended, state and military authorities remain convinced that the arms traffic exists, and the blockade is maintained throughout the war.

January 21. **Marines reinforce Fort Brooke.** A detachment of 57 marines under First Lieutenant Nathaniel S. Waldron arrive on a chartered brig to bolster the garrison of Fort Brooke, Florida. They were sent from Key West by Commodore Dallas.

March 16–30. The revenue cutter *Washington*, Captain Ezekiel Jones, U.S. Revenue Marine, reinforced by 15 seamen under Lieutenant William Smith, explores the shores of Charlotte Harbor for signs of the Indians and lands parties that push inland as far as 10 miles.

March 17–28. A boat expedition from the sloop *Vandalia*, 18, under Lieutenant Levin M. Powell makes a similar reconnaissance of the Manatee River and the keys around Tampa Bay.

April 1. **Action with the Seminoles.** On a second expedition from the *Vandalia*, Powell sends a detachment under Lieutenant Stephen C. Rowan to intercept a band of Seminoles who have plundered a fishing village on Josefa (probably present-day Useppa) Island. Rowan surprises the Indian encampment, killing two and capturing two others.

May 23. **Creek War.** President Andrew Jackson orders marine corps commandant Colonel Archibald Henderson to send all available men to aid the army in suppressing the Creek Indian uprising in Georgia and Alabama. Henderson personally leads two battalions—more than half the corps—into the field. On the conclusion of the campaign, late in the summer, the marines continue south to fight the Seminoles.

July 12. **First engineering officer.** Charles H. Haswell, who designed the engines for the second steamship built for the navy, the side-wheeler *Fulton* (II), is the first engineer to be commissioned in the U.S. Navy. He later becomes engineer-in-chief.

October 6–November 20. A force of 50 seamen and 95 marines under Lieutenant Levin M. Powell, with two chartered schooners and six boats, searches the coast of Florida from Charlotte Harbor to the St. Lucie River for Seminoles, without success.

November 21. **Battle of the Wahoo Swamp.** One of the relatively few pitched battles of the Seminole War is fought in eastern central Florida between the hostiles and a mixed force of regulars, volunteers, and friendly Creeks led by marine officers.

1837

January 27. **Battle of the Hatchee-Lustee.** Colonel Archibald Henderson, USMC, who has been given command of one of the two brigades of the army in Florida, fights a sharp action with the Seminoles at

Hatchee-Lustee Creek, on the edge of the Great Cypress Swamp near Lake Tohopekaliga. In 1843, Henderson is brevetted brigadier general for his services against the Creeks and the Seminoles, thus becoming the corps's first general officer.

December 13.   The sidewheel steamer *Fulton* (II), 4, the first seagoing steamship built for the navy, is commissioned at New York.

December 26.   Future admiral George Dewey is born in Montpelier, Vermont.

1838

January 15.   **Battle on the Jupiter River.** In December, Lieutenant Levin M. Powell leads a fourth expedition against the Seminoles. His aim is to penetrate the Everglades, where no troops have yet ventured, with a force of approximately 200 seamen, soldiers, and marines in flat-bottomed boats. Prior to reaching the Everglades, however, he discovers a trail near Jupiter Inlet and follows it to attack a Seminole encampment in a cypress swamp five miles from the coast. After an initial advance, his 75 men are driven back to their boats in some disorder. Four are killed and 22 wounded.

March 22.   A combined expedition of regulars and Tennessee volunteers under Colonel James Bankhead and a detachment of soldiers and sailors under Lieutenant Powell drive the Seminoles from an island encampment in the Everglades. This is one of the first times U.S. forces have penetrated the great swamp.

July 1.   James K. Paulding becomes the 11th secretary of the navy.

August 19–July 6, 1842.   **Wilkes Expedition.** An expedition consisting of the sloops *Vincennes*, 18, and *Peacock*, 18, brig *Porpoise*, 12, converted pilot boats *Sea Gull* and *Flying Fish*, and storeship *Relief,* under the command of Lieutenant Charles Wilkes, sails from Norfolk, Virginia, with orders to survey various parts of the Pacific and to explore the south polar regions. Officially designated the U.S. Exploring Expedition, it is the first large operation of its kind conducted by the navy. In voyages lasting nearly four years, the expedition sails approximately 85,000 miles, charts 280 is-

lands, collects thousands of scientific specimens, and discovers the Antarctic continent.

August 19.   A boat party of 24 men under Second Lieutenant John Faunce, U.S. Revenue Marine (now Coast Guard), from the revenue cutter *Campbell* surprises a band of Seminoles near Cape Florida, killing three and putting a dozen to flight. A few days earlier the Indians had massacred the crews of three New England fishing sloops and also the crew of a merchant brig that grounded in a gale.

1839

January 1–2.   **Second Battle of Kuala Batu (Quallah Battoo).** Commodore George C. Read, commander of the East India Squadron, launches an attack on the Sumatran village of Kuala Batu, which had undergone a similar experience in 1832, in retaliation for the murder of the captain of the merchantman *Eclipse.* Supported by the ships' fire, a landing party of 360 men under Commander T.W. Wyman from the frigate *Columbia*, 44, and sloop *John Adams*, 18, captures and destroys five forts and most of the village. An indemnity is collected and the inhabitants promise to mend their ways.

April 5.   **The Florida Expedition.** Convinced that the navy's blockade is not preventing a flow of arms to the Seminoles from Cuba and the Bahamas, in 1838 the War Department purchased two schooners, the *Wave* and the *Otsego*, and a number of barges to support the revenue cutters already under its orders in maintaining an in-shore blockade of the southern tip of Florida. These vessels are manned by navy crews. Command of this force, commonly referred to as the Florida Expedition and strengthened by the acquisition of the side-wheel steamer *Poinsett*, is now unified under Commander Isaac Mayo.

April 26.   The converted pilot boat *Sea Gull*, Midshipman J.W.E. Reid, a tender to the Wilkes Expedition, becomes separated from the *Flying Fish* en route from Tierra del Fuego to Valparaiso and disappears at sea. She carried a crew of 16.

The attack on Kuala Batu: a contemporary print (undated), in the caption of which the village is referred to as "Muckee." Courtesy Mystic Seaport, Inc.

May 18.   General Alexander Macomb concludes a preliminary treaty of peace with the Seminoles.

July 23.   **Harney Massacre.** The Seminole War resumes when a trading post on the Caloosahatchee River, established in accordance with Macomb's treaty by a 26-man detachment under Colonel William S. Harney, USA, is attacked by warriors led by Hospetarke and Chakaika. Harney and 13 men escape.

August 26.   The pirate schooner *Amistead* is captured off New London, Connecticut, by the brig *Washington*, 10, Lieutenant T.R. Gedney.

December 2.   **Genesis of the Mosquito Fleet.** Lieutenant John T. McLaughlin, whose ideas of carrying the war to the Seminoles in the Everglades are similar to those advanced earlier by Lieutenant L.M. Powell, succeeds Commander Isaac Mayo in command of the Florida Expedition. His force soon becomes known as the Mosquito Fleet.

1840

January 19.   **Discovery of Antarctica.** Lieutenant Charles Wilkes, sailing in the sloop *Vincennes*, flagship of the U.S. Exploring Expedition, discovers Antarctica, one day before d'Urville's French expedition sights the continent 400 miles to the west. Wilkes's observations, long contested, were con-

firmed by Sir Ernest Shackleton in 1908–09.

April 10.   In Florida a detachment of 24 sailors and marines from the Mosquito Fleet schooner *Otsego*, landed to examine the shoreline at Cape Sable, is attacked by a party of 50 to 80 Seminoles. The Indians withdraw upon the approach of boats bringing reinforcements from the schooners *Wave* and *Flirt*.

July 26.   At Malolo, in the Fiji Islands, Lieutenant Charles Wilkes leads a landing party that destroys the towns of Sualib and Arro in retribution for the murder of two of the exploring expedition's officers.

August 6–7.   **Indian Key Massacre.** Chief Chakaika makes the only Indian amphibious assault in history, leading a war party of about 135 Seminoles who paddle across 30 miles of open water after nightfall to attack the 70 settlers on Indian Key, Florida, only a few miles from the Mosquito Fleet's hospital on Tea Table Key. Most of the settlers manage to flee to a schooner anchored off the island and reach Tea Table Key, but 13 are killed. At the navy base, there are only five able-bodied men, commanded by Midshipman Francis K. Murray. This detail and seven patients load a pair of four-pounders on two barges and row to Indian Key, where Murray opens fire on the canoes drawn up on the beach, hoping to strand the Seminoles until the squadron's return. Both his guns recoil

The U.S. Exploring Expedition: Lieutenant Wilkes's flagship, the sloop *Vincennes*, in Disappointment Bay, January 25, 1840. Wilkes gave the bay the name he did because the ice shelf barred his approach to the newly discovered Antarctic continent. A lithograph of this painting, based on a sketch by Wilkes, appeared in his official *Narrative of the United States Exploring Expedition* (1845). Courtesy Peabody Museum of Salem.

overboard on the third shot; the Indians return fire with the settlement's six-pounder, and Murray retires.

September.   The pirate brig *Malek Adhel*, 4, is captured by the schooner *Enterprise*, 10, Lieutenant Louis M. Goldsborough, off Bahia, Brazil.

September 27.   Alfred Thayer Mahan is born in West Point, New York.

December.   **Harney's revenge.** Colonel W.S. Harney borrows 16 canoes from the Mosquito Fleet and, guided by a black slave who has recently escaped from the Seminoles, enters the Everglades with a detachment of 90 men to attack Chakaika's village. This time the troops, disguised as Seminoles, achieve surprise. Chakaika is killed and his band dispersed.

December 31–January 19, 1841.   **First crossing of the Everglades.** A combined force of 240 sailors, marines, and soldiers under Colonel Harney and Lieutenant John T. McLaughlin enter the Everglades from Fort

Dallas, on the Atlantic. Harney returns to the coast after several days, but leaves his guides with McLaughlin, who pushes on with 90 sailors and 60 marines to emerge on the Gulf on January 19. These men are the first whites to cross the Everglades.

1841

February 25.   The sloop *Peacock*, 18, a vessel of the Wilkes Expedition, lands 70 sailors and marines who burn three native villages on Upolu, in the Samoan Islands, in retaliation for the murder of an American merchant seaman.

March 6.   George E. Badger becomes the 12th secretary of the navy.

April 9.   A detachment of 80 men from the *Peacock* disperse 800 native warriors and burn two villages on Drummond Island in the Gilberts in an unsuccessful attempt to rescue a seaman who had been kidnapped from one of the ship's shore parties.

July 18.   The *Peacock*, Lieutenant William L. Hudson, wrecks without loss of life on a bar off the Columbia River, Oregon.

October 10–27.   A force of 200 sailors and marines of Lieutenant John T. McLaughlin's Mosquito Fleet enters the Everglades by Shark River to cooperate with an army detachment in an unsuccessful sweep for the band of Seminoles led by Chief Sam Jones.

October 11.   Abel P. Upshur enters office as 13th secretary of the navy.

November 3–December 23.   Lieutenant McLaughlin leads two more expeditions into the Everglades to harry the Seminoles. At the close of the operations almost 25 percent of McLaughlin's men are incapacitated by exhaustion or disease.

1842

February 11.   **Final operations in the Everglades.** Elements of Lieutenant McLaughlin's Mosquito Fleet execute a pincers movement through the Everglades. One party, under Lieutenant John Rodgers, enters the swamp from the east coast; the other, under Lieutenant John B. Marchand, from the west. The operation continues for 60 days, during which the men live in dug-out canoes and endure appalling hardships. Few Seminoles are encountered, but many fields and dwellings are destroyed.

May 10.   **End of the Seminole War.** Secretary of War John C. Spencer notifies Colonel William J. Worth, the army commander in Florida, that he may cease operations. It is estimated that there are at most 300 Seminoles left in the territory. A treaty of peace is never signed.

June 20.   The Florida Expedition (Mosquito Fleet) is disestablished.

June 29.   **Pathfinder of the Seas.** Lieutenant Matthew Fontaine Maury, disqualified for sea duty by a leg injury, is appointed superintendent of the Depot of Charts and Instruments. In this post, he will promote the research and collect the data that lay the foundations for the science of oceanography.

Lieutenant Matthew Fontaine Maury, from a photograph. Courtesy U.S. Naval Academy Museum.

August 9.   **Webster-Ashburton Treaty.** A treaty between the United States and Great Britain settles the long-standing controversy over disputed territories on the Canadian-American frontier and provides that each country will maintain a naval squadron off the west coast of Africa to prevent the slave trade from being carried on under its flag.

August 11.   The campaign against the Seminoles is officially concluded.

August 31.   **Bureau System.** The administrative organization under which the navy will operate for more than a century is established when Congress abolishes the Board of Navy Commissioners and creates five bureaus: Yards and Docks; Construction and Repair; Provisions and Clothing; Ordnance and Hydrography; and Medicine and Surgery.

October 2.   The sloop *Concord*, 24, Commander William Boerum, wrecks with the loss of three lives in the Mozambique Channel.

October 21–23.   **Occupation of Monterey.** Mistakenly believing that the United States has gone to war with Mexico, Commodore Thomas ap Catesby Jones, commander of the Pacific Squadron, seizes Monterey, in the Mexican province of Upper California, with landing parties from the frigate *United States*, 44, and sloop *Cyane*, 20. He is relieved of command for this excess of zeal in 1843, but reappointed to the same post in 1848.

December 1. **Somers Mutiny.** Commander Alexander Slidell Mackenzie hangs three men for conspiring to mutiny on the brig *Somers*: Seaman Elisha Small, Boatswain's Mate Samuel Cromwell, and 19-year-old Midshipman Philip Spencer, the son of Secretary of War John C. Spencer. Mackenzie learned of the plans for the mutiny when Purser's Steward James Wales reported that Spencer had asked him to join in it. A search of Spencer's possessions produced incriminating papers, and Mackenzie had Spencer, Cromwell, and Small put in irons on the quarterdeck. The attitude of the crew, composed mostly of impressionable, teenaged apprentice boys, grew threatening, however, and Mackenzie convened a court-martial composed of the *Somer*'s officers and midshipmen, who unanimously recommended that for the safety of the vessel the three men should be put to death. Mackenzie's decision to follow that council remains controversial to this day, even though Spencer confessed his intentions. The prominence of Spencer's father makes the incident the subject of national attention and generates debate on methods of officer selection and training. This is the only mutiny in the history of the U.S. Navy.

1843

March 11. The schooner *Grampus*, 12, Lieutenant A.E. Downes, sails from Charleston, South Carolina, for Norfolk, Virginia, and is lost en route with all hands.

July 24. David Henshaw assumes office as 14th secretary of the navy.

August 25. The side-wheel frigate *Missouri*, 10, Captain John T. Newton, arrives at Gibraltar to become the first steam-powered U.S. naval vessel to cross the Atlantic. The

next night fire breaks out in one of her storerooms, and the ship is destroyed.

September 9. The navy's first screw steamer, the *Princeton*, 14, is commissioned at Philadelphia, Pennsylvania, Captain Robert F. Stockton, commanding. All of the navy's previous steamers were side-wheelers.

December 5. **First iron ship.** The steamer *Michigan*, the navy's first iron-hulled vessel, is launched at Erie, Pennsylvania, to patrol the Great Lakes. She is also the navy's first prefabricated ship, having been built in Pittsburgh and transported to Erie for assembly.

December 15. Commodore Matthew C. Perry, commander of the newly reconstituted Africa Squadron, lands with a party of 200 sailors and marines at the village of Little Berebee on the Ivory Coast, where two years earlier the crew of the American trader *Mary Carver* had been massacred. A palaver with the native leader, King Ben Krako, ends in a scuffle in which the king is mortally wounded and made prisoner. The landing party then captures and fires Little Berebee.

1844

February 19. Thomas W. Gilmer enters office as 15th secretary of the navy.

February 28. **"Peacemaker" disaster.** Captain Robert F. Stockton invites President John Tyler and other dignitaries for a cruise down the Potomac on the *Princeton,* the navy's first screw streamer. During the voyage Stockton demonstrates the "Peacemaker," a 12-inch wrought-iron gun of his design. Unfortunately, his knowledge of metallurgy is not extensive. After several successful firings the gun bursts, cutting a swath through the bystanders. Eight persons are killed and nine wounded. Among the dead are Secretary of State (and former secretary of the navy) Abel P. Upshur, Secretary of the Navy Thomas W. Gilmer, Senator David Gardner, and Captain Beverley Kennon, Chief of the Bureau of Construction, Equipment and Repairs. Stockton is slightly wounded.

March 26. John Y. Mason becomes the 16th secretary of the navy.

March 29.   Uriah P. Levy, who had entered the navy during the War of 1812, is the first Jewish officer promoted to the rank of captain. In 1859 he attains flag rank as commander of the Mediterranean Squadron.

June 19–July 20.   A detachment of marines from the sloop *St. Louis*, 20, is landed at Whampoa Island, off Canton, China, where a mob has surrounded the American trading compound.

1845

March 1.   **Origin of the Mexican War.** President John Tyler signs a congressional resolution calling for the annexation of the Republic of Texas, which Mexico claims still belongs to her.

March 11.   **Genesis of the Naval Academy.** George Bancroft, the distinguished historian, becomes 17th secretary of the navy. Soon after he enters office William Chauvenet, a brilliant young mathematician in charge of the navy school at Philadelphia, sends him a plan, previously rejected by Secretary Mason, for transforming the existing cram course into a formal, two-year program. Bancroft likes the idea, but decides that the school should be located at Annapolis, Maryland, where an obsolete army post, Fort Severn, can be converted into a campus.

March 31.   Mexico breaks diplomatic relations with the United States.

July 25.   In anticipation of troubles with Mexico, an American army under General Zachary Taylor lands near Corpus Christi, Texas.

August 15.   At Annapolis, Fort Severn is transferred to the navy. Commander Franklin Buchanan, whom Secretary Bancroft had earlier asked to prepare a plan of organization for the naval school, is appointed superintendent on the same day.

October 10.   The U.S. Naval School, as it is originally known, commences classes at Annapolis, Maryland, with a student body of 56 and a staff of 7: Commander Buchanan, Lieutenant James H. Ward, Passed Midshipman Samuel L. Marcy, Surgeon John A. Lockwood, Chaplain George Jones and Professors William Chauvenet, Arsène N. Girault, and Henry H. Lockwood.

Henceforward, all midshipmen entering the navy will attend the school for two years, between which, however, they will serve a three-year apprenticeship at sea.

October 30.   **Gillespie mission.** President Polk personally directs First Lieutenant Archibald H. Gillespie, USMC, to carry a secret message to Thomas O. Larkin, U.S. consul at Monterey, California, instructing him to encourage the Californians to revolt against Mexico and to urge them not to accept assistance from any power except the United States.

December 29.   Texas is admitted to the Union.

1846

April 23.   **Beginning of the Mexican War.** Mexico declares war on the United States.

May 8.   A Mexican army that has crossed the Rio Grande into Texas is defeated by General Zachary Taylor's forces at the Battle of Palo Alto, the first major clash of the Mexican War.

May 13.   The United States declares war on Mexico.

May 14.   **Blockade of Mexico.** Commodore David Conner, commanding the U.S. Home Squadron, proclaims a blockade of the Mexican Gulf ports of Matamoros, Tampico, Alvarado, and Veracruz. Not a single Mexican naval vessel will put to sea during the war.

May 16.   Eleven Revenue Marine (Coast Guard) cutters are detailed to support the army and navy during the Mexican War.

May 24.   The Mexican schooners *Criolla* and *Amada* are captured by the sloop *Falmouth*, Commander Joseph R. Jarvis, and the brig *Somers*, Commander Duncan N. Ingraham, respectively. Although Commodore Conner releases both ships upon learning that Mexico allowed four American vessels caught in Veracruz by the outbreak of war to depart, they are the first numerous Mexican merchantmen taken by the U.S. Navy in the course of the conflict.

June 8.   The sloop *St. Mary's*, 20, Commander John L. Saunders, shells Tampico, Mexico.

June 14.   Boat parties from the *St. Mary's* make an unsuccessful attempt to cut out three Mexican gunboats at Tampico, Mexico.

July 4.   In California, American settlers proclaim the independence of the Bear Flag Republic.

July 7.   Commodore John D. Sloat, commander of the Pacific Squadron, lands a party of 140 seamen and 85 marines under Captain William Mervine of the sloop *Cyane*, 20, to occupy Monterey, in the Mexican province of California. The landing is unopposed.

July 9.   Seventy seamen and marines landed from the sloop *Portsmouth*, 20, Commander John B. Montgomery, take possession of the villages of San Francisco and Yerba Buena, California, also without encountering opposition.

July 10.   John Y. Mason becomes the 18th secretary of the navy. He had held the same position in 1844–45.

July 20.   Commodore James Biddle anchors in Edo (Tokyo) Bay with the *Columbus*, 74, and the sloop *Vincennes*, 18, in an unsuccessful attempt to open diplomatic relations with Japan. His vessels are the first American warships to visit that country.

July 29.   Commodore Robert F. Stockton relieves Commodore Sloat in command of the Pacific Squadron. His energetic leadership will make him the man most responsible for the conquest of California.

July 29.   The sloop *Cyane*, 20, Captain William Mervine, arrives off San Diego, California, having sailed from Monterey on July 25 with a battalion of California volunteers under Captain John C. Frémont, USA. A naval detachment commanded by Lieutenant Stephen C. Rowan lands unopposed and takes possession of the town, after which Frémont's men go ashore.

August 4.   A landing party from the frigate *Congress*, 54, Commander Samuel F. Du Pont, flagship of the Pacific Squadron, takes possession of Santa Barbara, California. No resistance is encountered.

August 6.   San Pedro, California, is peacefully occupied by a marine detachment under First Lieutenant Jacob Zeilin from the frigate *Congress*.

August 7.   **First attack on Alvarado.** On the Gulf coast of Mexico nine ships of Commodore Conner's Home Squadron, including the screw steamer *Princeton*, 13, Commander Frederick Engle, and the paddle-wheeler *Mississippi*, 10, Captain Andrew Fitzhugh, bombard the forts and gunboats guarding the mouth of the Alvarado River. Conner breaks off the attack when the weather turns threatening.

August 13.   A naval brigade of 360 men advancing from San Pedro under Commodore Robert F. Stockton occupies Los Angeles, California. Captain Frémont's California Battalion, which had taken another route, arrives an hour later.

August 14.   Mexican forces in California surrender.

August 14.   The brig *Truxtun*, 10, Commander Edward W. Carpenter, grounds without loss of life on Tuxpan Reef, off the east coast of Mexico, and surrenders to enemy forces ashore the next day. On August 22, a boat party from the steamer *Princeton* burns the empty ship.

September 2.   Lieutenant Stephen C. Rowan leads a landing party from the sloop *Cyane*, 20, which spikes 24 enemy cannons at San Blas, Mexico.

September 7.   A boat party of 69 men under Lieutenant William Radford from the sloop *Warren*, 20, cuts out the Mexican merchant brig *Malek Adhel* in the harbor of Mazatlán, Mexico. The prize is taken into U.S. service.

September 10.   The schooner *Shark*, 12, Lieutenant Neil M. Howison, wrecks without loss of life at the mouth of the Columbia River, Oregon.

September 23.   **Californian revolt.** Mexican army Captain José Maria Flores becomes the leader of an uprising by native Californians against the small and scattered American occupation forces. The first fighting occurs at Los Angeles, where Lieutenant Archibald H. Gillespie, USMC, commands a 48-man garrison from Frémont's California Battalion. He is compelled to surrender, but allowed to withdraw on September 29. Santa Barbara is evacuated soon afterward.

October 7.   The sloop *Cyane*, 20, Commander Samuel F. Du Pont, shells Guaymas, Sonora, destroying the Mexican gunboats *Anahuac* and *Sonorense*, and sends a boat expedition under Lieutenant George W. Harrison, which cuts out the merchant brig *Condor*.

October 7–8   Captain William Mervin advances from San Pedro with 225 men from the frigate *Savannah* and Lieutenant Gillespie's Californians to recapture Los Angeles. His column is forced back by California cavalry equipped with a cannon, of which he has none.

October 15.   **Second attack on Alvarado.** Seven vessels of the Home Squadron make another attempt to enter the Alvarado River. Commodore Conner orders them to withdraw when the side-wheel steamer *McLane*, 6, which is to tow three sailing ships into the river, proves unable to cross the bar.

October 23.   **First Tabasco Expedition.** A squadron of seven vessels under Commodore Matthew C. Perry enters the Tabasco River, capturing the coastal town of Frontera, and pushes 72 miles upstream to reach and briefly occupy the city of Tabasco (present-day Villahermosa) on October 25. Seven Mexican vessels are taken during these operations. No resistance is encountered until the next day, when Mexican troops reoccupy Tabasco and open fire on the ships. Perry shells the city until their firing ceases and returns to the coast.

November 14.   **Pánuco Expedition.** Commodore David Conner leads a force of six ships and boat parties from five others into the Pánuco River, on the Mexican Gulf coast. The port of Tampico is occupied without resistance that afternoon. Five vessels, four of which become U.S. gunboats, are also taken. On November 19, Commander Josiah Tattnall pushes 25 miles upstream with the side-wheel steamer *Spitfire* and schooner *Petrel* to capture the town of Pánuco, where he destroys a number of Mexican cannons. Tampico will be held by U.S. forces for the remainder of the war.

November 15.   The sloop *Boston*, 18, Commander George F. Pearson, wrecks without loss of life on Eleuthera Island in the Bahamas.

November 26.   After nightfall, the Mexican brig *Criolla*, which had slipped through the American blockade into Veracruz, is burned beneath the guns of Fortress San Juan de Ulloa by a boat party from the brig *Somers* consisting of Lieutenant James L. Parker,

Passed Midshipmen John R. Hynson and R. Clay Rogers and five men. Unfortunately, the *Criolla* was a spy ship that Commodore Conner had deliberately let pass.

December 8.   **Loss of the Somers.** Blockading off Veracruz, the brig *Somers*, 10, Lieutenant Raphael Semmes, is capsized by a sudden squall. Of her 76 crewmen, 32 are lost.

December 21.   A squadron of four ships commanded by Commodore Matthew C. Perry occupies Carmen, a Mexican port on the Bay of Campeche, without opposition.

1847

January 2.   **Action near the Mission Santa Clara.** A detachment of 101 marines and volunteers with one gun under Captain Ward Marston, USMC, defeats a Californian uprising led by Francisco Sanchez, former military commandant of San Francisco. Sanchez surrenders four days later.

January 8.   **Battle of San Gabriel.** Commodore Robert F. Stockton has planned a two-pronged offensive to recapture Los Angeles. While Captain J.C. Frémont, USA, moves south from Santa Barbara with his California Battalion, Stockton will advance north from San Diego with a naval brigade and a detachment of U.S. dragoons who have marched overland from Kansas under Colonel Steven W. Kearny. His force consists of 607 men and four guns. On this date it defeats the Californian army of 450 men and two guns under Captain José M. Flores, which had attempted to prevent it from crossing the San Gabriel River.

January 9.   **Battle of La Mesa.** Commodore Stockton's column defeats and disperses the remainder of Captain Flores's Californian army—perhaps 300 men—in an action of two-and-a-half hours south of the Los Angeles River.

January 10.   American forces reoccupy Los Angeles. Three days later the Californians sign the Treaty of Cahuenga, ending the war in California.

March 9.   **Landing at Veracruz.** Despite General Taylor's victories in northern Mexico, culminating in the occupation of Monterey, the Mexican government refuses to

The landing of General Scott's army near Veracruz: a lithograph published in Philadelphia in 1847 from a drawing by eyewitness Lieutenant Charles C. Barton, USN. Courtesy Beverley R. Robinson Collection, U.S. Naval Academy Museum.

make peace. Plans are then developed to land another American army under General Winfield Scott at Veracruz for an advance on Mexico City. Commodore Conner's Home Squadron lands 8,600 of Scott's men on Collado Beach, two-and-a-half miles south of the city, in less than five hours without the loss of a single life. This is the first major amphibious operation conducted by the U.S. Navy and a model of its kind.

March 10.   The paddle-wheel steamer *Spitfire*, 3, Commander Josiah Tattnall, shells Castle San Juan de Ulloa while Scott's army encircles Veracruz.

March 15.   Commander George P. Upshur becomes the second superintendent of the naval academy.

March 21.   Commodore Matthew C. Perry relieves Commodore Conner as commander of the Home Squadron.

March 22.   General Scott's three siege batteries, supported by fire from seven ships of the Home Squadron, begin to bombard Veracruz.

March 22.   **The Naval Battery at Veracruz.** Three 32-pounders and three 8-inch-shell guns are landed from ships of the Home Squadron to augment the army's heavy artillery in the bombardment of Veracruz. Commanded by Captain John H. Aulick of the frigate *Potomac*, the naval battery opens fire on the morning of March 24.

Two of its men are killed and three wounded in the course of the siege.

March 23.   **Tattnall and the Spitfire.** Directed to renew the bombardment of Veracruz, Commander Josiah Tattnall leads a flotilla consisting of the steamers *Spitfire*, 3, and *Vixen*, 3, towing the schooners *Petrel*, 1, *Tampico*, 1, *Bonita*, 1, and *Reefer*, 1, to a position only 600 yards from the Mexican fortifications. Perry orders him to open the range after an hour, during which Tattnall's ships suffer remarkably little damage, probably because they were too close for the Mexican guns to depress on them.

March 27.   Veracruz surrenders.

March 30.   In Baja California, the port of San José del Cabo is briefly occupied by a landing party of 140 men under Lieutenant Benjamin F. B. Hunter from the sloop *Portsmouth*.

March 31.   **Capture of Alvarado.** Following the surrender of Veracruz, General Scott lays plans for the capture of Alvarado, off which the Home Squadron had been repulsed in August and October 1846. On March 30, a brigade commanded by Brigadier General John A. Quitman marches south along the coast for Alvarado, where it is to be met and supported by twelve vessels under Commodore Perry. The steamer *Scourge*, 3, Lieutenant Charles G. Hunter, is sent ahead of the expedition. Arriving off Alvarado on March 30, Hunter

The naval battery at Veracruz. This lithograph, published by Sarony & Major in New York in 1848, was based upon a watercolor by eyewitness Lieutenant Henry Walke, USN. Courtesy Library of Congress.

shells the fort guarding the river mouth. It surrenders the next morning and Hunter crosses the bar, takes the city of Alvarado and three Mexican vessels, and pushes upstream to capture the village of Tlacotalpán on April 1. Perry is outraged. Averring that the *Scourge*'s actions allowed the Mexicans to destroy or withdraw supplies that could have been captured, he has Hunter court-martialled and dismissed from the Home Squadron.

April 3.   The marine detachment from the sloop *Portsmouth* briefly occupies the village of San Lucas in Baja California.

April 13.   A landing party from the *Portsmouth* under Lieutenant John S. Missroon occupies La Paz, the capital of Baja California.

April 18.   **Tuxpan expedition.** Commodore Matthew C. Perry enters the Tuxpan River with a force consisting of the steamers *Scourge*, 3, *Spitfire*, 3, and *Vixen*, 3, schooners *Bonita*, 1, *Petrel*, 1, and *Reefer*, 1, and 30 barges carrying a landing force of 1,519 men under Captain Samuel L. Breese. The forts of La Peña and La Palmasola, which oppose the flotilla's advance, are captured, and the city of Tuxpan is occupied. Perry withdraws from the river, having destroyed its fortifications, on April 22.

May 12.   **Coatzacoalcos expedition.** A flotilla of Commodore Perry's Home Squadron enters the Coatzacoalcos River, on the Gulf of Campeche. Two ships under Commander Abraham Bigelow push on to the village of Minatitlán, 24 miles upstream, to gather intelligence.

May 16.   Continuing south from Coatzacoalcos, Commodore Perry occupies the town and island of Carmen.

June 14.   **Second Tabasco expedition.** Commodore Perry leads an expedition into the Tabasco River to capture the city of the same name (present-day Villahermosa). His force consists of the steamer *Scourge*, 3, *Scorpion*, 4, *Spitfire*, 3, and *Vixen*, 3, the schooner *Bonita*, 1, the brigs *Etna*, 1, *Stromboli*, 1, *Vesuvius*, 1, and *Washington*, 1, and 47 boats carrying a landing force of 1,173 men and seven guns. The river defenses, considerably strengthened since Perry's expedition of October 1846, consist of four earthworks mounting eight guns and garrisoned by 900 Mexican troops. Perry lands the naval brigade which, with himself at its head, supports the ships in the capture of all four works and occupies Tabasco on June 16. An outbreak of yellow fever causes him to evacuate the town on July 22.

June 30.   Mexican troops occupying the village of Tamulté, four miles upstream from Ta-

The capture of the Mexican forts during the Tuxpan expedition, April 19, 1847. Another lithograph by Sarony & Major after an eyewitness painting by Lieutenant Walke. Courtesy U.S. Naval Academy Museum.

basco, are scattered by an expedition consisting of the steamers *Scourge* and *Vixen* and a land force of 200 men. The operation was mounted by Commander Abraham Bigelow, the military governor of Tabasco.

July 16.   **To the halls of Montezuma.** A marine battalion of 357 officers and men under Brevet Lieutenant Colonel Samuel F. Watson arrives at Veracruz to participate in General Scott's advance on Mexico City.

August 4.   Secretary of the Navy Mason instructs Commodore Perry not to occupy any more Mexican ports.

September 13.   **Storming of Chapultepec.** The marine battalion plays a leading part in the capture of Chapultepec Castle, the key to Mexico City. Lieutenant Colonel Watson having been given command of an army brigade, the marines go into action under Major Levi Twiggs, who is killed beneath the walls of the castle. Captain George H. Terrett's company, 67 officers and men, diverge from the battalion's advance and, joining forces with 24 men of the 4th Infantry under Lieutenant U.S. Grant, become the first American troops to enter Mexico City. Thirty-nine marines are killed or wounded in the day's fighting, and 13 of the 23 officers present receive brevet promotions for gallantry.

October 1.   A Mexican garrison is driven from the village of Mulejé in Baja California by a party of 50 men under Lieutenant T.A.M. Craven landed from Commander Thomas O. Selfridge's sloop *Dale*, 16.

October 5.   A landing party from the *Dale*, again led by Lieutenant Craven, seizes three cannons and other arms at the village of Loreto, Baja California.

October 20.   The frigate *Congress*, 54, Captain Elie A.F. La Vallette, and sloop *Portsmouth*,

Commodore Matthew C. Perry leads the landing party ashore at Seven Palms during the second Tabasco expedition, June 16, 1847. A third lithograph by Sarony & Major after a painting by Lieutenant Walke, published in 1849. Courtesy U.S. Naval Academy Museum.

22, Commander John B. Montgomery, bombard Mexican forces defending Guaymas, Sonora. The Mexicans withdraw after an hour, and the town is briefly occupied by a naval landing party.

November 11. **Capture of Mazatlán.** Mexico's most important Pacific port is occupied and garrisoned by a landing party of 730 men from the frigates *Congress* and *Independence* and the sloop *Cyane* under Captain Elie A.F. La Vallette of the *Congress.*

November 11. **Revolt in Baja California.** Anti-American sentiment in Lower California results in an uprising headed by Captain Manuel Pineda. It begins on this date with an unsuccessful surprise attack on the garrison of La Paz. Another assault is beaten off on November 17.

November 17. Informed of Mexican activity around Guaymas, Sonora, Commander Thomas O. Selfridge, commanding the sloop *Dale,* 16, lands with a party of 67

seamen and marines as a show of force. They are attacked by 250 troops. Selfridge is badly wounded, and his men are pinned down until the *Dale* disperses the Mexicans with her fire.

November 19–22. After the two attempts to recapture La Paz, Mexican forces in Baja California attack San José del Cabo, where a marine garrison of 24 men under Lieutenant Charles Heywood had been stationed on November 8. The marines hold out in a mission compound until the Mexicans, seeing the sails of two whaling vessels on the horizon, suppose that they are warships and withdraw.

November 20. A Mexican company at Urias, 10 miles south of Mazatlán, is routed in a dawn attack by landing parties under Lieutenants George L. Selden and Stephen C. Rowan.

December 12. After nightfall, a naval detachment of 43 men under Lieutenant Montgomery Lewis surprises and scatters a band of Mexicans 10 miles from Mazatlán.

December 13.   A patrol of 20 marines under Lieutenant William W. Russell disperses a group of Mexicans at Palos Prietos, near Mazatlán. This is the last skirmish in that area.

1848

January 12.   The guns defending the port of San Blas, on the west coast of Mexico, are removed by a landing party of 47 men from the bark *Whiton* and storeship *Lexington*, 6, under Lieutenant Frederick Chatard, the *Whiton*'s commanding officer.

January 17.   Lieutenant Chatard lands a party from the *Whiton* that spikes the guns at Manzanillo, Mexico. This leaves Acapulco the only defended Mexican port on the Pacific.

January 22–February 14.   In Baja California, the Mexicans again attack San José del Cabo, where Lieutenant Heywood's original garrison has been increased to 62 men. The siege is lifted by the arrival of the sloop *Cyane*, Commander S.F. Du Pont, who lands a detachment of 102 men. Before it can reach him, Heywood leads a sortie that drives the discouraged Mexicans from town.

January 30.   A Mexican detachment at Cochori, eight miles east of Guaymas, Sonora, is routed in a dawn attack by a landing party under Lieutenant T.A.M. Craven from the sloop *Dale*.

February 2.   **Treaty of Guadaloupe Hidalgo.** A treaty of peace between Mexico and the United States, ratified by the U.S. Senate on March 10, is signed at a village outside Mexico City. According to its terms, Mexico recognizes the American claim to Texas and cedes the United States an additional 500,000 square miles: all of present-day Arizona, California, Nevada, and Utah, most of New Mexico, and part of Colorado and Wyoming. The United States pays Mexico $15,000,000 and assumes all claims of American citizens against the Mexican government.

February 13.   A Mexican force at Bocachica-campo, four miles north of Guaymas, Sonora, is attacked and dispersed by a party of 60 of the *Dale*'s seamen and marines led by Lieutenant Fabius Stanly.

April 8–May 10.   **Dead Sea Expedition.** Lieutenant William F. Lynch leads a small party that surveys the Sea of Galilee (Lake Tiberias) and proceeds from there via the River Jordan to the Dead Sea.

April 9.   A landing party from the *Dale*, again commanded by Lieutenant Fabius Stanly, marches 12 miles inland to spike three Mexican guns near Guaymas, Sonora. On its return march, the detachment fights a short skirmish with Mexican forces. These are the last shots fired by the U.S. Navy in the war with Mexico.

1849

March 3.   The Nautical Almanac Office is established at Harvard University under the superintendency of 42-year-old Lieutenant Charles H. Davis, under whose able leadership it becomes America's first real scientific institute.

March 8.   William B. Preston becomes the 19th secretary to the navy.

August 16.   **U.S. Astronomical Expedition to the Southern Hemisphere.** Lieutenant James M. Gilliss, formerly chief of the Depot of Charts and Instruments, sails from New York to conduct astronomical observations that will aid navigators in determining the exact position of ships at sea. His work, performed in an observatory he builds near Santiago, Chile, is completed in the summer of 1852.

1850

May 26.   **First Grinnell Expedition.** Two brigs especially outfitted for the Arctic, the *Advance* and the *Rescue,* sail from New York to search for the British Arctic expedition of Captain Sir John Franklin, RN, which has not been heard from since 1847. Loaned to the government by Henry Grinnell, the ships are manned by navy volunteer crews under Lieutenant Edward J. De Haven. The site of Franklin's first winter quarters (and the graves of three of his men) are located on August 27, but little progress can be made thereafter, and on September 14 both vessels are frozen in. The expedition winters over, suffering considerable hardship, and renews the search, without success, in the summer of 1851 before returning to New York.

July 1.   Commander Cornelius K. Stribling becomes the third superintendent of the naval academy. On this same date the curriculum is extended to four years—still broken in the middle by three years at sea—and the institution is officially renamed the U.S. Naval Academy.

August 2.   William A. Graham becomes the 20th secretary of the navy.

September 2.   Congress abolishes flogging as a disciplinary action in the U.S. Navy.

September 6.   The ship sloop *Yorktown,* 16, Commander John Marston, wrecks without loss of life on Isla de Mayo in the Cape Verde Islands.

1851

May 21.   **Herndon Expedition.** Lieutenant William L. Herndon, Passed Midshipman Lardner Gibbon, and Master's Mate Henry J. Richards leave Lima, Peru, to explore the Amazon basin. Herndon reaches the city of Para (now Bélem), Brazil, after a journey of 4,366 miles on April 11, 1852; Gibbon and Richards, who follow a different route, arrive there in November. The primary purpose of the expedition, conceived by Lieutenant Matthew Fontaine Maury, was to determine the navigability of the Amazon River.

August 6.   The sloop *Dale,* 16, Commander William C. Pearson, anchors off Johanna Island in the Indian Ocean to demand an indemnity from King Selim for the temporary imprisonment of a New England merchant skipper. When the king refuses to comply, the *Dale* shells his town. The indemnity is paid the next day.

November 15.   The four-year curriculum at the Naval Academy is made continuous, the sea training for which it had been interrupted being provided by annual summer cruises.

1852

February 3.   Marines are landed from the Brazil Squadron, Commodore Isaac McKeever, to protect American citizens at Buenos Aires, Argentina.

July 26.   John P. Kennedy becomes the 21st secretary of the navy.

September 17.   The sloop *Jamestown* lands her marines to protect Americans at Buenos Aires, Argentina.

September 30–November 12, 1853.   The brig *Dolphin,* 10, Lieutenant S.P. Lee, sails from New York to verify the theories advanced by Lieutenant Matthew Fontaine Maury, the founder of oceanography, regarding the winds and currents of the Atlantic.

1853

January 19.   The paddle-wheel steamer *Water Witch,* Lieutenant Thomas J. Page, sails from Baltimore to explore and survey the River Plate and its tributaries. She returns home on February 3, 1856.

March 8.   James C. Dobbin enters office as 22nd secretary of the navy.

March 11.   The sloop *Cyane,* 20, lands her marine detachment to protect American citizens and property at San Juan del Norte, Nicaragua.

May 30.   **Second Grinnell Expedition.** An unofficial Arctic expedition privately financed by Henry Grinnell sails from New York in the steamer *Advance.* It is led by Dr. Elisha Kent Kane, a navy surgeon who had served under Lieutenant De Haven in the expedition of 1850–51. Trapped in pack ice later in 1853, the *Advance* remains imprisoned at the height of the Arctic summer in April 1855. Kane then abandons the vessel and leads his men on an 83-day sledge journey across the ice to Upernavik, Greenland, arriving there on July 24, 1855.

June 11–October 19, 1855.   **North Pacific Surveying and Exploring Expedition.** The coasts and islands of the Pacific are charted from the Aleutians to Japan and Hawaii by an expedition headed by Commanders Cadwallader Ringgold (1852–54) and John Rodgers (1854–55), the son of Commodore John Rodgers of the War of 1812.

June 21. **Koszta incident.** At Smyrna, Turkey, Martin Koszta, a naturalized American citizen who had participated in the Hungarian revolution of 1848, is seized by the Austrian consul and confined aboard the Austrian brig *Hussar*. The sloop *St. Louis*, 20, Commander Duncan N. Ingraham, is also at Smyrna. Upon learning what has happened, Ingraham clears his ship for action and sets a deadline for Koszta's release. The *Hussar* and another Austrian warship in harbor clear for action, too, but in the end Koszta is freed. Congress awards Commander Ingraham a gold medal for his determination in upholding the rights of American citizenship.

July 8. **Perry Expedition.** A squadron consisting of the side-wheel steamers *Mississippi*, 10, (flag), and *Susquehanna*, 9, and the 20-gun sloops *Plymouth* and *Saratoga* under the command of Commodore Matthew C. Perry enters Edo (Tokyo) Bay to establish relations with Japan. Perry had sailed from Norfolk, Virginia, on Novem-

ber 24, 1852. The Japanese have traditionally shunned contact with the outside world, but they are impressed by Perry's firm and dignified manner—as well as by the technological marvel of his steamships. Staunchly refusing to deal with subordinate officials, on July 14 he lands to meet the joint governors of Uraga, to whom he presents a letter from President Fillmore to the emperor of Japan. Three days later he sails for China, informing the Japanese that he will return to resume negotiations the following spring.

November 1. Commander Louis M. Goldsborough becomes the fourth superintendent of the Naval Academy.

1854

January 19. **Cyane expedition.** Lieutenant Isaac G. Strain leads a detachment of 12 officers and 13 seamen from the sloop *Cyane*, 20, on an expedition across the Isthmus of Pan-

The *St. Louis*, left, and the *Hussar* at Smyrna during the Koszta incident: a lithograph published in New York in 1853. Courtesy Beverley R. Robinson Collection, U.S. Naval Academy Museum.

ama from Caledonia on the Atlantic coast to Darien on the Pacific to reconnoiter a route for an interoceanic canal. The expedition undergoes extreme hardship, from which nine of its members perish. Lieutenant Strain pushes on alone to reach the coast on March 12 and leads a party back to rescue the others.

February 13.   Commodore Perry returns to Japan, anchoring off Yokohama with a squadron consisting of the side-wheel steamers *Mississippi* (flag), *Susquehanna,* and *Powhatan,* the sloops *Macedonian, Saratoga, Lexington,* and *Vandalia,* and the storeship *Southampton.*

March 8–31.   **Treaty of Kanagawa.** After three weeks' negotiations, Commodore Perry concludes a treaty of peace and amity with Japan. Although the Japanese still refuse to enter into commercial relations with the United States, these will soon be established. Japan has been opened to the western world.

April 4–5.   **Action at Shanghai.** The foreign concessions at Shanghai are threatened by the fighting between Chinese government troops and Taiping rebels. A landing party of 90 men under Commander John Kelly from the sloop *Plymouth,* 20, joins with a British naval detachment to avert the danger by driving both Chinese forces out of the city. One American is killed and three wounded.

Commodore Perry lands to meet the Japanese commissioners at Yokohama, March 8, 1854. This lithograph, by Sarony & Major, was one of the illustrations in the official *Narrative of the Expedition of an American Squadron to the China Seas and Japan* (1856). Courtesy Beverley R. Robinson Collection, U.S. Naval Academy Museum.

July 11.   **Treaty of Naha.** Commodore Perry concludes a treaty of peace and amity with the regency of the Loo Choo (Ryukyu) Islands.

July 13.   **Bombardment of Greytown.** The sloop *Cyane,* 20, Commander George N. Hollins, arrives at Greytown, Nicaragua, where the American ambassador had been arrested and held overnight, to demand an apology and an indemnity. When neither is forthcoming, Hollins gives the town a day's notice that he will bombard it and duly does so. Most of Greytown is consumed in the consequent fires. His robust initiative is subsequently approved by the State Department.

September 21.   The brig *Porpoise,* 12, Lieutenant William K. Bridge, disappears at sea after being sighted in the vicinity of Formosa on this date.

September 29.   The sloop *Albany,* 22, Commander James T. Gerry, and a crew of 193 sails from Aspinwall, Panama, for New York and is never seen again.

November 17.   The sloop *Vincennes,* 18, lands sailors and marines at Okinawa to enforce the provisions of the Treaty of Naha.

1855

May 19.   The side-wheel steamer *Powhatan,* Captain William J. McCluney, lands her marine detachment to protect American interests at Shanghai, China.

August 4.   Parties from the *Powhatan* and the British sloop *Rattler* destroy 17 pirate junks in Ty-Ho Bay, near Hong Kong, China.

August 28.   The sloop *Germantown,* 22, Commander William F. Lynch, lands her marines to safeguard Americans at Montevideo, Uruguay.

September 12.   The sloop *John Adams,* 18, Commander E. B. Boutwell, sends a party ashore at Nukulau in the Fiji Islands to obtain redress for damages to American citizens.

September 22.   A landing party from the *John Adams* seizes the native king of Viti Levu, Fiji Islands, and carries him back to the ship, where he is compelled to sign a treaty promising to compensate American citizens for the damage or destruction of their property.

October 28–31.   Returning to Viti Levu, Commander Boutwell finds that the Fijian king has not honored the treaty made the preceding month. The *John Adams* then lands a party of sailors and marines under Lieutenant Louis C. Sartori that burns three native villages at a cost of one man killed and three wounded.

November 27.   A detachment of 100 seamen and marines under Lieutenant Augustus S. Nicholson from the sloop *Germantown* joins landing parties from three other navies to guard the foreign consulates and customs house during an insurrection at Montevideo, Uruguay.

1856

January 26.   Fire support and a small landing party from the sloop *Decatur*, 14, Commander Guert Gansevoort, help the settlers of Seattle, Washington, repel an attack by 1,000 hostile Indians.

September 20.   The frigate *Independence*, 54, and sloop *St. Mary's*, 20, land a party of 160 sailors and marines under Captain Addison Garland, USMC, to protect American citizens during a period of disturbances at Panama City, in the Colombian province of Panama.

October 23.   A landing party of 150 men from the sloops *Portsmouth*, 20, and *Levant*, 22, goes ashore to protect American lives and property at Canton, China.

November 15–16.   The Chinese Barrier Forts commanding the Pearl River below Canton fire on U.S. vessels that have come to withdraw the detachment landed in October.

November 20–22.   **The Barrier Forts.** Following orders from Commodore James Armstrong, the ailing commander of the East India Squadron, Commander Andrew H. Foote lands with 287 seamen and marines to storm the Barrier Forts. In three days' fighting the landing party, supported by fire from the sloops *Levant* and *Portsmouth*, captures four modern forts mounting 170 guns, plus a six-gun battery, and repulses counterattacks from two Chinese columns, the first with an estimated strength of 2,000, the second of 4,000. All of the captured fortifications and cannons are de-

stroyed. American casualties number 42; approximately 400 Chinese are killed.

1857

March 7.   Isaac Toucey enters office as 23rd secretary of the navy.

September 15.   Captain George S. Blake becomes the fifth superintendent of the Naval Academy.

1858

January 2.   The marine detachment of the frigate *St. Lawrence* is landed to safeguard Americans during disturbances at Montevideo, Uruguay.

July 29.   **First Atlantic cable.** The steam frigate *Niagara*, Captain William L. Hudson, and HMS *Agamemnon* cooperate to lay a telegraph cable across the Atlantic. The work is completed on August 5 and the first message, from Queen Victoria to President James Buchanan, is sent on August 16. The cable fails weeks later, but the practicality of the project has been established, and a permanent cable will be laid by the giant British steamer *Great Eastern* in 1866.

October 6.   A punitive expedition of 44 men under Lieutenant C.H.B. Caldwell from the ship sloop *Vandalia*, 18, destroys a village on the island of Waya in the Fijis in retribution for the murder of two American traders.

October 17.   The largest U.S. naval squadron ever assembled, 19 ships under Flag Officer William B. Shubrick, commander of the Brazil Squadron, sails to obtain satisfaction from Paraguay for firing on the survey vessel *Water Witch* in the Paraguay River in February 1855. Schubrick performs his mission with great success. Entering the La Plata on January 25, 1859, he quickly secures an indemnity for the attack on the *Water Witch* and concludes a new commercial treaty with Paraguay.

1859

January 6.   Colonel Archibald Henderson dies after 39 years as commandant of the marine

The *Portsmouth* begins the bombardment of the Barrier Forts near Canton: a contemporary lithograph (undated). Courtesy Beverley R. Robinson Collection, U.S. Naval Academy Museum.

corps. He is succeeded by 66-year-old Lieutenant Colonel John Harris, a veteran of the War of 1812.

April 21.   At the mouth of the Congo, the ship sloop *Marion,* 16, Commander F.W. Blunt, captures the first of the five slavers that will be taken by U.S. naval vessels in the course of the year.

June 25.   **"Blood is thicker than water."** Britain and France are engaged in the Second Opium War with China. Commodore Josiah Tattnall, commander of the U.S. East India Squadron, is aboard the chartered steamer *Toey-Wan* when gunboats of the Royal Navy begin to remove obstructions the Chinese have placed at the mouth of Pei-Ho River. Seeing the British come under heavy fire from the Taku forts, Tattnall takes a boat party to the British flagship to help out, remarking, "Blood is thicker than water." One American seaman is killed, and an officer is wounded in the action. Later Tattnall uses the *Toey-Wan* to tow British reinforcements forward. The U.S. government subsequently approves his initiative.

July 31.   At the request of the U.S. consul, Captain William C. Nicholson lands a party from the side-wheel steamer *Mississippi,* 10, to protect American lives and property at Shanghai, China.

October 16–18.   **John Brown's Raid.** The fanatical abolitionist John Brown seizes the U.S. arsenal at Harper's Ferry, West Virginia, in hopes of igniting a slave uprising. The uprising does not occur, but several hos-

Commodore Josiah Tattnall: a woodcut from *Harper's Weekly* for October 22, 1859. Courtesy U.S. Naval Academy Museum.

tages are taken, and eight of Brown's men and a number of townsfolk are killed or mortally wounded in exchanges of fire. The first U.S. troops to reach the scene are a company of 86 marines sent from Washington under Lieutenant Israel Greene; they arrive shortly before midnight on October 17. The next morning army Colonel Rob-

U.S. Marines storming the engine house held by John Brown's raiders at Harper's Ferry, West Virginia: a contemporary woodcut from *Harper's Weekly*. Defense Department photo (U.S. Marine Corps).

ert E. Lee, to whom the suppression of the insurrection is entrusted, sends Lieutenant J.E.B. Stuart to demand the raiders' surrender. Upon Brown's refusal, a storming party of 26 marines breaks into the arsenal. Two of the raiders are bayoneted, Brown is wounded by a slash from Lieutenant Greene's saber, and five others are captured. One marine is killed and another wounded.

1860

February 6. **Antislavery operations.** Beginning on this date, in the course of the year U.S. naval vessels capture 13 slave ships.

March 1–2, 4.   A party of 50 seamen and marines from the ship sloop *Marion,* 16, Commander Thomas W. Brent, is landed to protect American property at Kissembo, in present-day Angola.

September 25.   The ship sloop *Levant,* 22, Commander William E. Hunt, sails from Hilo, Hawaii, bound for Aspinwall, Colombia, and disappears somewhere en route.

September 27.   The sloop *St. Mary's*, 20, lands a party of marines to help quell an insurrection in Panama City, Colombia (present-day Panama). A detachment from HMS *Clio* soon follows.

November 1.   Plans are announced to convert

seven of the navy's sailing ships to steam power. The cost of the conversion will be $3,064,000.

November 6. **Abraham Lincoln is elected president.** He has been viewed as the abolitionist candidate. Many Southerners regard his election as a sign that the time has come for their states to leave the Union.

December 20.   South Carolina becomes the first state to secede from the United States. Six other states of the Deep South follow by February 1, 1861.

December 26.   Major Robert Anderson, USA, commanding the defenses at Charleston, South Carolina, evacuates Fort Moultrie and moves his forces to Fort Sumter, on an island in the harbor.

1861

January 9.   At Charleston, South Carolina forces, including cadets from The Citadel, fire on the chartered steamer *Star of the West* as she attempts to enter the harbor carrying reinforcements and supplies for Fort Sumter. The vessel returns to New York.

January 10.   At Pensacola, Florida, Lieutenant Adam J. Slemmer, commanding Company G, 1st U.S. Artillery, transfers his men from the mainland to Fort Pickens, on Santa Rosa Island. Although the navy yard is soon occupied by Southern troops, Pickens remains in Union hands.

January 14.   The South Carolina legislature announces that any attempt to reinforce Fort Sumter will be regarded as an act of war.

February 8.   **The Confederacy is formed.** In Montgomery, Alabama, representatives of the seceded states adopt a constitution for the Confederate States of America.

February 9.   Jefferson Davis of Mississippi is chosen to be president of the provisional government of the Confederate States.

February 20.   The Confederate States Navy Department is established.

February 21.   Stephen R. Mallory of Florida, formerly chairman of the U.S. House Naval Affairs Committee, is appointed secretary of the navy of the Confederate States.

February 27.   Congress approves the construction of seven steam sloops.

March 7.   Gideon Welles, a newspaper editor from

Hartford, Connecticut, assumes office as the 24th secretary of the navy.

April 11.   Major Robert Anderson, USA, refuses a demand by General P.G.T. Beauregard, commanding Confederate forces at Charleston, South Carolina, to evacuate Fort Sumter.

April 12.   **First shots of the Civil War.** The Confederate batteries around Charleston Harbor open fire on Fort Sumter. Later in the day an expedition consisting of the steamship *Baltic,* USS *Pawnee,* and revenue cutter *Harriet Lane* under the command of Gustavus V. Fox, a former naval officer acting under special authority from the president, arrives off the harbor to reinforce Sumter, but it is too late.

April 13.   Major Anderson surrenders Fort Sumter. His garrison is evacuated by Fox's ships.

April 15.   President Lincoln calls for 75,000 90-day volunteers.

April 17.   Virginia casts her lot with the Confederacy.

April 17.   President Davis invites all interested parties to apply for letters of marque and reprisal.

April 19.   **The Blockade.** President Lincoln proclaims a blockade of the Confederate coast from Texas to South Carolina.

April 20.   **Seizure of the Norfolk Navy Yard.** Due in part to the lack of energy of its elderly commander, Captain Charles S. McCauley, Virginia forces seize this important installation almost intact. An expedition sent from Washington under the command of Captain Hiram Paulding on April 18 manages to burn nine of the vessels in the yard, tow away the sloop *Cumberland,* 32, and set fire to the facilities, but the Southern troops who burst into the yard upon its evacuation extinguish the flames. The dry dock and ordnance workshops are major gains to the Confederacy, as are hundreds of captured cannons that will soon be mounted in fortifications up and down the Atlantic coast. The Confederates are also successful in raising the screw frigate *Merrimack,* which had been burned to the waterline and sunk.

April 24.   **The Naval Academy leaves Annapolis.** Fearing that Maryland secessionists plan to attack the academy, Captain George S. Blake embarks the faculty and

midshipmen on the frigate *Constitution* and sails to New York. On May 9, the academy relocates at Newport, Rhode Island, where it will remain throughout the war. In Annapolis the academy yard is transformed into an army hospital.

April 27.   President Lincoln extends the blockade to include the coasts of North Carolina and Virginia.

May 2–3.   **The Anaconda Plan.** In letters to President Lincoln and General George B. McClellan, General Winfield Scott outlines a plan for "a complete blockade" of the Confederate coast and a "powerful movement down the Mississippi . . . so as to envelop the insurgent states." Coupled with army offensives on the Southern land frontier, this strategy—soon dubbed the Anaconda Plan—will be pursued through the four years of war to final victory.

May 3.   President Lincoln calls for the enlistment of 18,000 seamen.

May 6.   **Confederate privateering.** The Confederate Congress authorizes the issue of letters of marque and reprisal. Few Southern privateers ever put to sea, however, as blockade running offers greater profits at lesser risks; the Confederate war on Union shipping is waged almost exclusively by government cruisers.

May 6.   Arkansas leaves the Union.

May 7.   Tennessee indirectly withdraws from the Union by making an alliance with the Confederacy.

May 9.   **Bulloch to England.** Commander James D. Bulloch, CSN, is sent to England by Secretary Mallory to purchase and outfit the warships the Confederacy cannot build for herself. Because of neutrality laws, these purchases must be disguised. For almost four years Bulloch wages a brilliant battle of wits with U.S. Ambassador Charles Francis Adams. Although his plans to procure European-built ironclads are finally frustrated, the cruisers he commissions— the *Alabama,* the *Florida,* and the *Shenandoah*—sweep the Northern merchant marine from the seas.

May 10.   In a letter to the Committee on Naval Affairs of the Confederate Congress, Secretary Mallory calls for the construction of "an iron-armored ship as a matter of the first necessity."

May 10. The blockade of Charleston, South Carolina, is established by the screw frigate *Niagara,* Captain William W. McKean.

May 13. The blockade of Pensacola, Florida, is established by the frigate *Sabine,* Captain N.S. Adams.

May 20. North Carolina secedes from the Union.

May 24. **Capture of Alexandria.** Commander Stephen C. Rowan, captain of the screw sloop *Pawnee,* commands an expedition, embarked at the Washington Navy Yard, which occupies Alexandria, Virginia.

May 26. The blockade of New Orleans, Louisiana, and the mouth of the Mississippi is established by the screw sloop *Brooklyn,* Commander Charles H. Poor.

May 26. The blockade of Mobile, Alabama, is established by the side-wheel steamer *Powhatan,* Lieutenant David Dixon Porter.

May 29. The blockade of Savannah, Georgia, is established by the steamer *Union,* Commander John R. Goldsborough.

June 10. **Work begins on the CSS Virginia.** At Norfolk, Lieutenant John M. Brooke, CSN, is placed in charge of converting the former wooden frigate *Merrimack,* which was raised on May 30, into the ironclad ram *Virginia.*

June 27. **First naval officer killed in the war.** Union vessels on the Potomac have been engaging Confederate batteries on the Virginia shore since April. Commander James H. Ward, first commandant of midshipmen at the Naval Academy, becomes the first U.S. Navy officer killed in the Civil

War when he is picked off by a Confederate sharpshooter during an engagement at Mathias Point, Virginia.

June 27. **Blockade Strategy Board.** A board is convened to consider the implementation of the blockade and the seizure of advanced bases on the Confederate coast. It consists of Captain Samuel F. Du Pont, Commander Charles H. Davis, Major John G. Barnard of the army corps of engineers, and Professor Alexander D. Bache, superintendent of the coast survey.

June 28–29. **Capture of the St. Nicholas.** Confederates led by Captain George N. Hollins, CSN, and Colonel Richard Thomas, CSA, capture the passenger steamer *St. Nicholas,* which they have boarded disguised as passengers on her regular route from Baltimore to Georgetown, District of Columbia. They had hoped to encounter the screw sloop *Pawnee* in the Potomac, but are unable to locate her and put into the Chesapeake Bay, where they capture three merchant vessels.

June 30–January 18, 1862. **Cruise of the CSS Sumter.** Sailing from New Orleans, the screw steamer *Sumter* slips past the blockader *Brooklyn* at the mouth of the Mississippi and begins her career as a commerce destroyer under the command of the redoubtable Raphael Semmes. In six months she takes 18 prizes. Her cruise ends at Gibraltar, where Semmes is unable to obtain coal. The *Sumter* is soon blockaded by three Union vessels and in April 1862 Semmes

The CSS *Virginia:* a possibly contemporary out-board profile discovered in the files of the old Bureau of Construction and Repair, now in the National Archives. Official U.S. Navy photograph.

lays her up. He and his men receive the thanks of the Confederate Congress.

July 2.   The blockade of Galveston, Texas, is established by the screw steamer *South Carolina*, Commander James Alden.

July 8.   **First Confederate mines.** The screw tug *Resolute* picks up two floating "torpedoes"—mines—in the Potomac. In the course of the conflict the Confederates will show great resourcefulness in the development of this new type of naval weapon. More than 40 Union warships will be sunk or damaged by Confederate mines.

July 14.   The blockade of Wilmington, North Carolina, is established by the screw steamer *Daylight*, Commander Samuel Lockwood.

July 21.   **Battle of Bull Run.** Northern hopes for a short war evaporate when the Union army of General Irwin McDowell is defeated in the first major battle of the war. A detachment of U.S. Marines commanded by Major John Reynolds is present; 9 are killed, 19 wounded, and 16 missing. Union and Confederate naval batteries are also engaged, the former of which loses two guns.

July 24.   Congress passes an act "for the temporary increase of the navy" authorizing President Lincoln to expand the service by whatever extent appears necessary.

August 1.   Gustavus V. Fox, a former naval officer who had commanded the expedition to relieve Fort Sumter, is appointed assistant secretary of the navy. The legislation creating this position had been passed on July 24.

August 3.   **First "navy air."** The navy has its first experience with aeronautics when John La Mountain ascends in a captive balloon from the U.S. steamer *Fanny* to observe the Confederate batteries at Sewell's Point, Virginia, near Hampton Roads.

August 3.   **Ironclad Board.** Congress appropriates $1.5 million for the construction of iron- or steel-clad ships and appoints an Ironclad Board of three officers to evaluate designs.

August 7.   **Eads's Turtles.** James B. Eads of St. Louis is given a contract by the war department to build seven shallow-draft, ironclad gunboats for service on western waters. These vessels—the *Cairo, Carondelet, Cincinnati, Louisville, Mound City,*

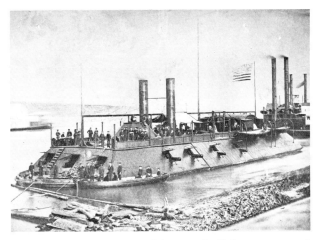

The gunboat *Cairo*, one of the "turtles" that penetrated the Confederacy's waterways. She was sunk by a mine on December 12, 1862. Courtesy Library of Congress.

Pittsburgh, and *St. Louis*—form the core of the gunboat flotilla that supports the Union army in breaching the defenses of the central Confederacy. Because of their humpbacked silhouettes, they are often referred to as "Eads's Turtles" or "Pooks's Turtles," after Constructor Samuel M. Pooks, USN, is responsible for their design.

August 28–29.   **Hatteras Expedition.** Confederate Forts Hatteras and Clark defending strategic Hatteras Inlet, North Carolina, are captured by a joint army-navy expedition consisting of 8 warships commanded by Flag Officer Silas H. Stringham and 2 transports carrying 900 troops under Major General Benjamin F. Butler. In addition to depriving the blockade runners of the most convenient entrance to Pamlico Sound, the occupation of this point provides the blockading squadrons with an advanced base. This is the first amphibious operation of the Civil War.

September 6.   **Capture of Paducah and Smithland.** In Kentucky, the gunboats *Tyler*, Commander John Rodgers, and *Lexington*, Commander Roger Stembel, support General U.S. Grant in the seizure of these strategic locations at the mouths of the Tennessee and Cumberland rivers.

September 14.   At Pensacola, Florida, a party of 100 men in four boats from the screw frigate *Colorado*, under the command of Lieu-

The second day's action at Hatteras Inlet; from left to right, the *Susquehanna, Cumberland, Minnesota,* and *Wabash.* A drawing by eyewitness Alfred R. Waud, a war artist for *Harper's Weekly.* Courtesy Library of Congress.

tenant John H. Russell, destroy the Confederate schooner *Judah.*

September 16.   In a report to Secretary Welles, the Ironclad Board enthusiastically endorses the concept of ironclad vessels and recommends the construction of designs it has considered for the *Monitor,* the *New Ironsides,* and the *Galena.*

October 1.   In Pamlico Sound, North Carolina, three small Confederate gunboats commanded by Flag Officer William F. Lynch capture the U.S. steamer *Fanny* with a detachment of troops aboard.

October 12.   **Action at Head of Passes.** A Confederate force consisting of the lightly armored ram *Manassas* and the armed steamers *Ivy* and *James L. Day* sails from New Orleans under the command of Commodore George N. Hollins, CSN, to surprise the Union blockading squadron near Head of Passes on the Mississippi. The latter consists of the steam sloop *Richmond,* sloops *Preble* and *Vincennes,* gunboat *Water Witch,* and storeship *Nightingale.* In a hot action, the *Manassas* rams the *Richmond,* which runs aground, as does the *Vincennes.* The Confederates then withdraw.

October 25.   **Work begins on the Monitor.** At Greenpoint, New York, the brilliant, Swedish-born engineer John Ericsson commences construction of his revolutionary ironclad.

November 7.   **Capture of Port Royal Sound.** The largest fleet yet assembled under the U.S. flag, 77 vessels, is put under the command of Flag Officer Samuel F. Du Pont to seize an advanced base for the Atlantic blockading squadrons at Port Royal Sound,

South Carolina, midway between Charleston and Savannah. It is accompanied by an army expeditionary force of 16,000 men under Brigadier General Thomas W. Sherman. The fire from Du Pont's ships forces the Confederates to evacuate Forts Walker and Beauregard, whose garrisons are ferried to the mainland by Commodore Josiah Tattnall's little Confederate squadron. U.S. forces land unopposed.

November 8.   **Trent Affair.** The screw frigate *San Jacinto,* Captain Charles Wilkes, stops the British mail steamer *Trent* in Old Bahama Channel and seizes James Mason and John Slidell, the Confederate envoys to Great Britain and France. Wilkes's action precipitates a major international incident. On December 27, Secretary of State Seward apologizes to Her Majesty's Government for Wilkes's conduct and orders the envoys released.

November 11.   Another aerial reconnaissance is made from shipboard when "aeronaut" Professor Thaddeus Lowe ascends in a captive balloon from the "balloon boat" *G.W. Parke Custis* in the Potomac River.

December 2.   Secretary Welles advises President Lincoln that since the establishment of the blockade the navy has captured 153 vessels.

December 17.   **Stone Fleets.** Seven old vessels laden with stones and concrete are sunk by the blockading squadron at the entrance to Savannah harbor in an attempt to impede navigation. "Stone Fleets" will be sunk at various other places and times in the course of the war by both Union and Confederate forces with the aim of preventing one another from getting in or out of particular ports or rivers. They are not especially effective.

December 21. **Medal of Honor.** Congress creates the Navy Medal of Honor to reward petty officers, seamen, and marines "as shall most distinguish themselves by their gallantry in action and other seamanlike qualities." Commissioned officers will not become eligible until 1915. A total of 375 medals are awarded for the Civil War. The Army Medal of Honor is instituted six months later, on July 12, 1862.

1862

January 9. Flag Officer David G. Farragut is assigned to command the West Gulf Blockading Squadron. His appointment reflects the government's decision that he is the man to carry out the single most important naval operation undertaken so far in the war: an attack on New Orleans, the South's largest city and principal seaport.

January 16. The Eads gunboats are commissioned.

February 4–6. **Capture of Fort Henry.** The defenses of the central Confederacy extend from the Mississippi to the Appalachians. The keys to the center of this position are Forts Henry and Donelson, which command the Tennessee and Cumberland rivers, respectively. Plans for a joint, army-navy attack on the forts by forces under General U.S. Grant and Flag Officer Andrew H. Foote are frustrated when rains delay Grant's advance and Foote decides to tackle Fort Henry with his ships alone. The attack is led by the ironclads *Carondelet*, *Cincinnati*, *Essex* (which is disabled during the action), and *St. Louis*, supported by the wooden gunboats *Conestoga*, *Lexington*, and *Tyler*. Their fire is so effective that all but four of the fort's guns are dismounted and its commander, Brigadier General Lloyd Tilghman, CSA, surrenders the position.

February 7–8. **Capture of Roanoke Island.** An army-navy expedition under Brigadier General Ambrose E. Burnside and Flag Officer Louis M. Goldsborough overwhelms the Confederate defenders to take Roanoke Island, on Albemarle Sound,

North Carolina. This victory completes the Union hold on the Carolina sounds.

February 10. **Battle of Elizabeth City.** Following the capture of Roanoke Island, the small Confederate squadron on Albemarle Sound—five "cottonclad" gunboats under Flag Officer William F. Lynch—withdrew up the Pasquotank River to Elizabeth City, North Carolina. There it is destroyed by a superior Union force under Commander Stephen C. Rowan.

February 14. **Attack on Fort Donelson.** In Tennessee the gunboats of Flag Officer Foote's flotilla cooperate with land forces under General U.S. Grant in operations against Fort Donelson, commanding the Cumberland River. In a sharp action, the flagship *St. Louis* and the *Louisville* are disabled, and Foote receives a wound from the lingering effects of which he will die in June 1863. The continued presence of the gunboats on the river greatly restricts the Confederates' freedom of action, however, and the fort surrenders to Grant's army on February 16. The loss of Forts Henry and Donelson opens western Tennessee to invasion and compels Confederate General Albert Sidney Johnson to withdraw from Kentucky.

February 17. At Norfolk, Virginia, the ironclad ram CSS *Virginia* is commissioned under the command of Captain Franklin Buchanan.

February 25. At New York, the USS *Monitor* is commissioned under the command of Lieutenant John L. Worden.

March 8. **Battle of Hampton Roads.** Accompanied by two small gunboats, the Confederate ironclad *Virginia* attacks the Union blockading squadron at Hampton Roads, Virginia. After ramming and sinking the sloop *Cumberland*, 32, Lieutenant George U. Morris, she attacks the frigate *Congress*, 52, Lieutenant Joseph B. Smith, which runs aground and is destroyed by the *Virginia*'s incendiary shells. Captain Buchanan is wounded in the course of the action, and the *Virginia*, which left part of her ram in the *Cumberland*, returns to Norfolk for repairs. For a few hours it appears that the South may be in possession of a means to break the blockade, but the *Monitor* reaches Hampton Roads that evening.

The CSS *Virginia* rams the *Cumberland*, whose crew's washing still hangs on the lines: a painting by Alexander C. Stuart. U.S. Marine Corps photograph.

The second day at Hampton Roads: the *Monitor* and the *Virginia* (ex-*Merrimack*) fight to a draw. This Currier & Ives lithograph was published in New York in 1862. Courtesy Beverley R. Robinson Collection, U.S. Naval Academy Museum.

March 9. **First battle between ironclads.** Returning to Hampton Roads to complete her work of destruction, the CSS *Virginia*, now commanded by Lieutenant Catesby ap R. Jones, is confronted by Lieutenant Worden's *Monitor*. The ensuing action, fought at close ranges over a period of four hours, ends in a draw. Strategically, too, the honors are even. The *Monitor* has preserved the blockade, but the *Virginia* prevents the McClellan's army from using the James River in its upcoming Peninsula Campaign.

March 13. Confederate forces evacuate New Madrid, Missouri, covered by three gunboats of Flag Officer George N. Hollins's squadron.

March 14. **Capture of New Bern.** Thirteen warships under Commander Stephen C. Rowan provide gunfire support for a force of 12,000 men under Brigadier General Ambrose E. Burnside in the seizure of New Bern, on the Neuse River in North Carolina.

March 16–April 7. **Struggle for Island No. 10.** Following the fall of Forts Henry and Donelson, the South sought to establish a western anchor for the defense of the central Confederacy by fortifying a large, wooded island in the Mississippi River on the northern border of Tennessee. The gunboats and mortar boats of Flag Officer Foote's flotilla engage the Confederate batteries there, but are unable to silence them. Then, on the stormy night of April 5, the ironclad *Carondelet*, Commander Henry W. Walke, runs the gauntlet past the island. The ironclad *Pittsburgh*, Commander Egbert Thompson, duplicates this feat on April 7. That same day they cover a Union army that crosses the river to the east to operate against Island No. 10. Confederate Brigadier General William W. Mackall thereupon surrenders the position and its defenders—more than 5,000 men and 20 pieces of heavy artillery.

March 22. The Confederacy's first British-built cruiser, the CSS *Florida*, sails under the command of Acting Master John Low from Liverpool for the Bahamas, where she will receive her guns. Her cover name is the *Oreto*.

March 28. **The America.** A boat party under Lieutenant Thomas F. Stevens returns to Jacksonville, Florida, after an expedition up the St. John's River, during which it has raised the famous racing yacht *America* (CSS *Memphis*). Purchased by the Confederacy from an English sympathizer for use as a commerce raider, she had been scuttled when Union forces trapped her in the river. She is taken into the U.S. Navy under her original name.

April 6. **Battle of Shiloh.** Confederate forces led by General Albert Sidney Johnson surprise Grant's army at Pittsburg Landing (Shiloh), Tennessee, and threaten to push it into the Tennessee River. Fire from the gunboats *Lexington*, Lieutenant James W. Shirk, and *Tyler*, Lieutenant William Gwin, is instrumental in stemming the Confederate advance.

April 14. On the upper Mississippi, Flag Officer Foote's mortar boats begin bombarding Fort Pillow, Tennessee, the next Confederate stronghold below Island No. 10.

April 18. **Beginning of the battle for New Orleans.** A flotilla of Union mortar boats under Commander David Dixon Porter begins to bombard Fort Jackson, on the Mississippi River below New Orleans.

April 20. In an effort to prevent Union forces from ascending the Mississippi, the Confederates have stretched an obstruction, consisting of hulks linked together by a huge chain, across the river under the guns of Forts Jackson and St. Philip. It is breached by the gunboats *Itasca* and *Pinola*, both under the orders of Captain Henry H. Bell.

April 24. **The Battle of New Orleans.** Concluding that the bombardment of Fort Jackson is getting nowhere, Flag Officer Farragut resolves to lead his fleet—17 vessels, all wooden, plus Porter's mortar schooners—upstream between the Confederate fortifications. The movement begins at 2:00 A.M. Miraculously, not a single one of Farragut's ships is disabled by the forts' fire. Upriver, a fierce, confused action is fought with Commander John K. Mitchell's Confederate flotilla, consisting of the thin-skinned ironclad ram *Manassas*, the gunboats *McRae* and *Jackson*, two armed launches, the Louisiana State gunboats *General Quitman* and *Governor Moore*, and six River Defense gunboats mounting 1 or

Flag Officer and soon-to-be Rear Admiral David G. Farragut still wears a captain's uniform in this *carte de visite* photograph made in New Orleans in 1862. Courtesy U.S. Naval Academy Museum.

2 guns apiece. The screw sloop *Varuna*, 10, Commander Charles S. Boggs, is rammed and sunk by the *Governor Moore*, 2, Lieutenant Beverley Kennon, and the *Stonewall Jackson*, 1, Captain George W. Philips, but she is the only Union ship lost. The Confederate forces are annihilated. The total number of Union casualties for the operations of April 18–26 is 39 men killed and 171 wounded.

April 25.   The city of New Orleans surrenders to Farragut. Its loss is the greatest blow the Confederacy has suffered. The unfinished ironclad *Mississippi*, the most powerful vessel ever put under construction in the Confederate States, is destroyed to prevent her capture.

April 26.   Am amphibious operation under Commander Samuel Lockwood and Brigadier General John G. Parke captures Fort Macon, North Carolina.

April 28.   The defenders of Forts Jackson and St. Philip, isolated by the capture of New Orleans, surrender to Farragut's fleet. The unfinished ironclad *Louisiana* is destroyed to prevent her capture, as are the CSS *Defiance* and *McRae*.

May 10.   Union forces capture Norfolk, Virginia, and reoccupy the Norfolk Navy Yard.

May 10.   Stunned by the news of Farragut's success in passing Forts Jackson and St. Philip, the Confederates evacuate Pensacola, Florida. It is promptly occupied by Union forces.

May 10.   **Action at Plum Point Bend.** Captain James E. Montgomery leads his Confederate River Defense Fleet of eight cotton-clad gunboats in a spirited attack on the Union gunboats and mortar schooners bombarding Fort Pillow on the Mississippi River. The CSS *General Bragg* rams and sinks the gunboat *Cincinnati*, Commander R. N. Stembel, and the *Mound City*, Commander A. H. Kilty, is rammed by the CSS *General Earl Van Dorn*, Captain Isaac D. Fulkerson, and runs aground to keep from sinking. The Confederates then return to Fort Pillow.

May 11.   **Destruction of the CSS Virginia.** The fall of Norfolk seals the fate of the Confederate ironclad. Finding that the vessel draws too much water to retire up the James River, Flag Officer Josiah Tattnall, who has replaced the wounded Buchanan, reluctantly orders her to be blown up.

May 15.   On the James River, Virginia, a Union squadron consisting of the *Monitor*, the ironclads *Galena* and *Naugatuck*, and the wooden gunboats *Aroostook* and *Port Royal* under the command of Commander John Rodgers pushes upstream to within eight miles of Richmond before being halted by Confederate batteries at Drewry's Bluff.

June 4–5.   Hammered by the fire of Union vessels on the Mississippi, Confederate forces evacuate Fort Pillow, the last fortification above Memphis, Tennessee.

June 6.   **Battle of Memphis.** Captain J. E. Montgomery's Confederate River Defense

The Battle of Memphis: a contemporary lithograph by Currier & Ives. Official U.S. Navy photograph.

Fleet is destroyed in a sharp, close action with the ironclad gunboats *Benton*, *Cairo*, *Carondelet*, *Louisville*, and *St. Louis*, Captain Charles H. Davis, and the rams *Monarch* and *Queen of the West*, Colonel Charles Ellet, Jr. The Confederate ships *General Beauregard*, *General Bragg*, *General M. Jeff Thompson*, *General Sterling Price*, *General Sumter*, and *Little Rebel* are captured, grounded, or sunk; only the *General Earl Van Dorn* escapes. Colonel Ellet is mortally wounded. Memphis surrenders to Davis, opening the Mississippi all the way to Vicksburg.

June 28.   Flag Officer Farragut's fleet runs past the batteries at Vicksburg, the last great Confederate bastion on the Mississippi.

July 1.   Farragut's fleet meets the Western Gunboat Flotilla of newly promoted Flag Officer Charles H. Davis above Vicksburg.

July 1.   **Malvern Hill.** In April General George B. McClellan exploited Union command of the sea to land the Army of the Potomac on the tip of the peninsula between the James and York rivers and launched an advance on Richmond from the rear. Defeated in a series of battles on the outskirts of Richmond by General Robert E. Lee, who had just assumed command of the Army of Northern Virginia, late in June McClellan begins to withdraw towards the James. Lee makes several unsuccessful attempts to intercept his retreat, the last at Malvern Hill on the bank of the river. Here the ironclad *Galena* and the gunboats *Aroostook* and *Jacob Bell* are able to enfilade the right flank of the Confederate line, materially contributing to the repulse of Lee's attack.

July 4.   The Confederate minelayer and balloon ship *Teaser*, Lieutenant Hunter Davidson, is captured by the gunboat *Maratanza*, Lieutenant T. H. Stevens, at Haxall's on the James River, Virginia. Her crew escapes ashore.

July 5.   **Bureau system reorganized.** The number of the Navy Department's bureaus is increased to eight by the creation of bureaus of Equipment and Recruiting, Navigation, and Steam Engineering.

July 14.   Congress abolishes the navy's daily spirit ration to enlisted men.

July 15.   **The Arkansas.** On a reconnaissance up the Yazoo River, Mississippi, the gunboats *Carondelet*, Commander Henry W. Walke, and *Tyler*, Lieutenant William Gwin, and the ram *Queen of the West* are met by the new Confederate ironclad ram *Arkansas*, Lieutenant Isaac N. Brown. The *Arkansas* pursues the three ships into the Mississippi, heavily damaging the *Carondelet* and *Tyler*, and proceeds to run through Farragut's fleet to take refuge beneath the guns of Vicksburg.

July 16.   **First rear admiral.** Congress creates the rank of rear admiral and first confers it on David Glasgow Farragut as a reward for the capture of New Orleans. The act also establishes the ranks of commodore and lieutenant commander.

July 19.   **Pension bill.** Congress provides that all naval personnel disabled in the line of duty will be granted lifetime pensions.

July 22.   Anchored beneath the guns of Vicksburg, the Confederate ironclad ram *Arkansas*, Commander Isaac N. Brown, fights off an attack by the ironclad *Essex*, Commander William B. ("Dirty Bill") Porter, and the ram *Queen of the West*, Lieutenant Colonel Alfred W. Ellet.

July 24.   Falling water forces Farragut's fleet to pull back downstream to Baton Rouge and New Orleans.

August 6.   **Destruction of the Arkansas.** Confederate Major General Earl Van Dorn orders Lieutenant Henry Stevens, temporarily commanding the ironclad ram *Arkansas* while Commander Brown is on sick leave, to support an attack on Baton Rouge, Louisiana. The ram's engines break down during an engagement with Commander W. B. Porter's ironclad *Essex*, and Lieutenant Stevens sets his ship afire to prevent her from being captured.

August 10.   At a secret rendezvous at Green Cay in the Bahamas, the cruiser *Florida* is armed and commissioned into Confederate service by Lieutenant John N. Maffit. She is the first of the Confederate cruisers Commander Bulloch has had built in England.

August 24–June 19, 1864.   **Cruise of the Alabama.** CSS *Alabama*, another of Commander Bulloch's British-built cruisers, is commissioned off Terceira, Azores, by Captain Raphael Semmes. She will become the most successful commerce raider of all time, capturing 68 merchantmen valued at more than $15,500,000 and sinking 1 warship on a cruise that lasts for 22 months and extends from the Gulf of Mexico to the China Sea.

August 26.   Captain Franklin Buchanan is promoted to become the first rear admiral in the Confederate States Navy.

September 4.   The CSS *Florida*, Lieutenant John N. Maffit, runs the blockade into Mobile Bay after yellow fever breaks out on board.

October 1.   The army's Western Gunboat Fleet is transferred to the Navy Department and renamed the Mississippi Squadron. Upon the recommendation of Farragut, who found Rear Admiral Charles H. Davis deficient in energy, Acting Rear Admiral David Dixon Porter is placed in command.

October 3–9.   The defenses and city of Galveston, Texas, are bombarded and captured by naval forces under Commander William B. Renshaw, consisting of the wooden gunboats *Clifton*, *Harriet Lane*, *Owasco*, and *Westfield* and the mortar schooner *Henry James*.

October 28.   In the Chesapeake Bay, the ship *Alleghanian* is captured and burned off the mouth of the Rappahannock by a Confederate boat party led by Lieutenant John Taylor Wood, CSN.

October 31.   **Mine warfare.** In the course of the month, Confederates establish a Torpedo Bureau under Brigadier General Gabriel J. Rains and a Naval Submarine Battery Service under Lieutenant Hunter Davidson. Both the "torpedoes" and the "submarine batteries" are what are now called mines. Several Confederate naval officers, most notably Commander Matthew Fontaine Maury, had experimented with mines. Davidson took charge after Maury was sent to Britain to second Commander Bulloch's efforts to buy warships abroad. The Confederates will make extensive use of mines in harbor and river defense.

December 12.   **First ship mined.** The ironclad *Cairo*, Lieutenant Commander Thomas O. Selfridge, Jr., is sunk by a mine in the Yazoo River, Mississippi. She is the first of more than 40 Union vessels that will be destroyed or damaged by mines during the war.

December 20–27.   **Beginning of the Vicksburg campaign.** With Memphis and New Orleans in Northern hands, Vicksburg is the principal Southern stronghold on the Mississippi. To capture it would fulfill one of the objectives of the Anaconda Plan, cutting the Confederacy in two and reopening the Northwest's outlet to the sea. The first advance on the city is made by two Union armies, one moving overland

The Confederate cruiser *Alabama* leaving Port Royal, Jamaica: a woodcut from the *Illustrated London News* for April 11, 1863. U.S. Naval Institute Collection.

under Major General U.S. Grant and the other down the Mississippi under Major General William T. Sherman. It ends in failure when Confederate cavalry destroy the railways and supply depots in Grant's rear (December 20), compelling him to retire, and Vicksburg's defenders repulse Sherman's landing at Chickasaw Bluffs, a few miles north of the city (December 27).

1863

January 1. **Recapture of Galveston.** A Confederate surprise attack by land and sea recaptures Galveston, Texas. The Union naval force anchored off the town consists of the wooden gunboats *Harriet Lane*, *Westfield*, *Clifton*, *Corypheus*, *Owasco*, and *Sachem*, and is under Commander William B. Renshaw. It is engaged by a Confederate flotilla commanded by Major Leon Smith, CSA, composed of the cottonclad gunboats *Bayou City* and *Neptune* and the tenders *John F. Carr* and *Lady Gwin*. The *Harriet Lane*, Commander Jonathan M. Wainwright, sinks the *Neptune*, but is captured by the *Bayou City* in a hard-fought boarding action in which Wainwright is killed. The *Westfield* runs aground. Commander Renshaw sets her afire to keep her

from being captured and is killed when she blows up before his boat party can get clear. The other four Union ships hurriedly put to sea.

January 4–11. **Arkansas Post.** A joint army-navy expedition, 30,000 men under Major General John A. McClernand and six gunboats under Rear Admiral David Dixon Porter, succeeds in the capture of Fort Hindman, at Arkansas Post. The Confederate garrison, 4,700 men commanded by Brigadier General Thomas J. Churchill, CSA, surrenders after a two-day bombardment in which Porter's ships disable every one of the fort's guns.

January 11. The Confederate cruiser *Alabama*, Captain Raphael Semmes, surprises and sinks the side-wheel gunboat *Hatteras*, Lieutenant Commander Homer C. Blake, in a sharp night action 30 miles off Galveston, Texas.

January 16–August 23. **First cruise of the Florida.** The Confederate cruiser *Florida*, Lieutenant John N. Maffit, runs the blockade out of Mobile, Alabama, to begin her career as a commerce raider. Operating primarily in the South Atlantic, she takes 22 prizes before entering port at Brest, France, to refit. It will be six months before she returns to sea.

January 21. At Sabine Pass, Texas, the small

The Confederate cruiser *Florida* at Brest, France: a woodcut from *L'Illustration*, 1863. U.S. Naval Institute Collection.

blockaders *Morning Light*, Acting Master John Dillingham, and *Velocity*, Acting Master Nathan W. Drummond, are captured by the Confederate cottonclads *Josiah Bell* and *Uncle Ben*, under Major Oscar M. Watkins, CSA.

January 30. The gunboat *Isaac Smith*, Acting Lieutenant Francis S. Conover, is captured by Confederate land forces while on a reconnaissance up the Stono River, South Carolina.

January 31. **Charleston sortie.** Flag Officer Duncan N. Ingraham, CSN, leads the ironclad rams *Chicora*, Commander John R. ("Handsome Jack") Tucker, and *Palmetto State*, Lieutenant John Rutledge, on a dawn attack on the blockading fleet off Charleston, South Carolina. The gunboat *Mercedita*, Commander H. S. Stellwagen, is rammed by and surrenders to the *Palmetto State*, while the *Keystone State*, Commander William E. Le Roy, is heavily damaged by the *Chicora*. The blockading squadron retires to the open sea, and Confederate authorities at Charleston try unsuccessfully to persuade the foreign consuls that the blockade has been broken.

February 3–March 17. **Yazoo Pass expedition.** Following the failure of his overland advance on Vicksburg (see December 20–

27, 1862), Grant moves his army down the Mississippi to Milliken's Bend, barely 10 miles above the city. Unusually high water adds to the difficulties of campaigning in the marshy lowlands around Vicksburg, but Grant is determined to retain the initiative. He has already decided that the only way to take the city is from the high ground to its east. His problem is how to get there. First he undertakes to cut a canal across the peninsula opposite the city, which would allow Porter's fleet to move south without having to run past the Vicksburg batteries. This project is finally abandoned on March 29. Simultaneously, two other attempts are made to open a passage south through the bayous west of the Mississippi, and two essentially naval operations are conducted east of the river with the aim of approaching Vicksburg from the north. The first, to which Porter commits eight light-draft gunboats under Lieutenant Commander William Smith, is to move down the Tallahatchie and Yazoo rivers from the Yazoo Pass, 325 miles upstream. To counter this threat, the Confederates hurriedly construct Fort Pemberton, just above the junction of the two rivers. There Smith's gunboats are halted on March 11. They are unable to silence the fort with their fire, and there is no place in the flooded countryside for the troops accompanying them to land. On March 17 the gunboats begin to fall back. By then the Steele's Bayou expedition is under way (see March 14–24).

February 3.   A Confederate attack on Fort Donelson, Tennessee, is repulsed with the help of a squadron of gunboats—the *Brilliant*, *Fairplay*, *Lexington*, *Robb*, *St. Clair*, and *Silver Lake*—under Lieutenant Commander Le Roy Fitch.

February 14.   The ironclad ram *Queen of the West*, Colonel C. R. Ellet, grounds under the fire of three enemy batteries while on a patrol up the Red River, Louisiana. Ellet abandons the ship, which is taken into Confederate service.

February 24.   Major Joseph L. Brent, CSA, leads a squadron consisting of the recently captured ironclad ram *Queen of the West*, the ram *Webb*, and the cottonclad *Beatty* to attack the ironclad *Indianola*, Lieutenant Commander George Brown, near Warrenton, Mississippi. Rammed by the *Queen of the West*, the *Indianola* fills with water, grounds herself, and surrenders. The Confederates immediately begin efforts to refloat her.

February 25.   **Porter's ruse.** The Confederates give up the attempt to salvage the *Indianola* and burn her to the waterline upon the approach of a large Union gunboat. This "gunboat" turns out to be a barge, rigged with dummy stacks, superstructure, and guns, which Admiral Porter sent floating downstream in hopes that it would produce the result it did.

February 28.   The Confederate blockade runner *Rattlesnake* (ex-CSS *Nashville*) is shelled and destroyed under the guns of Fort McAllister, on the Ogeechee River, Georgia, by the monitor *Montauk*, Commander John L. Worden.

March 13–14.   A Confederate night attack on Fort Anderson, on the Neuse River, North Carolina, is beaten off with the help of the gunboats *Ceres*, *Hetzel*, *Hunchback*, and *Shawsheen* and two small craft under Commander Henry K. Davenport.

March 14.   **Farragut at Port Hudson.** Rear Admiral David G. Farragut leads a squadron of seven ships up the Mississippi to estab-

Rear Admiral David Dixon Porter appears as a lieutenant commander in this *carte de visite* photograph made early in 1862. Courtesy U.S. Naval Academy Museum.

lish a blockade at the mouth of the Red River. This force must pass the powerful batteries the Confederates have emplaced at Port Hudson, Louisiana. The veteran side-wheeler *Mississippi*, Captain Melancton Smith, runs aground and is destroyed in the attempt, and several other vessels are damaged. Only Farragut's flagship, the *Hartford*, and the gunboat *Albatross*, which is lashed alongside, succeed in fighting their way through. Continuing upstream to Warrenton, Mississippi (just south of Vicksburg), Farragut establishes communications with Porter on the 20th and then begins to blockade the Red River, from which Confederate trade is entering the Mississippi.

March 14–24.   **Steele's Bayou expedition.** When the Yazoo Pass expedition is halted at Fort Pemberton (see February 3–March 17), Grant asks Porter to make another attempt to reach Vicksburg by the waterways east of the Mississippi, this time by pushing north from Milliken's Bend up Steele's Bayou to enter the Yazoo via Deer Creek, Rolling Fork, and the Sunflower River. Porter himself takes command of the expedition, which consists of the gunboats *Carondelet*, *Cincinnati*, *Louisville*, *Mound City*, and *Pittsburgh*, four mortar schooners and four tugs. Pushing through the tortuous river channels in the face of a resourceful defense, Porter reaches Rolling Fork on March 19. Obstructions in the channel stop the gunboats here, and when the Confederates begin felling trees across the river behind them it appears that they may be trapped. Union infantry, following the ships along the marshy river banks, press forward in a fatiguing night march to reach them on March 21. The expedition then retires.

March 25.   The ironclad ram *Lancaster*, Lieutenant Colonel John A. Ellet, is sunk and her sistership, the *Switzerland*, Colonel C. R. Ellet, is heavily damaged in an attempt to pass the Vicksburg batteries to reinforce Farragut at the Red River.

April 2.   **Final campaign against Vicksburg.** Meeting with Admiral Porter, Grant proposes a new plan of operations against the city. While Sherman distracts the defense by a feint at Haynes's Bluff, north of Vicksburg, Grant's army will march south along the western bank of the Mississippi. At the same time, Porter's fleet and the army's empty transports will run south past the Vicksburg batteries. The two forces will meet at Hard Times, 30 miles below the city, where the transports will carry Grant's men across the river to its eastern shore. This plan will bring victory.

April 7.   **First attack on Charleston.** Rear Admiral Samuel F. Du Pont, commanding the South Atlantic Blockading Squadron, attacks the fortifications of Charleston Harbor with an ironclad squadron of nine ships: the *New Ironsides* (flag) and the monitors *Catskill*, *Keokuk*, *Montauk*, *Nahant*, *Nantucket*, *Passaic*, *Patapsco*, and *Weehawken*. The defenses of Charleston are by far the strongest of any Confederate port, consisting of several forts, some of masonry construction, bolstered by underwater obstacles and large numbers of both contact and electrical mines. Du Pont's ships slug it out with the forts at point-blank range for 50 minutes. Little damage is done to the Confederate works, but the monitors take a hammering. The *Catskill* is hit 20 times; the *Passaic*, 35; the *Nahant*, 36; the

Patapsco, 47; the *Nantucket*, 51; the *Weehawken*, 53; and the *Keokuk*, which sinks the next morning, 90. Du Pont plans to renew the attack the following day, but his captains convince him that no good would come of it. Charleston cannot be captured by ships alone.

April 9–October 28.   **Cruise of the Georgia.** At a secret rendezvous off the coast of France, Commander William L. Maury commissions the former merchantman *Japan* into Southern service as the CSS *Georgia*. The vessel had been purchased in Scotland by Maury's father, Commander Matthew Fontaine Maury. The *Georgia* takes nine prizes on a cruise to the Cape of Good Hope and is sold upon her return to Europe, her sailing characteristics having proven unsuitable for commerce raiding.

April 16–17.   On the Mississippi, Admiral Porter's gunboats and the army's empty transports run south past the Vicksburg batteries under cover of darkness. Despite heavy fire from the bluffs, only one vessel—a transport—is sunk.

April 20.   Land and sea forces cooperate to capture a Confederate redoubt mounting five guns at Hill's Point, on the Nansemond River, Virginia.

April 20.   Confederate defenders of Fort Burton, at Butte à la Rose, Louisiana, surrender after being bombarded by a small naval force headed by the side-wheel *Estrella*, Lieutenant Commander A. P. Cooke.

April 29.   Porter's gunboats engage the Confederate batteries at Grand Gulf, Mississippi, enabling the empty army transports to pass safely in the night.

April 30–May 1.   **Grant crosses the Mississippi.** The transports that Porter has shepherded south ferry Grant's army across the Mississippi from Hard Times to Bruinsburg, 10 miles below Grand Gulf. This movement solves the strategic problem with which Grant has been contending since February. His army is on the east bank of the Mississippi, in position to advance on Vicksburg from the rear.

May 3.   Returning to engage the Confederate positions at Grand Gulf, Porter finds that the garrison, outflanked by Grant's advance, has withdrawn.

May 4.   Admiral Porter pushes up the Red River,

Louisiana, with a force consisting of the ironclads *Arizona*, *Benton*, *Estrella*, *Lafayette*, *Pittsburgh*, and *Switzerland* and the wooden gunboat *General Sterling Price*. Upon his arrival Admiral Farragut, who had been blockading the mouth of the Red River since late March, returns to New Orleans.

May 5.   Porter's squadron reaches Fort De Russy, Louisiana, which the Confederates have evacuated in the face of the Union advance.

May 6.   **"Savez" Read.** Off the coast of Brazil the CSS *Florida* captures the brig *Clarence*, which is commissioned into Confederate service under Lieutenant Charles W. ("Savez") Read, the "anchor man" of the Naval Academy Class of 1860. Commencing his operations off the mid-Atlantic seaboard between June 6–12, Read takes six prizes, to one of which, the bark *Tacony*, he transfers his crew, destroying the *Clarence*. Between June 12–24 he makes another 15 captures and again transfers his crew, this time to the schooner *Archer*, in which he sails into Portland, Maine, with the idea of cutting out the revenue cutter *Caleb Cushing*. The raiders succeed in getting the *Cushing* out of the harbor on the night of June 26–27 but are overtaken by five pursuing steamers the next morning. Read orders his men into the lifeboats and sets fire to the *Cushing*, which blows up just after their capture.

May 7.   Alexandria, Louisiana, is occupied by Porter's squadron.

May 16, 18.   **Grant's advance.** Having brushed away Confederate forces to the east of Vicksburg, Grant turns back towards the city. Lieutenant General John C. Pemberton, commanding the city's defenders, moves to block his advance and is defeated at the battles of Champion's Hill and Big Black River.

May 18.   Admiral Porter sends six gunboats under Lieutenant Commander John Grimes Walker up the Yazoo River to support Grant's army in the operations east of Vicksburg. The force reaches Yazoo City on May 21, compelling the Confederates to destroy three unfinished rams and a well-equipped navy yard.

May 19–July 3.   **Siege of Vicksburg.** After unsuccessful attempts to take Vicksburg by

Lieutenant Charles W. Read, CSN. This "class picture" was made upon his graduation from the U.S. Naval Academy in 1860. He stood last in his class. Nimitz Library Special Collections.

storm on May 19 and 22, Grant settles down to a regular siege. The vessels of Porter's squadron are active throughout the ensuing operations, firing a weekly average of almost 2,000 shells into the city. The gunboat *Cincinnati*, Lieutenant George M. Bache, is sunk in action with the Vicksburg batteries on May 27.

May 27–July 8.   **Siege of Port Hudson.** To the south of Vicksburg, a Union army under Major General Nathaniel P. Banks closes around Port Hudson, Louisiana, the other Confederate strongpoint on the Mississippi. Farragut's ships support the siege, bombarding the city for three to five hours each night.

June 7.   A Confederate attack on Union forces at Milliken's Bend on the Mississippi is repelled with the help of fire support from the ironclad ram *Choctaw*, Lieutenant Commander Francis M. Ramsay, and gunboat *Lexington*, Lieutenant George M. Bache.

June 8.   The steam tug *Boston* is captured at Pass à l'Outre on the Mississippi by a boat party led by Master James Duke, CSN. Putting to sea in their prize, the Confederates capture and burn the barks *Lenox* and *Texana* before running the blockade into Mobile on June 11.

June 17.   The Confederate ironclad ram *Atlanta*, Commander William A. Webb, runs aground and is captured while engaging the monitors *Weehawken*, Captain John Rodgers, and *Nahant*, Commander John Downes, in Wassaw Sound, Georgia.

July 4.   **Vicksburg surrenders.** Port Hudson follows on July 9. The Confederacy has been cut in two along the line of the Mississippi. These events, occurring almost simultaneously with Lee's defeat at Gettysburg (July 1–3), signal the beginning of the end of the Confederacy.

July 4.   Fire support from the gunboat *Tyler*, Lieutenant Commander James M. Prichett, aids the Union garrison in repelling a Confederate attack on Helena, Arkansas.

July 10.   **Beginning of the siege of Charleston.** The failure of the naval attack of April 7 to overcome the harbor defenses of Charleston, South Carolina, leads to the initiation of combined operations against the city. To conduct them, Brigadier General Quincy A. Gillmore is put in command of the Department of the South (June 12), and Admiral Du Pont is replaced as commander of the South Atlantic Blockading Squadron by Rear Admiral John A. Dahlgren (July 6). Gillmore believes that if the army can neutralize Fort Sumter, squarely in the mouth of the harbor, the fleet can enter and reduce the remaining fortifications. The first step must be the capture of Battery Wagner, on the northern end of Morris Island, from which the army's guns can reach Sumter. On this date one of Gillmore's brigades, covered by the fire of Dahlgren's ships, crosses the inlet from Folly Island, already in Union possession, to land on the southern shore of Morris Island.

July 11.   A Union attempt to storm Battery Wagner is repulsed with heavy losses.

July 13.   On the Yazoo River, Mississippi, Lieutenant Commander J. G. Grimes's gunboats land troops who capture Yazoo City.

July 14.   A squadron of eight gunboats under Rear Admiral Samuel P. Lee captures Fort Powhatan on the James River, Virginia.

July 16.   Commander James Bulloch, the Confederate purchasing officer in Europe, contracts with the Bordeaux firm of Lucien Arman for the construction of two double-turreted ironclad rams, one of which will eventually be commissioned as the CSS *Stonewall*.

July 16.   **Shimonoseki incident.** On June 25, the American merchant steamer *Pembroke* was fired on while passing through the Shimonoseki Strait, between the Japanese islands of Kyushu and Honshu, by ships belonging to a feudal lord, Prince Nagata. In retribution, the screw sloop *Wyoming*, Captain David McDougal, enters the straits and although outgunned, sinks all three of the prince's warships present and shells the forts ashore.

July 18.   At Charleston, South Carolina, a second assault on Battery Wagner, again supported by the ships of Admiral Dahlgren's fleet, is repulsed.

July 19.   **Morgan's raid.** On July 9, with a command of 2,400 cavalry, Confederate Brigadier General John Hunt Morgan crossed the Ohio River into Indiana and proceeded east into Ohio on his most audacious raid. Among the Union forces that begin to pursue Morgan's column is a squadron of gunboats under Lieutenant Commander Le Roy Fitch. Ten days later the Confederates attempt to recross the Ohio River into West Virginia at Buffington Island's, only to find their way blocked by a Union entrenchment supported by the gunboats *Allegheny Belle* and *Moose*. Most of the raiders are then captured by land forces coming up behind them.

July 21.   On the Mississippi, the transport *Sallie Ward*, disabled by Confederate artillery fire, drifts aground on Island No. 82 and is destroyed.

August 23.   A Confederate boat party led by Lieutenant John Taylor Wood captures the gunboats *Reliance*, Acting Ensign Henry Walter, and *Satellite*, Acting Master Robinson, at anchor off Windmill Point on the Rappahannock River, Virginia.

August 25.   Lieutenant Wood uses the *Satellite* to capture the schooners *Golden Rod*, *Coquette*, and *Two Brothers* at the mouth of the Rappahannock, after which he strips and burns all five of his prizes.

September 6. At Charleston, South Carolina, the Confederate garrison of Battery Wagner on Morris Island is evacuated under cover of darkness in barges manned by the crews of the rams *Chicora* and *Palmetto State*. Union picket boats, unaware of the movement until it is nearly completed, succeed in capturing the last three barges.

September 8. **Battle of Sabine Pass.** Ordered to establish a Union presence in Texas, Major General Nathaniel P. Banks, commander of the Department of the Gulf, organizes an amphibious operation to capture Sabine Pass. The expedition consists of 4,000 men under Major General William B. Franklin, in transports accompanied by four light-draft gunboats—the *Arizona*, *Clifton*, *Granite City*, and *Sachem*—under Acting Volunteer Lieutenant Frederick Crocker. To defend Sabine Pass the Confederates have erected Fort Griffin, an earthwork mounting five guns, for one of which there is no ammunition, garrisoned by 42 men of the Davis Guards commanded by 20-year-old Lieutenant Richard Dowling. Holding fire until the gunboats are well within range, the defenders open a well-aimed cannonade that soon disables the *Clifton* and *Sachem*. Both ships and their crews, approximately 315 officers and men, are captured. The expedition returns to New Orleans.

September 8–9. **Assault on Fort Sumter.** At Charleston, Admiral Dahlgren and General Gillmore plan to follow up the occupation of Morris Island with an amphibious assault on Fort Sumter, most of whose guns have been disabled by repeated bombardments by Dahlgren's monitors and Gillmore's artillery. Each service organizes its own separate landing party. The approach to the fort is made in small boats under cover of darkness. The navy's 500 sailors and marines under Commander Thomas H. Stevens have the misfortune to reach Sumter first. There they discover that, despite the damage done to the fort, the garrison is full of fight and the walls cannot be scaled. The guns of the other harbor fortifications and the CSS *Chicora* open up, and the landing forces draw off, leaving approximately 100 prisoners in Confederate hands.

September 19–23. In the Chesapeake Bay, a Confederate boat expedition commanded by Acting Masters John Y. Beall and Edward McGuire capture and destroy the schooners *Alliance*, *J. J. Houseman*, *Samuel Pearsall*, and *Alexandria*.

October 5. **The Davids.** In Charleston harbor the ironclad screw steamer *New Ironsides*, Captain Stephen C. Rowan, is damaged by a spar torpedo rammed into her side by the *David*, Lieutenant William T. Glassell, CSN. The *David*, which gives her name to a type of Confederate warship, is a small, cylindrical steamer with a very low silhouette, built specifically for delivering torpedo attacks. A number of such craft are subsequently constructed at Charleston and elsewhere.

October 9. **Seizure of the Laird rams.** Ceaselessly prodded by American Ambassador Charles Francis Adams and increasingly doubtful that the Confederacy will be able to sustain its independence, the British government seizes two nearly completed ironclad rams being built for Commander Bulloch by Lairds of Birkenhead. This action, though not entirely unexpected, is a great blow to Southern hopes of breaking the blockade. Unlike the primitive, casemated, strictly coastal rams that could be cobbled together in the Confederacy, the Lairds were sea-going, double-turreted, state-of-the-art ships.

October 26–December 4. **Bombardment of Fort Sumter.** At Charleston, Union batteries on Morris Island and Admiral Dahlgren's monitors begin an intensive, 40-day bombardment of Fort Sumter, which is reduced to little more than rubble.

October. **Confederate States Naval Academy.** The Confederate Congress had authorized the establishment of a naval academy on April 21, 1862. This month classes commence, with 52 of the Confederacy's 106 midshipmen in attendance, aboard the school ship *Patrick Henry* at Drewry's Bluff on the James River below Richmond. The superintendent is Lieutenant William Harwar Parker, formerly head of the Department of Seamanship at the U.S. Naval Academy.

December 6. The monitor *Weehawken*, Commander James M. Duncan, sinks with the loss of more than 20 lives while tied to a buoy outside Charleston harbor.

December 7.   A party of 15 Confederate sympathizers led by John C. Braine seize the steamer *Chesapeake*, which they had boarded as passengers, during her regular run between New York and Portland, Maine. The plot was organized by "John Parker" (real name: Vernon G. Locke, formerly captain of the Confederate privateer *Retribution*), who boards the ship from a pilot boat in the Bay of Fundy. The conspirators intend to run the blockade into Wilmington, North Carolina, but the *Chesapeake* is recovered by the U.S. gunboats *Annie* and *Ella*, Acting Lieutenant J. Frederick Nickels, while coaling near Halifax, Nova Scotia, on December 17. Braine, "Parker," and most of their followers escape ashore. Although Braine claims to be a lieutenant in the Confederate States Navy, in fact none of the men involved hold Confederate commissions, and the Confederate government disavows their actions.

1864

February 2.   Confederate boat parties led by Commander John Taylor Wood capture and destroy the Union gunboat *Underwriter*, Acting Master Jacob Westerveldt, in the Neuse River, near New Bern, North Carolina, Westerveldt is killed in hand-to-hand fighting on the deck of his ship, which was taken by surprise. For this and previous exploits, Wood receives the thanks of the Confederate Congress.

February 12.   **Second cruise of the Florida.** The Confederate cruiser *Florida*, Lieutenant Charles M. Morris, slips out of Brest, France, past the blockading screw sloop *Kearsarge*, Captain John B. Winslow. She takes 15 prizes between this date and her capture on October 7.

February 17.   **Sinking of the Housatonic.** The screw sloop *Housatonic*, Captain Charles W. Pickering, is sunk by the Confederate submarine *H.L. Hunley*, Lieutenant George E. Dixon, CSA, while at anchor on blockade duty off Charleston, South Carolina. The *Hunley*, operating on the surface, strikes the *Housatonic* with a spar torpedo and is

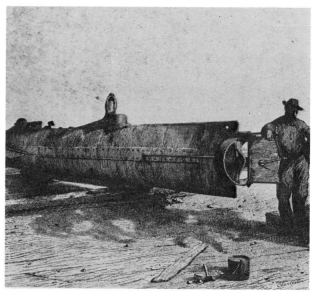

The Confederate submarine *Hunley*: an engraving of a sketch made at Charleston in December 1863. Official U.S. Navy photograph.

herself lost with all hands, probably as a result of the explosion.

March 5.   Commander John Taylor Wood, CSN, leads 15 men who cross the Chesapeake Bay at night in barges to seize and destroy the Union telegraph station at Cherrystone Point, Virginia. Wood also captures the small army steamer *Aeolus*, which he disables, and *Titan*, which he sails back across the bay into the Piankatank River and destroys.

March 6.   In the North Edisto River, near Charleston, South Carolina, the gunboat *Memphis*, Acting Master Robert O. Patterson, is struck twice by a spar torpedo mounted on a Confederate David commanded by First Assistant Engineer C.S. Tombs, but the torpedo fails to detonate.

March 12.   **Red River expedition.** Rear Admiral David Dixon Porter leads 13 ironclads, 4 tinclads, and 5 wooden gunboats of the Mississippi Squadron up the Red River to cooperate with land forces commanded by Major General Nathaniel P. Banks. The immediate object of the expedition is to capture Shreveport, Louisiana, after which it is to advance into Texas, thereby cutting the trickle of supplies that continues to reach the eastern Confederacy via the Red River and, by strengthening Union presence west of the Mississippi, to discourage French Emperor Napoleon III from meddling in Mexico.

March 16.   A landing party from the monitor *Osage*, Lieutenant Commander Thomas O. Selfridge, Jr., occupies Alexandria, Louisiana, on the Red River. Nine of Porter's vessels reach the town that morning.

March 25.   A Confederate attack on Union forces at Paducah, Kentucky, is repulsed with the help of fire support from the gunboats *Paw Paw*, Acting Lieutenant A. Frank O'Neil, and *Peosta*, Acting Lieutenant Thomas E. Smith.

April 1.   The army transport *Maple Leaf* is destroyed by a Confederate mine near Mandarin Point on the St. John's River, Florida.

April 3.   Nine of Admiral Porter's ironclads and three wooden steamers convoy transports carrying an army corps commanded by Major General A.J. Smith up the Red River from Alexandria to Grand Ecore, Louisiana. From Grand Ecore the troops are to march to Natchitoches to join Bank's army for the advance on Shreveport.

April 9.   Blockading off Newport News, Virginia, the steam frigate *Minnesota*, Lieutenant Commander John H. Upshur, is damaged by a spar torpedo in a night attack by the Confederate David craft *Squib*, Lieutenant Hunter Davidson.

April 10.   **Withdrawal from the Red River.** At Springfield Landing, only 30 miles below Shreveport, Louisiana, Admiral Porter finds that the Confederates have blocked the river by sinking a huge steamer, the *New Falls City*, across the stream. Before the obstruction can be removed, word is received that General Banks's army has been defeated at the Battle of Sabine Crossroads and is in retreat. Porter has no choice but to withdraw downstream. Falling water and the opposition of Confederate land forces make this a perilous operation.

April 12.   **Action at Blair's Landing.** Retiring down the Red River, Porter's fleet fights its way past Confederate batteries supported by dismounted cavalry under Brigadier General Thomas Green, CSA, who is killed in the action.

April 15.   The ironclad *Eastport*, Lieutenant Commander S. Ledyard Phelps, is crippled by a mine in the Red River near Grand Ecore, Louisiana. Her crew keeps her going for some days, but on April 26 Admiral Porter orders her destroyed.

April 16.   The army transport *General Hunter* is destroyed by a mine near Mandarin Point in the St. John's River, Florida.

April 17.   A Confederate attack on Plymouth, North Carolina, is repulsed with the help of fire support from the gunboats *Miami* and *Southfield*. The army steamer *Bombshell* is sunk during the action.

April 19.   **The Albemarle.** The new Confederate ironclad ram *Albemarle*, Commander James W. Cooke, attacks the wooden gunboats *Miami* and *Southfield* off Plymouth, North Carolina, Lieutenant Commander Charles W. Flusser, the senior Union officer, has lashed the two gunboats together in anticipation of the ram's appearance and boldly advances to meet her. The *Albemarle* rams and sinks the *Southfield* and drives away the *Miami*, the tinclad *Whitehead*, and the little steamer *Ceres*. Flusser is killed early in the action.

April 20.   Supported by the *Albemarle*, Confederate land forces recapture Plymouth, North Carolina.

April 21.   The tinclad gunboat *Petrel*, Acting Master T. McElroy, is disabled and captured by Confederate land forces near Yazoo City, on the Yazoo River, Mississippi.

April 26–27.   On the Red River, Admiral Porter's vessels reach Alexandria, Louisiana, after heavy engagements with Confederate land forces, during which the small steamer *Champion No. 3* is disabled, *Champion No. 5* is destroyed, and several other ships are damaged.

May 2–13.   **Passing the Red River rapids.** At Alexandria, Louisiana, Admiral Porter's squadron is trapped by falling water above the Red River rapids, and it appears as though he may have to destroy his ships to keep them from being captured and then withdraw overland. Fortunately, Lieutenant Colonel Joseph Bailey, an army officer in the brigade that has remained with the squadron, conceives the idea of building a dam across the river until the water reaches the necessary seven-foot minimum depth.

Admiral Porter's ironclads passing the dam at Alexandria, Louisiana, during the withdrawal from the Red River: a woodcut from *Harper's Pictorial History of the Civil War* for May 1864. U.S. Naval Institute Collection.

The dam would then be opened, and the ships could ride the torrent to safety. Bailey's first dam gives way on May 9, but four ships take advantage of the rush of water to pass through the rapids. A second dam is then constructed, and the remainder of the squadron makes its escape.

May 4–7.   A successful amphibious assault on Tampa, Florida, is supported by the steamers *Sunflower*, Acting Master Edward Van Sice, and *Honduras*, Acting Master John H. Platt, and the sailing bark *J.L. Davis*, Acting Master William Fales.

May 5.   The Confederate ironclad *Albemarle*, Commander James W. Cooke, enters Albemarle Sound in company with the gunboats *Bombshell* and *Cotton Plant* to engage the Union forces at the mouth of the Roanoke River. The *Bombshell* is soon captured, and the *Cotton Plant* retires upriver, but the *Albemarle* disables the wooden side-wheel gunboat *Sassacus*, Lieutenant Commander Francis A. Roe, and continues to engage the side-wheelers *Mattabesett*, Captain Melancton Smith, and *Wyalusing*, Lieutenant Commander Walter W. Queen, until nightfall brings an end to the action.

May 5.   In a sharp action near Dunn's Bayou on the Red River, Louisiana, Confederate forces ashore capture or destroy the wooden steamers *Covington*, Acting Lieutenant George P. Lord, and *Signal*, Acting Lieutenant Edward Morgan, and the transport *Warner*.

May 6.   The side-wheel steamer *Commodore Jones*, Acting Lieutenant Thomas Wade, is blown up by an electric mine while sweeping mines in the James River, Virginia. Forty of her crewmen are killed.

May 6.   The Confederate ironclad ram *Raleigh*, Flag Officer William F. Lynch, sorties from the Cape Fear River, North Carolina, and drives off the blockaders *Britannia* and *Nansemond*, allowing a blockade runner to slip out. After exchanging fire with other blockaders the next morning, the *Raleigh* grounds while attempting to enter the river and is destroyed to keep her from falling into enemy hands.

May 6.   The wooden steamer *Granite City*, Acting Master C.W. Lamson, and the tinclad *Wave*, Acting Lieutenant Benjamin A. Loring, are captured by Confederate land forces during an engagement at Calasieu Pass, Louisiana.

May 7.   Confederate land forces surprise and capture the side-wheel steamer *Shawsheen*, Acting Ensign Charles Ringot, near Chaffin's Bluff, on the James River, Virginia.

May 10.   The army transport *Harriet A. Ward* is sunk by a mine in the St. John's River, Florida.

May 23. The gunboat *Columbine*, Acting Ensign Sanborn, is attacked and captured at Horse's Landing on the St. John's River, near Palatka, Florida, by a party of 16 sharpshooters and two guns under the command of Captain J.J. Dickison, 2nd Florida Cavalry.

May 25. A boat party from the side-wheeler *Mattabesett*, Captain Melancton Smith, makes an unsuccessful attempt to destroy the Confederate ironclad ram *Albemarle* at her anchorage in the Roanoke River, near Plymouth, North Carolina.

June 3. Around 2:00 A.M., a Confederate boat expedition of 130 men led by Lieutenant Thomas P. Pelot surprises and captures the blockader *Water Witch*, Lieutenant Commander Austin Pendergast, at anchor off Ossabaw Island, Georgia. Pelot is killed in the boarding action.

June 10. Colonel Jacob Zeilin becomes the seventh commandant of the marine corps.

June 19. **Kearsarge vs. the Alabama.** The Confederate cruiser *Alabama*, Captain Raphael Semmes, which put into Cherbourg, France, on June 13, stands out to engage the screw sloop *Kearsarge*, Captain John B. Winslow, which appeared off the port the next day. Some of the *Alabama*'s shells fail to explode, and Semmes gives the order to abandon his sinking ship after a one-sided action of 70 minutes. Semmes and 40 of his officers and men escape captivity when they are rescued by boats from the English yacht *Deerhound*.

June 24. The paddle-wheel steamer *Queen City*, Acting Master Michael Hickey, is surprised and captured by Confederate cavalry with artillery on the White River off Clarendon, Arkansas.

August 5. **Battle of Mobile Bay.** Rear Admiral David G. Farragut advances to attack the defense of Mobile Bay, Alabama, with a squadron consisting of the monitors *Chickasaw*, *Manhattan*, *Tecumseh*, and *Winnebago* and 14 wooden ships, including his flagship, the screw sloop *Hartford*. To enter the bay his ships must pass through a narrow channel, the western side of which is mined, between Fort Gaines on Dauphin Island to the west and Fort Morgan on Mobile Point to the east. Inside the bay is a Confederate squadron under Rear Admiral Franklin Buchanan composed of the ironclad ram *Tennessee* (flag) and the small wooden gunboats *Gaines*, *Morgan*, and *Selma*. The column of the monitors is headed by the *Tecumseh*, Commander T.A.M. Craven. Upon sighting the *Tennessee*, Craven makes straight for her, skirting the edge of the minefield, where the *Tecumseh* strikes a mine and sinks in a matter of seconds, taking 90 of her 114 crewmen, including Craven, with her. The screw sloop *Brooklyn*, Captain

The *Kearsarge* vs. the *Alabama*: a lithograph published in Berlin in 1864. Courtesy Beverley R. Robinson Collection, U.S. Naval Academy Museum.

Rear Admiral Franklin Buchanan, CSN. Official U.S. Navy photograph.

James Alden, heading the wooden ships, then begins to back water, threatening to throw the entire column into confusion directly below the guns of Fort Morgan. At this critical moment, Farragut shouts to Flag Captain Percival Drayton: "Damn the torpedoes! Full speed ahead, Drayton!" and the *Hartford* surges past the *Brooklyn* to lead the wooden ships into the bay. Not a single vessel is disabled by the forts' fire. The CSS *Selma*, Lieutenant Peter U. Murphey, strikes her colors after a sharp action with the *Metacomet*, Lieutenant James Jouett; the CSS *Gaines*, Lieutenant John W. Bennett, is severely damaged and runs aground near Fort Morgan; and the CSS *Morgan*, Commander George W. Harrison, escapes up the bay to Mobile. Admiral Buchanan singlehandedly engages the Union fleet with the *Tennessee* for an hour before his battered flagship is compelled to surrender. This action effectively closes the last major port on the Confederacy's Gulf coast.

August 6–23.   **Cruise of the Tallahassee.** Commander John Taylor Wood, CSN, slips out of Wilmington, North Carolina, in the steamer *Tallahassee* to attack Northern shipping off the eastern seaboard. In a cruise of a little more than two weeks, he takes

31 prizes and, eluding a dragnet of Union warships, runs the blockade back into Wilmington.

August 9.   City Point, on the James River, Virginia, General Grant's headquarters and base of supply, is rocked by explosions that result when two members of the Conference Torpedo Corps, John Maxwell and R.K. Dillard, place a time-bomb aboard a Union army transport.

September 19.   **Confederates on the Great Lakes.** On Lake Erie, 28 men led by Acting Master John Yates Beall, CSN, seize and burn the steamers *Philo Parsons* and *Island Queen* before retiring into Canada. The seizure of the ships was the only successful part of a daring plan to free the Confederate prisoners of war confined on Johnson's Island, near Sandusky, Ohio. Beall is later captured and hanged as a spy.

September 29.   The steamer *Roanoke* is captured off the coast of Cuba by John C. Braine and a party of Confederate sympathizers who had boarded her as passengers in Havana. Braine sails the ship to Bermuda with the aim of running the blockade back into the Confederacy, but in the end decides to burn her.

September 29–October 1.   Confederate Flag Officer John K. Mitchell's James River Squadron provides fire support for southern forces ashore during the fighting around Fort Harrison, Virginia.

October 7.   **Capture of the Florida.** Commander Napoleon Collins, commanding the screw sloop *Wachusett*, attacks and captures the Confederate cruiser *Florida*, Lieutenant Charles M. Morris, in the neutral harbor of Bahia, Brazil. His action precipitates an international incident. Commander Collins is court-martialled and sentenced to be dismissed from the navy, but Secretary Welles quashes the verdict. The *Florida* is ordered to be returned to the Brazilian government, but mysteriously sinks at her mooring at Hampton Roads, Virginia.

October 19.   **The Shenandoah.** In the Madeiras the English steamer *Sea King*, secretly purchased by Commander James D. Bulloch, CSN, is commissioned as the Confederate cruiser *Shenandoah*. Under the command

"An August Morning with Farragut" at the Battle of Mobile Bay: the famous late nineteenth century painting by W. H. Overender. Official U.S. Navy photograph.

of Lieutenant James I. Waddell, she will take 38 prizes and virtually destroy the New England whaling fleet.

October 27. **Destruction of the Albemarle.** Lieutenant William B. Cushing sinks the Confederate ironclad ram *Albemarle* at her mooring in the Roanoke River near Plymouth, North Carolina. Approaching in a steam launch under cover of darkness, Cushing rams a spar torpedo into the ironclad's side. Thirteen of his fourteen men are captured or killed, but Cushing and one other swim safely away.

October 28–November 19. **Cruise of the Chickamauga.** The Confederate cruiser *Chickamauga*, Lieutenant John Wilkinson, runs the blockade out of Wilmington, North Carolina. Three weeks later she returns to Wilmington under cover of a dense fog, having taken seven prizes.

October 29–November 7. **Cruise of the Olustee.** The CSS *Olustee* (ex-*Tallahassee*),

Lieutenant William H. Ward, slips out of and back into Wilmington, North Carolina, on a brief cruise in which she takes seven prizes.

October 29–November 1. Exploiting the advantage gained by Cushing's destruction of the *Albemarle*, Union naval forces under Commander W.H. Macomb recapture Plymouth, North Carolina. The Carolina sounds are again closed to the south.

October 30. The gunboat *Undine*, Acting Master Bryant, and the transports *Cheeseman* and *Venus* are captured by Confederate land forces on the Tennessee River near Johnsonville, Tennessee.

November 4. The paddle-wheelers *Key West*, Acting Volunteer Lieutenant E.M. King, and *Tawah*, Acting Volunteer Lieutenant J. Goudy, and the steamer *Elfin*, Acting Master A.F. Thompson, support Union land forces in defending the supply depot at Johnsonville, on the Tennessee River,

The Confederate cruiser *Tallahassee*: a woodcut from the *Illustrated London News* for April 29, 1865. U.S. Naval Institute Collection.

Tennessee, against an attack by Confederates under Major General Nathan Bedford Forrest. The enemy batteries are overwhelming, and at the end of the engagement both the ships and stores are fired to prevent them from being captured.

November 27. The *Greyhound*, headquarters steamer of Major General Benjamin F. Butler, is destroyed by an unexplained explosion and fire in the James River, Virginia. Admiral Porter and Major General R.C. Schenk are also aboard at the time. Porter suspects that the explosion was caused by a Confederate "coal torpedo"—a bomb in a big lump of coal.

November 30. A naval brigade of 500 seamen and marines from the ships of the South Atlantic Blockading Squadron under Commander George H. Preble supports Union land forces in an action at Honey Hill, near Grahamville, South Carolina.

December 5–9. Commander Preble's naval brigade continues to support army units in a series of actions near Tulifinny Crossroads, Georgia, the objective of which is to reach and cut the Savannah-Charleston Railroad, thereby facilitating Sherman's March to the Sea. Confederate forces succeed in halting the advance just short of the railway.

December 7. The steam tug *Narcissus*, Acting Ensign William G. Jones, is sunk by a Confederate mine in Mobile Bay, Alabama.

December 9. The gunboat *Otsego*, Lieutenant Commander H.N.T. Arnold, and the tug *Bazely* are sunk by Confederate mines in the Roanoke River near Jamesville, North Carolina.

December 15–16. **Battle of Nashville.** Seven gunboats of the Mississippi River Squadron under Lieutenant Commander Le Roy Fitch provide fire support for forces ashore in this decisive battle, which virtually destroys the Confederate Army of Tennessee.

December 21. At Savannah, Georgia, Confederate naval forces destroy the *Savannah, Isondiga, Firefly*, and *Georgia* to prevent their capture by Sherman's army, then approaching the city.

December 23. The rank of vice admiral is created and conferred on David Glasgow Farragut.

December 23–27. **First Fort Fisher expedition.** Wilmington, North Carolina, is the last major port open in the eastern Confederacy. It is guarded by Fort Fisher, a large earthwork fortification commanding the entrance to the Cape Fear River. To capture the fort, the Union mounts a joint expedition consisting of the largest American fleet yet assembled—55 warships, including the ironclad screw steamer *New Ironsides* and the monitors *Canonicus, Mahopac, Monadnock,* and *Saugus,* and nearly 45 auxiliaries and transports, under Rear Admiral David Dixon Porter—and 6,500 troops poorly led by Major General Benjamin F. Butler. A ship loaded with explosives with which Butler expected to level the fortifications is blown up without effect on the evening of December 23–24. The fleet smothers the fort with shellfire on the 24th, and approximately 2,000 troops land under cover of the ships' guns on Christmas Day. Butler then decides that the bombardment has not damaged the fort enough to make an assault practical and has them reembarked.

1865

January 1. The screw frigate *San Jacinto,* Captain R. W. Meade, wrecks on No Name Cay in the Bahamas.

January 13–15. **Capture of Fort Fisher.** A joint expedition composed of 60 warships under Rear Admiral David Dixon Porter and 8,500 troops under Brigadier General Alfred H. Terry makes a second attempt to capture Fort Fisher, guarding the mouth of the Cape Fear River, North Carolina. The troops land on January 13 under intense covering fire from the fleet. A naval brigade of 1,600 seamen and 400 marines under Lieutenant Commander K. R. Breese is put ashore on January 15 to deliver a diversionary attack. Their three charges are repulsed with heavy losses—309 casualties—but absorb the defenders' attention so that Terry's troops can storm into the fort from the rear. Some 500 Confederates are killed or wounded and 2,083 taken prisoner; total Union losses are 691.

January 15. The monitor *Patapsco,* Lieutenant Commander S. P. Quackenbush, is sunk by a mine outside Charleston, South Carolina, with the loss of nearly half her crew.

January 23–24. **Action at Trent's Reach.** The Confederate James River Squadron, Commodore John K. Mitchell, makes a desperate attempt to fight its way through the Union obstructions at Trent's Reach and destroy Grant's supply depot at City Point. Mitchell's force consists of the ironclads *Virginia II, Fredericksburg,* and *Richmond,* the gunboats *Drewry* and *Torpedo,* and the torpedo boats *Hornet, Scorpion,* and *Wasp.* The *Virginia II* and the *Richmond* run aground on January 23, and the next day, while refloating the *Virginia,* the *Drewry* is destroyed by a hit that detonates her magazines. The *Scorpion,* severely damaged by this explosion, is abandoned. Fire from the monitors *Massasoit* and *Onondaga* then compels the squadron to retire.

January 28. The steam gunboat *Valley City,* Acting Master J. A. J. Brooks, provides fire support for a force of Union troops during a night attack on their encampment at Colerain, North Carolina.

January 28. Blockading off Mobile, Alabama, the side-wheel steamer *Octorara,* Lieutenant Commander William W. Low, is hit by a spar torpedo carried by the CSS *St. Patrick,* Lieutenant J. T. Walker. The torpedo fails to fire, and neither vessel is damaged.

February 17–18. **Fall of Charleston.** Confederate forces withdraw from Charleston, South Carolina, upon the approach of Sherman's army, first destroying the ironclads *Charleston, Chicora,* and *Palmetto State.* The city had withstood a siege of 567 days.

February 17–18. Fort Anderson, North Carolina, is shelled and captured by a Union squadron commanded by Rear Admiral David Dixon Porter.

February 25. The armed tug *Catalpa,* Ensign Allen K. Noyes, lands a party that drives off a force of Confederate cavalry and captures Georgetown, on the Peedee River, South Carolina.

February 29. The side-wheel steamer *Harvest Moon,* flagship of Rear Admiral John A. Dahlgren, commander of the South Atlantic Blockading Squadron, is sunk by a mine in Winyah Bay, South Carolina.

March 4. The side-wheel gunboats *General Burnside,* Lieutenant Moreau Forrest, and *General Thomas,* Acting Master Gilbert

Admiral Porter's fleet bombarding Fort Fisher, January 15, 1865: a lithograph published in New York in 1865. Courtesy Library of Congress.

Morton, attack and capture the encampment of a Confederate force commanded by Brigadier General Philip D. Roddey at Mussel Shoals, on the Tennessee River, Alabama.

March 24.   The French-built, Confederate ironclad ram *Stonewall Jackson*, Commander Thomas J. Page, sails from El Ferrol, Spain, for America. Two Union warships, the steam frigate *Niagara* and screw sloop *Sacramento*, present under the command of Commodore Thomas T. Craven, make no attempt to interfere with her departure. Craven is later court-martialled for failing to engage the enemy. Despite his plea that the ram constituted a clearly superior force, he is convicted, but Secretary Welles sets the verdict aside.

March 28.   The ironclad gunboat *Milwaukee*, Lieutenant Commander J. H. Gillis, is sunk by a mine in the Blakely River, Alabama.

March 29.   The monitor *Osage*, Lieutenant Commander W. M. Gamble, is sunk by a mine in the Blakely River, Alabama.

April 1.   The tinclad *Rodolph*, Master N. M. Dyer, is sunk by a mine in the Blakely River, Alabama.

April 2.   **Fall of Richmond.** Following the disastrous Battle of Five Forks, General Lee informs President Davis that his army can no longer defend the Confederate capital. The ships of the James River Squadron— the ironclads *Virginia II*, *Fredericksburg*, and *Richmond*, wooden gunboats *Hampton*, *Nansemond*, *Roanoke* (formerly *Raleigh*), and *Torpedo*, picket boat *Shrapnel*, and the

school-ship *Patrick Henry* are burned and their crews formed into a naval brigade under the squadron commander, Rear Admiral Raphael Semmes, who is given the twin commission of brigadier general, CSA. Almost the entire brigade is captured when Lee's rear guard is overwhelmed at the Battle of Sayler's Creek. The midshipmen from the *Patrick Henry* are chosen to guard the train containing the Confederacy's gold reserves during the disintegrating government's flight to the south.

April 9.   **Appomattox.** General Lee surrenders the Army of Northern Virginia to vastly superior Union forces at Appomattox Court House. Although President Davis still has hopes of fighting on and the Confederate forces in the Trans-Mississippi will not surrender until May, the Civil War is effectively over.

April 13.   The armed tug *Ida*, Acting Ensign F. Ellms, is sunk by a mine near Chocktaw Pass in Mobile Bay, Alabama.

April 14.   The gunboat *Sciota*, Volunteer Lieutenant J. W. Magune, is sunk by a mine in Mobile Bay, Alabama.

April 22.   The side-wheel steamer *Black Hawk*, Lieutenant Commander James A. Greer, burns and sinks at Mound City, Illinois.

April 25.   **The Webb.** The Confederate side-wheel ram *Webb*, Lieutenant Charles W. Read, is destroyed in a daring attempt to reach the sea. Running the Union blockade of the mouth of the Red River, through sheer bluff the *Webb* made her way down the Mississippi to New Orleans before being recognized. Below the city she came upon the steam sloop *Richmond*. Incorrectly assuming that the more powerful Union vessel is ready to contest his passage, Read runs the *Webb* ashore and sets her afire to keep her from being captured.

May 19.   Discovering that the war has ended by the time his ship reaches the Western Hemisphere, Commander Thomas J. Page turns the Confederate ironclad ram *Stonewall Jackson* over to the Spanish authorities in Havana, Cuba.

June 3.   The European (formerly the Mediterranean) Squadron is reestablished.

June 28.   **Last shots of the Civil War.** Using the time-honored technique of a shot across the bow, the Confederate cruiser *Shenandoah* halts and burns ten Union whaling ships in the Bering Sea. Some of their captains protest that the war is over, but Lieutenant Waddell does not believe them. On August 2, he learns from a British ship that the war is indeed over. Apprehensive that the victorious North will regard the *Shenandoah*'s operations as acts of piracy, Waddell decides to sail her to England for internment there.

September 9.   Rear Admiral David Dixon Porter becomes the sixth superintendent of the U.S. Naval Academy.

October.   The U.S. Naval Academy returns to Annapolis, Maryland, from Newport, Rhode Island, where it had been located during the Civil War.

November 5.   **Farewell to the Stars and Bars.** Lieutenant James I. Waddell brings the Confederate cruiser *Shenandoah* into Liverpool, England, after a voyage of 122 days entirely out of sight of land. The following day he hauls down the last Confederate flag still flying anywhere in the world.

1866

January 4.   The armed tug *Narcissus*, Acting Ensign Isaac S. Bradbury, is wrecked on Egmont Key, Florida, with the loss of her entire company of 32 men.

June 20.   A party of 100 seamen and marines under Lieutenant John W. Philip from the screw sloop *Wachusett* is landed at New Chwang, China, to seize a bandit leader

whose followers had assaulted the American consul. Local authorities were unwilling to arrest the man.

June 21.   Congress approves the establishment of a Hydrographic Office to take over the work previously performed by M.F. Maury's Hydrographical Office. The new bureau, the brainchild of Rear Admiral C.H. Davis, is given space in the Nautical Almanac Office, which had been moved to the capital earlier in the year.

July 25.   Congress creates the unique, new rank of admiral and confers it on David Glasgow Farragut in recognition of his great services in the late war. David Dixon Porter is promoted to become the navy's second vice admiral.

1867

March 2.   **Civil Engineering Corps.** Congress establishes the Civil Engineering Corps. On March 3, 1871, it directs that at the discretion of the president members of the corps will be given relative rank to line officers.

June 13.   **Formosan expedition.** The screw sloops *Hartford* and *Wyoming* land a naval brigade of 181 men under Commander George C. Belknap who attack the aborigines on Formosa in retaliation for the massacre of the crew of the American merchant bark *Rover*. Lieutenant Commander Alexander S. Mackenzie is mortally wounded in the action.

June 19.   **Loss of the Sacramento.** The screw sloop *Sacramento*, Captain Napoleon Collins, wrecks without loss of life off the coast of Madras, India.

December 28.   **Annexation of Midway.** The United States claims the central Pacific island of Midway, over which Captain William Reynolds of the screw sloop *Lackawanna* has raised the U.S. flag on August 28. The island is America's first overseas territory.

1868

February 4.   The screw sloop *Oneida* sends a party of seamen and marines ashore to protect

American citizens and property at Hiogo, Japan.

February 7–26.   Detachments from five ships of the South Atlantic Squadron, Rear Admiral Charles H. Davis, are landed to protect foreign nationals during an insurrection at Montevideo, Uruguay.

February 8.   A party from the screw sloop *Shenandoah* lands to safeguard Americans at Nagasaki, Japan.

April 4.   The steam sloop *Iroquois* and side-wheel gunboat *Monocacy* land 25 marines to protect American interests at Yokohama, Japan.

July 9.   **Loss of the Suwanee.** The side-wheel gunboat *Suwanee*, Commander Richard S. Law, strikes an uncharted rock and sinks without loss of life in Queen Victoria Sound off Vancouver Island, British Columbia.

July 27.   **Japanese midshipmen.** In response to a request from the government of Japan, Congress passes an act allowing Japanese nationals to attend the U.S. Naval Academy, providing their country pays the cost. The first Japanese midshipman, Jiunzo

Midshipman Jiunzo Matsumura, Class of 1873, the Naval Academy's first Japanese graduate. Nimitz Library Special Collections.

Matsumura, graduates in the Class of 1873. He will rise to the rank of vice admiral in the Imperial Japanese Navy. A total of 16 Japanese midshipmen attend the academy between 1869 and 1906.

August 13.   **Arica hurricane.** The side-wheel gunboat *Wateree*, Commander James H. Gillis, and storeship *Fredonia*, Captain G. W. Doty, are among the vessels driven ashore by a tidal wave at Arica, Peru. Twenty-seven of their crewmen are lost.

November 19.   **Globe and anchor.** The marine corps's emblem is approved by the secretary of the navy. The design was by a board consisting of Major G.R. Graham and Captains R.W. Huntington and C.F. Williams.

1869

March 9.   Adolf E. Borie succeeds Gideon Welles to become 25th secretary of the navy.

April 26.   **Good Conduct Medal.** Congress authorizes the Navy Good Conduct Medal to reward enlisted personnel for blameless service. The award was originally a nickel Maltese cross. Its design was changed to the present bronze medal in 1892.

June 9.   The Navy Department issues orders for the construction of a torpedo station—the navy's first—on Goat Island, at Newport, Rhode Island.

June 26.   George M. Robeson enters office as the 26th secretary of the navy.

June 28.   William M. Wood is named the navy's first surgeon-general.

December 1.   Commodore John L. Worden, the hero of the *Monitor*, relieves Vice Admiral David D. Porter to become the seventh superintendent of the U.S. Naval Academy.

1870

January 22.   Commander Thomas O. Selfridge, Jr., sails in the gunboat *Nipsic* on an expedition to ascertain the best location for an interoceanic canal across the Isthmus of Darien. His report, based on a survey of four possible routes, is completed in 1874.

January 24.   **Loss of the Oneida.** The screw sloop

Oneida, Commander Edward P. Williams, sinks off Yokohama, Japan, with the loss of 117 lives after being struck by the British P. & O. Steamer *City of Bombay*, which continues on her way.

June 17.   Lieutenant Willard H. Brownson leads a party of six boats from the screw sloop *Mohican* to attack a band of pirates in the Teacapan River on the Pacific coast of Mexico. The pirates are dispersed and their ship, the former British gunboat *Forward*, is burned.

August 14.   Admiral David Glasgow Farragut dies, aged 69, in Portsmouth, New Hampshire.

October 29.   **Loss of the Saginaw.** The sidewheel steamer *Saginaw*, Commander Montgomery Sicard, strikes a reef and breaks up off remote Ocean Island, in the mid-Pacific. The ship's company gets safely ashore, but the prospects of rescue are slight. On November 18 Lieutenant John G. Talbot, the *Saginaw*'s executive officer, sets out in the ship's gig with five volunteers to sail 1,500 miles to Hawaii for help. Approaching Kauai 31 days later the boat swamps in the surf. Talbot and four of his men are drowned, but Coxswain William Halford survives to bring aid to his stranded shipmates.

1871

March 3.   The Pay Corps is established by an act of Congress. In 1919 it is renamed the Supply Corps.

May 30.   **Korean expedition.** A squadron of five ships under Rear Admiral John Rodgers carries Frederick Low, U.S. minister to China, to negotiate a treaty of amity and commerce with the "Hermit Kingdom" of Korea, where the crew of the American merchantman *General Sherman* was massacred in 1866. The vessels are the screw frigate *Colorado* (flag), screw gunboat *Alaska*, screw sloop *Benicia*, side-wheel gunboat *Monocacy*, and screw tug *Palos*. They anchor at the mouth of the channel (then known as the Salee River) leading to the Han River, near Chemulpo (now Inchon) on May 30. The next day the *Palos* is fired on by one of the five forts along

the river. The ships reply, and two men are wounded before the fort ceases firing. Admiral Rodgers demands an apology. It is not forthcoming, and on June 10 he lands a naval brigade under Commander L.A. Kimberly consisting of 575 bluejackets led by Lieutenant Commander Silas Casey, Jr., and 109 marines under Captain McLane Tilton, Asiatic Squadron Marine Officer, with seven guns. The brigade's advance is supported by fire from the *Monocacy* and the *Palos*, and the defenders of the first two forts withdraw without offering serious resistance. The next day the brigade pushes on towards the principal fort, "The Citadel," and its two secondary works. Here the Koreans await the assault. The first man inside The Citadel, navy Lieutenant Hugh W. McKee, is speared, and there is fierce fighting before the position is won. Only 20 Koreans, some wounded, surrender; 243 are killed. The storming party has three men killed and seven wounded. Captured are 481 cannon of various calibers, hundreds of matchlock muskets, and 50 flags and standards. The expedition sails, without resuming negotiations, on July 3. Six of Captain Tilton's marines are awarded the Medal of Honor.

1873

May 7–12.   A landing party of 200 men goes ashore from the screw sloop *Tuscarora* to protect Americans during one of the recurrent revolutions in the Colombian province of Panama.

September 23–October 9.   Another revolutionary disturbance in Panama leads to the landing of 190 men from screw steamer *Pensacola* and screw sloop *Benicia*.

October 9.   **U.S. Naval Institute.** At Annapolis, fifteen officers assigned to the Naval Academy meet to establish a society "for the purpose of discussing matters of professional interest." The first issue of the Naval Institute *Proceedings* appears a little more than a year later, in 1875. In time this private organization, dedicated to "the advancement of professional, literary and scientific knowledge in the Navy," becomes the open forum of the American naval

Bluejackets and marines inside Fort DeConde (as they named it), one of the Korean positions captured on June 10, 1871. Courtesy the Naval Historical Foundation.

service and one of the foremost societies of its kind in the world.

October 31. **Virginius affair.** The steamer *Virginius*, a Cuban-owned vessel falsely registered under the American flag, is captured by the Spanish cruiser *Tornado* while carrying men and guns to support a rebellion in Cuba. The prisoners, including a number of Americans, are tried before a Spanish court-martial in Havana, and 50 are shot before American and British protests bring the executions to a halt. Among those killed is the *Virginius*'s captain, Joseph Fry, a Naval Academy graduate who had been an officer in the United States and Confederate navies. News of the incident provokes a storm of indignation in the United States, and for a time war with Spain appears distinctly possible.

1874

February 12.   Landing parties totaling 150 officers and men are put ashore at Honolulu,

Hawaii, from the sloop *Portsmouth*, Commander Joseph S. Skerrett, and screw sloop *Tuscarora*, Commander George E. Belknap, to protect Americans during the disturbances following the coronation of King Kalakaua.

July 31.   The first U.S. naval vessel armed with torpedoes, the 438-ton screw steamer *Intrepid*, is commissioned at Boston. She is not a success.

September 22.   Rear Admiral C.R.P. Rodgers becomes the eighth superintendent of the U.S. Naval Academy.

1875

May 6.   Future Fleet Admiral William D. Leahy is born in Hampton, Iowa.

June 18.   The 1,463-ton side-wheel sloop-of-war *Saranac*, Captain Walter W. Queen, strikes a rock and sinks in the Seymour Narrows, off Vancouver Island, British Columbia. No lives are lost.

1876

November 1. Colonel Charles G. McCawley becomes eighth commandant of the marine corps.

1877

March 13. Richard W. Thompson assumes office as 27th secretary of the navy.

November 24. The sloop-rigged iron steamer *Huron*, Commander George P. Ryan, is wrecked in a storm off Nags Head, North Carolina. Of her company of 132 men, 98 are lost.

1878

June 18. The U.S. Life-Saving Service is established by Act of Congress. In 1915 it will be combined with the Revenue Cutter Service to form the U.S. Coast Guard.

July 1. Commodore Foxhall A. Parker becomes ninth superintendent of the U.S. Naval Academy.

November 23. Future Fleet Admiral Ernest J. King is born at Lorain, Ohio.

December 7. The screw sloop *Ticonderoga*, Commodore Robert W. Shufeldt, sails from Hampton Roads, Virginia, to become the first steam-powered American naval vessel to circumnavigate the globe. During the voyage Shufeldt lays the foundations for the first American treaty of commerce with Korea.

1879

August 2. Rear Admiral George P. Balch becomes the 10th superintendent of the U.S. Naval Academy.

August 7–March 23, 1882. **Jeannette Expedition.** The steam bark *Jeannette*, presented to the navy by *New York Herald* publisher James Gordon Bennett, sails from San Francisco under the command of Lieutenant George Washington DeLong with the goal of reaching the North Pole through

Lieutenant G. W. DeLong, commander of the ill-fated *Jeannette* expedition, left this photograph "For my wife to look at when she is wondering where I am." Courtesy U.S. Naval Academy Museum.

the Bering Strait. Her all-volunteer crew consists of 28 navy officers and men and 3 civilians. Reaching the Arctic early in September, the *Jeannette* is almost immediately trapped in pack ice and remains imprisoned for 21 months. Throughout this trying period the members of the expedition carefully record scientific observations that will prove of value to later explorers. Finally, on June 13, 1881, the *Jeannette*'s specially reinforced hull is crushed by the tremendous pressure of shifting ice, and the expedition begins an agonizing journey over the ice to the west, toward Siberia. Arriving at the edge of the ice pack on September 12, they sail for the mainland in three boats they had hauled from the *Jeannette*. One broaches and goes down with all hands; the other two, commanded by Lieutenant DeLong and Chief Engineer George W. Melville, are separated. Melville's party lands on the western side of the Lena delta, where they are found and cared for by natives. DeLong's party lands on the uninhabited, eastern bank of the Lena and attempts to push on overland. As his men's physical condition deteriorates, DeLong makes camp and sends two of the strongest ahead for help. They encounter a caravan, but are unable to communicate that there are others in need. Eventually the two are united with Melville's party, but by then it is too late. Melville finds the frozen bodies of DeLong and his 14 companions, together with the expedition's records, on March 23, 1882.

1880

November 9.   The screw sloop *Ticonderoga*, Commodore Robert W. Shufeldt, returns to Hampton Roads, Virginia, completing the first circumnavigation of the globe by a steam-powered vessel of the U.S. Navy.

1881

January 7.   Nathan Goff, Jr., becomes the 28th secretary of the navy.

March 7.   William H. Hunt becomes 29th secretary of the navy.

June 13.   Rear Admiral C.R.P. Rodgers is appointed 11th superintendent of the Naval Academy, thus becoming the only man ever to hold that post twice.

November 14.   Captain Francis M. Ramsay becomes the 12th superintendent of the Naval Academy.

1882

March 23.   **ONI.** The Office of Naval Intelligence is established.

April 17.   William E. Chandler becomes 30th secretary of the navy.

May 22.   Commodore Robert W. Schufeldt completes the negotiation of a commercial treaty between the United States and the kingdom of Korea.

July 14.   **Maintaining order in Alexandria.** On July 11, the British Mediterranean Fleet bombards Alexandria, Egypt, where a nationalist revolution headed by Colonel Arabi Pasha has seized power. Three days later the U.S. gunboat *Nipsic*, screw sloop *Lancaster*, and screw steamer *Quinnebaug* land a detachment of 73 marines and 60

seamen under Captain H.C. Cochrane, USMC, to guard the American consulate and assist British landing parties to maintain order in the seething city. The conduct of this force is later commended by the British authorities.

October 30.   Future Fleet Admiral William F. ("Bull") Halsey is born in Elizabeth, New Jersey.

November 15.   **First naval attaché.** Lieutenant French Ensor Chadwick is accredited to the London embassy to report on technological developments in European navies.

1883

February 18.   The side-wheel gunboat *Ashuelot*, Commander Horace E. Mullan, grounds near Swatow, China, with the loss of 11 lives.

March 3.   **ABCDs.** Congress authorizes the construction of four steel warships—the protected cruisers *Atlanta*, *Boston*, and *Chicago*—and the dispatch-vessel *Dolphin*. The cruisers are "protected" by armored decks to prevent plunging fire from penetrating to their engine spaces. Later known as the White Squadron, they are the first really modern ships to enter the fleet since the Civil War. The decision to build them is

The protected cruiser *Atlanta*, one of the ABCDs: an engraving of a drawing by J. O. Davidson in *Harper's Weekly*, May 21, 1887. Courtesy Beverley R. Robinson Collection, U.S. Naval Academy Museum.

generally regarded as the beginning of the American naval renaissance.

1884

April 25–May 10. **Greely Relief Expedition.** A rescue expedition consisting of the steamers *Thetis*, *Bear*, Lieutenant William H. Emory, and *Alert*, Commander George W. Coffin, sails from New York for the Arctic under the command of Commander W.S. Schley to search for the 25-man Lady Franklin Bay expedition under First Lieutenant Adolphus W. Greely, USA, which had set out for the North Pole in 1881.

June 22. Schley rescues Lieutenant Greely and his six surviving companions, all near death from starvation, at Cape Sabine, Grinnell Land (Ellesmere Island).

July 7. Congress authorizes the organization of the Office of Naval Records (originally called the Naval War Records Office). The work is carried out by former Naval Academy Professor James Russell Soley, who had taken charge of the Navy Library in 1882.

October 6. **Naval War College.** Secretary of the Navy Chandler establishes the Naval War College at Newport, Rhode Island. Commodore Stephen B. Luce, who had long advocated the foundation of such an institution, is appointed its first president.

Commander W. S. Schley, fourth from left, and the officers of the Greely Relief Expedition in cold-weather gear aboard the *Thetis*. Courtesy U.S. Naval Academy Museum.

Rear Admiral Stephen B. Luce. Courtesy U.S. Naval Academy Museum.

1885

January 18. The gunboat *Alliance* lands her marines at Aspinwall (now Colón), on the Atlantic coast of the Colombian province of Panama, where a revolution has broken out. They are to guard the terminal of the trans-isthmian railroad and protect American interests.

February 24. Future Fleet Admiral Chester W. Nimitz is born in Fredericksburg, Texas.

March 7. William C. Whitney becomes the 31st secretary of the navy.

March 16–May 25. **Panamanian intervention.** The progress of the Panamanian revolution has blocked free transit of the isthmus, to which the United States is entitled by treaty with Colombia. On March 26, the screw sloop *Galena* puts her landing party ashore at Aspinwall (Colón), where it is soon joined by detachments from the *Iroquois*, *Shenandoah*, and *Swatara*. On April 12, a battalion of 232 marines under Lieutenant Colonel Charles Heywood, rushed from the United States, lands at Aspinwall and reopens the railway to Panama City, on the Pacific. Three days later Heywood's men are reinforced by a battalion each of bluejackets and marines under Commander Bowman H. McCalla, who is given command of U.S. forces ashore. McCalla concentrates his brigade at Panama City and maintains order until Colombian troops suppress the insurrection.

September 3.   The Naval War College holds its first formal classes.

1886

July 3.   Future Admiral Raymond A. Spruance, victor of the battles of Midway and the Philippine Sea, is born at Baltimore, Maryland.

August 6.   **First American battleships.** Congress authorizes the construction of the *Maine*, originally designated an armored cruiser, and the *Texas*, which is referred to as an "armored battleship" from the beginning. The two vessels are similar in displacement (6,682 and 6,315 tons, respectively) and design, having their two main turrets placed diagonally on the starboard bow and port quarter, but the *Maine* carries four 10-inch guns in contrast to the *Texas*'s two 12-inchers. The immediate impetus to the appropriation was Brazil's acquisition of the British-built armored cruiser *Riachuelo*, which was considered capable of defeating the entire U.S. fleet.

September 9.   Commander William T. Sampson becomes 13th superintendent of the Naval Academy.

1887

March 3.   The protected cruisers *Philadelphia* (C 4) and *San Francisco* (C 5) and two gunboats are authorized by Congress.

1888

May 17.   **Origin of the naval reserve.** Massachusetts becomes the first state to organize a naval militia. Others follow, and eventually these units are transformed into the naval reserve.

June 19.   Twenty-five men from the screw steamer

Essex land at Chemulpo (Inchon), Korea, under First Lieutenant Robert D. Wainwright and proceed to Seoul to protect American citizens.

September 7.   The first American armored cruiser, the *New York* (ACR 2), and six smaller cruisers, including the *Olympia* (C 6), are authorized by Congress.

November 14.   The gunboat *Nipsic* lands her marines at Apia, Upolu Island, Samoa, to protect American traders during a civil war.

December 20.   An American steamer seized by Haiti is released following the appearance of the screw sloop *Galena* and gunboat *Yantic* at Port-au-Prince.

1889

March 6.   Benjamin F. Tracy becomes 32nd secretary of the navy.

March 15–16.   **Samoan hurricane.** Because of their strategic location on the trade route to Australia, the 14 islands of the Samoan archipelago have long been of interest to the American shipping community as well as to the navy. In 1878 the United States executed a treaty with a native chieftain whereby it obtained the right to establish a coaling station at Pago Pago in return for a pledge to use its good offices should Samoa become involved in a dispute with a third power. Eight years later the newborn German Empire began to show a strong interest in the area, actively intervening in tribal politics. Great Britain also entered the controversy, supporting Germany's demand for a partition of the islands. An international conference sponsored by the United States failed to relieve the mounting tension, and Germany sent three warships to Apia harbor on Upolu Island in an exercise of gunboat diplomacy. President Grover Cleveland responded by ordering three American vessels to Apia, and Germany adopted a more conciliatory attitude. On March 15–16, the rivalry is abruptly defused by an act of nature when a hurricane strikes Apia, where one British, three American, and three German warships and six merchantmen are anchored. HMS *Calliope* is the only vessel that succeeds in getting out of the harbor.

The captain of the U.S. gunboat *Nipsic*, Commander D.W. Mullin, is able to beach his ship. The screw steamer *Trenton*, Captain Norman H. Farquhar (flagship of Rear Admiral Lewis A. Kimberly, commanding the Pacific Station), and screw sloop *Vandalia*, Captain Cornelius M. Schoonmaker, are sunk, together with the German warships *Adler*, *Eber*, and *Olga* and all six merchantmen. Approximately 150 seamen, including 49 Americans, lose their lives. The following month a conference meets at Berlin, where the three powers agree to a tripartite protectorate over Samoa. This arrangement endures until 1899, when the islands are partitioned between, and annexed by, Germany and the United States.

July 30.   Marines from the screw gunboat *Adams* are landed to protect the U.S. legation during disturbances at Honolulu in the kingdom of Hawaii.

1890

1890

April 23.   **First torpedo boat.** The *Cushing* (TB 1) is commissioned at Bristol, Rhode Island. One hundred and forty feet in length and only 15′1″ abeam, she carries a crew of 22 and has a top speed of 23 knots.

May.   **Command of the sea.** Captain Alfred Thayer Mahan's *The Influence of Sea Power Upon History, 1660–1783* is published by Little, Brown and Company of Boston. The most important strategic study ever written by an American, the work is an extension of Mahan's lectures as a professor at the new Naval War College. Using the long maritime struggle between Britain and France as an historical test case, Mahan argues that the traditional French (and American) strategy of commerce raiding is a recipe for defeat. Victory comes only when a navy concentrates its operations, as had the British, on vanquishing the opposing fleet to win command of the sea. Quickly recognized as a classic, the work provides renewed impetus and a strategic direction to the American naval renaissance.

June 13.   Captain Robert L. Phythian becomes the 14th superintendent of the U.S. Naval Academy.

June 30.   **More battleships.** Congress authorizes the construction of the three *Indiana*-class battleships: the *Indiana*, the *Massachusetts* and the *Oregon*. These 10,000-ton ships are a third again as large as the *Maine* and the *Texas* and carry their four 13-inch guns in what becomes the standard arrangement of centerline turrets. When hull numbers are retroactively assigned to battleships in 1920, they are respectively designated BB 1, BB 2, and BB 3.

Captain Alfred Thayer Mahan. U.S. Naval Institute Collection.

The torpedo boat *Cushing*. U.S. Naval Institute Collection.

July 30.   A detachment of marines is landed at Buenos Aires, Argentina, from the side-wheel steamer *Tallapoosa* to guard the U.S. legation during a period of unrest.

November 29.   **First Army-Navy game.** The Naval Academy football team travels to West Point to win the first athletic contest ever held between the service academies, 24-0.

1891

January 30.   Lieutenant Colonel Charles Heywood succeeds Colonel Charles G. McCawley to become ninth commandant of the marine corps.

February 13.   Vice Admiral David Dixon Porter dies, aged 77.

March 3.   The office of assistant secretary of the navy, held during the Civil War by Gustavus V. Fox, is revived. Its first occupant is former Naval Academy professor James Russell Soley.

May 1.   **First marine school.** The "School of Application" is established for newly commissioned marine officers at the Marine Barracks, Washington, D.C.

June 2.   The screw sloop *Kearsarge* lands her marines to preserve order on Navassa Island, Hawaii.

August 28.   The cruisers *Baltimore* (C 3) and *San Francisco* (C 5) land a party commanded by Captain William S. Muse, USMC, to guard the U.S. Consulate at Valparaiso during the Chilean civil war.

October 16.   **Incident at the True Blue Saloon.** Two sailors are killed and sixteen injured when a liberty party from the cruiser *Baltimore* becomes embroiled with a mob of Chileans at the True Blue Saloon in Valparaiso. Offensive remarks by the Chilean foreign minister aggravate the ensuing crisis so that by December war between the United States and Chile appears quite possible. Americans are chagrined to note that materially the Chilean fleet is superior to their own.

1892

January 21.   **Chilean crisis.** President Benjamin Harrison sends Chile an ultimatum threatening to break diplomatic relations unless an apology is made for her foreign minister's remarks (see October 16, 1891).

January 27.   The crisis is resolved when Chile apologizes and pays an indemnity of $75,000 to the families of the two dead sailors.

July 19.   Congress authorizes the construction of a sixth battleship, the *Iowa* (BB 4).

1893

January 16.   **Hawaiian intervention.** American settlers in Hawaii revolt against Queen Liliukalani, who has proclaimed a new constitution designed to reduce their influence in the islands' government. The success of the uprising is assured when U.S. Minister John L. Stevens has the cruiser *Boston*, then at Honolulu, land 150 sailors and marines, ostensibly to protect the American legation. The settlers want the United States to annex the islands, but the incoming, Democratic administration of President Grover Cleveland disappoints them, and in 1894 Hawaii becomes an independent republic.

March 7.   Hilary A. Herbert becomes the 33rd secretary of the navy.

August 1.   The navy's first armored cruiser, the 8,150-ton *New York* (ACR 2), is commissioned at Philadelphia.

1894   1894

February 2.   The old screw sloop *Kearsarge*, Commander Oscar F. Heyerman, wrecks without loss of life on Roncador Reef, off Central America.

July 6.   The cruiser *Columbia* (C 12) lands a detachment of sailors and marines to safeguard American lives and property at Bluefields, Nicaragua.

July 24.   A party of 50 sailors and marines under Captain George Fielding Elliott, USMC, is sent from the cruiser *Baltimore* (C 3) to guard the American legation at Seoul, Korea, during the Sino-Japanese War. The Japanese had landed troops in Korea.

September 17.   **Philo McGiffen at the Yalu.** A graduate of the USNA Class of 1882 serving in the Imperial Chinese Navy,

The armored cruiser *New York*. Official U.S. Navy photograph.

McGiffen becomes the first American to command a modern battleship in action when he takes over from the captain of the *Chen Yuen* at the Battle of the Yalu during the Sino-Japanese War.

November 15.   Captain Philip H. Cooper becomes 15th superintendent of the Naval Academy.

1895

February 25.   **Cuban insurrection.** Another of the recurrent revolts against Spanish rule breaks out in Cuba. This one will eventually lead to American intervention.

March 2.   Congress authorizes the construction of the battleships *Kearsarge* (BB 5) and *Kentucky* (BB 6).

March 8.   The cruiser *Atlanta* lands a party to protect American interests at Boca del Toro, Colombia.

August 15.   The *Texas* is the first American battleship to be commissioned.

September 17.   The battleship *Maine* is commissioned.

November 20.   The battleship *Indiana* (BB 1) is commissioned.

1896

May 2–4.   The gunboat *Alert* sends her landing party ashore to safeguard American citizens and interests at Corinto, Nicaragua.

June 10.   The battleship *Massachusetts* (BB 2) is commissioned.

July 15.   The battleship *Oregon* (BB 3) is commissioned.

July 20.   An act of Congress establishes the Marine Corps Good Conduct Medal to reward enlisted men for blameless service. It was personally designed by the corps's commandant, Major General Charles F. Heywood.

1897

March 6.   John D. Long becomes the 34th secretary of the navy.

June 16.   The battleship *Iowa* (BB 4) is commissioned.

1898

February 7.   The gunboat *Alert*, Commander Eugene H. C. Leutze, lands a detachment

The battleship *Maine*. Courtesy National Archives.

of bluejackets and marines to protect the U.S. Consulate during revolutionary disturbances at San Juan del Sur, Nicaragua.

February 9.   **De Lôme letter.** The American public is angered when the *New York Journal* publishes an intercepted private letter in which the Spanish ambassador to the United States, Dupuy de Lôme, makes a number of highly uncomplimentary references to President McKinley.

February 15.   **"Remember the Maine!"** The battleship *Maine*, Captain Charles D. Sigsbee, which entered Havana harbor for a good-will visit on January 25, is destroyed by an explosion of undetermined origin. More than half her complement—253 of 358 officers and men—are killed. After examining the wreck, a naval court of inquiry headed by Captain William T. Sampson finds that the effects of the blast "could have been produced only by . . . a mine situated under the bottom of the ship." A furious country concludes that the Spanish are to blame. (Recent research indicates that the explosion was caused by a fire in a coal bunker, which ignited an adjacent magazine.)

March 8.   Congress unanimously appropriates $50,000,000 for national defense, to be spent at the discretion of the president.

The wreck of the *Maine*. Courtesy Nimitz Library.

March 17.   Senator Redfield Proctor, a Republican moderate who has just returned from a visit to Cuba, delivers a powerful speech condemning the brutality of the methods by which the Spanish are attempting to suppress the insurrection there. Many persons who had opposed American intervention become convinced that it is a humanitarian duty.

March 18.   In view of the possibility of war with

Spain, a Flying Squadron is formed for the defense of the eastern seaboard. Commanded by Acting Commodore Winfield Scott Schley, it consists of the armored cruiser *Brooklyn* (ACR 3), flag, the battleships *Massachusetts* (BB 2) and *Texas*, and the cruisers *Columbia* (C 12) and *Minneapolis* (C 13).

March 19–May 24. **Voyage of the Oregon.** The battleship *Oregon* (BB 3), Captain Charles E. Clark, sails from San Francisco, California, to join the forces in the Caribbean. She arrives at Jupiter Inlet, Florida, after an unprecedented, 67-day voyage of 14,700 miles at an average speed of almost 12 knots. No other warship had ever approached this achievement.

March 24. Captain William T. Sampson relieves ailing Rear Admiral Montgomery B. Sicard in command of the North Atlantic Squadron.

March 26. Under great pressure from public opinion eager for war with Spain, President McKinley sends an ultimatum to the Spanish government demanding, among other things, independence for Cuba. The Spanish reply, received March 31, is conciliatory, but ignores the question of Cuban independence.

April 9. The Spanish government agrees to enter an armistice with the Cuban rebels, one of the demands of McKinley's ultimatum of March 26, but the concession comes too late.

April 11. **War message.** President McKinley asks Congress for authority to intervene in Cuba.

April 19. Congress authorizes the president to use force to expel the Spanish from Cuba.

The battleship *Oregon* immediately after the Battle of Santiago. U.S. Naval Institute Collection.

The Teller Amendment to the war resolution pledges the United States not to annex the island. McKinley signs the act on April 20.

April 22. **Blockade of Cuba.** President McKinley proclaims a blockade of the coast of Cuba from Havana to Cienfuegos. Acting Rear Admiral William T. Sampson's North Atlantic Squadron, concentrated at Key West, Florida, sails for Cuba early this morning.

April 22. **First shots of the war.** En route to Cuba with the North Atlantic Squadron, the gunboat *Nashville* (PG 7), Commander Washburn Maynard, captures the Spanish freighter *Buenaventura*. The two shots fired across her bow are the first of the Spanish-American War. Dozens of other Spanish merchantmen will be taken in the brief course of the conflict.

April 23. The North Atlantic Squadron establishes a blockade of the Cuban ports of Havana, Mariel, Matanzas, Cárdenas and Cienfuegos.

April 25. **War with Spain.** Congress declares that a state of war has existed with Spain since April 21. Secretary of the Navy Long cables Commodore George Dewey, commanding the Asiatic Squadron at Hong Kong, "Proceed at once to Philippine Islands. Commence operations . . . against Spanish fleet. You must capture vessels or destroy."

April 27. The U.S. Asiatic Squadron, four cruisers, two gunboats, and a revenue cutter under Commodore George Dewey, sails from Mirs Bay, near Hong Kong, for Manila, seat of the Spanish government in the Philippines.

April 27. **First action.** The armored cruiser *New York* (ACR 2), flagship of Admiral Sampson, cruiser *Cincinnati* (C 7), and monitor *Puritan* (BM 1) engage and silence two Spanish batteries at Matanzas, Cuba, without damage to themselves. The batteries had previously fired on the torpedo boat *Foote* (TB 3).

April 30. Arriving off the Philippine island of Luzon, the Asiatic Squadron searches Subic Bay for the Spanish fleet, which is not there.

May 1. **Battle of Manila Bay.** Certain that the enemy fleet is off Manila, Commodore

Dewey leads the Asiatic Squadron past the shore batteries into the bay under cover of darkness, accepting the risk that the channel may be mined. Most of the ships have passed the batteries before the Spanish open fire, and no damage is done. At dawn the fleet of Rear Admiral Patricio Montojo y Parasón is found lying at anchor off the Cavite Navy Yard. The odds are distinctly in Dewey's favor. His squadron consists of the protected cruisers *Olympia* (C 6), (flag), Captain Charles V. Gridley, *Baltimore* (C 3), Captain Nehemiah M. Dyer, *Boston*, Captain Frank Wildes, and *Raleigh* (C 8), Captain Joseph B. Coghlan, the gunboats *Concord* (PG 3), Commander Asa Walker, and *Petrel* (PG 2), Commander Edward P. Wood, and the revenue cutter *Hugh McCulloch*, Captain Daniel B. Hodgson, U.S. Revenue Cutter Service, plus the transports *Nanshan* and *Zafiro*. The combined broadsides of these ships is 3,700 pounds. The Spanish fleet is formed of one modern but unseaworthy steel cruiser, the *Reina Maria Cristina* (flag); an old wooden cruiser, the *Castillo*; and five small cruisers and gunboats, the *Don Antonio de Ulloa*, *Don Juan de Austria*, *Isla de Cuba*, *Isla de Luzon*, and *Marqués de Duero*. Its combined broadside is only 1,273 pounds. In view of this disparity, Admiral Montojo has elected to fight at anchor, where his vessels can be supported by the Spanish shore fortifications. His tactic is reasonable but unavail-

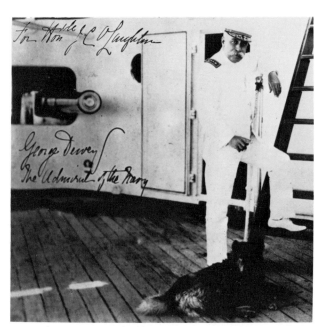

Commodore George Dewey aboard the *Olympia*, after his promotion to rear admiral, with his dog, Bob. Courtesy U.S. Naval Academy Museum.

ing. The *Maria Cristina*, *Castillo*, and *Ulloa* are sunk, the other vessels disabled, and the forts silenced. Three small Spanish gunboats that did not take part in the action—the *Elcano*, *General Lezo*, and *Velasco*—and the transport *Isla de Mindanao* are destroyed by shell fire in the navy yard. Spanish losses, afloat and ashore, are 91 men killed and 280 wounded. American casualties are two officers and six men slightly wounded. Informing the Navy Department of the victory, Dewey explains that he can take Manila at any time, but lacks enough men to hold it. Plans are then set in motion to dispatch an army expeditionary force from the West Coast.

May 1.   **Cervera's squadron.** In the United States it is learned that a Spanish squadron of four cruisers and three destroyers commanded by Rear Admiral Pascual Cervera y Topete sailed from the Cape Verde Islands on April 29. Admiral Sampson is confident that it is bound for the Caribbean.

May 2.   The Spanish naval arsenal at Cavite, near Manila, is occupied by a detachment from the gunboat *Petrel* (PG 2).

May 3.   A party under Lieutenant Dion Williams, USMC, from the cruisers *Baltimore*

The protected cruiser *Olympia*, flagship of the Asiatic Squadron at the Battle of Manila Bay. U.S. Naval Institute Collection.

(C 3) and *Raleigh* (C 8) lands on Corregidor in Manila Bay, captures the Spanish garrison, and spikes the island's guns.

May 11.   **Cable cutting at Cienfuegos.** To sever communications between the Spanish colonial administration in Cuba and the government in Madrid, the decision is made to cut the three underwater cables leading from Cienfuegos to Santiago and thence to Jamaica. (The cable running from Havana to Key West, Florida, has already been cut.) On this date, volunteer boat parties from the cruiser *Marblehead* (C 11) and gunboat *Nashville* (PG 7) commanded by Lieutenants C. M. Winslow and E. A. Anderson row to within 100 feet of the beach to dredge up the cables at Cienfuegos. Soon taken under small-arms fire by Spanish soldiers ashore, they persist in their work for two-and-a-half hours, during which they cut two cables at a cost of four men killed or mortally wounded and seven others hit. Some 54 Medals of Honor are awarded for this operation.

May 11.   **Action at Cárdenas.** Backed by the gunboats *Machias* (PG 5) and *Wilmington* (PG 8) and the revenue cutter *Hudson*, the torpedo boat *Winslow* (TB 5), Lieutenant John B. Bernadou, runs into the harbor at Cárdenas, Cuba, with the aim of cutting out one of three small Spanish gunboats tied up at the pier. During her approach the *Winslow* is struck three times by Spanish shore batteries, and her steering gear is disabled. The *Hudson*, Lieutenant F. H. Newcomb, U.S. Revenue Cutter Service, tows her to safety. Lieutenant Bernadou and two other men are wounded and four are killed. Among the dead is Ensign Worth Bagley, the only naval officer killed in the Spanish-American War.

May 12.   **The search for Cervera.** Assuming that the Spanish Cape Verde squadron will make for Puerto Rico, Admiral Sampson proceeds there with the armored cruiser *New York* (ACR 2), flag, battleships *Indiana* (BB 1) and *Iowa* (BB 4), the monitors *Amphitrite* (BM 2) and *Terror* (BM 4), the cruisers *Detroit* (C 10) and *Montgomery* (C 9), and two auxiliaries, arriving off San Juan before dawn. The Spanish squadron is not present. After bombarding the harbor fortifications for two hours, during

Ensign Worth Bagley, the only naval officer killed in the Spanish-American War. Nimitz Library Special Collections.

which one seaman is killed and six wounded, Sampson shapes course for Key West, which he reaches on May 18. Here he learns that Cervera's ships coaled at Curaçao, Netherlands West Indies, on May 14–15 and departed in the direction of Cuba.

May 19.   **The search for Cervera continues.** Upon the news that the Spanish squadron has appeared in the Caribbean, the Navy Department ordered Commodore Schley's Flying Squadron to Key West. Sampson finds that it has just arrived when he returns from Puerto Rico and directs Schley to establish a blockade of the southern Cuban port of Cienfuegos, certain that Cervera will appear at either Cienfuegos or Havana. Schley sails early on the morning of the 19th—the day Cervera slips into Santiago—with the armored cruiser *Brooklyn* (ACR 3), flag, the battleships *Massachusetts*

Rear Admiral William T. Sampson. Courtesy U.S. Naval Academy Museum.

(BB 2) and *Texas*, and the armed yacht *Scorpion*. Sampson promises to send the battleship *Iowa* (BB 4) to reinforce the Flying Squadron as soon as she can coal.

May 21.   Sampson sails from Key West to patrol the Nicholas Channel, off the northern coast of Cuba, in position to intercept Cervera should he attempt to reach Havana.

May 21–24.   **Schley off Cienfuegos.** Approaching Cienfuegos, whose harbor cannot be seen from the sea, Schley hears the sound of cannon fire, which he assumes to be a salute fired in honor of the arrival of Cervera's squadron. On May 23 he receives a dispatch from Sampson, reporting "Spanish squadron probably at Santiago" and instructing him to proceed there "if you are satisfied that they are not at Cienfuegos." Since Schley believes they are indeed at Cienfuegos, he stays where he is. The next day the cruiser *Marblehead* (C 11) arrives and informs him that a secret signal system, of which he was previously unaware, has been devised for communicating with Cuban insurgents ashore. Through these signals, Schley learns that the Spanish squadron is definitely not at Cienfuegos.

May 24–26.   **Schley's advance to Santiago.** Departing Cienfuegos around 6:00 P.M. on the 24th, Schley steams slowly down the coast towards Santiago. Twenty miles from the city he decides that his ships' need of coal and the difficulty of coaling at sea necessitate his return to Key West, and he reverses course. His decision is influenced by the fact that Captain Charles D. Sigsbee of the auxiliary cruiser *St. Paul*, which had been on patrol off Santiago for several days, reports having seen "absolutely nothing of the Spanish fleet."

May 27.   Around 9:30 A.M. the auxiliary *Harvard* reaches the Flying Squadron carrying a dispatch from the Navy Department, dated May 25, ordering Commodore Schley to Santiago to ascertain if the Spanish squadron is there. He replies, "Much to be regretted, can not obey orders of the department; forced to proceed for coal to Key West. . . ." That night, however, the sea abates. The battleship *Texas* succeeds in taking on some coal from the *Merrimac*, and Schley turns back towards Santiago.

May 28.   **Cervera is found.** Reaching Santiago this afternoon, Schley sends the cruiser *Marblehead* (C 11), Commander Bowman H. McCalla, to scout the mouth of the channel leading to the harbor. The ships of the Spanish squadron are clearly visible at anchor off the city. The next morning Schley makes an inshore sweep with his entire squadron, confirming the sighting, and institutes a blockage of the port. Admiral Sampson later terms Schley's conduct of the search for Cervera "reprehensible."

May 29.   Informed by dispatch boat that Schley has located the Spanish squadron, Sampson hastens to Key West to advise the Navy Department and starts for Santiago with the *New York* (ACR 2), collecting the battleship *Oregon* (BB 3), the torpedo boat *Porter* (TB 6), and auxiliary destroyer *Mayflower* en route.

May 31.   Commodore Schley conducts a long-range bombardment of the coastal fortifications at Santiago with the battleships *Massachusetts* (BB 2), flag, and *Iowa* (BB 4) and the cruiser *New Orleans*.

June 1.   **Sampson reaches Santiago.** Admiral Sampson arrives to assume command of U.S. naval forces off Santiago. For the moment, the strategic situation is stalemated. Sampson cannot enter the harbor, which is located at the end of a narrow, twisting channel commanded by powerful shore fortifications and presumably defended by minefields; and Cervera cannot leave without encountering Sampson's greatly superior fleet.

June 3.   **Dewey Medal.** Congress authorizes the award of a medal for the officers and men who participated in the Battle of Manila Bay. This is the first official American campaign medal.

June 3.   **Hobson and the Merrimac.** With no way of getting into Santiago harbor to attack Cervera's squadron, Sampson tries to bottle it up there. After nightfall a volunteer crew of seven bluejackets headed by Lieutenant Richmond P. Hobson sets out to sink the collier *Merrimac* across the channel. A hail of fire from the Spanish batteries disables the ship's steering before she reaches a blocking position, and she settles along the edge of the channel. Miraculously, all of her crew members survive and are rescued by a Spanish launch in which Hobson is surprised to find Admiral Cervera. The

Lieutenant Richmond P. Hobson, the hero of the *Merrimac.* Courtesy U.S. Naval Academy Museum.

seven enlisted men are awarded the Medal of Honor in 1899; as an officer, Hobson is ineligible for the honor at that date, but receives it through a special Act of Congress in 1933.

June 6.   The fortifications covering the channel into Santiago are shelled by Sampson's squadron, consisting of the battleships *Iowa* (BB 4), *Massachusetts* (BB 2), *Oregon* (BB 3), and *Texas*, the armored cruisers *Brooklyn* (ACR 3) and *New York* (ACR 2), the cruisers *Marblehead* (C 11) and *New Orleans*, the auxiliary cruisers *Suwanee*, *Vixen*, and *Yankee*, and the dispatch boat *Dolphin*. The Spanish cruiser *Reina Mercedes*, lying at the mouth of the harbor, is also engaged.

June 7.   The cruiser *Marblehead* (C 11), Commander Bowman H. McCalla, and auxiliary cruiser *Yankee*, Captain Willard A. Brownson, test the defenses of Guantánamo Bay, 40 miles east of Santiago, silencing a Spanish battery and driving the gunboat *Sandoval* into the inner harbor. Admiral Sampson has decided to seize the bay for use as a coaling station and advanced base.

June 10.   **Marines at Guantánamo.** Supported by fire from the battleship *Oregon* (BB 3), a marine battalion under Lieutenant Colonel R. W. Huntington lands at Guantánamo. Its members are the first American troops to set foot on Cuban soil.

June 11–14.   Beginning late in the afternoon of the 11th, the Spanish harass the marine encampment at Guantánamo with sniper fire. Three days later Lieutenant Colonel Huntington learns from Cuban guerrillas that Spanish forces in the area are dependent on a water supply point in the Cuzco Valley, two miles from his camp. Upon receiving this information, he sends two companies and 75 Cubans under his youngest company officer, 52-year-old Captain George Fielding Elliott, to destroy the enemy installation. The operation is supported by fire from the dispatch boat *Dolphin*. Elliott accomplishes his mission, defeating a Spanish detachment of 500 men and wrecking the windmill and well at a cost of 6 men killed and 16 wounded. The sniping ceases.

June 14.   **The army embarks.** The V Corps, a 17,000-man expeditionary force commanded by corpulent Major General Wil-

The bombardment of Santiago, June 6, 1898. This previously unpublished drawing was made by R. W. Bennett, a crewman on the cruiser *New Orleans*, on the back of a leaf from her log. Courtesy U.S. Naval Academy Museum.

liam T. Shafter, sails under naval escort from Tampa, Florida, to begin operations around Santiago. Sampson hopes that its appearance will force Cervera to leave the harbor.

June 15. The Spanish fort at Caimanera, on Guantánamo Bay, is destroyed by fire from the battleship *Texas*, Captain John W. Philip, the cruiser *Marblehead* (C 11), Commander Bowman H. McCalla, and the auxiliary cruiser *Suwanee*, Commander Daniel Delehanty.

June 20. Admiral Sampson and General Shafter meet to plan the strategy of the Santiago campaign. Sampson leaves the conference convinced that Shafter has agreed that the army's objective is the capture of the batteries commanding the channel into the harbor; Shafter believes that Sampson agrees its objective is the capture of the city itself.

June 21. **Seizure of Guam.** In the Pacific, the cruiser *Charleston* (C 2), Captain Henry

Glass, captures the island of Guam. The Spanish colonial authorities were unaware that there was a war under way.

June 22–25. **Landing at Daiquirí.** The V Corps goes ashore in an unopposed landing at the village of Daiquirí, 16 miles east of Santiago.

June 22. Arriving to establish a blockade of San Juan, Puerto Rico, the auxiliary cruiser *St. Paul*, Captain Charles D. Sigsbee, disables the Spanish destroyer *Terror* when she advances to attack her with the support of the light cruiser *Isabel II* and the guns of the shore batteries.

June 28. President McKinley proclaims a blockade of the southern coast of Cuba.

June 28. Off San Juan, Puerto Rico, the auxiliary cruiser *Yosemite*, Commander William H. Emory, manned by the Michigan Naval Militia, intercepts the transport *Antonio Lopez*, nearing port with supplies for the garrison. Despite efforts by the Spanish cruisers *Isabel II* and *Alfonso XIII* and a torpedo boat to cover the *Lopez*'s approach, the *Yosemite* drives her on a reef and wrecks her with gunfire.

June 30.   The auxiliary cruisers *Hist*, Lieutenant Lucien Young, and *Hornet*, Lieutenant J. M. Helm, and the armed tug *Wompatuck*, Commander Charles W. Jungen, sink two small Spanish warships in separate engagements off Manzanillo, Cuba.

July 1.   Escorted by the cruiser *Charleston* (C 2), transports carrying the first 2,500 men of the expeditionary force to the Philippines reach Manila Bay.

July 1.   **El Caney and San Juan Hill.** Advancing on Santiago, General Shafter's troops carry two strong Spanish positions by frontal assaults in which 1,572 of them— almost 10 percent of the entire expeditionary force—are killed or wounded.

July 2.   Alarmed by his casualties in the previous day's battles, Shafter sends Sampson a message urging him to force the entrance to Santiago harbor "to avoid losses among my men." Sampson is appalled. Instead of helping the navy by capturing the batteries, the army is asking the navy to help it capture the city. Sampson makes arrangements to confer with Shafter at Siboney, east of Santiago, the next day.

July 3.   **Battle of Santiago.** Shortly after his flagship, the armored cruiser *New York* (ACR 2), leaves the blockade line to carry Sampson down the coast to Siboney, the Spanish squadron solves his problem by a desperate attempt to escape. The orders for the sortie had been issued, over Admiral Cervera's objections, by the governor general of Cuba. The bow of the cruiser *Infante Maria Teresa*, Cervera's flagship, is sighted in the channel, leading the squadron out, at 9:31 A.M. On her approach Commodore Schley's flagship, the *Brooklyn* (ACR 3), turns to port, away from the Spanish vessel, a maneuver for which Schley later receives considerable criticism. Upon reaching deep water the *Maria Teresa* turns west on a course paralleling the Cuban coast. Cervera's other three cruisers follow. Smothered by fire from the battleships *Indiana* (BB 1), Captain Henry C. Taylor, *Iowa* (BB 4), Captain Robley D. Evans, *Oregon* (BB 3), Captain Charles Clark, and

Texas, Captain John W. Philip, and the *Brooklyn*, Captain Francis A. Cook, the Spanish flagship beaches herself six-and-a-half miles down the coast at 10:15. The *Almirante Oquendo*, the last cruiser in the Spanish line, is driven ashore at 10:35. The *Vizcaya* and *Cristobal Colón* continue their flight to the west, pursued by the *Oregon*— the only battleship to have all her boilers lit when the Spanish sortied—the *Brooklyn*, the *Texas*, and the *Iowa*, in that order. Around 11:00 the *Vizcaya* turns towards the coast with the evident intention of beaching herself, and Admiral Sampson, whose flagship has gradually overtaken the action, signals the *Iowa* to follow and finish her. The action then settles into a stern chase in which the *Colón* draws away from all her pursuers except the *Oregon*, "the bulldog of the fleet," and the *Brooklyn*. At 1:10 P.M. a 13-inch shell fired at maximum elevation from the *Oregon*'s fore turret strikes beside the *Colón*, whose speed has begun to slacken, and the cruiser runs aground off the mouth of Rio Tarquino. The two destroyers that followed the cruisers out of Santiago have already been destroyed: the *Pluton* by a direct hit from a battleship, probably the *Indiana*; and the *Furor* in a close action with Lieutenant Commander Richard Wainwright's auxiliary gunboat *Gloucester* (formerly J. P.

The smouldering wreck of the Spanish cruiser *Vizcaya* at the conclusion of the Battle of Santiago. U.S. Naval Institute Collection.

Morgan's yacht *Corsair*). Spanish losses are 323 dead and 151 wounded; the latter and most of the other 1,800 survivors, including Admiral Cervera, are rescued by Sampson's ships. American casualties are one man killed and one seriously wounded. Sampson opens his report of the action with the words, "The fleet under my command offers the nation as a Fourth of July present the whole of Cervera's fleet."

July 4.   After nightfall, the Spanish attempt to block the channel to Santiago by scuttling the cruiser *Reina Mercedes* across it. The movement is detected, and the Spanish ship is quickly sunk by fire from the *Massachusetts* (BB 2) and the *Texas*.

July 7.   The United States annexes Hawaii.

July 10.   The battleships *Indiana* (BB 1) and *Texas* and the armored cruisers *Brooklyn* (ACR 3) and *New York* (ACR 2) bombard Santiago.

July 15.   Rear Admiral Frederick V. McNair becomes 16th superintendent of the Naval Academy.

July 17.   **Fall of Santiago.** General José Toral, commanding the Spanish forces around Santiago, surrenders the city to General Shafter. Eight Spanish vessels, including the gunboat *Alvarado*, are captured in the harbor.

July 18.   A squadron consisting of the gunboats *Wilmington* (PG 8), Commander C. C. Todd, and *Helena*, Commander W. T. Swinburne, the auxiliary cruisers *Hist*, Lieutenant Lucien Young, and *Scorpion*, Lieutenant Commander Adolph Marix, and the armed tugs *Osceola*, Lieutenant J. L. Purcell, and *Wompatuck*, Commander Charles M. Jungen, enters Manzanilla harbor, where it destroys the Spanish gunboats *Cuba Española*, *Delgado Perado*, *Estrella de Guantánamo*, *Guardián*, *José Garcia*, *María Pontón*, and *Sentinel Delgado*, and the blockade runner *El Purísima Concepción*.

July 19.   A second contingent of American troops reaches Manila.

July 21.   The fortifications of Nipe, on the northern coast of Cuba, are shelled by the gunboats *Annapolis* (PG 10), Commander J. J. Hunker, and *Topeka*, Lieutenant Commander W. S. Cowles, the auxiliary cruiser *Wasp*, Lieutenant A. Ward, and the armed tug *Leydon*, Ensign W. S. Crosley. The

Spanish light cruiser *Jorge Juan* sorties to engage this force and is quickly sunk.

July 21.   **Expedition to Puerto Rico.** Major General Nelson A. Miles sails from Guantánamo for the invasion of Puerto Rico with 3,400 troops in eight transports escorted by the battleship *Massachusetts* (BB 2), Captain F. J. Higginson, the cruiser *Columbia* (C 12), Captain J. H. Sands, and the auxiliary cruisers *Dixie*, Commander C. H. Davis, *Gloucester*, Lieutenant Commander Richard Wainwright, and *Yale*, Commander W. C. Wise.

July 25.   Guánica, Puerto Rico, is seized by a landing party under Lieutenant Henry P. Huse from the *Gloucester*.

July 25.   Major General Wesley Merritt reaches Manila with a third contingent of troops, raising the strength of the American expeditionary force to 10,000 men, and begins operations against the Philippine capital.

July 26.   General Miles's expeditionary force lands at Guánica, Puerto Rico.

July 28.   Ponce, the largest city on the southern coast of Puerto Rico, surrenders to Commander C. H. Davis of the auxiliary cruiser *Dixie*.

August 12.   In Washington, D.C., representatives of the United States and Spain sign an armistice ending the Spanish-American War. Spain agrees to free Cuba and to cede Puerto Rico and Guam to the United States. The negotiation of the definitive treaty of peace is scheduled to begin in Paris in October.

August 12–13.   The port of Manzanillo, Cuba, is shelled and captured by a squadron consisting of the cruiser *Newark* (C 1), Captain Caspar F. Goodrich, the auxiliary cruisers *Hist*, Lieutenant Lucien Young, and *Suwanee*, Commander Daniel Delehanty, the captured gunboat *Alvarado*, Lieutenant Victor Blue, and the armed tug *Osceola* (AT 47) Lieutenant J. L. Purcell. Only afterwards is it learned that the war is over.

August 13.   **Capture of Manila.** Spanish authorities at Manila are anxious to surrender the city to American forces rather than to the insurrectionary Filippino army of General Emiliano Aguinaldo. The Belgian consul acts as an intermediary for secret negotiations between the Spanish and

Commodore Dewey, through which it is arranged that the city will surrender following token resistance to a naval bombardment and land attack. Accordingly, on this date the cruiser *Olympia* (C 6) and the gunboat *Petrel* (PG 2) shell Fort San Antonio, which does not return their fire, for an hour and a quarter. The Spanish then strike their colors and Dewey's Flag Lieutenant Thomas N. Brumby lands to raise the American flag over Manila. Six hundred troops go ashore from the transport *Zafiro* to begin the occupation later that afternoon.

August 14.   The last shots of the Spanish-American War are fired when the armed lighthouse supply ship *Mangrove*, Lieutenant Commander D. D. V. Stuart, engages two Spanish gunboats off Caibarién, Cuba. The Spaniards raise a flag of truce and explain that an armistice has been signed.

November 4.   A detachment of 15 marines under First Lieutenant Robert McM. Dutton from the cruisers *Baltimore* (C 3), *Boston*, and *Raleigh* (C 8), establish a U.S. Legation Guard at Peking, China.

December 10.   **Peace with Spain.** The definitive treaty is signed in Paris. It presents the United States with an instant empire consisting of the islands of Guam, Puerto Rico, and the Philippines, for all of which Spain is paid $20,000,000. President McKinley had not intended to keep the Philippines, but during the negotiations American opinion came out strongly in favor of annexation. These far-distant territories can be defended only by a battle fleet dedicated to the Mahanian concept of command of the sea. America's commitment to sea power is clenched.

December 23.   The Navy Department is assigned the responsibility of administering the island of Guam.

1899

January 17.   Commander E.D. Taussig, captain of the gunboat *Bennington* (PG 4), claims Wake Island for the United States.

February 4.   **Outbreak of the Philippine insurrection.** Disgruntled by the United States' annexation of the Philippines, the insurrectionary army of General Emiliano Aguinaldo attacks the American lines around Manila. In the ensuing conflict, which will last for more than two years, the navy plays an active role as a transport, patrol, bombardment, and landing force.

February 5.   The cruiser *Charleston* (C 2), monitor *Monadnock* (BM 3), and gunboats *Callao* and *Concord* (PG 3) provide fire support for the advance of American ground forces outside Manila.

February 11.   **Action at Ilo-Ilo.** The gunboat *Petrel* (PG 2) shells an insurgent fort on Panay, which is then occupied by a naval landing party.

February 22.   A landing party from the *Petrel* takes possession of the Philippine island of Cebu.

February 24.   The cruiser *Marietta* (PG 15) lands a detachment to protect American interests at Bluefields, Nicaragua.

March 2.   Admiral George Dewey is elevated to the rank of Admiral of the Navy. He remains today the only officer ever to have held that rank.

March 3.   President McKinley signs the Naval Personnel Act of 1899, which amalgamates the navy's engineers with its line officers and thereby eliminates the friction that had existed between the two groups since the advent of steam power.

April 1.   **Samoan uprising.** Late in 1898 intertribal warfare broke out in the Samoan Islands, which are jointly administered by the United States, Great Britain, and Germany. American and British landing parties, the former from the protected cruiser *Philadelphia* (C 4), are put ashore to guard their consulates. On April 1, an Anglo-American patrol is ambushed in the jungle near Apia, on Upolu Island. Four Americans and three British are killed and seven wounded. The dead include the American landing force commander, Lieutenant Philip Van Horn Lansdale, USN. The uprising is suppressed by April 25 by a combination of shore bombardments and punitive expeditions into the interior.

April 27.   The transport *Resolute* lands a party of 80 marines to preserve order in Havana, Cuba.

May 23.   **Marines to the Philippines.** Colonel Percival C. Pope's 1st Battalion of Ma-

Marines guard the residence of the U.S. consul at Matautu Point, Apia, Upolu Island, during the Samoan uprising. U.S. Naval Institute Collection.

rines, 275 strong, is landed to provide security for the naval base at Cavite, on the Philippine island of Luzon.

June 10.   A squadron consisting of the monitors *Monadnock* (BM 3) and *Monterey* (BM 6) and four gunboats gives fire support for a major army offensive south from Manila into Cavite Province.

June 13.   The six ships engaged on June 10 plus three additional vessels provide fire support for a successful army assault on the insurgent position along the Zapote River in Cavite Province.

September 18–23.   A squadron consisting of the monitor *Monterey* (BM 6), cruisers *Baltimore* (C 3) and *Charleston* (C 2), gunboat *Concord* (PG 3), and transport *Zafiro* shell and seize the insurgent positions at Olongapo, securing control of Subic Bay on the west coast of Luzon.

September 21.   The 2nd Battalion of Marines, 364 officers and men under future commandant Lieutenant Colonel George Fielding Elliott, arrives at Cavite.

September 25.   The armed patrol boat *Urdaneta*, Naval Cadet Welborn C. Wood (USNA 1899), is ambushed by insurgents in the delta of the Pampanga River near Orani on the island of Luzon. Cadet Wood and four of his eight men are killed in the ensuing fire fight; the others are captured in an attempt to escape ashore. The *Urdaneta* is the only naval vessel lost in the Philippine Insurrection.

October 8.   **Action at Novaleta.** Lieutenant Colonel G.F. Elliott's 2nd Marine Battalion cooperates in the capture of this insurgent stronghold between Manila and Cavite. The operation, in which the marines lose 11 men killed and wounded, is supported by fire from the gunboats *Callao* and *Petrel* (PG 2).

November 2.   The protected cruiser *Charleston* (C 2), Captain C.W. Pigman, wrecks without loss of life on an uncharted reef near Camiguin Island in the Philippines.

November 7.   A squadron of six ships under Commander Harry Knox supports the landing of 2,500 troops at San Fabian, on the Lingayen Gulf coast of Luzon.

November 26.   The battleship *Oregon*'s marine detachment, 49 men commanded by Captain Dion Williams, occupies Vigan, north of Lingayen Gulf, without opposition. It is relieved by army troops two days later.

December 10.   Landing parties from the *Oregon* (BB 3) and the cruiser *Baltimore* (C 3) take possession of the navy yard at Olongapo on Subic Bay. A company of marines arrives to garrison the town 10 days later.

December 15.   A third marine battalion, 340 men commanded by Major L.W.T. Waller, reaches the Philippines.

1900

Course of the Philippine Insurrection.
Throughout the year the navy continues to participate in the suppression of the insurrection. Most of its operations are carried out by gunboats, which frequently shell enemy positions, land detachments of sailors and marines to occupy coastal villages,

A marine patrol near Olongapo on Luzon during the Philippine Insurrection. Defense Department photo (Marine Corps).

and intercept insurgent vessels. Marine units also play an active role in the fighting ashore.

January 11.   The gunboat *Princeton*, Commander Harry Knox, takes possession of the Batan Islands in the northern Philippines.

February 10.   **American Samoa.** Commander Seaton Schroeder becomes the first naval governor of the American portion of the Samoan Islands, which were divided between the United States and Germany in 1899.

February 19.   President McKinley places the administration of American Samoa under the Navy Department.

February 20.   The battleship *Kearsarge* (BB 5) is commissioned.

March 13.   **General Board of the Navy.** A permanent board of senior officers is established under the presidency of Admiral Dewey to provide the secretary of the navy with professional advice on naval operations and policy.

March 15.   Commander Richard Wainwright becomes 17th superintendent of the Naval Academy.

May 15.   The battleship *Kentucky* (BB 6) is commissioned.

May 18.   **The Boxer Rebellion.** The Western penetration of China has provoked a violently xenophobic mass movement, the Righteous Society of Heavenly Fists, whose adherents foreigners refer to as Boxers. With the tacit approval of the Imperial Chinese government, in two years the movement spreads from outlying areas to the vicinity of Peking, seat of the foreign embassies to the Manchu Court. On this date, U.S. Minister Edwin Conger telegraphs a request to the Asiatic Squadron to send a force to guard the American legation. On May 28 his colleagues of the Corps Diplomatique send similar appeals to their navies.

May 31.   **Reinforcements reach Peking.** The foreign warships assembled off Taku Bar at the mouth of the Pei-Ho River send an international force of 337 American, British, French, Italian, Japanese, and Russian seamen and marines to guard the legations at Peking. The American contingent, landed from Captain Bowman H. McCalla's cruiser *Newark* (C 1), consists of 48 marines and

Heroes of the Boxer Rebellion: second from left, Captain Newt Hall, USMC; next to him, Captain Bowman H. McCalla, USN; far right, Captain John T. Myers. Defense Department photo (Marine Corps).

5 bluejackets under Captains John T. ("Handsome Jack") Myers and Newt H. Hall, USMC. A detachment of 89 Austrian and German sailors follow on June 3.

June 8.   The Boxers cut the telegraph line from Peking to Tientsin, isolating the legations.

June 10.   **Seymour Expedition.** Vice Admiral Sir Edward Seymour, KCB, the senior foreign officer in northern China, leads a force of 2,129 men representing eight nationalities from Tientsin to reopen communications with Peking. The expedition includes 112 American seamen and marines from the cruiser *Newark* (C 1) under Captain Bowman H. McCalla. First attacked by Boxers on June 13, the column is forced to retire four days later after pushing to within 25 miles of Peking.

June 15.   The Boxers besiege the international settlement at Tientsin, which is defended by 2,400 troops, mostly Russian.

June 19–20.   A detachment of 140 U.S. marines, rushed from the Philippines under Major L.W.T. Waller, and 440 Russian infantry are beaten back in an attempt to relieve Tientsin.

June 21–August 14.   **Defense of the Legations.** The three-quarters-square-mile Legation Quarter of Peking has been put in a state of defense in anticipation of the attacks that begin on this date. For 55 days, the 409 legation guards and 125 civilian volunteers defend the quarter against attacks by thousands of Boxes, intermittently aided by Chinese regular troops. Before their relief, 66 of the defenders are killed and 150 wounded. The conduct of Captain Myers's marines, who hold a key sector of the compound walls, is highly praised by all present.

June 22.   Retreating towards Tientsin, the Seymour Expedition captures Hsiku Arsenal, six miles from the city and, burdened by 250 wounded, prepares to defend itself there.

June 23.   **Relief of Tientsin.** An allied force of 2,000 men, including Major Waller's marines, fight their way through to Tientsin.

June 25.   **Relief of the Seymour Expedition.** Following the relief of Tientsin, the allies send out a strong column that escorts Seymour's battered expedition back to the city.

July 10.   The remainder of the First Marine Regiment, 318 men under Colonel Robert W. Meade (a Civil War veteran), reach Tientsin.

July 13–14.   **Capture of Tientsin.** The walled, native city of Tientsin, held by at least 20,000 Boxers, is stormed by 5,650 allied troops under British Brigadier General A.R.F. Dorward, DSO. The American contingent, commanded by marine Colonel R.W. Meade, consists of 1,021 men of the First Marines and Ninth Infantry. It is during this operation that the U.S. Marine Corps develops its friendship with the Royal Welsh Fusiliers.

August 3–14.   **Relief of the Legations.** An International Relief Expedition of 18,600 men commanded by Brigadier General Sir Alfred Gaselee, KCB, advancing from Tientsin, relieves the legations at Peking. This force includes 482 U.S. Marines and 2,000 soldiers under Major General Adna R. Chaffee.

October 11.   U.S. Marines are withdrawn from China.

October 12.   **The Holland.** The U.S. Navy's first submarine, the *Holland* (SS 1), is put in commission, Lieutenant Harry H. Caldwell, commanding. Privately built by John P. Holland, an Irish emigrant who devoted his life to submarine construction, she is 53'10" in length, displaces 64 tons, has four torpedo tubes, and carries a crew of seven.

The *Holland*, the navy's first submarine. Official U.S. Navy photograph.

October 16. The battleship *Alabama* (BB 8) is commissioned.

1901

January 2–3. Four boat parties under Lieutenant F.R. Payne capture 18 insurgent boats on the Imus River, near Cavite, in the Philippines.

January 17. The gunboat *Don Juan of Austria*, Commander T.C. McLean, shells insurgent positions and lands an army detachment at Donsol on the island of Luzon.

January 28. The *Don Juan of Austria* provides fire support for an army attack on Maringondon, Luzon.

January 31–February 3. Parties from the *Don Juan of Austria* capture the villages of Jamaruan, Calveria, and San Pascual on Luzon.

February 4. The battleship *Wisconsin* (BB 9) is commissioned.

February 23–March 3. The gunboat *Villalobos*, Lieutenant Henry P. Huse, supports army operations at Loorg Bay and Lubang Island in the Philippines.

March 18–28. The gunboat *Vicksburg*, Commander E.B. Barry, supports the army in operations on the Philippine island of Palawan.

March 23. **End of the Philippine Insurrection; Moro Insurrection.** General Emiliano Aguinaldo, the Filippino insurgent leader, is captured by American forces. Though operations continue on a diminishing scale for some months, for practical purposes the revolt has been extinguished. In the meantime, however, a new insurrection has broken out among the proud, Moslem Moros inhabiting the southern Philippine islands of Samar, Mindanao, and Jolo.

July 3–17. The armed patrol vessel *Basco*, Naval Cadet J.H. Comfort, fights a series of actions with insurgents on the Gandara River on the island of Samar.

July 4. The military government of the Philippines is replaced by a civil government headed by future president William Howard Taft.

September 16. The battleship *Illinois* (BB 7) is commissioned.

October 24. Four companies of marines under Major Littleton Waller Tazewell ("Tony") Waller are placed under the command of Brigadier General Jacob M. ("Hell-Roaring Jake") Smith, USA, to suppress Moro insurgents on the Philippine island of Samar, where a company of the Ninth Infantry was massacred on September 28. By November 12, Waller's columns have killed 39 and captured 18 insurgents and burned 255 huts at a cost of only two dead.

November 15. **Battle of the Sohoton River.** Major Waller's marines assault and capture a supposedly impregnable insurgent stronghold deep in the mountains of Samar.

November 16. **Sims writes the president.** Around 1890 a small number of progressive-minded naval officers, most notably the inventive Bradley A. Fiske, began to consider techniques and devices through which the quality of American naval gunnery could be improved. The record of the battles of Manila Bay and Santiago, after which it was found that only about 3 percent of the shells fired hit their targets, showed that improvement was needed. The results achieved by the Royal Navy's gunnery expert, Captain Percy Scott, proved that it was possible. Conservative senior officers in the Bureau of Ordnance were, however, slow to respond to the reformers' inventions and prescriptions. Finally, Lieutenant William S. Sims, to whom Scott has personally explained his system, takes the daring step of writing directly to President Theodore Roosevelt to condemn the navy's gunnery. His presentation converts the president to his cause. Sims is made inspector of target practice, and with the support of Fiske, Lieutenant Commander Albert P. Niblack, and the chief executive, sets out to revolutionize American gunnery methods. By the beginning of 1907 the navy has developed the elements of modern fire control.

November 16.   Three boat parties from the gunboat *Vicksburg* (PG 11), Lieutenant Commander J.H. Glennan, support a marine expedition against Philippine insurgents up the Basey River on the island of Samar.

November 24–December 4.   **Panamanian intervention.** Marines are landed in Panama at Panama City and Colón from the ships *Concord* (PG 3), *Iowa* (BB 4), *Machias* (PG 5), and *Marietta* (PG 15) to protect American interests—most particularly the trans-isthmian railway—during one of the recurrent revolts against Colombian rule. They are withdrawn after the *Iowa*'s Captain Thomas Perry negotiates an agreement between the opposing forces to respect American property.

November 28.   **Hay-Pauncefort Treaty.** A new agreement with Great Britain abrogates the Clayton-Bulwer Treaty of 1850 and provides that the United States may singly build, fortify, and control a canal across Central America. Diplomatically, the way is clear to the construction of the Panama Canal.

December 13.   **Sampson-Schley controversy.** During the Spanish-American War, Admiral Sampson and other officers thought that Commodore Schley's conduct of the search for Cervera was woefully lacking in energy and enterprise. Secretary of the Navy Long's agreement with this view was reflected in his postwar promotion list, which

proposed raising both Sampson and Schley to the permanent rank of rear admiral, but moving Sampson ahead of Schley, to whom he had been junior. After lengthy hearings, Congress voted to advance the two men the same number of places, thus preserving Schley's prewar seniority. This question was settled in April 1899. Controversy erupts again in the spring of 1901, when an updated edition of Edgar S. Maclay's *History of the Navy*, a book used as a text at the Naval Academy, presents Schley's actions at the Battle of Santiago as well as during the search for Cervera in a most unflattering light. Schley thereupon requests a court of inquiry into his conduct throughout the war. The court, of which Admiral Dewey is president, submits its opinion on this date—but its opinion is divided. The majority report condemns Schley's performance; a minority report, prepared by Dewey himself, commends it. Schley wants to continue the contest, but President Theodore Roosevelt, apprehensive of the disruptive effect of the quarrel on the service as a whole, declares the case closed. The spectacle of this unseemly squabble may be responsible for the almost obsessive discretion a new generation of naval leaders will observe in discussing the command decisions of World War II.

December 28.   **The ordeal of Samar.** With 54 marines, 2 Filipino guides, and 33 native bearers, Major L.W.T. Waller sets out to cross the interior of southern Samar. The march becomes a disaster as wrong turns multiply and rations dwindle. Eleven marines die of starvation and fatigue. Waller reaches his destination, the coastal town of Basey, on January 17, 1902. Three days later, certain that his Filipinos betrayed him, he holds a drum-head court-martial and executes 11 of them. Greatly to his surprise, he himself is then court-martialed on charges of murder. He is acquitted and eventually rises to the rank of major general.

1902

April 16–22.   The gunboat *Machias* (PG 5) lands a detachment of sailors and marines at Boca del Toro in the Colombian province of

Panama. This is the first of several landings that will be made in the course of the year to protect American lives and property during the revolution in Panama.

May 1.   William H. Moody becomes 35th secretary of the navy.

September 17.   A detachment of seamen and marines is landed from the cruiser *Cincinnati* (C 7) to protect American property at Colón, Panama.

September 18.   The survey ship *Ranger* lands seamen and marines to safeguard American interests at Panama City, Panama.

September 23–November 18.   A battalion of marines under Lieutenant Colonel B.R. Russell, landed from the transport *Panther*, occupies Colón, Panama. The commander of American naval forces off the Panamanian coast, Rear Admiral Silas Casey, refuses to permit Colombian troops to cross the isthmus to attack the rebels and arranges a compromise peace.

November 6.   Captain Willard H. Brownson becomes the 18th superintendent of the U.S. Naval Academy.

November 24.   **First U.S. destroyer.** The torpedo boat destroyer *Bainbridge* (DD 1) is commissioned. Of 420 tons displacement, she is 250 feet in length, carries a crew of 75, and has a speed of 29 knots.

December 22.   The battleship *Maine* (BB 10) is commissioned.

December–January 1903.   **Venezuelan crisis.** Germany, Great Britain, and Italy initiate a naval blockade of Venezuela, whose government has defaulted on the payment of debts owed to European investors, and the Germans go so far as to shell several Venezuelan forts. Determined to prevent European powers from intervening in the Western Hemisphere, President Theodore Roosevelt sends a naval force into the Caribbean and takes a leading role in negotiations that persuade the creditor nations to submit their case to the International Court of Justice at The Hague. In February 1904 the court rules that Venezuela must pay.

1903

January 22.   **Hay-Herrán Treaty.** U.S. Secretary of State John Hay and Colombian chargé d'affaires Tomás Herrán conclude a treaty whereby Colombia is to grant the United States a 100-year lease to build and control a canal across the province of Panama in return for a payment of $10,000,000 and an annual subsidy of $250,000. The U.S. Senate approves the treaty in March, but in August the Colombian Senate rejects it.

February 23.   **Gitmo.** The United States leases Guantánamo Bay, Cuba, where it will establish a major naval base.

March 21–April 16.   **Honduran Expedition-**

The destroyer *Decatur*, a sister ship of the *Bainbridge*. Courtesy Library of Congress.

ary Service. A peace-keeping force consisting of the cruisers *Olympia* (C 6), *Raleigh* (C 8), and *San Francisco* (C 5), gunboat *Marietta* (PG 15), and the transport *Panther* operates off the coast of Honduras during a revolution there. Marines are landed to protect the U.S. Embassy at Puerto Cortez.

April 1–19.   A detachment of marines from the cruiser *Atlanta* is landed to guard the U.S. Consulate at Santo Domingo during an insurrection in the Dominican Republic.

May 22.   A Cuban-American treaty is concluded, granting the United States the right to intervene in Cuba to maintain order or to preserve the island's independence.

September 7–13.   The cruiser *Brooklyn* (ACR 3) lands a party of sailors and marines at Beirut, in the Turkish province of Syria (present-day Lebanon), to protect U.S. citizens and the American University during a period of political disturbances.

October 3.   Colonel George F. Elliott becomes 10th commandant of the marine corps.

October 10–17.   Seamen and marines go ashore from the cruiser *San Francisco* (C 5) to safeguard American interests amid renewed disorders in Beirut.

November 3.   **Revolution in Panama.** According to the terms of the Hay-Herrán Treaty, the United States was to pay the stockholders of the French company that had tried to build a canal across Panama the sum of $40,000,000. The Colombian Senate's rejection of the treaty confronts these investors with the prospect of losing everything. At this point the company's chief lobbyist (and a major stockholder), Philippe Bunau-Varilla, goes into action. Justly confident that the Roosevelt administration will support his initiative, from a suite in the Waldorf-Astoria Hotel in New York Bunau-Varilla arranges for the Panama City fire department to stage a revolution against Colombia.

November 4.   **Enter the Nashville.** At Panama City, the rebels proclaim Panamanian independence. Simultaneously, the gunboat *Nashville* (PG 7) reaches Colón, on the Atlantic coast, where a force of 474 Colombian soldiers has landed and is preparing to cross the isthmus and crush the rebellion. The *Nashville*'s Commander John

Hubbard sends a small party ashore and, with the support of the American superintendent of the Panama Railroad, keeps the Colombians from taking the train to Panama City.

November 5.   The transport *Dixie* arrives at Colón carrying a marine battalion commanded by Major John A. Lejeune, who immediately puts two companies ashore. The Colombian troops concede the point and board a ship for home.

November 6.   The United States recognizes the independence of Panama.

November 18.   **Hay–Bunau-Varilla Treaty.** Secretary of State John Hay and Philippe Bunau-Varilla, who has promptly been appointed Panamanian ambassador to the United States, conclude a treaty for the construction of a canal in Panama. The United States is granted sovereign rights in perpetuity to a 10-mile-wide canal zone across the country, in return for which it agrees to pay a lump sum of $10,000,000, an annuity of $250,000, and to maintain the independence of Panama. (Another $25,000,000 will be paid to Colombia upon approval of the Treaty of Bogotá in February 1921.)

December 1.   The battleship *Missouri* (BB 11) is commissioned.

December 18–January 15, 1904.   **Journey to Addis Ababa.** A detachment of 19 marines under Captain George C. Thorpe, USMC, and Lieutenant Charles L. Hussey, USN, escorts a U.S. diplomatic mission hundreds of miles overland on an arduous journey to the capital of Emperor Menelik II of Ethiopia.

1904

January 3.   The cruiser *Detroit* (C 10) lands her marine detachment at Puerto Plata, Dominican Republic, to protect American interests during an insurrection.

January 5–April 23.   The transport *Zafiro* sends a party of 103 seamen and marines to guard the U.S. Legation at Seoul, Korea. Most of the party is withdrawn on the latter date, but 25 remain on duty until November 11, 1905.

January 7. **Marines in Panama.** In view of the unsettled relations with Panama, three marine battalions are sent to reinforce Major Lejeune, whose battalion has been in garrison there since December. They land on this date, and a provisional marine brigade is organized under Brigadier General Commandant George F. Elliott. This is the last time a commandant of the marine corps will take personal command in the field. It soon becomes evident that Colombia does not want war, and the brigade is disbanded on February 16.

January 7. The cruiser *Detroit* (C 10) lands a detachment at Sosúa, in the Dominican Republic, to safeguard Americans during a revolution in that country.

January 17. Seamen and marines from the *Detroit* and the old screw sloop *Hartford* land to protect American citizens at Puerto Plata, Dominican Republic.

February 11. Insurgent forces in Santo Domingo, Dominican Republic, fire on the steamer *New York*. A force of 300 bluejackets and marines from the cruisers *Columbia* (C 12) and *Newark* (C 1) commanded by Lieutenant Commander James P. Parker lands under covering fire from the *Newark* to expel the rebels from the city. It returns aboard ship, mission accomplished, that evening.

February 22. The U.S. Senate ratifies the Hay-Bunau-Varilla Treaty by a vote of 66–14.

February 25–27. The training ship *Yankee* lands her marine detachment to guard the U.S. Consulate at Santo Domingo, Dominican Republic.

March 12. The marine detachment of the cruiser *Cincinnati* (C 7) conducts the evacuation of American citizens, caught up in the Russo-Japanese War, from Seoul and Chemulpo (Inchon), Korea.

May 4. **Beginning the Panama Canal.** Lieutenant Mark Brooke, Corps of Engineers, formally takes possession of the canal works at Panama for the United States. Construction of the canal commences almost immediately, at first using the French equipment already present, in accordance with President Theodore Roosevelt's announced intention "to make the dirt fly." The work will take 10 years to complete.

May 30. **Landing at Tangier.** In Morocco, a naturalized American citizen, Ion Perdicaris, has been kidnapped by the bandit chieftain Raisouli. President Theodore Roosevelt informs the Moroccan government that he wants "Perdicaris alive or Raisouli dead" and lands Captain J. T. ("Handsome Jack") Myers's marine detachment from the cruiser *Brooklyn* (ACR 3) at Tangier. Raisouli releases Perdicaris.

July 1. Paul Morton becomes 36th secretary of the navy.

October 4. The battleship *Ohio* (BB 12) is commissioned.

December 6. **Roosevelt Corollary.** Determined to deprive European powers, especially the rambunctious German Empire, of a pretext for intervention in the Americas, President Theodore Roosevelt proclaims that "Chronic wrongdoing . . . in the Western Hemisphere . . . may force the United States . . . to the exercise of an international police power." Considered to be a corollary to the Monroe Doctrine, this proposition will lead to American occupation of Haiti, the Dominican Republic, and Nicaragua and the employment of the U.S. Marines as colonial infantry in a series of so-called banana wars in Central America and the Caribbean.

1905

January 20. **Dominican customs agreement.** U.S. Navy and Marine Corps officers assume control of the customs service of the debt-ridden Dominican Republic. A treaty, negotiated on the initiative of the Dominican president, is finally approved by the U.S. and Dominican senates in February and May 1907, respectively. By this time Dominican customs revenues, efficiently collected by American officers, had been used to reduce the country's public debt from $30,000,000 to $17,000,000.

April 7. After a search lasting six years, General Horace Porter, U.S. Ambassador to France, finds the body of John Paul Jones in Paris. The old Protestant cemetery in which Jones was buried had been abandoned and a Parisian suburb built on the site.

July 1. Rear Admiral James H. Sands becomes the 19th superintendent of the Naval Academy. He is the last Civil War veteran to hold that post.

July 7.   Charles J. Bonaparte becomes 37th secretary of the navy.

July 21.   Sixty men are killed by a boiler explosion aboard the gunboat *Bennington* (PG 4) at San Diego, California.

July 23.   **The return of John Paul Jones.** The body of John Paul Jones is brought ashore at Annapolis, Maryland, where, upon the urging of President Theodore Roosevelt, Congress has decided that it will be interred in the crypt of the Naval Academy Chapel. Jones's remains were escorted across the Atlantic by an honor squadron, commanded by Rear Admiral Charles D. Sigbee, of four cruisers—the *Brooklyn* (CA 5), *Chattanooga* (C 16), *Galveston* (C 17), and *Tacoma* (C 18)—and the French cruiser *Julien de la Gravière.* This squadron was joined off the Nantucket Shoals by the seven battleships of Rear Admiral Robley D. Evans's North Atlantic Fleet.

September 12.   **Legation guard.** By direction of President Theodore Roosevelt, the marine corps relieves the army in providing a guard for the U.S. Legation in Peking, China. A marine detachment will remain at the legation until 1941.

1906

February 19.   The battleship *Rhode Island* (BB 17) is commissioned.

March 8.   A naval landing under Ensign H.D. Cooke, Jr., joins an army detachment in storming a Moro position at Mount Dajo on the Philippine island of Jolo.

April 18.   **San Francisco earthquake.** Bluejackets and marines from the Mare Island Navy Yard assist in fighting fires and doing relief work following the disastrous earthquake that all but levels San Francisco, California.

April 21.   On his seventh Arctic expedition 49-year-old Commander Robert Peary, Civil Engineer Corps, reaches latitude 87°6' North, the nearest anyone has yet come to the Pole.

May 7.   The battleship *Virginia* (BB 13) is commissioned.

May 12.   The battleship *New Jersey* (BB 16) is commissioned.

June 2.   The battleship *Louisiana* (BB 19) is commissioned.

September 13.   **Cuban Pacification.** When a widespread revolution breaks out in Cuba following the elections of August 1906, President Theodore Roosevelt decides that the United States must intervene. A detachment of 120 bluejackets and marines from the cruiser *Denver* (C 14) lands at the request of the Cuban governor to maintain order in Havana on September 13–14; a battalion of marines under Major Albertus W. Catlin goes ashore from the transport *Dixie* to protect American interests at Cienfuegos on September 18; and five more marine battalions are rushed to Cuba.

September 24.   The battleship *Georgia* (BB 15) is commissioned.

September 29.   The battleship *Connecticut* (BB 18) is commissioned.

October 1.   Colonel L.W.T. Waller, USMC, arrives at Havana and organizes the two marine regiments in Cuba into a provisional brigade with a strength of 2,900 officers and men. This force, whose equipment comes to include an armored train, occupies 24 strategic ports throughout the island and begins to disarm the insurgent forces. The first units of an Army of Cuban Pacification land on October 10 and, with the situation well in hand, the marine brigade is soon disbanded. The First Marine Regiment is, however, retained in Cuba until the withdrawal of the army on January 23, 1909.

December 17.   Victor H. Metcalf becomes 38th secretary of the navy.

1907

March 4.   The battleship *Vermont* (BB 20) is commissioned.

March 9.   The battleship *Minnesota* (BB 22) is commissioned.

April 18.   The battleship *Kansas* (BB 21) is commissioned.

April 28–May 23.   The 12-man marine detachment of the gunboat *Paducah* (PG 17) is landed under the command of Ensign Lawrence P. Treadwell to safeguard

American interests at Laguna, Honduras, during a war between Honduras and Nicaragua.

May 24–June 8.   The *Paducah*'s marines move inland to protect Americans at Choloma, Honduras.

July 1.   The battleship *Nebraska* (BB 14) is commissioned.

July 15.   Captain Charles J. Badger becomes the 20th superintendent of the Naval Academy.

December 16–February 22, 1909.   **Voyage of the Great White Fleet.** Sixteen American battleships—the *Connecticut* (BB 18), *Georgia* (BB 15), *Illinois* (BB 7), *Kansas* (BB 21), *Kearsarge* (BB 5), *Kentucky* (BB 6), *Louisiana* (BB 19), *Minnesota* (BB 22), *Missouri* (BB 11), *Nebraska* (BB 14), *New Jersey* (BB 16), *Ohio* (BB 12), *Rhode Island* (BB 17), *Vermont* (BB 20), *Virginia* (BB 13), and *Wisconsin* (BB 9)—with colliers and auxiliaries, sail from Hampton Roads, Virginia, under the command of Rear Admiral Robley D. ("Fighting Bob") Evans on an unprecedented round-the-world cruise. Conceived by President Theodore Roosevelt, the voyage is undertaken as a dramatic demonstration of America's newly established naval power. No cruise approaching this length has ever been attempted by steam-powered, steel battleships, and it is freely predicted that it will prove technologically impractical. These forebodings are unfounded. Proceeding around Cape Horn to the West Coast of the United States, the fleet crosses the Pacific to visit Australia and New Zealand, steams north to the Philippines and Japan, turns south through the China Sea to enter the Indian Ocean, and returns to Hampton Roads via the Red Sea, the Suez Canal, the Mediterranean, and the North Atlantic to complete a voyage of 46,000 miles without a single serious breakdown. Admiral Evans falls ill before the fleet leaves the West Coast, and the major part of the voyage is made under the command of Rear Admiral Charles S. Sperry. The fleet takes its name from the battleships' dazzling white hulls.

1908

February 1.   The battleship *Mississippi* (BB 23) is commissioned.

March 19.   The battleship *New Hampshire* (BB 25) is commissioned.

April 1.   The battleship *Idaho* (BB 24) is commissioned. She is the last American predreadnought to enter service.

May 13.   The Navy Nurse Corps is established.

August 15.   The navy's first shipboard post offices are opened.

September 3–17.   Two official navy observers—Lieutenant George C. Sweet and Naval Constructor William McEntee—wit-

The Great White Fleet entering San Francisco Bay. Official U.S. Navy photograph.

ness the first military trials of the Wright brothers' aircraft. The tests are conducted by the U.S. Army at Fort Myer, Virginia.

November 12. **TR tries to remove the marines.** Influenced by the views of Commander William H. Fullam, who devotes much of his career to a crusade to remove marine detachments from the navy's ships, President Theodore Roosevelt signs Executive Order No. 969, "defining the duties of the United States Marine Corps." Shipboard service is conspicuous by its absence. The president had already directed Secretary of the Navy Metcalf to begin withdrawing the marines from ships on October 23.

December 1. Truman H. Newberry becomes 39th secretary of the navy.

1909

February 22. The Great White Fleet returns to Hampton Roads, Virginia.

March 3. **Congress upholds the marines.** President Theodore Roosevelt's plan to remove the marines from shipboard duty (see November 12, 1908) is thwarted when Congress attaches a rider to the naval appropriations bill stipulating that none of the funds allocated the marine corps are to be expended "unless officers and men shall serve as heretofore" on ships.

March 6. George von Lengerke Myer becomes 40th secretary of the navy.

April 6. **Peary at the Pole.** Commander Robert E. Peary, Civil Engineer Corps, is the first man to reach the North Pole, where he raises the American flag. With him are his faithful companion, Matthew Henson, a black, and four Eskimos. This is Peary's seventh Arctic expedition, and at the age of 52, previously having lost all but two toes to frostbite, he knows that it must be his last. Peary's distinction is immediately contested by Dr. Frederick H. Cook, who claims to have discovered the Pole several months earlier, but the National Geographic Society and other leading geographical and scientific organizations reject Cook's contentions.

June 10. Captain John M. Bowyers becomes the

Commander Robert E. Peary. U. S. Naval Institute Collection.

21st superintendent of the Naval Academy.

November 11. Plans are undertaken to build a naval base at Pearl Harbor, on the Hawaiian island of Oahu.

December 1. **The aide system.** Since 1900 Congress has rebuffed several attempts to establish a naval general staff. Through an initiative intended to rationalize naval administration in the absence of such a staff, Secretary of the Navy Myer divides his department into four divisions—fleet operations, materiel, inspections, and personnel—each headed by an "aide" who reports directly to him. The post of aide for operations foreshadows that of chief of naval operations, which will be created six years later.

December 18. **Revolution in Nicaragua.** A provisional marine battalion under Colonel E.J. Mahoney is embarked on the transport *Buffalo* for Corinto, on the Atlantic coast of Nicaragua, where it is joined by the Panama Battalion under Major Smedley D. Butler. The dispatch of these forces is occasioned by the outbreak of a revolution against Nicaraguan President José S. Zelaya, an ambitious dictator whose grandiose dreams of a Central American empire have kept the area in turmoil for 16 years. President William Howard Taft's predictable preference for Zelaya's opponents increased after two American citizens serving in the rebel forces were captured and executed by government troops. In December, while the marines remain aboard ship off Corinto, the United States formally withdraws recognition of the Zelaya regime and dismisses the Nicaraguan ambassador. American pressure persuades Zelaya to resign the presidency on December 20. The fighting gradually dies down, and in March 1910 the marines are withdrawn.

1910

January 4.   **The American dreadnought.** The battleship *Michigan* (BB 27) is commissioned. She is the first American dreadnought, the "all big gun" battleship that makes every earlier battleship obsolete overnight. The type is named for the first such ship to enter service, the British *Dreadnought*, which was commissioned in 1906. The plans, though not the construction, of the *Michigan* and her sistership, the *South Carolina* (BB 26), actually predate those of the *Dreadnought*, having been drawn in 1904. The American design is also the first to employ superimposed turrets, so that all eight of the ships' 12-inch guns can be trained to either side.

March 1.   The battleship *South Carolina* (BB 26) is commissioned.

April 4.   The battleship *Delaware* (BB 28) is commissioned.

April 11.   The battleship *North Dakota* (BB 29) is commissioned.

May 19.   Seamen and marines from the gunboats *Dubuque* (PG 17) and *Paducah* (PG 18) land at Bluefields, Nicaragua, to protect American lives and property when fighting flares up between government forces and rebel troops defending the city. Commander William W. Gilmer of the *Paducah* forbids the Nicaraguan gunboat *Venus* to shell Bluefields, declaring that the vessel is not a man-of-war and that there are no military targets for her to engage.

May 30.   Major Smedley D. Butler's marine bat-

The battleship *Michigan*, the first American dreadnought. Courtesy National Archives.

talion, which had just returned to Panama in March after three months aboard ship off Corinto, is rushed back to Nicaragua to establish a neutral zone around Bluefields. Butler and two of his companies land from the gunboat *Dubuque* (PG 17) on this date. Two other companies join them early in June. The battalion remains at Bluefields until September 4, by which time the rebel forces favored by the United States have gained control of the government.

October 13.   Secretary of the Navy Myer approves a recommendation that two officers should be detailed to examine and report on the progress of aviation.

October 22–30.   **Aviation advocate.** Captain Washington Irving Chambers, who as assistant aide for materiel has been assigned the duty of monitoring the progress of aviation, is an official observer at the International Air Meet at Belmont Park, New York. What he sees there makes him an enthusiastic advocate of the creation of a naval air service, the development of which he guides until his relief by Captain Mark L. Bristol in 1914.

November 14.   **First shipboard take-off.** Twenty-four-year-old Eugene B. Ely, a civilian barnstormer, becomes the first pilot to fly off a ship. He nurses his Curtiss pusher biplane into the air from a wooden platform erected over the bow of the cruiser *Birmingham* (CL 2) at Hampton Roads, Virginia.

November 29.   Aviation pioneer Glenn Curtiss offers to instruct a naval officer "in the operation and construction" of his aircraft.

December 23.   **First flight training.** In response to Curtiss's offer, the navy details Lieutenant T. Gordon ("Spuds") Ellyson to attend the course of instruction at the Glenn Curtiss Aviation Center at San Diego, California.

1911

January 18.   **First shipboard landing.** Civilian Eugene B. Ely, the first man to fly an airplane off a ship, becomes the first man to land on one when he brings his Curtiss pusher down on a wooden platform jury-rigged on the cruiser *Pennsylvania* (ACR 4) in San Francisco Bay. Killed in a crash ashore

later in the year, Ely is posthumously awarded the Distinguished Flying Cross in 1933.

February 1.   The cruiser *Tacoma* (C 18) lands a party to protect American interests at Puerto Cortez, Honduras.

February 3.   Colonel William P. Biddle becomes the 11th commandant of the marine corps.

March 4.   The first Naval Appropriations Act including funds for naval aviation ($25,000) is approved by Congress.

March 13.   A provisional marine battalion under Major George C. Thorpe is landed at Guantánamo Bay, Cuba, to defend American interests during a period of political tension.

April 12.   **Naval Aviator Number One.** Upon the completion of his training at the Curtiss Aviation Center, Lieutenant T. Gordon Ellyson becomes the navy's first pilot.

April 26.   **Marine Corps Association.** Alarmed by the consistent hostility of the Roosevelt and Taft administrations to the marine corps, Colonel F.J. Moses calls a meeting of the officers of the 1st Provisional Marine Brigade at Guantánamo, Cuba, "to discuss defenses against being abolished by the navy." This is the genesis of the Marine Corps Association, which adopts a written charter on April 25, 1913.

May 8.   **Beginning of navy air.** Captain Washington Irving Chambers completes the contract specifications for the first two naval aircraft. Although invitations to bid are not sent to plane builders until three weeks later, this date is officially considered to be the birthday of naval aviation. The contracts are awarded to Glenn Curtiss.

May 15.   Captain John H. Gibbons becomes the 22nd superintendent of the Naval Academy.

June 6.   The United States concludes a treaty with Nicaragua, whereby the latter is granted a large loan from American bankers to begin the repayment of the public debt and American officers are to collect Nicaraguan customs revenues to pay off the remainder.

July 1.   Glenn Curtiss successfully demonstrates his 80 h.p. A-1 Triad "hydroaeroplane," the first aircraft built for the navy, taking off and landing on Lake Keuka at Hammondsport, New York.

August 31.   The battleship *Utah* (BB 31) is commissioned.

Ely lands on the *Pennsylvania*. The sandbags on either side of the landing platform are connected by ropes meant to snag a hook on the bottom of the aircraft. They brought Ely to a halt a few feet short of a wooden barricade at the end of the little runway. Official U.S. Navy photograph.

September 15.   The battleship *Florida* (BB 30) is commissioned.

September.   **First naval air station.** An "aviation encampment" is established at the Navy Engineering Experiment Station at Annapolis, Maryland, across the Severn River from the Naval Academy.

October 10–January 19, 1914.   A battalion of marines under Major Philip M. Bannon is rushed from the Philippines to reinforce the legation guard at Peking during the Chinese revolution.

November 4–14.   Twenty-four marines are landed from the cruiser *Albany* (CL 23) and transport *Rainbow* to guard the cable station at Shanghai, China.

November 24.   The armored cruiser *Saratoga* (ex-*New York*) (ACR 2) carries a company of marines from Shanghai to protect American missionaries at Taku, China.

December 14.   The fleet base at Pearl Harbor, Hawaii, is ceremonially opened when the armored cruiser *California* (ACR 6) steams through the new channel.

1912

May 19.   The cruiser *Birmingham* (CL 2) begins the first American ice patrol in the North Atlantic. That such a patrol was needed had been made tragically evident by the sinking of the White Star liner *Titanic* the previous month. An International Ice Patrol is established in 1914 and the responsibility of the United States assumed by the coast guard.

May 22.   **Beginning of marine aviation.** Marine Second Lieutenant Alfred A. Cunningham reports to the aviation camp at Annapolis, Maryland, for flight training and soon qualifies as the first marine aviator.

May 28.   **Peace-keeping in Cuba.** A black revolution in Cuba leads to the hurried organization of the First Provisional Marine Regiment, which lands at Guantánamo from the transport *Prairie* on this date. A second regiment goes ashore on June 5, and a provisional marine brigade is formed under the command of Colonel Lincoln Karmany. The marines garrison 26 towns in the vicinity of Guantánamo and Santiago and also serve as railway guards. Order is restored by the end of July, and the brigade is withdrawn the following month.

July 16.   Rear Admiral Bradley A. Fiske patents the first aerial torpedo.

July 27.   The first radio communication between an aircraft and a ship is established over the

Chesapeake Bay near Annapolis, Maryland, when Lieutenant John Rodgers (Naval Aviator No. 2) and Midshipman Charles Maddox flying the Wright B-1 hydroaeroplane transmit the letter D in Morse code to the torpedo boat *Bailey* (TB 21) more than a mile away.

July 31.   The navy's first attempt to launch an aircraft by a compressed-air catapult is made by Lieutenant T. Gordon Ellyson in the Curtiss A-1 hydroaeroplane at the Santee Wharf at the U.S. Naval Academy. The plane, which is not secured to the track, cartwheels into the Severn River. Ellyson is unhurt.

August 3.   A permanent marine garrison of 250 men is established to provide security for the naval base at Guantánamo Bay, Cuba.

August 4.   **Intervention in Nicaragua.** In Nicaragua revolution has broken out against President Adolfo Díaz, who enjoys the support of the United States. On this date, a detachment of 100 bluejackets and marines from the gunboat *Annapolis* (PG 10) lands at Corinto and proceeds inland to guard the American legation in Managua. Major Smedley D. Butler's battalion is also ordered to Nicaragua—for the third time since 1909.

August 14.   Major Butler's Panama Battalion—354 officers and men—lands at Corinto, Nicaragua, and reaches Managua the next day.

August 17.   The cruiser *Tacoma* (C 18) lands a party of bluejackets and marines to maintain order at Bluefields, on the Atlantic coast of Nicaragua.

August 24 and 26.   A company of marines from the transport *Rainbow* is put ashore near Shanghai, China, to protect American lives and property during a period of revolutionary disturbances.

August 28.   A battalion of 364 bluejackets and marines from the armored cruiser *California* (ACR 6) lands at Corinto, Nicaragua.

August 30.   The cruiser *Denver* (C 14) lands a party of bluejackets and marines at San Juan del Sur, Nicaragua.

September 4.   The First Provisional Marine Regiment, 790 men under Colonel Joseph H. ("Uncle Joe") Pendleton, reaches Corinto from Philadelphia in the transport *Buffalo*. Pendleton assumes command of all U.S. forces ashore in Nicaragua.

September 5.   A battalion of 323 seamen and marines lands at Corinto from the armored cruiser *Colorado* (ACR 7), raising the strength of the forces available to Colonel Pendleton in western Nicaragua to approximately 2,000 men. He deploys them to take control of the railway from Corinto through Managua to Granada, which is, in effect, the artery of the revolution.

September 17.   The battleship *Arkansas* (BB 33) is commissioned.

September 22.   **Relief of Granada.** A column composed of two marine battalions and an artillery battery under Major Smedley D. Butler relieves the government garrison of Granada, Nicaragua, and disarms the rebel army of General Mena, by which the town had been besieged.

September 25.   The battleship *Wyoming* (BB 32) is commissioned.

October 2–4.   **Action at Coyotope.** A Nicaraguan rebel force of 1,000 men under General Zeledón is entrenched on two hills overlooking the railway near Masaya, roughly midway between Managua and Granada. It refuses to surrender when Major Butler's battalion, with which it had skirmished on September 19, returns from Granada. Butler shells the rebel position on Coyotope hill on October 3, during which Colonel Pendleton arrives with a third marine battalion and the *California*'s landing battalion. Coyotope is stormed at dawn on October 4. Afterwards marines count the bodies of more than 60 rebels, including that of General Zeledón, who is shot by his own men. The marines suffer 18 casualties.

October 6.   **Capture of León.** A force of 1,200 seamen and marines under Lieutenant Colonel C.G. ("Squeegee") Long captures the rebel-held city of León, between Corinto and Managua, at the cost of 6 casualties. Although mopping-up operations continue until November 2, the Nicaraguan revolution has been crushed.

November 12.   **First catapult launching.** Undeterred by his dunking on July 31, Lieutenant T. Gordon Ellyson succeeds in getting his new Curtiss A-1 hydroaeroplane into the air after a catapult launch from a barge anchored in the Anacostia River off the Washington Navy Yard.

November 21.   **Wind-down in Nicaragua.** The

revolution over, Colonel Pendleton's provisional regiment embarks on the transport *Buffalo* at Bluefields. A battalion under Lieutenant Colonel C.G. Long garrisons León until January 17, 1913, and a legation guard of 100 men at Managua remains until August 1925.

November 30. **First flying boat.** Lieutenant T. Gordon Ellyson tests the navy's first flying boat, the Curtiss C-1, at Lake Keuka in Hammondsport, New York.

1913

January 6. The navy's Aviation Detachment arrives at Guantánamo, Cuba, aboard the collier *Sterling* to take part in the annual fleet manuevers in the Caribbean. This will be the first time airplanes have participated in these exercises.

February 1. **PG School.** The Naval Postgraduate School opens at Annapolis Naval Academy's former Marine Barracks (later named Halligan Hall). After World War II, the school will be transferred to Monterey, California.

March 5. North Carolina newspaper editor Josephus Daniels becomes the 41st and perhaps the most controversial secretary of the navy.

June 20. **First aviation casualty.** Ensign W.D. Billingsley (Naval Aviator No. 9) falls to his death when he is thrown from the Wright B-2 hydroaeroplane by a violent down-draft while flying at an altitude of 1,600 feet over the Chesapeake Bay near St. Michael's, Maryland. Lieutenant John H. Towers clings to the plane and survives, with serious injuries, when it crashes into the bay. Neither man was wearing a safety belt.

July 7. The protected cruiser *Albany* (CL 23) lands her marine detachment to protect American interests during disorders at Shanghai, China.

August 30. The General Board of the Navy, still headed by Civil War veteran George Dewey, recommends the immediate establishment of "an efficient Naval Air Service."

September 5–7. A detachment of marines from the transport *Buffalo* conducts the evacu-ation of American citizens from Ciaris Estero, Mexico, during a period of revolutionary disturbances.

October 7. Secretary of the Navy Daniels appoints an Aeronautic Board to consider the future of naval aviation. Its recommendations include the establishment of an Aeronautic Center at Pensacola, Florida, and the attachment of an aircraft to every major battleship and cruiser.

December 19. By act of Congress, the tenure of the commandant of the marine corps is limited to four years, with the possibility of reappointment for a second term.

December 23. **Advanced Base Force.** A marine brigade of two regiments is organized under Colonel George Barnett to participate in the 1914 fleet manuevers. The professionalism with which this Advanced Base Force "defends" the Caribbean island of Culebra impresses naval observers and points the way to the amphibious mission the corps will adopt in the 1920s and '30s.

December 27. **Birth of marine corps aviation.** The Aviation Detachment, Advanced Base Force, is established with a strength of two officers, seven enlisted men, and two navy flying boats.

1914

January 20. **Pensacola.** Upon the recommendation of Captain W. I. Chambers, the navy's aviation detachment—9 officers and 23 men—is transferred from Annapolis, Maryland, to the unused navy base at Pensacola, Florida, where it is to develop a complete "aeronautical center." Lieutenant John H. Towers, the detachment commander, has a flight school in operation by the beginning of February.

January 28–February 9. The marine detachment of the battleship *South Carolina* (BB 26) joins British, French, and German landing parties to maintain order in Port-au-Prince during one of Haiti's recurrent revolutions.

February 7. Captain William F. Fullam becomes the 23rd superintendent of the Naval Academy.

February 25. Colonel George Barnett becomes 12th commandant of the marine corps. He

Early days at Pensacola: Lieutenant P.N.L. Bellinger at the controls of a Curtiss hydroaeroplane. Official U.S. Navy photograph.

is the first Naval Academy graduate to hold this post.

March 12. The battleship *Texas* (BB 35) is commissioned.

April 9. **Tampico incident.** Since October 1913, U.S. naval forces have been stationed off the Gulf Coast of Mexico to protect American lives and investments from the revolution raging in that country. On this date a boat party of eight seamen under Assistant Paymaster Charles W. Copp is seized and detained for approximately half an hour by Mexican government forces when it inadvertently enters a military zone on the Pánuco River. Although the local Mexican commander, General Ignacio Morelos Zaragoza, expresses regrets for the incident, Rear Admiral Henry T. Mayo, commanding the Fourth Division of the Atlantic Fleet, sends him an ultimatum demanding that he proffer a formal apology and fire a 21-gun salute to the American flag. Zaragoza obtains an extension of the 24-hour time limit originally set for a reply and forwards the admiral's message to Mexican President Victoriano Huerta. President Woodrow Wilson strongly endorses Mayo's action. Wilson has been trying to force Huerta, a military dictator for whom he feels a profound repugnance, to relinquish his office since August 1913.

April 11. Huerta apologizes for the arrest of Paymaster Copp's party, but declines to hoist and salute the American flag.

April 13. In Washington, President Wilson promises reporters "The salute will be fired."

April 14. The Mexican government agrees to fire the salute providing U.S. forces promise to return it round for round. Admiral Mayo had stated in his ultimatum of April 10 that the salute would be returned, but President Wilson rejects the condition. Huerta's compliance must be unqualified. The Atlantic Fleet is ordered to concentrate off the east coast of Mexico.

April 15. The battleship *New York* (BB 34) is commissioned.

April 18. **Enter the Ypiranga.** William W. Canada, U.S. consul at Veracruz, Mexico, notifies the State Department that a German steamer, the *Ypiranga*, is scheduled to arrive at the city on April 21 with an enormous cargo of arms and ammunition for the Mexican government. President Wilson determines that these arms must not be allowed to reach Huerta.

April 20. A final deadline set by the president for the salute having expired on April 18, Wilson goes before a joint session of Congress to request authority to employ armed force against Mexico. The measure passes the House of Representatives, but is delayed by debate in the Senate, which adjourns without taking action, placing it at the head of the agenda for April 22.

April 20. Secretary of the Navy Daniels sends a message to Rear Admiral Frank F. Fletcher, commanding the First Division of the Atlantic Fleet off Veracruz, Mexico, that the *Ypiranga* must not be permitted to land her munitions.

April 21. At 2:30 A.M. President Wilson is awakened and informed that the State Department has received a cable from the U.S. consul in Veracruz, reporting that the *Ypiranga* is to reach the city that morning and that three trains are in readiness to rush her cargo into the interior. Wilson directs Secretary of the Navy Daniels to order Admiral Fletcher to seize the customs house at Veracruz. This action will enable U.S. forces to intercept the *Ypiranga*'s arms as they come ashore, thereby avoiding diplomatic complications with Germany.

April 21. **The landing at Veracruz.** Admiral Fletcher receives Secretary Daniels's message at 8:00 A.M. The landing is made two-and-a-half hours later by a force of 787 men—502 marines from the transport *Prairie* under Lieutenant Colonel Wendell C. Neville and 285 bluejackets and marines from the battleship *Florida* (BB 30), all under the command of the *Florida*'s Captain William R. ("Wild Bill") Rush. In the meantime, Fletcher has sent officers ashore to advise Mexican authorities of the landing and to express the hope that no resistance will be offered. This hope proves to be in vain. Although the Mexican government orders the garrison to withdraw from the city, its commander, General Gustavo Maas, has already sent 100 men to the waterfront "to repel the invasion" and freed and armed the prisoners in the city jail. The cadets of the Mexican Naval Academy, members of the home guard, and assorted private citizens also take arms. Firing begins shortly after the landing is made. Ensign George M. Lowry's *Florida* company pushes on to take the customs house and by 3:00 P.M. American forces, reinforced by a battalion of seamen and marines from the battleship *Utah* (BB 31), are in control of the waterfront. Admiral Fletcher then makes an effort to arrange a cease-fire and when it fails, decides to await the arrival of the ships converging on Veracruz before resuming the advance. Meanwhile, the *Ypiranga* enters the harbor, where she will remain, without unloading her arms, until May 3. The cruisers *San Francisco* (C 5) and *Chester*

The landing at Veracruz: a bluejacket stands amid Mexican bodies at the corner of Calle Miguel Lerdo and Calle Morelos, where the firing broke out. U.S. Naval Institute Collection.

(CS 1) and the battleships *Arkansas* (BB 33), *New Hampshire* (BB 25), *New Jersey* (BB 16), *South Carolina* (BB 26), and *Vermont* (BB 20) arrive after nightfall and land detachments that are organized into the Second Seamen Regiment, commanded by Captain E. A. Anderson of the *New Hampshire*, and into the Third Provisional Marine Regiment under Major Albertus W. Catlin.

April 22. At 7:45 A.M. the naval brigade, now nearly 4,000 strong, pushes into Veracruz. The strongest resistance comes from the cadets at the Mexican Naval Academy, who repel the initial advance of the Second Seamen Regiment, but are overcome by accurate fire from Commander William A. Moffett's cruiser *Chester* (CS 1). The occupation of the city is completed by noon. American casualties are 17 dead and 63 wounded. At least 126 Mexicans have been killed and 195 wounded. A total of 55 Medals of Honor are awarded for Veracruz, the greatest number ever granted for a single engagement. The recipients include 37 navy and marine corps officers, who are made eligible for the medal by an act of March 3, 1915.

April 23. At 2:25 A.M., after hours of debate, the Senate passes the resolution authorizing President Wilson to use force against Mexico.

April 24. President Wilson accepts the offer of the ABC Powers—Argentina, Brazil, and Chile—to mediate the dispute between Mexico and the United States. U.S. forces at Veracruz are ordered not to undertake offensive operations.

April 24. The 1st and 2nd Aero Sections (of two aircraft each), commanded by Lieutenants John H. Towers and P.N.L. Bellinger, reach Veracruz aboard the cruiser *Birmingham* (CL 2) and battleship *Mississippi* (BB 23).

April 25. The first navy flight in a combat environment is made at Veracruz when Lieutenant P.N.L. Bellinger takes the Curtiss AB-3 flying boat from the *Mississippi* over the harbor to look for mines.

April 30. The naval forces occupying Veracruz are relieved by an army brigade commanded by Brigadier General Frederick Funston. The marines and the navy's Aero Sections stay on.

May 3.   The *Ypiranga* sails from Veracruz. Later in the month she succeeds in landing her arms at Puerto Mexico (now Coatzacoalcos).

May 6.   The Curtiss AH-3 hydroplane, Lieutenant P.N.L. Bellinger, pilot, and Lieutenant (jg) Richard C. Saufley, observer, is hit by rifle fire while on a reconnaissance flight inland from Veracruz. It is the first naval aircraft to be damaged by hostile fire.

July 1.   **The navy goes dry.** Secretary of the Navy Josephus Daniels abolishes the traditional officers' wine mess aboard naval vessels. U.S. warships have been dry ever since.

July 1.   The Office of Naval Aeronautics is established under the command of Captain Mark L. Bristol, who has replaced Captain W. I. Chambers as officer in charge of the navy's aviation program.

July 15.   The object of President Wilson's Mexican policy is attained when General Huerta resigns as provisional president of Mexico.

July 28.   **Outbreak of World War I.** Austria declares war on Serbia, beginning a chain reaction that will lead the world to war. Germany declares war on Russia on August 1 and on France on August 3, the same day on which she invades Belgium. Great Britain declares war on Germany on August 4.

August 5.   **Bryan-Chamorro Treaty.** U.S. Secretary of State William Jennings Bryan and Nicaraguan ambassador Emiliano Chamorro conclude a treaty whereby, in exchange for a payment of $3,000,000 and the promise to preserve Nicaraguan independence, the United States is granted the right to construct a canal across the country and to build naval bases on both coasts. The administration of the country's chaotic finances also passes under American control.

October 1.   **The Panama Canal is opened.** The collier *Jupiter* (AC 3) becomes the first U.S. naval vessel to transit the canal, October 10–12.

November 23.   Captain Mark L. Bristol is officially designated director of naval aeronautics.

November 23.   American forces withdraw from Veracruz, Mexico, after an occupation of seven months.

December 1.   Rear Admiral Alfred Thayer Mahan dies, aged 74, in Washington, D.C.

December 17.   **Haitian gold.** Rumors arise that the revolutionary government that took power in Haiti on November 20 plans to refill the country's empty treasury by seizing the gold reserves of the Banque Nationale d'Haiti, which is backed by the National City Bank of New York. Both banks and the U.S. State Department take a dim view of this prospect. To prevent its occurrence, the gunboat *Machias* (PG 5) is ordered to reclaim part of the reserve. Landing at Port-au-Prince on this date, the *Machias*'s marine detachment, 65 men under Major C. B. Hatch, secretly transfer $500,000 in gold to their ship, which then sails for New York.

1915

January 21.   The Bureau of Navigation issues the first seven "Navy Air Pilot" certificates.

January 28.   The German auxiliary cruiser *Prinz Eitel Friedrich* sinks the American schooner *William P. Frye*, whose cargo of wheat is consigned to an English firm. This ship is the first American merchantman to be lost in World War I.

March 3.   **First CNO.** The office of chief of naval operations is established. The creation of such a post, long advocated by navy reformers such as Admiral Bradley A. Fiske, had been fiercely resisted by Secretary of the Navy Josephus Daniels, who saw in it a threat to the primacy of civilian authority. As its first holder, on May 11 Daniels appoints Rear Admiral William S. Benson, a conventional officer who has never been identified with the cause of naval reform.

March 3.   **Naval Reserve.** The Navy Act of 1915, which creates the post of chief of naval operations, also establishes the U.S. Navy Reserve Force.

March 23.   The British passenger steamer *Falaba* is sunk by a German U-boat in St. George's Channel between Wales and Ireland. Although the U-boat surfaces and gives the liner's passengers and crew a few minutes to abandon ship, more than 50 lives are lost. Among the dead is Leon C. Thrasher, the first American citizen to die as a result of German naval action.

March 25.   The *F-4* (SS 23) becomes the first American submarine casualty, sinking with the loss of 21 lives off Honolulu, Hawaii.

May 1.   The American oil tanker *Gulflight* is torpedoed without warning by a German U-boat near the Scilly Isles, off the southwestern coast of England.

May 7.   **The Lusitania.** The British Cunard liner *Lusitania* is torpedoed without warning by the *U-20*, Kapitänleutnant Walther Schwieger, off Old Head of Kinsdale, 10 miles from the Irish coast, and sinks in 20 minutes; 1,198 of 1,959 passengers and crew are lost, 124 Americans among them.

May 13.   **Wilson protests.** President Woodrow Wilson responds to the sinking of the *Lusitania* with a stiff note to the Imperial German government. In it, he demands that Germany disavow the action, pay reparations for the American lives lost, and pledge that its submarines will conform to the rules of cruiser warfare, giving passengers and crew time to abandon a ship before sinking it. The president also asserts the right of American citizens to travel safely on merchant ships of belligerent nations. In the ensuing exchange of notes, which continues through the summer, the German government eventually expresses regret over the destruction of the *Lusitania* and admits liability for the incident.

July 1.   **Revolution in Haiti.** In March 1915 General Vilbrun Guillaume Sam, having led a successful revolution, was "elected" president of Haiti. Shortly thereafter, Dr. Rosalvo Bobo started a revolt against President Sam. On this date Rear Admiral William B. Caperton arrives at Cap-Haitien in the armored cruiser *Washington* (ACR 11) with orders from Secretary of the Navy Daniels to keep the peace. Caperton informs the government forces holding Cap-Haitien and the rebel troops outside it that there must be no fighting in or near the city. He also lands a detachment of marines to establish radio communication between the American consulate and his flagship.

July 27.   **Massacre in Port-au-Prince.** Hearing an outbreak of firing near the Presidential Palace, General Oscar Etienne, military governor of Port-au-Prince, elects to execute 167 prominent political hostages being held in the National Penitentiary. Upon the news of this massacre the capital goes wild. President Sam seeks refuge in the French embassy, General Etienne in the Dominican; both are dragged out and hacked to pieces. The Haitian government also ceases to exist.

July 28.   **Intervention in Haiti.** Learning of the events in Port-au-Prince, Admiral Caperton hurries to the scene, where he receives a message from Secretary Daniels to land troops and restore order. Two companies of marines and three of bluejackets under Captain George Van Orden, USMC, go ashore at the Haitian navy yard at Bizoton, three miles west of Port-au-Prince, and quickly take control of the capital. While this operation is under way, Caperton requests reinforcements. Back at Cap-Haitien, the gunboat *Eagle* lands a party of 20 men to protect the French consulate.

July 29.   The 24th Company of marines reaches Port-au-Prince from Guantánamo in the collier *Jason* (AC 12).

August 1.   The marine detachment from the gunboat *Nashville* (PG 7) occupies Cap-Haitien, Haiti's second-largest city, without opposition.

August 4.   Five companies of the Second Marine Regiment under Colonel E.K. Cole arrive at Port-au-Prince aboard the battleship *Connecticut* (BB 18) after a full-speed run from Philadelphia.

August 6.   Revolutionary elements are expelled from Port-au-Prince.

August 12.   Prompted by Admiral Caperton, the Haitian Congress elects Sudre Dartiguenave president—Haiti's seventh in seven years. On this same date, Caperton installs a military government at Cap-Haitien, where the locals' fear of Dr. Bobo prevents the formation of a civilian administration.

August 15.   Colonel L.W.T. Waller reaches Haiti aboard the armored cruiser *Tennessee* (ACR 10) with eight companies of the First Marine Regiment and the headquarters of the 1st Marine Brigade, of which he assumes command. Once ashore, Waller launches a vigorous campaign to suppress the *cacos*—bandit bands—which, by selling their services to would-be presidents, have effectively dominated Haitian politics for years. At the end of August, Waller's force numbers 2,029 officers and men.

September 1. **Arabic pledge.** Following the torpedoing of the British liner *Arabic*, in which two American citizens lose their lives, the German government promises President Wilson that no more passenger liners will be sunk without warning.

September 18.   The first shots of the Haitian intervention are fired when a marine patrol from Gonaïves skirmishes with a band of about 75 cacos.

September 20.   The 1st Battalion, First Marine Regiment, commanded by Colonel E.K. Cole, defeats the cacos in a sharp action outside Cap-Haitien.

September 20.   Captain Edward W. Eberle becomes the 24th superintendent of the Naval Academy.

September 27.   Five companies of marines under Colonel Cole capture Quartier Morin, Haiti, a bandit hangout a few miles from Cap-Haitien.

October 19. **New London.** A submarine base is established at New London, Connecticut.

October 24–25. **Butler's patrol.** A 40-man

Major Smedley Darlington Butler, USMC. Defense Department photo (Marine Corps).

marine patrol under Major Smedley D. Butler is ambushed in the dark after locating the caco stronghold at Fort Capois in northern Haiti. In this action Gunnery Sergeant Dan Daly, who had won his first Medal of Honor during the Boxer Rebellion, wins his second by slipping through the caco lines to retrieve a machine gun packed on a horse that had been killed at the beginning of the action. At dawn Butler counterattacks. The bandits break and the marines assault and destroy nearby Fort Dipité. By November 8, columns under Butler and Captain Chandler Campbell have captured three more forts, including Fort Capois.

October 28.   **Parris Island.** The marine corps establishes a recruit training depot, named Parris Island in 1917, at the former naval station at Port Royal, South Carolina.

November 5.   The first catapult launching from a ship under way is made by Lieutenant Commander Henry C. Mustin in the Curtiss AB-2 flying boat from the armored cruiser *North Carolina* (AC 12) in Pensacola Bay, Florida.

November 11.   **Treaty with Haiti.** Under pressure from Admiral Caperton, the Haitian Senate reluctantly ratifies a treaty, signed by President Dartiguenave on September 16, formalizing the American occupation of Haiti. According to its terms, American officials will take charge of the Haitian customs service, collecting revenues and allocating them to reduce the public debt, which cannot be increased without the approval of the United States; American officials will also administer the public works and sanitary services; and the Haitian government promises to raise an "efficient constabulary" commanded by Americans. This latter stipulation is the charter of the marine-led *Gendarmerie d'Haiti*, by which the existing Haitian army is speedily replaced. Ratified by the U.S. Senate on February 23, 1916, the treaty is to remain in force for 10 years and to be renewable for the same period at the desire of either country.

November 17.   **The storming of Fort Rivière, Haiti.** Major Smedley D. Butler is given three marine companies, the marine detachment from the battleship *Connecticut*

(BB 18), and a company of bluejackets from the same ship to assault the last caco bastion, Fort Rivière, an old, French-built masonry work on the crest of Montagne Noire about eight miles south of the town of Grande Rivière du Nord. At dawn, covered by his men's fire, Butler leads a storming party of 26 marines up the bare slope to capture the fort and win his second Medal of Honor. The two marines who precede him into the fort, Sergeant Ross L. Iams and Private Samuel Gross, are also awarded the coveted medal. More than 50 cacos are killed, and the fort is dynamited. This action brings the caco rebellion temporarily to an end.

1916

January 8.   A permanent, West Coast marine base (later named Camp Pendleton) is established at San Diego, California.

March 11.   The battleship *Nevada* (BB 36) is commissioned.

March 24.   **Renewed friction with Germany.** Several American citizens are injured when the *UB-29* torpedoes the French cross-channel steamer *Sussex*. This attack on an unarmed passenger ship clearly violates the German government's *Arabic* pledge of September 1, 1915.

April 16.   Outraged by the sinking of the *Sussex*, President Wilson hands German Ambassador Count Johann von Bernstorff a stiff note, warning that the United States will sever relations with his country unless it changes its way of conducting submarine warfare.

May 2.   The battleship *Oklahoma* (BB 37) is commissioned.

May 4.   **Sussex pledge.** The Imperial German government replies to Wilson's protest by promising that it will not sink merchant vessels without warning and due consideration for the safety of noncombatants aboard.

May 5.   **Dominican intervention.** In April civil war breaks out in the Dominican Republic when General Desiderio Arias, the minister of war, launches a revolt against President Juan Isidro Jiménez. After attempting unsuccessfully to negotiate a settlement be-

tween the two factions, the U.S. minister asks for marines to be landed. Two companies under Captain Frederick M. ("Dopey") Wise go ashore from the transport *Prairie* at Santo Domingo on this date. Besides protecting the American legation and consulate, he is to support President Jiménez, but that intention is frustrated by the president's resignation on May 6. Disorder persists, however, as government forces refuse to recognize Arias. Reinforced by 130 bluejackets and the marine detachment from the gunboat *Castine* (PG 6), Wise arranges a temporary truce.

May 12.   Rear Admiral William B. Caperton, commander of the Cruiser Squadron of the Atlantic Fleet, arrives at Santo Domingo in the dispatch vessel *Dolphin* (PG 24), and three marine companies land from the store ship *Culgoa*.

May 14.   Admiral Caperton meets with General Arias and demands that he disband his forces. Arias refuses to do so, but agrees to withdraw them from Santo Domingo. The marines complete the occupation of the city on May 15.

May 28.   By this date 11 companies of marines have been landed in the Dominican Republic. General Arias has withdrawn to Santiago, in the interior of the country, and it is obvious that the government forces are incapable of crushing the rebellion. That task is assigned to the marines.

June 1.   The port of Monte Cristi, on the northern coast of the Dominican Republic, is peacefully occupied by marines landed from the repair ship *Panther* (AD 6) and the destroyer *Lamson* (DD 18) under the command of Captain Frederick M. Wise.

June 1.   On the same day, two companies of marines and a small bluejacket battalion from the gunboat *Sacramento* (PG 19) seize Puerto Plata, 60 miles east of Monte Cristi, after a skirmish with rebel irregulars in which Captain Herbert J. Hirshinger becomes the first marine killed in action in the Dominican campaign.

June 12.   The battleship *Pennsylvania* (BB 38) is commissioned.

June 21.   Colonel Joseph H. Pendleton's Fourth Marine Regiment lands at Monte Cristi from the transport *Hancock* (AP 3). Pendleton assumes command of marine forces in the Dominican Republic, which become the 2nd Provisional Marine Brigade.

June 26. **Advance on Santiago.** The marines move on General Arias's stronghold in two columns: Colonel Pendleton's Fourth Regiment, with artillery—837 men in all—from Monte Cristi; and four companies, of which Major Hiram I. ("Hike 'em") Bearss takes command on June 28, from Puerto Plata.

June 27. **Action at Las Trencheras.** Rebel forces entrenched on two hilltops barring the road to Santiago are driven away by Colonel Pendleton's column, leaving five dead.

June 29. Major Bearss's Puerto Plata column breaks through 200 rebels entrenched across the railroad at Alta Mira at a cost of two men wounded.

July 3. **Action at Guayacanas.** The major engagement of the Dominican campaign is fought when Colonel Pendleton's column disperses a sizeable rebel force entrenched in heavy underbrush. The marines lose 1 man killed and 10 wounded; the bodies of 27 rebels are found on the field.

July 4. As planned, the two marine columns advancing on Santiago unite at Navarette.

July 5. **Occupation of Santiago.** As the marine column nears Santiago, General Arias sends a message to Colonel Pendleton that he is disbanding his army. The marines occupy the city without opposition the next day.

August 19. The U.S. Navy Reserve Force is formally organized.

August 24. **Gendarmerie agreement.** The United States and Haiti conclude an agreement detailing the organization and responsibilities of the *Gendarmerie d'Haiti*. Authorized strength of the force is set at 115 officers and 2,533 NCOs and men.

August 29. **A navy second to none.** Made apprehensive by the spectacle of the war in Europe, Congress approves President Wilson's request to build a navy equal to any other in the world. By the Naval Act of 1916, passed on this date, it authorizes almost $500 million for a three-year building program to produce 10 battleships, 6 battlecruisers, 10 scout cruisers, 50 destroyers, 9 fleet submarines, 58 coastal submarines, and 16 auxiliary vessels. Incomparably the greatest naval appropriation yet passed, the

Gendarmerie d'Haiti: inspection arms. U.S. Naval Institute Collection.

act also signifies the adoption of a new goal for American naval policy, one which has been adhered to ever since.

August 29. The cruiser *Memphis* (ACR 10), Captain Edward L. Beach, is wrecked by a tidal wave at Santo Domingo, in the Dominican Republic. Forty of her crewmen are killed and 204 injured.

September 7. **Shipping Board.** Congress establishes the Shipping Board, with powers to buy, build, and charter merchant ships for naval and military purposes. In 1917–18 this board will be instrumental in assembling shipping to supply American forces in Europe.

October 17. The battleship *Arizona* (BB 39) is commissioned.

November 29. Captain Harry S. Knapp is appointed military governor of the Dominican Republic, which is declared to be under the military jurisdiction of the United States.

November 29. Juan Perez, the governor of the Dominican province of San Francisco de Macoris and an adherent of General Arias, has refused orders to have his followers surrender their arms to American authorities. After nightfall two marine companies surround the fortress at San Francisco and First Lieutenant Ernest C. Williams leads 12 picked men to rush the gateway before it can be closed. Eight of the party are wounded in the performance of this mission, but the fort is quickly captured. Williams is awarded the Medal of Honor.

1917

January 13.   The cruiser *Milwaukee* (CL 21) strands off Eureka, California, while attempting to refloat the submarine *H-3* (SS 30). No lives are lost, but the ship is eventually wrecked.

January 16.   Admiral of the Navy George Dewey dies, still on active duty at age 79.

January 17.   The United States purchases the Virgin Islands from Denmark.

February 1.   **Unrestricted submarine warfare.** Accepting the risk of American intervention in the world war, the Imperial German government announces the initiation of a policy of unrestricted submarine warfare around the British Isles. The German navy believes that it can starve out Britain in six months, long before American belligerence could become effective. The U-boats come close, but are finally frustrated by the adoption of the convoy system in the summer of 1917.

February 3.   The United States severs relations with the German Empire.

February 24.   **Zimmermann telegram.** President Wilson is outraged when the British government gives him a copy of an intercepted cable in which German Foreign Secretary Alfred Zimmermann promises the Mexican government assistance in the recovery of her lost provinces—most of the American Southwest—in exchange for a military alliance in the event the United States enters the war against Germany. Wilson releases the message to the public, with predictable results.

February 25.   **"Sugar Intervention."** Marines begin to land from vessels of the Atlantic Fleet when revolution breaks out in eastern Cuba; they guard American property, mainly sugar plantations, while the Cuban Army engages the rebels. Withdrawn late in May, the marines return in August and remain in regimental and, briefly, brigade strength until August 1919. Two companies continue to garrison Camaguey until February 6, 1922.

February 25.   The British liner *Laconia* is torpedoed and sunk by a German submarine; three Americans lose their lives.

March 1.   President Wilson requests and receives from Congress authority to arm American merchantmen.

March 9.   Without consulting Congress, President Wilson assigns navy crews to man the deck guns being placed aboard American merchant ships.

March 14–21.   Five American merchant vessels are sunk by German submarines.

March 17.   **"Yeomanettes."** The navy is authorized to enlist women to perform yeoman's (clerical) duties. Some 11,275 women will serve during World War I.

March 26.   The Joint Army-Navy Airship Board is established to study the question of constructing rigid airships in the United States.

April 6.   **War with Germany.** Meeting in joint session, the Congress overwhelmingly approves President Wilson's request for a declaration of war on Germany. The strength of the navy at this time is 4,376 officers and 69,680 men.

April 7.   **Guardia Nacional.** Admiral Harry S. Knapp, military governor of the Dominican Republic, disbands the remnants of the Dominican Army and gives orders for the formation of a constabulary similar to the *Gendarmerie d'Haiti*, called the *Guardia*

Admiral William S. Sims. Courtesy U.S. Naval Academy Museum.

Nacional Dominica and officered by U.S. Marines.

April 8. The United States breaks diplomatic relations with Austria-Hungary.

April 9. Sims to London. Rear Admiral William S. Sims arrives in London to establish high-level contact with British naval authorities. In secret briefings at the Admiralty he is shocked to learn that, contrary to published information, the British are losing the war at sea; U-boats are sinking merchant ships faster than they can be built. Britain stands on the threshold of starvation. Sims responds to the crisis by urging the Navy Department to rush all possible destroyers and patrol craft to European waters and to suspend the capital ship construction called for by the Naval Act of 1916 in favor of a crash program of building antisubmarine vessels and cargo ships. His recommendations encounter considerable resistance, but in the end they prevail. Sims also supports the British officers advocating the adoption of a convoy system, which is tried on an experimental basis in May and proves an immediate success. The admiral remains in London as Commander, U.S. Naval Forces Operating in European Waters, throughout the war.

May 4. "The Return of the Mayflower." The first U.S. warships to reach the European war zone, the six vessels of Commander Joseph K. Taussig's Destroyer Squadron 8—the *Wadsworth* (DD 60), flag, *Conyngham* (DD 58), *Davis* (DD 65), *McDougal* (DD 54), *Porter* (DD 59), and *Wainwright* (DD 62)—arrive at the British naval base at Queenstown (now Cobh), Ireland. Asked by the British commander, Vice Admiral Sir Lewis Bayly, when his squadron will be ready for service, Taussig replies, "We are ready now, sir." The arrival of Taussig's force becomes the subject of Bernard Gribble's famous painting, "The Return of the Mayflower."

May 14. Quantico. The marine corps's need of its own East Coast base is filled by the establishment of the Marine Barracks at Quantico, Virginia.

May 24. The first American Atlantic convoy sails from Hampton Roads, Virginia.

May 29. Cruiser and Transport Force. Rear Admiral Albert Gleaves is made commander of the force, eventually numbering 45 transports and 24 cruisers, organized to carry troops of the American Expeditionary Force to Europe. It will move 911,047 soldiers—almost half the AEF—to France and England without the loss of a single life as a result of enemy action. (The other troops are carried in British transports.)

June 5–6. Navy air. The first naval aviation unit to reach France, Lieutenant Kenneth Whiting's 1st Aeronautical Detachment, arrives at Bordeaux and St. Nazaire aboard the colliers *Jupiter* and *Neptune* (AC 8). By the war's end the strength of navy air in Europe will have grown to 16,000 officers and men, with 500 aircraft, plus kite balloons and dirigibles, distributed between 26 naval air stations: 16 in France, 5 in Ireland, 3 in England, and 2 in Italy.

June 9. U.S. Patrol Squadron. Six armed yachts sail from New York for Brest, France, to form the nucleus of the U.S. Patrol Squadron. This force will relieve the escort vessels of the Cruiser-Transport Force of the responsibility for the security of American convoys upon the latter's entry into French coastal waters. Commanded after November 1, 1917, by Rear Admiral Henry B. Wilson, the patrol force will reach a strength of 38 destroyers and 16 armed yachts, plus minesweepers, tenders, and tugs.

June 14. The first ground combat units of the AEF, the 1st Infantry Division and Colonel Charles A. Doyen's newly organized Fifth Marine Regiment, sail for France.

August 14. The first experimental launching of a torpedo from an aircraft is conducted by Lieutenant Edward O. McDonnell at Huntington Bay, New York. The test was carried out on the initiative of Rear Admiral Bradley A. Fiske, who had been trying to interest the navy in the idea of a torpedo plane since 1912.

September 16. Gunner's Mate First Class Osmond K. Ingram becomes the first navy man to be killed in action in World War I when he is blown overboard from the destroyer *Cassin* (DD 43) by a German torpedo. Ingram saw the torpedo coming and was trying to roll a depth-charge over the side at the moment of impact. He is posthumously awarded the Medal of Honor,

"The Return of the Mayflower," by Bernard F. Gribble, shows British fishermen cheering the arrival of Commander Taussig's destroyers. Courtesy U.S. Naval Academy Museum.

and the destroyer *Ingram* (DD 255) is named after him.

October 17. The army transport *Antilles* is sunk by a U-boat while homeward bound from France.

October 23. **The Marine Brigade.** In France, the Fifth and Sixth Marine Regiments are organized as the 4th Marine Brigade under

The Cruiser and Transport Force safeguarded the passage of the American Expeditionary Force to France. Here, in November 1917, members of the Sixth Marine Regiment crowd the rails of the *Von Steuben* to view the *Agamemnon*, carrying troops of the 42nd ("Rainbow") Division. U.S. Naval Institute Collection.

the command of Brigadier General Charles A. Doyen. The 6th Machine Gun Battalion of Marines joins shortly afterwards.

October 28. The homeward-bound, army transport *Finland*, to which the survivors of the *Antilles* had been transferred, is torpedoed by a U-boat, but succeeds in making her way back to Brest, France.

November 5. The converted yacht *Alcedo* (SP 166), Lieutenant Commander William T. Conn, is torpedoed and sunk with the loss of 22 lives by the *UC-71* while patrolling off the coast of France. She is the first U.S. naval vessel lost in World War I.

November 17. **First U-boat kill.** Two of the destroyers based at Queenstown (Cobh), Ireland—the *Fanning* (DD 37), Lieutenant Arthur S. Carpender, and *Nicholson* (DD 52), Commander Frank D. Berrien—depth-charge the *U-58*. Kapitänleutnant Gustav Amberger brings his stricken submarine to the surface, and the crew is rescued before her final plunge.

November 18. Planes based at Le Croisic, France, at the mouth of the Loire, fly the navy's first patrols over European waters.

November 19. The destroyer *Chauncey* (DD 3), Lieutenant Commander Walter E. Reno, sinks with the loss of 21 lives after being rammed by the SS *Rose*, a British merchantman, 110 miles west of Gibraltar.

December 6.   The destroyer *Jacob Jones* (DD 61), Lieutenant Commander David W. Bagley, is torpedoed and sunk by the *U-53*, Kapitänleutnant Hans Rose, near the Scilly Isles. Sixty-four of her crewmen go down with her. The U-boat commander surfaces, takes two prisoners, and chivalrously radios the position of the sinking to the U.S. naval base at Queenstown (Cobh), Ireland, facilitating the rescue of the other 35 survivors.

December 7.   **Battleships to Britain.** The five dreadnoughts comprising Battleship Division 9—the *Delaware* (BB 28), *Florida* (BB 30), *New York* (BB 34), *Texas* (BB 35), and *Wyoming* (BB 32)—Rear Admiral Hugh Rodman, commanding, arrive at Scapa Flow in the Orkneys to reinforce the British Grand Fleet, in which they become the Sixth Battle Squadron.

December 17.   The submarines *F-1* (SS 20) and *F-3* (SS 22) collide off San Pedro, California, and the former sinks with the loss of 19 lives.

December 18.   The battleship *Mississippi* (BB 41) is commissioned.

1918

January 3.   **N.O.T.S.** The Naval Overseas Transportation Service is established under Commander Charles Belknap to control the shipment of supplies to American forces in Europe. Of the more than 450 cargo ships that eventually belong to the service, only 8 will be lost as a result of enemy action.

January 21.   The 1st Marine Aeronautics Company, Captain Francis T. Evans, lands at Ponta Delgada on São Miguel Island in the Azores, from which it will fly antisubmarine patrols. It is the first marine aviation unit to reach the European war zone.

March 4.   **Disappearance of the Cyclops.** The collier *Cyclops*, Lieutenant Commander George W. Worley, USNRF, puts out from Barbados, British West Indies, with a crew of 280 and is never seen again.

March 17.   **Into the trenches.** In France, marine units enter the front line for the first time.

March 19.   The destroyer *Manley* (DD 74),

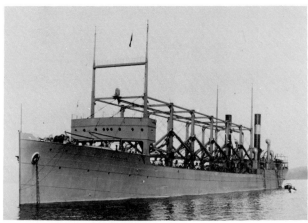

The *Cyclops*, whose disappearance remains a mystery. Official U.S. Navy photograph.

Commander Robert L. Berry, is severely damaged, and 56 of her crew are killed by the accidental detonation of 18 depth charges when she rolls against the British auxiliary cruiser *Motagua* off the Irish coast.

March 19.   **First aerial victory.** Ensign Stephen Potter (Naval Aviator No. 130) becomes the first navy pilot to shoot down an enemy aircraft, destroying a German seaplane near the island of Heligoland in the North Sea, while on a long-range patrol with the Royal Air Force. A little over a month later, on April 25, he is killed in an air battle with seven German aircraft off Felixstowe, England.

April 11.   The N.O.T.S. cargo ship *Lake Moor* is torpedoed by *UB-73* off the Corsewall Light, Scotland, and sinks with the loss of 46 lives.

May 8.   In the Mediterranean, the armed yacht *Lydonia* (SP 700), Lieutenant Commander Richard P. McCullough, collaborates with the British destroyer *Basilisk* to sink the *UB-70*.

May 12.   **Subchasers.** The first six of the new, 110-foot, wooden-hulled, American subchasers reach the European war zone. Before the war's end 121 of these little craft will be employed in British and French waters and in the Mediterranean.

May 20.   The battleship *New Mexico* (BB 40) is commissioned.

May 21.   The N.O.T.S. tanker *William Rockefeller*, Lieutenant Commander Richard E. Tull, USNRF, is torpedoed and sunk by the *UC-58* while en route from Lamlash to Rosyth, Scotland. All except 3 of her 51 crewmen are saved.

May 24.   **Intervention in Russia.** The outbreak of the Russian revolution and the Bolshevik's withdrawal from the war in March 1918 leaves huge amounts of arms and munitions, sent by the Allies to supply the czar's army, stockpiled at Archangel. To avert the possibility of these stores falling into unfriendly hands, the Allies decide to occupy Archangel, using Murmansk as a base. On this date the cruiser *Olympia* (C 6), Captain Bion B. Bierer, lands a detachment to cooperate with British forces in the unopposed seizure of Murmansk. In June, 55 of the cruiser's men participate in the advance on and occupation of Archangel.

May 25.   **U-boat operations in American waters.** *U-151*, the first of six long-range German submarines that will be sent into American coastal waters during the war, begins her operations by attacking three small schooners off Cape Charles, Virginia. Relatively little damage is done by these raids.

May 31.   The transport *President Lincoln*, Captain Percy W. Foote, is sunk by the *U-90* when two days out of Brest, France, bound for New York. Of the 715 men aboard, 26 are lost. The submarine surfaces after the sinking and takes Lieutenant Edouard V. Izac prisoner from a lifeboat. While aboard the *U-90* Izac gathers so much information regarding German submarine operations that upon his arrival in Germany he resolves to escape in order to put this intelligence at the disposal of the Allied navies. His first breakout ends in his recapture, but on the second he succeeds in making his way through the German lines. Lieutenant Izac's heroism and initiative is rewarded by the Medal of Honor.

June 5.   **Belleau Wood.** On May 27, a German offensive breaks through the French front in the Chemin des Dames, northeast of Paris. The 4th Marine Brigade, commanded by Brigadier General James G. Harbord, USA, is rushed to meet the threat. On this date, the marines repel German attacks along the Paris-Metz highway. The

Marines in France, riding the famous *hommes 40, cheveux 8* French railway cars. Courtesy National Archives.

following day they counterattack strongly fortified German positions in Belleau Wood, between the villages of Lucy-le-Bocage and Bouresches. As the marines advance towards the wood under heavy machine-gun and rifle fire, Gunnery Sergeant Dan Daly, winner of two Medals of Honor, encourages them with the shout, "Come on, you sons of bitches! Do you want to live forever?" The German resistance is tenacious. By June 26, the brigade has suffered 50 percent casualties (4,677 killed and wounded), but Major Maurice Shearer, commanding the 3rd Battalion, Fifth Marines, is able to report, "Woods now U.S. Marine Corps entirely." General Jean Degoutte, commander of the French Sixth Army, decrees that henceforth the wood will be known as the *Bois de la Brigade de Marine.*

June 8.   **North Sea mine barrage.** U.S. naval forces under the command of Rear Admiral Joseph Strauss begin the enormous task of laying a minefield across 240 miles of open sea from Scotland to Norway with the object of penning Germany's U-boats inside the North Sea. The British had considered undertaking such a project, but decided that it was technically infeasible. The belt is completed on September 20, and operations to increase its density and width continue until the armistice. A total of 70,263 mines are laid, including 13,652 by cooperating British forces. Many U-boats slip through the barrage, but as many as

U.S. minesweepers, painted in camouflage colors, laying the North Sea mine barrage. U.S. Naval Institute Collection.

six may have been destroyed in the attempt.

June 29–August 28. **Marines in Russia.** The cruiser *Brooklyn* (ACR 3), flagship of the U.S. Asiatic Fleet, lands her marine detachment to safeguard the American consulate at Vladivostok during the convulsions of the Russian Civil War. The marines remain ashore until relieved by an infantry brigade from the Philippines.

July 1. The transport *Covington*, Captain Raymond De L. Hasbrouck, is torpedoed by the *U-86* off Brest, France, and sinks while under tow the next day; 770 of the 776 men aboard are saved.

July 11. The cargo ship *Westover* is torpedoed by the *U-92* off the coast of France and sinks with the loss of 11 lives.

July 14. In France, Colonel Wendell C. ("Buck") Neville, CO of the Fifth Marines, is promoted to the rank of brigadier general and assumes command of the 4th Marine Brigade, General Harbord having been moved up to command the 2nd Infantry Division.

July 18–19. **Battle of Soissons.** The 4th Marine Brigade takes part in the counterattack that throws back the last German offensive of the war, advancing six-and-one-half miles and sustaining 1,972 casualties in 48 hours.

July 19. **Loss of the San Diego.** The cruiser *San Diego* (ex-*California*) (ACR 6), Captain Harley H. Christy, hits a mine laid by *U-156*, Kapitänleutnant Richard Feldt, off Fire Island, New York, and sinks with the loss

of 6 lives. She is the only major American warship lost in World War I. On her return voyage to Germany, the *U-156* will be sunk in the North Sea mine barrage.

July 21. Four seaplanes from the Naval Air Station, Chatham, Massachusetts, attack the surfaced German *U-156* that has sunk the tug *Perth Amboy* and four barges off Cape Cod. The submarine submerges after returning the planes' fire.

July 25. The navy is assigned the responsibility for developing rigid airships for the American armed forces.

July 28. In France, Brigadier General John A. Lejeune is given command of the 2nd Infantry Division. The first marine officer to command a formation larger than a brigade, he will be promoted to the rank of major general on August 7.

July 30. The 1st Marine Aviation Force, 100 officers and 657 men under Major Alfred A. Cunningham, lands in France from the transport *De Kalb*.

August 12. **Marinettes.** The marine corps is authorized to enlist women in the marine corps reserve to perform clerical duties. Mrs. Opha M. Johnson becomes the first woman marine.

August 21. One of a flight of three seaplanes from the Naval Air Station, Porto Corsini, Italy, is shot down in a dogfight with enemy land planes near the Austrian naval base at Pola, on the Adriatic. Ensign Charles H. Hammann, USNRF, becomes the first

Major General John A. Lejeune awarding decorations, a few weeks after the close of hostilities. Courtesy National Archives.

Marinettes (and two male marines) outside the corp's headquarters in Washington. Defense Department photo (Marine Corps).

naval aviator to win the Medal of Honor when he lands his plane on the water to pick up the downed pilot.

August 23. **More battleships to Britain.** A battleship division consisting of the *Nevada* (BB 36), *Oklahoma* (BB 37), and *Utah* (BB 31) under the command of Rear Admiral T. S. Rodgers reaches Bantry Bay, Ireland, to serve as a force in readiness in the event a German battlecruiser should break out to attack the North Atlantic convoys.

September 6. **Railway guns.** A naval battery of five 14-inch railway guns, commanded by Rear Admiral Charles P. Plunkett, goes into action in France, delivering a long-range bombardment of German positions north of Soissons. This unit is humorously known as the Woozlefinches.

September 12–15. **St. Mihiel offensive.** Brigadier General Wendell C. Neville's 4th Marine Brigade, still assigned to the 2nd Infantry Division, takes part in the first all-American offensive on the Western Front, the reduction of the German St. Mihiel salient. The Germans are in the process of withdrawing from the salient when the attack is launched, and American casualties are relatively light.

September 15. The transport *Mount Vernon*, Captain Douglas E. Dismukes, is torpedoed by a U-boat while homeward bound from Brest, France. Thirty-six men are killed, but the ship succeeds in returning to Brest.

September 16. The cargo ship *Buena Ventura*, Lieutenant Commander H. Fitzsimmons,

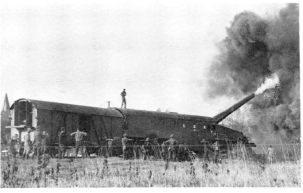

One of the navy's 14-inch railway guns in action on the Western Front. Courtesy National Archives.

USNRF, is torpedoed by the *U-46* two days out of Bordeaux, France, and sinks with the loss of 19 lives.

September 24.   **First navy ace.** Nineteen-year-old Lieutenant David S. Ingalls, flying a Sopwith Camel on temporary duty with No. 213 Squadron, RAF, in northern France, scores his fifth aerial victory, thereby becoming the navy's first and only ace of World War I.

September 26.   The coast guard cutter *Tampa*, carrying a crew of 115, is lost with all hands in the Bristol Channel, off the west coast of England, after being torpedoed by the *UB-91.*

September 29.   The battleship *Minnesota* (BB 22), Captain J. V. Chase, is slightly damaged by a German mine off the Delaware capes.

September 30.   **Ticonderoga vs. U-152.** The Naval Overseas Transportation Service Ship *Ticonderoga*, Lieutenant Commander James J. Madison, USNRF, is sunk in mid-Atlantic after an heroic, two-hour surface action with the *U-152.* Only 24 of the 237 men aboard survive, including Madison, who is awarded the Medal of Honor.

October 2.   **Durazzo raid.** In the Adriatic, 11 American subchasers under Captain C.P. Nelson screen an Allied British, French, and Italian force that bombards the Austrian naval base at Durazzo.

October 3–10.   **Blanc Mont Ridge.** In France General Lejeune's 2nd Infantry Division, including the 4th Marine Brigade, attacks Blanc Mont Ridge, a naturally strong and heavily fortified German position on the Champagne sector. The ridge and the village of Etienne, in its rear, are taken after a week's fighting, which costs the marines 2,538 casualties.

October 4.   **First armistice note.** The Imperial German government appeals to President Wilson to arrange an armistice.

October 14.   **First air raid.** Navy and marine corps aviation in northern France is organized as the Northern Bombing Group, consisting of a Marine Day Wing and a Navy Night Wing. The group's first major raid is made on this date when a marine squadron of eight DeHavilland DH-4s led by Captain Douglas B. Robin bombs the rail yards at Thielt, Belgium. Second Lieutenant Ralph Talbot and his observer, Gunnery Sergeant Robert G. Robinson, shoot down 2 of 12 German planes by which their aircraft is attacked. Both are awarded the Medal of Honor, the first marine aviators to gain that distinction.

October 17.   **Caco uprising.** The relative peace that has prevailed in Haiti since late 1915 is shattered when a band of approximately 100 cacos under the dynamic, new leadership of French-educated Charlemagne Péralte attacks the *gendarmerie* post at Hinche, in the central part of the country. The cacos are beaten off, leaving 35 dead, but hundreds more soon flock to Charlemagne's side. The second Haitian campaign has begun.

October 17.   The SS *Lucia* gains the unwanted distinction of being the last ship torpedoed by a German U-boat in World War I. She sinks the next day. On October 21, the German government accedes to President Wilson's demand for the cessation of submarine operations as a prerequisite to armistice negotiations.

October 29.   **The German Fleet mutinies.** Learning of plans for what they interpret as a death or glory sortie down the Belgian coast, the crews of the heavy surface units of the German High Seas Fleet mutiny. Their action sparks a spontaneous revolution among the war-weary civilian population ashore.

November 1.   **Marines in the Meuse-Argonne.** In a single day's fighting the 4th Marine Brigade penetrates the Germans'

The N.O.T.S. *Ticonderoga.* U.S. Naval Institute Collection.

Hindenburg Line, capturing the Brünhilde and Freya strongpoints, taking 1,700 prisoners and advancing more than four miles.

November 9. The Imperial German government is overthrown and a republic proclaimed. The Kaiser crosses the border into neutral Holland the next day.

November 9–10. The Fifth Marines cross the Meuse River against heavy resistance.

November 10. In Haiti, 60 cacos led by Charlemagne Péralte rout the 10-man *gendarmerie* garrison at Maissade, northwest of Hinche, and plunder the town.

November 11. **Armistice.** The cease-fire ending World War I goes into effect at 11:00 A.M.

November 21. **Surrender of the German Fleet.** In accordance with the terms of the armistice agreement, 14 German capital ships cross the North Sea to be interned at the British base at Scapa Flow in the Orkneys. The American battleships serving with the British Grand Fleet are present at the surrender.

December 1. At the Naval Air Station, Hampton Roads, Virginia, the dirigible *C-7* becomes the first American airship to be filled with helium, in place of the highly flammable hydrogen formerly used. Hereafter, all American lighter-than-air craft will use helium.

1919

February 4. The Navy Cross and the Navy Distinguished Service Medal are created by act of Congress.

February 12. Captain Archibald H. Scales becomes the 25th superintendent of the Naval Academy.

March 8. An upsurge of political banditry in the Dominican Republic leads to the reinforcement of the 2nd Marine Brigade by Colonel James C. Breckinridge's Fifteenth Marine Regiment and the 1st Air Squadron—six Curtiss JN6 "Jennies"—which land at Santo Domingo on this date. These arrivals increase the brigade's strength to 2,600 officers and men.

March 9. Lieutenant Commander E. O. McDonnell, in a Sopwith Camel, makes the first flight from a turret platform aboard

the battleship *Texas* (BB 35) at Guantánamo, Cuba.

March 16. **Second Haitian Campaign.** Major General (marine colonel) Alexander S. Williams, commandant of the *Gendarmerie d'Haiti*, notifies Brigadier General Albertus W. Catlin, commanding the 1st Marine Brigade, that the assistance of marine forces is needed to crush Péralte's caco rebellion. The number of hostile contacts since the first of the year make it evident that a full-scale rebellion is under way. Four companies are transferred from Guantánamo, Cuba, to reinforce the brigade later in the month, and approximately 1,000 marines are put into the field. From April through September the marines and *gendarmerie* are engaged in no less than 131 actions, large and small.

March 21. A *gendarmerie* patrol of five men led by Lieutenant (marine sergeant) Nicolas B. Moskoff is ambushed by around 100 cacos at Dufailly, Haiti. Moskoff is mortally wounded at the first fire, and his Haitian second-in-command is later killed, but the surviving *gendarmes* fight their way back to Mirebalais, carrying Moskoff with them.

March 24. The battleship *Idaho* (BB 42) is commissioned.

March 31. Squadron E, marine corps aviation, arrives at Port-au-Prince, Haiti, for service against the cacos.

May 8–31. **First across.** Three Navy/Curtiss ("Nancy") flying boats—the NC-1, NC-3, and NC-4—set out on the first transatlantic flight, with lay-overs at Trepassy, Newfoundland, and the Azores. Two drop out before reaching the latter, but the NC-4, piloted by Lieutenant Commander Albert C. ("Putty") Read, pushes on to reach

The NC-4. U.S. Naval Institute Collection.

Lisbon, Portugal, on May 27 and Plymouth, England, on the 31st. In 1929 Congress awards a gold medal to Read, his four crewmen, and their squadron leader, Commander John H. Towers. Today the NC-4 is on exhibit at the Smithsonian Institution in Washington, D.C.

May 28.   The General Board of the Navy recommends the completion of the great construction program projected by the Naval Act of 1916.

June 21.   The German fleet, interned at Scapa Flow in the Orkneys, is scuttled by its crews.

June 28.   The Treaty of Versailles is signed, officially ending World War I. Because ratification of the treaty would include acceptance of the covenant of the League of Nations, it will be rejected by the U.S. Senate.

July 11.   The navy pay corps is renamed the supply corps.

July 23.   Planes of the marine 1st Air Squadron attack a party of bandits at Meta de la Palma in the Dominican Republic.

July 30–August 1.   The marine detachment of the cruiser *New Orleans* (CL 22) lands to protect American interests at Tyutuke Bay, near Vladivostok, Russia.

August.   **Air-ground action.** In Haiti two marine aircraft—a Curtiss Jenny and a DeHavilland DH-4—support ground forces in a surprise attack on a caco encampment on a hilltop near Mirebalais. More than 200 bandits are killed. This is the first instance of the coordinated, air-ground action that will later become a marine corps specialty.

October 2.   Colonel John H. Russell assumes command of the 1st Marine Brigade in Haiti.

October 7.   **Attack on Port-au-Prince.** Charlemagne Péralte sends 300 of his followers to raid the Haitian capital. The cacos are repulsed and pursued by the marines and the *gendarmerie*.

October 31.   **The end of Charlemagne.** *Gendarmerie* Captain (marine sergeant) Herman H. Hanneken and First Lieutenant (marine corporal) William R. Button blacken their faces and lead a patrol of 16 hand-picked *gendarmes*, all disguised as cacos, through six enemy outposts to penetrate the camp of Charlemagne Péralte. Hanneken kills Péralte with two shots from his .45. The caco leader's corpse is later photographed,

and prints are distributed to convince his followers that he is indeed dead. Hanneken and Button are both awarded the U.S. Medal of Honor and the Haitian Médaille Militaire.

November 1.   Rear Admiral Robert E. Coontz becomes the second chief of naval operations.

November 2.   A detachment of *gendarmes* led by Captain Hanneken storms the caco stronghold of Fort Capois, effectively ending the insurrection in northern Haiti.

December 17.   The Eighth Marine Regiment is reconstituted and ordered to Haiti under the command of Lieutenant Colonel L. McCarthy Little.

December 25.   **Yangpat.** The American gunboats that have been operating on China's Yangtze River since 1903 are formally organized into the Yangtze Patrol under the command of Captain T.A. Kearney, first ComYangPat.

1920

January 1.   **Campaign against the cacos.** In Haiti Colonel John H. Russell, commanding the 1st Marine Brigade, intensifies efforts to suppress the cacos.

January 15.   **Second attack on Port-au-Prince.** Benoit Batraville, who has succeeded Charlemagne Péralte as the principal caco chieftain, sends a party of 300 men to assault the Haitian capital. The cacos penetrate the city before dawn, but are soon driven out, suffering 50 percent casualties.

YangPat: the *Guam*, a gunboat commissioned in 1927, on patrol on the Yangtze. Official U.S. Navy photograph.

April 4.   Climbing Morne Michel, near Las Ca-hobas, Haiti, a patrol led by *gendarmerie* Lieutenant (marine sergeant) Lawrence Muth is ambushed by cacos under Benoit Batraville. Muth, wounded and left for dead, is decapitated by Batraville.

April 10.   U.S. Marines enter Guatemala City, Guatemala, to protect the American embassy during a revolution.

May 19.   **Crushing the cacos.** A marine patrol led by Captain Jesse L. Perkins surprises Benoit Batraville's camp in Petit Bois Peine, near Las Cahobas, Haiti. Batraville is killed in the action. His death marks the end of the caco rebellion. By the close of the year, the pacification of the country is complete.

June 30.   The battleship *Tennessee* (BB 43) is commissioned.

July 1.   Major General John A. Lejeune becomes the 13th commandant of the marine corps.

July 12.   Naval forces afloat are organized into the Atlantic, Pacific, and Asiatic Fleets.

July 18.   The ex-German light cruiser *Frankfurt* is sunk by U.S. naval aircraft in bombing experiments off Hampton Roads, Virginia.

July 29.   The cruiser *St. Louis* (CA 18) and six destroyers are dispatched to Turkish waters to protect American citizens during the disturbances resulting from the Graeco-Turkish War.

October 14–November 1.   The obsolete battleship *Indiana* (BB 1) is sunk in Tangier Sound, in the Chesapeake Bay, after a series of air attacks and explosions designed to test the efficacy of her underwater compartmentation and double hull.

1921

February 26.   The destroyer *Woolsey* (DD 77) sinks with the loss of 16 lives after a collision with the freighter *Steel Inventor*.

March 5.   Edwin Denby becomes 42nd secretary of the navy.

June 21.   The formerly German battleship *Ostfriesland* is sunk off the Virginia Capes by aerial bombing supervised by Brigadier General "Billy" Mitchell, the controversial chief of the U.S. Army Air Service. Even though the planes have to break the prearranged rules of engagement to give the sta-

tionary old ship the *coup de grâce*, Mitchell proclaims that her sinking signals the end of the surface warship.

July 5.   Rear Admiral Henry B. Wilson becomes 26th superintendent of the Naval Academy.

July 21.   The battleship *Maryland* (BB 46) is commissioned.

July 23.   **Pete Ellis's plan.** Major General Commandant John A. Lejeune, USMC, approves Operation Plan 712, "Advanced Base Operations in Micronesia," prepared by Lieutenant Colonel Earl H. ("Pete") Ellis. This remarkable document, the marine corps's contribution to the Orange Plan prepared by the navy for use in the event of war with Japan, calls for the development of the amphibious capability the corps would demonstrate in World War II and accurately forecasts the general course of the Pacific campaigns. A brilliant, troubled man, Ellis will die of alcoholism while on a secret mission to reconnoiter Japan's island possessions in 1923.

August 10.   **BuAer.** Rear Admiral William A. Moffett is appointed chief of the newly established Bureau of Aeronautics. This is the first new bureau created since the Civil War.

August 10.   The battleship *California* (BB 44) is commissioned.

August 24.   **Loss of the R-38.** The dirigible *R-38* (ZR-2), built in England for the U.S. Navy, breaks up, burns, and crashes into the Humber River while on a test flight near Hull, England. Of the 17 Americans and 27 Englishmen aboard, all except 1 of the former and 5 of the latter perish in the disaster.

November 7.   **Marines guard the mails.** Two mail-train robberies spur President Warren G. Harding to detail 23 marine officers and 2,200 men to guard the U.S. mails. The robberies cease, and the marines are withdrawn in March 1922.

November 11.   **Washington Conference.** On the third anniversary of the armistice, U.S. Secretary of State Charles Evans Hughes welcomes the delegates of eight foreign nations—Great Britain, Japan, France, Italy, The Netherlands, Belgium, Portugal, and China—to the First International Conference on Limitation of Naval Armaments.

The idea had been championed by Senator William E. Borah, who feared the development of a naval race between the United States, Britain, and Japan, and in June a congressional resolution urging President Harding to organize such a conference passed by a landslide.

1922

January 25.   The cruiser *Galveston* (CL 19) lands her marine detachment at Corinto, Nicaragua, to reinforce the Managua legation guard during a period of political tension.

February 6.   **Washington Naval Treaty.** The United States, Great Britain, Japan, France, and Italy conclude the Five-Power Treaty of naval arms limitation, establishing a ratio of capital ships (battleships and aircraft carriers) of 5:5:3:1¾:1¾, respectively. This is the first time in recent history that Great Britain, traditional ruler of the waves, has conceded parity to any other naval power. To meet treaty limitations (which allow the United States 525,000 tons for battleships and 181,000 tons for aircraft carriers), the three principal powers agree to scrap more than 60 capital ships, completed or under construction. Other articles of the treaty provide for a 10-year moratorium ("naval holiday") on the laying down of new capital ships, which are defined as vessels of more than 10,000 tons with greater than 8-inch guns; they limit capital ships to 35,000 tons and 16-inch guns; and they compensate the Japanese for their inferiority in tonnage by a Non-Fortification Clause, whereby the United States and Great Britain pledge not to strengthen the fortifications of their Pacific possessions (Australia, New Zealand, and Singapore excepted), while the Japanese are free to increase the defenses of their Home Islands.

February 11.   To centralize the administration of the U.S. occupation of Haiti, Congress creates the office of U.S. High Commissioner, with ambassadorial rank. Brigadier General John H. Russell, commanding the 1st Marine Brigade in Haiti, is appointed to the post. He will serve in this capacity until November 12, 1930.

March 20.   **First carrier.** The U.S. Navy's first aircraft carrier, the *Langley* (CV 1), is commissioned at Norfolk, Virginia, Commander Kenneth Whiting, commanding. She was converted from the collier *Jupiter*.

April 22.   A spotter aircraft is assigned to every battleship and cruiser in the navy.

April 28.   The cruiser *Albany* (CL 23) lands her marine detachment to reinforce the legation guard at Peking amid the disorders of the Chinese civil war.

May 5.   A provisional battalion of marines, assembled from ships of the Asiatic Fleet, is landed at Taku, China, ready to advance to Peking should need arise.

July 1.   The conversion of the unfinished battlecruisers *Lexington* and *Saratoga* to aircraft carriers is authorized by Congress.

September 16.   **Evacuation of the Anatolian Greeks.** Following its victory in the Graeco-Turkish War, the Turkish government expels the 250,000 Greeks living in Asia Minor. On this date, Commander Halsey Powell, captain of the destroyer *Edsall* (DD 219), assumes control of the evacuation of this unfortunate population to Greece. Although most of the refugees are actually transported in Greek merchant ships, American destroyers also assist in the movement.

October 17.   **First take-off from a U.S. carrier.** Lieutenant Commander Virgil C. Griffin takes off from the flight deck of the newly commissioned carrier *Langley* (CV 1) in a Vought VE-7SF.

October 26.   Lieutenant Commander Godfrey DeC. ("Chevy") Chevalier becomes the first pilot to land on an American carrier while under way, setting his Aeromarine 39B down on the deck of the *Langley* off Cape Henry, Virginia.

November 18.   Another landmark event in the development of naval aviation occurs aboard the *Langley* when her commanding officer, Commander Kenneth Whiting, makes the first catapult launching from a U.S. carrier.

December 6.   The Atlantic and Pacific fleets are combined to form the United States Fleet.

1923

February 14.   The gunboat *Asheville* (PG 21) lands a small marine detachment to protect

The *Langley*, the navy's first carrier, affectionately known as "the old covered wagon." Official U.S. Navy photograph.

American citizens from bandits on Matsu Island, China.

June 2. The Naval Research Laboratory is established.

July 31. Admiral Edward W. Eberle becomes the third chief of naval operations.

August 30. The battleship *Colorado* (BB 45) is commissioned.

September 4. Under the command of Captain Frank R. McCrary, the airship *Shenandoah* (ZR-1) makes its first flight at the Naval Air Station, Lakehurst, New Jersey.

September 5. The U.S. Asiatic Fleet anchors off Yokohama, Japan, to assist in disaster relief following the great Kondo Plain earthquake that nearly leveled both Yokohama and Tokyo.

September 8. **Disaster at the Devil's Jaw.** Seven ships of Destroyer Squadron (Desron) 11 — the *Chauncey* (DD 296), *Delphy* (DD 261), *Fuller* (DD 297), *Nicholas* (DD 311), *S.P. Lee* (DD 310), *Woodbury* (DD 309), and *Young* (DD 312) — run aground in a heavy fog at Point Pedernales (often called the Devil's Jaw), off Santa Barbara, California. Twenty-two lives are lost, and the ships are completely wrecked.

November 15. A detachment of marines is landed to protect a group of American missionaries at Tungsham, China.

December 1. The battleship *West Virginia* (BB 48) is commissioned.

December 6. Destroyers from the U.S. Asiatic Fleet are ordered to join units of other navies off Canton to assist in safeguarding

foreign lives and property during the Chinese civil wars.

1924

January 16. The cruiser *Tacoma* (CL 20) wrecks on Blanquilla Reef, off Veracruz, Mexico, with the loss of four lives.

January 23. Marines from the gunboat *Sacramento* (PG 21) occupy Socorro, on Boca Grande Island in the Philippines, where the Moros are revolting against the local government. The insurrection is suppressed by mid-February.

February 28–March 2. Seamen and marines from the cruiser *Denver* (C 14) land at La Ceiba, Honduras, to protect American interests during the latest revolution in that country.

March 3. The destroyer *Billingsley* (DD 293) lands a detachment of bluejackets and marines to safeguard American property at Tela, Honduras.

March 4. The *Denver*'s landing battalion goes ashore to defend Americans at Puerto Cortez, Honduras.

March 9. Marines from the cruiser *Denver* (C 14) land to protect Americans at La Ceiba, Honduras.

March 17–19. A detachment of 176 officers and men goes ashore to establish a neutral zone around Tegucigalpa, Honduras.

March 19. Curtis D. Wilbur becomes 43rd secretary of the navy.

The ruins of Destroyer Squadron 11 off Point Pedernales, California. Official U.S. Navy photograph.

August 8.   The airship *Shenandoah* (ZR-1) secures to a mooring mast on the oiler *Patoka* (AO 9) while the latter is under way in Narragansett Bay. This is the first test of that maneuver.

September 10.   The cruiser *Rochester* (ex-*New York*) (ACR 2) lands 111 seamen and marines to safeguard American interests at La Ceiba, Honduras.

September 18.   **Withdrawal from the Dominican Republic.** The last elements of the 2nd Provisional Marine Brigade board ship at Santo Domingo, ending an occupation of eight years. A treaty signed on December 24 formally terminates the American protectorate over the Dominican Republic.

October 6.   **Guarding the International Settlement.** As the Chinese civil war approaches Shanghai, ships of the Asiatic Fleet land detachments to cooperate with contingents from other foreign navies in protecting the International Settlement at Shanghai.

October 7–25.   **Flight of the Shenandoah.** The airship *Shenandoah* (ZR-1), Lieutenant Commander Zachary Lansdowne, makes a transcontinental good-will cruise from the Naval Air Station, Lakehurst, New Jersey, covering 9,317 miles in 258 hours aloft.

November 25.   The navy's German-built airship *Los Angeles* (ZR-3) is christened by Mrs.

Calvin Coolidge at the Anacostia Naval Air Station, Washington, D.C.

1925

January 15.   The marine detachment of the gunboat *Sacramento* (PG 19) is landed to reinforce the defenders of the International Settlement at Shanghai during the tumults of the Chinese civil war. Several other marine units will land to serve briefly in the city in the course of the year.

February 17.   The five signatories of the Washington Naval Treaty—the United States, Great Britain, Japan, France, and Italy— report that they have scrapped all the ships necessary to comply with its terms.

February 23.   Rear Admiral Louis M. Nulton becomes 27th superintendent of the U.S. Naval Academy.

March 2–11.   The *Langley* (CV 1) is the first aircraft carrier to participate in a fleet problem.

March 4.   **NROTC.** The Naval Reserve Officers Training Corps is established by Act of Congress. Programs open at six universities in 1926.

April 1.   The first night landing on an American carrier is made by Lieutenant Commander

The airship *Shenandoah* at a mooring mast. U.S. Naval Institute Collection.

John D. Price on the *Langley* (CV 1) off San Diego, California.

April 20.   The cruiser *Denver* (C 14) lands marines to protect American interests at La Ceiba, Honduras.

August 1.   **Withdrawal from Nicaragua.** The 100-man marine legation guard is recalled from Managua, Nicaragua, where it had been established in January 1913.

September 1.   A four-engined PN-9 flying boat piloted by Commander John Rodgers runs out of gas 470 miles short of its goal after covering 1,841 miles on an attempted nonstop flight from San Francisco to Honolulu. Rodgers and his crew rig a sail from the airplane's wing fabric and reach a point only 20 miles from Hawaii when they are rescued by the submarine *R-4* (SS 81).

September 3.   **Loss of the Shenandoah.** The airship *Shenandoah* (ZR-1), Lieutenant Commander Zachary Lansdowne, breaks in two in a severe storm near Ava, Ohio, while on a second transcontinental goodwill tour. Lansdowne and 13 other of the ship's 43 crew members are killed.

September 25.   **Loss of the S-51.** The submarine *S-51* (SS 162) sinks with the loss of 33 lives after a collision with the SS *City of Rome* off Block Island, Rhode Island.

1926

May 7–June 5.   The marine detachment of the cruiser *Cleveland* (C 19) lands to protect American and other foreign interests at Bluefields, Nicaragua, when civil war breaks out between the Liberals and the Conservatives.

May 9.   **First over the Pole.** Piloting a Fokker tri-motor monoplane, Lieutenant Commander Richard E. Byrd and Chief Aviation Pilot Floyd Bennett become the first men to fly over the North Pole. Their roundtrip flight from Spitzbergen lasts 15½ hours.

August 27.   A flare-up of fighting in Nicaragua leads to the landing of 200 seamen and marines from the cruiser *Galveston* (C 17) to maintain a neutral zone around Bluefields. This force is subsequently relieved by detachments from the cruiser *Rochester* (ACR 2) (October 31) and *Denver* (C 14) (November 30).

October 10.   A detachment of seamen and marines from the cruiser *Denver* (C 14) lands at Corinto, Nicaragua, to preserve order during a conference between warring Liberal and Conservative leaders. The meeting proves unproductive.

October 20.   For the second time, a rash of robberies prompts the president to assign marine detachments to guard the U.S. mails.

October 22.   The first fleet exercise involving dive-bombing is held when a squadron of planes delivers a simulated surprise attack on the Pacific fleet as it stands out from San Pedro, California. The tactic is deemed highly satisfactory.

The wreck of the *Shenandoah*. Courtesy National Archives.

November 12. A detachment of 125 marines is landed from the transport *Gold Star* to protect American interests at Chingwangtao, China.

1927

January 6. A marine detachment landed from the cruiser *Galveston* (C 17) reestablishes the U.S. Legation Guard at Managua, Nicaragua.

January 10. The 2nd Battalion, Fifth Marines, lands to preserve order at Bluefields, Nicaragua. On January 18, all except one company proceed to Managua.

February 9. A battalion of marines is landed to protect the International Settlement at Shanghai, China, from the disturbances generated by the Chinese civil war.

February 9. Rear Admiral Julian L. Latimer, commander of the Special Service Squadron operating off the coast of Nicaragua, orders the marines to take control of the Corinto-Managua railway to prevent it from being disrupted by the civil war. This ac-

tion is accomplished by detachments from the cruisers *Galveston* (C 17), *Milwaukee* (C 21) and *Raleigh* (CL 7).

February 21. A battalion of 200 marines from the battleships *Arkansas* (BB 33), *Florida* (BB 30), and *Texas* (BB 35) reaches Nicaragua aboard the cruiser *Trenton* (CL 11) to guard the railway towns of Chinandega and León.

March 7. The remainder of the Fifth Marine Regiment and the headquarters of the 2nd Marine Brigade land at Corinto, Nicaragua. Marine Observation Squadron 1 arrived on February 28.

March 16. **China marines.** The Fourth Marine Regiment lands at Shanghai, China, to reinforce the battalion garrisoning the International Settlement. The regiment will remain there until 1941.

May 2. The Sixth Marine Regiment lands at Shanghai, China, and is combined with the forces already present to form the 3rd Marine Brigade under Brigadier General Smedley D. Butler.

May 4. **Peace of Tipitapa.** Former secretary of state (and future secretary of war) Henry L. Stimson negotiates a peace between the

Nicaraguan Liberal and Conservative parties. Under its terms, both factions are to lay down their arms, and the existing Conservative government will remain in office until American-supervised elections are held in 1928. In the meantime, U.S. marines will be responsible for maintaining order and training a national constabulary, the *Guardia Nacional.*

May 16.   More than 200 Nicaraguan bandits attack the railway town of La Paz Centro, garrisoned by a detachment of marines under Captain Richard B. Buchanan. The raiders are driven off after an action in which 14 of them and 2 marines, including Buchanan, are killed. He is the first marine officer to die in the Second Nicaraguan Campaign.

June 30–August 4.   **Geneva Naval Conference.** The United States, Great Britain, and Japan meet in an attempt to establish limitations on types of warships—principally cruisers—not covered by the Washington Naval Treaty. No agreement can be reached.

July 16.   **Action at Ocotal.** Augusto C. Sandino, a minor Nicaraguan Liberal leader, has refused to accept the terms of the Treaty of Tipitapa. At 1:15 A.M. on this date he leads a band of 800 rebels to attack a detachment of 37 marines and 47 *guardias* under Captain Gilbert D. Hatfield garrisoning Ocotal, the capital of Nueva Segovia Province. The marines hold out until daylight, when the Sandinistas are dispersed by five DH-4s led by Major Ross E. Rowell, the commander of Marine Observation Squadron 1, in the first actual dive-bombing attack in history. Approximately 300 rebels and 1 marine are killed.

August 28.   **Kellogg-Briand Pact.** Fifteen nations, including the United States, sign the Pact of Paris, renouncing recourse to arms as an instrument of national policy. Eventually almost every nation in the world subscribes. There are no enforcement provisions.

September 19.   **Action at Telpaneca.** A garrison of 21 marines and 25 Nicaraguan *guardias* under *Guardia* Captain (marine first lieutenant) Herbert S. Keimling at the village of Telpaneca, 10 miles from Ocotal,

is attacked by Sandinistas in the early morning hours. The enemy withdraws at dawn, having suffered 50 casualties to the defenders' 3.

October 10.   A marine patrol advancing from Jicaro, Nicaragua, under the command of First Lieutenant George J. O'Shea, to rescue the pilot and co-pilot of a DH-4 that had crashed the previous day, is ambushed by Sandinistas and compelled to withdraw. The fliers are captured and killed.

October 26–28.   Two marine patrols searching for the downed aircraft (which is finally found) are heavily engaged by Sandinistas near Sapotillal Ridge.

November 14.   Rear Admiral Charles Frederick Hughes becomes the fourth chief of naval operations.

November 16.   The carrier *Saratoga* (CV 3) is commissioned.

December 14.   The carrier *Lexington* (CV 2) is commissioned.

December 17.   While running submerged off Provincetown, Massachusetts, the submarine *S-4* (SS 109) sinks with the loss of 39 lives after being struck by the coast guard cutter *Paulding.*

December 30–January 8, 1928.   **Actions around Quilali.** In November, a marine reconnaissance flight locates Sandino's headquarters, a fortified mountaintop called El Chipote, near Sapotillal Ridge, Nicaragua, 26 miles from the Honduran border. On December 19, two marine columns—one of 115 men under Captain Richard Livingstone from Jinotega, the other of 65 men under First Lieutenant Merton A. Richal from Telpaneca—are sent to establish a base at Quilali and push on to take Chipote. Sandino, who is believed to have 300–500 men, actually has around 1,000. Both columns, heavily engaged on December 30–31, are besieged in Quilali on January 1, having had 8 men killed and 30 wounded, including both column commanders. Between January 6–8, 1928, Lieutenant Christian F. Schilt makes 10 flights to an emergency airfield laid out at Quilali, bringing provisions and evacuating the most seriously wounded. The combined columns then withdraw. Schilt is awarded the Medal of Honor.

A marine mounted patrol in Nicaragua. U.S. Naval Institute Collection.

The *Saratoga* during fleet maneuvers off Guantánamo, Cuba, in March 1930. Official U.S. Navy photograph.

1928

January 14.   In Nicaragua, Sandino's headquarters at El Chipote is bombed and strafed by a flight of four planes of Marine Observation Squadron 7 (VO-7M) led by Major Ross E. Rowell.

January 26.   **Capture of El Chipote.** Marine columns advancing from San Albino under Major Archibald Young occupy and destroy Sandino's base at El Chipote. No significant resistance is encountered.

February 27.   A packtrain escorted by 35 marines led by First Lieutenant Edward F. O'Day is ambushed by 600 Sandinistas near Bromaderos, Nicaragua. The marines fight off repeated attacks and are relieved the next day.

May 13. A column of marines engages the Sandinistas at the Cua River, northeast of Santa Cruz, Nicaragua.

June 16. Rear Admiral Samuel S. Robison becomes 28th superintendent of the Naval Academy.

August 7. **Cocos River Patrol.** Late in July, Captain Merritt A. ("Red Mike") Edson, USMC, starts up the Cocos River with 49 marines in native dugouts to penetrate the jungle highlands of northern Nicaragua, to which Sandino has withdrawn. On this date Edson's men defeat a body of 60 rebels who attempt to ambush them 60 miles above Bocay. Sandino's base camp near Poteca is captured without opposition 10 days later.

November. Free elections, supervised by 1,500 seamen and marines under the direction of army Brigadier General Frank R. McCoy, are held in Nicaragua. The Liberal candidate, General José M. Moncada, is elected president.

1929

January 19. The 3rd Marine Brigade is disbanded at Tientsin, China, and all units except the Fourth Marines and the Peking legation guard are withdrawn from the country.

January 23–27. **Fleet Problem IX.** The carriers *Lexington* (CV 2) and *Saratoga* (CV 3) participate in their first fleet problem. Rear Admiral Joseph M. ("Bull") Reeves, Commander Aircraft Squadrons, Battle Fleet, demonstrates the carrier's potential when he has the *Saratoga* make an end-run around the defending forces (which include the *Lexington*) to launch an air strike that "destroys" the Panama Canal.

March 5. Charles F. Adams becomes 44th secretary of the navy.

March 5. Major General Wendell C. Neville becomes 14th commandant of the marine corps.

May 8. **Momsen Lung.** The first test is made of the submarine escape lung developed by Lieutenant Charles B. Momsen, Chief

Gunner Clarence L. Tibbals, and Frank Hobson, a civilian engineer.

August 20. Marine troop strength in Nicaragua is reduced to 2,000. The marine-trained *Guardia Nacional* has been fully committed to action by this time, and Sandino had fled the country in June.

November 28. Lieutenant Commander Richard E. Byrd becomes the first man to fly over the South Pole. He had been first over the North Pole in 1926.

1930

April 22. **London Naval Treaty.** The signatories of the Washington Naval Treaty agree to extend its terms for five years. The United States, Great Britain, and Japan also establish a 10:10:7 ratio of cruiser tonnage.

May 15. **The Narwhal.** The navy's first streamlined submarine, the *Narwhal* (SC 1) is commissioned. She is 371′ in length, 33′ abeam, and displaces 2,730 tons.

June 19. Augusto Sandino, who has returned to Nicaragua from Mexico in May, is wounded in a marine air strike led by Captain B.F. Johnson on a body of 600 rebels. This is the marines' last major action with the Sandinistas.

July 9. Major General Ben H. Fuller becomes 15th commandant of the marine corps.

September 17. Admiral William V. Pratt becomes the fifth chief of naval operations.

1931

May 1. Rear Admiral Thomas C. Hart becomes 29th superintendent of the Naval Academy.

September 18. Following the Mukden incident, in which a Japanese railway line is very slightly damaged by a small explosion, Japan invades and conquers the Chinese portion of Manchuria. There it establishes the puppet Kingdom of Manchukuo, towards which the United States adopts a policy of nonrecognition. This is the first major international act of aggression since World War I.

1932

February 3.   The cruiser *Houston* (CA 30) lands her marine detachment to reinforce the Fourth Marines in protecting American interests at Shanghai, China, following a Japanese attack on the city.

April 12.   **Good Neighbor Policy.** In a speech to the Governing Board of the Pan-American Union in Washington, D.C., newly elected President Franklin D. Roosevelt inaugurates the "Good Neighbor Policy" towards the Latin-American countries. Eight months later the United States formally renounces the right of intervention at the Seventh Inter-American Conference. The result is the end of the marine corps's long involvement in the Caribbean and the termination of its role as colonial infantry.

June 30.   The dirigible *Los Angeles* (ZR-3) is decommissioned at the Naval Air Station, Lakehurst, New Jersey, after eight years in service. She was the navy's only rigid airship that did not meet a violent end.

September 20–30.   **Puller's patrol.** *Guardia* Captain (marine first lieutenant) Lewis B. ("Chesty") Puller and *Guardia* Lieutenant (gunnery sergeant) William A. Lee lead 41 men of the Nicaraguan *Guardia Nacional* on a classic patrol into the jungle northeast of Jinotega. During 10 days in the field, the force marches more than 150 miles, fights 4 actions, destroys 30 rebel camps, and kills at least 30 rebels, at a cost of 2 men killed and 4 wounded.

1933

January 2.   The last elements of the 2nd Marine Brigade leave Nicaragua.

March 4.   Claude A. Swanson becomes the 45th secretary of the navy.

April 4.   **Loss of the Akron.** The dirigible *Akron* (ZRS-4), Commander Frank McCord, crashes into the sea in a storm off Barnegat Light, New Jersey. Of the 76 men aboard, 73 are lost, including the Chief of the Bureau of Aeronautics, Rear Admiral William A. Moffett.

June 16.   President Franklin D. Roosevelt begins to rebuild the U.S. Navy by allocating for

Lieutenant Lewis B. ("Chesty") Puller, second from left, with Gunnery Sergeant W. A. Lee and two *Guardia* sergeants in Nicaragua in 1931. Defense Department photo (Marine Corps).

Rear Admiral William A. Moffett, facing the camera, in the control car of the airship *Akron*, with Commander C. E. Rosendahl, right. Official U.S. Navy photograph.

naval construction $238,000,000 from the National Industrial Recovery Act passed on this date. The program calls for 32 vessels to be laid down over a three-year period, including the carriers *Yorktown* (CV 5) and *Enterprise* (CV 6).

June 23.   The dirigible *Macon* (ZRS-5) is commissioned. She is the last airship of her type to be built for the U.S. Navy.

July 1.   Admiral William H. Standley becomes the sixth chief of naval operations.

October 28.   The development of the PBY Catalina flying boat, a workhorse of naval aviation in World War II, is begun by the award of a contract to the Consolidated Aircraft Company.

December 7.   The Fleet Marine Force is established.

1934

January.   **Tentative Manual for Landing Operations.** On November 14, 1933, Major General John H. Russell, acting commandant of the marine corps, suspended classes at the officers' schools and set the students to work to develop "rules and doctrines for landing operations." The *Tentative Manual*, based in part on a Joint Army-Navy Board study of *Joint Overseas Operations* and unpublished marine corps material, is completed this month. The concepts and procedures it sets forth, refined by subsequent training exercises, provide the foundation for the unparalleled amphibious capability that the corps will demonstrate in World War II.

January.   The marine detachment from the gunboat *Tulsa* (PG 22) is landed to protect the American consulate at Foochow, China, until Nationalist troops can restore order.

February 22.   In Nicaragua the marines' old adversary, Augusto Sandino, is executed by Colonel Anastasio Somoza, commander of the *Guardia Nacional*.

March 1.   Major General John H. Russell, Jr., becomes 16th commandant of the marine corps.

March 27.   **Vinson-Trammel Act.** Representative Carl Vinson, Chairman of the House Naval Affairs Committee, co-sponsors

legislation that authorizes the navy to be built up to the limits allowed by the Washington and London naval treaties over a period of eight years. Among the construction that immediately results is the carrier *Wasp* (CV 7).

June 4.   The first U.S. naval vessel built as a carrier from the keel up, the 14,500-ton *Ranger* (CV 4), is commissioned.

June 18.   Rear Admiral David F. Sellers becomes 30th superintendent of the Naval Academy.

August 15.   The last elements of the 1st Marine Brigade withdraw from Haiti, ending an occupation of 19 years.

November 18.   Development of the Dauntless dive bombers extensively used in World War II is initiated by the award of a contract to the Northrop Corporation.

1935

February 12.   **Loss of the Macon.** The dirigible *Macon* (ZRS-5), Commander Herbert V. Wiley, goes down in the sea off Point Sur, California, with the loss of two lives. This disaster ends the navy's operation of rigid airships.

July 30.   Lieutenant Frank Akers makes the first blind landing on a carrier, flying an OJ-2 observation plane aboard the *Langley* (CV 1).

August 31.   **Neutrality Acts.** As Japanese aggression in Asia and the rearmament of

The airship *Macon* over Manhattan. Official U.S. Navy photograph.

National Socialist Germany raise the specter of another great war, the U.S. Congress passes legislation intended to avert a recurrence of the circumstances that are believed to have led to America's involvement in the last one. On this date, it outlaws the export of arms and ammunition to any belligerent nation. Subsequent neutrality acts prohibit Americans from loaning money to belligerents (1936), traveling on vessels belonging to belligerents, and selling goods of any kind to them on other than a "cash and carry" basis (1937).

December 9. **Second London Conference.** A second naval disarmament conference between the United States, Great Britain, Japan, France, and Italy convenes at London to renegotiate the agreements reached at Washington in 1922 and London in 1930. It is a failure. Japan withdraws when the United States rejects her claim to parity; Italy remains, but refuses to sign the final agreement; and the treaty concluded between the United States, Great Britain, and France on March 25, 1936, contains so many contingency clauses that it is meaningless. The era of naval arms limitations has ended.

1936

March 25.   The London Naval Agreement is signed. (For details, see December 9, 1935.)

September 18.   A small navy squadron commanded by Rear Admiral Arthur P. Fairfield is sent to evacuate American citizens from Spain, at the time convulsed by an exceptionally ferocious civil war.

December 1.   Major General Thomas Holcombe becomes 17th commandant of the marine corps.

1937

January 2.   Admiral William D. Leahy becomes the seventh chief of naval operations.

July 7.   **War in the Far East.** Japan invades China proper, beginning a conflict that will flow into World War II.

September 30.   The carrier *Yorktown* (CV 5) is commissioned.

December 12.   **Panay Incident.** The Yangtze river gunboat *Panay* (PR 5), Lieutenant Commander James J. Hughes, is attacked and sunk by low-flying Japanese aircraft near Nanking, China, despite her prominently displayed American markings. Two crewmen are killed and 43 wounded. Japan apologizes for the attack, which it calls an unfortunate error, and pays a large indemnity.

1938

February 1.   Rear Admiral Wilson Brown becomes 31st superintendent of the Naval Academy.

April.   **Fleet Problem XIX.** In the course of this exercise, the carrier *Saratoga* (CV 3) launches a surprise attack on the fleet base at Pearl Harbor, foreshadowing the Japanese attack of December 1941.

May 12.   The carrier *Enterprise* (CV 6) is commissioned.

May 17.   The Navy Expansion Act authorizes a significant increase in the strength of the fleet and the procurement of 3,000 aircraft. Among the ships built as a result of this legislation is the carrier *Essex* (CV 9).

1939

May 23.   **The Squalus.** The submarine *Squalus* (SS 192), Lieutenant O.F. Naquin, sinks during a practice dive off Portsmouth, New Hampshire. Of her 85 crewmen, 59 are rescued by means of a diving bell. Raised in difficult salvage operations directed by Rear Admiral Ernest J. King, she is renamed the *Sailfish* and serves with distinction in World War II.

June 11–13.   Exercises conducted by the carrier *Saratoga* (CV 3) and the oiler *Kanawaha* (AO 1) off the west coast demonstrate the feasibility of underway replenishment. This technique, pioneered by the U.S. Navy, will prove to be of inestimable value during World War II.

July 7.   The Lighthouse Bureau is absorbed by the U.S. Coast Guard.

The Yangtze River gunboat *Panay*. U.S. Naval Institute Collection.

August 1. Admiral Harold R. Stark becomes the eighth chief of naval operations.

September 1. **Beginning of World War II.** Germany invades Poland. Two days later, Britain and France declare war on Germany.

September 5. **Neutrality Patrol.** President Roosevelt proclaims American neutrality and directs the chief of naval operations, Admiral Harold R. Stark, to establish a Neutrality Patrol of sea and air units to prevent belligerent acts in U.S. waters.

September 8. The existence of a "Limited National Emergency" is declared by President Roosevelt.

September 21. The president asks Congress to repeal the neutrality laws prohibiting the sale of arms and ammunition to warring nations on a cash-and-carry basis. As a consolation for isolationist opinion, he also requests authority to prohibit American ships from entering "danger zones," to be designated according to circumstances, where they are likely to be attacked.

October 2. **Act of Panama.** The Congress of American States, meeting at Panama, establishes a "neutral zone" extending 300 miles from the coast of the Americas, in which belligerent forces are not to conduct hostilities. The area from Maine to Trinidad will be patrolled by the U.S. Navy.

November 4. **Neutrality Act of 1939.** Congress accedes to the president's request of September 21. He immediately declares the waters surrounding the British Isles to be a danger zone.

1940

January 2. Charles Edison becomes 46th secretary of the navy.

April 25. The carrier *Wasp* (CV 7) is commissioned.

May 16. President Roosevelt asks Congress to appropriate $1.18 billion for national defense.

May 17. The president announces that 35 mothballed World War I destroyers are to be recommissioned.

June 14. The Naval Expansion Act of 1940 is signed by President Roosevelt, authorizing an 11 percent increase in the strength of the fleet.

June 14. **Fall of France.** The German Army enters Paris. The defeat of France, since 1918 regarded as the world's premier military power, probably does more than any other single event to convince American leaders that the United States must prepare to enter the war.

June 17. **Two-ocean navy.** Admiral Harold R. Stark, the chief of naval operations, appears before Congress to request funds to build a two-ocean navy: $4 billion, which will more than double the 1,250,000 tons of the existing combat fleet, and 15,000 naval aircraft. Congress approves the appropriation, and President Roosevelt signs the new Naval Expansion Act into law on July 19.

June 20.   The Bureau of Construction and Repair and the Bureau of Engineering are combined to form the Bureau of Ships, and the office of under secretary of the navy is created.

June 25.   The Naval Construction Corps is merged into the navy line, and its members given "engineering duty only" status.

July 2.   **Export Control Act.** Congress grants the president authority to control the export of war materials and related commodities. Three days later he prohibits the sale of such goods to Japan.

July 11.   Frank Knox becomes 47th secretary of the navy.

September 2.   **Destroyers for bases deal.** President Roosevelt and Prime Minister Winston Churchill conclude an agreement whereby 50 World War I destroyers, urgently needed by Britain to fight German U-boats in the Battle of the Atlantic, will be transferred to the Royal Navy in exchange for 99-year leases to British bases in the West Indies, Bermuda and Newfoundland.

September 16.   With the signing of the Selective Training and Service Act, the president establishes the first peacetime draft in American history.

September 27.   **Tripartite Pact.** Japan concludes an alliance with Germany and Italy.

1941

February 1.   The U.S. Fleet is divided into the Atlantic and Pacific Fleets, and the 1st and 2nd Marine Brigades are expanded into divisions.

February 1.   Rear Admiral Russell Willson becomes 32nd superintendent of the Naval Academy.

March 11.   **Lend-Lease.** Congress relaxes the provisions of the Neutrality Act of 1939 to permit the Allied Powers, which have run

short of cash, to obtain war materials on credit or loan.

March 27.   **ABC-1 Staff Agreement.** In Washington, D.C., naval and military representatives of the United States and Great Britain sign an agreement establishing the basis of Anglo-American cooperation in the event the United States enters the war. Its key provisions are that: (1) both countries will concentrate their war efforts on the defeat of Germany, deemed the most dangerous of the Axis Powers; (2) the British and American chiefs of staff will work together as the combined chiefs of staff; and (3) the U.S. Atlantic Fleet will begin assisting the Royal Navy in Atlantic convoy escort as soon as it is able. The latter provision is effective immediately.

April 9.   The battleship *North Carolina* (BB 55) is commissioned. She is the first American battleship to enter service since the *West Virginia* (BB 48) in 1923.

April 10.   The destroyer *Niblack* (DD 424), Lieutenant Commander E.R. Durgin, depth-charges a German U-boat while rescuing the crew of a torpedoed Dutch freighter. This is the first hostile action taken by an American naval vessel against the Axis Powers.

May 15.   The battleship *Washington* (BB 56) is commissioned.

May 21.   The freighter *Robin Moore*, torpedoed and sunk by a German U-boat in the South Atlantic, becomes the first American merchantman lost in World War II.

May 27.   President Roosevelt proclaims a state of "Unlimited National Emergency."

May 27.   **Destruction of the Bismarck.** On May 26, an American officer, Ensign Leonard B. Smith, flying as co-pilot in a PBY Catalina on loan to the Royal Navy, sights the German battleship *Bismarck* making for the coast of France. The next day another American officer, Lieutenant Commander Joshua H. Wellings, returning to the United States as a passenger on the British battleship *Rodney*, is present at the action in which the *Bismarck* is sunk.

June 12.   The U.S. Naval Reserve is mobilized.

June 20.   The submarine *O-9* (SS 70) sinks with the loss of all hands (33 men) in a test dive off Portsmouth, New Hampshire.

July 1.   **Sea Frontiers.** The American coastline

The battleship *North Carolina*. U.S. Naval Institute Collection.

is divided into six "sea frontiers" whose commanders will be responsible for convoy escort, antisubmarine warfare, and patrols in their designated areas. Two additional frontiers are established for Hawaii and the Philippines.

July 7.   Following agreement with the government of Iceland, U.S. naval forces assume responsibility for the defense of that country. Marines are landed at Reykjavik.

July 24.   Japanese troops move into French Indochina.

July 26.   **The last straw.** In response to the occupation of Indochina, President Roosevelt freezes Japanese assets in the United States and halts the sale of oil to Japan. Its utter dependence on imported oil is Japan's Achilles heel. The president's action confronts the Japanese with the necessity of either reaching an accommodation with the United States or striking out to obtain oil fields of their own by the conquest of the European colonies in Southeast Asia.

July 30.   The Yangtze River gunboat *Tutuila* (PG 44) is attacked by Japanese planes at Chungking, China. A day later, Japan apologizes for the incident.

August 9–12.   **Argentia conference.** President Roosevelt and British Prime Minister Churchill meet secretly at Placentia Bay, Argentia, Newfoundland. The president travels on the cruiser *Augusta* (CA 31), the prime minister on the battleship *Prince of Wales*. It is at this, their first meeting, that the two leaders agree on the principles set forth in the Atlantic Charter.

September 4.   **Greer incident.** Patrolling south of Iceland, the destroyer *Greer* (DD 145), Lieutenant Commander L.H. Frost, is attacked by the *U-652*. The submarine's torpedoes miss, whereupon the *Greer* drops depth charges, also without effect.

September 11.   **"Shoot on sight."** Following the *Greer* incident, President Roosevelt orders naval vessels to attack any ship that threatens American shipping or foreign shipping under American escort.

September 16.   **Beginning of convoy escort.** In accordance with the provisions of the ABC-1 Staff Agreement, the U.S. Navy joins the Royal Canadian Navy in escorting North Atlantic convoys to and from a Mid-Ocean Meeting Point (MOMP) with the Royal Navy.

September 27.   **Liberty ships.** The first Liberty ship, the *Patrick Henry*, is launched. These vessels and the Victory ships that follow in 1943 are built to replace the merchantmen sunk by Axis submarines.

October 2.   After almost two months of consideration, President Roosevelt rejects Japanese Prime Minister Prince Fuminaro Konoye's request for a summit conference. Konoye, who had hoped to avoid war, is then replaced by bellicose General Hideki Tojo.

October 17.   **Kearny incident.** The destroyer *Kearny* (DD 432), Lieutenant Commander

A.L. Danis, is torpedoed but not sunk by a U-boat while patrolling south of Greenland. Eleven of her company are killed.

October 20.   The carrier *Hornet* (CV 8) is commissioned under the command of Captain Marc A. Mitscher.

October 30.   The oiler *Salinas* (AO 19) is torpedoed in mid-Atlantic, but reaches port safely. There are no casualties.

October 31.   **Sinking of the Reuben James.** The destroyer *Reuben James* (DD 245), Lieutenant Commander H.L. Edwards, is torpedoed and sunk with the loss of 115 lives by the *U-562* while escorting a convoy from Halifax, Nova Scotia. She is the first U.S. naval vessel destroyed by the Axis Powers.

November 1.   The coast guard is placed under naval control for the duration of the National Emergency.

November 6.   **Odenwald incident.** The German blockade runner *Odenwald* is captured by the cruiser *Omaha* (CL 4) and destroyer *Somers* (DD 381) in the central Atlantic. She was disguised as the American merchantman *Willmoto*.

November 17.   Congress authorizes the arming of U.S. merchant ships.

November 20.   Japanese Special Envoy Saburo Kurusu presents U.S. Secretary of State Cordell Hull with Japan's final negotiating program. Agreement to its terms would concede Japan a free hand in the Far East. It is rejected.

November 26.   Secretary of State Hull hands

Japanese Ambassador Kichisaburo Nomura the American counterproposal for a general settlement in the Far East. Among other things, it calls for Japan to withdraw from both China and Indochina. There is little expectation that the Japanese will accept these terms, nor do they.

November 26.   A Japanese strike force consisting of six carriers, two battleships, three cruisers, nine destroyers, and three fleet submarines, plus tankers, secretly sails from the Kurile Islands under the command of Vice Admiral Chuichi Nagumo. Unless an agreement can be reached with the United States by December 5, it is to attack the Pacific Fleet at Pearl Harbor.

November 27.   The chief of naval operations, Admiral Harold R. Stark, sends a "war warning" message to the commanders of the Atlantic, Pacific, and Asiatic fleets.

November 27–28.   The Fourth Marine Regiment is withdrawn from Shanghai after 14 years' service in China.

December 7.   **Pearl Harbor.** At 7:55 A.M. Sunday morning the Pacific Fleet is attacked while at anchor at Pearl Harbor by 191 Japanese torpedo-bombers, dive-bombers, high-altitude bombers, and fighters from the carriers *Akagi, Hiryu, Kaga, Shokaku, Soryu,* and *Zuikaku* of Vice Admiral Chuichi Nagumo's strike force. The attackers withdraw at 8:25 A.M., but are followed by a second wave of 170 planes at 8:40 A.M. Fortunately, all three of the Pacific Fleet carriers—the *Lexington* (CV 2), *Saratoga* (CV 3), and *Wasp* (CV 7)—are elsewhere, and, overlooking the strategically vital oil tank farm, repair facilities, and submarine pens, the Japanese concentrate on the battleships anchored off Ford Island. The *Arizona* (BB 39) is destroyed by a bomb that detonates her forward magazine, killing 1,103 of 1,400 men aboard. The *Oklahoma* (BB 37) capsizes due to flooding, with the loss of 415 of her 1,354 officers and men; and the *California* (BB 44) is heavily damaged and settles to her superstructure, as do the *West Virginia* (BB 48) and the *Nevada* (BB 36)—the only battleship to get under way. The *Maryland* (BB 46), *Pennsylvania* (BB 38), and *Tennessee* (BB 43) are damaged, but can steam to the West Coast under their own power for repairs three weeks later. More than half of the army, navy,

The destroyer *Reuben James*. U.S. Naval Institute Collection.

The beginning of the attack on Pearl Harbor, photographed from a Japanese aircraft. Moored off the far side of Ford Island are, from left to right, the battleship *Nevada*, the battleship *Arizona* (with the repair ship *Vestal* outboard), the battleships *Tennessee* and *West Virginia* (outboard), *Maryland* and *Oklahoma* (outboard), the fleet oiler *Neosho*, and the battleship *California*. The *Oklahoma* has just taken a torpedo hit, probably from the plane banking above the *Neosho*. Courtesy National Archives.

and marine planes on airfields ashore are also destroyed. All except 29 of the Japanese aircraft involved return to their carriers. Altogether, 2,403 American servicemen are killed and 1,178 wounded, with the navy suffering by far the greatest losses. This "day of infamy," as President Roosevelt describes it, unites the American people in the determination to defeat Japan.

December 8.   At Shanghai, China, the Yangtze River gunboat *Wake* (PG 43) surrenders to the Japanese after an attempt to scuttle her fails. She is the only U.S. naval vessel to strike her flag in World War II.

December 10.   Off the coast of Malaya, Japanese aircraft sink the British battleship *Prince of Wales* and battlecruiser *Repulse*.

December 10.   Japanese forces occupy Guam.

December 10.   Japanese forces land on the Philippine island of Luzon.

December 10.   The marine detachments at Peking and Tientsin, China, approximately 500 strong, are taken prisoner by the Japanese.

December 11.   Germany and Italy declare war on the United States.

December 11.   **Defense of Wake Island.** The Japanese suffer their first reverse of the war when a sea-borne assault on Wake Island is repulsed by the 388 officers and men of Major James P. Deveureux's 1st Defense Battalion and the pilots of Major Paul A. Putnam's Marine Fighting Squadron (VMF) 211. Two destroyers, the first significant Japanese surface ships lost in the war, are sunk: the *Hayate* by the garrison's 5-inch guns and the *Kisaragi* by air attack; a transport is also destroyed, and a light cruiser, two destroyers, and a freighter are damaged.

December 15–23.   **Wake relief force.** A task force commanded by Rear Admiral Frank Jack Fletcher is sent to reinforce the garrison of Wake Island. Built around the carrier *Saratoga* (CV 3), it includes three heavy cruisers, nine destroyers, and the 12-knot oiler *Neches* (AO 5). Unfortunately, the *Neches* is allowed to dictate the force's speed, and the day of December 22 is spent refueling on a course that brings the force no closer to the island.

December 17.   Admiral Husband E. Kimmel is relieved as commander-in-chief, Pacific Fleet.

December 20.   Admiral Ernest J. King is appointed commander-in-chief, U.S. Fleet.

December 23.   **Fall of Wake Island.** After their repulse on December 11, the Japanese bomb the island daily. The marines' last 2 aircraft are destroyed engaging 39 enemy carrier planes on December 22. Before dawn the next day two Japanese patrol craft ground themselves to land approximately 1,000 men of the Special Naval Landing Force. After several hours of increasingly hopeless fighting Commander Winfield Scott Cunningham, the island commander, authorizes Major Deveureux to surrender. Admiral Fletcher's relief force, which has reached a point 425 miles from the island, is recalled.

December 31.   Admiral Chester W. Nimitz assumes command of the Pacific Fleet.

1942

January 2.   The Philippine capital of Manila and the Cavite Naval Base are occupied by the Japanese.

January 3.   **ABDA.** A unified American, British, Dutch, Australian command, formally activated on January 15, is established under General Sir Archibald P. Wavell for the defense of the southwest Pacific. Admiral Thomas C. Hart, CO of the U.S. Asiatic Fleet, is made naval commander. At this time the Allies still hope to stop the Jap-

Admiral Chester W. Nimitz. Courtesy National Archives.

anese at the "Malay barrier" extending from Malaya through the Netherlands East Indies, a hope that will be cruelly disappointed.

January 9.   On Luzon, the first strong Japanese attack on the American and Filipino forces holding the Bataan Peninsula is repulsed.

January 11.   The Japanese invade the Netherlands East Indies.

January 12.   Congress increases the authorized strength of the navy to 500,000 men.

January 14.   **Arcadia.** The first Washington Conference (Arcadia), which had begun on December 23, comes to an end. During it, President Roosevelt, Prime Minister Churchill, and key members of their staffs discussed the joint conduct of the war into which the United States has just been plunged. Although affirming the "Germany first" priority established at the ABC-1 Staff Conference (see March 27, 1941), it is agreed that Australia and the bases along its line of communications with the United States—New Caledonia, the Fijis, and American Samoa—must be held against Japan. The United States assumes the responsibility of conducting the war in the Pacific. Other important decisions reached are to mount an Anglo-American invasion of French North Africa in 1942 and to set up a combined chiefs of staff committee, anticipated in the ABC-1 accords, through which the U.S. joint chiefs of staff and the British chiefs of staff will concert the strategy of the Allied war effort.

January 20.   Off Darwin, Australia, the destroyer *Edsall* (DD 219), Lieutenant Joshua J. Nix, cooperates with three Royal Australian Navy corvettes to sink the *I-124*. The latter is the first Japanese submarine in whose destruction American surface forces play a part.

January 20.   On patrol in the poorly charted waters of the Makassar Strait, the submarine *S 36* (SS 141), Lieutenant John S. McKnight, Jr., runs aground and has to be scuttled. Dutch vessels rescue her crew.

January 24.   **Battle of Balikpapan.** In the first surface action fought by U.S. naval forces since the Spanish-American War, a division of four elderly destroyers under Commander Paul Talbot—the *John D. Ford* (DD 228) (flag), *Parrott* (DD 218), *Paul Jones* (DD

230), and *Pope* (DD 225)—surprise a Japanese invasion force of Balikpapan, Borneo, and sink 4 of 12 transports and a patrol boat in a night torpedo attack. None of the destroyers is seriously damaged. This engagement is also known as the Battle of the Makassar Strait.

January 27. The submarine *Gudgeon* (SS 211), Lieutenant Commander E. H. ("Joe") Grenfell, sinks the Japanese submarine *I-173* west of Midway Island. Of the 130 Japanese fleet submarines sunk by 1945, at least 23 will be destroyed by their American counterparts.

January 31. Rear Admiral John R. Beardall becomes the 33rd superintendent of the U.S. Naval Academy.

February 1. **Raid on the Gilberts and Marshalls.** The first American carrier strikes of the war are made under the command of Vice Admiral William F. ("Bull") Halsey. Task Group 8, formed around the *Enterprise* (CV 6), attacks Japanese bases on Kwajalein in the Marshall Islands, while Task Group 17, built around the *Yorktown* (CV 5), hits the Gilberts.

February 3. The submarine *Trout* (SS 202), Commander Frank W. ("Mike") Fenno, evacuates from Corregidor 20 tons of gold and silver taken from Manila banks. During the opening months of the war, submarines are frequently used to carry supplies to the Philippines and to evacuate key personnel.

February 4. An ABDA naval force consisting of the Dutch cruisers *De Ruyter* (flag) and *Tromp*, the American cruisers *Houston* (CA 30) and *Marblehead* (CL 12), and six American and four Dutch destroyers, under the command of Rear Admiral Karel Doorman, Royal Netherlands Navy, is attacked by Japanese aircraft while attempting to intercept a Japanese invasion fleet off Borneo. The *Marblehead* is so seriously damaged that she must return to the United States for repairs; the *Houston* loses her after 8-inch turret; and the *De Ruyter* is also hard hit. Operating in the absence of air cover, the ABDA force is compelled to retire.

February 7. The submarine *Shark* (SS 174), Lieutenant Commander Louis Shane, Jr., is lost in the vicinity of the Moluccas Passage, probably on this date.

February 14. Dutch and British pressure results in the replacement of Admiral Thomas C. Hart as commander-in-chief, Allied Naval Forces, Southwest Pacific, by Vice Admiral C.E.L. Helfrich, Royal Netherlands Navy.

February 15. **Fall of Singapore.** British Lieutenant General Arthur E. Percival surrenders the island and city of Singapore, supposedly "the Gibraltar of the East," and its 64,000 British, Australian, and Indian defenders to a numerically inferior Japanese army commanded by General Tomoyuki Yamashita.

February 19. The destroyer *Peary* (DD 226), Lieutenant Commander J. M. Bermingham, is sunk in a Japanese air raid on Darwin, Australia.

February 19–20. **Battle of the Badung Strait.**

The cruiser *Houston* as she appeared in 1935. Official U.S. Navy photograph.

A confused night action ensues when an ABDA force under Dutch Admiral K.W.F. Doorman—consisting of the Dutch cruisers *De Ruyter, Java,* and *Tromp,* one Dutch and six American destroyers, and five Dutch PT boats—attacks a Japanese invasion force that has just landed troops on the island of Bali. Three Japanese destroyers are damaged; the Dutch destroyer is sunk, and the USS *Stewart* (DD 224) is damaged.

February 20.   **Raid on Rabaul.** A task force consisting of the carriers *Lexington* (CV 2) and *Yorktown* (CV 5), seven American cruisers, and four British and one Australian, and 16 American destroyers under the command of Vice Admiral Wilson Brown, is sent to attack the Japanese air and naval base at Rabaul, on New Britain. The raid is cancelled when the force is spotted by the Japanese, but the largest air battle to date in the Pacific war develops. Lieutenant Edward H. ("Butch") O'Hare accounts for 5 of the 18 enemy planes destroyed, thus becoming the navy's first ace of World War II and winning the Medal of Honor. Only two American aircraft are lost.

February 23.   The oil refinery at Ellwood, near Santa Barbara, California, is shelled by the Japanese submarines *I-17.*

February 24.   **Wake Island Raid.** Japanese occupation forces are attacked by planes from the carrier *Enterprise* (CV 6) task force under Vice Admiral W. F. Halsey.

February 27.   The *Langley,* the navy's first carrier (CV 1), now redesignated an aviation transport (AV 3), is sunk by Japanese aircraft while ferrying army planes to Tjilatjap, Java.

February 27–28.   **Battle of the Java Sea.** Admiral Karel Doorman, RNN, leads the ABDA Strike Force—five cruisers: the Dutch *De Ruyter* (flag) and *Java,* USS *Houston* (CA 30), HMS *Exeter,* and HMAS *Perth,* and five American, three British, and three Dutch destroyers—on a sortie from Surabaja, Java, in an attempt to intercept two large Japanese invasion forces approaching the island. Instead, at 4 P.M. he encounters Rear Admiral Takeo Takagi's support force, consisting of 4 cruisers and 13 destroyers. In the course of an intermittent action lasting more than seven hours, the superiority of the Japanese Long

Lance torpedo and the ABDA squadron's lack of spotter aircraft prove decisive. Both Dutch cruisers and three of the destroyers are sunk. Only one Japanese destroyer is damaged. The Malay Barrier has been breached.

February 28.   **Battle of the Sunda Strait.** After nightfall, the cruisers *Houston* (CA 30), Captain Albert H. Rooks, and HMAS *Perth,* Captain H.M.L. Waller, RAN, survivors of the Battle of the Java Sea proceeding in company towards the Sunda Strait on the western end of the island of Java, encounter a Japanese landing in progress in Banten Bay. Three enemy transports are destroyed—two by friendly fire—and three are damaged in the melee before the cruisers are sunk by the Japanese covering force of three cruisers and nine destroyers under Rear Admiral Takeo Kurita.

February 28.   The destroyer *Jacob Jones* (DD 130), Lieutenant Commander H. D. Black, Jr., is sunk with almost all hands by a German U-boat off the Delaware Capes.

March 1.   Three other survivors of the Java Sea, the British cruiser *Exeter* and the destroyers USS *Pope* (DD 225), Lieutenant Commander W. C. Blinn, and HMS *Encounter,* are sunk by Japanese air and surface forces off Surabaja, Java. The destroyer *Edsall* (DD 219), Lieutenant J. J. Nix, is sunk in a separate action.

March 1.   The destroyer *Pillsbury* (DD 227), Lieutenant Commander H. C. Pound, gunboat *Asheville* (PG 21), and the Australian gunboat *Yarra* are destroyed off the coast of Java in a surface action with vastly superior Japanese forces.

March 1.   The German *U-656* is destroyed by aircraft of Patrol Wing 82 south of Newfoundland. She is the U.S. Navy's first U-boat kill of the war.

March 2.   The submarine *Perch* (SS 176), Lieutenant Commander David A. Hurt, is depth-charged and badly damaged by Japanese destroyers while on patrol off Surabaja, Netherlands East Indies. The next day she is forced to scuttle when a cruiser-destroyer group catches her limping along on the surface, unable to submerge. The Japanese rescue her crew.

March 4.   **Marcus Island raid.** Aircraft from Admiral Halsey's *Enterprise* (CV 6) task force strike the Japanese base at Marcus Island, in the central Pacific 800 miles northwest of Wake.

March 8.   The Japanese land forces at Lae and Salamaua on the northeastern coast of New Guinea.

March 10.   The Netherlands East Indies surrenders to the Japanese.

March 10.   **Lae and Salamaua raids.** More than 100 planes from the carriers *Lexington* (CV 2) and *Yorktown* (CV 5) of Vice Admiral Wilson Brown's task force strike Japanese positions on the northern coast of New Guinea.

March 11.   **MacArthur escapes from Corregidor.** General Douglas MacArthur, whom President Roosevelt has personally ordered to leave the Philippines, escapes from Corregidor with his family and selected staff members aboard the four boats of Lieutenant John D. Bulkeley's Motor Torpedo Boat Squadron 3. Eluding Japanese naval patrols, MacArthur reaches Mindanao on March 14 and continues his journey by air to Darwin, Australia, on March 17.

March 12.   The duties of chief of naval operations and commander-in-chief, U.S. Fleet, are combined under Admiral Ernest J. King,

although he does not officially relieve Admiral Stark as CNO until March 26.

March 17.   General MacArthur is appointed Allied Supreme Commander in the Southwest Pacific.

March 20.   The battleship *South Dakota* (BB 57), is commissioned.

March 25.   **Operations in European waters.** Task Force 39 is sent to reinforce the Royal Navy in European waters, where the British are temporarily weakened by the dispatch of an expedition to Madagascar. Originally commanded by Rear Admiral John W. Wilcox, Jr., who is lost overboard in mid-Atlantic and replaced by Rear Admiral R. C. Giffen, it consists of the battleship *Washington* (BB 56), carrier *Wasp* (CV 7), heavy cruisers *Tuscaloosa* (CA 37) and *Wichita* (CA 45), and a squadron of destroyers. In April and May this force, less the *Wasp*, will join the British Home Fleet in escorting convoys to Russia.

March 30.   To clarify command relations, the Pacific theater is divided into two zones: the Pacific Ocean Area, under Admiral Chester W. Nimitz, and the Southwest Pacific Area, under General Douglas MacArthur.

April 4–9.   **Indian Ocean raid.** A Japanese task force formed around five Pearl Harbor carriers under the command of Vice Admiral Chuichi Nagumo attacks Admiral Sir James Somerville's British Far Eastern Fleet in the Bay of Bengal, sinking the light carrier *Hermes,* cruisers *Cornwall* and *Dorsetshire*, and several smaller vessels.

April 9.   American and Filipino troops defending the Bataan Peninsula surrender to the Japanese. The garrison of Corregidor, "The Rock" in Manila Bay, continues to fight on.

April 18.   **Halsey-Doolittle Raid.** At 8:24 A.M., Vice Admiral W. F. Halsey's Task Force 16 launches a very special air raid. Sixteen twin-engined B-25 bombers commanded by Lieutenant Colonel James H. Doolittle, USA, take off from the deck of Captain Marc A. Mitscher's carrier *Hornet* (CV 8) to strike the first blows against the Japanese homeland. Tokyo, Yokohama, Kobe, and Nagoya are bombed. The B-25s fly on to China, where most reach friendly lines, only two crews being captured. The psycho-

Admiral Ernest J. King. Official U.S. Navy photograph.

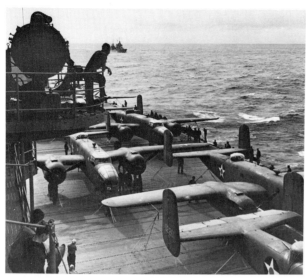

The Halsey-Doolittle Raid: B-25 bombers on the deck of the *Hornet*. Official U.S. Navy photograph.

logical effect of the raid is disproportionate to the relatively minor damage it does. The American people are thrilled that, after so many disasters, their armed forces have begun to hit back; the Japanese navy is deeply chagrined that it has failed to keep the Home Islands safe from attack.

April 20.   **The Wasp in the Mediterranean.** At the request of the Royal Navy, the carrier *Wasp* (CV 7), Captain J. W. Reeves, Jr., is used to stage 58 Spitfire fighters into Malta. The island, lying athwart the supply line to North Africa, is under siege by the German Luftwaffe. Returning to the Mediterranean with the British carrier *Eagle*, the *Wasp* launches another 47 "Spitties" on May 7. These reinforcements play a vital role in keeping the island's air defense in operation.

April 26.   The destroyer *Sturtevant* (DD 240), Lieutenant Commander C. L. Weigle, goes down in the Florida Keys after running into an American minefield of which no one aboard had been informed.

April 30.   The battleship *Indiana* (BB 58) is commissioned.

May 1.   The submarine *Drum* (SS 228), Commander Robert H. Rice, sinks the 9,000-ton seaplane carrier *Mizuho* off Honshu in the Japanese Home Islands.

May 6.   **Fall of the Philippines.** Lieutenant General Jonathan M. Wainwright surren-

ders the Philippines to Japanese Lieutenant General Masaharu Homma. Wainwright had intended to surrender only the fortress of Corregidor, in Manila Bay, but Homma insisted on a general capitulation before ceasing to attack on the island. Some garrisons initially ignore Wainwright's order, and it is June 9 before formal resistance ends.

May 7–8.   **Battle of the Coral Sea.** Japanese forces suffer their first strategic defeat of World War II when the Pacific Fleet codebreakers at Honolulu learn of a plan to seize Port Moresby, on the southeastern coast of New Guinea, through which the Australian forces fighting on that island are supplied, and the island of Tulagi in the Solomons. The Tulagi landing is unopposed, but Rear Admiral Frank Jack Fletcher's Task Force 17, formed around the carriers *Lexington* (CV 2) and *Yorktown* (CV 5), is on hand to intercept the units that enter the Coral Sea—an amphibious force of 12 transports screened by the light carrier *Shoho*, cruisers, and destroyers, and a Carrier Strike Force composed of the fleet carriers *Shokaku* and *Zuikaku* under Vice Admiral Takeo Takagi. The resulting action is the first carrier air battle ever fought. On May 7, planes of the Carrier Strike Force sink the fleet oiler *Neosho* (AO 23), Captain J. S. Phillips, and destroyer *Sims* (DD 409), Lieutenant Commander W. M. Hyman, which they mistake for a carrier and a cruiser. The next day American planes sink the light carrier *Shoho* and damage the *Shokaku*, while a Japanese attack destroys the *Lexington*, Captain Frederick C. Sherman. The *Zuikaku* is ordered to retire, and the Port Moresby Invasion Force, now lacking air defense, is recalled.

May 12.   The battleship *Massachusetts* (BB 59) is commissioned.

May 13.   The Bureau of Navigation is renamed the Bureau of Personnel, its scientific functions having already been transferred to the office of the chief of naval personnel.

June 2–6.   **Battle of Midway.** The turning point in the war with Japan comes in the Central Pacific. Admiral Yamamoto launches an operation of ill-advised complexity designed to extend the Japanese defensive perimeter by seizing the island of Midway,

The Japanese light carrier *Shoho*, already burning, is hit by an American torpedo bomber during the Battle of the Coral Sea. Official U.S. Navy photograph.

Abandon ship: the crew of the *Lexington* going over the side in the Coral Sea. Official U.S. Navy photograph.

1,100 miles west of Honolulu, thereby preventing a recurrence of the humiliating Halsey-Doolittle Raid. He also believes that an attack on Midway will bring the American carriers out to be destroyed, completing the job begun at Pearl Harbor. Numerically, the Japanese fleet appears to enjoy an insurmountable advantage in every class of vessel, from carriers (8 to 3) and battleships (7 to 0) to destroyers (55 to 33). Much of that advantage is dispelled, however, by the fact that at Pearl Harbor Commander Joseph J. Rochefort's basement codebreakers of the Communications Intelligence Unit have decoded the Japanese battle plans and are aware, for instance, that the diversionary assault on the Aleutians,

to which Yamamoto assigns two light carriers, is indeed a diversion. Thus it is that all three of Admiral Nimitz's carriers are waiting off Midway on June 4—the *Yorktown* (CV 5) in Rear Admiral Frank Jack Fletcher's Task Force 17, the *Enterprise* (CV 6) and *Hornet* (CV 8) in Rear Admiral Raymond A. Spruance's Task Force 16. Fletcher is officer in tactical command. In the course of a day's furious fighting, American carrier planes sink all four fleet carriers of Vice Admiral Chuichi Nagumo's Carrier Strike Force—the *Akagi, Hiryu, Kaga,* and *Soryu*. Aircraft from the *Hiryu,* last of the Japanese carriers to go down, severely damage the *Yorktown,* Captain Elliott Buckmaster, after which Admiral Fletcher transfers com-

The Battle of Midway: the *Yorktown* is hit by a Japanese bomber. Official U.S. Navy photograph.

mand to Admiral Spruance. That evening Spruance declines to pursue the Japanese to the west, apprehending that they might attempt to ambush his carriers in a night surface action, which is exactly what Yamamoto has in mind. The next day Spruance's planes sink the heavy cruiser *Mikuma*, and on June 6, a Japanese submarine sinks the crippled *Yorktown* and the destroyer *Hammann* (DD 412), Commander A. E. True.

June 7.   In the North Pacific, Japanese forces land unopposed on the Aleutian islands of Attu and Kiska.

June 18.   The obsolescent submarine *S 27* (SS 132), Lieutenant Herbert L. Jukes, runs aground off Amchitka Island while on a reconnaissance mission to investigate Japanese activity in the Aleutians. Her crew reaches shore safely and is rescued by PBY flying boats.

June 19–25.   **Second Washington Conference.** Prime Minister Churchill and the British chiefs of staff return to discuss op-

The Japanese heavy cruiser *Mikuma* afire and soon to sink, June 6, 1942. Official U.S. Navy photograph.

erations in the European theater in 1942. Despite the tentative agreement reached at the Arcadia Conference (see January 14) to invade North Africa in 1942, later General George C. Marshall, U.S. Army chief of staff, promoted the idea of establishing a beachhead in northern France instead. The British unenthusiastically assented in March, but by mid-summer their misgivings have increased. At Washington they advocate postponing the landing of France until 1943 and going ahead with the invasion of North Africa in 1942. No decision is reached, but on July 8, Churchill informs Roosevelt that the British War Cabinet is inflexibly opposed to invading France this year. Roosevelt then sends General Marshall and Admiral King to London to reach an agreement with the British on some joint action in the European theater in 1942. The American chiefs have no choice but to accept the British proposal for invading North Africa.

June 21.   Fort Stevens, Oregon, is shelled by a Japanese submarine.

June 26.   The German government announces the initiation of unrestricted submarine warfare off the American eastern seaboard.

July 20.   Admiral William D. Leahy, former chief

Admiral William D. Leahy. Official U.S. Navy photograph.

of naval operations (1937–1939) and ambassador to Vichy France (1941–1942), is appointed chief of staff to President Roosevelt. He also acts as chairman of the joint chiefs of staff, in which capacity he plays an important role in the formulation of American strategy.

July 21.   **Advance on Port Moresby.** The Japanese land at Buna, on the northeastern coast of New Guinea and launch an advance across the Owen Stanley Mountains on Port Moresby, the objective of the amphibious force that had been turned back at the Battle of the Coral Sea. The Japanese offensive is halted 30 miles short of its goal by Australian and American troops on September 13.

July 30.   **Waves.** The Waves (*Women Accepted for Volunteer Service*) are established. Lieutenant Commander Mildred H. McAfee receives the first Wave commission and becomes the new organization's commandant on August 2.

July 30.   The submarine *Grunion* (SS 216), Lieutenant Commander Mannert L. Abele, is lost on a North Pacific war patrol after being last heard from on this date.

August 4.   The destroyer *Tucker* (DD 374), Lieutenant Commander W. R. Terrell, is lost in an American minefield off Espiritu Santo in the New Hebrides.

August 7.   **Guadalcanal (Operation Watchtower).** Especially in view of the victory at Midway, Admiral King is determined to go over to the offensive in the Pacific. On July 2, the joint chiefs of staff approve his plan of employing Major General Alexander A. Vandegrift's 1st Marine Division, already en route to the Southwest Pacific, to seize Tulagi, where the Japanese are constructing a seaplane base, and nearby islands in the eastern Solomons. Rear Admiral Richmond Kelly Turner commands the amphibious force; Vice Admiral Frank Jack Fletcher, the attack force. Tulagi, the small adjacent islands of Gavutu and Tanambogo, and the much larger island Guadalcanal, on which the landing is unopposed, are secured by the evening of August 9. An airstrip, Henderson Field, becomes fully operational on Guadalcanal on August 17. In the meanwhile, however, the Japanese have won a stunning naval victory at the Battle of Savo Island (described below) and begun moving troops towards Guadalcanal, initiating a contest that will last for six months of the most concentrated combat in the history of the American sea services. During the hours of daylight, American land-based and carrier aircraft control the sea around Guadalcanal, but after darkness falls the Japanese Navy, which possesses a distinct advantage in night fighting at this point in the war, is able to move down "The Slot" through the Central Solomons to Guadalcanal to reinforce and resupply Japanese troops on the island and to bombard Henderson Field with such regularity that the marines call these runs the Tokyo Express.

August 8–9.   **Battle of Savo Island.** Vice Admiral Gunichi Mikawa sorties from Rabaul under orders from Admiral Yamamoto to break up the invasion of Guadalcanal with a force consisting of the heavy cruisers *Aoba, Chokai, Furutaka, Kako,* and *Kinugasa,* light cruisers *Tenryu* and *Yubari,* and destroyer *Yunagi.* Entering Ironbottom Sound shortly after midnight unobserved by American picket destroyers, Mikawa inflicts one of the worse defeats in the history of the U.S. Navy, sinking four heavy cruisers—the *Astoria* (CA 34), Captain W. G. Greenman, HMAS *Canberra,* Captain F. E. Getting, RAN, the *Quincy* (CA 39), Captain S. N. Moore, and the *Vincennes* (CA 44), Captain F. L. Riefkohl—without suffering significant damage to a single vessel of his own. Fortunately for his enemies, he then throws away the fruits of victory, leaving the scene without molesting the American amphibious forces that he has just rendered, defenseless.

August 9.   The destroyer *Jarvis* (DD 393), Lieutenant Commander W. W. Graham, Jr., damaged by an air attack on the 8th and hit again during the Battle of Savo Island, is sunk by Japanese torpedo planes with the loss of all hands.

August 10.   Off Kavieng, New Ireland, Lieutenant Commander John R. ("Dinty") Moore's antique submarine *S 44* (SS 155) sinks the Japanese heavy cruiser *Kako,* which is on her way home from the Battle of Savo Island. This cruiser is the first major warship put down by a U.S. submarine.

August 14.   The submarine *S-39* (SS 144), Lieutenant Commander Francis E. Brown, runs aground near Rossel Island on a Pacific patrol. An Australian naval vessel rescues her crew.

August 16.   The battleship *Alabama* (BB 60) is commissioned.

August 17.   **Makin Raid.** Lieutenant Colonel Evans F. Carlson's marine 2nd Raider Battalion ("Carlson's Raiders"), 222 strong, is landed by submarine on the island of Makin in the Gilberts. After destroying the 83-man Japanese garrison, the raiders reembark. The operation boosts morale on the American home front, but also alerts the Japanese of the need to reinforce their garrisons in the islands.

August 20–21.   **Battle of the Tenaru River.** On Guadalcanal the marines repulse the first major Japanese counterattack, destroying an elite regiment, the Ikke Unit, which had been landed on the night of the 18th.

August 22.   The destroyer *Blue* (DD 387), Commander H. N. Williams, is torpedoed by the Japanese destroyer *Kawakaze* in a night encounter off Guadalcanal and scuttled the next night.

August 23–25.   **Battle of the Eastern Solomons.** Admiral Yamamoto devises a characteristically complicated plan to defeat U.S. naval forces in the Solomons and reinforce Guadalcanal. The Combined Fleet moves south from Truk, in the Carolines, with the heavy carriers *Shokaku* and *Zuikaku,* three battleships, and supporting units to engage the U.S. carriers. At the same time three high-speed transports carrying 1,500 troops set out from the Shortlands, escorted by a cruiser-destroyer force commanded by Rear Admiral Raizo Tanaka and covered by a single-carrier task force formed around the *Ryujo* under Rear Admiral Chuichi Hara. These units are engaged by Vice Admiral Frank Jack Fletcher's Task Force 61, composed of the carriers *Enterprise* (CV 6), *Saratoga* (CV 3), and *Wasp* (CV 7), battleship *North Carolina* (BB 55), plus cruisers and destroyers. The result is an inconclusive American victory. Planes from the *Enterprise* sink the light carrier *Ryujo,* but the "Big E" is then damaged by a strike from the Japanese fleet carriers.

A marine patrol on Guadalcanal. Official U.S. Navy photograph.

U.S. aircraft also turn back the troop convoy, sinking the largest transport and the destroyer *Mutsuki.*

August 25.   A force of 1,500 Japanese troops land at Milne Bay, on the southeastern tip of New Guinea. Counterattacks by Australian infantry and Allied air strikes make the beachhead too hot to hold, however, and on September 5, the Japanese withdraw.

August 28.   The Japanese destroyer *Asagiri,* one of a three-destroyer Tokyo Express carrying reinforcements to Guadalcanal, is sunk off Santa Isabel Island by marine aircraft from Henderson Field.

August 30.   Japanese aircraft sink the fast transport (former destroyer) *Colhoun* (APD 2), Lieutenant Commander G. B. Madden, off Guadalcanal.

September 1.   **Seabees.** The 6th Naval Construction Battalion arrives at Guadalcanal, thereby becoming the first Seabee unit to enter a combat zone. The Seabees, who will perform sterling service throughout the Pacific War, had been organized by Rear Admiral Ben Moreell, Chief of the Bureau of Yards and Docks, in October 1941.

September 5.   The destroyer transports *Gregory* (APD 3), Lieutenant Commander Harry F. Bauer, and *Little* (APD 4), Lieutenant

Commander G. B. Lofberg, are sunk in a night gunnery action with the Japanese destroyers *Hatsuyuki, Murakumo,* and *Yudachi* while patrolling off Lunga Point, Guadalcanal.

September 12–14.   **Battle of Bloody Ridge.** The second major attack on the marine positions at Guadalcanal, made by a force of approximately 3,500 men under Major General Seikin Kawaguchi, is beaten off with heavy losses to the Japanese.

September 15.   **Loss of the Wasp.** While screening a troop convoy to Guadalcanal, the carrier *Wasp* (CV 7), Captain Forrest P. Sherman, is torpedoed by the Japanese submarine *I-19.* Efforts to save her are unavailing, and the flaming wreck finally has to be sunk by an escorting destroyer. Of her 2,247 crewmen, 193 are killed and 366 wounded.

September 27.   A gallant little action occurs in the South Atlantic when the Liberty Ship *Stephen Hopkins,* merchant marine Captain Paul Buck, is attacked by the German surface raider *Stier* (Ship 23) and the blockade runner *Tannenfels.* The *Hopkins* has only one 4-inch gun, manned by a naval armed guard under Lieutenant Kenneth M. Willett, USNR, against the raider's six 5.9-inchers, but in the end both ships go down.

The *Hopkins*'s 15 survivors reach Brazil after 31 days in a lifeboat.

October 12.   **Battle of Cape Esperance.** A Japanese force of three heavy cruisers and two destroyers under Rear Admiral Aritomo Goto is sent to escort a troop convoy to Guadalcanal and afterwards bombard Henderson Field. A few minutes before midnight it is intercepted by Rear Admiral Norman Scott's Task Force 64, consisting of the heavy cruiser *San Francisco* (CA 38) and light cruisers *Salt Lake City* (CL 25), *Boise* (CL 47) and *Helena* (CL 50), and five destroyers. The Japanese cruiser *Furutake* limps away from the action to sink a few hours later, as does the U.S. destroyer *Duncan* (DD 485), Lieutenant Commander E. B. Taylor.

October 15.   The destroyer *Meredith* (DD 434), Lieutenant Commander Harry E. Hubbard, is sunk by a Japanese torpedo plane off San Cristobal Island in the Solomons.

October 16.   Planes from the *Hornet* (CV 8) attack Japanese positions on Guadalcanal and San Cristobal.

October 18.   Dissatisfied with Admiral R. L. Ghormley's conduct of the Solomons campaign, Admiral Nimitz replaces him as commander of the South Pacific Area and South Pacific Force with fire-eating Vice Admiral William F. Halsey. The news of Halsey's appointment produces a wave of jubilation throughout the theater.

October 22–26.   **Battle for Henderson Field.** Lieutenant General Harukichi Hyakutake, commander of the Japanese Seventeenth Army, makes what proves to be the last big push against the marines on Guadalcanal, throwing 22,000 men into a two-pronged attack on the perimeter around Henderson Field. The Japanese are thrown back with heavy losses.

October 25.   Off Guadalcanal, B-17 bombers severely damage the Japanese light cruiser *Yura*, which is then sunk by the Japanese.

October 26–27.   **Battle of the Santa Cruz Islands.** Admiral Yamamoto sends the Combined Fleet—4 carriers, 4 battleships, 14 cruisers, and 44 destroyers—south again in another attempt to destroy the U.S. naval forces supporting the struggle for Guadalcanal. These forces, commanded by Vice Admiral William F. Halsey, consist

Admiral William F. Halsey. Official U.S. Navy photograph.

of 2 carriers—the *Hornet* (CV 8) and the *Enterprise* (CV 6)—the battleship *South Dakota* (BB 57), 6 cruisers, and 14 destroyers. In the ensuing battle, the Japanese win a tactical victory, sinking the *Hornet*, Captain Charles P. Mason, and damaging several other vessels, while the submarine *I-22* sinks the destroyer *Porter* (DD 356), Lieutenant Commander D. G. Roberts. No Japanese ships are lost, although the fleet carrier *Shokaku* and heavy cruiser *Chikuma* are heavily damaged. Strategically, however, the victory belongs to the Americans. The Southwest Pacific forces remain off Guadalcanal.

November 8–10.   **Invasion of North Africa (Operation Torch).** American ground forces under Major General Dwight D. Eisenhower enter combat in the European theater with a series of landings on the coast of French North Africa. Admiral Sir Andrew B. Cunningham, CO of the British Mediterranean Fleet, commands Allied naval forces, which are divided into three components: the Western Naval Task Force, Rear Admiral H. Kent Hewitt, which lands 35,000 American troops under Major General George S. Patton at three locations (Safi, Fedala, and Port Lyautey) around Casablanca in French Morocco; the Center Naval Force, Commodore Sir Thomas Troubridge, RN, which lands 39,000 Americans under Major General L. R. Fredenall around Oran, Algeria; and the Eastern Naval Task Force, Rear Admiral Sir H. M. Burrough, RN, which lands 10,000 American and 23,000 British troops around Algiers. Initially the French resist the landings, and a naval action is fought off Casablanca on November 8 when French destroyers and the light cruiser *Primauguet* bravely sortie to attack greatly superior American forces, including the battleship *Massachusetts* (BB 59). The *Primauguet* and the destroyers *Boulonnais, Brestois, Fougeux,* and *Frondeur* are sunk. A cease-fire is signed on November 10.

November 12–13. **Naval Battle of Guadalcanal: the Cruiser Action.** Admiral Yamamoto has determined to have Rear Admiral Raizo Tanaka's Tokyo Express carry the 38th Division to reinforce the defenders of Guadalcanal. First, however, he plans to soften up the American opposition by delivering a heavy bombardment of Henderson Field. This mission is assigned to Admiral Hiroaki Abe's Raiding Force, consisting of the battleships *Hiei* and *Kirishima*, light cruiser *Nagara*, and fourteen destroyers. At approximately 1:50 A.M. on the 13th, this force is intercepted off Lunga Point by Rear Admiral Daniel J. Callaghan's Task Force 67.4, composed of the heavy cruisers *Portland* (CA 33) and *San Francisco* (CA 38), the light cruisers *Atlanta* (CL 51), *Helena* (CL 50), and *Juneau* (CL 52), and eight destroyers. The ensuing action lasts less than a quarter-hour, but is one of the fiercest of the war as the U.S. force, steaming line ahead, literally sails through the wedge-shaped, Japanese formation. Callaghan and the other American flag officer present, Rear Admiral Norman Scott, are killed in the opening minutes of the engagement, Callaghan in the *San Francisco*, Scott in the *Atlanta*. Sunk or so badly damaged that they must be scuttled are, on the American side, the cruiser *Atlanta* and the destroyers *Barton* (DD 599), Lieutenant Commander D. H. Fox, *Cushing* (DD 376), Lieutenant Commander E. N. Parker, and *Laffey* (DD 459), Lieutenant Commander C. E. McCombs; on the Japanese side, the destroyers *Akatsuki* and *Yudachi*. The *San Francisco* is very severely damaged and several other vessels, Japanese and American, more or less so. Admiral Abe retires without having shelled Guadalcanal. The battleship *Hiei*, crippled by 30 hits, is sunk by American planes the next afternoon, hours after the Japanese

Bringing supplies ashore at St. Leu, near Oran, Algeria, November 8, 1942. U.S. Army photograph.

submarine *I-22* sinks the cruiser *Juneau*, Captain Lyman K. Swenson.

November 14.   **Naval Battle of Guadalcanal: the Air Action.** Admiral Tanaka's Tokyo Express sets out from the Shortlands with 11 destroyers escorting an equal number of high-speed transports to carry the 38th Division to Guadalcanal. American aircraft sink six transports and damage another, which turns back. Tanaka shepherds the last four to the island, where they begin unloading their troops under cover of darkness, but are destroyed by artillery fire the next morning. Only 2,000 of the 10,000 men originally embarked have reached the island.

November 14–15.   **Naval Battle of Guadalcanal: the Battleship Action.** To cover the landing of Tanaka's transports, Admiral Yamamoto sends another heavy surface force to shell Henderson Field. Commanded by Admiral Nobutake Kondo, it consists of the battleship *Kirishima*, two heavy cruisers, one light cruiser, and six destroyers. Approaching Savo Island it is intercepted by Rear Admiral Willis A. ("Ching") Lee's Task Force 64, formed of the new battleships *South Dakota* (BB 57) and *Washington* (BB 56) and four destroyers. In an action that begins shortly before midnight, the *Kirishima* and destroyer *Ayanami* are sunk and Kondo retires. The American destroyers *Preston* (DD 379), Commander M. C. Stormes, and *Walke* (DD 416), Commander T. E. Fraser, are sunk, the destroyer *Benham* (DD 397), Lieutenant Commander John B. Taylor, so badly hurt that she sinks the following afternoon, and the *South Dakota* heavily damaged.

November 30.   **Battle of Tassafaronga.** Off Guadalcanal, Rear Admiral Carleton H. Wright's Task Force 67.4—composed of the heavy cruisers *Minneapolis* (CA 36), *New Orleans* (CA 32), *Northampton* (CA 26), and *Pensacola* (CA 24), light cruiser *Honolulu* (CL 48), and six destroyers—encounters eight destroyers of "Tenacious" Tanaka's Tokyo Express. American gunfire obliterates the destroyer *Takanami*, but Tanaka's other ships launch a salvo of torpedoes that sink the *Northampton*, Captain W. A. Kitts,

and hit every other cruiser except the *Honolulu*.

December 11.   The last Pacific surface action of 1942 takes place off Guadalcanal when a force of PT boats attack a Tokyo Express of ten destroyers. HIJMS *Teruzuki* and *PT 44* are sunk in the engagement.

December 12.   The Japanese Navy recommends abandoning the struggle for Guadalcanal.

December 15.   **"Black Cats."** Night-flying PBY Catalinas—"Black Cats"—begin to operate off Henderson Field. Although the big planes are too slow for day combat, they prove extremely useful for nighttime bombing raids, searches, and attacks upon enemy shipping.

December 18.   The Japanese light cruiser *Tenryu* is sunk by the submarine *Albacore* (SS 218), Commander Richard C. Lake, off northern New Guinea.

December 31.   The carrier *Essex* (CV 9) is commissioned. She is the name-ship of a class of ten 27,100-ton carriers, all of which will enter service during World War II.

December 31.   Japanese Imperial General Headquarters concedes defeat and orders the navy to conduct a staged evacuation of Guadalcanal.

1943

January 10.   The transport submarine *Argonaut* (APS 1), Lieutenant Commander John R. Pierce, is sunk while attacking an enemy convoy between New Britain and Bougainville.

January 14.   The carrier *Independence* (CV 22) is commissioned.

January 14–23.   **Casablanca Conference.** President Roosevelt, Prime Minister Churchill, and the combined chiefs of staff meet to formulate Allied strategy for 1943. By now it is evident that the German and Italian forces in North Africa are destined for defeat. The Americans reluctantly defer their hopes for a cross-channel invasion of France in 1943 to the British proposal to maintain Allied momentum in the Mediterranean theater by landing in Sicily. Admiral King secures approval for opening a second line of advance against Japan, through the Central Pacific towards the Marshalls and Carolines. Other major agreements are to intensify the strategic bombing of Germany and the antisubmarine campaign in the North Atlantic. President Roosevelt surprises his confrères by announcing that the Axis powers will be required to surrender unconditionally.

January 14–February 7. **Mush Morton and the Wahoo.** Commander Dudley W. ("Mush") Morton, new skipper of the submarine *Wahoo* (SS 238), commands the most aggressive patrol to date in the Pacific War. Ordered to reconnoiter the harbor of Wewak, on the northern coast of New Guinea, Morton not only threads his way into the enemy anchorage, but torpedoes a destroyer with a dangerous "down the throat" shot. The next day he encounters a Japanese convoy of two freighters, a large transport, and a tanker en route to Palau. In a 10-hour, running battle, he sinks the first three vessels and damages the fourth. These exploits, for which he receives both the Navy Cross and the Distinguished Service Cross, serve as an example and an inspiration to the entire submarine service.

January 22. American and Australian troops commanded by General Douglas MacArthur crush the last pockets of Japanese resistance at Buna, on the northeastern coast of New Guinea, ending the Papuan campaign.

January 29–30. **Battle of Rennell Island.** Approaching Guadalcanal from the south, Rear Admiral Robert C. ("Ike") Giffen, commander of Task Force 18, leaves his two escort carriers because their slow speed will prevent him from making a scheduled rendezvous with another force and presses on with seven cruisers and six destroyers. At twilight he is attacked near Rennell Island by land-based Japanese planes, which torpedo the heavy cruiser *Chicago* (CA 29). The next day Giffen's ships come under the air umbrella of the *Enterprise* (CV 6), but Japanese bombers penetrate the screen to sink the crippled cruiser.

February. Three of the five submarines that leave Brisbane, Australia, on patrol this month fail to return. They are the *Amberjack* (SS 219), Lieutenant Commander John A. Bole, Jr.; *Grampus* (SS 207), Commander John R. Craig; and *Triton* (SS 201), Lieutenant Commander George K. MacKenzie, Jr.

February 1. The destroyer *De Haven* (DD 469), Commander C. E. Tolman, is sunk by Japanese dive bombers off Guadalcanal.

February 1–8. **Operation KE.** Despite opposition from American aircraft, destroyers, and PT boats, the destroyers of the Tokyo Express succeed in evacuating 11,706 troops from Guadalcanal. The U.S. command never realizes that an evacuation is under way, assuming that the Japanese are continuing to reinforce the island.

February 9. **Guadalcanal secured.** The Japanese are discovered to have withdrawn from the island. Of the 36,000 troops Japan committed to the struggle, 14,800 were killed, 9,000 died of disease, and 1,000 were captured. Casualties among the 60,000 Amer-

The *Wahoo* in July 1943. U.S. Naval Institute Collection.

ican soldiers and marines who fought on the island were 1,600 dead and 4,200 wounded. With the completion of this gruelling campaign, the tide of war in the Pacific turns in favor of the United States.

February 17.   The carrier *Lexington* (CV 16) is commissioned.

February 21.   American forces land unopposed on the Russell Islands, 30 miles northwest of Guadalcanal, beginning the advance through the central Solomons.

February 22.   The battleship *Iowa* (BB 61) is commissioned.

February 25.   The carrier *Princeton* (CV 23) is commissioned.

March 1–4.   **Battle of the Bismarck Sea.** A Japanese convoy of 16 ships—8 transports and 8 destroyers—under Rear Admiral Masatomi Kimura sets out from Rabaul on February 28 to carry 6,900 men to reinforce the garrison at Lae, New Guinea. Discovered by American aerial reconnaissance in the Bismarck Sea, it is attacked by Fifth Air Force planes flying from New Guinea. The convoy's air screen is overwhelmed, and all 8 transports and 4 destroyers are sunk. More than 3,000 troops drown.

March 1–20.   **Slaughter in the Atlantic.** The wolfpacks score their greatest success, sinking 85 Allied ships at a cost of only 6 U-boats. It appears as though the Germans may finally attain their goal of severing the North Atlantic sea lanes of communication.

March 5.   The *Bogue* (CVE 9) becomes the first escort carrier assigned to antisubmarine operations. Convoy escort groups formed around these little carriers will make a major contribution to victory in the Battle of the Atlantic.

March 6.   Three light cruisers and three destroyers under Rear Admiral A. Stanton Merrill shell Japanese installations at Vila, on Kolombangaro, and sink the Japanese destroyers *Minegumo* and *Murasame.*

March 15.   The practice, still followed, of numbering U.S. fleets is introduced by Admiral King.

March 26.   **Battle of the Komandorskis.** A classic, daylight gunnery action occurs in the Aleutians when Rear Admiral Charles H. ("Soc") McMorris's Task Group 16.6—consisting of the light cruisers *Richmond*

(CL 9) (flag), and *Salt Lake City* (CL 25) and destroyers *Bailey* (DD 492), *Coghlan* (DD 606), *Dale* (DD 353), and *Monaghan* (DD 354)—encounters a greatly superior Japanese force of two heavy cruisers, two light cruisers, and four destroyers escorting two transports to Kiska. After a bold attempt to reach the transports, McMorris is compelled to turn away. The Japanese pursue. For more than three hours the American ships evade disaster in a skillful running battle. The *Salt Lake City* is finally disabled, but Japanese Vice Admiral Boshiro Hosogaya has had enough and breaks off the action.

March 31.   The carrier *Belleau Wood* (CV 24) is commissioned.

April 1.   A bomber base, Carney Field, becomes operational on Guadalcanal. Aircraft based here will play an important role in the conquest of the Solomons.

April 7.   **Operation "I."** In hopes of slowing the American build-up in the Solomons, Admiral Yamamoto launches an air offensive, reinforcing the land-based Eleventh Air Fleet with carrier aircraft. The destroyer *Aaron Ward* (DD 483), oiler *Kanawaha* (AO 1), and the New Zealand corvette *Moa* are sunk at Tulagi on this date, and two Dutch cargo ships go down later. Japanese pilots greatly inflate their successes, however, and Yamamoto terminates the operation on April 16.

April 7.   On this date the submarine *Pickerel* (SS 177), Lieutenant Commander A. H. Alston, Jr., is lost in the vicinity of Honshu sometime after sinking a Japanese freighter.

April 9.   The rank of commodore is revived.

April 15.   The carrier *Yorktown* (CV 10) is commissioned.

April 18.   **Get Yamamoto.** Navy code-breakers learn that Fleet Admiral Isoroku Yamamoto, commander of the Japanese Combined Fleet, has planned a tour of inspection during which he will fly into Kahili, Buin, a point within range of U.S. aircraft. This intelligence is presented to Admiral Nimitz, who directs Rear Admiral Marc A. Mitscher, Commander Air Solomons, to arrange a reception. Sixteen Lockheed P-38 Lightnings from Henderson Field, Guadalcanal, are waiting when the two bombers carrying Yamamoto and his staff approach Kahili. The admiral is killed in the crash of his plane.

April 22. The submarine *Grenadier* (SS 210), Lieutenant Commander John Fitzgerald, is forced to scuttle after being damaged by a Japanese air attack off the coast of Malaya. Fitzgerald and his men are rescued by a Japanese freighter, and though cruelly treated, most are alive at war's end.

May. **Climax of the Battle of the Atlantic.** The turning point of the war in the North Atlantic comes with the passage of Convoy ONS 5, 43 merchantmen bound from the United Kingdom to Halifax, Nova Scotia. It is attacked by three wolfpacks totaling no less than 51 U-boats, almost half the number on patrol. Aided by aircraft from Greenland and Iceland, the convoy escort, a maximum of nine ships successively commanded by Commanders Peter W. Gretton, RN, and R. E. Sherwood, RN, destroys six U-boats. Only 13 merchant ships are lost. Subsequent convoys also take a heavy toll of their attackers, and on May 24 Grand Admiral Karl Doenitz, commander-in-chief of the German Navy, recalls his boats from the North Atlantic. Never again will the wolfpacks threaten to cut the lifeline of the Western Democracies.

May 8. In the Solomon Islands, the Japanese destroyer *Kuroshio* is sunk and the destroyers *Kagero* and *Oyashio* damaged by American mines laid a day earlier. The two cripples are then sunk by an air strike from Guadalcanal.

May 11–30. **Reconquest of Attu.** Rear Admiral Thomas C. Kinkaid's North Pacific Force lands 11,000 men of the 7th Infantry Division, Major General A. E. Brown, on the Aleutian island of Attu. The Japanese garrison of 2,500 fights almost literally to the last man. American casualties are 600 killed and 1,200 wounded.

May 13. **Victory in North Africa.** General Jürgen von Arnim surrenders the 238,000 German and Italian troops crowded into the Cape Bon Peninsula, Tunisia, to the Allies.

May 17–25. **Washington Conference (Trident).** President Roosevelt, Prime Minister Churchill, and the combined chiefs of staff meet at Washington, D.C., to frame a comprehensive strategic plan for the war against the Axis. General George C. Marshall, U.S. Army chief of staff, proposes an invasion of northern France in the fall of 1943; the British, still certain that a cross-Channel attack would be premature, advocate a landing on mainland Italy, which they believe would force that country out of the war. After earnest discussions, a compromise is reached: the Americans agree to commit limited forces to an invasion of Italy in 1943 in exchange for a British commitment to join in a landing in France on May 1, 1944. The British also accept Admiral King's arguments for intensifying the war against Japan.

May 20. **Tenth Fleet.** The Tenth Fleet is established under the command of Admiral Ernest J. King, chief of naval operations, to direct the American antisubmarine war in the Atlantic. There is no new fleet, however; the new organization is strictly an operational headquarters.

May 22. The *Bogue* (CVE 9), Captain Giles E. Short, is the first escort carrier to destroy a German submarine, sinking the *U-569* in the North Atlantic.

May 23. The battleship *New Jersey* (BB 62) is commissioned.

May 25. The carrier *Bunker Hill* (CV 17) is commissioned.

May 28. The carrier *Cowpens* (CV 25) is commissioned.

June 17. The carrier *Monterey* (CV 26) is commissioned.

June 30. **Offensive in New Guinea.** General MacArthur's forces begin their advance along the northern coast of New Guinea. The newly established Seventh Amphibious Force, commanded by Rear Admiral Daniel E. Barbey (who will soon become known as Uncle Dan, the Amphibious Man), lands army units at Nassau Bay on Huon Gulf slightly south of Salamaua, and in the Trobriand and Woodlark islands off the northeastern tip of New Guinea.

June 30–August 25. **Campaign for New Georgia.** The reconquest of the Solomons continues with the invasion of New Georgia (Operation Toenail), the primary objective being the capture of the airfield at Munda Point. Rear Admiral Richmond Kelly Turner commands the amphibious force (Task Force 31); support is provided by carrier and cruiser groups and two battleship divisions organized as Task Force 36 directly under Third Fleet commander Vice Admiral William F. Halsey. The operation begins on June 30 with a landing on Rendova Island, five miles from New Georgia, and on three other nearby islands. New Georgia itself, defended by more than 5,000 Japanese troops under General Noboru Sasaki, is invaded on July 2. Three infantry divisions and Colonel H. B. ("Harry the Horse") Liversedge's First Marine Raider Regiment are eventually committed to the struggle. The Munda airfield is taken after fierce jungle fighting on August 5, and organized resistance ceases on August 25.

July 5.   In a chance encounter between American and Japanese naval forces in Kula Gulf, between New Georgia and Kolombangara, the destroyer *Strong* (DD 467), Commander J. H. Wellings, is sunk shortly after midnight with the loss of 46 lives.

July 6.   **Battle of Kula Gulf.** Around midafternoon on July 5, the Third Fleet learns that a "Tokyo Express" is en route south from Bougainville with Japanese reinforcements for the central Solomons. Rear Admiral Walden L. ("Pug") Ainsworth's Task Group 36.1, consisting of the light cruisers *Honolulu* (CL 48) (flag), *Helena* (CL 50), and *St. Louis* (CL 49) and four destroyers, makes full speed to Kula Gulf to intercept the Japanese. It meets the enemy force— ten destroyers, seven of which are being used as transports, under Rear Admiral Teruo Akiyama—a few minutes past midnight. In a confused action that lasts almost until dawn, Admiral Akiyama's flagship, the *Niizuki*, is sunk and the *Nagatsuki* driven ashore, where she is destroyed by U.S. planes during the day; but the destroyer-transports succeed in unloading their troops on Kolombangara, and the *Helena*, Captain Charles P. Cecil, is sunk by three torpedoes fired by the *Suzukaze* and *Tanikaze*.

July 10.   **Invasion of Sicily (Operation Husky).** The largest amphibious assault in history, in terms of both the number of troops put ashore at one time and the extent of coastline covered, is made when eight American and British divisions are landed over a frontage of more than 100 miles on the southern and eastern coasts of Sicily. The naval forces involved—more than 1,400 ships and landing craft—are commanded by British Admiral Sir Andrew B. Cunningham, the land forces by General Sir Harold Alexander. Three American divisions of Lieutenant General George S. Patton's Seventh Army are put ashore in southern Sicily by the Western Naval Task Force, Vice Admiral H. Kent Hewitt, USN. Five British divisions of Lieutenant General Sir Bernard L. Montgomery's Eighth Army are landed on their right by the Western Naval Force, Vice Admiral Sir Bertram Ramsay, RN. A total of 470,000 men are committed to the operation. Sicily is defended by 300,000 Italian and 50,000 German troops under General Alfredo Guzzoni, but the Italians are sick of the war, and only the Germans show fight.

July 10   The destroyer *Maddox* (DD 622), Lieutenant Commander E. R. Sarsfield, is sunk with heavy loss of life by a German dive-bomber off Gela, Sicily.

July 11.   **Fire support on Sicily.** Fire from the light cruisers *Boise* (CL 47) and *Savannah* (CL 42) and eight destroyers helps defeat an armored thrust by the Hermann Goering Division on the Allied beachhead at Gela, Sicily. After their attempts to repel the landing are unsuccessful, the Germans fight an expert rear-guard action to the north towards the Straits of Messina.

The light cruiser *Boise* crosses the bow of the *LST 325* while providing fire support for U.S. forces ashore near Gela, Sicily, July 11, 1943. U.S. Army photograph.

July 13.   **Battle of Kolombangara.** On his fifteenth patrol up The Slot, Rear Admiral W. L. Ainsworth fights another night action with the Tokyo Express. This time he has the light cruisers *Honolulu* (CL 48) (flag), *St. Louis* (CL 49), and HMNZS *Leander*, and 10 destroyers. The Japanese force, commanded by Rear Admiral Shunji Izaki, consists of the light cruiser *Jintsu* (flag), five destroyers, and five destroyer-transports. The *Jintsu* is literally blown out of the water, and the *Leander* is badly damaged by a torpedo in the opening moments of the action. Then the failure to promptly identify the destroyers of the Japanese escort force allows them to reach a position to launch torpedoes that blow up the destroyer *Gwin* (DD 433), Lieutenant Commander John B. Fellows, and damage the cruisers *Honolulu* and *St. Louis*. The Japanese destroyer-transports succeed in landing their troops on Kolombangara.

July 19–20.   The Japanese destroyers *Yugure* and *Kiyonami*, members of a 13-ship Tokyo Express, are sunk by army and navy planes in The Slot north of Kolombangara.

July 20.   The submarine *Runner* (SS 275), Lieutenant Commander Joseph H. Bourland, is reported overdue and presumed lost in the Pacific.

July 22.   Navy planes sink the Japanese seaplane carrier *Nisshin* in Bougainville Strait.

July 23.   Patrol Squadron 63 arrives in Britain to participate in the Royal Air Force Coastal Command's offensive against German U-boats crossing the Bay of Biscay. It is the first U.S. Navy air unit to be based in Britain.

July 24.   The carrier *Cabot* (CVL 28) is commissioned.

July 25.   Following the Allied landings in Sicily, Benito Mussolini, *Il Duce* of Fascist Italy, is overthrown and imprisoned by a *coup d'état* organized around King Victor Emanuel III. German special forces led by Colonel Otto Skorzeny later rescue Mussolini, and he is installed as president of the German-backed Salò Republic in northern Italy.

July 28.   Undetected by U.S. forces, a Japanese task force commanded by Vice Admiral S. Kawase evacuates the 5,183-man garrison of the Aleutian island of Kiska.

August 1–2.   **PT 109.** After nightfall 15 U.S. torpedo boats engage a four-destroyer Tokyo Express off Kolombangara. The only loss on either side occurs when the *Amagiri* rams the *PT 109*, Lieutenant (and future president) John F. Kennedy, USNR. Eleven of the boat's thirteen crewmen survive. The next day they swim to a neighboring island, Kennedy towing a badly injured man. Friendly natives carry a message Kennedy carves on a coconut shell to an Australian coastwatcher on another island, and the party is rescued on August 7. Kennedy is awarded the Navy Cross.

August 3–17.   **Evacuation of Sicily.** Despite Allied air and naval superiority, a total of 39,500 Germans and 62,000 Italians succeed in crossing the Straits of Messina to reach the Italian mainland. A total of 167,000 Axis troops (37,000 German) are killed, wounded, or captured in the 39 days of the Sicilian campaign. American and British casualties amount to 25,000.

August 6–7.   **Battle of Vella Gulf.** The U.S. Navy wins its first unequivocal night-fighting victory of the Pacific war when seven destroyers under Commander Frederick Moosbrugger intercept four Japanese destroyers on a Tokyo Express run in Vella Gulf, between Vella Lavella and Kolombangara. The first spread of torpedoes launched by Moosbrugger's ships hit the *Arashi, Hagikaze*, and *Kawakaze*, all of which are soon sunk. Only the *Shigure* escapes. The American destroyers emerge from the action unscathed.

August 13.   Faced with inacceptable losses, especially of aircraft and destroyers, Japanese

PT 109. U.S. Naval Institute Collection.

Imperial Headquarters decides to cease reinforcing the Solomons.

August 14–24. **Quebec Conference (Quadrant).** The president, the prime minister, and the combined chiefs of staff meet to discuss plans for the landing in France—about which the Americans suspect the British still harbor reservations—and the future conduct of the war against Japan. May 1, 1944, is confirmed as the target date for the cross-Channel invasion; General MacArthur is to continue his advance up the coast of New Guinea, by-passing Rabaul; and the U.S. Navy will launch an offensive across the Central Pacific to the Marianas.

August 15. **Leapfrogging to Vella Lavella.** The Third Amphibious Force, Rear Admiral Theodore S. ("Ping") Wilkinson, lands 4,600 men under Brigadier General Robert B. McClure, USA, on the undefended Solomon island of Vella Lavella, bypassing and neutralizing strongly garrisoned Kolombangara.

August 15. **Anticlimax at Kiska.** After a heavy pre-invasion bombardment, Rear Admiral Thomas C. Kinkaid's North Pacific Force lands 34,400 American and Canadian troops on Kiska, in the Aleutians, which the Japanese had secretly evacuated on July 28.

August 16. The carrier *Intrepid* (CV 11) is commissioned.

August 27. The submarine *Grayling* (SS 209), Lieutenant Commander Robert M. Brinker, is lost in Philippine waters sometime after sinking a Japanese cargo ship on this date.

August 31. Japanese installations on Marcus Island, 800 miles northwest of Wake, are attacked by aircraft from the carriers *Essex* (CV 9), *Independence* (CVL 22), and *Yorktown* (CV 10) of Rear Admiral C. A. Pownall's Task Force 15.

August 31. The carrier *Langley* (CVL 27) is commissioned.

September 3. British troops of General Sir Bernard L. Montgomery's Eighth Army cross the narrows of the Straits of Messina to land at Reggio di Calabria on the Italian mainland opposite Sicily.

September 3. **Italian armistice.** An armistice is secretly signed with the new Italian government of Marshal Pietro Badoglio. It is to become effective on September 8. This date is chosen to coincide with the major

landings to be made by American forces at Salerno.

September 4. **Assault on Lae.** The Japanese positions at Salamaua, Lae, and Finschhafen on the northern coast of New Guinea must be eliminated before General MacArthur can continue his advance. On this date Rear Admiral Daniel E. Barbey's Seventh Amphibious Force lands the 9th Australian Division east of Lae. The next day American paratroopers capture an airfield at the village of Nadzab, west of Lae, and the 7th Australian Division is flown in. Faced by convergent attacks, the Japanese garrison withdraws on September 15.

September 8. **The Italian armistice is announced.** Simultaneously, the Italian fleet sorties to surrender to Allied naval authorities. The German Luftwaffe attacks the ships at sea and succeeds in sinking the battleship *Roma* and damaging other vessels, but most of Italy's active fleet escapes.

September 9. **Salerno.** Lieutenant General Mark Clark's American Fifth Army lands at Salerno, on the ankle of the Italian boot. The naval component of the operation is commanded by Vice Admiral H. Kent Hewitt. Simultaneously, the Germans react to the Italian armistice by seizing Rome (Septem-

This neat hole in the top of the Number 3 six-inch turret of the light cruiser *Savannah* was made by a radio-controlled glide bomb launched from a German aircraft off the Salerno beachhead. The bomb penetrated three decks to explode in the lower handling room, killing 197 men and seriously wounding 15 others. Official U.S. Navy photograph.

ber 10) and rushing reinforcements to the south. Between September 12 and 16, Field Marshal Albert Kesselring, commanding German forces in Italy, makes repeated and dangerous attempts to repel the invasion. Naval gunfire plays an important part in halting these thrusts. The Fifth Army links up with Montgomery's Eighth Army on the 16th, and Kesselring pulls back. For the next 19 months the Germans will exploit the defensive potential of the mountainous spine of the Italian peninsula to slow the Allied push to the north.

September 11.   The destroyer *Rowan* (DD 405), Lieutenant Commander Joel C. Ford, is sunk with the loss of 202 lives by a German PT boat off Salerno, and the light cruiser *Savannah* (CL 42) is damaged by radio-controlled bombs dropped by German aircraft.

September 18.   In the Pacific, the Tarawa Atoll, Gilbert Islands, is hit by carrier planes from Rear Admiral C. A. Pownall's Task Force 15.

September 19.   The submarine *Cisco* (SS 290), Commander James W. Coe, sails from Darwin, Australia, and disappears at sea. She was probably sunk by Japanese forces on September 28.

September 22.   **Finschhafen landing.** The last of the three Japanese positions on the Huon Gulf in northern New Guinea falls when Rear Admiral Barbey's Seventh Amphibious Force lands the Australian 20th Brigade at Finschhafen, taking the Japanese garrison by surprise. Despite stiff resistance by units of the Special Naval Landing Force, the village is secured on October 2.

September 25.   On this date, the submarine *Pompano* (SS 181), Commander Willis M. Thomas, is lost sometime after sinking a freighter off the Japanese coast.

October 3.   The destroyer *Henley* (DD 391), Lieutenant Commander A. R. Theobald, Jr., is sunk by a Japanese submarine off Finschhafen, New Guinea. Seventeen lives are lost.

October 4.   An American task force consisting of the carrier *Ranger* (CV 4), heavy cruiser *Tuscaloosa* (CA 37), and a destroyer division under the command of Rear Admiral Olaf M. Hustvedt participates in a raid by the British Home Fleet on German shipping at Bodö, Norway. Six enemy freight-

ers are sunk and four damaged by Allied air strikes.

October 5–6.   In the Central Pacific, Wake Island is attacked by carrier aircraft and shelled by cruisers of Rear Admiral A. E. Montgomery's Task Force 14.

October 6–7.   **Battle of Vella Lavella.** Another night action takes place in the Solomons when the Japanese send a force of 9 destroyers and 12 small craft under Rear Admiral Matsuji Ijuin to evacuate the 600 troops on Vella Lavella. It is intercepted by six destroyers commanded by Captain Frank R. Walker. One destroyer is sunk on each side—HIJMS *Yugumo* and the USS *Chevalier* (DD 451), Lieutenant Commander George R. Wilson—and two American destroyers are damaged. The Japanese small craft extricate the island's garrison. This is the last engagement fought in the central Solomons.

October 7.   The submarine *S 44* (SS 155), Lieutenant Commander Francis E. Brown, is sunk in a surface action with a Japanese destroyer at Paramushiro in the Kuriles.

October 9.   The destroyer *Buck* (DD 420), Lieutenant Commander Michael J. Klein, is sunk with the loss of 166 lives by the *U-616* off Salerno, Italy.

October 13.   Italy declares war on Germany.

October 13.   The destroyer *Bristol* (DD 453), Commander J. A. Glick, is sunk with the loss of 52 lives by the *U-317* off the coast of Algeria.

October 19–30.   **Moscow Conference.** U.S. Secretary of State Cordell Hull, British Foreign Secretary Sir Anthony Eden, and Soviet Foreign Secretary Vyacheslav Molotov confer. Hull and Eden assure Molotov that the western Allies will land in France in May 1944, satisfying Stalin's longstanding plea for the opening of a second front in northern Europe, and promise that they will not make a separate peace with Germany. Molotov intimates that the Soviet Union may enter the war against Japan.

October 24.   The submarine *Dorado* (SS 248), Lieutenant Commander Earl K. Schneider, is reported overdue and presumed lost in the Atlantic.

October 27–November 6.   **Landing in the Treasury Islands.** Mono and Stirling, the two little islands comprising the Treasury group, are seized for use as a base for the invasion of Bougainville.

October 27–November 4.   As a feint to distract the Japanese from the attack on Bougainville, the marine 2nd Parachute Battalion, Lieutenant Colonel Victor H. ("Brute") Krulak, is landed on and then withdrawn from Choiseul Island.

November 1.   **The Borie vs. U-405.** Seven hundred miles north of the Azores, the old destroyer *Borie* (DD 215), Lieutenant Commander Charles H. Hutchins, USNR, fights a night surface action with the *U-405*. After an hour's gunnery duel, the *Borie* succeeds in ramming the U-boat. The vessels are locked together for some minutes, during which the two crews exchange small-arms fire from their decks. Eventually the *U-405* wrenches away, crippled, to surrender shortly thereafter. The *Borie* sinks the following day as a result of the damage to her bow.

November 1.   **Bougainville.** Rear Admiral Theodore S. Wilkinson's Third Amphibious Force lands the 3rd Marine Division, Major General Allen H. Turnage, at Empress Augusta Bay on the west coast of Bougainville in the northern Solomons. Possession of an airfield here will put the Japanese stronghold at Rabaul, New Britain, within range of land-based planes. The beachhead is secured by nightfall. Later counterattacks by an enemy battalion brought down on the Tokyo Express from Rabaul and by Japanese forces garrisoned elsewhere on Bougainville are defeated. Marine casualties are 423 dead and 1,418 wounded.

November 2.   **Battle of Empress Augusta Bay.** Rear Admiral Sentaro Omori sorties from the Japanese fleet base at Rabaul with two heavy cruisers, two light cruisers, and six destroyers to break up the Bougainville landing. Arriving at the mouth of Empress Augusta Bay around 2:30 A.M., he is met by Rear Admiral A. Stanton ("Tip") Merrill's Task Force 39, consisting of four light cruisers and two destroyer divisions of four ships each under Captain Arleigh A. ("31-knot") Burke and Commander Bernard L. ("Count") Austin. The Japanese force, though greatly superior in firepower, is repulsed in an exemplary action, losing the light cruiser *Sendai* and destroyer *Hatsu-*

kaze. No American ships are sunk and only one, the destroyer *Foote* (DD 511), is seriously damaged.

November 5.   Still hoping to repel the invasion of Bougainville, Admiral Mineichi Koga, Yamamoto's successor as commander of the Japanese Combined Fleet, sends seven heavy cruisers, a light cruiser, and four destroyers under Vice Admiral Takeo Kurita to reinforce the Eighth Fleet at Rabaul. Admiral Halsey responds by ordering Rear Admiral Frederick C. Sherman's carrier Task Force 38 to raid the Japanese fleet base. Aircraft from the *Saratoga* (CV 3) and *Princeton* (CVL 23) deliver a devastating attack on the ships at Rabaul, seriously damaging the heavy cruisers *Atago, Chikuma, Maya, Mogami,* and *Takao.* This strike eliminates the possibility of further action by Japanese heavy surface units against the Bougainville beachhead. Only 10 of the 97 planes involved are shot down.

November 6.   The destroyer *Beatty* (DD 640), Lieutenant Commander W. Outerson, is sunk by German aircraft off Cape Bougaroun, Algeria.

November 9.   **Loss of the Wahoo.** Captain Dudley W. ("Mush") Morton's *Wahoo* (SS 238) is reported overdue and presumed lost on her fifth war patrol. She was probably destroyed by a Japanese aircraft on October 11 while exiting La Pérouse Strait after sinking four ships in the Sea of Japan.

November 13.   Daily air strikes on Japanese installations in the Gilbert and Marshall islands are begun by American carrier and land planes in preparation for the launching of the navy's offensive through the central Pacific.

November 16.   The submarine *Corvina* (SS 226), Commander Roderick S. Rooney, is sunk by the Japanese submarine *I-176*, which sights her running on the surface south of Truk. This is the only occasion in the war in which an American submarine is destroyed by a Japanese submarine.

November 17.   A Japanese air attack on a troop convoy to Bougainville sinks the destroyer transport *McKean* (APD 5), Lieutenant Commander Ralph L. Ramey, with the loss of 116 lives.

November 17.   The carrier *Bataan* (CVL 29) is commissioned.

November 19.   In the Central Pacific, the submarine *Sculpin* (SS 191), Commander Fred Connaway, is depth-charged, forced to the surface, and sunk by the Japanese destroyer *Yamagumo*. Aboard her, ready to form a wolf pack should the Japanese fleet sail from Truk, is Captain John P. Cromwell, commander of Submarine Division 43. Cromwell's duties ashore have made him aware of the vital role navy code-breaking plays in the success of the American undersea war. Deciding that he knows too much to permit himself to be taken prisoner, he deliberately stays in the *Sculpin* when she goes down for the last time. The testimony of the boat's survivors, who are rescued by the *Yamagumo*, will later result in the posthumous award of the Medal of Honor to Captain Cromwell.

November 20–23. **Tarawa (Operation Galvanic).** The navy launches its Central Pacific drive, in effect reviving the prewar War Plan Orange for a conflict against Japan, with landings on Betio, Makin, and Apamama islands of the Tarawa Atoll in the Gilberts. The operation is executed by Vice Admiral Raymond A. Spruance's Fifth Fleet. Rear Admiral Richmond Kelly Turner commands the assault force, Major General Holland M. ("Howlin' Mad") Smith, commander of the newly established V Amphibious Corps, the landing force. Makin and Apamama are taken against relatively light resistance. Betio, garrisoned by 4,836 naval troops (including 2,619 men of the elite Special Naval Landing Force) under Rear Admiral Meichi Shibasaki, is the linchpin of the Japanese defense. It is assaulted by Major General Julian C. Smith's 2nd Marine Division and secured after 76 hours of bitter fighting in which 990 marines are killed, 2,391 wounded, and only 17 defenders are taken prisoner. The landing demonstrates the basic soundness of the amphibious doctrines that the marine corps developed between the world wars. It also reveals the need for more intensive pre-landing bombardment, improvements in communications and air support, and the increased use of amphibian tractors (Landing Vehicles, Tracked).

November 22–26. **First Cairo Conference (Sextant).** President Roosevelt, Prime

Tarawa: landing craft, looking like waterbugs, make for the beach. Official U.S. Navy photograph.

184

longAMERICAN NAVAL HISTORY: 1943

Marines ashore during the savage struggle for Tarawa. Defense Department photo (Marine Corps).

Minister Churchill, and the combined chiefs of staff meet to finalize plans for 1944. Churchill's attempt to secure approval for an enlargement of the Allied war effort in the Mediterranean is rebuffed, as is the American idea of establishing a supreme Allied commander for the entire European theater. Generalissimo and Madame Chiang Kai-shek are also present and, with the Americans, urge the British to make a greater effort against the Japanese in the China-Burma-India theater.

November 24.   The escort carrier *Liscombe Bay* (CVE 56), Captain I. D. Wiltsie, flagship of Task Group 52.3, is torpedoed and sunk with the loss of 644 lives by the Japanese submarine *I-175* in the Gilbert Islands. Among those killed are Captain Wiltsie and the task group commander, Rear Admiral Henry M. Mullinnix.

November 24.   The carrier *Wasp* (CV 18) is commissioned.

November 25.   **Battle of Cape St. George.** Captain Arleigh A. Burke fights a brilliant night action when Destroyer Squadron 23 intercepts a Tokyo Express under Captain Kiyoto Kagawa transporting reinforcements to Buka, the island immediately north of Bougainville. The odds are even, five destroyers a side. Both ships of the Japanese screen, the *Onami* (flag) and *Makinawi* are hit by Burke's opening salvo of torpedoes. The former blows up; the latter

and the *Yugiri* are then sunk by gunfire. The two remaining enemies turn tail. Burke's ships do not take a single hit.

November 28–December 1.   **Teheran Conference (Eureka).** Leaving Cairo, the Western leaders fly to Teheran for their first meeting with Soviet Premier Stalin. Churchill renews his arguments for additional operations in the Mediterranean, but Stalin makes plain his preference for an invasion of France and is assured that it will be made in 1944.

November 29.   The destroyer *Perkins* (DD 377), Lieutenant Commander G. L. Ketchum, sinks following a collision with the Australian transport *Duntroon* off eastern New Guinea.

November 29.   The carrier *Hornet* (CV 12) is commissioned.

December 2.   On this date the submarine *Capelin* (SS 289), Commander Elliott E. ("Steam") Marshall, sails from Darwin, Australia, and is lost sometime after being sighted by the *Bowfin* (SS 287) in the Makassar Strait.

December 3–7.   **Second Cairo Conference.** Roosevelt, Churchill, and their staffs return to Cairo from Teheran to make plans for an invasion of southern France, Operation Anvil, which is to complement the cross-Channel assault. The number of landing craft needed for this operation necessitates the cancellation of Operation Buccaneer, a projected British assault on the coast of Burma.

December 4.   The submarine *Sailfish* (SS 192, originally *Squalus*), Lieutenant Commander Robert E. Ward, sinks the Japanese carrier *Chuyo* off the coast of Japan.

December 15.   **Landing at Arawe.** General MacArthur believes that to secure safe passage for naval forces through the Vitiaz and Dampier straits between New Guinea and New Britain it is necessary to occupy the western end of the latter island. The operation commences when Rear Admiral Barbey's Seventh Amphibious Force lands the 112th Cavalry Regiment (dismounted) at Arawe, on the southwestern shore of New Britain. Little resistance is encountered.

December 15.   The carrier *San Jacinto* (CVL 30) is commissioned. She is the last of the eleven fleet and four light carriers to enter service this year.

December 17. **Neutralizing Rabaul.** The Japanese fleet base at Rabaul, New Britain, the principal objective of the American drive through the Solomons, is taken under almost daily attack by land-based aircraft of the U.S. Army, Navy, and Marines and the Australian and New Zealand armed forces flying from nearby airfields. The usefulness of the base to the Japanese is destroyed.

December 24. Escorting a North Atlantic convoy, the destroyer *Leary* (DD 158), Commander James E. Kyes, becomes the third (and last) American destroyer to be sunk by a U-boat.

December 26. **Landing at Cape Gloucester.** Rear Admiral Barbey's Seventh Amphibious Force lands the 1st Marine Division, Major General William H. Rupertus, at Cape Gloucester on the western tip of New Britain. The airfield is taken on December 30, but it is not until January 16, 1944, that the Japanese are driven from the area.

December 26. The destroyer *Brownson* (DD 518),

Lieutenant Commander J. B. Maher, is sunk by Japanese dive-bombers off Cape Gloucester.

1944

January 1. Major General Alexander A. Vandegrift becomes 18th commandant of the marine corps.

January 2. **Landing at Saidor.** MacArthur's progress up the coast of New Guinea continues with the landing of an army regiment at Saidor, an undefended village at the western entrance of the Vitiaz Strait. This operation leapfrogs the 12,000 Japanese troops garrisoning Sio, 75 miles to the east.

January 3. The destroyer *Turner* (DD 648), Commander H. S. Wygant, Jr., sinks with the loss of 100 lives following an internal explosion in Ambrose Channel, New York.

January 22. **Anzio (Operation Shingle).** A stalwart German defense has held the Al-

Japanese shipping in harbor at Rabaul, New Britain, under attack by aircraft from the carriers *Princeton* and *Saratoga* on November 5, 1943. Official U.S. Navy photograph.

lied advance up the mountainous Italian peninsula to a snail's pace. Hoping to get the campaign moving, the Allies attempt an amphibious end-run around the German front by landing in the Anzio-Nettuno area, almost due west of Rome. From there, the assault force is to press on to occupy the Alban Hills, scarcely 20 miles inland, from which its artillery will dominate the roads carrying supplies to the German army in the south. The idea of undertaking such an operation had been indefatigably promoted by Prime Minister Churchill. The two divisions—one American, one British—comprising the VI Corps, Major General J. P. Lucas, USA, are put ashore by Rear Admiral Frank J. Lowry's Anglo-American Task Force 81 on this date. Surprise is achieved, but instead of striking for the Alban Hills, Lucas pauses to consolidate the beachhead, which may have been a blessing, since the German reaction is swifter and stronger than had been anticipated. Marshall Kesselring soon has more Germans surrounding the beachhead than there are Americans and British inside it. Naval fire support contributes to the frustration of his plans to hurl the invaders into the sea. As it is, the Germans succeed in containing the beach-

head, which is finally reached by Mark Clark's Fifth Army, pushing up from the south on May 25. Some 5,000 Allied troops have been killed, 17,000 wounded and 6,800 captured in the fighting.

January 29–February 6. **Softening up the Marshalls.** The aircraft and ships of Rear Admiral Marc A. Mitscher's Task Force 58 join land-based planes in bombarding Japanese positions on Kwajalein, Wotje, Eniwetok, and Taroa in the Marshall Islands.

January 30–February 9. Naval aircraft from Midway repeatedly attack Wake Island, neutralizing the Japanese airfield there in preparation for the invasion of the Marshalls.

January 31. The carrier *Franklin* (CV 13) is commissioned.

January 31–February 5. **The Marshalls (Operation Flintlock).** The Central Pacific offensive advances with a series of landings on the coral islands of Kwajalein Atoll. The operation is conducted by Vice Admiral Raymond A. Spruance's Fifth Fleet. The assault force is commanded by Rear Admiral Richmond Kelly Turner, the landing force (V Amphibious Corps) by Major General Holland M. Smith. Undefended Majuro Atoll, some 200 miles to the south-

Troops and equipment cross the beach at Anzio, Italy, on the day of the invasion. The column of smoke in the left background is from a burning LCI (Landing Craft, Infantry). U.S. Army photograph.

Admiral Raymond A. Spruance, left, and Admiral Chester W. Nimitz, center, aboard the battleship *New Jersey* off Majuro Atoll in the Marshalls, April 8, 1944. Official U.S. Navy photograph.

east, is occupied for use as an advanced base. Kwajalein, at the southern end of the atoll to which it gives its name, is stormed by the 7th Infantry Division, Major General C. H. Corlett, USA. Major General Harry Schmidt's 4th Marine Division lands on the Siamese-twin islands of Roi and Namur, on the northeastern angle of the atoll on February 1. The latter, defended by 3,600 Japanese naval troops, are secured by the afternoon of February 2. Only 91 members of their garrison are taken alive. Marine casualties are 195 killed and 545 wounded. These figures reflect the improvements in amphibious techniques made as a result of the experience gained at Tarawa. Kwajalein is secured on February 5.

February 15. **Landing in the Green Islands.** The 3rd New Zealand Division, Major General H. E. Barraclough, is landed on the Green Islands, 55 miles east of New Ireland, by Rear Admiral Theodore S. ("Ping") Wilkinson's Task Force 31. The purpose of the operation, ordered by Admiral Halsey, is to obtain another airfield for use against Rabaul.

February 17–18. **Attack on Truk.** Carrier task groups of Admiral Spruance's Fifth Fleet strike the Japanese fleet base at Truk, the cornerstone of the enemy position in the southwest Pacific. More than 1,200 sorties are flown. The light cruiser *Naka* and three destroyers are sunk and approximately 265 aircraft damaged or destroyed. Spruance's own Task Group 50.9, a surface action force

built around the fast battleships *Iowa* (BB 61) and *New Jersey* (BB 62), intercepts and sinks the fleeing light cruiser *Katori* and a destroyer. Numerous smaller vessels and cargo ships are also destroyed. The only serious damage to the U.S. fleet occurs when the carrier *Independence* (CVL 22) is hit by a Japanese torpedo plane.

February 18–23. **Capture of Eniwetok (Operation Catchpole).** It had not been necessary to commit the V Amphibious Corps reserve at Kwajalein. That force, composed of the Twenty-Second Marines and the One Hundred and Sixth Infantry, under Brigadier General T. E. Watson, USMC, is employed to attack Eniwetok, another Marshalls atoll some 360 miles northwest of Kwajalein. Rear Admiral Harry W. ("Handsome Harry") Hill is designated commander of the Eniwetok Expeditionary Force (Task Force 51.11). The marines capture Engebi and Parry islands—the army regiment, Eniwetok.

February 19. For the last time, a major air battle takes place over Rabaul. The air defense of the base, which has cost the Japanese more than 300 planes since November, is abandoned.

February 23. **First attack on the Marianas.** Six carriers of Rear Admiral Marc A. Mitsch-

Vice Admiral Marc A. Mitscher, right, and Commodore Arleigh A. Burke, his chief of staff, at the chart table, March 1944. U.S. Naval Institute Collection.

er's Task Groups 58.2 and 58.3 strike Japanese positions on Guam, Rota, Saipan, and Tinian in preparation for the invasion of the Marianas.

February 27. The submarine *Grayback* (SS 208), Commander John A. Moore, is sunk by a Japanese aircraft in the East China Sea.

February 29. The submarine *Trout* (SS 202), Lieutenant Commander Albert H. Clark, is lost sometime after successfully attacking a Japanese troop convoy en route to the Marianas, sinking one transport and damaging another. She may have been destroyed by the convoy's escort vessels.

February 29–March 9. **Landing in the Admiralties.** The strategic ring around Rabaul is strengthened when a Seventh Fleet amphibious force commanded by Rear Admiral William M. Fechteler lands elements of the 1st Cavalry Division on Los Negros Island in the Admiralty group, westward of New Britain. The beachhead is secured on March 5 and two days later LSTs ferry troops to nearby Manus Island. Meaningful enemy resistance ends on April 3.

March 6. The submarine *Scorpion* (SS 278), Commander Maximilian G. Schmidt, is reported overdue and presumed lost. She was probably destroyed in a minefield in the East China Sea.

March 9. The destroyer escort *Leopold* (DE 319), Lieutenant Commander K. C. Phillips, USCG, is sunk with the loss of 171 lives by the *U-255* while escorting a North Atlantic convoy.

March 13. The Japanese light cruiser *Tatsuta* is sunk off the Home Island of Honshu by the submarine *Sand Lance* (SS 381), Lieutenant Commander Malcolm E. Garrison.

March 20. In the Southwest Pacific, the Fourth Marine Regiment lands on unoccupied Emirau Island in the St. Matthias group, midway between New Ireland and the Admiralties, completing the encirclement of Rabaul.

March 26. The submarine *Tullibee* (SS 284), Commander Charles F. Brindupke, is sunk while attacking a Japanese convoy near the Palaus, probably by one of her own torpedoes making a circular run.

March 30–April 1. Japanese positions in the Palaus and the Carolines are attacked by the fast carrier forces of the Fifth Fleet.

April 15. The carrier *Hancock* (CV 19) is commissioned.

April 16. The battleship *Wisconsin* (BB 64) is commissioned.

April 19. Planes from the carriers *Saratoga* (CV 3) and HMS *Illustrious* of an Allied task force commanded by Admiral Sir James Somerville, RN, strike Japanese installations at Sabang in the Netherlands East Indies.

April 20. The destroyer *Lansdale* (DD 426), Lieutenant Commander D. M. Swift, is sunk with the loss of 49 lives by German aircraft in the eastern Mediterranean.

April 22. **Hollandia.** Rear Admiral Daniel E. Barbey's Seventh Amphibious Group lands two divisions of the I Army Corps, Lieutenant General Robert L. Eichelberger, around Humboldt Bay, on the border of Netherlands New Guinea 300 miles behind the Japanese front line. American planners refer to the area as Hollandia, the name of a tiny village on an arm of Humboldt Bay. Landings are made near it, on Tanahmerah Bay and at Aitape. This is one of MacArthur's most brilliant operations, bypassing the Japanese Eighteenth Army at Wewak, 90 miles to the east, and trapping it between the Americans at Hollandia and Australian forces advancing up the coast. Japanese resistance in the area is soon overcome and Hollandia becomes a major air and naval base for the next stage of the New Guinea campaign. Vice Admiral Mitscher's Fifth Fleet carriers are briefly loaned to MacArthur to support these landings.

April 27. The submarine *Bluegill* (SS 242), Commander Eric L. Barr, Jr., sinks the Japanese light cruiser *Yubari* near the Caroline Islands.

April 28. Secretary of the Navy Knox dies in Washington, D.C.

April 29–May 1. The Fifth Fleet attacks Japanese positions in the Carolines. Aircraft from Admiral Mitscher's carriers strike the fleet base at Truk and the port facilities at Ponape, the latter of which is also shelled by a battleship force commanded by Rear Admiral Willis A. Lee, and a cruiser-destroyer force under Rear Admiral Jesse B. Oldendorf shells the airfield at Satawan.

May 8. The carrier *Ticonderoga* (CV 14) is commissioned.

May 17. Japanese shipping and port facilities at Surabaja, Java, are attacked by carrier planes from an Allied task force commanded by Admiral Sir James F. Somerville, RN.

May 17–18. On the coast of New Guinea the Seventh Amphibious Force, temporarily commanded by Rear Admiral W. M. Fechteler, lands the 163rd Regimental Combat Team at the village of Toem and the offshore island of Wakde, 120 miles west of Hollandia.

May 19. James V. Forrestal enters office as 48th secretary of the navy.

May 19–20. Marcus Island, northwest of Wake, is attacked by the planes of the carriers *Essex* (CV 9), *San Jacinto* (CVL 30), and *Wasp* (CV 18) of Rear Admiral A. E. Montgomery's Task Force 58.6. Wake itself is hit three days later.

May 19. **The England.** In the Bismarck Archipelago, the destroyer escort *England* (DE 635), Lieutenant Commander Walton B. Pendleton, begins a phenomenal string of successes in which she sinks six Japanese submarines in twelve days: the *I-16* on the 19th, the *RO-106* on the 22nd, the *RO-104* on the 23rd, the *RO-116* on the 24th, the *RO-108* on the 26th, and the *RO-105* on May 30. No other American warship ever approaches this record.

May 27. Admiral Fechteler's Seventh Amphibious Force lands the 41st Infantry Division, Major General H. H. Fuller, on Biak, a sizeable island off the northern coast of New Guinea 150 miles west of Wakde, where

the previous landing had been made only 10 days before. The island is garrisoned by 11,500 well-led Japanese army and navy troops who retain control of its airfield until June 22.

May 29. **Loss of the Block Island.** Northwest of the Canary Islands the escort carrier *Block Island* (CVE 21), Captain Francis M. Hughes, is torpedoed and sunk by the *U-549*. The submarine also hits the *Barr* (DE 576), one of the four destroyer escorts screening the carrier, but is in turn sunk by another of them, the *Eugene E. Elmore* (DE 686), Lieutenant Commander G. L. Conkey. The *Block Island* is the only American carrier lost in the Battle of the Atlantic.

June 1. The submarine *Herring* (SS 233), Lieutenant Commander David Zabriskie, Jr., is sunk while attacking Japanese shipping at Matsuwa Island in the Kuriles on her eighth war patrol.

June 4. **Capture of the U-505.** Captain Daniel V. Gallery captures a submarine when his hunter-killer group, consisting of the escort carrier *Guadalcanal* (CVE 60) and five destroyers, encounters the *U-505* homeward bound off the Atlantic coast of North Africa. Depth-charged to the surface and abandoned by her crew, the *U-505* is boarded and saved by a party Gallery had organized in anticipation of just such an occasion. The only U-boat captured by the U.S. Navy in World War II, today she is exhibited at the Chicago Museum of Science and Industry.

The *England*. Official U.S. Navy photograph.

June 6.   **D-Day (Operation Overlord/Neptune).** The most fateful landings of World War II are made at dawn when five Allied divisions—two American, two British, and one Canadian—storm ashore on the beaches of Normandy. A few hours earlier, two American divisions, one British airborne division, and a Polish airborne brigade had been dropped behind enemy lines to create confusion and seize strategic points. The Germans are taken by surprise. Although well aware that the long-awaited cross-Channel invasion was imminent, they had expected the blow to fall to the north, in the Pas de Calais. General Dwight D. Eisenhower is Supreme Commander, Allied Expeditionary Force. The naval aspects of the assault (Operation Neptune) are commanded by Admiral Sir Bertram H. Ramsay, RN. The movement to the American beaches (Utah and Omaha) is conducted by the Western Naval Force, Rear Admiral Alan G. Kirk; to the British beaches (Gold, Juno, and Sword) by the Eastern Naval Task, Admiral Sir Philip Vian, RN. The strength of these two forces, in terms of vessels that cross the Channel on their own bottoms, is 911 and 1,796 ships, respectively. Resistance is fiercest at Omaha Beach, where fire support from destroyers running close inshore is instrumental to the success of the landing. By the morning of June 7, some 66,000 Allied troops have crossed the beaches. With the success of the invasion of Normandy, the defeat of Germany is assured.

June 7.   **"Mulberries."** Two artificial harbors are created off the Normandy beaches by sinking concrete caissons. The Norman coast's lack of port facilities was one of the reasons the Germans had believed landings would be made in the Pas de Calais. Mulberry A, off Omaha Beach, is destroyed by a great storm that scours the Channel, June 18–22, but by then more than 250,000 Allied soldiers are ashore.

June 7.   The submarine *Gudgeon* (SS 211), Lieutenant Commander Robert A. Bonin, is reported overdue and presumed lost on her 12th Pacific war patrol.

June 8.   Off the Normandy beaches, the destroyer escort *Rich* (DE 695), Lieutenant Commander E. A. Michel, is sunk with the loss of 89 lives and the destroyers *Glennon* (DD 620) and *Meredith* (DD 726) are damaged by German mines.

June 8–9.   In the Southwest Pacific, a force consisting of the cruiser HMAS *Australia*, the light cruisers *Boise* (CL 47) and *Phoenix* (CL 46), and 14 destroyers under Rear Admiral V.A.C. Crutchley, VC, DSC, RN, breaks up a Japanese attempt to reinforce Biak by sea.

June 9.   The destroyer *Meredith* (DD 726), Com-

D-Day: LCIs head for the landing beaches in the protective presence of the cruiser *Augusta*. Official U.S. Navy photograph.

mander George Knuepfer, damaged by a mine off the coast of Normandy, is sunk by a U-boat.

June 10.   A German shore battery sinks the destroyer *Glennon* (DD 620), Commander C. A. Johnson, damaged by a mine two days earlier, off Normandy.

June 11.   The battleship *Missouri* (BB 63) is commissioned.

June 15.   **Saipan.** The navy's Central Pacific offensive takes a giant stride across more than 700 miles of open water to assault the Marianas (Operation Forager), which Admiral King has long regarded as the key to that theater. Saipan is the first island to be attacked. As in the Marshalls, Admiral Raymond A. Spruance commands the Fifth Fleet; Vice Admiral R. K. Turner, the Joint Expeditionary Force (Task Force 51); and Lieutenant General H.M. Smith, the Expeditionary Troops. The assault is made by the 2nd Marine Division, Major General T. E. Watson, and the 4th Marine Division, Major General Harry Schmidt. In reserve is Major General Ralph C. Smith's 27th Infantry Division, which is landed on the night of June 17–18. The island is defended by 29,662 Japanese army and navy troops under Lieutenant General Yoshitsugu Saito and Admiral Chuichi Nagumo, who had commanded the Japanese carriers that attacked Pearl Harbor; both commit hara-kiri at the end of the struggle. Resistance is stiff. Marine Lieutenant General Smith, dissatisfied with the performance of the 27th Division, provokes a bitter, interservice controversy by summarily relieving army Major General Smith of command. The fighting ends on July 12. U.S. casualties are 3,426 killed and 13,099 wounded, three-quarters of them marines. Only 1,780 Japanese surrender. Possession of Saipan places Japan within range of land-based B-29 bombers.

June 19–20.   **Battle of the Philippine Sea (Marianas Turkey Shoot).** The Japanese fleet comes out in strength for the first time since October 1942 in an attempt to break up the invasion of Saipan. Commanded by Vice Admiral Jisaburo Ozawa, it includes 5 fleet carriers, 4 light carriers, and 5 battleships, plus cruisers (13) and destroyers (28). Admiral Spruance's Fifth Fleet, con-

A Japanese bomber goes down in flames in the Marianas Turkey Shoot. Official U.S. Navy photograph.

sisting of 7 fleet carriers, 8 light carriers, and 7 battleships, plus cruisers (21) and destroyers (69), is clearly a superior force—most notably, perhaps, in aircraft, 956 to 473 of all types. Ozawa hopes to offset the odds by exploiting his planes' greater range to remain beyond the reach of the American carriers. He also believes that his attack will be supported by land-based air in the Marianas and that it will be possible for his fliers to shuttle-bomb the American fleet, landing to rearm on Saipan and hitting the invaders again on the way back to their carriers. Most of these calculations go wrong. Vice Admiral Marc A. Mitscher's carrier planes have destroyed Japanese air power in the Marianas and made the islands' runways unusable. Even the plan of remaining out of range of the American carriers might have misfired had Admiral Spruance steered towards the Ozawa's fleet on the evening of June 18, when its approach was known to him, but he chose to remain within close supporting range of the beachhead, fearing that the Japanese might attempt to slip around his fleet to attack the amphibious forces. This con-

Japanese ships, including the carrier *Zuikaku*, center, maneuvering under attack from American aircraft at the Battle of the Philippine Sea. Official U.S. Navy photograph.

servative decision is later criticized by members of the aviation community. The air battle with the largely inexperienced Japanese pilots on June 19 is so one-sided that Mitscher's men call it "The Marianas Turkey Shoot." A total of 346 Japanese planes are shot down, against only 30 American. Meanwhile, the submarine *Albacore* (SS 218), Commander James W. Blanchard, sinks the 33,000-ton Japanese carrier and fleet flagship *Taiho*, and the *Cavalla* (SS 244), Lieutenant Commander Herbert J. Kossler, sinks the Pearl Harbor carrier *Shokaku*. The next day Spruance pursues the retiring enemy fleet, and four torpedo bombers from the *Belleau Wood* (CVL 24) sink the carrier *Hiyo*. Another 65 of Ozawa's planes are destroyed in this action, reducing the strength of the Japanese carrier fleet to 35 aircraft. As the American pilots return to their carriers after nightfall, Admiral Mitscher orders his ships to turn on their lights to help them land.

June 19. **Navy ace.** Commander David Mc-

Commander David McCampbell in the cockpit of his F6F Hellcat. This picture was taken after the Battle of Leyte Gulf, when his score of enemy aircraft had reached 30. Official U.S. Navy photograph.

A medium tank supports the advance of marine riflemen on Tinian, in the Marianas. Defense Department photo (Marine Corps).

Campbell's personal score in the Marianas Turkey Shoot is seven enemy aircraft. Four months later, during the Battle of Leyte Gulf, he will shoot down nine Japanese planes on a single day. For these actions, he is awarded the Medal of Honor. At war's end he is the navy's leading ace, with 34 confirmed victories.

June 25. German positions at Cherbourg, France, are shelled by a heavy surface force under Rear Admiral Morton L. Deyo. The battleship *Texas* (BB 35) and four destroyers are damaged in action with the enemy's shore batteries.

June 26. The garrison of Cherbourg capitulates.

July 2. **Landing at Noemfoor Island.** The next-to-last leap in MacArthur's advance along the coast of New Guinea is made to Noemfoor, an island approximately 50 miles west of Biak. The island's three Japanese-built airfields will be useful in supporting the invasion of the Vogelkop Peninsula on the western end of New Guinea. Rear Admiral W. M. Fechteler's Naval Attack Force conducts the landing of the 168th Infantry (reinforced), which secures the island at a cost of 409 casualties.

July 4. Aircraft and ships of the Fifth Fleet bombard Japanese installations on Chichi Jima, Haha Jima, and Iwo Jima in the Bonin Islands.

July 19. The Japanese light cruiser *Oi* is sunk by the submarine *Flasher* (SS 249), Commander Reuben T. Whitaker, in the South China Sea.

July 21. **Guam (Operation Stevedore).** The second of the Marianas is captured when Rear Admiral Richard L. Connolly's Southern Attack Force (Task Force 58) lands the 3rd Marine Division, the 1st Provisional Marine Brigade and the 77th Infantry Division, on Guam. Major General Roy S. Geiger, USMC, is the landing force commander. The largest of the Marianas, Guam is defended by 19,000 Japanese army and navy troops under Lieutenant General Takeshi Takashima. The island is secured by August 10, although some 9,000 of the enemy remain at large in the interior, and sporadic fighting continues until the end of the war. American casualties are 1,435 killed or missing and 5,648 wounded, nearly all marines.

July 24. **Tinian.** The island of Tinian, in the Marianas only five miles southwest of Saipan, is invaded by the 2nd Marine Division, Major General T. E. Watson, and the 4th Marine Division, Major General Clifton B. Cates. Rear Admiral Harry W. Hill commands the attack force (Task Force 51); Major General Roy S. Geiger, the landing force. Defending the island are 9,162 Japanese army and navy troops under Vice Admiral Kakuji Kakuta and Colonel Kiyochi Ogata. They are overcome by August 1 in what Lieutenant General H. M. Smith calls the best-executed amphibious operation of the war. Neither Admiral Kakuta nor Colonel Ogata survive the struggle; no Japanese island commander will ever be taken alive. Marine casualties are 328 dead and 1,571 wounded.

July 25–28. Japanese positions at Ulithi, Yap, Ngulu, and the Palaus are hit by carrier planes from Vice Admiral Marc A. Mitscher's Task Force 58.

July 26. The submarine *Robalo* (SS 273), Lieutenant Commander Manning M. Kimmel, is lost, probably by striking a mine, off the Philippine island of Palawan.

July 26–29. **The Philippines or Formosa?** President Roosevelt meets with General MacArthur and Admiral Nimitz at Honolulu to discuss the next steps in the war against Japan. Nimitz presents Admiral King's view that the Central Pacific drive should continue to Formosa, but both he and the president are convinced by

The Honolulu conference; from left to right, General Douglas MacArthur, President Franklin D. Roosevelt, Admiral Chester W. Nimitz, Admiral William D. Leahy. Courtesy National Archives.

MacArthur's argument that moral as well as military grounds dictate the United States must proceed at the earliest possible moment to liberate the Philippines, with successive landings on Mindanao, Leyte, and Luzon. The joint chiefs of staff take longer to make up their minds. The invasion of Mindanao and Leyte is not authorized until September, and the question of whether to go on to Luzon or Formosa remains unsettled even then.

July 28. The submarine *Golet* (SS 361), Lieutenant James S. Clark, is reported overdue and presumed lost on her second Pacific war patrol. She was probably destroyed by Japanese surface forces on June 14.

July 30–31. **Triumph in New Guinea.** The New Guinea campaign comes to a victorious conclusion when the 6th Infantry Division, Major General Franklin C. Sibert, is landed unopposed by Rear Admiral W. M. Fechteler's Seventh Amphibious Force at two villages near Cape Sansapor on the northern coast of the Vogelkop Peninsula. In the 14 weeks since the landing at Hollandia, MacArthur's forces have advanced 550 miles.

August 2. In the North Atlantic, the destroyer escort *Fiske* (DE 143), Lieutenant John A. Comly, USNR, is sunk with the loss of 30 lives while attacking the *U-804.*

August 4–5. Fifth Fleet carrier forces commanded by Vice Admirals Marc A. Mitscher and J. S. McCain attack Japanese installa-

tions on Chichi Jima and Haha Jima in the Bonin Islands.

August 6. The carrier *Bennington* (CV 20) is commissioned.

August 7. The Japanese light cruiser *Nagara* is sunk by the submarine *Croaker* (SS 246), Commander John E. Lee, off the Japanese Home Island of Kyushu.

August 13. The submarine *Flier* (SS 250), Commander John D. Crowley, is lost while running on the surface of the Balabac Strait, off British North Borneo. She probably hit a mine. Eight of her crewmen survive.

August 15. **Invasion of Southern France (Operation Dragoon).** Vice Admiral H. Kent Hewitt's Western Naval Task Force lands three American divisions between St.-Tropez and Cannes on the Mediterranean coast of France. Two French divisions follow. The beaches, lightly defended in the first place, are subjected to an intensive, daylight naval bombardment, and German resistance is weak. This landing originally had been planned to coincide with the invasion of Normandy, but had to be postponed because of a shortage of landing craft. General Eisenhower decided that it should still be made in order to gain the use of the port of Marseille for the campaign in France. Prime Minister Churchill argued unsuccessfully in favor of switching the site of the invasion to Trieste, at the head of the Adriatic, in hopes that an army landed there could beat the Russians into the Balkans.

August 24. **Loss of the Harder.** The submarine *Harder* (SS 257), Commander Samuel D. Dealey, is depth-charged and destroyed by a Japanese minesweeper off Luzon. One of the most aggressive sub commanders, in his five previous patrols Dealey had sunk 16 Japanese ships, including 4 destroyers and 2 frigates. He is posthumously awarded the Medal of Honor.

August 31–September 2. Ships and aircraft of Rear Admiral R. E. Davison's Task Group 38.4 bombard Japanese positions on Iwo Jima in the Bonin Islands.

September 6. Vice Admiral Marc A. Mitscher's Task Force 38, compri , 12 attack carriers, 1 light carrier, 6 ba leships, 3 heavy cruisers, and numerous light cruisers and

At Nisida, Italy, LSTs sheltered by barrage balloons load equipment for the invasion of southern France. Official U.S. Navy photograph.

destroyers, bombs and shells Japanese positions in the Palaus and the Carolines.

September 9–10.   The planes of Task Force 38 attack Japanese airfields on the southern Philippine island of Mindanao.

September 10–16.   Task Force 38 strikes Japanese positions in the Palau Islands, the Visayas, and Mindanao in preparation for and support of the landing on Peleliu, which is made on September 15.

September 11–16.   **Second Quebec Conference (Octagon).** President Roosevelt, Prime Minister Churchill, and the combined chiefs of staff meet. Held at Churchill's request, the conference deals primarily with the question of British participation in the war in the Pacific. The prime minister is anxious for the Royal Navy to play a role in the closing operations against Japan. Admiral King is adamantly opposed to the appearance of the British fleet in the Central Pacific, but President Roosevelt, more sensitive to diplomatic considerations, overrules him. The combined chiefs of staff also approve a recommendation initiated by Admiral Halsey and endorsed by Admiral Nimitz and General MacArthur to advance the date of the invasion of Leyte in the Philippines from December 20 to October 20 and to cancel the previously planned, intermediate landings in the Talaud Islands and on Mindanao. The question of whether to go on from Leyte to Luzon or Formosa remains unresolved.

September 13. The destroyer minesweeper *Perry* (DMS 17) strikes a mine and sinks off the Palau Islands.

September 15. **Landing on Morotai.** The Seventh Amphibious Force, back under the command of Rear Admiral Daniel E. Barbey, lands the 41st Infantry Division (reinforced) on the almost unoccupied island of Morotai, roughly midway between New Guinea and the Philippines. An airfield will be established there to support the invasion of Leyte.

September 15. **Peleliu (Operation Stalemate II).** From the Marianas the Central Pacific drive leaps 600 miles to the southwest to land in the Palaus. Peleliu, an island of 12 square miles, is defended by 10,700 Japanese troops under the tactical command of Colonel Kunio Nakagawa. The invasion is conducted by Vice Admiral T. S. Wilkinson's Third Amphibious Force and Major General Roy S. Geiger's III Amphibious Corps, composed of the 1st Marine Division, Major General W. H. Rupertus, and the 81st Infantry Division, Major General P. J. Mueller, which is left in reserve aboard ship. Japanese resistance, strong from the start, becomes even more deadly when the marines reach the complex of caves and tunnels along Umurbrogol Ridge. The First Marine Regiment is withdrawn after a week, having sustained 56 percent casualties, and the 81st Infantry Division relieves the marine division on October 20. Fighting finally ends on November 25. American casualties are 1,460 killed and 7,711 wounded.

September 15. The carrier *Shangri La* (CV 38) is commissioned.

September 16. The 20,000-ton, Japanese escort carrier *Unyo* is sunk by the submarine *Barb* (SS 220), Commander Eugene B. Fluckey, in the South China Sea. Another torpedo in the same salvo destroys the 11,000-ton tanker *Azusa*.

September 17–September 20. **Seizure of Angaur.** Amphibious forces (Task Group 32.2) commanded by Rear Admiral W.H.P. ("Spike") Blandy land the 81st Infantry Division on the southernmost of the Palau Islands. Although organized resistance is declared to have ended on September 20, fighting continues in the interior of the island until October 23. In the meanwhile, army engineers have constructed an airfield to support the invasion of the Philippines.

September 21–22. Aircraft from the three carrier task groups of Vice Admiral Marc A. Mitscher's Task Force 38 deliver devastating attacks on Japanese airfields and shipping at Luzon, in the Philippines.

September 23. **Ulithi.** The undefended atoll of Ulithi, halfway between and somewhat north of the Carolines and the Palaus, is occupied by a regiment of the 81st Infantry Division, landed by Rear Admiral W.H.P. Blandy's Task Group 32.2. This atoll replaces Eniwetok as the principal advanced base of the Pacific Fleet.

September 24. Vice Admiral Mitscher's Task Force 38 switches its attention to Japanese positions on the Visayan islands in the central Philippines.

September 29. In a meeting in San Francisco, Admirals Nimitz and Forrest P. Sherman finally persuade Admiral King that his plan of invading Formosa is impractical. The army cannot supply enough men. The next three objectives in the war against Japan will be Luzon, Iwo Jima, and Okinawa.

October 3. The destroyer escort *Shelton* (DE 407), Lieutenant Commander L. G. Salomon, USNR, is torpedoed and sunk by a Japanese submarine north of Morotai, Netherlands East Indies. The destroyer escort *Richard M. Rowell* (DE 403) and carrier aircraft then attack and destroy the American submarine *Seawolf* (SS 197), Commander Albert M. Bontier, under the impression that she is Japanese.

October 3. The joint chiefs of staff authorize General MacArthur to move on to Luzon and direct Admiral Nimitz to prepare to invade Iwo Jima and Okinawa.

October 9. The carrier *Randolph* (CV 15) is commissioned.

October 10–15. Aircraft of Vice Admiral Marc A. Mitscher's Task Force 38 deliver a series of heavy attacks against Japanese positions on Okinawa, the Ryukyus, Formosa, the Pescadores, and Luzon.

October 17. The submarine *Escolar* (SS 294), Commander W. J. Millican, is lost some-

Alligator amtracs churn towards Peleliu on D-Day while, at far right, an LSM(R)—Landing Ship Medium, Rockets—lays down a covering barrage. Official U.S. Navy photograph.

time after communicating with the submarine *Perch* (SS 313) on this date. She probably hit a mine.

October 17.   A task force commanded by Rear Admiral Arthur D. Struble lands the 6th Ranger Battalion to destroy small Japanese posts on Suluan and Dinagat islands in the mouth of Leyte Gulf. It was feared that these installations might give warning of the invasion, which is just what happens.

October 17.   **Operation SHO-1.** Informed by the unit on Suluan Island of the appearance of American ships in Leyte Gulf, Admiral Soemu Toyoda, commander-in-chief of the Japanese Combined Fleet, activates Plan SHO-1 for the defense of the Philippines. SHO is the Japanese word for victory.

October 17–18.   Third Fleet carrier planes pound Japanese positions on Luzon.

October 19.   Battleships and cruisers of the fire support units of Vice Admiral Thomas C. Kinkaid's Seventh Fleet shell the landing beaches on Leyte Gulf.

October 20.   **Invasion of the Philippines.**

MacArthur's promise to return to the Philippines is made good and the pincers of the dual advance in the Pacific close on the east coast of the island of Leyte. Shielded by the fast carriers and battleships of Admiral Halsey's Third Fleet, the Seventh Fleet ("MacArthur's Navy") lands four divisions of Lieutenant General Walter P. Krueger's Sixth Army on the shores of Leyte Gulf.

October 23.   Off Palawan, the submarines *Dace* (SS 247), Commander Bladen D. Claggett, and *Darter* (SS 227), Commander David H. McClintock, encounter the Japanese First Striking Force, the most powerful of the enemy fleet units coverging on the Philippines. The *Dace* sinks the heavy cruiser *Maya. Darter* sinks the heavy cruiser *Atago,* flagship of the force commander, Vice Admiral Takeo Kurita, and seriously damages the heavy cruiser *Takao,* which returns to port.

October 24.   The submarine *Darter* (SS 227), Commander David H. McClintock, is

Ships of the American armada assembled at Seeadler Harbor off Manus Island in the Admiralties prior to the invasion of the Philippines. Official U.S. Navy photograph.

scuttled after running ashore on Bombay Reef off Palawan. The *Dace* (SS 247) rescues her crew.

October 24.   **Loss of the Tang.** The submarine *Tang* (SS 306), Commander Richard H. O'Kane, is lost off the coast of Formosa when one of her own torpedoes circles back to sink her. The top-scoring American submariner of the war in terms of ships sunk (31 credited during the conflict, 24 according to a postwar survey), O'Kane survives to receive the Medal of Honor.

October 24.   The submarine *Shark* (SS 314), Commander Edward N. Blakely, is lost in the Philippines sometime after communicating with the submarine *Seadragon* (SS 194) on this date.

October 24.   **Beginning of the Battle of Leyte Gulf: Battle of the Sibuyan Sea.** In ac-

cordance with Plan SHO-1, the Imperial Japanese Navy stakes everything on the "decisive battle" to which its doctrine is devoted. There is really little choice in the matter. The loss of the Philippines would cut Japan off from her Southern Resources Area in Southeast Asia, without which her already crippled war economy will collapse. The Japanese hope to annihilate the American amphibious force, Admiral Kinkaid's Seventh Fleet, and thereby repel the invasion of Leyte. To do so, however, they must first destroy or decoy Admiral Halsey's Third Fleet. Realizing that their lack of carrier pilots makes the former impossible, they have decided to use their carriers as bait to accomplish the latter. A "Northern Force" (as the Americans name it) of four carriers, two hybrid battleship-car-

The Battle of the Sibuyan Sea: One of the two Japanese *Yamato*-class super-battleships of Admiral Kurita's Center Force under heavy attack from the planes of Task Force 38. Official U.S. Navy photograph.

riers, three light cruisers, and eight destroyers under Vice Admiral Jisaburo Ozawa is to advertise its presence off the northern coast of Luzon, luring Halsey away from the beachhead. Simultaneously, two powerful surface forces will converge on Leyte Gulf from the west—Vice Admiral Takeo Kurita's "Center Force" of the super-battleships *Musashi* and *Yamato*, battleships *Kongo*, *Haruna*, and *Nagato*, twelve cruisers, and fifteen destroyers via the San Bernardino Strait; and a "Southern Force" in two echelons of two battleships, four cruisers, and eleven destroyers under Vice Admirals Shoji Nishimura and Kiyohide Shima, via the Surigao Strait. The result of this strategy is four interlocking actions jointly comprising the largest naval battle ever fought. It begins around noon on this date, when planes from the Third Fleet attack Kurita's Center Force on its passage through the Sibuyan Sea, sinking the superbattleship *Musashi* and the destroyer *Wakabe* and disabling the cruiser *Myoko*.

October 24–25. **Battle of Surigao Strait.** After dark, Admiral Nishimura's Southern Force fights its way through the Surigao Strait under attack from 39 PT boats and the five destroyers of Captain Jesse G. Coward's Desron 54. The latter sink the battleship *Fuso* and the destroyers *Michishio* and *Yamagumo* and disable two other destroyers. Pressing on with the damaged battleship *Yamashiro*, heavy cruiser *Mogami*, and destroyer *Shigure*, Nishimura nears the eastern end of the strait to encounter a battle line composed of the six old battleships of the Seventh Fleet's fire support force—the *California* (BB 44), *Maryland* (BB 46), *Mississippi* (BB 41), *Pennsylvania* (BB 38), *Tennessee* (BB 43), and *West Virginia* (BB 48), under Rear Admiral Jesse B. Oldendorf. The *Yamashiro* is sunk and the *Mogami* seriously damaged. She and the *Shigure* withdraw. Vice Admiral Shima's echelon, two heavy cruisers, one light cruiser, and seven destroyers, enters the strait around this time, sizes up the situation and retires. Two of

The Battle off Samar: Japanese shells straddle the doomed escort carrier *Gambier Bay*. This official U.S. Navy photograph was taken from the *Kitkun Bay*, another of the escort carriers in Taffy 3.

Nishimura's cripples, the *Mogami* and destroyer *Asagumo*, are sunk after daybreak. Only one American ship, the destroyer *Albert W. Grant* (DD 649), is seriously damaged.

October 24. Land-based Japanese planes sink the carrier *Princeton* (CVL 23), Captain W. H. Buracker, off Luzon.

October 25. **Battle off Samar.** On the afternoon of the 24th (much later than the Japanese had hoped), Halsey's planes spot the Japanese Northern Force off Luzon. Accepting his pilots' exaggerated reports of the damage inflicted on the Center Force in the Battle of the Sibuyan Sea, Halsey takes the entire Third Fleet north after Ozawa's carriers. Because of a misunderstanding in communications, Admiral Kinkaid assumes that Halsey has left a force to guard San Bernardino Strait and does not try to cover it with the Seventh Fleet. Thus it is that at dawn Admiral Kurita's Center Force steams peacefully through the strait and opens fire on the six little escort carriers of Rear Admiral Clifton F. ("Ziggy") Sprague's "Taffy 3" off the island of Samar. Sprague launches his planes, makes smoke, and retires at his best speed, a paltry 18 knots, calling for help. Unfortunately, the only units near are other "taffies." As the Center Force gains on his carriers, Sprague sends his three destroyers and four destroyer escorts to deliver torpedo attacks against the enemy battleships, a death-ride in which the destroyers *Hoel* (DD 533), Commander L. S. Kintberger, and *Johnston* (DD 557), Commander E. E. Evans, and the destroyer escort *Samuel B. Roberts* (DE 413), Lieutenant Commander R. W. Copeland, USNR, are sunk. The damage is not all on the American side, however. The heavy cruisers *Chikuma*, *Chokai*, and *Suzuya* take bomb and torpedo hits to which they will succumb before noon; but Kurita keeps coming. The *Gambier Bay* (CVE 73), Captain W. V. R.

Vieweg, is the first of the carriers to be sunk by gunfire. Then, incredibly, Center Force reverses course. Admiral Kurita has mistaken the escort carriers for fleet carriers and, rattled by the attacks of the taffies' aircraft and destroyers, decides to break off the action. He may also be disoriented by the events of the last two days, during which he has lost two flagships. Shortly after noon, Center Force retires through San Bernardino Strait.

October 25. **Battle off Cape Engaño.** The planes of Admiral Halsey's Third Fleet have already begun attacking Ozawa's Northern Force when a message from Admiral Nimitz regarding the situation at San Bernardino Strait prompts Halsey to turn back south with his fast battleships. He leaves most of Mitscher's carriers with a cruiser-destroyer screen to pursue the Japanese. All four enemy carriers—the *Chitose*, *Chiyoda*, *Zuiho*, and *Zuikaku*—and the destroyer *Akizuki* are sunk in the course of the day. The cruiser-destroyer force overtakes and sinks the destroyer *Hatsuzuki*, and Commander Joseph B. Icenhower's submarine *Jallao* (SS 368) sinks the light cruiser *Tama*. This action concludes the Battle of Leyte Gulf, in which (including the approach and mopping up) the Imperial Japanese Navy loses four carriers, three battleships, eight cruisers, and eight destroyers and ceases to exist as an effective fighting force.

October 26. **First kamikaze attacks.** Japanese pilots in the Philippines fly the first deliberate suicide missions of the war. The escort carrier *St. Lo* (CVE 63), Captain F. J. McKenna, is crashed by a kamikaze in Leyte Gulf and so badly damaged that she must be sunk. Four other escort carriers are also hit. The kamikaze plane will prove to be the most effective anti-ship weapon of World War II.

October 26. Two destroyers of the Japanese Center Force retiring from the Battle of Leyte Gulf are sunk, the *Hayashimo* by air attack and the *Nowaki* in a separate, surface action.

October 26. Planes from Rear Admiral Thomas L. Sprague's Taffy 2 catch a Japanese force retiring through the Visayan Sea after landing reinforcements on Leyte and sink the light cruiser *Kinu* and the destroyer *Uranami*.

October 26–November 5. **Kamikaze attacks.** During this period off Leyte, Japanese suicide planes damage the carriers *Belleau Wood* (CVL 24), *Franklin* (CV 13), *Intrepid* (CV 11), and *Lexington* (CV 16), escort carrier *Suwanee* (CVE 27), light cruiser *Denver* (CL 58), and several destroyers and sink the destroyer *Abner Read* (DD 526), Commander A. M. Purdy. The destroyer escort *Eversole* (DE 404), Lieutenant Commander George E. *Marix*, is sunk by a Japanese submarine on October 28.

October 27. The Japanese light cruiser *Abukuma*, the only unit of Admiral Shima's force to be damaged in the Battle of Surigao Strait, is sunk by air attack off Negros Island.

November 5–6. Carrier aircraft from Vice Admiral J. S. McCain's Task Group 38.1 conduct heavy strikes against Japanese positions on Luzon and sink the heavy cruiser *Nachi* in Manila Bay.

November 7. The submarine *Albacore* (SS 218), Lieutenant Commander Hugh R. Rimmer, strikes a mine and is lost with all hands off the Japanese Home Island of Hokkaido.

November 8. The submarine *Growler* (SS 215), Commander Thomas B. Oakley, Jr., is destroyed while attacking a Japanese convoy on her 11th war patrol.

November 11. Third Fleet aircraft sink the Japanese destroyers *Hamanami*, *Naganami*, *Shimakaze*, and *Wakatsuki* off Ormoc Bay, Leyte.

November 13. The Japanese light cruiser *Kiso* and destroyers *Akebono*, *Akishimo*, *Hatsuharu*, and *Okinami* are sunk by Third Fleet air strikes in Manila Bay.

November 17. The 21,000-ton Japanese escort carrier *Shinyo* is sunk by the submarine *Spadefish* (SS 411), Commander Gordon Underwood, in the Yellow Sea.

November 21. **The Kongo.** Northwest of Formosa, the submarine *Sealion* (SS 315), Commander Eli T. Reich, sinks the Japanese battleship *Kongo* and destroyer *Urakaze*. The *Kongo* is the first enemy battleship to fall victim to an American submarine.

November 24. U.S. Army Air Force B-29 bombers make their first attack on Tokyo from the newly won airfields in the Marianas.

November 25.   The Japanese heavy cruiser *Kumano* and cruiser *Yashojima* are sunk during Third Fleet air strikes on Luzon.

November 26.   The carrier *Bon Homme Richard* (CV 31) is commissioned.

November 29.   **The Shinano.** The 59,000-ton Japanese carrier *Shinano* is sunk off Tokyo Bay on her maiden voyage by the submarine *Archerfish* (SS 311), Commander Joseph F. Enright. The largest carrier in the world, she had been laid down as a sistership to the superbattleships *Musashi* and *Yamato*. This single sinking makes the *Archerfish*'s patrol the most successful of the war in terms of tonnage destroyed.

December 2–3.   **Action in Ormoc Bay.** After nightfall three destroyers—the *Allen M. Sumner* (DD 692), *Cooper* (DD 695), and *Moale* (DD 693)—are sent to attack a Japanese convoy reported to be landing reinforcements at Ormoc Bay on Leyte. Despite heavy attacks by land-based enemy aircraft, they sink the destroyer *Kuwa* and several small transports. The *Cooper*, Commander M. A. Peterson, is torpedoed and sinks with the loss of 191 lives.

December 7.   The conquest of Leyte continues when Rear Admiral Arthur D. Struble's Task Group 78.3 lands two regiments of the 77th Infantry Division at Ormoc Bay. Enemy resistance ashore is light, but persistent kamikaze attacks damage the destroyer *Mahan* (DD 364), Commander E. G. Campbell, so badly that she has to be sunk. Several other vessels are also hit.

December 11.   The destroyer *Reid* (DD 369), Commander S. A. McCornock, is sunk by Japanese suicide planes off the Ormoc beachhead.

December 15.   **Fleet Admiral.** This new, five-star rank, created a day earlier, is conferred upon Admirals William D. Leahy, chairman of the joint chiefs of staff; Ernest J. King, chief of naval operations; and Chester W. Nimitz, commander of the Pacific Fleet. The Third Fleet's commander, William F. Halsey, is promoted to the rank after the war.

December 15.   **Landing on Mindoro.** Rear Admiral Arthur D. Struble's Visayan Attack Force lands a reinforced army division on the central Philippine island of Mindoro. The operation is unopposed except by kamikazes, which damage several ships.

December 18.   **Philippine typhoon.** Off the east coast of the Philippines, Admiral Halsey's Fifth Fleet is caught in a terrific storm. Three destroyers capsize—the *Hull* (DD 350), Lieutenant Commander J. A. Marks, *Monaghan* (DD 354), Lieutenant Commander F. B. Garrett, Jr., and *Spence* (DD 512), Lieutenant Commander J. P. Andrea—and numerous vessels, including eight small carriers, are damaged; 765 men drown. A court of inquiry finds Halsey principally responsible for failing to get out of the path of the typhoon.

December 19.   Commander Louis D. ("Sandy") McGregor's submarine *Redfish* (SS 395) sinks the Japanese escort carrier *Unryu* in the East China Sea.

December 21.   The submarine *Scamp* (SS 277), Commander John C. Hollingsworth, is reported overdue and presumed lost. She was probably sunk by a Japanese coast defense vessel south of Tokyo Bay on November 11.

1945

January 2–6.   **Advance to Lingayen Gulf.** Task Group 77.2, the support force for the invasion of Luzon, sails from Leyte Gulf to the landing site on Lingayen Gulf under the command of Vice Admiral Jesse B. Oldendorf. It consists of the battleships *California* (BB 44) (flag), *Colorado* (BB 45), *Mississippi* (BB 41), *New Mexico* (BB 40), *Pennsylvania* (BB 38), and *West Virginia* (BB 48), 12 escort carriers, 6 cruisers, 33 destroyers, and assorted other vessels. The movement is opposed by land-based Japanese kamikaze planes, which fatally damage the escort carrier *Ommaney Bay* (CVE 79), sink the destroyer *Hovey* (DD 208), and inflict varying degrees of damage on 23 other vessels. Rear Admiral Theodore E. Chandler, commanding Cruiser Division 4, is mortally wounded by a kamikaze crash on the *Louisville* (CA 28), and Lieutenant General Herbert Lumsden, the British liaison officer at General MacArthur's headquarters, is killed by a hit on the battleship *New Mexico* (BB 40).

January 2–9.   Admiral Thomas C. Kinkaid's Seventh Fleet attack force (TF 77) follows the same course taken by Admiral Oldendorf's task group to Lingayen Gulf. The kamikazes' concentration on the latter gives the attack force a relatively easy passage, although the escort carriers *Kadashan Bay* (CVE 76) and *Kitkun Bay* (CVE 71) are disabled by suicide planes.

January 3–9. In support of the Luzon landings, Task Force 38 of Admiral W. F. Halsey's Third Fleet delivers a series of carrier air strikes on Japanese airfields and other installations on Formosa (January 3–4 and 9) and Luzon (January 6–7). Despite consistently bad weather, more than 3,000 sorties are flown, and large numbers of enemy aircraft are destroyed, mostly on the ground.

January 5. Cruiser Division 5, Rear Admiral Allan E. ("Hoke") Smith, shells Japanese positions on Iwo Jima, Chichi Jima, and Haha Jima in the Bonin Islands, while far to the north, a similar force under Rear Admiral J. L. McCrea bombards Paramushiro in the Kuriles.

January 7–8. Vice Admiral Oldendorf's Bombardment and Fire Support Group (Task Group 77.2) delivers an intensive shore bombardment of the landing beaches on Lingayen Gulf. The destroyer minesweeper *Palmer* (DMS 5) is sunk by a conventional Japanese air attack, and the cruiser HMAS *Australia* is damaged by kamikazes.

January 9. **Invasion of Luzon.** The Seventh Fleet, Vice Admiral Thomas C. Kinkaid, lands four divisions of Lieutenant General Walter Krueger's Sixth Army at Lingayen Gulf. The beaches are lightly defended, Japanese General Tomoyuki Yamashita having withdrawn most of the island's 250,000 defenders to the mountainous interior, and 68,000 American troops are safely ashore by nightfall.

January 10–20. **Action in the South China Sea.** Following operations covering the invasion of Luzon, Admiral Halsey is authorized to penetrate the South China Sea, an operation he has long advocated. The Third Fleet's attacks commence with a spectacularly successful strike on the coast of Indochina, where approximately 132,700 tons of enemy shipping—29 merchantmen and 15 small naval vessels—are destroyed on January 12. Formosa, the Pescadores, Hong Kong, Hainan, and Canton are attacked on January 15–16.

January 12. The submarine *Swordfish* (SS 193), Commander Keats E. Montross, is lost sometime after exchanging signals with the *Kete* (SS 369) early this morning. She had been sent to conduct a photographic reconnaissance of Okinawa.

January 21–22. Carrier aircraft of the Third Fleet's Task Force 38, Vice Admiral John S. McCain, attack Formosa and Okinawa. The carrier *Ticonderoga* (CV 14) is badly damaged by a kamikaze, and the *Hancock* (CV 19) is hit by a torpedo plane during these raids.

U.S. troops landing ar Lingayen Gulf on the island of Luzon, January 9, 1945. Official U.S. Coast Guard photo.

January 25.   Japanese positions on Iwo Jima, one of the Bonin/Volcano Islands, are bombarded by surface forces, including the battleship *Indiana* (BB 58), under the command of Rear Admiral Oscar C. Badger.

January 26.   Admiral Raymond A. Spruance relieves Admiral William F. Halsey in command of the Third Fleet, which is redesignated the Fifth Fleet.

January 27.   The 1st Cavalry Division and the 32nd Infantry Division are landed at Lingayen Gulf to reinforce General Krueger's Sixth Army.

January 28.   The carrier *Antietam* (CV 36) is commissioned.

January 29.   The cargo ship *Serpens* (AK 97) blows up while being loaded with depth charges at Guadalcanal in the Solomons. Of 255 men aboard, all but 2 are killed.

January 29.   The Seventh Fleet's Amphibious Group 9, Rear Admiral Arthur D. Struble, lands Major General C. P. Hall's XI Army Corps—30,000 men—near San Antonio, at the neck of the Bataan Peninsula on Luzon. No opposition is encountered.

January 31.   The 11th Airborne Division, Major General J. M. Swing, is landed at Nasugbu, just south of the entrance of Manila Bay, by Rear Admiral William M. Fechteler's Amphibious Group 8.

February 1.   Prodded by General MacArthur, the XIV Army Corps, Major General Oscar W. Griswold, launches a strong attack towards Manila.

February 3.   **Liberation of Manila.** Supported by marine corps aviation, elements of the 1st Cavalry Division fight their way into Manila, liberating the 3,700 half-starved American POWs at the Santo Tomás camp. The capital's garrison, 18,000 mostly naval personnel under Rear Admiral Sanji Iwabachi, withdraw into the Old City, where more than 90 percent of them will die fighting. The last pockets of resistance are eliminated on March 4.

February 4–11.   **Yalta Conference.** The Big Three—Roosevelt, Churchill, and Stalin—meet in the Crimea to make plans for the postwar world. Upon Roosevelt's urging, Stalin agrees to enter the war against Japan in exchange for the southern (Japanese) half of the Sakhalin Peninsula, the Kurile Islands, and other Far Eastern

concessions. He also promises to hold "free and unfettered" elections in Poland and the other Eastern European countries occupied by the Red Army—a promise his subsequent disregard of which will precipitate the Cold War—and to send delegates to the charter meeting of the United Nations in San Francisco.

February 9–12.   The submarine *Batfish* (SS 310), Commander John K. ("Jake") Fyfe, sets a record by sinking three Japanese submarines in four days: the *RO-115* on the 9th, *RO-112* on the 11th, and *RO-113* on the 12th.

February 13.   Supported by the light cruisers of Rear Admiral R. S. ("Count") Berkey's Close Covering Group (Task Group 77.3), minesweepers begin to clear Manila Bay.

February 15.   Rear Admiral Arthur D. Struble's Amphibious Group 9 lands the 151st Regimental Combat Team, Major General W. C. Chase, at Mariveles, on the tip of the Bataan Peninsula. This unit pushes north against light opposition to link up with army forces advancing to the south. The peninsula is secured on February 21.

February 16.   The submarine *Barbel* (SS 316), Lieutenant Commander Conde L. Raguet, is reported overdue and presumed lost. She was probably sunk by a Japanese plane while on patrol in the Philippines on February 4.

February 16–27.   **Recapture of Corregidor.** A combined airborne and amphibious assault overcomes the 5,200 Japanese garrisoning "The Rock" in Manila Bay. Only 200 of the defenders are made prisoner. American casualties are 225 killed and 405 wounded.

February 16.   The pre-invasion bombardment of Iwo Jima is begun by the Fifth Fleet battleships and escort carriers under the command of Rear Admiral William H. P. ("Spike") Blandy.

February 16–March 1.   **Mitscher's raids.** Carrier aircraft of Vice Admiral Marc A. Mitscher's Task Force 58 strike Japanese installations around Tokyo (February 16–17), at Iwo Jima (February 19–23), Tokyo again (February 25), and in the Ryukyu Islands (March 1). An estimated 300,000 tons of enemy merchant shipping and 648 aircraft are destroyed. Mitscher's armada includes 11 fleet carriers—the *Bennington* (CV 20), *Bunker Hill* (CV 17), *Enterprise*

Before Iwo Jima: Lieutenant General Holland M. Smith, USMC, delivers a briefing attended by (front row, left to right) Rear Admiral Louis E. Denfeld, Vice Admiral Richmond Kelly Turner, Secretary of the Navy James V. Forrestal, and Rear Admiral Harry W. Hill. U.S. Naval Institute Collection.

(CV 6), *Essex* (CV 9), *Hancock* (CV 19), *Hornet* (CV 12), *Lexington* (CV 16), *Randolph* (CV 15), *Saratoga* (CV 3), *Wasp* (CV 18), and *Yorktown* (CV 10)—4 escort carriers, 8 battleships, 18 cruisers, and 75 destroyers.

February 19. **Iwo Jima (Operation Detachment).** The eight-square-mile volcanic island of Iwo Jima, approximately 660 miles south of Tokyo, is to be captured for use as a forward airfield to support the bomber offensive against Japan. It is defended by 21,000 Japanese troops ably commanded by Lieutenant General Tadamichi Kuribayashi. Although the beaches are strongly fortified, Kuribayashi has concentrated most of his forces in an intricate complex of static positions, containing more than 730 separate strongpoints, around Mount Suribachi on the narrow southern tip of the island and the high ground on the northern end. The assault is made by the V Amphibious Corps, Major General Harry Schmidt, USMC, from Task Force 53, Rear Admiral Harry W. Hill, under the overall command of Vice Admiral Richmond Kelly Turner, Commander, Joint Expeditionary Force (Task Force 51), and Lieutenant General Holland M. Smith, USMC, Commander Expeditionary Troops (Task Force 56). On this date the 4th and 5th Marine Divisions, Major Generals Clifton B. Cates and Keller E. Rockey, respectively, land on the east coast of the island. Despite 74 consecutive days of bombing by the Seventh Air Force from the Mariannas and 3 days of the heaviest naval bombardment of the Pacific War, the majority of the is-

Marines advance across the black sands of Iwo Jima, with Mount Suribachi looming in the background, February 19, 1945. Defense Department photo (Marine Corps).

land's dug-in defenses remain effectively intact. More than 2,300 marines are killed or wounded the first day. The corps is in for one of the hardest fights in its history.

February 21.   At twilight the escort carrier *Bismarck Sea* (CVE 95), Captain J. L. Pratt, is hit by a kamikaze plane off Iwo Jima. She sinks three hours later with the loss of 218 of her 943 officers and men.

February 23.   On Iwo Jima, men of the 2nd Battalion, Twenty-eighth Marines, raise the American flag over Mount Suribachi. Secretary of the Navy James V. Forrestal, who is present on the beach, assures Lieutenant General Holland M. Smith, "The raising of that flag means a Marine Corps for the next 500 years."

February 24.   The 3rd Marine Division, Major General Graves B. Erskine, enters the battle for Iwo Jima. One of its regiments had landed three days earlier.

February 28.   **Capture of Palawan.** Rear Admiral William M. Fechteler's Amphibious Group 8 lands the 186th Regimental Combat Team, Brigadier General Harold H.

Haney, at Puerto Princessa on the Philippine island of Palawan. The island is secured on April 22.

March 2.   Okino Daito (also called Borodino Island) in the Ryukyus is bombarded by a cruiser-destroyer force under Rear Admiral F. E. M. Whiting from Task Group 58.

March 10.   In the Philippines the 41st Division, Major General Jens Doe, is landed at Zamboanga, on the southwestern spur of the island of Mindanao, by Rear Admiral Forrest B. Royal's Amphibious Group 6. Organized resistance by the area's 8,300 defenders ends on March 24.

March 11.   **Crossing the Rhine.** In anticipation that the Germans will destroy the bridges over the Rhine and that the army's own assault boats may be unable to master the river's 8-knot current, four navy boat units have been organized under Commander William J. Whiteside to carry out the river crossings. Each of these units consists of 218 officers and men with 24 LCVPs (Landing Craft, Vehicle Personnel). A number of LCMs (Landing Craft, Mechanized) are later attached. Even though the bridge at Remagen is captured intact on March 7, the navy boats perform valuable service. Between March 11 and 27, Boat Unit 1 ferries 14,000 troops and 400 vehicles across the Rhine at Bad Neuenahr. Other crossings are made, often under heavy fire, at Boppard, Oberwesel, Oppenheim, and Mainz.

March 15.   **British Pacific Fleet.** The newly reconstituted British Pacific Fleet, under

The American flag floats over Mount Suribachi; in the right background, the landing beaches. Official U.S. Coast Guard photo.

LCMs ferrying tanks across the Rhine, March 24, 1945. Official U.S. Navy photograph.

the tactical command of Vice Admiral Sir H. Bernard Rawlings, RN, begins operations with the U.S. Pacific Fleet, into which it is incorporated as Task Force 113 (combat units) and Task Force 112 (service squadron). Its fighting ships include the battleships *King George V* and *Howe* and the carriers *Indefatigable*, *Indomitable*, *Illustrious*, and *Victorious*, which will serve with distinction off Okinawa and Japan in the closing months of the war.

March 18.   The 40th Infantry Division, Major General Rapp Brush, is landed on the island of Panay, in the Philippines, by Rear Admiral Arthur D. Struble's Task Group 78.3. The city of Ilo-Ilo is occupied the next day, and the island is secured on June 4.

March 18–21.   **Raids on the Home Islands.** Kyushu, southernmost of the Japanese Home Islands, is attacked by carrier planes from Vice Admiral Marc A. Mitscher's Task Force 58.

March 19.   **The ordeal of the Franklin.** Ninety miles off the coast of Japan the carrier *Franklin* (CV 13), Captain Leslie H. Gehres, flagship of Rear Admiral R. E. Davison's Task Group 58.2, is hit twice by an enemy bomber. One of the bombs penetrates her hangar deck, igniting armed planes, gasoline fuel and ready ammunition, and turning the interior of the ship above the engine spaces into a raging inferno. Of her approximately 3,450 crewmen, 724 are killed and 265 wounded, but through almost superhuman efforts, the ship is saved. No other American carrier has ever survived such punishment, and no other American warship has sustained such casualties and remained afloat.

March 20.   The submarine *Kete* (SS 369), Lieutenant Commander Edward Ackermann, is lost somewhere between Japan and Okinawa after making her last radio report on this date.

March 23–April 1.   Aircraft of Vice Admiral Marc A. Mitscher's Task Force 58 carry out pre-invasion strikes on Okinawa.

March 24.   **Iwo Jima secured.** The last Japanese positions on Iwo Jima are destroyed. Of the island's 21,000 defenders, only 216 survive its fall. The V Amphibious Corps has lost 5,981 men killed and 19,920 wounded.

These are by far the highest casualties ever suffered by the marine corps in a single battle. But they have not been in vain. Before the end of the war no less than 2,251 army air force B-29 bombers, carrying 24,761 crewmen, will make emergency landings on the island's airfields.

March 26.   **On to Okinawa.** The pre-invasion bombardment of Okinawa, in the Ryukyu Islands, is begun by Rear Admiral Morton L. Deyo's Gunfire and Covering Force (Task Force 54), consisting of 10 battleships—the *Tennessee* (BB 43) (flag), *Arkansas* (BB 33), *Colorado* (BB 45), *Idaho* (BB 42), *Maryland* (BB 46), *Nevada* (BB 36), *New Mexico* (BB 40), *New York* (BB 34), *Texas* (BB 35), and *West Virginia* (BB 48)—7 heavy and 3 light cruisers, and 32 destroyers and destroyer escorts.

March 26.   The destroyer *Halligan* (DD 584), Lieutenant Commander T. E. Grace, sinks with heavy loss of life off Okinawa after striking a mine.

March 26.   Rear Admiral I. N. Kiland's Task Group 51.1 lands the 77th Infantry Division, Major General W. H. Arnold, on six islands of the Kerama Retto group, approximately 10 miles off the southeastern coast of Okinawa. The occupation of these islands is virtually unopposed.

March 26.   **Capture of Cebu.** In the Philippines the Americal Division, Major General William H. Arnold, is landed by Captain Albert T. Sprague's Task Group 78.2 on the island of Cebu. The island is defended by 14,500 Japanese under Major General Takeo Manjome and Rear Admiral Kaku Harade. By April 12, 5,500 of these troops have been killed and the remainder driven into the mountains, where they are left until the end of the war. American battle casualties are 410 dead and 1,700 wounded.

March 27.   The submarine *Trigger* (SS 237), Commander David R. Connole, is lost on her 12th Pacific war patrol sometime after sinking a small Japanese merchantman on this date.

March 27–April 5.   Supported by destroyers and rocket-firing PT boats, a battalion landing team of the 151st Regimental Combat Team destroys the Japanese garrison of Caballo Island, in Manila Bay.

March 29.   Rear Admiral A. D. Struble's Task

The *Franklin* is wracked by one of the series of secondary explosions that followed the bomb hit on her hangar deck. Official U.S. Navy photograph.

Group 78.3 lands the 185th Regimental Combat Team under Major General Rapp Brush on the northwestern shore of Negros Island. The Japanese cease to contest the area, withdrawing into the mountainous interior, on June 4.

April 1. **Invasion of Okinawa (Operation Iceberg).** As a preliminary to and staging area for the anticipated invasion of Japan, American forces plan to seize Okinawa in the Ryukyus, some 325 miles south of Kyushu, nearest of the enemy's Home Islands. A narrow, mountainous island, 60 miles long and from 2 to 18 miles in width,

The *Franklin*, viewed from the cruiser *Santa Fe*. Official U.S. Navy photograph.

LSM(R)s—Landing Ship Medium, Rockets—fire a salvo at Japanese positions on Okinawa. Official U.S. Navy photograph.

Okinawa is garrisoned by more than 115,000 troops of Lieutenant General Mitsuru Ushijima's Thirty-Second Army and Rear Admiral Minoro Ota's naval base force. Shunning the traditional Japanese strategy of attempting to repel an invasion at the water's edge, Ushijima has concentrated his forces in the rocky southern third of the island. The invasion, the largest and most complex of the Pacific war, is conducted by Admiral Raymond A. Spruance's Fifth Fleet. As usual, Vice Admiral Richmond Kelly Turner commands the Joint Expeditionary Force (Task Force 51). The landing force, designated the Tenth Army, is commanded by Lieutenant General Simon Bolivar Buckner, Jr., USA. It consists of the III Amphibious Corps, under Major General Roy S. Geiger, USMC, and the XXIV Corps, under Major General John S. Hodge, USA—more than 183,000 men altogether. Little resistance is encountered during the first three days after the landing, and the 1st and 6th Marine Divisions continue to clear the northern end of the island without undue difficulty, but on April 4 the XXIV Corps, which has wheeled south,

comes up against General Ushijima's Machinato Line. The land battle for Okinawa has begun.

April 1.   **Awa Maru incident.** The *Awa Maru*, a Japanese passenger ship of 11,600 tons, has been granted safe conduct by the United States government to deliver Red Cross supplies to POW camps in Malaya and the Netherlands East Indies. On this date she is torpedoed and sunk in the Formosa Strait, en route back to Japan, by the submarine *Queenfish* (SS 393), Commander C. E. Loughlin. Loughlin delivered a radar attack in a dense fog under the misimpression that the ship was an enemy destroyer. Found guilty of negligence by a court-martial, he receives a letter of admonition, but still goes on to attain the rank of rear admiral.

April 6.   **Operation TEN-GO.** The Japanese respond to the invasion of Okinawa with Operation TEN-GO, a massed air attack on the American amphibious force. Admiral Soemu Toyoda, commander of the Japanese Combined Fleet, had hoped to concentrate 4,500 planes. In the event, he is able to assemble only 699, including 355

A marine flame-throwing tank douses a Japanese cave on Okinawa. U.S. Marine Corps photograph.

kamikazes; however, these succeed in doing great damage. The destroyers *Bush* (DD 529), Commander R. E. Westholm, and *Colhoun* (DD 801), Commander G. R. Wilson, and destroyer minesweeper *Emmons* (DMS 22), Lieutenant Commander E. N. Foss, USNR, and the cargo ships *Hobbs Victory* and *Logan Victory* are sunk, and 12 other vessels are damaged, 4 of them—the destroyers *Leutze* (DD 481), *Morris* (DD 417), and *Newcomb* (DD 586), and the destroyer escort *Witter* (DE 636)—so badly that they have to be scrapped. Nine more mass kamikaze attacks will follow in the course of the Okinawan campaign. The Japanese call these raids *kikusui*—"floating chrysanthemums."

April 7.   **Battle of the East China Sea.** As an element of Operation TEN-GO, on the afternoon of April 6 a Japanese surface force consisting of the 68,000-ton super-battleship *Yamato*, light cruiser *Yahagi*, and eight destroyers sets out from the Inland Sea on a suicide sortie to attack the American amphibious fleet off Okinawa. No air cover is provided. Attacked by successive waves of close to 300 carrier planes from Vice Admiral Mitscher's Task Force 58 on the afternoon of April 7, the *Yamato* capsizes after two hours' pounding, during which she is hit by at least five bombs and eleven torpedoes. Only 269 of her 2,767 crewmen survive. The *Yahagi* and four destroyers are also sunk. The force commander, Vice Admiral Seiichi Ito, and the *Yamato*'s captain, Rear Admiral Kosaku Ariga, go down with the battleship. This is the last sortie of the Imperial Japanese Navy. American losses are 10 aircraft and 12 men.

April 7.   The Japanese light cruiser *Isuzu* is torpedoed and sunk by the submarines *Gabilan* (SS 252), Commander William B. Parham, and *Charr* (SS 328), Commander Francis D. Boyle, off Bima Bay, Soembawa, Netherlands East Indies.

April 11.   **Capture of Bohol.** The 164th Infantry Regiment is ferried in landing craft from Cebu to the neighboring Philippine island of Bohol. Fighting ends with the destruction of the Japanese garrison on April 20.

April 12.   President Franklin D. Roosevelt dies of a cerebral hemorrhage at Warm Springs, Georgia. He is succeeded by Vice President Harry S Truman.

The Battle of the East China Sea: an enormous pillar of smoke marks the spot where the Japanese super-battleship *Yamato* has just gone down. Courtesy National Archives.

April 12–13. **Second kikusui raid.** A force of 185 kamikaze planes accompanied by 150 fighters and 45 torpedo bombers attack the American fleet off Okinawa. The heaviest blows fall on the destroyers of the radar picket screen. The *Mannert L. Abele* (DD 733), Commander A. E. Parker, is sunk by a piloted (*baka*) bomb and *LCS(L) 33* by a kamikaze; 9 other vessels are hit. Task Force 58's combat air patrol and the ships themselves claim to have downed 298 enemy aircraft.

April 12–20. The submarine *Snook* (SS 279), Commander John F. Walling, is lost in the vicinity of Formosa between these dates.

April 16. **Third kikusui raid.** Some 165 kamikazes attack the destroyer pickets off Okinawa. The *Pringle* (DD 477), Lieutenant Commander J. L. Kelley, is sunk. Commander Frederick J. Benton's *Laffey* (DD 724) is crashed by six aircraft and hit by four bombs. Every one of her guns is disabled, and 103 of her crewmen are killed or wounded, but almost miraculously, the ship is saved. The carrier *Intrepid* (CV 11), 4 destroyers, and 2 landing craft are damaged, some seriously.

April 16. Task Force 53, Rear Admiral L. F. Reifsnider, lands Major General A. D. Bruce's 77th Division on Ie Shima, a small island off the west coast of Okinawa. Determined Japanese resistance is crushed by April 21.

April 16. The carrier *Boxer* (CV 21) is commissioned.

April 17. **Mindanao campaign.** The X Army Corps, Major General F. C. Sibert, is landed by Rear Admiral A. G. Noble's Task Group 78.2 on the west coast of the Philippine island of Mindanao. The 41st Infantry Division had seized Zamboanga, on the island's southwestern spur, on March 10. Several unopposed, subsidiary landings are made before organized resistance by Mindanao's 43,000 Japanese defenders is overcome on June 30.

April 24. The destroyer escort *Frederick C. Davis* (DE 136), Lieutenant J. R. Crosby, USNR, is sunk in the central Atlantic by the *U-546*. The other destroyer escorts of the hunter-killer group to which the "Fighting Freddy" belonged then sink the U-boat.

April 24. On Okinawa, the army's XXIV Corps

breaks through the Machinato Line. General Ushijima withdraws to his next prepared position, where the American advance is halted on April 28.

April 26. In the Philippines, Task Unit 78.3.3, Commander W. V. Deutermann, lands the 164th Infantry Regiment on the southeast side of the island of Negros. The 40th Division had been landed on the northwestern coast on March 29. The last enemy resistance is overcome on June 12. This action completes the liberation of the Southern Visayas.

April 27–28. The cargo ship *Canada Victory* is sunk off Okinawa in the fourth mass kamikaze raid. Three destroyers and the hospital ship *Comfort* (AH 6) are damaged.

April 30. Adolf Hitler commits suicide in the *Fuehrerbunker* in Berlin. Grand Admiral Karl Doenitz, supreme commander of the German Navy, is his designated successor as chief of state.

May 1. On Okinawa, the III Amphibious Corps, having completed the conquest of the northern end of the island, is moved south to reinforce the XXIV Army Corps in attacking the Shuri Line.

May 1. **Back to Borneo.** General MacArthur has been directed to expel the Japanese from the oil-rich island of Borneo, now in the backwaters of the Pacific war. Australia agrees to furnish the necessary land forces. On this date Rear Admiral F. B. Royal's Task Group 78.1 lands the 26th Brigade of the 9th Australian Division, Brigadier General David A. Whitehead, on Tarakan, a small, oil-producing island off the northeast coast of Borneo. Organized resistance is overcome on June 14.

May 3. The submarine *Lagarto* (SS 371), Commander Frank D. Latta, is destroyed, probably by the minesweeper *Hatsutaka,* while attacking a Japanese convoy in the Gulf of Siam.

May 3–4. **Fifth kikusui attack.** Attacks by 124 kamikaze planes on the radar pickets off Okinawa sink the destroyers *Little* (DD 803), Commander Madison Hall, *Luce* (DD 522), Commander J. W. Waterhouse, and *Morrison* (DD 560), Commander J. R. Hansen, and three landing ships. The light cruiser *Birmingham* (CL 62), escort carrier *Sangamon* (CVE 26), destroyer *Ingraham*

(DD 694), the destroyer minelayers *Aaron Ward* (DM 34) and *Shea* (DM 30), and the destroyer minesweeper *Macomb* (DMS 23) are damaged.

May 7.   Germany surrenders unconditionally.

May 8.   **V-E Day.** President Truman and Prime Minister Churchill proclaim the end of the war in Europe.

May 9.   The destroyer escort *Oberrender* (DE 344), Lieutenant Commander Samuel Spencer, USNR, is sunk by a Japanese aircraft off Okinawa.

May 11.   Off Okinawa, 150 kamikazes deliver the sixth *kikusui* raid on the ships of the Fifth Fleet. Vice Admiral Mitscher's flagship, the carrier *Bunker Hill* (CV 17) is crashed by two planes and badly damaged, losing 396 men killed and 264 wounded. The destroyers *Evans* (DD 552) and *Hugh W. Hadley* (DD 774), and a landing ship are also hit.

May 13–14.   The carrier planes of Task Group 58.1, Rear Admiral J. J. ("Jocko") Clark, and Task Group 58.3, Rear Admiral Forrest P. Sherman, strike airfields on the Japanese Home Islands of Kyushu and Shikoku.

May 14.   The carrier *Enterprise* (CV 6), to which Admiral Mitscher had transferred his flag

The *Bunker Hill*, crashed by two kamikazes on the morning of May 11, 1945. Courtesy National Archives.

after the disabling of the *Bunker Hill* (CV 17) on May 11, is seriously damaged by a kamikaze plane off Okinawa.

May 16.   The Japanese heavy cruiser *Haguro* is sunk in the Malacca Strait by five British destroyers in the last surface action of the war.

May 18.   The destroyer *Longshaw* (DD 559), Lieutenant Commander C. W. Becker, is destroyed by enemy artillery fire after running aground off Okinawa.

May 21.   Ashore on Okinawa, advances by the 6th Marine Division and the 96th Infantry Division compel the Japanese to abandon the Shuri Line. General Ushijima executes a skillful withdrawal to his last line of defense, along the Yaeju Drake Escarpment.

May 23–25.   The seventh *kikusui* attack off Okinawa is made by 165 kamikazes. The high-speed transport *Bates* (APD 47) and a landing ship are sunk, and seven other vessels are damaged, the high-speed transport *Barry* (APD 29) beyond repair.

May 27–29.   The destroyer *Drexler* (DD 741), Commander R. L. Wilson, sinks with the loss of 158 lives after being crashed by two kamikazes during the eighth *kikusui* raid. Three other destroyers and several additional vessels are hit.

May 27.   Admiral Halsey relieves Admiral Spruance off Okinawa, whereupon the Fifth Fleet again becomes the Third Fleet. Vice Admiral J. S. McCain relieves Vice Admiral Mitscher in command of Task Force 38 the following day.

June 2–3.   Aircraft of Rear Admiral Arthur W. Radford's Task Group 38.4, consisting of the carriers *Intrepid* (CV 11) and *Yorktown* (CV 10) and the light carriers *Independence* (CVL 22) and *Langley* (CVL 27), with heavy surface forces, attack Japanese air bases on Kyushu.

June 3.   The carrier *Lake Champlain* (CV 39) is commissioned.

June 3–7.   The 50 kamikazes committed to the ninth *kikusui* attack at Okinawa achieve only meager results, damaging two minesweepers and a landing craft.

June 5.   **Okinawan typhoon.** Thirty-six vessels are damaged when the Third Fleet is caught in a typhoon off Okinawa. A court of inquiry finds that Admiral Halsey and Vice Admiral McCain exercised poor judgment on the approach of the storm, and Secretary of the Navy Forrestal seriously considers relieving Halsey of command.

June 8.   The Kanoya airfield on Kyushu, in the Japanese Home Islands, is attacked by aircraft from Rear Admiral Arthur W. Radford's Task Group 38.4.

June 8.   The British submarine *Trenchant,* Commander Arthur R. Hezlet, RN, sinks the Japanese heavy cruiser *Ashigara* off the northern coast of Java.

June 9–20.   **Operation Barney.** Vice Admiral Charles A. Lockwood, Commander Submarines, Pacific Fleet, sends "Hydeman's Hellcats," a wolf-pack of nine submarines under Commander Earl T. Hydeman in the *Sea Dog* (SS 401), to attack Japanese shipping in the Sea of Japan. Between these dates the Hellcats sink 28 Japanese ships totaling 54,784 tons, making this one of the most successful patrols of the war. One boat, the *Bonefish* (SS 223), Lieutenant Commander Lawrence Edge, is lost.

June 10.   **Landing on Brunei.** The reconquest of Borneo (see May 1) continues with the landing of a brigade of the 9th Australian Division, Major General G. T. Wooten, by Rear Admiral F. B. Royal's Task Group 78.1 at Brunei Bay, on the northwestern coast of the island. The area is secured by July 1.

June 10.   The destroyer *William D. Porter* (DD 579), Commander C. M. Keyes, sinks off Okinawa as a result of underwater damage sustained when a kamikaze crashes beside her. Not a single life is lost.

June 14.   On Okinawa, army and marine forces breach the final Japanese line of defense. Although the enemy continues to fight as fiercely as ever, it is obvious that the end is near.

June 16.   A kamikaze plane sinks the destroyer *Twiggs* (DD 591), Commander George Philip, off Okinawa. She is the 12th destroyer lost to date in the campaign. Every one of her twenty-two officers is killed or wounded.

June 18.   Lieutenant General S. B. Buckner, Jr., USA, is killed by an artillery burst at a forward observation post on Okinawa. He is succeeded in command of the Tenth Army by Major General Roy S. Geiger, the first marine ever to command a field army.

June 21.   **Okinawa secured.** General Geiger announces the end of organized resistance on the island. General Ushijima commits hara-kiri a few hours later. The battle for the island has cost the Tenth Army 7,613 dead and 31,807 wounded, almost equally divided between the army and the marines. Japanese losses are 107,500 killed and 7,400 captured. At sea, the U.S. Navy has had more than 4,900 men killed and 4,824 wounded, which makes the battle for Okinawa the bloodiest in its history. A total of 368 vessels have been damaged, and another 32 have been sunk, mostly by kamikazes.

June 21–22.   **Last kikusui attack.** The last mass kamikaze raid of the Okinawa campaign is made by 45 planes, which succeed only in sinking one landing ship and damaging four other vessels.

July 1.   **Landing at Balikpapan.** The last major amphibious operation of the war occurs when Rear Admiral A. G. Noble's Task Group 78.2 lands the 7th Australian Division, Major General E. J. Milford, at Balikpapan, on the southeast coast of Borneo, after a 16-day pre-invasion bombardment by an American, Australian, and Dutch cruiser-destroyer force under Rear Admiral R. S. Riggs. The town of Balikpapan, the center of Borneo's oil production, is captured on July 5, and Japanese resistance in the region ceases on July 22.

July 1.   **Operations against the Home Islands.** Task Force 38, Vice Admiral John S. McCain, sorties from Leyte Gulf to begin attacks on the Japanese Home Islands. It will operate in Japanese waters until the close of the war.

July 10.   Carrier aircraft of Task Force 38 strike Japanese airfields on the Tokyo plain. They have the sky to themselves, the Japanese having decided to husband their remaining aircraft for a mass attack on the anticipated invasion of the Home Islands.

July 14.   The first major shore bombardment of the Japanese Home Islands is delivered by Rear Admiral John F. ("Big Jack") Shafroth's Task Unit 34.81 against the Japan Iron Company plant at Kamaishi, Honshu. Engaged are the battleships *Indiana* (BB 58), *Massachusetts* (BB 59), and *South Dakota* (BB 57), heavy cruisers *Chicago* (CA 136) and *Quincy* (CA 71), and nine destroyers. The plant is put out of action.

A Japanese *Tone*-class cruiser under attack by the aircraft of Task Force 38 at the Kure Naval Base on Honshu, July 24, 1945. Official U.S. Navy photograph.

July 14–15.   Closing to within 80 miles of the Japanese coast, the carriers of Task Force 38 launch 1,391 sorties against targets in nothern Honshu and Hokkaido. These areas, outside the range of air force B-29s flying from the Marianas, have never before been attacked. Heavy damage is done, especially to merchant shipping.

July 16.   The Nihon Steel Company and Wanishi Ironworks plants at Muroran, Hokkaido, are shelled by Task Unit 34.8.2, Rear Admiral Oscar C. Badger, consisting of the fast battleships *Iowa* (BB 61), *Missouri* (BB 63), and *Wisconsin* (BB 64), two light cruisers, and nine destroyers. A total of 860 16-inch shells are fired during an hour's bombardment.

July 16.   The first atomic device is successfully exploded in a test at Alamagordo, New Mexico.

July 17–18.   Planes of Task Force 38 hit targets around Tokyo Bay, concentrating on the Yokosuka Naval Base.

July 17–18.   On this evening Admiral Badger's Task Unit 34.8.2, reinforced by the bat-

tleships *Alabama* (BB 60) and *North Carolina* (BB 55), bombards six industrial targets at Hitachi, 80 miles north of Tokyo.

July 24.   Off Luzon, the destroyer escort *Underhill* (DE 682), Lieutenant Commander R. M. Newcomb, USNR, is sunk with the loss of 112 lives, either by the Japanese submarine *I-53* or by a *kaiten* (piloted torpedo) released by the submarine.

July 24–28.   Task Force 38 launches some of the heaviest raids in the war against the Japanese naval bases at Kure and Kobe, on the Inland Sea, sinking the battleships *Haruna*, *Hyuga*, and *Ise*, the heavy cruisers *Aoba* and *Tone*, and the fleet carrier *Amagi*, and damaging the carriers *Katsuragi* and *Ryuho*.

July 25.   **Potsdam Declaration.** A statement issued by the Big Three in conference at Potsdam, Germany, calls upon Japan to surrender unconditionally or face "utter destruction." This is an implicit reference to the atomic bomb, the existence of which the Japanese (and the Russians) are yet unaware. Radio Tokyo rejects the ultimatum.

July 28.   The destroyer *Callaghan* (DD 792),

Commander C. M. Bertholf, is sunk by a kamikaze while on picket duty off Okinawa; 120 of her crewmen are killed or wounded. She is the 13th and last destroyer lost during the Okinawa campaign.

July 29. **The tragedy of the Indianapolis.** Two days after leaving Guam on an unescorted voyage to Leyte Gulf, the heavy cruiser *Indianapolis* (CA 35), Captain Charles B. McVay III, is sunk by the Japanese submarine *I-58*, Lieutenant Commander Mochitsura Hashimoto, or, it has been argued, by a *kaiten* released by this boat. Some 800 to 850 men succeed in abandoning the ship, but her SOS is unheard, and through a succession of tragic oversights, her loss goes unnoticed until August 2, when a group of survivors is accidentally sighted by a patrol plane. Only 316 men are then saved.

July 29–30. Three small naval vessels and 12 merchantmen are sunk by planes of Task Force 38 in attacks on the Maizuru Naval Base on the Sea of Japan, and on the northern coast of Honshu.

July 30. The British midget submarines *XE-1*, Lieutenant J. E. Smart, RN, and *XE-3*, Lieutenant I. E. Fraser, RN, attach charges that sink the Japanese heavy cruiser *Takao* (previously damaged by American aircraft) in the harbor at Singapore.

August 6. **Hiroshima.** The B-29 *Enola Gay* drops an atomic bomb on Hiroshima, a city of approximately 500,000 on southern Honshu. More than 70,000 people are killed.

August 6. The submarine *Bullhead* (SS 332), Lieutenant Commander Edward R. Holt, Jr., is sunk by a Japanese plane in the Lombok Strait.

August 8. The Soviet Union declares war on Japan.

August 9. More than 251 Japanese aircraft are destroyed and 141 damaged on airfields on northern Honshu by carrier strikes from Task Force 38.

August 9. **Nagasaki.** A second atomic bomb is dropped on Japan, this time on Nagasaki, a seaport on Kyushu. Approximately 20,000 people are killed.

August 10. Task Force 38 continues its strikes on northern Honshu.

August 12. The battleship *Pennsylvania* (BB 38) becomes the last major American warship to be damaged in World War II when she is hit by a Japanese torpedo plane in Buckner Bay, Okinawa.

August 13. Planes of Task Force 38 attack Japanese airfields on the Tokyo plain, destroying 254 enemy aircraft and damaging 149 more. Another 18 planes are shot down by the carriers' combat air patrol.

August 14. Japan surrenders unconditionally. The Japanese government, however, had been given to understand that no measures would be taken against the emperor.

August 15. **V-J Day.** The last air strike of the war is launched at 4:15 by the carriers of Task Force 38. News of the Japanese surrender leads to the recall of a second wave already approaching the Japanese coast.

August 16. Vice Admiral Aubrey W. Fitch becomes 34th superintendent of the Naval Academy.

August 28. The occupation of Japan begins when U.S. Army Air Force personnel land at Atsugi Airfield.

August 30. Covered by the guns of the Third Fleet, U.S. Army occupation forces begin landing in Tokyo Bay.

September 2. The Japanese instrument of surrender is signed aboard the battleship *Missouri* (BB 63) in Tokyo Bay. General Douglas MacArthur signs on behalf of the Allied Powers, Fleet Admiral Chester W. Nimitz for the United States.

September 10. The carrier *Midway* (CVB 41) is commissioned.

October 27. The carrier *Franklin D. Roosevelt* (CVB 42) is commissioned.

November 6. The first carrier landing by a jet aircraft is made by a Ryan FR-1 Fireball aboard the escort carrier *Wake Island* (CVE 65).

November 18. The carrier *Princeton* (CV 37) is commissioned.

The cruiser *Indianapolis*. U.S. Naval Institute Collection.

The Japanese delegation awaits the beginning of the surrender ceremony aboard the battleship *Missouri* in Tokyo Bay, September 2, 1945. Official U.S. Navy photograph.

December 8.   The carrier *Tarawa* (CV 40) is commissioned.

December 15.   Fleet Admiral Chester W. Nimitz becomes the 10th chief of naval operations.

1946

January 1.   The U.S. Coast Guard, which has operated under the navy since November 1941, is returned to the Treasury Department.

March 2.   The carrier *Kearsarge* (CV 33) is commissioned.

April 5–14.   The battleship *Missouri* (BB 63) calls at Istanbul, Turkey, and Athens, Greece, in a powerful demonstration of American interest in the eastern Mediterranean.

April 11.   The carrier *Leyte* (CV 32) is commissioned.

May 11.   The carrier *Philippine Sea* (CV 47) is commissioned.

July 14.   The carrier *Saipan* (CVL 48) is commissioned.

August 8–October 4.   The carrier *Franklin D. Roosevelt* (CVB 42) deploys to the Mediterranean. A visit to Athens, reinforcing that of the *Missouri* six months earlier, shows American support for the pro-Western Greek government, which is involved in a bitter civil war against Communist insurgents.

August 13.   **Holloway Plan.** At the end of World War II it was evident that the Naval Academy, as traditionally constituted, would be unable to produce the annual output of ensigns needed by a truly global navy. In August 1945 a board was convened under the presidency of Rear Admiral James L. Holloway, Jr., to consider the problem of officer education and training. It recommended retaining the Naval Academy in its existing format and developing a complementary source of junior officers by establishing a "regular" NROTC program with pay. Congress approved, and on this date President Harry S Truman signs the Holloway Plan into law.

October 1.   **Genesis of the Sixth Fleet.** A new command, U.S. Naval Forces, Mediterranean, is established. It will be redesignated the Sixth Task Fleet in 1948 and the Sixth Fleet in February 1950.

November 3.   The carrier *Valley Forge* (CV 45) is commissioned.

1947

January 15.   Rear Admiral J. L. Holloway, Jr., becomes 35th superintendent of the Naval Academy.

February 9.   The carrier *Wright* (CVL 49) is commissioned.

March 12.   **Truman Doctrine.** In an address to Congress requesting emergency funds to help the Greek government in its civil war against the Communists, President Harry S Truman declares that it should be the policy of the United States "to support free peoples who are resisting attempted subjugation by armed minorities or outside pressure." This concept will become one of the cornerstones of American foreign policy in the Cold War.

March 15.   Ensign John W. Lee becomes the first

black to receive a commission in the regular navy.

May 1.   The *Cusk* (SS 348) becomes the first U.S. submarine to launch a missile. The missile is a Loon, the American naval version of the German V-1.

June 5.   **Marshall Plan.** Secretary of State George C. Marshall, speaking at the Harvard commencement, announces that the United States will provide economic aid to assist the recovery of the war-torn nations of Europe. The Soviet Union and her satellites refuse to participate in the program.

July.   **"X." Article.** George F. Kennan, a foreign service officer at the Moscow Embassy and a veteran observer of Soviet affairs, considers the problem of Soviet-American relations in an article, "Sources of Soviet Conduct," in *Foreign Affairs* magazine. In view of Kennan's official position, the article is signed simply "X." It concludes that the United States should adopt a policy of "patient but firm . . . containment" of Soviet expansionism by the "application of counterforce at a series of constantly shifting geographical and political points corresponding to the shifts . . . of Soviet policy." Although Kennan will later insist that this concept has been misinterpreted as a purely military prescription, together with the Truman Doctrine and the Marshall Plan "containment" will form the foundation of American strategy in the Cold War.

September 6.   The carrier *Midway* (CVB 41) successfully conducts the first American launching of a V-2 ballistic missile.

September 18.   **NSA 47.** The National Security Act of 1947 becomes effective, unifying the departments of the army, navy, and air force under the aegis of a single Department of Defense (originally called the National Military Establishment).

September 18.   John L. Sullivan becomes 49th secretary of the navy, which the National Security Act of 1947 has made a subcabinet post.

September 23.   Former secretary of the navy James V. Forrestal enters office as the first secretary of defense.

October 1.   The carrier *Coral Sea* (CVB 43) is commissioned.

December 15.   Admiral Louis E. Denfeld becomes the 11th chief of naval operations.

1948

January 1.   Major General Clifton B. Cates becomes 19th commandant of the marine corps.

February 24.   **Czech coup.** The democratic, neutralist government of Czechoslovakia is overthrown by a coup conducted by native Communists with the evident support of the Soviet Union. For many Americans the spectacle of this once-free country being dragged behind the Iron Curtain confirms the existence of the Cold War.

March 31–May 12, 1949.   **Berlin Airlift.** Beginning on this date Soviet authorities progressively impede the flow of traffic to West Berlin, deep in the Soviet occupation zone, until on June 24 they halt all land transport to the city. The western powers respond to the blockade with a massive airlift, unprecedented in history, which successfully supplies the million-plus inhabitants of Free Berlin with the necessities of life. Two navy transport squadrons participate in this humanitarian operation.

May 6.   Fighter Squadron 17A, the first all-jet navy squadron, qualifies for carrier landings aboard the light carrier *Saipan* (CVL 48). It is equipped with FH-1 Phantoms.

1949

March 28.   Louis Johnson becomes the second secretary of defense.

April 4.   **NATO.** The North Atlantic Treaty Organization, a defensive military alliance, is established by the United States, Great Britain, France, Italy, Canada, Belgium, Portugal, the Netherlands, Denmark, Norway, and Iceland. This is the first peacetime military alliance into which the United States has entered.

April 23.   **Cancellation of the United States.** Secretary of Defense Johnson announces the cancellation of the supercarrier *United States* (CVA 58), a decision about which neither Secretary of the Navy Sullivan nor the chief of naval operations, Admiral Louis

E. Denfeld, were previously informed. Secretary Sullivan resigns in protest.

May 25. Francis P. Matthews enters office as 50th secretary of the navy.

June 3. Ensign Wesley A. Brown becomes the first black graduate of the U.S. Naval Academy.

August 9. An aircraft ejection seat is used for the first time when Lieutenant J. L. Furin ejects from an F-2H Banshee jet fighter traveling more than 500 knots.

October 1. **MSTS.** The army and navy transportation service are combined to form the Military Sea Transportation Service, which will operate under the control of the secretary of the navy.

October 5. **"Revolt of the Admirals."** Congressman Carl Vinson, chairman of the House Naval Affairs Committee, opens hearings on national defense policy in which the navy and marine witnesses assert that the needs of the sea services are being ignored, citing in particular the abrupt cancellation of the supercarrier *United States* (CVA 58). The highlight of the hearings is a forceful presentation by the chief of naval operations, Admiral Louis E. Denfeld. The committee's report, issued on March 2, 1950, supports the navy's position.

November 1. With the approval of President Truman, Admiral Denfeld is relieved of duty as chief of naval operations by Secretary of the Navy Matthews, to whom his testimony before the Vinson committee was most unwelcome.

November 2. Admiral Forrest P. Sherman becomes the 12th chief of naval operations.

1950

February 12. **Sixth Fleet.** The U.S. naval forces that have been operating in the Mediterranean since 1946 are officially designated the Sixth Fleet.

April 28. Vice Admiral Harry W. Hill becomes the 36th superintendent of the U.S. Naval Academy.

June 25. **Beginning of the Korean War.** Before dawn, six North Korean infantry divisions and three Border Constabulary brigades, supported by approximately 100 Russian-made T-34 tanks, invade the Republic of Korea.

June 25. The United Nations Security Council adopts a resolution condemning the invasion of South Korea.

June 26. The destroyers *De Haven* (DD 727) and *Mansfield* (DD 728) evacuate 700 American and foreign citizens from Inchon, South Korea.

June 27. President Harry S Truman authorizes General Douglas MacArthur, Commander-in-Chief, Far East, to use American air and naval forces in support of South Korea.

June 27. The United Nations Security Council issues a second resolution condemning North Korean aggression and recommends that U.N. members assist South Korea in repelling the attack.

June 28. North Korean forces occupy Seoul, the capital of South Korea.

June 29. **First fire support.** The cruiser *Juneau* (CL 119), Captain Jesse D. Sowell, delivers the first naval gunfire support of the Korean war, shelling an enemy troop concentration at Okkye on the east coast.

June 30. President Truman authorizes the employment of U.S. ground forces in Korea. Advance elements of the 24th Division are airlifted to the peninsula from Japan this same day. Ships of the Military Sea Transportation Service begin embarking the main body on July 1.

July 2. The only purely naval action in which an American warship is involved during the Korean War is fought off Chumunjin, on the east coast, when four North Korean torpedo boats attack the cruisers *Juneau* (CL 119) and HMS *Jamaica* and the frigate HMS *Black Swan*. Three of the torpedo boats are destroyed; none of the allied ships are hit.

July 3–4. **First air strikes.** Two units of Vice Admiral Arthur D. Struble's Task Force 77, the carriers *Valley Forge* (CV 45), Captain L. K. Rice, and HMS *Triumph*, Captain A. D. Torless, DSO, deliver the first naval air strikes of the Korean War, attacking military installations in the North Korean capital of Pyongyang. The F-9F2 Panther fighters launched by the *Valley Forge* are the first navy jets to enter combat. They

The light cruiser *Juneau* at anchor in Kagoshima Wan, Japan, on June 25, 1950. Official U.S. Navy photograph.

also score the first jet victories, downing two propeller-driven YAK-9 fighters.

July 4.   President Truman proclaims a blockade of the coast of North Korea.

July 7.   General Douglas MacArthur is appointed Supreme Commander of U.N. forces in Korea.

July 9.   The South Korean Navy is placed under the command of Commander Michael J. Luosey, USN.

July 11.   **First raid.** After nightfall, Commander W. B. Porter leads a party of 10 seamen and marines from the cruiser *Juneau* (CL 119) to successfully destroy a railroad tunnel at Rashin, North Korea. Many similar operations are carried out in the course of the conflict by U.S. naval forces and U.S., British, and South Korean marines.

July 18–19.   Amphibious Group One, Rear Admiral James H. Doyle, lands the 1st Cavalry Division at Pohang, on the southeastern coast of Korea. The arrival of this force is instrumental in halting the North Korean advance at an irregular, defensive perimeter extending 35 to 80 miles inland from the port of Pusan on the southeastern tip of the Korean peninsula.

July 18.   Aircraft from the *Valley Forge* (CV 45) destroy the oil refinery at Wonsan, North Korea.

July 25.   **Blockade of Korea.** Task Force 96.5 is organized to conduct the blockade of Korea. The U.S. Navy covers the east coast; the west coast is assigned to British Com-

monwealth forces (Task Group 96.53) under Rear Admiral William G. Andrewes, RN, who will be knighted in February 1951.

July 25.   **Close air support.** In response to an urgent request from Lieutenant General Walton H. Walker, commanding the U.S. Eighth Army, the carriers of Task Force 77 begin the unaccustomed task of providing tactical air support for the army forces holding the hard-pressed Pusan Perimeter. These operations, in which the carrier *Philippine Sea* (CV 47) joins on August 5, continue into September.

July 25.   The hospital ship *Benevolence* (AH 13) sinks with the loss of 13 lives following a collision with the SS *Mary Luckenbach* of San Francisco. She had been recommissioned to serve in the Korean War.

August 2.   The 1st Provisional Marine Brigade, Brigadier General Edward A. Craig, lands at Pusan. It had sailed from San Diego on July 14, the first unit to leave the United States for Korea.

August 7.   The marines enter action in Korea, counterattacking in the direction of Chinju and Sachon from the southwestern end of the Pusan Perimeter. Chinju is captured and the marines are poised to take Sachon when on August 12 they are diverted 75 miles to the north to repel an enemy offensive across the Naktong River. During this and subsequent actions the brigade receives valuable close air support from Marine Fighter Squadrons (VMF) 214 and 323, embarked on the escort carriers *Badoeng Strait* (CVE 116) and *Sicily* (CVE 118) of Rear Admiral Richard W. Ruble's Carrier Division 15. These squadrons also support U.S. and South Korean army units.

August 15.   **Battle of the Naktong.** The 1st Provisional Marine Brigade counterattacks the 4th North Korean People's Army Division, which has established a bridgehead south of the Naktong River, within the Pusan Perimeter, and hurls it back across the river, capturing 34 guns.

August 16.   The 3rd Republic of Korea Division, encircled while fighting a delaying action near Yonghae, on the east coast of Korea, is evacuated by four landing ships covered by the cruiser *Helena* (CA 75) and escorting destroyers.

August 23.   In a dramatic conference in Tokyo, General MacArthur persuades Admiral Forrest P. Sherman, the chief of naval operations, and General J. Lawton Collins, army chief of staff, to support his plan for an amphibious assault at Inchon, on the west coast of Korea.

September 3–5.   **Second battle of the Naktong.** Between September 1 and 3, a Communist offensive spearheaded by the 9th North Korean People's Army Division pushes back the U.S. 2nd Infantry Division and reestablishes a bridgehead across the Naktong. The 1st Provisional Marine Brigade, which had been withdrawn to take part in the planned Inchon invasion, is sent to seal the breach. The marines eliminate the bridgehead in three days of heavy fighting.

September 12.   **Task Force 95.** The units conducting the blockage of Korea are reorganized as Task Force 95, the United Nations Blockading and Escort Force. The blockade of the west coast remains a British Commonwealth responsibility, as it will throughout the war.

September 15.   **Inchon invasion.** General MacArthur launches an amphibious operation of unexcelled audacity at Inchon, the port of Seoul, 150 miles behind enemy lines. A less promising location for a landing can hardly be imagined: the tidal range at Inchon is in excess of 30 feet; the narrow, twisting channel through the mud flats to the harbor could be blocked by a single

The Inchon invasion: First Lieutenant Baldomero Lopez, a platoon leader in the Third Marines, leads his men over the seawall. He was killed minutes later, smothering a grenade with his body, and posthumously awarded the Medal of Honor. U.S. Marine Corps photograph.

ship; and the "beach" is a big-city waterfront. For these very reasons, MacArthur is confident that the invasion will achieve strategic surprise. His gamble works to perfection. A two-day preliminary bombardment is carried out by the naval attack force, Amphibious Group One, commanded by Rear Admiral James H. Doyle. The landing force, army Major General Edward M. Almond's X Corps, consists of the 7th Infantry Division and the hastily constituted 1st Marine Division, under Major General O. P. Smith. The marines spearhead the assault, capturing the offshore island of Wolmi-do on the morning tide and landing at Inchon at 5:30 P.M. By nightfall the marines have secured their objectives at a cost of 22 dead and 174 wounded. The 7th Infantry Division follows them ashore on the 17th. Simultaneously, the forces in the Pusan Perimeter begin a drive north.

September 17.   The 3rd Battalion of Colonel R. L. Murray's Fifth Marine Regiment cap-

tures Kimpo Airfield, midway between Inchon and Seoul.

September 18.   A detachment of 725 South Korean troops is evacuated from an unsuccessful east coast landing at Samchok by
auxiliary vessels supported by the battleship *Missouri* (BB 63), cruiser *Helena* (CA
75) and four destroyers.

September 21.   General George C. Marshall becomes the third secretary of defense.

September 21–22.   Colonel Lewis B. ("Chesty")
Puller's First Marine Regiment captures Yong-
dungpo, on the Han River opposite Seoul.

September 25.   **Capture of Seoul.** The 1st Marine Division and elements of the 7th Infantry Division enter Seoul.

September 25.   The carrier *Oriskany* (CV 34) is
commissioned.

September 26.   **Destruction of the North Korean Army.** At 11:45 P.M. the 1st Cavalry
Division, leading the Eighth Army's advance from the Pusan Perimeter, links up
with units of the 7th Infantry Division south
of Seoul. The North Korean Army, whose
principal supply lines ran through Seoul,
soon ceases to exist as an organized fighting force.

September 27.   The joint chiefs of staff authorize
General MacArthur to pursue the North
Korean Army north of the 38th Parallel.

September 29.   The minesweeper *Magpie* (AMS
25), Lieutenant (jg) Warren R. Person, is
destroyed by a mine off Chuksan, North
Korea. She is the first navy vessel lost in
the war.

October 1.   General MacArthur calls upon North
Korean Premier Kim Il Sung to surrender
his forces to avoid useless loss of life.

October 4.   The Political Committee of the U.N.
General Assembly resolves that all steps
shall be taken for the establishment of a
unified, democratic Korea.

October 9.   **Invasion of North Korea.** General
MacArthur issues a second surrender ultimatum to the North Korean government. U.S. forces cross the 38th Parallel
into North Korea this same day.

October 10.   **Wonsan: the battle of the mines.**
Minesweepers begin clearing the harbor of
Wonsan, on the east coast of North Korea,
in preparation for a landing by the U.S. X
Corps scheduled for October 20.

October 12.   The minesweepers *Pirate* (AM 275),

Lieutenant Commander Bruce Hyatt, and
Pledge (AM 277), Lieutenant Richard O.
Young, are sunk by mines in Wonsan harbor. It is learned that the harbor is defended
by approximately 3,000 mines, both contact and magnetic. Lanes through the
minefields are finally opened on October
25, five days behind schedule.

October 19.   U.S. forces occupy the North Korean capital of Pyongyang.

October 26.   The 1st Marine Division lands unopposed at Wonsan. The city had been captured by South Korean troops advancing
overland on October 10.

October 29–November 8.   The 7th Infantry Division, originally scheduled to land at
Wonsan, is put ashore at Iwon, where no
mines have been found.

November 1.   For the first time, Russian-built
MiG-15 jet fighters based in Manchuria cross
the Yalu River to attack U.N. aircraft.

November 2–7.   Colonel Homer L. Litzen-
berg's Seventh Marine Regiment, spear-
heading the 1st Marine Division's advance
towards the Yalu, shatters a series of attacks by the 124th Chinese Communist
Division.

November 2–20.   Minesweeping forces under
Commander Stephen M. Archer clear the
harbor of Chinnampo, the port city of
Pyongyang, without a single casualty.

November 5.   General MacArthur officially notifies the United Nations of the presence
of Chinese troops in North Korea.

November 8.   **Attacking the Yalu bridges.** The
aircraft of Vice Admiral Arthur D. Struble's Carrier Task Force 77 are ordered to
attack the Yalu River bridges near Chong-
sonjin. This is the first of many bridge-
busting assignments. All are complicated
by the fact that the aircraft are allowed to
attack only the Korean end of the bridges.

November 9.   **First MiG kill.** Lieutenant Commander W. T. Amen, flying an F-9F2
Panther jet from the *Philippine Sea* (CV
47), downs a MiG-15 to become the first
navy pilot to destroy an enemy jet fighter.

November 13.   The Seventh Marines reach the
village of Hagaru-Ri, on the southern end
of the Chosin Reservoir.

November 21.   The 7th Infantry Division's 17th
Regimental Combat Team reaches the
Manchurian border at Hyesanjin.

An F4U-4 Corsair from the *Philippine Sea* flies a combat air patrol over ships off Inchon, October 1950. Official U.S. Navy photograph.

November 24. **U.N. offensive.** U.N. forces launch an offensive intended to complete the occupation of North Korea.

November 25. **Chinese intervention.** Approximately 300,000 Chinese Communist regular troops have entered North Korea, largely undetected by the widely separated U.N. columns advancing along the roads on the eastern and western sides of the peninsula. On this date around 180,000 of these troops attack the American and South Korean forces in the west.

November 27–28. **Battle of the "Frozen Chosin."** Eight Chinese divisions attack 1st Marine Division positions to the west and south of the Chosin Reservoir. The marines hold their ground, but the Chinese cut the road between the marines' main body at Yudam-Ni, division headquarters 14 miles to the south at Hagaru-Ri, and from Hagaru-Ri south.

November 29. The X Corps commander, Ma-

A marine column during the breakout from the Chosin Reservoir. Defense Department photo (Marine Corps).

jor General Edward M. Almond, USA, orders the 1st Marine Division to fall back to Hamhung.

November 29. Task Force Drysdale, a composite formation of U.S. marines and infantry and 41st Independent Commando, Royal Marines—the whole under Lieutenant Colonel R.M. Drysdale, Royal Marines—fights its way north from Koto-Ri against heavy opposition to reinforce the marine battalion defending Hagaru-Ri.

December 3.   After 79 hours of almost uninterrupted combat, the main body of the 1st Marine Division completes its withdrawal from Yudam-Ni to Hagaru-Ri.

December 3–7.   U.S. naval forces evacuate 3,834 military personnel and 7,009 civilian refugees from Wonsan, on the east coast of North Korea.

December 4.   **Ensign Jesse L. Brown.** The navy's first black pilot, Ensign Brown is forced to make a crash-landing near Hagaru-Ri when his plane is hit by enemy ground fire while flying a close-support mission from the carrier *Leyte* (CV 32). Observing that Brown is unable to get out of his cockpit, one of his squadron mates, Lieutenant (jg) Thomas J. Hudner, fearlessly lands to help him. Brown dies before he can be removed from the wreckage. Hudner, who is rescued by helicopter, is awarded the Medal of Honor. Ensign Brown is posthumously decorated with the Distinguished Flying Cross.

December 5.   On the west coast of Korea, U.S. and British Commonwealth naval forces evacuate 7,700 U.S. and South Korean troops from Chinnampo.

December 6.   The 1st Marine Division begins its break-out south from Hagaru-Ri.

December 7.   U.S. naval forces begin the evacuation of Inchon. By the time the port is closed on January 5, 1951, some 32,400 troops and 57,700 tons of supplies have been transported to the south.

December 9.   **Marines break out.** Leading elements of the 1st Marine Division, attacking through Funchilin Pass, link up with marine units pushing north to meet them from Chinhung-Ni. The withdrawal from the Chosin Reservoir, one of the epic fighting retreats of all time, is complete. The marines have suffered 4,400 battle casualties, including 730 dead. Chinese losses are estimated at 37,500.

December 9.   General MacArthur orders the X Corps to be evacuated from North Korea

from the port of Hungnam. Vice Admiral C. Turner Joy, Commander, U.S. Naval Forces, Far East, assigns Rear Admiral James H. Doyle, Commander, Task Force 90, the responsibility of carrying out the operation.

December 10–24.   **Hungnam evacuation.** Rear Admiral Doyle's Task Force 90 conducts an exemplary amphibious operation in reverse, evacuating 105,000 U.S. and South Korean troops, including the 1st Marine Division, 91,000 civilian refugees, and 350,000 tons of supplies and equipment from the port of Hungnam. Air and fire support for the evacuation, with which the enemy does not try to interfere, is provided by the carriers *Leyte* (CV 32), *Philippine Sea* (CV 47), *Princeton* (CV 37), *Valley Forge*, (CV 45), *Badoeng Strait* (CVE 116), *Bataan* (CVL 29) and *Sicily* (CVE 118), and a surface force consisting of the battleship *Missouri* (BB 63), two heavy cruisers, eight destroyers, and three rocket ships.

1951

January 1–15.   Communist armies numbering approximately 500,000 men, mostly Chinese, push U.N. forces approximately 50 miles south of the 38th Parallel, recapturing Seoul.

January 29.   Carrier Task Force 77 is directed to begin a bombing offensive against the railway system and bridge network along the east coast of North Korea. Its commander, Vice Admiral Arthur D. Struble, had unsuccessfully protested the assignment, asserting that the carrier planes could best be used for close support.

February 2.   The minesweeper *Partridge* (AMS 31), Lieutenant (jg) B.M. Clark, is sunk by a mine while sweeping southeast of Wonsan. She is the last minesweeper lost in the Korean conflict.

February 16.   **Siege of Wonsan.** U.S. forces begin an unprecedented, 861-day naval siege of Wonsan, North Korea's principal sea port and a major communications center. A total of seven harbor islands are eventually occupied by U.N. forces—mainly South Korean marines—and U.S. warships maintain a constant presence off the

The end at Hungnam: demolition charges destroy harbor installations upon the completion of the evacuation. The ship in the foreground is the fast transport *Begor*. Official U.S. Navy photograph.

city, shelling traffic and batteries ashore. The position also offers a haven to damaged U.N. aircraft; helicopters from *LST 799* rescue 24 U.S., British, and South African airmen from Wonsan harbor or nearby locations between March 1951 and November 1952, and an emergency airfield is constructed on Yo-do Island in the summer of 1952.

March 7–31.   A U.N. counteroffensive, Operation Ripper, drives the Communists back to the 38th Parallel. Seoul is reoccupied on March 14.

March 8.   The North Korean port of Songjin is put under siege by U.N. naval forces.

April 1.   The bridge at Songjin, North Korea, is destroyed by the first navy jet bombing attack of the Korean War. It was delivered by Fighter Squadron (VF) 191 from the *Princeton* (CV 37).

April 7.   Covered by fire from the cruiser *St. Paul* (CA 73) and two destroyers, 250 men of 41st Independent Commando, Royal Marines, destroy a section of railroad near Chongjin, on the east coast of North Korea.

April 11.   **Relief of MacArthur.** President Truman relieves General MacArthur of command. MacArthur had made no secret of his dissatisfaction with the constraints the president established for the conduct of the war. He is succeeded by Lieutenant General Matthew B. Ridgeway.

April 22–May 1, May 14–20.   **Communist spring offensives.** Two successive enemy offensives are repulsed with heavy losses.

April 26.   U.S. naval forces put the North Korean port of Hungnam under siege.

May 20.   The battleship *New Jersey* (BB 62), recommissioned for the Korean War, reaches the theater of operations and delivers her first bombardment against the east coast town of Kangsong.

May 22–31.   **U.N. counteroffensive.** A general offensive by the U.S. Eighth Army, South Korean, and other U.N. troops

F9F Panther jets from the *Boxer* over Wonsan, July 1951. Official U.S. Navy photograph.

pushes the enemy back all along the front. By this time the Communist forces have sustained an estimated 200,000 casualties in a matter of months and are apparently on the verge of collapse. However, fear of widening the war leads the Truman administration to prohibit another all-out drive into North Korea.

June 5–September 20. **Operation Strangle.** The planes of Carrier Task Force 77 and the 1st Marine Air Wing are directed to support the Fifth Air Force in an attempt to choke the enemy frontlines by cutting eight key supply routes across a degree of latitude on the Korean peninsula. The effort is not successful.

June 12. The destroyer *Walke* (DD 723) is heavily damaged by a mine off Hungnam, North Korea, losing 26 men killed and 35 wounded.

June 23. Soviet U.N. Ambassador Jacob Malik proposes opening cease-fire negotiations in Korea. The Soviet initiative is often inter-

preted as a testimonial to how badly Communist forces had been hurt.

July 10. **Korean truce talks.** Negotiations begin at Kaesong, inside Communist lines. The chief U.N. delegate is Vice Admiral C. Turner Joy, commander of U.S. Naval Forces, Far East, since the start of the war. The talks break down in August, but are resumed at Panmunjon, a village between the lines, on November 12.

July 31. Dan A. Kimball becomes 51st secretary of the navy.

August 16. Admiral William M. Fechteler becomes the 13th chief of naval operations.

August 25. Fighters from the carrier *Essex* (CV 9) escort air force B-29 Superfortresses on an attack on Rashin, North Korea, a major rail center only a few miles south of the Soviet border.

September 17. Robert A. Lovett becomes the fourth secretary of defense.

November 6. A P-2V Neptune navy patrol plane is shot down on a routine mission over

The battleship *New Jersey* fires a full salvo in support of troops near the 38th Parallel, November 1951. Official U.S. Navy photograph.

international waters off the coast of Siberia.

1952

January 1. Lieutenant General Lemuel C. Shepherd, Jr., becomes 20th commandant of the marine corps.

January 11. **Projects Package and Derail.** The seaborne artillery of Task Force 95 and aircraft of Task Force 77 begin to concert attacks against selected targets on the coastal rail lines of North Korea.

January 29. LSTs of Task Force 90 complete the evacuation, begun in mid-December, of more than 20,000 civilians from islands off the west coast of Korea that have come under Communist attack.

February 19. Off Songjin, on the east coast of North Korea, an amphibious assault on the U.N.-held islands of Kil-chu and Myongchon by enemy troops embarked in 45 sampans is broken up by the destroyer *Shelton* (DD 790), the New Zealand frigate *Taupo*, and the minesweeping destroyer *Endicott* (DMS 35). Several sampans reach Kil-chu, but the landing force is killed or captured by the island's defenders, a company of South Korean marines commanded by First Lieutenant Jose ' Bartos, USMC.

April 21. Thirty men are killed by a powder fire in the No. 1 8-inch turret of the cruiser *St. Paul* (CA 73) off Kojo, North Korea.

April 26. **Hobson disaster.** The destroyer minesweeper *Hobson* (DMS 26), Lieutenant Commander W. J. Tierney, sinks with the loss of 176 lives following a collision with the carrier *Wasp* (CV 18) during exercises in the Atlantic.

April 28. The U.S. Navy decides to install the

Marines hug the side of their trench as an enemy mortar shell explodes on its lip, April 1952. Official U.S. Navy photograph.

steam-catapult aircraft-launching system developed by the Royal Navy in American carriers.

June 14.   The keel of the world's first nuclear-powered submarine, the *Nautilus* (SSN 571) is laid at the Electric Boat Company at Groton, Connecticut.

June 23.   **Suiho strike.** Thirty-five AD Skyraiders and an equal number of F-9F2 Panther jets from the carriers *Boxer* (CV 21), *Philippine Sea* (CV 47), and *Princeton* (CV 37) join air force Thunderjets in an attack on the heavily defended hydroelectric power plant at Suiho, North Korea, the fourth-largest such facility in the world. It is rendered unserviceable. The raid is part of a two-day aerial offensive against North Korea's 13 major power plants.

July 11.   **Pyongyang raid.** Ninety-one aircraft from the carrier *Bon Homme Richard* (CV 31) and *Princeton* (CV 37) collaborate with air force, marine, Australian Air Force and

Ordnance men arm Corsairs aboard the *Bataan*, summer 1952. Official U.S. Navy photograph.

British carrier planes to hit some 40 military targets in and around the North Korean capital of Pyongyang.

July 12–22.   Marine Major John H. Glenn, Jr., the future astronaut, destroys three MiGs while serving on exchange duty with the Fifth Air Force.

July 27–28.   Carrier aircraft of Task Force 77 strike two major industrial targets in North Korea, the lead and zinc mill at Sindok and the magnesite plant at Kilchu.

August 4.   Vice Admiral C. Turner Joy becomes 37th superintendent of the Naval Academy.

August 29.   **"All United Nations Air Effort."** Planes from the carriers *Boxer* (CV 21) and *Essex* (CV 9) participate in the biggest bombing raid in the war to date, an attack on Pyongyang by more than 1,000 U.N. aircraft.

August 30.   The ocean tug *Sarsi* (ATF-111) is sunk by a mine while patrolling off Hungnam. She is the last U.S. naval vessel lost in the Korean conflict.

September 1.   The oil refinery at Aoji, North Korea, only eight miles from the Soviet border, is destroyed by 144 planes from the carriers *Boxer* (CV 21) , *Essex* (CV 9), and *Princeton* (CV 37). This is the largest carrier raid of the war.

September 1.   The first prototype Sidewinder air-to-air missile is fired at the Naval Ordnance Test Station at Inyokern, California.

September 9.   Marine Captain Jesse G. Folmar destroys a MiG-15 with his F-4U Corsair. He is the first pilot to down an enemy jet while flying a propeller-driven aircraft.

October 8.   Twelve F-2H2 Banshee jets from the carrier *Kearsarge* (CV 33) escort 10 air force B-29 Superfortresses in an attack on the rail center at Kowon, North Korea. This is the second and last time in the Korean conflict that navy fighters cover B-29s.

October 9–July 1953.   **"Cherokee Strikes."** Dissatisfied with the scarcity of profitable targets in North Korea, Vice Admiral J. J. ("Jocko") Clark, the Seventh Fleet commander, initiates a battle-front bombing campaign against enemy supply facilities outside the range of U.N. artillery. The campaign, named after the admiral's Indian ancestry and enthusiastically welcomed by the Eighth Army, soon absorbs almost half

An AD Skyraider from the *Princeton* attacking marshalling yards near Kowon, North Korea, October 1952. Note the complete destruction of the bridge at lower left. Official U.S. Navy photograph.

the carrier air effort and continues until the end of the war.

November 1.   The first shipboard firing of the Regulus I missile is made from the missile ship *Norton Sound* (AVM 1) at the Naval Air Test Center at Point Mugu, California.

November 18.   **Dogfight off Chongjin.** Three F-9F5 Panther jet fighters from the carrier *Oriskany* (CV 34) engage seven, presumably Soviet MiG-15s 90 miles southwest of Vladivostok. Two of the MiGs are definitely destroyed. No American planes are lost.

1953

January 18.   A navy P-2V Neptune patrol plane is shot down by ground fire from a Communist-held island in the Straits of Taiwan.

January 22.   Landing tests begin on the navy's first angled-deck carrier, the *Antietam* (CV 36).

January 28. **Terrier.** The first shipboard launching of a Terrier surface-to-air missile is made by the *Mississippi* (AG 128, formerly BB 41) off Cape Cod, Massachusetts.

January 28. Charles E. Wilson becomes the fifth secretary of defense.

February 4. Robert B. Anderson becomes 52nd secretary of the navy.

March 6. The *Tunny* (SSG 282) is recommissioned as the navy's first missile-firing submarine. A veteran of World War II, she has been equipped with the navy's surface-launched Regulus I missile.

March 13. Aircraft from Task Force 77 deliver a devastating attack against the industrial section of Chongjin, North Korea.

June 11. With the truce talks apparently nearing a conclusion, the navy completes the evacuation of 19,425 Korean civilians from west coast islands north of the 38th Parallel.

June 16. The carrier *Princeton* (CVA 37) establishes a Korean War record by launching 184 sorties against enemy positions in a single day.

July 11. **Marine ace.** Major John F. Volt, a marine pilot flying an F-86 Sabrejet on exchange duty with the Fifth Air Force, shoots down his fifth and sixth MiG-15s.

July 16. **Navy ace.** Obsolete North Korean aircraft have begun nighttime, nuisance raids on Seoul. These planes, derisively known as "Bedcheck Charlies," fly so slowly and at such low altitudes that Fifth Air Force jets are unable to intercept them, and in June a detachment of navy night pilots and four F-4U5N Corsairs are lent to the air force to counter the raids. Between June 29 and this date, Lieutenant Guy P. Bordelon destroys five Charlies, thus becoming the only navy ace of the Korean conflict and the first navy nightfighter ace ever.

July 27. **Korean Armistice.** A cease-fire agreement, effective at 10:00 P.M. on this date, is signed by U.N. and Communist negotiators at the village of Panmunjon.

August 17. Admiral Robert B. ("Mick") Carney becomes the 14th chief of naval operations.

September 2. The navy announces plans to refit the *Midway*-class carriers with steam catapults and angled decks.

October 16. An explosion and fire wrack the

Bridge busting, summer 1953: the results of an air strike by Task Force 77. Official U.S. Navy photograph.

carrier *Leyte* (CV 32) in Boston Harbor, killing 37 men.

1954

May 3.   Charles S. Thomas assumes office as 53rd secretary of the navy.

May 26.   The carrier *Bennington* (CV 20) is damaged by an explosion and fire off Newport, Rhode Island; 103 men are killed and 201 injured.

May 27.   The chief of naval operations approves a program to completely modernize the *Essex*-class carriers by the installation of angled flight decks, enclosed bows, and other improvements.

July 26.   Near Hainan Island, in the South China Sea, two Communist Chinese LA-7-type aircraft attack two AD-1 Skyraiders that are searching for survivors from an Air Cathay flight shot down on July 24. Return fire from the Skyraiders destroys both planes.

August 11.   Chinese Communist Foreign Minister Chou En-lai declares that Nationalist-held Formosa must be "liberated." President Eisenhower replies that it will be necessary to "run over the Seventh Fleet" to do so.

August 12.   Rear Admiral Walter F. Boone becomes 38th superintendent of the Naval Academy.

August 16–May 18, 1955.   **Operation "Passage to Freedom."** According to the terms of the Geneva Accords, which ended the French Indochina War, Vietnamese who do not wish to live in the Communist-controlled north may move to the south. U.S. Navy units under Rear Admiral Lorenzo Sabin assist that emigration, transporting 293,002 civilians and 17,846 military personnel.

September 4.   Two MiG fighters shoot down a P-2V Neptune reconnaissance aircraft of Patrol Squadron 19 on a routine flight over international waters off the coast of Siberia. Nine of the plane's ten crewmen are rescued.

September 8.   **SEATO.** In Manila, the United States and seven other nations—Great Britain, France, Australia, New Zealand, Pakistan, Thailand, and the Philippines—

sign a collective defense treaty that provides the basis for the Southeast Asia Treaty Organization. Cambodia, Laos, and South Vietnam are later included in its protocols. Unlike NATO, however, SEATO does not establish an allied army or an integrated command.

September 13.   President Eisenhower orders the Seventh Fleet to provide logistic support to the Nationalist Chinese forces defending the coastal islands of Matsu and Quemoy.

September 30.   **The Nautilus.** The navy's first nuclear-powered ship, the submarine *Nautilus* (SSN 571), is commissioned at Groton, Connecticut.

1955

January 17.   **"Underway on nuclear power."** With these words, Commander Dennis Wilkinson reports the successful start of the first trial run of the *Nautilus* (SSN 571).

February 6–13.   **Evacuation of the Tachens.** The Seventh Fleet, Vice Admiral A.M. Pride, evacuates 29,000 Nationalist Chinese civilians and troops from the Tachen Islands, off the coast of China. The operation is covered by a carrier task force consisting of the *Essex* (CV 9), *Kearsarge* (CV 33), *Midway* (CVB 41), *Wasp* (CV 18) and *Yorktown* (CV 10).

June 22.   A P-2V Neptune reconnaissance plane of Patrol Squadron 9, damaged by fire from two Soviet MiG-15 fighters while over international waters, crashes without loss of life on St. Lawrence Island in the Bering Strait.

August 17.   Admiral Arleigh A. Burke becomes the 15th chief of naval operations.

September 13.   President Eisenhower directs the Department of Defense to develop a ballistic missile with a range of 1,500 miles and the capability of being launched from both land and sea.

October 1.   **New carriers.** The *Forrestal* (CVA 59), lead ship of a class of six new carriers—the first built since World War II—is commissioned at Norfolk, Virginia. Specifically designed to operate jet aircraft, these "super carriers" displace 59,630 tons.

November 8.   The Joint Army-Navy Missile

The *Forrestal* on maneuvers in the Caribbean in February 1956. Official U.S. Navy photograph.

The *Nautilus* on her sea trials. Official U.S. Navy photograph.

Committee is established to oversee development of the intermediate range ballistic missile later designated the Jupiter.

November 17.   The navy creates a Special Projects Office under Rear Admiral William F. Raborn, Jr., to direct the development of a shipboard launching system for ballistic missiles.

November 28.   Secretary of the Navy Thomas sets a target date of 1965 for the completion of a solid-fuel ballistic missile for use by submarines.

1956

January 1.   General Randolph McC. Pate becomes 21st commandant of the marine corps.

January 10.   **Nuke school.** The navy's first nuclear power school is established at the submarine base at New London, Connecticut.

March 12.   Attack Squadron 83, the first to be equipped with air-to-air missiles, deploys to the Mediterranean aboard the carrier *Intrepid* (CVA 11). Its F-8 Crusaders carry Sparrow missiles.

March 16.   Rear Admiral W. R. Smedberg III becomes 39th superintendent of the Naval Academy.

April 14.   The carrier *Saratoga* (CVA 60) is commissioned.

June 25.   Fleet Admiral Ernest J. King dies in Portsmouth, New Hampshire, at the age of 77.

July 20.   The first amphibious assault ship, the *Thetis Bay* (CVAH-1, later redesignated LPH-1) is commissioned. Vessels of this type carry a marine battalion (approximately 2,000 men) and helicopters to land them on hostile coasts.

August 22.   A Japan-based P-4M Mercator reconnaissance plane is shot down while flying a routine patrol over international waters off the coast of China. There are no survivors.

October 29–November 3.   **Suez Crisis.** Ships of the Sixth Fleet join U.S. military aircraft in evacuating American citizens from Egypt, Israel, and Syria when war breaks out in the Middle East. A total of 2,213 Americans are extracted, 1,680 by sea and 533 by air.

October 31.   Seven officers and men headed by Rear Admiral G. J. Dufek, Commander Naval Support Force, Antarctic, become the first persons to set foot at the South Pole since Captain Robert Scott, RN, reached there in 1912. They land in the R-4D twin-engined transport *Que Sera Sera*.

December 3.   **Polaris approved.** The navy is authorized to pursue the development of the compact, solid-fuel Polaris missile and to withdraw from the liquid-fuel Jupiter missile project to which the army is committed. Approval for this program had been requested on November 9.

December 18.   The Joint Army-Navy Missile Committee is disbanded.

December 19.   Admiral William F. Raborn's Special Projects Office is assigned the responsibility of developing the complete Polaris missile system, which is accorded the navy's highest priority.

1957

February 8.   The Chief of Naval Operations, Admiral Arleigh Burke, sets a deadline of January 1965 for the deployment of a solid-fuel missile with a 1,500-mile range suitable for launching from a submerged submarine. A few months later the deadline is moved up to January 1963.

March 11.   Rear Admiral Richard E. Byrd dies at the age of 68. He was the first man to fly over both the Poles.

March 17.   **Vanguard I.** The navy's first satellite is launched from Cape Canaveral, Florida. It weighs 3½ pounds.

April 1.   Thomas S. Gates becomes the 54th secretary of the navy.

August 10.   The carrier *Ranger* (CVA 61) is commissioned.

August 12.   Lieutenant Commander Don Walker lands an F-3D Skyknight aboard the carrier *Antietam* (CV 36) in the first test of the automatic carrier landing system.

October 9.   Neil H. McElroy becomes the sixth secretary of defense.

December 9.   Secretary of Defense McElroy advances the deadline for the development of the Polaris submarine missile system to 1960. The preliminary design of the submarine itself has just been completed.

1958

January. The first three Polaris fleet ballistic-missile submarines are put under construction. The lead ship, the *George Washington* (SSBN 598), had been laid down as the nuclear-powered attack submarine *Scorpion*. To accommodate Polaris missile-launching tubes, she is cut in two and lengthened by the insertion of a 130-foot section amidships.

March 7. The *Grayback* (SSG 574), the first submarine designed with the capability of launching guided missiles, is commissioned. She must surface to fire her jet-powered Regulus II missiles, however, and the program is abandoned in favor of Polaris.

May 28. The *Galveston* (CLG 3, originally CL 93), the first cruiser equipped with the Talos antiaircraft missile, is commissioned.

May 28. The submarine *Stickelback* (SS 415) is sunk without loss of life in a collision with the destroyer *Silverstein* (DE 534) off Pearl Harbor.

June 27. Rear Admiral Charles L. Melson becomes the 40th superintendent of the Naval Academy.

July 15. **Lebanon landing.** At the request of Lebanese President Camille Chamoun, U.S. forces commanded by Admiral J.L. Holloway, Jr., land at Beirut to support his government, which is threatened by both civil war and the prospect of foreign invasion. Two of the Sixth Fleet's three marine battalion landing teams are ashore within 24 hours. The third follows shortly. Within a few days the marines are joined by a reinforced airborne brigade flown from West Germany, and a USAF composite strike group arrives from the United States to support the Sixth Fleet carriers *Essex* (CV 9), *Saratoga* (CVA 60) and *Wasp* (CV 18). Peace is maintained. The feared invasion does not materialize, and American negotiators bring the civil war to an end by arranging an election satisfactory to all parties. The last American troops are withdrawn on October 25.

August 3. **First under the ice.** The nuclear submarine *Nautilus* (SSN 571), Commander William R. Anderson, becomes the first ship to reach the North Pole, beneath which she passes on a 4-day, 1,830-mile voyage under the polar ice from the Pacific to the Atlantic, where she surfaces on August 7.

August 11. **Surface at the Pole.** At 6:47 P.M., the *Skate* (SSN 578), Commander James F. Calvert, becomes the first submarine to surface at the North Pole. She does so again on August 17 in the course of an Arctic voyage of exploration that lasts from July 30 to September 22.

August 23. **Matsu and Quemoy crisis.** Communist China begins an intensive artillery bombardment of the Nationalist-held offshore islands of Matsu and Quemoy. Pres-

Marines go ashore near Beirut, Lebanon, July 15, 1958. Defense Department photo (Marine Corps).

ident Eisenhower orders the Seventh Fleet to assist the Nationalists in supplying the 100,000-man garrison of Quemoy, which it does by escorting their transports to the three-mile territorial limit. The president also reminds the Communists of a congressional resolution authorizing him to defend Formosa and deploys a six-carrier task force around the island. The crisis has cooled by December.

October 24.   The transport *Kliensmith* (APD 134), supported by the carrier *Franklin D. Roosevelt* (CVA 42), evacuates 56 American citizens and 3 foreign nationals from Nicara, Cuba, as Castro's revolution nears a climax.

1959

January 10.   The carrier *Independence* (CVA 62) is commissioned.

February 24.   The navy announces plans to scrap 43 obsolete warships, including the battleships *California* (BB 44), *Colorado* (BB 45), *Maryland* (BB 46), *Tennessee* (BB 43), and *West Virginia* (BB 48). The four fast battleships of the *Iowa* class are retained.

June 8.   William B. Franke becomes 55th secretary of the navy.

June 16.   Two MiG fighters attack and damage

a P-4M navy reconnaissance plane during a routine mission over international waters off the coast of Korea.

July 20.   Fleet Admiral William D. Leahy dies, aged 84, at Bethesda, Maryland.

August 16.   Fleet Admiral William F. ("Bull") Halsey dies at the age of 76.

December 1.   **Antarctic Treaty.** Twelve nations, including the United States and the Soviet Union, pledge that they will not undertake any kind of military activities in Antarctica.

December 2.   Thomas S. Gates, Jr., becomes the seventh secretary of defense.

December 31.   **First fleet ballistic-missile submarine.** The *George Washington* (SSBN 598) is commissioned.

1960

January 1.   General David M. Shoup becomes 22nd commandant of the U.S. Marine Corps.

April 13.   Navy Transit IB, the navy's first navigational satellite, is launched from Cape Canaveral, Florida.

May 6.   The Cuban cutter *Oriente* fires on the submarine *Sea Poacher* (SS 406) in San Nicholas Channel.

May 10.   **Around the world submerged.** The nuclear-powered submarine *Triton* (SSN 586), Commander Edward L. Beach, becomes the first vessel to circumnavigate the earth submerged. Her voyage, which lasts

The launching of the *George Washington* at Groton, Connecticut, June 9, 1959. Courtesy General Dynamics Corporation.

Captain Edward L. Beach on the bridge of the *Triton*. Official U.S. Navy photograph.

for 84 days and covers 41,519 miles, closely follows the route taken by Magellan in the first conventional circumnavigation almost 350 years before.

June 22.   Rear Admiral John F. Davidson becomes 41st superintendent of the Naval Academy.

July 19.   The destroyers *Ammen* (DD 527) and *Collett* (DD 730) collide off Long Beach, California. Eleven of the *Ammen's* crewmen are killed, twenty injured, and the ship is damaged beyond repair.

July 20.   **First Polaris launch.** Off Cape Canaveral, Florida, the *George Washington* (SSBN 598) successfully conducts the first submerged launchings of the new Polaris A-1 missile.

September 10.   The *Charles F. Adams* (DDG 2), the lead ship of a new class of 4,500-ton general-purpose destroyers, is launched.

The second of the two Polaris missiles launched by the *George Washington* on July 20, 1960, breaks the surface. The upright object at lower right is the tip of a radio antenna temporarily mounted on the submarine to receive telemetry data from the missile. Official U.S. Navy photograph.

The first ships equipped with Tartar missiles, 23 of them will join the fleet between 1960 and 1963.

November 1.   Prime Minister Harold Macmillan announces the British government's decision to allow Polaris submarines to be based at Holy Loch, Scotland.

November 15.   **First Polaris patrol.** The *George Washington* (SSBN 598) sails from Charleston, South Carolina, on the navy's first operational Polaris submarine patrol. She carries 16 Polaris A-1 nuclear missiles, which have a range of 1,200 nautical miles.

November 19.   The carrier *Constellation* (CVA 64) is swept by fire while under construction at the Brooklyn Navy Yard. Fifty workers are killed and 150 injured. Damage to the ship is estimated at $75,000,000.

1961

January 12.   In the budget proposed for Fiscal Year 1962, President Eisenhower projects a navy of 817 ships (625,000 personnel) and a marine corps of three divisions and three air wings (175,000 personnel).

January 20.   President Kennedy names Robert S. McNamara the eighth secretary of defense and John B. Connally, Jr., the 56th secretary of the navy.

April 17–20.   **The Bay of Pigs.** A force of 1,400 Cuban exiles, secretly trained by U.S. personnel in Guatemala and equipped with obsolete American equipment, lands at the Bay of Pigs, on the southwestern coast of Cuba, to overthrow the Communist government of Fidel Castro. Due in part to the failure of preliminary air strikes to eliminate the Cuban air force, the invasion is a disaster. Virtually the entire exile brigade is killed or captured. American naval units are standing offshore, in position to assist the exiles, but President Kennedy decides that to intervene would only worsen the situation. The debacle is a heavy blow to American prestige. Some months later the captured Cubans are ransomed with American medical supplies.

April 29.   The first missile-armed aircraft carrier, the *Kitty Hawk* (CVA 63), is commissioned at Camden, New Jersey.

May 5.   **First man in space.** Commander Alan

Commander Alan B. Shepard, Jr., soon after landing from his suborbital flight. Courtesy National Aeronautics and Space Administration.

B. Shepard, Jr., reaches an altitude of 116.5 miles in the Mercury capsule Freedom 7 on a suborbital flight from Cape Canaveral, Florida. He is picked up in the Atlantic, 302 miles downrange, by a helicopter from the carrier *Lake Champlain* (CVS 39).

August 1.   Admiral George W. Anderson, Jr., becomes the 16th chief of naval operations.

August 26.   The *Iwo Jima* (LPH 2), the first vessel built from the keel up as an amphibious assault ship, is commissioned.

September 10.   The world's first nuclear-powered, guided-missile cruiser, the *Long Beach* (CGN 9), is commissioned.

October 23.   The first firing of the Polaris A-2 missile from a submerged submarine takes place aboard the *Ethan Allen* (SSBN 608). The range of this new missile is 1,500 miles.

October 27.   The carrier *Constellation* (CVA 64) is commissioned.

November 16.   **Increased aid to South Vietnam.** Acting upon a report by General Maxwell D. Taylor, President Kennedy decides to increase the number of American military advisors to the Republic of South Vietnam, whose existence is threatened by a Communist insurgency sponsored by North Vietnam.

November 25.   **First nuclear-powered carrier.** The *Enterprise* (CVAN 65) is commissioned at Newport News, Virginia. Truly termed "the largest moving structure ever built by man," she is 1,123 feet in length, displaces 85,830 tons and carries a crew of 4,600. Her flight deck covers four and one-half acres. On trials she achieves a speed of more than 35 knots.

November 28.   **ASROC.** The antisubmarine rocket (ASROC) weapons system is formally approved.

1962

January 1.   **Creation of the SEALs.** Two Sea Air Land (SEAL) operating teams are es-

The *Enterprise*. Official U.S. Navy photograph.

tablished for the purpose of conducting unconventional warfare at sea and in coastal and riverine areas.

January 4.   Fred Korth becomes the 57th secretary of the navy.

February 8.   The U.S. Military Assistance Advisory Group (MAAG) in South Vietnam, which had been established in 1956, is reorganized as the U.S. Military Assistance Command, Vietnam (MACV), under the command of Lieutenant General Paul Harkins.

February 20.   **First American orbital flight.** Lieutenant Colonel John H. Glenn, Jr., USMC, makes three orbits of the earth, at an average speed of 17,400 miles per hour in the Project Mercury capsule Friendship 7. He travels 81,000 miles, attaining a maximum altitude of 162 miles, in 4 hours and 55 minutes. Landing in the Atlantic, he is recovered by the destroyer *Noa* (DD 841).

April 12.   Three ships of the Seventh Fleet Amphibious Group, the *Valley Forge* (LPH 8), *Navarro* (APA 215), and *Point Defiance* (LSD 31), land marines in Thailand to help support the independence of that country.

May 24.   **Second orbital flight.** Lieutenant Commander M. Scott Carpenter completes three orbits in the Aurora 7.

August 7.   **First Polaris A3.** The first flight model of this missile, capable of traveling 2,500 miles, is launched at Cape Canaveral, Florida.

August 17.   The *Long Point* (PC(H)1), the navy's first hydrofoil patrol craft, is launched at Seattle, Washington.

August 18.   Rear Admiral Charles C. Kirkpatrick becomes the 42nd superintendent of the U.S. Naval Academy.

August 31.   **The end of LTA.** The decision to terminate the navy's lighter-than-air program was announced on November 30, 1961. Almost a year later, the last airship flight is made from the historic Naval Air Station, Lakehurst, New Jersey.

October 3.   Commander Walter W. Schirra completes an orbital flight of more than 160,000 miles in 10 hours and 46 minutes in the Mercury-Atlas Sigma 7 capsule.

October 6.   **First nuclear-powered, guided-missile frigate.** The *Bainbridge* (DLGN 25) is commissioned.

October 14.   **Beginning of the Cuban Missile Crisis.** An American U-2 reconnaissance plane photographs a Soviet nuclear missile site under construction at San Cristóbal, 100 miles west of Havana, Cuba.

October 16.   The U-2 photographs are presented to President Kennedy. Soon afterwards it is also learned that Soviet Il-28 bombers are being assembled on Cuban airfields.

October 16-20.   **What to do?** The president's closest advisors, later designated the Excomm (Executive Committee of the National Security Council) hold marathon meetings to frame an appropriate response to the Soviet challenge. The joint chiefs of staff are unanimous in recommending a surgical air strike, a course a number of the civilians also urge. Kennedy's reluctance to adopt so drastic a decision is reinforced by his military advisors' admission that they cannot guarantee to eliminate all of the missiles with a first strike. In the end, he chooses the more flexible option of imposing a naval blockade, which, since the United States and Cuba are not at war, will be called a quarantine.

October 22.   **Quarantine of Cuba.** President Kennedy appears on national television to announce that he is imposing a naval quarantine, effective October 24, to block the entry of Soviet offensive weapons into Cuba. To carry out the quarantine, Task Force 136 is organized under Vice Admiral Alfred G. Ward, Commander, Second Fleet, and Commander, Strike Fleet Atlantic. It consists of the support carrier *Essex* (CVS 9), the heavy cruisers *Newport News* (CA 148), and *Canberra* (CAG 2), several squadrons of destroyers, and the necessary support ships. At the same time, Task Force 135 is established under Rear Admiral John T. Hayward, Commander, Carrier Division Two. Formed around the nuclear carrier *Enterprise* (CVAN 65), it stands ready to come to the defense of the U.S. naval base at Guantánamo. Rear Admiral Robert J. Stroh's Carrier Division Six, with the *Independence* (CVA 62), is also in position to intervene.

October 23.   The United Nations Security Council holds an emergency session to consider a charge by the United States that the Soviet Union is threatening the peace. On the same day, the Organization of American States approves the use of force in carrying out the quarantine of Cuba by a vote of 19-0, Uruguay abstaining.

October 24. The quarantine goes into effect. Reconnaissance has revealed that 25 Soviet vessels are en route to Cuba, but at mid-morning all but one of those nearing the blockade line stop dead in the water. Several hours later, they reverse course.

October 25. On the quarantine line, the destroyer *Gearing* (DD 710) stops the Soviet tanker *Bucharest*, but allows her to proceed to Cuba upon learning that she is carrying only oil.

October 26. The destroyers *Joseph P. Kennedy, Jr.* (DD 850) and *John R. Pierce* (DD 753) halt and board a Soviet-chartered, Lebanese-flag freighter, the SS *Marucla*. After her cargo is inspected, she is allowed to continue to Havana.

October 26. At 6:00 P.M. President Kennedy receives an emotional letter from Soviet Premier Khrushchev, which states that the missiles had been placed in Cuba only to deter an American invasion and promises to remove them if the United States will pledge to lift the blockade and not attack Cuba.

October 27. Before Kennedy has replied to Khrushchev's letter, an American U-2 is shot down over Cuba by a surface-to-air missile, and a second letter is received from Khrushchev. In this communication, the Soviet leader couples a demand for the withdrawal of American missiles from Turkey to his previous terms for the withdrawal of Soviet missiles from Cuba. For several grim hours it appears as though the situation has reached an impasse. Then the president's brother, Attorney General Robert F. Kennedy, suggests that the president agree to the conditions of Khrushchev's first letter and simply ignore the second. This is done. At the same time, Robert Kennedy privately informs Soviet Ambassador Dobrinin that the president was already planning to remove the missiles from Turkey.

October 28. **The crisis resolved.** Khrushchev notifies Kennedy that he is ordering the

The Soviet ship *Volgoles*, closely observed by the radar picket *Vesole* and a navy P2V Neptune patrol plane, on her way home with a deckload of missiles at the conclusion of the Cuban Missile Crisis. This official U.S. Navy photograph was taken on November 9, 1962.

Soviet missiles and bombers in Cuba to be withdrawn. The most dangerous, direct Soviet-American confrontation to date in the Cold War is over.

November 8. The Department of Defense announces that the Cuban missile bases have been dismantled.

November 20. President Kennedy states that, having received Premier Khrushchev's promise to recall all Soviet bombers from Cuba within 30 days, he has ended the quarantine of the island.

1963

April 10. **Loss of the Thresher.** The nuclear submarine *Thresher* (SSN 593), Lieutenant Commander John W. Harvey, is reported overdue and presumed lost with all hands, 129 officers, men, and civilian technicians, approximately 240 miles east of Cape Cod, Massachusetts. Apparently the disaster resulted from a reactor shut-down during a dive. The boat's auxiliary engines were unable to check her descent, and she was crushed by the pressure of the ocean depths. On October 1, 1964, the navy announces that the main wreckage has been located by the deep-submergence vehicle *Trieste II.*

The *Thresher*. Official U.S. Navy photograph.

April 23.   The *Lafayette* (SSBN 616), the lead ship of a new class of fleet ballistic-missile submarines, is commissioned.

August 1.   Admiral David L. McDonald becomes the 17th chief of naval operations.

October 26.   A Polaris A-3 missile is fired from a submerged submarine for the first time by the *Andrew Jackson* (SSBN 619).

November 1–2.   President Ngo Dinh Diem of South Vietnam is overthrown and killed by a military coup, leading to 18 months of political instability that greatly complicates American efforts to aid the country in resisting the Viet Cong insurgency.

November 29.   Paul H. Nitze becomes the 58th secretary of the navy.

December 4.   **SUBROC.** The navy announces that it is developing a rocket-powered guided missile, capable of being fired underwater from a conventional torpedo tube and armed with a nuclear depth bomb to destroy enemy submarines at long range.

1964

January 1.   General Wallace M. Greene, Jr., becomes the 23rd commandant of the marine corps.

January 11.   Rear Admiral Charles S. Minter, Jr., becomes the 43rd superintendent of the U.S. Naval Academy.

January 13.   During a revolution in Zanzibar, the destroyer *Manley* (DD 940) evacuates 55 American citizens and 36 other persons.

February 1.   **Admiral Rickover is extended.** Vice Admiral Hyman G. Rickover, assis-

tant chief of the Bureau of Ships for Nuclear Propulsion and Director of Naval Reactors in the Atomic Energy Commission, reaches the mandatory retirement age of 64, but at the request of the president remains on active duty as a retired officer. He will receive biennial extensions for the next 15 years.

May 13.   **First nuclear-powered task group.** In the Mediterranean, the Sixth Fleet forms the world's first task group of nuclear-powered ships. Commanded by Rear Admiral Bernard M. Strean, it consists of the attack carrier *Enterprise* (CVAN 65), the guided-missile cruiser *Long Beach* (CGN 9) and the guided-missile frigate *Bainbridge* (DLGN 25).

June 6.   An RF-8 reconnaissance plane piloted by Lieutenant Charles F. Klusmann from the carrier *Kitty Hawk* (CVA 63) is shot down by Communist insurgents over the Plaine des Jarres, Laos. Lieutenant Klusmann parachutes to safety, but later waves off a rescue helicopter, fearing that it will also be shot down. Captured by the Communists, he escapes on September 1 and is awarded the Distinguished Flying Cross.

June 7.   An F-8 Crusader fighter from the *Kitty Hawk* is shot down while escorting a reconnaissance plane over the Plaine des Jarres, Laos.

July 31.   **Operation Sea Orbit.** All-nuclear Task Force One, consisting of the carrier *Enterprise* (CVAN 65), guided-missile cruiser *Long Beach* (CGN 9) and guided-missile frigate *Bainbridge* (DLGN 25), departs Gibraltar for a 30,565-nautical-mile unre-

Operation Sea Orbit: from left to right, the frigate *Bainbridge*, cruiser *Long Beach*, and carrier *Enterprise*. Official U.S. Navy photograph.

plenished circumnavigation of the globe. The exercise concludes when the task force enters Charleston, South Carolina, on October 1.

August 2.   **Tonkin Gulf incident.** The destroyer *Maddox* (DD 731), Captain Herbert L. Ogier, is attacked at 3:08 P.M. local time by three North Vietnamese patrol boats while operating in international waters 30 miles off the coast of North Vietnam. The *Maddox* opens fire and calls on the carrier *Ticonderoga* (CVA 14), which sends four F-8E Crusaders to her assistance. The engagement lasts 21 minutes, during which the *Maddox* evades two torpedoes and one of the enemy boats is sunk.

August 4.   **Second Tonkin Gulf incident.** Be-

The *Maddox*. Official U.S. Navy photograph.

ginning at 9:30 P.M., the *Maddox* and the *Turner Joy* (DD 951), Commander Robert C. Barnhart, patrolling together in the Gulf of Tonkin, pick up radar contacts that are identified as North Vietnamese patrol boats. The contacts persist for four hours, during which both ships take them under fire and maneuver to evade torpedoes. Aircraft launched from the *Ticonderoga* are unable to locate the enemy in the darkness. Afterwards there is speculation that the contacts were only radar blips.

August 5.   **First naval strike on North Vietnam.** In retaliation for the attacks on the *Maddox* and the *Turner Joy*, President Johnson orders aircraft from the *Constellation* (CVA 64) and *Ticonderoga* (CVA 14) to attack naval bases, patrol boats, and oil depots along 100 miles of the North Vietnamese coast. A total of 64 sorties are flown, during which 25 patrol boats are damaged or destroyed and an estimated 90 percent of the petroleum in the target areas is set ablaze. The strikes last for four hours. The *Constellation* loses two planes: an A-1H Skyraider, whose pilot, Lieutenant (jg) Richard A. Sather, is the first navy pilot to be killed in Vietnam, and an A-4E Skyhawk, whose pilot, Lieutenant (jg) Everett Alvarez, becomes the first navy POW.

August 7.   **Tonkin Gulf (Southeast Asia) Resolution.** Congress relinquishes its warmaking powers to the president by authorizing him to "take all necessary measures to repel any armed attack against the forces of the United States . . . [and] to assist any member or protocol state" of the Southeast Asia Treaty Organization. The resolution passes in the House of Representatives by a vote of 416–0 and in the Senate by 88–2. It is on the basis of this legislation that President Johnson will commit U.S. forces to an ever-expanding role in Vietnam.

September 18.   After nightfall in the Gulf of Tonkin the destroyers *Morton* (DD 948) and *Parsons* (DD 949) open fire on four radar contacts believed to be attacking torpedo boats. The destroyers are undamaged; the effect of their fire is unknown.

September 28.   The first deployment of the Polaris A-3 occurs when the *Daniel Webster* (SSBN 626), armed with these missiles, departs Charleston, South Carolina, for a two-month patrol.

November 1.   **Bien Hoa incident.** The Viet Cong mortar the South Vietnamese air base at Bien Hoa. Four American servicemen are killed, 72 are wounded, and 28 American aircraft are damaged or destroyed.

December 6.   The completion of the last of three salt-water conversion plants makes the U.S. naval base at Guantánamo Bay, Cuba, independent of any outside water supply. The government of Fidel Castro had cut off the flow of fresh water to the base on February 6 and offered to restore it on March 4, but the offer was refused.

December 24.   A Viet Cong bomb explodes outside the Brink Bachelor Officers' Quarters in Saigon, killing two Americans and wounding 51 Americans and South Vietnamese.

December 26.   The first fleet ballistic-missile submarine patrol made in the Pacific begins when the *Daniel Boone* (SSBN 629) departs Guam armed with the Polaris A-3.

December 31.   At year's end, there are 23,000 U.S. servicemen in South Vietnam.

1965

January 23.   The aircraft carrier *America* (CVA 66) is commissioned.

February 7.   Eight American servicemen are killed and 126 wounded by a Viet Cong attack on a barracks at Pleiku, South Vietnam.

February 7.   **Flaming Dart I.** In retaliation for the Pleiku incident, barracks and facilities near Dong Hoi, North Vietnam, are attacked by 83 planes from the carriers *Coral Sea* (CVA 43), *Hancock* (CVA 19), and *Ranger* (CVA 61). One aircraft is lost. Simultaneously, the South Vietnamese Air Force hits North Vietnamese installations at Vinh.

February 10.   Twenty-three Americans are killed and twenty-one injured when the Viet Cong bomb an enlisted men's barracks at the helicopter base at Qui Nhon.

February 11.   **Flaming Dart II.** North Vietnamese military installations near Chan Hoa are attacked by 99 aircraft from the *Coral Sea* (CVA 43), *Hancock* (CVA 19), and *Ranger* (CVA 61), while the South Vietnamese Air Force strikes Vit Thu Lu. An F-8D Crusader from the *Coral Sea* is lost.

March 2.   **Rolling Thunder.** U.S. Navy and Air Force planes begin sustained bombardment of military targets in North Vietnam. These raids are an application of the strategic theory of graduated response, according to which pressure will be incrementally increased until the North's "ouch level" is reached, and it will terminate its support of the Viet Cong. The campaign continues until October 31, 1968. Unfortunately, the pressure applied does not produce the desired result. North Vietnam's "ouch level" will not be reached until the Linebacker II B-52 strikes of December 1972.

March 8.   **Marines land at Da Nang.** Using the authority conferred on him by the Tonkin Gulf Resolution, President Johnson orders the 9th Marine Expeditionary Brigade, 3,500 men commanded by Brigadier General Frederick J. Karch, ashore to assume responsibility for the security of the air base at Da Nang, South Vietnam. This is the first commitment of American ground combat troops in the Vietnam war. Without realizing it, the United States has entered its longest foreign war.

March 11.   **Operation Market Time.** The operation that will be named Market Time begins when the Seventh Fleet destroyers *Black* (DD 666) and *Higbee* (DD 806) are ordered to the coastal zone of Vietnam to inspect native junk traffic in order to prevent the infiltration of men and arms to the south. Many more vessels as well as patrol planes are soon assigned to this mission, Task Force 71 (the Vietnam Patrol Force) being established to conduct it. By the end of November, Market Time ships have made 73,000 junk sightings, of which approximately 15,000 have been visually inspected at close quarters and another 6,000 boarded and searched.

March 15.   Aircraft from the *Hancock* (CVA 19) and *Ranger* (CVA 61) attack an ammunition depot at Phu Qui, 100 miles south of Hanoi. One plane and its pilot are lost.

March 23.   The first two-man Gemini space capsule, the *Molly Brown*, completes three orbits of the earth. Aboard are Lieutenant Colonel Virgil Grissom, USAF, and Lieutenant Commander John Young.

March 26.   Four radar sites in North Vietnam are attacked by 40 planes from the *Hancock* (CVA 19) and *Coral Sea* (CVA 43). Two aircraft are lost, but both pilots are rescued.

From April on.   **Naval air war in Vietnam.** From this time forward, strikes involving from 4 to 100 aircraft are flown almost daily from carriers at Yankee Station in the South China Sea, attacking military targets, transportation facilities, and power

An A-1 Skyraider on the catapult of the *Hancock*, ready to be launched on a strike against North Vietnam, March 1965. Official U.S. Navy photograph.

stations in North Vietnam. Altogether, in the course of the year navy planes will fly more than 55,000 sorties in Vietnam. The U.S. Air Force will fly 50,000.

April 9.   Four F-4 Phantom fighters, flying cover for a raid on North Vietnam, are attacked by several MiG-17s, nationality undetermined, about 35 miles south of Hainan Island. One MiG is believed downed, and one F-4 fails to return.

April 10.   **Marine air to Vietnam.** Marine Fighter Attack Squadron (VMFA) 531 is based at Da Nang. Other squadrons soon follow.

April 14.   The 3rd Battalion, Fourth Marines, lands near Da Nang, bringing the strength of American ground combat troops in South Vietnam to 8,000.

April 15.   Navy and marine aircraft from the *Coral Sea* (CVA 43) and *Midway* (CVA 41) join U.S. and South Vietnamese air force planes in attacking Viet Cong positions in South Vietnam. This is the first time naval aircraft have been used against targets inside the country.

April 15.   Ten aircraft from the same two carriers fly the first reconnaissance mission over North Vietnam.

April 22.   **First ground action in Vietnam.** Near Da Nang, marines engage in a fire fight with the Viet Cong. No marines are killed or seriously wounded.

April 28.   **Dominican intervention.** A 400-man expeditionary force of the 3rd Battalion, Sixth Marines, is airlifted into Santo Domingo, the capital of the Dominican Republic, where a revolution that began on April 25 is believed to endanger American citizens.

April 29.   Reinforcements raise the strength of marine forces in the Dominican Republic to 1,600. They will be organized as the 4th Marine Expeditionary Brigade.

May 3.   **First army combat unit to Vietnam.** Leading elements of the 173rd Airborne Brigade begin to land at Saigon. The arrival of this unit will raise the total number of U.S. personnel in South Vietnam to 36,000.

May 3–7.   **III MAF.** In Vietnam the 9th Marine Expeditionary Brigade is reinforced and reorganized as the III Marine Amphibious Force, under Lieutenant General Lewis W.

Walt. The marines will be responsible for the northernmost of the four military districts into which the country is divided, five provinces comprising the I Corps Tactical Zone.

May 5.   Mediators of the Organization of American States persuade the warring Dominican factions to sign a cease fire, despite which fighting continues in Santo Domingo.

May 7.   **Chu Lai airfield.** The 1st and 2nd Battalions, Fourth Marines, and several hundred seabees land at Chu Lai, South Vietnam, and commence construction of a marine field. It becomes operational on June 1.

May 11.   With the arrival of elements of the army's 82nd Airborne Division, the number of U.S. troops in the Dominican Republic rises to more than 11,000, including 6,000 marines.

May 12–18.   **First Vietnamese bombing pause.** President Johnson suspends air attacks on North Vietnam and calls upon its government to negotiate. There is no response.

May 16.   **Dixie Station.** A single-carrier station is established approximately 100 miles southeast of Cam Ranh Bay, from which strikes can be launched in support of allied forces inside South Vietnam. It is discontinued 15 months later, following the build-up of air strength ashore.

May 20.   **First shore bombardment of the Vietnam conflict.** Units of the Seventh Fleet begin to deliver the navy's first fire-support missions since the Korean War. The use of naval gunfire in South Vietnam had been authorized on May 14.

May 26–June 6.   **Dominican wind-down.** Arrangements having been made through the Organization of American States to have an Inter-American peace-keeping force replace U.S. troops in the Dominican Republic, the marines are withdrawn. In the course of the crisis they have lost 10 men killed and 26 wounded in scattered street fighting in Santo Domingo. Elements of the 82nd Airborne remain to form part of the Inter-American force.

June 9.   **Development of Cam Ranh Bay.** The army's 35th Engineer Group lands to begin construction of a major port facility at Cam Ranh Bay, South Vietnam.

June 12.   Rear Admiral Draper L. Kauffman be-

comes the 44th superintendent of the Naval Academy.

June 17.   **First confirmed MiG kills of the Vietnam War.** Some 50 miles south of Hanoi two F-4B Phantoms of the *Midway's* VF-21 are attacked by four MiG-17s and shoot down two with Sparrow air-to-air missiles.

June 19.   Youthful Air Vice Marshall Nguyen Cao Ky becomes premier of South Vietnam, effectively ending the political instability that has plagued the country since the overthrow of President Diem in November 1963.

June 20.   Over North Vietnam, two MiG-17s attack four propeller-driven A-1H Skyraiders (popularly known as Spads) from the *Midway* (CVA 41). A Skyraider destroys one of the enemy with 20-mm cannon fire.

July 20–August 1.   **The coast guard in Vietnam.** Seventeen 82-foot coast guard cutters, organized as Coast Guard Division 1, arrive in South Vietnam and begin monitoring coastal shipping as part of the campaign (Operation Market Time) to prevent the infiltration of supplies to the Viet Cong. Each boat carries a crew of two officers and nine men.

July 28.   In a television address to the nation, President Johnson announces that he has ordered 1st Cavalry Division (Airmobile) and other, smaller units to South Vietnam. The arrival of these forces will increase the American commitment to approximately 125,000 men.

August 1.   The responsibility for the conduct of Operation Market Time is transferred to Rear Admiral Norvell G. Ward, Naval Component Commander, Military Advisory Command, Vietnam, and the units involved are reorganized as Task Force 115 (Coastal Surveillance Force).

August 11—12.   **First SAMs.** The first navy plane definitely known to have been downed by a surface-to-air missile, an F-4 Phantom II from the *Midway* (CVA 41), is lost over North Vietnam. The first American aircraft destroyed by a SAM was an Air Force F-4 on July 24.

August 13.   Five aircraft—an A-1 Skyraider, two A-4 Skyhawks, and two F-8 Phantoms—from the *Coral Sea* (CVA 43) and *Midway*

(CVA 41) are shot down over North Vietnam by conventional ground fire while searching for SAM sites in the worst day of the naval air war to date.

August 18. **Operation Starlite.** The marines launch their first large-scale amphibious assault in Vietnam on the Van Tuong Peninsula 14 miles south of Chu Lai. Supported by marine air and naval gunfire from the cruiser *Galveston* (CLG 3) and two destroyers, 4,000 men of the Third, Fourth, and Seventh Marines go ashore over the beach and by helicopter. Regimental Landing Team 7 virtually destroys the Viet Cong 1st Regiment, killing 964 of the enemy and taking 125 prisoner. This is the first major action between U.S. troops and the Viet Cong main force and the largest battle Americans have fought since the Korean War. Marines losses are approximately 50 killed and 125 wounded.

August 28. **Aquanauts.** Three teams of 10 men each spend 15 days in Sealab II, 205 feet below the surface off La Jolla, California. Commander M. Scott Carpenter, who is also an astronaut, remains in the capsule for 30 successive days.

October 15. The U.S. Naval Support Activity, Da Nang, is organized under the Commander, Service Force, Pacific Fleet, to provide logistic support for the war effort in South Vietnam.

October 17. An A-6 Intruder and four A-4E Skyhawks from the *Independence* (CVA 62) destroy a North Vietnamese SAM site at Kep 50 miles north of Hanoi without loss to themselves. This is the first successful strike on an enemy missile site.

October 31. **Swift Boats.** The first two Swift Boats to arrive in Vietnam exchange fire with the enemy within hours. These are 50-foot, aluminum-hulled fast patrol craft (PCF) armed with three .50-caliber machine guns and an 81-mm mortar. They carry a crew of one officer and four enlisted men. By the end of the year the navy has ordered 104 of these craft. They will be used mostly in Operation Market Time.

December 2. **First nuclear-powered ship at war.** The *Enterprise* (CVAN 65) launches 118 sorties against targets in South Vietnam, thus becoming the first nuclear ship to engage in hostilities.

An A-4 Skyhawk releasing bombs over Vietnam, November 1965. Official U.S. Navy photograph.

A Swift Boat (PCF) of the brown-water navy on a river north of Saigon during Operation Giant Slingshot in February 1969. Official U.S. Navy photograph.

December 4. The Gemini VII space capsule carries Commander James A. Lovell, Jr., USN, and Lieutenant Colonel Frank Borman, USAF, on a record-breaking orbital flight of 14 days.

December 15. **First meeting in space.** The Gemini VIII capsule, manned by Captain Walter Schirra, USN, and Major Thomas P. Stafford, USAF, is launched and makes a rendezvous with Gemini VII. This is the first meeting of manned space vehicles in orbital flight.

December 18. **Birth of Operation Game Warden.** The U.S. Navy River Patrol Force (Task Force 116) is activated in South Vietnam with the mission of patrolling the Mekong Delta and the swampy area between Saigon and the sea designated the Rung Sat Special Zone. Initially its equipment consists of four large patrol landing craft (LCPLs). Later it is given control of the navy's river patrol boats, which begin to arrive in April 1966, and its activities are designated Operation Game Warden.

December 22. The North Vietnamese thermal power plant at Uong Bi is hit by 100 aircraft from the *Enterprise* (CVAN 65), *Kitty Hawk* (CVA 63), and *Ticonderoga* (CV 14). Two planes are lost. This is the first raid on a purely industrial target in the enemy country.

December 24. **Bombing halt.** President Johnson orders the second pause in the air war against North Vietnam, which will not be resumed until January 31, 1966.

December 31. On this date, there are 181,000 American troops in South Vietnam. A total of 1,365 U.S. servicemen have been killed in action there in the course of the year.

1966

January 31. **End of the bombing halt.** After a 37-day pause, during which the U.S. government has tried unsuccessfully to open negotiations with North Vietnam, raids against military targets in that country are resumed.

February 14. Off the coast of South Vietnam, *PCF 4* becomes the first Swift Boat lost in action when she is destroyed by an underwater explosion. Four of her crewmen are killed and two are wounded.

February 16. The hospital ship *Repose* (AH 16) begins operations at Chu Lai, South Vietnam.

February 20. Fleet Admiral Chester W. Nimitz, the navy's last five-star admiral, dies at the age of 81 at his home on Yerba Buena Island in San Francisco Bay.

February 26. Nine more coast guard cutters reach South Vietnam. Organized as Coast Guard

Division 13, they will be based at Vung Tau. There are now 26 cutters in the combat zone.

March 1. The 5th Marine Division is reactivated. In the next 12 months the personnel strength of the corps is to be increased from 190,000 to 278,000.

March 31. The 1st Marine Division joins the 3rd Marine Division in Vietnam. This is the first time since World War II that two marine divisions have been committed to the same war zone.

March 31. **Arnheiter affair.** Lieutenant Commander Marcus Aurelius Arnheiter is abruptly relieved of command of the destroyer picket *Vance* (DER 387) on the gun line off Vietnam. Subsequently he protests that he has been victimized by a cabal of disloyal junior officers, and the incident attracts nationwide publicity. Hearings and suits continue for several years.

April 1. A new command, U.S. Naval Forces, Vietnam, is created to control the operations of naval forces inside South Vietnam and certain coastal units. Its first chief is Rear Admiral Norvell G. Ward, formerly Naval Component Commander, Military Advisory Command, Vietnam. The latter title is abolished.

April 10. **PBRs in Vietnam.** Two of the navy's new 31-foot, water-jet-propelled river patrol boats (PBRs) begin operating in Vietnam. They are assigned to Operation Game Warden.

April 11. **First B-52 raids on North Vietnam.** U.S. Air Force B-52 bombers attack tar-

A PBR in the Long Tau River, the main shipping channel between Saigon and the sea. This official U.S. Navy photograph was taken in January 1968.

gets near the Mu Gia Pass, 65 miles south of Vinh.

April 17.   Off Vietnam, the heavy cruiser *Canberra* (CAG 2) becomes the first U.S. Navy vessel to relay an operational message via communications satellite, using the Syncom III to reach the Naval Communications Station in Honolulu, 4,000 miles away.

May 1.   **Administrative reorganization.** Four of the navy's traditional bureaus—Naval Weapons, Ships, Supplies and Accounts, and Yards and Docks—are reconstituted into six commands under the Office of Naval Material: Ordnance Systems, Air Systems, Ship Systems, Electronic Systems, Supply Systems, and Facilities Engineering. At the same time, the Office of Naval Material, the Bureau of Naval Personnel, and the Bureau of Medicine and Surgery are placed directly under the chief of naval operations.

May 9.   **First operations in the Mekong Delta.** Ten river patrol boats (PBRs) begin to patrol the Bassac River. By June 1967 the Mekong Delta River Patrol Group has grown to include 80 PBRs, six UH-1B Seawolf helicopter gunships, and three platoons of SEALs.

May 9.   **First operational air-cushion craft.** Three air-cushion patrol vehicles (PACVs), capable of more than 50 knots, join Operation Market Time off South Vietnam. They carry one .50-caliber machine gun. These are the first vessels of their kind to become operational in the U.S. Navy.

May 11.   **Market Time action.** The *Brister* (DER 327), coastal minesweeper *Vireo* (MSC 205), and coast guard cutter *Point Grey* (WPB 82324) concert action with the South Vietnamese Air Force to destroy a 120-foot steel freighter caught running arms to the Viet Cong. The vessel carried 50 tons of supplies.

May 22.   Swift Boat *PCF 41* is sunk by 57-mm recoilless rifle fire on the Dinh Ba River in the Rung Sat Special Zone.

June 3.   **Gemini IX.** Lieutenant Commander Eugene A. Cernan, USN, on a three-day mission with Lieutenant Colonel Thomas P. Stafford, USAF, becomes the second American to walk in space.

June 12.   **First F-8 kill.** The navy scores its first aerial victory of the year and the first ever won by an F-8 Crusader when Commander Harold L. Marr, flying off the *Hancock* (CVA 19), destroys a MiG-17 over North Vietnam with a Sidewinder air-to-air missile.

June 20.   **More Market Time action.** Near the Co Chien River at the mouth of the Mekong Delta, the coast guard cutters *Point League* (WPB 82304) and *Point Slocum* (WPB 82313) encounter and receive fire from a 120-foot, steel-hulled trawler, which they drive aground ablaze. The Communist Chinese vessel is found to be carrying 250 tons of munitions destined for the Viet Cong. The *Point Slocum* takes a hit from a mortar shell in the course of the action.

June 29.   Forty-six planes from the *Constellation* (CVA 64) and *Ranger* (CVA 61) strike oil-storage plants on the outskirts of Hanoi and Haiphong, beginning a campaign to cripple the petroleum and oil storage and distribution system of North Vietnam. This is the nearest American bombs have fallen to either city.

July 1.   **Minesweeping.** Twelve 57-foot mine-sweeping boats (MSBs) of Mine Squadron 11 are constituted as Detachment Alpha, with the responsibility of keeping the Long Tau River shipping channel to Saigon clear of mines.

July 13.   Six Mig-17s are shot down, one by an F-4 Phantom from the *Constellation* (CVA 64) and five by air force planes. This raises the total of U.S. aerial victories in the war to 15.

July 15–August 3.   **Operation Hastings III.** In Quang Tri Province Task Force Delta—8,000 men of the III Marine Amphibious Force and 3,000 South Vietnamese troops—launch a sweep to intercept the movement of the North Vietnamese 324B Division south across the Demilitarized Zone. The enemy offensive is spoiled after heavy fighting in which 824 North Vietnamese are killed.

August 3.   Aircraft from the *Constellation* (CVA 64) deliver another attack against the oil depots at Haiphong. The Soviet Union later charges, and the United States denies, that the Soviet merchantman *Medyn* was hit by bullets fired by the planes.

August 6–22.   **Operation Colorado.** In a sweep through Quang Nam and Quang Tri provinces, a reinforced battalion of the Fifth Marines kills 170 Viet Cong.

August 7.   Seven U.S. aircraft, including a navy A-1 Skyraider, are lost over North Vietnam in the worst day of the air war to date.

August 20–29.   **Operation Allegheny.** A battalion of the Third Marines kills 117 Viet Cong in a drive in Quang Nam Province.

August 23.   The SS *Baton Rouge*, a freighter chartered by Military Sea Transport Service (MSTS), strikes a mine in the Long Tau channel 20 miles east of Saigon. Seven crewmen are killed, and the ship is beached. She is the third vessel mined in or near Saigon since 1964.

August 29.   A-4 Skyhawks and A-6 Intruders from the *Constellation* (CVA 64) damage two enemy torpedo boats and sink a third. Communist China later protests that the ship sunk and one of those damaged were Chinese merchantmen. The United States replies that the vessels were not attacked until they fired on the planes.

August 30.   Navy crews are placed in the armed UH-1B Seawolf helicopters being used in support of Operation Game Warden. Previously the Hueys had been flown by army personnel.

September 11.   Navy and air force pilots fly a record 171 missions over North Vietnam without losing a single plane. The previous record of 156 missions was set on August 26.

September 11.   The Viet Cong ambush two river patrol boats on the Co Chien River. One crewman is killed. He is the first American fatality in Operation Game Warden.

September 15.   **Gemini XI.** Navy astronauts Commander Charles Conrad and Lieutenant Commander Richard F. Gordon are recovered in the Atlantic by the USS *Guam* (LPH 9) after a 71-hour spaceflight.

September 17–27.   **Operation Golden Fleece 7-1.** A battalion of the Seventh Marines kills 244 Viet Cong and protects villagers harvesting an estimated 7,620 tons of rice in Quang Ngai Province.

September 22.   The Mine Force suffers its first casualties when two minesweeping boats come under recoilless rifle and rocket fire on the Long Tau River. One crewman is killed and eleven wounded by a hit on the pilothouse of *MSB 15*.

Operation Market Time: a Swift Boat examines two Vietnamese junks. Official U.S. Navy photograph.

October 9.   **Two MiG kills.** A MiG-21 is shot down by an A-1 Skyraider from the *Intrepid* (CVS 11) over the Phy Ly Bridge, 35 miles south of Hanoi, and a second MiG-21 is downed by an F-8 Crusader from the *Oriskany* (CVA 34).

October 25.   **Operation Sea Dragon.** The Seventh Fleet begins to attack supply vessels on the coast of North Vietnam. Some 230 enemy watercraft are sunk in a month. By the end of the first year of the operation this figure has risen to 2,000.

October 26.   **Fire on the Oriskany.** Off Vietnam, a parachute flare ignites a fire on the hangar deck of the *Oriskany* (CVA 34), in which 44 officers and men are lost.

October 31.   **Largest riverine action.** On the Mekong River, 10 miles west of My Tho, eight Operation Game Warden river patrol boats supported by navy Seawolf helicopter gunships destroy 51 junks and sampans and capture 6 more in an engagement lasting three hours. There are no American casualties.

October 31.   *MSB 54* becomes the first U.S. minesweeping boat lost in the war when she is sunk by a mine in the Long Tau River. Of her seven crewmen, two are missing and four wounded.

November 15.   **Gemini XII.** The last space flight of the Gemini series is completed by Captain James A. Lovell, USN, and Lieutenant Colonel Edwin E. Aldrin, Jr., USAF.

November 18.   For the first time in the Vietnam

war, navy ships shell a target that has not fired first when the destroyers *John R. Craig* (DD 885) and *Hamner* (DD 718) bombard a radar site two miles north of the Demilitarized Zone.

November 23. The destroyers *Mullany* (DD 528) and *Warrington* (DD 843) sink or damage 47 of a convoy of 60 supply barges off the coast of North Vietnam.

December 11. **Fight in the Mekong Delta.** In the second-largest riverine action to date, two patrol boats discover 40 sampans in a canal off the Mekong River west of My Tho and observe large numbers of uniformed Viet Cong ashore, evidently waiting to cross. In the ensuing engagement the patrol boats sink 28 sampans and kill 9 enemy soldiers.

December 23. **First hit by a North Vietnamese shore battery.** Two men are killed and four wounded when the destroyer *O'Brien* (DD 725) is hit twice by shore batteries approximately three miles north of Dong Hoi. Although ships have been fired on before, and the *Ingersoll* (DD 652) was struck by fragments from near misses on December 5, this is the first time a U.S. vessel has taken a direct hit.

At year's end, there are 385,000 U.S. troops in South Vietnam.

1967

January 13. **Master chief petty officer of the navy.** Master Chief Gunner's Mate Delbert D. Black is appointed the first Senior Enlisted Advisor of the Navy, a position analogous to the Sergeant Major the Army. The title is soon changed to master chief petty officer of the navy.

January 27. **Apollo tragedy.** At Cape Kennedy, a flash fire in a training session in the Apollo 1 spacecraft results in the death of three astronauts: Lieutenant Colonel Virgil I. Grissom, USAF; Lieutenant Colonel Edward H. White, USAF; and Lieutenant Commander Roger B. Chaffee, USN.

February 1–March 18. **Operation Prairie II.** Three marine battalions, later increased to five, make a sweep through northern Quang

Tri Province, killing 693 enemy troops. Marine losses are 93 dead and 483 wounded.

February 4. River patrol boat *PBR 113* becomes the first of her class lost to enemy fire when she is damaged beyond repair by a grenade while patrolling the Co Chien River.

February 16. **Operations in the Rung Sat Special Zone.** In cooperation with units of the U.S. 9th Infantry Division, River Assault Squadron 1 begins offensive operations in the Rung Sat Special Zone.

February 16–March 3. **Operation Deckhouse VI.** In a two-phase operation beginning 60 miles south of Chu Lai, the Seventh Fleet Special Landing Force accounts for 280 enemy dead.

February 26. **First mining of North Vietnam.** A-6 Intruders from the *Enterprise* (CVAN 65) drop mines in the rivers in the panhandle of North Vietnam. The United States announces that the mines pose no danger to "deep water maritime traffice."

February 28. The Mekong Delta Mobile Riverine Force (Task Force 117) is established.

March 9–11. **Gunnery duels.** The heavy cruiser *Canberra* (CAG 2) and destroyers *Ingersoll* (DD 652) and *Keppler* (DD 765) engage and silence numerous shore batteries while shelling coastal targets around Vinh, North Vietnam. The *Keppler* is hit on March 11, but none of her crewmen are killed.

March 11. **Walleye.** The first television-guided

Marines advance along a stream bed south of the Cam Lo River on Operation Prairie III, in late March 1967. Defense Department photo (Marine Corps.)

air-to-surface glide bomb (Walleye) used in combat is employed by aircraft from the *Oriskany* (CV 34) in an attack on the barracks at Sam Son, North Vietnam.

March 14.   A steel-hulled North Vietnamese trawler carrying arms to the Viet Cong is spotted by a P-2 Neptune on Market Time patrol and beaches herself after being intercepted by the *Brister* (DER 327), USCG cutter *Point Ellis* (WPB 82330) and *PCF 78*. Tons of munitions are captured.

March 20–April 1.   **Operation Beacon Hill I.** In the third amphibious landing of the year, a Special Landing Force of the 1st Battalion, Fourth Marines, attacks enemy positions in northern Quang Tri Province, a few miles south of the Demilitarized Zone. The Viet Cong and North Vietnamese lose 334 dead.

April 1.   **Coast guard transferred.** The coast guard is incorporated into the newly established Department of Transportation after 177 years as part of the Treasury Department.

April 10.   The *Sanctuary* (AH 17) becomes the second hospital ship to commence operations in Vietnam.

April 20.   Aircraft from the *Kitty Hawk* (CVA 63) and the *Ticonderoga* (CVA 14) attack power plants 2.1 and 1.1 miles from the heart of Haiphong. This is the closest planes have ever struck to the center of the city.

April 21–May 12.   **Operation Beacon Star.** A sweep through Thua Thien Province by the Special Landing Force of the Seventh Fleet leaves 764 enemy dead.

April 24–May 5.   **Battle for Hill 861 and Hills 881 North and 881 South.** A major battle erupts when North Vietnamese troops attack the Third Marine Regiment at Khe Sanh, just south of the Demilitarized Zone near the Laotian border. The marines count 554 enemy dead and estimate that another 600 have been killed and carried off. They lose 138 dead and wounded.

April 24.   **First attacks on enemy airfields.** A-4 Skyhawks, A-6 Intruders, and F-4 Phantoms from the *Bon Homme Richard* (CVA 31) and the *Kitty Hawk* (CVA 63) hit the North Vietnamese jet base at Kep, 37 miles northeast of Hanoi, while air force planes hit Hoa Lac, 19 miles to the west of it. At

Kep, two MiG-17s are downed while attempting to take off.

April 27.   At Saigon Rear Admiral Norvell G. Ward is relieved by Rear Admiral Kenneth L. Veth as Commander, U.S. Naval Forces, Vietnam.

April 28–May 13.   **Operation Beaver Cage.** The 1st Battalion, Third Marines, lands to sweep a long-established enemy stronghold 25 miles south of Da Nang. More than 200 Viet Cong are killed.

May 1.   A-4 Skyhawks from the *Bon Homme Richard* (CVA 31) and *Kitty Hawk* (CVA 63) destroy two MiG-17s in aerial combat and four more on the ground in a second attack on the jet field at Kep.

May 13–July 16.   **Operation Crockett.** In Quang Tri Province, the Twenty-six Marines account for 206 enemy dead.

May 15.   The number of coast guardsmen in Vietnam is doubled by the arrival of three 311-foot cutters, each of which carries a crew of 150 officers and men: the *Barataria* (WHEC 381), the *Bering Strait* (WHEC 382), and the *Gresham* (WHEC 387).

May 19.   Four MiG-17s are downed by F-8 Crusaders from the *Bon Homme Richard* (CVA 31) flying cover for A-4 Skyhawks attacking a thermal power plant 1.1 miles from the center of Hanoi.

May 20–28.   **Operation Hickory.** In Quang Tri Province, battalion 5 of the 3rd Marine Division kills 445 enemy troops.

May 27.   The *Truxtun* (DLGN 35), the navy's second nuclear-powered, guided-missile frigate is commissioned at Camden, New Jersey.

May 31.   **Operation Prairie IV.** Another sweep through Quang Tri Province by the 3rd Marine Division yields 489 enemy dead. Marine casualties are 164 killed and 999 wounded.

May 31.   At Da Nang, Lieutenant General Robert E. Cushman relieves Lieutenant General Lewis W. Walt as commander of the III Marine Amphibious Force. There are 75,000 marines in South Vietnam at this time.

June 1–July 14.   **Operations Cimarron and Buffalo.** The Thirtieth Marines, 3rd Marine Division, launch a major drive in Quang Tri Province—Operation Cimarron—

which continues after July 2 as Operation Buffalo. Some 1,290 of the enemy are killed.

June 2. **Soviets protest.** The Soviet Union complains that the Soviet merchant ship *Turkestan* was attacked by American aircraft in port at Cam Pha, North Vietnam. One crewman is said to have been killed and several wounded.

June 5. **Operation Union II.** At its conclusion, a drive through Quang Nam and Quang Tin provinces by two battalions of the Fifth Marines has killed 701 enemy soldiers.

June 8. **Attack on the Liberty.** During the Arab-Israeli War the technical research ship *Liberty* (AGTR 5) is repeatedly attacked by Israeli fighters and torpedo boats while operating in international waters north of the Sinai Peninsula. Of her 297 crewmen, 34 are killed and 75 wounded. Israel apologizes for the attack, claiming that the *Liberty* was mistaken for an Egyptian vessel, and pays $3,323,500 compensation to the families of the men killed. Captain William L. McGonagle, the ship's commanding officer, is awarded the Medal of Honor for his conduct during the attack.

June 25. Swift Boat *PCF 97* is sunk by recoilless rifle and automatic weapons fire on the east coast of the Ca Mau Peninsula. Miraculously, only one man is wounded. This is the third Swift Boat lost in action.

June 30. The Soviet government protests that the Soviet merchant ship *Mikhail Frunze* has been hit by bombs during an American bombing raid on Haiphong the previous day.

July 15. A 120-foot, steel-hulled trawler that ignores the challenge of navy and coast guard vessels on Market Time patrol is driven ashore at Cape Batangan, 11 miles north of Quang Ngai City. She is found to be carrying arms and ammunition for the Viet Cong.

July 21. Three MiG-17s are shot down by F-8 Crusaders from the *Bon Homme Richard* (CVA 31) during a raid on the oil storage plant at Ta Xa, 30 miles north of Haiphong. Pilots from this carrier have now knocked down nine MiGs.

July 29. **Fire on the Forrestal.** Off the coast of Vietnam, a conflagration breaks out on the flight deck of the *Forrestal* (CVA 59) when a rocket goes off as aircraft are being readied for launching. Fires burn for eight hours, during which 134 crewmen are killed and 21 aircraft destroyed. The carrier had begun operations on her first Vietnam deployment on July 26.

August 1. Admiral Thomas H. Moorer becomes the 18th chief of naval operations.

August 1. **The New Jersey to be reactivated.** The decision is made to bring the battleship *New Jersey* (BB 62) back into service to add the weight of her shells to the gun line off Vietnam. The four mothballed *Iowa*-class battleships possess the last 16-inch naval guns in the world.

August 10. Two MiG-21s are downed by F-4 Phantoms from the *Constellation* (CVA 64) during an attack on a truck park south of Hanoi.

August 30. The carriers of Task Force 77 begin a campaign to isolate the port of Haiphong with an attack by the air wing of the *Oriskany* (CV 34) on one of four major bridges linking the city to Hanoi.

September 1. Paul R. Ignatius becomes the 59th secretary of the navy.

September 3. General Nguyen Van Thieu is elected president of South Vietnam. He will remain in power until the fall of the country in April 1975.

September 28. A PBR is sunk by a single rocket hit in a canal off the Mekong River. Two of her crewmen are killed and four wounded.

October 25. Carrier pilots destroy or damage at least 10 MiGs on the ground in a strike on the Phuc Yen airfield.

October 26. An F-4 Phantom from the *Constellation* (CVA 64) downs a MiG-21 south of Hanoi.

October 30. Some 35 miles northeast of Hanoi two F-4 Phantoms from the *Constellation* (CVA 64) have a dogfight with four MiG-17s. One of the MiGs is dropped by an air-to-air missile.

November 1–February 28, 1969. **Operation Kentucky.** In 16 months, this 3rd Marine Division operation produces 3,821 enemy dead. American casualties are 520 killed and 3,079 wounded.

November 5–December 9, 1968. **Operation**

Operation Sea Dragon: the cruiser *St. Paul* is taken under fire while shelling the railway yard at Cong Phu, 25 miles south of Thanh Hoa, on August 4, 1967. Official U.S. Navy photograph.

A monitor, the capital ship of the riverine assault force, engaging an enemy position in the Mekong Delta with her 40-mm cannon, October 6, 1967. Official U.S. Navy photograph.

Napoleon Saline. Battalions of the Third Marine Division, the army's 196th Light Infantry Brigade and the 1st Brigade, 5th Infantry Division (Mechanized) kill 3,495 enemy troops in operations east of Gio Linh. American losses are 395 killed and 1,680 wounded.

November 14.   Major General Bruno Hochmuth, commander of the 3rd Marine Division, is killed when his UH-1E helicopter crashes five miles northwest of Hué.

December 4.   In Dinh Tuong Province, 66 miles south of Saigon, the Mobile Riverine Force kills 235 Viet Cong in a day's fighting.

December 14.   A MiG-21 is downed by an air-to-air missile launched by an F-8 Crusader from the *Oriskany* (CVA 34) in a dogfight between four MiGs and four navy planes.

December 31.   As of this date, the strength of American forces in South Vietnam is 486,000.

1968

January 1.   General Leonard F. Chapman, Jr., becomes the 24th commandant of the marine corps.

January 1–5.   Five naval aircraft are downed over North Vietnam in one of the worst weeks of the air war.

January 15–18.   President Johnson suspends the bombing of targets in the vicinity of Haiphong, North Vietnam.

January 21.   **Siege of Khe Sanh.** In western Quang Tri province the combat base at Khe Sanh, garrisoned by the 3,500 men of Colonel David E. Lownds's Twenty-sixth Marines, is isolated from overland access when North Vietnamese forces cut Route 9. In the following days the 1st Battalion, Ninth Marines, a South Vietnamese Ranger battalion, and two additional 105-mm batteries are air-lifted in to reinforce the defense. By January 29, Khe Sanh's garrison is 6,000 strong. Surrounding it are 15–20,000 troops of the North Vietnamese 324B and 325C divisions. At least superficially, the situation bears a worrisome resemblance to that which resulted in the French disaster at Dienbienphu in 1954. The key difference is air power. The North Vietnamese never succeed in closing Khe Sanh's airfield; only four transports are shot down in the course of the siege, which lasts until early April; and American aircraft,

The western perimeter of Khe Sanh. Defense Department photo (Marine Corps).

ranging from air force B-52s to Seventh Fleet F-4s, drop 100,000 tons of bombs on enemy positions ringing the base.

January 22. **Pueblo affair.** The intelligence collection ship *Pueblo* (AGER 2), Lieutenant Commander Lloyd M. Bucher, is surrounded and fired on by North Korean

The *Pueblo*. Official U.S. Navy photograph.

patrol boats in international waters off the east coast of North Korea. One crewman is mortally wounded and three others, including Bucher, are hit. The *Pueblo*'s only weapons, a pair of .50-caliber machine guns, are frozen fast beneath their tarpaulins on the ship's bridge, and there are no U.S. naval or air forces close enough to come to her assistance. Bucher accedes to the North Korean boats' demand to follow them into Wonsan harbor.

January 30–31. **Tet offensive.** North Vietnam chooses the most important Vietnamese holiday, the lunar new year (Tet), to launch its largest offensive of the war. In the past a tacit truce has been observed during this period, and about half of South Vietnam's 730,000-man army is on leave. Within a period of 48 hours, attacks are made on Saigon, Hué, Quang Tri, Da Nang, Kontum, and virtually every other major city in South Vietnam—36 of 44 provincial capitals (10 of which are briefly occupied), 5 of 6 autonomous cities, and 23 military airfields and installations. Television coverage centers American domestic attention on Saigon, where a suicide squad of 15 sappers penetrates the U.S. embassy, killing five servicemen before being wiped out. In purely military terms the effort ends in a major defeat for North Vietnam. Some 32,000 North Vietnamese and (mostly) Viet Cong troops—at least half the attacking force—are killed and 5,800 captured, against 1,000 American and 2,800 South Vietnamese combat deaths. A popular uprising against the Americans, for which Tet was expected to provide the impetus, fails to occur, and Hué is the only important position the attackers succeed in holding for any length of time. But the offensive's psychological impact on the American people, as transmitted by their television screens, transforms North Vietnam's military defeat into political victory. American public opinion turns strongly against the continuation of the war.

January 31–March 2. **Recapture of Hué.** A battalion of the Fifth Marines aids South Vietnamese troops in bitter street fighting to recover the former imperial capital. Marine casualties are 142 dead and 857 wounded. While they held the city the North Vietnamese had executed 5,000 civilian "political enemies."

March 1. Clark M. Clifford becomes the ninth secretary of defense.

March 31. **Bombing limitation.** In a television address to the nation President Johnson declares that he will not seek reelection and calls for the beginning of peace talks. As a token of good faith, he orders the bombing of North Vietnam to be restricted to the panhandle area south of the 20th parallel.

April 3. Radio Hanoi announces the willingness of the government of North Vietnam to discuss conditions for holding peace talks.

April 6. The battleship *New Jersey* (BB 62) is recommissioned.

April 10. **Farewell to the Skyraiders.** The propeller-driven A-1 Skyraider, which entered service in 1945, is removed from the navy's aircraft inventory.

April 14. **Relief of Khe Sanh.** The U.S. 1st Air Cavalry Division and a South Vietnamese airborne battalion reestablish overland contact with the marine garrison of Khe Sanh in Operation Pegasus/Lam Son

A UH-1B Seawolf helicopter provides air cover for a squadron of PBRs on the Cho Gao Canal in the Mekong Delta. Official U.S. Navy photograph.

207. Route 9 is reopened on April 12, and action around Khe Sanh ends two days later. It is estimated that in the course of the siege approximately 10,000 North Vietnamese have been killed; the defenders' casualties are 205 dead and about 800 wounded.

April 15–February 28, 1969. **Operation Scotland II.** In Quang Tri Province this operation by the 3rd Marine Division claims a total of 3,304 enemy dead. American losses are 463 killed and 2,553 wounded.

May 3. The government of North Vietnam agrees to begin preliminary peace talks in Paris.

May 18–October 23. **Operation Mameluke Thrust.** A major search-and-clear operation is launched by units of the 1st Marine Division and the 26th Marine Regimental Landing Team in an area 25 miles to the west and south of Da Nang. In its course 2,728 enemy troops are killed. Marine losses are 267 killed and 1,730 wounded.

May 21. **Loss of the Scorpion.** The nuclear-powered attack submarine *Scorpion* (SSN 589), Commander Francis A. Slattery, returning to Norfolk, Virginia, from training operations with the Sixth Fleet in the Mediterranean, is last heard from at 11:03 P.M. EDT. She is reported overdue on May 27 and declared to be presumed lost with all hands (99 officers and men) on June 5. Wreckage of the boat is finally located and photographed in more than 10,000 feet of water 400 miles southwest of the Azores by the Military Sea Transportation Service oceanographic research ship USNS *Mizar* (T-AGOR 11) on October 30. The cause of the disaster cannot be determined, but foul play is ruled out.

June 10.   The South Vietnamese Navy assumes responsibility for sweeping command-detonated mines from the Long Tau River channel to Saigon. Fourteen U.S. vessels are turned over to it for this purpose. This event marks the beginning of the turn-over program through which the South Vietnamese Navy is to be trained and equipped to fight the brown-water war on its own.

June 16.   The cruiser *Boston* (CAG 1) and the Australian guided-missile destroyer *Hobart* are slightly damaged and Swift Boat *PCF 19* is sunk by U.S. Air Force planes that mistake them for low-flying enemy helicopters.

June 22.   Captain Lawrence Heyworth, Jr., becomes 45th (temporary) superintendent of the Naval Academy.

June 26.   **Dogfight.** Three F-8 Crusaders from the *Bon Homme Richard* (CVA 31) tangle with two MiG-21s over North Vietnam. One MiG is downed by an air-to-air missile.

July 6.   The first North American OV-10A Broncos, small, propeller-driven aircraft especially designed for counter-insurgency warfare, begin operations with marine squadrons at Da Nang.

July 9.   The Army-Navy Mobile Riverine Force, now 18 months old, commences operations on the Co Chien River, the only branch of the Mekong on which it was not already active.

July 12.   **The last seaplane.** The navy's last operational seaplane, a P-5 Marlin, is retired in ceremonies at Patuxent Naval Air Station.

July 20.   Rear Admiral James F. Calvert becomes 46th superintendent of the Naval Academy.

July 22.   **306 missions.** Commander Samuel R. Chessman, 42, commanding officer of Attack Squadron 195 aboard the *Ticonderoga* (CVA 14), flies his 306th Vietnam combat mission, breaking the record of 305 set by his predecessor, Commander Charles Hathaway, in April 1967. Chessman also flew 77 combat missions in Korea.

July 29.   **Operation Game Warden expanded.** Patrols are extended to the upper reaches of the Mekong and Bassac rivers, so that Game Warden now covers the delta waterways from the Cambodian border to the sea.

July 29.   Four F-8 Crusaders from the *Bon Homme Richard* (CVA 31) engage an equal number of MiG-17s in a five-minute dogfight northwest of Vinh. One MiG is shot down.

September 7.   The *John F. Kennedy* (CVA 67), a conventionally powered, *Forrestal*-class carrier, is commissioned.

September 18.   In Quang Tin Province, 35 miles south of Da Nang, Swift Boat *PCF 21* destroys or damages 44 junks and 4 sampans and kills four Viet Cong.

September 19.   An F-8 Crusader from the *Intrepid* (CVS 11) kills a MiG-21 northwest of Vinh. This victory, the navy's 29th and the last officially credited to an F-8, is the 110th scored by U.S. forces so far in the war.

September 29.   **Back to the war.** The battleship *New Jersey* (BB 62) begins operations off the coast of Vietnam, firing 20 of her 16-inch shells at enemy positions north-northwest of Con Thien near the northern boundary of the Demilitarized Zone.

September 29.   Vice Admiral Elmo R. Zumwalt, Jr., relieves Rear Admiral Kenneth L. Vest as Commander, U.S. Naval Forces, Vietnam.

October 6–19.   **Operation Maui Peak.** More than 350 enemy are killed in a search-and-clear operation around An Hoa by battalions of the 1st Marine Division and the South Vietnamese 51st Regiment.

October 15.   **Operation Sealords.** The previously independent efforts of Operation Game Warden forces and the Army-Navy Mobile Riverine Force are concerted in a joint operational plan against the enemy in the Mekong Delta. Sealords stands for "South East Asia Lake, Ocean, River, Delta Strategy."

October 23–December 7.   **Operation Henderson Hill.** Battalions of the 1st Marine Division kill 700 enemy troops and detain 94 suspects in a sweep a few miles west of Hoi An. Marine losses are 35 killed and 231 wounded.

October 29.   Seven Swift Boats, the Market Time support ship *Washoe County* (LST 1165), coast guard cutter *Wachusett* (WHEC 44)

A monitor leads two armored troop carriers along a canal in the Mekong Delta. U.S. Naval Institute Collection.

and South Vietnamese Air Force A-1 Sky-raiders cooperate in a surprise attack against enemy positions in the Cua Lon–Bo De river areas at the extreme southern tip of South Vietnam. In five hours 242 enemy junks and sampans and 167 structures are damaged or destroyed. U.S. casualties are five wounded.

October 31.   **Bombing halt.** President Johnson orders a complete cessation of all air, sea, and land bombardment of North Vietnam, effective at 8:00 A.M. EST November 1. Previous to this announcement there had been nine separate bombing pauses since June 1965. After each pause American pilots found that the North Vietnamese had used the respite to repair and improve their air-defense system.

November 1–30.   **The New Jersey on the gun line.** In her first full month in action, the battleship *New Jersey* (BB 62) destroys 182 enemy bunkers, more than 800 other structures, 15 cave complexes, and 9 sampans.

November 20–December 9.   **Operation Meade River.** In a sweep through Quang Nam Province, battalions of the 1st Marine Division kill 841 enemy soldiers and detain 2,710 suspects. U.S. losses are 107 killed and 385 wounded.

December 6.   **Operation Giant Slingshot.** The brown-water navy's activities are ex-panded by the initiation of regular patrols on the Vam Co Dong and Vam Co Tay rivers, which extend westward from their divergence 23 miles south of Saigon in a Y- or slingshot-shaped configuration to enclose the "Parrot's Beak" of the Cambodian border. In the first year, forces committed to the operation kill 1,894 enemy troops and capture 517 tons of supplies.

December 7–March 8, 1969.   **Operation Taylor Common.** Battalions of the 1st Marine Division conduct a search-and-clear operation 10 miles west of An Hoa. Losses of 1,398 dead are inflicted on the enemy at a cost of 151 killed and 1,324 wounded.

December 23.   The 82 crewmen of the intelligence ship *Pueblo* (AGER 2), which was seized by North Korea on January 22, are released.

December 23.   Attacking enemy base camps in An Xuyen Province, never previously disturbed by naval forces, a task force of four Swift Boats supported by army gunship helicopters destroy or damage 167 sampans, 125 structures, and 8 bunkers.

1969

January 13.   **Operation Bold Mariner.** The

Two A-6A Intruders from the *Constellation* on a bomb run. Official U.S. Navy photograph.

largest amphibious assault of the Vietnam War is made when more than 2,500 marines from the Seventh Fleet Amphibious Force land on the Batangan Peninsula, a Viet Cong stronghold 10 miles north of Quang Ngai City in the I Corps area. The operation is supported by fire from the battleship *New Jersey* (BB 62) and two destroyers. U.S. Army and South Vietnamese troops are positioned inland in an attempt to trap the enemy on the peninsula. Some 12,000 Vietnamese are screened, and 239 Viet Cong are killed.

January 14. **Fire on the Enterprise.** Seventy miles south of the Hawaiian island of Oahu, fire breaks out when a rocket ignites on the flight deck of the nuclear-powered carrier *Enterprise* (CVAN 65). The blaze is brought under control in 45 minutes, but 28 crewmen have been killed and 65 injured.

January 22. Melvin R. Laird becomes the tenth secretary of defense.

January 22–March 19. **Operation Dewey Canyon I.** More than 1,600 of the enemy are killed during an extremely successful sweep through the Da Krong valley in southwestern Quang Tri Province by Colonel Robert H. Barrow's Ninth Marines.

January 25. **Truce talks.** In Paris, representatives of the United States and North Vietnam begin formal negotiations to end the Vietnam War.

January 31. John H. Chafee becomes 60th secretary of the navy.

January 31. The strength of U.S. forces in Vietnam reaches a peak of 542,000.

February 1. In the Mekong Delta, twenty-five U.S. river gunboats, representing two complete river assault and interdiction divisions, are transferred to the South Vietnamese Navy.

March 5. The *Ticonderoga* (CVA 14) begins her fifth tour off Vietnam, the first carrier to reach this number.

March 15. **Operation Maine Crag.** The Third Regiment, 3rd Marine Division, begins a search-and-clear operation six miles south of Khe Sanh. By the time the operation ends on May 2, marines have killed 157 Viet Cong, detained 52 suspects, and captured 465 weapons. Their losses are 17 killed and 104 wounded.

March 25. The air component of the River Patrol Force is reinforced by the arrival of Light Attack Squadron (VAL) 4, which is based at Vung Tau and Binh Thuy. Its OV-10A Broncos will fly in support of the river patrol boats.

March 26. Lieutenant General Herman Nickerson, Jr., relieves Lieutenant General Cushman as commander of the III MAF.

March 27. In her most effective single day's shelling, the battleship *New Jersey* (BB 62) destroys or damages 72 enemy bunkers around Phan Thiet in the II Corps area.

March 31. The *New Jersey* (BB 62) leaves the gun line at the conclusion of a six months' tour off Vietnam.

March 31–May 29. **Operation Oklahoma Hills.** The Seventh Marines search and clear an area 20 miles southwest of Da Nang. The enemy loses 596 dead; marine casualties are 53 killed and 482 wounded.

April 14. **EC-121 Incident.** An unarmed, four-engined EC-121 aircraft of Fleet Air Reconnaissance Squadron One carrying a crew of 31 is shot down by North Korean aircraft while on a routine mission over the Sea of Japan. She disappears from U.S. radar screens at 11:50 P.M. EST, in a position approximately 90 miles southeast of Chongjin. An intensive air-sea search is mounted. Two bodies, as well as wreckage, are found on April 17, but there are no survivors.

April 18. The *Bon Homme Richard* (CVA 31) begins her fifth tour off Vietnam.

April 20. **Show of force.** In response to the North Korean attack on the EC-121 aircraft, Task Force 71 is organized under the command of Rear Admiral Malcolm W. Cagle to make a naval demonstration in the Sea of Japan. Initially it consists of 23 combatant vessels, including the carriers *Enterprise* (CVAN 65), *Ranger* (CVA 61), *Ticonderoga* (CVA 14), and *Hornet* (CVS 12), and is strengthened on April 23 by another six destroyers. The *New Jersey* (BB 62), en route home from Vietnam, is ordered back to Japan.

April 26. At the end of its demonstration, Task Force 71 passes through the Straits of Tsushima into the Yellow Sea and is soon deactivated.

May 3. **The Triton (SSN 586) is decommissioned.** The first submarine to circumnavigate the globe submerged and the largest nuclear submarine built to date is decommissioned at Groton, Connecticut.

May 5. **Operation Daring Rebel.** Marine Battalion Landing Team 1/26 joins South Vietnamese and South Korean forces in an amphibious operation 20 miles south of Da Nang. Commanded by the Seventh Fleet's Amphibious Force Alfa, the operation terminates on Barrier Island on May 20. The marines kill 105 Viet Cong at a cost to themselves of 2 dead and 51 wounded. Overall, 7,000 Vietnamese are detained for questioning, and 200 enemy cadre are captured.

May 15. The *Guitarro* (SSN 665), a nuclear submarine being built at the San Francisco Bay Naval Shipyard (Vallejo) sinks at dockside in 35 feet of water. The report of Special House Armed Service Subcommittee convened to investigate the accident charges "culpable negligence" on the part of shipyard workers responsible for it.

May 16. The *Point Garnet* (WPB 82310) and *Point League* (WPB 82304) become the first coast guard cutters to be transferred to the South Vietnamese Navy. They raise to 101 the number of vessels turned over to the South Vietnamese since June 1968.

June 1. **Progress of Vietnamization.** The South Vietnamese Navy assumes full responsibility for patrolling the Fourth Coastal Zone, which extends more than 400 miles along the South China Sea and the Gulf of Thailand.

June 2. Lieutenant General Lewis W. Walt, assistant commandant of the marine corps, is promoted to full general. This is the first time in its history that the corps has been authorized two four-star posts.

June 2. **Evans disaster.** The destroyer *Frank E. Evans* (DD 754) is struck and cut in two by the Australian aircraft carrier *Melbourne* (R 21) in the South China Sea approximately 650 miles southwest of Manila at 4:15 A.M. June 3, Philippine time. The two ships are engaged in a SEATO naval exercise. The bow section of the *Evans* sinks in two minutes with the loss of 74 of her 273 crewmen. Her aft section is quickly secured alongside the *Melbourne*. There are no Australian casualties. On June 9, a Joint Board of Investigation composed of three American and three Australian naval officers begins hearings at the Subic Bay Naval Base. It finds that primary responsibility for the collision rests with the destroyer, but that the carrier is partly to blame. The *Evans*'s captain and officer of the deck are court-martialed, found guilty of dereliction in the performance of duty, and reprimanded. The commander of the *Melbourne*, Captain J. P. Stephenson, is honorably acquitted by a Royal Australian Navy court-martial. In September, Australia donates $32,500 to the 26 children whose fathers were lost on the *Evans*.

June 8. **First troop withdrawals from Vietnam.** While meeting with South Vietnamese President Nguyen Van Thieu at Midway Island, President Nixon announces that 25,000 U.S. combat troops will be withdrawn from Vietnam by August 31.

July 1. **Strength of the fleet.** At the start of Fiscal Year 1970 the U.S. Navy has 886 vessels in active commission. Their average age is 17 years.

July 10. OV-10A Bronco aircraft attached to the River Patrol Force sink six Viet Cong boats that are seeking to evade river patrol boats off Kien Giang Province in the Gulf of Thailand. Twelve of the enemy are killed.

July 20. **Moon landing.** The Apollo 11 capsule lands on the moon. The first man to walk on the lunar surface is former navy fighter pilot Neil A. Armstrong. On its return to earth the spacecraft is recovered by the carrier *Hornet* (CVS 12).

August 5. **First POWs released.** North Vietnam releases the first three American prisoners of war: Lieutenant Robert F. Frishman, USNR; Seaman Douglas B. Hegdahl, USN; and Captain Wesley L. Rumble, USAF. Lieutenant Frishman, a pilot in Attack Squadron 121, was shot down and captured on October 24, 1967; Seaman Hegdahl was captured on April 6, 1967, after falling overboard from the cruiser *Canberra* (CAG 2) in the Gulf of Tonkin. In a press conference at Bethesda Naval Hospital on October 3, they report that American POWs are being beaten and tortured by the North Vietnamese.

August 21. **Defense cuts.** Secretary of Defense Laird announces that up to $3 billion will be shaved from defense expenditures for Fiscal Year 1970. Part of the savings is to be realized by deactivating more than 100 naval vessels, including the battleship *New Jersey* (BB 62).

September 16. **Troop withdrawals.** President Nixon announces that 35,000 more troops

OV-10A Broncos of Light Attack Squadron (VAL) 4 over the Rung Sat Special Zone. Official U.S. Navy photograph.

will be withdrawn from Vietnam by December 15. This figure includes 5,200 navy personnel and 18,500 marines. The number of American forces left in Vietnam will be 484,000.

October 10.   Eighty U.S. Navy river patrol boats (PBRs) are turned over to the South Vietnamese Navy. The largest single transfer to date, this raises to 229 the total number of vessels turned over to the Vietnamese since June 1968.

October 26.   The carrier *Coral Sea* (CVA 43) begins her fifth tour off Vietnam.

November 14.   **Apollo 12.** America's second moon-shot is manned by an all-navy crew: Commander Charles Conrad (mission commander), Commander Richard Gordon (command module pilot), and Lieutenant Commander Alan Bean (lunar module pilot). Their capsule is recovered in the Pacific by the *Hornet* (CVS 12) on November 24, and all astronauts are promoted to the rank of captain by President Nixon during a telephone conversation aboard the carrier.

November 15.   The antiwar movement's "November Vietnam Moratorium" produces massive demonstrations in Washington and San Francisco.

November 29.   In the Mekong Delta, the U.S. My Tho Naval Base is turned over to the navy of South Vietnam. This is the first naval base to be transferred.

December 13.   Admiral Raymond A. Spruance, commander of the American naval forces at the Battles of Midway and the Philippine Sea, dies at his home in Pebble Beach, California, at the age of 83.

December 15.   President Nixon directs the withdrawal of another 50,000 men from Vietnam, bringing the total ordered home in 1969 to 110,000.

December 17.   **The New Jersey (BB 62) is decommissioned.** The ceremony occurs at the Naval Inactive Ship Maintenance Facility at Bremerton, Washington. In his address, the ship's commanding officer, Captain Robert C. Peniston, enjoins the battleship to "rest well but sleep lightly." His words are prophetic. Thirteen years later the *New Jersey* will return to service.

December 30.   In a typical riverine action, a patrol boat on the Saigon River surprises a body of enemy troops making a crossing 17 miles north of the capital. She takes them under fire and also calls for a helicopter gunship. Twenty-seven of the enemy are killed and one captured. American casualties are nil.

1970

January 1.   On the Saigon River, 25 miles northwest of the city, U.S. and South Vietnamese naval forces fight throughout New Year's night to defend a sunken South Vietnamese river patrol boat from the enemy, whose swimmers make six attempts to destroy it. Later, twelve enemy dead are counted, and the patrol boat is salvaged.

January 9.   A Sealords patrol encounters enemy forces estimated at battalion strength in Tay Ninh Province. Navy Seawolf helicopter gunships and OV-10 Bronco aircraft are called in. A total of 32 Viet Cong are killed.

January 28.   Near Vung Tau, in South Vietnam's III Corps area, the destroyer *Mansfield* (DD 728) heavily damages enemy positions while firing in close support of the 1st Australian Task Force.

February 3.   Merchant shipping on the Long Tau River in the Rung Sat Special Zone comes under enemy small arms and rocket fire for the first time in six months. No serious damage is done.

February 14.   Three 82-foot coast guard cutters are transferred to the South Vietnamese Navy. Six others follow later in the year.

February 28.   At Da Nang, 11 Swift Boats are transferred to the South Vietnamese Navy, which now takes over all coastal patrols operating off the country's five northern provinces.

March 7.   In the IV Corps area, the South Vietnamese Navy assumes control of operation Tran Hung Dao I, which had been established in February 1969 to interdict the infiltration of enemy personnel and supplies from Cambodia.

March 9.   Lieutenant General Keith B. McCutcheon relieves Lieutenant General Nickerson as commander of the III MAF.

March 14.   The hospital ship *Repose* (AH 16) leaves South Vietnam after four years of almost uninterrupted service there.

March 16.   Four U.S. Navy support ships and two more coast guard cutters are transferred to the South Vietnamese Navy at Da Nang. The coast guard decommissions the second of the three divisions it had operated in Vietnam. Only the 13th Division, which operates in the Mekong Delta, remains active.

March 18.   The left-leaning, neutralist Cambodian government of Prince Sihanouk is overthrown in a bloodless coup by General Lon Nol, whose anticommunist stance attracts the sympathy of the Nixon administration.

March 28.   **MiG kill.** An F-4 Phantom fighter escorting an unarmed reconnaissance plane, both from the *Constellation* (CVA 64), destroys a MiG-21 near Thanh Hoa, North Vietnam. This is the navy's first aerial victory in 16 months, as enemy aircraft seldom venture into airspace in which U.S. planes are authorized to operate.

March 28.   On the gun line, the destroyer *Orleck* (DD 886) damages or destroys 44 enemy structures while firing in support of the South Vietnamese 21st Infantry Division near Rach Gia in the IV Corps area. In the course of the week ending April 3, the *Orleck*, other Seventh Fleet destroyers, and the coast guard cutters *Chase* (WHEC 718) and *Dallas* (WHEC 716) hit 105 enemy structures, 48 bunkers, and 22 sampans.

April 20.   **Troop withdrawals.** President Nixon announces plans to withdraw 150,000 U.S. servicemen from Vietnam during the next 12 months. This will leave approximately 285,000 in the country.

April 29–June 30.   **Invasion of Cambodia.** American and South Vietnamese forces launch spoiling attacks into six Communist staging areas, one no more than 33 miles from Saigon, inside the Cambodian border. Great quantities of munitions and supplies are captured or destroyed.

May 4.   **Kent State.** The invasion of Cambodia sparks antiwar demonstrations throughout the United States. At Kent State University, where the Ohio National Guard has been sent to maintain order after the burning of the ROTC building, a detachment of guardsmen open fire on a group of protesters. Four students are killed. The tragedy provokes a new wave of campus

disorders. By the week's end, 450 colleges or universities are closed by student or faculty strikes.

May 5.   Operation Giant Slingshot, the joint U.S.–South Vietnamese navy patrol of the Vam Co Dong and Vam Co Tay rivers north of Saigon, is turned over to the South Vietnamese in ceremonies at Ben Luc. Since its inception in December 1968, forces in the operation have engaged in 1,200 fire fights and killed more than 2,400 enemy troops.

May 6.   **The navy in Cambodia.** A flotilla of 40 U.S. river patrol boats enters Cambodia on the Kham Span River, some 65 miles northwest of Saigon. It comes under fire less than two miles inside the border.

May 8.   A force of 100 U.S. and South Vietnamese patrol boats move up the Mekong River into Cambodia. The U.S. boats are to stay inside the 21.7-mile limit President Nixon has established for the American penetration of Cambodia.

May 12.   In the Gulf of Thailand, U.S. and South Vietnamese vessels establish a blockade of the Cambodian coastline west to Sihanoukville to prevent North Vietnamese and Viet Cong vessels from reaching Cambodia.

June 23.   **Vietnamization of the riverine force.** The U.S. transfers 273 river patrol craft to the South Vietnamese Navy, raising the total of vessels turned over to date to 525. The 125 boats still being operated by the U.S. Navy are scheduled to be transferred in December.

July 1.   Admiral Elmo R. Zumwalt becomes the 19th chief of naval operations, relieving Admiral Thomas H. Moorer, who has been named chairman of the joint chiefs of staff. At the age of 49, Zumwalt is both the youngest four-star admiral and the youngest CNO in the history of the navy. He will also become one of the most controversial.

July 22.   Sixty South Vietnamese are graduated from the U.S. Navy's Officer Candidate School at Newport, Rhode Island. They are the first class of South Vietnamese to attend.

August 3.   **Poseidon.** The first submerged launching of the navy's new, multi-warhead Poseidon nuclear missile is made by the fleet ballistic submarine *James Madison* (SSBN 627) off Cape Kennedy. A Russian surface ship closely observes the proceedings.

September 14. A Pentagon report places the strength of the South Vietnamese Navy at 35,000 men and 1,500 vessels, including 600 U.S. river patrol boats transferred since the beginning of Vietnamization.

September 17. The navy announces plans to deactivate 58 ships, including the carrier *Shangri-La* (CVS 38). Together with previous deactivations, this raises the number of ships retired from active service since January 1969 to 286.

October 29. Secretary of the Navy Chafee states that under current projections the U.S. Navy will have less than 700 ships in July 1971, a net reduction of 234 vessels since his entry into office, and warns that any further reduction would be dangerous.

November 20. **POW rescue mission.** A U.S. commando force lands from helicopters 23 miles west of Hanoi in an attempt to free American POWs. Unfortunately, the POWs had been moved from the area a few days earlier.

December 15. The State Department announces that a $19 million naval communications facility will be constructed on the British island of Diego Garcia in the Indian Ocean.

December 31. **Repeal of the Tonkin Gulf Resolution.** Having passed the Senate by a vote of 81–10 on June 24, the repeal of the resolution through which President Johnson introduced U.S. troops into Vietnam is approved by the House. President Nixon signs the bill into law on January 14, 1971.

1971

January 6. **Harrier.** The marine corps accepts the first of its new, close-support, V/STOL aircraft, the British-built AV-8A Harrier.

February 8–March 25. **Attack into Laos (Operation Lam Son 719/Dewey Canyon II).** A force of 16,000 South Vietnamese troops cross the Laotian border slightly south of the Demilitarized Zone in an operation designed both to disrupt a Com-

munist build-up in the area and to demonstrate the capability of the South Vietnamese Army. No American ground troops enter Laos, but many South Vietnamese units are lifted into (and out of) the country in U.S. army helicopters, and the U.S. Air Force and 1st Marine Air Wing provide massive air support. The results of the operation are mixed. Although the South Vietnamese inflict heavy losses on the enemy and capture large quantities of arms and ammunition, their withdrawal, begun on schedule on March 10, is often disorderly, and they suffer roughly 50 percent casualties.

February 11. The navy's traditional practice of enlisting Filipinos to serve as mess stewards is abolished by Admiral Zumwalt.

February 11. The United States and the Soviet Union sign a treaty prohibiting the deployment of nuclear weapons on the ocean floor.

April 1. **First Poseidon deployment.** The *James Madison* (SSBN 627) departs Charleston, South Carolina, on an operational patrol armed with the new missiles.

April 7. President Nixon announces that 100,000 troops will be withdrawn from South Vietnam in the course of the year.

April 12. A navy gunboat, two coast guard cutters, a South Vietnamese patrol craft, and two navy aircraft collaborate to sink a 160-foot North Vietnamese trawler discovered attempting to slip through the surveillance line off the southernmost coast of South Vietnam.

April 14. The wind-down of the marines' war in Vietnam is symbolized by the deactivation of the Third Marine Amphibious Force (III MAF) and the withdrawal of the 1st Marine Aircraft Wing from Da Nang.

April 24. Approximately 200,000 protesters stage a giant antiwar rally in Washington, D.C.

April 28. **First black admiral.** The navy announces the selection of 49 new rear admirals, including Captain Samuel L. Gravely, Jr., the first black to reach that rank.

May 1. The hospital ship *Sanctuary* (AH 17) sails from Da Nang for home after four years in Vietnam.

June 26. **Marine withdrawal completed.** The 3rd Marine Amphibious Brigade, the last marine combat unit in South Vietnam, departs from Da Nang.

August 19. In Vietnam, ships of the Seventh Fleet shell enemy rocket and mortar positions in the southern half of the Demilitarized Zone.

August 26. America's first man in space, astronaut Alan B. Shepard, is promoted to the rank of rear admiral. His selection had been announced on April 28.

October 1. The carrier *Constellation* (CVA 64) sails from San Diego on her sixth deployment off Vietnam. The antiwar movement had staged a well-publicized campaign to "Keep Connie Home."

November 12. President Nixon announces that another 45,000 troops will be withdrawn from Vietnam by February 1, 1972. At the end of 1971 there will be fewer than 175,000 American servicemen still in the country.

December 11. Full-fledged war began between India and Pakistan on December 4. On this date, a task force formed around the *Enterprise* (CVAN 65) is ordered from the coast of Vietnam to the Bay of Bengal, where, if necessary, it can evacuate American citizens from East Pakistan.

December 31. The ropewalk at the Boston Naval Shipyard, the navy's only rope-making activity, is closed after 147 years in operation. Hereafter the navy's rope will be made by private firms.

1972

January 1. General Robert E. Cushman, Jr., becomes 25th commandant of the marine corps.

January 13. President Nixon announces that another 70,000 U.S. troops are to be withdrawn from South Vietnam. Only 69,000 will be left there by May 1.

January 19. Over North Vietnam, an F-4 Phantom from the *Constellation* (CVA 64) downs a MiG-21. This victory, the navy's first since March 1970, is also the first scored by the team of Lieutenant Randall F. Cunningham, pilot, and Lieutenant (jg) William Driscoll, radar intercept officer, who will become the first American aces of the Vietnam War.

March 28. Two F-4 Phantoms from the *Coral Sea* (CVA 43) destroy a MiG-17.

March 30. **Spring offensive.** North Vietnam launches a massive conventional invasion of the south, sending three divisions across the Demilitarized Zone.

April 1. The navy's last in-country combat unit, Light Attack Squadron (VAL) 4, is withdrawn from South Vietnam.

April 6. In response to the North Vietnamese invasion, the United States resumes the aerial bombing and naval bombardment of North Vietnam. Marine air squadrons are sent to Da Nang to provide close support for the South Vietnamese.

April 17. **Linebacker.** Following orders from President Nixon, B-52s hit North Vietnam above the 20th parallel for the first time since March 1968.

April 25. John W. Warner becomes the 61st secretary of the navy.

April 27. **First woman admiral.** Captain Alene B. Duerk, a nurse, is the first person of her sex selected for promotion to the rank of rear admiral.

May 1. The North Vietnamese capture Quang Tri City.

May. Navy pilots have their best month of the war, downing a total of 16 MiGs. In addition, the cruiser *Chicago* (CG 11) knocks down an unidentified enemy aircraft with a Talos surface-to-air missile.

May 8. **Mining of North Vietnam.** Confronted by North Vietnamese intransigence at the Paris peace talks and the continuation of the enemy spring offensive, President Nixon orders the navy to carry out existing plans for mining the harbors of North Vietnam. A-6 Intruders from U.S. carriers sow mines at Haiphong, Hon Gai, Cam Pha, Thanh Hoa, Vinh, Quang Khe and Dong Hoi. Neutral shipping is given a grace period to clear North Vietnamese waters by a 72-hour delay in the activation of the mines. The flow of seaborne supplies to North Vietnam ceases overnight.

May 8. Rear Admiral Rembrandt C. Robinson, commander, Cruiser-Destroyer Flotilla 11, becomes the first flag officer killed in the Vietnam War when his helicopter crashes in the Gulf of Tonkin.

May 8. Lieutenant Randall J. Cunningham and Lieutenant (jg) William Driscoll score their

Lieutenant Randall F. Cunningham and Lieutenant (jg) William P. Driscoll in the office of Secretary of the Navy John W. Warner in June 1972, a month after scoring their fifth victory. Cunningham holds a model of the F-4 Phantom they flew. Official U.S. Navy photograph.

second aerial victory, destroying a MiG-17 with a Sidewinder air-to-air missile.

May 10.   **Navy aces.** Carrier pilots shoot down seven MiGs, three of which fall to Cunningham and Driscoll, making them the first American aces of the war.

May 15.   The United States relinquishes Okinawa, which it has ruled since World War II, to Japan.

May 26.   **SALT I.** The United States and the Soviet Union conclude two strategic arms limitations agreements. The first limits each country to the construction of two anti-ballistic missile (ABM) systems; the second establishes ceilings on the number of land- and sea-based intercontinental ballistic missiles (ICBMs) to be deployed during the next five years. Strategic Arms Limitation Talks between the two countries had begun in November 1969.

June 16.   Vice Admiral William P. Mack, former commander of the Seventh Fleet, becomes 47th superintendent of the U.S. Naval Academy.

June 25.   **Success in South Vietnam.** South Vietnamese troops break the siege of An Loc, in the III Corps area, signaling the defeat of the North Vietnamese spring offensive. Although no U.S. ground forces have been engaged, American air power has made a crucial, perhaps decisive, contribution to the victory.

June 30.   The nomination of Admiral Thomas Moorer to serve a second, two-year term as chairman of the joint chiefs of staff is approved by the Senate.

July 26–27.   Congress authorizes the construction of a fourth nuclear-powered carrier.

August 27.   **Shelling Haiphong.** A four-ship surface action group with the Seventh Fleet commander, Admiral James L. Holloway III, embarked delivers a night bombardment of the North Vietnamese port of Haiphong. Two enemy torpedo boats that engage the force are sunk.

September 22.   Commander Denis R. Weichmann sets a naval aviation record when he returns from his 501st combat mission over Vietnam.

October 11.   Nineteen sailors are killed and ten wounded (one mortally) by an explosion in an 8-inch turret on the all-gun cruiser *Newport News* (CA 148) during a fire mission off the coast of Vietnam.

October 23.   Bombing raids on North Vietnam above the 20th parallel are halted by order of President Nixon in anticipation of peace.

October 26.   Presidential Advisor Henry Kissinger, who has been conducting the Paris peace talks, announces that "peace is at hand"; the remaining differences between the United States and North Vietnam should be resolved in one more negotiating session.

December 6.   The last scheduled moon flight is made by Captain Eugene A. Cernan, Commander Ronald E. Evans, and a civilian, Dr. Harrison H. Schmidt.

December 18.   The American anticipation of imminent peace is confounded when the North Vietnamese delegation walks out of the Paris peace talks.

December 19–30.   **Linebacker II.** President Nixon bombs the enemy back to the negotiating table by the resumption of B-52 strikes throughout North Vietnam. In eleven days, the B-52s fly a total of 729 sorties—389 from Guam and 340 from U Tapao airfield in Thailand. By this time, the air defenses of the Hanoi-Haiphong area are probably the densest in the world and 15 B-52s are lost, all to SAM missiles, six on December 20 alone. The enemy defenses are gradually overcome, however, and no planes are downed during the last three days of the raids.

1973

January 3.   In Paris, the North Vietnamese delegation announces its readiness to resume peace talks.

January 5.   In a personal letter to South Vietnam President Thieu, President Nixon promises that the United States will take "swift and severe retaliatory action" should North Vietnam violate the terms of a peace accord.

January 12.   **Last MiG kill.** Lieutenant Walter Kovaleski and his radar intercept officer, Lieutenant James Wise, flying an F-4 Phantom off the *Midway* (CVA 41), score the last American aerial victory of the Vietnam War, destroying a MiG-17 with two Sidewinder missiles over the Gulf of Tonkin. In the course of the conflict, navy pilots have shot down 59 MiGs and 2 AN-2 biplane transports. By a twist of fate, two days later Lieutenant Kovaleski and another RIO, Ensign Dennis Plautz, become the last American fliers downed in the war when their plane is hit by antiaircraft fire. Happily, they eject over the ocean and are rescued by a navy helicopter.

January 15.   In anticipation of peace, President Nixon suspends all offensive operations against North Vietnam.

January 27.   **Paris Accords.** Dr. Henry Kissinger, and Le Duc Tho, chief North Vietnamese negotiator, formally sign the agreement ending direct American participation in the Vietnam War. The terms call for a cease-fire throughout South Vietnam; the withdrawal of U.S. forces; and the release of all American prisoners of war within 60 days.

January 30.   Elliot L. Richardson becomes the 11th secretary of defense.

February 17.   **Return of the POWs.** The first group of American POWs released by North Vietnam arrive in California as the nation celebrates their return. A total of

591 U.S. servicemen are repatriated; more than 800 remain missing.

February 24–July 18.   **Operation Endsweep.** In conformity with the terms of the Paris Accords, a squadron of four ocean minesweepers and Helicopter Mine Countermeasures Squadron 12, organized as Task Force 78, sweep North Vietnamese waters of the mines laid in May 1972.

March 20.   American air power covers a convoy of eight supply ships that proceed up the Mekong River to the besieged Cambodian capital of Phnom Penh.

March 29.   The last American troops leave South Vietnam.

April 10.   U.S. forces begin airlifting gasoline and oil into Phnom Penh.

May 25.   **Skylab I.** An all-navy crew, consisting of Captain Charles P. Conrad, Jr., Commander Joseph P. Kerwin, and Commander Paul J. Weitz, begins a 28-day mission aboard America's first space laboratory. The unmanned Skylab capsule was launched on May 14.

June 22.   The three Skylab I astronauts splash down in the Pacific.

June 29.   Congress passes a resolution banning the continuation after August 15 of bombing in Cambodia, where American air power is being used to support the government against the Communist Khmer Rouge.

July 3.   James R. Schlesinger assumes office as the 12th secretary of defense.

August 15.   With the cessation of bombing in Cambodia, in accordance with the congressional resolution of June 29, American military operations in Southeast Asia come to an end.

September 1.   The last American combat unit is withdrawn from the Southeast Asian mainland when a marine F-4 squadron leaves Thailand.

September 5.   **Skylab II.** A new record for time in space is set by navy Captain Alan L. Bean in the second Skylab mission. The previous record of 49 days, 3 hours, and 37 minutes had been held by Captain Charles P. Conrad, Jr.

November 7.   **War Powers Act.** In a measure intended to prevent the president from conducting undeclared wars, Congress passes a resolution requiring that the president notify it within 48 hours of committing American forces to combat or "situations where imminent involvement in hostilities is clearly indicated by the circumstances," and that such forces must be withdrawn within 60 days unless it declares war or authorizes an extension of the 60-day period.

November 19.   Vice Admiral Hyman G. Rickover, USN (Retired), is promoted to four-star rank.

1974

February 8.   **Skylab III.** The three Skylab III astronauts are recovered by the *New Orleans* (LPH 11) in the Pacific approximately 150 miles west of San Diego.

April 24.   **Clearing the Suez.** U.S. Task Force 65 begins clearing the Suez Canal of mines and vessels laid and sunk in it by Egypt during the 1972 Mideast War. The mine-sweeping is completed on June 3, and most major obstructions have been removed by mid-December.

June 20.   J. William Middendorf II is nominated by the president to become 62nd secretary of the navy.

July 1.   Admiral James L. Holloway III becomes the 20th chief of naval operations.

July 1.   The Boston Naval Shipyard is closed after

174 years in operation. It was the navy's oldest facility.

July 2.   Admiral Thomas C. Moorer retires after four years as chairman of the Joint Chiefs of Staff. His successor is air force General George S. Brown.

July 22.   U.S. Marine and Royal Navy helicopters evacuate more than 400 American, British, and other foreign citizens from the British base at Dhekelia on the southern coast of Cyprus. Turkish forces had invaded the island on July 20.

July 25.   **Trident.** The General Dynamics Corporation is awarded the contract to begin construction of the first nuclear-powered, fleet ballistic-missile Trident submarine.

November 24.   The *Constellation* (CVA 64) becomes the first American aircraft carrier to enter the Persian Gulf since 1948.

1975

March 3.   The Navy Department announces that as of 30 June 1976 the strength of the fleet will have dropped to 490 ships.

March 5.   **North Vietnamese spring offensive.** North Vietnam launches a strong conventional offensive in the central highlands of South Vietnam. The early success of the attack leads South Vietnamese President Thieu to order his forces to withdraw from Kontum, Pleiku, and Darlac provinces. The retreat quickly degenerates into a rout, and in a few weeks the northern two-thirds of the country is abandoned to the North Vietnamese.

March 25.   Army Chief of Staff General Frederick C. Weyland is sent to South Vietnam to evaluate the military situation.

April 1.   General Lon Nol, head of the Cambodian government, flees the country as Communist forces tighten their grip on Phnom Penh.

April 8.   General Weyland, returned from his fact-finding mission to South Vietnam, reports to Congress that without major American military assistance the country will fall. No such assistance is authorized.

April 9–11.   In Laos, heavy fighting breaks out between government forces and the Communist Pathet Lao.

April 10–15.   **Fall of Xuan Loc.** Thirty miles

Vice Admiral Hyman G. Rickover is congratulated on his promotion to four-star rank by President Richard M. Nixon and Secretary of the Navy Warner. Official U.S. Navy photograph.

east of Saigon the town of Xuan Loc, where the best remaining South Vietnamese Army units have made a strong stand, is overrun by numerically superior enemy forces.

April 12. **Operation Eagle Pull.** American embassy personnel are evacuated from Phnom Penh, Cambodia's besieged capital, by the CH-53 Sea Stallions of Heavy Marine Helicopter Squadrons (HMH) 462 and 463.

April 17. Phnom Penh falls to the Khmer Rouge.

April 21. South Vietnamese President Thieu resigns in an emotional television address, during which he denounces the United States for abandoning his country.

April 26–27. In anticipation of the fall of Saigon, some 6,000 Americans, South Vietnamese whose associations with Americans would compromise them in enemy eyes, and other nationalities are flown out of Tan Son Nhut airfield on C-130 and C-141 transports.

April 29. North Vietnamese artillery opens fire on Tan Son Nhut airfield, making further evacuation flights impossible.

April 29–30. **Operation Frequent Wind.** In 18 hours, navy and marine helicopters from Seventh Fleet carriers evacuate almost 9,000 people from Saigon: 1,373 Americans and 6,422 of other nationalities, plus 989 marines who were inserted to cover the operation. A-6, A-7, and F-14 fighter aircraft and A-1 and AC-119 gunships from the *Coral Sea* (CVA 43), *Enterprise* (CVAN 65), *Hancock* (CVA 19), and *Midway* (CVA 41) provide air support. The final flights are made from the rooftop of the American embassy, where U.S. Ambassador Graham Martin is among the last to leave.

April 30. **Fall of Saigon.** As North Vietnamese tanks roll into the city, General Duong Van Minh, who succeeded President Thieu on April 28, announces the unconditional surrender of South Vietnam.

May 3. The 81,600-ton, nuclear-powered carrier *Nimitz* (CVAN 68) is commissioned. America's second nuclear-powered carrier, she carries approximately 100 aircraft and helicopters and has a speed in excess of 30 knots.

May 12–15. **Mayaguez Incident.** On May 12, the American container ship *Mayaguez* is fired upon and seized while en route from Hong Kong to Sattahip, Thailand, by a gunboat of the Cambodian Communist (Khmer Rouge) regime. President Gerald F. Ford warns that "serious consequences" will follow unless the ship and her 40 crewmen are released immediately, and a battalion of marines is flown from Okinawa to U Tapao air base in Thailand. On May 15, a rescue operation is mounted. It centers on Koh Tang Island, 34 miles from the Cambodian coast, off which the *Mayaguez* is anchored and on which her crew is believed to be held. While planes from the *Coral Sea* (CVA 43) hit air and naval bases on the Cambodian mainland, a party of 60 marines and sailors from the *Harold E. Holt* (DE 1074) board the *Mayaguez*, which is discovered to be deserted, and a company of marines in helicopters from U Tapao assault Koh Tang. In the meanwhile, the Cambodians have decided to release the American seamen, who are being carried back to their ship when the attack begins. The marines meet strong resistance at Koh Tang. By the time they are withdrawn that evening, 15 servicemen have been killed, 3 are missing, 50 have been wounded, 3 of their helicopters have been shot down, and 2 have been damaged. The *Mayaguez* resumes her voyage.

June 5. **Reopening of the Suez Canal.** The guided-missile cruiser *Little Rock* (CLG 4), flagship of the Sixth Fleet, is the only foreign naval vessel in the official flotilla that first transits the canal. U.S. forces had cleared the waterway of the mines and hulks that had kept it closed since the mideast war. The clearing operation officially ends on July 23.

July 1. General Louis H. Wilson, Jr., who won the Medal of Honor on Guam in 1944, becomes the 26th commandant of the marine corps.

August 1. Rear Admiral Kinnaird R. McKee becomes the 48th superintendent of the Naval Academy.

August 23. **Fall of Laos.** The Pathet Lao complete the conquest of Laos. All of the states of Indochina are now under Communist rule.

September 20. **Spruance class.** The *Spruance* (DD 963), lead ship of a new class of 30 destroyers, is commissioned at Pascagoula,

The *Nimitz* during her sea trials. Official U.S. Navy photograph.

The *Mayaguez* incident: marines landing on Koh Tang Island. U.S. Air Force photo.

Mississippi. These 7,400-ton vessels are the navy's first gas turbine-powered destroyers.

November 20.   Donald H. Rumsfeld becomes 13th secretary of defense.

November 22.   **Belknap disaster.** On exercises in the Mediterranean, the guided-missile cruiser *Belknap* (CG 26) collides with the carrier *John F. Kennedy* (CV 67). Six of the *Belknap*'s sailors are killed, one dies later, and 24 are injured seriously enough to require hospitalization. One man is killed on the *Kennedy*. In the ensuing investigation, the *Belknap*'s officer of the deck is found guilty of negligence and disobedience of orders. The *Belknap* is recommissioned, after extensive repairs, on May 10, 1980.

1976

February 12.   Captain Fran McKee becomes the navy's first woman line officer selected for promotion to the rank of rear admiral.

March 28.   **Tomahawk.** The first successful launch of the navy's Tomahawk cruise missile is made from an A-6 Intruder off the coast of California. A second, successful 315-mile flight is made over the Pacific on April 26.

July 6.   **First women at the Naval Academy.** At Annapolis, 81 women are sworn into the Academy's Class of 1980.

August 28.   In the Ionian Sea, a submerged Soviet Echo II-class submarine collides with the frigate *Voge* (FF 1047). Both vessels suffer damage: the *Voge* to her propeller, the submarine (which surfaces) to her sail. One American sailor is injured. A U.S. Navy investigation concludes that the submarine was at fault.

September 14.   The carrier *John F. Kennedy* (CV 67) and the destroyer *Bordelon* (DD 881) collide during night operations 100 miles north of Scotland. Six of the destroyer's crewmen are injured. The cost of repairing the *Bordelon* is deemed uneconomical, and she is decommissioned in February 1977.

October 7.   **Naval districts consolidated.** The number of naval districts is reduced from twelve to four. Their headquarters are located in Seattle, Washington; Great Lakes, Illinois; Philadelphia, Pennsylvania; and Washington, D.C.

November 13.   **Los Angeles class.** The *Los Angeles* (SSN 688), lead ship of the navy's newest class of nuclear attack submarines, is commissioned at Newport News, Virginia. The largest SSNs built to date, these

vessels—360 feet in length—have a submerged speed of more than 30 knots and are armed with Tomahawk, Sub-Harpoon, and Subroc missiles.

1977

January 10.   Admiral Arleigh A. Burke, former chief of naval operations, is awarded the Medal of Freedom, the United States' highest civilian decoration.

January 18.   The first successful launch of the navy's new, long-range Trident ballistic missile is made at Cape Canaveral, Florida.

January 21.   Dr. Harold R. Brown becomes the 14th secretary of defense.

February 14.   W. Graham Claytor, Jr., enters office as 63rd secretary of the navy.

May 9.   The navy announces that during Fiscal Year 1978 the strength of the fleet will reach a low of 462 active vessels.

June 28.   The guided-missile cruiser *California* (CGN 36) and submarine *Billfish* (SSN 676) are among 150 British and foreign vessels

The *Los Angeles*. Courtesy Newport News Shipbuilding Company.

that participate in Queen Elizabeth's Silver Jubilee Naval Review off Portsmouth, England.

September 7.   **Panama Canal Treaty.** President Jimmy Carter and Panamanian President Omar Torrijos sign treaties that recognize Panamanian sovereignty over the Canal Zone and provide for the transfer of the canal to Panama.

October 3.   **SALT I expires.** The 1972 Strategic Arms Limitations Agreements between the United States and Soviet Union expires, but both countries declare that they will continue to adhere to its provisions during the negotiating of a second treaty.

October 18.   The *Dwight D. Eisenhower* (CVN 69) is commissioned. She is the navy's third nuclear-powered carrier and the second of the *Nimitz* class.

December 17.   **Perry class.** The *Oliver H. Perry* (FFG 7), lead ship of a new class of 50 guided-missile frigates, is commissioned. The most numerous class of U.S. warships built since World War II, the *Perry*s are designed primarily for convoy escort and related duties.

1978

February 1.   The first submarine launch of a Tomahawk cruise missile is made from the *Barb* (SSN 596) off the coast of California.

February 9.   A new era in naval communications begins with the launching of the first satellite of the navy's Fleet Satellite Communications System.

March 11.   The *Abraham Lincoln* (SSBN 602) becomes the first ballistic-missile submarine to complete 50 operational patrols. In the 17 years since her commissioning, she has spent more than 8½ years submerged and steamed more than 420,000 miles.

April 6.   Colonel Margaret A. Brewer is nominated by President Carter to become the first woman brigadier general in the marine corps.

July 1.   Admiral Thomas B. Hayward becomes the 21st chief of naval operations.

August 28.   Rear Admiral William P. Lawrence becomes 49th superintendent of the U.S. Naval Academy.

October 20.   The commandant of the marine corps is designated a full member of the joint chiefs of staff.

October 20.   **Cuyahoga disaster.** The coast guard training cutter *Cuyahoga* (WIX 157) is sunk in a collision with the 521-foot Argentine freighter *Santa Cruz II* in the Chesapeake Bay. Eleven coast guardsmen lose their lives; the freighter rescues eighteen others. The captain of the *Cuyahoga*, found guilty of dereliction of duty, receives a letter of reprimand and is demoted 200 places on the seniority list.

November 1.   **Women at sea.** Nine women ensigns are assigned to five non-combatant vessels of the Atlantic Fleet. This is the first time in history women have been assigned to vessels other than hospital ships and troop transports. Such assignment was authorized by the Department of Defense appropriations act for Fiscal Year 1979, which also allowed for the assignment of women to temporary duty of up to 180 days on combat ships provided no combat is foreseen.

1979

February 6.   Six U.S. vessels evacuate 200 American citizens and 240 other persons from the ports of Bandar Abbas and Char Bahar in revolution-wracked Iran.

April 1.   Twenty-six-year-old Lieutenant (jg) Beverly Kelly, USCG, becomes the first woman ever to captain a U.S. warship when she assumes command of the coast guard cutter *Cape Newagen* (WPB 95318).

June 18.   **Salt II.** In Vienna, Austria, the second Strategic Arms Limitations Treaty is signed by President Jimmy Carter and Soviet President Leonid Brezhnev. It is later rejected by the U.S. Senate.

June 28.   General Robert H. Barrow becomes the 27th commandant of the U.S. Marine Corps.

September 30.   At midnight, the United States relinquishes the Panama Canal Zone to the Panamanian government.

October 25.   Edward Hidalgo becomes 64th secretary of the navy.

November 4.   **Iranian hostage crisis.** A mob of Muslim "students," adherents of the Ayatollah Khomeini's fundamentalist revolution, storms the U.S. Embassy at Teheran and seizes the Americans in the compound, including 14 marine guards. The students announce that they will release their hostages if the United States will extradite the deposed shah, who is undergoing medical treatment in New York, for trial by a revolutionary tribunal.

November 19.   The Iranians occupying the Teheran embassy free three American hostages: a woman and two black marines.

November 20.   Ten more of the Americans taken hostage at the Teheran embassy are freed. Fifty-three remain in captivity.

November 21.   A marine guard and an army warrant officer are killed when a mob burns the U.S. Embassy at Islamabad, Pakistan.

December 2.   A mob storms the U.S. Embassy at Tripoli, Libya. The embassy personnel escape unharmed.

December 5.   **RDF.** The marines announce that the corps is organizing three brigades to form part of a joint-services Rapid Deployment Force (RDF), which is to be maintained in instant readiness for operations anywhere on the globe. Later in the month marine Major General P. X. Kelley is designated force commander.

1980

January 10.   Ensign Roberta L. McIntyre becomes the first woman to earn the badge of a surface warfare officer.

January 28.   **Blackthorn disaster.** The coast guard buoy tender *Blackthorn* (WLB 91) sinks with the loss of 23 lives following a collision with the tanker *Capricorn* in Tampa Bay, Florida. The National Transportation Safety Board rules that the *Blackthorn* was chiefly at fault.

March 1.   The repair ship *Vulcan* (AR 5) completes the first regular, six-months' deployment of a U.S. naval vessel in which women formed part of the ship's company. There were 57 females in her crew.

April 7.   As the hostage crisis enters its fifth month, the United States severs diplomatic relations with Iran.

April 24.   **Operation Blue Light.** A daring attempt to rescue the hostages ends in disaster. Six Air Force C-130 transports from

Egypt and eight navy RH-53D helicopters from the *Nimitz* (CVN 68) carry a joint services commando to rendezvous at Desert One, a staging point 200 miles from Teheran. Unfortunately, two of the helicopters are forced to turn back as a result of mechanical difficulties, and a third conks out at Desert One. As a minimum of six helicopters are needed for the rescue, the mission commander, Colonel Charles Beckwith, USA, cancels the operation. During the withdrawal from the landing site, a helicopter and a transport collide on the ground, and five airmen and three marines are killed.

May 28.   Fifty-five midshipmen of the 770-strong Class of 1980 become the first women to graduate from the U.S. Naval Academy.

December 22.   The nuclear-powered carrier *Dwight D. Eisenhower* (CVN 69) and her escorts, the nuclear-powered, guided-missile cruisers *South Carolina* (CGN 37) and *Virginia* (CGN 38), return from the troubled Indian Ocean-Persian Gulf area after the navy's longest deployment since World War II—251 days. At one point the *Eisenhower* was at sea for 152 consecutive days.

1981

January 20.   After 444 days of captivity, the Americans remaining hostage from the seizure of the Teheran embassy are released by Iran on the day Ronald Reagan takes office as president of the United States.

January 20.   The Senate confirms the appointment of Caspar M. Weinberger as the 15th secretary of defense.

February 5.   John F. Lehman, Jr., assumes office as 65th secretary of the navy. In testimony before the Senate Armed Forces Committee he states that the navy must build back to an active fleet of 600 ships, including 15 carrier groups.

March 4.   **Defense build-up.** Secretary of Defense Weinberger unveils the Reagan administration's defense budgets for Fiscal Year 1981 and 1982, proposing increases of 11 percent and 15 percent, respectively, over the previous administration's proposals. The 1981 budget includes funds for the reactivation of the battleships *New Jer-*

sey (BB 62) and *Iowa* (BB 61) and the carrier *Oriskany* (CV 34).

April 9.　While running submerged, the fleet ballistic-missile submarine *George Washington* (SSBN 598) collides with the 2,350-ton Japanese merchantman *Nissho Maru* approximately 110 miles south of Sasebo, Japan. The submarine is essentially undamaged; the merchant ship sinks with the loss of two of her fifteen crewmen. A navy investigation finds that the submarine was at fault. Her captain is relieved of command and issued a letter of reprimand.

April 27.　The 37-year-old carrier *Intrepid* (CVS 11), which has served in World War II, Korea, and Vietnam, is transferred to the Intrepid Museum Foundation of New York City for conversion into a sea-air-space museum.

May 28.　Fourteen men are killed and forty-eight injured when a twin-engined, marine EA-6B Prowler crashes while attempting to land on the carrier *Nimitz* (CVN 68) off the coast of Florida.

June 27.　The navy's 2,000th fleet ballistic-missile patrol is completed by the *James K. Polk* (SSBN 645).

August 19.　**Gulf of Sidra incident.** Two F-14 Tomcats from the carrier *Nimitz* (CVN 68) shoot down two Libyan SU-22 Fitter fighters that open fire on them over international waters some 60 miles off the coast of Libya. The Libyan government of Colonel Omar Khadafi has claimed the entire Gulf of Sidra as its territorial waters, a pretension the United States refuses to recognize.

August 22.　Vice Admiral Edwin C. Waller III becomes 50th superintendent of the U.S. Naval Academy.

An F-14 Tomcat. Official U.S. Navy photograph.

October 1.　The last Polaris missile patrol is completed by the *Robert E. Lee* (SSBN 601).

November 11.　**Ohio class.** The first of the navy's new, nuclear-powered, fleet ballistic-missile submarines, the *Ohio* (SSBN 726), is commissioned at Groton, Connecticut. She was originally scheduled for delivery in April 1979. Seven others of her class are under construction or on order. These ships are by far the largest submarines ever built, having a submerged displacement of 18,700 tons. They are armed with 24 Trident I nuclear missiles, each of which carries more than 14 independently targeted reentry vehicles (MIRV) and has a range of more than 4000 nautical miles.

November 13.　**Admiral Rickover is retired.** The navy announces that 81-year-old Admiral Hyman Rickover, head of the navy's nuclear propulsion program for more than three decades, has been appointed presidential advisor on nuclear science and will not be retained on active duty when his current extension ends on January 31, 1982. He is succeeded by Admiral Kinnaird R. McKee.

1982

January 17.　The submarine *Ohio* (SSBN 726) successfully fires her first Trident I missile while submerged off Cape Canaveral, Florida.

March 1.　**The last Polaris.** The navy's last Polaris fleet ballistic-missile submarine, the *Robert E. Lee* (SSBN 601), is redesignated as an attack submarine (SSN 601), marking the end of the Polaris system after 21 years in service.

March 13.　The *Nimitz*-class supercarrier *Carl Vinson* (CVN 70) is commissioned, giving the navy a total of 14 carriers.

June 6.　Israel invades Lebanon with the object of eliminating the Palestine Liberation Organization (PLO), an action that brings the Middle East to a boil.

June 20.　In the South China Sea, an unidentified vessel opens fire with a machine gun on three U.S. naval vessels—the guided-missile cruiser *Sterett* (CG 31) and destroyers *Lynde McCormick* (DDG 8) and *Turner Joy*

(DD 951)—which are returning from the U.S.-Thai exercise Cobra Gold '82. The *McCormick* responds with her machine gun, deliberately aiming high, and the foreign craft ceases fire. She is probably Vietnamese.

June 24–25.   Nearly 600 American and foreign citizens are evacuated from Juniyah, near Beirut, Lebanon, where the Israeli Army is engaged in pitched combat with the PLO, by the amphibious transport *Nashville* (LPD 13) and landing ship *Hermitage* (LSD 34).

July 1.   Admiral James D. Watkins becomes the 22nd chief of naval operations.

July 6.   President Reagan states that he has conditionally approved the deployment of U.S. Marines to join a Multinational Peace-Keeping Force in Beirut, Lebanon, to safeguard the evacuation of the PLO in the event a cease-fire agreement is reached.

August 25.   **Peace-keeping in Lebanon.** A force of approximately 800 marines from the 32nd Marine Amphibious Unit lands at Beirut, Lebanon, under Colonel James M. Mead to cooperate with French and Italian detachments in supervising the departure of the PLO. More than 12,000 Palestinians are evacuated in a 10-day period ending September 10. The merchant ships in which they sail are convoyed by 11 cruisers, frigates, and destroyers of the U.S. Sixth Fleet.

September 10.   The evacuation of the PLO completed, the 32nd Marine Amphibious Unit is withdrawn from Beirut.

September 15.   The battleship *Iowa* (BB 61) enters the Avondale Shipyards, at Pascagoula, Mississippi, for modernization. She is scheduled to join the fleet in June 1984.

September 20.   President Reagan announces that U.S. forces will return to Beirut in a peace-keeping mission to assist the Lebanese government in retaining control of the city.

September 29.   **Return to Lebanon.** The 32nd Marine Amphibious Unit, 1,200 men under Colonel James M. Mead, lands at Beirut, where 2,200 French and Italian troops are already present, to form a Multinational Peace-Keeping Force.

December 28.   **The New Jersey.** The battleship *New Jersey* (BB 62), a veteran of World War II, Korea, and Vietnam, is recommissioned at Long Beach, California. Her

Marines on patrol in Beirut, Lebanon, October 1982. Official U.S. Navy photograph.

modernization includes the installation of 16 Harpoon missiles with a range of 50-60 miles and 32 Tomahawk cruise missiles with ranges up to approximately 500 miles.

1983

January 1.   **USCentCom.** The U.S. Central Command is activated to respond to threats to American security interests in the Middle East, including the Persian Gulf. An extension of the Rapid Deployment Force, its contingent authority includes the deployment of marine forces.

April 18.   A truck bomb explodes outside the U.S. Embassy in Beirut, Lebanon, killing 61 persons. A marine is among the 17 American dead, and 8 other marines are wounded.

May 17.   Israel signs an agreement with Lebanon, providing for the withdrawal of foreign armies from the latter country; but Syria, which also has moved sizeable forces into Lebanon, refuses to join the accord.

June 26.   General Paul X. Kelley becomes 28th commandant of the marine corps.

July 26.   **Naval demonstration.** The carrier *Ranger* (CV 61) leads a battle group that conducts a two-week demonstration off the west coast of Central America, where the United States is attempting to check the spread of Communism. Later in the summer another carrier group headed by the *Coral Sea* (CV 43) exercises off the east coast and the battleship *New Jersey* (BB 62) off the west.

August 29. The first two marines to die in Lebanon as a result of enemy fire are killed during a rocket, artillery, and mortar attack on the marine positions around the Beirut International Airport.

August 31. Rear Admiral Charles R. Larson becomes 51st superintendent of the U.S. Naval Academy.

September 1. **KAL atrocity.** Soviet fighters shoot down Korean Air Lines Flight 007—a Boeing 747 jetliner—en route from Anchorage, Alaska, to Seoul, Korea, after it strays into Soviet airspace over the Kamchatka Peninsula and Sakhalin Island. All 261 persons aboard, including U.S. Representative Larry McDonald, are killed. U.S. naval forces participate in the search for survivors and, after it is clear that there are none, for the wreckage of the plane.

September 8. **Fire support in Lebanon.** The Sixth Fleet frigate *Bowen* (FF 1079) becomes the first vessel to fire in support of the marines at Beirut, using her 5-inch gun against a position from which the Syrian-supported Druze militia had shelled marine positions.

September 19. What will be widely perceived as a major shift in U.S. policy in Lebanon occurs when the nuclear guided-missile cruiser *Virginia* (CGN 38) and destroyer *John Rodgers* (DD 983) fire 338 rounds from their 5-inch guns in support of Lebanese Army forces defending the strategically important village of Suq el Gharb in the Shouf Mountains east of Beirut. Until now Sixth Fleet ships had fired only in response to attacks on U.S. positions.

September 25. The battleship *New Jersey* (BB 62) takes station off Beirut, Lebanon.

October 23. **Beirut bombing.** Around 6:25 A.M. on this Sunday morning a Mercedes truck loaded with at least 2,000 pounds of high explosive crashes through the barricades outside the headquarters building of the 24th Marine Amphibious Unit assigned to the Multinational Peace-keeping Force in strife-torn Lebanon. Inside the lobby of the building the suicide-driver detonates the charge. A total of 241 marines die and 70

are wounded as a result of the blast. Minutes later, 58 members of the French contingent are killed when a second truck rams into their quarters.

October 25. **Landing on Grenada (Operation Urgent Fury)** On October 19, a radical Marxist military coup overthrows the government of the 133-square mile, eastern Caribbean island of Grenada, a former British colony and Commonwealth nation. This event and subsequent developments arouse official apprehension over the safety of the approximately 1,000 U.S. citizens on the island, mostly students at St. George's University Medical School. A task force of 12 ships, including the carrier *Independence* (CV 62) and the amphibious assault ship *Guam* (LPH 9), en route to Lebanon with 1,900 men of the 22nd Marine Amphibious Unit to relieve the troops there, is diverted to the area. On October 22, the Organization of Eastern Caribbean States, fearful that Grenada will become a Cuban-Soviet outpost, formally asks the United States to intervene. Two days later, President Reagan orders American forces to occupy the island. The mission commander is Vice Admiral Joseph Metcalf III. Operations begin before dawn on October 25 when a SEAL team infiltrates the Grenadan capital of St. George's to secure Government House, where Governor General Sir Paul Scoon has been held since the coup. At 5:36 A.M., 400 marines from the *Guam* land in helicopters to seize Pearls Airport, Grenada's only operational airfield. Half an hour later, C-5A and C-130 transports from Barbados drop army ranger parachutists over the unfinished 9,000-foot airstrip being built by Cuban forces at Point Salinas. Despite unexpectedly stiff resistance from some of the 784 Cuban troops on the island, the airfield and the medical school's True Blue campus are secured by 8:50 A.M. At 7:50 P.M., 250 marines from the *Guam* make an amphibious landing at Grand Mal Bay, just north of St. George's. By nightfall 1,900 American troops have reached the island.

October 26. At 7:12 A.M., marine forces reach Government House at St. George's, where the SEALs, landed the day before, have been besieged. Governor General Scoon

Marines on Grenada. Courtesy History and Museums Division, Headquarters, U.S. Marine Corps.

and 32 other government officials are, at their own request, flown to safety on the *Guam*. American medical students from the True Blue campus begin to be evacuated from the Point Salinas airfield at 9:00 A.M. Resistance from several hundred Cubans and an unknown number of Grenadan troops outside the medical school campus at Grande Anse is overcome around 4:00 P.M. None of the students have been harmed.

October 27. **Grenada secured.** Admiral Wesley McDonald, commander of the Atlantic Fleet, announces that all major military objectives on the island have been secured, though pockets of resistance remain. Some 638 Cubans have been made prisoner. By this time the flow of reinforcements has raised the strength of U.S. forces on Grenada to 500 marines, 500 rangers, and 5,000 paratroopers of the 82nd Airborne Division. American casualties in the course of the operation are 18 killed and 116 wounded. The Cubans lose 24 dead and 59 wounded; 45 Grenadan soldiers are also killed. The results of the operation prove that the concerns prompting this action were fully justified. American students and foreign service officers on the island testify that they felt their situation to be distinctly dangerous, and evidence of a Communist military build-up is unmistakable. Discoveries include the presence of 49 Russian, 24 North Korean, and 13 Eastern European diplomats and advisors; warehouses crammed with arms and military equipment; and documents revealing plans for a garrison

of 6,800 Cuban troops. The majority of Grenadans greet the Americans as liberators.

November 1. Six men are killed and thirty-five injured when fire breaks out in the engine room of the carrier *Ranger* (CV 61) in the Arabian Sea.

November 1. Retired Admiral Hyman G. Rickover receives his second congressional gold medal. He and President Zachary Taylor are the only persons ever to be awarded two congressional medals.

November 17. The Soviet Krivak I-class guided-missile frigate *Razyashchiy* collides with the destroyer *Fife* (DD 991) in the Arabian Sea. The *Fife* had moved to head off the Soviet ship when she approached too near the carrier *Ranger* (CV 61). No one is injured on the destroyer, which suffers minor damage. The *Razyashchiy* appears unharmed.

November 28. The Navy Department announces that the battleship *New Jersey* (BB 62), which has been diverted to Lebanese waters from a Western Pacific cruise originally scheduled to end in September, will be retained off Beirut, although her crew may be rotated.

December 4. **Action in Lebanon.** On December 3, Syrian antiaircraft and surface-to-air missile batteries fire on U.S. naval reconnaissance aircraft over the Bekaa Valley, 20 miles east of Beirut. In retaliation, 16 A-6 Intruders and 12 A-7 Corsairs from the carriers *Independence* (CV 62) and *John F. Kennedy* (CV 67) strike six Syrian positions in the mountains overlooking the valley. Two aircraft are lost. Later, eight marines are killed when the Syrian-sponsored Druze militia shell their perimeter around the Beirut International Airport. U.S. warships respond by bombarding the Druze positions.

December 14. The *New Jersey* (BB 62) fires 11 shells from her 16-inch guns at hostile positions inland of Beirut. These are the first 16-inch shells fired for effect anywhere in the world since 1969.

1984

January 3. Lieutenant Robert O. Goodman, the bombadier-navigator of one of the carrier planes (an A-6E Intruder) shot down by Syrian forces in Lebanon on December 4, 1983, is released from captivity following a meeting between the American Reverend Jesse Jackson and Syrian President Haffez Assad. Goodman's pilot, Lieutenant Mark A. Lange, was mortally wounded in the crash of their plane.

February 7.   **Redeployment in Lebanon.** President Reagan announces his decision to withdraw the 1,600 U.S. Marines, who form part of the Multinational Peace-keeping Force in Beirut, to ships standing off the Lebanese coast.

February 7.   Navy Captain Bruce McCandless uses the manned maneuvering unit (MMU) to make the first untethered walk in space from the Challenger space shuttle.

February 8.   The battleship *New Jersey* (BB 62) fires almost 300 16-inch shells at Druze and Syrian positions in the Bekaa Valley east of Beirut. Some 30 of these massive projectiles rain on a Syrian command post,

killing the general commanding Syrian forces in Lebanon and several other senior officers. This is by far the heaviest shore bombardment conducted since the Korean War.

February 26.   The 22nd Marine Amphibious Unit completes its withdrawal from Beirut, leaving only the marine embassy guard.

March 21.   The carrier *Kitty Hawk* (CV 63) collides with a submerged, Soviet Victor-class nuclear attack submarine in the Sea of Japan. The carrier sustains minor damage. A Soviet salvage vessel tows the submarine to the Vladivostok naval base.

April 2.   At midday in the South China Sea the Soviet carrier *Minsk* fires eight signal flares at the frigate *Harold E. Holt* (FF 1074) when the latter passes along her starboard side at a distance of approximately 300 meters. Three of the flares strike the *Holt*, but no one is injured.

April 28.   The battleship *Iowa* (BB 61) is recommissioned.

Glossary

Brig   A sailing vessel having two square-rigged masts

Caique   A type of sailing vessel common to the eastern Mediterranean, characterized by a high bow and rounded stern

Carronade   A short-barreled, short-ranged naval gun used in the late eighteenth and early nineteenth centuries, which was extremely destructive at close quarters

Gundalow   A barge with a single mast; sometimes spelled *gondola*

Felucca   A lateen-rigged coasting vessel found principally in the Mediterranean

Frigate   In the Age of Sail, a ship having a single enclosed gundeck. (The upper deck would also carry a number of guns, but it was not counted as a gundeck.) These vessels were designed to carry from 28 to 44 guns; resourceful captains often added others.

Lugger   A Northern European coasting vessel distinguished by her rig, each mast carrying a single, four-sided sail, called a lug sail, suspended from an oblique spar

Master   An obsolete naval rank between midshipman and lieutenant, introduced in 1837 and replaced by that of lieutenant (junior grade) in 1883

Master Commandant   Another obsolete naval rank, intermediary to lieutenant and captain, replaced by that of commander in 1838

Naval Cadet   The term used in lieu of midshipman from 1882 until 1902

Polacre   A three-masted, Mediterranean vessel on which the foremast is lateen-rigged and the main and mizzen-mast are square-rigged; sometimes spelled *polacca*

Schooner   A sailing vessel with two or more masts rigged fore-and-aft

Ship   In strict sailing terminology, a vessel having three or more square-rigged masts and a bowsprit

Ship of the line   In the Age of Sail, naval vessels were divided into six "rates" or classes according to the number of guns they carried. The first three classes, vessels considered sufficiently powerful to take their place in the line of battle, were called ships of the line (first, second, or third rate). These vessels had two or three gundecks and carried at least 64, but usually more guns. Frigates were fifth and sixth rates.

Ship sloop   A ship-rigged sloop of war

Sloop   A small sailing vessel having a single mast rigged fore-and-aft

Sloop of war   A generic term used during the Age of Sail to describe any small, cruising naval vessel, regardless of her rig, carrying fewer guns than a frigate, usually under 20.

Spar torpedo   A weapon used by small craft, mostly Confederate, during the Civil War. It consisted of a powder charge with a percussion fuse—in effect, a contact mine—mounted on a spar protruding from the bow of its carrier, which aimed to ram it into an enemy ship.

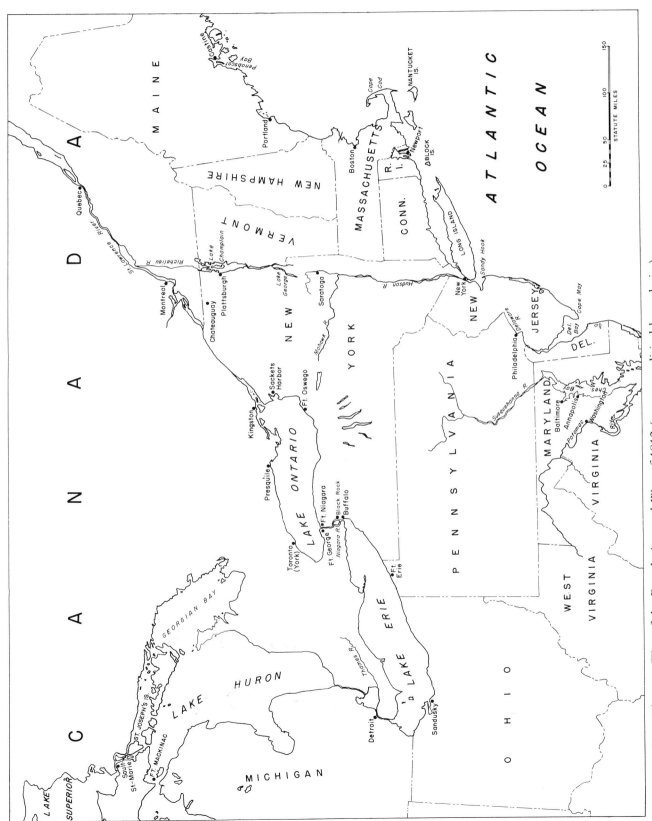

I. The Northern Theater, War of the Revolution and War of 1812 (present political boundaries)

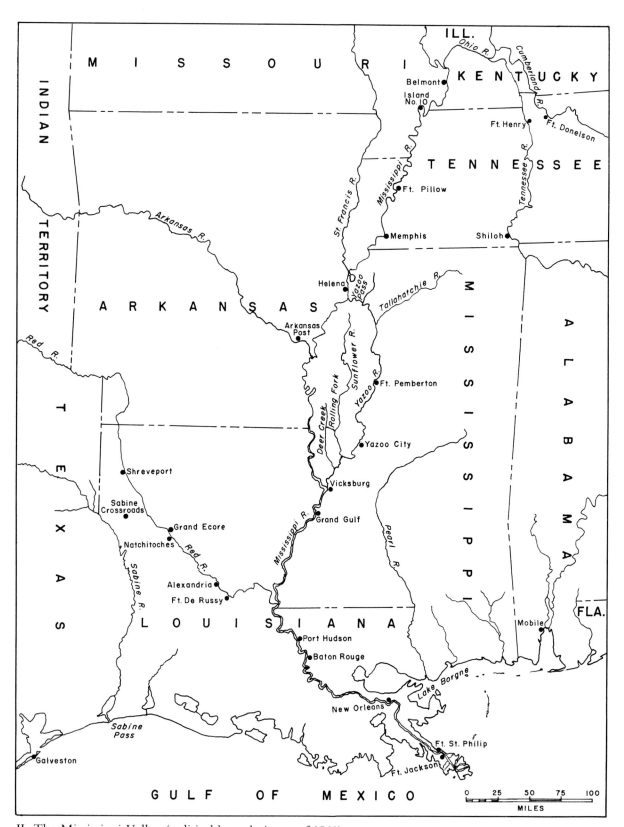

II. The Mississippi Valley (political boundaries as of 1861)

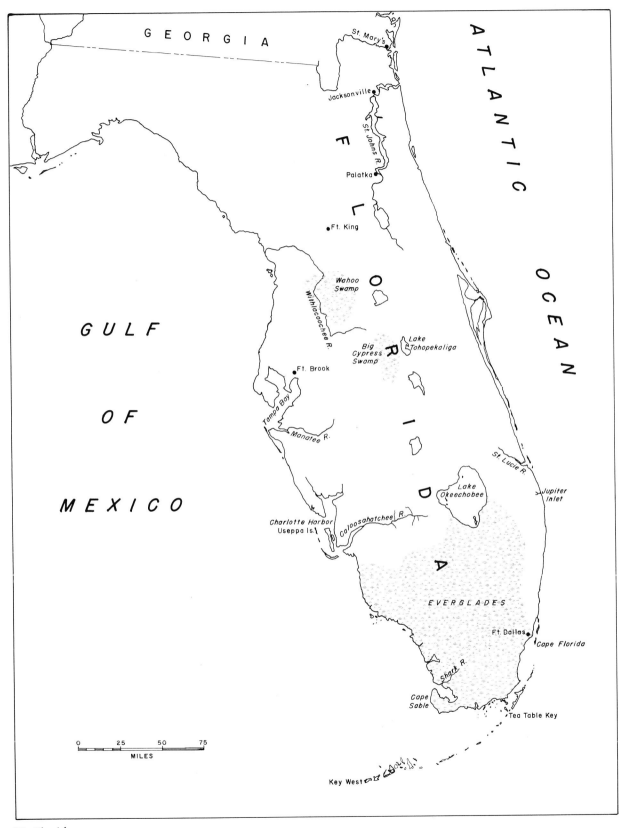

III. Florida

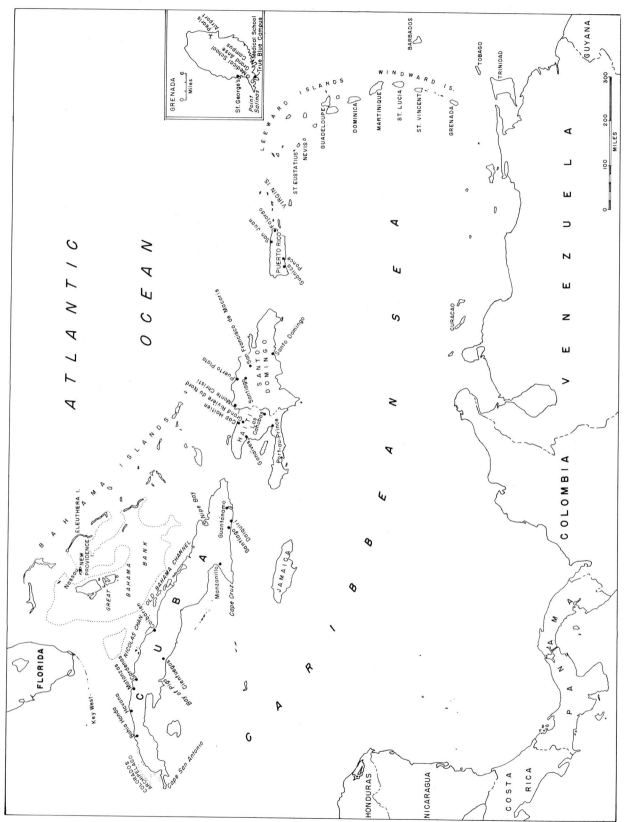

IV. The West Indies

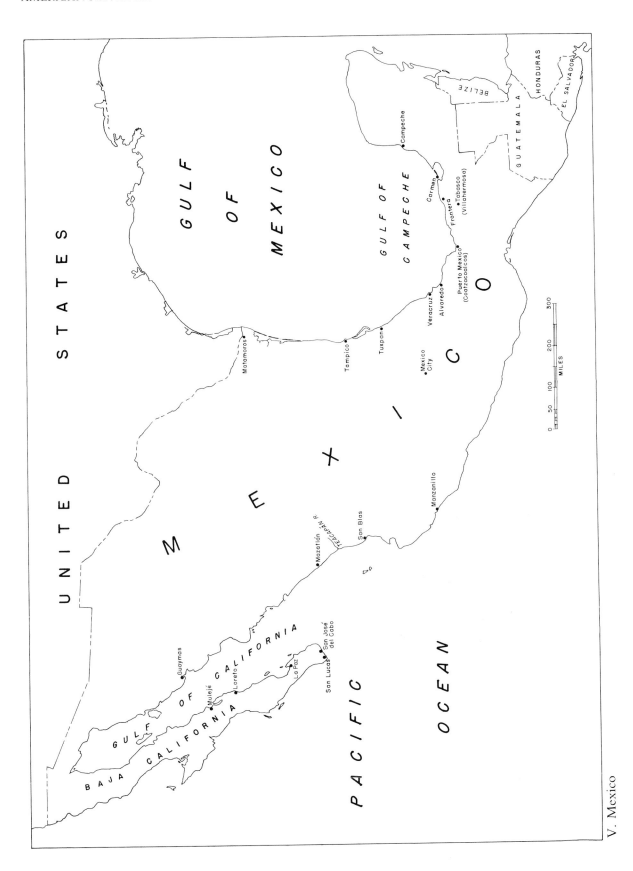

V. Mexico

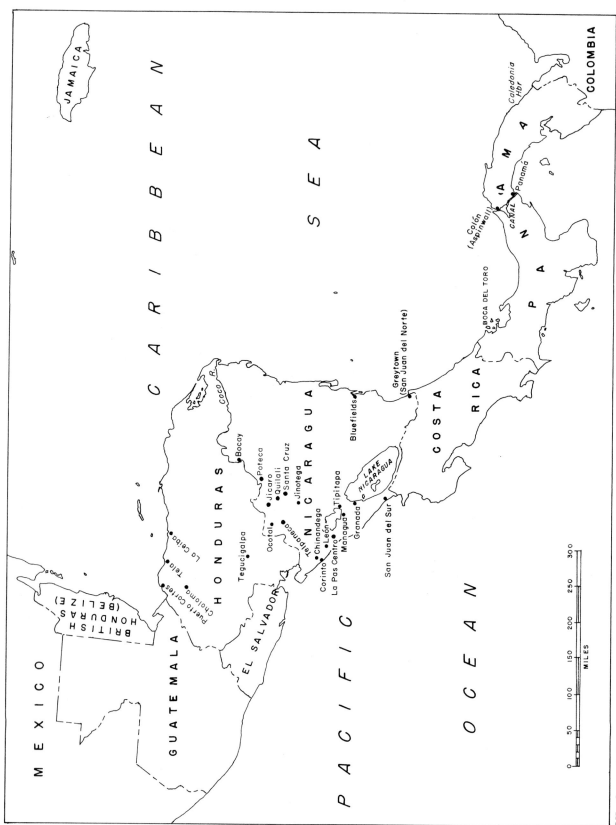

VI. Central America

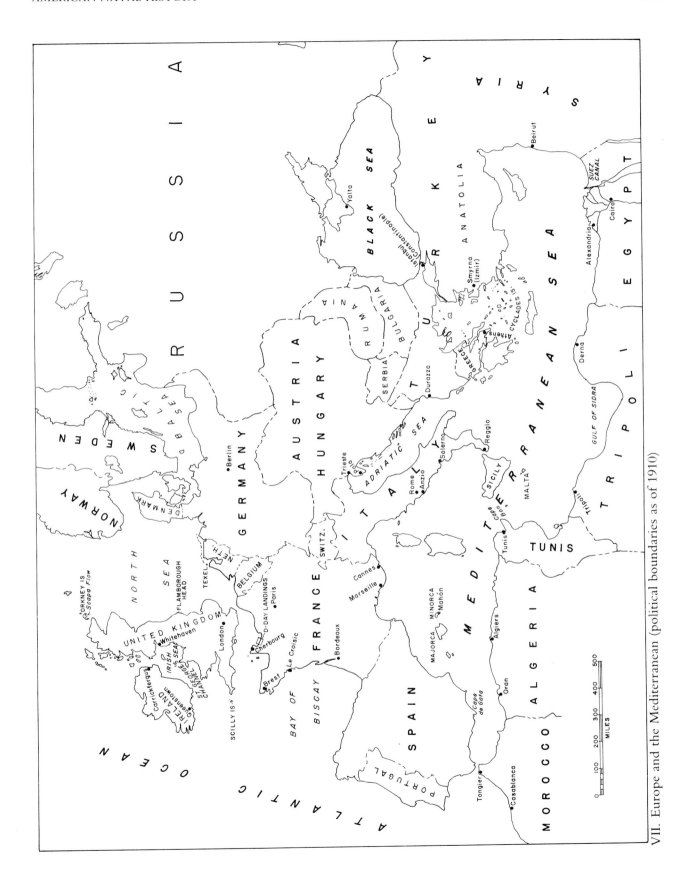

VII. Europe and the Mediterranean (political boundaries as of 1910)

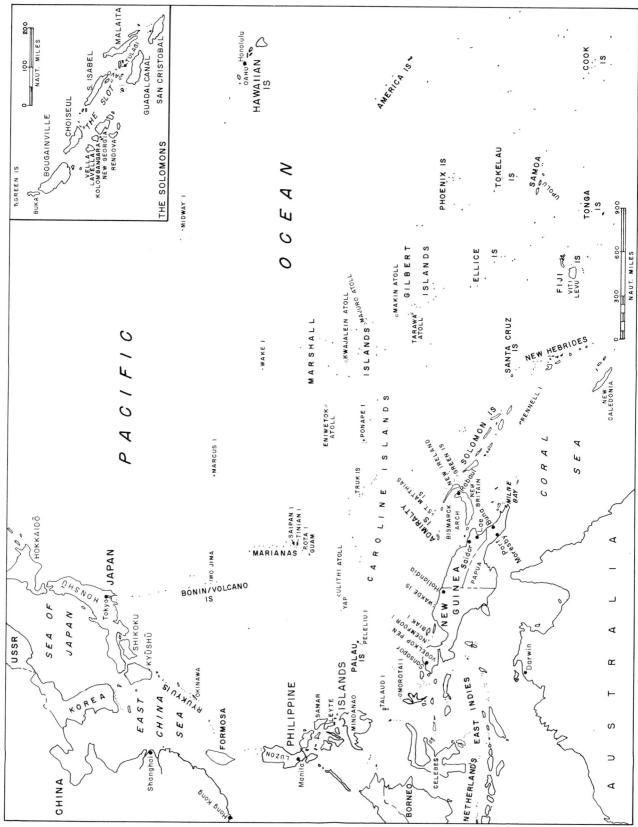

VIII. The Pacific (political boundaries as of 1941)

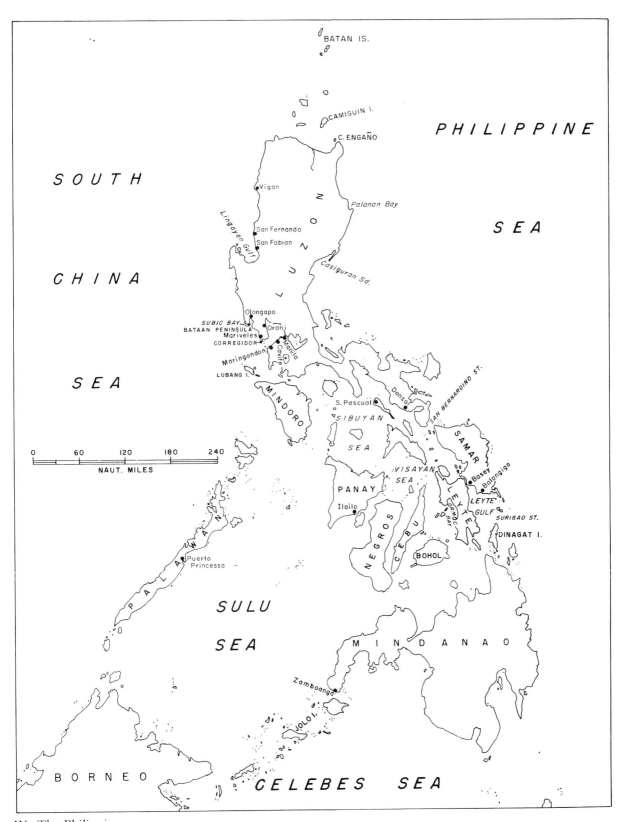

IX. The Philippines

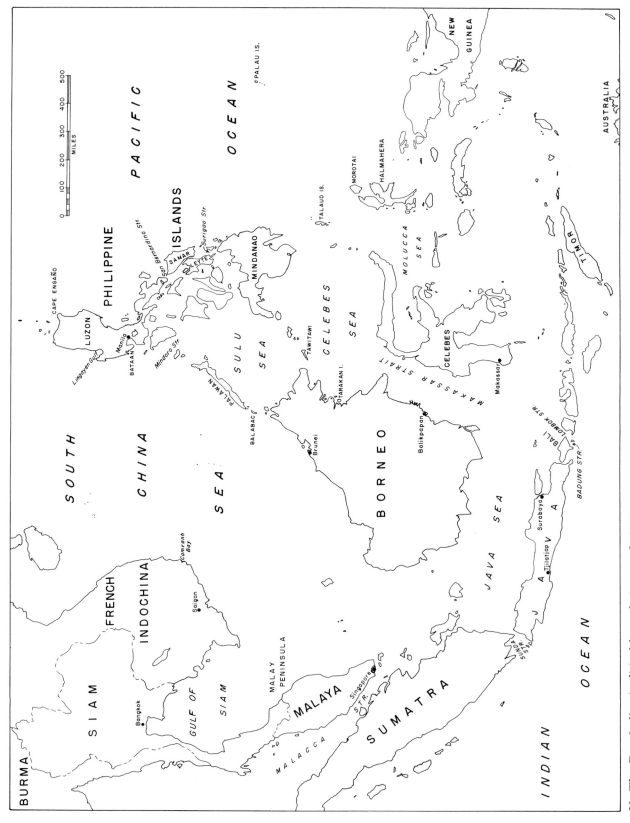

X. The East Indies (political boundaries as of 1941)

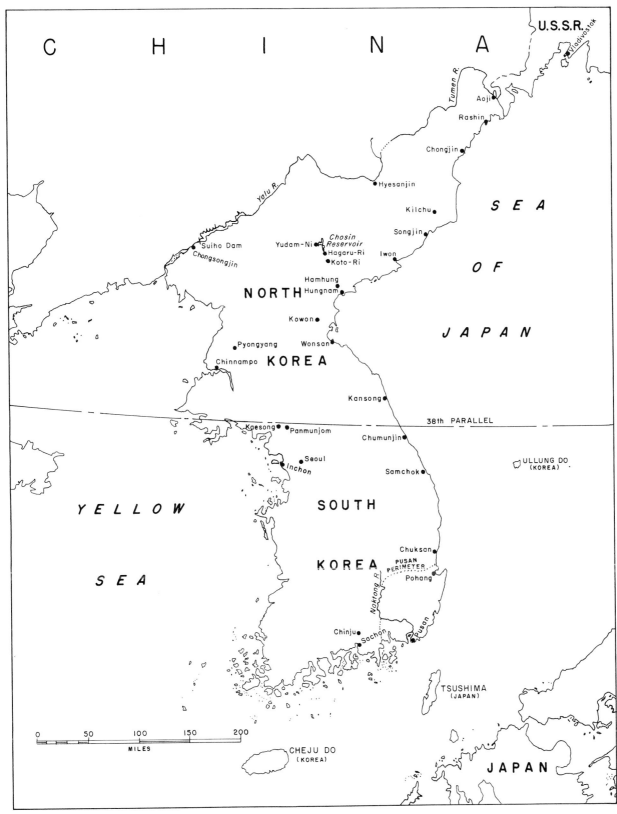

XI. Korea

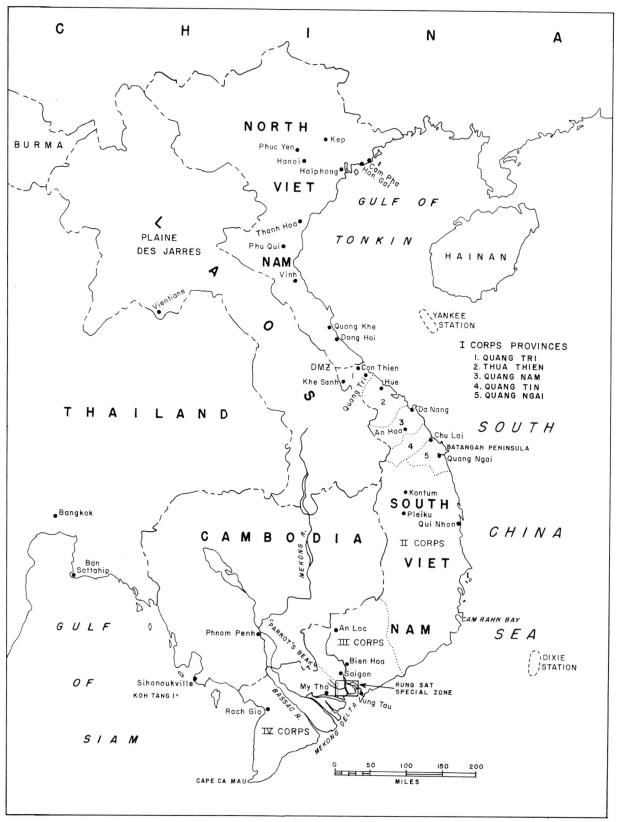

XII. Southeast Asia

Bibliography

Naval and Maritime Chronology, 1961–1971. Annapolis: Naval Institute Press, 1973.

Allen, Gardner W. *Our Naval War with France.* Reprint, n.p.: Archon Books, n.d.

――――. *Our Navy and the West Indian Pirates.* Salem, Mass.: Essex Institute, 1929.

Anderson, R.C. *Naval Wars in the Levant, 1559–1853.* Princeton, N.J.: Princeton University Press, 1952.

Bauer, K. Jack. *Surfboats and Horse Marines: U.S. Naval Operations in the Mexican War, 1846–1848.* Annapolis: U.S. Naval Institute, 1969.

Blair, Clay, Jr. *Silent Victory: The U.S. Submarine War against Japan.* Philadelphia: J. B. Lippincott, 1975.

Boatner, Lieutenant Colonel Mark M., III. *The Civil War Dictionary.* New York: David McKay Company, 1959.

Bonds, Ray, ed. *The Vietnam War.* New York: Crown Publishers, 1979.

Bonnel, Ulane. "The French Navy and the Independence of the United States." New York: Service de Presse et de l'Information, Ambassade de France, n.d. [1976].

Breemer, Jan S. *U.S. Naval Developments.* Annapolis: The Nautical & Aviation Publishing Company of America, 1983.

Buell, Thomas B. *The Quiet Warrior: A Biography of Admiral Raymond A. Spruance.* Boston: Little, Brown and Company, 1974.

――――. *Master of Sea Power: A Biography of Fleet Admiral Ernest J. King.* Boston: Little, Brown and Company, 1980.

Buker, George E. *Swamp Sailors: Riverine Warfare in the Everglades, 1835–1842.* Gainesville, Florida: The University Presses of Florida, 1975.

Bureau of Aeronautics, Department of the Navy. *A Calendar of Significant Events in the Growth and Development of United States Naval Aviation, 1898–1956.* N.p. [1957].

Cagle, Commander Malcolm W., and Commander Frank A. Manson. *The Sea War in Korea.* Annapolis: U.S. Naval Institute, 1957.

Cagle, Vice Admiral Malcolm W. "Task Force 77 in Action off Vietnam." U.S. Naval Institute *Proceedings*, vol. 98, no. 831 (May 1972).

Callahan, Edward W., ed. *List of Officers of the Navy of the United States and of the Marine Corps, from 1775 to 1900.* New York: L. R. Hamersly and Company, 1901.

Chapelle, Howard I. *The History of the American Sailing Navy: The Ships and Their Development.* Reprint, New York: Bonanza Books, n.d.

Churchill, Winston S. *The Second World War.* 6 vols. Boston: Houghton Mifflin, 1948–53.

Clowes, William Laird. *The Royal Navy: A History from the Earliest Times to the Present.* Five volumes. London: Sampson, Low, Marston and Company, 1899.

Coletta, Paolo E. *Admiral Bradley A. Fiske and the American Navy.* Lawrence, Kans.: The Regents Press of Kansas, 1979.

――――. *The American Naval Heritage in Brief.* Second edition. Washington, D.C.: University Press of America, 1980.

Cooney, Commander David M. *A Chronology of the U.S. Navy, 1775–1965.* New York: Franklin Watts, 1965.

Dull, Paul S. *A Battle History of the Imperial Japanese Navy (1941–1945).* Annapolis: Naval Institute Press, 1978.

Dupuy, R. Ernest, and Trevor N. Dupuy. *The Encyclopedia of Military History.* Revised ed. New York: Harper & Row, 1977.

Ellsworth, Captain Harry Allanson, USMC. *One Hundred Eighty Landings of United States Marines, 1800 to 1934.* Washington, D.C.: History and Museums Division, Headquarters, U.S. Marine Corps, 1974.

Emmons, Lieutenant George, USN. *The Navy of the United States, From the Commencement, 1775 to 1853…* Washington: Gideon & Company, 1853.

Esposito, Colonel Vincent J., chief ed. *The West Point Atlas of American Wars.* 2 vols. New York: Frederick A. Praeger, 1959.

Fleming, Peter. *The Siege at Peking.* New York: Harper and Row, [1959].

Fowler, William M., Jr. *Rebels under Sail: The American Navy during the Revolution.* New York: Charles Scribner's Sons, 1976.

Frost, John. *The Pictorial Book of the Commodores; Comprising Lives of Distinguished Commanders in the Navy of the United States.* New York: Nafis & Cornish, 1845.

Fuller, Captain Stephen M., USMCR, and Graham A. Cosmas. *Marines in the Dominican Republic, 1916–*

1924. Washington, D.C.: History and Museums Division, Headquarters, U.S. Marine Corps, 1974.

Goralski, Robert. *World War II Almanac, 1931–1945.* New York: G. P. Putnam's Sons, 1981.

Gray, Edwyn, *The Killing Time: The U-Boat War 1914–1918.* New York: Charles Scribner's Sons, 1972.

Griffing, Midshipman D. A. "Vanished Ships of the United States Navy." First Class term paper, U.S. Naval Academy, 1952.

Guttridge, Leonard F., and Jay D. Smith. *The Commodores.* New York: Harper & Row, 1969.

Hagan, Kenneth J., ed. *In Peace and War: Interpretations of American Naval History, 1775–1978.* Westport, Conn.: Greenwood Press, 1978.

Heinl, Colonel Robert Debs, USMC. *Soldiers of the Sea: The United States Marine Corps, 1775–1962.* Annapolis: U.S. Naval Institute, 1962.

Hobbs, William Herbert. *Peary.* New York: Macmillan, 1936.

Holmes, W. J. *Double-Edged Secrets: U.S. Naval Intelligence in the Pacific during World War II.* Annapolis: Naval Institute Press, 1979.

Hook, Thom. *Shenandoah Saga.* Annapolis: Air Show Publishers, 1973.

———. *Sky Ship: The Akron Era.* Annapolis: Airshow Publishers, 1976.

James, William. *A Full and Correct Account of the Military Occurrences of the Late War between Great Britain and the United States of America.* London: the author, 1818.

Johnson, Robert Underwood, and Clarence Clough Buel, eds. *Battles and Leaders of the Civil War.* 4 vols. New York: Century Company, 1884, 1887–88.

Knox, Captain Dudley W. *A History of the United States Navy.* New York: G. P. Putnam's Sons, 1936.

Langley, Lester D. *The Banana Wars: An Inner History of the American Empire, 1900–1934.* Lexington, Ken.: The University Press of Kentucky, 1983.

Long, David F. *Nothing Too Daring: A Biography of Commodore David Porter.* Annapolis: U.S. Naval Institute, 1970.

Love, Robert William Jr., ed. *The Chiefs of Naval Operations.* Annapolis: Naval Institute Press, 1980.

McCrocklin, James H. *Garde d'Haiti, 1915–1934: Twenty Years of Organization and Training by the United States Marine Corps.* Annapolis: U.S. Naval Institute, 1956.

McCullough, David. *The Path Between the Seas: The Creation of the Panama Canal, 1870–1914.* New York: Simon and Schuster, 1977.

McKee, Christopher. *Edward Preble: A Naval Biography, 1761–1807.* Annapolis: Naval Institute Press, 1972.

Mersky, Peter B., and Norman Polmar. *The Naval Air War in Vietnam.* Annapolis: The Nautical & Aviation Publishing Company of America, 1981.

Miller, Nathan. *The U.S. Navy: An Illustrated History.* New York and Annapolis: American Heritage Publishing Co., Inc., and Naval Institute Press, 1977.

Miller, Colonel William M., USMC, Major John H. Johnstone, USMC, and Carolyn A. Tyson, *A Chronology of the United States Marine Corps,* vols. I–II (1775–1946), Washington, D.C.: History and Museum's Division, Headquarters, U.S. Marine Corps, 1965.

Millett, Alan R. *Semper Fidelis: The History of the United States Marine Corps.* New York: Macmillan, 1980.

Morison, Samuel Eliot. *History of United States Naval Operations in World War II.* 15 vols. Boston: Little, Brown and Company, 1947–62.

———. *John Paul Jones: A Sailor's Biography.* Boston: Little, Brown and Company, 1959.

———. *"Old Bruin": Commodore Matthew C. Perry, 1794–1858.* Boston: Little, Brown and Company, 1967.

Moskin, J. Robert. *The U.S. Marine Corps Story.* New York: McGraw-Hill, [1977].

"Naval and Maritime Events," 1972–1981. This compilation appeared in the annual Naval Review issue of the U.S. Naval Institute *Proceedings.* Those for 1972–1976 (*Proceedings,* vol. 100, no. 855–vol. 103, no. 891, May 1973–May 1977) were written by Commander J. B. Finkelstein; for 1977–1981 (*Proceedings,* vol. 104, no. 903–vol. 108, no. 951, May 1978–May 1982), by Captain Brent Baker. In 1983 the feature was replaced by four separate articles on the past year's operations of the U.S. Navy, Marine Corps, Coast Guard, and Merchant Marine.

Naval History Division, Navy Department. *Civil War Chronology, 1861–1865.* 5 vols. Washington, D.C.: Government Printing Office, 1961–65.

———. *Dictionary of American Naval Fighting Ships.* 8 vols. Washington, D.C.: Government Printing Office, 1959–81.

Navy Department. *Official Records of the Union and Confederate Navies in the War of the Rebellion.* Series 1 and 2 (27 + 3 vols.). Washington, D.C.: Government Printing Office, 1894–1927.

———. *Register of the Commissioned and Warrant Officers of the United States, including Officers of the Marine Corps...* Washington, D.C.: various printers and editions, 1814–.

Neeser, R. W. *Statistical and Chronological History of the United States Navy, 1775–1907.* 2 vols. Reprint, New York: Burt Franklin, 1970.

Nixon, Richard. *The Memoirs of Richard Nixon.* New York: Grosset & Dunlap, 1978.

Paullin, Charles Oscar. *Paullin's History of Naval Administration, 1775–1911.* Annapolis: U.S. Naval Institute, 1968.

Ponko, Vincent, Jr. *Ships, Seas and Scientists.* Annapolis: Naval Institute Press, 1974.

Potter, E. B. *The Naval Academy Illustrated History of the United States Navy.* New York: Thomas Y. Crowell, 1971.

———. *Nimitz.* Annapolis: Naval Institute Press, 1976.

———— and Fleet Admiral Chester W. Nimitz, eds. *Sea Power: A Naval History*. Englewood Cliffs, N.J.: Prentice-Hall, 1960.

Quick, John. *Dictionary of Weapons and Military Terms*. New York: McGraw-Hill, 1973.

Rappaport, Armin. *A History of American Diplomacy*. New York: Macmillan, 1975.

Reilly, John C., Jr., and Robert L. Scheina. *American Battleships, 1886–1923*. Annapolis: Naval Institute Press, 1980.

Reynolds, Clark G. *Famous American Admirals*. New York: Van Nostrand Reinhold, 1978.

Robertson, Bruce, ed. *Air Aces of the 1914–1918 War*. 2nd ed. Letchworth, Herts.: Harleyford Publications, Ltd., 1959.

Rohwer, Jürgen, and G. Hummelchen, trs. Derek Masters. *Chronology of the War at Sea, 1939–1945*. 2 vols. London: Ian Allen, 1972–74.

Roscoe, Theodore. *United States Destroyer Operations in World War II*. Annapolis: U.S. Naval Institute, 1953.

Scharf, J. Thomas. *History of the Confederate States Navy*. Reprint, n.p.: Fairfax Press, 1977.

Schley, Rear Admiral Winfield Scott. *Forty-five Years under the Flag*. New York: D. Appleton, 1904.

Seager, Robert, II. *Alfred Thayer Mahan: The Man and His Letters*. Annapolis: Naval Institute Press, 1977.

Sheehan, Neil. *The Arnheiter Affair*. New York: Dell Publishing Company, 1973.

Spears, John R. *The History of Our Navy*. 5 vols. New York: Charles Scribner's Sons, 1899.

Sprague, John T. *The Origin, Progress and Conclusion of the Florida War*. Reprint, Gainesville, Fla.: University of Florida Press, 1964.

Sweetman, Jack. *The Landing at Veracruz: 1914*. Annapolis: U.S. Naval Institute, 1968.

————. *The U.S. Naval Academy: An Illustrated History*. Annapolis: Naval Institute Press, 1979.

Symonds, Craig L. *A Battlefield Atlas of the Civil War*. Annapolis: The Nautical & Aviation Publishing Company of America, 1983.

Tolley, Rear Admiral Kemp. *Yangtze Patrol: The U.S. Navy in China*. Annapolis: Naval Institute Press, 1971.

"U.S. Marine Corps in . . ." This is one of the articles that replaced the "Naval and Maritime Events" chronology in the U.S. Naval Institute *Proceedings*. That for 1982 (*Proceedings*, vol. 109, no. 953, May 1983) was written by Danny J. Crawford and Ann A. Ferrante; for 1983 (*Proceedings*, vol. 110, no. 975) by Anne A. Ferrante and Colonel John G. Miller.

"U.S. Naval Operations in . . ." Another of the articles that replaced "Naval and Maritime Events" in the Naval Institute *Proceedings*; those for 1982 and 1983 (*Proceedings*, vol. 109, no. 953 and vol. 110, no. 975, May 1983 and May 1984) were written by Christopher C. Wright.

U.S. Senate, Subcommittee on Veterans' Affairs. *Medal of Honor Recipients, 1863–1963*. Washington, D.C.: Government Printing Office, 1964.

Van Deurs, Rear Admiral George. *Wings for the Fleet*. Annapolis: U.S. Naval Institute, 1966.

Wright, Arthur Reginald. *Contact! Careers of U.S. Naval Aviators Assigned Numbers 1 to 2000*. Wshington, D.C.: Naval Aviation Register, 1967.

Calendar Index

Index of American Naval Vessels

Numbers in italics in the following three indexes represent photographs.

This index includes airships, ships of the Continental, Confederate, and state navies, privateers, the U.S. Coast Guard and its precursors, the Naval Overseas Transportation Service (NOTS), the Military Sea Transportation Service (MSTS), and vessels operated by the U.S. Army. Ships for which no other service is cited are U.S. Navy.

In cases of two or more vessels having the same name prior to the introduction of hull numbers, the type of each vessel is specified.

Note on hull numbers: The practice of identifying vessels by hull numbers, prefaced by a letter designator indicating their class, was adopted by the U.S. Navy in 1920. These numbers were assigned, retroactively, to almost every vessel then in inventory, as well as to all subsequent construction. It is possible, as a result of reclassification, for a ship to have more than one hull number in the course of her career. For example, the *Princeton* began life as a simple aircraft carrier, CV 37, in 1945. In 1952 she was redesignated an attack carrier, CVA 37; two years later she was converted into an antisubmarine warfare carrier, becoming CVS 37; and in 1959 she underwent another conversion, this time into an amphibious assault ship, to end her days as LPH 5. The meaning of the letter designator (some obsolete) of every class of ship listed in the index appears below.

AC	Collier
ACR	Armored Cruiser
AG	Miscellaneous Auxiliary
AGER	Environmental Research Ship
AGTR	Technical Research Ship
AH	Hospital Ship
AK	Cargo Ship
AM	Minesweeper
AMS	Motor Minesweeper
AO	Oiler
AP	Transport
APA	Attack Transport
APD	High-speed Transport
APS	Minelaying Submarine or Transport, Submarine
AR	Repair Ship
AT	Ocean Tug
ATF	Fleet Tug
AV	Aviation Transport
AVM	Guided-missile Ship
BB	Battleship
BM	Monitor
C	Cruiser
CA	Heavy Cruiser
CAG	Guided-missile Heavy Cruiser
CG	Guided-missile Cruiser
CGN	Guided-missile Cruiser, Nuclear-powered
CL	Light Cruiser
CLG	Guided-missile Light Cruiser
CS	Scout Cruiser
CV	Aircraft Carrier
CVA	Attack Aircraft Carrier
CVAN	Attack Aircraft Carrier, Nuclear-powered
CVB	Large Aircraft Carrier
CVE	Escort Aircraft Carrier
CVHA	Assault Helicopter Aircraft Carrier
CVL	Small Aircraft Carrier
CVN	Attack Aircraft Carrier, Nuclear-powered (replaced CVAN)
CVS	Antisubmarine Warfare Aircraft Carrier
DD	Destroyer
DDG	Guided-missile Destroyer
DE	Destroyer Escort
DER	Radar-picket Destroyer Escort
DLG	Guided-missile Frigate
DLGN	Guided-missile Frigate, Nuclear-powered
DM	Destroyer Minelayer
DMS	Destroyer Minesweeper
DSV	Deep-submergence Vehicle
FF	Frigate
FFG	Guided-missile Frigate
LCSL	Landing Craft, Infantry (Support)
LPD	Amphibious Transport, Dock
LPH	Amphibious Assault Ship
LSD	Landing Ship, Dock
LST	Landing Ship, Tank
MSB	Minesweeper, Boat
MSC	Minesweeper, Coastal
PBR	Patrol Boat, River
PCF	Patrol Craft, Inshore
PCH	Patrol Craft, Hydrofoil
PG	Patrol Gunboat
PR	River Gunboat
PT	Motor Torpedo Boat
SC	Submarine Chaser
SP	Motor Patrol Boat
SS	Submarine
SSBN	Ballistic-missile Submarine, Nuclear-powered
SSG	Guided-missile Submarine
SSN	Submarine, Nuclear-powered

Index of Other Vessels

The following abbreviations are used:
HIJMS   His Imperial Japanese Majesty's Ship
HMS   His/Her Majesty's Ship (Great Britain)
HMAS   His/Her Majesty's Australian Ship
HMNZS   His/Her Majesty's New Zealand Ship
HNMS   Her Netherlands Majesty's Ship
KM   Kriegsmarine (Germany, Third Reich)
SMS   Seiner Majestät Schiff (Imperial Germany)

General Index

★ *Note*: The following army, coast guard, marine, and navy units are listed in a generally ascending order of magnitude. Changes in the composition and titles of forces over the years make the progression approximate.